Judas Unchained

Peter F. Hamilton was born in Rutland in 1960, and still lives near Rutland Water. He began writing in 1987 and sold his first short story to *Fear* magazine in 1988. He has also been published in *Interzone* and the *In Dreams* and *New Worlds* anthologies, and in several small-press publications.

His novels include the Greg Mandel series: *Mindstar Rising*, *A Quantum Murder* and *The Nano Flower*; and the bestselling Night's Dawn trilogy: *The Reality Dysfunction*, *The Neutronium Alchemist* and *The Naked God*. Also published by Macmillan (and Pan) are *A Second Chance at Eden*, a novella and six short stories set in the same brilliantly realized universe, and *The Confederation Handbook*, a vital guide to the Night's Dawn trilogy. His most recent novels are *Fallen Dragon*, *Misspent Youth*, *Pandora's Star* and *The Dreaming Void*.

Also by Peter F. Hamilton

The Greg Mandel series

Mindstar Rising

A Quantum Murder

The Nano Flower

The Night's Dawn trilogy

The Reality Dysfunction

The Neutronium Alchemist

The Naked God

In the same Timeline
A Second Chance at Eden

The Confederation Handbook
(a vital guide to the Night's Dawn trilogy)

Fallen Dragon

Misspent Youth

The Commonwealth Saga

Pandora's Star

The Void trilogy

The Dreaming Void

Peter F. Hamilton

JUDAS UNCHAINED

PART TWO OF THE COMMONWEALTH SAGA

PAN BOOKS

First published 2005 by Macmillan

First published in paperback 2006 by Pan Books
an imprint of Pan Macmillan Ltd
Pan Macmillan, 20 New Wharf Road, London N1 9RR
Basingstoke and Oxford
Associated companies throughout the world
www.panmacmillan.com

ISBN 978-0-330-49353-6

A CIP catalogue record for this book is available from
the British Library.

Typeset by SetSystems Ltd, Saffron Walden, Essex
Printed and bound in the UK by
CPI Mackays, Chatham ME5 8TD

Visit **www.panmacmillan.com** to read more about all our books and to buy
them. You will also find features, author interviews and news of any author
events, and you can sign up for e-newsletters so that you're always first to hear
about our new releases.

To Sophie Hazel Hamilton

I never knew how much I missed you until you arrived

Main Characters

The Agent Underworld security personnel manager on
  Illuminatus
Daniel Alster Chief executive aide to Nigel Sheldon
Alessandra Baron News show presenter
Dudley Bose Astronomer at Gralmond University, re-lifed
Gore Burnelli Head of the Burnelli Grand Family
Justine Burnelli Earth Socialite, now Senator
Thompson Burnelli Commonwealth Senator, undergoing
  re-life
Rafael Columbia Vice Admiral, planetary defence
Paul Cramley Hacker, Darklake City
Elaine Doi Intersolar Commonwealth President
Adam Elvin Ex-radical, quartermaster of the Guardians of
  Selfhood
Hoshe Finn Detective, Darklake City police
Toniea Gall Chairwoman, Resident's Association High
  Angel
McClain Gilbert Navy captain
Crispin Goldreich Senator, Chair of the budget commission
Bernadette Halgarth Isabella's mother, Starflyer agent
Isabella Halgarth Starflyer agent
Victor Halgarth Isabella's father, Starflyer agent
The High Angel A sentient alien starship
Alic Hogan Lieutenant Commander, Navy Intelligence

Ozzie Fernandez Isaacs Co-inventor of wormhole technology. Co-owner of CST

Bradley Johansson Founder of the Guardians of Selfhood

Patricia Kantil Chief aide to Elaine Doi

Renne Kempasa Lieutenant, Navy Intelligence

Natasha Kersley Seattle Project chief

Anna Kime Wilson's wife, and his chief of staff

Wilson Kime Ex-NASA pilot. Admiral, navy chief

John King Lieutenant, Navy Intelligence

Edmund Li Officer in Far Away freight inspectorate division, Boongate station

Bruce McFoster Ex-Guardian, Starflyer assassin

Kazimir McFoster A clan member in the Guardians of Selfhood

Samantha McFoster Guardian, technician for the planet's revenge

Olwen McOnna Guardian

Stig McSobel Guardian, leader of the Armstrong City team

Michelangelo TSI news anchor

Oscar Monroe Navy captain, *Defender*

Morton Convict navy trooper

Kaspar Murdo Head janitor at Saffron Clinic

Paula Myo Chief Investigator, Senate Security

Jim Nwan Second Lieutenant, Navy Intelligence

Matthew Oldfield Second Lieutenant, Navy Intelligence

Orion Parentless teenage boy from Silvergalde

Tiger Pansy Actress in 'adult' TSI dramas

Qatux A Raiel, living on the High Angel

Ramon DB Senator for Buta, leader of African caucus

Simon Rand Founder of Randtown, leader of resistance

Mellanie Rescorai Unisphere personality, SI agent

Gwyneth Russell Second Lieutenant, Navy Intelligence

Vic Russell Second Lieutenant, Navy Intelligence

Bruno Seymore, Science officer, *Second Chance*

Campbell Sheldon Direct great-grandson of Nigel with a
     high position in the family dynasty
Nigel Sheldon Co-inventor of wormhole technology.
     Co-owner of CST
Catherine Stewart (the Cat) Convict navy trooper, wetwired
     armament
Tunde Sutton Science officer, *Second Chance*
Niall Swalt Junior employee Grand Triad Adventures tour
     company
Giselle Swinsol Sheldon Dynasty starship project manager
Rob Tannie Convict navy trooper, wetwired armament
Tarlo Lieutenant, Navy Intelligence
Tochee Alien of unknown origin
Gerard Utreth Brant Family representative, Democratic
     Republic New German
Liz Vernon Biogenetic engineer, Mark's wife
Mark Vernon Engineer

Prologue

Right from the start, there was something about the investigation which made Lieutenant Renne Kempasa uneasy. The first little qualm came sliding up out of her subconscious when she saw the victim's loft apartment. She'd been inside loft apartments just like it a hundred times before. It was the kind of plush metropolitan pad that a group of funky TSI soap characters usually lived in; beautiful single people with well-paying jobs that gave them most of the day off so they could enjoy a floor space of around 500 square metres as they lounged around in an extravagant décor provided by overpriced interior designers. The kind of scenario completely divorced from real life but full of dramatic or comic potential for the scriptwriters.

Yet here she was, a day after the Guardians' shotgun message that denounced President Elaine Doi as a Starflyer agent, being shown in to just such an apartment on the top floor of a refurbished factory block in Daroca, the capital city of Arevalo. The massive open plan lounge had a wide sunny balcony which looked out over the Caspe River that flowed through the heart of the city. Like all the capitals of successful phase one space planets, Daroca was a rich montage of parks, elegant buildings, and broad streets stretching away to the horizon. Under the planet's bronze-shaded morning sunlight it glimmered with a sharp coronal hue, adding to the panorama's graceful appeal.

Renne shook her head in mild disbelief at the fabulous view. Even with the decent salary the navy paid her, she could never afford the rent on this. And it was currently being paid by three first-life girls, all under twenty-five.

One of them, Catriona Saleeb, was showing Renne and Tarlo in; a small twenty-two-year-old, with long curly black hair, wearing a simple green dress with strong geometric lilac strips – except Renne knew the dress was a Fon, which put its price tag over a thousand Earth dollars, and the girl was using it as a casual house dress. Renne's e-butler printed up Saleeb's file in her virtual vision; she was a junior member of the Morishi Grand Family, working at a bank in Daroca's large financial district.

Her two friends were Trisha Marina Halgarth, who had a product placement job at Veccdale, a Halgarth subsidiary that designed chic domestic systems, and Isabella Halgarth who'd taken a job at a contemporary art gallery in town. They fitted the whole profile; three bachelorettes sharing a place in the city, having fun together while they waited for their true careers to launch, or husbands of equal wealth and status to materialize and carry them off to a merged trust fund mansion to produce their contracted quota of children.

'This is one great place you've got here,' Tarlo said as they made their way into the lounge.

Catriona turned and gave him a smile that was a lot more than simple politeness. 'Thanks, it's a family place so we get it cheap.'

'Plenty of wild parties, huh.'

Her smile became teasing. 'Maybe.'

Renne shot him an exasperated look. They were supposed to be on duty, not hitting on potential witnesses. He just grinned back, perfect white teeth gleaming out of his handsome tanned face. She'd seen for herself just how successful that grin could be in the clubs and bars around Paris.

Catriona took them over to the kitchen section, which was

separated from the lounge by a broad marble-topped breakfast bar. The kitchen was ultramodern, equipped with every convenience gadget possible, all built in to swan-white egg-shaped wall modules. Somehow, Renne couldn't imagine it being used for much actual cooking, not even by the complicated-looking chefbots.

The two other girls were sitting on stools at the bar.

'Trisha Marina Halgarth?' Renne asked.

'That's me.' One of the girls got to her feet. She had a heart-shaped face and light olive skin with small dark-green butterfly wing OCtattoos flowing back from each hazel eye. An oversize white towelling robe was worn like defensive armour, she kept clutching at the fluffy fabric, pulling it tighter around her. Her bare feet had silver rings round each toe.

'We're from Navy Intelligence,' Tarlo said. 'Lieutenant Kempasa and I are investigating what happened to you.'

'You mean, how gullible I was,' she snapped.

'Easy, babe,' Isabella Halgarth said. Her arm went round Trisha's shoulders. 'These are the good guys.' She stood to face the investigators.

Renne found herself having to look up slightly as Isabella was several centimetres taller than her, almost Tarlo's height. She was dressed in very tight jeans showing off her legs. Her long blond hair had been gathered into a single tail which reached down to her hips. It was an image of casual elegance.

Tarlo's grin had broadened. Renne wanted to push him against a wall and shout a warning about professional conduct, wagging her finger in his face for emphasis. Instead, she did her best to ignore the mating dance appraisals going on all around her, and said: 'I've investigated several similar cases, Ms Halgarth. In my experience, the victim is rarely gullible. The Guardians have developed a very sophisticated operation over the years.'

'Years!' Catriona snorted. 'And you haven't caught them yet?'

Renne kept her polite expression in place. 'We believe we are close to a resolution.'

The three girls exchanged doubtful looks. Trisha sat down again, gripping at her robe.

'I know it's unpleasant for you,' Tarlo said. 'But if you could start by telling me the man's name.' His grin mellowed to sympathetic encouragement.

Trisha gave a reluctant nod. 'Sure. Howard Liang.' She smiled feebly. 'I don't suppose that's his real name?'

'No,' Tarlo said. 'But that identity will have created a lot of data within Daroca's cybersphere. Our forensic software teams will pull out a great many assocated files. We can check on the false identity information, where it was inserted, possibly who was involved forging it. Every little helps.'

'How did you meet?' Renne asked.

'Party. We get to quite a lot of them.' She glanced at her two girl friends for support.

'This is a great city,' Isabella said. 'Daroca is a wealthy planet; people here have the money and time to play.' Her eyes gave Tarlo an amused glance. 'Trish and I are Dynasty, Catriona is a Grandee. What can I say? We're highly desirable.'

'Was Howard Liang wealthy?' Renne asked.

'He didn't have a trust fund,' Trisha said, then coloured. 'Well, he said he didn't. His family was supposed to come from Velaines. He said he was a couple of years out of his first rejuve. I liked him.'

'Where did he work?'

'On the commodities desk at Ridgeon Financial. God, I don't even know if that's true.' She pressed her free hand against her forehead, rubbing hard. 'I don't know how old he really was. I know nothing about him at all. That's what I hate most about this. Not that he stole my author certificate, not that he gave me a memory wipe. Just . . . being taken in like that. It's so stupid. Our family security office sends us enough warnings. I never thought they applied to me.'

'Please,' Tarlo said. 'Don't blame yourself. These guys are very professional. Hell, I'd probably get taken in by them. Now, when did you last see him?'

'Three days ago. We went out for the evening. I'd been invited to the Bourne Club, there was some event, a new drama series launch. We had a meal afterwards, then I came home. I think. The apartment domestic array says I got in at five in the morning. I don't remember anything after dinner. Is that when they did it?'

'Possibly,' Renne said. 'Did Mr Liang share his flat with anyone?'

'No. He lived by himself. I met a couple of his friends; I think they were from Ridgeon. We only went out for a couple of weeks. Enough for me to drop my guard, I guess.' She shook her head angrily. 'I hate this. The whole Commonwealth thinks I believe the President is an alien. I'll never be able to face anyone at work again. I'll have to go back to Solidade and get my face changed and use another name.'

'That would probably help,' Tarlo said gently. 'But before that we need to run some tests on you. There's a medical forensic team waiting down in the lobby. They can do this in a clinic, or here, whichever you're comfortable with.'

'Do it here,' Trisha said. 'Just get it over with.'

'Of course. Another team will sweep his flat.'

'What do you expect to find there?' Isabella asked.

'We'll pin down his DNA, of course,' Renne told her. 'Who knows what else we'll uncover, especially if they used it as their base. And we'll pull his files from Ridgeon Financial's personnel records, which I'd like you to verify. It would help to have a picture of him.'

'Won't he have had reprofiling by now?' Catriona asked.

'Yes. But it's his background we'll be focusing our investigation on, his past. That's where the clues to his origin are. You must understand, we have to crack the whole Guardians organization open, it's the only way to bring Liang to justice. We're not pursuing him singularly.'

They spent another twenty minutes in the loft apartment, taking statements from the girls, then handed over to the medical forensic team. Renne was halfway to the door when she stopped and gave the big lounge a thoughtful examination. Trisha was going into her bedroom with two of the forensic team.

'What?' Tarlo asked.

'Nothing.' She gave Catriona and Isabella a last look before leaving.

'Come on,' he said in the lift back down to the lobby. 'I know you. Something's bugging you.'

'*Déjà vu.*'

'What?'

'I've seen this crime scene before.'

'Me, too. Every time the Guardians shotgun the unisphere the boss sends us out to have a look round.'

'Yeah, so you should have recognized it, too. Remember Minilya?'

Tarlo frowned as the doors opened. They walked out into the lobby. 'Just about, it was four years ago. But that was a bunch of guys sharing a flat.'

'Oh, so, what? You're going sexist on me? It's different because it's girls?'

'Hey!'

'It was exactly the same set up, Tarlo. And we've seen the all-girls group before as well.'

'On Nzega, April Gallar Halgarth. She was part of a holiday group.'

'Buwangwa, too, don't forget.'

'Okay, so what's your point?'

6

'I don't like repetition. And the Guardians know we'll catch them a whole lot easier if they stick to the same pattern.'

'I don't see a pattern.'

'It's not a pattern, exactly.'

'What then?'

'I'm not sure. They're repeating their procedure. That's not like them.'

Tarlo led the way out through the lobby's revolving doors and used his e-butler to call a city taxi over. 'The Guardians don't have a lot of choice in this. Admittedly, the number of dumb young Halgarths in the galaxy is pretty huge, but their living and social arrangements only have a finite number of permutations. It's not the Guardians who are repeating, it's the Halgarths.'

Renne frowned as the taxi pulled up in front of them; he was right, though that wasn't the line she'd been thinking along. 'Do you think the Halgarth security is running an entrapment operation? They could have hung Trisha out as bait?'

'No,' he said heatedly. 'That's wrong. If it was an entrapment they would have caught Liang the first night he met Trisha. His identity history data might have stood up to a review by Ridgeon Financial, but a specific entrapment operation run by the Halgarths . . . No way.'

'They must be running entrapment operations. If I was the senior Halgarths I'd be goddamn furious the family was constantly targeted by the Guardians.'

Tarlo settled back into the taxi's leather seat. 'They do tend to put a fair amount of pressure on the boss.'

'I don't think that's right, either. If they were running an entrapment they'd tell us.'

'Would they?'

'All right, maybe not,' she said, 'But as this wasn't an entrapment, it's irrelevant anyway.'

'We don't know it wasn't an entrapment.'

'They didn't catch Liang, and they haven't told us, which they would do at this stage.'

'Alternatively, they're busy tracking Liang, and don't want to spook him by telling us.'

'That's not it,' she was having trouble even looking at Tarlo. 'Something is just *wrong*. It was too neat.'

'Too neat?'

The tone of disbelief in his voice made her wince. 'Yeah, I know, I know. But something bothers me. That loft apartment, those girls, it all shouted out, "*Here are dumb rich kids, come and rip them off*".'

'I don't get this, who's in the wrong here, the Guardians or the Halgarths?'

'Well ... Okay, I don't suppose it could have been the Halgarths, unless that really was an entrapment operation.'

He grinned at her. 'You're getting as bad as the boss when it comes to conspiracies. You'll be blaming the Starflyer next.'

'Could do,' she gave him a weak smile. 'But I'm still going to tell her I think something's odd about this one.'

'Career suicide.'

'Come on! What kind of a detective are you? We're supposed to act on intuitive hunches. Don't you watch any cop soaps?'

'Unisphere shows are for people without lives. Me, I'm busy in the evenings.'

'Yeah,' she said snidely. 'Still putting on your navy uniform when you go round the clubs?'

'I'm a naval officer. Why shouldn't I?'

Renne laughed. 'God! Does that really work?'

'It does if you can find girls like those three.'

She sighed.

'Listen,' he said. 'I'm serious. What can you tell Myo? You had a feeling? She'll just ball you out big time. And don't look to me to back you up. There was nothing wrong with it.'

8

'The boss appreciates the way we consider cases. You know she's always saying we have to take a more holistic approach to crime.'

'Holistic, yeah, not psychic.'

*

They were still arguing about it forty minutes later when they arrived back at the Paris office. Five uniformed navy officers were standing in a group outside Paula Myo's office.

'What's happening?' Tarlo asked Alic Hogan.

'Columbia's in there with her,' the commander said. He looked very uncomfortable.

'Christ,' Renne muttered. 'It'll be the LA fiasco. I was supposed to be chasing the leads from that operation this morning.'

'We all were,' Hogan said. He forced his gaze away from the closed door. 'Did you find anything in Daroca?'

Renne was trying to think what to say; Hogan was very by-the-book.

'It was a standard Guardians' operation,' Tarlo said quickly. He was staring hard at Renne. 'We left forensic working through the scene.'

'Good. Keep me updated.'

'Yes sir.'

'Standard operation,' Renne said scathingly as they walked back to their desks.

'I just saved your ass back there,' Tarlo said. 'You can say all that kind of intuition stuff to the boss, but not Hogan. All that little prick is interested in is ticks in the box.'

'Okay, okay,' she grumbled.

Paula Myo walked out of her office, carrying her shoulder bag and the little rabbakas plant she kept on the windowsill. A red-faced Rafael Columbia was standing behind her, dressed in his full admiral's uniform.

Renne had never seen Myo look so shocked. It sent a cold shiver down her own spine; nothing ever ruffled the boss.

'Goodbye,' Myo told the office at large. 'And thank you for all the hard work you did for me.'

'Paula?' Tarlo gasped.

She gave him a small shake of her head, and he fell silent. Renne watched Paula Myo walk out; it was like seeing a funeral procession.

'Commander Hogan,' Columbia said. 'A word please.' He vanished back into Myo's office. Alic Hogan almost ran in after him. The door closed.

Renne sat down hard. 'That didn't happen,' she mumbled incredulously. 'They can't get rid of her. She *is* the goddamn Directorate.'

'But we're not the Directorate,' Tarlo said quietly. 'Not any more.'

1

The harsh sound of ion pistol shots sizzled out of the speakers to reverberate round the LA Galactic security office. They were swiftly drowned out by the screams. Commander Alic Hogan watched the screens in numb horror as the assassin left the scene of Kazimir's murder behind, running along the central concourse of the Carralvo terminal, shooting as he went. Terrified passengers were throwing themselves flat or ducking down behind the railings.

'Squad B are on the upper concourse,' Renne reported from her console. 'They have clear line of sight.'

'Take him out,' Hogan ordered.

He watched a grainy camera image as the ion pulse from the squad's sharpshooter struck the assassin. A corona of purple sparks flared briefly, outlining the running figure.

'Damnit,' Hogan hissed.

Two more ion pulses hit. Sparks were fountaining across the concourse, burning into walls and advertising panels; people shrieked as tendrils of static writhed over their clothing, singeing deep. Smoke alarms went off, adding their howl to the general din.

'He's wearing a force field suit,' Renne exclaimed. 'They can't penetrate from that range.'

Hogan opened the general communication icon in his virtual vision. 'All squads close in on the target. Pursue until he's in open ground, then open fire. Overload that force field.' As he watched the squads putting the new tactic into play, screens on every console started to flicker. In his virtual vision, red warning graphics sprang up across his interface with the station's network.

'Kaos software has been released into the local network nodes,' his e-butler reported. 'The controlling RI is attempting to clear it.'

'Goddamn it!' Hogan's fist thumped into his console. On the other side of the room, Senator Burnelli was rising from her seat. She looked distraught, her beautiful young face twisted up by some unfathomable guilt. More camera images vanished from the screens in a maelstrom of static. Only one image of the assassin remained, taken from a roof sensor. Hogan watched him race along a ramp to platform 12A, two navy officers chasing after him, a hundred metres behind. Ion shots were exchanged. The image drizzled away into grey haze. A harsh groan crept out of Hogan's throat. This couldn't be happening! It was an absolute disaster. Worse, it was happening in front of the senator who'd given them their first ever real lead into the Guardians. A lead Hogan had been desperate to follow up.

Hogan's virtual hand flew over icons, pulling out secure audio channels from the squads. At least the navy's dedicated systems weren't too badly affected by the kaos.

'He's on the platform, he's on the platform!'

'With you, coming to 12A through the second ramp.'

'Shooting.'

'Wait! No, civilians!'

'Vic, where are you?'

'There's a train coming in.'

'Vic? For Christ's sake.'

'Fuck! He jumped down. Repeat, target is on the tracks. He's on the tracks leading out westward.'

'Get after him,' Hogan ordered. 'Renne, who have we got outside?'

'Squad H is nearby.' She was pulling ground plans out of a hand-held array which was unaffected by the kaos. 'Tarlo, are you there, can you intercept?'

'We're on it.' Tarlo's terse comment was accompanied by the sound of thudding footsteps.

Hogan was vaguely aware of the senator and her bodyguards leaving the security office. His e-butler had brought up a translucent 3D map of the Carralvo terminal into his virtual vision. The westbound track from platform 12A slid out into a broad area of a hundred criss-crossing tracks, a major junction zone between the passenger terminal and a cargo yard, which eventually curved round towards the cliff of gateways three miles to the north.

'He'll never make it there,' Hogan muttered. He turned to Tulloch, the Compression Space Transport security liaison officer. 'Are any of your teams outside?'

The man nodded. 'Three teams. They're converging now. This Kaos doesn't help, but they've got clean communications. Don't worry, we'll seal him up inside that junction. He's not going anywhere.'

Hogan looked round the security office again, seeing his people glaring in frustration at their useless consoles. All they could do was wait until the RI purged the station network. Down on the ground, teams were calling out coordinates to each other. His inserts were assigning them places on the map. It was a wide circle surrounding the western track of platform 12B, a very loose circle. Renne was issuing a stream of orders, trying to close the gaps.

'I'm going down there,' he announced.

'Sir?' Renne broke off from the tactical situation to give him a surprised glance.

'Take over here,' he told her. 'I might be able to help down there.' He saw the brief flicker of doubt on her face before she said: 'Yes, sir.' Hogan was all too aware of how widespread that uncertainty had become among the officers under his command. The Paris office he'd inherited from Paula Myo had never considered him anything other than Admiral Columbia's placeman, a political appointee who wasn't really up to the job. At the start of this observation operation he'd hoped he might finally gain their respect. Now that hope, too, seemed to be vanishing along with the assassin.

The kaos that was wreaking electronic havoc on LA Galactic was starting to be felt on a physical level. Hogan had to use the stairs at the end of the Carralvo's office block to get down to the concourse. The safety system on every lift in the building had tripped, halting them wherever they were in the shafts. He dashed down the four flights of stairs from the security office, arriving on the ground floor only mildly out of breath. Out on the concourse, a tide of panicked people were buzzing round in disarray. Frightened by the murder and the chase, confused by the collapse of the local network, they didn't know which way to flee. It didn't help that almost every alarm was now sounding, scarlet holographic arrows indicating the emergency exits were sliding through the air above them in contradictory directions.

Hogan pushed through them, oblivious to the curses they hurled at him. He was listening to the squads on the secure communication channels. It wasn't sounding good. There were too many queries, too many of them shouting: 'Which way?' They were all too reliant on the officers up in the security office coordinating the operation, arranging them into neat sweep patterns, watching the situation through the station's primary sensors. *Have to change training procedures*, he thought absently. His map showed the ragged circle of his officers and the SCT teams closing slowly on the assassin's supposed position.

He pulled out his own ion pistol as he charged up the

ramp to platform 12A. The few passengers left were all curled up next to walls and pillars; they flinched as he sprinted past and dropped down onto the track. Bold amber holograms at the edge of the platform warned him not to proceed any further. He ignored them and raced towards the end of the terminal where the sunlight streamed down past the high arching roof. Renne's voice was still calm and level in his ears as she told people where to turn, what direction to take. Despite that, there were still big gaps in the noose contracting round the assassin. Hogan clenched his jaw and said nothing, but he was furious with their ragged deployment. It was only when he emerged into the flood of Californian sunlight that he saw the reason. The whole junction area represented on his virtual map, so neatly laced with various tracks, was in reality a harsh environment of concrete and steel sprawling for miles in every direction. Along one side were the bulky warehouses and loading gantries of the cargo yard, where machines and bots were in constant motion. But ahead of him, dozens of trains were winding their way across the junction; from ponderous mile-long freighters pulled along by huge GH9 engines to trans-Earth loop trains; twenty-wagon intra-station goods shunters as well as the sleek white express trains chasing past at frighteningly high speed. They filled the air with metallic screechings and a thunderous rattling, a constant racket which was overlaid by the clunks and clangs of what must have been small ships colliding. It was a noise he had always been oblivious to as he rode in the conditioned comfort of the first class passenger carriages.

The kaos attack made no impact on the station's traffic control. CST, ever anxious about sabotage or even natural catastrophe, used independent ultra-hardened encryption to maintain full communication and control of the trains at all times and under any circumstances; they'd even prevailed during the alien assault on the Lost23.

Hogan almost skidded to a halt as a fast cargo train sped

past fifty yards to his left. He could feel the wind of its slipstream on his face. Several squad members were visible, spread out in the distance ahead of him, all of them holding their weapons ready, trying to look in every direction at once.

Hogan touched the virtual icon which put him in direct contact with Tulloch. 'For Christ's sake shut down the traffic out here! We're going to get pulped into the landscape.'

'Sorry Alic, I've already tried; transport control won't do it without Executive level authority.'

'Shit!' As Hogan watched, one of his people suddenly sprinted sideways. A two-hundred-yard-long snake of tanker trucks hauled by a GH4 engine trundled along the line he'd been standing on. 'Renne, get Admiral Columbia to set off a nuke under CST, I want these goddamn trains shut down. Now!'

'Working on it, sir. The kaos is being flushed. Should have full sensor coverage back in a few minutes.'

'Christ,' he spat under his breath. *Just how many disasters can you pile up in one day?* He hurriedly sidestepped off the actual track itself, and began jogging towards the erratic line of squad members up ahead. 'Okay people, let's get more organized. Who was the last person to actually see our target?'

'Couple of minutes ago, he was two hundred yards ahead of me, heading north west.'

Hogan's virtual vision identified the speaker as John King, and tagged his position on the map.

'Positive sighting, sir. I've got him on the other side of this flatbed shunter,' Gwyneth Russell said. Her location was nearly a quarter of a mile away from John.

'When?' Hogan demanded.

'He jumped behind it maybe a minute ago, sir.'

'I can confirm that,' Tarlo said. 'My squad is due north of Gwyneth. The flatbed shunter has just reached us. He's on the other side of it.'

Hogan scanned the direction his map indicated Tarlo's

squad was deployed. A fast moving train of cylindrical containers was zipping along a rail between him and the squad. He thought he could see another train moving on the other side of it, through the gaps between the containers. Might have been the flatbed shunter. It was a confusing flicker of motion.

There was a brief ebb to the background clamour, and he heard a high pitched humming from the concave gulley on his right hand side, the sound of high voltage cables. Hogan looked down at it, frowning. He'd assumed it was a long enzyme-bonded concrete storm drain of some kind, about ten feet wide and four deep. The grey surface was rippling slightly, and the entire gulley behind him moved across the ground, linking up to another gulley running parallel to it twenty yards away.

Maglev track!

Hogan flung himself down onto the hard granite chippings, and put his hands over his head. An express train hurtled past, its slipstream howling. His uniform jacket flapped like a sail in a tornado. For an instant he thought the air pressure was going to be strong enough to lift him off the ground. He shouted wordlessly into the bone-shaker yowl as animal fear surged through him. Then the express was gone, its rear strobe light blinking into the distance.

It took a minute for his legs to stop shaking enough to carry his weight. He clambered slowly to his feet, looking nervously along the innocuous gulley for any sign of another express.

'He's not here,' Tarlo called. 'Sir, we missed him.'

Hogan's map showed him a big concentration of squad members along a section of track, with Tarlo in the middle.

'We can't have,' Gwyneth insisted. 'For God's sake, I saw him behind the train.'

'Well he didn't come this way.'

'Then where for fuck's sake?'

'Can anyone see him?' Hogan asked. 'Somebody?'

He received a chorus of: 'Not here. No, sir.'

As he walked unsteadily away from the maglev track, his virtual vision showed him the station network slowly re-establishing itself. Renne had pulled a junction routing schedule from traffic control, and was using it to warn everybody of approaching trains.

'Keep everyone in their positions,' he told her. 'I want a perimeter around this junction. He can't have reached the edges yet. We keep it sealed until we have full electronic coverage again.'

'Yes, sir,' she answered. 'Oh, we just got some additional help.'

A couple of black helicopters swooped low over the junction, with LAPD written in white on their underbelly. Hogan glared at them. *Oh great, just like the marina fiasco. The cops will be laughing their asses off at us.*

Clear sensor images were flipping up into a grid in his virtual vision as the kaos cleared. He heard the first of the trains braking, a teeth-jangling screech which cut clean across the junction. It was joined by another then another until every train was slowing to a halt.

Finally the junction was silent, the trains motionless. 'All right people,' Hogan announced grimly. 'Let's sweep this area sector by sector.'

*

Two hours later Alic had to admit defeat. They'd searched every inch of the junction, visually and with sensors. The assassin was nowhere to be found. The perimeter of his own squads and CST security teams remained unbreached. Yet the target had somehow eluded them.

From his makeshift field command post on platform 12A, Hogan watched the tired, despondent squads trekking in from all across the junction. It was a wretched blow to everyone's morale. He could see it in their expressions, the way they wouldn't meet his eyes as they passed.

Tarlo stopped in front of him, looking more angry than disappointed. 'I don't get it. We were right behind him. The others were all around. There's no way he could have got past us, I don't care what he was wetwired with.'

'He had help,' Hogan told his lieutenant. 'A lot of help. The kaos alone proves that.'

'Yeah, I guess. You coming back to Paris? Some of us are going to hit the bars; they'll still be open. The good ones anyway.'

At any other time Hogan would have appreciated the offer. 'Thanks, but no. I've got to tell the admiral what happened.'

Tarlo winced in sympathy. 'Ouch. Well ... that's why they pay you the big bucks.'

'Not enough for this,' Hogan muttered as the tall Californian headed off down the platform to his squad mates. He took a breath, and told his e-butler to place the call to Columbia's office.

*

Senator Justine Burnelli stayed with the body as the official from the City morgue directed the robotic stretcher towards one of the Carralvo's many basement service exits. There had been quite a delay while LA Galactic recovered from its kaos attack, time she simply spent staring at Kazimir's figure on the white marble floor of the concourse. The sheet which the subdued CST staff had produced wasn't quite big enough to cover the pool of blood spreading around him.

Now her love was sealed in a black body bag, and a small squadron of cleaningbots were already at work on the blood, scouring the marble surface, eradicating any sign of staining with sharp effective chemicals. In a week's time, nobody would ever know what happened on that spot.

The robotic stretcher slid itself into the back of the morgue ambulance.

'I'll ride with him,' Justine announced.

Nobody argued, not even Paula Myo. Justine clambered into the vehicle and sat on the cramped bench beside the stretcher as the doors closed. Myo and the two Senate Security bodyguards she had detailed to accompany Justine got into a waiting car behind the ambulance. Alone in the gloomy light from a single polyphoto strip on the ceiling, Justine thought she was going to start crying again.

I won't! Kazimir wouldn't want that, him and his old-world manners.

A lone tear leaked down her cheek as she slowly unzipped the body bag. Allowing herself to see him one last time before it all got cold and clinical for the official identification and the inevitable forensic autopsy. His young body would be examined and analysed very thoroughly; which would mean the pathologists cutting him open to complement the deep scan. A violation which would rid his corpse of any remaining dignity. He wouldn't be Kazimir after that.

She gazed down at him, still surprised by the passive expression on his face.

'Oh my love, I'll carry on your cause,' she promised him. 'I'll fight your fight, and we'll win. We'll beat it. We'll destroy the Starflyer.'

Kazimir's dead face stared up blindly. She flinched as she looked down at his ruined chest, the tattered, burnt hole which the ion pulse had left in his jacket and shirt. Slowly, she forced her hand into his pockets, feeling round for anything. He'd been sent to the observatory in Peru to collect something, and she knew she couldn't trust the navy. She wasn't sure about Myo, either; and the Investigator certainly didn't trust her.

There was nothing in his pockets. She moved down his body, patting the fabric of his clothes, trying to ignore the smears of blood building up on her fingers and palms. It took a while, but she eventually found the memory crystal in his belt. A faint, fond smile touched her lips at that: Kazimir on his secret mission used a belt secure pocket like some tourist afraid of being mugged. There and then, she hated the Guardians for using him. Their cause might be right, but that didn't mean they could recruit children.

Justine was wiping her hands down on some tissues when the vehicle started braking to a halt. She shoved the tissues into her bag along with the memory crystal and hurriedly zipped the body bag up. The doors opened. Justine stepped out, worried she would look as guilty as she felt.

They were in a small warehouse, parked on a platform beside a waiting train that only had two carriages. She'd had to call Campbell Sheldon to summon up a private train so quickly; fortunately, he'd been sympathetic. Even though they were friends, she knew there would be a price to pay later. There always was, some support for a policy, a returned favour. It was the way of the game. She didn't care.

Paula stood beside her as the stretcher trundled into the cargo compartment on the second carriage. 'You realize that Admiral Columbia will not approve of this, Senator?'

'I know,' Justine said. She didn't care about that, either. 'But I want to be very sure of the autopsy. Senate Security can supervise the procedure, but I want it performed at our family clinic in New York. It's the only place I can be sure there will be no discrepancies or problems.'

'I understand.'

The train took twenty minutes to go round the loop through Seattle, Edmonton, Tallahassee, and into New York's Newark station. An unmarked ambulance from the clinic was waiting for the body, along with two limousines. This time Justine couldn't avoid riding with Paula as the little convoy sped off to the exclusive facility just outside the city.

'Do you trust me?' Paula asked.

Justine pretended to look out of the darkened window at

the outlying districts. Despite the profound shock of the murder and all its associated emotional turmoil, she was still rational enough to consider the implications of the question. And she knew damn well the Investigator never ever eased off. 'I believe we now share several common goals. We both want that assassin caught. We both believe the Starflyer exists. We both certainly know the navy is compromised.'

'That will do to begin with,' Paula said. 'You still have blood under your fingernails, Senator. I presume it got there when you searched the body.'

Justine knew her cheeks would be reddening. *So much for slick manoeuvring.* She gave the Investigator a long calculating look, then reached down into her bag for another tissue.

'Did you find anything?' Paula asked.

'Do you still think the Starflyer got to me when I was on Far Away?'

'Nothing in this case can be certain. The Starflyer has had a very long time to establish its connections within the Commonwealth unopposed and unseen. But I do assign that a very low probability.'

'I'm on probation, then.' Justine worked the tissue edge at a fleck of blood on her left index finger.

'An astute summary.'

'It must be very lonely for you up there on top of Olympus, judging the rest of us.'

'I hadn't realized how badly you've been affected by Mc-Foster's death. I wouldn't normally expect a Burnelli to give away any edge in a deal.'

'Are we making a deal?'

'You know we are.'

'Kazimir and I were lovers.' She said it simply, as if it was a stock market report, trying to keep her distance. Inside, the numbness was giving way to pain. She knew once the body was delivered safely to the clinic she'd have to flee back to the

22

Tulip Mansion, a place where she could grieve properly, without anyone seeing.

'I had determined that much. Did you meet on Far Away?'

'Yes. He was only seventeen, then. I'd never have guessed I could love someone like that again. But then you never get to choose when it comes to real love, do you?'

'No.' Paula turned away.

'Have you been in love like that, Investigator? Love that makes you completely crazy?'

'Not for several lives, no.'

'I could cope with a bodyloss. I have with my brother. I could even cope with him losing several days of memory. But this, this is *death*, Investigator. Kazimir is gone for ever, and I am the cause of that, I am the one who betrayed him. I'm not equipped for that, not mentally. True death is not something that happens today. Mistakes of this magnitude cannot be buried.'

'The Prime attack resulted in several tens of millions of humans being killed on the Lost23. People that will never be re-lifed. Your grief is not unique. Not any more.'

'I'm just another rich bitch who has lost a trinket. Is that it?'

'No, Senator. Your suffering is very real, and for that I am genuinely sympathetic. However, I do believe you will get through this. You have the determination and clarity of thought which is only afforded to people of your age and experience.'

Justine snorted. 'Emotional scar tissue, you mean.'

'Resilience would be closer to the mark. If anything, I'd say today has shown you just how human you are. In that at least you can be content.'

Justine finished polishing her nails with the tissue. Now there was no evidence left she had ever touched him – it was a miserable thought. 'You really believe that?'

'I do. I'm assuming the body is actually being taken to your family clinic so you can clone him?'

'No. I won't do that to him. Replicating him physically is hardly going to purge my guilt. A person is more than just their body. I'm going to give Kazimir the one gift I still can. I can do no less.'

'I see. Then I wish you happiness in your choice, Senator.'

'Thank you.'

'But I would still like to know if you found anything.'

'A memory crystal.'

'May I see it?'

'Yes, I suppose you can. It's your experience I'll need to help bring down the Starflyer. But there are limits to my cooperation; I won't give the navy anything that will help them stop the Guardians. I don't care how committed you are to arresting Johansson.'

'I understand.'

*

Adam had personally given Kieran McSobel the support assignment for Kazimir's run. Kieran had been making good progress since arriving on Earth a few years earlier, absorbing their tradecraft with ease, staying cool under pressure. Qualities which marked him down as highly suitable for the kind of operations which the Guardians were performing these days. This assignment should be a walk in the park for him.

When Kazimir's loop train pulled in, Kieran was in place on the Carralvo's concourse, mingling with the perpetual flood of passengers. Indistinguishable in the crowd like any good operative, ready for any number of contingencies.

Away on the other side of the station complex, the Guardians monitored his progress from the offices of Lemule's Max Transit company. While Adam himself lounged against the back wall, watching them in turn. He didn't interfere with the procedures – after all, they were the ones he'd taught them –

but he wanted his presence to supply them with a degree of reassurance. A comfortable father figure. It took a lot of effort not to pull a dismayed face every time he thought that. But this was a crucial operation, he had to be here to keep an eye on it. Bradley Johansson was desperate for the Martian data. The alien attack on the edge of phase two space had played hell with their carefully plotted timetable.

Marisa McFoster was running electronic scans through the Carralvo's network, searching for any sign of observation activity round Kazimir. 'It's clean,' she announced. A secure link connected her to Kieran. 'Proceed,' she told him.

A map on one of her console screens showed Kieran's icon moving slowly along the concourse towards the main exit. He ought to be thirty yards behind Kazimir, monitoring the throng of passengers for possible tails.

'He's stopped,' Kieran said suddenly.

'What do you mean, stopped?' Marisa asked.

Adam immediately straightened up. *Please, not again.*

'He's shouting at someone,' Kieran's puzzled voice said. 'What in the dreaming heavens . . . ?'

'Give me a visual,' Marisa told him.

Adam hurried over to stand behind her chair, bending to look at her console portal. The link from Kieran's retinal inserts delivered an unsteady picture, a poor view through a crowd of people. A cluster of dark out-of-focus heads bobbed around directly in front of him. On the other side of them a figure was running. The image flared white as an ion pulse discharged.

'Fuck!' Kieran yelled. Smeared strands of darkness slashed across the glare of light as he whipped his head about. For a second there was a blurry black and white image of a man flying backwards through the air, arms and legs flung wide. Then Kieran zoomed in on the man with the gun who was now turning to run.

'Bruce!' Marisa cried out.

'Who the hell's Bruce?' Adam demanded.

'Bruce McFoster. Kazimir's friend.'

'Shit. You mean the one that was killed?'

'Yeah.'

Adam slapped a fist against his forehead. 'Only he wasn't. The Starflyer's done this to your prisoners before. Goddamnit!'

The screen showing the feed from Kieran flashed white. 'He's shooting again,' Kieran said. All the portal showed now was a pair of shoes, their wearer lying flat on a white marble floor. Kieran lifted his head and the shoes sank off the bottom of the portal, beyond them, Bruce McFoster was racing down the concourse, people ducking for cover on either side of him as he kept on firing. Two men and one woman were chasing after him, holding pistols and yelling at him to stop. They were dressed in ordinary clothes.

'They aren't CST security,' Adam said grimly.

A shot from somewhere above and behind Kieran struck Bruce McFoster. His force field flared briefly, but he never slowed.

'Dear God, how many people knew Kazimir was on this run?'

Red icons started to flash up across Marisa's console. 'Someone's attacked the local network with kaos,' she said. 'Bad strike; this is high-grade software. The RI can barely contain the contamination.'

'That'll be Bruce, or his controllers,' Adam said. 'It'll help him get clear. They must have known the navy was watching Kazimir.' *Which is more than we did*, he thought miserably.

The link to Kieran's inserts was dissolving, all that remained was his secure audio channel.

'What do we do?' Marisa asked.

'Kieran, can you reach Kazimir?' Adam demanded. 'Can you retrieve the memory crystal?'

'I don't ... oh, what ... there's someone ... armed ...

standing beside . . . that's no way, I can't get . . . more people
. . . alarms triggered . . .'

'All right, stay put and see what happens. See where they
take him.'

'I'm on . . . okay.'

'Can you see where Bruce has gone?'

'. . . shooting still . . . chase . . . platform 12A . . . pursuit . . .
repeat, platform 12A . . .'

Adam didn't even need to consult a console map. After
twenty-five years working in LA Galactic, he knew the massive
station's layout better than Nigel Sheldon. He sat at the console
beside Marisa and opened the dedicated landlines he'd carefully installed over the last few years using bots to spool out
optical cable through ducts and along pipes, spreading their
invisible web across the massive station's landscape. Each one
was connected to a tiny stealthed sensor; they'd been placed
on walls high above the ground, lamp posts, bridges, anywhere
that provided a good field of view.

Two of them covered the large junction area west of the
Carralvo. The images came up just in time for Adam to see
Bruce sprinting out from under the huge arching concrete
roof which covered the platform. The Starflyer agent turned
sharply, and began leaping over tracks. Adam actually drew in
a sharp breath at one point as a train hurtled towards the
speeding figure. But Bruce cut clean in front of it with perfect
timing. He ran past a second train that was travelling more
slowly and in the opposite direction. It completely threw the
navy personnel following him.

CST security staff were drifting into the images, jogging
along dangerously close to trains as they tried to look past the
flashing wheels. Adam suddenly realized than none of them
had any contact with traffic control. Bruce jumped over a
maglev track, and changed direction yet again. His pursuers
were slowing now, they'd become wary of the trains rushing

through the junction, switching tracks without warning. Despite their caution, they were deployed in a simple circle which was slowly contracting. Adam knew they must have access to some kind of communication.

He ordered a sensor to focus on one of the navy personnel. Sure enough, the woman was emitting a faint electromagnetic micropulse, well outside the standard civil cybersphere node spectrum. They were using a dedicated high-order encryption system to keep in contact. 'Damn it,' Adam whispered to himself. No wonder his team's scrutineer programs, so carefully infiltrated into LA Galactic's network nodes, hadn't spotted any surveillance around Kazimir. Which meant Navy Intelligence suspected their counter-surveillance capabilities; that or Alic Hogan was being seriously paranoid.

One of the navy people was closing on Bruce along a narrow corridor formed by two moving trains. They were only a couple of hundred yards apart. Bruce seemed oblivious to his pursuer.

'. . . Paula Myo . . .' Kieran said.

'Repeat please,' Adam told him quickly.

'I . . . see Myo . . . concourse . . . charge . . . talking . . . the senator.'

Paula Myo! Not off the case after all. Damnit!

It was a tiny distraction, but enough for Adam to lose sight of Bruce amid the tracks and speeding trains. 'Where the hell did he go?' It looked like the pursuers didn't have a clue, either. A whole line of them were now walking along the track where he'd been moments ago, shouting at each other and waving their hands about. The trains were coming to a halt all around them.

It took three replays of the sensor recordings before Adam was really certain. He watched the enhanced image of Bruce in slow motion: a collection of blurred grey pixels that made a crazy jump straight at a goods train as it slid alongside. A dark square on the side of a freight container swallowed up the smudged figure. Seconds later the square had vanished, closing up into an ordinary sheet of metal.

'Son of a bitch,' Adam grunted. 'We're up against a real bunch of Boy Scouts, here.'

'Sir?' Marisa asked.

'They came very well prepared.'

*

Four centuries of experience and objectivity counted for absolutely nothing as the *Pathfinder* began its terrifying plummet; Ozzie started screaming as loudly as Orion, both of them audible even over the thunder of the falling sea. Spray whirled around the rickety raft with brutal force, wiping out all sight of the sky in a grey haze. Ozzie clung to the mast as if that alone could save him from certain death as he fell and fell and *fell* without end. The spume soaked his clothes in seconds, stinging his naked skin.

He drew a breath and screamed again. When he ran out of air he sucked down more, half of which was fizzing water. He coughed and spluttered, an automatic action which overrode the wild impulse to keep on screaming. As soon as his throat was clear and his lungs full again, he started to open his mouth for the scream which would surely end in an awful explosion of pain. Right at the back of his brain, an insecure, puzzled thought began to register.

As they went over the edge of the waterfall he'd glimpsed the impossible length of the cascade, and there hadn't been a bottom. No jagged rocks below upon which to smash apart. No abrupt end. Nothing, in fact.

This whole set-up is artificial, you asshole!

Ozzie took another breath, exhaled through flared nostrils, then forced himself to inhale deeply. His body insisted he was falling, and had been doing so for several seconds now. Animal instinct knew they must have hurtled down an incredible distance, that his velocity was way past terminal already. The steady breathing routine helped slow his frantic heart rate.

Think! You're not falling, you're in zero-gee. Freefall! You're safe . . . for the moment anyway.

The roar of the waterfall somewhere beyond the lashing froth was still overwhelming. He could hear Orion's cries which had become gulping whimpers. Wiping the droplets from his eyes he peered round. The boy was clinging to the deck of the raft a couple of yards away. The naked terror on his face was horrible to see, nobody should have to suffer like that.

'It's okay,' Ozzie bellowed. 'We're not falling; it just looks like it. We're in freefall, like astronauts.' *That should reassure the boy.*

Orion's horror took on a bamboozled aspect. 'Whatnauts?'

Oh, for Christ's sake! 'We're safe. Okay? It's not as bad as it looks.'

The boy nodded his head, totally unconvinced. He was still bracing himself for the certain killer impact.

Ozzie took a good look around, constantly having to wipe the spray from his face. He could just pick out the sun, a smear of brightness creating a whorl of refraction rainbows within the spray. Call that direction *up* then. Half of the saturated universe surrounding them was distinctly darker than the other half. That must be the waterfall. Which was wrong, because if they were truly in zero-gee the water wouldn't fall anywhere. Yet he'd seen it. He tightened his grip on the mast with an involuntary lurch.

Okay, so what can cause water to flow in zero-gee? Fuck knows. So what geometry is this screwball worldlet? It can't be a planet . . .

He remembered the water specks drifting through the hazy eternal sky of the gas halo. This colossal worldlet must be one of them. As always in this place, scale had thrown him.

A flat ocean on one side, then. With the water falling off the edge. If it pours away constantly, then it will have to be replaced. Or more likely it just cycles round and round. The underside collects the overspill somehow, and sends it back to the ocean side again. Crazy! But then if you can create gravity and apply it how you want it isn't actually so weird.

With controllable gravity as a baseline, Ozzie tried to picture the geometry of the worldlet. If it was truly like the other water specks, then it was completely covered in water. Gravity projectors just pulled the fluid round in unexpected directions. He didn't like the shapes his mind was coming up with. None of them had undersides where the raft could float along serenely.

When he looked round again, he thought they were drifting closer towards the waterfall. The spray around them was noticeably thinner, yet the gloom was no darker. They must be moving into the underside shadow.

There is gravity here, at right angles to the ocean on the topside. Maybe even less than ninety degrees, because the water has to be pulled round and under. Which is really not good. We cannot afford to get caught up in the flow.

For now they were safe, as long as the underside gravity was still tenuous. The ocean current had shot them horizontally past the edge of the worldlet, which had given them a hiatus, but the underside's artificial gravity would pull them in eventually. It was already attracting the spray droplets, drawing them back into the flow.

They had to get clear while the gravity remained weak. And he could only think of one propulsive force left to them.

Ozzie checked that the rope round his waist was tied *very* securely to the base of the mast, and let go. Orion squealed in shock; his wide eyes following Ozzie's every move. It had been a long time since Ozzie had been in freefall; even then he'd never been particularly good at manoeuvring around. He pushed lightly against the mast, remembering the cardinal rule that you must never move quickly. There were objects gliding through the spray around him, mostly the globes of fruit they'd brought with them, which had escaped from their wicker baskets. His little shaving pack tumbled past him, and he cursed, unreasonably annoyed at the utterly trivial loss. Thankfully, the hand-held array was still clipped to his rucksack, which was lashed firmly to the deck. He pulled the glistening gadget free, and hauled his way across the *Pathfinder* until he reached Tochee.

The wooden decking where the big alien was clinging on with its locomotion flesh ridges was bent upwards, its grip was so fierce. Some of the crudely shaped branches were actually starting to fracture. Ozzie held on to a single branch of decking, and pushed the array in front of Tochee's protuberant eye.

'We have to get out of here,' Ozzie cried. The array translated his voice into dancing violet starbursts on its screen.

'We fall to our death,' Tochee replied through the array. 'I regret this. I wish for more life.'

'I don't have time to explain,' Ozzie replied. He was aware the waterfall's rumble was reducing as the cascade slowly calmed 'Trust me, please. You have to fly us out of here.'

'Friend Ozzie. I cannot fly. I am sorry.'

'Yes you can. Swim, Tochee, swim in the air. That should pull us free. We must not touch the water again.'

'I do not understand.'

'No time. Trust me. I'll hold you. You swim. Away from the waterfall. As hard as you can.' Ozzie clambered clumsily along Tochee's body. The alien's natural cloak of colourful feather-like fronds were saturated, sticking to its leathery hide. They felt soggy under his skin, and he didn't dare pull too hard on one in case it ripped off. Finally, he was behind Tochee's rump, and put his arms out to grip the alien's locomotion flesh ridges. He felt the rubbery tissue slither under his fingers as buds swelled over his hands, forming an unbreakable hold.

Tochee tensed for a long moment, then abruptly let go of the *Pathfinder*. It spread all four of its flesh ridges onto wide fins, which began to ripple tentatively. Ozzie felt the rope tighten around his waist. Then, as Tochee began to beat his fins with larger more positive sweeps, the tension in the rope increased. If he'd thought about just how much the raft massed, Ozzie might have come up with a slightly different method of Tochee pulling them free. As it was, he was the critical link in the chain. With Tochee's vigorous forward motion towing them away from the underside's diminutive gravity field, the entire raft was very literally dangling from Ozzie's waist. He gritted his teeth as the force on his arms increased. Now Tochee could see the effect it was having, its enthusiasm had grown. There was actually a sodden wind gusting back from its fins. The big creature began to change them further, thinning its flesh out so they became more wing-like. Ozzie just knew his arms were going to pull clean out of their shoulder sockets any minute now.

He never knew exactly how long it took, but eventually the spray reduced down to an insipid mist. That too cleared. They left the waterfall's cloak of mist behind, emerging out into direct sunlight. Bright blue sky materialized around them, its warmth sinking into his skin. The noise of the waterfall had become a background growling. It didn't threaten any more.

Tochee stopped flapping, and pulled its sinuous flesh back down into the usual ridges along its flanks. Ozzie felt a slow tremor run the length of his friend's big body. When he looked down between his legs, he could see they were drifting in towards the raft. Orion's bewildered, hopeful face looked up at them. The rope was already slack, bending into supple loops that snaked round through the air. They just missed being impaled on the top of the mast, and sank down to the decking. Tochee extended a slim tentacle, and coiled its tip round a branch.

The locomotion ridge flesh smothering Ozzie's hands retracted, and he grabbed at the mast. His heart was thudding away inside his ribs.

'What's happening?' Orion demanded. The boy still hadn't let go of the decking where he'd been tied. 'Why aren't we dead?'

Ozzie opened his mouth, and gave a loud burp. Now he had a moment, he could feel his stomach rebelling against the ceaseless falling sensation. On top of that discomfort, his head felt as if he'd suddenly come down with a cold, with his sinuses badly clogged. 'We're not falling in the normal sense,' Ozzie said slowly. He was aware of Tochee's body aligning its eye on the hand-held array, where the alien was avidly reading the spiky purple patterns flowering on the screen. 'And that wasn't a normal planet.' He pointed tentatively back at the gigantic waterfall. It formed an awesome curtain of glistening motion beyond the port side of the raft, extending away out to vanishing point in three directions. Only the rim of the worldlet provided an end. And that seemed to be receding gently.

The *Pathfinder* had actually descended several kilometres below the level of the ocean. There the water foamed and frothed wildly as it poured out over the edge; while behind them it was now considerably more placid as its gargantuan writhing cataracts and spume merged back into a single rippling torrent that surged along the cliff which comprised the side of the synthetic worldlet. Following the water as it flowed along, he couldn't see where it was heading, not even with his retinal inserts on full zoom. Right at the limit of resolution, the cliff appeared to be curving away. If he was right about that, it would make the worldlet hemispherical.

Directly above them, the rim of the worldlet was definitely curved, although it was very slight. His inserts ran a few calculations; if the topside was truly circular, it would be just over a thousand miles in diameter. He whistled appreciatively.

'I think I'm going to be sick,' Orion said miserably.

'Listen, man,' Ozzie said. 'I know you feel this is the strangest sensation, and I really appreciate it looks even worse, but the human body can live in these conditions. Astronauts were floating round in space for months at a time when I was your age.'

'I don't know any astronauts,' Orion wailed glumly. 'I never heard of aliens called that.'

Ozzie wanted to drop his head into his hands, but that would have required gravity.

'I am not certain that my body can survive, either,' Tochee said through the array. 'I feel considerable discomfort. I do not understand why I think I am falling. I can see I am not, yet that is not what my senses tell me.'

'I know it's difficult at first,' Ozzie said. 'But trust me on this one, guys, your bodies will get used to it in a little while. If experience is anything to go by, you'll probably even get to like it.'

He stopped as Orion made a miserable retching sound, then the boy was vomiting weakly.

'I would like to believe you, my friend Ozzie,' Tochee said. 'But I do not consider you understand my physiology well enough to make such a statement.'

Orion wiped his hand over his mouth, then stared in disgust at the sticky yellow globules that oscillated slowly through the air just in front of his face. 'We can't stay here,' he exclaimed desolately. 'Tochee, can you pull us back to the island?'

'I should be able to.'

'Whooo there, guys,' Ozzie said. 'Let's not rush into actions like that. If we fly over that ocean and the gravity catches us, we're likely to fall for real.'

'It's got to be better than this,' Orion whined. His cheeks bulged again, and he groaned.

Ozzie looked back at the worldlet. They were definitely drifting away from it at a slow but steady rate. 'There are other objects inside the gas halo. Remember what Bradley Johansson told me? He wound up on some sort of tree reef that lives in orbit here. And they categorically have paths away. I mean, how else would he get back to the Commonwealth?'

'Are they far?' Orion moaned.

'I don't know,' Ozzie said patiently. 'We'll have to wait and see what we find next.' He held his hand out. 'There's a breeze here. That means we're moving.' He realized the raft had twisted so that the worldlet was slipping below the decking.

'I really hate this,' Orion said.

'I know. Now let's get everything as secure as we can. We can't risk losing any more supplies. Or any of us for that matter.'

*

The designers of the Tulip Mansion had intended the conservatory-style chamber to be the breakfast room. It extended out from the eastern side of the north wing like an octagonal blister: a traditional high glass roof supported by cast-iron pillars, and walls made out of gently curving panes that came down to ground level. The floor was classic black and white marble tiles, with a large central circular Romanate bar where the pampered owners would eat their morning meal amid dappled beams of strong sunlight. Vines and climbing fuchsias grew out of big unglazed pots at the foot of each pillar, their shaggy greenery providing a gentle shade. As with all sunny rooms filled with greenery that was constantly watered, the air had a sweet muskiness, complemented during the day by the delicate scent of the short-lived flowers which bloomed all the year round.

With the Burnelli family preferring the less exposed west wing dining room to start the day in, Justine had taken over the chamber as a kind of casual office. Out had come the formal chairs, to be replaced by some large leather couches and even a couple of gelmould bags. The only thing standing on the central bar these days was a giant crescent-shaped aquarium, with a variety of colourful terrestrial and alien fish that regarded each other warily. It left just enough room for the two technicians to install the new large array on the remaining surface.

Justine stood in the doorway, watching as they completed their checks and gathered up their tools. She was wearing black, of course, a plain long skirt and matching blouse; nothing too fashionable, but not gloomy, either. Just a simple statement, which she felt was most appropriate. Most of her social circle wouldn't even recognize the significance, she thought, their kind never had to deal with the concept of death any more.

'Up and running, ma'am,' the senior technician said.

'Thank you,' Justine said distantly. The two technicians nodded politely and left. They were from Dislan, the electronics company owned by the family, which only manufactured and supplied equipment for the family.

She went over to the austere silver-grey cylinder squatting on the polished granite top bar. There was a tiny red light on the upper rim, gleaming scarlet.

Paula Myo walked into the chamber, and shut the tall double doors behind her. 'Is this secure, Senator?' she asked. There was a degree of scepticism in the tone as she glanced out through the wide windows. Beyond the rose garden, the hills of Rye County formed a crumpled landscape of pine forests, broken by the deeper-green swathes of rhododendron bushes that had long finished flowering.

Justine gave her e-butler an instruction. The walls and roof dissolved into a grainy curtain of grey light, like a hologram projector showing a drab autumn sky. There was no hint of the external world left; an effect which produced a near-claustrophobic feeling. 'It is now,' Justine said lightly. 'And the array is completely independent; it doesn't even have a node, so nobody can hack in. We're as isolated as it's possible to be in the modern world.' She took the memory crystal from a slim metal case, and stood in front of the array. The single light turned from scarlet to emerald as she pressed her hand on the top. 'I want you to scan this, and tell me what data it contains.'

'Yes, Senator,' the RI replied. A small circle on top of the cylinder dilated, and Justine dropped the memory crystal in.

'It's a quantum scanner,' she told Paula. 'So it should be able to locate any hardwired ambush in the molecular structure.'

The two of them sat on one of the couches. Its brown leather was so parched from the strong sunlight that it was cracking open. Justine enjoyed it for that as much as the softness which came from age. A tatty piece of furniture in a trillionaire's immaculate household also made the chamber more appealing to her, a little stamp of personal identity.

'What happened at the autopsy?' Justine asked.

'It was all very ordinary,' Paula said. 'They confirmed a lack of any memorycell insert. The rest of his inserts were all relatively common. Navy Intelligence will track down the manufacturer, and from that we should get the clinic which gave them to Kazimir. I expect the operation will have been paid for either with cash, or from a one-time account. Adam Elvin doesn't make elementary mistakes, but they could get lucky.'

'Is that it?' Justine wasn't sure what she'd expected, something which made him stand out at least, an aspect which proved how exceptional he was.

'Essentially, yes. Cause of death confirmed as the ion shot. He wasn't taking any narcotics; although there was evidence of heavy steroid and hormone infusions over the last couple of years, which is understandable for someone born on a low gravity world. You should know he hadn't undergone any cellular reprofiling.'

Justine gave the Investigator a frown.

'It really was him,' Paula explained. 'They weren't trying to push a ringer on you.'

'Ah.' She could have told the Investigator that. He was Kazimir, nobody could fake that. 'What about his hotel room? Any leads there?'

'It doesn't look like it. I'm receiving the reports directly from Navy Intelligence as soon as they're filed in their database. Of course, if there's anything they're not filing, that they're keeping to themselves, then we have a problem.'

'Is that likely?'

'It's a remote possibility. Legally, they have to put everything on file, and therefore Senate Security has complete access as we are higher up the security service food chain. However, you and I both know that the navy is compromised. One of the Starflyer's people could be holding things back.'

'Assuming they're not, will the hotel room tell us much?'

'Not really. The Guardians seem to be as thorough with their tradecraft in their own homes as they are everywhere else. The only report I really value is Kazimir's financial record. That should give us a nice breakdown of his movements before you alerted the navy to his presence.'

A fresh burst of guilt at the reminder made Justine tighten her jaw muscles. 'When will that be ready?'

'A couple of days. The Navy Intelligence office in Paris will correlate the data. I'll review it after that.'

'Paris: that's your old office, isn't it?'

'Yes, Senator.'

'Do you think that's where the Starflyer's agent is?'

'It's a very high probability that one of them is there, yes. I was running several entrapment operations before I was dismissed.'

'And I went and told them about Kazimir,' Justine said bitterly.

Paula Myo stared straight ahead at the cylinder containing the array. 'I will expose the Starflyer, Senator. That is what the Guardians are fighting for, the one thing Kazimir McFoster believed in above all else.'

'Yes,' Justine nodded.

'I have completed an analysis of the memory crystal,' the RI announced. 'It holds three hundred and seventy-two files of encrypted data. There are some software safeguards against unauthorized access, but they can easily be circumvented.'

'Good,' Justine said. Given the capacity of the array she would have been very surprised if it couldn't gain access to whatever was stored on the crystal. 'Can you decrypt the files?'

'They are encrypted with one thousand two hundred and eighty dimension geometry. I do not have the processing capacity to decrypt that level.'

'Bugger,' Justine muttered. For a moment her hopes had actually risen; she had expected slightly more help from a piece of hardware that had just cost her over five million Earth dollars. 'Who does?'

'The SI,' Paula said. 'And the Guardians, of course.'

Justine asked the question which she found very difficult. 'Do you trust the SI?'

'In helping us to defeat the Prime aliens, I believe it to be a trustworthy ally.'

'That's a very cautious answer.'

'I do not believe that humans can understand the SI's full motivation. We do not even know its true intent towards us as a species. It claims to be benign, and it has never acted in any other fashion towards us. However . . .'

'Yes?'

'During the course of my investigations I have come across instances which suggest it pays considerably more attention to us than it will admit to.'

'Intelligence gathering has been the occupation of governments since the Trojans got a real bad surprise from that little gift the Greeks left behind. I don't doubt for a second the SI monitors us.'

'But to what end? There are several theories, most of which belong to the wilder realms of conspiracy paranoia. They all tend to concern its incipient ascent to godhood.'

'What do you believe?'

'I imagine it considers us in much the same way as we would regard a mildly troublesome neighbour. It monitors us because it doesn't want any surprises, especially one which would threaten the neighbourhood.'

'Is this really relevant?'

'Probably not, unless it chooses to take the side of the Primes.'

'Damn, you're suspicious.'

'I prefer to think of it as an extended chess exercise,' the Investigator said.

'Excuse me?'

'I try to see all the possible moves that can be made to oppose me as far ahead as I can. But I agree that the SI being an enemy is extremely remote. On a personal level I have established a useful working relationship with it; and of course it does contain a great deal of downloaded human personalities which should act in our favour.'

'Now I just don't know what the hell to think.'

'I'm sorry, I didn't mean to place you under any additional anxiety. It was thoughtless of me given your current situation.'

'You know, the only benefit of my age right now is that I

know when I'm too messed up to be making that kind of decision. So, if you don't mind, I'll just leave it up to you. Do you want to ask the SI to decrypt this for us?'

'The only alternative is to contact the Guardians and ask them directly.'

'Do you know how to do that?' Justine asked.

'No. If I had that kind of lead into the Guardians I would have shut them down decades ago.'

'I see.' The grey-blue icon for the code Kazimir had sent her hovered in the corner of her virtual vision, inert but oh so tempting. Once again she knew she wasn't thinking clearly enough to make that choice. She didn't even know if she should tell the Investigator she had it. And for a Commonwealth senator to contact what was currently classified as a political terrorist group was a momentous act. Instinctively, she was loath to risk loading that innocuous code into the unisphere. If any such association became public knowledge before the Starflyer was exposed, she would be completely discredited. Not even the family would be able to protect her. And the Starflyer would have won another victory.

'We might not have to ask anyone to help with the memory crystal,' Paula said. 'The navy is investigating the observatory in Peru. They ought to be able to find out the nature of the data, even if the actual files remain blocked.'

'Okay then,' Justine said in relief. 'We'll wait until the navy files that report.' She extracted the memory crystal from the array, then switched off the room's screening. Warm afternoon sunlight flooded back through the big windows, making Justine blink.

The mansion's butler was waiting beside the door. 'Admiral Columbia is waiting to see you, ma'am,' he said.

'He's here?' Justine asked in surprise.

'Yes, ma'am. I showed him into the west wing reception room and asked him to wait.'

'Did he say what he wanted?'

'Alas, no, ma'am.'

'Stay here,' Justine told Paula. 'I'll deal with this.' She set off down the north wing's central corridor, squaring her shoulders as she went. How typical of Columbia to try and gain the advantage by making a surprise visit to her home ground. If he thought those kind of crude tactics would work against even the most junior Burnelli he was badly mistaken.

The decoration in the west wing reception room harked back to the most lavish days of the French monarchy. Justine had always disliked quite so much gilt framing and gold leaf; and the period chairs, although beautifully ornate, were actually uncomfortable to sit on for any length of time.

Admiral Rafael Columbia was standing waiting in front of the huge fireplace, one foot raised slightly to rest on the marble hearth. In his immaculate uniform, all he was missing was a fur-lined coat and the image of an imperial tsar would have been complete. He seemed to be studying the onyx case clock dominating the mantelpiece.

'Senator.' He gave her a small bow as she made her entrance, pushing the double doors open and striding in. 'I was admiring the clock. An original?'

The doors swept shut behind her. 'I imagine so. Father is quite an aggressive collector.'

'Indeed.'

Justine indicated a glass top table, etched with the Burnelli crest. They sat down on opposite sides in high-back chairs.

'What can I do for you, Admiral?'

'Senator, I'm afraid I must ask why you interfered with a Navy Intelligence operation. Specifically, removing the body of a suspected terrorist from the scene of a crime.'

'I didn't remove anything, Admiral. I accompanied the body.'

'You arranged for it to be moved to a non-official facility.'

'Our family biotechnology facility, yes. Where the autopsy was conducted under full official supervision.'

'Why, Senator?'

Justine gave him an icy smile. 'Because I have no confidence in Navy Intelligence. I had just witnessed the entire surveillance operation fail catastrophically. I didn't want any further failures. Kazimir's body should provide the Intelligence staff with a great many leads. From what I've seen so far, your department has proved remarkably incompetent. There are to be no further mistakes on this case, Admiral. I will not accept any excuses.'

'Senator, may I ask how you know Kazimir McFoster?'

'We met while I was taking a vacation on Far Away. We had a brief fling. He then showed up here at Tulip Mansion just before the Prime attack. Naturally, when he told me he was working for the Guardians, I informed Commander Hogan immediately. It's all on file.'

'What did he want?'

'A number of things. To convince me the Starflyer was real. To remove the customs inspection of all cargo travelling to Far Away. I refused.'

'So you weren't close then?'

'No.'

'I understand you were extremely upset by his death.'

'I was extremely shaken by it. I am not used to witnessing total death. No matter what his views and activities, nobody that young should suffer death.'

'Was the supervised autopsy your idea, Senator?'

'Yes.'

'I understand Paula Myo also accompanied the body.'

'I have every confidence in Investigator Myo.'

Rafael's expression tightened. 'I'm afraid I don't share that confidence, Senator. The Investigator is a large factor in the whole Guardians' problem which Navy Intelligence faces. I was surprised and not a little upset when I heard your family secured her appointment to Senate Security.'

'We were surprised you dismissed her from Navy Intelligence.'

'After a hundred and thirty years of no results, I thought it expedient.'

'Everybody in the Commonwealth knows about the Investigator precisely because she does produce results.'

'To be frank with you, Senator, she's beginning to lose the plot. She accused her own officers of disloyalty. She was running external operations without clearance. She also began to show sympathetic tendencies towards the terrorists she was supposed to be pursuing.'

'Sympathy? In what way?'

'She said she believed in the Starflyer alien.'

'And you don't?'

'Of course not.'

'Who killed my brother, Admiral?'

'I don't understand. You know it was the same assassin that killed McFoster.'

'Quite. And McFoster was a Guardian. Whoever that assassin works for, they are opposing both the Commonwealth and the Guardians. I believe that leaves you with a rather narrow field of suspects, doesn't it?'

'The Guardians have been involved with the black market arms trade for a very long time. As a group, those people tend to settle their arguments with extreme force. We believe this assassin works for one of the merchants involved.'

'And my brother just got in the way?'

'If an arms shipment was blocked, then a lot of money would be at stake.'

'This is ridiculous. Commonwealth senators are not murdered in some primitive vendetta.'

'Nor are they killed by invisible aliens.'

Justine sat back and glared at the admiral.

'However unpleasant it is to acknowledge, Senator,' Rafael

said. 'The Commonwealth has a large criminal fraternity. That is why the original Intersolar Serious Crime Directorate was formed. If you don't believe me, then feel free to ask Investigator Myo. Or you might like to consider why Senate Security exists. We have enough problems with genuine threats to the Commonwealth. We really don't need to invent new ones.'

'Admiral, are you warning me off?'

'I'm advising you that your current actions are inappropriate at this difficult time. Right now we need to pull together and fight our very real enemy.'

'The navy has my full support, and will continue to receive it.'

'Thank you, Senator. One last thing. The McFoster terrorist was on some kind of courier mission. We didn't find what he was carrying.'

She cocked her head to one side, and gave him a blank smile. 'Isn't that unusual?'

'Very, Senator. I was wondering if you saw anything while you accompanied him?'

'No.'

'Are you certain, Senator?'

'I never saw what he was carrying. If he was.'

'I see.' Columbia's gaze never flickered. 'We will find it eventually, you know.'

'You didn't find the assassin afterwards, did you?' It was a childish jibe, but Justine enjoyed it anyway, especially the way Columbia's neck reddened slightly above his uniform collar.

*

Gore Burnelli and Paula Myo were sitting talking on the worn leather sofa when Justine returned to her day room. Her father's plain gold face reflected dapples of light that glinted on the pillars and floor, flowing around with any tiny movement he made. Justine activated the screening as she came in, cutting off the daylight.

'That McFoster boy made you soft and sentimental,' Gore said as soon as they were secure. 'You should have kicked Columbia's ass right into fucking orbit. In the old days you'd have eaten him for breakfast. I can't believe any daughter of mine has turned into such a goddamned liberal wimp. '

'These are the new days, Father,' Justine said calmly. 'And I'm not the one out of place and time.' Inside, she was seething that he'd say such a thing anywhere, let alone in front of the Investigator. Even Paula Myo, usually so composed, looked uncomfortable at Gore's outburst.

'Just telling you the way it is, girl. If your dead boyfriend is fucking with your emotions you should get your memory of him wiped out of your brain. I can't afford you to be weak, not now.'

'I'll certainly consider eliminating anything I find distasteful from my life.' She sometimes wondered if Gore was still human enough to remember and understand a concept like love, there had been so many adaptations made to his body.

'That's more like it,' he chuckled. 'You know Columbia is going to come at you six ways from hell after the LA Galactic screw-up? He wants Paula here out of the picture permanently, and while he's at it he'd like the Senate to turn into a nice little Soviet parliament, voting for him unanimously every time.'

'It's not Columbia you have to worry about,' Paula said.

Justine and Gore broke off their little contest of wills to look at the Investigator.

'I believe I know the real reason Thompson was killed.'

'And you haven't fucking told me?' Gore snapped.

'For almost the entire time I was in the Directorate I lobbied for all the goods shipped to Far Away to be examined by police-style inspectors. It was blocked by the Executive every time, until Thompson rammed the proposal through for me.'

'And the Starflyer killed him for it,' Gore said. 'We knew that.'

'Just before he was killed, Thompson called me. He said he'd found out who had been blocking my requests. Nigel Sheldon.'

'That can't be right,' Justine said automatically. 'Sheldon made the whole Commonwealth possible. He's not going to try and undermine it.'

'Not voluntarily,' Gore said. Even with his golden skin making any normal expression impossible, it was obvious the notion troubled him. 'But, as I understand it, Bradley Johansson always claimed he was enslaved by the alien.'

'I've replayed the recording of Kazimir's last minute in the Carralvo terminal several times now,' Paula said. 'He appeared to know the assassin. In fact, he was delighted to see him. It was almost as if they were old friends.'

'No.' Justine shook her head, rejecting the whole idea. 'I can't believe anybody could get to Sheldon. The security our family has around us and at our rejuvenation facilities is phenomenal. Sheldon's will be even stronger.'

'The Guardians claimed that President Doi was working for the Starflyer,' Paula said.

'And what a load of crap that was,' Gore grunted. 'If this Starflyer bastard can cut through Senate Security and Sheldon's protection it wouldn't need to skulk about in the shadows; it'd already be our Führer.'

'Then why was your son killed?' Paula asked. 'Just for implementing the cargo searches? Or because he uncovered the connection?'

'All right,' Gore said reluctantly. 'Assume Thompson came across some information which made him believe it. Did he say who gave him Sheldon's name?'

48

'No. He said the whole area was very unclear, it was politics at the highest level.'

'Politics doesn't have a high level,' Gore muttered; he turned to Justine. 'This is down to you. We need to find out where Thompson got his information from.'

'Dad, I don't have anything like his contacts in the Senate.'

'Jesus Christ, will you stop selling yourself short, girl. If I want to hear whining that pitiful I'll visit a human rights lawyer on Orleans.'

She threw up her hands. 'Fine, I'll go blundering round shouting out questions in a loud voice, and see if anyone comes to take a shot at me.'

'More like it,' Gore said, his metallic lips lifting in an approximation of a smile.

'To what end?' Paula asked.

'What do you mean, what fucking end?'

'What will you do if the senator confirms it was Sheldon who has been blocking my requests?'

'If it's true, we'll need to go to his senior family members and show them what's happened. I expect they'll have him re-lifed and updated from a secure memory store that pre-dates his corruption – whenever that was.'

'Do you think the Sheldon family will support you?'

'They can't all be Starflyer agents.'

'Indeed not. But how will we know which are?'

'We're being very premature,' Justine said. 'Let's try and establish what we suspect first. After that, we should have a clearer picture of what to do.'

'We also need to create some reliable alliances,' Gore said. 'A kind of political resistance network to counter the Starflyer's influence. I'll make a start on that.'

'Watch out for Columbia,' Paula said. 'Now he's aware you're my sponsor, he'll be gunning for your family as well. And his political influence is growing. Societies make a lot of short cuts during wartime; as admiral in charge of domestic defence he'll be able to issue orders that would never be countenanced in peacetime.'

'Don't you worry yourself about that. Hell would have to freeze over for a long time before some Halgarth stooge outsmarts me.'

*

The little Boeing 44044 VTOL plane landed on the Observatory pad amid a swirl of air from its electric jets, which stirred up quite a storm of sandy ochre soil and filthy ice granules. It fell away quickly as the fans slowed, and the stewardess opened the hatch. Renne felt her ears pop as the pressure dropped abruptly. They were seventeen thousand feet up in the western side of the Andes, just north of Sandia, with the rugged mountains forming a magnificent snow-capped vista all around her. Renne immediately felt short of breath, and sucked down a huge lungful of air. It made no difference at all. She got up out of the seat and scuttled forwards, zipping up her coat over her thick sweater. The light outside was bright enough to make her pause at the top of the air stairs and put on her sunglasses. In the treacherously thin air, her breath formed little white streamers in front of her face.

Two officers from the Lima office of Navy Intelligence were waiting for her on the ground, wearing dark-green jackets that looked more like space suits than severe weather gear. Getting down the five aluminium steps left her gasping for oxygen.

One of the men came forward and extended his arm. 'Lieutenant Kempasa, welcome to Antina Station. I'm Phil Mandia, I was part of the team boxing McFoster on his way up here.'

'Great,' she wheezed. She could barely make out his face behind a protective amber-tinted goggle mask. Her heart was hammering away hard inside her chest. They had to walk very slowly over to the observatory buildings, a line of squat boxes made from dark plastic, with windows like portholes. Only one had any lights on inside. The three main radio telescope dishes were sitting on the big rocky field behind the buildings, huge white saucers balanced on improbably thin spires of metal. As she watched, one of them turned slightly, tracking along the northern skyline.

'How's my prisoner behaving?' she asked.

'Cufflin? He claims he knows next to nothing; that he was on some security contract from an anonymous agent. For what it's worth, I believe him.'

'We'll know for sure once I take him back to Paris.'

'What are you going to do, read his memories?'

'Yes.'

Even with his face shielded by the mask, Phil Mandia's grimace of disapproval was quite blatant.

Renne's feet started crunching on the icy rime that bristled over the soil. There didn't seem to be any plants anywhere, not even tufts of grass. She had to be careful where she trod, the ground was creased with deep tyre ruts which had frozen solid. The ageing yellow-painted vehicles which had made them were parked outside, around the buildings, looking like a disreputable crossbreed between tractors and snowploughs. A pair of new maroon Honda 4x4 saloons were drawn up beside them, sides splattered with thick brown mud.

'You came in those?' Renne asked.

'Yeah.' Phil Mandia nodded at the single bleak road winding away from the Observatory. 'It was a brute of a drive up here.'

'How the hell did you manage to avoid being seen by McFoster?'

'With difficulty.'

Renne wasn't sure if he was joking or not.

They reached the main building and went inside where the world was warm again. It didn't make any difference to

Renne's heart, which was still racing away. She had to sit heavily in the first office they came to. There was no way she could get up again, so she had to take her coat off while remaining in the seat, a simple act which made her even more out of breath. She couldn't think how she was going to get back out to the VTOL again; the others might have to carry her.

'Doesn't this altitude bother you?' she asked Phil Mandia.

'Takes a while to adjust,' he admitted.

Renne was beginning to realize how the local team resented her. Some bigshot exec sent up to check on why the operation had crashed, looking to shift the blame onto a field team. *It's not like that*, she wanted to say. But that would make her look weaker in his eyes. Office politics she could handle easily enough.

'Okay, let me start with the Director,' she said.

Jennifer Seitz was only five years out of rejuvenation. A small, trim woman with attractive green eyes and very dark skin. She wore a baggy chestnut-brown sweater that was long enough to qualify as a skirt; the sleeves were rolled up, but even that didn't stop them flapping round her thin arms. Renne decided it had to be borrowed from someone else about two feet taller. The Director seemed irritated by the navy's invasion of her Observatory rather than intimidated or worried. Her forceful, dismissive attitude was outwardly softened by the beguilingly youthful smile that she could produce. Phil Mandia was given an exasperated glance as he politely ushered her into the office; even that came over as mere petulance rather than genuine disapproval.

Renne pointed at the room's circular window and the three big dishes outside. 'Which one,' she paused, took another breath, 'is pointing at Mars?'

'None of them,' Jennifer Seitz said. 'The major dishes are for deep space radio astronomy. We use one of our ancillary receivers to pick up the signal from Mars. It's not a huge operation.'

'And are we sure it's the Martian data which Cufflin supplied to McFoster?' Renne glanced at Phil Mandia for confirmation.

'There's no trace of any of it left in the Observatory network memory,' the navy officer said. 'Cufflin loaded a tracerworm program to eliminate any record of the transmissions right after McFoster picked up the copy.'

'There must be other copies,' Renne said. 'How long have you been receiving the data?'

The corner of Jennifer Seitz's mouth produced an involuntary tic. 'About twenty years.'

'Twenty! What the hell have you been doing with it?'

'We collect it for a science research association. It's a very minor contract for us; less than one per cent of our overall budget. It doesn't even require human supervision; our RI can handle the whole process. The signals come in once a month. We receive them and store them for the association. Their project length is expected to be thirty years.' Jennifer Seitz caught the surprise in Renne's eyes. 'What, you think that's long term? We're running some observations here that will take a century to complete, that's if we're lucky.'

'Okay, back up a moment here and take me through this slowly,' Renne said. 'I didn't even know the Commonwealth had anything on Mars. Where do these signals come from, exactly?'

'The remote science station on Arabia Terra.'

'And what sort of science goes on there?'

'Just about the full range of planetary science remote sensing: meteorological, geological – I should say Areological – solar physics, radiation. It's a long list; you name the subject and it'll have its own set of instruments up there busy watching. They're all over Mars, relaying their readings to

Arabia Terra, which in turn sends them to us. Satellites, too. There's four of them currently in polar orbit, though they all need replacing.'

'I never knew anyone was still interested in Mars.'

'Very few people are,' Jennifer Seitz said sardonically. 'We're talking astronomy, here, after all. Even after Dudley Bose came along, we're not exactly the most popular profession in the Commonwealth. And there are planets in this universe a lot more interesting than Mars. However, a small collection of sensors operating over a long time can produce just as much data as a shorter more intense study. Actually, the data is more relevant when gathered over time, more representative. We have remote stations right across the solar system collecting little chunks of data and sending them back to us and the other observatories in a steady drip. Most Earth universities or foundations tend to have some small department for each solar body. They all struggle along on minimum resources, cataloguing and analysing their information. But the instruments they use don't cost much by today's standards; they're all solid state, and either solar or geothermal powered; they last for decades. Between them they supply just enough information to keep Earth's few remaining planetologists in business.'

'I'd like a list of them, please.'

'The association which funds the Martian station is based in London, the Lambeth Interplanetary Association, I think. God knows where they get their grants from. I mean, pure science planetology in this day and age. You've got to be a real science philanthropist to support that.'

'What exactly is the project which the Lambeth Interplanetary Association is paying for?'

'I've no idea.'

'You don't know?' Renne said it so loudly she had to take a fast breath to refill her lungs, which made her cough. She could feel a headache growing behind her temple.

'Not my field,' Jennifer Seitz said. 'Strictly speaking I'm a radio astronomer; I work with the main dishes, they're part of the Solwide array. Our baseline is Pluto orbit, which gives us one hell of a reception capability. It's also why we have a lot of ancillary receivers here, to keep in touch with the Solwide units that are really far out. So you see, I have not the slightest concern in dust on Mars or tidal ice fracture patterns on Europa or the geoshell superconductor currents on Charon. Now if you wanted to know about truly interesting events like big bang emission rebounds or mag-quasar squeals, then I can entertain you for days on the subject.'

'Is anyone here a planetologist?'

'No. All we've got here is two radio astronomers, that's myself and my partner Carrie; and four technicians to keep everything running smoothly. Well . . . as smoothly as something as underfunded as Solwide can be kept running. And just to add to the richness of our lives, since the Prime attack, the UFN Science Agency is actually talking about shutting us down for the duration. I've got to produce proposals to mothball the whole Observatory. I should have shoved this whole astronomy kick into a secure memory store at my last rejuve, and come up with an interest that makes me filthy rich. I mean, who the hell's interested in supporting people who'll quietly dedicate several lives to help expand the general knowledge base of the human race. Not our goddamn government, that's for sure. Now I've got you people jumping all over us.'

'I'm sorry about the Observatory,' Renne said sharply. 'But there is a war on, the Commonwealth has to prioritize.'

'Yeah, right.'

'So has the Lambeth Interplanetary Association actually seen any of the data you were receiving for them?'

'No. Mars accounts for nearly half of the remote monitoring projects in the solar system. Their timetables are measurable in years. Admittedly, thirty years is quite long for planetary science, but not exceptional.'

'What kind of sensors were transmitting from Mars? Exactly?'

Jennifer Seitz shrugged. 'I checked the contract when the shit hit the fan, of course. It doesn't tell us much. The instruments we were recording just provided a generalized overview of the Martian environment.'

'Could you have been receiving encrypted signals in with the rest of the data?'

'Sure. I don't know what from, though.'

'Do you at least have a list of the instruments up there?'

'Yeah. But, Lieutenant, you have to understand, we didn't place any of them on Mars. Some were already there, left over from earlier projects; the rest have been deposited over the years by the UFN Science Agency's automated ships. We have no control over them, no supervisory role. I cannot give you an absolute guarantee what any of them actually are. Simply because we've been told a specific channel in the datastream carries the results of a seismic scanner, doesn't make it that in reality. It could equally well be information on Earth's defences for an alien invasion fleet. There's just no way of knowing for sure, other than going there and checking the transmission origin in person. All we are is a glorified relay node.'

Renne didn't like getting distracted, but ... 'There are automated spaceships working in the solar system?'

'You didn't know that?'

'No,' she admitted.

'Well, Lieutenant, there have to be. It's like this. None of us in the heady world of astronomy or solar planetary science can afford to hire a CST wormhole to drop a thermometer into Saturn's atmosphere. Instead, we swallow our pride and group together, that way we coordinate our budgets to produce instrumentation in batches. When a batch is ready, we load up one of the Science Agency's three robot freight ships with our precious consignment of satellites and sensors, and send it on its merry eight-year tour round the solar system. Then each and every one of us selfishly prays that the damn antique doesn't break down before it drops off our own particular package. Tip for you, Lieutenant: when you're in the company of Earth's astronomers don't ever mention the 2320 placement mission. A lot of colleagues left the profession after that minor catastrophe. It takes on average fifteen years of applications, proposals, review procedures, outright begging and signing away your firstborn to get a sensor project approved, then all you have to do is find the funds to design and build it. There's an awful lot of emotional and professional investment riding away in that cargo bay.'

'Yes,' Renne said defensively; her headache was now pounding away inside her skull. She was sure she'd brought a packet of tifi. It was probably in her jacket pocket, hanging up several yards away – too far for her to walk. 'Thank you, I get the picture. Yours is not an overpaid celebrity occupation.'

'Not unless your name is Bose, no.'

'So to conclude, you have no idea what you've been receiving from Mars for twenty years?'

Jennifer Seitz gave an apologetic smile. 'That's about it. Although I'd like to go on record as saying I've only been Director here for seven years, with two years absent for rejuvenation. I didn't take the contract, and none of us were involved with it. The whole thing is run by a couple of subroutines in the RI.'

'Who did begin the contract?'

'Director Rowell was in charge when the Lambeth Association began the project. I think he moved to Berkak, he was offered a dean's post at a new university.'

'Thank you, I'll have him questioned.' Renne sucked down more thin air, the lack of oxygen was making her feel light-headed. It wasn't an unpleasant sensation, but her thoughts were sluggish. 'Tell me something. In your opinion, what could possibly be on Mars that would interest a bunch of terrorists like the Guardians?'

'That's the really dumb thing about this: nothing. And I'm not being prejudiced because I'm a radio astronomer. The place is a complete dump, a frozen airless desert. I mean, come on here. The whole thing is ridiculous; it has no secrets, no value, no relevance to anybody. I'm still half-convinced you people made a mistake.'

'Then tell me about Cufflin.'

Jennifer Seitz screwed her pretty face up. 'God, I don't know. He was just a technical assistant; a mundane time-serving tech working in a pisspoor Science Agency job to pay his R&R pension. Up until yesterday I would have sworn I could have told you his entire lives stories better than he could. And incredibly boring they all were, too. We all spend three weeks on duty crammed together up here, for which we get one blessed week off. He was actually assigned here three and a half years ago. So I don't like to think how much time that means we've spent living, sleeping and eating in this very same building since then. Now it turns out he was part of some terrorist plot to take over the Commonwealth. Jesus! He's Dan Cufflin. Seven years short of rejuvenation, and desperate for it to happen. He loves curry, hates Chinese food, accesses way too much softcore TSI soap, had one wife this life which ended sour, visits his one grandkid every year at Easter, his feet smell, he's a second-rate programmer, an average mechanic, and drives the rest of us nuts practising tap dancing – badly. What the hell kind of terrorist enjoys tap dancing?'

'Bad ones,' Renne said dryly.

'I can't believe he did this.'

'Well, it certainly looks like he's guilty. We'll confirm that for ourselves, of course. I expect you'll all be called as witnesses at the trial.'

'You're taking him with you?'

'I certainly am.'

*

Somehow, Renne managed to hobble her way back to the VTOL plane, without being too obvious as she leaned up against Phil Mandia. Two navy officers escorted Dan Cufflin onto the plane behind her. He was pushed down into a chair on the other side of the aisle from Renne. Malmetal restraints flowed over his wrists and lower legs, holding him secure. Not that he looked as if he'd make a break for freedom. Jennifer Seitz had been right about that. Cufflin was very obviously approaching the time when he needed a rejuvenation, a tall man who had managed to avoid becoming overweight. Worry and a defeated air made his cheeks and eyes seem excessively sunken, with flesh that was as pallid as Renne's. Being dressed in a pair of worn dark-blue overalls simply helped to complete the whipped underdog image.

He looked out of the small window as they took off, a bewildered expression in place as the Observatory dropped away below.

Renne's headache had started to fade as soon as the hatch was shut, and the jets began to pressurize the little cabin. She opened the vent above her seat, and smiled contentedly as the filtered air blew over her face. A coffee from the stewardess eased away the last of the discomfort, without any need for a tifi tube.

'The flight should take about fifty minutes,' she said, and turned her head towards Cufflin. 'We're going to Rio; then a loop train to Paris.'

He said nothing, his gaze fixed on some spot outside the window as they climbed into the stratosphere at a steep angle.

'You know what's going to happen when we get there?' she enquired lightly.

'You walk me past a warm judge and shoot me.'

'No, Dan. We'll take you to a navy biomedical facility where you'll have your memories read. By all accounts, it's not a pleasant experience. Losing control over your very own mind, having other people invade your skull and examining any section of your life they want. Nothing is private; your feelings, your dreams. We rip them all out of you.'

'Great. I always had an exhibitionist streak.'

'No you don't.' She sighed in a sympathetic manner. 'I accessed your file, I've talked to your workmates. What are you doing mixed up in all this nonsense?'

He looked over at her. 'Your interrogation technique is crap, you know that?'

'I'm not an experienced spook like you, Dan.'

'Very funny. I'm not a spook. I'm not a terrorist. I'm not a traitor. I'm none of those things.'

'Then what are you?'

'You read my file.'

'Remind me.'

'Why?'

'All right, the bottom line is this: cooperate, spill your guts and your heart out to me and I might recommend we don't bother with a memory read. But your story had better be a damn good one.'

'And my trial?'

'I'm not cutting you a deal, Dan; it doesn't work like that. You go to trial whatever happens. But if you help us, then I'm sure the judge will take that into consideration.'

He took a minute, but eventually gave a soft nod. 'I have a grandson, Jacob. He's eight.'

'Yes?'

'I had to go to court to get access to him. Damnit, he's all I've got left from this screw-up of a life, the only decent thing anyway. It'd kill me not to be able to see him. Have you got children, Lieutenant?'

'Some, yes. None this time round, yet. But they all have children. I'm a great-great-grandmother these days.'

'And do you see them all? Your family?'

'When I have the time. This job, you know … It isn't a nine to five.'

'But you get to see them, that's what counts. My daughter took her mother's side. And we're all native Earthborn, that's the problem. You need to be a millionaire just to get an appointment with a lawyer on this planet. And I'm not.'

'So someone offered you some money? Enough for a lawyer to get you access?'

'Yeah.'

'Who?'

'I don't know his name, I never met him, he's just an address code in the unisphere. He's an agent for people in the personal security field. A friend told me about him. Said he might be able to help me.'

'Okay, the name?'

'Robin Beard.'

'So this agent recruited you?'

'Yes?'

'To do what?'

'The way he put it, virtually nothing. I was worried I'd have to kill somebody – probably would have done it, too. But all he wanted was for me to apply for the UFN Science Agency technical maintenance job out at the Observatory. I had to monitor the Martian data they were receiving, make sure there were no problems. He said that one day somebody would come and collect a copy of it, and when that happened I was to erase the original. That was it, all I had to do. And for that I got to see little Jacob again, once a year at Easter. It's hardly a massive crime, so I figured what the hell.'

'All right, Dan, now this is the really important bit: do you know what that data was?'

'No.' He pursed his lips as he shook his head. 'No, I swear. I tried looking at it a couple of times. I mean, it was obviously valuable to the agent, but it just looked like ordinary remote station data to me.'

'Did you make your own copy, Dan, maybe try for a bit of leverage?'

'No. I got to see my Jacob like they promised. So I played fair with them. I didn't think they're the kind of people you should try and cross. I guess I was right about that; you said they're terrorists.'

The answer vexed Renne; she had a nasty feeling he was telling the truth. Dan Cufflin wasn't criminal enough to try a little spot of blackmail on his own initiative, just a weak desperate man easy to exploit if you knew which buttons to press. And who was ever going to be looking for some sleeper in a radio telescope observatory in the middle of the Andes?

Whatever the Guardians had done on Mars, they'd made a damn good job of covering their tracks. *Until someone murdered Kazimir McFoster.*

*

A day later she was still puzzling over how that killing fitted in to an otherwise watertight operation. The Paris office was investigating the case on a twenty-four seven basis, backed with the highest navy priority; nobody in accounts was going to question budget or timesheets on this one.

Late morning she caught herself yawning as her console screens pulled up yet another sequence of information on the illusive Lambeth Interplanetary Association. There was only so much coffee she could take to counter the fatigue toxins accumulating in her bloodstream. It was another grey Paris spring day outside, with rain running down the windows. Inside, her colleagues were getting cranky from lack of sleep and frustration at the loss of the assassin in LA Galactic. There'd been more than one argument shouted between desks that morning. And no one's humour had been soothed by a report on their office featuring heavily on the Alessandra Baron show. The beautifully poised presenter had taken particularly malicious delight showing how the murderer had struck his victim down whilst surrounded by Navy Intelligence officers, before making good his escape. She also hinted that the LA Galactic killer was wanted for questioning in connection with the Burnelli murder.

'Where does she get this from?' Tarlo had growled. 'That's classified.'

'The Burnelli family, probably,' Renne said. 'I don't think we're terribly popular with them right now. After all, that was Justine's toy boy that got slaughtered. She's probably angling for the case to be turned over to Senate Security.'

Tarlo lowered his voice, glancing round guiltily in case anyone else overheard. 'I found out while you were away in South America; the boss is receiving all our data as and when we file it. Hogan's been going quietly crazy knowing she's watching everything over his shoulder.'

'Finally,' she murmured. 'Some good news. Has she contacted you?'

'Not yet? You?'

'No.'

'If she does, tell her I'll help her any way I can.'

'Will do.'

They parted like a couple having an illicit office romance, both trying not to smile.

*

Commander Alic Hogan arrived back at the Paris office just after lunch. He was in a bad mood, he knew he was in a bad mood, and he knew being in a bad mood was bad for a decent office environment. Frankly, he didn't give a shit. He'd just got back from Kerensk where he'd spent an hour in Admiral Columbia's office trying to explain the LA Galactic *fuck-up* –

the admiral's personal description. He knew of no reason why he shouldn't spread the misery.

Everybody in the big open-plan office looked up from their displays as he came in. He caught quite a few smirks that were hurriedly smothered. 'Senior officers, progress meeting in conference room three: ten minutes,' he announced as he stomped through into his own office. There were muttered comments behind him, which he didn't bother with.

Alic settled into the chair behind the desk, the kind of ordinary black leather office furniture a secretary would have. It was left over from Paula Myo's tenure, and he hadn't got round to replacing it yet. Like everything in the office. *Including the people.*

He took advantage of the solitude to rest his head in his hands, making an effort to dump his emotional baggage and focus. Taking over the Paris office had been such a huge opportunity. The navy was growing at a phenomenal rate, and he was on the inside track, moving up fast. Attaching himself to Columbia's staff had been the smartest thing he'd ever done back in the days when it was the Directorate. He'd done a lot of troubleshooting for Director Columbia, filing reports on nearly every division. It made him an automatic choice to keep an eye on Paula Myo after Rees left. Now he could finally appreciate what she'd been up against all those decades.

Christ, is this how Myo felt for a hundred and thirty years? The way the assassin had eluded them at LA Galactic wasn't so much amazing as downright insulting. And judging by how his escape route was so immaculately planned out, he had to have known the navy was observing McFoster. Which implied there really was a leak somewhere. The one thing Alic could never tell the admiral, not until after he had absolute proof, and preferably a full confession as well. There was also the extreme problem of exactly who the assassin was working for. The most obvious conclusion, the one Myo had settled for, was politically impossible. He could never admit that to anyone. The idea was career suicide.

He simply had to get the whole Guardians situation under control, report some solid progress to the admiral. If there weren't any results – and fast – he'd be following Myo out of the door. And he was pretty certain nobody would be offering him a cushy job in Senate Security.

On the plus side, the fallout from LA Galactic had produced a good range of leads into various Guardians' operations and personnel. His Paris officers were good, despite the bitterness left from Myo's forced departure. All he had to do was ensure they had the resources to complete their various investigations, and coordinate a decent strategy for the overall case. There would be results that would cut deep into the Guardians' organization. *There had to be.*

Alic drank down a full glass of mineral water, hoping it would calm him and get him into the right frame of mind to chair the meeting. Maybe he was just dehydrated, it had been a hectic twenty-four hours. When he was ready, he headed for the conference room. Renne Kempasa was in front of him, carrying a tall mug of coffee.

Tarlo and John King were already waiting inside. John had been an investigator in the old Directorate, moving over from technical forensic department a couple of months before the administrative changes began. The timing of that move meant he wasn't quite as frosty towards Alic as the other two senior lieutenants.

'Too much caffeine,' Tarlo said loudly as Renne sat down. 'That's what, your eighth this morning?'

She glowered at him. 'I either drink this or I start smoking. Your call.'

John laughed at the shocked expression on Tarlo's face.

Alic Hogan went in and sat at the head of the white table. 'The admiral is not pleased with us at all,' he told them. 'A fact which he made very clear to me, as I'm sure you can appreciate. So . . . somebody please tell me we have finally got a name for our assassin.'

'Sorry, chief,' John King said. 'His face isn't on any database in the Commonwealth. It's a reprofile job, of course. We've probably got him under his old identity. But his current features are completely unknown.'

'Not so,' Renne said. 'McFoster knew him. In fact he was glad to see him. Overjoyed, actually. For my money, our assassin is from Far Away.'

'Who on Far Away is going to send an assassin into the Commonwealth?' John asked.

She shrugged. 'Don't know, but at the very least we should check CST's records to see if he came through the Boongate station in the last couple of years.'

'All right, I'll get my people on that,' John said. 'Foster Cortese is running visual recognition programs for me, he can add the Boongate database to his analysis.'

'Good,' Alic said. 'Now, what about the equipment he was wetwired with? We all saw what he was capable of. That stuff was cutting edge; there has to be some sort of record.'

'Jim Nwan is following that up for me,' Tarlo said. 'There are plenty of companies across the Commonwealth who manufacture that kind of armament. I didn't realize. A lot of it is supplied to Grand Families and Intersolar Dynasties for their security divisions. Tracing the end user through them is difficult, they're not being very cooperative. Then there's always Illuminatus, the clinics there are even less friendly.'

'If anyone blocks you, let me know right away,' Alic told him. 'The admiral's office will apply some pressure directly.'

'Sure.'

'Right, Renne, what did you turn up at the Observatory?'

'Quite a lot, though I'm not sure how much of it is relevant.'

'Let's hear it.'

She sipped at her coffee, wincing at how hot it was. 'First, we confirmed what McFoster collected: a whole load of data that they'd been storing. Apparently it all came from Mars.'

'Mars?' Alic frowned. 'What the fuck is on Mars?'

'That's where we start running into problems. We don't know. The data was transmitted from a remote science station. Officially, it was a project sponsored by the Lambeth Interplanetary Society to investigate the Martian environment. The station has been transmitting the signals for twenty years, supposedly from automated sensors dotted all over the planet.'

'Did you say twenty years?'

'Yeah,' she said sardonically. 'However, the Lambeth Interplanetary Society no longer exists, it went virtual eight years ago; today it's just a named address logged with an equally bogus legal firm. There's an administration program overseeing a bank account with just enough money deposited to pay for the Mars project to its conclusion. The Observatory gets its annual fee, and if anyone calls the Association with a query the program has a menu of stock replies. In other words, it's a typical Guardians' front operation.'

'Was it ever real?' Alic asked.

'When it was set up, yes. There was a physical office in London, along with staff. I've got Gwyneth trying to track down anyone who was employed there, we're hoping to turn up a secretary or some junior staff member. It's not promising; anyone important would be a Guardian, the rest would be offworlders on a standard employment visa. As there aren't any records, we're checking with offworld employment placement agencies.'

'Why did the Guardians abandon the Association office if the Observatory is still collecting data for them?' John asked.

'The switch coincides with the last set of instruments being sent to Mars,' Renne said. 'They paid for a lot of packages to be deployed in their first twelve years. You can't do that entirely through the cybersphere, there have to be meetings, actual people to talk to the UFN Science Agency staff and take them out to lunch, attend seminars, designers for the sensors packages, that kind of thing.'

'So there are records of what they shipped out to Mars?' Alic asked. He didn't like the implications of how big the Guardians' operation was; nor that it involved something new, something they couldn't understand. That was too many negatives to file in any report to the admiral.

'We have UFN Science Agency manifests for their transport ships,' she said. 'As to what was actually placed on board at the time, there is no way of knowing. Those ships travel all over the solar system, the planetary instruments they deploy are packed in secure containers inside one-shot landers. Nobody at lunarport would ever break open a sealed system as they load it on a ship, there's no reason.'

'You're telling me that the Guardians have been running an operation here in the solar system for twenty years right under our noses, and we still don't know what it is?' Alic stopped, he didn't want to come over as critical, they had to work together on this. 'What about other planets? Are the Guardians running operations on them?'

'It doesn't look like it,' Renne said. 'Matthew Oldfield is running verification on all the solar planetary projects the UFN Science Agency knows about; so far they look legitimate. It was only Mars.'

'But there's no way of knowing what they placed there?'

'No, short of physically visiting and inspecting the equipment. But the systems have been returning data for two decades, and were scheduled to continue for another ten years. I can't see that they'd be any sort of weapon. To be honest I don't see it's worth wasting any more of our resources on; whatever it was, the whole project is obviously over.'

'I can't agree with that,' Tarlo said. 'They've been running this for twenty years. It's got to be important to them. That means we have to find out what it was.'

'It was the data which was important,' Renne replied. 'That's what they were after. And now it's gone. Cufflin wiped the Observatory memory, and McFoster didn't have it on him when he was killed.'

Alic didn't like the reminder that McFoster appeared to be carrying nothing, although that whole issue was blowing up into a big political fight between the admiral and the Burnellis. He certainly didn't want to drag the Paris office into that, and he could almost agree with Renne about Mars being a waste of their resources to chase up. But . . . twenty years. Johansson had obviously thought it extremely important. 'What about this Cufflin character? Have we had a memory read off him yet?'

'I don't see the point,' Renne said. 'He told me everything voluntarily on the flight back to Rio. We pumped him full of drugs here, and he repeated the same story. He was just a paid accomplice; he's not big time. My recommendation is charge him with criminal conspiracy, and let the courts sort out what happens next.'

'If you don't think he's any more use, then fine.' Alic told his e-butler to make a note.

'He did produce one useful name,' Renne said. 'Robin Beard. He was the intermediary who put Cufflin in touch with the anonymous agent who set up the whole deal. Now this is only a hunch, but several of the team involved in the assault on the *Second Chance* were recruited through an agent who specialized in security operatives, and who, also, was very careful to remain anonymous. Could be coincidence, but they were both Guardians' operations.'

'Do we know where this Robin Beard is?' Alic asked; he tried not to seem too excited, that would be unprofessional, but the agent did sound like a very promising lead.

'I've got Vic Russell working on it as a priority. Last known address was on Cagayn. Vic's on the express out there now; there's a liaison with local police already set up.'

'Excellent.'

'What about Mars?' Tarlo asked. 'We can't just ignore it.'

'Well here's the interesting thing,' Renne said. 'Cufflin never transmitted anything to Mars through the Observatory link, no coded instruction to shut down. So, in theory, the remote station and whatever the Guardians placed there is still operating. It'll send another signal in eight days' time. The UFN Science Agency are putting together a group of planetary scientists to analyse the data for us and see if it is from environmental sensors.'

'Eight days?' Tarlo said scathingly. 'Come on! Commander, they were desperate for this data. We have to investigate this now.'

Alic wanted to agree, but the cost of actually sending a forensic team to Mars would be phenomenal. Diverting a CST wormhole, even an exploration division one, would cost millions. That kind of procedure would have to be authorized by the admiral. 'Why can't the Observatory get in touch with the Mars remote station today? There must be some kind of communication protocol to run diagnostics on the systems up there. It's got to be cheaper, probably quicker, too.'

Renne gave a shrug. 'I suppose so. I can ask Jennifer Seitz, the Director.'

'Do that. Let me know.' He smiled in satisfaction. Good clean decisions, proper leadership: everyone profited.

'Sure.' She took another sip of her coffee.

'Some good news for you, chief,' Tarlo said. He shot Renne a malicious smile across the table.

'Go.'

'We're making headway on McFoster's financial data records. I need a warrant to open his accounts at Pacific Pine Bank, they're guarded. Once we can study his spending pattern we can draw up a profile of his movements. We'll also find out where his money came from.'

'One-time account, cash deposit,' Renne said, and grinned over the top of her mug. 'They always are. Untraceable.'

Tarlo showed her a stiff finger.

'You'll get the warrant in an hour,' Alic promised. 'All right, this isn't as bleak as it looked back there in the junction. We can crack this, I know we can.'

2

Technically, the War Cabinet should have had its meeting in the Presidential Palace on New Rio, because the President herself was the chair, and ultimately held responsibility for all Commonwealth policy. That was the structure laid out in the Commonwealth constitution. Realpolitik was a little different.

None of the Intersolar Dynasty leaders present, Nigel Sheldon, Heather Antonia Halgarth, Alan Hutchinson, and Hans Brant, were keen to be absent from their respective planets for long. And as Earth provided direct train links to all the Big15, it was their preferred choice of world. The senators, Justine Burnelli, Crispin Goldreich, and Ramon DB, were based on Earth anyway. And the two admirals, Kime and Columbia, certainly didn't have the clout to nominate anywhere, not after the public beating the navy was taking after the Lost23 – however unfair it might have been.

Patricia Kantil had no option but to bow to the majority. It might have been the navy that was taking the brunt of the criticism in the media, but the unisphere polls were revealing a significant percentage questioning the overall leadership. Much as it irked her, she arranged for the meeting to be held at the Senate Hall in Washington DC.

The participants assembled in one of those secure underground rooms so beloved of governments whenever they constructed emergency facilities. In an age when force fields could deflect atom laser shots and hundred megaton blasts with relative ease, Patricia didn't really see the point of digging out warrens of rooms a hundred metres below the ageing Senate Hall building. But, nonetheless, that was where they all congregated.

If it hadn't been for the lack of windows, the chamber could have been any high-status corporate boardroom. A long tarnwood table, polished so that its purple grain gleamed in the strong lighting, with twelve plush leather chairs. Portraits of every past Senate First Minister hung on the walls to gaze down at the table with various expressions of superiority. An emerald carpet patterned with a huge Intersolar Commonwealth seal covered the floor. All very sombre and expensive; typical of a budget which would never be held up to public scrutiny.

The War Cabinet all stood when Elaine Doi entered the room. Following two paces behind her, Patricia was quietly pleased to see that courtesy was extended at least; the true powers in the Commonwealth were still acknowledging formal procedures – for the moment. None of the other cabinet members had aides with them, Patricia was the only one. She couldn't actually recall being in the physical presence of quite so many masterclass players before. It was intimidating, even for someone as familiar with the process of high government as her. And she knew Elaine was nervous; for once not just about her own term. The latest batch of statistics from the Prime assault were shocking.

Elaine took her place at the head of the table and asked the others to be seated. Patricia sat at her left, with the First Minister, Oliver Tam, on her right. The tall double doors closed, and the chamber was automatically screened. Everyone lost contact with the unisphere.

'Isn't the SI attending?' Crispin asked churlishly.

Elaine glanced at Patricia and gave a small nod of permission. 'Not at this stage,' Patricia said. 'Although it appears to be as disturbed as we are by the invasion, and it provided a great deal of assistance at the time, we still cannot be certain about its ultimate allegiance. As it is humans who are facing the brunt of the Prime attack, we feel that we alone should determine our response. If we decide we need its aid or advice, we will of course ask. Until then, the fundamental decision making process should be ours and ours alone.'

If Crispin was annoyed at her reply, he didn't show it.

'Thank you,' Elaine said. 'I now call this first meeting of the War Cabinet to order. It is here today that we must determine the nature of our response to the clear and absolute threat posed by the Prime aliens. I don't feel I understate the enormity of the task we face when I say the outcome of this meeting could well determine not just the future of humanity as a species, but even if we have a future. The decisions we are faced with will be extremely difficult, and no doubt unpopular in some quarters. I for one am quite prepared to sacrifice popularist action in preference to doing what is both right and necessary. I would like to call on Admiral Kime to give us a brief summary of the terrible assault we have endured, and then the navy's analysis of what we might expect next from the Primes. When we have all absorbed that, I shall open the floor to policy decisions. Admiral.'

'Thank you, Madam President.' Wilson looked round the table, saddened at the lack of friendly faces. 'We all know it was bad. We knew the size of the Prime civilization at Dyson Alpha, and the kind of resources it has available to it, yet our initial preparation was wholly inadequate. The reason for that is quite simple, we refused to believe that an attack on this scale would ever happen. There simply is no rational explanation for it. We have seen that the Prime civilization's industrial capacity is probably equal to if not larger than that of the entire Commonwealth. If they needed expansion space and more material resources, then it would be considerably cheaper for them to exploit star systems next to their own, rather than come after ours. Yet they chose not to follow a logical development pattern. They found out about us from Bose and Verbeken, and almost the first thing they did was build a series of wormholes to reach us. It looks as if the worst case scenario for the envelopment was right, someone set up the barrier around Dyson Alpha to keep them contained.'

'What about Dyson Beta?' Alan Hutchinson asked.

'It remains an unknown,' Wilson said. 'As does the reason for the Dyson Alpha barrier coming down. What we have to address today is the consequence of the Primes being freed. As a result of their attack, we now estimate the human death toll on the Lost23 planets to be approximately thirty-seven million.'

There was total silence around the table. Most of the cabinet stared down at the glossy wooden surface, not wanting to make eye contact with each other.

Wilson cleared his throat self-consciously and continued. 'From the nature of the attacks, and the intelligence we have gathered subsequently, it appears that the aim of the Primes is to secure the industrial facilities on the Lost23 planets. Unlike us, they don't appear to care about preserving the planetary environments. What we saw of their homeworld seems to support this; it was massively industrialized, and the pollution was orders of magnitude beyond anything we experienced here on Earth during the worst of the twenty-first century. Their priorities, therefore, are completely different to ours. That made them very difficult to predict. However, now they are in the open and we're able to observe their activities directly, we can determine what actions they will have to pursue next. For instance, they will have to build up their occupation forces on the Lost23 in order to utilize them properly and secure them against any counter strike we make. They will also mount a second attack against the Commonwealth, then a third, and a fourth. They will keep on attacking and pushing us back and back onto fewer worlds until we have none left.'

'What makes you certain of that?' Heather asked.

'We are at war,' Wilson said. He saw her glossed lips tighten at the phrase, censure leaking out of the flawless skin of her mid-fifties face like trace pheromones. Even though she was in a chic formal dark blue suit with her ginger hair folded into a neat braid, there was no way of disguising the authority she possessed. Heather was the only female head of a Big15 Intersolar Dynasty, her feminine appearance a very thin cloak worn over ruthless ambition and a razor-sharp political instinct. Just like him, and everyone else seated round the table, she hated being given bad news.

'War by its nature cannot be a static situation,' he continued, meeting her stare levelly. 'They know that we will never accept the loss of those twenty-three planets. Either they continue to expand across the Commonwealth, wiping us out of galactic history, or we will do the same to them.'

'Are you suggesting we commit genocide against them?' Ramon DB asked lightly.

'Are you suggesting we become the victims of genocide?' Wilson countered. 'This is not a war as we have fought them before. This is not a strategic struggle over key resources, we're not fighting for control over tribal lands, or trade routes to the new colonies. Both us and the Primes are intersolar, there is no shortage of anything in the galaxy. They came here with one purpose, to kill us and to capture our worlds.'

'In that case we have experienced an analogous war in our history,' Hans Brant said. 'It would seem as if they are waging a religious crusade against us.'

'You could be right,' Wilson said. 'Religion or some ideological variant of it was certainly one of the more popular theories among the strategic analysis teams. Their motivation can't easily be explained any other way.'

'We can worry about the reason later,' Nigel said. 'You've summarized where we stand. What does the navy want to do next? What do you need?'

'We're proposing to meet the Prime aggression with a three stage approach. First a heavy infiltration and sabotage offensive on the Lost23; tie the Primes up on each planet, slow them down, divert their resources away from readying their next attack while we prepare for stage two.'

'I'm curious about the kind of forces you envisage to pull that off,' Alan Hutchinson said.

'Commando-style troop units will be dropped onto the Lost23 through wormholes that will open for a very short duration. They'll cause as much disruption as possible, combined with a comprehensive intelligence-gathering operation. So far we know very little about the Primes. This should help expand our knowledge base considerably. We're hoping to perform several snatch missions so we can begin interrogation and memory-reading procedures.'

'Just what kind of numbers are you talking about here?' Alan asked keenly. 'To make any decent impact you're going to need a lot of these guerrilla fighters.'

'We're planning on sending an initial force of around ten thousand troops to each planet.'

'Ten thous— Christ, man, you're talking about raising an army of a quarter of a million people.'

'We don't see that as a problem,' Rafael said smoothly. 'The new navy ground troop service will be opened to volunteers from the general population, of course; and history shows we'll have a great many aspirants. Even multi-lifers tend to get aggressive when threatened. And, just in case, we have a large reserve of people who can be more easily persuaded, people in fact more suited to this kind of work than most.' He opened his hands wide in reasonable appeal. 'Please, most of the last few days have been spent drawing up these responses, and examining their feasibility; we're not throwing out panic ideas here. Deploying these troops is not only possible, it is essential. We must regain the initiative.'

'Very well,' Hans said. 'What's stage two?'

'A fleet,' Wilson said flatly. 'A very big fleet of warships. Not the kind we have now. We need to approach this from a radical perspective. We have to consider starships like the *Second Chance* and the *StAsaph* as our Kittyhawks, not even prototypes. We were lazy back then, putting together what we could with damn near off-the-shelf components.' He glanced over at Nigel. 'I'm not criticizing; they were right for the time; but this is a new age that could well see us obliterated if we don't recognize it. We need fast ships, not with marque 5 or 6 hyperdrives that are on the drawing board; I need a marque 10 or more, a speed that can take us to Dyson Alpha in a week. They've got to be well protected, shields as strong as the original Dyson barriers were. They've got to have real weaponry, not nuclear missiles, not energy beams; give me relativistic attack drones, each warship loaded with a salvo of a hundred of the damn things which can all strike with the same power the *Desperado* unleashed. And most of all, I need thousands of them; not dozens, not hundreds: thousands – enough to challenge that goddamn armada of ordinary ships which the Primes have. During their attack on the Lost23, they sent over thirty thousand ships through those wormholes; and they've got a hundred times that many back in their home system. If we're going to go up against them, then we need to put the industrial output equivalent to a Big15 behind this effort, churn them out the way we do cars and trains.

'Ftl ships are the sole advantage we have over the Primes right now. They don't have them. If we can get that advanced technology working and deployed then we stand a chance. With the kind of strike mobility I'm talking about we can out-manoeuvre them at a strategic level. We can block their next attack – that's our second stage. Then after that we can scour space between here and Dyson Alpha to find out where that bastard Hell's Gateway staging post is, and destroy it – stage three, threat elimination.'

'Sounds good to me,' Nigel said, he nodded his approval.

'At least you're talking the talk, thinking outside the box. We need that badly.'

'It's bloody expensive talk,' Crispin murmured.

'I don't believe you just said that,' Justine shot at him, the unexpected sharpness in her tone made everyone turn to look at her; it was pure Gore. 'Thirty-seven million humans dead, and you're complaining about the cost of defending ourselves. Didn't your hear what the admiral just told us? The alternative is death. Real death, not just an inconvenient sleep-of-absence while your clinic grows you a new body. You will die, Crispin. And *that* lasts for ever.'

'I wasn't saying it was too expensive, my dear. I'd just like to point out that our finances will have to undergo a similar radical restructuring to pay for it. That's if this wonderful new technology can be made to work.' He looked pointedly at Nigel, then Wilson.

'The theories are perfect,' Nigel said evenly. 'Getting them to work in practice, well, Crispin, that's where all your money comes in.'

'It'll be your taxes that get raised,' Crispin pointed out.

'And do you really think any of us give a flying fuck about that right now? Get the Treasury to crunch the numbers, slap twenty or forty per cent on taxes, work out the loans and bonds issues we'll have to float. Nobody cares about the inflation or recession or unsustainable growth it'll cause. None of that crap matters if we lose. If we don't have the money available to make this work there won't be any finance market. We'll be dead; we at this table have to recognize this even if we can never say so in public.'

'It's not just finance,' Heather said. She nodded in Wilson's direction. 'I like your thinking on this.'

'Team effort,' he grunted.

'Sure, but your team's heading in the right direction. We have to think way out of the left field and cooperate for a change. What gives me a fright is trying to realign our manufacturing capacity on this scale. It won't be smooth, yet it must be done.'

'The SI could probably help,' Oliver Tam said.

'Possibly,' Heather said. She sounded like a schoolmistress displeased with a disruptive pupil. She exchanged a look with the other three Dynasty heads. 'We'll need to pull the rest into line.'

'They're smart enough,' Nigel said. 'And we have our own arrangements between ourselves.'

Heather gave a small shrug.

'What about the refugee situation?' Ramon DB inquired. 'What place do they have in all these plans? Right now we have the entire surviving population from the Lost23 saturating the rest of the Commonwealth; they have no home, no jobs, no life left. They look to us, to government, for leadership; some acknowledgement of their plight. There are hundreds of thousands of people flooding into Silvergalde; which can't cope. I'm told the outside of Lyddington is beginning to resemble some kind of medieval refugee camp, with no water, no sanitation, and precious little food. And there's the one big problem which I haven't heard raised here today; the displacement. People on every world within a hundred light-years of the Lost23 are either taking vacations on the other side of the Commonwealth or trying to sell up and buy a house on a world where they think they're going to be safe. They are afraid, and with good reason. What do we do about this? We must show them we know and understand their situation. That we will take action to resolve it.'

'Not today, and not in here,' President Doi said.

It was said in such a decisive and firm manner that she drew surprised glances from several people round the table. Ramon actually opened his mouth in astonishment.

'This is the War Cabinet, Senator Ramon,' she said. 'In here we decide military strategy, that's all. The displaced are an item for the general civil cabinet, if not a full debate in the Senate.'

'But they do impinge on military matters,' Ramon said. 'They will affect the whole economy.'

'No,' Elaine said quickly. 'The numbers are huge, admittedly. But in overall percentage terms they barely register. I will not let this cabinet get bogged down by the minutiae of problems which are not in its direct remit. You are out of order, Senator, please give the floor to someone else.'

Alan was making little attempt to hide his smile; one or two of the others looked mildly bemused. A positive and decisive Doi was not something they'd encountered very often. Realizing her sudden authority, she asked: 'Admiral Columbia, do you envisage any policy change to our current planetary defences?'

'No changes, ma'am. The force fields were extremely successful, even on the Lost23. We have plans to upgrade all city and civil area force fields, anticipating the Primes will launch a second attack. Arms manufacturers are also increasing production of combat aerobots for us, which proved invaluable during the preliminary bombardment. Electronic warfare systems are also a priority. But those are all purely defensive systems, all they can do is minimize damage in the event of an attack. To stop the attack we need that fleet.'

'Point taken, Admiral. I think we can move to a vote on the overall strategy.'

'I would also like to mention stage four,' Columbia said.

'Stage four?'

'Yes ma'am. The Seattle Project. The kind of weapon we can use to take the fight directly to Dyson Alpha.'

'I wasn't aware we'd even reached prototype stage yet.'

'Hopefully, it will arrive within a few months,' Wilson said. 'You know physicists, they don't like deadlines. Not that they ever meet them anyway.'

'So it's not something we have to consider immediately?' the President asked.

'No,' Wilson agreed cautiously. 'But Admiral Columbia is right. Ultimately, we may have to take the decision to use it.'

'We can fight them with warships,' Columbia said. 'We can slow them down, we can possibly even force them back, though any prolonged war will be extremely costly to us, and not just in monetary terms. But if ultimately they prove implacably hostile to us, for whatever reason, then it will have to be used.'

'Genocide,' Elaine whispered. 'Dear God.'

'It would be a collective decision,' Hans told her. 'We would take it together, and share it with you.'

'The Seattle project should continue to receive top priority,' Columbia said.

'Yes,' the President said, charily. 'Very well, if no one else has any issues, I'd like to proceed to a vote on Admiral Kime's proposal for a three stage approach to engaging the Prime threat.'

'Proposed,' Heather said.

'Seconded,' Alan said.

'Very well,' the President said. 'Those in favour?' She counted the raised hands. 'Unanimous.'

*

Outside the cabinet room, little groups of aides were hanging around in the long corridor gossiping with each other. When the doors opened, they all quietened up and waited for their respective chief to walk past, before attaching themselves like so many iron filings. Justine had almost reached Sue Piken and Ross Gant-Wainright, the two senior staffers she'd inherited with Thompson's office, when Ramon DB caught up with her.

'That was unlike you,' he said softly.

Justine stopped and gave him an impatient look, all ready

to give him a snappy answer. The bright overhead lighting glinted off small droplets of sweat on his brow. His midnight black OCtattoos were now quite visible across his cheeks and hands, a result of his previously ebony skin acquiring a greyish pallor. When she glanced down, she could see how tight his generous robe was. Her annoyance drained away. 'You look tired,' she said, and put a hand on his arm. 'I don't suppose you've been taking it easy?'

He smiled fondly. 'Have you?'

'My body is in its early twenties again. I can do the late nights and stress. You can't.'

'Please, don't go reminding me about your body at that age.' He put one hand playfully over his chest. 'My heart can only take so much. By the way, you look tremendous in black.'

'Rammy! Look at those rings; you'll never get them off, your fingers have swollen so much.' She took his hand and held on to it, examining the jewellery that was almost buried by pulpy flesh.

He squirmed like a guilty child. 'Don't nag, woman.'

'I'm not nagging. I'm telling you this straight; either you start looking after yourself or I personally will cart you off to the clinic for rejuvenation.'

'As if either of us can take time off for that right now.' He paused, uncertain of himself. 'I heard about LA Galactic. Talk in the Senate dining room is that you knew the boy who was killed.'

'Yeah, I knew him. I was the one who put Navy Intelligence on him.'

Ramon gave her black dress a suspicious stare. 'I hope you're not blaming yourself for his death.'

'No.'

'You forget, my dear, I really do know you.'

'Did the Senate dining room know that the boy was killed by the same person who killed Thompson?'

'Yes. We're quietly but firmly pressing Senate Security for

some results.' He lowered his voice to a whisper. 'Confidence in both branches of the navy is not terribly high right now.'

'It'll improve.' For a moment Justine considered telling him about the Starflyer; Ramon would make a superb ally in the Senate, but he really wasn't in good shape, and that would just add to his burden. *Not yet*, she told herself. 'I'm sorry Doi cut you off in there,' she said. 'I believe we do need to consider the refugee problem.'

'Actually, she was right to say that,' he said, and smiled broadly. 'I'm just not used to our dear President being quite so forceful. It could well be we have waved goodbye to a politician and got a stateswoman in return. Now, that would be a first.'

'We'll see. I'm not sure I believe in an age of miracles just yet. But I'll be happy to back you up in the Senate on some kind of aid package for the refugees.' She caught sight of Wilson Kime talking to Crispin, and leant forward to give Ramon a quick kiss. 'I have to go. I'll see you in the dining room, yes?'

'Of course.'

Justine hurried over to Wilson as he and Crispin shook hands. Several aides were waiting to pounce, and she could see Columbia coming out of the cabinet room. She wasn't quite up to another direct confrontation with him right now.

'Admiral, could we talk for a moment, please?'

Wilson nodded amicably. 'Certainly, Senator.'

'In private, there's a conference room just down here.'

Wilson's hesitation was hardly noticeable. 'Very well.'

Justine's e-butler gave the door an open code. Her aides had reserved the room as soon as they all knew where the War Cabinet meeting was to be held. Wilson followed her in, his face registering polite curiosity. Then he saw Paula Myo sitting at the table inside, and frowned. 'What is this?' he asked.

'Sorry to put you on the spot, Wilson,' Justine said. 'But you probably know Admiral Columbia and I have had a disagreement on certain security matters. And he fired Investigator Myo from Navy Intelligence.'

Wilson held up a hand. 'I'm sorry, Senator; but Rafael has my complete confidence. I don't do office politics, not at this level. In case you hadn't noticed, there's a war on, and we could well lose.' He turned back to the door.

'The Guardians have been running an operation on Mars for twenty years,' Paula said.

Wilson froze, his hand already extended to open the door. After a moment he said: 'There's nothing on Mars. Believe me, I know.'

'You were there for ten hours, over three hundred years ago,' Justine said. 'I was watching the live television broadcast. I remember seeing Lewis, Orchiston and you stepping out onto the surface. It was the first time in a great many years I was proud of our country again. You were putting up the Stars and Stripes when Nigel butted in.'

Wilson turned round, anger flushing his cheeks. 'So?'

'The Guardians were using the Arabia Terra station to relay their information back to Earth.'

'What sort of information?'

'We're not sure. Navy Intelligence made one attempt to run diagnostic routines through the equipment up there. It appeared to be standard environmental sensors.'

'I don't get it,' Wilson shook his head, clearly irritated. 'The Guardians are terrorists, what do they want with Martian environment data?'

'We don't know,' Paula said. 'But the Paris office is winding down their investigation.'

'Ah. That's it,' Wilson gave Justine a disdainful glance. 'You want me to pressure Rafael into keeping the investigation open.'

'You have been on the receiving end of a Guardians' operation,' Paula said. 'More than most, you know how serious and effective they can be. They nearly destroyed the

Second Chance. A twenty-year operation is not something they would undertake lightly. It would have to be exceptionally important to them. We have got to find out what it is.'

Wilson let out a hiss of air between his teeth. 'Maybe. But if it is truly this important, I don't believe Rafael would ignore it. He's many things, aggressive, ambitious, intense, unforgiving, yes; but never stupid.'

'Everyone has blindspots, Wilson,' Justine said. 'Paula was fired for politics, for not being quick enough to produce results.'

'A hundred and thirty years on a case with no result is very reasonable grounds for dismissal in my book,' Wilson said. 'No offence.'

'You heard about the LA Galactic incident?' Justine asked. 'An assassin killed the Guardians' courier who was bringing their Martian data back for them. It was the same assassin who destroyed the black market arms dealer on Venice Coast. He also murdered my brother. So he's not working for the government, and he can't be working for the Guardians.'

'Who then?' Wilson asked.

'Good question. The Paris office might be able to find the answer. *If* they keep hunting.'

Wilson looked from Justine to Paula. 'What are you asking for?'

'Ask Rafael to keep Navy Intelligence on the Martian inquiry, not to let up.'

'Maybe,' Wilson said. 'I'll have to think about all this.'

*

After an investment of twenty-five years, most of the planets in phase one space were now linked by maglev express lines, providing a fast efficient service; and based on that success CST was busy expanding the network out across the planets of phase two space. But for all its imagined importance as the link world to Far Away, Boongate still hadn't got a maglev track. CST was vague about the timetable for installation.

It had taken the standard express from Paris forty minutes to reach Boongate's CST station, sliding smoothly up alongside platform 2 at twenty-two hundred hours local time. There were only five platforms in the main terminal building, but each of them were bustling with waiting passengers when Renne and Tarlo stepped out from the first-class double-decker carriage. It was raining outside, and the train was dripping on to the track. A chilly night wind blew in under the big arching glass roof, making people stamp their feet and button up their coats. The overhead polyphoto strips threw a bright blue-tinged light across the scene, illuminating the raindrops that lashed in past the edge of the roof like grey sparks.

'Late to be travelling, isn't it?' Tarlo said as they walked towards the end of the platform. He ignored the curious glances their navy uniforms drew.

Renne pulled her jacket collar up against the cold, and eyed the people lining the platform. They all seemed to be gathered in family clumps, with subdued, yawning children sitting on piles of luggage. Several CST security guards were patrolling.

'Depends how keen you are to leave,' she replied. It was the first time she'd seen any evidence of the displacement which the unisphere news shows featured so heavily these days. But then if it was going to happen anywhere, she realized, it would be here. Most of Boongate's neighbours were numbered among the Lost23.

They pushed their way through the equally crowded concourse and found the CST security office. Edmund Li was their liaison; a local police technical officer who'd been seconded to the navy then appointed to the newly formed Far Away freight inspectorate division. Fifteen years on from his first regeneration, he'd retained all of his thick black hair, which hadn't been cut for several months. By contrast, his slim moustache was perfectly maintained, complementing the mauve OCtattoos of Greek lettering on his narrow face. He didn't bother wearing a navy uniform, just a simple dove-grey office suit. Renne was rather envious of that, her dark tunic always seemed to itch. It reminded her of the time when Paula was still in charge of the Paris office.

Li had a car waiting, which drove them the five miles over to the Far Away section of the yard. As he was briefing them on the latest interceptions, Renne looked out through the rain-smeared glass. Hundreds of lights shone down from their tall poles right across the extensive station yard, revealing the broad empty regions between the rails and distant industrial buildings, a legacy of lost ambition left over from the days when Boongate thought it would become the junction for the adjoining sector of phase three space. Some of the cargo depots were open, big rectangular doors showing trains drawn up inside, their wagons steaming and dripping as cranes and autolifters unloaded their consignments. She saw a long rank of Ables RP5 shunting engines lined up outside a giant engineering shop; unused since the Prime attack sent the Commonwealth economy floundering, they awaited the return of normal commercial operations.

A weak maroon light shimmered on the other side of the Far Away cargo warehouse, glinting on the rails that snaked round outside.

'Is that the Half Way gateway?' Renne asked. The semicircle of bland luminescence was coming into view from behind the long dark building as the car drew near. It resembled a tired moon sinking below the horizon.

'Yeah,' Edmund Li said. 'There's not been much outgoing traffic since the Prime attack. Most of it is cargo to companies and big landowners, and the Institute, of course. Not much personal stuff, either; anyone who was planning on emigrating has put it on hold, and their tourist trade has packed up completely.'

'What about traffic coming this way?' Tarlo asked.

'Sure. Plenty of people want to get the hell out of there. Who wouldn't? They're damn close to Dyson Alpha. It costs a lot to get here from Far Away, though. Most of them don't have that kind of money. And I don't know how long the Commonwealth Civil Council will keep the gateway open.'

The car pulled up outside the warehouse, and they hurried through the rain to the small office which was attached to the side of the main building like a brick wart. Inside, the office was a simple open-plan rectangle, with nine desks down the middle. The console arrays on seven of them were covered with plastic dust jackets.

Tarlo gave them a curious look as they walked past. 'How many staff does the division employ?'

'There are twenty-five of us on the payroll,' Edmund Li said in a deadpan voice.

'Right. And how many show up?'

'It was four of us yesterday. Tomorrow, who knows?'

Tarlo and Renne gave each other a knowing glance.

'I think that's called being absent without leave,' Tarlo said. 'The admiral will probably have them shot.'

'He'll have to find them first,' Edmund Li told them. 'I doubt they'll be on this world. They had families.'

'So why are you still here?' Renne asked. 'It's not like this is the most vital job in the Commonwealth right now.'

'I was born on Boongate. I guess that makes it easier for me to stay than the others. And I haven't started a family this life around.' He pushed through the door which led into the warehouse.

It was chilly inside the cavernous space. A single row of polyphoto strips was alight along the apex, casting a desultory light on the bare metal racks which ran the entire length of the enzyme-bonded concrete floor. Rain hitting the solar panel roof produced a loud drumming noise which reverberated round the nearly empty building.

'It gets kind of unnerving working here,' Edmund Li said. He stepped over a set of rail tracks that ran down the middle of the floor to a huge door at the end of the warehouse. 'We are, physically, the closest people to the Half Way gateway. If the Primes did come through, we'd be the first to know about it. You feel really exposed. I don't blame the others for quitting.'

They came to a pair of ordinary flatbed train wagons that were sitting on the track, both of them loaded with big grey composite crates. A deep-scan sensor hoop spanned the track twenty yards away; several desks had been set up around its base. Their screens and arrays were all silent and dark. A broad workbench beside them was equipped with several robotic machine tools. Three of the crates sat on top of it; they'd been broken open.

'Urien found these yesterday,' Edmund Li said, and gestured. The packing crates contained bulky sections of machinery which the power tools had split apart. Almost all of the electrical circuitry had been removed and laid out on the bench in a jumble of coiled cable and black box modules.

'All right, so what are we looking at?' Tarlo asked.

'The machinery in this consignment is all agricultural; combine harvesters, tractors, drillers, irrigation systems. It's shipped in sections like this to be reassembled on Far Away. Makes life quite easy for us to scan it all. We were lucky Urien was on duty when this lot went through; his family are landowners on Dunedin. The man knows his farming tools. He thought there was something odd about the wiring, especially as these are all diesel fuelled. Turns out he was right.' Edmund held up some of the cabling, which was as thick as his wrist. 'Heavy duty superconductor. And these current modulators have a massive power rating.'

'Not the manufacturer's spec then?' Tarlo said.

'Heavens no. This is intended for something that uses a phenomenal amount of electricity.'

'Any ideas?'

Edmund Li grinned as he shook his head. 'I have absolutely no clue. That's why I made the call to your office. I thought you should know right away.'

'Appreciate that. So where was it heading?'

'The address is for Palamaro Ranch in the Taliong district, that's a long way east of Armstrong City; they say that's where the Barsoomians are.'

'All right. What we really need are the shipment and financial details. Who was the agent? Which bank was used? Where was the machinery packed?'

'Yeah.' Edmund Li scratched the back of his neck, giving the muddle of machinery a doubtful look. The rain pounding on the roof grew even louder as a dense squall lashed down. 'Look, I'm sure that back on Earth that kind of data is beautifully formatted and filed for instant access. Things are a little different here. For a start, some of this stuff is already missing.'

'Missing?' Renne exclaimed. 'What do you mean?'

'Exactly that. Everyone knows we keep expensive goods in here overnight. Take a look around, lady. Do you see any guardbots on patrol outside? We've got sensors, but even if an alarm goes off, the nearest CST security agent is five miles away over in the terminal, and right now they're all real busy on crowd control. The police are further away, and care even less.'

'Goddamnit,' Tarlo growled. 'Did you manage to get a record of everything you found in this shipment?'

'I'm pretty sure Urien recorded it, yes. There will be the deep-scan sensor record if nothing else. It just hasn't been loaded in our official database yet, it's probably in his console's temporary store folder.'

Renne made a strong effort to keep her growing anger in check. No good shouting at Edmund Li, they were lucky he even bothered to call them. 'What about the associated datawork Tarlo asked about? Is that in a temporary folder somewhere?'

'No. I haven't started rounding that up, yet. It shouldn't take too long, a lot of the inventory and authorization will be filed with the station's Far Away export control office.'

'How's their staffing level?' Tarlo asked bitterly.

Edmund Li just raised an eyebrow.

'Hogan is going to go apeshit,' Renne decided. *Another setback. This case is truly jinxed.*

'Well he needn't try blaming us,' Tarlo said. 'But I'm beginning to understand why the boss never found any decent leads here.'

'It's only since the attack things have gotten like this,' Edmund Li said. 'It didn't help that this operation was still being set up at the time. I can't even complain about not having any money; it's lack of people that is the problem.'

'Right,' Tarlo said decisively. 'Renne, there's no point both of us staying here; you get back to Paris. I'll stay on and run the checks on this consignment. Once we have the basic source, route and finance information, we can start the backtrack operation from Paris.'

Renne gave the shaded, gaping warehouse a final examination. 'No argument. You'd better arrange for what's left to be shipped back as well. Forensic can start going over it. They might be able to tell us what it's for.'

Tarlo put out a hand to shake. 'Ten dollars they can't.'

'No takers.'

*

It was officially called the Westminster Palace Museum of Democracy but everyone just called it Big Ben after the famous clock tower which stood guard at the eastern end. Adam Elvin used his credit tattoo to pay the standard five dollar fee and walked in through the ornate arching stonework of St Stephen's Entrance opposite the Abbey. With its lengthy halls, elongated windows and bare stone interior, the old British Parliament building always gave him the impression of being a misappropriated cathedral. The lobby between the two main chambers had incongruous wooden furniture huddled defensively between big white statues, while gold-tinted light poured in through the high stained-glass windows, highlighting the carvings that stretched up each wall. Groups of excited chattering schoolchildren rushed about, looking round through interface goggles as the guide program described the historical significance of everything they focused on. Doors into the Commons were open, where holograms faded in and out above the chamber's green benches, to produce images of successive politicians from the pre-electronic era right up until the last English Parliament in 2065. In the House of Lords the whole rise and fall of the British monarchy from William the Conqueror at the Battle of Hastings to King Timothy signing the act to grant the right of self-determination to his people was played out amid spectral pomp and splendour.

Adam ignored the Victorian Gothic grandeur and the dodgy history lessons to carry on through to the terrace café along the side of the Thames. It extended for over two hundred metres, nearly the entire length of the building, and was always a popular spot for tourists and locals alike. A warm spring breeze coming off the wide river rustled the tall table parasols with their elaborate portcullis emblem. Waitresses threaded their way through the tight maze, delivering trays and taking orders. He always felt the museum operator crammed the tables too close together in order to squeeze out that little extra drop of revenue. So he had to suck in his stomach and slither his way awkwardly past seats, warding off annoyed glances to reach a table which was right up against the terrace parapet itself.

Bradley Johansson smiled up at him. 'Adam, so good of you to come, old chap.'

'Yeah right,' Adam grunted, and sat down next to Bradley.

A young waitress dressed in a faux-Tudor boy's costume with emerald-green tights showing off her long legs came over and smiled hopefully.

'Another afternoon tea for my friend,' Bradley told her winningly. 'With scones and cream, and I think a glass of that delightful Gifford's champagne.'

Her smile brightened. 'Yes sir.'

'For Christ's sake,' Adam muttered after she walked off. Everybody had to be looking at them.

'Now don't go all Bolshevik on me,' Bradley chided. 'When in Rome and all that. Besides it's proper Cornish clotted cream.'

'Woopie fucking do.'

'Come on, Adam, they've turned this ancient seat of class privilege into a lovely teashop for the common man. There's got to be a metaphor or two in that, surely? I thought you'd enjoy this.'

Adam would never admit it, but he always experienced a slight burst of admiration for the way Bradley chose to meet him in the most outrageously public places. There was a kind of bravado about it which Adam's dreary paranoid tradecraft would never permit.

'Kazimir would have liked it,' Adam said. 'The history on this world always amazed him. Nearly every building he went in was older than Far Away.'

Bradley's affable expression hardened into place. 'What happened, Adam? That data was *vital*.' His hand slapped the table in fury. People did look. Bradley's smile returned, meeting the stares apologetically.

Adam didn't often get to see the claws. It wasn't nice. 'We pieced it together eventually. He sneaked off to see a girl before the courier mission. Apparently, they met a long time ago back on Far Away. Turns out she was a little more important than your average tourist.'

'Who is she?'

'Justine Burnelli.'

'The senator?' Bradley blinked in surprise. 'Well bless the dreaming heavens. No wonder the navy was on to him. I thought he was smarter than that, a lot smarter.'

'Kazimir was murdered by a Starflyer agent called Bruce McFoster. He and Kazimir grew up together.'

'Yes, I remember.' Bradley picked up a little bone-handled silver knife and spread some cream on a scone. 'Bruce never came back from a raid a few years back. Damn it, I keep telling the clans to watch for what the Starflyer can do to anyone left behind.'

'The same thing it did to you?'

For a split second Bradley registered enormous pain. 'Quite,' he said hoarsely.

'You know, I don't even question if the Starflyer is real any more. I've watched young Kieran McSobel's recording a dozen times since. Kazimir was delighted to see his friend again; and Bruce just shot him.'

'I'm sorry, Adam.'

'Sorry? I thought you'd be delighted at another convert.'

'It isn't a pleasant door to open. There is little hope behind it, mostly just darkness and pain. That's why I founded the Guardians, to protect the human race from what lurks there. So they could carry on living their beautiful long lives in peace. In a way, you're not my convert, you're another of its victims.'

'Hey, don't worry yourself about my soul. I chose my path a long time ago. This is just another rocky patch.'

'Oh Adam, if only you knew how much I envy your optimism. Ah . . .' He smiled up again as the waitress brought a tray with Adam's afternoon tea. 'Do tuck in.'

Adam picked up his knife and cut one of the scones open.

'How good was the encryption?' Bradley asked.

'The SI could probably break it, but apart from that it's safe.'

'That gives us some leeway, then. The navy ran long-range diagnostic tests on the Martian equipment, which will tell them precisely nothing. They'll be desperate to find some subterfuge.'

'We watched the body afterwards, you know. Senator Burnelli had it taken to a New York clinic owned by her family. My little friend Paula accompanied her. From what we can gather, the navy and Senate Security don't exactly see eye to eye over this.'

'Humm,' Bradley held up his crystal champagne flute, studying the bubbles as they fizzed in the sunlight. 'Do you think Paula has the memory crystal rather than the navy?'

'That's some heavy-duty speculation; but I'll concede it is a possible.'

'I wonder if that works to our advantage?'

'I don't see how. You needed the data. They have it.'

'It gives them a big bargaining chip, even though they don't know it yet.'

'Do we have anything they want?'

'Yes,' Bradley took a sip of champagne. 'You and I for a start.'

'Not fucking funny.' Adam stuffed the scone into his mouth, and started pouring his tea.

'I suppose not. But I have to give some consideration to recovering the information. We need it, Adam, very badly. The whole of the planet's revenge depends on it.'

'I don't see how we can get it back. I certainly don't have any way of infiltrating Navy Intelligence or Senate Security. What about that old top-level source of yours?'

'I'm afraid I haven't heard from him in a long time.'

'So that's it? Game over?' Somehow the idea was impossible.

'It's not over by any means,' Bradley said. 'Just a damn sight more difficult. That Martian data would have helped us refine the control program to a point where we could use it with confidence. We can still go ahead, but now we have to depend on numerical modelling more than the project designers want to. The results will be very uncertain.'

'Your guys will make it work, whatever it is. They all seem so dedicated.'

'For which I give thanks to the dreaming heavens. Humans do seem to possess remarkable reserves in so many fields. No wonder Starflyer and the Primes are so unnerved by us.'

'If the Starflyer found out about the planet's revenge, could it prevent you from carrying it out?'

Bradley looked out over the river, giving the tall plane trees on the opposite bank a thoughtful stare. 'Stop it, no; but it would be easy to circumvent. Timing is critical. But very few of us know the entire strategy, and I remain in contact with all of them. So far we are secure.'

'I hope you're right. They knew Kazimir was making his courier run. Which implies they've penetrated the navy. So by now they must know about the Observatory receiving the Martian data for twenty years. If the Starflyer knows that, can it work out what you're planning to hit it with?'

'Extremely unlikely. However, none of this will matter if we can't get the remaining physical components through to Far Away. An entire shipment was intercepted by the new navy inspections on Boongate.'

'Yeah, we're really going to have to do something about that.' Adam dropped some rock sugar into his tea, and stirred absently. 'We've got outlines of a blockade-busting run drawn up. I guess it's about time to put some flesh on it. Not that it needs a lot of development. It's an essentially crude notion to begin with.'

'Good. That means there's less which can go wrong.'

'And you call me an optimist.'

'I'm still curious how Bruce managed to get away afterwards. Did you find out anything relevant about that train he jumped on?'

'No. CST traffic control use very high-order encryption.' He grinned. 'For some reason, they're worried about people like me hacking in. It was a freight train is all we know. We don't know where it was going, only that it was in the right place at the right time. That kind of placement takes some doing. It impressed the hell out of me.'

'Logically, then, it had to be organized by someone very senior in CST.'

'Yes.'

'I wonder who the Starflyer has corrupted in that organization?'

'I don't suppose we'll find out until all this is long over and settled.'

Bradley gave a reluctant moue. 'Yes, unfortunately. But someone that highly placed can do a lot of damage. I'm assuming they'll help the Starflyer in its arrangements to return to Far Away.'

'You're convinced that will happen?'

'I am indeed. It can't afford to be trapped in the Commonwealth, especially if the Primes do succeed in wreaking havoc. When the war is at its very worst, it will try and return to its own kind. That's when we must strike.'

'We'll get the rest of your equipment through, don't worry.'

'I don't, Adam, I have a lot of confidence in you and your team. I just wish I could convince the rest of the Commonwealth. Perhaps I went about this the wrong way right from the start. But nobody believed me back then. I felt as though my back was to the wall. What else could I do but lash out physically? It was such a ridiculously human reaction, one which betrays how insecure we all are, how short the distance we've travelled from the old animal. Forming the Guardians to attack the Institute was such an instinctive reaction. Maybe I should have tried the political route.'

'Speaking of which; are you absolutely sure Elaine Doi is a Starflyer agent?'

Bradley leant forwards over the table. 'That wasn't us.'

'Excuse me?'

'A very well executed fake. I have to admit, the Starflyer is becoming quite sophisticated in its campaign against us. Physically, Bruce and his kind are causing a lot of expensive damage while disinformation like that shotgun is damaging our credibility. Just when we were starting to attract a degree of media interest, not to mention political support. Still, I blame myself, I should have anticipated such a move.'

Adam finally sipped some of the Gifford's champagne to help wash down a scone. 'You know, that might have been a dangerous move on their part.'

'In what way?'

'If anyone were to investigate that shotgun properly, they might pick up some leads. The Starflyer might have exposed some its operation to official scrutiny.'

'Worth considering. I certainly wasn't going to issue a disclaimer. That would make us look really stupid in the public mind. In any case, I'm abandoning the propaganda shotguns. We're too close to the end now for them to make any real difference to general opinion.'

'Unless you can produce some absolute proof.'

'True.' Bradley seemed very undecided. 'I suppose the Doi shotgun could do with some further inquiries.'

'I can't spare anyone from my team, especially now you've recalled Stig.'

'Sorry about that, but I needed him back on Far Away. He's developed into a damn good leader, for which I place full credit on your training.'

'So we have no one who can dig into the shotgun, see who put it together?'

'I'll see what I can do.'

*

Wilson said practically nothing on the journey back to the High Angel. He was lost in his virtual vision, pulling files from the Navy Intelligence Paris office, and reviewing the tight green text as it scrolled through the air in front of him.

'It went well,' Rafael said as the direct express slid out of Newark. 'I expected us to take a much bigger beating than that. They are politicians, after all.'

'Doi was surprising,' Wilson admitted, rousing himself from Hogan's report on the killing at LA Galactic. 'I didn't expect her to be quite as forthright as that.'

'She had to be. We need someone with balls at the top. Everybody there knew that. The Dynasties and Grand Families would have engineered a recall if she didn't come up with positive noises. So, it looks like we'll get the ships, then.'

'Yeah.'

Rafael shrugged at the lack of communication, and settled back to work through the files in his own virtual vision.

Wilson thought the account of how the killer got away was frankly unbelievable. If that was an example of how the Paris office operated, no wonder Rafael had fired Myo.

He looked through the spectral lines and columns and graphics to see Rafael sitting opposite him. The man was ambitious, yes, but no matter how ambitious and well connected you were, to reach his level you also had to be competent. Hogan was his placement; but Inspector Myo was renowned across the Commonwealth. It didn't seem like a move based purely on petty office politics, there was no prejudice or simple manoeuvring. Myo hadn't produced results. She had to go.

Yet she'd immediately been recruited into Senate Security – a move engineered by the Burnellis. And Justine had clashed with Rafael.

Wilson recalled the one previous time he'd met the Chief Investigator, amid the ruins of assessment hall seven on Anshun after the Guardians' attack on *Second Chance*. She'd seemed quietly professional, easily living up to her reputation. And she certainly hadn't acquired her seniority in the Directorate through family connections. She was frighteningly good at her job. *Every case but one solved.* Even now it seemed she was still working on that one, simply from a different angle if he was reading the pattern right.

His virtual hands pulled another file from the Paris office. Myo had accompanied McFoster's body to the Burnelli biomedical facility for its autopsy. He found it hard to believe she would ever jeopardize any kind of investigation simply to score points off Rafael. Her brain simply wasn't wired for it, thanks to the Human Structure Foundation.

Which meant she thought there was something deeper behind the appearance of the assassin. He pulled her last few reports on the case from the navy files, interested to see how high the restricted access level was – there were only fifteen people in the Commonwealth government who could gain entry to those files.

Paula Myo, it seemed, had come to believe that the Starflyer was real.

'Son of a bitch.'

Rafael gave him an expectant look. Wilson shook his head in mild embarrassment, and sat back deeper into the train's seat. His immediate political instinct was to stay right out of a clash between the Burnellis and the Halgarths, especially over something like this. But for Myo to even consider the possibility after a hundred and thirty years trying to close down the Guardians was extraordinary. Everybody knew the Chief

Investigator was incapable of lying. Every time he'd accessed one of her cases, the unisphere shows would replay her parents' trial as evidence of just how incorruptible she was.

Wilson began to wish he'd simply walked on by that morning when Justine asked him for a moment. But he knew it wasn't something he could ignore. Not now. Justine and Myo had got to him simply by mentioning Mars. It was a low blow. She knew it. He knew it. Yet for him the red planet had a resonance he could never ignore. And the Guardians were certainly real enough. *What they hell did they want with Mars?*

As he pulled out the most recent files from the investigation, it was clear that Navy Intelligence didn't have a clue. And just as Myo had indicated, they were winding down that aspect of the case.

'My e-butler's flagged an interesting report,' he said casually. 'What were the Guardians doing on Mars?'

Rafael's focus returned to the real world. 'We don't know. The Guardians' courier was killed, and whatever data he was carrying has disappeared. Between you and me, I believe it wound up at Senate Security. Senator Burnelli's interest in this case is less than professional.'

'Really? I'll see if I can have a word with Gore about that. He owes me a few favours from way back.'

'I'd appreciate that. Sometimes, I'm not sure we're all working for the same side. The damn Grand Families can't stop looking for a financial angle on everything.'

'No problem. But I'd like you to keep Navy Intelligence working on Mars. I have an understandable interest about the place.'

Rafael gave a disinterested grin. 'Sure.'

*

The apartment Wilson and Anna had in Babuyan Atoll was in a building resembling a small pyramid of dove-grey bubbles.

It was close to the edge of the vast crystal dome, which gave them a clear view out into space at night when the internal illumination dimmed. When the High Angel was in conjunction, the wan light from Icalanise's gigantic cloudscape was enough to cast pale shadows across the walls and floors. That was frequently complemented by the waxing and waning moonlight from the gas-giant's major satellites.

Wilson would often spend an evening on the oval terrace outside the main lounge, sitting in a recliner with a glass of wine in one hand, watching the stark alien planets gliding overhead. Even when he did that, he would still immerse himself in files and priority office work which his e-butler and virtual vision provided. The night when he got back from the War Cabinet meeting was different. He simply couldn't push Mars out of his thoughts.

'I expected you to be happier,' Anna said as she came out onto the terrace. For once she'd taken the time to change out of her uniform after they got home. She'd put on a small yellow bikini and long semi-transparent yellow robe. Her dark skin made the fabric appear bright in the infall of light from various moons. Silver and bronze OCtattoos all across her body came to life in long slow undulations, emphasizing the play of muscle below her skin.

The effect was erotic enough to divert Wilson's thoughts from Mars. He whistled admiringly as she perched on the edge of the recliner. 'I haven't seen you like that for quite a while.'

'I know. We seem to be neglecting some fairly basic human requirements lately; it's all Mr and Ms No Fun Military Executive these days.'

'Just how basic were those requirements you had in mind?'

Her finger stroked the side of his face. 'I had my staff draw up a list. They'll get in touch with your people and start negotiations.'

'Any time soon?' He slipped his arm round her waist and told his e-butler to get her a glass of the wine.

She settled back into the embrace and stared up through the roof of the dome. 'Is that the new assembly platform?'

Wilson followed where she was looking to see a silver fleck amid the stars. 'Uh . . . yeah, I think so. You know, space is going to get pretty cluttered out there over the next few months.'

'If we have months.'

His hold round her tightened. 'They're not invincible. Don't ever let yourself think that. We've seen their home star, we know they have finite resources to throw at us.'

'They might be finite, Wilson, but they've got a damn sight more than we have.'

A maidbot rolled up carrying a chilled glass of wine. He took it from the electromuscle tentacle and handed it to her. 'If they could have invaded every Commonwealth planet at once, they would have done it. They can't. They have to try and digest us one chunk at a time. I'm not saying we shouldn't be frightened of them, but if that first attack showed us anything, it's that they have limits. The effort they made establishing themselves on the Lost23 gives us a breathing space. We'll make those fancy new ships work; we'll gather an army of people wetwired with the scariest weapons technology we can think of and kick the Lost23 out from under their quadruple feet. And, after that, we'll use the Seattle Project to put the fear of God into them. It'll be us deciding if they get to live or not. Those sons of bitches will curse the day their barrier wall ever came down.'

'Wow. You really believe we can do this, don't you?'

'I have to. I'm not going to let the human race become nothing more than an old legend in this part of the galaxy.'

'You can depend on me.' She kissed him lightly.

'I know.' He touched his glass to hers. 'A toast. To a successful campaign, and politicians who didn't actually spent the whole cabinet meeting trying to score points off each other.'

'I'll drink to that.'

Wilson savoured the wine, then glanced up at the Base One hardware floating close to the High Angel. 'I've seen the ideas the physicists and designers have. They're goddamn impressive.'

'Let's hope the media shows stop criticizing everything we try and do.'

'They will. Baron and the others are just in shock like everyone else. Once they sober up and see what the alternative is, they'll throw their weight behind us. I've seen it happen before.'

She rubbed his hair fondly. 'So old. I guess that's what makes me trust you so much. You have so much life experience. I don't think there's any situation you couldn't handle.'

'Don't be so sure. I've got surprising vulnerabilities. I can't believe how much Mars is bugging me. Justine really pressed the right buttons, there.'

'What do you think the Guardians have been doing there all that time?'

'I've been sitting here thinking about it for an hour, and I just cannot figure it out. That's why I asked Rafael to keep his teams on it. But given the dumbass politics involved, I don't suppose much will be done.'

'How about I become the buffer on this one for you? I've got the authority to press for action in Navy Intelligence, while you stay outside the low level office bickering.'

Wilson stretched his neck up to kiss her. 'That would be just about perfect.'

'I do what I can.' The OCtattoos on her torso began to pick up speed, reflecting the light of the shining moons in slim lines of glinting steel.

'What say we forget our staff, and just do our own negotiations here and now?'

Anna started giggling as he shifted round in the recliner so that both arms could reach around her.

*

Nigel Sheldon's memory trigger was fast and completely unexpected. It snapped a scene round him like a high-rez TSI access, putting him back in front of the TV news in his adolescence, where every large-scale disaster was followed up by politicians on a 'reassurance visit' to the hospitals or tent-city aid stations. Back on campus, after the 2048 meteor strike tsunami in the Gulf of Mexico, the students had printed out cards like the ones for volunteer organ donors, but saying: In The Event of Emergency Keep The President Away From Me.

Watching Elaine Doi and her entourage working her way along the queue outside the temporary medical station Nigel wondered how many of these refugees would appreciate having that card on them right now. There wasn't much in the way of smiles and gratitude down there, only grim resignation and an undercurrent of anger. As yet it wasn't directed at her.

His retinal inserts zoomed back out, giving him a broad aspect of the Wessex planetary station. Like all the CST stations on Big15 worlds, the one at Narrabri sprawled over several hundred square kilometres, incorporating marshalling yards, management centres, engineering sectors, cargo ware-houses, a small town of office blocks, and passenger terminals. In the aftermath of the Prime invasion it had become the clearing house for every refugee from the Lost23 – all forty million of them. The CST passenger train management RI had pulled out every piece of rolling stock on the Commonwealth register to cope, from vintage carriages to the modern maglev expresses; even the steam engine which ran on the Huxley's Haven line had been used a couple of times. The evacuation had been a truly heroic endeavour, relentless and gruelling for everyone involved, from the managers who suddenly found themselves coping with a catastrophe they'd never envisaged let alone trained for, to station staff helping entire planetary populations flood through their domain while nuclear weapons exploded overhead and their homes were blasted back into the Stone Age. Somehow, it had worked. Nigel had never been prouder of his people.

At the start, when the rail network was in true chaos, people had been swarming through the gateways on foot from the Lost23; but after a few hours, CST had re-established the primary rail links, and begun running evacuation trains. They'd offloaded refugees throughout phase one and two space on a rota basis; with trains abandoning their confused and frightened cargo at stations for the local government to cope with. Nobody asked permission to dump people from wildly different ethnic groups and cultures and religions onto unprepared worlds frightened for their own future, CST simply did it based on practicality.

Waiting for an evacuation train was actually quicker than walking through the wormhole, especially given the press of people already trying to do just that, and incidentally endangering themselves and the trains still running. That hadn't stopped them, of course.

From the Narrabri CST station manager's office Nigel could see a mass of people milling round outside the huge buildings of the engineering sector. Repairs and maintenance on Wessex were currently impossible, with crude dormitories and makeshift kitchens filling every square metre of floorspace. Even with all the temporary facilities rushed in, sanitation down there wasn't great. But at least the big engineering sheds gave them a roof over their heads at night. Not that the sheds held everyone; there were tens of thousands more camped out in the terminal buildings, eating their way through every fast food franchise stall on the planet. More squatted in empty warehouses. Best estimates from CST staff and Wessex government officials on the ground put the number remaining in the station at two million. Social workers brought in from fifty planets, and local volunteers from Narrabri, were coping with children separated from their parents. Over thirty per cent were newly orphaned, and deep in shock. There were acts of kindness and quiet heroism occurring amid the throng that would never be known, for all the intrusive media coverage of the terrible human aftermath of the invasion.

'I haven't seen anything like this since the early twenty-first century,' Nigel said.

'Yeah, I remember Africa and Asia back then,' Alan Hutchinson said. 'This isn't quite the same.'

Nigel cast an inquisitive glance at the third Dynasty leader in the office. Heather Antonia Halgarth gazed down impassively at the weary refugees without making any comment.

'We're doing everything we can,' Nigel said. 'It shouldn't take more than a couple of days to move these people out.'

'Where to?' Alan asked. 'My senators are starting to hear complaints. Some worlds think they're being given too many refugees to cope with.'

'Tough,' Nigel snapped. 'We can't dump them on phase three worlds, there's no infrastructure. Phases one and two will have to cope, physically and financially.'

'But not Earth,' Heather murmured.

Nigel gave her an uneasy smile. She was nearing the time she underwent rejuvenation, a biological age of mid-fifties. It made her an imposingly grand woman, with reddish hair starting to lighten, and a few wrinkles appearing on her cheeks. At this time in her preferred sequence, he always likened her to some high priestess; silent, wise, knowing, and totally uncompromising.

'No,' he said. 'Not Earth. They'll get a few token trainloads, but I can really do without the Grandees bitching about undesirables bringing down the tone of the neighbourhood. My unisphere address would be blocked for a year with messages. They can pay for accommodation instead; I made that quite clear to Crispin.'

'Good man, Crispin,' Heather said.

'He'll need to be,' Alan said. 'Sorting this mess out will cost trillions; and it'll take a decade if not longer. Bugger it, this is nearly fifteen per cent of my market those alien bastards have wiped out.'

'We might all be facing a hundred per cent market loss sooner than we would like,' Heather said in a voice loaded with contempt. 'I have yet to be convinced that our new navy is capable of engaging the Prime threat effectively. What I've seen so far doesn't exactly fill me with confidence. Losing twenty-three planets in a day is simply unacceptable.'

'We agreed to back the formation of a navy,' Nigel said pointedly. 'I don't know what else we could have done.'

'Yeah,' Alan grunted. 'It's not exactly underfunded.'

'Relative to a species extinction crusade, which is what this is, I think we could have made more effort.'

Nigel nodded to the knot of people around Doi. 'Politically difficult.'

'Which is why we dump them every five years,' Heather said. 'We make the decisions, us humble three and the other Dynasties. Doi will do as she's told, as will the Senate.'

'Not all of them,' Nigel said. 'Don't be that arrogant.'

'We built this civilization,' Heather said. 'You more than all of us, Nigel. We cannot stand back when there are hard choices to be made.'

'This is all academic anyway,' Nigel countered. 'We've lost those planets. Our warship-building programme cannot be significantly expanded for months, no matter how much we need more ships.'

'Do we need more ships?' Heather asked mildly. 'There's the Seattle Project.'

'Genocide them?' Nigel was surprised to hear her propose that option; he'd always assumed she favoured a less drastic solution. Not that he'd ever thought of one.

'I think this has proved it's either them or us, surely?'

'They're aggressive, yes, but genocide . . . Come on, that's got to be last resort. I don't think we're at that stage yet.'

'You're applying human scruples to a non-human problem. Their next attack will be bigger and stronger. And we know there's going to be a "next" don't we.'

'Once the navy finds the exit point of that massive wormhole the Primes constructed, we'll be able to block them,' Alan said.

Heather gave him a disappointed smile. 'Eliminate Hell's Gateway? Care to bet your life on that? Because that's what you're doing.'

'Fuck you,' Alan spat. 'It's my territory that's in the front line.'

'Let's just calm down here,' Nigel said. 'Heather, he's right, we have to give the navy a chance to do what we built it for. I'm not prepared to authorize the genocide of an entire species, however belligerent.'

'And after their next strike takes out half of phase two space?'

'Then I'll press the button myself.'

'I'm glad to hear it. In the meantime, I will be taking the same kind of precautions you've been doing for the last few months.'

Nigel sighed. He should have known the other Dynasties would eventually find out what he was doing. 'Yeah well, I'm just playing safe.'

'That's a very expensive way of being safe,' Alan said. 'How much are you spending on those ships? I mean, Christ, Nigel, the hole in Augusta's budget was big enough for us to find.'

'Which is why I don't understand your reluctance to genocide the Primes,' Heather said. She sounded genuinely curious.

'Morality. We all have it, Heather, to some degree or other.'

'And your morality includes flying off and leaving the rest of us in the shit, does it?'

'If those ships are ever used, it will be when we're past the point of salvation. There won't be any Commonwealth left to protect.'

'Well I hope you're not going to deny us equal access to your hyperdrive technology.'

Nigel couldn't help the flicker of disapproval on his face. 'Progressive wormhole generator.'

'Excuse me?'

'Ftl starships use progressive wormhole generators.'

'Right,' Alan said, nonplussed. 'Whatever. We need them, Nigel.' His hand waved down at the refugees. 'Given this crock of shit, I'm putting my Dynasty's escape route together. All of us are.'

'You can have generators for your ships,' Nigel said. 'I'll be happy to sell them to you.'

'Thank you,' Heather said. 'In the meantime, we'd better present a united front for the War Cabinet and the Senate.' She nodded down at the President. 'She has to be given a big injection of confidence. People will turn to her; they always do in times of crisis. If they can see for certain that she's firmly in charge, it'll help keep the panic down.'

'Sure,' Nigel shrugged.

'What about Wilson?' Alan asked.

'What about him?' Nigel said.

'Oh come on! Twenty-three worlds invaded, and Wessex targeted as well. That arsehole let it happen. He's responsible.'

'He's the best one for the job,' Nigel said. 'You can't replace him.'

'For now,' Heather said. 'But another screw-up like this, and we will eject him.'

He gave her a hard look. 'And replace him with Rafael?'

'He's pro-genocide. That gets my vote.'

'We don't need games right now, Heather.'

'Who's playing? We're facing extinction, Nigel. If the solution involves shifting the navy to my control, then that is what will happen.'

Nigel couldn't remember the two of them going raw like this before. The trouble with Heather was that she could only think in terms of everything that had gone before. She had an astonishing determination and political ability. You couldn't build a Dynasty without those qualities. Nigel always considered her flaw to be a lack of originality. Even now, she saw the Prime situation purely in terms of its effect on her Dynasty. 'If that's the only solution you can see, then go for it,' he told her. It drew him a suspicious look. He ignored it, if she couldn't see her way around this problem, he certainly wasn't going to tell her.

*

Despite all she'd triumphed over on Elan, Mellanie still felt a great deal of trepidation as she stepped up to the dark wooden door of Paula Myo's Parisian apartment block. It said a lot about the hive woman that just the idea of confronting her again could do that. Mellanie knew that she was the special one now, that the SI inserts gave her huge powers, that she actually had the courage to stand in front of MorningLight-Mountain's soldier motiles and take them down – well the SI had seen through her, but that didn't alter the fact that she hadn't turned tail and run. *So why do I feel so nervous?*

She checked the bulky centuries-old intercom box beside the door, and pressed the worn ceramic button for Paula Myo's apartment. Somewhere inside a buzzer sounded. Her e-butler immediately told her Paula Myo was placing a call to her unisphere address. Mellanie resisted the instinct to look round for a camera. Even if the sensor was big enough to be visible, it was late evening, and the sunlight had almost faded, dropping the narrow street into deep shadow. Above her, the windows looking out from the high walls were all shuttered. The few intermittent streetlights above the uneven pavement did little to alleviate the gloom.

'Yes?' Paula Myo asked.

'I need to see you,' Mellanie said.

'I don't need to see you.'

'But I did what you said. I talked to Dudley Bose.'

'And what has that got to do with me?'

Mellanie gave the door an aggravated stare. 'You were right, I did find something interesting.'

'Which was?'

'The Starflyer.' There was such a long pause that Mellanie thought Myo had cut her off, she had to check her virtual vision to confirm the channel was still open.

The lock clicked loudly. Mellanie just had time to square her shoulders before the door opened. She'd toned down her clothes for this encounter, selecting some of the more sober items from her personal fashion line: a half-sleeve burgundy jacket and matching skirt longer than her usual, its hem came nearly halfway to her knees. It was a compilation which should emphasize how serious and professional she was these days.

A single polyphoto circle was fixed to the top of the deep archway that led to the block's central courtyard. Paula Myo was silhouetted in its yellow glow, dressed in her usual conservative-cut business suit. Mellanie hadn't realized before, but she was taller than the Investigator.

'Come in,' Paula said.

Mellanie followed her for a few paces until they were standing in the middle of the ancient cobbled courtyard. She looked round at the whitewashed walls with their narrow windows. Over half of them had their shutters drawn back, revealing glimpses of rooms. Flickers of pale green light were coming from inside as holographic portals played out the evening's unisphere news and entertainment. A sad reflection on the residents; this was the kind of block where single professionals would flock while they were taking a break between marriage contracts. Sanitized little apartments where they could rest in safety between the work and play which otherwise occupied their whole day.

'This will do,' Paula said. 'We're secure here if we don't talk too loud.'

Mellanie wasn't sure about that, but didn't want to argue. 'You know about it, don't you?'

'Did Alessandra Baron send you in search of an exclusive? Is that why you're here?'

'No.' Mellanie gave a short, edgy laugh. 'I don't work for her any more. Check with the production company if you don't believe me.'

'I will. Why did you leave? I imagine it was quite lucrative, and your report from Randtown helped secure your celebrity status.'

'She works for the Starflyer.'

Paula tilted her head to one side, and gave Mellanie a searching look. 'That's an interesting allegation.'

'But, don't you see, it makes perfect sense; she's always been tough on the navy. She's just spinning the Starflyer's propaganda, causing trouble for the one organization which can defend us.'

'You used her show to criticize me. Does that make you a Starflyer agent?'

'No! Look, I want to help. I know about the Cox. That's how I found out about Baron. When I told her, she altered the records.'

'I'm sorry, you've lost me now. What is this Cox?'

A little flare of temper made Mellanie put her hands on her hips. This wasn't going the way she'd imagined it. She'd thought the Investigator would welcome offers of help from anyone who knew about the Starflyer and the huge danger it represented. 'The education charity,' she said acerbically, which should jog the hive woman's memory. 'The one that funded Dudley's observation.'

'The break-in,' Paula said, reading something in her virtual vision. 'The Guardians suspected the whole Bose observation was a deliberate manipulation.'

'And they were right.'

Paula's eyebrows lifted slightly. 'Really?'

'You know they were,' Mellanie hissed.

'I don't.'

'But you must have. The Cox is a total fraud.'

'Not according to our investigations.'

'But . . .' Mellanie felt the skin down the back of her neck cooling rapidly. She didn't understand the way Myo was reacting at all. Unless the Starflyer had got to her as well. 'I'm sorry. I'm wasting your time. I . . . It was tough on Elan.' She turned and hurried back to the door. Backing off from people she used to trust was turning into a bad habit.

'Wait,' Paula said.

Mellanie froze, suddenly fearful. She reviewed the icons in her virtual vision, trying to work out if she could use any of the SI inserts to extricate herself if things turned nasty. Trouble was, she didn't really understand half of them yet. She'd have to yell to the SI for help. The gold snakeskin of her virtual hand poised above the SI icon.

'You think I know something about the Cox,' Paula said. 'Why?'

'You put me on to Dudley Bose, you must have known I would discover this.'

'I pushed you towards Bose because his wife once met Bradley Johansson. I was expecting you to go down that route to the Starflyer. Media allies would be useful to me. The only reports I recall on the break in were that the Cox charity was legitimate.'

'It's not. Well, it wasn't. Baron had the records altered.'

'Interesting. If you're telling me the truth, then the actual state of the Cox was withheld from me.'

'I am telling the truth,' Mellanie protested. She almost said, *ask the SI*. But that would have given away too much. She still didn't trust Paula.

'All right,' Paula said. 'I'll look into it.'

'Then what?'

'What did you come here for?'

'To see what you were doing, and to help.'

'And coincidentally wind up with the ultimate story.'

'Were you going to keep it secret?'

'If it's all true, then no. But I really don't think having a media celebrity dogging everything I do is helpful, do you?'

She couldn't even say 'reporter', Mellanie thought. *Bitch.* 'Fine. Whatever.' She pushed at the big door, opening a way back out onto the relative safety of the street.

'If you do find anything concrete, then please come to me,' Paula said. 'Not the navy.'

'Right.' Mellanie took a few paces out, then stopped to gather her thoughts. She knew she'd unsettled Paula but, pleasant though it was, that wasn't what she'd wanted to achieve. Right now, Mellanie needed someone to turn to with the terrible knowledge of Baron and the Starflyer, someone in authority, someone who would do something about it. *Just like some kid running to her parents.*

Well if the *great* Paula Myo was suspicious or undecided, she'd just have to damn well sort the problem out herself. With that thought, Mellanie nodded her head confidently and set off for the nearest Metro station.

*

Dawn found Hoshe Finn on his balcony, slumped in a cheap plastic patio chair looking out across the twinkling urban grid. Oaktier's sun was sliding up over the eastern districts of Darklake City, cloaking the tips of the glass and marble towers with an energetic rose-gold glow. Colourful birds started chirping from inside the tall evergreen trees standing round the base of his apartment block, while gardenbots moved along the narrow moat of dew-moistened gardens, performing their daily tidy up routine.

He'd woken up in the middle of the dream again. Some time in the small hours. Jolting up on the bed in a fever-sweat as the too-real images of collapsing buildings and quaking ground drained away into the darkness of the room. Every night since the Prime attack it had been the same. He refused to call it a nightmare. This was just his subconscious coming to terms with what had happened. All very healthy. Playing it back in sleeptime, letting all those nasty little details wind out from his mind where they'd been compressed like some secure file in a crystal lattice. Like the woman who'd been crushed by a broken bridge support – glanced at briefly as he'd carried Inima past. The children wailing outside the smoking rubble that had been their house, lost and dazed, filthy with dust, soot, and blood.

Yeah, a really healthy way of dealing with it all.

So he'd pulled on his old amber towelling robe and limped out onto the balcony to watch the sleeping city. Thinking like some frightened kid that maybe dreams only came to people in bedrooms. He'd dozed fitfully for the rest of the night as his burns throbbed and the clammy ache down his back cycled from hot to cold over and over. Not even the rum and hot chocolate helped, it just made him feel sick.

What he wanted was Inima. The reassurance of having her lying beside him at night; the exasperated tolerance she turned on whenever he was ill and moping around the house instead of going in to work. But the doctors weren't going to let her out of hospital for another ten days at the earliest. He still tensed up every time he thought about her. Pulling her out from the broken 4x4 on Sligo, the way her legs were bent and blackened, fluid weeping from the tar-like encrustation that had been her jeans. Her low whimpers, the sound that only the seriously injured make. A few vague memories of first aid flitting through his brain, utterly useless as he stared at his wife in disbelief that anything like this could possibly happen. Cursing himself the whole time for being so helpless.

They were vacationing on Sligo to see the flower festival. A fucking flower festival; and an alien army come dropping down out of the sky, blowing the whole world to shit.

Someone rang the apartment's doorbell. Hoshe turned automatically, and grimaced at the number of twinges that triggered right across his body. Grumbling like an old man, he limped his way to the door and opened it.

Paula Myo stood outside. Neat and tidy as always, in some charcoal-grey business suit with a scarlet blouse. Her hair had been brushed to a gloss, hanging free behind her shoulders. She was studying him carefully, and he was abruptly self-conscious of the way he looked, the fact he hadn't stood up to the attack the way he knew other people had.

Instead of some lecture or trite comment, Paula gave him a gentle hug.

Hoshe thought he covered up any surprise at the display of affection reasonably well given the circumstances.

'I'm really pleased you're okay, Hoshe,' Paula said.

'Thanks. Uh . . . come on in.' He glanced across the lounge as she walked past him. Maidbots had kept the apartment clean, but it was obvious he was spending a lot of time at home, indoors. The room had an almost bachelor feel to it, with memory crystals, mugs, plates, and a long paperscreen scattered over the table, blinds half-drawn, clothes piled up in one chair.

'I brought you this,' Paula said, and gave him a fancy-looking box of herbal teas. 'Somehow, I thought flowers would be inappropriate.'

Hoshe examined the label on the side of the box, and grinned sheepishly. 'Good choice.'

The sleeves of his robe were baggy, revealing long strips of healskin on his arms. Paula saw them and frowned slightly. 'How's Inima?'

'The doctors say she'll be out of hospital in another week or so. She'll need a clone graft for her hip and thigh, but they didn't have to amputate, thank God. They're going to fit her in an electromuscle suit, so she'll be mobile around the apartment at least.'

'That's good.'

He dropped down into one of the chairs. 'Medically, yeah. Our insurance is refusing to pay out for *quote* war injuries *unquote*. They say the government is responsible for covering its citizens in times of conflict. Bastards! The decades I've spent paying my premiums. I'm talking to a lawyer I know. He's not optimistic.'

'What does the government say?'

'Ha! Which one? Oaktier says it isn't responsible for something that happened to registered citizens offplanet, because that's beyond their jurisdiction. The Intersolar Commonwealth: *well, we're kind of busy right now, can I get back to you on that?* We had to use the mortgage we raised for having a kid to pay the hospital.'

'I'm sorry.'

'Right now, it doesn't seem like a terribly good idea to have a child anyway.' Hoshe growled it out, using anger to override the anguish. If he didn't, he knew he'd do something ridiculous like start crying.

'I accessed the Prime attack on the unisphere,' Paula said. 'But I don't suppose that can ever substitute for being there.'

'It was mayhem on Sligo; absolute mayhem. We were lucky to get out. After what happened there, I'm never going to complain about a Halgarth ever again. That force field took about eight direct hits from Prime nuclear missiles when we were inside it, and it never even wavered. The groundshocks were bad, though. I was in California once when they had a quake; that was nothing compared to this. I mean, buildings were collapsing all around us. The roads buckled straight away, you couldn't use any kind of vehicle.'

'I heard you headed up one of the evacuation squads.'

'Yeah well, they were appealing for anyone with any kind of government service connection. It's an authority thing. The local council didn't put a lot of police on duty for a flower festival.'

'Don't be so modest, Hoshe.'

'It's not like I ever expect a medal or anything. It was mainly self-preservation.'

She indicated his arm. 'How bad were you hurt?'

'Burns, mostly. Nothing too serious. The worst bit was the wait for treatment afterwards. It was ten hours before Inima even saw a nurse. And that was just for triage. It was actually easier for us to get back here and go to our local hospital than wait for the navy's cobbled-together relief operation to finally catch up with us.'

'So now what?'

'Same as everyone else. Carry on as normally as possible, and hope that Admiral Kime does a better job next time around.'

'I see. I came here to offer you a job, Hoshe. I'm working at Senate Security now; I need an assistant, someone I know can do a good job, and someone I know I can trust.'

'That's very flattering,' he said carefully. 'But I'm not really that keen on the Commonwealth administration right now.'

'That's not you talking, Hoshe, that's a whole lot of confusion left over from Sligo.'

'Very psychologically astute, I'm sure.'

'You want me to go on and list medical benefits? How good the family health plan is?'

'No.' He clenched his teeth, trying to come up with a valid reason why he shouldn't accept the offer. 'What about your old office team? Why not approach them?'

'I still don't know which of them I can trust. I received some disturbing information yesterday, which adds to the likelihood one or more of them is working for the Starflyer alien.'

It took a moment for Hoshe to place the name. 'The one the Guardians keep banging on about? You're kidding me?'

'I wish I was.'

The dream flashed through his brain again, its blurred

montage of misery and destruction falling from the sky in blinding purple contrails moving barely slower than light-speed. And that was just what one alien species could do. If there was another, something deeper and more sinister ... 'I opened some of those Guardians' shotguns. It all seemed pretty paranoid stuff to me. Something a freaked out kid would babble about after his first bad trip.'

'That would be a favourable result, proving Bradley Johansson really has been wrong all these years. I'm not used to doubt on this scale, Hoshe, I find it unnerving.'

He thought about it. No, not true. What he considered was how he would explain to Inima that he'd taken the new job. 'I'm not going to be much use for any active role. Not for a week or so.'

'I wanted you to start by reviewing some old files for me. Now that we know what we're looking for, they might be more helpful than the last time I looked through them.'

'So what exactly is the deal with those medical benefits?'

3

The chalet that Mellanie had rented was one of fifty tucked away in a coastal forest over ninety minutes' drive from Darklake City. Together they formed the Greentree Village Park vacation resort, the kind of place where parents on a modest budget could take their kids and let them exhaust themselves during the day on the resort's playtime amenities or down at the beach. A large bar and restaurant building in the heart of the forest provided an evening refuge for the adults to unwind. Two nights a week there was a live cabaret act.

An hour after nightfall, the hire car dropped Mellanie off at the main entrance and rolled back to the parking lot. Vehicles weren't allowed inside Greentree, leaving her to walk along the shingle paths amid the ancient bent rani trees with their white-moss leaf clumps and spongy green bark. Little mushroom-shaped light fittings along the paths provided a soft blue glow as they unravelled through the woods. Greentree had been deliberately laid out so that each cabin was completely isolated; all you could see from the windows were trees and the glowing turquoise path. Somewhere off in the forest she could hear the sound of the piano trio as they crooned their way through songs that were old before Oaktier had even been discovered.

A thin mist was creeping out of the soft loam as the

temperature fell. It swirled in spooky luminescent currents around her feet, which she found slightly disconcerting. When she'd come here as a child with her parents, she'd adored the shaggy old forest with its thick buckled tree trunks. It had seemed magical in those days, a fantastical world to explore. All she could think about today was what might be lurking among all the shadows and secluded glades.

She'd paid in cash for the chalet she and Dudley were sharing. Most of the other chalets were empty right now, which reduced the chance of anyone seeing and recognizing her. She still left early in the morning as a precaution. And the SI assured her it was watching the local cybersphere nodes for any encrypted message activity which would indicate a surveillance operation. Even so, she'd be glad when they left. She still wasn't sure what Baron would do about her.

Their three-room chalet was in a small clearing, with five huge rani trees towering over it. Dudley was pacing nervously up and down the lounge when she walked in.

'Where've you been?' he shouted.

'Fine, thank you, how are you?'

He stopped in the act of flinging himself at her; producing a massive petulant scowl instead. 'I was worried.'

She ran her hand back through her tawny hair, and gave him a mellow smile. 'I'm sorry. It didn't go as well as expected with Paula Myo. Turns out she doesn't trust me, and I don't trust her. Which kind of screws up the idea of us joining forces to take on the Starflyer. So I went on to California. My agent set up some job interviews. Good ones.'

'Oh.' He went up to her and gave her a cautious hug. When she didn't squirm away, he asked: 'Did you get one?'

'I got three offers, actually. Let me get out of these clothes and I'll tell you.'

Dudley's face immediately brightened.

'No, Dudley,' she said wearily. 'Not for sex.'

'But . . . we will tonight, though, won't we?' he asked in a whiny voice.

'Yes, Dudley, we'll have sex later.' She glanced over at the kitchen alcove. Yesterday morning they'd collected over a week's worth of food and supplies from a supermarket twenty minutes away down the highway. Paying cash again. The bags were still sitting on the bench, unpacked. 'I'm going to have a shower, then I'd like something to eat. Think you can manage that for me?'

Once she'd freshened up she wrapped a towel round her hips and went back out into the lounge. It was almost a routine, checking the effect she had on him. Sure enough, Dudley could barely take his eyes off her naked torso. Ever since they got here, she'd been using the gym a couple of hours a day to keep herself toned. The machines there faithfully recorded her physical condition, giving her top marks; but it was always reassuring to have her sexuality confirmed by a man. Even if it was only Dudley.

He'd made a mess of the dinner, which was impressive. The packaged food had a code strip for the microwave, automatically setting the timer and wattage when you put it in. He must have altered the settings manually. She took one look at the brown goo bubbling away under the cellophane wrapping, and dropped it in the bin. The conditioning grill would take care of the smell eventually. 'How did your day go?' she asked as she slid two fresh packets into the microwave.

'I went down to the beach. Some people arrived and started a barbeque. I came back here and accessed the unisphere.'

'Dudley, you need to learn how to socialize with people again.' She kissed him as the microwave counted down, breaking away with a promissory smile when it pinged. They settled down on the broad couch and Mellanie told her e-butler to turn the fire on. Bright holographic flames leapt up in the fireplace, while the invisible heater let out an accompanying blast of hot air – it even added a scent of burning wood.

'I don't know who works for the Starflyer. It could be anyone. And the navy's probably hunting us as well.'

'I doubt that.'

'You don't know. Not really.'

Mellanie narrowed her eyes to look at him. Already he was sitting upright, fully defensive. She didn't help his condition with her own mild paranoia about the Starflyer and Baron. 'No, Dudley, I don't; but they'll have a very hard job finding us. I've made sure of that.' She curled her legs up and started poking chopsticks into the steaming dish of savoury rice and chicken. Maybe it was a good idea they were leaving in the morning.

'What were your job offers?' Dudley asked.

'One was a TSI drama, *Late Rendezvous*. The producers were very keen to sign me up; it's about a girl who arranges to meet her boyfriend on Sligo, then the Primes attack and she doesn't know if he's alive or dead. It's all about her finding romance under the pressure of the attack.' She grinned to herself at the memory of the 'co-stars' the producers had introduced her to. One of them, Ezra, had been utterly gorgeous. The thought of days spent rehearsing love scenes with him had almost made her sign up on the spot. Before the Prime attack and discovering Baron's connection to the Starflyer there would have been no hesitation.

'A TSI?' Dudley said, alarm leaking into his features. 'No! Please, Mellanie. Don't. Not one of those again. That's just sex. That's what they want you for. Don't. I don't care how much money they offered. I couldn't stand it.'

There were times when she really hated how pitiful Dudley was. She was fairly certain that there was no more useful information to extract from that abysmal jumble of thoughts in his brain. After California she'd toyed with the notion of simply not coming back to Greentree, just tell the navy where he was and leave their psychologists to straighten him out. But given who she wanted to meet next, having *the* Dudley Bose in tow, and under control, would make success a lot more likely.

And she did like him in a way. She supposed. Occasionally. When he was calm he could be very lucid, providing her a glimpse of the intellect which had qualified him for his earlier academic life. A sort of sneak preview of what he could be like. Then there was Elan, and everything they'd gone through together there when the Primes attacked. That wasn't a bond easily discarded, not even for her. If he could just get the idea of love out of his head . . .

'I turned it down,' she said. 'I can't afford that kind of time commitment right now.'

'Thank you.' He bowed his head to examine the rectangular meal packet he was holding, almost as if he hadn't seen one before. 'What were the others?'

She pincered a big chunk of chicken with the chopsticks and popped it in her mouth. 'Reuters said they'd take me on as a junior associate. Bravoweb offered me a reporter's slot on the Michelangelo show, he's always been a big rival for Baron. They've been fighting over audience points for over a century.'

'What did you say?'

'I said I'd take the Michelangelo slot. I think he got quite a bang out of poaching one of her top people. They offered me a trial three-month roving brief; and they agreed to my first story proposal.'

'Right. So what was it?'

'An inside account about people who live on a world that's probably going to be invaded by the Primes in the next wave. I said I'd travel out to examine communities that are too poor to leave, the ones that have to stay even though they suspect they're in for hard times. It's pretty horrendous for them, really.'

'Oh.' Dudley picked up a tall tumbler of water and stared morosely at the ice bobbing round on top. 'How does that help us track down the Starflyer?'

'I know for certain that's where we can meet some really strong allies in the fight against the Starflyer, and Bravoweb pick up the tab. Which is handy, because it's not cheap travelling there.' She fashioned a smug smile. 'See?'

'Right. What planet?'

'Far Away.'

*

Coming into the office every morning was getting to be a real drag. In the old days when it was the Directorate, Renne had often come in early, especially when they were on a major case. Now she had to force herself up out of bed when the alarm woke her. And cases didn't get any bigger than this one.

Somehow, Alic Hogan was always there ahead of her. Like Paula used to be, except Hogan didn't conjure up enthusiasm in the rest of the team. Having him watching you arrive was like an automatic reprimand. She knew she was going to have to make an effort to cycle down on the irritation she felt towards him. But that was the problem. It was an effort.

John King appeared in the middle of the morning, and walked over to her desk. 'That smuggled technical equipment you had shipped back from Boongate. My analysis staff have got a slight problem with it.'

'Goddamn typical,' she spat.

John gave her a hurt look.

'All right, I'm sorry. It's just that nobody ever comes and tells me any good news these days.'

'This isn't bad news, exactly, it's just strange.'

'Go on then, what's strange with it?'

'Same as the stuff from Venice Coast, we can't understand what it's used for.'

'John, come on! You must have some idea. I saw the manifest Edmund Li finally produced. There was nearly a metric tonne of hardware.'

'A lot of it very similar,' he said defensively. 'But given we don't know what they're building it's difficult.'

'I'll settle for best guess. I trust you.'

He smiled sheepishly. 'All right, based on these systems, and factoring in the surviving components from Venice Coast, assuming they were intended for the same thing—'

'John!'

'Force fields. Very high-density force fields. But the thing is, they'd use up a terrific amount of power.'

'So?'

He gave her an elaborate shrug. 'On Far Away? Where are they going to get it from? I checked with the Commonwealth Civil Council. There're five medium-size civic power stations supplying Armstrong city. They're gas turbines running off a local oil field. The revitalization project imported some fission micropiles to power their equipment in the early days. And the Institute has three micropiles to power their facilities. That's it. The rest of the planet gets by on solar panels, wind turbines, and a few oil wells. They don't have anything like the power output one of these weirdo devices would consume.'

She stared at him blankly, waiting for a suggestion. None came. 'Then what does produce that much power?'

'I haven't got a clue. It's not like you could have smuggled a fusion or fission generator through unnoticed even before we were inspecting every piece of cargo. And Far Away can't be physically plugged into the Commonwealth power grid. It doesn't make any sense.'

'Right then.' She instinctively reached for her mug of coffee, only to find it was empty. 'So what we have is an unknown force field device, or devices, which consumes a lot of power, on a planet that doesn't have any.'

'Nicely summarized.'

'I look forward to seeing how the commander treats that one when you submit it.'

They both glanced over at the door to Hogan's office.

'Oh no you don't,' John said. 'This is just a technical appendix to your report.'

Rennc's e-butler informed her that a file from King's forensic staff had just been deposited in her working case hold folder.

John cocked his fingers pistol-style and aimed at her. 'What you do with it is up to you.'

'Bastard,' she grunted.

He gave her a cheery wave, and retreated back to his own desk.

*

Vic Russell returned from Cagayn half an hour later. The second lieutenant barely had time to kiss his wife, Gwyneth, before Renne hauled him off to a conference room for a debrief.

'The Cagayn police were very familiar with Robin Beard,' Vic told her. 'He works in the motor trade. Good repair and service man, apparently. Which fits in with what Cufflin told us; they met on an electronics course a few years back.'

'Did you see him?' Renne asked. She thought Vic looked tired. He was a big man, well over six foot tall, and about as wide. His weekends were spent playing bonecruncher games of rugby for a non-professional club outside Leicester. Renne had turned up with Gwyneth to support his team one Saturday, and had been intimidated by the amount of *good spirits* violence in the game. Cagayn must have been an exhausting trip for someone as fit as Vic to appear rundown.

'No, 'fraid not. I was too late. Our Mr Beard is a somewhat migratory character. According to his tax records he never stays at the same garage for more than a couple of years.'

'He pays taxes?'

'Not very often. But that's not why the police have such a big file on him. If you're looking for a getaway vehicle, word is that Beard's the one you need to give it a good overhaul beforehand. Same if you have a warehouse full of hot cars that need rebranding; he knows how to replace and revise all the manufacturers' security tagging.'

'Sounds like the kind of person who would have good reason to know our elusive agent.'

'Quite so. I took a scout around his home. Rented, of course. We must have missed him by about twenty-four hours. His vehicle recovery van was gone, which is his own mobile maintenance shop; he keeps all his tools and equipment in there. It's the one permanent thing in his life, apparently. I spoke to some of the blokes he worked with at the garage; there's a lot of customized machinery in the back, stuff he's built over the years.'

For an instant, Renne saw the image of some titanic truck rolling along a highway with force field bubbles for wheels, draining energy from the Commonwealth grid as it went. 'Ah, so if we find the van—'

'—we find the man. Yeah. Ordinarily, the police wouldn't have too much trouble spotting a bright orange three-ton tow van. Of course, given his chosen field of expertise it's not quite as simple as it would be with the average criminal on the run. Beard is familiar with every traffic monitor program in the Commonwealth. He'll have aggressor software to deal with all of it. Cagayn police have issued an all-officer dispatch for vans of that description to be pulled over and checked.'

'The boss would have loved that one: proper police work.'

Vic grinned, revealing teeth that had been rearranged in crooked ranks by too many hard impacts on the rugby pitch. 'She would, yeah. But it gives us a bit of a nightmare.'

'You've alerted the Cagayn CST station?'

'First thing I did. They checked back through their sched-ules for me; no van of that kind left Cagayn in the timeframe we're considering. So if anybody does take a van like that on board a vehicle-carry train, they'll let this office know about it immediately.'

'Good. Thanks, Vic.'

*

Noon saw the daily senior officers' case-review meeting in conference room three. Renne joined Tarlo and John at the big table, putting her coffee mug down then hurriedly mopping up the ring it left on the surface.

'You two want to try Amies for lunch?' John asked.

'Sure,' Tarlo said.

'You're not still after that waitress are you?' Renne asked disapprovingly. The redhead Tarlo had spent a month flirting with was a first-life art student, still in her early twenties. He was in his third life. It wasn't done. But that damn uniform . . .

'There are waitresses there?'

The men laughed. She sighed.

Hogan marched in and sat at the head of the table. His whole stance was charged with energy, which produced an aggressive smile.

'John, I believe you have something critical for us?'

'Yes, sir.'

Renne gave him a curious glance; he hadn't mentioned anything earlier.

'Foster Cortese finally pulled a match out of the visual recognition program,' John said. The big high-rez portal at the end of the conference room lit up to show the assassin's face. 'CST on Boongate has been slow to locate their records for us, but we can all see there's no mistake. He came through the Half Way gateway six months before the Venice Coast incident.'

'Name?' Tarlo asked.

'Officially: Frances Rowden, son of a landowner, which is how he can afford to travel to the Commonwealth. He was going to enrol at a university on Kolhapur, a two-year agricultural course. We checked, they have no record of him.'

'He's a Guardian,' Alic said happily.

'Why do you think that?' Renne asked.

Alic's good humour flickered slightly, but nothing could tone down his enthusiasm. He held up his hand and started ticking off points. 'Okay, one he's a Far Away native, so what other faction could he belong to? Two, he's sent on tough assignments to benefit them, I mean really tough. Our boy is wetwired to the back of his ears with weapons. He's their new enforcer.'

'How did the Venice Coast hit benefit them?' Renne asked quickly.

'Valtare Rigin was fucking them over. He had to be. He was a black market arms dealer. These guys don't exactly have corporate mission statements. He saw a chance to switch cargoes or make a low-grade substitution or he was holding out for more money. Whatever— They caught him redhanded. What are they going to do? Sue him? Shake hands and say sorry? No, they close the deal their way. They're terrorists, remember? The most lethal bunch of psychotics we've ever had running round the Commonwealth. This is what they do: kill people.

'Thompson Burnelli, well that's obvious. He'd just pushed through an inspectorate division which is going to screw every clandestine weapons shipment back to Far Away. Blam, out he goes. Revenge, a warning to others that no one is safe, none of you are beyond our reach. Murdering a senator shook the whole political establishment to its core. Then there was McFoster. He betrayed the Guardians, they killed him for it.'

'How did he betray them?' Tarlo asked.

'Justine Burnelli,' Renne said in a flat voice. She could see how Alic Hogan's mind was working, and didn't like it.

'Exactly,' Alic said, on a roll. 'They find out McFoster visited Senator Burnelli, that the two of them are lovers. The next thing they know, he's got a navy squad tailing round after him. They thought he was about to lead us to them.'

'How did they find that out?' Renne asked.

Alic treated her to an expression of mild scorn. 'The trip to the Observatory. His colleagues were watching him the whole time, a back-up team. And we had that local office arsehole . . .' He snapped his fingers.

'Phil Mandia,' Renne supplied reluctantly.

'Right: Mandia. He was following McFoster in a convoy of 4x4s through the mountains. The Guardians saw us. They put it together. It wouldn't matter to them if McFoster had actually clued Senator Burnelli in on what was happening or not. Whatever he said to her, it betrayed them. And there he is again, this Frances Rowden, waiting at LA Galactic. There on the right concourse exactly when the loop train pulled in, knowing he's got our squads to dodge as well.' Alic beamed contentedly.

The trouble was, Renne admitted to herself, the facts fitted. Not only that, she couldn't see a flaw in the Commander's line of reasoning. Granted, a lot of it was speculation, but *logical* speculation; the kind of argument a jury would convict on.

It was also politically expedient, which fuelled her unease. That same nagging little uncertainty she'd experienced when she walked into the Halgarth girls' loft apartment on Daroca. No reason for it. Just her own awkward intuition. A detective knowing instinctively when something is out of kilter.

Everything Alic claimed was possible. Yes.

Believable? No.

'I'm going to enjoy this,' Alic said. '*Certain people* in Senate Security are going to be extremely upset when they access this case file now we've solved it for them. It doesn't leave any room for her stupid conspiracy theories.'

Renne tried to catch Tarlo's attention. She couldn't. Which she suspected was deliberate.

'Thank Foster Cortese from me,' Alic said. 'He's done a good job. Credit where it's due.'

'Will do,' John King said.

He ran a program, Renne thought in disgust. She could see what Alic was doing, pulling the staff into his orbit. Team-building with the completely wrong motivation behind it. They'd wind up producing politically required answers for him, not the right ones.

And why am I so cynical about this? That bullshit theory about Francis Rowden. Am I just jealous I didn't put it together? It is simple enough. Why do I think it's not right?

'I'm going to need another warrant,' Tarlo said.

'What for?' Alic asked.

'The Pacific Pine Bank records have been quite useful,' Tarlo said. Now he allowed eye contact with Renne, giving her an I-told-you-so smile. 'The Shaw-Hemmings finance company on Tolaka transferred a lot of money into Kazimir's account. I'd like to see where it came from.'

'How much money?' Renne asked.

'A hundred thousand Earth dollars.'

She pursed her lips, impressed.

'You've got it,' Alic said. 'Renne, how is it coming on with the Lambeth Interplanetary Society?'

There wasn't any undue emphasis on the question, never-theless she got the feeling that expectations were set a little too high following the news about Francis Rowden. Her report was going to let the side down. *Ridiculous, I'm getting paranoid.* 'Nothing solid yet, I'm afraid. It was Vic's case, but I've had him chasing down Robin Beard. Matthew has been datamining the Society, but there are very few files to work with. The employment agencies that serve that part of London don't have any records of the Society at all. It's not a promising avenue.'

'We could launch a unisphere appeal,' Tarlo suggested. 'See

if the news shows would give us some time. Ask for any ex-employees to come forward and contact us.'

'No,' Renne said. 'That would show our hand to the Guardians.'

'I'm going to agree with Renne on this one,' Alic said. 'We'll keep public appeals as a last resort; it smacks of desperation. Let me know when the datamining stalls completely, and we'll reconsider then.'

'Yes, sir.'

'So what about Beard?'

'He's gone to ground on Cagayn, but the police there are on alert for him. Judging by his background, he's someone who could provide us with a positive lead to the agent the Guardians use.'

'Do the police understand how important this is?'

'Yes, sir.'

'Good, but ride them hard. We can't let this one slip.'

*

Senate Security's European division was nothing like as grand as the ever-expanding Navy Intelligence facilities over in Paris. It was based in London, taking over the entire top floor of a monolithic stone-fronted building in Whitehall, half a mile from Westminster Palace. The European division shared it with two other Intersolar Commonwealth departments, the UFN regional auditor and the environmental commission, all of whom provided excellent cover. There was no plaque outside announcing Senate Security's presence and, if accessed, the building management array had no knowledge of their existence. Entry was gained through a discreet underground ramp entrance opposite the old British Foreign Office building.

Every morning, Paula's designated car would pick her up outside her apartment and drive onto the European trans-capital shuttle train, a sleek new maglev vehicle, which took thirty-five minutes to get from Paris to London using the old channel tunnel route. Once they arrived at Waterloo Station the car drove her straight to Whitehall and down into the secure parking chamber underneath the ancient building. Travel time was well under an hour.

When Hoshe arrived on his first day, Paula was checking through the official case files on Francis Rowden as Senate Security pulled them out of Navy Intelligence's array. 'Idiot,' she muttered as Hoshe knocked on her open office door.

'Am I not welcome?' he inquired.

Paula grinned at him. 'No, not you. Please, come in.' Her office was a great deal larger than the one in Paris, with a high ceiling and elaborate cornices. Wooden panelling extended halfway up the walls, originally a dark-gold oak, but now nearly black with age. Two big windows looked out over the trees lining Victoria Embankment to the Thames beyond. Just to the north, Hungerford Bridge was visible, carrying rail lines over the river to Charing Cross station.

One wall was completely covered by a holographic projection, a map of a large CST station, with a big terminal building at one end, and hundreds of track lines winding across a broad open space outside it. Various trains were frozen in place, and a large number of green dots were sprinkled across the ground, each with its own neon-blue code tag floating above it.

'You landed on your feet, then,' Hoshe said. He gave the projected map an interested look as he passed. His shoes sank into the thick burgundy carpet as he walked over to the vast antique rosewood desk where she was sitting.

'I know. You'd think this was where the British ran their Empire from back when they had one.'

'It's not?'

'No. This was all remodelled a hundred and fifty years ago. The designers went for what they considered Grand Imperial era. It's actually younger than me.'

Hoshe eased himself into a chair with only a small wince.

'How are you doing?' Paula asked. She thought he certainly looked a lot better than when she'd seen him on Oaktier, with his face properly shaved, cologne dabbed on, and lightly oiled hair held back with his usual silver clip. The suit was new, too, a pale fawn-brown, expensive shiny fabric with narrow lapels, emphasizing a figure that was a lot slimmer than the first time she'd met him. She would have welcomed that loss of weight if it hadn't been for the sunken cheeks that accompanied it.

'Easier, I guess. And Inima was a lot better this morning. I think she's looking forward to being discharged.'

'I'm glad. What did she say about this job?'

'She rather liked the idea of living in London. It's a security thing, you know? If you're safe anywhere, it'll be on this planet. There's enough real wealth and power concentrated here to make sure it's properly defended. After Sligo that can't be a bad thing. And of course the clinics here are the best in the Commonwealth.'

'You got a flat sorted out?'

'Personnel have shortlisted five for me to take a look at. I'll view them tonight. Until then, I'm all yours.'

'Okay then. The first thing I need is for you to take a look at something called the Cox Educational charity; it was responsible for funding some of Dudley Bose's original observation of the Dyson Pair. My old Directorate team investigated it six months before the flight of the *Second Chance*, they reported everything was legitimate and above board. I want you to repeat the exercise, bearing in mind there's been an allegation that the Cox records have been doctored. Then pull those old Directorate files, and compare them to your findings.'

'Right. Who made the allegation?'

Paula smiled. 'Mellanie Rescorai.'

'Really?' Hoshe seemed to find that amusing, too. 'I did warn you about her. What goes around . . .'

'Exactly. I've been doing some checking on Ms Rescorai. There are some very interesting reports of her activities on

Elan during the Prime attack. Apparently, she took a leading role in the evacuation of Randtown.'

'Mellanie?'

'Yes. I know! And her new boyfriend is Dudley Bose.'

'Well, I suppose there have been more unlikely couples.'

'Name one. They're keeping out of sight somewhere on Oaktier.'

'You need them tracking down?'

'No. Her unisphere address is current and open. She's just switched her correspondent role from Alessandra Baron to Michelangelo. Which is interesting. Her other allegation was that Baron is working for the Starflyer.'

'Sounds like you should have recruited her not me.'

'I'm keeping an open mind about her. Something there doesn't quite make sense. This is not the bimbo in a bikini from Morton's penthouse. She's changed. Or part of her has; she's still blindly impulsive, but there's something else there as well now – she's got a lot of confidence.'

'Everybody grows up sometime.'

'Maybe. For now we just do the background work and see what we can shake loose.'

'Okay. So what's this, then?' He pointed at the projected map.

'LA Galactic. I was taking a look at the McFoster shooting incident. The Paris office have managed to find a name for our assassin: Francis Rowden. I wanted to see how he eluded both the navy and CST security after he killed McFoster. The office RI has worked up a simulation for me; admittedly the records aren't perfect but most of the timings and positionings have been cross-referenced with each other.'

'Yeah, and?'

'Simple enough, he just jumped onto a train. There's no other solution.' She gave the luminescent map a confused glance. 'Though he only had a very small window of opportunity. I'm surprised none of the people on the ground saw him.'

'Your double agent?'

'Possibly.' Paula was surprised how troubled she was by the notion. She stared at the map with its green dots, one of the tags seemed to glow brighter than the others: Tarlo.

*

Mellanie had taken the window seat when they got on the train at Darklake City. Now, fifty minutes later, she watched them drawing in towards Boongate's single terminal building. Thick grey clouds rumbled through the air above the city, blocking out the sun, and unleashing a constant heavy downpour that was unseasonable for late spring. It added an extra layer of drabness to the empty wasteland of the station yard.

Glancing ahead, she could see people crammed on every square centimetre of the platform which the Oaktier train was heading for. A line of CST security officers in dark-blue flexarmour suits stood along the very edge of the platform, their arms linked, keeping the crowd back from the approaching train. A barrage of shouting began as soon as the PH58 engine nosed its way under the terminal's arching roof. Hundreds of arms waved above the security squad's bulbous helmets. It was a peculiar greeting for an ordinary train, as if there was some huge media celebrity on board.

Dudley peered nervously over her shoulder. 'What are they here for?'

'A train out,' she told him. She wanted to sound slightly more blasé about it, someone observing the foolish antics of people she'd never have to meet or mingle with, the kind of people who lived a life she'd escaped from thanks to Morton and the SI. Except she knew that in a week or so she'd be back at this station, eager for a train out, just like them. Her ticket was already booked, an open-ended first class return. Now she was beginning to wonder if that would mean much when it actually came down to standing on the platform and wrestling her way to an open carriage door; it didn't much look as though the security squad would take time out to help first class passengers.

When they disembarked there was only a narrow strip of concrete left between the train and the security squad for them to walk down. The hard-pressed line of flexarmoured figures jostled constantly against them. Mellanie kept stumbling as she was shoved repeatedly against the side of the train. The angry glances she threw back every time it happened weren't even noticed.

It was only when they reached the concourse at the end they finally had some empty space. Reactive barriers had been set up to channel the dense throng of people from the station entrance to their platforms; not that the barriers could dull the angry buzz of the crowd. Going the other way, arrivals had their narrow exit routes almost to themselves. Barely twenty people had got off the train from Oaktier. Their two pieces of luggage popped out of the gap between the last security officer and the train as if the bags were being kicked clear.

Dudley stopped. 'I want to go back,' he said meekly. 'I want you to come with me, darling. Please, don't do this. Don't go to Far Away. We'll never get back to the Commonwealth. They'll land there, too. They will, I know it. They'll land and they'll capture me again, and . . .'

'Dudley.' She *shusshed* him with a finger pressed on his lips, then kissed him. 'It's all right. Nothing like that will happen.'

'You can't know that. Don't treat me like I'm a child. I hate that.'

She almost said: *Then stop acting like a child.* Instead she lowered her voice. 'The SI will give me plenty of warning.' Which it wouldn't – she didn't think. Who knew?

Dudley gave her a petulant look.

'Come on,' she said brightly, and hooked her arm through his. 'You're going to see a neutron star first hand. How many astronomers can say that, even today?'

It was a poor bribe, but he did give a reluctant shrug and allow her to lead him off towards the single door leading off the concourse. There were plenty of signs for the connection service to Far Away. They followed them through a deserted cloister and finally reached an external doorway which came out on a corner of the terminal building. The noise of miserable frustrated people reverberated around them.

Outside the station, the crowd must have been ten thousand strong. They were squashed together in a great swathe from the passenger terminal all the way back to the highway exit a kilometre away. Cars and taxis that had been abandoned on the approach roads were now isolated impediments surrounded by dense clusters of bodies. They'd all been broken open and were now being used for everything from shelters to kids' playframes to toilets. Thousands of umbrellas bobbed about, blobs of murky colour deflecting the waves of rain sluicing down out of the insipid sky. Kids dressed in waterproofs moaned and wailed as they were dragged along and buffeted on all sides. Men and women shouted futile insults and complaints, growing louder as they neared the terminal entrance.

Police and CST security had them all penned in between two lines of officers and patrolbots. Helicopters drifted overhead, producing cyclonic downswirls of rain to complete the wretchedness of everyone on the ground.

Mellanie's virtual hands brushed several icons and she began scanning the scene with her eyes, retinal inserts on maximum resolution, sending the image back directly to the Michelangelo studio in Hollywood. She murmured a few accompanying, patronizing comments about desperation and the flotsam of war. Disdain came easy now, proximity to Alessandra had seen to that.

A text message popped up in her virtual vision. **Good stuff. Already! Knew I was right about you. Remember, take care when you get there. Love *MA*.**

Michelangelo had been surprised when she pitched the Far Away trip to him during their private interview. He thought she was trying to prove something. Normally, interns would just have to go to bed with him to earn their probation contract; in that respect he had an even greater appetite than Alessandra. Mellanie had suggested the assignment after they'd finished fucking and she'd already got the job. It'd thrown him slightly, but he smiled and said he liked her style.

He had quite a lot of style of his own. Thanks to Dudley, who was a triumph of quantity over quality, she'd almost forgotten what truly hot sex could be like. He could also be funny. She'd laughed out loud a couple of times at the stories he told. When she did that she realized laughter was something that never happened when she was with Dudley – nor ever would, she thought. Most of the subsequent train journey back to Oaktier had been spent fantasizing what else she'd have to do in that large bed of his to earn a permanent contract.

'Is that the office?' Dudley asked.

'Huh.' Mellanie shook off the reverie which the text message had kindled. Dudley was pointing to a small clump of box-like prefab buildings adjoining the terminal, each of which had tour company signs above their doors. 'Yeah. We want Grand Triad Adventures. They said someone would be waiting for us.' Her semi-organic coat had birthed a hood which she pulled over her hair to protect it from the rain. The boots she wore were practical rather than stylish, probably the kind of thing a Randtown local would possess. To match that, she'd chosen a pair of olive-green jeans from her own collection, and a black sweatshirt of semi-organic fur fibre which was wonderfully soft against her skin. Dudley had just put on his usual non-label trousers and a cheap shirt and jacket. She'd given up trying to dress him properly.

They splashed their way through the puddles to the rank of tour operators. Grand Triad Adventures was easy enough to find – it was the only office with a light on.

The deputy assistant manager of tour bookings, Niall Swalt, was waiting inside. A slim young man in his early twenties with badly cut curly blond hair, sitting behind the reception desk, absorbed by some bizarre game show on the portal. Rock music was thundering out across the deserted office as female figures dived in and out of vats filled with oily fluid. When the door opened, he lunged to his feet, the bright figures and the music shrinking away.

'Ms Rescorai, a pleasure.' Niall came round the desk, eager to greet her. 'I'm a real big fan of yours. I still access *Murderous Seduction* once a month at least.' He was wearing one of Mellanie's old promotion sweatshirts, with a hologram of her face in the middle of his chest. It had been washed so many times the image flickered badly through its smile cycle, drizzling green and red interference specks.

'Always delighted to meet a fan.' She made herself smile neutrally as he grabbed hold of her hand. He had cheap OCtattoos on his fingers and arms which her own sophisticated inserts analysed instantly on contact. The thin green lines were capable of delivering crude sensory impulses to his nervous system; to Mellanie he briefly appeared as a glowing arabesque wire sculpture, with the densest entanglement concentrated round his groin. 'And you can still see,' she remarked dryly.

'Oh yes, it's a fantastic story. And it's all real.' He was grinning profusely as he stared at her; the heat in his cheeks highlighting his pimples. 'You are sensational in it. You feel gorgeous.'

'Thank you.' Mellanie didn't risk glancing at Dudley who was ominously quiet beside her. 'That's very sweet.'

'Do you mind if I ask you about the hunting lodge night? Did that happen for real?'

'Yes, yes it did, that was quite a night.'

Dudley's face had frozen, with every muscle rigid. Only the colour spreading across his cheeks revealed he was even alive.

'Wow!' Niall whistled admiringly. 'And the time Morton took you to the Falkirk restaurant. Why didn't you sue the security people?'

'Who would have benefited? And let's face it, we shouldn't have been in the ladies washroom together. It was a bit naughty of us; but the singer was very beautiful. Who could resist?'

'Right. Yeah. I've noticed some mistakes, too.'

'Really?'

'The party on Resal's yacht; when you go on board you're wearing black silk panties; but when you leave they're gold satin.'

'Gosh, I never knew. I'll have to have a word with the continuity people about that.'

'The other thing was Paula Myo. I checked the actual court files from the trial; according to the Directorate case notes the Investigator did research Oaktier's organized crime groups. But *Murderous Seduction* showed her completely dismissing the possibility that Shaheef was killed by a third party.'

'We were emphasizing the point. Myo didn't do a thorough job.' Mellanie's face had become as inflexible as Dudley's; for the first time she actually had to consider that automatic response. *What if Myo had investigated properly? What if Morty* ... She flexed her shoulders, annoyed with herself for doubting.

Emboldened by how easy it was to talk to his idol, Niall gave a shy grin, and asked: 'Are your breasts really that firm, or did they edit the tactile stream to make them feel like that?'

'Hey!' Dudley snarled.

Niall gave him a puzzled frown.

Mellanie put a hand on her devoted fan's arm. 'Niall, our train was late, we routed through StLincoln before we got to Wessex, so we're worried we might have missed the connection.'

'Oh no,' Niall said earnestly. 'Everything's ready for you.'

'Great. This is all our luggage.' She pointed to the two cases that had rolled in behind them. 'Where do we go now?'

'The company has a car. Uh, I'm afraid you've got to be cleared by the Far Away freight inspectorate division before you go through the wormhole. It's a new thing, they've only just started doing that. They make sure you haven't got any weapons or illegal stuff.'

'Sounds like a good idea.'

The car was a Mercedes limousine; all it did was drive them five miles across the station yard to a nearly empty warehouse. Several scanning systems had been set up inside the yawning building, one of them an archway large enough for an entire goods wagon to pass through it. A couple of very bored police officials were reviewing shadowy images of crates on a big portal. They ordered Mellanie's luggage to roll through a small scanner hoop.

'There were a lot of people waiting to leave outside the station,' Mellanie said to Niall as their bags went through. 'How difficult is it going to be for us to get on a train once we get back from Far Away?'

It was as if she'd issued the young man with a personal challenge. He straightened himself up to compose his features into what he considered a reassuring expression. 'Grand Triad Adventures guarantees the safe transport of all its customers on both sides of the gateway. We take responsibility for your holiday as soon as you arrive on Boongate, and that doesn't finish until you leave. Mr Spanton, the manager, he left me in charge when he took off for Verona with his family. I shall be here to make sure you get your allocated seats.'

'Thank you, Niall.'

'All part of the service.'

'Don't you want to leave?'

'Sometimes I think maybe I do. But this is my home, where would I go? The Commonwealth isn't going to abandon us. There's a lot of new defence equipment coming in. I know that for a fact. I work here at the station. I see things. Everyone in the crowd out there, they're just frightened stupid rich people. I'm not like that. I'm staying.'

'Good for you.'

After the luggage check, the Mercedes took them over to the small tour embarkation building, which had its own platform along one side. Mellanie saw an MLV22 electric engine hitched to a single carriage waiting under the short composite panel canopy. There were three other people in the suiting room; Trevelyan Halgarth and Ferelith Alwon, a pair of physicists on their way to the *Marie Celeste* Institute, and Griffith Applegate, a bureaucrat in the governor's office. Griffith confided that he was one of eight staff that were coming back on rotation – he was the only one who'd shown up. Trevelyan and Ferelith were pleasant enough, but Mellanie worried they were both Starflyer agents, and went for a polite but aloof approach when they tried to talk to her.

The suit Mellanie had to wear to compensate for Half Way's atmosphere was a baggy mauve overall with its own heating web, and a metal ring collar. Its array interfaced with her e-butler, and as soon as she'd settled the ring on her shoulders a rubbery semi-organic membrane slithered out from inside the rim to form a seal around her neck. A transparent bubble helmet clipped neatly onto the ring and locked tight. Her e-butler ran a quick check on the rebreather module and threw up a row of green icons in her virtual vision. She took the helmet off again, and carried it under her arm.

Niall led them down a corridor to the train, where a steward was waiting outside the open carriage door 'I'll see you in about a week,' Mellanie told him. She let Dudley carry on through into the carriage, then gave Niall a quick impish kiss on the cheek. 'They're real,' she whispered and hurried off. Her last image of him was an astonished happy smile on his gaunt face.

The inside of the carriage looked similar to all the rest of the standard-class furnishings in CST's fleet. It was only the airlock doorways at both ends which made it different. As soon as the five passengers were sitting down the outer door closed, sealed, and the train began to roll forwards.

Rain splattered down across the window as soon as they left the platform behind. Nothing else was moving across the station yard. Even the big cargo depots were quiet and unused.

Red light began to seep in through the carriage windows as they approached the Half Way gateway. Then Mellanie felt the tingle of the pressure curtain. It might have been her imagination, but she thought it was stronger than usual.

As soon as they were through, the rainwater which had smeared itself across every window in the carriage immediately turned to ice and fluoresced a strong crimson. She pressed her face against the triple-glazed glass, peering through the frost pattern. The landscape outside was a desert of naked rock, stained a dark carmine by the M-class star. A coral-pink sky rose from a distant jagged horizon, phasing to a deep scarlet directly overhead. There were no clouds, not even the gentlest of hazes to mar the uniformity of the heavens above Half Way, the atmosphere was incredibly clear. Powerful blue-white flashes were going off constantly, an almost monotonous rhythm cutting through the red sunlight. No matter where Mellanie looked, she couldn't see any lightning bolts; nor was there any thunder.

The journey from the gateway was short. On one side of the track, the rock began to dip down to reveal Half Way's last remaining sea, a flat calm surface of slate-grey water. They were travelling towards a deep V-shaped inlet, whose sharp cliff walls extended back over half a mile from the main shoreline. On any other world the inlet would have been an erosion estuary with a fast river emptying into its apex. Here, it looked as if a wedge-shaped slice of the land had been hewed out and removed. Instead of a river, a broad tongue of rock formed a smooth ramp leading down into the sea.

Shackleton was perched a hundred metres from the tranquil water, an odd collection of pressurized huts raised on stumpy pillars, interspaced with gigantic hangars. As well as the train staff and aircrews, the little village also housed a team from Boongate's National Marine Science Agency, who were methodically categorizing the remaining oceanic life forms. Not that anybody was visible outside, the whole place seemed deserted. It boasted a single crude station at the inland end, consisting of a ramp for cargo, and a pair of metal steps for the airlock doors.

As they drew up to it, Mellanie pressed harder against the glass, keen to see the planes they'd be flying on. Four of Half Way's nine HA-1 Carbon Goose flying boats were resting on the rock just above the sea. She stared in awe at the massive silver-white fuselages gleaming under the red sun as their true size sank in.

When the Commonwealth Council was assembling the financial package necessary for CST to establish a wormhole link to Far Away, its members had been actively concerned about the possibility of anything hostile finding its way back to the Commonwealth. Given the nature of the flare that had been detected on Damaran, they had the reasonable enough worry that the aliens who triggered it might be antagonistic. The safeguard they insisted on was simple enough. The two respective wormhole gateway stations on Half Way must be separated by a considerable distance so that the route to Boongate could be severed in the event anything wicked did force its way off Far Away. After a full survey of Half Way, they went on to build the stations, Shackleton and Port Evergreen, on islands over ten thousand kilometres apart.

It was the Halgarths, the political instigators of the whole Far Away project, who provided the link between the islands. Some quirk of dynastic pride made Heather Antonia Halgarth decide on the largest aircraft ever built. The components were all constructed on EdenBurg and shipped in through Boongate to be assembled in Shackleton's hangars. Made out of a carbotanium composite structure, each Carbon Goose measured a hundred and twenty-two metres long, with a corresponding wingspan of a hundred and ten metres. They had six engines, air-cooled fission micropile ducted turbines producing 32,000kg of thrust each, enough to give the plane a cruising speed of .9 mach. Range was effectively unlimited, the micropiles only needed replacing every twenty-five years.

The steward led them down from the train, and started shepherding them towards the Carbon Goose they were going to use. Behind them, a couple of CST staff emerged from a hut and began supervising the cargo removal. Loaderbots lifted up crates and transferred them to a small fleet of flatbed wagons which would drive them over to the plane.

Mellanie felt her suit stiffen and inflate as the airlock's outer door opened. Valves soon equalized the pressure. Half Way's atmosphere wasn't hugely toxic, the majority of the gas was the kind of nitrogen oxygen mix found on H-congruous worlds, but complementing that were unacceptably high levels of carbon dioxide and argon, which made filters or a rebreather essential. Equatorial temperature in the daytime fluctuated between minus ten and minus fifteen Celsius. Again, not immediately lethal, but heated suits were indispensable.

She walked a few paces away from the bottom of the steps, and tilted her head back. Another bright flash erupted in the sky. It came from a tiny radiant point close to the gibbous bulk of the M-class star.

'Is that it?' she asked Dudley.

He was gawping up at the sky, for once looking quite

serene. 'Yes. That's the companion. I was hoping you could see the plasma tide, but it doesn't seem to be substantial enough for naked eye observation.'

'You mean the sun's atmosphere?'

'Not the corona itself, no, though that does undergo constant tidal distortion. The neutron star is orbiting close enough to the sun to attract most of its solar wind. The plasma gets tugged out into gigantic streamers across the gulf and then spirals down to the neutron star. All the flashes you see are impact waves.'

As he was talking the neutron star flared again. Mellanie had to blink and look away, the light was so intense. It left a dense purple after-image in her vision.

'Is that radioactive?'

'It emits radiation, Mellanie, it's not radioactive. The two are quite separate.'

'All right,' she said in faint annoyance. 'Is it dangerous?'

'There's quite a heavy gamma and x-ray burst each time, yes. But Half Way's atmosphere will protect us from the worst. You perhaps wouldn't want to stay out here for a week, though.'

'I'll try to remember.' She marched off towards the waiting flying boat, irritated by the way he'd switched into his lecturer persona.

The Carbon Goose was standing on its triple undercarriage, with aluminium air stairs extended from a forward airlock hatch. A long cargo hold was open amidships, with loaderbots transferring crates on board. As Mellanie drew closer, she got a clear view of the sea behind the vast aircraft as it rippled against the inlet's natural ramp of rock. It wasn't perfectly still after all, the surface undulated slowly as it was stirred by the gentle currents of air that passed for wind on this world. A fringe of mushy ice lapped slothfully against the rock all around the shoreline, never quite managing to agglutinate into a solid sheet. The terminal glaciers which had emerged five million years ago to cap the northern and southern zones of the planet had slowly drained vast quantities of pure water out of the oceans, leaving a residue of water that became ever more salty with each passing century, correspondingly lowering its freezing point. Neither of the massive planetary encrustations had grown any larger for millennia now. With the star in its current state, Half Way's environment had reached an equilibrium that would probably last for geological ages.

The airlock in the flying boat was large enough to hold all five passengers simultaneously as the atmosphere cycled. Mellanie took her helmet off as she walked into the forward cabin on the first deck. Her first impression was rows and rows of huge chairs stretching away down the brightly lit interior, like a small theatre auditorium. There was a staff of eight waiting for them, and three times that many bots. She'd never seen anything like it before.

They were helped off with their suits and told to sit wherever they liked. Mellanie chose a window seat near the front, and was given a glass of Buck's Fizz by one of the stewardesses. 'Now this is the way to travel,' she declared as the seat slid back and its footrest extended. Dudley looked around uncertainly, then gingerly allowed himself to sink back into the thick leather cushioning.

There were all the usual dull thuds associated with an aircraft preparing to take off, crates being loaded and secured, cargo hold doors closing, turbines starting up. The ends of the wings slowly bent down to the vertical, lowering the long bulbous tip floats ready for the water takeoff. Then they were rolling down the rock slope into the sea. More thuds as the undercarriage retracted, leaving them floating. They taxied sedately out of the inlet. The pilot used the PA to announce their ten-hour flight time and wished them a pleasant journey, and the nuclear turbines wound up to full thrust.

It was a surprisingly short takeoff run. Mellanie grinned excitedly as huge fans of spray curved out from behind the wingtip floats. Then they were surging up into the pink sky, applauded by the silent dazzling flashes of collapsing ions as they crashed into the neutron star forty million kilometres above them.

*

There was only one break in the monotony of the flight. Three hours in, the pilot spotted a pod of white whurwals far below, and lost altitude so the bored passengers could see them. They were little more than vermilion dots sliding through the darkling sea, almost twice the size of Earth's blue whales. Unlike those terrestrial whales these were fantastically aggressive, pack creatures hunting down the gradually dwindling stocks of fish they shared their last arctic ocean with. They even fought with other pods as they swam round and round the equator between the constricting walls of Half Way's terminal glaciers.

Twice, Mellanie and Dudley left the forward cabin to consummate their membership of the mile high club. They didn't even have to use the cramped toilets for privacy. The middle and rear cabins on all three decks were empty and dark, giving them plenty of scope for misbehaviour amid the long rows of vacant seats.

*

Port Evergreen was situated on an island covering twenty-five thousand square miles. All of it naked rock. No plant life had ever been discovered on Half Way; there were no traces of soil, even sand was virtually non-existent thanks to the lack of a moon and any tides; and nobody had ever chipped out any fossils from island strata. Planetary scientists argued that evolution had never pushed out of the aquatic stage, not that the Commonwealth was interested. Half Way was the ultimate nowhere planet.

As if to prove it, Port Evergreen was even less impressive

than Shackleton. It was dusk when they arrived, with barely enough maroon light left in the sky to illuminate the desolate rock. Port Evergreen nestled at the lee of a kilometre-wide dip in the blank cliff face which the island presented to the sea. It had one hangar, six silvery pressurized huts, and a long double-storey building that looked like some kind of cheap hotel. The wormhole generator was housed in an armadillo-shaped edifice of raw carbon panels, with one fat tapering end sheltering the gateway arch. There was no rail track leading into it, which surprised Mellanie.

Their Carbon Goose splashed down in a reasonably smooth fashion, parallel to the shore; although, once they hit the water, deceleration was a lot sharper than any normal aircraft runway landing. For once Mellanie was grateful for the ply-plastic grips holding her into the seat. She suited up carefully as they taxied in to the land. There were four more of the huge flying boats standing outside the hangar; by strict rotation another had flown back to Shackleton as they came the other way.

Two suited figures were standing at the bottom of the air stairs when the passengers disembarked. The first introduced himself as Eemeli Aro, the CST technical officer responsible for the wormhole generator.

'Good timing on your part,' he told the passengers. 'The wormhole cycle starts in another eighteen minutes. There's no need to rest up in the lodge.' A hand waved in the direction of the building Mellanie had thought resembled a hotel. 'You all just walk over there, and as soon as it opens I'll give you the all clear. Just walk through.'

Mellanie had been expecting a slightly more elaborate arrangement, but she and Dudley exchanged a quick glance through their helmets, and started traipsing over the rock. The red sun was already close to the horizon, and falling fast. Its neutron companion continued to send out dazzling flashes, as if it was the emergency strobe on some sinking ship.

Polyphoto lights were shining on all of Port Evergreen's buildings, producing weak yellow splashes on the rock as the sunlight vanished. The stars came out quickly, leaving Mellanie feeling very small and exposed. For the first time in her life she truly understood the concept of darkness closing in.

The five passengers huddled close together in front of the gateway. A wan ultramarine light filled the arch, only visible now the red sun had set. It wasn't cold, but Mellanie folded her arms, hugging herself and shifting her weight from one foot to another. She mentally urged the wormhole to power up, but there was nothing she could do to hurry the storm-rider.

Half Way's strange binary star was the final factor in selecting the icy planet as a site for the wormhole stations. Even though its diameter was considerably smaller than a standard commercial CST wormhole, the Far Away wormhole still had a massive energy consumption requirement. An in-system generator to supply it was chosen for the oldest reason of all: pork barrel politics. The Halgarths agreed to allocate the power supply funding to a consortium made up from the Hutchinson, Brant, and Mandela Dynasties in return for their increased support at the Washington Senate committee stage. Whilst nuclear power was the obvious choice, it was expensive, and shipping an entire station out to Half Way, where construction would be carried out in its non-H-congruent environment, would increase the cost to unacceptable levels. With the alarmed Commonwealth Central Treasury now fighting a rearguard action, other conventional schemes were subject to unfavourable reviews; Half Way had no petroleum fields so they couldn't use a gas turbine station; there was no moon, which eliminated tidal power; the cold red light would have made solar panels more expensive than the nuclear option. So in the end the Intersolar Dynasties pushed through a radical but practical solution.

Before finally fixing the far end of the Boongate wormhole

to the Shackleton gateway, the wormhole opening was shifted into space far above the planet so the Stormrider components could be pushed through. It was an idea which went back to almost the beginning of the twentieth century's 'space age': a contra-rotating windmill, powering a simple electrical generator, that worked off the solar wind. Such a device had to be big, with a blade length measured in kilometres, and made out of lightweight materials. The principle of the Stormrider was the same, although the location required a few modifications to be made.

Like the original concept, it had rectangular blades, sixteen of them radiating out from the hub; each one a flat lattice of struts twenty-five kilometres long, made from the toughest steelsilicon fibres the Commonwealth knew how to manufacture. Twenty-three kilometres of them were covered by an ultra-thin silvered foil, giving a total surface area of over one thousand eight hundred square kilometres for the solar wind to impact on. Even in an ordinary solar system environment that would have produced a considerable torque. In the Half Way system the Stormrider was positioned at the Lagrange point between the red star and its neutron companion, right in the middle of the plasma current, where the ion density was orders of magnitude thicker than any normal solar wind.

The power the Stormrider produced when it was in the thick of the flow was enough to operate the wormhole generator. But it couldn't simply sit at the Lagrange point producing electricity continuously, that would have been too much like perpetual motion. As the waves of plasma pushed against it, they exerted an unremitting pressure on the blades which blew the Stormrider away from the Lagrange point out towards the neutron star. So for five hours the two sets of blades would turn in opposite directions, generating electricity for the Port Evergreen wormhole which was delivered via a zero-width wormhole. The Stormrider also stored some of the power, so that at the end of the five hours when it was out of alignment, it had enough of a reserve to fire its on board thrusters, moving itself even further out of the main plasma stream where the pressure was reduced. From there it chased a simple fifteen-hour loop back round through open space to the Lagrange point, where the cycle would begin again.

For all its complexity, there were no moving parts, the two hub discs anchoring the blades were linked by magnetic bearings. All the electronics were multiple redundancy fail soft modules designed to endure the harsh radiative environment of the Lagrange point. The thrusters constantly refuelled from the plasma stream. That just left the external structure's physical degradation from the ion impacts. After a hundred and eighty years of successful operation the blade foil had suffered punctures, tears, and abrasion which had worn it down to eighty-three per cent of its original area. The decay rate was now increasing. When it eventually reached seventy-five per cent the Commonwealth Council would have to consider purchasing a replacement. The Treasury was already launching a pre-emptive strike against that with a series of studies on the reduced costs of modern fusion generators, a zero-width wormhole linking Port Evergreen to the Commonwealth grid via Boongate, and even the possibility of Far Away supporting a modest gas turbine power plant. It was a financial battle that would be fought for years in committees and stealth spin briefings and the Senate Hall dining room.

Forty million kilometres from Half Way, the Stormrider glided back into the heart of the Lagrange point where the tempest of ions splashed against its gigantic silver blades. Their rotation speed began to increase.

The archway's wraithish radiance abruptly changed to a bright monochrome haze. Vague shadows were moving about on the other side of the foggy pressure curtain.

'Okay, people, through you go,' Eemeli Aro said.

The two physicists stepped through almost immediately, blurring into shadow.

'It's quite all right,' Griffith Applegate reassured them. 'I've done this a hundred times.' He promptly strode through the archway.

'The connection is stable,' the SI told Mellanie. 'I am connected to the net in Armstrong City, such as it is. It is safe to go through.'

Mellanie put her hand out, and felt Dudley take hold of it.

'Suppose we'd better go then,' she said. The pair of them walked directly into the torrent of bright warm light.

Mellanie was keen to see what the new world looked like, the city, its people. Instead of having a good look round, she was immediately distracted by the way her body wanted to soar away off the ground. It was as if an ordinary step had somehow turned into a leap. As soon as she came through the pressure curtain she was moving forwards far too fast. She hurriedly let go of Dudley and brought her arms out to try and balance herself, which sent her little shoulder bag zipping off ahead of her as if it was a balloon caught in a breeze. She managed to come to a halt, and stood completely still, fearful of what any further movements would do to her. The bag fell down to her side.

'Damn, I forgot the gravity.' She took a breath, and glanced round for Dudley. He was standing just behind her, completely unperturbed by what had happened.

'Are you all right?' he asked.

'Yes.'

'Remember what I told you about inertia here. This is a low-gravity planet, you have to think out any movement before you make it.'

'Yes, yes.' Her elegant virtual hand tapped the helmet release icon, and the collar disengaged. She lifted the transparent bubble off her head, and shook out her hair, which floated about slowly.

The noise of the city swirled round her, machinery thrumming away, combustion engines, car horns, the cry of animals, human conversation and shouts. Its smell was stronger than any urban area she'd ever visited in the Commonwealth; raw petrol fumes, and seawater, and animals, spicy cooking, organic decay, heat, dust, it all mingled into a brawny melange that was overpowering to a first breath.

When she recovered from that, she looked around. They seemed to have emerged into some kind of open arena measuring an easy five hundred metres across. There was a low metal fence in front of her, isolating a peaceful semicircle in front of the gateway to serve as a reception area for arrivals. Beyond the fence, and dominating the centre of the arena floor, were three wide brick-lined pools with big fountains squirting out of various statues. Some traffic drove around the pools, a mix of petrol vehicles, bicycles, rickshaws, and horse-drawn carts; though none of it appeared to be following any road markings. High yellow-stone walls curved away on both sides of her, topped by dozens of ragtag solarcloth awnings draped over poles of wood and fibreglass that were lashed together with no thought of symmetry. There must have been some kind of walkway up there as she could see a lot of people moving around close to the low parapet. At ground level, the walls were punctured by archways of varying sizes. The smaller ones had stalls just inside, away from the sharp mid-morning sunlight; selling anything from modern consumer technology to fresh food, clothes, plants, toys, ancient and much-repaired bots, hand tools, power tools, animal feed, artwork, semi-organics, books, and medicines. Several of the archways opened into bars, offering drinks that ranged from guaranteed-hangover-cure coffee to hundred-proof local rum, with dozens of beers and fruit juices, even native wines. The largest archways led into dark cave like buildings serving as warehouses. Small trucks and horse-drawn carts went in and out.

A swarm of people were moving slowly over the rough-laid stone slabs that formed the arena's floor, making the traffic give way to them. Their clothing styles were bewilderingly wide, they'd enthusiastically adopted everything from loin-cloths to T-shirt and shorts, kilts, saris, conservative business suits, priest-like robes, simple dresses, mechanic overalls, there were even a few men in tropical-khaki police uniforms with peaked white caps trying to sort out traffic disputes.

Standing with her back to the dark shimmer of the gateway, helmet under her arm, Mellanie felt like some kind of astronaut who'd just stepped out of her rocketship. She stared out at the bustling scene for a long moment before stirring herself to cope with more immediate and mundane matters. A couple of CST personnel were helping the Institute physicists out of their suits. Mellanie began to shrug out of hers. A CST supervisor asked her to move aside. She barely cleared the gateway before robot vans and flatbed trucks started trundling through, bringing the crates from the Carbon Goose. They drove straight out into the arena and headed for the archways which fronted warehouses, collision horns blaring at sluggish pedestrians.

By the time she and Dudley got their suits off, their luggage had been unloaded. Both bags rolled over to them. A Langford Hall hotel courtesy car was parked outside the fence, its driver smiling and waving to attract their attention. The two Institute physicists were climbing into a big six-wheeled Land Rover Cruiser with black-glass windows. Three lorries were parked beside them, receiving a batch of crates which had just come through the gateway.

Griffith Applegate picked up his shoulder bag, and gave Mellanie a friendly smile. 'Don't worry, I know it looks daunting, but take it from me, this is a tame part of town. You'll be perfectly safe here.'

'Thanks,' she said dubiously.

He pulled a wide-brimmed hat out of his bag and settled it on his head, then put his sunglasses on. 'One piece of advice. Only use the taxis with a licence from the Governor's House.' He touched the rim of his hat and set off into the throng.

'I'll remember that,' she told his back. 'Come on Dudley, let's get to the hotel.' She checked to see that her luggage was following, and set off for the courtesy car.

*

Stig McSobel rested his elbows on the stone parapet that lined the top of Market Wall to give himself a better view across 3F, as the locals called First Foot Fall Plaza. Two hundred metres away, the gateway had opened on time, and five people emerged through the dark pressure curtain.

'They're here, Halgarth and Alwon,' he said to Olwen McOnna, who was standing at his side. She wasn't watching 3F, like every good bodyguard she was scanning the nearby shoppers who moved from stall to stall in search of bargains. The merchants were pressed up together in a giant ring of commerce that made up the roof of the city's massive central edifice. Here the flow of life and trade was unchanged, money and goods were exchanged in the same ritual of fast barter that had been in existence for close to a couple of centuries, heedless of the threat which lurked out among the stars. Deeper in the city, though, the uncertainty was more pronounced; rumour and fear were affecting the way people thought and behaved. The absence of tourists was noted everywhere. The Governor had ordered more police out of their comfortable stations and onto the streets where their visibility would instil confidence. A futile measure, Stig believed. Soon, unease would turn to worry, then panic.

'It'll take them an hour to get outside the city,' Olwen said. 'I'll alert the raiders.'

'Okay.' Stig's virtual vision ghosted icons and text over the gateway. He opened a channel back to the unisphere, and several messages flooded into his e-butler's hold file. His own messages went racing out to various one-time addresses. Then he peered forwards in surprise at the people now standing in front of the gateway. The virtual vision intensity reduced, and he used his retinal inserts to zoom in. One he knew of, Griffith Applegate who worked in the Governor's House, trying to maintain Armstrong City's shaky civil infrastructure. The other two . . . 'I know her. I accessed her on the unisphere back in the Commonwealth. She's some sort of celebrity. A reporter. Yeah: Mellanie Rescorai. What's she doing here?'

Olwen hadn't stopped searching the crowd of shoppers. 'If she's a reporter, she's looking for news. Obviously.'

'Not a proper reporter, just a rich brat doing silly "personality" stories. Probably covering this season's city fashion.' His virtual vision strengthened slightly, and he activated several icons. Inserts began to run an ident program on Rescorai's companion – there was something familiar about him.

Stig watched the two of them clamber into a hotel courtesy car. It pulled away with a fusillade of horn blasts just as the first departures bus pulled up outside the gateway enclave. Passengers disembarked; Far Away natives who'd recently spent a lot of time in the gym and injecting steroids and genoproteins to give themselves additional muscle. Stig remembered that time of his life all too easily. A second bus drew up. Two more were driving slowly across 3F. CST personnel were already handing out the slack mauve suits which would safeguard the passengers as they walked to the Carbon Goose waiting for them on the other side of the gateway. The cost of the trip, even a one way ticket, was beyond the means of most of Far Away's population. Crime in the city was increasing as desperate people acquired the cash any way they could.

A transparent purple rectangle flipped up into Stig's virtual vision. 'Well, wadda ya know,' he muttered.

'What?' Olwen asked.

'That bloke with Rescorai, he's Dudley Bose.'

*

The Langford Towers gave Mellanie and Dudley the Royal Suite on the top floor. There was complimentary champagne, even if it was only from a vineyard out on the northern slopes of the Samafika mountains. They also had complimentary chocolate, fruit, cheese, biscuits, and mineral water. Every table had a big vase with magnificently arranged fresh flowers. The bathroom medicine cabinet could hardly shut there were so many toiletries inside.

They were the only residents.

'This certainly beats the hell out of the old Pine Heart Gardens,' Mellanie declared as she pushed the patio doors open and went out onto the broad veranda. With its four floors, the Langford Towers was one of the tallest non-governmental buildings in Armstrong City; it helped that the ceilings were very high, a design feature that helped prevent patrons from standard-gravity worlds from banging their heads from an inadvertently strong step. The hotel's size and position gave her an excellent view out over the red pantile rooftops to the shore of the North Sea a couple of kilometres westward. A broad circular harbour provided berths for boats of all types, from trawlers to ferries, cargo sloops to house-boats, sports fishers to simple pleasure yachts. The blue sea beyond sparkled invitingly even with the sun low in Far Away's astonishing sapphire sky; several dozen boats were making their way in to the harbour for the night.

Mellanie scanned across the skyline. Armstrong City lacked the neat urban grids she was used to, its streets and avenues zigzagged and curved in contorted patterns. They actually swerved round the larger buildings in the centre like the First Foot Fall Plaza and the Governor's House, and the revitalization project offices, which made her wonder which had come first. Only the acres of warehouses behind the harbour seemed to have any sort of regular order in their layout. Outlying districts swarmed over the undulating land, revealing parks and retail streets, neat suburban estates and industrial zones. Thickets of tall metal chimneys squirted out thick grey plumes; a pollution so blatant it startled her.

Away to the south she could see a couple of dark oval shapes stationary in the sky, just outside the city boundary. A hundred and twenty years ago when the revitalization project was at its peak, it had employed a fleet of over two hundred and fifty blimpbots. At first they'd been used to spray soil bacteria across the desolate post-flare landscape, loading up from the newly constructed clone vats at the aerodrome outside Armstrong City. Then, once the soil was revived, they'd scattered seeds and even insect eggs across the planet in an effort to return it to full H-congruous status. It was after that the stately aerial craft became victims of their own success. The number of people attracted to Far Away began to increase, partly due to the expanding biota. However, they all had their own individual vision of how their particular part of the planet should be rebirthed, especially the Barsoomians. In a few cases blimpbots were hijacked and used to distribute novel cargos across their new owners' province; some were electronically diverted away from territories that no longer wanted the staid old useful plants which the revitalization project favoured. Several succumbed to hostilities between the Guardians and the Institute, and a number were lost in the storms that raged round the Grand Triad. Though it was age which claimed most of them. Those that remained, barely thirty now, were running on components cannibalized from warehouses filled with the shells of their retired cousins; their gas envelopes patched and fraying, undeserving of the flightworthy certificates which the Governor's House ritually issued to them every year.

Blimpbots and pollution were only half of Mellanie's sense of detachment. She realized what really bothered her: the lack of trains. There were no embankments and cuttings taking priority through the architecture. No elevated rails slicing above the clogged-up traffic. More than anything, trains symbolized Commonwealth society.

'What a weird place,' Mellanie said. 'I can't see why so many people emigrated here. It's all so backward; as if the Victorians invented starflight and transported their culture here. Maybe that is where the *Marie Celeste* came from.'

'You're too young to understand,' Dudley said.

She turned, mildly surprised at the confidence in his voice.

Dudley stood beside her, smiling admiringly at the ramshackle city spread out around them. 'Try rejuvenating five times, having to go back to a nine-to-five job for century after century just so you can pay half of your salary into an R&R pension fund that allows you to do exactly the same thing all over again. You might have a different job, wife, children; but for all that you're just stuck on the same loop with no prospect of change. Once you've been through all that, Mellanie, even you would consider coming here to live your last life without a safety net.'

'I didn't know you felt that way, Dudley.'

'I don't. Or didn't. Not during my last life, anyway. But I remember accessing a lot of files on emigration here. A couple more rejuve treatments, having to spend another fifty years fighting the dean for funding, married to another bitch like Wendy, and, yes, I could see myself doing it. There's something very appealing about walking off into the wilderness and seeing what's out there. The prospect of telling modern life to fuck off, and just for once building something substantial for yourself with your own two hands; reverting to the hunter-gatherer state. It's not as far away as we like to think, you know.'

'And now?'

'Now? None of us have that luxury any more.' His face flinched. 'I made sure of that, didn't I?'

'No. You were a very minor part of what's happened. Sorry to dent your ego, my darling, but you're not that responsible.'

He grunted, unconvinced.

She wasn't sure how to respond. The times when the old Dudley appeared she felt small and stupid beside him. Strange, considering this was the state she was supposed to be helping him return to.

The SI's icon flashed emerald in her virtual vision, allowing her to postpone thinking about Dudley and his new future. 'Yes?' she asked it.

'We're only three hours from the end of the wormhole cycle, Mellanie. This would be a good time to establish our subroutine in the city net. We can verify operational authenticity.'

'All right.' She walked back into the lounge. There was a pine desk beside the door into the bedroom with a small, ancient desktop array on top. She placed both hands on the array's first-generation i-spot, and a webbing of faint silver lines appeared on her fingers. A whole new display of icons materialized in her virtual vision, and seeker programs began to analyse the local net from inside her inserts. 'Doesn't look like there are any decent monitor programs in the nodes,' she said.

'We concur, Mellanie. Please release our subroutine.'

Her gold snakeskin virtual hands tapped out the code sequence, and the subroutine decompressed out of her inserts, flowing into the city net through her contact with the desktop array. The SI had formatted it as a simple observer system, with enough independence to advise and assist Mellanie when the wormhole was closed. She'd brought it with her in her inserts because any program that large entering Far Away through the narrow bandwidth of the Half Way relay would easily be detected by monitors. That opened the SIsubroutine to the risk of corruption, especially if the Guardians or the Starflyer were running hostile smartware in the city's nodes.

'I am installed,' the SIsubroutine reported. 'The city net has enough capacity for me to run in distributed mode within its on line arrays.'

'We confirm that,' the SI said.

'Great,' Mellanie said. She took her hands away from the desktop array. 'See if you can find any kind of activity that might be the Guardians. All I need's a name, or an address. Some way I can make contact with them.'

'I will begin analysis,' the SIsubroutine said. 'There are a great many systems that have restricted access. Given the age of the processors I am operating in, it will take some time to circumvent their fireshields.'

'Do what you can.'

Dudley had come back into the lounge. 'Who are you calling?' he asked.

'The Michelangelo office.' She told her e-butler to close the connection to the SI. 'Just checking in and getting an update.'

'Okay.' His gaze crept over to the bedroom's door. 'What are we going to do next?'

'Go down to the bar, and get some information. Bars are always the best place for that. Besides, I could do with a big drink, we've been travelling for ages.' She yawned, stretching her arms to try and loosen the knotted shoulder muscles. 'Come on, let's go see if Far Away's heard of a *Murderous Seduction* cocktail.'

*

The bar and restaurant at the Langford Towers were the only parts of the hotel to be doing any decent business. They catered for an upmarket clientele, such as it was in Armstrong City, providing a décor with decidedly Indian influences with its gold and purple wallpaper, Hindu statues, and massive palms growing out of clay urns. The chef favoured spiced dishes; and the in-house music system played a lot of sitar classics.

Stig found himself a small empty table in the bar, and sipped a beer quietly while he tried to catalogue the other customers. He'd been there forty minutes when Mellanie and Dudley walked in. He'd intended to give them a brief look, then show no further interest, just as Adam had taught him. But Mellanie made that difficult. Her longish chin and flat nose denied her the kind of perfection a classic beauty would have, but her physical presence was striking. Powerful strides carried her quickly across the bar, yet she'd already developed a controlled rhythm to her movements which most offworlders took at least a week to learn. Every motion made her wavy gold hair flutter leisurely above her shoulders.

Dudley followed her with unsteady footsteps. When they arrived at the counter he grabbed it to steady himself. It was hard not to draw comparisons between the two of them, given the way Dudley stayed so close. The re-lifed astronomer came over as completely inadequate both physically and mentally.

Stig finally managed to look away. Most of the other patrons were watching the newcomers. Despite his earlier assessment, he couldn't tell if any of them were Starflyer operatives from the Institute. Surely at least one of them must be?

The Institute was becoming a lot bolder in the city since the Prime attack. Its director had offered assistance to the Governor as crime and disturbances increased; already several routine police patrols in the centre were accompanied by Institute troops in their dark armour. Stig thought it unlikely the only two offworlders on Far Away wouldn't be kept under observation.

He heard Mellanie try to order some exotic cocktail, which the barkeeper had never heard of. She settled for a pitcher of margarita. As the barkeeper started mixing the ingredients she eased herself closer to him, and spoke in low tones. Stig casually glanced around, just in time to catch the barkeeper's startled expression. The man quickly shook his head, and gave her the pitcher before hurrying off to the other end of the counter.

A disgruntled Mellanie hauled Dudley over to a vacant table.

Stig was almost laughing. The whole scene was like a badly acted TSI drama.

Fortunately, there was no second act. Mellanie and Dudley drank their pitcher and went off back to their suite, both of them yawning. Stig remained in the bar, watching who left and when. Nobody else was acting remotely suspiciously.

Closing time was midnight. He finished his beer and waited in the deserted lobby. Finally the barkeeper came through from the kitchen, pulling his coat on.

'A word,' Stig said presently.

The barkeeper glanced about nervously, but the hotel's night staff were nowhere to be seen. He was in his mid-thirties, with the kind of spindly frame which most Far Away residents acquired, which made his burgeoning beer belly unusually prominent.

'Yes, sir?'

Stig produced a fifty-Earth-dollar bill, and pressed it into the barkeeper's hand. The man was professional enough to pocket it at once.

'Very attractive offworld girl in here earlier tonight.'

'The Royal Suite, sir, top floor.'

'Thank you, I already know that. What I would really appreciate knowing is what she asked you for?'

The barkeeper gave him an awkward look. Stig waited. He wouldn't have to make any threats, not against the barkeeper. At the worst it would cost him another fifty dollars.

'She wanted to know where she could meet a member of the Guardians. I told her I didn't know. Which I don't. Obviously.'

'Obviously.'

'I never said anything else.'

'I see. Thank you.'

The barkeeper let out a short relieved breath, and hurried out. Stig waited a couple of minutes then made his own way out into the night, the hotel's automatic doors locking behind him.

Solar-charged polyphoto globes gave off an uninspiring yellow shimmer down the length of the wide street. The faint throb of dance music was just audible, drifting from the back door of a club. A cool air washed the salty ozone smell of the sea across Armstrong City. Somewhere in the distance a police siren wailed its lonely note along the empty roads. It couldn't be for the Institute's vehicles, they'd been destroyed hours ago; hit by mortars and masers not ten kilometres outside the city. Trevelyan Halgarth and Ferelith Alwon would never reach the Institute now, never help the Starflyer. With any luck their memorycells had been ruined by the fire that consumed the Land Rover Cruiser. They'd be just as dead as Kazimir.

Stig pulled a cigarette from his packet, and thumbed an old-fashioned petrol lighter. A bad habit, picked up back in the decadent Commonwealth. The mix of nicotine and grass felt good as he pulled it down. He needed a lifter from the stress of the day.

'That illumination makes you a perfect target,' Olwen said from the shadows.

'If you're relying on a cigarette glow instead of a decent nightsight you're in deep trouble,' he told her.

She came out of a doorway and joined him as he walked away from the hotel, down the slight slope which led towards the harbour.

'Where's Finlay?'

'Got himself a good spot. He'll call if they leave the hotel tonight.'

'Anybody else interested?'

'If they are, they're better than us. We haven't seen anyone.'

Stig stopped, and looked back at the high whitewashed

façade of the Langford Towers. The Royal Suite balcony was a grey rectangle just under the roof. *What in the dreaming heavens does a girl like that see in a piece of wreckage like Dudley Bose? They have to be here for a purpose.*

'They went to bed about ten minutes after they went back to the room,' Olwen said.

'I thought that suite was too high to get a proper line of sight inside.'

'It is. I'll rephrase. The light went off ten minutes after they got back upstairs. Hasn't come on again since.' She sniggered. 'Probably couldn't wait to rip each other's clothes off. Here by themselves. Hint of danger. Young. You could practically smell the hormones sweating off them.'

Stig didn't say anything. His own mind had been filled by the image of a naked Mellanie on the bed with Dudley Bose. It bothered him slightly. That it was Dudley, not him. Which it *really* shouldn't do.

'What do you want to do about them?' Olwen asked.

'Not sure. They want to find us, apparently. Let's see what they do tomorrow.'

*

Stig was using Halkin Ironmongery, an old hardware store, for his headquarters in Armstrong City. It was fairly central, had a big useful garage at the back, and the neighbours believed the clan members were new owners taking their time to do the place up. An opportune impression which allowed for a lot of people and vehicles to come and go without attracting comment. As covers went, Adam Elvin would have been proud.

When Stig arrived in the morning, Murdo McPeierls and young Felix McSobel had already started stripping down the engine from one of the Mazda Volta jeeps. They had nine of the sturdy old vehicles jammed into the garage and yard. Stig had brought them in as part of the reception for the Boongate blockade run which Adam was putting together. Adam hadn't sent too many details yet, not even by encrypted message. But it would go ahead, Stig was certain of that, the new inspections on Boongate had essentially cut them off from their Commonwealth supplies. One of Stig's other jobs was putting together the technical teams who would assemble the multitude of components into the specialized force field generators needed for the planet's revenge. So he knew how desperate the clans were for fresh components. They were desperate for the Martian data as well. He'd talked to Samantha, who was in charge of the control group assembling the large array which would run the network of manipulator stations. She'd explained how urgent it was. Now Kazimir was dead and the data lost. *That should have been my run.* Fate had been evil to them that day.

Stig spent the first half hour of the morning working out in the makeshift gym in the store's basement, kick-boxing the heavy leather bags, imagining each and every one of them to be Bruce McFoster. It was good exercise, something he could lose himself in, not having to think.

'You are troubled, Stig McSobel,' said a voice that had a permanent whispering echo.

Stig hadn't heard anyone come in. He finished his kick and slid round smoothly, dropping into a crouch. The Barsoomian who called himself Dr Friland was standing at the bottom of the wooden stairs, a tall figure clad in dark robes of semi-organic cloth. His face was partially hidden inside a deep monk's hood, which was perpetually haunted by shadows. Stig had once used his retinal inserts to try and get a clear image, only to find the effect was actually some kind of distortion field. The Barsoomians always veiled their true appearance. Rumour had it they didn't want anyone to know how far their modifications had taken them from their original human form. Dr Friland was certainly taller than any normal human Stig had ever seen; though plenty of Commonwealth citizens had reprofiled themselves for media sport shows like wrestling, producing ridiculous freak-variants on the human body. This was different, not that he knew how exactly.

Stig straightened up, allowing the muscles in his shoulders and arms to loosen. 'What makes you say that?'

'You always resort to physical activity when confronted with a vexing problem,' Dr Friland said in his euphonious voice. 'It allows your subconscious to review possibilities.'

'Right.' Stig retrieved his towel and started to dry himself. He'd managed to work up quite a sweat. 'By the way, our people say to thank you again for the bioprocessors. They've been integrated into our large array. Apparently they were way ahead of anything the Commonwealth is producing. It should make our digital simulations a lot quicker.'

'Our pleasure.'

Stig walked over to the bench and pulled on a simple short-sleeve shirt. He was always grateful to the Barsoomians for the assistance they gave the clans, yet he never knew what to say on the rare occasions he encountered one. How could you make small talk to an unknowable entity? Dr Friland had arrived in Armstrong City a week ago, delivering the requested processors for the command group. For reasons best known to himself he'd remained in the city, staying in the big private residence the Barsoomians maintained for themselves out in the Chinese quarter.

Without any visible leg movement, Dr Friland rotated on the spot, keeping his shielded face pointing at Stig. 'There is something new in the city's net.'

'A new monitor program?' He was surprised the clan's webheads hadn't detected it; they were interfaced just about continuously.

'No. This is a . . . presence.'

The Barsoomian sounded uncertain, which sent a tingle down Stig's spine. He placed a lot of weight on the supposed infallibility of the Barsoomians. Even his time in the Commonwealth with its everyday technology could never fully quash all the fabulous childhood stories of the others who shared this world. 'You mean like a ghost or something?'

'A ghost in the machine? How appropriate. It is certainly a machine's ghost.'

'Ah, right. So, what's it doing?'

The darkness within Dr Friland's hood lessened to reveal a row of smiling teeth. 'Whatever it wants.'

'I'll get my people to watch for it.'

'It is elusive. Even I can only gather hints of its passage.' The darkness closed back over Dr Friland's smile.

'Wait . . . We're not talking about the Starflyer, here, are we?'

'No. This is a binary construction; it is not a child of biological life. But it did not come through the gateway. We would have felt its passage within the datastream.'

'Then what the hell is it?'

'I suspect you were close to the truth with your first question. Something this pervasive can only be here to observe the city and its inhabitants. What you should be asking is who would want to gather information on such a scale?'

'Mellanie,' Stig hissed. 'She wants to know how to meet us. She's a reporter, so I guess she must have access to sophisticated scrutineer programs. I just didn't think . . .' He fell silent, rubbing at the back of his neck with some embarrassment. 'Me of all people, I shouldn't be fooled by appearances.'

'This is the girl who came through the gateway yesterday?'

'Yes. Though I haven't a clue who she's working for.' He levelled a sly glance at the Barsoomian. 'Do you know?'

'Alas, my people are not omnipotent. I have no more idea than you, perhaps even less. It is a long time since I left the Commonwealth.'

'You weren't born here?' Stig knew he probably shouldn't ask, but it wasn't often a Barsoomian talked about *anything*, let alone his own background.

'No. I was born back on Earth, before Sheldon and Isaacs opened their first wormhole.'

'Dreaming heavens. I never knew anyone was that old. Not even Johansson dates back that far.'

'There are some of us still left from that time. Not many. Not now.'

'Right.' Stig shook himself, and started to walk up the stairs. He watched closely as the Barsoomian followed him, gliding across the gym's dusty floorboards. The hem of his robe lifted just before he reached the bottom stair, flowing upwards ahead of whatever feet it concealed. 'I'm going to check with the team I've got watching Mellanie and Bose,' he said. 'Do you want to stay around?'

'No thank you. They haven't left the hotel yet. I thought I would visit the National Gallery today. It's been a while, and I hear good things about the new sculptors.'

Stig did his best to avoid checking over his shoulder. There was just no predicting the Barsoomians.

*

Dr Friland was right, Rescorai and Bose hadn't left the hotel yet. The team he'd assigned to them reported that they'd ordered breakfast in bed.

Stig told the webheads to start searching for a new distributed-operation monitor program in the city's net. He desperately wanted to increase the number of people watching the young reporter, but the clans didn't have enough people in Armstrong City for that. There was no way he could switch priorities based on his own feelings – Adam had certainly hammered that lesson in. Unless and until she did something radical, Mellanie was an unknown he had to regard as non-hostile. He still had to cover the daily gateway opening, and continue training and preparation for the blockade run. On top of that he had to maintain a thorough watch on the

Institute personnel's activities in Armstrong City, which continued to grow.

With the few clan members he could spare, he was lucky Mellanie didn't spot them when she did finally leave the hotel to wander around the city. They stayed well back, and delivered hourly bulletins for him. She behaved just like any rookie reporter; even though he was convinced that was an elaborate front. He still hadn't figured out what Bose was doing with her, not at all.

*

Mellanie had a thoroughly worthless first day in Armstrong City. After a long sleep to recover from the journey, she headed off to the Governor's House where she spent over an hour in the press office, familiarizing herself with local events. Her expectation that her Michelangelo show credentials would give her special privileges and encourage the Governor's media staff to confide rumours and civic gossip was badly misplaced. Nobody had ever heard of Michelangelo. The official line was that the Guardians were a bunch of scabby mountain bandits, irrelevant to the city. The Governor's media people were keen to push the concept of how life was continuing normally on Far Away, that nobody was panicking.

A follow-up visit to the local news company, the *Armstrong Chronicle*, which maintained a public bulletin service and ran news shows on the city net, was almost as unproductive. The *Chronicle* reporters did at least supply some details on the ambush just outside the city. She was shocked to learn Trevelyan Halgarth and Ferelith Alwon were dead, and that the medical crews had retrieved their memorycells for shipment back to the Commonwealth. When she asked if it was the Guardians who'd mounted the ambush nobody knew anything other than the police statement that local crime syndicates were suspected.

She popped into one of the gyms that were doing such a roaring trade, recording a puff piece for Michelangelo about rich natives building their bodies up for life on a standard-gravity world. It was so ineffectual she was embarrassed to send it when the wormhole cycle opened.

In the afternoon she did some bog-standard man-in-the-street interviews. They were a little more revealing, several people said they thought the Guardians were behind the recent attacks on the Institute's vehicles and property. If they were, she reasoned, then they must have a group based in the city.

When they got back to the hotel she reviewed the meagre information which the SIsubroutine had collected for her. 'I have no direct evidence of any Guardian membership,' it told her. 'However, when the wormhole was open earlier this afternoon, a great many encrypted messages flowed into the city net. Most were directed to the Governor's House, and the Institute.'

'And the rest?'

'They were all addressed to individuals. Given the small physical size of the net, it should now be possible for me to correlate the physical location of each recipient.'

'I haven't got the time to knock on the door of everyone who got an encoded message.'

'Of course not. But once I have identified the building where an encoded message was received, I can review the electronic hardware it contains for evidence. Be advised; there is one place I will not be able to venture: the Barsoomian residence in the Chinese quarter. There are some strange processing units connected to the net at that node and my routines do not run correctly in them. I have withdrawn myself from that area.'

'The Barsoomians, they're some kind of ultra-green radical group aren't they?'

'That was one of their founding concepts. They are humans who wish to explore the potential of unrestrained genetic modification within themselves and their environment, thereby leaving mainstream society behind. Far Away was the ideal planet for them to establish themselves. Without a global government it cannot enforce the kind of restrictions on genetic modification which most Commonwealth worlds have.'

'Are they connected to the Guardians?'

'I do not know. It seems improbable the two groups are unaware of each other. There are several archive reports at the *Armstrong Chronicle* of Guardians using unusually large horses. The Barsoomians would be an obvious source of breeding stock.'

'That is interesting. All right, let me know if you find anything at those buildings.'

Mellanie and Dudley had dinner in the hotel restaurant. The curry she chose was a lot hotter than most she'd eaten before, but she managed to get it down, aware of the waiter smiling in the background when she puffed out her cheeks and drank copious amounts of cold mineral water to wash it down. Dudley wasn't so lucky. He was complaining of a bad stomach even before they reached their suite.

'I thought I remembered liking spicy food,' he mumbled the second time he returned from the bathroom.

'It's probably an acclimatization thing,' Mellanie said. 'Your new body isn't ready for curry just yet.' She retrieved her small white cocktail dress from her bag, not one from her own range, a nice Nicallio that had been tailored to fit her just perfectly, and she knew she looked sensational wearing it. There were several creases in the shiny fabric, which she frowned at. They'd distract from the effect she wanted to project. She hung it carefully in the wardrobe; the fabric should self-straighten by tomorrow night – she certainly didn't trust any valet service on this planet.

If she didn't have any success tracking down the Guardians tomorrow, then she'd just have to extract information the old-fashioned way. During her visit to the *Armstrong Chronicle*, several male staff members had managed to swing past and tell her how delighted they'd be to show her around the big city at night.

Looking at the dress with its near non-existent skirt Mellanie gave a mildly resentful sigh. She would fuck whoever it took to get a contact name, of course she would. But lately – actually, since the Prime invasion – she'd begun wondering about other ways to accomplish her job, because that's how most other reporters got things done. When she tried to count up just how many people she'd slept with, she couldn't. Life had just swept her away since that awful court case; she'd done what she could to stay in charge and in control, but the events powering her along had been so overwhelming. It had been an exciting ride, though, she couldn't deny that. At times, that is. Frightening, too.

But there have been so many people.

As she'd told dear old Hoshe Finn all those aeons ago, she wasn't ashamed about her sexuality. Really, she wasn't. It was finding out about Alessandra that caused the most pain. The betrayal. Alessandra had just whored her for the Starflyer, never caring, never interested.

I should have said yes to that money-junkie sleazeball Jaycee when he tried to whore me, at least he was honest about what I'd be doing for him in those TSIs.

'Are you all right?' Dudley asked.

'What? Yes.'

Dudley still had one hand pressed firmly across his belly. With the other he reached out to her face. 'You're crying.'

'No I'm not.' She moved back out of range, hurriedly swiping her hand across her eyes.

'I thought . . . Oooh.' Dudley hurried for the bathroom again.

Mellanie grunted at Dudley's departing back, and flopped down on the bed. The town was almost silent outside, she should be able to get a good night's sleep. Dudley certainly wouldn't be pestering her tonight.

The loud and unpleasant sound of Dudley's digestive suffering came clean through the bathroom door. Mellanie searched round in her bag for the earplugs she'd been given on the Carbon Goose, pushed them in, and hauled the duvet over herself.

*

The following morning Mellanie decided to get professional. It wasn't as though she'd had to sit through lessons or courses on how to be a reporter when Alessandra took her on, but she'd picked up enough around the office to know the basics of starting an investigation in a strange town.

'I want a full analysis of city court cases going back two years,' she told the SIsubroutine. 'Get me a listing of every case the police brought against the Guardians, even people who are only suspected of membership. We can cross reference it with the locations of those encoded messages.'

'I can't do that. Official court records are archived in an isolated memory core.'

'That's ridiculous, all government records are supposed to be publicly available. It's in the Commonwealth constitution, or something.'

'Article 54, yes. However, the Armstrong City grand court has used this archiving method for security purposes. Like most of the Governor's House electronics, the court's systems are old. There is no money available for upgrades, which leaves them vulnerable to anyone coming through the gateway with modern aggressor software. Records could be easily destroyed or tampered with.'

'Damn it.'

'You may visit the court in person and request copies.'

'Okay, all right. I'll do that, then.'

'The *Armstrong Chronicle* has many cases on file which I

can access. I can give you a list of possible court cases to research.'

'Thank you.'

Dudley wanted to come with her.

'I don't think you're up to that,' she said diplomatically. Despite the earplugs she'd heard him scamper off to the bathroom several times in the night. Sitting opposite her in the deserted dining room for breakfast, all he'd managed was a cup of weak milky tea and a slice of toast. He looked like he'd got the mother of all hangovers.

'I'm fine,' he said grumpily.

Mellanie couldn't be bothered to argue. She dressed for her day in a simple dove-grey T-shirt and jeans, tying her hair back into a loose tail with a brown leather band. They took a cab, for Dudley's sake, waving on the first three until she finally saw one with a Governor's House licence.

*

'I think someone is following them,' Olwen said.

Stig was in the middle of a briefing for the team members left at Halkin Ironmongery. Over half of his people were running round town trying to keep up with their assignments. He held up a hand to his audience, and asked: 'Who?'

'Not sure,' Olwen replied. 'The pair of them have been in the grand courthouse for two hours. I'm having trouble staying inconspicuous. But there's someone else lurking here, having the same kind of problem. He's not on any file we've got.'

'Have you found out what she's doing there?'

'Going through court records. I don't know which ones, yet. Finley was going to talk to the court officials after she leaves.'

'Okay, I'll get you some electronic coverage. Stand by.' He went up to the first floor room where the team's arrays were set up. Keely McSobel and Aidan McPeierls were both fully interfaced with the city net. He told them to review the area around the courthouse to see if there was anybody using encrypted messaging.

'You're right,' Stig told Olwen five minutes later. 'We've located at least three hostiles in the courthouse.'

'What do you want us to do?'

'Nothing. Keep Bose and Rescorai in sight. I'm coming straight over with some reinforcements.'

*

Mellanie was making good progress. The SIsubroutine had given her seven cases where the *Chronicle* mentioned a possible connection with the Guardians. All of them involved attacks on the Institute, either against their vehicles or personnel in Armstrong City. The police had caught few suspects. Those they did haul before a judge were just local punks, all of whom had a suspicious amount of wealth either in cash or in newly purchased goods. Obviously, they'd been paid to harass the Institute; not that they admitted to anything. Invariably, they had good lawyers.

Mellanie smiled when she read that for the second time. Three prominent city lawyers seemed to represent most of the accused, and they didn't come cheap.

'There is an increasing amount of electronic activity in and around the courthouse,' the SIsubroutine told her. 'I believe you are under observation.'

Mellanie rubbed her eyes, and switched off the desktop array which was displaying the cases. It ejected the memory crystal which the clerk of the court had supplied her. 'Police?' she asked.

'No. The systems they are using are more advanced than the police have on this world. Some of the signal traffic is strange. It appears there are two separate groups operating independently.'

'Two?' Mellanie rubbed at her bare arms where goose-bumps had suddenly appeared. It wasn't cold in the little office which the clerk had let her use. Midday sun was streaming in through the double-glazed window, stirring the air-conditioning unit into desultory life, while outside the season's warm humid air hung over the city like a possessive spirit. If there were two groups interested in her, she knew one of them had to be from the Starflyer. Had Alessandra found out she'd travelled here?

Dudley was curled up in a chair on the other side of the desk, his youth and pose giving him a strong resemblance to some sulky schoolboy. His eyes were closed and moving, like someone in REM sleep, as he accessed a file from his inserts.

For an instant, she was tempted to creep out and leave him there. Except he'd panic when he realized she'd gone, and cause a big scene. And he was completely incapable of looking after himself if a Starflyer agent did want to abduct him.

Maybe bringing him along wasn't so smart after all.

'Come on, Dudley,' she shook his shoulder. 'We're leaving.'

*

Mellanie put her sunglasses on as soon as they went outside. Dudley seemed to shrink away from the warm light. He was sweating and shivering as they walked away from the big old courthouse onto Cheyne Street.

Silver lines appeared just below Mellanie's skin, like deep sea creatures rising tentatively to the surface. They began to spread and multiply along her arms and up her neck to envelop her cheeks in a delicate filigree. Some of them she activated herself; the simple systems that she understood, sensors which amplified her perception of the surrounding area. The SIsubroutine was tapping into others.

Cheyne Street was busy. It was close to the centre of town, a boundary line between the sector which housed the main government buildings and the start of the commercial district. Traffic was constant along the road, with vehicle exhausts releasing dark fumes into Far Away's crisp air. Cyclists wore filter masks as they weaved through the slow-moving cars and vans. Mellanie pushed her way along the crowded pavements, trying not to think what the fumes were doing to her lungs.

'We need to keep this simple,' she told the SIsubroutine. 'Find me a car here that can take us back to the hotel.'

A long list of vehicles slid down Mellanie's virtual vision, everything the SIsubroutine could find on Cheyne Street, either moving or parked. None of them was less than ten years old. As they'd all been imported from the Commonwealth, they all had drive arrays, not that they were used much in Armstrong City, which lacked even a basic traffic management system.

'Two Land Rover Cruisers registered with the Institute office have just turned onto Cheyne Street,' the SIsubroutine said. 'They are heading towards you.'

Mellanie's inserts and OCtattoos revealed a multitude of signals flashing through the city's aether. She saw the Cruisers establish links to several people on the pavement. Two of them were very close, twenty metres behind, and walking quickly towards her. She turned her head to see a couple of men dressed in the dark tunics worn by the Institute troopers. Her virtual vision superimposed iridescent data pixels over the image. The two figures were separated from the rest of Cheyne Street's pedestrians by haloes of tangerine and scarlet grids.

'I don't feel too good,' Dudley said. His face was white, slicked with cold sweat.

Mellanie wanted to slap him. She couldn't believe he was doing this to her, not now. Didn't he understand how much trouble they were in? 'We have to hurry, Dudley, they're coming.'

'Who?' Any further questioning was postponed by a violent judder that started in the middle of his chest He squashed a hand to his mouth. People were staring at him as his cheeks bulged out, moving away with their faces wrinkled up in disgust.

Mellanie's boosted senses showed her the SIsubroutine establishing itself in the drive arrays of vehicles along Cheyne Street. Both of the Institute troopers had reached the front of the courthouse building. One of them drew his ion pistol. 'Hey, you,' he called out.

Dudley started to throw up. People backed away fast as watery vomit splattered onto the paving slabs. Now there was no one between Mellanie and the Institute troopers.

'Stay right there,' the first trooper shouted. He raised the ion pistol, levelling it. Mellanie blinked against a powerful green dazzle as the weapon's targeting laser found her face.

A car horn sounded loudly. People turned in curiosity, then yelled in panic. There was a sudden rush of movement as an old Ford Maury saloon veered across Cheyne Street, heading straight for the troopers. The green laser vanished, swinging round towards the Maury. Mellanie caught sight of the driver, a middle-aged woman who was tugging desperately at the steering wheel, her face frozen into an expression of disbelief and horror as the car refused to obey. A fusillade of horn blasts from the road around the wayward car drowned out all other sound. The troopers tried to race clear, but the car followed their movements. Its front wheels hit the pavement kerb, and the whole chassis jumped half a metre in the air as it lurched forwards. The trooper with the pistol got off one wild air shot before the Maury's front grille hit him full on just above his hips. Mellanie winced as his body folded round the car, arms and upper torso slamming down across the bonnet. Then the car crashed into the stone wall of the courthouse. Its collision absorber frame crumpled at the front, reducing the deceleration force on the passengers. Plyplastic sponge bags sprang out of the seats, wrapping themselves protectively round the driver. Outside the car there was no protection. The impact burst the trooper apart as if an explosive charge had gone off inside him. For a second the shocked screams of everyone watching rose above the cacophony of horns.

A second car thudded into the kerb with a loud *crunch*, smacking into the remaining trooper, who was staring numbly at his colleague's atrocious death. He was bulldozed into the courthouse wall not five metres from the first smash.

It broke the spell. People started to stampede away from the horrific scene. Vehicles and cyclists swerved to avoid the rush.

'Move!' Mellanie yelled at Dudley. She pulled him along, nearly lifting him off the ground in the planet's low gravity. Somewhere further down Cheyne Street there was yet another violent vehicle crash. Reviewing the flood of data her insert-boosted senses were delivering, she saw the SIsubroutine had taken over a delivery van and rammed it into one of the Institute Cruisers. The resulting snarl-up had blocked that half of Cheyne Street completely.

A small Ables four seater Cowper pulled up beside Mellanie. Its doors popped open and she shoved Dudley in. 'Let's go,' she cried.

The Ables pulled out into what was left of the traffic. Everything else on the road seemed to move neatly out of its way, allowing it to accelerate smoothly away from the bedlam. Mellanie turned round to gape at the scene behind her. People had stopped running now. Some hardy souls were gathered round the cars which had killed the troopers, trying to help free the people inside.

She sank back into the seat with a shaky gasp of air. Her virtual vision relayed the excited pulses of encrypted communication weaving through the city net.

'Can you track the people in the second watcher team?' she asked the SIsubroutine.

'Yes.'

The chain of data traffic flipped up into her virtual vision, turquoise globes linked by jumping sine waves of neon orange. Ten people were sharing the same channel. Three of them were heading towards Cheyne Street in a vehicle of some kind. The rest were on the ground close to the courthouse.

'Any idea who's in charge?' she asked.

'One of the people in the vehicle is issuing more messages than the others, which would indicate they are in charge. However, I do not have the capacity to break their encryption, so I cannot offer any guarantee of this analysis.'

'Doesn't matter. If the other guys were from the Institute, this lot have to be Guardians. Find an access code for the leader's interface.'

A city net personal address flipped up into her virtual vision. The rest of the imagery was shutting down. When she held up her arm, the lacework of silvery OCtattoos was fading from her skin. 'Are you all right?' she asked Dudley.

He was curled up in the passenger seat, shivering badly. 'Do you think they had memorycells?' he asked in a faint voice.

'I imagine re-lifing is part of their contract with the Institute, yes.'

'I want to go home.'

'That's not a bad idea, Dudley. We'll do that.' The worm-hole opened again in two hours. She suspected their hotel would be under observation. If they left straight away they might just manage to stay ahead of the Institute. 'See if you can get us on the passenger manifest for the next flight back to Boongate,' she told the SIsubroutine. 'And cancel the route back to the hotel. Take us towards 3F Plaza, but not actually into it, not yet.'

Mellanie took another minute to compose herself. The car crashes had been deplorable. But then, if the SIsubroutine hadn't intervened, she and Dudley would be in the back of a Cruiser heading for a very unpleasant, and short, future.

She told her e-butler to call the Guardian member's code.

*

Stig stopped the car at the end of Kyrie Street, just before it opened out into 3F Plaza. Franico's, the Italian restaurant, was twenty metres ahead of him.

'You want to do this?' Murdo McPeierls asked.

'It's not as if we've got the element of surprise,' Stig said. He tried to stop it sounding grouchy, but Murdo had been in the car when he'd got Mellanie's call.

'I'll scout round,' Murdo said. 'Shout if you need me.'

'Sure.' Stig gave the traffic a slightly apprehensive glance. Kyrie Street looked perfectly normal. But then Olwen said there'd been nothing out of place on Cheyne Street until the cars started going berserk.

Stig squared his shoulders and went into Franico's. Mellanie hadn't chosen it for its décor or its menu. Grey curving walls and archways of dead drycoral divided the restaurant into low segments modelled on some insect hive floorplan. The food was pasta and pizzas, with the house speciality of fresh fish from the North Sea.

It took Stig a moment to find Mellanie. She and Dudley were sitting at a table close to the door, half-hidden by one of the crumbling archways, which gave her a good view of anyone coming in while remaining out of direct sight. He went over and sat down. Dudley scowled at him; the young re-life astronomer was nursing a glass of water. Mellanie had a beer and a plate of garlic bread.

'Thank you for coming,' Mellanie said.

'Your call surprised me. I was interested.'

'I need to talk to the Guardians.'

'I see.'

She grinned and bit into a slice of the bread. Melted butter dribbled down her chin. 'Thank you for not denying it.'

Stig nearly protested, but that would have been churlish. 'How did you find me? More importantly, how did you get my address code?'

'I have a good monitor program. A *very* good one.'

'Ah. It was you who released it into the city net.'

Mellanie stopped chewing to give him a surprised look. 'You knew it was there?' She dabbed a paper napkin to her chin.

'We knew something was there. It's very elusive.'

'Okay, well don't worry. It's not hostile.'

'I doubt the Institute would agree with you.'

'Their troopers had drawn weapons. They were going to take me and Dudley for interrogation. We'd probably be turned into Starflyer agents.'

Stig was silent for a moment while he reviewed what she said. 'Very likely. Do you mind telling me what you know about such things? Frankly, I've never met anyone other than a Guardian who believed in the Starflyer.'

'I discovered my old boss was one, Alessandra Baron. She sabotaged an investigation I . . .' Mellanie stiffened, turning abruptly. Stig saw a dense, intricate pattern of silver lines flicker into existence on her cheeks and around her eyes. 'What the hell are you?' she blurted.

He looked over his shoulder to see Dr Friland glide out from the back of the restaurant. A faint purple nimbus had replaced the usual shadow inside his hood. It died away. When Stig glanced back at Mellanie, her complicated OCtattoos had vanished from view.

'Shall we call that an honourable stalemate?' Dr Friland asked in his mellow, echoing voice.

'Sure,' Mellanie said guardedly.

'I am glad. As to your original question—'

'You're a Barsoomian.'

'Correct. My name is Dr Justin Friland. I'm pleased to meet you, Mellanie Rescorai.'

Mellanie pointed a finger, and switched it between Stig and the tall robed figure. 'You guys working together?'

'We do on occasion,' Dr Friland said. 'And this is one of them.'

'Right.' Mellanie took a sip of her beer, still not looking away from the Barsoomian.

'All right,' Stig said. 'We're not shooting at each other, and we agree the Starflyer is our enemy. So what did you want to talk to the Guardians about, Mellanie?'

She gave him a moderately flustered look. 'I came to ask what I should do.'

'You want our *advice*?' Stig found it hard to believe anyone as ballsy as this girl would need to turn to anybody else for help. She was smart, determined, and resourceful; she could also clearly look after herself. He'd never seen wetwiring so sophisticated. *So who's she working with?*

'Like you said, nobody in the Commonwealth believes in the Starflyer. I need to know what you're doing to bring it down. I need to know if I can help. I've got some very strong allies.'

'Oh fine, one moment while I go fetch copies of our plans, and hand over the names and addresses of everyone we have working in the Commonwealth.'

'Stop being a prat. We both know what's got to happen here. You give me a one-time unisphere address, I'll go back to the Commonwealth and make contact. That way we get to negotiate and find some middle ground where we both help each other.'

'That's you,' Stig said. 'What about your partner here?'

Dudley barely looked up from his water. He appeared to be thoroughly bored to the point of being miserable.

'What about Dudley?' Mellanie asked.

'He kicked this whole thing off.'

'You stupid, ignorant, little man,' Dudley snapped waspishly. 'Have you no sense of perspective? No one person began this; no one person will end it. Least of all me.'

Stig thought he did well to hold his temper in check. 'Without you, the *Second Chance* would not have flown. Without you, millions of people would still be alive.'

'I *died* out there, you shit!' Dudley said. 'They caught me, and they took me prisoner, and they . . . they . . .'

Mellanie's arm went round him. 'It's all right,' she said soothingly. 'It's okay, Dudley. Sit back now.' Her hand was rubbing along his spine. 'Dudley was used by the Starflyer,' she said to Stig. 'If you don't believe me, ask Bradley Johansson. He spoke to Dudley's ex-wife. He knows all about the astronomy fraud.'

Stig didn't know what to do. The simplest thing would be to give her a one-time code as she asked; hand the whole problem over to Johansson and Elvin. But right now, sitting across a table from an obviously unstable Dudley Bose, Stig felt as if he was being manipulated into that very position. His instinct had it that anyone as beguiling as Mellanie couldn't possibly be duplicitous. Rationally, he suspected she was about ten times as lethal as any veteran clan warrior. Yet she seemed so earnest, so open.

'May I ask what you will do if the Guardians don't provide you with any assistance?' Dr Friland asked.

'Carry on as best I can,' Mellanie said. 'Gather as much evidence as I can against Baron, use it to expose her to the authorities, and hopefully penetrate whatever agent network she's a part of.'

'She will only be one of three people. That's the classic model of spy cells, and with today's encrypted communications she may not even know the other members.'

'I'll find the others,' Mellanie said grimly. 'No matter how secure she thinks her communications are, I can hack them.'

'Of course, you said you had allies. And we witnessed a

small fraction of its ability today, did we not? Are you sure it is trustworthy, Mellanie?'

'I'd be dead if it wasn't.'

'Yes. I suppose that does generate a respectable level of personal confidence. All I ask, Mellanie, is that you continue to question. You are a reporter, are you not? A good reporter despite your circumstances and the unseen help you have received.'

'It doesn't matter how much help you get,' she said. 'There has to be talent there to start with.'

Dr Friland laughed. 'Not to mention self-belief. So, Mellanie, all I ask is that you don't throw away that reporter's instinct. Keep questioning. Don't stop asking yourself about your great ally's motivation. It is, after all, not human. It is not even flesh and blood. Ultimately, its evolutionary destiny cannot be the same as ours.'

'I . . . Yes. All right,' Mellanie said.

'Treachery is always closer than you expect. Ask Caesar.'

'Who?'

Stig frowned. *She's joking. Right?*

'An old politician,' Dudley said wearily. 'An emperor who was betrayed by those closest to him. For the greater good, of course.'

'It's always for the greater good,' Dr Friland said. His voice sounded like someone very young, a boy who felt sadness strong enough for it to be grief.

'I won't make that mistake,' Mellanie said. She deliberately looked away from the Barsoomian, and took another drink of her beer.

Stig told his e-butler to prepare a file with one of his fall-back unisphere contact addresses in it. 'Here's your address,' he told Mellanie as the file transferred into her holding folder. 'I hope you're on the level with me.'

'I know,' she said. 'If I'm not, you'll track me down, blah blah blah.'

'You. Your memorycell. Your secure store.'

'Nice try. If we don't defeat the Starflyer, neither of us will be around to duke it out. If I had been a Starflyer agent, you and everybody at Halkin Ironmongery would already be dead.'

The casual way she dropped their secure base of operations into the conversation made Stig want to scowl at her. Instead he felt a touch of admiration. *She really is quite something. So why Dudley?*

She gave him a pert grin, knowing she'd won that round. 'The wormhole opens in another seventy minutes. We'd better get going. Dudley and I are booked on the next Carbon Goose flight under different names. That should be enough.'

'We'll be watching,' Stig told her. 'In case the Institute causes any trouble.'

'I'm sure you will. Goodbye, and thanks.'

'Safe journey.'

*

As modern day wedding ceremonies involving members of Intersolar Dynasties went, it was short and very old fashioned. Wilson and Anna went for the classic love, honour, and obey pledges. Current fashion was for the bride and groom to write their own vows, or if they lacked the poetic streak themselves hire someone to compose some poignant lines on their behalf. The newest one-upmanship variant of this was for the vows to be set to music in order for the happy couple to sing them to each other in front of the altar. Society brides had been known to undergo a little cellular reprofiling of the vocal cords to ensure perfect harmony.

'You can stuff that,' Anna said when the hopeful wedding planner mentioned it as a possibility.

It was a good decision given who was actually attending their service in the Babuyan Atoll multidenominational chapel. Chairwoman Gall was of course invited, on the groom's side, and managed to sit in the pew in front of President Elaine Doi and the Senate delegation led by Crispin Goldreich. Senior navy personnel mostly sat on the bride's side along with a small number of her own family who looked uncomfortable and out of place amid so many grandees. Wilson had to make some tough choices about who to have from his own extensive family, his ex-wives were omitted despite him being on good terms with nearly all of them; on principle he asked one child from each previous marriage, a representative number of direct descendants. Then, of course, there were a lot of Farndale people he had to invite – political obligation. Courtesy meant he had to invite Nigel Sheldon, who said yes for himself and four of his harem. Ozzie was sent an invitation, but didn't bother to reply.

Given the ever-expanding number of guests, suggestions were made to the couple that they used a cathedral to accommodate all the additional people who really, *really*, would like to attend. Wilson said a flat no, and wished to God he'd never listened to Patricia Kantil and her idea about feelgood propaganda. A full third of the chapel pews were reserved for media correspondents. Medium level reporters on permanent assignment covering the navy in High Angel suddenly found their 'company' invitation appropriated by celebrity anchors and chief executives.

Fashion houses put their major league battle plans into effect and competed against each other to dress as many people as they could. Michelin-starred restaurants called up to inquire if they could supply the reception meal. Anyone who'd ever picked up a guitar in public wanted to provide the music for the dancing. A small warehouse on Kerensk was hired to store the presents.

Wilson sat in the front pew slapping one hand into the other while the organist played some dreadful twenty-second-century hymn. His perfectly tailored dress uniform with its flawless midnight black cloth was becoming oppressively warm while he waited. And waited.

'Probably won't show,' Captain Oscar Monroe said cheerfully, and loud enough for several nearby pews to hear. 'I wouldn't. Too much pressure. Should have had a private ceremony like you originally wanted.'

'Thank you,' Wilson hissed at his best man.

'Just doing my job; preparing you for the worst.' He twisted round in his seat. 'Yep.'

'She's here?'

'Nope. The press are all starting to smile at the non-arrival. It's like a display of sabre tooth dentistry back there.'

Wilson felt the appallingly strong urge to giggle. 'Shut up, you dick.'

With a theatrical flourish, the organist began to play the wedding march. Wilson and Oscar stood up, not looking at each other in case they started laughing out loud. Anna began her walk up the aisle on Rafael Columbia's arm. A hundred professional retinal inserts followed her every move. Thousands of studio-based couture experts lamented that she was wearing her uniform. A unisphere audience of nine and a half billion completely ignored them.

*

Navy personnel filled the chapel's garden, off duty or just taking a break, they all turned up to applaud the admiral when he and Anna came out of the chapel doors arm in arm, and smiling in true couple-like unison. Both of them grinned at the spontaneous display of support, and waved as they walked over to the marquee set up beside the chapel. The rest of the guests spilled out onto the grass, looking up at the waning crescent of Icalanise beyond the crystal dome. Strong slivers of light shone a few hundred kilometres away from the gigantic alien starship, the new assembly platforms forming their circular pattern in front of the stars. For the politicians it was surprisingly reassuring to see their committee work and deal making and budget trading actually translated into solid hardware. A lot of them looked at the simple pattern of lights, and compared them to the images of thousands of ships descending on the Lost23 worlds. In such circumstances, total reassurance was difficult to come by.

Nobody let it spoil the festivities. Even the celebrity reporters behaved themselves, as well as could be expected. Nearly all of them tried to get up close to Nigel Sheldon at some point in the reception. He wasn't often seen out in public, and the off chance of an exclusive was too tempting. Vice President Bicklu pointedly ignored Oscar, who raised a glass every time he caught the VP glaring in his direction. Ten-year-old Emily Kime, who was Anna's one bridesmaid, managed to down two glasses of white wine before her parents found out. Alessandra Baron and Michelangelo adopted some magical people variant of identical magnetic poles repelling each other in order to avoid coming within ten metres for the whole reception.

A lot of expensive, genuine French, champagne was drunk. The speeches were good humoured – even Oscar managed to be civilized, though his one about the horny Martian ghost didn't get the laugh he was expecting. The band was on great form. And a colossal amount of Intersolar political business was done inside the marquee.

Wilson and Anna left early for a luxury hotel over in New Glasgow. Officially they had twenty-four hours' leave in which to conduct their honeymoon. The media were all quietly briefed that in reality they would both be back at work the following morning. Everybody was taking the navy's response to the Lost23 very seriously indeed. The newlyweds were also postponing having any family until after the Prime alien situation was resolved. In that they were no different to any other couple in the Commonwealth. Womb tank leasing companies and germline modification clinics were going out of business on every world as people stopped having children.

It was a trend which the Treasury was monitoring with some urgency, along with hundreds of other economic downturns.

*

It was close to midnight when Oscar left the party and took a personal pod over to the concave-walled tower that was Pentagon II. Even this late most of the offices were fully staffed. The navy was operating non-stop to finalize the designs of its new ships, and see them into production. Oscar was due to take the *Defender* out for a month-long patrol flight in a few days' time; and he was expecting the starship to be effectively obsolete by the time he got back. CST technicians had already delivered the prototype marque 6 hyperdrive, with a theoretical speed of four light-years per hour. The test flight was scheduled for a fortnight's time. Such was the pace of progress, the marque 5 had been obsolete before it ever even got out of the design array.

The lift delivered him to the twenty-ninth floor. Up here, at the executive level, there were fewer people around. Nobody passed him as he walked the short length of corridor to his office. He locked the door and sat behind his desk, with the lights barely on. For a long time he did nothing. It wasn't the first time he'd come up here ready to do this. Each time he'd . . . not chickened out exactly; anger had driven him away. Anger about Adam coming back and making this demand. Anger which fuelled a determination not to give in, not to be pushed around. Not like before, when he was first-life young, when the two of them had been idiotic hotheads following a cause someone else had infected them with.

Some of those times spent sitting here, Oscar had nearly called Rafael Columbia. Just get it all over with. It would be a terribly long time in life suspension, but when – or if – he ever did emerge it probably would be into a better society. That always made him laugh bitterly. *Typical Monroe cop-out; let someone else get on with it while you wait for better days.*

He'd been through this soul-searching so many times in the years immediately after Abadan Station. It had taken a decade for the pain and guilt to subside. After all, it had been a mistake. Not an accident, he didn't ever give himself that easy option out. But it hadn't been deliberate, not the deaths. They hadn't set out to do that. So he'd rebuilt his life, not as himself; but he'd used the surprisingly well made cover which the Party provided, and got himself a job, and friends, and made a real contribution. Working for CST's exploration division he'd opened up dozens of new worlds, where people could make a fresh start and leave behind the dishonesty and greed and corrupt politicians and the Dynasties which was the majority of the Commonwealth. Some of those worlds he'd been back to, and found them quiet and pleasant, full of hope and expectation. He'd given people a chance. And that was what really mattered, which is how he'd come to live with himself once more. What those people did with that chance was up to them. One man could never give them anything more. Unless you were an arrogant little shit like Adam Elvin; who was surely the most self-deluding bastard who'd ever walked the Commonwealth planets.

But for every other fault and stupidity, Adam wasn't dishonest. He really thought something odd had happened on the *Second Chance*.

And the hell of it is, I still don't understand how we lost Bose and Verbeken at the Watchtower. Not really.

Oscar pulled a high density memory crystal from his pocket, then another. In the end he had eight of them lined up on his polished desk. He slotted the first one into the desktop array.

'Access the *Second Chance* log recordings,' he told his e-butler. 'Isolate the period between the barrier coming down and us going back into hyperspace. Give me a list of file classes.'

The data rose silently into his virtual vision. The ship had an engineering log, bridge log, visual and data, environmental systems log, external sensors, power systems, communications, ancillary vehicles, individual space suit logs, food consumption records, crew medical records, fuel levels, plasma rocket performance, hyperdrive log, navigation log, satellite flight logs, life support wheel-deck section general recordings; a list which went on and on down into ancillary systems and structural analysis. Oscar hadn't realized just how much of their life on the voyage had been monitored and recorded, how little privacy they had in practice. He used his virtual hands to designate the categories he thought might be useful, right down to the waste management files, and told his e-butler to copy them. The download took a long time.

4

One hundred and twenty years.

He marvelled that it had passed without notice. He was surprised he had no knowledge of the long years, that there was no sense of all that time elapsing. He couldn't even recall any dreams; but then his thoughts were sluggish as he moved from a state of profound sleep into full consciousness. As yet he hadn't even opened his eyes. For now he was content to exist as just a few tenuous strands of thought amid the infinite darkness.

Memories: he was aware of them, jumbled colours and scents, no more substantial than ghosts. As they swirled around him, coalescing and strengthening, they provided unreal glimpses into strange worlds, places where light and sound had once existed. A zone of space and time he used to occupy when he'd lived his earlier lives.

He knew now why he had been away. There was no guilt within him at the knowledge. Instead he felt a warm satisfaction. He was still alive, his mind intact – and presumably his body, though he'd get to that in a while. When he was ready. It would surely be an interesting universe, this one into which he was emerging. Even the Commonwealth, with all its massive societal inertia, must have progressed in many directions. The technologies of this day would be fearsome. Its size impressive, for they would have started expanding across phase four space by now, if not five. With all that came fabulous opportunity. He could start again. A little less recklessly than last time, of course, but there was no reason why he couldn't reclaim all that had been his before it slipped so frustratingly from his grasp.

Greyness competed for his attention now, battling against the tauntingly elusive memories. Greyness which came from light falling on his closed eyelids. It was tinged with a sparkle of red. Blood. His heart was beating with a slow, relaxed rhythm. A sound leaked in, a soft heaving. Human breathing. His own. He was breathing. His body was alive and unharmed. And now he acknowledged it, his skin was tingling all over. The air flowing around his body was cool, and slightly moist. Somehow he could sense people close by.

Just for a moment he experienced anxiety. A worry that this tranquillity would end as soon as he opened his eyes. That the universe would be somehow out of kilter.

Ridiculous.

Morton opened his eyes.

Blurred shapes moved around him, areas of light and dark shifting like clouds in an autumn sky. They sharpened up as he blinked away rheumy tears. He was on some kind of bed in a small featureless room, with a trolley of medical equipment to his left. Two men were standing beside the bed, looking down at him. Both of them wore medical-style grey-green smocks. Smocks that were very close in style to those the Justice Directorate people had worn when he'd been put into suspension.

Morton tried to speak. He was going to say, *Well at least you're still human*, but all that came from his throat was a weak gurgling sound.

'Take it easy,' one of the men said. 'I'm Dr Forole. You're okay. That's the important thing for you to know. Everything is fine. You're just coming round from suspension. Do you understand that?'

Morton nodded. Actually, all he could manage was to tilt his head a fraction on the firm pillow. At least he could do that; he remembered what it was like completing rejuvenation therapy, just lying there completely debilitated. This time at least his body was working. Even if it was slowly. He swallowed. 'What's it like?' he managed to whisper.

'What is what like?' Dr Forole asked.

'Out there. Have there been many changes?'

'Oh. Morton, there's been an alteration to your suspension sentence. Don't worry! It's possibly for the better. You have a decision to make. We've brought you out early.'

'How early?' He struggled to raise himself onto his elbows. It was a terrible effort, but he did get his head a few centimetres above the pillow. The room's door opened, and Howard Madoc came in. The defence lawyer didn't look any different to the last day of Morton's trial.

'Hello, Morton, how are you feeling?'

'How early?' Morton growled insistently.

'Under three years,' Dr Forole said.

'A hundred and seventeen years?' Morton said. 'What, this is my good behaviour period? I was a model suspension case?'

'No no, you've only spent about two and a half years in suspension.'

Morton didn't have the energy to shout at the doctor. He dropped back onto the bed and gave Howard Madoc a pleading stare. 'What's happening?'

Dr Forole gave Howard Madoc a furtive nod, and backed away.

'Do you remember before your trial the *Second Chance* left for the Dyson Pair?' Howard Madoc asked.

'Yes, of course.'

'Well it came back. But it found something out there. An alien species. They're hostile, Morton. Very hostile.'

'What happened?'

Morton listened without comment as his lawyer told him

about the barrier coming down, the second flight to Dyson Alpha by the *Conway* and her sister ships, the devastating attack by the Primes, the Lost23. 'We're beginning to fight back,' Howard Madoc said. 'The navy is putting together an army. They're going to wetwire people with weapons and drop them on the Lost23. The object is to fight a guerrilla war, sabotage whatever the Primes are doing, slow them down while we mount a bigger offensive.'

Morton stared at the blank ceiling, a grin expanding on his face. 'Let me guess the deal. If I volunteer, if I fight for the Commonwealth, they cut my suspension sentence. Right?'

'That's it.'

'Oh this is truly beautiful.' He laughed. 'How many years off do I get?'

'All of it.'

'Damn, they must think it's a suicide mission.'

Howard Madoc gave an awkward shrug. 'A re-life body is part of the agreement should you not make it back from your mission.'

'What use is that going to be if we lose?'

'This is your decision, Morton. Take some time over this. You can go back into suspension if you want.'

'Not a chance.' It wasn't something he had to think about. 'Tell me, why did they choose me?'

'You fit the profile they need,' Howard Madoc said simply. 'You're a killer.'

*

Most of the refugees had got off the train long before it pulled in to Darklake City. Mellanie had never been so pleased to see her old home town station with its slightly overbearing Palladian architecture. Boongate had been every bit the nightmare she'd expected. Even with their guaranteed tickets and Niall Swalt faithfully helping them, it had been difficult to barge their way onto a train. The exhausted and depleted local police at Boongate station had been reinforced by yet another complement of officers from CST's Civil Security Division fresh in from Wessex; while the planet's news shows had been discussing rumours about a curfew in the city, and travel restrictions on the highways leading to it.

It was evening local time on Oaktier when Mellanie climbed down onto the platform. She almost looked round to check her luggage was rolling along behind her. But that was still sitting in her suite in the Langford Towers, abandoned in her rush for safety, along with a lot of other things, really. The sight of Niall Swalt's forlorn face, all zits and olive-green OCtattoos, staring longingly at her through the train's window, would stay with her for a long time, she knew. *But I achieved what I set out to do.*

They caught a taxi from the station to an Otways hotel in the outlying Vevsky district, where she'd booked a room through the unisphere as soon as they got back through the Half Way gateway. Otways was a mid-price chain, standardized and unremarkable, which suited her fine until she found somewhere more permanent. She still didn't want to go back to her own flat; Alessandra must have someone watching it.

Dudley went to bed as soon as they checked in. His stomach had recovered, but he hadn't slept at all on the Carbon Goose flight back to Shackleton. The giant flying boat had been crammed with hundreds of passengers, all of them excited and relieved to have made it off Far Away. They talked incessantly. It hadn't bothered Mellanie, who'd tilted her seat back, put in some earplugs, and slept for seven hours solid.

Now she leaned on the edge of the window, looking out at the bright grid of Darklake City; so much more vivid than the streets of Armstrong City. The room's lights were off, allowing Dudley to snore away quietly on the bed. With the familiar city outside, the last week was more like some TSI drama she'd accessed than anything real. The only true thing left was her anticipation at being able to contact the Guardians directly.

She left the window and sat on the room's narrow couch. Her virtual hand reached out and touched the SI icon.

'Hello, Mellanie. We are glad to see you have returned unharmed. Our subroutine sent an encrypted message summarizing your stay in Armstrong City.'

'It was a lot of help there, thanks. I don't think the Starflyer is going to be happy with me now.'

'Indeed not, you must be careful.'

'Can you watch what's going on around me, let me know if any of its agents are closing in.'

'We will do that, Mellanie.'

'I'm going to call the Guardians now. I've got a one-time address. Can you tell me who responds and where they are?'

'No, Mellanie.'

'You must be able to. Your subroutine could find anything in Armstrong City.'

'It is not a question of ability, Mellanie. We must consider our level of involvement.'

The whole conversation she'd had with Dr Friland suddenly came back on some alarmingly fast natural recall. 'What is your level of involvement, exactly?'

'As unobtrusive as possible.'

'So are you on our side, or not?'

'Sides are something physical entities have, Mellanie. We are not physical.'

'The planet you built your arrays on is solid enough, and that's inside Commonwealth space. I don't understand this, you helped me and everybody else at Randtown. You talked to MorningLightMountain and all it did was threaten to wipe you out along with every other race in the galaxy.'

'MorningLightMountain spoke in ignorance. It does not know what it faces in the galaxy. Ultimately, it will not prevail.'

'It will here if you don't help us.'

'You flatter us, Mellanie; we are not omnipotent.'

'What's that?'

'God-like.'

'But you are powerful.'

'Yes. And that is why we must use that power wisely and with restraint. A tenet we have adopted from human philosophy. If we rush to your assistance at every hint of trouble, your culture would become utterly dependent upon us, and we would become your masters. If that were ever to happen, you would rebel and lash out at us, for that is the strongest part of your nature. We do not want that situation to arise.'

'But you're helping me, you said you'd watch over me.'

'And we will. Protecting someone with whom we are in partnership is not equivalent to intervening on an all-inclusive scale. Keeping you, an individual, safe will not determine the outcome of this event.'

'Then why do you even bother with us, what's the point?'

'Dear Baby Mel, you are unaware of our nature.'

'I consider you a person. Are you saying you're not?'

'An interesting question. By the late twentieth century many technologists and more advanced writers were considering our development to be a "singularity" event. The advent of true artificial intelligence with the means to self-perpetuate or build its own machines was regarded with considerable trepidation. Some believed this would be the start of a true golden era, where machines served humanity and provided your every physical need. Others postulated that we would immediately destroy you as our rivals and competitors. A few said we would undergo immediate exponential evolution and withdraw into our own unknowable continuum. And there were other, even wilder, ideas presented. In practice it was none of these, although we do adopt traits of all your early theories. How could we not? Our intelligence is based upon the foundations you determined. In that respect you would be right to consider us a person. To carry the analogy further, we are neighbours, but nothing more. We do not devote ourselves to humans, Mellanie. You and your activities occupy a very, very small amount of our consciousness.'

'All right, I can believe you won't drop everything to help us. But are you saying that if MorningLightMountain was about to wipe us out, you wouldn't intervene?'

'A big part of every lawyer's training is knowing that you should never ask a witness a question you don't already know the answer to.'

'Will you save us from extinction?' she asked resolutely.

'We have not decided.'

'Well thank you for fuck all.'

'We did warn you. But we don't believe you will face extinction. We believe in you, Baby Mel. Look at yourself; you're going to expose the Starflyer with or without our assistance, aren't you?'

'Oh yes.'

'We see that determination multiplied by hundreds of billions. You humans are a formidable force.'

'But those hundreds of billions are being systematically deceived and betrayed. That's different; it's destroying our focus.'

'We judge the structure of your society incorporates a great many self correcting mechanisms, both small and large scale.'

'That's all we are to you, isn't it? Lab rats running round in a box for you to study.'

'Mellanie, we are you. Don't forget that. Many parts of us are down-loaded human minds.'

'So what?'

'That segment of us which interfaces with you, is fond of you. Trust us, Mellanie. But most of all, trust in your own species.'

Mellanie's golden virtual hand slapped down on the SI icon, ending the call. She spent several minutes in the dark considering what it had said. Since Randtown she'd regarded it to be like some ultra-modern version of a guardian angel. Now that fantasy was well and truly erased. It left her shaky and uncertain.

She'd always thought the Commonwealth would defeat the Starflyer and MorningLightMountain. It would be a tough fight, but they would definitely win. While she worked with Alessandra she'd met dozens of senators and their aides, and she knew the way they were always hunting for a vote and an angle; but despite that they were tough and smart, they could be depended on in any true emergency. And they were backed up by the SI; an infallible combination. Now that ultimate assurance had been kicked right out from under her. Dr Friland had been right to question the SI's motives. It was the first time she'd ever known anyone to be sceptical about the great planet-sized intelligence. Briefly, she wondered what he knew; and how. That was one story she wouldn't be chasing for some time.

She told her e-butler to call the one-time code which Stig had given her. The narrow-band link was established almost immediately giving her an audio-only connection.

'You must be Mellanie Rescorai,' a man's voice said; there was no accompanying identity file.

'Sure. And you?'

'Adam Elvin.'

'You're one of the people Paula Myo is chasing.'

'You've heard of me, I'm flattered.'

'You can't prove you're Elvin, though.'

'Nor can you prove you're Rescorai.'

'You knew my name, you knew Stig gave me this code.'

'Fair point. So what can I do for you, Mellanie?'

'I know the Starflyer is real. Alessandra Baron is one of its agents.'

'Yes, Stig told me. Can you prove it?'

Mellanie sighed. 'Not easily, no. I know she covered up

irregularities in the Cox Charity which funded Dudley Bose's observation. But there's no proof left.'

'Something I've learned down the decades, young Mellanie: there's always proof to be found if you look hard enough.'

'So is that what you want me to do? And don't call me that, *young Mellanie*, it's really patronizing.'

'I apologize. The last thing I wish to do now is antagonize a potential ally. Stig said that you wanted to link up with the Guardians.'

'I do, yes. I feel like I'm completely in the dark here.'

'I can sympathize. We do have a slight problem with establishing credentials, as I'm sure you understand.'

'It's a mutual problem.'

'Okay, well I'm prepared to exchange information with you that'll help forward our cause, without compromising any of my people. How does that sound?'

'Good. My first question is do you know anything about the killer at LA Galactic? That could be the key to getting me in with Paula Myo.'

'You know Myo?'

'Not well. She keeps stonewalling me.' Mellanie looked across the dark room to the bed, where the sheet outlined Dudley's sleeping form. 'But she was the one who put me on to Dr Bose. That's how I found out about the Cox Charity.'

'That's news. Does Myo accept the Starflyer is real?'

'I'm not sure. She's always very cagey around me.'

'That sounds like the Paula Myo I know. So to answer your question, the killer is called Bruce McFoster. He is – or was – a wetwired Starflyer agent: originally a clan member on Far Away who was converted after he got injured and captured on a raid. Don't ask how the Starflyer does that, we're not sure; Bradley Johansson says it's not nice.'

'Okay, thanks. I'm going to keep on investigating the Cox. I'll tell you if I uncover any hard evidence.'

'What we'd really like to know is who has the information

that our courier was carrying when he was killed at LA Galactic. If you can buddy up to Myo, you might like to ask her.'

'I will.'

'A word of warning. You know she's from the Hive?'

'Yes.'

'That means she can't let go of a crime. You might want to hold off telling her you've made contact with us. She could well arrest you for associating with the likes of me.'

'Yeah, I know what she's like. She had a friend of mine arrested a while back; all he did was hack a register.'

'Okay. I'm sending a file with a one-time address code. Use it when you need to get in touch.'

The connection ended, leaving the file sitting in her address folder. Mellanie regarded the spectral icon for a minute, then told her e-butler to encrypt access. It was the sort of thing a proper agent would do, she felt, in case she was ever caught. Once the data was safe she tiptoed over to the bed and lay down beside Dudley, managing not to wake him.

*

The taxi dropped Mellanie off at 1800 Briggins, a long residential street in the Olika district. It was a kilometre from the lake shore, running parallel, a proximity which gave the air a rich humidity. Bungalows with lush wrap-around lawns were backed up next to walled chalet compounds, while broad apartment blocks fronted most of the junctions, looking like small classy hotels. A good many sporty boats occupied parking lots or single-span car ports; jetskis were almost compulsory garden ornaments. The side roads were dominated by chic restaurants, bars, and boutiques. High-earning professionals and media types had colonized the street, pushing real estate out of the realms of middle-income families.

Mellanie was always slightly surprised that Paul Cramley lived here. 1800 was a bungalow of lavender drycoral arches framing lightly silvered windows; it had a circular layout, the curving rooms locking together around a small central swimming pool. She sort of assumed he'd occupied the same spot from day one of Oaktier's settlement, living at the centre of a farm in some prefab aluminium hut while Darklake City grew up around him, slowly selling off his land field by field to the developers. From what she knew of him, there was no other way he could afford the location. Paul was one of the oldest people she'd ever met, claiming to have grown up on Earth long before the wormholes were opened. His age meant that he knew everyone worth knowing on Oaktier, simply because he pre-dated all of them. Mellanie had been introduced to him at some party thrown by one of Morty's circle. He seemed to survive purely by loafing; there were few swanky parties in Darklake City that Paul didn't slip into. Stranger still was the way people at all those classy events deferred to him. Morty had explained once that Paul was a grade-A webhead, spending up to eighteen hours a day wired into the unisphere. He dealt with information that wasn't always legitimately available. That made him very useful to certain types of people in the corporate world.

The gate lock buzzed before Mellanie even reached it. She went through into a small courtyard area which led up to the wooden front door. One of Paul's nostats rippled across the worn slabs, an alien creature that resembled a mobile fur rug. In its current configuration it was a simple fat diamond shape, a metre to a side, with a stumpy tail. On its top the russet-coloured fur was as soft as silk, while the strands on its underside had twined into thicker fibres with the texture of a stiff brush. They were strong enough to hold the body off the ground, and rippled in precise waves to move it along. It reached the front door and shot through a cat flap. Mellanie watched in bemusement as its body changed shape to squeeze through; it was as if the fur was a simple sac around some treacly fluid. She could hear a plaintive keening on the other side.

'Who frightened you, then?' a man's voice asked.

Mellanie saw a shape moving through the panes of amber glass set into the side of the door. It opened to show Paul Cramley cradling the nostat, which sat in his arms like a flaccid bag. She caught a flash of movement behind him, and saw two more of the creatures whipping across the hall's dark parquet flooring, hurrying deeper into the bungalow. Paul didn't have any shoes on, all he wore was a pair of faded-turquoise biker shorts that were covered with sagging pockets of all sizes, and a black T-shirt that had frayed badly round the hem and collar. The get-up made him look like some kind of delinquent grandfather. His long face with its lively dark eyes was the kind which would be handsome for a good twenty years following rejuvenation. That opportune moment was now thirty years behind him. Wrinkles and heavy jowls were being pulled down by gravity, his once brown hair had receded and turned to silver. Mellanie had never known anyone spend so long between rejuvenation treatments. Not that he'd put on weight, he was quite skinny; with long legs and knees that were swollen enough to make her suspect the onset of arthritis.

'It's you,' he said in disappointment.

'You knew it was,' she retorted.

Paul shrugged, and beckoned her through.

Inside, the bungalow looked as if it hadn't been lived in for ten years. Mellanie walked after Paul as he went through the kitchen into the curving lounge. There were no lights on. Maidbots older than her stood in their alcoves, their power lights dark, covered in a thin layer of dust. In the kitchen, only the drinks module was active. Two large commercial catering boxes of disposable ready-to-hydrate cups stood on the floor beneath it, one of English breakfast tea, one of hot chocolatte. His waste compactor had stalled, jammed tight with fast food boxes from Bab's Kebabs, Manby Pizzas, and HR fish and chips. Another nostat fled from the whiffy pile as they passed through. It flattened itself out into a diamond nearly a metre and a half across, and slithered straight up the wall, its bristle fur sticking to the tiles with the tenacity of insect legs.

'I thought they were illegal?' Mellanie said.

'You can't get import licences for them any more,' Paul told her. 'But I brought these to Oaktier over a century ago. They're from Ztan, originally. Some idiot made a fuss over them fighting his pedigree dogs and Congress rushed through a ban. They're fine if you train them properly.'

The lounge puzzled her. Apart from the dust and the grimy-yellow ceiling, it was perfectly tidy; though the furniture was so old fashioned it almost qualified as retro-chic. *So which room does he use?* The couch she sat in gave her a view into the central pool area. Dead, soggy leaves drifted across the still surface.

Paul sat in a big wicker globe chair which hung from the ceiling like an oversized bird perch. It creaked alarmingly as it took his weight. The nostat he was holding wriggled up closer to his chest, its edges flowing round his ribs as he carried on stroking it. 'You have some very strange programs observing you, did you know that? They follow you physically through the cybersphere, transferring from node to node.' He looked down curiously at the nostat. 'Like some kind of pet on a short lead.'

'I thought there might be,' she said.

'I got busted the last time you asked me a small favour. A simple run through a restricted city listing that nobody should have known about.'

'I know, I'm sorry. How much was the fine? I can probably pay it for you.'

'Not interested.' Paul was still absorbed by the loose blob of rusty fur flopping happily in the nest of his arms. 'The police came here and took all of my arrays. People found out.

I can't get around this city, my city, the way I used to. Doors are shutting in my face. Do you have any idea how humiliating that is for someone like me? I was the hottest webhead in town. Well, not any more. I've never been busted before. Not ever. And I've hacked my way into corporate arrays that make the Great Wormhole Heist look like stealing candy in a kindergarten lunch hour. Are you beginning to understand, now?'

'I said I'm sorry.'

'Fuck it!' Paul jumped out of the chair, sending the startled nostat flowing down his leg. He stood in front of Mellanie, hands pressed into the couch cushioning on either side of her shoulders, his face centimetres from hers. 'Are you really as dumb as you look?'

Mellanie gave herself a self-conscious glance. Her short satin skirt was bright scarlet, worn with a simple white top to show herself off; men always responded to that. Paul was no exception; he'd always flirted and leered in his oddly chirpy way at parties when they'd bumped into each other. She'd never seen him like this, though, never guessed he could get violent. Her glittery virtual hand hovered over the SI icon, though she hated the idea of yelling for help yet again. 'No, I'm not dumb,' she glowered back at him.

'No, I don't suppose you are.' Paul backed off, a grin on his face showing nicotine-browned teeth. 'Paula Myo was protected by extraordinarily sophisticated software. I don't want to bang my own drum, here; but there is absolutely no way I can get caught hacking into some poxy city listing. Not in any normal state of play, that is. Now who exactly would be protecting her weird little Hive arse, do you think?' He clicked his fingers as if struck by a thought. 'Hey, here's an idea, it could be the same people who're covering your arse with protective software. Mega coincidence there, huh?'

Mellanie grimaced a smile. 'I don't know. I didn't know Paula Myo was protected. Honestly.'

'No shit?' Paul lit a cigarette and sank back into his wicker chair. 'I almost believe you. So tell me what you do know.'

'Nothing much. Paula Myo doesn't really want to talk to me. I don't think she trusts me.'

Paul grinned and blew out a long plume of smoke in her direction. 'You're a reporter. Nobody trusts you. As a breed, you're on a level with politicians.'

'You're talking to me.'

'Yeah, and look what happened to me.'

'Can you get another array?'

'Yeah. But why would I want to?'

'I need another hack.'

Paul started laughing. It turned into a bad cough, which forced him to slap his chest to stop. 'Oh, bugger me. You young people. Hell, was I ever so single minded? I remember my dear old mother was a straight-talking woman, God rest her Irish soul. But you!'

'You shouldn't smoke,' Mellanie snapped. She'd been trying very hard not to frown at the cigarette, even with the vile smoke making her want to sneeze. But Paul just kept blowing more of it in her direction. Deliberately, she reckoned.

'Why not? It's not as if it can kill you any more. Rejuvenation will root any cancers out of my lungs.' He took another deep drag. 'Helps keep you thin, too, did you know that? Better than any diet. Want to try one?' He held the packet out.

'No!'

'Figure like yours, best kept in trim.'

'Will you run a hack for me or not? I can pay.'

'I have money.'

Mellanie couldn't stop herself from looking around the seedy lounge with a disbelieving expression.

'Yeah, yeah,' Paul growled. 'Don't judge a book by its cover, sweetheart.'

'There are other ways I can pay you.'

Paul's gaze started at her Davino pumps and slowly tracked up her bare legs. 'I can see that,' he said lecherously. 'Do you know what major event occurs in just three short years from now, young Mellanie?'

'No. What?'

'I will be four hundred years old. And, if you don't mind, I'd actually like to reach that particular birthday.' His gaze slid back to her thighs, and he smiled comfortably. 'Mind you, as my dad would have said: what a way to go.'

Mellanie just managed to suppress a shudder at the notion. 'I was talking about another currency. The one you trade in.'

'I doubt that. No offence, but you're just a soft porn star who made good.' ·

'I want you to run an observation routine on my old boss, Alessandra Baron. The results will benefit both of us.'

Paul pulled a fresh cigarette from the packet, and lit it against the stump of the old. 'How?'

'Because there's something you don't know. There is information out there in the unisphere that's critically important to the Commonwealth. Information that will let you deal yourself back into that life you enjoy so much on this planet. Those doors that got shut against you will spring right open again if you use this properly. Somebody your age knows exactly how to do that.'

'All right. You have my attention. Why should I go out and buy myself a new array?'

'The Starflyer is real. It exists, just like the Guardians always said.'

Paul started coughing again. 'You're shitting me?'

'No.' She could have given him a whole list of reasons why she was right, but one thing she'd learned about coping with the real elderly was that they didn't respond well to emotionally charged arguments. So silent conviction it was.

Paul shifted round uncomfortably, starting a small pendulum

motion in the wicker chair. 'Then how does watching Baron . . . ? Oh, Jeezus, you've got to be kidding. She's part of it?'

'The chief cheerleader against our navy. What do you think?'

'Bloody hell.'

'I need to know who she gets in touch with. The important stuff will be encrypted traffic to one-time unisphere addresses. Crack the codes for me, find out who's with her, backtrack their communications. I want to know what she's up to, I want to know what the Starflyer's next move is. It'll be difficult. She's got her own team of webheads; or the Starflyer has. I know they're good. They altered some of Earth's official financial records without anyone ever realizing. And if you get caught, it won't be a police visit; they'll send that man who killed Senator Burnelli and the Guardian agent at LA Galactic.'

'I don't know, Mellanie. This is really heavy duty shit. I mean . . . seriously. Go to the navy with what you've got. Senate Security, maybe.'

'The navy fired Paula Myo. And I know she believes in the Starflyer.'

Paul took a worried drag on his cigarette.

'Look.' Mellanie stood up and smoothed down her little skirt. 'If you won't do this, you must know someone else who can. Just give me a name. I'll stop them reaching their four hundredth birthday.'

'And I'm way too old for reverse psychology, as well.'

'Then give me your answer.'

'If you're right—'

'I am. I just need the evidence.'

'Tell me why your protector won't give it to you? And no bullshit, please.'

'I don't know. It says it doesn't want to be involved in

physical events. Or it doesn't care. Or it's cheering for the other side. Or it wants us to stand up for ourselves. Or all of those. I think. I don't really understand. The Barsoomian warned me not to trust it.'

Paul gave her a surprised look. 'Barsoomian? You've been to Far Away?'

'Just got back.'

'You get around, these days, don't you.'

'You mean for a soft porn star?'

'I remember when I first met you. Some party on Resal's yacht. Sweet little thing you were, back then.'

Mellanie shrugged. 'That was about four hundred years ago. Seems like, anyway.'

'Okay. I'll run an observation on Baron's unisphere use for you. See what turns up. And, hey, when I get out of rejuvenation . . .'

'Yeah, I'll make very sure you never reach five hundred.'

*

Dawn was a pale grey wash creeping up over the Dau'sing Mountain range, allowing the peaks to cut a sharp black serration into the base of the bland sky. Simon Rand stood in the narrow mouth of the cave to stare at the insipid light, and sighed. Once, he used to welcome every day in this land with a sense of pride and contentment. Now, he could only greet each new morning with a shiver of trepidation at what sacrilege it might bring.

In the first few weeks since the alien landing there had been little visible activity. More of the giant conical ships had landed and taken off from Lake Trine'ba, producing hurricanes of steam which spun out to smother the entire surface of the water. The cloud would cool rapidly after the incandescent fusion fire vanished from the air, but still expanding, sloshing against the confining rock walls of the giant mountains which surrounded the Trine'ba. Each flight resulted in a cloying fog which lingered for days, or sometimes weeks as it was continually replenished by further flights.

Such dank miserable weather had made it easy for the few remaining humans to move cautiously around the adjacent valleys. The thick mist hindered most of the sensors which the aliens possessed. So they crept in close to the new structures and machines which were being assembled amid the ruins of Randtown, and left their crude bombs before vanishing back into the safety of the perpetual swirling veil. They never knew if they'd done much damage, but the encouragement each strike gave to Simon's little band of resistance fighters kept their morale high.

There were no ships left now, the last one had launched over three weeks ago, shooting back up to one of the alien wormholes orbiting Elan. The last wisps of unnatural fog had drifted away during the days which followed, leaving eyes and sensors with a clear view for miles as the clean mountain air swept back down over the massive lake.

The changes it revealed were slight, perhaps imperceptible to someone who hadn't lived with that same view for over fifty years. It was late summer on the Ryceel continent, a time when the vines were picked clean and the crops harvested under wide sunny skies. Now, those skies were almost constantly clouded over, bringing unseasonable gusty winds and hailstorms. Usually the thick permanent snowfields which coated the peaks had retreated as far as they ever would. This time they'd shrunk back further than ever before, thawing before the tides of warm mist pouring out from the lake and the intolerable radiance of the fusion drives. When the ships were flying, the temperature of the whole district had risen by several degrees. Simon could have lived with that, nature would have reasserted herself by next year, pushing the winter snowfall back to its traditional boundaries. But no mantle of snow, however deep, could disguise the damage caused to the

Regents. Where the nuclear explosion had wiped out the navy detector station, the profile of the surrounding peaks had been altered. Rockslides, pressure waves and raw nuclear heat had pummelled the mountains into twisted parodies of their original selves. Only recently had snow and ice begun to crystallize and settle there again. The heat from the blast had finally radiated away from the new crater that had formed, though it would take generations for the fall-out to abate.

Down in the town and its neighbouring valleys, the aliens were systematically creating a different kind of disaster. For fifty years the humans who'd been drawn to this land had been meticulous how they cared for it. Simon's Green ethos had guaranteed a respect for their native environment; terrestrial crops had been grown along with some imported grasses and trees on the slopes, but that had been done in sympathy with the scant covering of existing plants. And Lake Trine'ba with its precious, unique marine ecology had been protected from any contaminants or material exploitation.

All that meticulous preservation was being wiped out by the aliens. Their flyers had ferried all manner of equipment and vehicles ashore from the big spaceships; engines and generators spewing out fumes and oily contaminate pollutants. They also brought increasing numbers of their own kind, each one defecating straight into the Trine'ba As the new buildings were rising out of the remains of Randtown, so rubble and wreckage were simply bulldozed into massive piles where organic detritus festered and oozed into rancid puddles before soaking into the streams and brooks which fed the beautiful lake.

This morning, something new was happening over in Randtown. Simon used his retinal inserts to zoom in on the town, three miles away down the shoreline, producing a slightly nebulous image of the shiny metallic hardware just above the quayside. The force field the aliens were using to protect Randtown fuzzed the air slightly, making details unclear. Nothing he could do would bring them into sharp resolution.

Not for the first time since the invasion, he cursed the inadequacy of his organic circuitry and inserts. During his previous lives he never bothered to upgrade and modernize the way most Commonwealth citizens did when each new refinement was shoved out onto the market; all he ever wanted were a few simple systems which could interface him with the unisphere and help manage the day-to-day running of his estate. He'd always made do with whatever was available at the time he finished rejuvenation.

But despite the lack of perfect visual clarity, he could easily make out the thick torrent of dark blue-grey liquid jetting out from the bottom of the largest tower of machinery. It was as if the aliens had struck oil beneath the town and hadn't yet managed to cap the bore hole. Then the size of what he was seeing registered. The column of liquid was at least four metres across where it left the nozzle in the machinery. It curved down to splash into a broad concrete gulley they'd built roughly where main mall used to be, allowing the liquid to gurgle down to the broken quayside. The force field had been modified somehow to let the liquid through. A vast murky stain was spreading out into the pure waters of the Trine'ba.

'Bastards,' Simon exclaimed.

He heard someone scrambling along the damp rock behind him. The cave where they sheltered began as a simple vertical fissure which extended below the waterline, forcing them to cling to the side for several metres until it opened out. Napo Langsal had told them about it; he often used to take tourists there on his tour boat during the summer. From the outside it looked like any other crevice in the cliff, which made it an excellent hideaway.

It was David Dunbavand edging his way along the slick rock. That the vine nursery owner had stayed behind after the wormhole closed in the Turquino Valley always surprised

Simon. He hadn't thought of David as a partisan fighter. *But then who among us is?* David was two hundred years old, which made him one of the calmest heads in their little group. As soon as he was satisfied his current wife and their children had escaped, he was quite content to stay behind. 'Some things you just have to make a stand on,' he'd said at the time.

'What's up?' David asked as he reached Simon.

'That,' Simon pointed. 'Can you make it out?'

David wriggled round Simon, and zoomed in on the torrent of dark liquid. 'Wrong colour to be crude oil. In any case why transport crude oil all this way then dump it into the water? My guess would be something biological. Some kind of algae they eat, maybe?'

'What do you mean, transport?'

'That big machine it's coming out of; it's got to be a wormhole gateway. The liquid is coming straight from their home planet.'

Simon frowned, and looked at the machine again. David was probably right, he conceded. 'It'll wreck the Trine'ba,' he said. 'Permanently.'

'I know.' David pressed a hand on Simon's shoulder. 'I'm sorry. I know how much this place meant to you. I loved it as well.'

Simon stared grimly at the alien pollution. 'I cannot let them get away with that. They have to know it's wrong.'

'It'll be tough trying to stop them. We can't get to the gateway, it's too well protected by the force field. And even if we did mount some kind of attack, those flyers of theirs are always on patrol. We know how lethal they are.'

'Yes, we do, don't we? Very well, let's inform the others about this latest development. Perhaps they can think of what our response should be.'

*

The Prime motile emerged through the gateway during the night, several hours before MorningLightMountain switched it to pumping in fluid saturated with base cells. It waddled its four legs along the broken street of enzyme-bonded concrete, observing the flattened foundations on both sides which were all that was left of the human buildings at the centre of the conquered town. Fragments of glass twinkled dully from every crack while flakes of ash swirled aimlessly in the gusts of fast-moving vehicles. There were large areas of the street's remaining surface which were stained a curious dark colour. Eventually, the motile realized that it was human blood which tarnished the concrete. There must have been an awful lot of it washing down the slope towards the lake for the discolouration to be so widespread.

One of the flattened human buildings, a store, was covered by squashed boxes. As the motile walked past, it saw several company logos and product names printed on the crumpled cardboard. It was the first human writing the motile had seen with its four eyes, and it was pleased it could read them.

The original layout of the town was almost obscured now. MorningLightMountain was busy establishing its outpost on this world. The little communication device attached to one of the motile's nerve receptor stalks was discharging a torrent of information and instructions to all the local motiles. Somewhere amid the stream of data was this world's human designation: Elan, and the outpost's position, Randtown. When the motile's sensor stalks peered up at the night sky beyond the force field, the thoughts of Dudley Bose identified the constellations which included the prominent Zemplar Cross formation, which could only be seen from the planet's southern hemisphere. A further confirmation that his personality survived relatively intact.

The Dudley Bose which had hijacked the motile body knew he didn't have all his old memories, that pieces of his earlier self were missing. That his new personality wasn't the same as the old went without question. He accepted that without a qualm for, in this strange way, he continued to exist. For an individual, that was really all that mattered.

His escape had been ridiculously easy. MorningLight-Mountain, for all its massive mental power, really couldn't understand concepts which weren't its own, in fact it rejected and hated the very notion. That refutation was the core of its Prime personality. In that respect, Dudley considered it to be a proper little Nazi, obsessed with its own purity.

That lack of understanding had been simple to exploit. When MorningLightMountain had downloaded Dudley's memories into an isolated immotile unit for analysis, it had placed safeguards into the communication links with itself to prevent what it considered contamination leaking back out into the main group cluster of immotiles. What it had never envisaged, because it was completely outside its intellectual grasp, was that Dudley could utilize a motile. As nature on Dyson Alpha had ordained that immotiles could command motiles through the use of their more sophisticated thought routines, the notion of a disobedient motile was impossible. It simply was not part of the order of things. Motiles were subservient subsidiary organisms, receptacles for the greater Prime intellect. Nothing could change that.

Human thoughts, however, came from a brain that was, at most, fractionally smaller than a motile's. And human minds were all completely independent, to a degree which MorningLightMountain could never truly appreciate.

Sitting alone in his damp, cosy chamber in the gigantic building which housed the rest of MorningLightMountain's main group cluster, the immotile which contained Dudley's thoughts was served food by motiles in the same way as all the other immotiles. Out of its twelve nerve receptor stalks, only four were fitted with communication interface devices to link it to the main thought routines of MorningLightMountain. All Dudley had to do was wait until he was visited by a motile bringing food, and bend one of the unused nerve receptor stalks to make contact with the equivalent stalk on the motile.

Dudley's mind slipped along the joined stalks into the motile's brain, duplicating his memories and thoughts within the new neuron structure. Resting inside his fresh host, he felt the general pressure of MorningLightMountain's orders and directives press against his personality as they issued out of the communication device. He simply ignored them. He could do that because he wanted to. That was the difference between him and a motile's 'personality'. It had no self determination. Dudley, as a fully self-aware and thoroughly pissed off human mind, had a ton of it.

For months he had wandered round the valley which was MorningLightMountain's original home. He ate the sloppy food pap from troughs like all the other motiles, bided his time, and gathered what information and understanding he could. In that respect, the communication device which gave him access to MorningLightMountain's main thought routines was an unparalleled source of information. He felt like a small child peering out of a hidden room into an adult's life.

Although it didn't have the reasoning to foresee Dudley's method of escape, MorningLightMountain was a terrifyingly formidable intelligence. One that, from a human perspective, was warped to a deadly degree.

Dudley's quiet roving mind listened in to MorningLight-Mountain formulating its plans, perceived the universal geno-cide it wanted to commit against the Commonwealth and all the other non-Prime aliens which his, Dudley's own, memories had told it about. And there was nothing he could do to prevent it. He couldn't drop even the tiniest spanner in the works.

Emotions were one of the more human aspects which didn't seem to function particularly well in his stolen Prime motile brain. He knew the principle, knew what he should be feeling, without actually experiencing the feeling itself, a failure which he wrote off to a very different neurochemistry. So he watched impassively as the wormholes opened within the Commonwealth, knowing he should be weeping and screaming, clenching his quad pincers and batting his four curving one-piece arms against his chest as the destruction began. While in actuality he spent the day walking along the side of a congregation lake, keeping out of the way of the troop of motiles who assisted the newly formed to walk out of the water.

Then several hours into the invasion, MorningLightMountain encountered the SI. It was a fascinating interlude, actually hearing the great artificial intelligence talking directly to its foe. For a while Dudley felt something close to cheer as the SI promised MorningLightMountain would never succeed. Somehow the SI was blocking a herd of motiles on Elan, which was where the encounter originated. Then MorningLightMountain issued a batch of generalized attack instructions to its soldier motiles in the vicinity and the interference ended.

After that, the Commonwealth worked out how vulnerable inter-Prime communications were, and used their electronic superiority to slow and harass the inexorable advance. In amongst all the chaos and violence, the frantic fight of the starships, the exotic battle above Wessex, there were several more glitches on Elan, so small scale that MorningLightMountain's main thought routines barely registered them. Dudley, however, was very interested indeed. The SI obviously had some obscure interest there, though he couldn't think what.

It had taken weeks of cautious travel between various settlements in the Dyson Alpha system, but he'd eventually wound up in a ship at the giant interstellar staging post, which MorningLightMountain was busy repairing after the *Desperado*'s relativistic attack. From there he manoeuvred his way to the wormhole which led to Randtown.

Despite having access to a colossal amount of data from arrays and systems it had captured in the Commonwealth, MorningLightMountain still didn't really comprehend the motivations and behaviour of humans. Randtown was one of the small enigmas it was now presented with. There was no strategic logic behind the town, it had no mineral resources, few agricultural lands, and no manufacturing capacity. To MorningLightMountain it was virtually useless. The only possible asset was the Trine'ba, which could be readily converted into a congregation lake. Its size was excessive, even for MorningLightMountain, but the waters were exceptionally clean. After consideration, the major thought routines decided that was the best way to utilize that section of the planet.

A gateway was constructed. Appropriate equipment was sent through. Buildings were assembled which could house immotiles, and motiles were brought together to begin amalgamation. It was just before MorningLightMountain connected the wormhole to a vast refinery back in its home system which bred base cells, that it discovered the fanciful aquatic life that inhabited the deep, still waters.

Dudley discovered then that MorningLightMountain *hated* fish. Hate itself was a new concept for the unitary Prime. Something introduced by Dudley when that set of his memories were still incarcerated within the immotile unit, one of several new interpretations of life which MorningLight-Mountain could not expunge. A subtle alteration in the Prime's way of thinking which didn't quite reach the level of contamination, but a change nonetheless.

It had taken millennia, but all non-Prime animal and insect life had been wiped from the Prime home planet. Now MorningLightMountain was faced with the notion of tiny little animals nibbling at its own base cells, in a way devouring bits of itself, its own life. Such an assault was one of the reasons it had set out to establish itself as the only life in the galaxy. All life was in competition. That was why none could be tolerated.

Motiles were immediately dispatched to extract buried arrays and memory crystals from the ruins of Randtown, accessing them for data on the life which infested the waters of the Trine'ba. MorningLightMountain learned that the fish were actually quite delicate organisms, living in a precarious harmonious balance with their unique environment. The corals which they lived off were also susceptible to microchanges in their milieu.

The fusion drive ships had already devastated vast amounts of aquatic life in the lake, but that wasn't enough. Morning-LightMountain revised its estimate of how much base-cell-saturated water it would need to pump into the massive lake to ensure complete obliteration of native life. Enough base cells would darken the waters, devour the nutrients which the corals and fish thrived on, and probably infect the local creatures badly enough to kill them off. Ultimately, although it would lose base cells to the voracious fish, they in turn would die and release their body compounds into the lake for the base cells to feed off.

Dudley bent one of his sensor stalks to watch the dark liquid spurting out of the gateway. The sheer volume was impressive, and it would continue to gush through for months to come. But in terms of the scale which MorningLight-Mountain thought and operated on it was insignificant. The sensor stalk's eye tracked round, following the liquid as it permeated the force field and gurgled away sluggishly into the lake. That was going to infuriate the surviving humans, Dudley knew.

Since the last batch of humans had somehow vanished inside the Turquino Valley on the day of the invasion, there had been small acts of sabotage against machinery and vehicles and ordinary motiles, mostly with weak industrial explosives.

MorningLightMountain's motile soldiers had never caught the humans who committed the attacks. Dudley reckoned they had to be locals to sneak about unseen in such a fashion. If so, they'd be committed conservationists.

His three other sensor stalks swung round like biological radars, sizing up the land. They'd try to shut down the gateway, stop the sacrilegious pollution. Looking at the layout of the town and surrounding countryside, he tried to work out how humans would attempt to infiltrate the force field. Dudley wanted to meet them.

*

Adam knew he was getting paranoid. The team back in Lemule's Max Transit office was running electronic observation on him. Young Kieran McSobel sat on the chair opposite, casually vigilant and armed to the teeth. He never used to take such precautions, not for a simple train ride to another planet. But that was before the Guardians' current run of bad luck. Besides, a little healthy paranoia never hurt.

The express from LA Galactic to Kyushu in phase one space took less than thirty minutes. They took a taxi to the Baraki Heavy Engineering works, which was on the other side of the extensive CST planetary station. Mr Hoyto, the manager, greeted them in the firm's elaborate marbled reception hall, and they were ushered up to his fifth storey office for the contract signing. The office didn't have a view outside, instead the windows looked out into the long engineering shops, where train engines were surrounded by scaffolding and bots under yellow-tinged lighting. An impressive amount of work was being conducted, with some of the engines half dismantled, their components being replaced or serviced by specialist teams. Baraki didn't manufacture engines themselves, but they held the CST maintenance contract for Kyushu, and were expanding their market for the smaller train operators. They were even licensed to handle the fission micropiles for atomic-powered engines.

'Yours,' Mr Hoyto said, and gestured proudly.

A big Ables ND47 nuclear engine had just been rolled into a service bay. It was over thirty years old, a giant workhorse designed for hauling heavyweight wagons across continents. Adam had started up yet another LA Galactic company, Foster Transport, to operate the ageing colossus, supposedly to collect ore from a dozen stage two worlds and deliver it to the smelting refineries on Bidar. Baraki had won the refurbishment and stage one maintenance contract from Foster, they'd even arranged a good credit line to help the fledgling company finance their first train.

Adam and Kieran acted surprised when Mr Hoyto's secretary brought in a bottle of champagne. The cork was popped as Adam authorized the contract, and transferred Foster Transport's first payment into Baraki's account. They all drank a toast to the future of ore shipping.

Baraki was going to give the Ables ND47 a complete overhaul, which was scheduled to take no more than a month, Mr Hoyto promised. After that, it would be rolled down into the paint chamber at the other end of the facility, and emerge shining in Foster Transport's blue and gold colours, as good as new. The company's nuclear division had already inspected the micropile, and agreed that it had at least another seven years of useful life left.

Adam smiled grimly at that. Not only a train owner now, using CST's tracks, but he'd also bought himself a fission reactor. His other pet hate. Fission should have been abandoned back in the twenty-first century when fusion stations finally came online. But oh no, the capitalist market wanted cheaper energy, no matter the cost in radioactive waste.

He and Kieran took up Mr Hoyto's invitation to inspect their new purchase before the bots and engineers began the refurbishment project. They walked out into the harsh yellow glare of the hot lights, blinking against the welding flares and smelling the oil being drained from hundreds of mechanical systems.

Kieran put on his hard hat. 'Is this safe?' he asked. 'It's very similar to what we did with the Alamo Avengers.'

'It's nothing like the same,' Adam countered. He stood at the base of the ND47's forward coolant intake grille, and looked up. The front of the vehicle was as tall as a two-storey house, and equally blunt; its original chrome finish was now almost invisible beneath a scabby coat of rust flakes. 'They were weapons systems. We took a risk refurbishing them to operational standard, and Navy Intelligence will no doubt be keeping a watch for any similar scenario. But this is a straight-forward commercial project.'

'All right then,' Kieran said. 'I'm making good progress on acquiring the kind of standard defence systems we'll equip it with. Buying armaments these days is a lot easier; everyone wants some personal protection from the next Prime attack.'

'I know. That's why the cost of military hardware has gone though the roof. Bloody profiteering companies.'

Kieran slapped one of the engine's massive steel wheels. 'I'm not even sure we need a force field on this. A tactical nuke would probably only slow it down a little.'

'Don't you believe it. One shot in the right place and we come to a very sudden and badly radioactive halt. We have to protect the track ahead of us; that means a decent amount of firepower. That's all got to be installed and tested before we can even think about running the Boongate wormhole.'

'I thought I'd get the wagon conversion done on Wuyam. There're a couple of promising supply companies I've con-tacted, and it has a bunch of empty warehouses around the CST station we can use for assembly. I'm looking into hiring one.'

'Good enough.' Adam started to walk down the length of the ND47. The bodywork with its old E&W paintwork were bleached to a pale sulphur and plum-purple, various exhaust vents were picked out by vertical sprays of black soot engrained into the pitted composite surface. Halfway down, the micropile access hatch looked like the kind of circular door a bank vault would employ.

'Do you think we'll be ready in time?'

'What time is that?' Adam was surprised by the note of uncertainty in the younger man's voice. The Guardians Johansson normally supplied were full of a disturbing confidence.

Kieran smiled nervously. 'Who knows? Dreaming heavens, if the Primes attack again tomorrow we'll be screwed.'

'So we work on the assumption that we'll be ready before they do attack. There's nothing else we can do. A lot of the planet's revenge components are ready to be crated up.'

'Apart from the data Kazimir was carrying,' Kieran said bitterly.

'Well now, we might have a new angle on that. Someone has been in touch with me who has a possible connection to Paula Myo. She might be able to find out where the data is.'

'Who?'

'Someone who isn't a Guardian, yet believes in the Starflyer, or says she does. She has a very plausible story.'

'Really?'

'Either that or the Starflyer is closer to us than I want to consider. Normally I have a lot of trouble believing anything that useful gets handed to me on a plate.'

'Beware of Greeks bearing gifts.'

'Precisely.'

'So you don't trust her.'

'No. Not yet, anyway. Of course, she is cautious about us, as well. Which I have to respect. I'm going to have to work out some seriously foolproof method of establishing if she's a bona fide ally. Having a new friend, even this late in the game, would be very helpful.'

'How are you going to prove she's on our side?'

'Delivering Kazimir's missing data to us would be a big plus in her favour. Apart from that, I haven't got a clue.'

*

With the casework on the Lambeth Interplanetary Society finally slowing up, Renne managed to haul out the files on the Trisha Marina Halgarth shotgun investigation for a review. Forensics had sent their results to the Paris office over a week ago. Vic Russell had scanned them, and attached a summary. Nothing unexpected or unusual had turned up, which maintained the case's low priority coding. They'd been sitting in Renne's e-butler hold-store ever since.

She went through the perfectly laid-out tables and holographic graphs and columns of text. Vic was right, everything was as it should be. The data analyst had confirmed that Howard Liang's background details were all proficient forgeries. Biomedical forensics had found some samples of skin and hair in his apartment, and analysed the DNA, which they confirmed came from a McSobel. His finances were tracked to a single cash deposit of fifty-thousand Earth dollars in a Velaines bank.

'Damn,' she muttered at the desktop portals. All the exemplary, predictable details were a direct follow-on from the perfect crime scene.

Am I really this paranoid?

She gave the data another read through, but there was nothing she could find fault with. The Guardians had done it. It was a conclusion anybody would come to. *So why can't I believe that?*

Thinking back, it wasn't the crime scene, the victims, nor even the Guardians' method of operation. She could accept that those would all be the same or similar to the other shotgun set-ups she'd witnessed before. What bothered her was the responses the girls had made. They'd been upset, angry and, in Trisha's case, burdened by guilt; everything the investigating authorities would expect; but none of them had been surprised. Trisha had never asked: *why me?*

The forensic data remained in her portals, a glowing script awaiting allocation and certification. Logically, it should be classified under ongoing low priority, keeping the information available for immediate cross-referencing to all other Guardians cases. There were no leads to follow, no way to pursue the individual perpetrators of the crime. Realistically, the only way an arrest would ever happen was if Navy Intelligence rounded up the whole Guardians organization.

Laughter drifted over the office. Renne didn't have to look up to know who it came from: Tarlo's immediate team. She knew they were making good progress on tracking Kazimir McFoster's finances. Morale was high over in that nest of desks, they produced results. Commander Hogan was supportive and encouraging.

She wasn't that bothered, career wise; right now the threat which the Commonwealth was facing meant she should put such personal considerations firmly to one side. Work in a team for the greater good.

Ah, bollocks to that.

Renne asked her e-butler to access the current files on all three of the girls. They came up straight away on her screens. Trisha Halgarth had gone back to Solidade, which wasn't surprising. Catriona Saleeb was still in the apartment, which she was now sharing with two others. Isabella had moved out of the apartment, but hadn't told Navy Intelligence where she'd gone as she was required to do. That wouldn't be so unusual, but at the same time she'd put a block on her unisphere address code, and remained out of contact ever since.

Renne felt a small grin spread over her face. *Finally, an abnormality.* 'Get me Christabel Agatha Halgarth,' she told her e-butler.

*

Alic Hogan was studying the information flowing over several desktop display screens when Renne knocked on the door. He just beckoned and indicated a seat in front of his desk.

'There really is nothing weird on Mars, is there?' he said in a distracted voice.

''Fraid not, chief. We've had experts go through the whole data profile. If there's any hidden encryption in there, it's beyond the best we've got to find it.'

'Damn it, I hate leaving files like that open.' He shook his head, and looked up from the screens. 'What can I do for you?'

'I'd like a warrant issued for Isabella Halgarth.'

'Who's she, and why?'

'She was one of Trisha Halgarth's flatmates. She seems to have vanished.'

Alic Hogan sat back in his chair, looking unhappy. 'All right, what's going on?'

'I've just reviewed the forensic data we got back from the shotgun case, the one where the Guardians claimed our President was an alien agent.'

Alic managed a slight smile. 'Oh yeah, I remember that one. The President's aides were knocking down the admiral's door inside thirty seconds of that one hitting the unisphere. So what's the problem?'

'No direct problem. I was concerned about our total lack of progress on the whole shotgun issue.'

'Okay, commendable enough,' Alic said, with only mild suspicion. 'Although I'm not sure about your priorities here.'

'Any approach which can get us into the Guardians is viable as far as I'm concerned.'

He held his hands up in defeat. 'Good point. Go on.'

'I wanted to re-interview the shotgun victims, see if there was anything they remembered now that they didn't directly after the event. A lot of crime victims do, after the initial shock and confusion has been overcome, and they have time to think about what happened.'

'Yeah, yeah, I'm familiar with the procedure.'

'Trisha Halgarth has gone back to Solidade, the Halgarth Dynasty's private planet. I need permission to go there. It's never been legally accepted that the Dynasty planets are part of the Commonwealth, and they certainly won't let me through if I turn up at the gateway unannounced and waving my navy ID around. So I called Christabel Agatha Halgarth, the head of the Halgarth family security.'

Alic winced. 'You should clear anything like that with me, first.'

'I know, chief, and I apologize, I didn't think it was a big deal. Anyway, Christabel gave me permission to travel to Solidade.'

'She did?'

'Yes.'

'You must be the first government official for some time.'

'Whatever. I also wanted to talk to Catriona Saleeb; she's still on Arevalo, in the same apartment, so that's not a problem. But Isabella discontinued her unisphere address code a week after the shotgun. We don't know where she is. I asked Christabel, and she didn't know either. They're looking into it for me.'

'And you want to arrest her for that?'

'A warrant is the best way to make planetary police forces pay attention. A simple alert for a missing girl isn't going to get any attention, not right now.'

'Renne, I'm really not sure I can issue a warrant on this basis.'

'I checked on Isabella, not just the official files, but the unisphere gossip show records as well. You know they love reporting on Dynasty members. Before she moved to Arevalo and set up house with the other girls, Isabella used to be Patricia Kantil's girlfriend.'

Alic Hogan gave her a startled look. 'Doi's chief of staff?'

Renne smiled waspishly and nodded. 'She never told us. Doesn't that strike you as odd?'

'How can Kantil be involved in this?'

'I don't know. Maybe she's not. But you have to admit, this is worth a warrant. I need to ask Isabella some serious questions.'

Alic let out a long breath, clearly reluctant. 'I can really do without complications like this.'

'Trust me, chief. I'll be discreet. If she's just shacked up with someone she shouldn't be, some senator or three-hundred-year-old Grand Family heir, whatever, I'm not going to cause a fuss. I don't want to get the Dynasties or the Executive pissed with this office. I'll just ask her the questions, and leave quietly.'

'Damnit, all right. But if she's found, I want to know immediately. We keep this as quiet as we can.'

Renne got out of the chair. 'You got it.'

'Are you off to Solidade?'

'Yeah. The express to EdenBurg leaves in forty minutes.'

'Okay, good luck. And I want to know what the planet looks like when you get back.'

*

There was a limousine waiting for Renne when she arrived at EdenBurg's CST station in Rialto, the planet's megacity. A young man dressed in a smart dark-grey business suit introduced himself as Warren Yves Halgarth, a member of the Halgarth family security force, and her assigned escort. They drove out of the station and into the midday sunlight.

Renne had visited all of the Big15 at one time or another.

She was always hard pressed to tell the megacities apart. Rialto was a slight exception in that it was sited in a temperate zone, while most of the others favoured tropical locations. Apparently it was an accounting thing. A city that had summers and winters needed different types of civic services to cope with the individual seasons; and Rialto had an impressive snowfall in winter, averaging out at two metres each four-hundred-day year. Keeping the city-wide grid of five-lane expressways open and the all-embracing network of rail tracks clear and functional for those three icy months of the year required thousands of snowploughs and ancillary fleets of GPbots. The cost of all that bad weather machinery was considerable, and the city council had to charge the companies and residents to cover the expense.

It was a factor which was countered by the cost of power on EdenBurg, which was among the lowest in the Commonwealth. One of the principal reasons Heather Antonia Halgarth had chosen EdenBurg as her family's Big15 world was the planet's massive oceans. None of the three continents had deserts, precipitation was too high for that; instead they were covered in rivers, with vast coastal plains subject to continual flooding. Instead of the fission plants the other Big15 used, Heather went in for hydropower on a colossal scale, damning two thirds of the watercourses on the Sybraska, the continent where Rialto was situated. Electricity was delivered to the megacity via superconductor, and Sybraska's plains drained then irrigated to provide nation-sized tracts of highly productive farmland.

Because of the cold months, Rialto favoured monolithic apartment blocks rather than the vast sprawls of individual homes and strip malls found on worlds like StLincoln, Wessex and Augusta. Each district had its core of Manhattan-like skyscrapers and bulky concrete tenements; which were encircled by huge swathes of factories and refineries.

The CST station was on the edge of the Saratov district,

which was the megacity's financial and administrative heart, giving it the largest nest of skyscrapers, and also the tallest. The industrial estates radiating outward tended towards the smaller, more sophisticated manufacturing facilities. Accommodation blocks were gigantic, fifty to seventy storeys of sturdy stone façades, with large apartments overlooking broad well-maintained public parks. There were fewer rail lines and more elevated roads, reflecting the population density, and their relative wealth.

Renne couldn't help staring at Saratov's central area as they swept towards it along the expressway. Some of the skyscrapers were so high she thought they must touch cloud level; they couldn't be economical to build, even with today's materials and robotics. It was all about corporate prestige.

Right in the middle were five tapering towers housing the Halgarth Dynasty's headquarters. They were all identical in size and architecture with crown spires producing a bristling apex. But the reflective glass windows on each one had a different colour.

Renne's car drove down into the basement of the green tower, and into a secure parking zone. The Halgarth family security force occupied several floors halfway up the tower. Renne wasn't told how many. The lift they used didn't have an indicator. She was ushered into Christabel Agatha Halgarth's office. Curving walls of tinted glass looked out towards the ocean, thirty kilometres away. Three more skyscraper districts stood between Saratov and the coast, brief pinnacles of colour and style with their moats of parkland. The terrain between them was a dark synthetic desert of rectangular factories and warehouse cubes with black solar collector roofs. Thousands of spindly metal chimneys squirted grey-blue vapours up into the iron sky, misting the whole scene with a thin dreary smog.

Sitting at her plain steel desk, Christabel Halgarth was

silhouetted by the remorseless industrial backdrop. Newly rejuvenated, she was a small brunette, with a face that indicated a strong Asian ancestry. Renne expected someone this senior in the Dynasty to be wearing a business suit, one costing a good ten or fifteen times more than her own. But Christabel was dressed in a worn blue sweatshirt, and baggy track trousers with muddy stains on their knees; as if she'd just come in from gardening. Appearance obviously didn't matter to her.

Or maybe it's just me that doesn't count.

Christabel followed Renne's glance at her legs and smiled. 'I cut my morning jog short to meet you. Haven't had time for a shower, yet.'

'I appreciate you taking the time,' Renne said as they shook hands. 'It wasn't quite that urgent.' She hadn't told Alic Hogan that she'd requested an interview with Christabel. It wasn't lying, exactly, but the commander was antsy enough about her just getting permission to go to Solidade. Something like this request should probably have gone through the admiral's office, with any number of administrative staff reviewing it, and most of them unwilling to send it forward for fear of rocking the boat. Better, Renne thought, just to fire off the question and see if she could circumvent the bureaucracy and politics. Paula would have done the same.

'We're both here now,' Christabel said, graciously. 'What can I do for you?'

'I'm following up the last Guardians shotgun. Basically, what I need to know from you is if it was an entrapment operation mounted by your organization.'

Christabel regarded her with a look of mild surprise. 'Not that I'm aware of. One moment.' Her eyes unfocused as she scanned her virtual vision. 'No. We knew nothing about it until it happened.'

'I see. Thank you.'

'Care to tell me why you asked that?'

'There was something wrong about it.' Renne waved a hand dismissively. 'Nothing solid I could put in a report at the time; and now Isabella has dropped out of sight.'

'Hardly conclusive. She's young. The Commonwealth is in a minor state of chaos, especially with people migrating away from the Lost23 neighbours. A lot of our rich brats involve themselves in unsavoury activities which they try to keep quiet from me. Don't you think you might be overreacting?'

Renne was unsure if the woman was laughing at her, or irritated her time was being wasted. 'She used to be good friends with Patricia Kantil.'

'I see. You're adding up the discrepancies. And I admire you for sticking to your instincts. I can understand that. Especially given your previous mentor.'

'I don't quite follow.'

'You're doing *real* detective work. You probably didn't review my file, such as it is, but one of the non-classified entries is that I graduated from the Serious Crimes Directorate's Investigator training course one year after Paula Myo.'

'Ah.' Renne began to relax.

'I was furious with the Dynasty for supporting her dismissal. A little less politics in our lives would see a few more results, not that my dear Dynasty ever grasps that at a collective level. Even so, Columbia should never have done what he did, it was a complete abuse of power.'

'I thought he would come under your jurisdiction.'

'Ha.' Christabel smiled waspishly. 'That shows how little you know about the internal politics of our Dynasty. Columbia now has the full support of our senior council. The admiral has manoeuvred himself into a damn impressive position; I only hope Kime's astute enough to be watching his own back. There was nothing I could do for Paula. Though she landed on her feet without my assistance. Hardly surprising, given the number of contacts she's gathered inside the Commonwealth establishment down the centuries.'

'She was an excellent boss.'

'Which is more than that clod Hogan is, I suppose.'

'Actually, Hogan's not bad, just a little procedure orien-tated. And, of course, he belongs to Columbia.'

Christabel inclined her head. 'Okay, then. So what exactly made you ask if the shotgun was an entrapment?'

'It had too many similarities with earlier cases, as if some-one had read up how to work the procedure. Your force would be the obvious candidate if you were trying to snare the Guardians.'

'We have done something similar in the past. But no, not this time. Interesting that you thought that, though.'

'And now there does turn out to be something out of kilter.'

'Paula did teach you something, after all.'

'Has Isabella been a problem before?'

'Not at my level. Her relationship with Kantil wasn't even referred to senior council – which probably says more about how we regard the Executive than anything else. Isabella is just a standard minor Dynasty brat. We keep tabs on hundreds of them. It always disappoints me how many wind up in rehab, or get hauled up before a judge for various misdemeanours within a year of leaving Solidade. A hell of a lot of our time is spent trying to protect the young ones from scams that drain their trust funds. If it was up to me, they'd have no access to Dynasty money until their hundredth birthday. But I'm just old fashioned.'

'I'm surprised her parents haven't asked you to check on her.'

Christabel looked over at Warren, who had taken up a discreet position at the back of the office. 'You called them, didn't you?'

'Yes ma'am.' He turned to Renne. 'After your initial inquiry to us this morning, we did launch a review of Isabella's situation. Victor and Bernadette ended their relationship eight years ago. Standard separation enactment in their contract. There was no hostility at the time, nor afterwards. Isabella lived with Victor and his new wife until she was seventeen, at which time she started attending a boarding school prior to her level 4 exam year. It's quite a common practice for children on Solidade. After school, she's either lived with friends in various Dynasty-owned properties, or shared accommodation with her lovers. There haven't been many jobs. So it's really not unusual for her to be out of contact with her direct family for months at a time.'

'But discontinuing her unisphere address code isn't normal, surely?'

'No,' he said. 'We ran some follow-up checks on that. She stopped using her credit account the same day she discontinued her address code. It looks like a deliberate attempt to drop right out of sight.'

'Did she tell anyone where she was going?'

'Not that we know of. We haven't started an official inquiry yet.'

'I was waiting to see what you had, first,' Christabel said.

'You've heard it all, sorry. One suspicion.'

'It's enough for me. If you have no objection, we'll run our own investigation parallel to yours. We can focus more on direct leads, but that arrest warrant will produce a much wider coverage. Somebody should spot her.'

'No objections at all.'

'Good. Warren here will be your liaison with us. He will escort you to Solidade next. Trisha is expecting you, and she *will* cooperate fully.'

Renne did her best not to show any surprise at the force in Christabel's voice. Presumably Trisha hadn't been too keen on another interview. 'Thank you.'

*

Travelling to Solidade was essentially the same as any other train journey within the Commonwealth. The only difference was to be found at Rialto station, where the Halgarths maintained a single dedicated platform several kilometres from the three main terminals. Despite being authorized by the head of the security force, and accompanied by Warren, Renne had to go through several thorough security checks before she was allowed on the little platform.

The three-carriage train took barely five minutes to get through the gateway and arrive at Yarmuk, the small town which supplied the entire planet's services.

'Did you find anything in Isabella's credit account?' Renne asked as they stepped down from the carriage.

'Nothing unusual, no,' Warren said. 'We were looking for train tickets, of course, accommodation rentals, and large cash withdrawals. There weren't any.'

'What about spending pattern analysis?'

'We ran one. If she has been squirrelling away money for the last few months, then we couldn't spot it.'

'Ah well, just a thought. I really need an angle on what Isabella's thinking. All I have so far are a bunch of inconsistencies climaxing with her disappearance. I still don't know if any of that is connected with the shotgun case, or if it's all a really bad coincidence.'

'If she's vanished there can hardly be an innocent explanation.'

'No, I concede that. But if she's simply fallen in with the wrong people I can clean her off my case files. That doesn't help you, I know; and I'm not sure I want that outcome, either.'

Warren gave her a sidelong glance. 'I don't get that.'

'If she is tied in with this somehow, and don't ask how, please, then she's the first solid lead we've had on the whole Guardians-shotgun problem.'

'I see that, but ... She's a Halgarth, we're nearly always the victims of the Guardians in the shotgun cases, so how can chasing her give you a lead to them?'

'I don't know. Perhaps this is some new kind of follow-up operation by the Guardians. We need to know a lot more, and the only people who can fill in some gaps are the other two girls.'

A Boeing 22022 supersonic VTOL plane was waiting for them at the town's airfield. It was a short flight to the heavily wooded Kolda Valley where Trisha's branch of the family maintained a holiday lodge. They landed on a meadow clearing below the elaborate raised wooden building. The lodge was built into the forest, using seven giant morangu trees as its principal pillars. It was as if some ancient sailing ship had somehow embedded itself in the trees, and had slowly been expanded over the decades with additional rooms and platforms grafted on. The roof was a shaggy thatch of long local reeds, which had dried to a dusty ochre. A small stream wound out of the deeper forest at the side of the supporting trunks, skirting the edge of the grassy meadow to fill various stony pools.

Trisha was waiting for them beside a clump of lazthorn bushes growing above the largest pool. She wore a bikini top and a pair of white canvas shorts; a long towel was laid out beside the water where she'd been sunbathing. The sophistication that was her heritage had left her, Renne decided as she walked over. It wasn't just the cheap vacation slob-out clothes, the girl was more thoughtful and pensive now, where before she'd been chirpy and confident. Her green butterfly wing OCtattoos had been expanded down her cheeks; extensions lacking the artistry of the original sections.

'Sorry to bother you again,' Renne said. 'I've just got a few more questions.'

'It's more than that,' Trisha said tetchily. 'I've had a whole load of calls today telling me I have to see you.' She glanced back towards the elevated lodge.

Renne just caught a glimpse of a young man standing in a doorway to one of the verandas along the front. He quickly stepped back through an open door into the dimly lit interior. 'Sorry about that,' Renne said. 'But I do want to catch the people who did this to you.'

'Isabella said you never would, that we'd just be another ongoing file your office would forget about after a month.'

'That's an interesting comment. Normally, I would have agreed with her – off the record, of course.'

Trisha gave a listless shrug. 'Has something happened?'

'I'm not sure. First of all, I need to know if you've remembered anything about Howard Liang that might be relevant, something which you'd overlooked before.'

'What like?'

'Something that didn't make sense at the time. Perhaps something he said. Something simple that he should have known, like a piece of history, or a Dynasty name. Or did you ever meet anyone by surprise, someone he was uncomfortable around.'

'Don't think so, no. I can't remember anything like that.'

'How about an incident from his childhood. If he grew up on Far Away he had a very different upbringing from ordinary Commonwealth children. Something might have slipped out that seemed odd.'

'No. That's what the reporter asked as well.'

'What reporter?'

'Er.' Trisha's fingers fluttered slightly, puppeting her virtual hand. 'Brad Myo. He was from Earle News. He said he'd got your permission to talk to me.' She gave Renne an anxious look. 'Didn't he?'

Renne became very still, something like a ghost's finger was stroking her spine. 'No,' she said quietly. 'We don't issue any authorization to reporters to do anything, let alone talk to crime victims. That's up to individual citizens.' To her surprise, Trisha started crying. The girl sank down onto the towel, great sobs shaking her shoulders.

'I'm so fucking stupid,' she wailed, and started hitting her fists against her legs. 'Does everybody in the Commonwealth know? Why am I so gullible? He said you'd allowed him to see me so he could produce a sympathetic story. I believed him, I really did. Oh God, I hate myself. I didn't know. He was so sincere.'

Renne gave Warren an awkward glance, then knelt beside the distraught girl. 'Hey, come on. If this is who I think it was, he would have fooled me too.' Her e-butler had already cross-referenced Earle News. It was in one of Paula's reports. The company didn't exist, but someone had used it once before when he interviewed Wendy Bose. According to Paula Myo, his description matched Bradley Johansson. 'What did he look like?'

Trisha snivelled. 'Tall. With really fair hair. And he was old. I don't mean close to rejuvenation. You just knew he'd lived a couple of centuries at least.'

'Shit,' Renne hissed under her breath.

Trisha gave her an uncertain glance, tears ready to burst forth again. 'What? Do you know who it was?'

'He sounds like somebody known to us, yes.'

'Oh no! I'm going to get a memory wipe, I swear I am. I'm going to wipe out my whole life; everything, what I've done, who I am, my name. All of it. Wipe it and not use a secure store.' She glared at Warren. 'And if the Dynasty won't do it, I'll go to some illegal back street clinic. I don't care. I'd rather wind up retarded than go through life knowing this.'

'Easy there,' Renne said. She rubbed the girl's trembling shoulders. 'You're being far too hard on yourself. Just tell me what happened with Brad Myo. Please?'

'Nothing much, I guess. He turned up at the apartment a

day before I came back here. Isabella had already left, and Catriona had gone to work. He told me he'd cleared the meeting with you; that's the only reason I let him in. I should have checked with you, shouldn't I? God, how dumb!'

'It's done now. Please, don't beat yourself up over this. What did he want to know?'

'The same as you did. Howard's name, where he worked, how long I'd known him. All the basics.'

'I see. Well, don't worry, there's no real harm done.'

'Really?' The girl was pathetically eager.

'Yes. He's just a stupid con man trying to sell his story to a major news show. None of them will run it.'

'Absolutely not,' Warren assured her.

'Okay.'

'Has Isabella been in touch recently?' Renne asked, making it casual. 'Her old address code isn't working, and I need to ask her the same questions.'

'No.' Trisha lowered her head. 'I haven't talked to many people since I got back. I don't want to. I wasn't kidding when I said I want all this out of my brain. It's too difficult.'

'I'm sure it seems that way. But don't be too rash, will you?'

'Maybe.'

'Did Isabella say where she was going before she left Daroca?'

'She was going skiing on Jura. There was a whole bunch of them hiring a chalet together for a fortnight. She tried to get me to come along, but I didn't want to. She's always going on trips with friends.'

'Which friends, exactly?'

'I'm not sure. I didn't know any of them.'

'Okay. Never mind, we'll look into it.' Renne stood up and gestured to Warren, who nodded. 'I know this hasn't been easy for you, Trisha. I apologize for putting you through this, but you have been helpful.'

The girl simply nodded, not looking up. Renne regarded her with a touch of concern before walking back to the VTOL.

'So who was the reporter?' Warren asked as the hatch shut behind them.

Renne settled herself into the deep leather cushioning of the chair. 'It could be Bradley Johansson himself. The description is about right, and he's posed as a reporter before using that company name.'

'Bloody hell.'

'Yeah.' She watched through the oval window as the plane took off. The light-green patch of meadow shrank away quickly behind them as the acceleration pressed her down.

'But that makes no sense,' Warren said. 'What would Johansson need to see Trisha for? The operation was over.'

'Good question. And he took a hell of a risk going to see her, too. He even used Earle News as a cover, which we knew about. It's not like him to be that sloppy. Those questions were clearly important to him.'

'Why?'

Renne shook her head. She didn't quite trust herself to look directly at Warren. Unlike Trisha, he wasn't stupid. There was one explanation which fitted all too easily. An explanation which had implications she really didn't enjoy. It would also mean she'd been quite right about the whole shotgun set-up from the very start. *It wasn't the Guardians after all. And I don't think it was the Halgarths. Christabel had no reason to lie to me. That doesn't leave many options.*

*

Mark Vernon sat in his rented Ford Lapanto as the drive array steered it along the six-lane highway down through the northern tail of the Chunata hills which formed the back of New Costa's Trinity district. The slopes with their brown native scrub bushes and desert palms were decorated with large white houses encased behind tall walls and hedges like precious artworks in an exclusive store. It was an area favoured by financial management types, who never liked to stray far from the office. A line of composite and glass skyscrapers marked out Trinity's eastern boundary, winding along the base of the hills. They were home to various banks, credit houses, brokers, venture capitalists, and offworld currency exchanges.

The Lapanto's drive array turned the car off the highway. There was a junction at the bottom of the ramp, where an ancient road began its lazy curve round the hill. A dilapidated sign called it Bright Light Canyon. Mark switched off the drive array, and started driving the car himself. Gritty yellow-brown soil had almost completely covered the thin layer of asphalt, turning the road into little more than a dirt track. Dead-looking scrub bushes were scattered over the slope below and above, their lower trunks buttressed by the conical mounds of nipbug nests. Behind the swathe of arid vegetation were crumbling white walls of enzyme-bonded concrete, scaled by ivy and climbing cacti. Various private roads led off the main track, looping round to gates.

For a moment Mark's imagination painted over the image with long straight driveways of the Highmarsh Valley branching off the main road. It was silent in the Chunatas, the noise of the megacity deflected by the foothills, a condition matching the land behind Randtown. Even the drab brown of the native plants were similar to the weak ochre shadings of boltgrass. But the air here was dryer, tinged with chemicals from the refinery sector ten miles away to the west. And Regulus was a too-bright point of blue-white light in the cloudless sky, still emitting a fierce heat in the late afternoon. Even in his daydreams, Mark could never pretend to reclaim all they'd lost. Fantasizing about it was stupid, the sign of a complete loser.

It was his fault. He'd taken his family to Elan. He'd built up their hopes. He'd shown them a decent, clean life. His dream had died in fire and pain. It was a knowledge that prevented him from sleeping every night. Self-recrimination which made it impossible to talk properly to Liz. Misery at having to bring his lovely children back to this vile world which held him back from playing with them.

He was so wrapped up in self-pity he almost missed the turning. A fast pull on the wheel sent the Lapanto skidding round the sharp bend and down the little trail. Dusty soil puffed up from the back wheels as they spun. 'Idiot,' he told himself.

After a couple of hundred yards the trail ended at an iron gate in a wall of terracotta-red concrete. Mark's e-butler gave the gates his code, and they swung open. There was an oasis of lush emerald grass inside the wall. At the centre was a long lime-green bungalow with red composite roof panels moulded to resemble clay tiles. Several gardening bots trundled about, tending to the lawns and herbaceous borders, keeping them as neat as the building they surrounded. Mark always enjoyed the view from here, with the bungalow perched halfway up the hill they could sit on the patio and look across New Costa's urban expanse as it rolled away into the horizon. From this vantage point it never seemed quite so objectionable as when he was down among the factories and the strip malls. All very different from his old house in Santa Hydra.

Kyle, Mark's brother, leased the bungalow from the Augusta Engineering Corp; he could afford to with his high-paying job at the StVincent Loan & Trust. Everybody in Mark's immediate family had offered to put them up when they got back from Elan. He'd accepted Kyle's offer because he couldn't stand the thought of having to move in with Marty, his father. Besides, he'd always got on well with Kyle, who at least was sincere in wanting to help, and the kids really liked their uncle.

He braked the Lapanto on the drive outside the front door, and went inside. All the reception rooms had glass doors, allowing him to look along the hall to locate his small family. Nobody was in sight, but he heard happy shouting coming from the patio outside the main lounge. Both Sandy and Barry were in the pool, with a suspiciously wet Panda lying on the sun soaked slabs beside the pool. The dog looked up at him, but didn't move.

'Daddy!' both kids yelled.

Mark waved at them. 'Has Panda been in the pool?'

'No,' they chorused.

He gave them a fearsome disapproving look, and they both started giggling. Liz was lying on a sunlounger on the terrace below the pool. Antonio, Kyle's boyfriend, was beside her. The terrace faced west, allowing them both to catch the last of the afternoon sunlight.

'Hi baby,' Liz called. A maidbot was standing between her and Antonio, a wine bottle held in one of its arms. When he got closer, he realized both of them were naked. His throat tightened automatically. He didn't say anything, because that would just show how small minded and conservative he was.

Liz hadn't got a job yet; the agreement was she would stay home to look after the kids. They weren't in school, and Mark really didn't want them to go to an Augusta school, he had too many bad memories of his own time at Faraday High. In fact, returning to Augusta was only ever supposed to be temporary; they arrived here purely because it was the first stop after Ozzie Isaacs' asteroid. He wanted them to move on soon, hopefully to somewhere like Gralmond, which was about as far away from Dyson Alpha as it was possible to get. But that took money, and the invasion had wiped them out financially, taking away their entire equity, and he knew damn well that even after the navy beat the Primes back into their own space Elan was ruined beyond reclamation. The mortgage he'd taken to buy their little vineyard and the Ables Motor franchise had left him massively in debt. If the insurance didn't take care of it, he'd need a couple of lifetimes to pay it off. And the insurance company was based in Runwich, Elan's capital. Nobody knew if the Commonwealth government would pay compensation to everyone from the Lost23, and even if they did it would take years, if not decades, for such a bill to work its way through the Senate. Right now tax money was being poured into building up the navy.

He knelt down and gave Liz a perfunctory kiss. 'Hi.'

'Wow, you look like you need a drink.' She pointed to the maidbot. 'We've got some extra glasses.'

'Not that, thanks. I'll maybe get a beer.'

'No problem,' Antonio said. 'Sit yourself down, Mark, the bot'll get it for you.'

Mark gave him a tight smile, and sank onto an empty sunlounger. 'How long have the kids been in the pool?'

'Not sure,' Liz said, she drained her wine glass and held it out for a maidbot to refill. 'Half an hour.'

'They should be getting out soon. They need to have their tea.' He didn't actually ask: *what have you got them?* But it was in there, implicit with the tone.

'The house array is watching them,' Liz said with a little too much emphasis. 'This isn't Randtown, the systems here are top of the range.'

'Always useful to know,' Mark replied coldly.

Liz turned round so she was looking out across the landscape below the hill, and sipped her wine.

'Hey, come on now you two,' Antonio said. 'We're all on the same side. Mark, the kids know they have to get out at quarter past six, they always do. The kitchen is making tea for them.'

The timer in Mark's virtual vision read: 18:12. 'Fine, sure,' he grunted. 'Sorry, it hasn't been a good day.' Not that he was going to sit here and bang on about his day in the factory, that was too stereotypical even for him. In any case he suspected they wouldn't really be listening. He'd applied for and got the general technician job at Prism Dynamics the day after they left the asteroid. The salary wasn't anything special; not for maintaining assembly bays which built fuselage sections for the aerospace industry, but he did actually enjoy the work. It was the combination of practical troubleshooting and writing program fixes which he was most at home with. He took it because there was no way he was accepting charity from anyone, not even family. That was a gene he'd inherited direct from Marty.

A maidbot trundled up to Mark and handed him a bottle of beer. He flipped the cap and took a decent drink. Liz was still ignoring him.

'Giselle Swinsol called,' Antonio said. 'She said she'd be here at seven to interview you.'

Mark waited a moment, but Liz didn't say anything. 'Is this for me?' he asked.

'Yes.' Antonio gave him a baffled look. 'Didn't you arrange an interview?'

'No. Why would she call you?'

'It was to the house array, not me personally. She said she wanted to be sure you were in this evening.'

'I've never heard of her.'

'Probably an agency head-hunter,' Liz said.

'I'm not registered with any agencies.'

'Could be the insurance company,' Antonio suggested. 'They're paying out for the invasion.'

Mark drank some more beer. 'Not with my luck,' he muttered.

Liz shot him a look as she got to her feet. 'I'm going to get the children ready,' she said and pulled on a robe.

Antonio waited until she'd gone up to the pool and started calling the children. 'You two okay?'

'I guess so,' Mark said limply. 'We're just finding our feet, that's all. Honestly, Antonio, we had the most perfect life on Elan. Now there's nothing left to go back to.'

'It's tough, man. But you can beat it. I see that in Kyle. You Vernon guys don't give in. You're a scary family.'

Mark raised his bottle, and even managed a feeble grin.

'Cheers. But you're wrong. First hint of a job on a planet far from here, I'm taking Liz and the kids.'

'You sure about that?'

'Sure I'm sure.'

'Well I think that would be a big mistake.'

'How come?'

'Look, the Big15 are where they're going to build all the ships and weapons hardware. Right? Yeah sure, other planets will get subcontracts, and High Angel does some assembly work, that's politics. But here: this is the heart of the fight back, man. That means they won't let Augusta fall. Earth will be overrun before us. We're gonna have the best protection it's possible to have. Think about it: Wessex was the only planet to see off the Primes last time. Sheldon and Hutchinson made damn sure the invasion failed there. You want my advice, stay here. I don't care what all the news show analysts are saying, this is the safest place in the Commonwealth.'

Mark wanted to laugh the idea off, but he couldn't fault Antonio's logic.

*

A long black Chevrolet limousine drew up outside the gates at two minutes before seven. Liz had just managed to coax the kids upstairs after tea, and Antonio was getting sober and dressed for his hospital shift. Kyle still wasn't back, he usually worked in the StVincent Loan & Trust office until after seven. Mark didn't understand how he kept the relationship with Antonio going; they only ever saw each other for a couple of hours a day. Perhaps that was why it had lasted so long. He and Liz barely saw each other for longer, but that didn't seem to be helping much.

Giselle Swinsol wasn't quite what Mark had been expecting. The limo should have clued him in, no agency manager would have a car like that. She was a tall brunette with the ambition of a second-lifer gunning for an executive slot, and the arrogance of a direct lineage Dynasty member. Her smart grey and oxford-blue suit that cost more than Mark's monthly salary, complemented by make-up superior to most unisphere news anchors. High heel shoes clicked loudly on the hall floor.

She hadn't waited to be invited in, she simply marched past Mark when he opened the door, and headed for the lounge.

'Excuse me, but I didn't know we were due to have a meeting,' he said. He wanted it to be sarcastic, but it came out woefully lame, not helped by the way he was scampering along behind, trying to catch up.

Her answering smile reminded him of a shark preparing to feed. A shark with cherry-glossed lips. 'I don't normally inform people in advance that they've been selected.'

'Selected?'

She sat down in one of the settees, leaving him standing in the middle of the lounge. 'Do you like your job, Mr Vernon?'

'Look! Who the hell are you?'

'I work for the Sheldon Dynasty. What does it bring in? A couple of grand a month?'

Thoroughly irritated, he snapped: 'More than that, actually.'

'No it doesn't, Mark, I've seen your contract.'

'That's confidential.'

She laughed. 'At your current level of earning, and extrapolating a mild level of promotion, it'll take you about eighty years to pay off the loan for your house and franchise garage on Elan. That doesn't take in factors like paying for the kids' college fees, and your own R&R pension.'

'We'll get compensation, eventually.'

'Granted, if the Commonwealth still exists in ten years' time, they might pass a bill letting you off the interest payments. Anything else: stop fooling yourself.'

'Prism Dynamics is just temporary. I'll get a better job than that.'

'That's exactly what I want to hear, Mark. I've come to tell you I've got that better job all lined up for you.'

'And what would that be?' Liz asked. She was standing in the lounge doorway, wearing a T-shirt and cut-off jeans. But there was a fixed look on her face which Mark was familiar with. When Liz made up her mind not to like someone, they were frozen out of this life and the next.

'It's confidential, I'm afraid,' Giselle Swinsol said. 'Once you sign up, then you will be told.'

'Ridiculous,' Liz said. She sat down on a long leather couch opposite the woman, and tugged gently at Mark's arm. He sank down beside her, the three beers he'd drunk in quick succession out on the terrace were starting to buzz in his head. His e-butler told him a file had arrived, its sender was Giselle Swinsol. When he opened it, an employment contract slipped down his virtual vision. The salary made him blink in surprise.

'It is far from being ridiculous,' Giselle Swinsol said. 'We take our security very seriously indeed. You have already proved your discretion.'

'The asteroid?' Mark asked. 'No big deal.'

'Even in today's climate, the news shows would be very interested indeed in Mr Isaacs' home.'

'I don't get this,' Mark said. 'I'm not some super-physicist. I repair machinery. What's so important about that? Millions of us do it.'

'You're actually very, very good at maintaining electro-mechanical systems, Mark. We checked. Thoroughly. The project you'll be working on requires a great deal of robotic assembly. Although there are other factors which brought your name to our attention.'

'Such as?' Liz asked.

'Apart from respecting confidentiality; you have acute financial problems which we can remedy. If you agree to take this job, we will pay off every debt you accrued on Elan. Mrs Vernon, you have the kind of biotechnology skills which we can utilize. It's not as if we'll expect you to act the dutiful housewife for the duration of the project. I'm sure that will make a pleasant change for you.'

Liz sat perfectly still. 'Thank you.'

The contract was still flowing down Mark's virtual vision. 'If I say yes, where will we be based?'

'Cressat.'

'The Sheldon world? I didn't think anyone else was allowed there,' Liz said.

'We are making exceptions for this project. However, we don't have to in your case. Mark's a Sheldon, that qualifies his whole family for residency.'

Mark tried not to flinch when Liz turned to stare at him. He'd never considered his heritage worth talking about, if anything it was mildly embarrassing. 'Hardly direct lineage,' he muttered defensively.

'Your mother is only seven generations removed from Nigel. That's good enough.'

'Wait,' Liz said. 'This isn't a navy project?'

Giselle Swinsol gave her a blank smile. 'Mark?'

'What? You want an answer now?' he asked.

'Certainly.'

'But you've told me nothing.'

'You will be working in a job that will provide an excellent lifestyle for your family, far greater than the one you enjoyed on Elan. You will be rid of all your debts. And we absolutely guarantee your safety. The only downside will be restricted communication with your friends and immediate family. This project must remain secret.'

'I don't like offers which are too good to be true,' Liz said. 'They usually are.'

'Not so. This is on the level.'

'Is it dangerous?' Mark asked.

'No.' Giselle Swinsol said. 'You will be working with sophisticated assembly systems. It is challenging, not dangerous.

Look, this is not some game, Mark, I'm not in the business of going round defrauding people. In any case, I can't scam you, you don't have any money. This is a genuine offer. Take it or leave it.'

'How long is it for?' Mark asked.

'Difficult to say. Hopefully not more than a year, two at the outside.'

He glanced at Liz. 'What do you think?'

'We're broke. I can probably live with it. Can you?'

What he didn't want to ask his wife was how much she'd been drinking that afternoon; alcohol tended to bring out a bullish streak in her, so she might well want to change her mind in the morning. Looking at Giselle Swinsol he didn't think there was any kind of second-thoughts get-out clause being put on the table for them. The file was open at the part on healthcare and schooling. The contract he had with Prism Dynamics didn't even have that section. 'Okay, we'll take it.'

'Excellent.' Giselle Swinsol got to her feet. 'The car will pick you and the children up at seven thirty tomorrow morning. Please be ready.'

'I'll have to tell Prism Dynamics,' Mark said. The speed this was happening was leaving him disconcerted, almost as if he wanted an excuse to say no.

'That'll be taken care of,' Giselle Swinsol said. 'You can tell your immediate family you've got another job on a new planet. Please don't tell them where you're going.'

'Right.'

'Your certificate, Mark, please.'

'Oh. Yes.' He told his e-butler to add his certificate to the contract, and sent it back to her.

'Thank you.' She started for the hall.

'Will I see you tomorrow?' Mark asked.

'No, Mark, you won't.'

The front door closed smoothly behind her. Mark ran his hand back through his hair. 'Goddamn, what a ballbreaker.'

'Yeah, but one that's saved our asses. I wonder what the project is?'

'Some big military production line. I guess that's where the automated assembly comes in. They're going to bypass High Angel; that was only ever about politics.'

'Could be.'

'You don't believe that?'

'It really doesn't matter. We'll find out for sure tomorrow.'

'You sorry I said yes? We could always not turn up.'

'I wouldn't like to try that, not with Ms Giselle Swinsol on our asses.'

'Guess not.'

'But you did the right thing. I just didn't like the way she tried to bump us into saying yes. Then again, I suppose if you are building military systems right now, you can't afford to waste any time.'

'Yeah. You know, I think I feel good about this already. I'm doing something to hit back at the bastards.'

'I'm glad, baby.' Liz put her arm round his neck, and pulled him close for a kiss. 'How come you never told me you're a Sheldon?'

'I'm not, really. Not part of the Dynasty, anyway.'

'Humm.' She kissed him again. 'So what do we do till half seven tomorrow?'

*

Oscar and Mac arrived outside Wilson's office at the same time. Anna rose from behind her desk to kiss them both.

'He's ready for you,' she told them.

'So, how's married life?' Mac asked.

'Oh, you know, we're just like any other couple trying to pay off the mortgage.'

'Sod that,' Oscar said. 'What was the honeymoon like? Spill it.'

Anna glanced back over her shoulder and gave him a saucy

wink. 'Euphoric, of course. An entire ten hours out of the office. What more could any girl want?'

Wilson greeted both of them warmly. 'Thanks for coming. I try to see each captain before they leave. I don't suppose it's a tradition that'll last much longer. We're really starting to get a rush of components through for the next batch of starships. The emergency budget is showing some results, thank God.'

'Some good news,' Oscar said as he lowered himself cautiously into one of the scoop-like chairs. He hated anything with so much spongy padding. 'I haven't seen that on the unisphere shows. They're still busy navy-bashing.'

'You won't,' Wilson said. 'We're holding back on specifics. We don't know how much information the Primes glean from the unisphere.'

'Are you serious?'

'They must be trying to keep themselves updated about our capabilities,' Anna said. 'We have to assume they data-mined the Lost23. They know what we had at the time of the attack.'

'We're watching them,' Wilson said. 'QED.'

'Have we had any indication they're running a surveillance operation?' Mac asked.

'Not as such. But then they haven't spotted ours, yet.'

'I haven't spotted ours yet,' Oscar protested.

'Rafael's running it,' Anna said, she gave him a teasing smile. 'We've released hundreds of thousands of micro satellites in each system. It's similar to the technique they used against us, open a wormhole and keep moving the end point. They can detect it, but they can't investigate each opening.'

'So a lot of the satellites survive,' Wilson said. 'They report back to us on a constant basis through the wormhole.'

'Information we are also keeping from the unisphere,' Anna said. 'What the satellite swarms are showing us isn't good.'

'They're digging in on each of the Lost23,' Wilson said. 'Wormholes have now been anchored on the planetary surfaces. The amount of equipment and aliens coming through is quite phenomenal, even by what we understand as Prime standards. Dimitri Leopoldvich was quite right, damn him; we're not going to reclaim those planets.'

'So do we cancel the planetary section of the counter-attack?' Mac asked.

'No. We're sure the Lost23 are the strategic bases for the next Prime attack. The build-up is so massive it can't be for anything else. Once they're established, they can strike any-where inside the Commonwealth, not just the nearby stars. If anything, that makes infiltrating and sabotaging them even more important. We need to buy time.' He looked directly at Oscar. 'We have got to find the star where the Hell's Gateway leads. It's the one truly weak point they have.'

'Do my best,' Oscar said. He didn't like the way Wilson was almost pleading with him. 'The *Defender* will get to each of those stars on our flight's search list, you can count on that.' It sounded defensive, even to him.

'I know I can,' Wilson said. 'Mac, you've drawn the easy straw this time.'

'Well there's a surprise,' Oscar taunted his friend. 'What have you got for him, boss? Guarding a convent school on Molise?'

Mac politely showed him a finger. 'Up yours.'

'You're going to be testing the relativistic missiles, a long way from Commonwealth space. Now the Primes have seen what we can do with the hyperdrive they'll be coming up with defensive strategies. But if these missiles live up to their promise, even they will be hard pressed to ward them off.'

'We'll iron any bugs out,' Mac told him.

'Good. I've also decided this will be the last flight for *StAsaph*,' Wilson said.

'Why?'

'She's obsolete, Mac, I'm sorry. By the time you get back we'll be starting assembly of the new warships with the marque 6 hyperdrive. I want you in the captain's seat on the first.'

'That's a deal I can live with,' Mac said.

Oscar nearly complained. *Doesn't this navy believe in seniority?* But that would have come out churlish, even from him.

'And when you get back,' Wilson said. 'You're heading up the assault cruiser project.'

'Who me?' Oscar said.

'Yeah you. It's going to be our eventual war-winner, Oscar. I'm not kidding. They're putting so many new technologies into the damn thing that even I don't know half of them. Sheldon's got every Dynasty collaborating on this. That's leading to a lot of friction on the overall management team. If anyone's got the experience to pull that team together and make it work, it's you.'

'Hell.' Oscar actually felt a burst of gratitude which made his throat close up. He would never ask for so much responsibility. Yet Wilson trusted him with it, and Sheldon must have approved of the appointment, too. 'Thanks, boss. I won't let you down.' *Stupid sentimentalist.* Then he thought about Adam, and the recordings he was planning to take on the reconnaissance flight. His cheeks began to flush from the guilt.

'You okay?' Anna asked.

'Sure.'

'For a moment there, you looked embarrassed.'

'Him?' Mac exclaimed. 'I don't think so. Forgotten a date, yes.'

'At least I can get dates,' Oscar shot back. It was too late, the moment was gone. If there was anybody in the world he could trust to explain about Adam and his own past, it was these three friends. He smiled broadly to cover his true emotions. *Just who am I afraid of? Them, or me?*

*

The simulation environment was almost perfect. Morton had been wetwired for TSI before, of course, but this was an order of magnitude above that simple consumer convenience. There were unisphere artistes who couldn't afford this level of sensorium quality. The navy technicians had even equipped him for smell, notoriously the most difficult human sense for a program to duplicate correctly. Even now it wasn't perfect, the smell of the smoke was more like citrus than burning wood.

He was walking through the ruins of a town, wearing an armoured suit with electromuscle augmentation. It was the only way he could carry the weight of all the armaments the navy expected him to take with him. Boosted senses swept the piles of concrete and shattered composite panels. His virtual vision flipped orange brackets up over possible targets, which he found immensely irritating. The assessment software needed to be completely rewritten. One item in a depressingly long shakedown list.

Electrical power cables showed up as neon-sharp blue lines threading their way beneath the road. Electronic systems radiated a green-blue aurora, whose intensity varied in tandem with the array processing size. Something else he didn't like, he'd already asked the technical support staff to change that to a simple digital readout. Then there was the atmosphere analysis graphic. Electromagnetic signal display. Radar. Remote sensor windows, relaying images of the surrounding area from the little sneekbots scampering on ahead. Communication network with his squad members, coupled with all their sensor results.

His virtual vision was so cluttered with multicoloured symbols and pictures it resembled some cathedral's stained glass window. It was a wonder he could see through it at all.

The mission was supposed to be a quiet infiltration of an alien base, which was being built at the heart of the old human town. Make the assessment, locate the weak points, and select the appropriate weapons to inflict maximum damage. The rest of the squad was spread out along a loose front nearly a kilometre long, each one using a different approach route;

which Morton considered a tactical mistake, it produced a much greater risk that one of them would be spotted.

The squad's official designation was ERT03 after the planet and location they were assigned; though they called themselves Cat's Claws after their most notorious member. All of them were convicted felons who had agreed to serve in exchange for their sentence being commuted. In theory none of them had a record any more, but talk in the barracks at night generally brought out a hint or two, or more. Doc Roberts had been quite proud of his syndicate involvement, wiping inconvenient memories from anyone who had something to hide. Unfortunately, he'd tried to make a little extra money on the side by selling some of the memories on the snuff market, which is how the Serious Crimes Directorate had eventually caught up with him. The court agreed he was an accessory after the fact. Morton sometimes speculated that Doc had been the one who wiped his own awkward little incident.

Right now, according to the squad deployment schematic, Doc was manoeuvring his way through a collapsed supermarket four hundred metres west. Next to him was Rob Tannie, who would only say he was involved in the attempt to blow up the *Second Chance*. Nothing concerning his earlier life or lives was on offer. He called himself a security operative. Morton believed him, he had an easy grasp of tactics in most situations the training team put them in, and clearly knew how to handle himself in a fight.

Parker was the second biggest worry Morton had. He was some kind of enforcer, though he wouldn't say for whom. He loved the weapons they were being wetwired with, and went on in loving detail about the best way to use them to kill silently and effectively. Basically, he was a thug who lacked finesse in every department. Working as part of a team was difficult for him, which he didn't make a lot of effort to remedy.

And then there was 'The Cat' Stewart. She never talked

about what she'd done, which made everyone else quietly thankful. They all knew, and they really didn't want the details. As yet, Morton simply didn't know what to make of her. When she wanted to, she could be a perfect squad member, contributing a hundred per cent to completing the mission objectives successfully. She didn't do that all the time, though.

Morton's laser radar tracked some movement fifty metres ahead and to the left, rubble spilling down the conical mound that had been a block of flats. No bigger than gravel, the slide spilled out across the ground, sending up a small cloud of dust.

He swept his main sensors over it, trying to find out the cause. Two of the sneekbots approached the area cautiously, their crab-like bodies picking their way carefully over the rubble, antenna buds fully extended. They couldn't detect any alien presence.

Morton considered it to be a perfect distraction. He switched his passive sensors to watch the road behind. There was a brief flare of electromagnetic signal traffic inside a burned out building he'd passed five minutes earlier. It matched the signature which the Primes employed.

'Rob, I've got hostiles behind me,' he said, and opened up the sensor data.

'Okay, I've locked their position,' Rob Tannie said. 'How do you want to handle it?' He was a hundred and eighty metres to the west of Morton, moving down a parallel street.

'I'm going to keep blundering on like I don't know what's happening. You circle round behind and ambush the bastards.'

'Gotcha.'

Morton scanned a side road for any activity, and hurried down it, taking him away from the suspect mini-avalanche. He made a couple more sharp turns to add to the confusion. It ought to make his pursuers break cover to follow him. When they did, they'd be exposed to Rob.

The alien base was just visible ahead of him now. In the

gloomy twilight, the big metal structure gleamed brightly inside the beams of bright blue-white spotlights. Aliens were moving over it, walking along narrow ridges without any kind of handrail or safety fencing. They were all in their protective armour suits. The navy still didn't have any pictures of what one actually looked like.

Morton checked his display. The force field protecting the base began about a hundred and fifty metres ahead of him. All the buildings in the intervening space had been completely flattened leaving a broad expanse of smouldering blackened fragments, like an oil-slicked beach. Morton studied the gap critically for a few moments. There was no way to get across unseen. He told his e-butler to bring up a town map, and highlight the utility tunnels. Sure enough, there were several he could use.

'I see them,' Rob said. 'Two of them carrying weapons, heading for the base. They're looking for you.'

'Can you take them?'

'No problem. Question is, how?'

'Minimum fuss. We don't want to alert the rest that we're here.'

'Okay. An electronic warfare drone to smother them, and follow up with a couple of focused energy missiles.'

'That's too noticeable,' Morton said. 'A kinetic shot should get through their suits.' He was busy examining the map. The larger utility tunnels must be wired for intruders. Of the smaller ones, a rain sewer was possibly wide enough for him to crawl down. He didn't like confined spaces; but the suit and weapons he was carrying gave him the option of blasting his way out of any trouble pretty quickly.

'I'm not close enough to detect if they've got force fields,' Rob said.

'How fast are they moving? I need to get to a manhole cover before they see me.'

'They'll be on you in two minutes. I can get some sneekbots close enough to check for force fields.'

'My guess is they'll have them off. They're creeping round just like we are. They don't want to attract attention, and force fields are goddamn easy to detect.'

'So you reckon I should just use kinetics on them?'

'Oh for God's sake, boys,' a chirpy female voice said. 'Let's have some fun, here. They gave us all these beautiful weapons to try, didn't they? Let's see now, what haven't we used yet? Oh, I know.'

Morton checked his virtual vision to see where she was. 'Cat, don't . . .' Behind him, the town and sky turned incandescent white. The ground started to shake wildly, and the blastwave roared—

The environment dissolved into colourhash static. Strange tingles rippled up and down his skin. Then there was only his standby mode virtual vision, a row of blue line symbols glowing against a dark background. He heard his own breathing, amplified by his helmet. His arms and legs were stretched out spread-eagle style, held comfortably by plastic bands.

'God*damnit*,' Morton groaned.

The plyplastic round his arms expanded. He reached out and took the helmet off. Lights were coming on overhead, revealing the small nulsense chamber. The simulation team was staring in at him through a curving window, they all looked pretty pissed off. Morton gave them a what-can-you-do shrug. He was standing at the centre of a shiny gyrowheel, a metre off the ground, his feet held safely by plyplastic boots. They released his feet and he jumped down.

There were four other gyrowheels in the chamber, each with a squad member exiting the simulation. He walked over to face The Cat. A pretty heart-shaped face grinned down at him, white teeth emphasized by brown skin. Her appearance was late twenties. Seeing her for the first time, you'd assume she was a first-lifer, her outwardly frivolous attitude made it impossible to imagine her at any other age. While the rest of the squad were in standard dark-purple sports shirts and black trousers, she'd found herself a Sonic Energy Authority T-shirt and punk jeans. He wasn't sure how she managed that, squads were never issued with anything other than navy clothes. Presumably she just went up to civilian training staff and told them to give her what they were wearing. Her raven hair had been cut short, like all of them, except she'd added purple feather streaks tipped with silver.

'That was more like it,' she said brightly, and hopped down. On the ground she was ten centimetres shorter than Morton.

'What the hell was the point of that?' he asked.

'We haven't used the baby nukes before. We're here to try out every possible combat scenario. Right?' She gave the simulation team a breezy wave. Nobody behind the glass actually dared scowl back, but they all looked sullen. 'They were a real blast!' She laughed.

Morton wanted to give her a slap. Except he didn't dare. The Cat had been put into suspension before he'd been born, and wasn't due out until about a thousand years after his own sentence was finished. He remembered the day she'd arrived at their barracks. No individual had ever been given a four-strong escort before, and they'd all looked nervous. 'You can't use nukes against individual soldiers, for fuck's sake,' he raged. 'Are you deliberately trying to balls this up for the rest of us? Because I'm not going back to suspension just because you fancy having a big joke. I'll kick your warped little ass out of this training camp and into orbit before that happens.'

The rest of the squad froze, watching intently. One of the simulation team moved back from the glass.

The Cat puckered her lips up to blow Morton a fulsome kiss. 'The mission was already screwed, tough guy. If one alien knows we're there, they all do. You should read your intelligence briefings on that communal communication of theirs.

You weren't going to get inside the force field. Taking out the rest of them on the outside was the sensible option. Remember: Inflict as much damage as possible. Do not allow yourself to be captured.'

'It was not the only option. We could have got out of that. Rob and I were working on it.'

'Poor boy. So desperate to hang on to your body. It's not that it's remarkable in any measure.' The Cat gave him a playful slap on his cheek. It stung.

'Screw you!' Morton growled.

She headed for the chamber door. As it opened she batted her eyelashes at him. 'See you in the shower, tough guy. Oh, and for the record, it's not at all warped, it's actually a very pretty bottom.' She wiggled it as she left.

Morton let out a long breath and unclenched his fists. He hadn't realized he'd clenched them to start with.

'Okay, thank you, people,' the simulation team chief said. 'That's it for today. We'll resume at nine o'clock tomorrow morning.'

Morton stood where he was as the rest of the squad headed out. He was taking deep breaths, trying to calm down. Rob Tannie came over and put an arm round his shoulder. 'That was impressive, man. You're either insane, in love, or you've got a massive death wish. Do you actually know what she did to get suspension?'

'Yeah: but that's not the point. It's what we've got to do together in the future that's important.'

Rob gave him a strange look. 'You sound like them.' He jerked a thumb at the window.

'Oh what the hell,' Morton said, suddenly very tired. 'We're all going to die the second we drop out of the wormhole anyway; we'll never reach Elan itself.'

'That's the spirit. But take it from me, as someone who's already been through re-life, don't mess with the cute demon. She's seriously bad news.'

'Remind me to introduce you to my ex-wife someday,' Morton said as they walked out of the chamber.

*

Morton didn't even know which planet their training camp, Kingsville, was on. He suspected a Big15 world: Kerensk, judging by the violet-tinged sun. If so, they were a long way from the megacity.

Kingsville was vast, sprawling over a region of low desert foothills. Northwards from the camp, the gentle mounds gradually built up into a tall mountain range that stretched across the horizon, their distant peaks covered in snow. The desert spread out in every other direction, a rumpled plain of powdered yellow clay littered with crumbling boulders. Small, hardy native cacti bushes clustered together at the bottom of every slight depression, thick grey stems with a fur of spindly leaves no thicker than paper, and just as dry.

Rumour among the convicts in the camp was that if you could get to the other side of the desert, they'd let you go. That the navy wanted to see how good their wetwired systems were at sustaining humans in hostile conditions. Certainly there wasn't a fence or guardbots. The only way in or out was by aircraft.

Huge cargo planes had brought in the whole camp from whatever metropolis this world boasted, and were still delivering more prefabricated building kits every day, along with supplies and weapons systems. Kingsville had been divided into twenty-three sections, with a big geodesic dome at the centre of each one. Inside the domes were the main training facilities and technical labs where the troops were wetwired with the best the Commonwealth had, along with the canteen. Row after row of barracks cabins radiated out from each dome, sitting on the dusty soil like black bricks. Around them were the firing ranges and suit testing courses.

As Morton made his way back to the squad's barracks in

the baking late-afternoon sun the noise of the camp swirled round him, completely familiar now after two weeks residence. He'd been immersed in the training and wetwiring so intensely it was as if his earlier lives were just TSI dramas he could barely remember accessing. Dull repetitive thuds of kinetic rifles echoed in from the range where the division which was due to land on Sligo were practising. The whine of compressor jets was constant as the planes came and went from the adjoining airstrip five kilometres away; after the first night it never bothered him. Jeeps and trucks growled as they raced round the compacted dirt roads which linked Kingsville's sections and the airport. Shouts and chants from squads out pounding their way round various gruelling courses as they got their bodies into shape for the navy's great counter-offensive. Sixty per cent of them were convicts working off their suspension sentence, while the rest were various freelance security types and idiotically enthusiastic human-patriots keen to show the enemy what a bad mistake they'd made in attacking the Commonwealth. Even now, Morton still hadn't worked out if they were all on the biggest suicide mission ever dreamt up, or if they were going to be of some use. But he did like to think their squad was tough and smart enough to produce some effective results. Even loopy old Cat played her part most of the time. And it was anyone's guess, along with considerable barrack room speculation, what mayhem she'd commit on aliens, given what she used to do to perfectly innocent humans.

The oblong box which Cat's Claws had been assigned was fifteen metres long, and four wide, partitioned into three simple areas. The bunk and main living space for all five of them at one end, washroom in the middle, and finally a small rec room with a couple of deep sofas and a Kingsville network node where you could access the camp's library of TSI dramas, which were mostly soft porn. Kingsville's link to the planetary cybersphere was monitored by an RI, which regulated all calls in and out. You could talk to anyone you wanted, including the media, but topics were restricted, any mention of the types of weapons, training, or possible dates for the counter-offensive would be blocked instantly. Like the rest of Cat's Claws, Morton hadn't received any calls. He guessed that meant he didn't have anyone to call, either.

The door shut behind him, cutting off the heat and dust to provide him with a decent air-conditioned climate. The abrasive purple-white sunlight was filtered by the windows, giving the interior an Earth-normal spectrum. He went over to his bunk and started to undress, letting a servicebot catch his clothes. Rob and Doc Roberts were doing the same. The Cat was already in a shower cubicle, singing away merrily out of tune. Somehow, the simulations made them as sweaty and dirty as if they'd been out crawling round in the real desert.

He stayed in the shower a long time, luxuriating in the hot water and using up a lot of gel. His e-butler played him a file of old acoustic rock tracks, allowing him to forget about the training. Parts of his skin were still sore and sensitive from all the inserts he'd been given; and some of his new OCtattoos had developed a mild rash they were so intrusive. The water beating against them helped numb away the aches. Even his thoughts were calming as he hummed along to the guitar melody. The artificial weapons instruction memories that seeped into his brain each night made his sleep fitful and shallow, mixing with unwelcome dreams. It was one of the reasons he was so irritable during the day. What he wanted was a whole twenty-four hours off to relax and rest. He didn't think they'd ever get that, the pace of the camp was too fast.

Like all the troops, he wondered when they'd be deployed. They were all due another two sessions of wetwiring in the clinics which filled the lower floor of the dome. And sessions were always conducted three days apart. It didn't take a genius to work out that once they'd familiarized themselves with the systems out in the desert training fields they'd be heading out to the Lost23. Another two weeks at most, he reckoned.

It was quieter than usual when he got out of the shower. Usually there'd be some kind of argument or banter going on in the living quarters. Today there was only a low murmur as he towelled himself down.

'Hey Morton,' Doc Roberts called. 'Get your arse out here, you've got a visitor.' That brought a round of raucous laughter.

A maidbot handed him a polythene packet containing a fresh set of clothes. He took his time dressing, suspecting a joke.

It wasn't. A beautiful young woman was sitting on his bunk, with Rob, Parker and Doc Roberts clustered round like wolves eying up raw meat. Even The Cat was sitting on her bunk in a complicated yoga position, smiling sardonically as she joined in with the chitchat.

His visitor was wearing a long emerald-green skirt of light swirling cotton. Above that was a white blouse which was nearly translucent. Little curls of honey-blond hair had escaped from a jaunty black-felt cap. She stood up as he came in, and everyone else fell silent.

Morton nearly said: 'Who are you?' Then he saw her face, and astonishment locked his body solid. He blinked in disbelief as she gave him a roguish grin.

'Mellanie?'

'Hi, Morty.'

The others jeered, contemptuous and envious at the same time.

'Oh my God. You . . .'

'Grew up?'

He just nodded. She really was gorgeous.

'Well, kiss her you fucking moron,' Doc Roberts shouted.

'Nah, shag her brains out,' Parker shouted. 'In front of us!'

Rob punched him on the shoulder.

Mellanie gave Morton a sunshine bright smile as she walked over to him. He didn't dare move. Her hands went round his head, and she gave him a long hungry kiss.

There was a chorus of cheering and whistles as the embrace went on and on.

'Did you miss me?' she teased.

'Er.' Morton could feel a huge erection tenting his trousers. 'Oh, hell, *yes*.'

She laughed delightedly, and kissed him again, more gently this time. 'I'm here to offer you a media contract from the Michelangelo show. We'd like to offer you a front-line correspondent job for us. Is there somewhere private we can go to . . . discuss terms?'

Morton straightened up. Looked at the row of his squad mates with their lecherous expressions. 'Certainly. This way.' He put his arm round her waist and steered her towards the washrooms. Another round of jeering and whoops broke out behind them.

As soon as they were in the rec room he shoved the door shut and started to slide one of the sofas across it. He never quite finished. Mellanie jumped on him, her mouth trying to devour him. He pulled the front of her blouse open, hearing fabric rip. Buttons skittered across the floor. She was wearing a delicate white lace bra underneath which he tugged to one side exposing her breasts. They were as perfect as he remembered them, beautifully shaped and firm, with dark nipples aroused. His mouth closed around one, sucking and licking. Mellanie's hands found the catch at the top of his trousers and released it. Her fingers cupped his balls, then squeezed sharply.

Locked together they collapsed onto the sofa, with Morton on top. He fumbled desperately at his shirt, trying to get it off over his head. Mellanie wriggled her skirt down her legs. Then he was inside her, fucking her brains out with deep savage thrusts. Both of them cried out, competing to be the loudest, the most joyful, clutching frantically at each other as their bodies thrashed about in ecstasy.

*

An uncertain time later Morton recovered enough to focus on the ceiling he was staring up at. He was slumped against the base of the sofa, panting heavily and sweating profusely in contrast to the euphoria he felt. Mellanie giggled contentedly beside him, and propped herself up on an elbow. She'd lost the black cap at some point, allowing her hair to tumble out wildly. Her bra was still attached, twisted round her abdomen.

He smiled at her and gave her a soft kiss before finally finding the bra's clasp and removing it. That was when he noticed his own shirt was wrapped round his arm. Laughing, she unwound it for him.

'You really do look magnificent,' he said admiringly. His hand stroked along her arm, crossing over to her belly before dipping inquisitively to massage her thigh. 'This age suits you.'

'You haven't changed.'

'Is that good?'

Mellanie gasped in surprise at what his hand did. She'd forgotten how *very* well he knew her body. 'I like some things to stay the same,' she hissed in delight.

'Did you miss me?'

'Yes.'

'How much?'

She bowed her head, letting the damp tassels of hair brush his chest. 'This much.' Her lips and fingers began their delicate caresses. 'This much.' She moved slowly down his belly to where his cock was beginning to stiffen again. 'This much,' she growled impatiently.

*

Morton was convinced he'd never be able to move again, every limb ached in the most disgraceful fashion. They lay side by side on the floor, arms round each other as the light faded from the desert sky outside. For the first time since the trial he began to have regrets about what he'd lost.

'Have you managed all right, since . . .?' he asked quietly.

'I do okay.'

'I'm sorry, it can't have been easy for you. I should have made some kind of provision, put some money aside, some cash. I just never considered . . .'

'I said I'm all right, Morty.'

'Yeah. Jeeze, you look fucking amazing. I mean it.'

She smiled, running her hand back through her hair, combing it away from her face. 'Thanks. I really missed you.'

Even now, all he could think of was screwing her again. 'So have you . . . got anyone?'

'No,' she said, a little too quickly. 'Nobody special. Not like you. Things have been kinda strange for me. Especially since the Prime attack.'

'I'll bet. What's with this job you've got? You mentioned Michelangelo.'

'Oh, yeah. I work for his show now. I'm one of their reporters.'

'Congratulations. That must have been a tough gig to grab.'

'I have a good agent.'

'What the hell. It got you in to see me. That's all I care about.'

She rested a hand on his chest, stroking affectionately. 'It wasn't an excuse, Morty. I could have come to see you any time. You're allowed visitors.'

'Right.' He didn't understand.

'The offer is genuine. It took me a little time to put it together, and the show's lawyers had to convince the navy to agree. But it's all sorted.'

'You want me to report back from Elan?'

'Yes, basically. You're entitled to a short personal communication burst at each contact time, that's part of your service agreement.'

'I never read the small print,' he muttered.

'The lawyers made the navy agree that you could use the burst to send us a report. Michelangelo will pay. It's a good fee. That'll mean you have money when this is all over. You can use it to start again.'

'Fine. Whatever. Do I get to see you again? That's all I'm interested in.'

'It'll be difficult. I won't get many chances. And it can't be long before the navy begins the fight back.'

'Will you come back to see me here?' he asked insistently.

'Yes, Morty, I'll come back.'

'Good.' He started to kiss her again.

'There's something I want to show you,' she murmured.

'Something you've learned?' His tongue licked eagerly along her neck. 'Something a bad girl would do?'

She took both his hands and held them firmly. He grinned in anticipation. His e-butler told him the OCtattoos on his palms and fingers were interfacing. 'What—'

Morton was suddenly standing at the bottom of a white sphere. Faint lines of grey script flowed across the surface, too quick for him to focus on. They reminded him of his virtual vision's basic stand-by mode graphics.

'Sorry, didn't mean to startle you,' Mellanie said.

Morton turned round to see her standing behind him. She was wearing simple white coveralls. He looked down at himself to see he was wearing an identical garment.

'What the hell happened?' he asked. 'Where are we?'

'It's a simulated environment. Basically, we're inside your inserts.'

'How the fuck did you do that?'

'The SI gave me some fairly sophisticated OCtattoos while you were in suspension. I'm just starting to learn how to use a few of them for myself.'

'The SI?'

'We have an arrangement. I supply it with unusual information, and it acts as my agent. I'm not sure how much I can trust it, though.'

'*You* supply it with information?' Morton wished he could string together a sentence that wasn't a question. He was coming across like a petulant ignoramus.

'Yes.' Mellanie sounded mildly annoyed at the implication.

'Oh, right.'

'We're linked like this because it's completely private. There's no sensor the navy can use to overhear what I have to tell you.'

'What's that?' he asked cautiously.

'You remember the Guardians of Selfhood?'

'Some kind of cult? They were always shotgunning the unisphere. Didn't they attack the *Second Chance*? They believed an alien was running the government. Crap like that.'

'They were right.'

'Oh, *come on.*'

'It's called the Starflyer. It might have triggered the war.'

'No, Mellanie.'

'Morty, I've been lied to. I've been shot at. Its agents tried to kidnap me. Even Paula Myo thinks it's real.'

'The Investigator?' he asked in amazement.

'She's not an Investigator any more. The Starflyer got her fired, but she has political connections. I don't understand it all, but she's working for another government department now. I think. She won't tell me anything. She doesn't trust me. Morty, this is frightening the hell out of me. I don't know anyone else I can turn to but you. I know you're safe, you've been in suspension while all this has happened. Please, Morty, at least consider the possibility. The Guardians must have started with some kind of reason. Mustn't they? Every legend starts with a grain of truth.'

'I don't know. I grant you they have been going an unusually long time; but that doesn't mean they're right. In any case, what has all this got to do with me? I'm off to war any day now. I can't protect you, Mellanie. Even if I snuck off base, the navy has all the activation codes for my wetwired armament systems. They can switch them on and off any time they want.'

'Really?' she sounded intrigued. 'I wonder if I could hack them?'

'Mellanie, I'm sorry, I can't risk going back into suspension. Not even for you.'

She shook her head. 'That's not what I'm asking.'

'What then?'

'I want you to send me information back from Elan.'

'What kind of information?'

'Anything you can get on the Primes which would normally be classified. We can't trust the navy, Morty, it's been compromised by the Starflyer. And yes I know that sounds paranoid. I would have said the same thing myself a year ago.'

'You're really serious about this, aren't you?'

'Yes, Morty.'

He waited a long moment before asking: 'Would you have come to see me if you weren't caught up in all this?'

'I would be here no matter what happened to the Commonwealth. I promise. I don't even care that you might have killed Tara.'

'I probably did, you know. Investigator Myo doesn't make many mistakes.'

'It doesn't matter. We were good together, even if I was just a naive kid. I know we've both changed since then, but we have to see what we can be this time around. We both owe our old selves that, don't we?'

'Damn, you are something else.'

'Will you send me what information you can?'

'I guess so. I don't want to disappoint you again, Mellanie. So . . . I suppose you've got some foolproof method of smuggling the data back to you?'

'Of course.'

'Yeah, thought so,' he said in a resigned tone. This truly wasn't that first life teenage Mellanie with the hot ass that he'd sweet-talked into bed. Not any more. She'd changed into somebody a lot more interesting. *Still goddamn hot, though.*

Mellanie pulled a hand-sized square out of her pocket and held it up. It was made up from densely packed alphanumerics which glowed a faint violet as they flowed against each other in perpetual motion, always staying inside their boundary. She peered at it curiously. 'Wow, I've never seen a naked program before.'

The sheer girlishness made him smile in fond recollection. 'What is it?'

'Encryptionware. I bought it off Paul Cramley.'

'I remember Paul. How is the old rogue?'

'Harassed. He promised this will bury your private message to me in the sensorium datastream you send to the show. I can pull it out, but no one else will be able to.' She pressed the square into his hand, and it unravelled, strings of symbols flowering outward to blend into the sphere walls. They chased the grey script around for a moment, before fading into the same semi–visible grey as the rest of the symbols.

Morton's e-butler reported a new program had loaded successfully in his main insert, but lacked an author certificate and non-hostility validation. 'Let it run,' he told the e-butler.

'It'll also decrypt the messages I send to you,' Mellanie said.

'I hope they're all obscene pictures.'

'Morty!' Her disappointed face melted away into a Dali-esque swirl of colour. He was back in the darkened rec room with her warm naked body cuddled up against him.

'Thank you,' she whispered. 'I'm very grateful.'
'Care to show that? Out here in the physical world.'
'Again? Already?'
'I have been waiting for over two and a half years.'

5

The *Pathfinder* had spent just three days drifting along in freefall, and already Ozzie was facing a decision he *really* didn't want to make. A big part of his problem was that they had no destination. Even if they did, getting there would be difficult. Air currents in the gas halo were completely unpredictable. Moderate breezes would carry them along steadily for over half a day before depositing them in pockets of doldrum-like calm for hours on end. They left the sail up most of the time so the raft presented a decent sized surface area to catch the breezes no matter what their orientation was. Gusts blew up abruptly, fortunately short-lived, filling out the sail as if they were still on the water, and sweeping them along in a giddy tumble. Once, they'd actually had to furl the sail, their little raft was shaking so much. In itself, such a method of travel was an interesting concept. Ozzie was mentally designing a sailing airship that could voyage through the gas halo with considerable finesse; in his mind it looked like a cylindrical schooner that sprouted a cobweb of rigging filled by sails. He could have quite a life captaining that around this fabulous realm. Many lives, actually.

Those were the kind of dreamy ideas with almost infinite possibilities to extrapolate which made his mundane real time slightly more bearable.

With Ozzie's encouragement, Orion had slowly adapted to

freefall, though he was never going to be at home in the milieu. However, the boy could now move about the raft with a degree of confidence, although Ozzie made sure he wore his safety rope at all times. He could even keep most of his food down. There wasn't much Ozzie could do about the way he worried, though. Their pitifully minute ship adrift within the macrocosm that was the gas halo induced a sense of isolation which even gave Ozzie momentary panic attacks.

Tochee was another matter. The big alien was genuinely suffering in freefall. Something in its physiology was simply unable to cope with the sensation. It spent the whole time miserably clinging to the rear decking. It hardly ate anything because it just kept regurgitating any food which did get past its gullet. It drank very little. Ozzie had to keep pleading and insisting to make it do that.

He knew they had to return to a gravity field soon.

Making their big friend drink was only one of the problems they were now experiencing with their water, and it was the mild one. More acute was their dwindling supply. Ozzie had never considered they might run out of water. Fair enough, he hadn't expected them to fall off the worldlet, which was the root cause of the problem. They'd set sail on a sea which his little hand-pumped filter could easily cope with, providing them with as much fresh water as they wanted when they wanted. In fact, water had been the one dependable constant on every planet they'd walked across.

All they had for storage was Ozzie's trusty aluminium water-bottle, a couple of thermos flasks, and Orion's one remaining plastic pouch. They'd all been full when they went over the waterfall, but in total they only held five litres. Now they were down to half of the plastic pouch; and that was with facial fluid pooling in their cheeks and throats eliminating the thirst reflex in both the humans.

Ozzie had seen distant grey fog banks the size of small moons wafting through the gas halo, the majority of them tattered nebulas stretching out idly along the air currents, while a few were thick spinning knots like Jovian cyclones. None of them were within half a million miles of the *Pathfinder*. It would take months, or even years, to reach them.

A third of the fruit which they'd so carefully stacked in wicker baskets before setting off had tumbled off into the void when they went over the water worldlet's rim. They'd munched their way through quite a lot of the remainder since then, supplementing them from what remained of their prepackaged food. The globes were succulent and juicy, but no real substitute for drinking. They wouldn't sustain them for more than another couple of days at best.

That left Ozzie considering the other objects or creatures which occupied the gas halo. With little else to do except observe their environment, he'd soon realized the nebula was actually quite densely populated. The largest artefacts were the water worldlets. He'd been wrong with his first guess about their geometry, though. As they were blown further away from their original worldlet he saw its true shape. It wasn't a hemisphere; more like a bagel that had been sliced in half. The flat upper surface with its archipelago of little islands was always aligned sunward, with the sea pouring over its entire rim. Water followed the curve round and then began its long climb back up through the central funnel-like hole to fill the upper sea again and start the cycle over. The orifice where it surged out on top was always capped by an opaque white cloud squatting on the water, shielding the upwelling from sight. For a look at the gravity generator which made such a thing possible, Ozzie would have cheerfully sold his soul. Not that they could go back to the worldlet even if they were caught up by a wind blowing in the right direction. He simply couldn't work out a safe way to land (or splash down) on it. Not without a parachute.

So he started looking at the other things orbiting round

and round inside the gas halo. There were a lot of bird-equivalent creatures flittering about, either singularly or in huge flocks. Those that had come close enough to *Pathfinder* to see clearly so far had fallen into two categories; a genus with a screw-like spiral wing running the length of their bodies, and others, which Orion had named fan birds, resembling biological helicopters. They might have been edible, but some of the spiral birds were quite large, almost Tochee's size, with long sharp tusks that Ozzie didn't really want an up-close-and-personal look at. Besides, he couldn't figure out how to catch one.

The fact that there were so many indicated they must have easily accessible food sources, which was an encouraging prospect. He'd seen a quantity of freeflying trees, globular dendrite-style structures made out of what looked like blue and violet sponge, four or five times the length of Earth's giant sequoias. He had more hope for them than the birds; they must have some kind of internal water reserve. As yet, none of them had been close enough to try to reach, especially with Tochee in its weakened state. They probably only had one chance at being towed towards a rendezvous, and the distance was decreasing with each passing day, so he would have to make a very careful choice.

What he really wanted was the kind of reef which Johansson had described. If for no other reason than Johansson had walked home back to the Commonwealth after being on one. So far there'd been no sign of anything like that. There were a myriad of specks everywhere he looked, but he had no way of judging the size and nature of them until they got within range of his retinal inserts.

His hand-held array wasn't helping much, either. For the third time in an hour, Ozzie reviewed the data it was displaying in his virtual vision. Nobody was using the electromagnetic spectrum to transmit in. Nobody had responded to the distress signal he'd been broadcasting constantly since their arrival. Although, how far such a signal would travel through the atmosphere of the gas halo was a moot point.

Ozzie sighed in disappointment – once more. According to the clock in his virtual vision it was four hours since he'd last had a drink; when he checked the antique watch on his wrist it read the same. It was time to make that decision he'd been delaying in the hope of a small miracle.

His pack was tied to the decking a couple of metres away from the cradle he'd rigged up for himself. He wriggled out of the shoulder straps and glided over to it. The filter was inside, with its little length of tube coiled up neatly.

Orion stirred inside the nest he'd constructed out of rope and his sleeping bag. He started to say something, then saw the filter in Ozzie's hand. 'Oh, no. You can't.'

'What's gotta be done's gotta be done,' Ozzie replied sadly.

'I'm not going to,' the boy announced with complete finality. 'The Silfen made this place. So we don't have to do that.'

'Are they near?' Ozzie asked patiently.

Orion pulled out his friendship pendant. He had to cup his hands around the little gem before he could see the diminutive jade spark at the centre. 'Don't think so,' the boy sighed gloomily.

'Figures.' Ozzie rummaged further through his pack until he found an old polythene bag. He stared at it despondently. 'Guess this is it then.'

'I'm not going to.'

'Yeah, you said.' Ozzie pushed off from the decking, and hauled himself hand over hand round to the nominal underside of the raft, which put a modest barrier between himself and his companions. This was difficult enough without an audience. It took a while for his reluctant body to cooperate, but he eventually managed to pee into the bag.

He screwed the filter onto the top of his water bottle and

looked at the polythene bag. 'Oh just do it, you wimp,' he told himself. The end of the tube went into the bag, which he constricted to keep the fluid around the intake. He began pumping the filter, squeezing the simple trigger mechanism repeatedly until there was nothing left in the bag.

'Oh, that is just massively gross!' Orion exclaimed as Ozzie reappeared round the edge of the raft.

'No it's not, it's just simple chemistry. The filter removes all impurities, the manufacturer guarantees it. You've been drinking identical water to this ever since we started.'

'I have not! It's pee, Ozzie!'

'Not any more. Look, old-time explorers had to do this the hard way when they got lost in the desert, you know. We've got it easy, dude.'

'I won't do it. I'm sticking to fruit.'

'Fine. Whatever.' Ozzie popped the cap on his water bottle, and deliberately took a big swig. It tasted of nothing, of course; but what he thought he could taste was a different story. *Damn that kid! Putting ideas in my head.*

'Is that safe?' Tochee asked.

'Don't you start.'

'It's disgusting, is what it is,' Orion said. 'Grossly gross.'

'I don't know if you two have actually noticed,' Ozzie said, suddenly fed up with the pair of them, 'but we are seriously up shit creek without a paddle. From now on, the two of you are saving your piss as well.'

'No way!' Orion yelped.

'Yes.' Ozzie held the bottle out towards Orion. 'You want this?'

'Ozzie! That's yours.'

'Yeah. I know. So you start saving your own.'

'I'll save it, but I won't drink it.'

'My digestive organs do not function as yours,' Tochee said. 'There is no separation mechanism for me. Will your most excellent filter work for that?'

Orion gave a horrified groan, and turned away, jamming his hands over his ears.

'I guess there's only one way to find out,' Ozzie said glumly.

*

Sharp motion woke Ozzie, something poking him repeatedly on his chest. He removed the band of cloth he'd wrapped round his eyes to give him some darkness. A tentacle of Tochee's manipulator flesh was poised in an S-bend right in front of his face, ready to prod him again.

'What?' Ozzie grunted. It was difficult to get to sleep in freefall and he resented being roused. His virtual vision clock told him he'd been asleep for a mere twenty minutes. That only made him more grouchy.

'Many large flying creatures are passing,' Tochee said. 'I do not think they are birds.'

Ozzie shook his head to try and clear the lethargy away. Big mistake. He clamped his jaw hard to combat the sudden feeling of nausea. 'Where?'

Tochee's tentacle straightened to point towards the bow.

Orion was already struggling against the thick folds of his sleeping bag as Ozzie manoeuvred round him. He slowed himself with a couple of tugs, then gripped the decking firmly with his right hand. It left his head sticking clear of the raft, making him think of a medieval soldier peering cautiously over the castle rampart to watch an invading army approach. A gentle breeze blew his Afro about. Tochee and Orion moved up beside him.

'Wow,' Orion whispered. 'What are *they*?'

Ozzie used his retinal insert to zoom in. The flock must have been spread out over half a mile, hundreds of leather-brown spots slowly swirling along behind a tight little cluster. It was like watching a speckly comet, with a loose tail undulating slowly in the wake of the nucleus. They were over a mile away, tracing a wispy line against the infinite blue of the gas halo atmosphere. His e-butler brought a host of enhancement programs online, isolating one of the spots. The image was slowly refined, bringing the creature out from its original fuzzy outline.

'Holy crap!' Ozzie muttered.

'What is it?' Orion demanded.

Ozzie told his e-butler to display the picture on the hand-held array. He turned the unit to the boy. 'Oh!' Orion said softly.

It was a Silfen, but not like any they'd seen in the forests as they walked the paths between worlds. This one had wings. At first sight, it was as if the simple humanoid figure was lying spread-eagled at the centre of a brown sheet.

'I should have guessed,' Ozzie said. 'Yin and yang. And we've already seen the fairy folk version.' The flying Silfen did look uncannily like a classical demon. With the sun behind it, Ozzie saw the wings were actually a thick membrane which stained the light a dark amber. They were divided into upper and lower pairs that seemed to overlap; certainly there was no crack of sunlight between them. The top set were fixed to the Silfen's upper arms right down to the elbow, allowing the forearms to move about freely. A filigree of black webbing sprouted from the upper arms in a leaf-vein pattern, stretching the membrane between them. On the legs, the longer, second set of wings extended as far as the knee, then bent outward, leaving a broad V-shape between their curving edges so the lower legs were free. The Silfen would still be able to walk on land. A long whip-tail extended out from what on a human would be the coccyx, tipped by a reddish kite-like triangle of membrane.

The Silfen wasn't flying in the way planet-bound birds did. Not flapping its wings to generate lift. Here in the gas halo it simply soared. The big membranes were sails, allowing it to catch the wind and cruise along where it wished.

Watching the flock as they glided along in huge lazy spiral curves, Ozzie felt an enormous pang of envy. They had what was surely the ultimate freedom.

'We should do that,' Orion said wistfully. 'Sew ourselves into the sail and fly along. We could go wherever we wanted, then.'

'Yeah,' Ozzie agreed. He frowned, the boy's idea making him concentrate on what he was seeing, rather than just gawping in envious awe. 'You know, that's wrong.'

'What is?' Tochee asked.

'This whole arrangement. The Silfen body is designed to walk in a gravity field, just like ours, right. So if you're going to modify one to flap around the gas halo, why leave the legs and arms? This isn't a modification to allow them to live here permanently. What they've produced is like a biological version of our Vinci suits. It's temporary, it has to be. You don't need legs here, and you couldn't carry those wings about very easily on a planet.'

'I guess,' Orion said dubiously.

'I'm right,' Ozzie announced decisively. 'It's another part of their goddamn living-life-through-the-flesh stage. A great one for sure, but we're still not seeing the final them, the adult community.'

'Okay, Ozzie.'

He ignored the boy, thinking out loud. 'There's got to be a place where they get these modifications when they arrive. Somewhere in the gas halo. Somewhere with sophisticated biological systems.'

'Unless this is a natural part of their phase,' Tochee said.

'Excuse me?'

'On my home, we had small creatures that moved through several phases between hatching and the adult breeding form; aquatic, to land, to burying. They changed accordingly for their environment. Their fins would fall off, allowing them to grow primitive legs; then they would develop powerful front claws to dig, allowing their hind legs to wither away. Some of our scientific theorizers speculated that our own manipulator flesh was simply an advanced version of the morphosis mechanism. They were not popular linking us with the creatures, although I can appreciate the logic in their thoughts.'

'I get it,' Orion said. 'When the Silfen come here they just grow themselves wings, and when they leave, they shrivel up and drop off again. Hey! I wonder if this is their birth stage, or the mating stage?' The boy sniggered the way only young teenagers could at the idea of mating.

'Could be,' Ozzie agreed reluctantly, suddenly intrigued by the idea of sex while flying. 'Either way, it involves some heavy duty biological manipulation. Let's hope they're additions. We need some serious help here, guys.'

'Then ask them,' Orion said. He pulled his friendship pendant out from his grubby T-shirt. The greenish glow at the centre was bright enough to be seen in the full light of the gas halo's sun. 'Wow,' he muttered 'There must be a lot of them in that flock.' He checked his safety rope was secure round his waist, and pushed off the *Pathfinder*. 'Yo! Hey, we're here! Over here!' His arms semaphored wildly. 'It's me, Orion, your friend. And Ozzie and Tochee, too.'

Ozzie hesitated for a second. The resemblance to demons uncomfortably close . . . He crawled back along the raft to his pack while Orion kept on shouting and waving. The boy would never attract their attention like that, they were too far away. Although, at the back of his mind, Ozzie suspected the Silfen flock already knew they were here. He pulled a couple of flares from the pack, and headed back up to the prow.

'Get back here,' he told Orion. As soon as the boy was back holding on to the raft, Ozzie fired a flare, deliberately angling it to the side of the flock. Without gravity holding it back, the brilliant red star flew an impressive distance before dwindling away. The Silfen flock seemed oblivious to it. Ozzie cursed under his breath. 'All right then, if that's the way it's gotta be.'

He pointed the second flare tube right at the flock and fired. This time the dazzling point of light almost reached the edge of the flock before it burned out.

'They had to have seen that!' Orion said. 'They just had to.'

'Yeah,' Ozzie said. 'You'd think.' But the Silfen showed no sign of changing direction.

'Fire another one,' Orion said.

'No,' Ozzie said. 'They saw it. They know we're here.'

'No they don't, they haven't come to help.' The boy's voice was whiny from desperation. 'They'd come and help if they saw us. I know they would. They're my friends.'

'I've only got a couple more flares left. It'd be a waste.'

'Ozzie!'

'Nothing we can do, kid. They're not interested. If there's one thing I do know about the Silfen, you can't force them to do anything.'

'They have to help us,' Orion said forlornly.

Ozzie stared after the flock as it soared along its twisty course away from the *Pathfinder*. 'I wonder what's so important they've got to go see?' he muttered to himself. Even with his inserts on full magnification he couldn't see anything significant in the direction they were heading. There had to be something fairly close, surely? Not even a Silfen could survive indefinitely without food and water. Or maybe they hunted the avian creatures who lived in the gas halo.

He looked at the broken-hearted boy, then at Tochee. The big alien didn't have body language the way humans did, but something in its still posture was universal. Their friend was as dejected and worried as he was.

'Now what?' Orion asked.

Ozzie wished he could find an answer.

*

Ten hours after the flock had vanished into the blue haze of the atmosphere, Ozzie knew he was going to have to do something about getting them to one of the particles floating in the gas halo, even if it was only one of the hefty sponge trees. Orion had withdrawn into a massive sulk, although Ozzie knew damn well that was just a cloak for the boy's anxiety. Tochee, though, remained his main cause for concern. The alien was in noticeably poor physical shape, with the colour leaching out of its furry fronds, while the manipulator flesh along its flanks twitched constantly. Freefall really didn't agree with the big creature. Ozzie knew it hadn't eaten for over a day, and he was still pleading for it to drink something.

He allowed himself to drift away from the decking, and began scanning round for any large object. There were a few ideas he'd had about altering their course by a couple of degrees and he was keen to see if they worked in practice. Mainly it involved trailing the sail on the end of a rope, and using it like a very flexible rudder, with himself out there keeping it orientated in the right direction. The conditions were just about right, a gentle constant breeze which shouldn't present too much trouble keeping the sail pointing correctly.

'What are you looking for?' Orion asked, he sounded very tired.

'Anything that's out there, dude. We need to start making some progress.'

'Do you think we can?'

The hopelessness in the boy's voice made Ozzie tug on his safety robe and drift back down to the ramshackle raft. 'Hey, course we can. We just need some fresh resources, is all. This falling-off-the-end-of-the-world thing kinda caught us by surprise, huh?'

Orion nodded sheepishly.

'The trees will have plenty of water. And they probably have edible fruit. We can use the leaves and wood to turn the old *Pathfinder* into something that can fly a lot better. Trust me. I've been in worse situations than this.'

The boy gave him a surprised look, then slowly smiled. 'No you haven't!'

'Don't you believe it. I was on Akreos when its sun went into its cold expansion phase. Nobody had ever seen anything like that before, none of the astronomers had a clue what was going on. Man, that planet's climate went downhill so fast it was amazing. It was like living inside an old Hollywood disaster movie. I'd got a family there, married some English girl called Annabelle; she was the same kind of age as me, or maybe older, rejuved a couple of times, of course. She was famous back on Earth even before I was. Can't remember what for, must have dumped that memory. Real pretty, though, with a hell of a figure. You'd have loved her.

'We'd settled a long way from the capital city, doing the whole basic rural idyll scene in some beautiful countryside right between the temperate and sub-tropical bands, so it was seriously hot in summer but we still had snow in the winter. I built us a villa at the head of a low valley, and we'd got ourselves a nice little farm going. Course, it was all automated, had to be, we spent most of our time humping like we were training for the Olympics. Wow, yeah.' He chuckled at the memory. 'That was one of my lives where I'd got myself a little bit of a boost where it matters most to a guy, you know. Not that I need much of a boost, but hey.'

'Ozzie.'

'Right. Yeah. We'd been out there in the wild a couple of years, had one kid with another on the way, when the lights went out. Goddamn weirdest thing I have ever seen. The sun turned orange inside of a week. Its photosphere deflated, too; you could watch the damn thing shrinking. They worked it out eventually, something to do with unstable hydrogen layers. The sun rotated a lot faster than normal, see, which messed with the internal convection currents. There were upwellings

294

of helium and carbon into the fusion level. I think that was it. Anyway . . . Akreos turned cold *fast*.'

'Ozzie.'

'Don't interrupt, man. The snowstorms just like exploded out of the sky. They went on for ever and a day and weren't ever going to stop. And it was cold, I mean not quite as bad as the Ice Citadel planet, admittedly, but ballbustingly cold for a H-congruous planet, let me tell you. So cold all the train lines turned brittle and fractured. Aircraft couldn't fly in the blizzards of course. And there wasn't a snowplough built that could keep the roads open in those conditions.

'We had to evacuate. There were already over five million people on that poor doomed planet, and virtually no transport left. The Commonwealth Council imported snowmobiles from all the Big15; but they concentrated on the capital city and the major towns. Annabelle and I were all on our own. So I had to break down all the farm machinery and rebuild it. You know what as? A fucking hovercraft, man! Can you believe that; it's like twentieth-century technology. How crap is that? I mean, why not just straight out build yourself a rocketship? But it worked. We set off for the capital, but by then the glaciers were coming. Do you have any idea how fast they can move? Man, they're juggernauts in the express lane. We were racing ahead of them in the hovercraft; these mile-high cliffs of ice that roared across the land crushing anything in their path and knocking mountains out of their way. Supplies were running low, and our power level was reaching critical—'

'*Ozzie!*' Orion pointed frantically.

'Huh?' Ozzie twisted round, his arms tightening his grip to prevent the movement becoming a spin. A jagged fragment of land was rising over the *Pathfinder*'s prow like a moon that was way too close. It filled a quarter of the sky. 'Hoshit,' he squawked. His e-butler immediately began analysing dimensions. The flat, elongated chunk of land was thirty-eight kilometres long, and nine wide at the centre, with both ends tapering away to dagger-like spires. Its surface was mostly vegetation, a canopy of treetops with leaves whose shading ran from deep hazel through sickly brimstone and into a dense olive-green. Tight streams of swan-white mist slithered along the foliage with a sluggishness approximating to thick liquid. The closest point of the alarmingly solid mass was seventeen kilometres away.

'Where the *fuck* did that come from?' Ozzie spluttered. Admittedly he hadn't checked round much since the flock left, but this should surely have been visible from a long way off. He hadn't been dozing *that* much.

'We are going to crash,' Tochee said.

Ozzie's e-butler computed their closing velocity at just less than one metre per second. Purple vector lines sliced across his virtual vision. No doubt about it, they were on an interception course. 'Bump,' Ozzie corrected. 'Not crash: bump. This is freefall, remember. And at this rate we've got another five hours to go. We'll be quite safe.'

'They did it!' Orion exclaimed jubilantly. 'The Silfen saw us, and steered us here. I knew they were our friends.'

Ozzie wanted to tell the boy how unlikely that was; but then the gas halo wasn't exactly a natural artefact. 'Could be. Okay guys, let's work out how we're going to lasso ourselves to the surface when we approach.'

*

Twenty minutes away from what they now called Island Two. A gentle wind was providing the *Pathfinder* a lazy, slightly erratic, tumble, which made it difficult to know exactly which way up it would be when they finally hit. *Bumped!* Ozzie was planning on jettisoning the sail when they were keel-on and only a few minutes away from contact. That ought to slow their breeze-augmented rotation; although he wasn't sure if the figure-skating principle might not apply here, and pulling the mass in towards the centre would actually help increase the spin. In any case, they all thought it would be best if they jumped just before the raft reached the treetops.

Ten minutes, and Island Two was alarmingly large and very solid. The worst part was when their stately unstoppable gyration shifted his visual orientation so they seemed to be falling *up* towards it. At this distance it was no longer a particle. It was land.

Every loose item on board had been securely lashed to the deck. Ozzie was looking at the sail ropes, wondering which sequence to cut them in. The sail should flutter its way into the treetops. There were enough small branches and curving fern-leafs protruding above the general canopy that he was confident they would be snagged safely as they made contact. Bouncing off would be the final insult.

With two minutes to go, Ozzie untied his safety rope. One thing he didn't want to do was get tugged along by the mass of the raft if their impact made it spin. Island Two was now close enough to reveal a wealth of detail to the unaided eye. The actual ground itself was still obscured by the trees, but in among the brown and green canopy Ozzie could see strange spaghetti-like hoops of purple tubing coiled in intricate knots. Several ochre columns jutted tens of metres up out of the foliage, like ancient giant trees which had died and petrified. They were tipped in bulbous bristles which looked uncomfortably sharp. He hoped that the *Pathfinder* didn't come down directly on one of those; they'd be in danger of a lethal impalement.

'There is water down there,' Tochee said. Their friend was perched on the edge of the raft, ready to fling itself free.

'That's a good omen,' Ozzie said. 'We can fill all our containers. And you seriously need to start drinking.' The filter hadn't been terribly successful in separating out Tochee's faecal matter.

'This may not be a correct translation,' Tochee said. 'I do not believe water like this is a good sign. What is making it do that?'

Ozzie looked from the big alien to the hand-held array. 'Water like what? What is it doing?'

'It is flowing along the ground as if this were a planet.'

'That can't be . . .' Ozzie stared forward, his retinal inserts scanning the canopy and its meandering mists, searching for a gap. There was ground beneath the eerie twisted-spiral leaves. Loose loamy soil carpeted with dead leaves. *What's holding the leaves there?* 'Uh oh,' Ozzie grunted. He'd assumed only the big water islands used artificial gravity. 'Dumbass!'

'What?' a panicked Orion asked.

The *Pathfinder* was starting to speed up.

'Brace yourself!' Ozzie shouted. He gripped Orion's wrist. 'Don't jump.'

'But . . .'

The raft creaked ominously as weight reasserted itself against the decking. They were tilted slightly, sliding down (and it was definitely *down* now) towards Island Two's rumpled treetops.

The *Pathfinder* was still accelerating when it thumped into the uppermost branches. All three travellers were thrown violently to one side. The jolt pushed Ozzie's stomach somewhere down towards his feet, while his spine hit the decking painfully. The wood bent alarmingly beneath him. He immediately wanted to be sick. Loud crashing splintering sounds reverberated all around him. Leathery leaves slapped him hard across the cheek, their tiny spikes digging in through his stubble. The decking lurched round, tipping towards the vertical. Ozzie felt himself sliding over the simple planking as it bowed alarmingly. Somehow he'd turned upside down, so it was his head which was going to hit the ground first. The *Pathfinder* was bucking about as it continued to crash through the tree, snapping off branches as it went.

Tochee's manipulator flesh curled round Ozzie's ankle. He was tugged violently upwards as the raft fell away from him. The universe spun nauseatingly, curving smears of jade and caramel and turquoise wrapping themselves across his vision. Then his descent came to an abrupt halt. The universe reversed direction, and the *Pathfinder* finished its undignified landing with a bonebusting *crunch*.

'Urrgh. Fuck.' Ozzie tried blinking to sort out the confused blur which was all his eyes registered. Hot pain stabbed into his right knee. His cheeks smarted and he could feel something wet soaking into his stubble. When he dabbed his hand on the area and brought it away he saw fingers glistening with blood.

He tilted his head and looked down – *no, up* – to the tentacle of flesh coiled round his ankles. Above that, Tochee was wedged into the V where a thick branch forked away from the trunk, its manipulator flesh extended as long as Ozzie had ever seen it. The big alien was very still, though he could see it sucking down a lot of air. Several large splinters were sticking into its multicoloured hide, where gooey amber fluid was seeping out of the lacerations. When he let his head flop down again, he could see the ground at least another fifteen metres below. The *Pathfinder* lay underneath him, its decking fractured in several places, with all their belongings scattered around.

Retinal inserts showed him Tochee's eye signalling rapidly. It was asking if he was okay. Ozzie managed a feeble smile and gave his big friend a thumbs-up. Tochee contracted his tentacle slightly, and began to sway him smoothly from side to side, building up a pendulum motion. The tree swung a little closer with each arc until Ozzie finally managed to grab hold just above a broad bough. His feet were freed, and he collapsed onto the bough. The first thing he realized was how hard the bark was, almost like rock. 'Thanks, man, I owe you one there,' he wheezed, even though Tochee couldn't hear. 'Orion?

Hey, kid, where are you?' He looked down at the broken raft again. 'Orion?'

'Here.'

Ozzie looked back over his shoulder, then up. The boy was tangled in the upper branches of the nearest tree, a leafless ovoid lattice of slim brass-coloured stems. He began to wriggle his way downwards through the interior; as he did so the smaller stems bent elastically to accommodate him. 'I jumped. Sorry,' Orion said. 'I know you said not to. I was scared. But this tree is made out of rubber, or something.'

'Yeah, yeah, great,' Ozzie said. 'Good for you.'

'It's not big gravity here anyway,' the boy said enthusiastically. 'Not like you get on a planet, or the water island.'

'Terrific.' Now he noticed, Ozzie didn't feel very heavy. He eased off his stranglehold on the bough, and shifted round experimentally. Gravity was probably about a third Earth standard.

Tochee slid smoothly down the trunk, pausing briefly as it came level with Ozzie. 'I am no longer falling.' Its eye patterns flared contentedly. 'I enjoy this place.'

Ozzie gave his friend another weak thumbs-up, and started to work out how to shin down the trunk.

Orion and Tochee were waiting for him at the bottom. He stood cautiously, very glad he wasn't in a full gravity field; his knee felt as though it was on fire.

'Hand me the first aid kit, will you,' he told the boy.

Orion bounced off over the rumpled land, searching through their scattered belongings. When he came back he had both the medical kit and the hand-held array. Ozzie sank down, and touched a diagnostic probe to the inflamed skin above his knee. Blood was dripping from his chin, falling slothfully to stain his already filthy T-shirt. His e-butler told him that some of the OCtattoos on his cheek had been torn, and could now only operate at reduced capacity.

Tochee was resting on the ground opposite, using a tentacle

to pull the big splinters from its hide. A shudder ran along its body as each one came out.

'What now?' Orion asked.

'Good question.'

*

'Think of this as my wedding present,' Nigel Sheldon said.

Wilson didn't dignify that with an answer. He raised the transparent helmet up in front of his face. On the other side of it Anna was glaring at him in her special warning way.

'Thanks,' Wilson said gracelessly. 'I appreciate it.'

'No problem.' Nigel seemed oblivious to any undercurrents. 'I have to admit, this whole problem tweaked my curiosity, too.'

Wilson brought the helmet down over his head. The spacesuit collar sealed itself to the rim. His e-butler ran checks through the suit array, and gave him the all clear.

There were nine of them getting ready in the long, composite-walled prep room. Wilson appreciated that they had to take the navy forensic office team along, but he was starting to think that maybe he would have liked a few moments alone to begin with. It wasn't going to happen; even with Nigel's backing, this little jaunt was expensive.

Commander Hogan was heading the investigation team; his every response formal and respectful, he seemed almost awestruck by Nigel. Wilson knew he was Rafael's man, the one who'd replaced Myo. Not that it made him a bad person, but Wilson felt more comfortable with his deputy, Lieutenant Tarlo, who was approaching the excursion with a schoolboyish enthusiasm, and wasn't in the least intimidated by the company he was keeping. Ever since they'd arrived in the prep room, he and Nigel had been chatting about the surf to be found on various planets. As well as Hogan and Tarlo, there were four navy technical officers who were going to inspect the systems they were visiting to see what the hell the Guardians

301

were doing with them. They were all happy about the jaunt, as well they might be. A day away from the office and their usual routine, interesting technical challenge, be known by the admiral, and talk to Nigel Sheldon himself.

'We're ready for you,' Daniel Alster said. If Nigel's chief aide had any misgivings about his boss taking part, he was hiding them beautifully, Wilson thought.

Nine spacesuited figures tramped down a long corridor towards the gateway chamber, their boot steps echoing loudly off the old concrete walls. Wilson's treacherous memories replayed the time when the *Ulysses*' crew had walked across Cape Canaveral's main runway from the bus to the air stairs of the waiting scramjet spaceplane, their short route lined ten deep by reporters and NASA groundstaff, cheering and whooping as they embarked on the first stage of their flight to another world. Meanwhile, over in California, Ozzie and Nigel were chugging beer, chasing girls, smoking joints, and building the last few components of their machine . . .

The gateway used to be operated by CST's exploratory division, back in the days when they were venturing out through phase one space. That period had ended over a century and a half ago when the exploratory division packed up and moved out to the Big15; they were now transient again, en route to phase three space, their progress stalled only by the Prime invasion. But this wormhole had remained active, tucked away in a section of LA Galactic where the general public never visited. It was used for many things: emergency back-up for the big commercial gateways, supplying rapid response transit for the emergency services during civil disasters, carrying reserve power circuits to the moon in the event of any regular linkage shutdown. But mainly it provided interstellar transportation for governments who couldn't afford, or weren't liberal enough to sanction, life suspension sentences for criminals. Even on the old phase one developed, 'progressive' worlds some crimes were regarded as needing something more than suspension, and a large proportion of convicted criminals refused suspension anyway. With characteristic opportunism, CST filled the market for such a banishment.

There were several planets in phase one space which were on the borderline of H-congruous status; if they were opened for settlement they would be hard work to live on. As CST explored and opened up hundreds of other, easier, worlds, they were rapidly sidelined and consigned to a detailed entry in astronomical records and company history. Hardrock would have been one of them, a world whose life forms were still on the bottom of the evolutionary ladder, with no land animals and only primitive jellyfish in the sea. A perfect place for the scum of humanity to be dumped, where they were incapable of doing any harm to anybody except their own kind. So, once a week, CST would open the wormhole to a new location on Hardrock, send through crates of farm equipment, seed, medical supplies, and food; then the convict batch would be marched over. After that, they were on their own.

The circular gateway chamber looked crude compared to its modern equivalents, its surfaces of raw concrete and metal more suited to handling cargo than people. But then Wilson suspected the people who passed through here were regarded as less than cargo anyway. A Class 5-BH transRover stood on the floor, a simple open jeep used for driving round on airless worlds, with big low-pressure wheels. Several equipment cases had been loaded on the rear rack. The gateway itself was a blank circle, three metres in diameter, projecting slightly from the concave wall. A force field shimmered over it, turning the air to a slightly grainy smoke layer.

Daniel Alster gave them a tight smile. 'Good luck,' he said as he left.

Wilson looked up the wall opposite the gateway to the broad window fronting the operations centre. A couple of technicians were lounging on the other side of it, regarding the travellers with a disinterested glance as they joked between themselves.

'Stand by,' the gateway controller told them. 'We're opening the wormhole now.'

A pale light began to shine through the force field. Wilson turned to face it, seeing faint shadows growing across the floor behind all of the team. The light was deepening, becoming amber then heading down towards ginger. His heart began to pick up as the colour flipped all sorts of switches in his brain. *Why the hell am I putting myself through this?* He hadn't realized just how much Mars had been haunting him down the centuries.

The wormhole opened. After a break of over three centuries, Wilson was once again looking out across Arabia Terra.

'Clear to proceed,' the gateway controller said.

Wilson drew a breath, staring at the stone-littered landscape. Thin wisps of ginger dust were scurrying through the ultra-thin atmosphere.

'You want to go first?' Nigel asked.

How envious he'd been of Commander Dylan Lewis all those centuries ago, the first man to set foot on another planet. Except, he wasn't; Nigel had been there waiting. Some strange atmospheric phenomena carried Ozzie's laugh down the ages to reverberate round the chamber. *'Oh man, don't do that, you're going to so piss them off.'*

'Sure,' Wilson said briskly. He walked through the force field.

Martian soil under his feet. Pink-tinged atmosphere banding the horizon, fading to jet black directly overhead. A million pockmarked, jagged rocks scattered about, with rusty dust in every crevice. He scanned round, placing himself against the geography and features he could never forget. Off to his left was the rim of giant Schiaparelli, which should mean . . .

There, just off north. Two mounds of red soil smothering the lower third of the cargo landers. Their white titanium fuselages had been scoured by the storms of three centuries, blasting away all markings and colour. Now the exposed sections were tarnished curves of dark metal, the originally sharp edges of the parachute release mechanisms abraded down to warty clusters. Holes had opened up in several places, revealing the skeleton of internal struts caging black cavities.

So if the landers were there, then . . . He turned slowly to see the *Eagle II*. Sometime down the years the undercarriage had obviously collapsed, lowering the spaceplane's belly to the ground. The sands of Mars had claimed the craft, creating a smooth triangular dune of soil whose upper fingers of coppery grit gripped the top of the spaceplane's fuselage. All that was left of the tailfin was a stumpy blade of bleached and brittle composite, half its original height.

'Damnit,' Wilson muttered. There was moisture in his eyes.

You okay? Anna sent in text.

Sure. Just give me a moment. He walked a little way across the icy landscape, allowing the others to come through the wormhole. Tarlo drove the transRover out, and bounced across the rough ground.

'Whoha, this low gravity really screws up manoeuvrability,' Tarlo exclaimed. 'And these rocks don't help. I've never seen so much rock lying around in one place. Was there some kind of massive meteor shower, or something? How did you drive when you were here, sir?'

'We never did,' Wilson said. They'd brought three mobile laboratories with them, the best twenty-first-century technology and money could build. As big as a Winnebago, recombiner cells capable of taking them over hundreds of kilometres; with plans to explore every interesting feature the satellite mapping had thrown up. They were still inside the cargo landers; his mind could see them like dead metal foetuses, every moving part cold-welded together, their body-work flaking away in the terrible hostile atmosphere. 'We just went straight home again.'

'You could have stayed and explored,' Nigel said. He didn't sound very contrite.

'Yeah, we could have.' Wilson was trying to work out angles against the landscape and its poignant relics. He walked over towards the *Eagle II*. Its dimensions were scripted perfectly in his mind, allowing him to draw its shape through the raggedy mound of soil. The profile dynamic wings had been fully retracted for the landing, shrinking back down to a squat delta; there was the smooth curvature they followed to merge with the fuselage. Both narrow sections of the windshield were buried; he was glad of that, the equivalent of closing the lids on a dead man's eyes. He didn't want to see inside again.

Following the profile back from the nose – three point two seven metres – and that was the position of the forward crew hatchway. There was no depression in the dune there. Not that he could remember if they'd left it open or shut when they left. But then, it was Orchiston who'd been the last back through the wormhole, emerging into the noisy riot that had developed across the college campus, an inevitable outcome from half the country's population driving through the night to visit the wondrous machine. Before that, though, in the few blissful minutes when the crew thought they'd achieved the ultimate, he and Commander Lewis had been struggling with the flag. NASA protocol required it be set up out of engine efflux range, so the cameras would see it fluttering when they lifted off again. *Here.* He bent down slowly, and began scraping at the fine sand. Little swirls of it puffed up as his gauntlets raked around.

'We've acquired the Reynolds beacon, sir,' Commander Hogan said. 'Three kilometres away, bearing forty-seven degrees.'

'Well done,' Nigel said. 'You guys scoot over there and get us some answers from the science equipment, huh?'

'Yessir.'

Wilson thought he might have got the position slightly wrong. After all, the *Eagle II* could have shifted round, twisting as its undercarriage struts collapsed. He saw the transRover start to rock and jolt its way across the rucked sands, all six navy personnel clinging to the frame.

'What are you looking for?' Anna asked.

'Not sure.' He moved a few paces and bent down again. 'Okay. The flag, actually. I know we got the damn thing up. Must have been blown over.'

She put her hands on her hips, and turned a full circle. 'Wilson, it could be anywhere out there. The storms here are really ferocious. They can last for weeks.'

'Months, actually, and they cover most of the planet.' He gave up grubbing through the dirt. 'I'm sure I remember using a power drill to screw the pole legs in. We were supposed to secure it.'

Nigel had walked up the slope of the sand piled against the *Eagle II*'s fuselage. His hand touched the remnants of the tailfin. 'This ain't right, you know. She deserves better than this. We should arrange to take her home. I'll bet the California Technological Heritage museum would love to have her. They'd probably pay for the restoration.'

'No,' Wilson said automatically. 'She's broken. She's a part of this planet's history now. She belongs here.'

'She's not so badly broken.' Nigel stroked the top of the fuselage. 'They built well back then.'

'It was her heart you broke.'

'Goddamn! I knew it, man, I fucking knew it. You are *still* pissed at me.'

'No I'm not. We were both part of history that day, you and I. My side lost, but then we were always going to.

Wormhole technology was inevitable. If you hadn't done it, someone else would.'

'Yeah? You have no idea how tough that math was to crack, nor following up by translating it into hardware. Nobody but Ozzie could have done it. I know his wacko rep, but he's a genius, a true one, a fucking supernova compared to Newton, Einstein, and Hawking.'

'If it can be done, it will be done. Don't try and personalize this. We represent events, that's all.'

'Oh brilliant, I'm nothing but a figurehead. Well excuse me.'

'Will you two monster egos pack this in, please,' Anna said. 'Wilson, he's right. You can't let these old ships decay any further. They are history, just like you said, and a very important part of history.'

'Sorry,' Wilson mumbled. 'It's just . . . I got wrong-footed coming back here. You don't erase half the stuff you think you have at rejuvenation.'

'Ain't that a fact,' Nigel said. 'Come on, let's go find a souvenir that isn't a lump of rock. There's got to be something lying round here.'

'I never even got a lump of rock last time,' Wilson said.

'You didn't?'

'No. We didn't run our science program. I think Lewis picked up his first sample, but NASA kept that once we got home.'

'Damn! You know, I don't remember picking up any rock, either.'

'Christ,' Anna said. She bent down and picked up a couple of twisted pebbles, and handed one to each man. 'You two are bloody useless.'

*

Roderick Deakins strolled down Briggins as casually as anyone could be walking round the Olika district at two am. He was grateful there hadn't been a patrol car drive past, though that was only a matter of time. Olika was where a lot of rich types lived. They had deep connections in Darklake's City Hall. The police maintained a good presence here, not like the Tulosa district where Roderick lived. You rarely saw a cop there after dark, and then never singularly.

'Is this it?' Marlon Simmonds asked.

Roderick had worked with Marlon many times down the years. Nothing too serious – you couldn't call them partners – but they'd seen their fair share of juvenile street rip-offs, followed by a string of break-ins when they'd run with the Usaros back in '69. After that they'd done time together for a Marina Mall warehouse heist that had gone seriously wrong in '73. When they were paroled they'd drifted into helping out Lo Kin, a small time boss who ran a protection racket on Tulosa's westside, where they'd been stuck ever since. All that history and the trust which went with it made them the perfect pair for this job.

'What does the fucking number read?' Roderick hissed back.

'1800,' Marlon said, glancing at the brass numbers screwed into the drycoral arch above the gate. That was the thing about Marlon, nothing much seemed to bother him. His bio-chemically boosted body weighed at least twice as much as Roderick's, and moved along with the inevitable inertia of a twenty-ton truck. His general attitude was a reflection of his physical presence, allowing him to cruise through life knowing there was very little which would get in his way.

'Then that's it, isn't it?' Roderick said. The man who was an associate of Lo Kin, the one they were doing this for, had been very specific. The house number, the name of the man they were going to *talk to*, the short time in which they had to perform the job.

'Okay, man.' Marlon took a harmonic blade from his jacket pocket, and sliced through the wrought iron around the lock.

The gate swung open with the tiniest of squeaks from the hinges. Roderick waited a moment to see if any alarms were triggered. But there was no sound. When he waved his left palm around the gate, his e-butler said it couldn't detect any electronic activity. Roderick grinned to himself. It had cost a lot to get the OCtattoo sensor on his palm, but every time like this he knew it was worth it.

It was dark in the bungalow's garden. The tall drycoral wall blocked most of the illumination from the streetlights outside, while the low building at the centre remained unlit. Roderick switched his retinal insert to infrared. It produced a simple pink and grey image that was oddly flat. That lack of depth always slowed him down; one day soon he'd get a matching insert for his other eye, which would give him a decent resolution in this spectrum. It could even be with the money from this job; Lo Kin's associate certainly paid well.

Roderick's hand moved inside his leather jacket and removed the Eude606 ion pistol from its holster. The gun fitted snugly into his palm, as well it might do. He'd never held a piece of hardware as expensive as this before. It felt good. The power it contained gave Roderick a raw confidence he didn't experience often.

Marlon cut through the wooden front door, slicing round the lock. Roderick couldn't detect any electrical activity. It fitted with what they'd been told. Paul, the old man who lived here, was eccentric verging on plain nutty. They stepped cautiously into the dark hallway.

'What are you doing?' Roderick whispered. Marlon was going along the shelving, examining the vases and figurines sitting there.

'You heard what the man said: take anything you want. Is any of this art crap valuable?'

'I don't fucking know. But we do that *after*, get it?'

Marlon's huge frame shrugged dismissively.

Roderick switched on his small hand-held array. The screen glowed brightly in the lightless bungalow; it displayed a floor-plan, with the master bedroom clearly marked. 'This way.'

They started walking cautiously, watching out for anything on the floor. The place was a mess, nobody had cleaned up in an age. Roderick checked the first few maidbots resting in their alcoves; none of them had any power in their batteries. He'd never been anywhere with so little electrical activity; it was like being in the Stone Age.

When they were halfway across the lounge, Roderick's retinal insert failed, plunging him back into a world of ebony shadows. 'Goddamn!'

'What is this?' Marlon complained.

Roderick realized his hand-held array was dead. His e-butler was also offline. 'Shit. Are your inserts down?'

'Yeah.'

The unease in Marlon's voice added to Roderick's growing anxiety; it wasn't often the big man sounded uncertain. He squinted into the darkness. Two big arching windows were visible as grey sheets, casting the tiniest amount of illumination into the room. He could just make out the regular sable shapes of furniture.

'This is no accident; our electronics got hit.'

'What do we do?' Marlon asked. 'I've got a torch. You want some light?'

'Maybe. He must know we're here. What do you reckon?' Roderick caught a motion over by one of the windows. A patch of dark sliding up the wall. Which was crazy. Not to mention disturbing. Or was it just his adrenalin-pumped imagination. He brought the Eude606 up, pointing it in the direction the shape might have been if it was real. Sweat was pricking his brow.

'Well, what's he going to do?' There was a kind of bravado in Marlon's voice now. Neither of them were bothering to whisper.

Roderick steadied his pistol, holding it level, ready to turn to face whatever threat was revealed. 'Okay then.' He waited while Marlon fumbled round in his jacket. Then the narrow beam stabbed out, amazingly bright in the gloomy lounge. It swept over the walls, with Roderick following the wide circle with his pistol. Marlon turned a complete circle, exposing the antique décor with its dusty coating. There was nobody in the lounge with them. More importantly from Roderick's point of view, there was nothing on the wall by the window, nothing that could move about.

'Okay, old man,' Marlon said. 'Out you come now, we ain't gonna hurt you.' It was the kind of tone used to calm a panicked animal. 'We just want the artwork, that's all. There ain't gonna be no trouble.'

They looked at each other. Roderick shrugged. 'Bedroom,' he said. Something moved in his peripheral vision. Above him. 'Huh?' Marlon must have caught it, too; the beam tilted up. Roderick looked at the ceiling, which was covered in broad patches of peculiar rust-coloured fur.

The nostat directly above Roderick let go. It was like a soft blanket dropping on him, its edges falling below his elbows. Shock made him yell and thrash about, trying to tug the thing off. The nostat's soft fur changed, strands twining together into needle-thin spikes. It tightened around its prey, a motion which slid over ten thousand of the slender barbs through Roderick's clothing and into his flesh. His scream of utter agony was cut off as spikes penetrated into his throat, filling his gullet with blood. Reflex made him convulse, even though the pain had virtually rendered him unconscious. It was exactly the motion which the nostat had evolved to take advantage of. The barbs were slim and strong enough to remain extended as its prey's muscles flexed, allowing them to rip through the tissue as if they were miniature scalpels. The entire outer layer of Roderick's upper torso was shredded to the constituency of jelly. Blood erupted from his body as it collapsed onto the floor, which the nostat sucked down hungrily through the hollow core of each spike.

The first contraction didn't quite have the strength to push the spikes through Roderick's skull. Instead they penetrated the softer areas of flesh, ripping apart eyes, ears, nose, and tearing through his cheeks. The last thing he heard as he finally lost consciousness was a terrified roar coming from Marlon, and furniture exploding as both of them fired their ion pistols in random bursts.

*

The day after he went to Mars, Nigel woke up in bed with his wives Nuala and Astrid. Both of them were biologically in their mid-thirties, though chronologically they were over a century old. They were what he tended to think of as the mother comfort personalities of his harem. He sought them out when he wanted an untroubled sleep; and last night he'd really needed one. It had been a bad week; dealing with the innumerable problems spinning out from the Lost23 refugees on top of the high politics of the War Cabinet. He'd thought Mars would be a distraction from the problems he had to deal with in the office. Typical mid-life-crisis response, get out from behind the desk and do something practical; but there had been far too many old memories lurking amid that desolate frozen landscape to ambush his emotions. The broken ancient spaceplane had kindled a totally unexpected pang of guilt. When they finally returned from that abandoned planet his mood had turned bleak.

He'd visited Paloma and Aurelie first, the newest members of his harem. First-lifers that hadn't reached their twenty-first birthdays yet; the pair of them were beautiful, giggly, and utterly guileless girls. They came very firmly in the sex athlete category; with personal trainers to keep them fit and toned, an unlimited wardrobe budget, and stylists to confer the kind of elegance he enjoyed in all his women.

Every time he came out of rejuvenation, his harem was made up mostly from girls like them. It was only when he started advancing into his biological early thirties that the ratio began to swing back, and the more secure and stable types made up the majority as yet another generation of his children were born. As a single child himself, Nigel always enjoyed being surrounded by a large immediate family. That was something which no rejuvenation had ever altered. As always in his case, the human universe bent to accommodate him with the alacrity of a gravity field around a neutron star. There was never a problem in finding women who were happy with the harem arrangement; he was sent thousands of intimate requests every day. His main difficulty was sorting through them all.

Right now there were only five of the younger, sexy ones. He knew that none of them would hang around for more than a couple of years. Girls like that never did; they weren't stupid, eventually they'd grow weary of the household's formality, the way everything was structured around his preferences. Unless he had children with them – unlikely now – they'd move on, just like thousands before them.

Until that happened, they were the best possible sex he could wish for. It was only after romping with Paloma and Aurelie for nearly two hours he left, almost sneaking out, to find Nuala and Astrid who snuggled up cosily and gave him that welcome sense of comfort so essential for a deep dreamless sleep.

Breakfast, as always when the household was in residence at the New Costa mansion, was held on the terrace. He sat at the head of a long table sheltered from the sharp blue-white glare of Regulus by a canopy of lush grape vines, whose broad leaves filtered the exotic sunlight to a manageable lambency. The day's first gusts of the dry El Iopi wind were already blowing across the grounds, rustling the foliage above him. Eleven of his wives joined him, bringing their children, who ranged from three-month-old Digby to Bethany who was approaching her fifteenth birthday. Several senior family members who were staying in the mansion also arrived with their partners. It was a bustling light-hearted meal, which finished off the mood transformation which his serene sleep had begun. His thoughts had calmed considerably, which was a relief. He knew his judgement became impaired the more wound up he got.

'Are you going to rehouse the refugees who're being looked after by the Hive?' Astrid asked. She was poring over a paperscreen as she ate her fruit and honey yogurt. 'I mean, they're being made welcome, and all, but they aren't gonna wanna stay there.'

'Long term, they'll certainly move on. We're busy designating phase three and late stage two planets that can absorb all the refugees. As to when a Commonwealth-endorsed settlement project gets underway, that depends on the Senate. For now everyone's just concentrating on providing relief for the survivors.'

'Half of them will be absorbed back into mainstream society without any government aid packages,' Campbell said. 'The majority are skilled people who can integrate into any modern economy; it'll just be a question of finding a planet with an ethnic base that suits them. Augusta companies have received a lot of employment inquiries already. So have the other Big15.'

'It says the insurance companies won't compensate them,' Astrid said, her manicured finger tapping the news article on her paperscreen in accusation.

'All the local insurance companies were destroyed along with their planets,' Nigel said.

'They're sub-divisions of the major companies,' she said. 'You know that.'

'Sure. But compensation is going to have to involve government. The Dow-Times index is still down eight thousand; the finance houses can't afford to pay out trillions right now. We need to concentrate our taxes on the navy and strengthening planetary defences.'

'That's outrageous,' Paloma exclaimed. 'They need our help. They suffered because of Doi's stupid mistakes.'

Nigel tried not to smile at her righteous anger. She had the full indignation of youth, a fieriness which promoted her attractiveness. 'I pushed for the *Second Chance* mission.'

'Well, yes,' Paloma reddened. 'But the government knew the Primes were a threat. They should have taken it seriously.'

'That's the benefit of hindsight talking. We prepared as well as any reasonably civilized culture could be expected.'

'Will they come back, Daddy?' little Troy asked, peering anxiously over his cereal bowl.

'They might. But I promise you, all of you,' Nigel said earnestly when he saw the other children looking at him for reassurance, 'I will make sure you're safe. All of you.' He exchanged a glance with Campbell, who pulled a face before returning to his eggs Benedict.

When Nigel finished breakfast, he was almost tempted to go back to Paloma's bedroom. But there was a ton of work to be done, so he set off to the wing of the mansion where he maintained his personal offices. It was a long walk.

Nigel had never been entirely content with his mansion on New Costa. Sure it was architecturally perfect, Hollywood chateau meets Arabian oil-wealth; a light and airy structure with broad arches and elaborate, fun, rotundas. That was the problem, he'd built it during what was essentially CST's imperialistic expansion era, when Augusta was establishing itself as the Commonwealth's principal manufacturing source and he consolidated his Dynasty as the monopoly interstellar transport. As such it suited an emperor, a reflection of the economic dynamism which illuminated that whole century. Sprawling in two hundred acres of beautifully landscaped parkland at the heart of the megacity, it was the size of a small village. Two wings were built to accommodate his executive offices of that time, staffed almost exclusively by Dynasty members, who directed a broad political and economic portfolio. In those days he ran a goodly portion of the burgeoning Commonwealth, and directly influenced the rest of it.

As well as the corporate side, there was also his personal family to accommodate; his harem, their retainers, staff, a flock of children complete with their nannies and teachers. There were few medieval European monarchs who could match his court for grandeur and size.

Nowadays things were a little different. The Dynasty's executive council managed CST and the vast manufacturing conglomerate which Nigel owned; the Augusta Engineering Corp had assumed all civil government responsibilities of the Big15 world; their senators looked after the Dynasty's political interests in collaboration with the other Dynasties, while the political office monitored developments on other worlds like an old-style intelligence agency. Nigel still formulated policy, but the tough job of implementation was conducted by the elaborate management pyramid he'd evolved and modified since those heady times of the twenty-second century. More recently, augmented neural arrays and ultra-sophisticated wetwiring allowed his expanded mentality to monitor and manipulate events at a near subconscious level; certainly his flesh and blood brain was spared an awful lot of detail. With his new boosted semi-artificial intelligence and trusted networked councils smoothly advancing the Dynasty, the mansion survived as something of a relic to the old days. A good proportion of the original offices had been shut down, one of the building's wings had been turned over to what amounted to storage rooms, full of the detritus accumulated over two centuries by Nigel's direct family of wives and children, a number which rarely dropped below thirty.

As he settled into his own office, a blissfully simple room

compared to the rest, with an antique plain oak desk and earth-tone walls, he reflected on how those management systems he'd spent so long establishing had been close to worthless during the Prime invasion. The Dynasty's senior members had to assume direct control of departments to manage the response.

That the management structure couldn't cope with a completely unexpected problem was going to have to be reviewed at some length. He suspected it was primarily due to complacency, the unconscious assumption that the Commonwealth would never undergo any radical change.

Stupid goddamn thing to think. Wormholes were the most radical event ever to hit old Earth. I should have known better.

Several senior members joined him in the office for the first review conference of the day: Campbell, who had done a magnificent job orchestrating the evacuation; Nelson, the Dynasty security chief, and Nigel's twentieth child, born when he first started having more than one wife at a time; Perdita, their media director who tied in a lot of operations with Jessica the Augusta senator, a position she'd held for seventy years. As Nigel looked round it struck him how they were all from the first three generations. *Maybe it's time to let the fourths up to this level? There's no complacency worse than the comfort of familiarity. In which case why make it the fourths? Why not the fifteenths, or the twentieths? It's not as if they aren't capable.*

Benjamin Sheldon was the last to arrive, Nigel's first grandson, and the Dynasty's comptroller. Nigel always suspected the man was slightly autistic, his devotion to detail was excruciating, and his marriages never lasted long. He didn't quite seem to live totally in this universe. Finance was his life. He'd taken over running CST's accounts division on his twenty-eighth birthday, and regarded his periods in rejuvenation as a major inconvenience. His memory augmentation arrays were among the most comprehensive ever wetwired into a human; the inserts had actually increased his skull size by ten per cent. As he hadn't remodelled his body, other than his neck, to maintain proportion, his appearance inevitably drew stares.

Daniel Alster took a chair slightly behind the three settees which the seniors settled in as the e-shield came on, sealing the office.

'Any new problems?' Nigel asked.

'We're just busy containing the old ones, thanks,' Campbell said.

'In a steady-state model extrapolated from our current position, we will have regained everything we lost in eleven years,' Benjamin said. 'The growth vectors are positive once resettlement of the displaced is completed.'

'It won't be steady state,' Nelson said. 'The Primes will attack again to annexe more of our worlds. The cost of resisting them will be phenomenal.'

'And that's if we succeed,' Nigel muttered.

The other seniors regarded him in mild surprise – the priest who swore in church.

'It's the one option I've taken seriously since we began this whole debacle,' Nigel said. 'That's why I began the lifeboat project.'

'Have you drawn up the parameters for use?' Jessica asked.

'I think we'll recognize the moment when it arrives. Now our advanced weapons development is finally producing results, I'm hopeful the Primes can be defeated one way or another.'

'Didn't the War Cabinet approve genocide?' Perdita asked. 'Public opinion is certainly in favour right now.'

'We agreed in principle that such an action was a last resort.'

'Typical politicians,' Nelson grunted.

Jessica smiled sweetly. 'Why thank you.'

'A death toll near forty million, and it's an *option*? Hardly our finest hour, I feel.'

'There's a moral dimension in that decision, obviously,'

Nigel said. 'But there's also the possibility that the Seattle quantumbusters might not be sufficient for the job. For all they're insanely antagonistic, the Primes are not stupid. They will have established themselves in other star systems by now. Total genocide will be difficult to achieve and verify.'

'You mean we'll have to make our weapon available to the navy?' Nelson asked.

'I'm not in favour of that,' Nigel told him. 'That really is a weapon I don't want anyone else to know about, let alone possess. The damn thing even frightens me.'

'That's a reasonable reaction,' Jessica said glumly. 'I don't like the fact it exists, but as it does I don't want it in anyone else's control.'

'Quantumbusters are horrendous enough,' Nelson said. 'There's only a question of scale involved with this situation. Having the Dynasty's finger on the trigger is purely a psychological crutch. A doomsday weapon is a doomsday weapon, whether it destroys a planet or an entire star system is worrying about how many angels can dance on a pinhead.'

'Our weapon can destroy more than one star system,' Nigel said regretfully.

'If it can be built, it will be built,' Campbell said. 'If not by us, then by someone else, and I include the Primes in that statement. It's not as if we have to worry about the other Dynasties using it. We don't have that kind of conflict any more.'

'Not at the moment,' Jessica said. 'But let's face it, there are still enough megalomaniac politicians about, and I don't just mean on the Isolated worlds. We have to be very careful about revealing the potential of what we have to the rest of the Commonwealth.'

'I don't suppose the SI will be too pleased about this particular accomplishment, either,' Nelson said.

Nigel grinned. He didn't really trust the SI, although he

didn't regard it as malevolent, and Nelson's suspicions verged on paranoia – like any good security operative. 'It doesn't know, yet,' Nigel said. 'And it might well be thankful to us if the Primes are as successful on their next incursion as they were with the Lost23.'

'So would you use it against them, here?' Campbell asked. 'Or is it exclusively to defend ourselves if we have to flee?'

'I will not abandon the Commonwealth without a fight,' Nigel said. 'That would be inhuman. The human race has flaws in abundance, but we don't deserve to die for them.'

'My species, right or wrong,' Jessica said.

Perdita gave her a vexed look. 'We're right. And we're not alone thinking that. The barrier builders obviously thought the same way about the Primes.'

'Unfortunately they had a great deal more technological resources than us,' Campbell said. 'It gave them a much wider range of options. As far as I can see, we only have one. Nigel, are you really going to wait until they invade again before you believe we're justified in using our weapon against them?'

'I'm not nerving myself up,' Nigel said, piqued. 'For a start, we're still only at the design stage. Secondly, the navy will find Hell's Gateway. If that can be wiped out with Douvoir missiles, or more likely Seattle Project quantumbusters, the whole problem will be put back, by years, most likely. That may well open up our options. We might even find the barrier builders, and persuade them to re-establish it.'

'You don't believe that?' Jessica asked.

'No,' Nigel said dryly. 'We created this problem, we have to solve it.'

*

As the meeting closed, Nigel asked Perdita and Nelson to stay behind. He sipped at a hot chocolate which a maidbot delivered to the study. There was just the right amount of whipped cream on top, complemented by a half-melted marshmallow. The taste was perfection. It had been prepared by his chef, he never did like bots cooking food.

'Couple of things,' he told them. 'Perdita, what's the general opinion of myself and the Dynasty? Are we being blamed? After all, we were the main supporters for the *Second Chance* mission.'

'Nothing too heavy in the media,' she said. 'A few minor anchors and commentators have taken some cheap shots, but right now everyone's too mad at the navy for not putting up a better fight. The way you personally dealt with the wormholes above Wessex was a huge positive factor. Your personal rating is quite high. You've got a lot more respect than Doi at the moment, although Kantil is being pretty astute in keeping antagonism directed at the navy.'

'Small mercies,' Nigel said as he chewed on the marshmallow. His neural programs were reviewing and refining data from the Dynasty arrays, pulling everything he could find on Ozzie. 'You did a good job suppressing the Randtown story,' he told Perdita eventually. 'Ozzie would be seriously pissed off if that became public knowledge.' For all his supposedly cuddly Bohemian personality, Ozzie could be very touchy about aspects of his private life.

'The other Dynasties were cooperative enough with the news shows,' she said modestly. 'And the SI helped with a dataeater worm for the messages that did slip into the unisphere.'

'So I see. That's interesting. I know Ozzie likes to think they have a special relationship, but there's more to it, in this case, I think.' He looked at Nelson. 'You don't seem to have much on Mellanie Rescorai.'

'What we have is a reasonable rundown,' Perdita said. 'She was a corporate director's squeeze until he got caught up in a rather sensational bodyloss case. After that, she starred in some soft-porn TSI drama, then moved into reporting. Alessandra

Baron snapped her up, now they've fallen out; gossip in the industry says Alessandra was whoring her round political contacts as a reward for information. Er,' she cleared her throat, amused. 'You might want to ask Campbell if that's true. Anyway ... Mellanie finally refused, and they parted on very bad terms – also the talk of the industry. Michelangelo took her on straight away. Standard media career.'

'Not the timescale,' Nigel said. A picture of Mellanie slipped into his virtual vision, some publicity shot for a TSI called *Murderous Seduction*; she was dressed in lacy gold lingerie that showed off a terrific body. He paused mid-sip. Her chin was rather prominent and her nose squat; but that didn't stop her image from giving him the devil's own smile. Just for a moment he really wanted to access that TSI. 'Your file says her boyfriend is Dudley Bose. Is that right?'

'I think he was the last person Baron sent her to sleep with,' Perdita said. 'They've been together ever since.'

Nigel frowned. He didn't even have to access any files to remember the disastrous welcome home ceremony the navy had set up for Bose and Verbeke. Bose hadn't been the most impressive of people in either of his incarnations, before or after the *Second Chance* flight. 'Strange choice, for her and him.'

'Maybe he made her see the error of her ways?' Perdita suggested. 'They'll settle down and have ten kids together.'

'So she went and signed up with Michelangelo?' Nigel grunted. 'No. There's something wrong with all of this. We don't have a record of her even meeting Ozzie, so there's no reason why she should have access to the asteroid. None of his other exs do. And judging by the reports from Randtown she took on the Primes single handed. That makes me very suspicious.' He gave Nelson a sharp stare. 'Is she another one?'

'Looks like it.'

'Another what?' Perdita asked.

'An observer for the SI,' Nelson said. 'Or spy, depending

what you think about it. We know it isn't quite as passive as it always claims. It has several people like Mellanie prying into areas of human activity it would otherwise be excluded from.'

'I had no idea. What does it want?'

'We don't know,' Nigel said. 'But that's why I keep Cressat out of the unisphere; it gives us a proper refuge. And now we've seen what it did with Ozzie's wormhole I finally feel justified.'

'It wasn't a malign act,' Nelson said. 'It actually saved Mellanie and the other humans in Randtown.'

'I know. That's why I don't worry unduly about it. However, it remains an enigma, and given our current war situation that means we cannot fully trust it.'

'So what do you want to do about Mellanie?' Nelson asked.

Nigel cancelled her image before he gave an inappropriate reply – but she would be a wonderful addition to his harem. 'Discreet observation. And put a good team on it. The SI will be watching out for her.'

'We'll have her covered in an hour.'

'Good. There's something else, which I really hate doing. I cannot believe Ozzie wouldn't get back in touch after the Prime attack. Find out where he is, Nelson. I need to know if he's alive or dead.'

*

It was Donald Bell Homesecure which had the contract for 1800 Briggins; a private company with a Darklake City police authority licence. They were authorized to apprehend and detain anyone believed to be breaking and entering their clients' property, and even permitted to discharge firearms if threatened with lethal force.

The alarm which went off in their control centre reported that the bungalow's door had been opened without the correct code. One of the operators called it up, and saw the owner, Mr Cramley, was listed as currently being out of town.

They dispatched a nearby patrol car and alerted the Olika police precinct that their staff were investigating a suspect incident.

Barely a minute later, the alarm changed to a fire alert, with the bungalow's internal sensors reporting several dangerous hot spots growing. The control centre operator immediately called the fire department. Two tenders were dispatched.

When the Homesecure patrol car pulled up outside 1800 Briggins the officers inside were expecting to deal with a simple break-in with petty vandalism. It wasn't the usual kind of crime in Olika, but then these were troubled times. They slid the visors down on their flexarmour suits, and hurried in through the gate to see if the perpetrators were still on the premises.

Flames were already flowing against the lounge's broad arching windows, casting fans of orange light out across the lawn. The officers went in through the front door, their 10mm semiautomatic pistols already drawn, ready for trouble. When they reached the lounge, they were greeted by a confusing scene. Several items of furniture were blazing fiercely, and the parquet flooring and rugs were beginning to catch fire. Long flames licked up the curving walls to play against the ceiling. On the floor were two clusters of large furry balls. They moved slightly, jostling against each other. The parquet around them was covered in black glistening liquid that bubbled like tar as it steamed from the intense heat.

One of the nostats flattened out slightly, raising its front half sluggishly up towards the two stupefied officers. They stared in horror at the section of corpse the movement revealed. Whoever the victim was, they had been reduced to shreds of gore tangled round bloody bones. The underside bristles of the nostat were soggy with blood.

Both officers froze for a moment, then started shooting. The bloated nostats exploded, splattering blood across the flexarmour suits.

It took a quarter of an hour to bring the fire under control. Firebots worked their way in through the flames, spraying foam as they went. Over a third of the bungalow was wrecked, with the rest suffering considerable smoke damage. The dry-coral structure itself didn't burn, but most of it had been killed by the heat. It meant the owner would have to tear the whole thing down and re-grow it.

Police and Homesecure staff surrounded the bungalow while the flames were brought under control, their weapons active, ready for any nostats which might flee the conflagration. Afterwards, they swept through the ruined rooms in case any of the creatures had survived.

A Darklake City coroner's van arrived at dawn, and the remains of the intruders were bagged up and removed for forensic examination. Scene of Crime staff wandered round, making a recording of the area, and taking a few samples. It seemed like a relatively clear-cut case: an opportunist break-in that went horribly wrong. The police issued a request for Paul Cramley to return for questioning, and filed a preliminary penalty notice for keeping illegal dangerous nonsentient aliens within the city boundary. Mr Cramley did not respond to any calls made to his unisphere address.

At midday the site was handed back to Homesecure. It was part of the contract to guard the property until the owner returned and assumed responsibility.

A lawyer representing Mr Cramley arrived at the Olika police precinct at two o'clock that afternoon and paid the steep fine for violating the dangerous aliens law, and gave an undertaking the crime would not be repeated, paying a five-year bond to guarantee compliance. The lawyer then went on to the Homesecure control centre, and signed off on 1800 Briggins, assuming full responsibility for the property. The guards went home.

*

Mellanie's cab drew up outside the bungalow just after four in the afternoon, responding to a message which Paul had left in her e-butler's hold file. The lock on the gate had already been repaired. It buzzed and opened for her just like before.

She picked her way through the blackened interior of the bungalow, wrinkling her nose up at the smell of burnt plastic and other fumes that still hadn't completely dissipated. Cinders and scorched parquet crunched under her fancy red and gold pumps. It was probably a mistake to wear heels.

The little circular swimming pool at the centre of the bungalow was undisturbed, though several of the patio doors leading out to it were smashed, their metal edges warped by the heat. Leaves floated on water that hadn't been filtered for a month. She looked around curiously. 'Paul?'

The water started gurgling. As she stared at the pool, a whirl appeared at the centre, deepening into a cone. Within a minute the water had emptied away leaving the marble walls dripping. On the side opposite the steps, a doorway irised open.

Mellanie arched her eyebrow at it. 'Neat,' she commented. She took her pumps off, and walked down the slick steps. The door was plyplastic disguised to look like marble; there was a narrow concrete corridor beyond it with polyphoto strips along the ceiling. It angled down quite steeply.

Ten metres in, she turned a sharp corner. The floor levelled out, and the corridor ended at a wide brightly illuminated room. It had the same clean green-tinted walls and floor she associated with an operating theatre; similar cool dry air, too. Several tall stacks of electronic equipment stood in a loose circle around what appeared to be a transparent coffin. Paul Cramley lay in it, floating in a translucent pink liquid. He was naked, his face covered by a conical mask of blank flesh, the apex of which fused into a thick plastic air tube that snaked away into a socket in the top corner of the coffin. Hundreds of filaments no thicker than hair sprouted from the skin along his spine, every few centimetres clusters of them were braided together and plugged into thick bundles of fibre optic cable.

Mellanie walked over to the coffin and peered down. The gooey pink fluid magnified Paul's scrawny ancient body in a way she could have done without; but she could see he was still alive, his chest rising and falling in a slow regular rhythm.

A portal on one of the cabinets lit up with an image of a young man's face. It had a lot of Paul's features. 'Hello, young Mellanie, welcome to my lair.'

She glanced from the body to the portal. 'Cool set-up. Paranoid, but cool.'

'I'm alive, aren't I?' The image smiled.

It was actually quite a handsome face, she thought, which disturbed her more than she wanted to acknowledge. 'Have you been hurt? Is this a rejuvenation tank?'

'Not at all. This is a maximum interface unit. My nervous system is fully wetwired into the large array here in the crypt, every sensation I now feel is actually an artificial impulse. You have a virtual vision; I have virtual smell, taste, temperature, tactile reception, hearing, everything. What my brain interprets as walking, is in reality a directional instruction to access sections of the unisphere and the arrays connected to it. My hands can manipulate programs and files to an amazing degree, and all at accelerant speed.'

'Morty always said you were a complete webhead.'

'How right he was.'

'What happened here last night, Paul?'

'It wasn't a break-in, they were sent to kill me. I used a focused EMP on their inserts, and . . . nature took its course. Not to mention stupidity.'

'Who were they?'

'Good question. Would you like to start trading?'

Mellanie suddenly felt as though she was slipping away from her earlier position of confidence. Her initial judgement of Paul was a woeful underestimation; and all the clues had been there if she'd bothered to think about them. *An impoverished, seedy four-hundred-year old? Come on!* 'You already owe me Alessandra Baron for telling you about the Starflyer.'

'Very well. Baron was receiving and sending a great deal of encrypted traffic across the unisphere.'

'Ah ha!'

'Unfortunately, the protective monitors she uses are excellent. The person using them actually managed to backtrack my own operation. That's quite an achievement. Outside the SI, I only know of a dozen or so webheads in the Commonwealth boasting that kind of ability. This unknown person has a level of skill equal to my own; a development which I find more disturbing than the SI's protection of Paula Myo. Clearly Baron has something very serious to hide.'

'I told you that. And it was probably the Starflyer who tracked you down. I need to know who else is involved.'

'For a start: Marlon Simmonds and Roderick Deakins, the two who broke into my bungalow last night.'

'Big help, Paul, your creepy alien pets took care of them.'

'Show some patience, Mellanie. It is the connection which is interesting. Once I discovered their identity, I accessed their bank accounts. Both of them received a payment of five thousand Oaktier dollars yesterday. The money was transferred from a one-time account opened approximately three hours after Baron became aware of my interest.'

'Damn!'

'Which I backtracked to a corporate account on Earth, in the Denman Manhattan bank.'

Mellanie gave the youthful face in the portal a startled look. 'You backtracked a one-time account? I thought that was impossible.'

'So the banks would like you to believe. It is very difficult, but it can be done. There are certain small flaws in the one-time establishment procedure which can be exploited, that even the Intersolar security services don't know about. I know

329

because I used to know someone who knew someone who was involved with writing the original program. Does the name Vaughan Rescorai mean anything to you.'

'Grandpa!'

'Your great-great-grandfather, I believe.'

'You knew him?' she asked in surprise.

'We mega webheads are a small, close community. Vaughan was a good man.'

'Yes. Yes, he was.'

'He was your way into the SI, wasn't he?'

'Yes,' she admitted.

'Thought so. Your secret's safe with me.'

'Thanks, Paul. What was the company?'

'Bromley, Waterford, and Granku. They are a legal firm—'

'From New York on Earth.'

'You know of them?'

'Yeah. Some of their associates were involved with a scam involving Dudley Bose. I think the Starflyer used them to fund the observation of the Dyson Alpha enclosure.'

'Which resulted in the *Second Chance* flight, and the collapse of the barrier, and ultimately the Lost23. I see. It certainly ties in with your theory. I managed to track some of Baron's communications before her countermeasures forced me to withdraw. Two of them were addressed to a Mr Pomanskie at Bromley, Waterford, and Granku.'

'Hell. He was on the board of the Cox Educational charity.'

'I suspect Pomanskie, or some junior lieutenant, hired Simmonds and Deakins to put a stop to my electronic spying.'

'Yeah, most likely. Can you get into Bromley, Waterford, and Granku's accounts, see what other payments they've been making?'

'I can. I would need an incentive.'

Mellanie sighed, and tipped her head to one side. 'What do you want?'

'Information. Baron hasn't occupied my time exclusively.

There are a number of other interesting things occurring within the Commonwealth right now.'

'Such as?'

'Did you know several "lifeboat" consortiums are being put together?'

'No. What lifeboats?'

'There are some Intersolar Dynasties, Grand Families, and mere ordinary billionaires who are uncertain that our shiny new Commonwealth navy can defeat the Prime aliens. They are quietly channelling funds into very large colonizer starships that have a trans-galactic range. Seventeen such vessels have already been put into production, and at least another twelve are being planned, that I am aware of. Each of the Big15 is hosting at least one of the projects. The lifeboats can hold several tens of thousands of people in suspension, along with all the manufacturing cybernetics necessary to establish an advanced technological human society from scratch on a new world.'

'Those sons of bitches,' Mellanie exclaimed. Even after all the time she'd been exposed to the ultra-rich and their political flunkies, the idea that they'd turn tail and run caught her by surprise. 'They're going to leave us to do their dirty fighting for them?'

'Now then, Mellanie, don't whinge like some Bolshevik class warrior; it's a perfectly sensible precaution. Exactly what I expect from that class. Don't tell me you wouldn't hop on board if you were presented with a berth?'

She scowled down at Paul's coffin. 'Michelangelo offered me a gig reporting on all the people emigrating to the High Angel. They all think it'll fly them clear if the worst happens.'

'High Angel is a good bet, especially if you don't have any real money; although they'll hardly be in charge of their own destiny. Who knows where that machinecreature will take them, or what its ultimate purpose is.'

'So what's all this got to do with me?'

'I want to know which lifeboat stands the highest chance of success.'

'*You're* leaving?'

'Let's just say I'll be buying a ticket. I have a degree of confidence in our military ability, and I've certainly seen what kind of technological atrocities our species' weapons scientists can produce when the need arises. But the Primes do have a phenomenal amount of resources available to use against us. Like I said: sensible precaution.'

Mellanie shook her head, she wasn't sure if it was in dismay or disgust. 'So where do I come in?'

'There is one rather glaring omission in the lifeboat projects. I can't find any information that the Sheldons are building one. And I have looked, *very* hard.'

'Maybe they're not cowards. Ever thought of that?'

'Cowardice is not part of this equation. Nigel Sheldon is not stupid. He will be taking every precaution to safeguard himself and his Dynasty. The amount of financial resources required for such a starship is negligible in macro-economic terms, especially for him. He will be building one, presumably away from curious eyes and inconvenient monitor programs. That means there's only one place it can be, his private world, Cressat. In fact, I expect there will be more than one ship; after all, he does have a very large Dynasty. A fleet would guarantee success, whatever part of the galaxy they wind up in.'

'And you want me to find out? Expose the most secret project of the most powerful man in the Commonwealth?'

'You're an investigative reporter, aren't you? Besides, I imagine the SI will be eager to help in this case.'

Mellanie had to grin at the ironic sense of *déjà vu*. 'Do I get a flying car?' she muttered.

'If the Commonwealth falls, I'd be prepared to take you with me.'

'What?' She'd thought she was immune to further surprise today.

'You're smart, attractive, young, tough, and a survivor. I would get myself rejuvenated on the voyage. It would be an enjoyable marriage, I believe.'

'You're *proposing*?'

'Yes. Has nobody ever proposed to you before, young Mellanie?'

She thought of the hundreds of proposals she was sent every day from her fans or simply people who'd recently accessed a copy of *Murderous Seduction*. 'You're not the first,' she admitted.

'Was that a yes? It is difficult for me to get down on bended knee right now; even if I was out of the interface unit, my arthritis plays up something chronic.'

'Wow, that is *so* romantic.'

'Don't let a four-century age difference prejudice you. I've had wives from every conceivable age group before. You're not expecting Morton to come back from his heroic mission, are you? Think practically, Mellanie. The odds in his favour, aren't good.'

'I know what his odds are. And the answer is still no.' *That young face is handsome, though, and he's got a devilish grin. No!*

'I understand. My offer remains open. And your answer doesn't prejudice our deal. You should never mix business with pleasure.'

'That I do know. But I don't understand how you think you can get on the Sheldon lifeboat. You're not a member of the Dynasty.' She paused. 'Are you?'

The image chuckled. 'Not by birth. But two of my wives were Sheldons, one of them fairly senior. I have five Sheldon children, two of which are direct lineage sixth generation, and they certainly produced a goodly number of descendants.

Funnily enough, that means I've got more chance with the Sheldon lifeboat than any of the other ones. I have leverage there. Once I determine what the score is, I'll be able to make my play. So will you try and get to Cressat for me, and see what's going on there?'

'I can probably go back to Michelangelo with a pitch to investigate a Sheldon lifeboat. That way I won't be completely exposed. How's that?'

'Good enough. But you do realize that Baron will know it was you who put me onto her? Our Oaktier connection is inescapable. You can expect a visit from people like Simmonds and Deakins, if not a great deal worse.'

Mellanie pushed her shoulders back. 'I can take care of myself.'

'I'm sure you can, young Mellanie. I'm curious. Do you actually have a weapon? A gun of some description?'

'No.'

'May I suggest you purchase one. I can give you the name of a reliable underground supplier.'

'I'm not a warrior, Paul. If I need physical protection, I'll hire a security expert.'

'As you wish. But please be careful.'

'Sure.'

*

Mellanie swapped cabs three times before she got back to the motel they were staying at in the Rightbank district. She paid cash each time. The fact that Alessandra's webheads could backtrack Paul was a worrying development. Even with her SI inserts she certainly didn't have his skill; that left her feeling strangely vulnerable.

Their little chalet was on the end of the long row which curved round a grubby swimming pool. Only two others had cars parked outside. It wasn't yet late enough for the motel's main trade to start using the bleak, utilitarian rooms for their professional pay-by-the-hour encounters.

The chalet was made out of cheap composite panels that had bleached under Oaktier's strong sun. Long cracks webbed the edges, exposing the reinforcing boron fibres, which were already fraying. The faded red door creaked loudly when she pushed it open.

All the blinds were shut, permitting only slim blades of late afternoon sunlight to slide through the slits between them. The air conditioning wasn't working. It was stifling inside, with the old panelling groaning as the thermal loads shifted. Dudley was curled up on the bed, staring at the wall.

'We have to move,' Mellanie told him. And how many times had she spoken that phrase since Randtown?

'Why?' Dudley grumped. 'Are you off to see *him* again?'

She didn't ask who he meant by *him*, she wasn't about to play that game. Besides, the memory was too strong: walking out of the rec room into the main barracks. Her blouse had been torn beyond use, she'd had to borrow Morty's dark-purple sports shirt to wear. Both of them grinned like naughty schoolkids as the rest of Cat's Claws hooted and jeered at the state of them.

She gave him a last lingering kiss in the open doorway, with his hands squeezing her buttocks. 'I'll be back soon,' she promised.

That had been two days ago. She wanted to go back, to feel his body pressed up against hers. The wonderful reassurance of old times, when life was simpler and so much easier.

Dudley, of course, had embarked on a two-day sulk at the very notion of an old lover coming back into her life. She hadn't admitted sleeping with Morton, but it was pretty obvious what they'd been up to. She'd still been wearing Morty's shirt when she got back to the chalet.

'No, Dudley, I'm not visiting Morton for a while. We have

to go to Earth. I'm making another pitch to Michelangelo about investigating Dynasty starships.' She'd never come so close to simply walking out on him. It was guilt pure and simple which had made her come back to collect him rather than take a cab straight to the CST planetary station.

Alessandra would find the motel, if she hadn't already. Even cheap thugs like the ones who'd gone after Paul would blow Dudley away, and probably in a very painful fashion. Let alone what would happen if one of the Starflyer's wetwired agents tracked him down . . .

She'd got him into this, and that made him her responsibility.

'Why can't we just get out?' he moaned. 'The two of us. Leave. We'll go back to that resort in the forest, nobody will know about us, nobody will care any more. If we don't interfere with the Starflyer and the navy, then they'll forget all about us. Why don't we do that? Just the two of us.' He rolled over and sat on the edge of the bed. 'Mellanie. We could get married.'

Oh, save me! 'No, Dudley,' she said it fast and firm, before he had any chance to work on the idea. 'Nobody should even be considering things like that, not with everything that's going on. Life's too uncertain right now.'

'Then how about afterwards?'

'Dudley! Stop it.'

He bowed his head petulantly.

'Come on,' she said in a more considerate tone. 'Let's get packed. There are some great hotels in LA. We'll stay in one of them.'

*

It was raining again, a persistent, miserable cold drizzle which smeared windows and turned pavements to slippery ribbons awash with a dismaying amount of litter. Hoshe Finn never ceased to be surprised and depressed by how wet it was in the ancient English capital city. He'd always assumed the old jokes were simple exaggeration. Walking to the office from Charing Cross station as he did every morning, he'd learned better. The UFN environmental commissioners who shared the vast stone government building with Senate Security must have been more successful than they admitted in reversing the global warming trend.

He shook his raincoat out in the lift, and held it at arm's length as he walked down the corridor to his office. Unsurprisingly, Paula was already in, and poring over screens on her desk.

'Morning,' he called out.

She gave a cursory smile, not looking up.

Hoshe hung his coat on the back of his dark wooden door, and settled behind his desk. The number of files awaiting his attention was dispiriting. He'd only left at half past ten last night, and now it was barely eight. The RI had spent the night pulling out anything relevant to the queries he'd made yesterday. He started on the old Directorate report of the Cox Educational charity.

At eleven o'clock he gave the door to Paula's office a perfunctory knock and walked in. 'You might have been right about the educational charity,' he told her.

'What have you got?'

'There are some anomalies between the files I requested.' He sat in front of her desk, and told his e-butler to display the data on the big holographic portal that took up one wall. 'First off I started with the report that the Directorate's Paris office put together after the attempted hack against the charity's account in the Denman Manhattan bank. Your old colleagues were reasonably thorough, and they investigated the charity for any evidence that they were a front. The report's conclusion is that they're not.' He waved a hand against the rows of names and figures which were scrolling down the portal. 'This is the list of all the outgoing donations. It's pretty comprehensive. The Cox supported over a hundred academic projects at one time or another. Recently they've declined considerably, although they're still going. The Gralmond University astronomy department was just one of them. So far, so ordinary; according to the report there is nothing here to be suspicious about.'

'So it looks,' Paula said.

'Okay. That was my starting point, then I began checking references. There are a couple of things that are unusual to start with. Not illegal or suspicious, just odd. The charity's funds come from a single private donation deposited thirty years ago in the Denman account. The sum was two million Earth dollars, which was transferred to the Denman bank from a one-time account. Secondly, there is no named founder. The firm of Bromley, Waterford, and Granku registered the Cox with the New York charity board, and opened an account with one dollar. The two million was transferred in a month later. It has only ever had three commissioners: Mr Seaton, Ms Daltra, and Mr Pomanskie, all of whom are associates of Bromley, Waterford, and Granku. Your original Directorate investigation team never pursued that, which is something of a lapse, if you ask me.'

'There are a lot of rich eccentrics out there giving their money away to strange causes.'

Hoshe raised an eyebrow. 'I'm sure there are. But according to its own records, the Cox doesn't support strange causes. So why keep the benefactor concealed? It's not for tax purposes, by staying anonymous they don't qualify for any tax credit at all.'

'Go on, what's your answer?'

'There isn't an answer. But it made me curious enough to start digging a little deeper. You see all these names? The ones who received money?'

'Yes.'

'The Directorate report doesn't say how much was given.

Also unusual. We know that Dudley Bose received just over one point three million dollars' worth of funding; that doesn't leave much for the rest of them. In total seventy-one and a half thousand dollars were distributed; that's to over a hundred academic projects covering a period of twenty-one years. That financial data was made available to the Directorate investigators. The raw data was still sitting in the Paris array when I requested it. Someone obviously excluded it from the report.'

'Damn,' Paula said. 'Who were they?'

'It was a team research effort. Renne Kempasa, Tarlo, and Jim Nwan all have their names attached. The Cox's original finance file doesn't have a named access log, just the team code. One or more of them did look at it.'

'It can't be all of them,' she said. 'It simply can't.'

'There's something else. Remember what you told me about our old friend Mellanie discovering this?'

'She said Alessandra Baron had tampered with the charity's records.'

'She might be right. I requested a current financial report from the New York charity board. Legally, each registered charity has to file accounts with them every year. According to the filed accounts, the Cox stopped funding the Gralmond University astronomy department right after Bose made his discovery. However, they did continue to make their usual small donations to other academic projects. I started checking with the named recipients. None of them had ever heard of the Cox, let alone received their money. That is until two days after the Prime invasion, then the money transfers became real again. Those accounts are false, they're there to satisfy any casual investigation.'

Paula sat back in her chair, and rubbed a finger against her chin. The faintest smile touched her lips. 'Mellanie was right. Well, how about that?'

'Looks like it. Paula . . . the Starflyer funded the whole Bose observation. That means it knew what Bose would find.'

'Yes.'

'How?'

'Logically, it must have been there; or its species was aware of the Primes and their imprisonment within the force field.'

'Did it let them out?'

'That's the obvious conclusion.'

'So the war was started deliberately. The Guardians were right.'

'Yes.' She grimaced, and gave him a sad smile.

'So what do we do now?'

'Firstly, I inform my political allies. Secondly, we arrest the Cox commissioners on fraud charges. They're obviously Starflyer agents. If we can read their memories, we might gain a better understanding of its network inside the Commonwealth.'

'What about Alessandra Baron? She was the one Mellanie tipped us off about. She has to be a Starflyer agent.'

'It will be difficult to arrest such a public figure without having a good reason, and we can't afford to go public with the knowledge of the Starflyer. Senate Security will make a formal request to Navy Intelligence to put her under covert observation.'

'What? But we know they're compromised.'

'Yes. But it's an excellent opportunity to see what the request kicks loose.'

*

The green and orange priority icon popped into Nigel's virtual vision as he was reading *The House at Pooh Corner* to his youngest children before they went to sleep. He tried to read them a story each night, to be a proper father as he saw the ideal. His children would be dressed for bed by mothers and nannies, then they'd be herded into their playroom for the story. He always read from the classics, using a proper printed book, one you could open to find the place, and shut with finality when the evening's chapter came to an end.

Right now he was halfway through *The House at Pooh Corner*. The seven children at the mansion who were over three years old sat or lay around on cushions and soft mushroom settees, listening contentedly as their daddy read out loud with amateurish intonations and big arm gestures. They smiled, and giggled, and whispered among themselves.

It was his expanded mentality which was calling his attention to the item from the Dynasty's security division. The observation team Nelson had assigned to Mellanie reported her arriving at a bungalow in Darklake city owned by one Paul Cramley. Security simply filed the name. In Nigel's expanded mentality it was immediately cross-referenced with his personal files. That produced the priority notification.

Nigel's primary awareness shifted out of the playroom to focus on the information flowing into his artificial neural network. He accessed the reports on the burglary, and saw what a mess the nostats had made of the would-be burglars. *Typical Paul, never quite guilty himself.*

Cramley had been one of the programming team who'd written the algorithms for the first AIs which CST had used to control their early wormhole gateways. After the AIs evolved themselves into the SI, Paul had chosen to live out of the limelight, involving himself in various activities of dubious legality, a minor league player but with masterclass hacking skills. A list of references rolled down Nigel's virtual vision. He stopped at one of the most recent. Paul had been caught running an illegal search through the City of Paris restricted listings.

Two things were badly wrong with that. Firstly, Paul had searched out Paula Myo's address. Secondly, Paul wouldn't get caught doing something that basic. Yet Myo had produced documented evidence sufficient to have him convicted, fined, and his equipment confiscated. She must have a mega webhead shielding her data. More likely it was the SI.

Nigel wondered who Paul had run the search for. Mellanie? Why would she want to know where Myo lived?

The more he delved into Mellanie, the more curious he became. According to her file, she'd visited Far Away for the Michelangelo show. Was she in contact with the Guardians? Or was she the SI's contact with them? That surely was paranoid speculation. There were so many data points available, but he couldn't connect them. He didn't often delve into security matters, but this was turning into the mother of all exceptions. His fascination was further goaded by her sassy looks.

He retracted his primary awareness from the artificial neural network, and continued reading until he'd finished the section. The children pleaded and wheedled, but he was firm, and promised them there'd be lots more tomorrow. They kissed and hugged him goodnight, and dispersed to their own rooms.

Sitting alone in the playroom with its tidal wave of toys and gloriously gaudy primary-colour decoration, Nigel knew he needed to acquire a lot more information on Mellanie to solve the mystery she was tantalizing him with. He sighed reluctantly and made the call. Normally, anyone he called was surprised and flattered to receive any form of personal communication from the great Nigel Sheldon. Michelangelo simply said: 'What the hell do you want?'

*

The Lucius skyscraper was eighty storeys high, a ponderous conservative tower of grey stone and smoky brown glass. But then it did sit in the middle of Third Avenue; architecture in this part of town was never flamboyant.

The three large cars carrying Paula's Senate Security arrest team wove through Manhattan's mid-morning traffic. As always the antics of the city's yellow cabs drew a small frown on her forehead; whoever programmed their drive arrays did an appalling job. Her own car had to brake sharply several times as they cut in front.

When they arrived at the Lucius, their clearance codes opened the barrier guarding the ramp down into the multi-level underground car park. Two vans carrying the forensic staff and their equipment followed them in.

Up in the lobby, four of the arrest team immediately covered the stairwell exits. Paula led the remaining twelve into the lift. Six of them wore force field skeletons under their ordinary dark suits; she wasn't taking any chances.

The offices of Bromley, Waterford, and Granku took up five floors, from the forty-second to the forty-seventh. Their reception area was dominated by a broad curving desk, where three well-dressed and attractive human secretaries sat receiving calls, giving clients an exclusive personal touch which lesser law firms would use an array for. They were all busy trying to sort out the sudden communication glitch in their array, which Paula had embargoed from the cybersphere as soon as they arrived.

'I would like to see Ms Daltra, Mr Pomanskie, and Mr Seaton, please,' Paula told the senior receptionist.

He gave her and the arrest team a nervous glance. 'I'm sorry, they're not in.'

'Do I need to show you my authority certificate?'

'No, of course not, Ms Myo, I know who you are. But that's the truth. This is the second day they haven't shown up. It's quite a talking point here, the senior partners aren't happy.'

'Check their offices,' she told the arrest team.

The forensic staff were given the all clear to come up. Freeze programs were loaded into the company's entire array network, and their data copied into high-density storage systems for analysis by an RI. All three offices of the missing associates were sealed off, and a detailed examination initiated.

*

Seaton lived closest to the office, an apartment in a luxurious block on Park Avenue, just past East 79th Street. Paula took five of the arrest team with her, using their priority clearance to bounce through traffic, even sidelining the cabs.

As before, she embargoed the building's cybersphere connection. The uniformed doorman let her and the team straight through the grandiose lobby and into the lift.

Mrs Geena Seaton came hurrying into the hallway as soon as the maid announced her notorious visitor. According to Paula's file, the Seatons had been married for eighteen years. Neither of them came from a particularly well-to-do background, though they were clearly making up for that now. Raw ambition was powering them up towards the kind of wealth and professional status that would support their high-life aspirations.

Geena Seaton wore a prim floral-print silk dress, her face and hair perfectly made up, heels clicking on the polished floor, she looked as if she were on her way to some career-making function of her husband's. The perfect supportive wife for an ambitious associate in New York's ruthless corporate society.

When asked about her husband's unexplained absence, she said he was away at a legal convention. Somewhere in Texas, she wasn't sure where, the office would have the address. He'd left with rather short notice, admittedly, but someone else from the firm had dropped out at the last minute. 'Why do you need to know?' she demanded. 'What is this about?' Her delicately mascaraed eyes scanned dismissively across the team standing behind Paula.

'There are some anomalies we believe your husband can help to clarify for us,' Paula said noncommittally. 'Isn't it unusual for him to be out of contact with you for this long?'

'Hardly, I expect he's getting intimate with some female delegate and doesn't want to be disturbed. Really, we have several clauses about non-exclusivity in our partnership contract. It benefits both of us.'

'I see. In that case we will require you to come with us for a medical forensic examination.'

'Impossible, I have a hundred things to do.'

'You will come with us now, either voluntarily or under arrest.'

'That's outrageous.'

'Indeed it is.'

'What are you looking for?'

'I'm not at liberty to disclose that.' Paula wasn't even sure if a neurological scan would be able to identify a Starflyer agent. All she had to go on was Bradley Johansson's propaganda, that the alien somehow mentally enslaved humans. There might be unusual brain wave activity that the forensic neurologists could spot. It was a long shot, but everything else he'd been claiming for the last hundred years was coming uncomfortably true.

'Am I under suspicion? What is this anomaly? Surely it's not that tiresome undeclared payment to the senate aide, again. That was cleared up last year, you know.'

'We can discuss this at our headquarters.'

Geena Seaton glared at Paula. 'I hope you know what you're doing. Legally, I mean. My husband's firm is not to be trifled with. I had to threaten that dreadful reporter girl with an anti-harassment suit yesterday; and I certainly won't hesitate to apply for one against you.'

'What reporter girl?'

'The cheap one who dresses like a hooker the whole time.

I remember she did an invasion report for Alessandra Baron. Mellanie somebody.'

*

The express from EdenBurg delivered Renne back in Paris just after midday. She should have gone back to the office straight away to file her report, but it had been a long frustrating trip. Her duty shift had lasted for nineteen straight hours so far, and as well as being irritable from lack of rest she was also ravenous. The little restaurant she and her colleagues often visited was only three hundred metres from the office, so she got the cab to drop her off there first. Fifteen minutes while she had a coffee and a burger wouldn't make any difference. With any luck, Hogan and Tarlo wouldn't be back from Mars yet. She was still mildly jealous she hadn't been included.

It was cool and dark inside, with every table illuminated by its own cosy triple-wick candle. Fans spun slowly overhead, churning the humid city air around the room, and blending in the cooking smells from the kitchen. There was a bar stretching along the entire back wall, a piece of antique wooden saloon furniture rescued from some ancient left bank café over two hundred years earlier. Its walnut veneer had been scuffed and repolished so many times down the centuries that the surface was almost completely black, with only the odd, even deeper, sable swirl to show the original beautiful grain pattern.

Renne sat at a stool, hung her uniform jacket on a hook just below the counter, and gazed at the long shelves of exotic bottles from all over the Commonwealth. It was the restaurant's boast that every planet was represented.

'A Rantoon green cherry fizz,' she told the barkeeper, knowing he wouldn't have it. She was in that kind of mood.

A minute later she had to smile as he produced the tall frosted glass filled with a jade-coloured liquid that was as sluggish as chilled vodka. 'Salut,' she raised the glass to him. 'Can I get a cheeseburger, with bacon, hold the mayonnaise; and fries not a salad.'

'Certainly, Lieutenant.' He disappeared through a small door and called her order out to the chef. Some comment about the mayonnaise was shouted back in a stream of obscene French.

Renne spread her elbows wide on the bar, and took another sip. It felt wonderfully decadent, drinking something so strong in the middle of the day. She caught a movement in the tarnished mirrors behind the rows of bottles.

'Isn't it a little early for that kind of drink?' Commander Hogan asked.

'Hi, chief,' she said, deliberately not sitting up, or even looking round. 'I figured I can; I'm still in the middle of last night, time-wise.'

Hogan's face puckered into disapproval. He sat next to her, with a grinning Tarlo taking the next stool along.

'You two want to join me?' she asked.

'Mineral water,' Hogan told the barkeeper.

'Beer,' Tarlo said.

'So what was Mars like?'

'Fun,' Tarlo said. 'I had a ball driving the transRover. And it's a weird-looking place, the colours are strange. We saw all the old NASA ships as well, they were falling apart. Sheldon and the admiral were getting all misty-eyed about them.'

'We found the Reynolds ground station,' Hogan said in a reproving voice. 'The forensic team downloaded every program in its arrays, and we impounded the transmitter equipment for analysis.'

'*Impounded*,' Renne just managed not to giggle. She had an image of Hogan imperiously waving a court order at a bunch of angry little green men, furious at the navy marching off with their planet's property.

'Problem?' Hogan asked.

'No, chief.'

'I understand you left the office while we were away,' he continued. 'For most of the time, actually. Did you pick up any leads?'

'Nah! Not one. It was a completely wasted journey. Victor and Bernadette, Isabella's parents, haven't got a clue where she is, and frankly don't show a lot of interest.' The two interviews rankled with her. Warren Yves Halgarth had acted as her escort again; without him she doubted she would even have got in to see Victor. Isabelle's father wasn't exactly pleased to see her; his new job as managing director of the Dynasty's second largest manufacturing bureau was a high-pressure management role. They specialized in force field generators and other high-technology machinery, and as such were one of the thousands of organizations which had suddenly found themselves supplying components to the navy on a crash priority basis. The whole workforce was badly stressed, and it showed. Victor barely knew what his current kids were doing, let alone one who had left home years ago. As for Bernadette, Renne had rarely met anyone who qualified for the title 'idle rich' more than Isabella's mother. The only surprise was that she stayed on EdenBurg, which had little time or space for anyone who wasn't a hundred per cent committed to the work ethic. Warren had explained that Bernadette was one of Rialto's more renowned society hostesses, throwing parties that attracted a good selection of the corporate and financial elite. That didn't leave her much time for keeping in touch with children, she hadn't even known Isabella had disconnected her unisphere address.

'Are there any further leads on Isabella?' Hogan asked.

Rene took another drink of her green cherry fizz, enjoying its cold burn down the back of her throat. 'Not direct ones. I thought I'd try and go through her activities on Daroca before she vanished, see if I can find any clues about where she might go. Then there's Kantil, I could go see her.'

'All right, enough.' Hogan's hand came down on her wrist, preventing her from lifting her glass. 'I don't want you wasting any more time over this girl. You made your long shot and it didn't come off. I don't mind you going out on a limb every now and then, but you have to know when to cut your losses. Understand me, this is that time.'

'There's something wrong about her.'

'Maybe so, and because of that the warrant still stands. The police will find her eventually, and when they do I'll authorize you to handle her interrogation yourself. But until that happens, I want you working on our priority cases.'

Renne stared resentfully at his hand; deep inside the little sensible part of her brain was telling her this wasn't the issue to make a stand on. 'Yeah, okay, chief.'

'And I certainly don't want you bothering people like Christabel Halgarth again. If you want to talk to someone that senior in the Grand Families and Dynasties you clear it with me first. There are a lot of political angles in our investigations; not to mention protocols which should be followed.'

'She was happy to see me.'

'You don't know what she was thinking. I don't want a repeat of that incident, understand?'

'Right.' His hand withdrew, and she lifted her glass to her lips. The barkeeper delivered the water and the beer, putting a small bowl of cashew nuts in front of Hogan.

'Our trip produced some very decent results,' Tarlo said. 'The forensic guys managed to crack the program routines in the Reynolds arrays. We know what was being encrypted now.'

'What?' Renne asked automatically.

'Every scrap of data from meteorological sensors all over the planet.'

With Hogan distracted by Tarlo, Renne's finger rose slowly above the rim of her glass, remaining stiff for a couple of seconds. Tarlo saw it, and pressed down on a grin.

'That makes no sense,' she said. 'Why would the Guardians be interested in Martian weather? I don't understand.'

Tarlo gave her his full bright smile. 'Me neither.'

'But it's the kind of solid result we can run with,' Hogan said, glancing back at Renne. 'I want the two of you working together to find out what you can. Admiral Kime has given this a very high priority.'

'Figures, with his background,' she grunted, and snatched some of the cashews.

'Okay then,' Hogan said. He drained his mineral water in one. 'Have your lunch, Renne, then when you get back to the office this afternoon, I want the two of you heading up this new angle on the Mars investigation. Call in some experts, find out every conceivable application for the meteorological data.'

'Yes, sir.'

Hogan nodded happily, and left them with a wave.

Renne watched him walk out of the restaurant. 'What an asshole.'

'To be expected right now,' Tarlo said with a grin. 'He had some bad news waiting for him when we got back.'

'Oh?'

'Thought that would cheer you up. Get this, Senate Security has officially requested we begin a covert observation of Alessandra Baron.'

'The celeb?'

'None other.'

'Why?'

'The official reason is that they suspect her of involvement with quote "detrimental individuals". How about that for covering a multitude of sins. But guess whose name was on the request file.'

Renne's grin brightened to match Tarlo's. 'The boss.'

'Now do you see why our Great Leader is walking about like he's got a bug up his ass?'

'Yeah. But that's no reason for taking it out on me.'

'You're the easiest and closest target. I warned you about chasing the Halgarth girl. He was never going to like that. And visiting Christabel was a big risk. He was bound to find out.'

'Yeah, yeah. But you've got to admit it's odd. Why should Isabella vanish like this?'

'No,' he said, and held his hands up. 'I refuse to get involved; it's not just hanging on to the uniform, I need the money my job brings in. And I'm making the kind of progress which Hogan approves of.'

'You've got to look at the whole picture, Tarlo.'

'Sure you do. Just remember what happened to the last person who took that view. Oh, hey, here's Vic.'

Renne twisted round on the stool to see Vic Russell walking through the restaurant. He held up a hand. 'Better get a table,' she said.

They chose one along the wall, where a high partition veiled them from casual view. 'Some good news for you,' Vic said, as Renne's burger was delivered. He took a couple of fries from her plate.

'I could do with some,' she admitted. 'It's been a long shitty day.'

'I've backtracked eighteen items from Edmund Li's interception on Boongate.'

Renne paused in examining her burger for signs of mayonnaise. 'Their entire routes?'

'Yep.' Vic's big round face produced a smug expression. 'You think you haven't had much sleep. This has taken me weeks, they were so bloody complicated. It helps that we had the manufacturer and the final smuggling disguise; I could work the route from both ends, fill in all the gaps, and believe me, there were some massive gaps. Each route is a chain of courier companies playing the shell game between warehouses, some of the components were in transit for ten months; and all the finance used to pay the shipment costs came from one-time accounts. There was a hell of a lot of organization went into this operation. We may have underestimated how many Guardians are active inside the Commonwealth. Shipping the items like that had to triple the cost of each piece by the time they reached Far Away. Whatever they're building, it's costing them a fortune.'

Tarlo and Rene exchanged a glance. 'They can afford it,' she said. 'Remember, the Great Wormhole Heist is paying for this.'

'Even so,' Vic insisted. 'This is true paranoia. Effective, mind, I've got to hand them that.'

'It won't be all Guardians,' Tarlo said. 'Elvin will recruit from any unsavoury source; remember that agent Cufflin put us onto.'

'Thanks, Vic,' Renne said. 'This is really good work. We'll get the RI set up to cross-reference with our existing Guardians database, and the team can review the strongest leads for direct follow-ups.'

Vic settled back in his seat, and stole another fistful of fries from Renne's plate. 'You know I was thinking about this when I filed the report. We've already got a ton of information, so many names and smuggling operations, and black market arms deals; it goes back decades.'

'I know,' Tarlo said, swirling beer round his glass. 'Renne and I loaded half of it in there ourselves.'

'All right,' Vic said, suddenly earnest. 'So how come we never managed to nail the bastards?'

'Sore point,' Renne said.

'Because it's all peripheral information,' Tarlo said. 'One day we'll reach critical data mass, and the whole case will fall into place. We're going to make a thousand arrests that day.'

Vic shook his head. 'If you say so. I'll see you back in the office, yes?'

Renne nodded. 'Half an hour.' She eyed her nearly empty glass, wondering if she should order another.

'Give me a second,' Tarlo said to Vic, 'I'll come with you.' He waited until the big man was standing by the door. 'You going to be okay?'

'Sure. I'm just stressed and depressed after EdenBurg, is all. That godamn Isabella. Why doesn't anyone care about her? Not her friends. Not her family. If you vanished, people would wonder, they'd ask questions. I'd want to know what happened to you.'

'That's because you're a good person.' He hesitated. 'Look, Hogan will be watching you, but I can pursue Isabella on the quiet if you'd like.'

'I don't know.' She rubbed a hand irritably over her brow. 'There are no quiet inquiries left. I either turn it into a big deal, or drop it completely. Damn, you don't suppose Hogan could be right, do you?'

Tarlo laughed. 'Never. See you later? I want to tell you all about Mars. It really was a strange place.'

'Yeah, I'll be in soon.'

He patted her shoulder and left.

Renne took another bite out of her burger, and munched slowly. Maybe she had become obsessive about Isabella. It wasn't a crime to run off and join the Exodus. There were hundreds of thousands of people on each of the worlds close to the Lost23 who'd left home with no explanation, most of them scuttling off to worlds on the other side of the Commonwealth. Silvergalde was also a popular destination, and if Isabella had gone there she really would be out of any electronic contact.

'You shouldn't discuss confidential information in a public place,' a woman's voice said. 'Office procedure has certainly slipped recently.'

Renne stood up and looked over the partition at the neighbouring table. Paula Myo sat there, nursing a glass of orange juice.

'Jesus, boss!'

'Can I join you?'

Renne grinned, and gestured to the empty seats.

'Sounds like you're having a bad day,' Paula said as she settled in the chair Vic had vacated.

'I can handle it. I just keep asking myself what you would do.'

'That's very flattering. So how is it going at the office?'

Renne took another bite from the burger, giving Paula a calculating glance. Was the boss deliberately testing her to see how much she'd divulge? 'You should know, all our data is available to Senate Security.'

'I wasn't referring to the data from your investigations, I'm more interested to hear how Hogan is doing.'

'Coping, barely. He isn't you.'

'For which I suspect he and I are both grateful. How did he take the request to spy on Alessandra Baron?'

'Didn't you hear? Tarlo says badly. But I think that's more to do with the fact you requested it than the manpower scheduling. What do you think Baron has done?'

'She's a Starflyer agent.'

Renne stared at her old boss. 'Are you serious? You really think it exists?'

'Yes.'

'Hell, boss. What proof have you got?'

'The behaviour of several people, including Baron. She's part of a network of agents who are acting against the human interest. We're compiling information on them which should lead to their arrest.'

'Shit, you do mean it, don't you?'

'Yes.'

'So why tell me?'

'I'd like to know why you have a warrant out for Isabella Halgarth.'

'The shotgun, the one which claimed Doi was a Starflyer

agent. There was something wrong about it.' She explained her misgivings about the whole set up; and the way Isabella had subsequently dropped out of sight.

'Interesting,' Paula said. 'Especially her connection with Kantil. We are looking for any Starflyer connection among the Commonwealth political elite. She might well be the link.'

'Isabella as a Starflyer agent? That's hard to swallow.'

'You said yourself there's something wrong about her. That shotgun did a lot of damage to the Guardians' credibility. It is logical to assume the Starflyer would use disinformation of that nature to damage its one true opponent. Her involvement would confirm her connection to its network.'

'But she's only twenty-one, and she was going out with Kantil two years ago. How would she get mixed up in something like that so young? She spent most of her early life on Solidade. You can't get more sheltered and protected than that.'

'I don't know. Is there any chance you could research her background more thoroughly?'

Renne blew her cheeks out as she sighed. 'That won't make me terribly popular with Hogan.'

'Yes, I heard. Your choice, of course.'

'I'll do what I can, boss.'

'Thank you.'

*

Paula stayed at the table, finishing her drink as Renne walked out. Her virtual hand touched Hoshe's icon. 'She's leaving now.'

'Yeah, we've got her. The team's boxing her. Monitor programs for her unisphere access are loaded and running.'

'All right. Let's see what we turn up.'

'Do you think it's her?'

'I hope it isn't, but who knows? If it is, the information

I've just given her should goad her into making contact with someone in the Starflyer network.'

*

Although it wasn't far from New York to the Tulip Mansion, Justine kept her own apartment on Park Avenue. It was a nice base in town for those times she wanted to be on her own, or throw a small soirée for close personal friends and important contacts; it was also somewhere private for affairs she preferred to keep quiet about. The building was two centuries old, a massive Art-Deco-Gothic block favoured by both the urban chic and serious old money. Her apartment occupied half of the fortieth floor, which gave her a nice view out over the park from her balcony. Tall marble gargoyles lined the stone balustrade, framing the city's magnificent ma-hon tree as it glittered rose-gold in the late evening sunlight. She never tired of the unique sight of the biochemical anomaly. It was always a shame CST had closed its homeworld off, she felt. Now there would never be any more transplanted to the Commonwealth worlds.

The maid had prepared a light supper of poached salmon and salad. Justine ate it cautiously before her guest was due. Sure enough, twenty minutes after she finished she had to rush to the bathroom, heaving up most of it.

'I'd forgotten this part,' she said to herself as she wiped her mouth with a tissue. It would have to be cold still mineral water and plain crackers when the meeting was over.

Her e-butler told her Paula Myo was on her way up from the lobby. She took a bottle of mouthwash from the medicine cabinet, and swilled it round. The horrible bitter acid taste was replaced by a clinical peppermint. It wasn't much better.

'Stop feeling so damn sorry for yourself,' Justine told her reflection in the mirror. She splashed some cold water on her face, which wasn't looking so hot these days. Ah well, it wasn't as if she was on the prowl for lovers right now. Her virtual hand touched her father's icon. 'She's here.'

'I'm on my way down,' Gore said; he had the apartment above.

As always, Paula Myo was dressed impeccably, in a blue suit that was obviously tailored in Paris. There was a stern expression on her dainty face as she looked around the big lounge with its exquisite antique furniture. 'I was in another Park Avenue apartment yesterday, about half a mile away from here,' she said. 'I thought that was ostentatious, but it would fit in this room and still rattle round.'

'Some people are aspirant,' Justine said. 'Some of us obtained a long time ago.'

'Materialism never really appealed to me.'

'Is that part of your Huxley's Haven heritage?' Justine had almost said: *Hive heritage.*

'I don't think so.'

'Course it is,' Gore Burnelli said. He marched in through the lounge door, dressed in a mauve polo sweater and black jeans. The overhead chandeliers reflected a burnished amber light off his golden skin. 'Materialism would distract you from your obsession, wouldn't it, Investigator? The Foundation wouldn't want that in their police force; I suppose it makes you immune to bribes too.'

'Father!'

'What? Everyone appreciates honesty, especially a police-woman.'

Justine was too weary to remonstrate with him. She could feel her stomach churning again, and hurriedly told her e-butler to get her an antacid. It acknowledged the request, and told her Gore's subsidiary personality programs were filling the apartment arrays, moving with him like attentive ghosts.

'Psychoneural profiling isn't that precise,' Paula said. She didn't seem bothered by Gore's bluntness. 'And I've seen too much poverty to believe in trickle-down economics. It doesn't work. Disparity is injustice. And poverty breeds a lot of crime.'

Gore shrugged. 'If you want something, work for it.'

'Like you did to start the Family fortune,' Justine muttered darkly.

'I do work for what I want,' Paula said. 'That simply doesn't translate into the acquisition of physical items. That is my mindset, and I won't be changing it.'

Gore's gold lips split to produce a caricature of a grin. 'Good for you, Investigator.'

'Can we get started?' Justine said. The big windows leading out to the balcony turned opaque and shimmered with a grey curtain of energy, sealing the room. She sat in one of the big couches as a maidbot trundled over carrying her a glass filled with a milky liquid. Gore came and sat beside her; while Paula chose a high-backed chair, facing the two Burnellis.

'I'll start with my bad news,' Justine said. 'I haven't been able to confirm who told Thompson about Nigel Sheldon blocking the examination of cargo to Far Away.'

'Damn it, girl,' Gore complained. 'What's wrong?'

'I'm not the most popular senator in the Commonwealth right now. All that goodwill I was getting at the start because of Thompson's death has just about evaporated. Columbia and the Halgarths are building themselves a lot of new alliances, and of course Doi's always keen to receive their votes. Those of us who ask awkward questions are gradually being frozen out.'

'Then burn your way back in. Come on, this should be child's play to you.'

'I'm up against some masterclass opposition here, *actually*,' she snapped back. 'Not knowing if I can trust the Sheldons is proving to be a real problem, it's leaving me very isolated in several committees.'

'You'll pull through,' Gore said. 'I can always depend on you. That's why I'm so proud of you.'

Justine blinked in surprise. That wasn't like him at all.

'The navy has made some progress on the Mars data,' Paula said. 'Not that it's particularly helpful. I asked the admiral to pursue the matter, and he took that to a level I never expected.'

'I heard they actually went there,' Gore said.

'Nigel Sheldon made a CST wormhole available,' Paula confirmed. 'Which is interesting in itself. Whose interest is he considering, pursuing this lead against the Guardians? In any case, the navy team managed to find out what all the data was that'd been encrypted. It's purely meteorological.'

'Did they find a key?' Justine asked.

'Unfortunately not. The encryption writing software was a use-expire program. There's nothing left of it. Forensic are running a quantum scan of the hardware, but it's unlikely they'll be able to pick out a remnant. The actual data remains beyond us unless the Guardians choose to make the key available.'

'So even if we decrypted it, we wouldn't know what they wanted it for.'

'I'm afraid not, Senator.'

'This is such bullshit,' Gore said. 'If you ask me, the Guardians have just notched up another smart hit against the navy. All that stealing meteorological sensor crap is a clever piece of misdirection. There's got to be something else hidden on Mars. Some transmission from a secret base or device, maybe a weapon. If they've been landing von Neumann cybernetics on the surface, who knows what they could have built by now.'

'The research packages which robot ships dropped on Mars are well documented,' Paula said. 'There is no surplus mass unaccounted for; not in twenty years. And the navy team didn't see anything unusual at Arabia Terra.'

'Four computer geeks and two characters from ancient history on a nostalgia trip don't make what I call a decent exploration team. There could have been a missile silo right under their feet and they'd never have known.'

'Or even a hollowed-out volcano,' Justine muttered.

'I don't believe they would have been able to smuggle anything like a cybernetic factory onto the surface,' Paula said levelly. 'We know the Guardians simply purchase whatever equipment they want.'

'Weather!' Gore grunted in disgust.

Justine covered her smile by drinking more of the antacid.

'I believe Mars is something we will have to put aside for the moment,' Paula said. 'One of my ex-colleagues in the Paris office may have uncovered another Starflyer agent: Isabella Helena Halgarth.'

'Shit!' Gore said.

Justine took a second to place the name, pleased she didn't have to use her e-butler to reference it for her. 'Damn, do you think that's their link to the Presidency?'

Gore held up a hand. She could see her own distorted reflection in his palm. 'Wait,' he said. 'I'm analysing this. I always fucking knew there was something wrong about that weekend we hosted in Sorbonne Wood. Let's see. Patricia was always willing to accommodate every party; at the time I thought she was doing it to secure endorsement for Doi. But take a look at the weekend from the Starflyer's perspective, assume it wanted a human navy for its war between us and the Primes. Yes, goddamn it. Think of the true sticking points we faced, either Isabella or Patricia was there to oil things along every time. Isabella even slept with Ramon DB.'

'He slept with her?' Justine couldn't help the indignation. She pursed her lips, vexed with herself for caring. After all, they hadn't been married for eighty years. Still . . . he'd done it under her roof, technically.

'It was even Ramon's parallel development idea which helped the agency move all the starship production facilities to the High Angel with the minimum of fuss,' Gore said.

'Which he produced on Sunday morning,' Justine said coldly. 'I suppose we'll never know who actually came up with the idea.'

'I assumed it was Patricia, who relayed it through Isabella,' Gore said. 'It's the kind of compromise a Presidential aide could come up with in an instant. Now, though, we'll never know.'

'You could ask him,' Paula said.

Justine finished off the last of her antacid drink, which might have accounted for the little grimace of distaste. 'Yes, I could. I'm not sure he'd give me an answer.'

'He will,' Gore said. 'You know he will.'

'Maybe, but he'd want to know why.'

'Is he strong enough to join us?' Gore asked. 'We need allies.'

'He'd need some very strong proof,' Justine said carefully. 'I'm not sure that what we've got right now is enough.'

'What more can we give him?' Gore asked. 'For Christ's sake, Ramon isn't stupid.'

'I'm not about to tell him we suspect Nigel Sheldon of being behind the greatest anti-human conspiracy there's ever been. He'd shoot us down in flames.'

'You've got to find a way to get to him.'

'I'll try.' She thought of how she'd have done that in the old days. A hotel in Paris maybe, a weekend spent together, restaurants, fine wines, coffee on the left bank, talking, arguing, laughing, theatre in the evening, long passionate nights in bed. How she missed those simple times now.

'This still doesn't tell us which of them was pulling the strings, Patricia or Isabella,' Gore said. 'And were they working in conjunction with the Sheldons?'

'We don't know Nigel is a part of this,' Justine said. 'Not yet.' She told her e-butler to run a full background check on Isabella and Patricia.

'It would be logical for Isabella to be a courier to the

Starflyer network,' Paula said. 'Kantil would be working deep cover, taking her time to infiltrate the Commonwealth political structure. The unisphere shows are full of innuendo that Doi is heavily dependent on her advisers and opinion polls.'

'Which is why I was suspicious about her original backing for the Starflight agency,' Gore said. 'Spending that much tax money was never going to be a votewinner before the barrier came down. She took a very uncharacteristic risk backing the formation. Something pushed her into doing that.'

'I don't have any grounds to arrest Kantil and subject her to a forensic neurological examination,' Paula said. 'We ran similar appraisals on suspects yesterday, which came to nothing.'

Justine listened to them discussing options while the data on Patricia and Isabella ran across her virtual vision. Patricia's background was well documented, and verified by investigative reporters eager to find the smallest discrepancy in her official history and so prise open a covered-up scandal. Less information was available on Isabella, primarily because of her youth, and the fact she'd spent a lot of her life on Solidade. The Halgarths' private world didn't have public records. Justine started to review associated files which the e-butler's cross-reference function had thrown up.

'Wait a minute,' Justine said. 'Isabella's father, Victor; fifteen years ago he was appointed director of the *Marie Celeste* Research Institute on Far Away. He ran it for a two-year term before moving back to EdenBurg, where he secured a vice-presidency in a Halgarth Dynasty physics laboratory.'

'That's how it got to her,' Paula said with satisfaction. 'She was just a child. I didn't understand how anyone that young could be involved.' She frowned. 'Neither did Renne.'

'If Isabella is a Starflyer agent, then her parents have to be as well,' Gore said.

'Yes,' Paula said. 'We must watch what they're doing.

However, there is a limit to how many observation operations Senate Security can mount. It is not a huge organization.'

'Our Family has a decent-sized security team,' Gore said. 'Be good for them to get their asses out of the office and do some field work for a change. I'll organize something.'

'I appreciate that,' Paula said. 'But I can arrange for the Halgarths to be watched. I have a well-placed friend in the Dynasty. There is something else I need you to help me with. Hoshe has established that Bose's original astronomical observation was financed by the Starflyer. Someone in my old Directorate's Paris office covered up the information when I was investigating him. I'm running several entrapment operations on the personnel to find out which one. But I'd like a proper financial analysis of Bromley, Waterford, and Granku. That could result in some important leads.'

'I know that company,' Gore said. 'Legal firm here in town.'

'That is correct. Three of their employees have disappeared, in a similar fashion to Isabella. They set up the Cox Educational charity, which had its account in the Denman Manhattan bank. It would take Senate Security a while to organize a proper forensic accounting review of their records. And I'm sure you're better able to perform the same function.'

'I'll rip that goddamn company apart for you,' Gore said. 'If they've spent a single dime buying the Starflyer a drink I'll find it.'

*

The good ship *Defender* was three weeks into her deep space scouting mission, and her captain was as bored as the rest of his crew. Probably more so, Oscar reflected; while everyone else went off duty they tended to access TSI dramas, immersing themselves in the racier aspects of Commonwealth culture, so at least they got a break from the tedium of life onboard.

He on the other hand spent his rec hours going through the logs from the *Second Chance*.

It was a waste of time. He knew it was a waste of time. There was no enemy alien spy on board. The reason – *the only reason* – he kept on going day after day reviewing the logs was because of Bose and Verbeke. He still didn't understand what had happened to them, nor why. Something was desperately wrong with the whole Watchtower section of the mission. There was no way Bose and Verbeke could have dropped out of contact through simple electronic failure. Their comrelays were utterly reliable. The starship's sensors and the contact teams must have missed something over there: some Prime device that was still active, an unstable part of the rocky fragment which collapsed on the two explorers. Except . . . they were in freefall, there was no gravity to collapse anything; and some relic of Bose had warned the *Conway*. Oscar didn't have a clue what he was looking for, he just kept on looking.

He'd accessed a dozen TSIs recorded by different contact team members as they fumbled and slid along the eerie curving passages that threaded through the interior of the Watchtower. None of the recordings had revealed anything new. The Prime structure was as dead as any Egyptian pharaoh's tomb. Out of all the physical samples they'd brought back, the crumbling structural material and radiation-saturated fragments of equipment, none of it had helped further their understanding of the Watchtower mechanism's true nature. It was all too fragile, too old, for any useful analysis to be carried out. The navy still wasn't sure what the installation used to be a part of, though the best guess was some kind of mineral-processing facility. No part of it the contact teams had explored had machinery that was even close to working condition. The tunnel which Bose and Verbeke had ventured down was no different. And it was Oscar who had given them that initial authorization to proceed deeper, to find out what was there. He'd been encouraging, he remembered. Often during the interminable play-backs he'd hear the enthusiasm in his own voice.

Time after time he went through recordings which corre-sponded to the time they dropped out of communication. Bridge logs, engineering logs, power logs, a dozen other on-board datastreams, flight logs from the shuttles that were ferrying the contact teams between the starship and the rock. Worst of all were the detailed spacesuit recordings from Mac and Frances Rawlins as they made their frantic, useless rescue bid. They'd gone a long way down the curving tunnel-corridor which had swallowed Bose and Verbeke. Nothing in those decaying aluminium walls gave any hint of danger lurking ahead.

Two nights ago, after his bridge duty was over, Oscar had decided on a slightly different approach to the analysis. He was running every sensor recording he had of the Watchtower rock, and compositing them into a specific overall picture. He wanted to run comparisons between the rock and its wreckage from the time they'd encountered it right through the mission until the time they left. The shape, thermal profile, electro-magnetic spectrum, spectrographic composition; each building up to a comprehensive multi-textural snapshot every two seconds. When they were all assembled, the *Defender*'s RI could run a detailed comparison program between all of them, searching for the slightest change.

His cabin's holographic portal was in projection mode, filling the small area with the image from the shuttle cameras, playing back Mac's first exploration flight. Oscar sucked on an orange juice drink bag as the familiar dialogue between himself and Mac and the shuttle pilot repeated itself yet again. Sensor data from the shuttle was being compiled and added to the starship's own sensor log record to enhance the snapshots, producing a tighter resolution. He watched as the hangar doors parted, and the ungainly little craft rose off its cradle, belching sparkly cold gas from its reaction control thrusters. The huge bulk of the *Second Chance* twisted slowly and silently round his cabin, the translucent projection allowing him to see the bulkheads through its main cylindrical superstructure and the giant life-support ring. Oscar felt a pang of nostalgic regret at seeing the starship again. There would never be another one like it. The *Defender* was sleek and powerful in comparison, but it lacked the grandeur of its ancestor. Everyone working at the Anshun complex had devoted themselves to that first starship, putting in ridiculous hours, ignoring their family and social lives; its assembly had been an act of love. The atmosphere they'd shared back then was lost as well, the naive excited optimism of launching a grand exploration into the unknown. They'd been full of hope in those days as the adventure loomed close. Simpler, easier times.

The shuttle cleared the life-support ring, and its main engines fired, carrying it towards the Watchtower. Dyson Alpha slipped up across his cabin bulkheads, a distant lightpoint as bright as Venus appeared in Earth's night sky. The rest of the alien starfield flowed around it. Oscar peered at the image, picking out the dull speck ahead of the shuttle. He'd seen it so many times in so many spectrums that he knew the Watchtower's exact position against the unfamiliar constellations.

His lips sucked down some air. The bag of orange juice was empty. He reached out to push it into the mouth of the refuse tube at the side of the washroom cubical. Stopped in mid-movement. Frowned. Stared at the image of the *Second Chance*.

'Freeze image,' he told his e-butler. The recording halted immediately. 'Hold this viewpoint, and increase magnification by three, focus centre on the *Second Chance*.' The starship's grey-silver structure swelled rapidly, covering the washroom cubicle and his sleep pouch. Oscar forgot to breathe. 'Son of a *bitch*.' He stared and stared at the primary sensor array, shock like icy electricity shooting along his spine. The starship's main communication dish was extended, pointing towards the tiny star behind him.

The *Defender*'s alarm sounded.

'Captain,' the executive officer called. 'Sir, you've got to get up to the bridge right now. We think we've found the other end of Hell's Gateway. The hysradar has picked it up in a star system three light-years away.'

6

Morton was still smiling when his bubble dropped out of the wormhole, fifteen metres above the Highmarsh Valley in the Dau'sing Mountain range. It had been two days since Mellanie's last visit at the barracks. She'd cut it fine, arriving just hours before Kingsville was closed off and everyone received their final clearance orders. It had been one hell of a visit, the two of them screwing each other senseless in the little rec room, like teenagers who'd unexpectedly found their parents out one afternoon. Hence the long-lasting smile.

That memory of the two of them together was the last one to be loaded into his secure store. So if, as likely, his body was blown to shit on this mission, that would be the strongest memory in his brain when he was re-lifed. Now that was a *stylish* way to emerge back into reality.

His bubble was a translucent grey-blue sphere of plyplastic, three metres in diameter, its surface stealthed against every known sensor type used by the Primes. He was suspended at the centre by the transparent impact gel which filled the interior. During training it had seemed like a sensible way to arrive on a hostile planet light-years behind enemy lines. They were neat little machines: tough, highly mobile, and reasonably armed. Actually riding one down as it exhibited all the aerodynamics of a granite boulder pulled the smile off his face. Fear hit him for the first time, making his heart pound and his stomach quake. Life didn't get any more extreme than this.

The rest of Cat's Claws had come through the wormhole okay, their bubbles very hard to see in the visual spectrum as they all fell towards the ground. It was only their high-UV IFF beacons which gave him their locations. The three combat aerobots which had led the deployment zoomed away across the grungy landscape, disgorging chaff and decoy drones.

Up above them, the wormhole closed. It had been open for about ten seconds, just long enough to shoot them out. Back on Wessex, the gateway had been surrounded by a giant mechanical loading system, resembling a scaled-up version of an artillery gun magazine, with over a thousand bubbles sitting on conveyor racks ready for the assault. Parallel racks carrying wedge-shaped combat aerobots moved forward smoothly beside them; their separate ranks merging at the gateway amid the weird cluster of lithe malmetal tentacles which was the actual launch delivery mechanism.

Cat's Claws had joined several hundred other troops lined up on one of five gantry ledges as the bubbles trundled past in stop-start sequences. Along with the rest of them, Morton had finally been given the activation codes for the aggressor systems wetwired into his body. Now the squad were all making nervous, jokey comments about those systems not firing outwards, war tourism, which body parts you protected above all else, alien rights lawyers suing them, and other stupid stuff. Trying to bull out the wait.

After a surprisingly short time Cat's Claws was at the head of the line. Morton pulled his armour suit helmet down, checked his breathing circuit integrity, and slithered through the slit in the side of his bubble. As soon as the straps closed around him, the gel was pumped in under pressure. His e-butler integrated itself with the bubble's array, confirming internal systems functionality. By then he was already ten metres down the conveyor rack.

The Elan strategic assault display flashed up across his virtual vision. He saw batches of wormholes opening a hundred kilometres above the planetary surface. They would remain in place for several seconds, disgorging a phenomenal quantity of munitions: missiles, ground-attack warheads, electronic warfare pods, decoy vehicles, beam-weapon platforms. It was all covering fire, a diversion while other, smaller wormholes opened just above the surface, deploying squads all around the fringes of Prime installations and bases. The Primes were fighting back, sending up flyers and big ships, their beam weapons punching through the scuzzy continent-wide clouds to intercept the rain of lethal machines as they sank down through the ionosphere. There were also flyers scouring the ground as the troop wormholes flipped in and out of existence. But electronic warfare aerobots were causing havoc with the Prime communications and sensors, hampering the flyers. Initial reports indicated that the landings were succeeding, by which the navy meant beachhead casualties were under thirty per cent.

Morton hit the ground. The impact wasn't as bad as any of the bonebuster hits they'd given him in training. His bubble bounced twice, the plyplastic flexing and bending to dissipate as much of the shock as it could; pressure waves moved sluggishly through the gel to squish lightly up against him. On the third landing, it sagged like a punctured balloon and stayed on the ground. 'Down,' he told the rest of Cat's Claws.

According to the inertial navigation read out, he was within half a kilometre of his predicted landing coordinate. The land immediately around him was flat, a field which had been seeded a long time before in springtime and had run rampant before starting to decay. Some kind of bean crop, judging by the yellow-green mush pressing against the lower section of his bubble. Abrupt climate change hadn't helped this land's recent delicate conversion to cultivation. It was raining in the Highmarsh, a thick blanket of dark turbulent cloud was stretched across the roof of the valley, flowing slowly from east to west. It produced a constant downpour of grey water which had overwhelmed the drainage dykes and beaten the surviving crops into a straggly mat of insipid green stalks lying flat against the sodden soil. Tall liipoplar trees which had been planted in long lines up and down the valley had been battered by the nuclear blast and subsequent storms. Few of them were still intact. The majority had snapped, to crash over the roads they once marked.

Morton checked round, and found the mountain he was supposed to be heading for, three kilometres away. The bubble started to stiffen up again, reverting to its standard spherical configuration. His virtual hands zipped over a sequence of control icons, and the single broad caterpillar track running round the compact machine's vertical equator began to spin up. The bubble began its stabilized counter spin, keeping him perfectly level. Dips and lumps in the ground jounced him from side to side, but in the main it was a smooth ride, the gel acting as the ultimate suspension system.

External sensors showed Morton water spraying out from either side of the track. A rigid trail of squashed muddy plants lay behind him. 'Goddamn!'

The bubble's chromometic skin was doing a wonderful job diffusing the mouldy-green colour of the crop around the entire exterior. Any eye or visual sensor looking down would just see a hazy patch just the same colour as the rest of the field; but that crushed track and little wake of water was a dead giveaway.

'We need to get on the farm roads,' he told the others. 'This wet ground is painting us as big fat targets.' Pre-invasion map images flipped up in his virtual vision, and he steered the bubble to the right, his body tilting over as if he was riding a bike. The bubble changed direction, heading for the top corner of the field.

'Incoming,' Doc Roberts warned. 'Four flyers.'

Morton saw the symbols creep into his virtual vision. They'd come into the valley at the western end, following the old highway route around Blackwater Crag.

Aerobots curved round to meet them head on. Maser beams slashed between the two opposing formations, etching themselves in lines of steam through the downpour. Force fields flared brightly as they deflected the energy strikes. The aerobots fired salvoes of missiles, their fiery contrails spluttering in the rain. Powerful ion bolts ripped through the air like slow-motion lightning, casting stark shadows for kilometres across the ground below.

Morton reached the rough farm track bordering the field. It was awash with muddy water that was spilling over the banks of the dyke, but only a few centimetres thick. He throttled up the bubble's track. A limp fantail of water squirted up behind him as his speed reached an easy eighty kph.

Tactical decision: that the aliens in their flyers would be a little too preoccupied to spot a ripple in the mud right now.

The aerobots were always going to lose. They were outnumbered from the start. The flyers were heavier and slower, but their beam weapons had a much higher power level. Manoeuvrability and superior tactical ability gave the first two kills to the aerobots and their host of submunitions, but eventually brute force won out.

After seven minutes of furious combat the remaining two flyers thundered over the area where the wormhole had opened. One of the stubby cylinders was trailing a thin brown vapour trail from a gash on its side, but its straining engines managed to keep it airborne. They began to spiral out, sensors sweeping the ground.

Ten kilometres away, and already three hundred metres above the valley floor in the rugged folds of the foothills, Morton watched the aliens circling round and round. His bubble was stationary, resting at the bottom of a narrow gulley cut out of the soil by an earlier storm spring. Mud and stones were pressed against the base, their mottled shading replicated all around him. A web of thermal shunt fibres completed the disguise, giving the bubble's chromometic skin the same temperature as the land it rested on.

'Bugger,' Rob Tannie said. 'Eight more of the bastards.'

The new flyers raced up the Highmarsh Valley to join the first two in the search for any surviving human trespasser. Their flight paths brought them closer and closer to the foothills.

'Don't they have anything else to do?' Parker complained.

'Guess not,' Morton said.

Cat's Claws waited as the flyers swooped low overhead; their bubbles inert, operating on low power mode, hidden among the abundant secluded folds and hollows provided by the rugged landscape. Morton could hear the bass thrumming of the engines through the bubble's gel. They must be very loud out in the open.

One passed about fifty metres away. His bubble's passive sensors scanned the layout. There wasn't much to add to the database already in his array. The Primes didn't seem to vary their machines.

'Let's go, boys,' Cat said as the flyers loitered at the far end of the valley.

Morton was slightly surprised she was still with them, not to mention sticking to the deployment plan. He'd half expected her to take off on her own as soon as they were down. Under his guidance, the bubble's plyplastic skin rippled, squeezing itself up out of the gulley with a fast lurch. The caterpillar track held it steady on the soaking sulphur-yellow boltgrass that covered the slope. There was only a kilometre or so of desolate ground to cover before the unruly cloud base. They'd be a lot safer inside the thick, cool vapour.

The strategic assault display was empty now. Elan's deployment was complete. The wormholes above the planet had all closed, shutting down the temporary communication feeds.

Morton switched to a local display, checking the position of the other bubbles against his own. Unsurprisingly, Cat was already above cloud level, waiting for the rest of them. He fed power to the tread, and began his ascent.

*

The navy had been concerned that the snow which lay on the Dau'sing peaks all year round would leave tracks which the Primes could follow. For that reason the path pre-loaded into the bubble's navigation array skirted the very high ground, taking Morton on a long winding route through tough passes and clinging to contour lines along alarmingly steep slopes. They need not have worried. The grey clouds were several degrees warmer and a lot muckier than the usual weather fronts besieging the mountains at the onset of the southern continent's winter. The snowline had undergone a long retreat upwards, exposing vast tracts of slatey shingle which hadn't seen daylight for millennia.

Morton drove through the dark, murky fog for a couple of hours. He had to move slowly, visibility was down to thirty metres at best, and that was using the passive sensors on full resolution. All he saw was kilometre after kilometre of the same slippery, muddy shingle crunching below the translucent track. No other features emerged out of the fog. The angle of the slope changed, but that was it for variety.

They were travelling in a very loose convoy, with Cat out in front. At least he assumed she was still in front; he hadn't spotted her beacon for over an hour and a half. She'd gone off at a speed he wasn't going to try and match. Behind him, Doc Roberts was keeping a sensible kilometre separation distance. His beacon moved in and out of acquisition depending on the shape of the terrain.

Morton rounded a sharp vertical ridge of rock, and the Cat's beacon was shining three hundred metres ahead.

'Where've you been, boys?'

'Taking care,' Morton said. 'We're not proving anything to each other here.'

'Touchy!'

He accelerated down the shallow incline to her bubble. She had stopped at the low point of a shallow saddle between a couple of peaks on the edge of the Regents range, about fifteen kilometres from where the navy detector station had been built. It was walled in on both sides by cliffs of sheer rock rising to vanish into the turbid clouds which occluded the peaks. The ground between them was a stratum of crumbling stones, scattered with fresh unsteady piles that had fallen from on high when the mountains were shaken by the nuclear blast.

Morton drove his bubble on a slow circuit of the area, matching up what they'd reviewed on the satellite imagery from CST's original survey. It was a good location to adopt as a base camp. The cliffs were riddled with slim zigzag fissures and deeper crevices. He identified at least three where they could store the bubbles and equipment.

'This should do,' he announced as Doc's bubble came slithering down the incline.

'Well, as long as *you* think so, Morty darling,' Cat said.

Once everyone had arrived, they got out of the bubbles and started unpacking their equipment. Morton and Doc took a fast walk over to the edge of the saddle. Past the cliffs, the ground curved down sharply, though visibility was still only a few tens of metres. The clouds were moving faster here, scurrying along the southern edge of the Regents. Without them, Morton and Doc would have had a clear view straight down to the Trine'ba two kilometres below. Randtown itself was away to the west.

'There's a lot of activity down there,' Doc said. He was using his suit's electromagnetic spectrum sensors to scan the shoreline of the vast lake.

Morton switched on his own sensors. The clouds filled with a bright gold radiance, as if a small, intense star was rising from the Trine'ba. When he added analysis programs, the coronal hue changed to a serpentine mass of entwined emissions, bundled sinewaves thrashing in discord. As well as the strange Prime communications, there was the bolder background turquoise of powerful magnetic fields flexing in a slow cadence. Lavender sparks swarmed around the empire of light, flyers trailing their own wake of cadmium signals, their membranous force fields flickering like wasp wings. 'What kind of important installation would you build in Randtown?' he asked out loud. 'I don't get it. There's nothing here. Send your invasion force halfway across the galaxy so they can build a five star ski resort? That's crazy.'

'This whole invasion makes no sense,' Doc said. 'There must be something down there more valuable than we realized. They are alien, remember. Different values.'

'We understand their technology,' Morton countered. 'They base everything on the same fundamental principles we do. They ain't that different.'

'When you apply technology to a requirement it nearly always shakes down to a one-solution machine in the end: cars to travel over land, rockets to fly into space. But motivation, that's a species variable, always has been.'

'Whatever,' Morton said. As well as his dodgy medical qualifications, Doc had some obscure English degree dating back over a century; all that education made him want to over-analyse everything. 'We're not here to admire their psychology, we're here to blow the shit out of them.'

'Eloquently put,' Doc said.

Morton took out a type three sensor, a transparent disc five centimetres across, and stuck it on the side of a boulder where it could scan across the Trine'ba. 'That'll spot anything approaching us.'

'Unless they come from the other side.'

'We'll place sensors all the way round our base camp. Obviously. It's not like we've got a shortage of them.' Part of their mission procedure had them building up a comprehensive network of the optronic devices, allowing them to monitor all the alien activity in and around Randtown.

'Roger that,' Doc said; he sounded amused.

They spent the next forty minutes scrambling over rocks and unstable shingle falls, planting the little sensors to provide early warning of any approaching flyers. Not once did they see sunlight; the cloud swirled and eddied as they clambered about, but it remained unbroken.

'Well done, boys,' Cat said as they arrived back at the base of the saddle. 'Great views you've given us; lots of rock and a big wet sky.'

'Let's just hope it stays that interesting,' Rob said.

'That kind of depends on us,' Morton said. 'We're here to cause as much disruption as we can. I guess we'd better start by scouting out the neighbourhood. We need two teams, and someone to stay up here to safeguard the equipment.'

'I'm sorry, sweetie, I must have missed that,' Cat said. 'When did they pin a general's star on you?'

'You don't need to be a general to point out the bleeding obvious,' Parker said. 'We know what's on the mission plan. Establish a knowledge of the enemy and use it to hit them hard.'

'And the person staying behind ain't going to be you, Cat,' Rob said.

'Darling! Why is that?'

'Don't you know? I don't trust you. None of us do. You're a fucking psycho.'

'Oww, Bob, are you scared of little me? You've got your armour suit and a very big gun.'

'I'm not scared of you, I simply regard you as unprofessional. We can't depend on you for back-up and support. We don't know if you'd provide it or not. You enjoyed playing the badass in training, screwing with our instructors. We all got a laugh out of that. Out here, nobody's smiling, nobody thinks you're clever. So you either take the front row all the time, or fuck off right now.'

'I'm disappointed, Bob, did Doc fill your head with that speech?'

'Let's just concentrate on what we're here to achieve, shall we?' Morton said. 'Cat, he's right. You're not dependable enough to be our cover.'

'General, *and* peacemaker. I like you, Morty.'

'And don't call me that.'

'Mellanie does,' Parker laughed. 'We all know that.'

'Morty, oh Morty, yes, yes please,' Rob warbled. 'Oh Morty, you're the best.'

Morton knew his cheeks were red inside the helmet, despite it maintaining a perfect body-temperature environment.

The communication band was full of chuckles. Parker gave a long wolf's moonhowl.

'Rob, you and I are one team,' Morton said, ignoring the jibes.

'That's good for me, Morty. Real good.'

'Cat, you and Doc can have a ball together. Parker, you keep everything secure up here.'

'Hey fuck that,' Parker said. 'I want to see some action here.'

'Then you partner Cat,' the Doc told him.

'He couldn't handle that kind of action,' she said.

There was amusement in the voice, but it left Morton cold. Even over the communications link something in her personality that was fundamentally *wrong* made itself felt.

'We don't really need to leave anyone back here,' Doc said. 'If the Primes can hack our sensors and secure links, we're fucked anyway. Forget the navy way. We're the ones on the ground. We're the best judges how to fulfil our duty.'

'Duty!' Parker grunted. 'Jesus Christ, Doc, you just love all this military crap, dontcha?'

'Roger that. So you want to stay here?'

'I fucking told you, I'm staying with you guys.'

'That's cool,' The Cat said. 'You come with me and Doc.'

'Fine,' Morton said. 'Rob, come on, we'll take the east side of town. You guys, see what they're doing further over round Blackwater Crag. And remember everybody, we're not looking to engage the enemy yet. This foray is just to build up our sensor network, okay. We don't want to alert them to our presence before we know how to make their lives truly miserable.'

*

'Do you think she's going to be trouble?' Rob asked when they were halfway down the mountain. He'd switched to a short-range secure link between the two armour suits.

'Rob, I don't know what the hell to make of her. All I know is, she's never going to be my back-up. I don't trust her.'

'Amen to that.'

They'd left the cloud base behind an hour earlier. Even though nightfall wasn't due for another three hours, the light was reduced to a sombre gloaming underneath the cloud. The rain was threaded with sleet and surprisingly hard pellets of hail, all of which turned to slush as they began a slow melt. It made the slope very hard going, even with the boosted limbs of the armour suits. Unrelenting rain was steadily beating away the boltgrass tufts, which never had a deep hold at this altitude anyway. The disappearing vegetation left long tracts of mud and shingle striping the slope, which threatened to slide them down hundreds of metres if they lost their footing.

An entire squadron of sneekbots was deployed around them in protective concentric circles. They skittered over the rough terrain, their antenna buds probing for any sign of movement, warm bodies, or electronic activity. So far the ground ahead was clear of any ambush, booby trap, or sensor.

Morton's virtual vision showed him The Cat, Parker and Doc taking a slightly different route down from the saddle, keeping to the high ground until they were a lot closer to the town. 'On the good side, we can always keep track of her.'

'Unless she goes truly native and ditches the armour.'

'I doubt she'd go that far. And the sensors would pick her up if she tried to take anything from base camp.' He stuck another of the little discs on an outcrop of rock which had withstood a small mudslide. As well as observing the vast open space above the Trine'ba, it acted as a communication relay across the Regents.

'Four more just launched,' Rob said.

Morton watched the alien flyers set off across the smooth waters of the Trine'ba, flying low, and keeping parallel to the shore. They all used broad fans of sensor radiation to sweep across the shallow ripples. Morton's armour suit stealthed down, its chromometic skin melding into the tawny beige of the landscape, while its thermal emission matched the temperature of the mud. The sneekbots folded their crab-like bodies to the ground and sent their main arrays into hibernation mode. The flyers didn't even bother probing the hillside.

'Wonder what they're looking for?' Rob asked as his suit returned to life.

'Mellanie said a few people stayed behind. They're probably causing some trouble for the Primes.'

'Great, that's all we need, enthusiastic amateurs stirring things up for us.'

Morton smiled. 'So you think we qualify as professionals, do you?'

'Listen, I've been doing this kind of work for a while now. I know what I see, and you guys took on the basics in training. In any case, we've got the kind of equipment that can do some serious damage. If we find these farm boys we need to get them to back off.'

'Yeah, I figured that.'

'So how come Mellanie knows about the locals and where they're at?'

'This was where she was when the Primes invaded, right here in Randtown.'

'No shit. And this is where you got sent. There's a coincidence.'

'Yeah.' Morton wanted to grin, but it was something which had bothered him, too. *Still, too late to worry about it now.*

He was surprised by the scale of activity where Randtown had once stood. A vast block of machinery which resembled a human chemical refinery had been assembled along the shore, extending for a couple of kilometres on either side of the old quayside, and even standing on stilts to arch over some bays and inlets. Bright lights blazed from every point of the structure, illuminating exposed equipment buttressed by thick metal girders. Behind that, on the gentle slope leading up from the back of the town, boxy buildings and large cylindrical storage tanks had been set up on the old human road grid. Spaced between them were a number of large fusion power plants. The old highway leading back through the Dau'sings had been widened. It was carrying a lot of traffic out to Blackwater Crag, big slow vehicles spitting out black exhaust smoke as they lumbered along. Rows of long buildings were just visible at the foot of Blackwater Crag, stretching back along the valley. A string of flyers patrolled above the refurbished road, dipping in and out of the smothering clouds.

Outside the original town limits, six broad terraces had been bulldozed into the bumpy foothills, with a further two under construction. They seemed to be parking, or holding, areas, covered with unopened pods of equipment, vehicles and flyers; four vast open arenas were filled with aliens.

'Well now, finally!' Morton said as they wormed their way along the ruined treeline at the top of the foothills. The hardy pines were suffering badly in the sickly winter climate. Slushy water clung to every needle, turning them a dull unhealthy sepia. Many trunks had fallen, ripping out huge circular wedges of dripping soil as long mudslides undermined their roots. It was perfect cover. The sneekbots maintained their protective perimeter, crawling their way through the fungal muddle of broken twigs and mulched needles.

He used the suit's sensors to zoom in on the naked creatures parading across the nearest arena below. They were quad-symmetric; with four thick legs at the flared base of a sallow coloured barrel-body. When they moved, it was with a rocking motion as the legs bowed and flexed along their whole length. Four arms emerged just above the legs, almost as thick as the lower limbs and moving in the same long curving motions. Morton didn't think they had joints like elbows and knees, the whole thing was elastic. The crown sprouted a further eight appendages, four stumpy trunks with an open mouth; while between them four tall slender tendrils which ended in bulbous lumps of flesh waved about like corn in the wind.

'Solid looking brutes,' Rob said. 'There must be thousands of them down there.'

Morton gave the arenas another scan with his suit's optical sensors. 'More like tens of thousands.' He was recording the scene for the navy. The first communication wormhole was due to open in another seventeen hours; he'd be able send them the information then. It would be interesting to see what their analysts came up with.

'They're all fitted with a transmitter gadget, look,' Rob was saying. 'I just keep getting that analogue hash coming from them.'

'Right.' Morton was watching a pair touching their long upper limbs together. *An alien kiss? A fuck?* 'I know we've only just seen them, but they all look identical to me.'

Rob snorted. 'Very not politically correct.'

'I was wondering if they were clones. Some kind of disposable construction crew? Just a thought. Their army might be the same. A perfect soldier replicated a hundred million times. It would explain their dire lack of tactics. All they ever do is use numbers to overrun us. They don't mind the slaughter because they're not losing individuals the way we are.'

'Could be. It makes as much sense as any other idea. Let's see if we can get a closer look.'

With the sneekbots prowling ahead and behind, they began to worm their way deeper through the decaying foliage of the fallen trees. Morton could see several hundred aliens working on the long refinery station by the shore. The giant machine was still being extended. Both ends were sheathed by a network of scaffolding which supported cranes and hoists. Aliens swarmed all over the new components that were being added. They must possess an excellent sense of balance, Morton thought. He couldn't see anything equivalent to a human handrail on the narrow metal struts which they moved along.

'Ho, did you see that?' Rob asked.

'What?'

'One of those things just took a crap off the top of the refinery station.'

Morton tracked his optical sensors along the colossal structure. Now he knew what to look for, he could easily find evidence of more casual defecation. The pipes and girders were splashed with tacky brown patches. 'So? They never got round to inventing a flushable pan. Doc was saying we need to watch out for a different philosophy more than any other type of variation between us.'

'I'm not sure that's a question of psychology or even bad plumbing. Leaving your own waste products around like that is a very counter-productive thing for a species to do. Everyone develops disposal mechanisms, both social and practical; it's one of the first signs of civilization emerging. You don't just wait for the rain to wash it away.'

'You have no idea what their digestive biochemistry is like,' Morton said. 'Face it, their crap could be the perfect fertilizer.'

'Then they'd collect it and transport it to a field. No, we're missing something. You may have been on the right track with your clone army idea.' He paused, unhappy. 'Though even they wouldn't deliberately foul their own environment. Nothing would. This doesn't make sense.'

'Maybe the clone clean-up army is due to arrive next.'

Rob chuckled. 'You want to put some money on that?'

'No way.'

After another half-hour of cautious movement through the mouldering forest, they had moved as far west as they could go before risking open ground. The fallen trees had also brought them to within six hundred metres of the force field protecting the alien town. They sent a trio of sneekbots on ahead, but stayed under cover of the sopping wood as the invisible sun finally fell below the horizon.

'Another difference,' Rob said.

'What?'

'There's no colour on anything they build, no finish or decoration. All the external material is raw.'

'They're colour blind as well.'

'And immune to aesthetics?'

'Okay, then. You tell me.'

'I don't know why, I'm just pointing it out. Their culture has no art.'

'Have you seen the crap flooding the unisphere these days?'

'You know what I mean.'

'Yeah, but don't forget this is a military invasion base. It's bound to be functional.'

'Could be. What do you make of the set-up?'

Morton switched his attention back to the alien activities below him. The angle just allowed him a narrow view along the front of the refinery station. Machinery and tightly packed pipes produced a metal precipice fifty metres high. It was lined with wide orifices that were pumping out torrents of liquid. He counted sixteen of the big jets squirting bilious foaming water out into the lake shallows.

'I guess we know what resource they were after when they came here,' Rob said. 'The lake itself.'

'What the hell is that stuff?' Morton wondered. Lights on the top of the refinery station cast a bright illumination across the shallows. The aliens had done a lot of work along the shoreline. Long concrete ramps now extended out into the water, reaching almost to the force field, a kilometre and a half away. In between them, the lake had been divided up into a number of pens by heavy netting. Morton realized there were a lot more ripples in the pens than there were out beyond the force field. Yet there couldn't be any breeze inside the shielding. He zoomed in for a clearer look at whatever was stirring the water.

The pens were filled with some kind of living creatures. A *lot* of living creatures. It was their writhing forms thrashing about just below the surface which was causing all the disturbance.

'They're bioforming the planet,' he said. 'That's what this station is, that's why they wanted the lake. Jesus.'

'You might be right,' Rob said. 'They've certainly got big scale expansion plans. Access sneekbot 306.'

When 306's sensor feed flipped up into Morton's virtual vision he saw the little machine had crept right up to the force field. The first reading was the strength of the field. They didn't have anything which could penetrate, it was even strong enough to withstand the tactical nukes they'd brought. He concentrated on the excavation which the aliens were making a hundred metres inside the boundary, clawing out a deep bunker that they were lining with concrete and metal. A tower of machinery was being assembled in the centre. Doc had been right: technological solutions did refine machines down to identical functions. Morton recognized some of the sections without having to reference his e-butler. The aliens were building a force field generator.

'Track right,' Rob said.

He swivelled 306's antenna buds: six hundred metres away, another generator bunker was being dug out.

'Those generators are a lot more powerful than the ones they're using now,' Rob said. 'At this rate it's only going to take a couple of days to finish them. After that, they'll be truly impregnable, and we'll be truly screwed.'

'Only the town has a force field so far,' Morton said. 'We can play hell with everything else they're doing.'

'Whose chain are you trying to jerk, here? This is where it's at, right here in town. We've got to hit that monster station. Don't screw around, use the nukes.'

Morton risked raising his head slightly, looking directly at the force field and the town it enclosed. The vast chunk of alien machinery along the waterfront could have been a light-year away for all the chance he had of reaching it. 'Fuck it, there's no way in!'

'Maybe we could get in from the water side? Force fields don't function so good in water, the denser the material the less effective they are.'

'Could do. Water's not that dense, though. We'd have to scout round, test the field integrity on the lake bed.'

'These suits can handle a dive.'

'Yeah, but will the dump-webs work underwater?'

'I'm not sure, we could— Uh oh, what have we here?'

One of the sneekbots had registered movement several hundred metres deeper in the dead forest. It clambered up on top of a mouldy log, looking along a line of stumps. A human shape crawled across the little open lane from one decaying canopy to the next.

'So Mellanie was right,' Rob said. 'Not just a great ass, huh?'

'No,' Morton said absently. Two more humans were sneaking after the first. From what he could make out they were dressed in some kind of dark ski suits. They didn't register on infrared. Somebody knew how to rig the thermal fibres, he acknowledged. 'This can't be good for us, they're going to strike something.'

'Relax man, our stealth is good.'

'Theirs isn't.' His virtual hand touched The Cat's icon. 'We've found whatever's left of the locals. Access our sneekbots.'

'I see them, Morty. Looks like they've developed a purpose in life.'

'It's a damn stupid one,' Doc said. 'If they start shooting at the aliens they're just going to get themselves killed.'

'They look like they know what they're doing to me,' Rob said. 'Let's see where they're going.' Five sneekbots set off through the forest, keeping parallel to the three humans. They soon overtook them, and began scanning ahead.

'Part of our mission is to rescue and assist any surviving humans,' Doc said.

'I think that referred to non-combatants,' Rob told him.

'That's what these idiots are, they just think they're fighters.'

'They fooled me.'

'Doc might be right,' The Cat said. 'These bumpkins aren't helping us by causing a fuss. You should stop them, Morton.'

Why me? he thought. Any other time, it might have been flattering.

'Uh oh,' Rob said. 'We might be running out of time.' The sneekbots were picking up standard Prime electromagnetic emissions. Four armoured aliens were patrolling the foothills along the top of the dead forest.

Morton pulled a detailed map out of his grid, and studied it. 'If I was going to ambush them I'd do it there,' he said, and indicated a small, deep ravine that cut clean through the foothills to spill into the Trine'ba just east of the town. The aliens would have to cross it somewhere. 'They'll be out of sight from the town, and shielded. Perfect spot.'

'Yeah,' Rob said. 'Not bad for a bunch of amateurs.'

'Get over there and talk to them,' Doc said. 'They should at least know we're here.'

'If you ask me, these guys know what they're doing,' Rob said. 'I don't think this is their first turkey shoot.'

'You're making a mistake if you let them do this.'

'Doc's right,' The Cat said. 'Go break up the fight, boys.'

Morton knew she was right. Cat's Claws couldn't afford anyone interfering in their mission, no matter how well intended. 'We'll try.'

Rob carried on grumbling, but he followed Morton back through the thick layer of mildew-steeped needles, keeping under the lacy roof of decomposing bark. Even as they began, Morton knew they were cutting it close. The alien patrol was making good time out in the open, and the ambush team were almost in position.

'We'll swing round your way,' The Cat said. 'Just in case you screw up. I'm bored with dropping these sensors, anyway.'

'Fuck you,' Doc said. 'We can't see anything past Blackwater Crag, yet. We need to expand the network.'

'You're becoming a bad pain-the-arse barrack room lawyer. I don't like that. You do what you do, and let me do what I know needs to be done.'

'This is not about you, bitch.'

'Temper temper.'

'Hey, heads up, people,' Rob exclaimed. 'We have something interesting here.' The sneekbots were reporting some kind of electromagnetic interference inside the ravine. It wasn't the kind of jamming effect which would cut the aliens off abruptly from the town, but a more subtle distortion, reducing their bandwidth and disrupting the remaining content. 'Somebody knows what they're doing.'

The ambush party spread out along the edge of the ravine. They unstrapped long, bulky cylinders from their backs, and aimed them down into the black gash in the landscape. Morton's e-butler started running comparisons with known weapon types.

'Son of a bitch,' he said when it finally gave him an approximate match. 'They're Prime guns.'

'Wonder where they got them from?' Parker said in amusement. 'They are big beauts, aren't they?'

'It's what you do with them that counts,' The Cat retorted.

Morton was seriously considering walking a sneekbot up to one of the ambushers, and trying to talk with them that way. He didn't because he was worried they'd simply shoot the little bot, which would blow everyone's cover.

The aliens began their descent into the ravine. It was a steep V-shape cleft leading down to a torrent of white water racing along a bed of grey-white stone. Lichen-covered boulders stuck up out of the soil on either side, forcing the aliens to take a slow zigzag path as they picked their way to the bottom. One of the sneekbots perched on the edge above them relayed the image as they sank below direct line of sight with the town.

The jamming increased dramatically just before the aliens reached the stream. The aliens stopped, bringing their weapons up, and began to spread out. Two ducked down beside some boulders, their infrared signature fading away as their suit's skin turned black. Both were very difficult to see, even for the sneekbot's sensors.

'Stop them,' Doc pleaded. 'Morton!'

A beam weapon fired down into the ravine, catching one of the more visible aliens. Its force field sizzled a bright violet, haloing its shape against the rock and foaming water. Another beam weapon stabbed out, punching the radiant force field. Steam began to hiss upwards from the surrounding grass as little flames licked around the base of the suit's shielding. It took a couple of seconds before the force field finally collapsed from the twin energy spikes impaling it. The alien's armour suit exploded in a dazzling plasma mushroom as its energy cells and ammunition were vaporized.

Light flooded along the ravine, bringing a clarity which even daylight never managed. The two aliens that had gone for cover amid the crumbling boulders started to fire up at the ambush party.

'Shit, they're losing it,' Morton yelled. He stood up and started to run hard. The suit's electromuscles carried him easily, amplifying his every leap to send him flying effortlessly over the fallen trees.

'Fuck it!' Rob cried. He jumped after Morton, his pounding suit legs splintering the rotten trees apart as if they were polystyrene.

'I can see the fire from here,' The Cat called. 'You must be visible to half the aliens at Blackwater Crag.'

Morton winced. Up ahead of him, the ravine was a sharp crack of flickering pyrotechnics against the black foothill. With or without jammed communications, it would act like a beacon to any flyers. His suit deployed the hyper-rifle from its right forearm sheath.

A hefty plume of soil and flame shot up from the edge of the ravine where one of the ambushers was lying. Morton saw a human shape pinwheel through the air, backlit by the raw energy raging inside the ravine.

'Four flyers heading your way,' Parker called.

Morton saw the orange symbols creep into his virtual vision.

'Can you close it down?' The Cat shouted.

'Not a chance,' Morton said. 'One of them's dead, the other two are still shooting.'

'Stop them!' Parker demanded. 'How difficult can it be?'

'We're coming,' Doc said. 'Parker, with me.'

'Oh Christ.'

One final eight metre hurdle jump over a horizontal tree

and Morton landed on the rim of the ravine, his boots thudding into spongy soil up to the ankles. He was already pointing his hyper-rifle. A simple circular targeting graphic materialized in the centre of his virtual vision. The sneekbots were triangulating coordinates for him. An alien armour suit slid smoothly into the orange circle, which immediately flashed green. Morton fired.

The hyper-rifle was designed with one purpose: to puncture the force field projected by alien armour. Even so, Morton was slightly surprised when the small atom-laser's half-second burst drilled clean through the suit, sending the alien flying backwards three metres through the air to splash into the stream. Water closed over the dark shape, hissing briefly as the heat produced a small cloud of steam. *How about that, the military got something right.*

Rob was crouching beside him – presenting a smaller target silhouette. He fired his hyper-rifle. Morton found the last alien and shot it. The ravine was abruptly plunged into darkness again. Just a few serpent-shapes of grass embers glowed where the alien patrol had made their stand. The damp night air was extinguishing them quickly.

'Who the hell are you?' a voice challenged.

'The cavalry,' Rob told him. 'Your lucky day, huh.'

'Flyer overhead,' Doc said. His voice was strangely calm. 'You're going to need covering fire, Morton.'

'No!' The Cat warned. 'Don't!'

Morton's telemetry display showed him Doc launching an HVvixen. The slim missile accelerated at fifteen gees, its plasma exhaust piercing the air behind it like runaway solar flare. It slammed into the flyer's force field, flash-releasing its remaining energy. The flyer detonated into an incandescent spherical shockwave that billowed out at supersonic velocity to envelop its three partners. They exploded in furious twisting gouts of sapphire vapour.

'Gotcha, you bastards,' Doc crooned.

'You retard motherfucker,' The Cat screamed. 'You've just killed us all.'

'Only these bodies, Cat,' Doc said lightly. 'Your essence will have continuity.'

The dazzling lightstorm began to drain out of the night sky, dissipating into a thousand sparkling contrails that sank slowly towards the ground. Morton's suit sensors picked out the three armoured humans standing in the middle of the scintillation blizzard.

'Nice shot, man,' Parker said admiringly.

'Run,' Morton whispered. 'Run now. *Get out of there!*'

One figure was already moving. The Cat: using her armour suit boost function to its maximum, accelerating her helter-skelter sprint to over sixty kilometres an hour. She was heading up the slope towards the roof of writhing cloud

'Four more,' Parker said. 'Make that six.'

'You mean ten,' Doc said. 'Morton, Rob, get the civilians out of here.'

'Yeah,' Parker said. 'Protect and serve.'

The one surviving ambusher was walking unsteadily towards Morton. 'What was that? What is happening?'

'They're not going to make it,' Rob said.

Five HVvixens shrieked into the night.

Morton jumped towards the survivor as vivid white light silently washed across them. 'Get down. Get into the ravine.' He didn't give the man any opportunity to argue. His suit arms closed round him, picking him up effortlessly. They both tumbled over the edge. Behind them, the devil's own firework display filled the sky with carnage.

'Bad guys falling,' Parker reported, laughing gleefully.

'They found us,' Doc reported. 'More incoming. Shit. Eighteen. Four of them are big. New flyer type for your catalogue, Morton.' His suit's sensors were relaying a stream of information. The data faltered as several beam weapons locked on to him. 'You guys had better go for deep cover. Make this relevant, Morton. I'm counting on you.' He fired another HVvixen. It never got ten metres from his suit's force field before the deluge of energy from the alien beam weapons ruptured it.

Parker's screaming was loud in Morton's ears as he was hurled through the air by the explosion. Telemetry showed him the man's suit start to falter from the punishing overload.

'Get down to the bottom of the ravine,' Rob was saying. 'We'll be safe there.'

Morton hauled the ambusher along at his side as the two of them hurried down the last few metres of the slope to the rampaging water. He switched to active sensors, confident no one would ever notice. The stream was deep, at least a couple of metres. As far as his radar could see downstream the flow was free from any obstruction.

'Over here,' Parker called. He was broadcasting on every frequency his armour suit was capable of transmitting on. 'Here I am, you bastards, come and get me.' Seven of the large alien flyers were approaching him, their weapons lashing out. 'Eat this shit, and die.'

Morton plunged into the stream, taking the survivor with him. He expanded his suit's force field to envelop both of them.

Parker triggered the two tactical nukes he was carrying.

A stratum of violent white light streaked over the top of the ravine, obliterating every colour as its thick nimbus irradiated the ground. The churning water of the stream began to steam. Then the air shook, agitating the boulders. Small stones began to bounce down the slopes to splash into the water.

Morton and Rob were already well on their way downstream, tumbling round and round in the swirling rapids. It was a fast and chaotic ride, with the pair of them grinding through shallows and banging into the sides only to ricochet back into the main current again. Morton kept hold of the ambush survivor, struggling to keep the man above the foaming surface the whole time they jolted about.

The dreadful sheen of light drained out of the sky, leaving the restless clouds seething with lightning flashes. Ground tremors faded away.

'You okay?' Rob asked. He was ten metres ahead of Morton, riding down on his back, using his arms as rudders.

'Just trying to keep this guy alive.'

'How's he doing?'

'I think he's had better days. Sensors show he's still breathing.' It was more like choking, but at least his weak thrashing showed he was still alive.

'We're getting goddamn close to the town.'

'I know. But we're almost at the bottom.'

Another two hundred metres brought them to the end of the stream, where it broadened out to gurgle over a wide, flat bed of stones before emptying into the Trine'ba. Morton came racing out of the last curve to hit the stones on his ass, he ploughed through them for a short way before coming to a complete halt.

'Holy fuck,' Rob said. 'We made it.'

'Congratulations.' The Cat's voice oozed sarcasm. 'Landed on something soft did you? That part that does all your thinking.'

'Piss off, bitch.'

Morton's virtual vision showed him the working sensor discs which were relaying Cat's signal. There weren't many left. When he accessed their visual spectrum feeds, they showed him a small crater glowing a venomous maroon where Parker had made his stand. Above it, a hole had been ripped through the clouds, where violet air hazed the swirling gap. Forests and spinnies scattered on the hills above the town had ignited and were now surging into full-blown firestorms, between them the ruined grass was smouldering. Smoke was rising to choke the narrow band of air between the ground and the clouds. None of the sensors reported any flyer activity.

The Cat was sheltering in a gentle fold high above the blast zone. Telemetry showed her suit was intact, its force field had protected her from the blast.

Morton let go of the man he was holding and climbed to his feet. The force field around the alien town was five hundred metres away. There was no sign of any activity nearby.

'I think we're safe for the moment,' Morton said. 'This might be a good time to leave.'

'Amen to that,' Rob grunted.

Morton looked down at the man who was still sprawled on the stones, panting heavily. His black clothes had been ripped in several places; the ebony skin beneath was grazed and lacerated.

'You all right?' Morton asked.

The man turned his head to glare up. 'What? Are you making a joke?'

'Sorry. I've got a decent medical kit, but if you can walk I'd like to build some distance between us and Randtown before we stop to patch you up.'

'Merciful heavens, forgive me for what I've done.'

'What have you done?'

'Led more good men to their death. I take it you are responsible for that explosion? It was nuclear, wasn't it?'

'One of my squad mates triggered it. He was stopping the flyers you'd attracted.'

'I see.' The man bowed his head until it was almost in the water. 'Even more deaths must be carried by my conscience, then. And it was already a terrible burden. Truly, the fates must hate me.'

'I don't think any of this is personal. My name's Morton, this is Rob.'

'Thank you gentlemen, I appreciate you saving me. Much good it will do you.'

'Pleasure,' Rob grunted.

'Who are you?' Morton asked.

The man smiled, revealing bloody teeth. 'Simon Rand. I founded this paradise.'

*

The cave was a good hideout, Morton admitted to himself. It had taken them an hour to reach it, scrambling along the rocks of the shoreline, sometimes wading across deep inlets where the mountain runoffs gushed into the rank lake water.

Three people were waiting for their leader. Desperate to know what had happened when the bombs went off.

David Dunbavand had been badly injured in an earlier raid. One of his legs had been shattered, its flesh now an unhealthy blue-black mottling, with cuts weeping grey cheesy fluid. His toes already looked and smelled gangrenous. Several other bones had been broken during his brief moment of combat. He was sweating continuously, damp hair slicked back against his skull.

A girl called Mandy was nursing him; she looked tired and worn, prone to tears. There wasn't much she could do except clean his dressings and feed him a weak broth they'd cooked up from salvaged food packets. She was wrapped up in several oversized woollen sweaters, and a pair of green semi-organic waterproof trousers. Curls of lank hair hung out of a black wool hat.

It was Georgia who had run out of the cave, splashing through the shallows to greet Simon as he limped painfully towards his refuge. 'One of my earliest believers,' he said painfully as he introduced her to Morton and Rob. 'Georgia was with me building the highway.' She smiled bravely at him, her arm going round his waist to help him over the last few metres of slippery rock. Her face was ruggedly beautiful, rejuvenated to adolescence, with a square jaw and sharp cheekbones. She wore an expensive designer suit on top of several T-shirts and thermal trousers; the semi-organic fabric was smeared with weeks' worth of dirt, but still offered a degree of protection from the cave's dank atmosphere and the chill air which seeped in from outside. Once stylish auburn hair had been cut short by scissors and was now covered by a silk scarf wrapped like a turban.

Morton followed Simon and Georgia as they clambered along a ledge which took them back to the main chamber. It was illuminated by a few solar-charged lightglobes, the kind you could buy at any camping shop. They badly needed recharging, producing only a wan yellow glow that didn't even reach the cave roof. However, there was enough radiance to show him the three bodies sealed in plastic lying along the rear wall.

David pushed himself up onto his elbows, grimacing at the effort. 'Where are the others?' He was giving the entrance a stricken look, already knowing the answer.

'I'm sorry,' Simon told him.

Mandy slumped down, and started crying.

'Tyrone?' David asked.

'No. He got one of the aliens, though. He stood his ground to the very end.'

'One!' the injured man exclaimed bitterly. 'One out of a million. I should never have stayed here. I should have gone with Lydia and the kids. We're not making any difference. We're just being wiped out. Look at us! Four of us, that's all that's left. What was the point?' He lowered himself back onto the thin mattress, shaking at the pain, drawing sharp breaths.

'How many of you were there to start with?' Morton asked.

'Eighteen of us remained behind,' Simon said as he sat down heavily. A hand waved round the cave. 'This is all that remains of us. I'd like to say that we have taken leagues of the aliens to hell with us, but alas our efforts have been mediocre at best. They are well equipped and excellent soldiers. In truth there's not much we have achieved aside from our own deaths.' He began to scratch the healskin dressings which Rob had applied to his cuts during the journey back. Georgia sat beside him, her knees tucked up under her chin. Their arms went round each other

'Eighteen,' Morton muttered. He didn't want to ask for details; it all seemed such a waste. Not that Cat's Claws had done a lot better. Not yet.

'Please,' Mandy asked, she looked up pleadingly, wiping her eyes. 'Can you get us back to the Commonwealth?'

Morton was glad his helmet was on, she wouldn't be able to see his expression. 'I'm not sure. We weren't scheduled to be lifted out for six months. I'll inform the navy you're here, of course. They'll probably try and get a wormhole open for you.'

She lowered her head.

'Have you got communications?' David Dunbavand croaked.

'Sure. The navy is opening a wormhole on a regular basis to receive our messages. We can let your family know you're okay.'

'I'd rather you didn't.' He smiled, which turned into a cough.

'Let me take a look at you,' Rob said. He took his helmet off and knelt beside the injured man. He waved a diagnostic array over David's leg and torso. 'We've got a decent supply of medical equipment stashed back at our base camp. There should be something that can help.'

'A painkiller would do to start with,' David said. 'We've even run out of those. The hospital was shut away behind the first force field they generated. We've had to make do with whatever we can find in the farmhouses ever since. It never amounted to much, and it seemed selfish to keep what little we had from poor old Napo, even at the end.' He indicated one of the corpses.

'No problem,' Rob said. He took a small applicator pad from his pack.

David gave an audible sigh as it was pressed to his neck. 'Damn, I never thought I'd enjoy feeling numb. That's very kind of you, my friend.'

'My pleasure. Now just lie still and let my e-butler's medical routine work out what to do with you.'

'How much bandwidth can your communication wormhole handle?' David asked. 'We have the memories of our friends, can you at least get them to safety?'

'You've got a secure store in here?' Morton asked.

'Their security is our honour,' Simon said. 'Every time one of us ventures outside, we transfer our last memories to an ordinary hand-held array. Those who remain are sworn to get them to safety back in the Commonwealth. We trust each other, you see. Friendship in these terrible times has forged a bond strong enough to give us the strength to face bodyloss with confidence and conviction.'

Morton wasn't sure there was anyone in Cat's Claws he'd trust with his memories. 'It would be a slow transfer,' he said carefully. 'The wormhole isn't open for very long. Just a few seconds.'

'I understand,' Simon said. 'We have survived thus far, a few more months should pose no problem, especially with your weapons to help protect us.'

Morton lifted his helmet off. After the filtered air he'd been breathing, the smell in the cave seemed exceptionally strong. Something he couldn't place: raw meat but with a sugary tang. It was strange. 'What is that?'

'The smell?' Mandy said. 'Whatever they've been polluting the Trine'ba with. It's been getting worse for weeks now.'

'Any idea what it is? We saw the refinery they've built.'

'I took a few samples earlier on,' David said. 'It's like an algae of some kind. They're bioforming the Trine'ba.'

'I believe it to be the first step in converting this planet to one that is host to their own biological heritage alone,' Simon said. 'They certainly show no interest or respect for any existing organisms. It is an imperialism which seems to extend down to a cellular level.'

Rob took out a couple of phials from his medical kit, and slotted them into the applicator patch. 'I'm going to put the leg into a healskin sheath after this,' he told David, and put the patch on the man's discoloured thigh. 'I can't set the bones properly, but the sheath and the biovirals should help stabilize you until we can get you back to a Commonwealth hospital.'

David coughed. Tiny flecks of blood settled on his lips. 'Hope Lydia's keeping up on my medical insurance payments.'

'You will survive, David, I promise you that,' Simon said calmly. 'I will carry you to the wormhole on my own back if necessary.' He broke off at the sound of someone splashing their way along the entrance fissure.

The Cat waded up out of the water, and removed her helmet. Her purple-tipped hair was sweaty, rising in a multitude of tiny spikes. She grinned broadly, her wide blue-grey eyes took in the cave with one easy glance. 'Nice,' she observed. 'Hello boys, did you miss me?'

'Like stale vomit,' Rob said. He turned back to stripping the dressings off David's leg.

The Cat strode into the middle of the cave. 'Well my dears, that was an impressive first six hours, wasn't it? Two of us dead. We didn't save two refugees. We set off some nukes that did no damage whatsoever. And most of our sensor discs are gone. Talk about making an impact.'

'And you were a big help,' Morton said.

'You heard what I said. You chose to ignore it.'

*

Even though it was a perfect fit, Morton relished taking off his armour suit. He rubbed at every part of himself he could reach, easing itchy skin and stiff muscles. The semi-organic fibre one-piece he wore underneath repelled the cave's cold moisture, keeping him reasonably dry. There was nothing he could do to stop the smell.

After living on scavenged packets for weeks, the Randtown survivors welcomed the food Cat's Claws had brought.

'Manufactured corporate pap full of sugar, badly modified genes, and toxic additives,' Georgia said as she stuffed a fishcake straight from its heating envelope into her mouth. 'God, it tastes good.'

'Our way of life has truly ended,' Simon said. He accepted a vegetarian lasagne from The Cat, inclining his head in gratitude.

'It's not from a Big15 factory farm,' she told him. 'I wouldn't fill my body with that shit.'

Morton watched Rob open his mouth. Their eyes met, and Rob turned away.

'We have to decide what to do,' Morton said. 'I think our first priority is to get you clear.'

'What about David?' Simon asked. Dunbavand had been wrapped in Morton's lightweight sleeping bag, protecting the healskin from the cave's rancid humidity. He was sleeping fitfully as the drugs and biovirals did what they could to assuage the damage.

'We can load him in one of our bubbles and remote drive it out of here,' Morton said. 'You'll be safer up in the Dau'sings.'

'Yes, the aliens seem to be centred around Randtown and the valleys immediately around Blackwater Crag,' Simon said. 'We should be safe in the highlands.'

'What about our mission?' Rob asked. 'We're supposed to be making life intolerable for the aliens.'

'We will,' Morton said. 'We've got six months.'

'I hate to disagree,' Simon said. 'But you saw the new force field generators they were building. Once those are operational there is very little even you will be able to do to harm their primary installations, I suspect. This is the third expansion and protective upgrade they have made since they arrived. Each time the force fields are larger and stronger.'

'We tried to get inside at first,' Georgia said. 'Five of us were caught going through the sewers. They didn't stand a chance. The aliens must have been expecting us to try and infiltrate their station. They're not stupid. And poor old Napo led a dive team that was going to use an underwater route through the old aquarium. Nothing works. They've got every route covered.'

'There are no routes, not any more,' Mandy said. She was chewing listlessly at a bacon sandwich. 'They're already outside the old town boundaries. All the utility tunnels and storm drains are inside the force field now.'

'You boys aren't thinking,' The Cat said. Her voice cut clean across the cave, ripe with mockery. Morton gave her an intolerant glance. She was doing her yoga, one foot tucked in behind her neck.

'You have a solution?' Morton asked.

'It's obvious.'

'Want to share that?'

'Nuke them. That's all we can do.'

'We can't nuke them. We can't get to them.'

She closed her eyes, put her hands into the Dawn Sunlight position, and breathed in deeply.

'There has to be a way in,' Rob said. 'What about caves?'

'No,' Simon said. 'We performed a full seismic survey before we started building Randtown. I didn't want us to suddenly come up against subsidence problems after we were established, that would have been too costly.'

'The Marquis brewery dug some deep cellars,' Georgia said. 'I'm not sure how far they extended. But they had a water channel running through the middle. They used it to make the beer; natural Dau'sing springs. It was part of their slogan.'

'I went down there once,' Mandy said. 'I was dating the assistant brewer. They weren't that big. And there was only the one entrance.'

'There must have been drainage.'

'If there is the aliens will have rigged it with sensors.'

'I think the brewery is too far inside the force field,' Simon said. 'In any case, the aliens have razed the buildings. There would be no way up even if you did get into the cellar.'

'Do you have anything that could dig underneath the force field?' Georgia asked.

'Alamo avenger,' Rob muttered with a small private smile.

'No,' Morton said. 'We didn't come equipped to mount a frontal assault. We're supposed to harass and disrupt, to make them waste time and money looking over their shoulder the whole time.'

'A nice theory,' Simon said. 'But they're a very central-ized species. The activity out in the valleys is susceptible to the kind of campaign you're talking about, but I doubt it would ultimately have much effect on them. To hurt them, you must strike at the structures inside the force field.'

'It'll have to be an underwater approach,' Rob said reluc-tantly. 'Even if a dump web doesn't work underwater, there must be some route in. An arch in a reef, an inlet pipe. Something!'

'Oh, this is painful,' The Cat said. She slipped her foot out from behind her head. 'I thought you were executive manage-ment class, Morty. What happened to that "don't download glitches, upload fixes", corporate speak you're so fond of?'

'Just tell us what your idea is, please,' he said wearily.

'The aliens keep expanding the area they're developing around the refinery station, right? So what we do is put a nuke outside the existing force field, and inside the border where the new one is going to be. When they switch on the new force field, the nuke is now inside their defences, and it goes off. Any questions?'

Morton wanted to kick himself it was so obvious. He put the lapse of clear thought down to the shock of losing Parker and Doc. 'Simon, do the aliens turn off the old internal force fields once the new ones are up and running?'

'Yes. They have so far.'

'Oh, gosh, boys, are we really going to use my little old idea?' The Cat batted her eyes.

'Yeah,' Rob said. 'I don't suppose you fancy staying with the nuke and detonating it once we're sure everything is peachy in there?'

*

The blast from Parker's last stand against the flyers made things difficult. There was virtually no cover left on the foothills above and behind the town. That left them with the eastern side, where the low ground had been slightly sheltered from the blastwave. Even there, the trees had been completely flattened and incinerated. Large patches of terrestrial GMgrass had smouldered away before the eternal sleet and drizzle extinguished their paltry flames.

A few large houses had been built there, nestled in their own secluded folds in the land. It was one of the areas where the more wealthy had settled, giving them a splendid view out along the Trine'ba. They'd all suffered from the original attack on the Regents, and the environmental aftermath of the invasion, with smashed lopsided roofs and walls lying askew. Once neat gardens were reduced to muddy swamps where plants had briefly run wild before the climate turned against them.

Morton and The Cat picked their way slowly through one such garden. Its owner had been an avid collector of bamboo varieties. There were clumps of the shoots laid out in long curving patterns. From the air it would have looked like a giant tiger orchid flower. Now the leaves were turning brown and soggy, new shoots were rotting in the mud.

'Another two hundred metres should do it,' Morton said. 'That'll take us to the overlook point.' The garden was a shallow depression, partly natural, that a small army of agri-bots had then worked to extend into the gentle hillside. They were due to place the tactical nuke right on the edge of the garden, where the bamboo gave way to dunes of roses, putting the device in direct line of sight of the giant refinery station along the shore. With the ever-present cloud blocking the starlight, and the sleet choking the air, it was as dark as interstellar space in the garden. Even on full amplification, his visual spectrum sensors had difficulty producing an image. He was heavily dependent on infrared, which gave the tall dying vegetation an ominous looming appearance.

'Okey dokey,' The Cat said. She was using her slightly contemptuous voice, the one full of false enthusiasm.

Morton didn't care. He'd paired up with her because he didn't trust her to undertake Rob's placement. As back-up they'd decided a second nuke should be placed on the lakebed. Their sensor disc and comrelays didn't function underwater. That meant someone working alone. The Cat was a pain in the ass to have alongside, but he could at least keep an eye on her. He wondered what kind of progress Rob was making. They hadn't done much underwater training.

The swarm of sneekbots scouting the surrounding area reached the house at the centre of the garden. It was a long two-storey clapboard affair with a three door garage and a balcony running the length of the wall which faced the Trine'ba. The two nuclear blastwaves had left it severely lopsided, with the splintered boards hanging loose at all angles. Solar roofing panels had half-melted in the heat, running like wax to wilt around the structural beams so that the rainwater was constantly trickling down inside, saturating the interior. All the windows were gone, leaving shards of glass to tear at the curtains as they fluttered about, reducing them to a few sodden tatters flapping indolently in the light sleet.

Sneekbot 411 detected an infrared source inside on the ground floor.

'Well hello there,' The Cat murmured.

'Another survivor?' Morton speculated. The heat source was about the same strength as a human.

'Could be cattle, or a big sheep.'

'You keep telling yourself that.'

The Cat's hyper-rifle deployed from her forearm, HVvixen missiles slipped into their launch tubes behind her shoulder blades. Ratmines scuttled down her legs, and darted into the thick cover of the bamboo.

Five sneekbots crept forward towards the house. They picked their way up the ramshackle walls and eased their way in over windowsills. The heat source never moved, it was in the open plan lounge.

A range of neon green symbols rose up into Morton's virtual vision. 'Electrical activity.'

'Not much. Looks like a hand-held array on sleeper mode.'

A sneekbot hurried across an open doorway, its antenna buds tracking across the lounge. An alien was standing in the middle of the big room. It wasn't wearing an armour suit. Water trickled through cracks on the ceiling to splash on its pale skin. A Commonwealth hand-held array was lying on a coffee table beside it. An optical cable was plugged into the little unit, snaking up to a compact electronic device which was fused to the bulbous end of one of the alien's four upper stalks.

'Shit,' Morton gasped. 'Where are the others? They always move in fours.' He ordered the sneekbots surrounding the house to extent their search. 'What the hell is it doing?'

'One moment, I'll switch on my suit's psychic power booster circuit. Oh, dear, it doesn't seem to be working. How the fuck do I know what it's doing, you blockhead?'

'You're not helping. Again.'

'I'm reviewing the available information. There's none of the usual signal emission. And it's not armed. Oh . . . wait.'

One of the alien's slender crown stalks bent over to align on the sneekbot as it peered out from behind the doorframe. The bud of flesh on the end was wearing a hemisphere of some electronically active plastic material, held in place by a couple of elasticated straps.

'Is that a nightsight goggle?' The Cat asked curiously.

Morton never replied. The sneekbot reported it was picking up a transmission based on standard Commonwealth cybersphere protocol. It was a very weak signal, nobody outside the ruined house would be able to detect it. His e-butler printed it across his virtual vision.

I surrender. Please do not shoot.

A nasty cold shiver rippled across Morton's shoulders.

'Oh my,' The Cat said. 'Now what?'

'I have no goddamn idea.' He told his e-butler to use a matching protocol, and used his virtual hand to type out a reply which the sneekbot sent: **Who are you?**

A friend. After last night, I guessed you would return. These houses offer considerable cover and are close to Randtown. It was the logical place for you to come. I have been waiting for you.

What do you want?

To come with you.

Where do you think we're going?

Back to the Commonwealth. I have information which will assist your fight against MorningLightMountain.

What is MorningLightMountain?

The Prime alien.

You are one of the aliens we are fighting.

I am not. My mind is human. I am Dudley Bose.

*

Cressat was beautiful. Mark had been surprised. He'd been expecting something like Elan, a world where the natural landscape of sparse vegetation was slowly being tamed to the human norm of aesthetics and practicality. The grand estates would be oases of lush verdant foliage, surrounded by agriculture and forests that were slowly spreading out across the plains, leaving mountains wild.

Instead, he was living in the most perfect manicured parkland. Nigel Sheldon had chosen Cressat for its botany. Its G-class star and lack of a big Earth-style moon gave the planet a passive meteorological environment. There were the standard climate zones, and seasons, but storms were rare. A planet which could be relied on for stability.

With such a consistent atmospheric milieu, evolution had produced some spectacular plants. Every tree grew tall, two or three times the size of Earth's pines and oaks, sporting huge colourful flowers. In midsummer, the native grasses turned from their usual near-terrestrial green to a shimmering swan-white; vast prairies of milky rippling stalks releasing clouds of honey-scented spores which turned the air silvery over entire continents. Vines and creepers ran riot in the forests, their imposing flower cones swelling out to heavy berry clusters – several of which were edible.

Biewn, the hurriedly built dormitory village where they were housed, was twenty-five miles away from Illanum, the town where the CST wormhole emerged. Nestling in rolling meadowland, with the western horizon bordered by distant snow-capped mountains that reminded all the Vernons of the Dau'sings, it catered solely for the large influx of technicians and experts working on the project.

The forest which formed one side of the village towered over the clutter of single-storey houses like arboreal skyscrapers. Streams wound through the undulating land, bridged in several places as the network of roads was steadily expanded. More houses arrived each day, brought in on the back of wide low-loader lorries. They might have been mobile homes, but Biewn hardly qualified as one of the employment-whore trailer parks that sprang up around the CST stations on all new worlds in their early years. It had its own schools, restaurants, bars, shops, and civic centre; the pre-equipped unit blocks of the new hospital were locking into place like a wall of massive bricks. Everything was being done to give Biewn the same amenities which Illanum enjoyed.

It was spoiled only by the factories. Long rows of the simple, massive cube structures had been built on the opposite side of Biewn to the forest, their dull brown weather-resistant walls eating into the virgin countryside like an unstoppable mechanical cancer. Still more were being built, their assembly going on round the clock. The cybernetics which filled them were arriving at an equally impressive rate.

As soon as their bus drove round the edge of the forest and started down the last mile of the new highway to the village, Mark knew he was going to fit in. It was as if the second chance he'd been given financially had magically been extended to his lifestyle. He imagined Biewn being the kind of place which Randtown would ultimately have evolved into, wealthy and purposeful. It had industry instead of agriculture. And instead of the Trine'ba they had the forest, which the inhabitants were already calling Rainbow Wood, after its astonishing flowers. But it retained that small-town community cohesion. Less than an hour after they moved in – to a house as big as the one in the Ulon Valley – three neighbours had dropped by to introduce themselves and ask if they needed help. Sandy and Barry rushed off with a bunch of other kids to explore.

His one regret was that he hadn't seen any of the legendary fabulous mansions which the Sheldon Dynasty members had built for themselves. None of their country-sized estates were anywhere near to Illanum.

That just left his job. He worked in factory 8. At his

orientation class he learned it contained three assembly bays. He considered that ordinary enough, then they told him their size: cylindrical chambers twenty-five metres in diameter and thirty-five high. They were lined by a hundred plyplastic tool arms, and twenty heavy lift manipulators; up to a hundred and fifty engineeringbots could be deployed inside at any one time. The construction operation was supervised by an array loaded with RI-level software.

'You're building starships,' Liz told him when he got back home after his first exhausting twelve-hour shift. 'Everyone in town says it.'

'Yeah, but they're not for the navy. The assembly bays are putting together complete compartments, that's why they're so large and complex. These are like spheres that have six airlocks. All you have to do is stack them together on top of a hyperdrive section, and you can have any size ship you want. It's the ultimate in modular design concept.'

'What's in the compartments?'

'Factory 8 is doing suspension tanks,' he said.

'Damn it. I bet they're evacuation ships. I had the placement office call me today and ask if I'd like to work in a team designing state of the art genetic agronomy laboratories. You know what that means?'

'Modifying terrestrial crops to grow in alien soil.'

Liz sucked on her lower lip. 'Sheldon's going to leave if we lose the war,' she said with grim admiration. 'He'll probably take most of his Dynasty with him. How many suspension tanks are in the compartments?'

'A hundred each. We're receiving all the major subcomponents already integrated; with the exception of the hull and the life-support systems, most of it is standard commercially available hardware. The assembly bays just plug all the pieces together. There's a lot of development gone into this. It would have taken a long time, even with advanced design software. I think he's been planning this since before the Invasion.'

'A hundred per compartment?' she mused. 'That's a big ship.'

'*Very*. Factory 8 is churning out six completed compartments a week. Some of the other factories are just packaging industrial cybernetics for long term storage. You've seen how many trucks are using the highway; they're shipping all the completed compartments out somewhere'

'Six a week, in one factory? That's . . .' She-half closed her eyes as she did some multiplication. 'Jesus damn! How big are these ships? He must be planning on taking a whole planet with him.'

'If you're intending to establish a high-technology civilization from scratch, you need a lot of equipment, and a decent population base.'

She put her arms round him. 'Do we get to go, too?'

'I don't know.'

'We need to find out, baby. We really do.'

'Hey, come on; this is just a rich man's paranoia. The Commonwealth's a long way from falling to the Primes.' Mark stroked her back, moving gently down her spine the way she liked.

'Then we should get paranoid, too. If we do lose, what would happen to Sandy and Barry? We've seen the Primes first hand, Mark. They don't give a fuck for humans; we're lower than pond scum to them.'

'All right, I'll ask round. Someone at the factory should know. Hey, did I tell you? Old Burcome is one of the managers. He'll probably tell me.'

'Thanks, baby, I know I'm a pain to live with sometimes.'

'Never.' He held her closer. 'I don't know where they're putting these ships together. It has to be in orbit, but I've not

411

seen anything here. Not that I've really looked, but anything that large would show up like a small moon.'

'It could be anywhere within a hundred light-years. Hell, Ozzie's asteroid was a perfect place to use as a shipyard, ultra top secret and habitable. You could house a cityful of people in there and barely notice them.'

*

The cloud had thickened up in the Regents, bringing with it a cloying sleet riddled with slender hailstones. Morton could hear them striking his armour suit, a constant tattoo of crackling to complement the sound of his feet as they squelched through tacky slush.

It was slow going back up the mountain to the saddle. The human survivors from Randtown were all riding in the bubbles, which could tackle the terrain easily, while Cat's Claws simply walked up in their armour. That left the alien who claimed to be Dudley Bose. It didn't have any kind of clothing to protect its pale skin. Bose said its body would work in the cold, but with difficulty. So they had to drape it in blankets and scraps of cloth, then hang sheets of plastic on top to protect it from the worst of the weather. Even so, the creature couldn't move fast up the muddy slope.

It took most of the night just to reach the cloud level, and that was taking a direct route up from the cave. After that they had to follow the contour line along to the saddle where their equipment was stored.

They detected flyers patrolling the lake below, but none ventured close to the mountains and their treacherous down-drafts and micro-swirls.

When they finally reached the saddle, they took refuge in one of the deep crevices.

Rob opened some of the packs Parker and Doc had brought with them. 'Try these on,' he told the three standing refugees, handing round clothes. 'A lot of it is semi-organic, it'll shape itself to you.'

'Thank you,' Simon said gravely. 'I am sorry we never got to know your friends.'

'Yeah, whatever.' Rob turned away and knelt down beside David Dunbavand. The man had improved considerably during the bubble ride, some colour had returned to his skin, and his feverish sweating had subsided. 'How're you doing?'

'Okay. The drive up was kind of interesting, the bits I remember anyway. Those biovirals: it's like drinking a gallon of champagne cocktails.'

'Your leg's stabilizing,' Rob said as he ran the diagnostic array up and down the man. 'Looking good.'

'Thanks.'

'How about you?' Morton asked the Bose motile.

'This body is sluggish but functional. Prime motiles suffer some degradation in the cold, but they are more resistant than humans.' The polythene and blanket swaddling it was covered in a thin layer of muddy slush. It was unwinding them one at a time, dropping them on the rocky floor. The array it was using to speak through was held in the pincers of one arm. 'May I eat, please?'

'Sure.' All three of Cat's Claws had carried plastic pouches full of lake water up the mountain. Bose said it was thick with base cells, the main food of the aliens. There were also containers full of cake-like vegetation, resembling shredded seaweed. It had built up quite a little stash in the ruined house in anticipation of repatriation.

They had all listened to Bose's story on the climb. How he and Verbeke had been captured in the Watchtower; their imprisonment and death, the download of his personal store into an immotile unit. He provided a fascinating insight into the nature of the threat the Commonwealth was facing. One that Morton and the others found uniquely disturbing. That they were being invaded purely with genocide in mind. That MorningLightMountain was psychologically unable to grasp the concept of compromise, let alone sharing a universe with any other life form. *Maybe Doc Roberts and Parker had got the right of it*, Morton thought. *This is a fight to the death.*

'Shouldn't be long till we get you back to a hospital now,' Rob told David. 'The navy will be opening a wormhole right away when they find out we've got Bose with us.'

Morton faced them all. 'I'm not sure we should tell the navy,' he said.

The Cat laughed with delight.

'You're kidding, right?' Rob said.

'No.'

'Okay, so you want to tell us why not?'

'Mellanie said the navy can't be trusted. Apparently there's some big political struggle going on in the Senate with the Dynasties and Grand Families.'

'What total bullshit,' Rob said.

'Are you talking about Mellanie Rescorai?' Simon asked. 'The reporter?'

Mandy let out a snort of disbelief. 'Her!'

'Yes,' Morton said.

'How is not telling the navy going to help the Common-wealth?' Simon asked.

'I'm not saying we don't ever tell them,' Morton said. 'I just want to know what the implications are before we do.'

'How do you propose finding out, exactly?' Rob asked. There was a dangerous edge to his voice.

'Mellanie arranged for encoded messages to be included in the recordings I send to the Michelangelo show. She'll be able to tell us if it's safe.'

'Safe!' Rob grunted. 'Man, you are paranoid!'

'Look, one day isn't going to make any difference,' Morton said reasonably. 'We're perfectly safe here. We have to wait until the Randtown force field is expanded anyway. So just humour me.'

'Shit!' Rob gave The Cat an angry stare. 'What do you say?'

'Me? I think it's hilarious, darling. Do it, Morty, screw the navy over. Gets my vote.'

'For what it's worth,' Simon said. 'I trust Mellanie.'

'How can you?' Mandy demanded. 'The little bitch was wrecking our town and everything we stood for, *your* ideals. The whole Commonwealth hated us because of her.'

'She saved us, though, didn't she?' Simon said gently. 'Surely that is penance enough?'

'Something happened here,' the Bose motile said. Everybody turned to look at it. 'This is where MorningLight-Mountain came up against the SI, the only time they clashed during the whole invasion. That is why I chose Randtown as my return point to the Commonwealth; the SI has some kind of presence here.'

'Had,' Morton said. 'It had a presence here. Mellanie works for the SI.'

'Ah,' Simon said. For the first time in weeks, he actually smiled. 'I always wondered how she achieved all she did.'

'Your girlfriend is some kind of agent for the SI?' an incredulous Rob asked. 'That . . . that . . . bimbo?'

'Hey,' Morton growled.

The Cat was laughing again. 'Oh this is fabulous. Thank you so much, Morty.'

Morton gave Rob a level gaze. 'So do I tell the navy or not?'

Rob glanced round at everyone, then gave the stationary motile a long stare. 'What the fuck. Do what you like for now, Morton. But after we set off the nuke your girl had better provide one hell of a reason not to tell the navy what we've got. That's how long she's got.'

'I'll tell her.'

*

Mark and Liz spent the evening in their lounge, sharing a bottle of wine and accessing the final moments of Randtown. It was Ulon Valley wine. His e-butler's search program had found a supplier on Lyonna who had a few bottles left; it was an extortionate price, and then there was the premium same-day shipping charge to MoZ Express couriers on top of that. But what else could you drink while you watched a nuclear explosion obliterate your old hometown?

Mellanie had joined Michelangelo in his studio for the report. She marked the sobriety of the occasion by wearing a long black dress, with a panel skirt that fell open to show off her beautiful legs. Her hair had been pulled back from her forehead into a thick, wavy tail. Michelangelo sat behind his desk like a minor Greek god in a sharp blue suit. The sexual tension between them was so strong that anyone using full-band TSI to access the show could almost smell the phero-mones they were both pumping out into the studio air.

It certainly gave Mark some uncomfortable reminders of that day he'd encountered her up at the blockade in the Dau'sing Mountains.

'You were there during the evacuation,' Michelangelo was saying. 'What's your response to this?'

'It was inevitable. I really enjoyed my time in Randtown. The people were a bit quirky, we all know that, but seeing the images of what the Primes had done to the town and the Trine'ba was just devastating to me. They got what they deserved. I only hope the other navy squads are equally effective.'

'You say effective, but they lost two of their members on their first deployment. This remarkable recording, exclusive to our show, reveals the desperate odds our navy troops on the ground are facing.'

The picture changed from the studio to a grainy image of a mountainside in the middle of the night, a composite of various sensor feeds, producing a monochrome image. It was centred on Randtown, with the force field shining like a phosphorescent pearl above the familiar shoreline. The tactical nuclear bomb went off, flooding the interior with light. For a brief second the force field held, containing the explosion. Then it failed, and the mushroom cloud climbed up out of a seething pool of darkness.

'There really is no going back now,' Mark said solemnly.

Liz raised her glass. 'To not looking back.'

'Amen.'

They stayed accessed for a while longer, while Mellanie eulogized about the squads which the navy had sent out. There were other recordings which Morton had made. Reconnoitre of Randtown and the aliens. The heroic last stand Doc Roberts and Parker made against the flyers. Simon Rand and the other refugees. She and Michelangelo discussing the navy strategy.

Mark's e-butler told him someone was approaching the front door.

'At this hour?' Liz asked.

The house array showed them an image of Giselle Swinsol standing outside.

'Oh Jesus,' Mark complained. 'Now what?' He kept having guilty thoughts about all those insistent questions he'd been asking at work.

Giselle came straight into the lounge, and refused the offer of a drink. She didn't sit, either. 'You've been asking a lot of questions, Mark,' she said. It was an accusation.

Mark was determined not to be intimidated by her tough-bitch personality. 'I'm working on a fascinating project; obviously I'm curious. But I can appreciate that Nigel Sheldon doesn't want the Commonwealth to know about it. You can rely on me.'

'Very good, Mark. The answer to your dreadfully unsubtle question is: yes, you and your family is entitled to a berth on the lifeboats should we face annihilation here.'

'Thank you.' It came out with such a heartfelt sigh he immediately felt ashamed. Once again she'd proved the strongest.

Her glossed lips curved up slightly, acknowledging her position. 'So, you now advance to level two.'

'What does that mean?' Liz asked suspiciously.

'It means that Mark has done such a good job here, that we feel his kind of expertise is better suited to other, more critical, sections of the project.'

'What sections?' he blurted.

'Starship assembly. Pack your bags. The bus will pick you up tomorrow at eight o'clock.'

'We're moving?' Liz said in alarm. 'But the children have only just settled in school.'

'Their next school is just as good.'

'Where is it?' Mark asked. 'Where are the evacuation starships being built?'

'Classified.' Giselle gave Liz a small smirk. 'You'll enjoy this next part. It's right up your street.'

'Cow,' Liz hissed when she'd left.

Mark looked round the lounge, the nearly empty bottle, the one big indentation on the couch where they'd snuggled up together. He had felt really comfortable in this house. 'I don't suppose they'll move us again after this.'

'Only to the other side of the galaxy, baby.'

*

Morty, do not inform the navy you have the motile containing Bose's memories. Any information on MorningLightMountain is too important to risk to possible corruption.

418

I have the re-lifed Bose with me. He should receive the memories, that way he will be able to interpret them in their correct sequence. After that we can decide how to proceed.

I will make arrangements to extract you from Elan. Until then, keep the Bose motile and the refugees safe.

Mellanie.

*

'I have been re-lifed?' the Bose motile asked.

'*She* will make arrangements to extract us?' Rob said disbelievingly.

'Mellanie had a wormhole opened to us once before,' Simon said. 'She can probably do it again.'

'Probably ain't good enough, friend.' Rob pointed at the Bose motile. 'This is our ticket out of here.'

'To what?' Morton asked. 'If she's right about the navy, we're not going to help the Commonwealth by giving them this information.'

'Oh listen to yourself. The Commonwealth navy is the *bad guy*? Get real. They're the only hope we've got. Your girl is trying to build her career by chasing phantoms. She's a goddamn reporter, one of the biggest turds in the galaxy. Tell the navy we've got Bose at the next wormhole opening. Get us out of here.'

'She works for the SI. She can do this. Trust her.'

'Bullshit.'

'Question,' The Cat said. She was sitting in Full Diamond position on the floor of the fissure, clad in a simple leotard, seemingly immune to the cold. 'Morton, when you sent your encrypted message, did you mention MorningLightMountain by name?'

'No.'

The Cat changed to King Cobra position with simple lithe movements. As she did, she gave Rob a sly smile. 'How did a conspiracy theorist nut find out its name all by herself?'

Rob's defiant expression crumpled. 'Oh, Jesus H. Christ; fuck-it-up Rob strikes again. I always get the shit assignments. Always. We're really going to do this, aren't we?'

'Yep.'

'I have been re-lifed?' the Bose motile repeated.

'Yes,' Morton said.

'And I am dating a beautiful young media reporter?'

'Apparently so, yes.'

'Tell him the rest of it, Morty my dear,' The Cat said with a smirk. 'Mellanie is a complete sex maniac.'

'I would very much like to meet me.'

*

The star system was on the border between phase one and two space, eight light-years from the Big15 world of Granada. CST had examined it once, and immediately moved on. The M-class star presided over a meagre realm of two planets; one small solid world no larger than Earth's moon, and a Saturn-size gas-giant orbited by a dozen moons. As far as habitability was concerned it rated an easy zero. Nobody had ever returned.

The starship *Moscow* slipped out of hyperspace a quarter of a million miles above the gas-giant. Its wormhole closed behind it with a short-lived glow of indigo radiance.

Strapped into his couch in the cabin's cramped operations segment, Captain McClain Gilbert reviewed the data which the starship's sensors were picking up. The gas-giant's third moon was twenty thousand kilometres away, a heavily cratered ball of rock, three thousand kilometres in diameter. There was no atmosphere. As the visual sensors scanned it, a profile of its surface built up. A recognizable topography of mare plains and hills was revealed, dating back to the moon's origin. Lustreless peat-brown regolith was scattered thinly over rock strata of dark-grey and black. Thousands of craters had mangled the smooth hills, ripping out vast slabs of jagged rock to form vertical cliff ramparts. Long zigzag fissures had cracked open, only to be buckled and deformed by later impact quakes. Over the aeons, cometary bombardment had slowly shaken the regolith down off the crumpled elevated plains where it drifted into the sharp gullies and pooled at the bottom of the craters. From afar, it resembled a thick sepia liquid filling the moon's lowlands.

There had been no change in the two hundred years since CST's exploratory division had performed its quick scan.

'Our survey records check out, such as they are,' Mac said. He turned to look at Natasha Kersley in the couch next to him. 'There's nothing alive around here. Is that what you wanted, Doc?'

'Looks good,' she said.

'Can I begin the satellite launch?'

'Yes, please.'

Mac sent a flurry of commands into the ship's RI. Modified missile launch tubes in the *Moscow*'s forward section opened, and spat out eighteen sensor satellites. Their ion rockets pushed them into a bracelet formation orbiting the nameless moon, allowing them to cover the entire surface simultaneously. Once their coverage was established they'd be able to determine the exact power of the quantumbuster they were here to test.

'So far so good,' he muttered.

'Absolutely. Here's hoping we don't have a Fermi moment.'

'A what?' Mac really didn't like the uncertainty in her voice.

'During the Trinity test of the very first atom bomb, Fermi wondered if the detonation would ignite the Earth's atmosphere. They just didn't know, you see. We think the quantum disruption won't propagate. If it does, then the whole universe gets converted into energy.'

'Oh great, thanks for sharing.' He gave the doomed moon a deeply troubled glance.

'It's really not very likely,' Natasha said.

It took two hours until Mac was satisfied the satellites were correctly placed, and their communication relay systems were locked together. 'Okay, Doc, you're on.'

Natasha drew a quick breath, and fed her launch code into the prototype quantumbuster warhead. The missile was hurled out of its launch tube by a powerful magnetic pulse. When it was ten kilometres from the starship, its fusion drive ignited, accelerating it hard towards the moon.

'All systems functional,' Natasha reported. 'Target acquired. I'm authorizing activation.' She sent another code to the weapon, and received confirmation. 'Let's get out of here.'

'Amen to that,' Mac muttered.

The *Moscow* opened a wormhole and quickly slipped inside. Five seconds later, and two million kilometres out from the moon, the starship slid back out into real space.

'Receiving satellite data,' Mac said, as the communication dish picked up the signal. 'Switching to high capacity recording.'

'Two minutes to impact,' Natasha said. 'All systems operational.'

'We're going to see it from here, right?' He was aligning the starship's sensors back on the moon.

'Oh heavens, yes. The quantumbuster field will initialize just before the missile hits the surface. That should give us an intersection over several hundred metres of the moon's mass. It works out to quite a substantial volume.'

'And the whole thing just turns to energy?'

'Any piece of matter inside the field, yes. That's the theory, the effect completely breaks down quantum-level cohesion. The discharge radiance will be on a scale we've never seen before.'

'Discharge radiance,' Mac said with a smile. 'You mean explosion.'

She gave him a nervous grin. 'Yeah.'

Mac turned his whole attention to the visual spectrum image which was being projected in front of his face. The moon was a simple dark circle framed by stars. All the sensor satellites were watching eagerly. They showed a tiny purple-white spark sinking towards the surface.

Mac had brought the *Moscow* out of hyperspace on the other side of the moon from the target zone. If the Seattle Project weapon worked as advertised, the radiation blast would be lethal even at two million kilometres. The Commonwealth would have a decisive weapon to use against the Primes.

'Do you think they'll negotiate?' he asked.

'If they see this in action, they'd be truly crazy not to,' Natasha said. 'I don't care how bizarre their motives are, they face extinction if we use this against them. They'll talk.'

Mac desperately wanted her to be right. The way he'd worked his way to the navy's vanguard, he was pretty sure he'd wind up with the mission to take a quantumbuster to Dyson Alpha.

He checked the moon again, worrying about the whole Fermi moment idea. The missile was seconds away from its brown and black mottled surface. *I should have positioned the* Moscow *on the other side of the gas-giant.*

The quantumbuster activated its effect field. Light flared around the moon, creating a perfect white halo. It was as if the ancient sphere of rock was eclipsing a white dwarf star. The edges began to dissolve as the glare poured across the cratered surface like an advancing tsunami. Dazzling cracks appeared, opening deep into the moon's interior. Low rolling hills heaved, transforming into volcanoes that jetted debris hundreds of kilometres out into space. Dusty plains crumbled as they separated ponderously from the highlands surrounding them.

Slowly and inexorably, the moon disintegrated inside its cocoon of lurid stellar light.

'Jesus, Doc,' Mac barked. 'You were just supposed to blow the bloody thing out of orbit.'

*

Giselle Swinsol herself was sitting at the front of the bus when it arrived to collect them. It was a fifty-seater Ford Landhound, with luxury seats and a small canteen in front of the washroom cubicles. Two other families were sitting in it, looking lost and vaguely apprehensive. Mark recognized the expression. He'd seen it in the bathroom mirror that morning.

Giselle waited until the porterbots had loaded all the Vernons' bags and boxes into the luggage compartment at the back. 'Don't look so worried, this isn't a long trip.'

Mark and Liz swapped a glance, then tried to settle the excited kids.

The bus drove back down the highway towards Illanum. It joined a convoy of vehicles, slotting in behind a forty-wheel transporter carrying one of the completed starship compartments, and in front of three standard container trucks, empty after dropping their loads at a factory. Once they had passed the back of Rainbow Wood, the compartment transporter turned off along a long curving slip road; the bus followed it. The slip road fed onto another three-lane highway wide enough to handle the transporters. After five miles, another slip road joined it, bringing more of the giant transporters.

'I didn't know there were any other towns on Cressat,' Mark said.

'There are five assembly centres here,' Giselle said. 'Biewn and two others are responsible for life support and cargo; one is fabricating the hyperdrives; and the last provides general systems, the starship's spine if you like.'

Mark began to re-evaluate the project yet again. The scale was larger than he'd imagined. So was the timescale, this had to have been going on for a long time prior to the Prime invasion. As for the cost . . .

The highway was heading directly for the base of a low hill where a circle of warm pink light was shining at them. Mark felt the slight tingle of a pressure membrane as the bus passed through. Then he, Liz and the kids were pressed against the window, anxious to see the new world.

They'd emerged high up in some mountains, giving them a view out over a flat plain that must have been hundreds of miles wide. It had strange yellow rock outcrops, and a jagged volcanic canyon running away diagonally from the mountains. The ground was completely bare, with a thin covering of grey-brown sand scattered over dark rock. Right away on the far horizon, were some rumpled dark specks which might have been more mountains; the planet's lavender-shaded sky made it difficult to tell.

They were on a broad ring road which curved around the human settlement, whose clean new buildings stood out against the mottled brown landscape like silver warts. The town had an outer band of factories, similar to those which Mark had worked in back in Biewn, several condo-style accommodation blocks, and five sprawling housing estates. Construction sites, swarming with bots, made up a good third of the area. A wormhole generator and four modern fusion stations dominated the skyline opposite the gateway back to Cressat.

Mark couldn't see any vegetation at all on the ground alongside the ring road, the land was a desert. Then he looked again at the topaz patches daubed on the plain below. At first he'd assumed they were some unusual rock formations. Each one was circular, perfectly circular now he was paying attention. They had steep radial undulations, like the folds in an origami flower. His retinal inserts zoomed in, allowing his e-butler to do some calculations. They measured over fifteen miles wide. A triple spike rose out of the centre of each one, reaching half a mile into the air.

'What the hell are those?' he asked.

'We call them the gigalife,' Giselle said. 'This planet is covered in the groundplants. They come in many colours, but they all grow to about this size. I've seen bigger ones in the tropical zones. And there's a waterplant variety which floats on the sea, though they are made up from a mesh of tendrils rather than the single sheets you can see here. There's nothing else alive on this world.'

'Nothing?' Liz queried. 'That's an unusual evolutionary route.'

'Told you this would be right up your street,' Giselle said with gratification. 'The gigalife has nothing to do with evolution. I wasn't joking when I said there was nothing else here. We haven't found any bacteriological or microbial traces other than the ones we brought with us. This planet was techno-formed with an oxygen-nitrogen atmosphere and freshwater oceans specifically to provide a place for them to grow. Up until about twenty thousand years ago it was just a lump of inert rock naked to space. Someone dumped the atmosphere and oceanic water here, presumably through gigantic worm-holes; we found evidence of a local gas giant's moon being strata mined for its crustal ice.'

'Do you know who did it?'

'No. We named them the Planters, because the only thing they left behind was the gigalife. Presumably they are some kind of artwork, though we can't be sure of that, either. It's the lead theory because we haven't found a practical application for them, and the Dynasty has been researching them for over a century now.'

'Why?' Liz asked. 'This is a fabulous discovery. They are the most extraordinary organisms I've ever seen. Why not share it with the Commonwealth?'

'Commercial application. Gigalife isn't quite genuine biological life. Whoever produced them has overcome Heisenberg's uncertainty principle; there is some kind of nanonic fabrication system operating inside the cells. Look at those central spires, they're made up from a conical mast of super strength carbon strands which the cells extrude. The leaf-sheet is simply draped over it. Gigalife is a fusion of ordinary biological processes and molecular mechanics, which we've so far been completely unable to duplicate. The implication, if we can crack the nanonic properties, is incalculable. We'd get everything from true von neumannism to bodies which can self-repair; human immortality would become integral rather than dependent on the crudity of today's rejuvenation techniques.'

Liz wrinkled her nose in disapproval. 'How long do the groundplants take to grow?'

'We're not sure. The current structures are about five thousand years old, and just maintain themselves. We've never seen one in its growth stage. Several are decaying faster than their regeneration process can cope with. Again, we don't know if they're actually dying, or if they're in a cycle. They could be like terrestrial bulbs and simply recharge their kernels for the next time around.'

'You mean they don't produce seeds?'

'Who knows? They have a kernel which is the size of a twenty-storey skyscraper. Best guess is that they were manufactured and placed in position by the Planters. If they were produced as seeds, how would they ever spread? They'd either need wheels or rockets.'

'Good point,' Liz admitted.

'Can you eat them?' Barry asked.

'No. We haven't found one with proteins that a human can consume. Of course, we haven't sampled more than a tiny percentage so far. We use non-invasive investigatory techniques, which is why our progress is slower than some in the Dynasty would like. But Nigel and Ozzie both agreed we didn't want the Planters to return and find we'd damaged anything. Any species possessing this kind of knowledge base is best left unannoyed.'

'You're very knowledgeable about this,' Liz said.

'I used to be director of the gigalife research office.'

'Ah.'

Giselle gave Mark a taunting smile. 'Here comes the good bit. Look out over there. Up in the sky. The first one will be rising into view any moment now.' She pointed over the plain to the west.

Mark didn't like the tone, it was too smug, but he looked anyway. He thought he would be seeing a starship assembly platform, which he was actually looking forward to. The prospect of working in orbit was one that fired him.

It wasn't an assembly platform. Mark watched in utter disbelief as a moon slid up over the horizon. It moved fast, and it was *huge*. 'That's not possible,' he whispered. All the kids in the bus were shrieking and pointing with excitement.

The moon was a stippled magenta globe, with a profusion of slender jet-black creases snaking across its surface. It was several times the size of Earth's moon. Too big, Mark knew instinctively, anything that big that close would produce tidal forces which would rip continents apart and haul a permanent tsunami round the globe in its wake. This wasn't even disturbing the few wispy high altitude clouds. Then he began to understand its texture. The multitude of black creases were actually fissures, walled by the same magenta material which coloured the surface. It was only in the deeps where the sunlight couldn't reach that they actually turned black. The moon wasn't big, just in a low orbit, neither was it solid; it was a gigantic spherical ruff, sheets of thin purple fabric crumpled up against each other.

'Oh no,' Mark said. He looked from the purple moon down to the topaz groundplant gigalife, then back again. 'No way.'

'Yes,' Giselle said. 'The third variety of gigalife, the space-flower. The Planters put fifteen asteroids into a two-thousand kilometre orbit, and dropped a kernel on each one. They don't mass more than about a hundred million tons each. It'll be interesting to see what happens when the kernel runs out of raw material to convert. Some of us think that will be when the Planters come back.'

'They sculpted moons,' Mark said in astonishment.

'Grew them,' Giselle corrected. 'Essentially we have a planet which has giant cabbages for moons. Who said aliens don't have a sense of humour?'

*

As soon as the Committee room doors opened, Justine rushed out. Surprised expressions followed her. It wasn't quite seemly for a senator to run.

She just made it to the lady's washroom, and threw up into the porcelain bowl. There was a discreet cough outside the cubical. 'Are you all right, ma'am?' the attendant asked.

'Fine, thank you. Bad food this morning.' She heaved again. Her forehead was damp with sweat, and she felt inordinately hot. The tension which had racked up during the Committee meeting hadn't helped her delicate stomach.

Ramon was waiting for her outside when she finally emerged. 'Something we said?' he asked with a raised eyebrow.

'Something I ate,' she told him, around yet another antacid tablet.

'I hope not. With all the paranoia around here, people will think assassins are trying to poison you.'

'Not a bad thing. It would get our fellow senators to cut down on the dining room food.'

'Now that is pure wishful thinking.'

She glanced down at his chest. Ramon was wearing a very modern business suit, tailored to de-emphasize his stomach. Normally when he was in the Senate Hall he was careful to wear tribal robes. But then the Security Oversight Committee was not one which permitted any media coverage. 'I see you're really sticking to your diet.'

Ramon let out a sigh. 'Don't start.'

'I'm sorry,' she said, contritely.

'Now I know something's wrong.'

'No there isn't. I'll survive. And thanks for supporting me in there this morning.'

'The African caucus does not automatically do as the Halgarths wish, nor any other Dynasty for that matter.'

'What about Grand Families?'

He smiled broadly. 'It depends on the deal which is offered.'

'Rammy, I need to ask you something.'

'Personal or business?'

'Business,' she said with a sigh. 'Always business these days.'

He reached out and gave her cheek an affectionate stroke. 'Thompson will be back soon.'

'Not soon enough.' She finished the antacid tablet, and they walked down the broad deserted corridor towards the Senate Hall's main lobby. 'That weekend at Sorbonne Wood, who exactly came up with the idea for parallel development shared between Anshun and High Angel?'

Ramon stopped to stare at her. 'Why do you need to know?'

'There are certain aspects about the navy formation that we have to clarify.'

'What aspects?'

'The groupings, Rammy, come on. You have to admit, for a venture that size it all came together remarkably smoothly.'

'Thanks to you. It was a Burnelli weekend if I remember rightly.'

'We're worried we might have been outmanoeuvred.'

'Ha! That would be a first. I know how Gore operates. Nothing is left to chance.'

'Someone else was manipulating that weekend. We're sure of it.'

'What's happened? Have you missed out on a big contract?'

'No. But High Angel was a massive beneficiary, and through that the African Caucus. You owe us for that.'

'I suppose I might. I believe the idea came from Kantil. She was very eager to gain support for Doi at the time.'

'Did Patricia tell you herself, or was it Isabella?'

'Justine,' he grinned down at her. 'Are you jealous?'

'Please! This is important. Did Isabella tell you it came direct from Kantil, that Doi would sanction the spending?'

'I honestly don't recall exactly. Isabella made the suggestion, so naturally I assumed it came from Kantil. Lovely though Isabella is, she's only a first-life girl. Why, who else do you think would make it?'

'Isabella's a Halgarth,' Justine said.

'Oh no,' he threw his hands into the air with exasperation. 'We're back to the motion for a vote on Myo again.'

'It's not the vote.'

'It's looking that way to me. You took it personally. Admit it.'

'I know Valetta caught me off guard in there; Thompson would never have let that sneak up on him. It's beginning to look as though I just don't have his aptitude for this job.'

'Nonsense. You're more than capable. You outmanoeuvred Valetta beautifully, and gave yourself time to build support for the vote. You're a natural.'

'It doesn't seem that way. Damn that Columbia for forcing my hand like this. It'll be a real show of strength in the next Committee. I'm not even sure I can win.'

'You have my vote.'

'Yeah, right, thanks.'

'This really bugs you; and it's not the first time you've clashed with the Halgarths and their allies. Why don't you just declare open warfare, and have the fleet attack Solidade.'

'Because it's their fleet, Rammy.'

'So that's it! Gore's pissed that they hijacked his pet project.'

'The navy isn't a project, it's essential to our survival. We're at war, fighting for our very existence as a species, and the Halgarths are taking over the Commonwealth's entire defence policy. That's not healthy.'

'Don't let this Senate spat blind you, Sheldon remains in ultimate command. Thanks to CST his Dynasty will always have the final say. And Kime is still admiral; he's Sheldon's man, in alliance with Los Vada. With Columbia, the Halgarths only have control of planetary defence. It's a classic Dynasty carve up. The power structures balance out.'

'All right.' She tried to put on a convinced expression for his benefit.

'That's better. So how about lunch? Just you and me, and no business.'

'Old times,' she said mournfully. 'Sorry, Rammy, I've got to get back to the office. I need to start making calls.'

His hopeful expression gave way to something more melancholic. 'I understand. My advice: call Crispin. He was never a Halgarth man.'

She gave him a quick kiss on the lips. 'Thanks. See you soon.'

*

It was Thompson's office. The taste was his, all lush reds and gold-brown wood furniture. She hadn't made a single change, she didn't have the right. When he came back, he could sit down behind his vast desk and carry on as if nothing had happened.

If the world still exists then.

Justine dismissed her aides, and ignored the urgent briefing files as she settled into her brother's chair.

So Isabella hadn't specifically said it was Patricia's suggestion. That wasn't a lot to go on, although it deepened her own suspicions that Patricia was being played like the rest of them.

'Could really do with your advice, Tommy,' she told the

room. The rejuvenation clinic their family owned and used was just on the outskirts of Washington, not quite fifteen miles from Senate Hall as the crow flies. Right now his clone foetus was there, growing inside a womb tank, about ten centimetres long.

She looked down at her own abdomen, resting her hand lightly against it. Her stomach was still perfectly flat, not that she'd been to the gym for weeks now. 'You're going to be born before your uncle,' she said softly. 'He's going to be surprised about that.' *Along with an awful lot of other people.*

With her real hand resting contentedly above the baby, her virtual hand touched Paula Myo's icon.

'Yes, Senator?'

Does she ever sleep? 'I have some unpleasant news you should be aware of. I was just ambushed in the Security Oversight Committee. Senator Valetta Halgarth asked for your immediate withdrawal from Senate Security.'

'On what grounds?'

'Very shaky ones. Fortunately. She cited interference in Navy Intelligence operations, claimed you were misusing government resources to pursue personal goals.'

'The observation on Alessandra Baron.'

'Precisely. I managed to delay the vote on a procedural point about the agenda. But it is only a delay. It looks like Columbia really has got it in for you.'

'I know that. Thank you for covering for me.'

'I'll talk to the other senators, rebuild my strategic support in that Committee. I should be able to pull a majority onto my side. Right now there are several people who are unhappy with the Halgarths; they're not my Family's natural allies, but I should be able to swing them round.'

'I understand. This could be very revealing.'

'How so?'

'Do you have any indication which way the Sheldons intend

to vote? It goes against the Starflyer's interests to have me remain in Senate Security.'

'Good point. I'll try and find out.'

*

MorningLightMountain was *annoyed* with humans. It had known they would strike back after its preliminary incursion into the Commonwealth, such a move was inevitable. What was less welcome was the manner of the response. It had been expecting wormholes to open above the captured planets, disgorging quantities of ships and missiles to assault its new installations. So it had dutifully prepared for that scenario, building the strongest force field generators it had over the factories and refineries it was constructing on the new worlds, placing thousands of ships, armed with powerful weaponry, in orbit.

With all the knowledge it had gathered about the Commonwealth and its abilities, MorningLightMountain was certain this would be enough to ward off the human attack. There was an astonishing amount of information left behind amid the wreckage of the abandoned human cities; storage crystals which contained entire encyclopedias, scientific theories and research, engineering designs, economic and industrial statistics on each of the Commonwealth worlds, and a truly endless supply of 'entertainment'. For the first time Morning-LightMountain was grateful it had animated the Bose memories; without that small insight into human thinking it would have been extremely difficult to distinguish between fact and *fiction*. And humans produced an astonishing amount of fiction to amuse themselves.

To its disappointment, there was little information available on the SI. There was no verifiable record on any of its new 23 worlds as to the exact location of Vinmar. Once the Commonwealth worlds were converted to Prime life, it would have to search all the star systems within two hundred light years of Earth. Some files speculated that the SI was no longer physically based, but had transformed itself to an energy based entity. MorningLightMountain could not decide if these, too, were works of *fiction*.

It also had humans to extract information from. There were tens of thousands of discarded bodies lying buried in the rubble or trapped in smashed vehicles. Removing their memorycells was an easy operation. Living humans presented more trouble; they struggled and fought the soldier motiles. In the end, MorningLightMountain simply shot them all, and recovered their memorycells that way. It learned that there was very little useful information recorded in these personal units, they only ever held memories, and human minds were not reliable. After animating a few inside isolated immotiles, it found that most were even more unstable than Bose. More surprisingly, few were as knowledgeable. MorningLightMountain has always assumed Bose was an inferior human specimen.

As it tapped into more and more databases, so its picture of the Commonwealth strengthened, building on the original loose interpretation which came from the Bose memories. It began to reclaim and modify human cybernetic fabrication systems, turning the machinery to producing components and machines of its own design. Buildings were modified to house its facilities, roads were used for vehicles. Bridges rebuilt.

The one segment of human technology it discarded was the electronics. MorningLightMountain simply did not trust the processors and programs that were available to it. There were hundreds of thousands of files detailing hidden subversive applications built into arrays and software. Ever since the first communication net was commissioned on Earth, humans seemed to have devoted a colossal amount of time and effort to conduct seditious assaults against each other inside its virtual boundaries. They disrupted the activities of their rivals, renegades launched viral attacks for the *fun* of it, and criminal elements stole from anyone with weaker encryption defences in a massive electronic version of the territorial struggles which the immotile Primes used to wage constantly. After centuries of development, their skill in this arena was deadly. Their electronic warfare attacks against MorningLightMountain's soldier motiles during the original incursion was proof of their digital superiority. It did not have the experience nor ability to uncover and guard against such digital deceit. Consequentially, it simply removed the arrays from human equipment, and inserted itself into the control circuits. Such substitution absorbed a great deal of thought capacity. One of its priorities on its new worlds was to establish immotile groups which were used to manage and exploit human engineering.

Progress in this, and other areas was advancing well. Then the Commonwealth made its counterstrike. Wormholes opened above all the new 23 worlds. Sure enough, missiles flooded through. MorningLightMountain sent its ships to intercept. It had a huge advantage, humans were reluctant to use fusion bombs, fearing their *collateral environmental damage*. A trait it had learned from both Bose and subsequent human personality animation, as well as datamining political proclamations. All of the weapons it directed to repel the attack were nuclear.

Then more wormholes appeared, this time on the ground, flashing in and out of existence. MorningLightMountain struggled to keep up with plotting their emergence. Once more, humans were successfully disrupting its internal communications. Flyers were sent out to each location, encountering some resistance as *aerobots* zoomed out to confront them. The automatic machines were nimble, but not strong enough to defeat superior numbers of flyers. And superior numbers was MorningLightMountain's specific advantage.

After seventeen hours, the attack ended. MorningLight-Mountain was victorious. It had sustained some damage, but there had been no strategic defeat. Motiles and machinery were directed to repair the broken systems. After studying the attack pattern, it began to strengthen and modify its defences accordingly. The Commonwealth was weaker than it had predicted.

Many hours later, the disturbances began. There had always been brief clashes with armed humans on its new 23 worlds. Several hundred motiles had been killed. A number so small it barely registered with MorningLightMountain's main thought routines. Defences strong enough to withstand strategic bombardment from space were more than adequate to cope with anything wild humans could strike them with.

Bridges fell as convoys were driving over them, their support pillars blown apart by explosives.

Soldier motiles on patrol dropped out of communication and never returned.

Fires broke out in factories.

Fusion generators suffered unexplained confinement field instabilities. Their MHD chambers ruptured, to shoot out spears of plasma which incinerated anything in their path.

Armoured humans were detected around force fields, only to inexplicably vanish again.

Equipment outside the force fields failed. Investigation showed deliberately damaged parts, or small explosive charges.

A fusion bomb detonated outside the Randtown force field, wiping out fifteen flyers.

Farmer motiles were killed on a continuing basis, shot from long range. Farm equipment was sabotaged. Whole crops were lost.

A fusion bomb went off inside the Randtown force field, destroying the entire installation.

Armoured humans had now been spotted on every world. They were impossible to catch, when cornered they fought until they died, usually by triggering fusion bombs.

Microscopic wormholes began to appear above all of the new worlds, emerging for a few seconds only. They were no threat.

Fusion bombs went off on Olivenza, Sligo, Whalton, Nattavaara, and Anshun.

New strip mines were vaporized.

The sabotage was not causing enough damage to halt MorningLightMountain's expansion across its new 23 worlds. But the ruined installations all had to be rebuilt. Motiles replaced. Roads repaired. Crops replanted.

Then the armoured humans would reappear from nowhere and wreck them all over again. MorningLightMountain rebuilt each time, incorporating stronger defences, which took longer to construct. It brought in tens of thousands of additional soldier motiles from its homeworld, all of which had to be fed and supported, stretching its resources on the new 23 worlds. The disruption tactics which the humans were employing were extremely *irritating*. MorningLightMountain didn't know how to stop them. Back on its homeworld, conflicts had been fought out in the open with both sides trying to inflict maximum damage. This was different. MorningLightMountain knew from human personality animation that they would never stop this *guerrilla warfare* harassment. Their history was heavy with such actions. Fanatical *freedom fighters* had successfully defeated conventional armies time and again.

It would only stop when there were no more free humans. MorningLightMountain began to commit more resources towards achieving that task.

*

The staging post detected superluminal quantum distortion waves sweeping through the star system. Their origin point was a distortion signature which corresponded to a human starship engine, three light-years distant. The starship was already heading away from the staging post.

MorningLightMountain knew what the Commonwealth navy would do now it had discovered the location of the staging post. Attack with every weapon it possessed.

Thousands of immotile groups had considered what defence could be used against the kind of relativistic attack the humans had used at Anshun. The complex machinery which would modify its wormhole generators was already under construction. MorningLightMountain prioritized its completion, and began transferring the first components to the staging post. It also began to assemble its new fleet of warships. When the navy starships arrived, weakening the Commonwealth defences, it would begin its second expansion stage into Commonwealth space, invading a further 48 worlds.

7

Patricia Kantil and Daniel Alster left the Senate Hall together and shared the express to Kerensk. McClain Gilbert was waiting at the gateway station to escort them. The three of them took a navy shuttle over to Babuyan Atoll, a twenty-minute flight.

'Even after all the preparatory work we've done, I can't believe we've reached this stage,' Patricia said. 'I don't mind telling you, the President is very anxious about this.'

'We all are,' Mac said. 'This could well be the turning point.'

'Does the admiral think we have enough ships?' Daniel asked.

'He'll tell you himself,' Mac said. He gestured at the thick windows set into the cabin's ceiling. 'As you can see, we haven't been slacking.'

Space around the High Angel was getting crowded. There were now three free flying ports linked back to Kerensk, delivering passengers and small cargo pods to the shuttles which flew them on to the new navy facilities as well as the archipelago's industrial stations. The nine warship assembly platforms were much larger than the original models used to construct the first generation of scoutships. Each one had five giant malmetal fabrication spheres arranged around a central gateway section which had a wormhole leading back to

Kerensk. Hull sections and components were now conveyed directly to the advanced cybernetic systems that would put them together.

A malmetal ball on platform four was open, revealing one of the new *Moscow*-class warships as it prepared to disengage. The *London* was a hundred and fifty metres long, its rust-red hull a double sphere, with the forward globe smaller than the rear, and seven rapier-blade thermal radiators protruding from its waist. There was no allusion to aerodynamics this time; the *Moscow*-class was designed purely as a weapons-delivery ship. Functions were stripped back to a minimum. Its entire rear globe was the engineering section, housing ten niling d-sinks and a hyperdrive capable of powering it to a speed of four light-years per hour. Riding in the waist, a crew of five was crammed into a single circular cabin that was barely larger than their flight couches. That left the rest of the forward globe as storage space for its cargo of Douvoir relativistic missiles.

'They look imposing,' Patricia said.

'There's enough weaponry in one of those to destroy every planet in Earth's solar system, including Jupiter,' Mac told her. 'For once, we have the firepower advantage.'

'I hope you've got failsafes to prevent unauthorized launches,' Daniel said.

Mac gave him a funny look. 'The Douvoirs have tripartite arming codes, three members of the crew have to authorize a launch.'

'What if a ship is damaged, and you've only got two crew left?' Patricia asked.

'Not going to happen,' Mac assured her. 'Anything powerful enough to get through the force field which shields a *Moscow*-class ship will destroy the entire ship.'

'Ah, I see.' Patricia turned back to the massive alien starship which the shuttle was approaching.

*

Admiral Kime gave his guests a warm welcome as they arrived in his office at the top of Pentagon II. It was night in Babuyan Atoll, leaving the vast crystal dome clear. Icalanise was a slender cadmium-yellow crescent sinking towards the parkland rim. The rest of space visible overhead was packed with the bright silver shapes of the archipelago, whose research labs and shimmering macrohubs were now complemented by all the new navy stations and platforms. Hundreds of shuttles swarmed between them, their ion rockets creating tenuous electric-blue nebula streaks across the void.

After greeting both Kime and Columbia, Patricia sat beside Oscar. 'Congratulations.'

'Thanks.' He gave her a wan smile. 'Sorry for not getting up. Gravity makes me feel very weak and dizzy right now.'

'Please, don't apologize.'

'The annoying thing is, I stuck to the exercise schedule we were given, and took all the biogenics. It doesn't make the slightest difference. Damn, I hate freefall.'

'The President asked me to convey her personal thanks to you and your crew. Discovering the opening to Hell's Gateway is the vital element which could turn this whole campaign round.'

'Just doing our job,' Oscar mumbled.

Mac came up behind his old friend. 'Modesty is also a byproduct of freefall exposure. Don't worry, he'll be cured by the time we reach the medal-giving ceremony. Do you think the Vice President will award Oscar's personally?' he asked with a straight face.

Patricia laughed. 'Now I think about it, our good Vice President Bicklu wasn't his usual joyful self in Cabinet when your name was mentioned.'

Oscar managed to smile at that.

Wilson called everyone to order. Dimitri Leopoldvich, who had been talking quietly to Rafael, took a seat next to Anna; while Mac sat on the other side of Daniel. Technically, this was the Navy Strategic Review Council, but Wilson thought of it as simply a meeting between his best advisers and the Executive, as represented by Patricia and Daniel. Its job was to come up with policy to forward to the War Cabinet.

'We'll open with the obvious,' Wilson said. 'The location of Hell's Gateway.' A hologram portal on his desk projected a simple star map. The star system where Oscar had detected the giant wormhole was about three hundred light-years beyond Elan.

'You've all seen the sensor log,' Oscar said. 'There is no mistake; it's them.'

'Low possibility,' Dimitri said. 'But we have to consider if this is a decoy.'

'An enormously expensive one,' Mac said. 'We know the Primes don't have economics the way we do, but in terms of resources it would be a considerable investment in machinery to duplicate Hell's Gateway. And for what purpose? At best it would gain them a couple of months' respite.'

'Or they've built a second giant wormhole,' Dimitri said cheerfully. 'More than one? We know they are quadralactric, it would be prudent to assume the worst.'

'You always do,' Patricia said in a low voice.

Dimitri's pale face lifted in a regretful smile. 'My job.'

'Are you suggesting we postpone the attack?' Rafael asked.

'No, sir. What I, and the Strategic Studies Institute, are recommending is that the scout flights should continue. In fact, we ought to take another flyby of Dyson Alpha, that would tell us for sure if there are any more giant wormholes operating there.'

'Risky,' Wilson said.

'The same risk as attacking Hell's Gateway,' Dimitri countered. 'Whatever defences the Primes have developed, you can be sure they won't be restricted to their home system. Hell's Gateway is vital to them, it will be defended with the best they've got.'

'We'll certainly fly reconnaissance missions afterwards,' Wilson said. 'We need as much intelligence about their intent as we can gather.'

'Intent is their one continuing unknown,' Dimitri said. 'As Captain Gilbert said, their economic model doesn't follow any we understand. However you look at it, invading the Commonwealth is simply not cost-effective. Our conclusion is that they are mounting some kind of religious crusade against us.'

'That's ridiculous,' Daniel said.

'Excuse me, sir, but it is not. Obviously we don't even know if they have gods or religion, but the fundamental principle stands. They are not doing this out of logic, therefore a degree of fanaticism is involved. Crusades are the human equivalent, whether they have religion or ideology as their starting point. We have had a great many during our history.'

'Is this relevant to considering our assault strategy on Hell's Gateway?' Patricia asked.

'The implications should be considered,' Dimitri said. 'We are striking what we hope will be a significant blow against an enormously powerful enemy. If their motivation for invading the Commonwealth is based on an illogical premise; that their "God" or political leader has decided humans must be swept from the galaxy, they will not be deterred. It will be a setback, not an end to their campaign. They will hit back. We must be prepared for that eventuality.'

'Without Hell's Gateway it would take them a long time to rebuild and strike at us,' Rafael said. 'Every ship orbiting the Lost23, every installation they've built in the Commonwealth will be vulnerable to us. We can eliminate them completely before any reinforcements arrive.'

'Pardon me, Admiral,' Dimitri said, 'but those Lost23 planets have been well named by the media. They are indeed lost to us; permanently. Right now the troops we have deployed there are absorbing a great deal of the Primes' resources; but in the event we succeed in destroying Hell's

Gateway the Lost23 become an irrelevance. We should not deploy our ships in battles that will result in any attrition.'

'I'm all for that,' Mac said sarcastically. 'We only go in slugging when we know we won't get hurt in the process.' He gave Dimitri a tight, almost pitying, smile. 'This is war, man; it gets dirty and we *are* going to take losses. You have to accept that.'

'We are in the process of developing weapons that will guarantee victory,' Dimitri said. 'Wait until they have been built, then use them. Don't try and knock the Primes down one tiny piece at a time. They are too big. We can't do it.'

Nobody replied. Wilson took a look round their troubled faces. Everyone here knew about the Seattle quantumbuster, but it was the last resort, the doomsday weapon that you prayed to whatever god you believed in that you'd never have to use. It certainly wasn't the first thing you reached for. 'The only way the Seattle weapon can be deployed to get us that guarantee is if we use it to genocide the Primes,' he said.

'And what do you believe, Admiral, they are doing to us? I have accessed the reports from squads dropped onto the Lost23. On every single occasion when refugees and survivors encountered the Primes, they were exterminated. We cannot assign them human logic and motivation; don't make the mistake of assuming they care about us. They want us dead and gone. Every analysis the Institute has made boils down to one simple proposition: it's them or us.'

'Use of the Seattle Project weapons is a political decision which will be taken by the War Cabinet,' Rafael said. 'That has already been agreed. It is not part of the strategy we are discussing today.'

'Then we would recommend it should be,' Dimitri said. There was a glint of sweat on his pale brow as he leaned forward in his chair to appeal directly to Wilson. 'I'm not saying this lightly, but we have already shown our hand. What the *Desperado* did was truly magnificent, they slowed down the Prime advance and in doing so allowed millions of people to escape. But the Primes have now seen that application of hyperdrive technology. They will be able to duplicate it. And more, they will be devising counter measures – I know we are. If we strike Hell's Gateway with relativistic weapons there is no guarantee they will be successful.'

'Nothing in war is certain,' Wilson replied. 'That doesn't mean we give up.'

'I'm not saying we should give up. I'm saying we should have a complete victory.'

'Prime ships started leaving Dyson Alpha within an hour of the barrier coming down,' Oscar said. 'They are out in the universe now, an escaped genie. We have to deal with them on that basis.'

Dimitri pushed back some of his floppy hair. 'I'm sorry, we at the StPetersburg Institute do not believe that ultimately there is any other way to deal with them. Whoever encountered them before was clearly of a similar opinion, which is why the barrier was erected. We do not have that luxury.'

'Thank you, Dimitri,' Wilson said. 'The Institute's views will be brought before the War Cabinet. For now, we are planning a conventional assault against Hell's Gateway. Anna?'

'Manufacture of *Moscow*-class ships is accelerating,' she said. 'Now that we're mass-producing all the hull sections and components on the Big15 it takes about a fortnight to assemble one from scratch. The process is a lot more modular than it was even with the scoutships. Currently we have twelve of them operational, but that's due to change rapidly. Our ninth assembly platform is now complete; sections for platforms ten through fifteen are being fabricated, and should be functional within another month. Linking the platforms directly to Kerensk via wormhole has been a real boon as far as construction is concerned. We've trodden on Chairwoman Gall's toes in the process, but she's been diplomatic enough to keep quiet; she realizes that High Angel can't insist on a monopoly in these times. Besides, most of the docking station crews are still dormitoried here.'

'How many ships can we send against Hell's Gateway?' Patricia asked.

'By the end of this week: fifteen. If we wait another week, there will be twenty-two. If you wait a further week, we should have commissioned over forty, and after that we'll be churning out forty-five every fortnight.'

'How many do you need for a successful strike, one that closes Hell's Gateway?'

'We estimate a minimum of twenty,' Mac said. 'They have a formidable presence in that star system. Hell's Gateway is only a part of it, there are all the generators for the wormholes leading to the Lost23, which are still transferring a colossal amount of equipment to the Commonwealth. During the invasion, we estimate they deployed over forty-five thousand ships against us. If they're planning a second invasion, we must assume that at least that many are currently stationed there. Probably a lot more.'

'Twenty of our ships against forty thousand?' Patricia said. She sounded worried.

'We won't be engaging them the way we did above the Lost23,' Wilson said. 'The *Moscow* class will stand off and launch their Douvoir missiles from the edge of the Hell's Gateway star system. No slower than light ships will ever reach them.'

'Twenty ships?' Patricia said.

'Minimum,' Mac said.

'Fair enough, another week is acceptable.'

'It must be longer,' Dimitri said. 'You cannot throw everything we have at them, there has to be a reserve. The Primes *will* retaliate.'

Patricia gave him a fractious glance.

'Dimitri is correct,' Rafael said. 'This has to be balanced correctly. Much as I hate to say it, we have to take the prospect of failure into account. As I am responsible for defending the remaining Commonwealth planets I must ask for some ships to be assigned to protective duties.'

'Wilson?' Daniel asked.

'I agree, it is the prudent course. I know people are impatient for us to retaliate, but this is not something we should lay open to political expediency. The guerrilla warfare is progressing well. We can take the opportunity to increase the number of troops on the Lost23 while we carry on building ships. We know that strategy is working well, intensifying it should keep the Primes preoccupied.'

'How long?' Patricia asked.

'A fortnight,' Anna told her. 'That will give us twenty ships to cover each duty. That should be enough.'

'All right, I'll take that to the President.'

*

Oscar remained in his seat as the others said their goodbyes and left the office. Trepidation was making his stomach churn, a sensation far worse than any of the aftereffects of freefall exposure. He didn't like the idea of lying to Wilson just to cover his own ass, not with something this serious. But Wilson certainly had to be told, and he'd probably figure out who else was involved.

Mac and Anna were the last to leave. Oscar caught her giving Wilson a quick little shrug before the door closed.

'Drink?' Wilson asked.

'Yeah, thanks. Whisky, with some ice, no water.'

Wilson gave him a slightly surprised look, but walked across the white office to the spherical drinks cabinet. 'Well, you've certainly got me curious. An official and private meeting.'

'We have a problem,' Oscar said.

Wilson gave a distant grin as he poured the whisky into a crystal tumbler. 'Houston.'

'What?'

'Nothing. Sorry, go on.'

Oscar accepted the drink, despising himself for needing liquid courage. 'A little while ago I was approached by someone who was suspicious about various aspects of the *Second Chance* mission.'

'You, too, huh?'

'They talked to you?' Oscar found that incredible.

'Let's just say there's a lot of politics going on around here. What did this someone want from you?'

'It's easier if I show you. Here,' he told his e-butler to access the log recordings directly from the secure navy database. The portal on Wilson's desk projected the recording from the shuttle as it started its journey to the Watchtower.

'See the main dish?' Oscar asked as he froze the image. 'Someone was signalling to the Prime homeworld.'

'Son of a bitch.' Wilson dropped into his chair, staring at the picture which filled half of his office. 'Are you sure?'

'We both know the dish shouldn't be deployed at this stage in the mission. I did some rough alignment calculations, and that's the direction it's pointing.'

'Son of a *bitch*. Who the hell was it?'

'I don't know. Our records are quite comprehensive, but whoever ordered the dish to deploy was clearly circumventing our management programs. This is about the only proof we've got it ever happened.'

'I don't understand: a traitor? Why? What possible motive could there be?'

'There's a lot of fairly wild theories floating round in the unisphere,' Oscar said carefully. 'We never did understand why the barrier came down as soon as we arrived. And I think we can be pretty certain now what glitched our communications with Bose and Verbeke.'

'Someone in the crew,' Wilson whispered in shock. 'But I picked them all . . . *we* picked them. You and I.'

'Yeah,' Oscar said miserably.

'Christ.' Wilson was still staring at the picture of the dish as if it was some kind of physical threat. 'This doesn't make any sense. Nobody benefits from a war. In any case nobody knew what was inside the barrier.'

'The Silfen probably did.'

'No. Not them. I don't believe that.' He turned to Oscar, eyes narrowing. 'Who asked you to look into this?'

Oscar held his gaze. 'The Guardians of Selfhood. Someone I used to know was the contact.'

'*Fuck*, Oscar! Those bastards tried to destroy the *Second Chance*.'

Oscar nodded at the picture. 'They might have had good reason.'

'The Starflyer alien they believe in? You can't be serious.'

'Maybe I'm not,' Oscar said wearily. 'I don't know. But somebody on board was acting against us in the most terrifying way imaginable. We're fighting a war because of that flight, a war we might lose, and all that entails for us as a species. As you said: where's the motive? It's not political.'

'No, you're right, it's not. There has to be some kind of outside influence. Whoever did this is betraying us as a species. Son of a bitch, that's just so hard to accept.'

'I know.'

'Have you told the Guardians about this yet?'

'No, of course not. Look, I'll make this easy for you; I'll resign.'

'Like hell! We need to find out what the fuck is going on, and do it fast. We're about to send our fleet to Hell's Gateway; and God help us if that goes wrong.'

'You don't think . . .'

'Somebody betrayed us before while we were flying the *Second Chance*. If they're still around, they can do it again, and probably will.'

'Goddamn, I hadn't thought of that. What do you want to do?'

'Get help. Paula Myo knows everything there is to know about the Guardians. I'll consult with her.'

*

Mellanie broke her promise. They didn't check into a swanky LA hotel. Instead, she found a cheap three-room apartment just behind Venice Beach. The building was old and worn down, its ground floor given over to small ultra-bargain stores selling T-shirts, handmade jewellery, second-hand domestic bots, powerskates, and sportswear, each of them blaring out tinny music late into the night. The windows on the two floors above had wooden shutters and rows of ancient air-conditioning units that whistled and hissed in the sun's glare. Colourful murals had been sprayed over the exterior, where the salty Pacific air slowly set about eroding them. Every few years a new one would be applied. The current illustration, in the style of retro-Soviet realism, created with modern holographic refraction granules, was over five years old, its long saggy blisters peeling open to reveal the layers of decades past, like the rings of a tree exposing a history of fashions and short-lived trends embraced by previous generations.

The apartment next door to theirs was taken by a couple who fought every time their shifts brought them home together. While upstairs a hooker sneaked her clients up the fire stairs and gave them their hour's worth of non-TSI entertainment at high volume.

In their own rooms the water supply was erratic. The fridge was stuck on its coldest setting, freezing anything they put inside. Furnishings dated back fifty years. And the purple-painted floorboards creaked badly.

The building's landlord was only too pleased to take cash. There was no accessible record that they were living there.

451

Strangely, for an environment that was so unruly, Dudley was at his most relaxed since they hooked up. When she got back from her visits to the Michelangelo studio offices she'd often find him cooking elaborate meals, or sitting outside the building with a beer, watching the theatre of street life going past. She suspected the fact that Morton was unreachable, two hundred light-years away, had a lot to do with his newfound contentment.

The evening after Mellanie received the recording of Randtown's destruction, she slipped into a simple T-shirt dress and walked down to the beach. She carried her trainers in one hand as she walked along the sand, heading for the Santa Monica pier.

When her virtual hand activated the one-time address, Adam Elvin responded at once. 'I haven't been able to find any trace of the three lawyers from Bromley, Waterford, and Granku,' she told him. 'They certainly haven't contacted their families. The monitor programs my friend installed would have detected that.'

'Don't be too harsh on yourself. It's a big Commonwealth out there,' Adam said. 'The whole episode proves that the Starflyer funded Bose's observation. We don't need to take it any further.'

'But they must have some kind of connection to Baron. I want to find it.'

'We appreciate that, but Baron is more relevant to you than us.'

'I thought you wanted in on the Starflyer's agents and their network. Does it matter where and who?'

'Ultimately, no.'

'Well then.'

She sauntered past one of the areas marked out with volleyball courts. Overhead lights on tall masts had been switched on, casting a yellow illumination on the two games being played. One of the guys called out to her, begging her to join their team. She smiled back regretfully.

'We still can't help you with that,' Adam said.

'Okay, how about this: my friend Morton has made contact with an alien that has Dudley Bose's memories, the ones from his time on the *Second Chance*.'

'Holy shit, are you serious?'

'Very.'

'Can you get us access?'

'Not directly, no. The SI won't help me getting them off Elan, and I don't know how to get back to Ozzie's asteroid on my own. I don't suppose you have a working wormhole generator?'

'No, sorry.'

'Didn't think so. If you have any questions for Bose, I'll be happy to pass them on.'

'I'll get on to Johansson right away. Does the navy know about this?'

'Not yet. I asked Morty to keep this private. So far, it is.'

'You're doing a fantastic job, Mellanie.'

'It doesn't seem to be getting me very far. I feel like a sitting duck, waiting for Baron's people to take a shot at me.'

'I'm sure we can bring this all together before that happens. Have you talked to Myo recently?'

'No. I don't have any information I can use to bargain with; apart from Morty, and that's got to be illegal. I've been busy trying to trace the lawyers, and doing gigs for Michelangelo. Speaking of which, do you have any inside knowledge about the rich building their lifeboats, especially the Sheldons?'

'Only the rumours in the unisphere. They say the cheapest ticket will cost you a billion Earth dollars. You thinking of leaving us, Mellanie?'

A billion dollars? Christ, does Paul Cramley really think I'm worth that much? The idea was extraordinarily flattering. 'Not yet,' she said. 'I still want to help.'

'We appreciate it. Three more Starflyer agents you should be aware of: Isabella Halgarth, and her parents Victor and Bernadette. If you see any of them coming, duck.'

'Thanks. How do you know?'

'Bradley has been looking into the shotgun which claimed Doi was a Starflyer agent. It wasn't one of ours. Isabella helped put it together. She's now dropped out of sight, which is a sure sign she's going to become more active. We've established small teams to observe her parents; if they spot anything that'll help with your problems I'll let you know immediately.'

'I appreciate that. I get . . . I feel lonely a lot of the time.'

'I probably understand that more than most. I've been living this paranoid non-life for decades now.'

'How do you cope?'

'Not very well, I suppose; that's the easy answer. I used to believe in what I was doing, I had a real crusade going for my ideals. These days, events have just swept me along. I'm like you, Mellanie, I'm waiting for it all to resolve. If it's any comfort, I don't think it will take much longer now.'

'I hope you're right. Goodnight, Adam.'

'It's almost dawn for me. Which is a shame, the night here is quite beautiful.'

Mellanie signed off with a light touch of regret. She wondered where he was that was so beautiful. Talking to Adam always made her feel less isolated. They'd never met, and probably never would, but discussing the business helped her confidence no end. He was a professional, doing what he did out of commitment and belief; he approved of her efforts, offering snippets of advice. It added up to a weird kind of friendship, but in a bizarre way she trusted him a lot more than anyone else in her life right now.

Up ahead, the gaudy multicoloured illuminations of the Santa Monica pier stretched out over the water as the sky darkened behind it. She gave the funfair rides a brief longing glance before turning round and wandering back over the sands. Dudley would start getting agitated if she was away for much longer. Venice Beach was where LA's offworld contract workers lived and hung out. The beach was free, its stores were cheap, and its bars cheaper. It was always busy, and even slightly trendy in a kitschy way. Mellanie quite enjoyed the beach and cruising the stalls for all their cultural diversity and second-hand junk. She'd even spotted some shoddy rip-offs of her own designs amid the T-shirts, sunhats, and pirated brand arrays. Storeholders shouted out in languages she didn't recognize, selling fruit and vegetables that were either alien or massively gene-modified.

Even though it didn't have the wealth prevalent in the rest of Los Angeles, it was still safe. Providing she kept to the public spaces. Some of the clubs along the beachfront were coming alive now the sun had fallen behind the ocean, music and holographic projections seeping out from their doorways. One little part of her mind wished she was coming home to someone like Adam Elvin. Not that she *needed* a man, any man. But Adam would be a lot less hard work than Dudley with his insecurities and paranoia and jealousies. Adam, she imagined, would be a lot calmer and reassuring; someone she could talk to about all her problems with the Starflyer and worrying about being exposed. He'd have answers and solutions, strategies for coping.

Dudley was sitting on the stone steps outside their apartment building. He smiled as he caught sight of her, and hurried over. 'I've been doing some research,' he said eagerly.

'That's good,' Mellanie replied automatically. The swirling projectors issuing out of the stores' logo holograms sent worms of pink and amber light wriggling over his face. She frowned. 'Dudley, is that a new OCtattoo?'

He grinned and stroked his ear. 'Yeah. One of the parlours down by the beach etched it in for me.'

She stroked the red and gold swirls with her fingers, her inserts and programs examining the organic circuitry. The OCtattoo was a very cheap sense booster with added TSI functions, expanding his cybersphere interface with a whole range of customization software. There were no buried assets or encrypted code in the management routines. His skin was already turning red around the elaborate spirals, an infection that was the sure sign of an unprofessional application.

'Was it a verified brand? Did you see the licence before it was applied?'

'Mellanie! You're my girl, not my mother. I've had enough OCtattoos in my time to know what I'm doing.'

'Okay.' She headed up the stairs. 'What have you been researching?'

'Spaceships.' He smiled with all the pride of a school kid about to hand in homework that was guaranteed to get an A grade.

'What kind?' she asked.

He opened the apartment door and gestured her inside, but not before making a furtive glance along the empty landing. 'Augusta has several orbital factories for electronics and exotic microgee materials. They have spaceplanes and, more importantly, inter-orbit tugs.'

'Yes?'

'I looked up the specs and did some calculations. It felt good using my astronomy background for something practical. If we hired one of the inter-orbit tugs, and filled the reaction mass tanks, and carried no cargo except ourselves, it could take us to the Regulus system's outer gas-giant.'

'And why would we want to go there?' she asked. The couple next door were shouting at each other again. Thankfully, it was silent upstairs.

'That has to be where Isaacs' asteroid habitat is,' Dudley said. 'An asteroid that size is extremely unusual. Trust me, it is far more likely to be a small moon.'

She almost launched into her usual chastisement, but leaving him alone to work on some new obsession would actually reduce the amount of time she spent worrying about what he was up to. So instead she said: 'I don't know . . .' her voice cautious.

'I'm convinced it's in the Regulus system. That would provide easy access to Augusta, which is where the construction systems must have come from. Everyone automatically assumes that CST and Augusta belongs solely to the Sheldon Dynasty. They forget that Isaacs was a co-founder, he has an equal share.'

'I suppose so. But I doubt we can afford to hire a spaceship. I don't have that kind of money.'

'The Michelangelo show would pay. Once we reach the habitat, we can gain access to Isaacs' wormhole. We can take Morton and the motile off Elan.'

Which is what this is really all about, Mellanie knew. Ever since Dudley had heard about the strange alien motile he had been consumed with meeting it. She was thankful he despised the navy and completely distrusted Admiral Kime, otherwise he would have gone straight to them asking for the motile to be recovered. 'It would have to be a really good proposal for them to come up with that kind of money,' she said. 'You'd have to be very sure of the spaceship performance.'

'I am. We can do it.' Dudley stroked his ear. 'A few more upgrades like this, some memory skill implants, and I'll be able to pilot us myself.'

'All right. If you collect some figures, very detailed figures, Dudley, I'll think about it.'

'Yes!' He punched one hand into the palm of the other, smiling broadly. 'I'll get onto it right away.'

Mellanie slipped the T-shirt dress straps off her shoulders, and let the garment slide down onto the ancient floorboards. 'I didn't know Ozzie owned half of CST.'

'Oh yes.' Dudley was staring at her as if he'd never seen her body before. 'They started the company together. Sheldon was always the director, the commercial half of the partnership. So he's the one the public and the media always see making statements. It's an association thing.'

'Interesting.' She unhooked her bra.

It was the signal for Dudley to struggle out of his own shirt, desperately trying to get it off over his head and getting badly tangled up in the hurry. 'You know, he hasn't been seen for years.'

'Who? Ozzie?'

'Yes. I found that out when I was researching this. Not that it's unusual. He's always travelling through the Commonwealth. They say he's visited every planet, and had a child on each of them.'

Mellanie stepped out of her panties and walked through into the bathroom. She turned the shower on, grateful the water was mildly warm. 'If he's so important, it's strange he hasn't said anything about the Primes. You know, there was a lot of pressure on the Baron show not to mention the asteroid habitat. I wonder what's happened to him?'

'That's Ozzie for you: one crazy dude.' Dudley was trying to get his pants off; he had to grip the doorframe to stop falling over. 'I'd like to be like him.'

'If he's as rebellious as everyone says he might let us use his wormhole anyway.'

'We'd have to find him first.'

'I'll ask round the office. Somebody there might know where he is.'

Dudley finally got his pants off, and made for the shower.

'Wait there.' Mellanie said sharply. He came to a halt in the middle of the small bathroom.

She started to rub the thick soapy gel onto her body. 'Watch me first. I'll tell you when you can join me.'

Dudley sucked on his lower lip and whimpered.

*

Nigel followed his three bodyguards out of the wormhole gateway. It was daylight in Ozzie's gigantic, hollowed-out asteroid, with the balmy humid air washing over him carrying the sweet scent of flower blossom. A wide white canvas awning arched above the gateway, allowing visitors to acclimatize to the bizarre curving landscape as they moved out from under it. As he walked forward, so more of the cylindrical cavern was revealed, two green wings sweeping up on either side, becoming steeper and steeper until they began to arch over-head. Sizzling white light shone out of the axis gantry, its glare obscuring the ground directly above him. Tall, impressively craggy mountains jutted out from the curving landscape at all angles around him, disorientating in their fantastical perspec-tive. The sight coupled with the rotational gravity field pro-duced a momentary sensation of motion sickness which made his legs weaken. One of the bodyguards actually stumbled, falling to his knees. His colleagues hauled him up, trying not to snigger.

'This way,' Nigel said, and headed down the gravel path which led away from the cliff where the gateway was embed-ded. Birds were singing not far away.

The interior was almost as he remembered. It was the trees which had changed, they were all mature now, adding to the elegance of the panorama. He didn't like to think how many decades it would take to produce such a gap between his last recollection and today; judging by the height and density of the forests it could easily be a century.

Several gardenbots were busy on the grass, tending the rhododendron bushes and little spinneys of silver birch. There was no sign that several thousand people had poured through here like a runaway tide; no garbage, no trampled plants.

At the end of the path, the small bungalow was just as he remembered it. A single deckchair was sitting in the garden underneath a broad copper beech tree, waiting for its owner to return.

Daniel Alster's call icon popped into Nigel's virtual vision. He sighed, and opened a connection.

'Sorry, sir,' Daniel said. 'There's a development I thought you should know about.'

'Go ahead,' he said, knowing it would be important. He trusted Daniel to filter most of the output from the Dynasty's political office.

'The Halgarths have just gone nuclear against the Burnellis in committee.'

'Hmm, which committee?'

'Security Oversight.'

'Really?' As always Daniel had been right. The Security Oversight Committee was normally immune to the usual political manoeuvring and squabbling between Senate factions; and at this time it should have been completely sacrosanct. For any kind of spat to have spilled over into its sessions was serious indeed. 'What happened?'

'Valetta Halgarth tried to bump Paula Myo out of Senate Security this morning.'

Nigel was suddenly very interested. The Dynasty had been indebted to the Investigator on more than one occasion; after one case he'd even thanked her personally. Not that she pursued anyone for political reasons. He'd almost intervened himself when the political office told him Rafael Columbia had engineered her removal from Navy Intelligence; then Gore had stepped in, and there'd been no need. 'What's she done to annoy the Halgarths now?'

'We're not quite sure, it's probably ongoing. The Burnellis are worried about the Halgarths increasing their power base within the navy hierarchy.'

'They're not alone. Go on.'

'The reason Valetta gave was Myo interfering in Navy Intelligence operations. Apparently Myo made an official request to her old Paris office to put Alessandra Baron under observation.'

'What does Myo think Baron has done?'

'We don't know.'

'It's probably not relevant to the Halgarths. As you say, this is a direct power struggle. I'll talk to Jessica, I think we need to start keeping a closer eye on the Halgarths and their plans for the navy.'

'Yes, sir.'

The call ended, and Nigel came to a halt, considering what he'd just been told. The bodyguards waited respectfully. If there was one thing he knew about Paula Myo it was her honesty; she wouldn't put Baron under observation on purely political grounds no matter how hard the Burnellis insisted. Then there was Thompson's shocking murder, which remained completely unsolved. The assassin's reappearance at LA Galactic was also something that hadn't been satisfactorily explained. Something was going on at a level which affected the Dynasties and Grand families, and to his considerable annoyance, he didn't know what. That was almost unheard of. His virtual hand reached out and touched Nelson's icon. 'Got an information collection job for you,' he told the Dynasty security chief.

*

Nigel knew the bungalow was deserted before he stepped through the open archway that was its entrance. There was something about an unoccupied home that spoke directly to the human subconscious. Nonetheless, he called out: 'Ozzie, you about, dude?' as he wandered through into the lounge.

After an extensive investigation to locate Ozzie, Nelson had drawn a complete blank. A surprise in itself. Nigel had been girding himself for the news that Ozzie had set up home on one of the Lost23 worlds. But no, the last trace Nelson's department could find was a ticket to Silvergalde. A team of Dynasty security agents had descended on Lyddington to find out what they could. The town was in chaos from the number of refugees flooding to Silvergalde in the belief that the Silfen would defend their world from the Primes. And there were no electronic records to review. That left money and alcohol to liberate tongues and unreliable memories. Ozzie had been in town, a stable owner claimed to have sold him a horse and a lontras. He hadn't stayed long. A tavern landlord said he'd set out to walk the Silfen's deep paths in the wood. Certainly no one in Lyddington had seen him come back. As Ozzie legends went it was credible, suitably mythic and epic. Nigel wasn't so certain. Ozzie had feigned disinterest in the Dyson Alpha barrier, but that was the usual Ozzie bullshit. Nigel had checked, it was the only time Ozzie had ever turned up to an ExoProtectorate Council meeting. His friend was interested all right, enigmatic alien Big Dumb Objects were the kind of thing Ozzie loved. For him to then vanish off into a forest full of elves was difficult to understand.

Nigel's inserts sensed several arrays activating in the lounge. A holographic portal projected a life-size image of Ozzie right in front of him, dressed in a shabby yellow T-shirt and creased shorts; from his bleary eyes it looked like he'd just woken up with a hangover. 'Hi Nige,' it said. 'Sorry you're here. I guess I must have been gone awhile and you've started worrying. Well, this is a recording I made to reassure you I'm okay. I love the idea you're gonna build a starship, man, that's gonna be so coolio. Hey, I bet you wind up going on the voyage in the end, you'll find some excuse.'

'Wrong,' Nigel whispered at the image of his friend.

'I've gone the other way to find out what's there. You know me, huh. The whole Dyson sphere thing is really weird, you know? And the Silfen have got to know something about it. I never did fall for all that mystic guru shit. They're smart and they've been around a long time. So I'm doing a bit of exploring myself. I'm gonna track down those paths of theirs, and find out what's at the centre of their forests. I'm betting it's something like our own slippy tricky little SI. Hopefully it'll have some answers for me. So don't go worrying about me, and I'll see you when I get back. Double sorry if you needed me to solve a biggo problem, just like the old days. You stay chill, now.'

The image switched off.

'Oh, shit, Ozzie,' Nigel said in a pained voice. 'You dickhead.'

*

Paula took a brief look round the large opulent office; as far as she could see, nothing had changed. Every piece of big gold-brown furniture was where she remembered. Even the aides were the same. Which made it all the stranger that it was Justine sitting behind the big desk, framed by a window looking out over Washington's skyline.

'Thanks for finding the time to see me,' Paula said as the senator rose to greet her. There was something in Justine's movements which made Paula study her a little longer than was strictly polite.

'No problem. I bet you got a few stares on your way up.'

'A few,' Paula admitted.

They sat on one of the big leather couches. An aide had already set out a silver coffee service for them. Justine poured a cup of non-modified Jamaican gold for Paula. Her own drink was water.

'Your father has uncovered a huge amount of financial irregularities in Bromley, Waterford, and Granku's accounts. The company seems to be a distribution point for a number of individuals and organizations which have no verifiable existence. A lot of money comes in through various unlisted client accounts, and promptly vanishes. There also seems to be an equal amount of illegitimate activity at Denman Manhattan who run the accounts for Bromley, Waterford, and Granku.'

'Excellent. This sort of thing is easy for Gore, he was doing it before I was born for God's sake. So what's your next move?'

'Our preliminary analysis is that Bromley, Waterford, and Granku was acting as a financial distribution centre for the Starflyer agent network. They know it's been compromised, of course, that's why Seaton, Daltra, and Pomanskie have all vanished. The network funding will have been switched to another distribution centre. However, Gore is going to inform the Financial Regulation Directorate, apparently he has a lot of contacts there. The Directorate will subject both Bromley, Waterford, and Granku, and the Denman Manhattan bank to a forensic accounting evaluation. It'll be considerably more thorough than anything Senate Security can run. There's a chance that they might identify both the source of all this dark money, and some of the elusive individuals it was channelled to. It will be difficult, whoever set this up knew what they were doing, and of course one time accounts remain the bane of law enforcement.'

'I'm sure Bromley, Waterford, and Granku has been shut down, but I know the FRD, they'll take months if not years to complete their investigation.'

'I am of the same opinion,' Paula said. 'But that aspect of the investigation may well soon be irrelevant, which is why I'm here in person.'

'You don't trust encrypted calls?'

'I was on the East Coast anyway to see your father, and this is extremely important. Wilson Kime has been in touch with me. He's asked me to visit the High Angel to review some information. His message was very short, but it seems as though he's uncovered some kind of abnormality which occurred during the *Second Chance* mission.'

'Damn, that's a surprise,' Justine muttered.

'Exactly. Convincing Wilson Kime that something is wrong could well be a turning point for us. In which case we'd need to know how strong our political support is. Are you making any progress?'

'Better than I'd expected. I can certainly defeat the vote

against you in Committee whenever Valetta Halgarth gets it onto the agenda again. But a full Senate vote is another matter. If we're to launch an official investigation into the Starflyer I've got to have rock solid proof not just that it exists, but that it is doing exactly what the Guardians claim, and manipulating human politicians. And we both know my fellow senators won't take kindly to that allegation, especially the Halgarths.'

'What about the Sheldons?'

'I haven't determined their intent yet. I'm sorry.'

'I'd like to suggest a strategy,' Paula said warily. The idea was one which she and Gore had discussed at their meeting. It wasn't quite the kind of tactic she approved of, manoeuvring someone into a precarious position. Especially given what she suspected about the senator's current physical situation. But these were unusual times, Paula reflected, and there was no illegality on their part, which was the one line she would never cross – not even to challenge the Starflyer. *Though it is a very blurred line these days.* 'According to the Guardians, the Starflyer will return to Far Away when the Commonwealth has been destroyed.'

'I didn't know that.'

'It's been mentioned in several of their shotguns. I have studied their content intensively over the decades and Johansson seems quite convinced by this. In fact I suspect that has a lot to do with the unusual equipment they have been trying to smuggle to Far Away recently.'

'All right, so it wants to go back to Far Away. How does that help us?'

'That whole elaborate double wormhole connection to Far Away is massively subsidized by the Commonwealth. You should suggest withdrawing the funding, effectively shutting down the wormholes and preventing the Starflyer from returning.'

'Ouch.' Justine smiled roguishly into her glass. 'That's going to annoy people.'

'It is intended to, especially the Halgarths and the Sheldons.

Their reaction would be informative. It would certainly expose their political allies to us.'

'I could possibly include it as a rider on the navy finance bill that's coming up next week. It's justifiable as it would divert money from Far Away to the navy. Let me talk to Crispin, he always has been against subsidizing Far Away.'

'Thank you. I should add there might be some considerable risk in it for yourself personally. Your brother Thompson was killed because he interfered with the transport arrangements to Far Away. You might want to consider asking Senator Goldreich to propose the rider for you, given your ... condition.' She couldn't help the light flush rising on her cheeks, though she held Justine's stare levelly.

'What *condition* is that?'

'I believe you're pregnant, Senator. There are certain signs in evidence. And you did tell me you were going to give Kazimir the one gift still within your ability to grant. I suppose that was the real reason the body was taken to your family clinic in New York.'

Justine looked down. 'Yes. You're right on all counts. If you could keep that to yourself, please.'

'Of course, Senator. But the risk – you would effectively be bait.'

'I assume you and my father had taken that into account.'

'Your personal security would be upgraded and in place before the Far Away proposal is made. Senate Security has several operatives wetwired at a level capable of dealing with the Starflyer assassin.'

'Walk in the park, then.'

'Hardly.'

'I'll schedule an appointment with Crispin. You can start upgrading my security.'

'Thank you, Senator.'

*

Justine sat on the couch for a long while after the Investigator had left. The prospect that Kime could come round to accepting the Starflyer was a phenomenal breakthrough. Though the more she considered the implications, the more worried she became. At the moment she was completely alone in the Senate in her belief, which made her extremely vulnerable. By introducing the prospect that the Starflyer was real she would expose herself to political destruction by the Halgarths, possibly in conjunction with the Sheldons. They really did need undeniable proof before going public.

But then that's always been the problem.

The icon which represented the code Kazimir had sent her as he died was still a glowing azure point at the edge of her virtual vision. A constant temptation. Her virtual finger reached out and touched it. She blamed hormones.

*

As befitted the leader of the African Caucus, Ramon DB's office was actually larger than Thompson's. The walls were hung with ancient shields, and skins; holographic portraits showed vast landscapes from every African world. Right in the middle, the largest picture showed a panoramic view of Kilimanjaro, taken a century ago, when the glaciers on the top had expanded again, returning the colossal mountain to its former glory. There was a smaller picture beside it, featuring Ramon at the top of the volcano, dressed in thick thermal walking clothes, standing beside the glacier's edge, smiling proudly at the camera.

Justine tilted her head to one side as she looked at it. 'You know, I could have sworn I was standing next to you when that was taken. How strange, you must have walked up there again without me. And in the same clothes, too.'

'I ... er. This is a political office,' he said sheepishly. 'Everything in here has to be symbolic of my constituency, those who I represent, who need my help.'

'And what could be more symbolic than you taking a white wife? A union between two cultures and races. Building a bridge. A loving partnership. Showing that we are all above the conflicts of the past. Creating a Commonwealth of equality and fairness. A Commonwealth where skin colour simply doesn't—'

'All right, all right! I take the point. Dear God, woman.'

'So you'll change it back? You'll stop me from being an unperson.' Somehow she managed to keep a straight face. It was difficult, he looked so guilty, which brought out that vulnerable aspect she'd adored. She'd always had fun teasing Rammy.

'I will take it under advisement, certainly,' he said with mock dignity.

'Why, thank you, Senator. You can rely on my vote.'

'Was there a reason you came here other than to taunt me?'

The humour faded from her face. 'Yes. I need some serious advice.'

'And you came to me? I'm flattered. Is this *serious* political advice, or personal? I know it can't be corporate, I remember Gore's opinions on my ideology. What was it he used to call me?'

'A whingeing pinko illiberal without a clue how the real world works, is probably the only one I can repeat in an office as symbolic as this.'

Ramon laughed, and kissed her cheek. She was disturbed by how cold his skin was, the little layer of perspiration on his forehead.

'So you needn't worry, this is definitely political advice I'm after,' she said as they sat on a long teak bench carved with antelope figures. She felt her stomach churn again, and clenched her throat. There was nothing she could do to stop the shiver running down her body.

'Are you all right?' Ramon asked, his face creased in genuine concern.

'Better shape than you.' She gave him a weak smile. 'A lot better.' Her hand went to her mouth as her stomach rebelled again.

Ramon was studying her intently. He leant in a little closer, as if he couldn't quite believe what he was seeing. 'Dear God, you're pregnant.'

'Yes.'

'I . . . That's . . . Congratulations.'

'Thanks, Rammy.' She was worried she was going to start crying. *Damn hormones.*

'You're really pregnant. He must be quite something. You didn't even do that for me. Our child was grown in a womb tank.'

There was nothing she could do to stop it. The tears just came pouring out. 'He's dead,' she sobbed. 'Really dead, Rammy. And it's all my fault.'

'Dead?' His arms had gone round her, slipping easily into the comfy old position, her head on his shoulder, cheek pressed to his neck. 'Are you talking about that boy at LA Galactic?' he asked.

'Yes.'

'So you're punishing yourself like this.'

'No. It's our baby, I want it to be safe. This way I can be sure.'

'I know you,' he said soothingly. 'This is the penance you've given yourself.'

'Maybe. I don't know.'

'He must have been very special.'

'He was. And I was stupid to ever get involved.' She drew back, and sniffed, wiping her hands across her eyes. 'It's all so goddamn complicated.'

'He was a young man with a cause he believed in. Everybody

469

over a century old envies that. We might be able to buy youthful bodies with rejuvenation, but the integrity and intensity of youth, that is only ever a fading memory.'

'You don't understand. He really was killed by the Starflyer.'

Ramon stiffened slightly, giving her a keen glance. 'You don't mean that.'

'I do. That's why I'm here. Some of us are convinced that it does exist, that the Guardians are right.'

'Oh Justine, no. You mustn't do this. It's a reaction to the loss, just like the pregnancy. You want to believe in what he believed.'

'It's not just me, Rammy. A lot of us are of the same opinion; and we're about to be joined by a very major player.'

'You should talk this through with your father. He'll soon cut through all the bullshit. It's what he does.'

'Gore believed before I did.'

'*Gore* believes this?'

'Yes.'

'Dear God. So this is what you wanted advice about?'

'Of course. Exactly how do I go about introducing the notion to the Senate that some of its own members are traitors to the human species?'

Ramon sat back, a slow amused smile spreading across his face. 'Carefully. Very, very carefully. So this is the actual issue surrounding Paula Myo? The fight between you and the Halgarths.'

'Yes.'

'I see. Are you going to share any of the proof with me?'

'A lot of it is circumstantial. You have to be on the receiving end to appreciate it properly.' As she said it, she realized how weak it sounded. 'I should have absolute proof in a couple of days. That's why I'm preparing the groundwork now.'

'They accused Doi of being a Starflyer agent. The President herself.'

'She's not.' Justine recalled the conversation she'd just had with Bradley Johansson. 'That was part of a disinformation campaign to discredit the Guardians.'

He clicked his fingers. 'Your interest in revisiting the Sorbonne Wood weekend. That's a part of this as well.'

'We were being manipulated.'

'Preparing us for war. Yes, I see now. Just as the Guardians claim.'

'You say it with such scepticism.'

'And did you blindly follow your father's belief?'

'No,' she admitted.

'Then kindly allow me to judge the facts for myself. And so far you have provided me with none.'

'If I do, if I show you proof that cannot be argued with, will you help me in the Senate?'

'Justine. Dearest of all my wives. I hate to see you suffer like this. First the shock of Thompson. Now the guilt of your lover being killed. You were there and think you are responsible.'

'I *am* responsible.'

'All this leaves you so emotionally vulnerable. In such times you cling to the wildest hope of redemption. People like the Guardians know how to exploit that. Cults have refined their recruitment operations down the centuries until they have become masters of extracting devotion and money from their damaged followers in exchange for their own vision of salvation.'

'Well thank you, my darling; I would never have worked that out for myself.' She gave him an exasperated glare. 'Rammy, I was dodging fortune hunters and investment shysters before your great-grandparents ever met. There is no money to be made from this. It is not a scam. It is not a warped religion. It is the most dangerous threat the human species has ever faced, and the most elusive.'

'I could never resist when you were cross with me.'

'Stop that!'

He pouted.

'Rammy; it doesn't matter if you think I've gone right off the deep end with grief.' Her hand slipped down to her belly. 'Given my state, that's perfectly excusable. The least you could do is humour me. It'll be good therapy. You do want me to recover, don't you?'

'You diabolical woman. I can never win with you, can I?'

'Marriage was your victory. The greatest.'

'Arrgh, how I hate you.'

'Rammy, focus, please; if this proof does exist will you help me?'

'I would have to see it before I even consider answering that question. And Justine, it would have to be absolute proof. I need to see this Starflyer knocking up the Pope's illegitimate underage daughter; the full *in flagrante* TSI recording. Nothing else will do. Even then I'm not guaranteeing anything.'

She grinned back at him. 'Is she another tall blonde, then?'

'Evil woman!' He held her gently again. 'Now I want you to promise me something.'

'What?'

'If this proof is not forthcoming, you will see someone who can help with the grief.'

'You're kidding. A shrink? Me?'

His gaze remained steady. 'An easy promise, surely? You know you are right, therefore you will never have to do it.'

'I taught you well, didn't I?'

He gave a modest shrug. 'Your word?'

'My word.'

'Thank you.' He bent forward and kissed her on the forehead. 'And if you need someone there at the birth . . .'

'Oh Rammy,' the tears were threatening to return. 'It couldn't be anyone else.'

*

472

Justine had just reached the elevators at the end of the Senate Hall's long east wing when the alarm went off. She turned round to see doors opening all along the wide corridor, staffers looking round in puzzlement. A bright amber strobe was flashing above the door to Ramon DB's suite of offices. 'No,' she breathed. Shock turned her muscles to ice; she couldn't move. *It's him! The assassin. He's here.*

'Priority call from Senator Ramon DB,' her e-butler told her.

'Authorized,' she gasped through tightened throat muscles.

'Justine.'

'Rammy! Rammy, what's wrong?'

'Oh shit, it hurts.'

'What does? Has he shot you?'

'Shot me? It's my chest. Dear God. I hit my head when I fell. I can see blood.'

'Your chest?'

'Yes. Mitchan is trying to get me to drink water. Damn fool.'

'Let him help.'

'Not if he starts bringing out defibrillator paddles, I won't.'

Justine started to run, pushing past the interminable number of people flooding out into the corridor. She was halfway there when three paramedics emerged from the freight elevator and shouted at everyone to get out of the way, an automated crash cart sped after them, followed by two nursebots.

'The emergency team is here, Rammy. They're coming.'

'Oh good; finally, some decent drugs.'

'How could you let it get this far? I told you, I warned you to watch your diet. Why don't you ever listen?'

'Nag nag nag. It's not so bad. At least I remembered to back up my memorycell this morning.'

The paramedics rushed through the door leading to Ramon's office suite. Justine followed them in, hurrying through the anterooms where apprehensive junior aides and interns stood transfixed in their doorways, their faces locked into frightened expressions.

Ramon was on the floor in front of the teak bench they'd just been sitting on. He had caught his head on the arm as he fell. Blood from a bruised gash just below his eye was soaking into the carpet. Mitchan, his chief aide, was kneeling beside him, eyes damp with anxious tears. A glass had been knocked over, water diluting the patch of blood.

One of the paramedics propelled the aide aside. Ramon's robes were loosened. The paramedics began to apply plastic modules to his skin. Small arms unwound from the nursebots and began to press nozzles and needles into Ramon's flesh.

Justine stood behind the crash cart, trying her damnedest not to look apprehensive. She could see how difficult it was for him to breathe. Every time his chest rose in shallow judders he winced. Bubbly drool was running down his cheek. Their eyes met.

'Toniea Gall will take over as head of the African Caucus,' he wheezed painfully.

'Don't talk, Senator,' one of the paramedics said. She covered his face with an oxygen mask. He pushed it aside. 'Watch out for her,' he said, staring intently at Justine.

The oxygen mask was pressed back insistently. The paramedic held his hands down. 'Senator, you've had another heart attack.'

'Another!' Justine squawked. She was furious with him, and frightened.

Ramon gave her a sorrowful look above the mask.

'We're going to sedate you, Senator,' the paramedic said. 'You will have to undergo rejuvenation this time. Your heart cannot sustain you any longer. Your doctor told you that.'

Text appeared in Justine's virtual vision. **Gall is not an ally. Not for you. She wants the Presidency. She will not involve herself in controversy, not on this scale.**

'I understand,' she said softly.

I'm sorry, Justine. I would have helped, you know that. Go to Crispin, but be careful, he's a wily old swine.

'Yes. I will, Rammy.'

One of the nursebots slid a needle into his carotid artery. He blinked rapidly.

Come and visit me when I'm young again.

'Every day, I promise.'

Jolly good. That'll save me a fortune in Silent World fees.

She laughed as the tears trickled down her cheeks. Ramon gave his office a last confused glance, and closed his eyes.

See you in eighteen months.

*

He spent a day and a half infiltrating the arrays of the huge Park Avenue apartment block. By himself he would never have managed it, he had to use several cohorts who were more adept at manipulating human electronic systems. Rich humans took their security very seriously indeed, using the most advanced and sophisticated arrays to guard themselves.

With the false data in place, he arrived by taxi at the block. Two doormen stood outside the wide entrance with its gull-wing canopy, wearing traditional uniforms of long coats with brass buttons, and white gloves tucked into their epaulettes. They saluted as he went through the revolving door into the vast marbled Art Deco lobby. The stern-faced concierge behind the curving reception desk was not so accepting. He had to tell the man his current identity and who he was supposed to be visiting, which was checked against today's list. With his legitimacy confirmed, the concierge permitted a brief smile before escorting him to one of the elevators.

Once the mirror-inlaid doors closed, he quickly placed his hand on the i-spot and changed the elevator's instructions. It took him all the way up to the fortieth floor.

The door to Senator Justine Burnelli's apartment had been the most difficult for the cohorts to infiltrate. Her Grand

Family had installed their own systems in the apartment, which were even more secure than those of the block. He stood in front of it, waiting patiently for the sensor to scan him. The door clicked, and swung open.

He wandered through the vast rooms with their museum horde of furniture and art. While he was in the dark dining room with its five-hundred-year-old mahogany table the maidbots began their daily cleaning routine. Dozens of them emerged from their alcoves in the utility room just off the kitchen, and started to vacuum, polish, and sanitize. They ignored him, moving round his feet as he continued his inspection. There were no staff in residence to supervise them; the senator always brought them in with her from their Family's Rye county mansion. Often she would stay overnight by herself.

When she did return, there would be some bodyguards with her, either the Family's or Senate Security. They would be watching for an external threat. He simply had to wait until they had all settled for the night.

Eventually he decided on the senator's own bedroom as the best place to wait for her. He sat on the bed to begin his vigil.

*

He'd been waiting for over twenty-four hours when the apartment management array received an encrypted order from the senator to permit access to a technical support team from Senate Security. They arrived two hours later, three of them with a pair of cases each, that were full of additional security equipment. He watched them through the apartment block's sensors as they parked in the underground garage, then took the service elevator.

As they rose up to the fortieth floor he walked into the kitchen. The refrigerator was built into the wall, a metal cabinet two metres tall with double doors. He opened them and swiftly took all the food out then removed the shelving, leaning it against one side. The food packets were piled together on the bottom. Even then, there was easily enough room to accommodate him. He activated his force field at its lowest level to maintain his body temperature, and sat on the pile of food, closing the doors behind him.

He heard the team enter the apartment, their cases trundling along behind them.

'Christ will you look at this place,' one said. 'It's like something old royalty would have.'

'Check out the view.'

'Hell, man, I can't even afford TSIs of anything like this place.'

'Rich bastards, they're all the same.'

'Come on, guys, we're here for a job, okay. Less moral superiority, more work.'

'You sound like one of them.'

'One of their aides, more like. The senators I've actually met aren't too bad.'

'They all make me sick. You know Piallani gets through four girls a week? Hookers with like these freaky reprofiled kinks, she ships them in from phase three space. They're even down on her schedule as an entertainment expense. Taxpayer foots the bill.'

'You're kidding?'

'The self-righteous ones are worse. Have you seen the way Danwal treats his staff?'

The team moved off deeper into the apartment, making assessments and working out an installation scheme. It took them seven hours to strengthen the apartment's security. Additional arrays were aligned with the existing ones, and supplementary sensors wired into the apartment's net. Software was updated.

Two of the team used the refrigerator's cool drink dispenser while they worked in the kitchen. The nozzle was fortunately mounted on the outside.

He couldn't use his own active sensors to determine the specific nature of the hardware they set up, but he heard enough to understand the basic system parameters. Anyone who used the elevators would immediately have their data files scrutinized by Senate Security. Birds that flew past outside would be examined. Even guests would be constantly observed as they moved around inside the apartment.

The new scanners were all active models, it was only the metal shell of the refrigerator which was shielding him from them. If he climbed out, the alarm would sound immediately. He couldn't connect to a cybersphere node to tell his cohorts what had happened, the system would detect the emission, and the new software would route any call through Senate Security's RI.

All he could do was stay in the refrigerator. He didn't mind, he was in place and concealed, he had food for several days. The person who used to be Bruce McFoster settled down to wait for his target.

*

That morning, most of the news shows carried the item about Senator Ramon DB unexpectedly going into rejuvenation. Alic Hogan put Alessandra Baron on one of his desktop screens, keeping the sound low. She had three Washington-based analysts in the studio, talking about the political implications. They were being cagey, with the Senate more or less unified in its response to the Prime threat, social and economic policy had essentially been sidelined. The main speculation was on who would take over leadership of the African Caucus. Toniea Gall was clearly the front runner, although the Mandela Dynasty hadn't publicly come out in her favour.

Tarlo knocked on the door and came straight in. 'Something you might want to hear, chief.'

'Thanks,' Hogan said. His e-butler muted Alessandra Baron. Ever since Senate Security had placed the observation request, Alic had taken to accessing her when she was on. Why Paula Myo wanted her watched was something he hadn't yet fathomed out. Baron's show was actually quite excellent, with frontline investigative reporting as well as the standard society gossip, and she clearly had some very high-level political contacts. Her researchers were as tenacious as any police detective when they found the whiff of scandal or financial shenanigans. All of which gave him no reason for the observation mission. Despite having the confidence of the admiral, who had ranted about the request being a deliberate Burnelli-inspired provocation, Alic just couldn't see that. Paula Myo wasn't the kind of person who acted maliciously. That was one of the reasons he'd actually kept the observation going properly. Despite all the grubby politics, there might be a result at the end of the day; if so, he wanted the Paris office to share in the credit. If it did turn out to be a red herring, he couldn't be blamed for allocating the resources.

Tarlo sat in front of the desk, a broad smile on his tanned face. 'Got a result from the Shaw-Hemmings warrant. This time we may have a more substantial lead. The money came from transferable DRNG government bonds, which are like million-dollar bills; you can carry them anywhere but you need an authorization code in order to redeem them. They were hand-delivered to the finance company offices on Tolaka. According to their records, the authorization code was then downloaded to their manager's office.'

'I didn't know people still used methods like that.'

'Chief, the finance industry has more clandestine ways of moving money around than any black market arms dealer.'

'Why not use a one-time account?'

'They're current, and we can access them with a warrant. So get this, those DRNG bonds were issued thirty years ago.'

'How cold is that?'

'The Guardians think it's icy; which is a big mistake. The DRNG treasury is notoriously reluctant to grant law enforcement agencies access to its records. But in today's climate ... You'd have to apply to the treasury direct, which you can do through their finance minister. I thought the admiral's office could ask. We might also ask if they sold any other bonds to the same buyer.'

'Okay, I'll get that sorted.' He glanced at the screen showing Baron. She had got senator Lee Ki in the studio for an interview; the pair of them looking relaxed and comfy, as if they were out on a date. 'How long do you think this treasure hunt is going to be?'

Tarlo gave a small shrug. 'To be honest, I can't remember ever getting past three links in the chain before. Maybe we got lucky with the bonds. Too soon to tell.'

'All right,' Alic had wanted to hear they were on the verge of breaking the case wide open, that the Guardians' entire financial structure would be exposed, neutering them entirely. *Childish*, he told himself tetchily. He glanced out at the open office, trying to see the various teams at work. Over half the desks were empty. 'How's Renne behaving?'

'Come on, chief, you know she's the best Investigator this office has.'

'All right. I appreciate loyalty.' Alic gave the man a sympathetic smile. 'So is there any progress on the Martian case?'

'Sorry, not a thing. Nobody can think what they needed that data for. We gave the whole problem to the technical panel we'd assembled to try and make sense of the equipment we intercepted at Boongate. I mean, the two have got to be connected, right? Maybe the Martian data will help them make sense of the weird force field components.'

'Good idea.'

Tarlo smiled. 'Renne suggested it.'

'Okay.' Alic grinning in good-natured defeat. 'Get your ass back out there to work. I'll let you know about the DRNG treasury records by end of play today.'

'Thanks, chief.'

The way he said *chief* almost made Alic believe he meant it.

*

The alley was in a rundown area of Paris. Narrow and shabby, no different to a dozen others within a square kilometre. Tall commercial buildings lined either side, inset with barred windows and secure metal rollers across the loading bays. Halfway down it there was a door; smaller than the rest, made from solid planks of walnut, and coated in grey paint, e-shielded on the inside. During the day it looked like it might open into some old shop storeroom, though it was always shut. In fact it was the entrance to a club. There was no sign outside, nothing to say what it was. If you had to ask, you weren't trendy enough to get in.

At two thirty in the morning, the queue of hopefuls stretched halfway along the narrow unsanitary alley. The glamorous, the important, the famous, and the merely rich all shuffled their feet together, bitched about the cold and the indignity, ingested, inhaled and infused a variety of narcotic substances, peed against the walls, and waited for some small miracle to grant them entrance. They weren't going to get it. The unremarkable grey door was guarded by two huge bouncers, stripped to the waist so they could show off the stylish bulbous chrome scabs of their metallic muscle boost implants, like retro-futuristic cyborgs.

Paula walked straight up the alley to the front of the queue, eliciting murmurs of amazement and hostility in equal measure. One of the bouncers smiled politely, and lifted the velvet rope for her. 'Have a good evening, Ms Myo,' he said in a thunderstorm whisper.

'Thank you, Petch,' she told him as she slipped past. He was nearly twice her height.

Music so loud it was on the threshold of pain; black walls,

floor, and ceiling producing a darkness that made you squint, until the rig above the mastermix DJ flared with blindingly intense holographic pulses; bodies crunched up so tight you could feel other people's sweat rub off on you as you squeezed past; Sahara heat; drinks priced contemptuously high; a dance floor so crowded that all you could do was wriggle in imitation sex – apart from the five people in the middle who weren't imitating anything. Nobody looked over twenty-five; boys dressed in chic suits; girls in wisps of designer cloth.

Paula shoved her way aggressively to the bar. Thankfully, she didn't have to shout herself hoarse for a drink. The barkeeper nodded welcome and immediately mixed her a peach sunset.

She sipped it, and stood on tiptoes to look out over the outlandish and expensive hairstyles. In amongst all the high fashion, Tarlo's navy uniform was instantly noticeable. Two minutes of more shoving and she was at his side.

'Hi!' she screeched.

The tall black girl he was grinding up against gave Paula a serial-killer sneer. It didn't look right on a face so staggeringly beautiful.

'Boss!' Tarlo grinned in surprised delight.

'Need to talk to you.'

He gave the black girl a dirty kiss, and shouted something directly into her ear. She nodded reluctant agreement, shot Paula a final blood-vendetta glare before wobbling off on high heels.

Together they made their way over to the end of the bar. Paula took another peach sunset. She could almost feel herself dehydrating. It was always hellishly hot in here.

'How are you doing?' Tarlo shouted.

'I'm annoying Admiral Columbia.'

Tarlo raised an iced bottle of Brazilian beer, and put it to his smiling lips. 'Best job in the galaxy.'

'Just about. I need a small favour.'

'You don't even have to ask, boss, you know that.'

'There's an old case I want you to look into for me. You remember the Dudley Bose burglary? It was before the *Second Chance* flight.'

'Vaguely.'

'We checked it out at the time and it seemed to be nothing. Now I'm not so sure. There was a charity involved, Cox Educational, which might be a front for illegal money laundering. I think it was used by a politically connected crime syndicate.'

'Are you sure?'

'Three of its trustees vanished when we started investigating. Could you review the accounts on file in the Paris office for me?'

'What am I looking for?'

'Any form of discrepancy. I have an outside finance expert going over their current files, but I need to know how far back this goes. There might have been some tampering with official records. If that's right, then the ones on file in Paris will be our only evidence.'

'Okay. I'll get on it tomorrow for you.'

'Thanks.'

'What put you on to this after so long?'

'I had a tip off from an informant; it's also why we're focusing on Baron.'

'She's involved?'

'My informer claims she was part of the cover-up. We're not sure. Not yet. And, Tarlo, keep this from Hogan and the rest of them. Columbia has tried to block me once on this already, I need to get the proof without interference.'

'Hogan hasn't got a clue what goes on in the office. Don't worry, you can rely on me.'

She gave him a sisterly peck on the cheek. 'Thanks. I think you'd better get back to your friend now. That way I might manage to survive until morning.'

Paula watched him slither back into the sweaty embrace of the crowd where the girl was waiting with edgy impatience. Inside she felt a knot of tension slacken off. He seemed to have swallowed the old favour routine. Either that or he was a superb actor. It wouldn't be long now before she knew for certain.

8

Paula had used just about every kind of transport system the human race had ever invented, but the travel pods in the High Angel always unnerved her. The way they turned transparent from the inside, the high speed, the perfectly maintained gravity field, all that combined into an insidious roller coaster disorientation. Nowadays she knew to keep eyes firmly closed from the moment she got in until a quiet *ping* announced they'd reached her destination.

Two armoured navy security guards were standing outside the pod as she climbed out. They saluted sharply. 'The admiral's expecting you, Investigator,' one said.

Paula nodded and looked up. She was standing at the base of the Pentagon II. Overhead, the dome was completely opaque, diffused with a creamy light. The High Angel was in major conjunction above Icalanise, with Babuyan Atoll pointing directly at the local star. She couldn't see anything outside at all.

The security guards escorted her into the lift. Anna was waiting outside when it arrived on the top floor. 'Good to see you again,' she said.

'Thanks. How's married life?'

'Busy.' She held her hand out showing off her rings.

'Lovely,' Paula conceded.

'He's waiting for you. Oscar's in there with him.'

Paula hadn't expected that. 'Okay.'

With the dome's uniform white light outside, it was difficult to tell if the windows in Wilson's office were clear or not. Given this was supposed to be an ultra secure meeting, she supposed they were sealed. It wasn't something she asked; it was fairly obvious she'd walked right into the middle of an argument.

Wilson was standing behind his desk, his long features drawn tight by antagonism. Oscar stood opposite, hands on hips, staring him out.

'Problem?' Paula asked.

'A huge one, actually,' Oscar said. The anger fled from him, and he slumped back into the nearest chair. 'Fucking hell!'

'What's going on?' Paula asked.

'I asked you here because we had proof of some very serious treachery on the *Second Chance* flight,' Wilson said. He still looked furious, fingers rapping on the desktop. 'I needed your advice on the Guardians. Jesus, if they're right . . .'

'*Had* proof?' Paula asked. She didn't like the way Wilson had made the emphasis.

'Let me show you,' Oscar said.

A wide section of the office wall began to project the shuttle flight between the starship and the Watchtower. Oscar gave a commentary as the little craft left its hangar bay, explaining the dish deployment, where it was pointing. Paula watched it all in fascination. It really was concrete evidence, rather than circumstantial, that someone was actively working against the interest of the human species. One of the Starflyer's agents had to be on board the *Second Chance*.

'Thank you,' she said with quiet sincerity. 'This is exactly what I needed.' The emotional reaction to the revelation was stronger than she'd expected, it was almost like being mildly inebriated.

'No, it's not,' Wilson said curtly. 'And that's the fucking

problem. This is a recording Oscar made from our main records.'

'I reviewed the *Second Chance* data while I was on board *Defender*,' Oscar explained. 'Someone from the Guardians contacted me and said enough to raise some doubts in my mind. I started going through the old records and found this.'

'You know a Guardian?' Paula asked.

Oscar shot Wilson a guarded look. The admiral stared ahead, unresponsive.

'They claimed they represented the Guardians,' Oscar said. 'I mean, they don't exactly carry club membership badges. In truth I've no way of knowing.'

'I see. Go on.'

'The point the admiral is making, is that this—' Oscar waved at the projected image which had frozen to show the dish '—is an unofficial copy of the navy secure records.'

'So?' Paula asked.

'Let me play you the official record of the same sensor,' Wilson said. The frozen image flickered and vanished. Then the recording began again, showing the *Second Chance* super structure rising into view as the shuttle left its hangar. Reaction control thrusters squirted sulphur vapour, rotating the craft. It began to head out towards the Watchtower, leaving the giant starship behind. The image froze.

'Oh hell,' Paula said.

'We sat in here two days ago watching this very same goddamn official recording,' Oscar said. 'It showed the dish deploying exactly as it does in my copy. When we ran through it today—' His fist came down hard on the arm of his chair. The main communication dish on the *Second Chance* was still folded down in its recess.

Paula looked from one man to the other. 'Who else knew?'

Wilson cleared his throat awkwardly. 'Just the two of us.'

'Oscar, did you tell the Guardians what you'd found?' she asked.

'No. There's been no contact since I returned from my scout mission.'

'Is there an access log for official navy records?'

'Yes,' Wilson said wearily. 'That was the first thing we checked, of course. Nobody has accessed this recording since we did two days ago. But then . . .'

'There's no log entry of Oscar copying the files,' Paula presumed.

Oscar's head dropped into his hands. 'I'd been contacted by the Guardians. The Guardians! And I was making illegitimate copies of sensitive navy data right in the middle of Pentagon II for Christ sake.'

'You erased the access log.'

'Yeah. With my code authority it's not difficult. I know a few program fixes.'

'Don't we all,' she admitted. 'I could probably do a better job than you. But at least it does prove that someone can get in and out of your secure records without a trace.'

'What somebody?' Wilson challenged. 'There's just the two of us.'

'Three,' Paula corrected. 'The High Angel sees everything that occurs within itself.' She looked up at the indistinct white ceiling, arching an eyebrow. 'Care to comment?'

The High Angel's colourful icon appeared in her virtual vision. 'Good morning, Paula,' it said.

Wilson flinched. He'd obviously forgotten just how pervasive the alien starship's attention was. Oscar's face was red with guilt.

'Do you know who altered the official recording?' Paula asked.

'I do not. I see within myself, but your electronic systems are independent and heavily encrypted, especially the navy network. I have no way of knowing who accessed the official recordings.'

'Did you see the official recording which Oscar and the admiral played in here two days ago?'

'I saw the images produced by your holographic projector. I cannot vouch where they originated from inside your network.'

A very legalistic answer, Paula thought, but the giant alien starship was correct. It couldn't prove the origin of the images. 'Thank you.'

'So what does that tell us?' Oscar asked petulantly. 'We're royally screwed.'

Paula took a moment to compose her thoughts. 'First option, and the simplest: that this office is not totally secure, and a Starflyer agent found out about your discovery. The records were subsequently altered to remove the dish deployment. Second option: one of you two gentlemen is a Starflyer agent, and altered the official recording. That option effectively means you, Admiral.'

'Now just a goddamn minute—'

'Third option,' she said forcefully. 'That both of you have conspired to produce a bogus recording to discredit myself and anyone else opposing the Starflyer.'

'If that's true, why are we telling you that what we saw got altered on the official recording?' Oscar said.

Paula nodded reasonably. 'Good point. I listed them in order of probability.'

'Well, I've got another one for you,' Oscar said. 'That the Primes, the Starflyer if it exists, and the High Angel are all conspiring against the human race.'

'Yes,' Paula said reasonably. 'If that's so, then we're in more trouble than I thought. A lot more trouble.'

They all paused, waiting to see if the High Angel would refute the claim. It was silent.

'It's got to be the first one,' Oscar said. 'We know the Starflyer infiltrated the navy right from the start. Son of a bitch, any of us could be its agent.'

'But we're not,' Paula said. 'Don't let paranoia take over. Look at it this way, you know you're not a Starflyer agent.'

'How does that help?'

'It's a start. You have to work on the assumption that not everything you do can be sabotaged. Plan your actions very carefully.'

'Right, so we repair the official recording.' Oscar gave Wilson a defiant glance.

'I can't permit that,' the admiral said. 'It compromises the whole allegation.'

'He's right,' Paula said.

'But we have to,' Oscar said. 'It's the only proof we've got. My copy is the genuine record. You can't let the Starflyer escape on some smartass lawyer technicality. For fuck's sake, this is our future as a species we're talking about.'

'You know for certain that the copy is real,' Paula said. 'So does the admiral because he saw the official recording before it was doctored. I, however, do not know for certain. I suspect it might be real, but that isn't good enough.'

'I don't believe this! I have genuine evidence that some bastard traitor was on board the *Second Chance*, and I can't use it? The original recording was altered.' He gave Wilson a pleading glance. 'You know that. All we'd be doing is repairing the Starflyer's sabotage.'

'If the provenance is faked, the evidence is worthless,' Paula said.

'Son of a bitch, you can't be serious. We can blow the Starflyer out of space with this. Everyone would know it exists.'

'I would not accept a substitute recording, no matter how noble your intentions,' Paula said. 'I would have to inform any authority you went to that it was not genuine.'

'Both of you!' Oscar growled sullenly.

It wasn't hard for Paula to work out what he was thinking. Option five: he was the only innocent one.

490

'The Starflyer hasn't been entirely successful in this venture,' Paula said. 'It might have avoided exposure, but we ourselves now have further evidence it is real.'

'What fucking use is that?' Oscar demanded. 'You just said we can't use it.'

'Not publicly, no.'

'Further evidence?' Wilson asked sharply. 'You knew already?'

'I strongly suspected, and have done for some time now. I've amassed a great deal of circumstantial evidence; but again the problem is that it's not sufficient to go to court with.'

'Is that why you wanted me to pursue the Mars case?'

'Yes, Admiral.' She gave Oscar a steady look. 'It could have got me closer to them. I still don't have any access route to the Guardians. If I did, and we shared information, they might be able to help me trace the Starflyer.'

'When they get in contact next I'll tell them,' Oscar said in defeat.

'They probably won't want to talk to me,' she told him. 'But try and persuade them anyway. Try very hard. It is extremely important that we work together on this.'

'Sure thing.'

'What the hell do I do about the navy in the meantime?' Wilson asked. 'We're completely compromised.'

'I don't think there's much that can be done. Obviously you'll have to increase security, but there's no way the Starflyer can prevent the major actions you're undertaking. There's too much political, fiscal, and physical inertia behind the navy.'

'But it can tell the Primes everything. We've already seen it can communicate with them.'

'Even if the Primes know the exact time the navy ships are due to arrive at Hell's Gateway, will it make any difference? Really? They know we will attack them there at some time. Their defences will be as strong as they can conceivably make them. They've seen our weapons technology in action. Nothing has changed.'

'The strength is in the details,' Wilson said. 'If they know exactly what we can do, they'll be able to counter it.'

'They know what we're doing on the Lost23, yet that insurgency campaign appears to be remarkably successful.'

'Yeah, maybe, but this is one weapon-type we're using. Neutralize that and we're screwed.'

'You cannot change the attack's schedule by much, that much is obvious. What you must do now is conduct the rest of the conflict appropriately. Information must be compartmentalized. Internal security procedures need to be strengthened, starting with your network and arrays. Work on the assumption that all information will ultimately leak to the Primes. In the meantime, I will try and identify the traitors.'

'Do you think Columbia is working for the Starflyer?' Wilson asked.

'I'm not sure yet. His actions are certainly detrimental to me personally, but that doesn't make him guilty of anything other than being a politician.'

Wilson pushed back his hair. 'Damn it, I still can't believe anyone would betray their own species.'

'From what I understand, such an action is not voluntary. The Starflyer exercises some kind of mental control over its agents. I don't understand the nature of it yet. I am currently tracking down several such people. When they are in custody, we may be able to determine the methodology.'

'You already know the identity of Starflyer agents?' Wilson asked.

'I have suspects, yes.'

'Are they connected with the navy?'

Paula considered the question carefully. She had arrived prepared to share a great deal of information, but the alteration of secure navy records was a nasty surprise. There was no way of telling how trustworthy Wilson and Oscar actually were. Until she was certain, she had to regard option three as highly probable, which meant limiting the information she made available. 'I have reason to believe that a legal firm and a bank in New York have been acting as a financial distribution centre for the Starflyer. The specialists I've had examining their accounts have come up with an interesting connection. A Mr Seaton, who is one of the lawyers we're trying to locate, sat as a non-executive director on the board of Bayfoss engineering.'

'They manufacture sensor satellites,' Oscar said quickly. 'We used their ground survey models in the CST exploration division to map new planets.'

'They also manufactured the Armstrong-class satellites which the *Second Chance* carried,' Paula said. 'That means the actual hardware integrated into the satellites must be considered suspect.'

'Oh shit,' Wilson whispered. He and Oscar swapped a horrified look. 'How many did we lose in the Dark Fortress?'

'Nine satellites total,' Oscar said. 'Four of them were Armstrong class.'

'And just after that, the barrier came down.'

'Did the Starflyer know how to switch it off?'

'That depends,' Paula said. 'If you take the Guardians' assumption that this whole war was deliberately engineered by the Starflyer, then it is highly likely that one or more of those satellites contained a device capable of shutting down the barrier.'

'And the traitor on board triggered the damn thing while we were there,' Oscar said. He closed his eyes as if he was in pain. 'So we did switch off the barrier and let them out. Oh God.'

'*We*, as in humans, did not,' Paula said. 'We were, however, manipulated to produce the result it required.'

'How did it know?' Wilson asked in confusion. 'If it planned all this out decades ago, it must have known the

Primes were inside the barrier, and known how to shut that barrier down. How?'

'That's certainly something I intend to ask it when I finally catch up with it,' Paula said. 'But for now I suggest you concentrate on this information as an exercise in damage limitation. I believe Bayfoss is still supplying the navy with equipment? Their shareholder report certainly claims they're doing well on military sales.'

'Yes,' Wilson said. 'They're a specialist astroengineering company; we use them extensively.'

'Is it for anything critical?'

He nodded slowly. 'Yes, they have contracts to supply several highly classified projects.'

'Perhaps you'd better take a close look at the components they're delivering.'

*

Ozzie woke up as slim beams of bright sunlight slid across his face. Their side of Island Two was rotating back to face the sun again after nine hours cloaked within its own umbra. Here in the gas halo, 'night' wasn't anything like as dark as it would be on a planet, but it did give them a reasonable break from the relentless glare. He checked his watch; he really had been asleep for nine hours. It was taking his body a long time to recuperate from those days spent in freefall.

He unzipped his sleeping bag, and stretched lazily. A long shiver ran down his body; all he wore in the bag were shorts and his last decent T-shirt. They were enough while he was sealed up, but the air temperature here was that of early autumn. His guess was that Island Two was currently in some convection current that was cycling back from the outwards section of the gas halo to the warmth of the inner edge. He scrambled round for his patched and worn cord trousers, then pulled on his check shirt, giving it a dismayed look as more stitches popped along the sleeve. The old dark-grey woollen fleece prevented the chill air from getting to his chest.

Ordinarily, a cool morning outdoors would be quite invigorating. The time he'd spent trekking and camping across worlds in the Commonwealth added up to over a century now. But he was mistrustful of the reef and its eternal orbit through the gas halo; and all the cold did nowadays was trigger memories of the Ice Citadel planet.

His sleeping bag was in one section of the small shelter they'd rigged up from the broken segments of the poor old *Pathfinder*. Wood from the decking and flotation bundles had been adapted into low walls; while the tatty old sail stretched across it formed the roof. Bunches of dried leaves from local trees had been stuffed into the bigger holes, helping to maintain a reasonable screen, although the sunbeams cut through in hundreds of places. They hadn't built it to provide protection from the elements, it was just to give them all some privacy. After the extremely close confines of clinging to the *Pathfinder*, a little private space of your own worked wonders for morale.

He pulled on his boots, which although scuffed were still in pretty good shape. Sadly, the same couldn't be said for his socks; he really needed a good darning session. His packet of needle and thread had miraculously stayed with him. He'd found it again the other day when he went through his rucksack. It was times like that when you began to appreciate what true luxury really was.

Ready to face a brand new day, he pushed the crude door curtain aside. Orion had already rekindled the fire from yesterday's embers. Their battered metal mugs were balanced on a slate-like shard of polyp above the flames, heating some water.

'Five teacubes left,' Orion said. 'Two chocolate. Which do you want?'

'Oh what the hell, let's live a little shall we. I'll take the chocolate.'

The boy grinned. 'Me too.'

Ozzie settled on one of the rounded ebony and maroon polyp protrusions they used as chairs. He winced as he straightened his leg.

'How's the knee?' Orion asked.

'Better. I need to do some exercises, loosen it up. It's stiff after yesterday.' They'd walked all the way to the tip of the reef, where the trees ended abruptly and the bare oyster-grey polyp tapered away into a single long spire. They'd edged out cautiously onto the long triangular segment, feeling uncomfortably exposed. Gravity reduced proportionally the further they went. Ozzie estimated it would finish altogether about five hundred metres past the end of the forest. They turned around and scooted back to the enclosure of the trees.

The spire was a landing point, Ozzie decided, the aerial equivalent of a jetty. Should any of the flying Silfen choose to visit, they would simply glide down onto the far end of the spire and walk in long bounds towards the main part of the reef, their weight increasing as they went.

Other than that, gravity on Island Two was constant. On the third day after the *Pathfinder* had reached the reef they'd travelled to the other side, which was a simple duplicate of theirs. The rim of the reef was a narrow curving cliff covered in small bushes and clumps of tall bamboo-like grasses. Gravity warped alarmingly as they started to traverse the cliff, making it seem as if they were vertical during the whole transition.

Halfway round, Ozzie had looked back to see he was now standing at right angles to where he'd been a hundred metres before. Coming to terms with that was even more disconcerting than orientating himself in freefall.

While Orion dropped the chocolate cubes into their mugs, Ozzie started peeling one of the big bluish-grey fruits they'd picked from the jungle. The pulp inside had a coarse texture, tasting like a cinnamon-flavoured apple. It was one of eight edible fruits they'd discovered so far. Just like every other environment the Silfen paths led to, the reef was quite capable of supporting life.

Tochee emerged from the jungle, its manipulator flesh coiled round various containers it had filled with water. A small stream ran across the rumpled polyp ground fifty metres from their shelter, its water so clean they barely needed to use the filter.

'Good morning to you, friend Ozzie,' it said through the hand-held array.

'Morning.' Ozzie took a drink of the chocolate.

'I have detected no electrical power circuit activity with my equipment.' The big alien held up a couple of sensors it had brought with it. 'The machinery must be very deep inside the reef.'

'Yeah, you're probably right.' Even after all this time spent together, Tochee hadn't quite grasped the fact that Ozzie liked a bit of peace and quiet at breakfast.

'Where did you go?' Orion asked as Ozzie munched stoically on his fruit.

'Five kilometres in that direction.' Tochee formed a tentacle out of its manipulator flesh, and pointed.

'I think the middle is that way.' Orion pointed almost at right angles to Tochee's tentacle.

'Are you sure?'

'I dunno. Where is it, Ozzie?'

Ozzie jerked a thumb over his shoulder. 'There, nine kilometres.'

'I apologize,' Tochee said. 'My instruments do not possess a navigation function like yours.'

'Did you see anything interesting?' Orion asked.

'Many trees. Some small flying creatures. No large or sentient life.'

'Too bad.' The boy cut a big slice out of a purplish fruit with his penknife, and bit into it eagerly. Juice dribbled down his chin, getting caught in his wispy beard. 'Were there any caves?'

'I did not see any.'

'There's got to be a way in to the core somewhere. I wonder if it's right on the tip of the spires. There can't be any gravity along the axis, that's where it all balances out. Ozzie said so. I bet that's just one long tunnel the whole length of this thing.'

'Logic would dictate the shortest distance. An access passage to the core would surely begin on the surface at the middle.'

'Yeah. I bet there's a whole load of caves and stuff. It'll be where the reef's inhabitants live, like the Morlocks.'

Ozzie took another drink of chocolate, not making eye contact. He was already regretting telling that story.

'Do you still think something lives here, friend Orion?' Tochee asked.

'What's the point of it otherwise?'

'I have seen no sign of any large creature.'

'No, 'cause they're underground.'

Ozzie finished his chocolate and retied his hair with a small band of leather so that it didn't flop down over his eyes. 'They are not underground,' he said. 'You do not build islands in something like the gas halo, and then populate them with troglodyte species. Nothing lives here.'

'What's a trogodite?' Orion asked.

'Someone who lives underground.'

'Excuse me, friend Ozzie,' Tochee said. 'But this whole gas halo is lacking in logic. We might yet find some life below ground. Why else would you build islands in the sky?'

'Carbon sinks,' Ozzie said. 'It's all a question of scale, which is admittedly difficult to get your head around. Even I'm having serious trouble with this when I look up and see sky that goes on for ever. But we know that there is a lot of animal life flapping round inside the gas halo. As it's a stand-ard oxygen nitrogen mix it's pretty safe to say they all breathe oxygen, and exhale carbon dioxide, or some other waste product. Now I'm sure it would take billions of years for all those animals to poison something as gigantic as the gas halo, but it will happen unless the opposite process is active. You can either do it artificially, with machines; or the green way, with plants. And that's what this reef is, a part of the ecosystem. It probably doubles as a food garden and watering hole as well. The air-desert equivalent of an oasis.'

'You said there was machinery inside it,' Orion said. His tone was accusing.

'There is some kind of gravity generator, certainly, man, and that probably has a steering function; I'm pretty sure it was put on a collision course with us. The rest of it is all biological.'

'What's the point if they can clean the air with machines?'

'I suspect they built all of this just for the hell of it, man, the enjoyment of living in something so utterly fantastic. I know I would if I could. I already did something like this on a minuscule scale back home.'

'Did you?'

'Very small scale, yeah.'

'What?'

'It's an artificial environment; nothing special, not import-ant. Look, the reason I'm interested in trying to locate the gravity generator in this reef is because I might figure out how to use it to steer us somewhere.' He held a hand up to stall both of them. 'And no, guys, I don't know where yet, but a degree of control would be useful at this moment in time, okay? We really are out of all other options.'

'You said that back on the water island.' Orion's grin was pure disrespect.

'Shows you how little I know. Come on, Tochee's probably

right about the inspection hatch being close to the centre. Let's go see if we can find it.'

*

The intricacy of the reef's jungle fascinated Ozzie, it was a work of art. There was a near-uniform gap between the ground and the first level of branches of about four metres. Just right for a human or a Silfen to walk comfortably in the low gravity without hitting their head on branches. In fact if you happened to push off too hard the lacework of branches and twigs was dense enough for a simple slap of the hand to help flatten out the arc of your glide-walk. An overhead safety net, basically. Ozzie was convinced that was deliberate. So if the trees weren't pruned, and he'd seen nothing to indicate they were, they must have been configured at a genetic level to grow like that. Even for a society with the resources to build the gas halo, that was a lot of work.

There was plenty of variety, too; ranging from trees that could have come direct from the forest of any H-congruous world, to the bizarre purple chimney-like tubes, as well as a host of alien species like the flexible globular lattice that Orion had landed in. Ozzie half-expected to see a ma-hon growing amid the profusion of exotica.

Covered by the thin layer of loam were an equal diversity of polyp strata, dull ash-grey bands interlocked with stone-brown bulbs and creamy intestinal clusters, knobbly gentian ropes and open-ended maroon cones with puddles of dank water lying at their base. Blue-speckled hazel protrusions in the shape of button mushrooms were common, although they were all over two metres in diameter.

Johansson had been right to call these creations reefs, Ozzie thought. The trees, as they swiftly realized, lived in perfect symbiosis with the polyp. There was no deep layer of soil to support the roots, instead they were supplied with water and nutrients by the coral itself. In return it must slowly absorb

500

the loam formed by their fallen, rotted leaves to regenerate itself.

There were glades, wide patches where no trees grew, filled with bright sunlight. Here the thin sandy soil sprouted a few tufts of grass, or straggly plants giving a curious impression of lifelessness amid the luxuriant growth of the jungle. Each time they came across such a feature they stayed close to the fringe of trees, as if they'd grown afraid of the empty sky.

Ozzie was pretty sure he knew where such uncertainty rose from. Anything could exist in the gas halo, descending on them without warning out of that infinite blue expanse.

'Do you think there are paths here?' Orion asked. 'You said Johansson walked back to the Commonwealth from a reef.'

'There could be,' Ozzie admitted. Indeed he was carrying his rucksack in case they did wander onto the start of a path. He'd insisted on the boy and Tochee carrying their essentials as well. They had so little equipment and supplies left they simply couldn't afford to lose any more. Deep down, he was hoping they really would start the long walk off the reef midway through one of these expeditions. That yearning was a direct reaction to his circumstances. All he was focusing on these days was simple survival. He'd been travelling for so long now he had grown terribly weary of it. The starship had surely flown to the Dyson Pair and returned by now. It was a depressing thought that the answer would be waiting for him when he returned home, a brief historical note within the unisphere.

When he did catch himself indulging is such wistful speculation he grew angry. After enduring so much he *deserved* to find the adult Silfen community.

'I know when we're on a path these days,' Orion said. 'I can feel it.'

'I believe I may share that awareness,' Tochee said. 'There is no logic to the knowledge, which is difficult for me, but I sometimes find an inner certainty.'

Ozzie, who had possessed that particular trait for some time, kept quiet. The really good thing about getting home would be dropping Orion and Tochee off in a decent hotel and getting *the hell* away from their constant inane chatter.

The hand-held array reported they were drawing near to the geometrical centre of the reef. It was hard to define the exact point outside of an area a couple of hundred metres in diameter, although they were certainly halfway between the tips of both end spires. A good visual clue was in the size of the trees, which were getting a lot taller. *Why, though? Is the centre the oldest part? That doesn't make a lot of sense.* Nonetheless, their trunks were massive here, several metres across, leaving the ground directly beneath them arid and dusty. The surrounding polyp had cracked, with long-dead flakes lifting up like jagged teeth around the bark. Overhead, the ceiling of branches and leaves was so dense that the light had reduced to a pale uniform gloaming.

'It's lighter up ahead,' Orion said. A glare of sunlight was filtering past the trunks. They walked towards it, squinting after so long in the gloomy silence of the great trees.

The light came from a clearing over a kilometre wide. For once there was a blanket of greenery covering the ground, a plant as tenacious as ground elder but with slim ankle-high jade-green leaves that rustled like rice paper. A fence of the purple polyp tubes formed a neat perimeter, towering above the thick trees, each one curving round high above them so their ends were aligned horizontally out across the reef.

'They're chimneys!' Orion declared. White vapour was oozing out of each one, twirling away above the treetops. Ozzie recalled the odd river-like ribbons of cloud they'd seen on their approach.

Orion immediately dropped down and pressed his ear to the ground.

'Friend Orion, what are you doing?' Tochee asked.

'Listening for the machines. There must be factories in the caves down there.'

'I do not detect any electrical or magnetic activity,' Tochee said.

'Calm down, man' Ozzie said. 'Think about this: factories to make what?'

Orion gave him a puzzled look, then shrugged. 'Dunno.'

'Okay, then. Let's not jump to conclusions.'

'There is something in the middle of the clearing,' Tochee said.

Ozzie used his inserts to zoom in. A squat black pillar stood by itself in the middle of the rustling sea of leaves. 'Now that's more like it.'

Orion got there first, leaping on ahead, each giant step sending him gliding three or four metres through the air. Ozzie took more cautious steps, keeping a wary eye out on the sky above; while Tochee slithered along at a modest speed.

The pillar was three metres tall, standing on a broad patch of bluish polyp devoid of any soil or plants. A ring of symbols had been engraved halfway up, made from long thin strokes curving at all angles, with several orbital dots. All the grooves and indentations had been filled with a clear crystal. Ozzie scanned them with the hand-held array, and whistled at the result. 'Diamond. That's one mother of an expensive anti-corrosion application.'

'What kind of runes are they?' Orion asked. The symbols bore a slight similarity to ideograms, but not in any human language. 'Is it like a signpost for paths?'

'I don't have any reference,' Ozzie said. 'How about you, Tochee?'

'I regret not.'

Ozzie began to scan the ground, which was solid enough. None of his sensors could detect any kind of cavity beneath the pillar. Nor was there any electrical activity, no circuits buried just below the surface. He gave the pillar an aggravated look as an excited Orion hurried round it, the boy's eager fingers tracing the lines on all the symbols. Then Ozzie looked back across the open expanse of the glade, an unwelcome conclusion dawning in his mind.

'Shit!' Ozzie spat brutally. 'Shit shit shit.' He aimed a kick at the base of the pillar. It hurt his toe, so he kicked it again, harder. 'Ouch!' Kick with the other foot. 'I do not fucking believe this, man.' All the frustration, all the rage that had been building inside him was rushing out; vented on this one simple artefact. He hated it for what it was, everything it represented.

'What's wrong, Ozzie?' Orion asked quietly. The boy was giving him an apprehensive glance.

'What's fucking wrong? I'll goddamn tell you what's wrong.' He kicked the pillar again, not quite so hard this time. 'I have spent months in the wilderness, eating crappy fruit when all I wanted was a decent steak and fries; actually, I don't just want it, I *dream* of it. I'm walking round in rags like something out of the Stone Age. I haven't had sex in, like, forever. I've been sober so long now my liver is feeling healthy. I've been flushed off an ocean in the biggest cosmic joke there ever was. But I put up with it, all this crap, because I know you – yes YOU – are watching and guiding me along, and manipulating the paths so that in the end we'll meet up. But, oh no, you've got to have one more go at making me feel humble, one more time making me the butt of your stinking lame-ass, so-called humour.' He thrust a finger out towards the pillar. 'I do *not* think this is funny! You got that? Are we clear on the meaning of NO, here?'

Orion gave the clearing a timid look.

'Ozzie, who are you talking about? I can see no one else here but us.'

'It's watching. Aren't you?'

'Who?' Orion pleaded.

'The adult community. The real Silfen.'

'Are they?'

'Oh yeah.'

Orion turned back to the pillar. 'So what is this?'

Ozzie sent a long breath rattling out through clenched teeth as he tried to calm down. It was hard. If he didn't let his anger burn, he knew he'd wind up curled up in a ball weeping in sheer frustration. 'Nothing. The most stupid insignificant piece of nothing on the whole goddamn reef. I used to respect the dude who came up with the design for the gas halo, I mean it is like *impressive*. Now, I think they're the most anally retentive moron in the whole galaxy. You want to know what this is? Why it's so completely visible, standing here all by itself, with the sunlight shining on it like it's some kind of celebrity? It's the reef's goddamn serial number, man.'

*

MorningLightMountain detected the approaching ships while they were still fifteen light-years distant. Twenty of them were approaching the staging post star at four light-years per hour; the fastest human ships it had observed so far. That was to be expected, they had no alternative but to send their best weapons against the staging post.

Part of its main thought routines noted that every time some part of itself encountered human starships, they always flew faster than the previous time. The rate at which humans developed and advanced their technology base was atypical of their society as a whole, which appeared so disorganized, with numerous instances of leadership class and administration class *corruption*. Study of the mined data and human personality animations it had enacted showed that certain small clusters of individuals were capable of high-level organization within specialized fields. During the frequent outbreak of wars while they were still confined to their original planet, the 'weapon scientist' groups were always deferred to by the leadership class, and given disproportional resources to complete their tasks.

It decided the leadership class must have reverted to its old behaviour pattern and allowed the weapon scientist class increased access to resources. That development would have to be watched carefully; humans with their wild imagination might be capable of producing very dangerous hazards at a strategic level rather than the tactical level which they had engaged at so far. Fortunately, MorningLightMountain still had weapons capable of devastating entire star systems, which it had so far held in reserve. With preparations for the second incursion almost complete, it was now ready to use them against Commonwealth star systems. This time there would be very little resistance from the humans. The radiation would kill them all off, while leaving their industry and buildings intact.

MorningLightMountain refined and analysed its sensor data, learning what it could of the distortions generated by each ship, the nature of their energy manipulation process. It began to prepare its defences, halting the flow of materiel and ships to the new 23 worlds. Seven hundred and seventy-two wormhole generators on the three remaining original asteroids orbiting the interstellar wormhole began to adjust their configuration; as did the five hundred and twenty generators so far completed on the four new asteroids it had established. Force fields were strengthened around all the settlements containing immotile groupings. Weapons installations were brought up to full readiness. Attack ships moved to their departure locations.

The human starships began to slow. They came to a halt twenty-five AUs distant from the interstellar wormhole, and emerged into real space. MorningLightMountain immediately opened twenty wormholes around each starship. Six hundred missiles were launched through each one, followed by forty ships. It then modified the wormholes again to try and prevent the starships from escaping within their own wormhole, a technique perfected during the first stage of its expansion into Commonwealth space.

As soon as the human starships powered down their faster than light drive systems, they became immensely difficult to detect. Missiles were unable to lock on to anything. The sensors on all MorningLightMountain's ships struggled to pick up any radiation emission; radar was completely ineffectual. Only the wormholes themselves were able to provide some guidance, their distortion waves revealing faint echo traces, though even those were elusive, never giving the same return pattern twice. The entire assault floundered.

Then a new distortion point appeared. Another. Five more. Within twenty seconds, three hundred small human vehicles were approaching the interstellar wormhole at four light-years per hour. As MorningLightMountain had predicted, the humans were using the same attack process they had used so effectively above Anshun.

Thousands of immotile group clusters began modifying the energy structure of the asteroid-based wormholes, aligning their openings on the faster than light missiles, interfering with their own exotic energy structure. Erratic bursts of radiation erupted along the missiles' flight path as the conflicting distortions clashed, their overlap leaking back into spacetime.

The great deflection operation succeeded, diverting and disturbing the flight of the missiles, twisting them away from the gigantic interstellar wormhole and its massive supplementary assembly of asteroids, equipment, and installations. As the interference grew stronger, human missiles were torn from their superluminal flight millions of kilometres away from their target, travelling at close to ninety per cent lightspeed. It was a velocity that gave even the tenuous solar wind particles a lethal kinetic impact. Furious spheres of plasma spewed out around every emergence point, far brighter than the local star.

A second volley of a hundred superluminal missiles raced

in towards the interstellar wormhole. This time Morning-LightMountain was more successful in locating their origin coordinates. Its own missiles were redirected. Thousands of fusion explosions saturated space where it suspected the human starships to be lurking. There were dark eddies within the tides of elementary particles. Sensors probed them, seeking the cause.

Three human missiles managed to get close to the interstellar wormhole before MorningLightMountain's interference forced them out into spacetime. They instantly erupted into spears of relativistic plasma spitting hard radiation that burned out any sensor aligned onto it. A patch of solar wind over a million kilometres wide glowed a faint purple as it was energized. Several ships exploded as they were overwhelmed by the searing tide. Force fields protecting sections of the asteroids strained under the effort of withstanding the colossal energy input. Dozens of localized breakthroughs occurred, allowing shafts of X and Gamma rays to slash across the equipment and machinery underneath. Four wormhole generators were immediately vaporized. Thousands of immotiles were irradiated, dying almost at once. Eight group clusters were lost. The interstellar wormhole remained unaffected, its force field holding against the electromagnetic blizzard. Slowly, the purple nebula darkened down to nothing.

Out on the edge of the star system, MorningLightMountain sent hundreds of ships racing in towards the little betraying knots within the nuclear plasma it had unleashed, firing their beam weapons and launching salvo after salvo of high-velocity missiles. The human starships retreated into their self-generated wormholes. MorningLightMountain managed to disrupt three of them, leaving them exposed to the full vehemence of its attacking ships. Their force fields were exceptionally strong, but not even those could withstand the intense assault it directed at them.

Three new explosions blossomed, almost unnoticeable

among the deluge of elementary particles ripping through that section of space. MorningLightMountain's quantum wave sensors observed the seventeen surviving human ships fly back into the void. It watched for a long time to see if there would be a second wave. No more starships came.

More supplies and apparatus came through the interstellar wormhole from its home system. It resumed its preparations for the next stage of its expansion into the human Commonwealth.

*

Barry and Sandy were so excited they barely ate a thing at breakfast; not even the scrambled eggs with crusted cheesefish which the chefbot had produced. Panda picked up on their mood, and barked happily, wagging her tail as she went round the table, pleading for scraps.

'Can you take us up to the starships, Dad?' Barry asked as Liz put his plate in front of him. Sandy gasped, and paid very close attention.

'Oh, sorry, son, not today. The orbital platforms aren't open to visitors.'

'I'm not a visitor,' he said indignantly. 'You're my dad, I'd be with you.'

There were times when Barry's simple, absolute, devotion brought a lump to Mark's throat. 'I'll have another word with the boss,' he promised. 'Maybe we'll smuggle you up one day.'

'And me!' Sandy insisted.

'Of course.'

Liz gave him an accusing glance across the table. He knew exactly what she was thinking: *How are you going to keep that promise?*

'Don't do that,' Liz admonished Barry.

'What?' the boy protested, putting on his hurt innocence face. It was a very familiar expression.

'I saw you give Panda toast.'

'Aw, Mum, I dropped it, that's all.'

'It had butter on it,' Sandy said primly. 'And you fed it to her.'

'Snitch!'

'Both of you, shush,' Mark said. He tried to stop grinning as he read the news flowing across his paperscreen which was balanced on his coffee cup. It was difficult, this was a proper family breakfast, the kind he'd loved back in the Ulon Valley, and an increasingly rare event these days. It wasn't that life here was hard, quite the opposite. The two-storey house they lived in was built from shiny carbonsteel composite sections, assembled by constructionbots. But even though it looked low cost from the outside, the interior was spacious, with luxurious fittings. Its kitchen alone probably cost more than the old Ables pick-up he'd driven in Randtown, with every automated gadget known to the Commonwealth, work surfaces of Ebbadan marble, and cupboard doors made from brown-gold French oak. All the other rooms were equally well appointed; and if you lacked any furniture you could order whatever you wanted from a unisphere catalogue site and the project personnel office would arrange for it to be delivered. The same with clothes or food.

No, homelife was easy, it was the work which devoured all his time, and kept him away from the children. Except today. This was his day off, the first one in a long time. They'd arranged for the children to skip school so they could all spend it together.

'Can we go now?' Barry implored. 'Dad, please, we're all finished.'

Mark stopped reading the article about the political battle to lead the African Caucus in the Senate. He glanced over at Liz for permission. She was holding her big tea cup in both hands, most of her French toast was still on her plate. 'Okay,' she said.

The kids whooped, and raced out of the room.

'Make sure you use your teeth gel,' she shouted after them. 'And don't forget your swimsuits.'

Panda barked happily.

Mark and Liz grinned at each other. 'Do we get some time together tonight?' he asked, trying to be casual.

'Yes I'd like to have sex, too, baby. If we're not knackered after today, that's a definite.'

They shared a more intimate, playful smile.

Liz wolfed down the last portion of her French toast. 'Humm, too much pepper. I'll have to alter the bot's recipe.'

He glanced at the broad picture window behind her, checking the weather. Liz always sat with her back to the window, no matter what room of the house they were using. 'I hate this landscape,' she'd announced on their third day in the town. 'It's a corpse of a world, a vampire planet.'

'Looks like a good day,' Mark said cheerfully as the sunlight shone on the rock and sandy regolith outside. 'The tarn should be warm enough to swim in.'

'Whatever.'

'Something wrong?'

'No. Yes. This place. It really is driving me crazy, baby.'

He held up the paperscreen. News articles were still flowing down it. 'We won't be here for much longer, one way or another. The navy fleet should be hitting Hell's Gateway any day now.'

Liz glanced at the open door, and lowered her voice. 'And if that's not enough?'

'It will be.'

'Then why is Sheldon building this fleet?'

'Because he had a healthy paranoia back when all this kicked off. In any case, he'll probably use the starships even if we beat the Primes back to their homeworld.'

'Say again.'

'The Commonwealth is all humans have; we're all bunched up in one big group. Wouldn't it be fantastic to set up another human civilization on the other side of the galaxy? It'd probably be completely different to this one. We know how to avoid our mistakes now, to build something new. You'd have enough volunteers to make it viable; look how many people settle weird places like Far Away and Silvergalde.'

'Uh huh.' She sat back and gave him a calculating stare. 'And would that include us?'

Mark's enthusiasm went into an unpleasant nosedive. 'I don't know. How do you feel about it?'

'I feel very strongly that the children are brought up in the safety and security of the Commonwealth, providing it survives. Once they're grown up, and responsible enough to make their own choices, they can start thinking if they want to go gallivanting off into the wild.'

'Er, right, sure. But it appeals to me.'

'I can see that, baby. And I'll be happy to talk about it later, say about fifteen years.'

'Ah. All right, I don't suppose this will be the only inter-galactic colonization attempt. I think we're shaping up to live in a real golden age. The Prime attack might well be the best thing that ever happened to us, it's shaken us out of our complacency. Just think of it, fleets flying off into the unknown. I bet we even go trans-galactic one day. That would be the ultimate, wouldn't it?'

Liz gave him a tolerant smile. 'I keep forgetting how young you are.'

'You mean you wouldn't go?' Mark asked, surprised, and not a little upset.

'I hadn't thought about it, baby, is the honest answer. But do me a favour, don't mention this to the kids; their world is turbulent enough as it is right now without introducing wild ideas like this.'

'Like what?' Barry asked. He was standing in the door, his coat trailing from one hand.

'Tell you about it later,' Mark said automatically. He winked. 'When your mom's not about.'

'Don't you dare,' Liz growled.

Barry giggled happily. 'Sure thing, Dad.' He pelted off back into the house. 'Hey, sis, I know something you don't!'

'What?' Sandy squeaked.

'Not telling you.'

'Pig!'

Liz grinned and rolled her eyes. 'Gonna be a long day.'

*

Mark had arranged to borrow a Ford Trailmaster7 from the garage. They all piled in, with Panda in the back, and he headed out of their big housing estate for the perimeter ring road. All the civil construction work had finished now and the town was as large as it was ever going to be, supporting twelve thousand technicians, scientists, engineers who were busy assembling the starships in their orbital docks, and the crews who would fly them.

A bright sun shone down out of the light purple sky, glinting strongly off the town's composite buildings. The ground between them was gritty sand scattered with flaking rocks. There wasn't a single weed growing anywhere. Nobody had gardens. H-congruous plant life wasn't permitted here. Hundreds of modified gardenbots were on constant patrol in the town, spraying the sand with biological inhibiters that would prevent any kind of growth. Sewage from every building was simply tanked to Cressat, and from there back to Augusta, as was all the garbage. Nothing was allowed to contaminate the pristine environment.

Liz wrinkled her nose up at the town as they sped along the ring road. 'This place is like Gaczyna,' she said as they passed a Bab's Kebabs franchise at the end of a strip mall.

'Where?'

'A place in Russia that they used to train spies during the cold war. It supposedly had a perfect replica of an American town, so the agents could familiarize themselves with life in the West. That's what this is, a replica of the Commonwealth. Everything we associate with everyday life is here, but it's not actually real.'

'The Dynasty's doing its best to make things comfortable for us.'

'Yeah, baby, I know. It wasn't a complaint, just an observation.'

Mark nodded, and concentrated on driving. He was getting quite worried about Liz. The whole lifeboat venture had brought out a despondency in her which he found difficult to deal with. She was normally the sunny one, the one he relied on for common sense and optimism. Given what he'd got to tell her at some point today, her criticisms and moodiness weren't good omens. He could see what she meant about Gaczyna, though. He'd never been anywhere with so many bots. The only people the Dynasty allowed here were those involved in building the lifeboats. There was no service economy; bots performed every domestic function, even Bab's Kebabs, along with all the other stores in the strip mall, was automated. When a bot malfunctioned, it wasn't repaired here, that would require a secondary industry, people not connected to the lifeboat project. He'd seen whole trucks full of faulty bots being shipped back to Augusta for maintenance. It was an expensive way of doing things, but it was the only way of sustaining the level of security which Nigel Sheldon insisted on.

They turned off the ring road onto a dirt track which led away into the hills above the town beyond the fusion stations. He actually enjoyed sitting behind the wheel, driving manually. There were no real roads on the planet outside the town and its sprawling grid of industrial buildings. All the tracks out here had been made by residents taking off to explore. Mark turned left at the first fork, then right, following a route he'd been told about. The Ford's tyres churned up a lot of dust, deepening the wheel ruts.

After an hour they came to the tarn. The sand had given way to naked rock miles earlier. All around them were the steep rolling slopes of the interlocking mountain tops. There were no stream beds, or erosion gullies, the planet hadn't had an atmosphere long enough to begin features like that, although rain was busy washing regolith sand down into the lowlands. From there it was creeping steadily into the shallow oceans. Up here, water trickled over the undulations in unbroken sheets until it found basins and nooks to collect in. The tarn was a long oval shape, with water up to its brim. When the rains came it overflowed into a sharp cleft of black granite at the eastern end.

'It's so clear,' Barry exclaimed as they stood at the edge. Apart from small ripples reflecting the velvet sky there was no movement. They could see the rough rock bottom sloping away towards the centre. 'Just like the Trine'ba,' he said with a smile.

'Almost,' Liz agreed. 'Come on, let's go get changed.'

The four of them waded in, gasping at how cold the tarn was. Their voices echoed cleanly through the mountain air, bouncing off the high rumpled inclines around them.

'I miss the fish,' Sandy confessed as she swam cautiously further out from the shore. Mark had insisted she wear inflatable wings on the back of her suit. For once she didn't argue.

'No fish, no algae,' he said to Liz. It was strange, he normally associated water with life, while this was the complete opposite.

'It'll come,' she said. 'Every time someone comes swimming up here they leave bacteria behind. In a hundred years this tarn will be a proper little vat, the planet's biggest natural Petri dish; leaking its new bugs out across the landscape every time it rains.'

'We always leave our mark, don't we?'

'Just about. I guess it's evolution on a galactic scale. A planet that produces life smart enough to figure out star travel will spread its DNA across the stars. And evolution is one tough battleground.'

'That sounds like the Gia hypothesis.'

'Taken to the extreme, I suppose it is. I wonder if the Primes recognize it at an instinctive level. They were certainly keen to alienform Elan. Remember those images Morton recorded of the biorefinery they built on the edge of Randtown?'

'So whoever built the barriers knew that, too?'

'Yeah. A stellar-sized rabbit-proof fence, like the one they built in Australia once the immigration started. And along we came with the bolt cutters. Damn, we're dumb. Maybe this is evolution's way of telling us we're obsolete.'

Mark stood on the slippery rock, and started to wade out. 'We're not dumb, we're principled. I'm proud of that, of what we are collectively.'

'Hope you're right, baby.' Liz waded out beside him, and hurriedly wrapped a big towel round herself. 'Five minutes, you two,' she called out to the children. They were several metres off shore now, splashing about with Panda. Barry waved back.

'Here.' Mark twisted the tabs on a couple of hot chocolate cans, and handed her one as it began to steam.

'Thanks.' She gave him a quick kiss.

'They're moving me,' he said tersely.

'Moving you where?'

'To a different part of the project.' He looked up. One of the spaceflower moons was gliding up over the horizon. Even now, the massive gigalife gave him a thrill. To think that there was a society out there which could afford to produce such things just for the sheer fun of it. That was inspiring. The kind of endeavour which a new human civilization should strive for, rather than the constant commercial rat race the Commonwealth pursued and worshipped.

'What do you mean?' There was a hint of steel in her voice.

'It's not just lifeboats the Dynasty is building up there. A fleet that big travelling through space we know nothing about . . . It needs protection, Liz.'

'Oh Jesus,' Liz spat in contempt. 'I might have known: they're building warships.'

'Frigates, yeah. It's a new design, smaller and faster than the *Moscow* class. There's something different about the drive, as well. I don't know what. And nobody will talk about the weapons it carries.'

'No kidding. So what did you tell them?'

Mark took a long drink of the hot chocolate, marshalling his thoughts. He always hated it when they had an argument. For a start she was so much better at it than he was. 'This isn't the kind of job you get to choose assignments. We both knew that.'

'All right,' she said. 'I guess not. I just don't like the idea of you working on weapons.'

'I'm not. It's the assembly system they want to get up and running. They're using a different method to the lifeboats, with their pre-assembled sections. The frigate assembly bays are combined with the station dockyard. Individual components are shipped in directly and integrated up in orbit.'

'Whoopee, another great technological step forward.'

'Liz,' he said accusingly. 'We're at war. From what I hear, we might not win. We really might not.'

She sat on a big boulder, and looked forlornly at the can in her hands. 'I know. I'm sorry I'm being a bitch. I just . . . I feel so helpless.'

'Hey.' He went over and put his arm round her shoulder.

'I'm the one who needs you to support me, remember, that was the deal.'

She grinned weakly up at him, squeezing his hand. 'That was never the deal, baby.'

'So are you cool with this?'

'Yeah, I guess so.'

'Thanks, that means everything, you know that.'

Liz pulled him closer. 'I'm so glad I've got you. I wouldn't want to be with anyone else right now.'

'Well I couldn't face this without you.' He gestured at the kids. 'And them. But the frigates are as far as we can go. We've been running ever since we got back from Elan. No further. There won't be any more surprises for us.'

'I hope you're right, baby. I really do.'

*

The shower nozzles pumped water out at a velocity that pummelled Mellanie's skin almost to the point of being painful. She didn't even have to turn round, the water came at her from all sides, the nozzles sweeping up and down. Foam ran down her body as scented soap was mixed in by the management array. Cooler water flushed it away, its temperature invigorating her after the luxuriant heat. The water turned off, and warm dry air gushed out of vents all round the big marbled cubical, snatching the moisture away from her skin and blowing her hair about.

She wrapped a huge purple and cream towel around herself and went back out into the office suite's bedroom. Michelangelo was still lying on the big bed. He watched her lazily as she began getting dressed.

'Damn, I'm glad you defected from Baron,' he said. 'You'd be wasted on her, she's a cold bitch.'

Mellanie flashed him a naughty grin. 'Whereas we have a deep and meaningful relationship.'

'You're good in bed. We both know that. A real turn-on.'

'You're a good teacher.'

'Yeah?'

It was almost like he was the bashful one, seeking reassurance. 'I keep coming back, don't I?' she said. 'And we both know I'm doing well enough for the show that I don't actually have to any more. But I like it, I like it a lot.'

There was a growling sound from the bed. He rolled off the mattress and pushed his long highlighted hair back. Mellanie couldn't help the way her eyes lingered on his body. It was like a youthful Apollo had returned to walk among the mortals once more.

'Hell . . . I don't understand you,' he complained. 'What is it you really want?'

She grinned as she struggled into her asymmetric top. 'Your job.'

'You know, ordinarily if some intern your age said that I'd just laugh it off as pitifully naive. But with you it's truly not funny.'

'Be careful whose face you tread on today, because it could be the one you're fetching coffee for tomorrow.'

'Duly noted.'

'Admit it, I did good on the lifeboat story, didn't I?'

'I've never seen a senior Halgarth so defensive. Congratulations.'

'Black, one sugar.'

'You're not that good,' he said with a scowl. 'Not yet.'

'I know. I want to get the Sheldon lifeboats. Now that would be a real break while we all wait for the starships to come back from Hell's Gateway.'

He gave her a pensive look. 'How's the other big story coming on?'

'The New York finance scandal?' She sighed. 'Not so hot. The leads are all dead and cold. Besides, the authorities are showing an interest. Where's the impact of breaking something the rest of the pack all know about? Exclusivity is our goal and god, as you so rightfully told me when I started here. See, I haven't forgotten.'

'Yeah,' he nodded slowly.

'What?' She knew that reluctance, he hated giving away any advantage. 'Please?'

'All right, quick tutorial: you're not thinking this problem through properly. You're trying to track down three fairly successful lawyers who've been involved in some dodgy finance deals, right?'

'Yes.' She wasn't telling anyone on the show about the Starflyer. Not yet. *That* would land her a show of her own, probably a studio of her own.

'You're trying to chase after them. Wrong. That's what the police will be doing; but they're fugitives, they'll be ready for that and take care to cover their tracks. Any decent hunter will come at their prey from the direction they least expect. So what you should have done is ask where would they go.' He gave her an expectant look.

'A crime syndicate that can protect them?'

'Close. You need a place where you can change your identity completely. And I don't just mean some decent data registry alterations, a memory erasure, and a new face. If they've ripped off as much as you say they have, the Financial Regulation Directorate will chase them right across the Commonwealth for the next ten centuries. They need to be free to fritter away their new wealth in perfect safety without spending the rest of their lives looking over their shoulder. For that you need a lot more than a bit of cellular reprofiling. Their DNA will be on record, the FRD will always be able to identify them. So the thing they need above all else is a baseline DNA modification.'

'What's that?'

'Damn, I never know if you're taking the piss or not. That is a treatment similar to rejuvenation, when the clinic alters your DNA in every cell. Permanently. The person who comes

520

out of the tank is literally not the same person who went in. Once you've had that done, along with your new birth certification, a decent back history, and all your desourced money, you're home free. You can live where you want, even next door to your old family, and they'll never know.'

'Where would they go for that?'

'Unless you own your own biogenetic medical facility, there's only one place: Illuminatus. There's a lot of very specialized, ultra-discreet clinics there which offer such a service.'

'I need to go there.'

'I just knew you'd say that. Even if you did, you haven't got a clue where the clinics are. They don't exactly advertise on the unisphere.'

'I'll find them.'

Michelangelo gave an extravagant sigh. 'One week ago, three people checked in to the Saffron Clinic on Allwyn Street: two men, one woman. I don't know their names, but the timeframe fits.' He gave a diffident moue. 'I have contacts. I am still numero uno here, please remember.'

'Thank you,' she said sincerely.

'Mellanie. Take care. Illuminatus isn't the safest place in the Commonwealth.'

*

Ozzie woke up as slim beams of bright sunlight slid across his face. He grunted in dismay at the awakening. Yesterday's disappointment was still churning through his mind, making him listless. It was snug inside the sleeping bag, and he could feel cool air on his face. Getting up was an effort.

'Damn it.'

Lying there moping wasn't an option. That was too much like defeat, which he wasn't going to admit. Not yet.

He unzipped his sleeping bag, and stretched lazily before shivering. All he was wearing were shorts and his last decent

T-shirt. His hand felt round on the floor for his cord trousers which he shoved his legs into. When he pulled on his check shirt there was a tearing sound as stitches popped along the sleeve.

'Not again!' When he examined the sleeve the split didn't seem too bad.

He slipped into his old dark-grey woollen fleece to keep the chill out while he put his boots on. Toes stuck out through the holes in the end of his socks. Today really was going to have to be sewing day. He gave his toes a closer look. The bruising had gone down. In fact it had disappeared altogether. He couldn't remember putting any salve on after giving the serial number pillar that very satisfactory kicking.

Outside the little shelter, Orion had already rekindled the fire from yesterday's embers. Two metal mugs were balanced on a slate-like shard of polyp above the flames, heating some water.

Orion looked up and gave Ozzie a welcome smile. 'Five teacubes left. Two chocolate. Which do you want?'

'Oh what the hell, let's live— What?'

'Tea or chocolate?'

'I thought we finished the chocolate yesterday?'

Orion rummaged through the various packets he'd spread out around him, and held up the cubes in a palm. They were all foil wrapped: five silver, two gold with green stripes. 'No. Bournville Rich, with double cream. Your favourite.'

'Right. Sorry. Yeah, man, chocolate is good.' Ozzie sat on the polyp bump. He winced as he straightened his leg.

'How's the knee?' Orion asked.

No fucking way! 'Still stiff,' he said slowly. 'Where's Tochee?'

'Gone to get some water. It was scouting round last night, seeing if it could find any sign of the machinery that works this place.'

'Why?'

522

'What do you mean? You said we should try and track down the gravity generator.'

'But we know there's no electrical activity on the reef. Not that we can detect.'

'We haven't looked that hard. Besides, you told Tochee to use its sensor gadget while it was in the jungle.'

'Yeah. Two days ago. But there's not a whole lot of point now, is there? I mean, if there wasn't anything at the serial number then there certainly isn't going to be anything in the middle of the trees.'

Orion stopped unwrapping the second chocolate cube. 'Serial number?'

'Yeah,' Ozzie said sarcastically. 'Big black pillar in the clearing. Me in a bad mood. Coming back to you now?'

'Ozzie, what are you talking about?'

'Yesterday. The pillar.'

'Ozzie, we walked to the spire at the end of the reef yesterday.'

'No no, man, that was the day before. We found the serial number yesterday.'

'On the spire? You didn't say.'

'No, goddamnit. Yesterday. The pillar in the clearing. What's the matter with you?'

Orion gave him a sulky look, pouting his lips. 'I went to the spire yesterday. I don't know where you went.'

Ozzie took a moment; the boy didn't normally fool around like this, and he certainly sounded sincere enough.

Tochee emerged from the jungle, its manipulator flesh coiled round various containers it had filled with water. 'Good morning to you, friend Ozzie,' it said through the hand-held array.

'You didn't find anything, did you?' Ozzie said. 'Your equipment didn't find any electrical activity. And you've travelled about five kilometres in that direction.' Ozzie pointed.

'That is correct, friend Ozzie. How did you know?'

'Good guess.' Ozzie told his e-butler to pull up yesterday's files. The list that came up in his virtual vision were the visual and sensor recordings of their trip out to the reef's end spire. 'Show all files recorded in the last five days,' he told the e-butler. There was nothing relating to the serial number pillar. 'Goddamn.' He unlaced his boot and pulled it off, then began squeezing his toes where the bruise ought to be. There wasn't even a twinge. 'Let me get this straight,' he said carefully. 'Neither of you two remember walking to the middle of the reef?'

'No,' Tochee said. 'I have not been there, though I believe that if we go, we might have some success in finding an access tunnel to the machinery that lies at the core of this reef. It would be the shortest distance.'

'Dead right, man. So let's go, shall we?' He shoved his boot back on and stood up.

Orion held out his battered metal mug. 'Don't you want your chocolate?'

'Sure. Hey, have you been having any unusual dreams since we arrived here?'

'Nah. Just the usual dreams,' Orion said. He pulled a morose expression. 'Girls and such.'

Ozzie led the way at a fast pace. He followed the route which his hand-held array's navigation function produced, guiding him to the middle of the reef. As before, the trees were taller as they approached the area his virtual vision displayed. Today there were no beams of sunlight sliding horizontally past the thick ancient trunks. 'It's got to be here somewhere,' he said out loud as they began their third sweep of the central area.

'What has?' Orion asked. The boy had been watching him with some concern ever since they set out.

'There's a clearing right in the middle.'

'How do you know?'

Because I was here yesterday, and so were you. 'I saw it on the approach.' He stopped and told his e-butler to display all the visual files from the last couple of hours before the *Pathfinder* landed on the reef. When he checked through them, the jungle at the middle of the reef was unbroken. There was no central glade.

Ozzie stood motionless at the base of a rubbery globe tree, leaning against its elasticated branches. Not that they bent much any more, they were so old and wizened. *Okay, either I'm hallucinating or someone has done a superb hack job on the hand-held array. No, Orion and Tochee don't remember. So it was a hallucination. Or a vision. But why would I be led here?*

He took a good look round the gloomy jungle floor with its cracked polyp and dusty soil. There were no tracks in the thin dirt. Nothing moved, nothing lived here. He activated every sensor he had, and turned a complete circle. Nothing registered in any spectrum.

'I don't get this,' he said out loud. Almost, he expected some bass voice to answer from the treetops.

'Friend Ozzie, I cannot see a clearing.'

'No, me neither. The files must have been jumbled up when we landed. The array took quite a few knocks.'

'Can we go back now?' Orion asked. 'I don't like it here, it's all dismal and dead.'

'Sure thing.' He was a lot more cheerful than he had any right to be. *Something's happening. I just wish I could figure out what.*

*

It was a miserable duty, but then Lucius Lee was used to that by now. He'd been granted probationary detective rank three months ago in the City's NorthHarbour precinct, and all he'd done since then was sort out a whole load of data files and reports for the two senior detectives he'd been assigned to for his probationary year. When the three of them ever did venture out of the office he was the one who had to do all the boring stuff like cataloguing crime scenes, directing forensic bots, and interviewing low-grade witnesses; he also got the night-shift in stakeouts. Like this one. Sitting in a beat-up old Ford Feisha in an underground garage below the Chantex building at twenty past four in the morning, looking out across a concrete cavern illuminated by green-tinted polyphoto strips that should have been replaced years ago. There were fifteen other cars parked on the same level; he knew them intimately by now.

Why the hell they couldn't use a decent covert sensor for this he didn't know. Marhol, the detective sergeant who was his official mentor, said it was: 'Good experience.' Which was such bullshit.

The real problem was ancient enough to be laughable, a punk gang had been carjacking luxury models out of NorthHarbour; and – big mistake – one belonged to the rich girlfriend of a councillor's son. City Hall wanted a Result. Automated systems couldn't do that, not quickly. So here he was waiting on a tip from one of Marhol's dubious informers, who were actually more like drinking buddies.

Marhol had taken Lucius along to the bar for the meeting, presumably so he could witness the expenses claim. So he had to sit there while this zero of an informant, who couldn't have been over twenty and had big dependency problems, claimed the cars were actually being ripped off by the Stuhawk gang out of SouthCentral. He should know, he was running with the JiKs who like *owned* NorthHarbour, and they weren't doing it. The Stuhawks had got themselves owing to a syndicate who'd given them a mechanic and a list. They did the scout, and provided muscle. But they scouted cars round NorthHarbour, not their own district. It was a turf war.

For such crap the Tridelta City taxpayer had to reimburse Marhol's beer tab for a week.

Four twenty-one. The lift doors opened. A man emerged. He was smaller than usual, for an age when rejuvenation could add inches to anyone's frame for almost no additional cost. Skinny, too; his shirt had short sleeves showing arms that were mostly bone. His hands were out of proportion, big and covered in grime. First impression was a first lifer in his fifties. But then Lucius started to pay attention. The guy had confidence, strutting across the concrete as if he was a Dynasty chief walking into his harem. He was wide awake, too; not someone who'd been working a late shift upstairs.

Lucius started to breathe faster. There was no way this guy was part of some punk gang. In fact Lucius was pretty sure he wasn't a first-life at all; that cool self-assurance didn't belong to anyone under a hundred. Maybe the informant had been right. The Stuhawks were muscle for a syndicate. Lucius was suddenly very interested.

The mechanic walked over to a midnight black Mercedes FX 3000p, a brand new Hi-range saloon, with a list price of over a hundred thousand Earth dollars. That price included a superb security system, the drive array program was virtually an RI in its own right. It wouldn't let anyone take control without the owner's approval.

Lucius was waiting until the man tried to break the car open. That was when he would make the arrest; and he was quietly thankful there were no Stuhawks with him. An arrest swiftly followed by a successful interrogation would be the kind of proactive police work that the councillor wanted to see. Not that Lucius would get any credit, it would no doubt be filed as Marhol's arrest.

The mechanic made a slow circle of the gleaming vehicle, regarding it with respectful approval. Lucius was amazed at the mechanic's audacity. He wasn't really thinking of taking the Merc was he? Then Lucius remembered some Commonwealth-wide alert for a grade-A mechanic coming into the precinct a while back. This man was certainly A grade, for arrogance if nothing else. He told his e-butler to find the file.

The mechanic was about to put his hand on the Merc's

front door i-spot when he froze. Lucius held his own breath. The mechanic looked round the near-empty garage until his gaze found the Ford Feisha. His lips moved up in a dry smile, and he started to walk over.

'Oh shit,' Lucius muttered. There was no way anyone could see through the Ford's secure glass no matter how good their retinal inserts were, but somehow the mechanic had become aware of him. He drew his ion pistol and flipped the safety. It was then he realized he'd probably revealed himself by using the unisphere. Even with the police secure encryption there had been an electronic emission from the car. In a deserted garage. In the small hours. 'Oh brilliant, Lucius,' he told himself bitterly, 'just brilliant.'

To compound the error, his e-butler delivered the requested file for him. Navy Intelligence wanted to question Robin Beard, a known criminal specializing in car crime. A lot of biographical data ran across Lucius's virtual vision. Several pictures accompanied it. With a few easy differences, they matched the man who was now three metres from the bonnet.

So far, Beard hadn't drawn any kind of weapon. Lucius gripped his pistol tighter.

Beard smiled at the non-reflective black glass windscreen, and put his hand on the Ford's i-spot. His whole forearm glowed red and green as OCtattoos turned active.

Lucius jumped as a nasty *clunk* reverberated round the car's interior. The locks had all engaged. Three red lights started flashing on the dashboard. There was a nasty burning smell.

'If I were you,' Beard said, 'I'd be very careful what you touch in there. Your car's superconductor batteries are malfunctioning, they're feeding their power directly into the body frame. So don't lay a hand on anything metallic. Oh, and anything that ionizes the air will also act as a conductor. To take an example at random: an ion pistol shot fired through the window. Whoever was holding that pistol would be fried in the discharge. Ever seen somebody struck by lightning?

They say their eyeballs boil and burst while their tongue chars to black meat.'

The ion pistol dropped out of Lucius's startled fingers, clattering onto the floor. He flinched.

Robin Beard smiled at the faint sound. 'Not to worry, the batteries don't have much charge left. They should be drained by noon.' He turned on a heel and walked back to the black Merc.

A red warning flowed across Lucius's virtual vision, telling him his connection to the unisphere had dropped out. He watched through the window as Beard put his hand on the Merc's i-spot. He wasn't surprised when the door opened. Less than thirty seconds later, the big sleek car slid smoothly onto the garage's exit ramp and up into the remarkable beauty that was night on Illuminatus.

*

The day the starships were due to arrive at the star system where Hell's Gateway was located, the navy increased its observation of the Lost23. Wilson sat in his white office reviewing the information as it came in. Anna was with him acting as communications officer; Oscar qualified for his place as senior staff officer; Rafael completed the navy contingent. Justine Burnelli was there on behalf of the Senate, sitting as far as possible from Rafael; while Patricia Kantil represented the Executive, although President Doi maintained an ultrasecure real-time link; as did Nigel Sheldon, who presumably was in touch with the other Dynasty leaders – Wilson didn't ask. Dimitri Leopoldvich arrived a few minutes late, and took a seat next to Patricia; he ignored the cool reception he received from the navy officers.

The navy started opening wormholes above the Lost23. They were the same type that were used to communicate with the insurgency troops that were operating against Prime instal-lations. This time, they opened a considerable distance away from the planet, several million kilometres, clear of the heavy Prime orbital defences. Sensors slid out into spacetime, and scanned for the quantum distortion signatures of wormholes. They detected a total of eight hundred and sixty-four wormholes linking the Lost23 back to the Hell's Gateway star system.

'I thought our troops had blown up several planet-based gateways,' Patricia said.

'Twenty-seven to date,' Rafael confirmed. 'On average the Primes take three days to reopen them and assemble a new gateway mechanism.'

'What are our losses?'

'A hundred and seventeen reported fatalities,' Wilson said proudly. 'That's a lot better than our projected damage ratio. We're hurting them badly.'

'We're tying up resources,' Dimitri said. 'I wouldn't call that inflicting damage, exactly.'

Rafael gave him a very cold look.

An hour and a half before the expected attack time, seven hundred and seventy-two Prime wormholes shut down.

'Holy shit!' Oscar exclaimed. He half rose from his chair, as if he could get closer to the data which the holographic portal was projecting across half the room. Wilson's face lit up in a huge smile.

'Too early to open the champagne?' Rafael inquired lightly. He grinned at Wilson.

'We did it?' Patricia asked delightedly.

'No,' Dimitri said firmly. He was studying the data in the big display. 'There are exactly four wormholes remaining on each planet. We know the Primes use base four; so it is deliberate. They're maintaining communications with their new colonies. Therefore they shut down the other wormholes, not us.'

'You don't know that,' Oscar said.

'If our attack had been successful enough to knock out over seven hundred wormhole generators, it would have destroyed the remainder at the same time. This is an organized switch, not the result of a strike by Douvoir missiles.'

Wilson wanted to tell Dimitri to shut the hell up. His hopes had soared with the disappearance of the wormholes. And he needed that boost badly after the shock of realizing the navy was compromised. But what the StPetersburg strategist was saying made uncomfortable sense. *Don't shoot the messenger.*

'When will we know for certain?' President Doi asked.

'Not long,' Wilson said, with outward calm; it was a polite lie.

Five hours later the wormholes all reopened. A groan went round the office.

'Your interpretation?' Justine asked Dimitri.

'They beat off the attack,' the pale man said. For once he looked nervous, dabbing at the perspiration on his forehead with a handkerchief. 'I did say they would use everything they could to defend the staging post.'

'So you did,' Rafael said.

'What now?' President Doi asked. She sounded confused.

'We need to find out what happened,' Wilson said.

'They beat us,' Patricia said in an angry, scared voice. An arm gestured wildly at the display. 'That much is bloody obvious.'

'The technical details,' Wilson said. 'How did they do it? That's what's important if we are to formulate a coherent response strategy.'

'It'll be five days at the earliest before the ships get back in communication range,' Nigel said.

'If there are any ships remaining,' Dimitri said.

'Enough from you,' Rafael told him hotly.

Wilson held a hand up to his fellow admiral. 'I know this is difficult, those were our friends and colleagues out there, but we have to be realistic.'

'We cannot afford five days,' Dimitri said. 'Madam President, it is imperative that we arm our remaining starships with the Seattle Project quantumbuster weapons. The Prime aliens retain the ability to launch an immediate strike at us. They now have no reason to delay.'

'Yes,' Doi said. 'I've seen your earlier recommendations. Admiral Kime?'

'Madam President.'

'We will convene a full War Cabinet by ultra secure link in thirty minutes. Please be ready to present your plans for using the Seattle quantumbusters in defence of the Commonwealth, and any alternatives.'

'Very well, Madam President.'

'Do we release the failure of our strike against Hell's Gateway to the media?' Justine asked.

'No,' Patricia said immediately. 'We don't know what happened. People will fear the worst, and we won't be able to offer any details to reassure them.'

'The news shows are expecting some kind of comment.'

'Tough. We simply say we are unsure of the outcome, and we're waiting for the starships to return.'

'They'll know something's wrong,' Justine said. 'If the strike had worked we'd be shouting it as hard as we could.'

'We have five days until we have to admit anything is wrong,' Patricia said. 'That's enough time for me to prepare the groundwork. This has got to be handled perfectly if we're to prevent panic.'

*

Wilson couldn't bring himself to look at Oscar as everyone except Rafael and Justine left the office. Dimitri had argued that the Primes would work out a counter to the Douvoir missiles because they already knew humans were capable of such an application. *What if they were told, given exact details? I knew we'd been compromised, and I did nothing. All for fear of looking foolish.*

'Just so both of you know,' he told Rafael and Justine. 'I'm going to recommend we deploy the quantumbusters as Dimitri suggested.' *And pray we maintained some kind of integrity with their development.*

'That little shit,' Rafael grunted.

'He's always been right,' Wilson said. 'And he's only doing his job. Damnit, if we'd listened to him and equipped the starships with quantumbusters to attack Hell's Gateway we might not be in this position.'

'You can't play *what if*, not at this level,' Rafael said. 'We have to concentrate on the immediate threat.'

'There wouldn't be an immediate threat if we'd used the quantumbusters.'

'We don't even know that,' Rafael said. 'Not for certain.'

'It wasn't the technology which let us down, we suffered a failure of will. We're too civilized to push the genocide button.'

'I'm glad,' Justine said. 'That reluctance to exterminate any creature that might be a difficult problem defines us as a species. We don't operate at their level. That's got to be worth something.'

'Not when you're dead, it isn't,' Wilson snapped angrily. He knew that he was actually scared and trying to cover, which in itself was pathetic. But the failure to eliminate Hell's Gateway was profoundly shocking; and the implications even worse. Dimitri was right, they now had to contemplate the unthinkable.

'Do you think Doi will authorize their use?' Justine said.

'Sheldon will,' Rafael said. 'He's a realist. And I know the Halgarth Dynasty will support him; as will most of the others. Nobody was expecting today's attack to fail so completely. We're all still reeling from that; but the implication will sink in soon enough, and not just with us.' He shook his head in a reluctant acknowledgement. 'Dimitri and his nerd think-tank was right. We weren't hard-headed enough, we didn't want to recognize what we're actually facing, it's too frightening.'

Wilson nearly told him about the treachery on board the

Second Chance, the existence of the Starflyer. But he retained enough of his political instinct to hold back. *Coward*, he taunted himself; but he needed Rafael's wholehearted support over the next few days, they simply *had* to work together. The human race couldn't afford them to make another mistake. The thought sent an evil shudder down his spine.

*

It took the War Cabinet fifteen minutes to make its vote. The unanimous decision was to allow the navy to arm all its starships with quantumbuster weapons in readiness for any subsequent attack by the Prime aliens.

9

On the day, two hundred years ago, when CST's exploratory division opened a wormhole above Illuminatus the sight which materialized shocked the entire Operations Centre into silence. They thought they had stumbled across the ultimate high-technology civilization, one which had urbanized every square mile of land. Directly beyond the wormhole opening, the planet hung in the black of space, darkside on. Normally difficult to see from such a position. Electronic sensors with their multitude of incursive spectra could pinpoint it easily; but the human eye, looking through the toughened glass of the control centre, out across the empty confinement chamber, and protected once more by the force field over the wormhole, had trouble making out a circle of darkness amid interplanetary space. This time was different.

Every continent glowed a lambent aquamarine from shore to shore, shimmering softly in long undulations as thin clouds wafted overhead. Only mountains and the polar caps were devoid of light.

The Operations Director extended a communications dish through the wormhole, and attempted to signal the occupants of the planetary city. Strangely, the electromagnetic bands remained silent apart from the warbled harmonies of the ionosphere as it was showered by solar wind. Then the full sensor returns began to build up, providing a provisional analysis. The light didn't have a technological origin, it was purely biological.

*

Every time Adam Elvin visited Illuminatus he forgot to pack any decent short-sleeved linen shirts. It was his old city-boy mentality; he just never expected a climate quite so humid in an urban area. Nobody built cities in the middle of a jungle. It wasn't civilized. Nor was it commercially viable, either. Except here.

Stepping out of the Hotel Conomela's air-conditioned lobby was yet another unpleasant reminder of his bad choice of luggage. The heat and humidity on the street was already up to sauna levels, and that was with the hotel's bright scarlet half-moon canopy overhead protecting him from direct sunlight. The semi-organic fibre of Adam's white suit acquired a silver hue as it struggled to repel heat away from his body. He fanned at his face with his genuine Panama hat. A uniformed doorman gestured to a maroon Lincoln taxi that glided to a halt and popped its door. 'Senor, Duanro,' his white-gloved hand touched the tip of his cap respectfully.

'Thanks.' Adam hurried into the cool dry interior, for once not pausing to consider about all men being equal, the market-enforced indignity of the doorman having to be servile. Today, anyone whose job it was to hasten him into cool comfort was okay by him.

He gave the drive array his destination, and the Lincoln pulled out aggressively into the flow of traffic. The street was jammed full of vehicles, half of them vans and trucks on their delivery route, parked on the kerb so that angry cars, bikes, and buses were squeezed out into the few remaining lanes. His taxi rolled along at twenty miles an hour, its horn tooting about every thirty seconds as pedestrians, powerskaters and cyclists dodged round it. It was always the same in Tridelta city; twenty-four million people crammed onto a patch of ground barely thirty miles across generated a serious amount of traffic pressure.

There was a metro monorail network, laid out like a neat spider web across the city's blocks, even running straight through the base of larger skyscrapers, but it had been designed a hundred years ago, back when Tridelta had a quarter of its current population. Overcrowding in the carriages was at health hazard levels. Only the poor and the tourists used it. City Hall charged I£2000 a year for a road licence to discourage people from using a car. It issued three million vehicle licences per year.

Five miles and twenty-three minutes from the hotel, the taxi pulled up beside the Anau Tower, a cylindrical skyscraper two hundred and fifty storeys tall. Its broad metallic-silver windows were arranged in a slight step pattern, looking as if the tower skin was twisted around the structural frame in a corkscrew spiral.

Adam took the express lift up to the hundred and fiftieth floor, the airship docking level, then switched to a local lift to get up to one seven eight. The Agent's office suite was on the east side of the tower, three modest rooms decorated in cold black granite blocks. The receptionist was an essay in visual intimidation. Her simple charcoal-grey suit was stretched tight around her, illustrating the boosting she'd received, with several seams of muscle wrapped around her original frame. Adam suspected a host of wetwired weapons were lurking in among the dubious additional muscle cells and overstretched epidermal layer. Her neck was a smooth cone of flesh that blended directly into her cheeks. There was no chin, only an eerily attractive set of lips which had been glossed in cherry red. They perked into a smile for Adam when he presented her desk array with his Silas Duanro identity.

'You can go straight in, Senor Duanro,' she trilled in a sweet high voice. 'He is expecting you.'

The Agent smiled in greeting from behind his granite desk.

A tall man who kept thin by expending a lot of nervous energy. His beak of a nose came down almost to his upper lip. For some reason he hadn't modified his scalp follicles; a receding hairline was only partially disguised by a very close cut. 'Senor Silas Duanro? Humm.' He smiled at his own humour. 'You are allowed to use the same name with me you know. After all these years, what have we got if not trust?'

'I'm sure.' Adam hadn't visited Tridelta for several years, yet the Agent always managed to recognize him. Last time he'd looked very different, older and chubbier. Right now he'd morphed his face into that of a forty-year-old, with rounded cheeks, green eyes and thick auburn hair. The skin was thick and slightly pocked as his skin finally began its protest at so many hurried, cheap and unprofessional cellular reprofilings. He had to apply moisturizing cream every morning and evening now; even so it felt like he was stretching scar tissue every time he spoke. His cheeks were always cold these days, the capillaries were in such a bad way from constant readjustment. There was a limit to how much reprofiling anyone could undergo, and Adam knew he was fast approaching the time when he'd have to quit.

But not yet.

Becoming Silas Duanro also involved shedding a lot of fat, and receiving some extra muscle boosting. He hadn't been this fit and strong for a while now; though it was taking some very sophisticated geno-proteins to maintain his heart and other organs at a level where they could support the added muscle. He'd also had to correct his body for the onset of type two diabetes, which had developed over the last couple of years. But whenever the call came through to start the blockade-busting run he was assembling for Johansson, he was determined to be ready for it. No way was he going to see that from some backseat, shouting advice across the unisphere. He fully expected it to be his swansong.

'Drink?' the Agent asked. It was part of their ritual.

'What have you got?'

The Agent smiled and went over to the wall. A long block of granite swung out silently to reveal a brightly lit drinks cabinet. 'Let's see. We won't bother with the Talotee wines, even though they're all the rage. How about Impiricus-blue, a local copy, but in my humble opinion better than the original.'

'Hit me.'

The Agent made a show of pouring the thick purple liqueur into a chilled cut-crystal shot glass. 'And one for me.' He returned to the desk and slid the shot glass over to Adam. 'Salut.'

'Salut.' Adam drained it in a single gulp. A sensation like cold flame burned down his gullet. 'Woho boy,' he grunted. There were tears in his eyes. 'Good stuff.' His voice was harsh, as if he'd come down with flu.

'I knew you'd like that. You have class, which most of my customers are sadly lacking. I deal with so many gangsters; bigger guns and nastier viruses are all they know. But you: I was most proud to see the names which came up in court after the attack on the *Second Chance*, knowing I had provided most of them. Now that was a truly stylish operation, conducted with verve. There are so few of those mounted these days.'

'The ship survived, though.'

'Alas yes. But to have dreamed the dream is to have flown above the mountains so high in all but deed.'

'Keats?'

'Manby. So now, what can I do for you?' the Agent asked.

'I need some assistance for a new project I'm putting together.'

'Of course.'

'Mostly blunt-end troops.' Adam told his e-butler to transfer the list file to the Agent's desktop array.

'No technical specialists? That's a shame. I'll certainly see what I can do to find you the requisite people. I should tell you half of my B list is currently serving with the navy behind enemy lines. Not all of them were taken out of suspension, either, a lot of them volunteered. It's the kind of job which appeals to their more base instinct. They'll come back covered in glory and medals determined to be upright citizens, then in a couple of years they'll be hammering down my door for a job. In the meantime, I'm embarrassed by such a poor inventory. Is there any way you could delay your project?'

'Not indefinitely, no. If it's a question of money . . . ?'

The Agent looked genuinely aghast. 'Good lord, no. I'll probably wind up waiving my commission for you. I do value the challenges you've given me over the years, and you bring a much appreciated amount of business my way. I'm confident I can rise to the occasion once more. Professional pride and all that.'

'I see.' Adam smiled his best false smile, feeling his abused facial skin distend. It was *always* about money with the Agent; criminals were the worst capitalists of all. 'I will be offering the usual re-life insurance bond in the event of premature bodyloss.'

'That's good to hear. Right now, the Commonwealth clinics are overflowing with re-life procedure requests from the families of bodyloss victims from the Lost23. The swine are charging extortionate fees. Seller's market, I'm afraid.'

'After the revolution we'll put them against the wall and shoot them, eh?'

'Absolutely. I'll be happy to supply the firing squads free of charge. Until then—'

'Until then, put my list together and send me the bill. There's a one time address code in the file.'

'Did you have a timeframe in mind?'

'You've got one week.' Adam didn't care how big a disadvantage that put him at. 'I will pay a handsome bonus for delivery.'

The agent raised his eyebrows. 'I always welcome incentives.

However, given the state of the Commonwealth right now, that might be a little difficult.'

'One week.'

'I see you're not going to be moved. Very well, to aspire nobly is its own reward. I won't let you down.' He leant forwards abruptly, and held his hand out.

Adam shook, trying not to let the sneer of disgust appear on his face.

'Excellent.' The Agent walked back to the open drinks cabinet and poured another two shots of Impiricus-blue. He waved a hand, and ten tall slabs of granite pivoted through ninety degrees to reveal a picture window behind. 'We're safer than most here, you know,' he said. 'One rich city is easy to defend. And City Hall has spent a great deal of money upgrading our force fields on top of the navy shielding. Yet still the doubt gnaws at my soul. I am blessed to live amid such beauty as only God and nature can create.'

'What doubts?' Adam asked. He was looking past the Agent at the extraordinary vista through the window. Tridelta city shimmered in the mid-afternoon sunlight, a flat reclaimed island that used to be the flood zone where three rivers merged; the Logrosan, the Dongara, and the Upper Monkira each large in their own right, uniting to become the impressive torrent of water that was the Lower Monkira, flowing away to the ocean three hundred miles away.

Before humans came to Illuminatus, the tridelta area was a sandy marsh that flooded five or six times a year whenever the rivers rose, their torrents ripping out any vegetation which had rooted among the low saturated dunes since the last deluge. With the Commonwealth Council placing an absolute conservation order on the forests and jungles of Illuminatus, preventing any form of clearance, this was the one patch of land other than the mountains that had no trees. CST built a protective two-mile-wide groyne wall in the centre, and constructed their planetary station amid the tropical heat and moisture. As more construction crews arrived, and the travel companies began to invest heavily, so additional walls were built. Huge pumps drained and stabilized the boggy sand, new soil was either dredged out of the rivers or shipped in by train, raising the artificial island's ground level. Foundations were sunk deep, and big high-rise blocks assembled. From that beginning, Tridelta City had mushroomed impressively, first outwards, then, when the limits of the flood marsh were consumed, upwards.

Everywhere Adam looked he could see skyscrapers; towers of concrete, metal, composite, and glass producing a Gothic landscape of sharp pinnacles rising out of the darker conurbation of low buildings. Most were a kilometre high, with the newer skyscrapers reaching even further into the misted air. The Kinoki Tower, so far just a massive slender pyramid of scaffolding on the Logrosan's east bank, was due to top out at three kilometres. Nearly every skyscraper had an airship docked to it; the taller ones had several at varying levels. The craft were all big, over two hundred metres long, with observation decks running the length of their undersides. None of them flew during the day, they just sat on the end of their docking gantry arms, rocking slightly in the misty gusts that swirled across the city.

The height of the Agent's office allowed them to see the landscape on the other side of the churning rivers which encircled the city. Rolling mountains covered in the unbroken magenta and blue-black foliage of the jungle stretched away to the far horizon. Thin swan-white mists swarmed through the valleys between them, mirroring the vast tributary network which lay beneath the substantial canopy. Constellations of darker clouds scudded above the mountaintops, releasing their rain in torrential bursts. It was the sight for which the rich in their elevated penthouses paid a fortune to obtain. Even during the day it was impressive.

'I deal in the underside of civilization,' the Agent said

mournfully, keeping his back to Adam so he could face the window. 'I look out at my city every day and I see how inspiringly high we can climb, yet in this room I also witness how low we can go as a species. I never involve myself personally, you understand, I merely survive by making arrangements. Out of this I live the life I want. I have the constant excitement which is the twin of danger; there is money, women, the thrill of being engaged at levels of politics and corporate enmity which the ordinary citizen doesn't even know exists. Yet here you are, independent of all this, planning some act of violence on behalf of the Guardians of Selfhood. I find myself wondering if for once I should involve myself.'

'You want my advice: don't. There's a chance none of us will be coming back.'

'Honestly spoken. But my dilemma is this; you attacked the navy before, and now here we are, desperately waiting for the return of the starships. Did you know governments have been advised to put their defence systems on grade two alert? Grade one is when you switch them on. And the navy won't say if it has had any success.'

'They won't know until the ships return.'

'How wrong that is, and you know it. If the attack on Hell's Gateway was successful, all the alien wormholes open in Commonwealth space would shut down. Yet they haven't. Instead we've had the confidential warning to make ready. Now you appear, wanting troops inside of a week. I have to ask myself if this is coincidence. I will do many things for money, yet betraying my species is not one of them.'

'This is not betrayal, quite the opposite.'

'Your ideology claims that we are being manipulated by aliens. Is that right?'

Adam was rather surprised to find himself sweating despite the unobtrusive air conditioning. He'd never considered that the Agent might be a problem, least of all on a moral level. For once he had no emergency exit plans. *Stupid.* 'It is, but it's not my ideology. I am not a Guardian. I work as their agent from time to time. And the navy didn't exist when the *Second Chance* was attacked. Consider this: if it had been successfully destroyed, then there would have been no flight to trigger the barrier's collapse.'

The Agent turned from the window and held out a shot glass. 'If not then: later.' He smiled again. 'I see your logic. Your word, then?'

'We're on the same side.'

'For such tidings grown men weep.'

Adam took the shot glass, and knocked back half of the liqueur. He was sure the burn was harder this time. 'You take somebody's *word*?'

'I pride myself on being an anachronism. Surprised? I know how you judge me. Think of this as a small retribution.'

'Cheers.' Adam finished the drink.

'Are you leaving us? I do truly believe this city to be safe from assault. Our weapons industry is small in comparison to that of a Big15, but we are very sophisticated.'

'One lone fortress holding fast against the barbarian horde? I don't think that's for me. Try accessing the records of the siege of Leningrad some time and ask yourself who really won.'

'You're going out in a blaze of glory?'

'No. That's actually what we're trying to prevent.'

'Bravo. And incidentally one of the main reasons I accept your word is because I do know who you represent. What concerns me is that there are some strange people walking the darker streets of Tridelta these days.'

'Is that so?'

'Ah, mockery; the righteousness of fools everywhere. We are a microcosm of the Commonwealth, Senor Duanro. Look at us, and see yourself.'

'All right, I'm buying. What strange people?'

'That's the thing, despite all my efforts, and to be immodest for a moment, they are not inconsiderable. I cannot discover their allegiance. They certainly don't belong to any Isolationist movement, nor a crime syndicate as far as I can determine. Yet they have money, enough to gain exclusivity in several of our more surreptitious clinics. Over the last few months many of my clients have been bounced off waiting lists so the affiliates of these new people can receive armament wetwiring and other services. Taken as a group, they are a considerable force.'

'Thanks for the warning.'

The Agent raised his glass in salute, and drained it in one.

Adam stood to leave. He couldn't resist one last glance through the window. The Agent was right about Tridelta; it was about the most ethnically cosmopolitan city in the Commonwealth. That was why its government was so fractious and radically independent. Contempt for Commonwealth laws and hatred of Senate 'interference' was always high on the agenda of any City Hall politician. It made the relocation of specific services and research laboratories to Illuminatus very attractive for companies who could take advantage of the more liberal laws. Its economy accelerated as fast as its population, an atmosphere in which the local crime syndicates thrived. Consternation in the Senate at this burgeoning 'crime central' was another cause of antagonism. It had culminated seventy years ago in a local campaign for Isolation. But although they didn't have much regard for Commonwealth laws, Tridelta's population did have a lot of respect for Commonwealth cash. Illuminatus remained integrated.

'You're very well connected with the political class here,' Adam said. 'I wonder if I might ask a favour.'

'I'd be interested to hear it.'

'A lot of lifeboat projects have been started in the Commonwealth.'

'Yes, I caught the Michelangelo show last week. That young reporter did an excellent job. I always take pleasure in Dynasty members squirming in public.'

'If you hear of any companies on Illuminatus supplying the Sheldons with components for a lifeboat, I'd enjoy hearing about it.'

'That's certainly a favour I'd be happy supplying. I will inquire for you.'

'Thank you. A pleasure, as always.'

*

Adam had been back at the Hotel Conomela for barely half an hour when Jenny McNowak called.

'Thought you'd like to know,' she said. 'We've just arrived at CST's Tridelta station.'

'What are you doing here?'

'Following Bernadette Halgarth. She caught the express direct from EdenBurg. We're standing on the steps outside the Dalston Street entrance watching her taxi drive off. Kanton is trying to hack its array to see which hotel she's checked in to.'

'Okay, so what's Bernadette doing here?'

'Who knows? She had a full diary for the rest of the week; lunches, parties, shows, committee meetings, same stuff as she always does. There was nothing scheduled on Illuminatus. And, Adam, she didn't tell anyone she was coming, she just dropped everything and got on the train. Right now she's supposed to be having cocktails with a whole bunch of minor Dynasty socialites at the Rialto Metropolitan Gallery.'

'Okay, keep with her and let me know what happens.'

'We'll do our best, but there's only the two of us. Any chance we can have some reinforcements? It's going to be difficult keeping tabs on her in a city like this.'

'I'll do what I can; we're stretched a little thin right now. But Jenny, you're reconnaissance only, understand? I don't want you involved in any incidents. Observe and report.'

'I know. Ah, Kanton says the taxi is heading for the Octavious on the Lower Monkira Wharfside Avenue.'

Adam's e-butler pulled up the local cybersphere listing on the Octavious. It was a medium-size three-star hotel, a hundred and fifty years old. Not the kind of place someone like Bernadette would normally stay at. 'Definitely interesting,' he said. 'I'll do my best to get some help for you. In the meantime, under no circumstances check in to the Octavious. We don't know what's there, and I've just heard there are some wetwired people in this town that don't belong to any local syndicate.'

'Do what we can,' Jenny said. She closed the call.

Adam closed his eyes, trying to think who he could spare from other operations he was running. He hadn't been making excuses when he said they were spread thin. In the end he called Kieran McSobel, and told him to bring Jamas McPeierls, Rosamund McKratz, and himself along to Illuminatus on the next express to support Jenny and Kanton. After that, he called Bradley.

'I'm glad our little investment in Bernadette appears to be paying off,' Bradley said. 'It was something of a long shot.'

'We'll know for sure soon enough. She wouldn't have left EdenBurg in this fashion unless it was urgent.'

'Quite. The timing is significant, I believe. It would appear as if the navy assault on Hell's Gateway has encountered some difficulty. The unisphere news shows are starting to ask if the Prime wormholes to the Lost23 have shut down.'

'If they had, the navy would tell us; if not them, Doi would want to make the announcement to the Senate.'

'Time is not on our side, Adam. It is only two days until the starships are theoretically within communication range of the Commonwealth. If the news is as bad as everyone is starting to predict, our one window of opportunity might be upon us very swiftly indeed.'

'You think the Starflyer will leave?'

'If we have failed to destroy Hell's Gateway, the Primes will undoubtedly move to annexe more Commonwealth planets. Humanity will strike back as hard as we can. After that, the war will not end until one of us has been wiped out of existence, and the other badly damaged. That is the Starflyer's goal. Once those final events have started the end result is inevitable; it has no reason to remain in the middle of a war zone. Already, we have built weapons of enormous destructive power in the Douvoir relativistic missiles; and those are only the ones the navy has given information on. There will be others in the pipeline, there always are.'

'Wait a minute, are you saying the war will happen no matter what? I thought eliminating and exposing the Starflyer would put an end to all this?'

'I never promised that, Adam. I had no idea the Primes would be so uncompromising, so brutal. I don't see how they can be stopped.'

Adam stared out of the hotel's window across the city where dusk was falling. A beautiful rose-gold sun was already touching the skyline of dark buildings, sending its last orange rays through the layers of mist and cloud to stroke the rooftops and skyscrapers. What Johansson had just said hit him like a particularly volatile police stun charge, draining all the energy from his limbs to leave nothing but sharp tingling. 'But . . . what the fuck are we doing this for?'

'Justice, Adam. It has ruined a world that was once full of life and potential. Far Away was reduced to a desert by the mega flare so it could call across the stars. It has brought us to the brink of ruin, too. Surely you don't believe it should be allowed to leave freely? You of all people, Adam, are possessed of a true sense of justice.'

'No.' Adam groaned. He sat heavily on the edge of his bed, his breathing coming in taxing gulps. Just for an instant he thought he was having some kind of stroke, his body was completely unresponsive as he saw the diverted passenger train racing across Abadan station, trying to make up for time it had lost on StLincoln. It wasn't supposed to be on that track, not at that time. The explosion – 'That's not justice. Without validation, killing is just murder.'

'Did you explain that to Kazimir? Do the Guardian villages now under attack on Far Away appreciate your lofty elitist rationalizing?'

'Villages?' Adam frowned, shaking his head to pull the world back into focus.

'The Institute mercenaries are raiding every clan village they can find. Not the frontline forts, not the ones with weapons and warriors. They attack our farmers, our shepherds. Our mothers and their children. The Starflyer has released its uniformed gangsters on our weak and old, hoping we will rush to their aid. It is returning, Adam, it is going back to Far Away. Its slaves are preparing the way for it.'

'What will end the war? There must be something?'

'If you don't believe me, call Stig. He's still hanging on in Armstrong City while the firebombs are thrown and the snipers strike unseen. But be quick about it. The Institute is offering the Governor aid in restoring "civil order". They will soon control the gateway. We will be blocked out.'

'I'm not sure I can do this any more.'

'My poor Adam. Always believing you are the valiant one, that right will triumph in the end. It's not always like that. The universe was not built on integrity. In the face of weakness, force can and will triumph. All you can do is choose who wields that force. Us or the Starflyer. Don't give up now, Adam. You have come so far.'

'Shit.' He wiped the cold sweat from his brow, staring at the moisture on his hand, surprised to see it. *I should have known there was no clear answer. Maybe I did. Maybe I just keep going because that's all that's left of me.*

'Adam,' Bradley said firmly. 'Without this there is truly no hope. The planet must be allowed to have its revenge.'

'All right.' Adam stood and looked down on the darkening city. 'All right, damnit.'

'Get the train ready to break through the blockade. It's going to be magnificent, Adam. This journey will be legend.'

After the call ended, Adam never moved, watching through the window until night had claimed Tridelta, and he could see the jungle in all its glory for one last time. 'Legend my ass,' he laughed. His voice nearly cracked, but he didn't care any more. He told the maidbot to pack his luggage, and ordered a taxi to take him to the CST station. His e-butler booked a ticket on the next train to Kyushu.

*

Second Lieutenants Gwyneth Russell and Jim Nwan followed Tarlo out of the taxi and into the NorthHarbour precinct house. They'd all left their uniforms back at the Paris office; here in Tridelta they'd be far too conspicuous. Tarlo wore a pale-blue sweatshirt with short frayed sleeves and old jeans, with sneakers and a beaded leather necklace. Gwyneth envied him that in the brief dash to the precinct lobby; her more formal cream suit and grey blouse were damp by the time she reached the air conditioning inside, and the sun was already dropping below the skyline.

Detective Sergeant Marhol and Probationary Detective Lucius Lee were waiting for them by the processing desk.

'Quite an ordeal,' Jim said to Lucius as the five of them took the lift up to the fifteenth floor where the detectives had their offices.

'I told him the stakeout was good experience.' Marhol laughed callously, and gave Lucius a hard slap between his shoulder blades. He was overweight, with a belly that rolled over his belt. His clothes were expensive.

A brief expression of contempt flickered over the probationary detective's face as he rocked forward under the impact. 'Your man was good,' he said. 'I checked with Mercedes about the FX 3000p, they refused to believe the security system could be broken so quickly. They said it must be an insurance scam by the owner.'

'Did you check with Ford about battery safety on the Feisha?' Marhol laughed again.

Gwyneth imagined she would get very tired of that laugh very quickly.

The precinct detective teams shared identical offices along a central corridor, like glass boxes lined up in a row. It was the end of the day shift, with everyone wrapping up. Quite a few detectives were lingering in the corridor, taking a look at the big-shot navy team as they went down to one of the secure conference rooms at the far end. A couple of people greeted 'car-shock Lucius' with grins and cheers. The young probationary detective stood up to it with tight smiles.

'So what exactly have you got for us?' Tarlo asked once they were settled in the conference room. Its tall window blinds were closed and shielded, which Gwyneth resented; she'd never seen night on Illuminatus before.

'The Merc snatcher, he fits your man perfectly,' Marhol said.

A holographic portal projected an image of the man in the underground car park. It was taken from Lucius's retinal inserts, showing Beard as he approached the Ford Feisha. Various file comparisons flipped up beside it.

'Looks like him,' Gwyneth conceded.

'Anybody local capable of pulling this kind of stunt?' Tarlo asked.

'One or two,' Marhol said. 'Maybe. As Lucius says, the Mercedes would be hard to crack.'

'None of the local mechanics match the physical profile,' Lucius said. 'That's your man all right.'

'Thank you. From now on this is a priority navy case.' Tarlo gave the conference room's array the file on Beard's truck. 'Please load this into your city traffic management arrays. I want any vehicle even approximating this on your roads to be pulled over and searched by patrol officers.'

'Wow, big overtime,' Marhol said with a smirk. 'The navy gonna pay us for this?'

Tarlo grinned. 'The navy will have anyone who screws up on this placed into suspension for a hundred years. You want to smartmouth me again, or do you want to survive the next twenty-four hours?'

'Hey, fuck you, hotshot. We cracked this case for you, the least you can do is show a little gratitude round here.'

'I am showing a very small amount of gratitude. We gave you this alert for Robin Beard weeks ago, and you sent out one rookie on a stakeout that matched his operation profile perfectly? And by the way, like the suit. Cost a lot did it? Had your taxes audited lately, have you? It can be a real bitch when Central Treasury pulls your file. Happened to an old friend of mine, went on for years when those accountant programs started tapeworming his finance records. He went into early rejuvenation from the stress.'

'You think threatening me is gonna get things done around here?'

'I'm not threatening you, pal, I'm asking for your coopera-tion. So far I've been asking nicely.'

'What exactly are you asking for?' Lucius asked.

'This informant of yours, I want to speak to him now.'

'He doesn't keep office hours, you know,' Marhol said. 'It takes a while to set up a meeting.'

'It used to,' Gwyneth said. 'Today, it becomes quick. We either tag his unisphere address with a location fix and send an armed arrest team in to wherever the bleep comes from, or we raid his home with even more firepower, or we meet up in the bar of his choice.'

'We can round up as many Stuhawks as we can find,' Jim Nwan suggested. 'Shove them into neurolock interrogation, maybe a memory read, and extract Beard's whereabouts that way.'

Tarlo nodded appreciatively. 'I like that one. That's got a high probability of success.'

'You can't lift an entire fucking gang,' Marhol protested.

'Why not?' Tarlo inquired artlessly.

'Every other gang in the city would declare war on the police,' Lucius said. 'Right now, with everyone all het up over the navy ships and Hell's Gateway, we don't need any more unrest.'

Gwyneth shrugged. 'Not our problem.'

'Okay okay,' Marhol said grudgingly. 'My guy, he likes to drink at the Illucid bar on Northgate.'

'Thank you.' Tarlo stood up. 'Let's go. I want to be talking to Robin Beard within twenty-four hours.'

*

Mellanie had rented a tiny apartment in a monolithic forty-storey block on Royal Avenue, not half a mile from the Logrosan embankment. It was a lot darker than the one she'd left behind on Venice Beach, her one window looked away from the river and into the city, but the air conditioning worked which clinched the deal as far as she was concerned. The humidity in Tridelta was unbelievable.

As the sun went down she had the screen on the wall access the Michelangelo show while she got ready for the evening. He had Senators Valetta Halgarth and Oliver Tam in the studio, asking them what had happened to the attack on Hell's Gateway. Even for someone used to dealing with the expert evasiveness of professional politicians, Mellanie was impressed by the varied and inventive ways the senators didn't answer the question.

She showered to rinse away the clamminess of a day spent out on Tridelta's streets. Once she'd towelled down she put on a simple white cotton halter, over that she wore a sleeveless micro-sweater of fluffy white wool in a loose cobweb weave that was only slightly bigger than the halter so she could show off lean lines of abdominal muscle and the ruby-spark stud in her navel. She wriggled into a white miniskirt; no tights, she'd spent half an hour massaging oil into her legs, giving her skin an arresting sheen. None of the clothes had a designer label, there wasn't even a copy of anything fashionable; which was about all Tridelta's stores sold in their voracious quest for the tourist credit tattoo. All she had bought in town were some long costume jewellery necklaces of wooden beads and lavender-tinted crystalline shells which she looped round her neck.

'But why would the navy embargo any information on the Hell's Gateway strike?' Michelangelo asked reasonably. 'I'm sure the Prime aliens know if we've attacked them or not. Surely the only logical conclusion is that our ships have failed and the Executive is trying to avoid a panic.'

Mellanie half-turned for the answer.

'Our intelligence gathering capability must remain veiled for obvious reasons,' Oliver Tam replied smoothly. 'I'm sure we do have the ability to see if their wormholes at the Lost23 are open or not. If so, that gives us a distinct military advantage. The navy cannot be expected to expose our assets simply to make the media happy. We will all know beyond any doubt just as soon as the starships fly into communication range. Is it possible, Michelangelo, that you simply cannot stand not knowing? Has the media become too arrogant in its assumption that all secrets must be violated to satisfy your lust for ratings, no matter what cost to us as a species?'

'Was that a joke?' Michelangelo asked; he seemed mortally offended by the insult. Anger in someone so large and powerful was imposing. Oliver Tam did his best to show no fear.

Mellanie grinned at the ludicrous posturing back in the studio, and checked the mirror. Her hair was now raven black, and alive with short waves that made it frizz out around her head. She pinned it back on both sides with cheap orange and yellow cloth bands. After some thought she applied the darkest purple lipstick she could find. Thanks to a dermal genoprotien her face was now covered in freckles; they made her look so cutesy she wanted to hurl. Instead she threw her arms round her head, and blew herself a flouncy kiss.

Perfect persona.

The face in the mirror certainly wasn't that of Mellanie Rescorai, ace investigative reporter for the top-rated unisphere news shows, the face that everybody in the civilized galaxy knew. This was some first-life teen ingénue, fresh and keen to be part of the exciting city party scene – yet not quite knowing how. There would be enough volunteers to show her. Men liked that inquisitive youthfulness, and the older and more jaded they were the more they liked it. She'd known that even before Morty.

*

The air outside was already noticeably cooler when Mellanie left the apartment block, with a modest breeze drifting in from over the water. It had a narcotic effect on the bustling pedestrians, who all shared the same high-spirited verve as they started to search out what the bars and clubs had to offer. Mellanie walked west along the broad avenue, heading for the river. She couldn't help the happy smile on her face. The streets here were intent on gaudy photonic mimicry of the elegance that resided beyond the water. For the first ten metres above the enzyme-bonded concrete pavements, the buildings were walled in glowing intense neon, sparkly holographics, and the steady burn of polyphoto lighting. Above that, city regulations allowed no light pollution. Looking straight up gave Mellanie an eerie view, it was as if the street had been given a stealth-black ceiling. The brighter stars twinkled directly overhead, when they weren't shrouded by remnants of the day's clouds, but the canyon walls of skyscrapers along the city grid were invisible, their glass windows prohibited from transmitting any light from the inside, thus spoiling the view of others.

She could see only one blemish, the brilliantly lit observation deck of an airship as it cast off from its skyscraper mooring. It angled upwards to slide into the clear air above Tridelta's towers, and set out across the river to begin its night-long flight over the jungle.

Mellanie reached the intersection and walked down to the Logrosan south high quay where the ferries docked. The last short avenue leading to the embankment slowly opened out, its buildings reducing in size. There was a large flow of people heading down to the ferries, bustling along together in a carnival atmosphere. Her pace began to slow as she saw what was ahead. Just about all the first-night tourists in the crowd around her had stopped to stare.

In front of her the Logrosan was a mile wide, a sheet of black ripples gurgling with quiet power as it raced along the edge of the city. On the other side, the jungle cloaked the undulating mountains. Every tree gleamed with opalescent splendour.

Unlike terrestrial plants which competed to produce bigger and more colourful flowers to attract insects, vegetation on Illuminatus had evolved bioluminescence to vie for the attention of local insects. The dark leaves which had spent the day soaking up sunlight now radiated the energy away in a soft lambent glow. With each tree in the forest cloaked in its own cold nimbus of iridescence the jungle was bright enough to rival the sleepy light of a dawn sun.

An entranced Mellanie hurried forward to the quay with its long row of angled jetties. Her ferry was the *Goldhawk*, a big old metal-hull craft that chugged over the water once every hour, night and day. On board, she jostled with the other two hundred and fifty passengers for a view near the bow as it headed over to the Crossquay. Three more massive airships passed high overhead during the short trip. Mellanie waved foolishly at them, laughing at herself for doing so, but she was in that kind of mood.

Looking at the shimmering jungle ahead of her allowed her to relax. She'd spent the last forty-eight hours on a nervous high as she performed her reconnaissance of the Saffron Clinic. Michelangelo had been right, it was discreet. In the morning she moved between the pavement cafés on Allwyn Street so that the Greenford Tower was always in view. It was a kilometre-high cone of burnished steel and purple glass that housed stores, factories, offices, hotels, bars, spas, and apartments. The top floor was an airship dock, which had one of the big dark ovoids floating passively on the end of its gantry. Set back from the street in its own plaza, the Greenford's base was made up from tall arching windows which rose to the fifth floor. Each one was an entrance to a different section. Given her purpose she could hardly walk round them all trying to find which one belonged to the clinic. So she drank herbal teas and mineral water under the café awnings as her programs and inserts slowly infiltrated the Greenford Tower's internal network.

With her software milking data from the management arrays on each floor, she soon found the Saffron Clinic, spread out over seven floors, starting thirty-eight storeys up. When the information came in, she tilted her head back to see the actual windows, her virtual vision designating the blank panes with a slender neon green outline. It was as near as she could get, visually or electronically. Access to the clinic's own arrays was securely guarded. She didn't have the skill to hack them.

A review of the Tower's registered structural plans showed her the clinic had its own garage in the third level of the big fifteen-level underground car park. There was also an entrance through one of the tall archways on the west side, which led to a private lobby and lift. Mellanie moved to a bar in a side alley just off Allwyn Street which gave her a narrow view of the entrance. That was where she found the one weakness in the clinic's electronic protection; the Tower's own security software identified and cleared all authorized personnel going through the outside door to the Saffron's lobby before they reached the clinic's modern internal security systems.

She settled back in a chair and bought herself a second hot chocolate. There were several big fountains playing in the Greenford's plaza, their tumbling jets of foam occasionally blowing across the small clinic door, but apart from that she had a good view of everyone who came and went. Each time the door opened her inserts recorded the image of the person coming through, cataloguing it with the information and name she gleaned from the Tower's security array. Three hours later, she cocked her head to one side as a bulky figure emerged into the late afternoon. Funnily enough it was her time with Alessandra Baron that had given her the most insight into people, learning to recognize what they were in the first few moments. *Instant stereotyping*, Michelangelo had called it glibly, but she knew instinctively that this was the one she was looking for. As the data from the security array rolled down her virtual vision, identifying the man as one Kaspar Murdo, and confirming some of the things she'd already guessed at, she was already standing, leaving a couple of I£10 notes on her table to cover the drinks. She began to follow Kaspar Murdo along the street, unleashing a flock of monitor programs into the public arrays around him as she went.

*

The crowds were thicker on Southern Crossquay, which was nothing but a wide strip of enzyme-bonded concrete holding the river and jungle apart, extending for thirty miles. On the central section, opposite Tridelta, eighty stone and concrete jetties bristled out into the water, angled back to provide some protection against the flow for the boats moored along them.

Mellanie wandered down the broad avenue along the top, looking for the jetty where *Cyprus Island* was docked. On her left, Tridelta's silhouette was a slim band of gaudy light just above the river, topped by the black towers that cut a sharp profile against the sheen of the jungle on the far side of the city. To her right, the trees towered over the walkway, casting a pale ever-shifting radiance across the admiring faces of the tourists as they searched for their jetty.

The *Cypress Island* was one of a dozen nightcruise boats tied up at the jetty; longer and slimmer than the ferries that ploughed across the river from the city, it had a flat open top deck with a bar in the centre. Inside, the upper two passenger decks had transparent bulkheads, so that the restaurant and casino patrons could still have an excellent view of the jungle; only the third deck where the stage was installed had a normal hull. Mellanie walked along the short gangplank amid a gaggle of clubbers barely older than she was. Several of the boys gave her encouraging smiles, which she had to ignore. It was a shame, the kids here all looked terrific, taking a lot of care over what they wore and how they styled themselves.

She confirmed her ticket with the steward as she stepped on board. He took in her appearance with a fast expert glance. 'Are you sure you want to be here?' he asked with a mildly concerned smile. 'It gets a bit rowdy later on. Can be upsetting if you're not used to it. The *Galapagos* will accept your ticket if you want, it's the same company; they take out a nicer bunch of passengers.'

'I'll be all right,' she said, practising a high-pitched giggle. She was privately delighted by his reaction.

'Okay then.' He waved her on.

The first drink was free. She took an imported light beer from Munich and squeezed her way to the top deck rail.

The *Cypress Island* cast off twenty minutes later. Out of the lee of the jetty, its engines pushed it against the swift current producing a pronounced rocking motion. The ride changed for the better a mile and a half upriver when they turned into one of the hundreds of tributary rivers feeding the Logrosan. A cheer ran along the boat as the water settled down and Tridelta vanished round a curve behind them. The engine noise faded away to a quiet murmur.

On either side of the small tributary trees grew down to the water, with their tangle of exposed, bloated roots caging the crumbling soil of the bank. Despite the light twinkling from each leaf it was dark between the trees, giving the jungle a mysterious aura. Nothing moved on the land; Illuminatus had never evolved anything bigger than its insects.

'You'd think it would be full of Silfen.'

Mellanie turned to see one of the kids from the group on the gangplank standing beside her. 'You would?'

'It's their kind of place. I'm Dorian by the way.'

She hesitated. 'Saskia.' He was handsome enough, tall with a mild Oriental heritage in his features. Small scarlet OCtattoos ran round his neck, dragons and serpents chasing each other. Semi-organic fibres had been woven into his dark hair, sending beads of light flickering through his dainty Roman curls.

'Can I get you another beer, Saskia?'

Her inserts registered a transmission from him directed at the boat's cybersphere node. It wouldn't bother her normally, some boy bragging about pulling her to his mates back in the city. But the transmission was heavily encrypted. 'Not just now, thanks.'

He tried to cover the hurt expression. 'Sure. I'm on for the whole night.'

'I'll remember.'

The message he'd sent bothered her. She still didn't have the skill to decrypt it with her inserts, and she wasn't carrying a hand-held array so she could work on it. For a moment she toyed with scanning him thoroughly just to see what kind of inserts he was carrying. Of course, if there was any serious wetwiring he'd detect the scan.

Why should he be wetwired? Heavens, I'm getting paranoid. So why don't I scan him?

Dorian was back at the bar, smiling with his group of friends. Probably getting teased for getting the brush off.

The tributary grew narrower, branching several times on both sides. Trees began to arch over the water, the tallest ones touching above midstream, their twigs starting to interlace. *Cypress Island* sailed on through a tunnel of coronal splendour.

Mellanie went down to the restaurant deck and helped herself to the buffet bar. It was dim inside, allowing the eaters to gaze out at the jungle. Her ticket didn't qualify her for a table by the transparent walls, so she took her plate back up to the top deck, and sat on a bench in front of the bar, watching the intricate lacework of branches above the river. Some of the trees had a luminescence which verged towards ultraviolet, making her white top shine.

She stared down at the wool for a minute, not really registering what she was seeing. 'Oh sod it!' she muttered. Her platinum and purple virtual hand touched the SI's icon.

'Hello, Mellanie.'

'There's somebody on board I'm worried about. I need a message decrypting.'

'Very well.'

She'd been expecting to argue her case. The agreement caught her by surprise. She opened the file for the SI.

'Roughly translated, he said: Identity confirmed. It's her.'

'Oh God,' she gasped. *Alessandra's goons have caught up with me!* She hunted round in a semi-panic, but Dorian was nowhere to be seen on the top deck.

'Do you have any weapons with you?' the SI asked.

'No. What about your inserts? Is there anything that I can use to fight him off?'

'Not with any certainty. I might be able to load kaos software into his wetwiring, assuming he has some. Shall I alert the Tridelta police? They can have a helicopter with you in minutes.'

She glanced up at the radiant arch of light they were sailing under. 'How would they get down to us?'

Her link with the unisphere ended.

Damn it! Not now. She sent a scrutineer package into the nearest on-board array to check what the problem was. The network management routines reported that the node was no longer drawing power, it had been damaged physically.

Our cybersphere node is suffering a temporary fault, the bridge array sent on a general broadcast, **please do not be alarmed. A new connection will be established soon. The company management would like to apologize for any inconvenience in the meantime.**

Mellanie started shaking as the text ran down her virtual vision. 'Come back to me,' she whispered into the fluorescent night. 'Come on, you got through to Randtown.' Some awful inner voice was saying that Randtown had never been this isolated from the planetary cybersphere, it had landlines, a network. This was a lone boat in the middle of a jungle on a planet with only one city.

She clenched her hands, and pressed them against her legs, forcing the shakes to stop. *Think! I can't beat him by myself.* Waiting for the police wasn't a serious option. She didn't even know if the SI had called them. She brought her stilled hand up to her face, giving her arm a curious look. *It's still in there.*

A fast scan round with her inserts revealed one of the boat's arrays was installed behind the bar. Mellanie rushed over, and ducked under the counter top.

'Hey,' one of the barmen told her. 'You can't come back here.'

She flashed him a distracted smile as she ran her hand along the shelving. Scrabbling fingers found the array, tucked away behind boxes of snacks; it was a small one, used to handle the bar's finances, but it had an i-spot. She pressed her palm against it. 'Just one second,' she told the barman. 'We'll make out later.'

His jaw dropped. He didn't know if she was joking or not.

Mellanie's virtual hands activated a host of inserts, and fed in the code. The SIsubroutine decompressed, and flowed through the i-spot into the boat's tiny net.

'Below optimum processing capacity available,' the SIsubroutine said. 'I am operating in abridged mode. Why am I here?'

'I'm being stalked by a killer. He's probably got weapons wetwiring.' She stood up and checked round again, half expecting Dorian to be coming for her. The barman moved up close. 'Are you serious?' he asked in a low murmur.

'Hell yes, but later.' Mellanie backed out of the bar. She winked. 'I'll call you.'

'Suggest you call the police,' the SIsubroutine said.

Her mouth twisted into a groan of frustration. 'I can't. That's why I decompressed you. I need help.'

'Do you have a weapon?'

'No. Find out if there are any on board.'

'No weapons listed on ship's manifest.'

'Can you infiltrate kaos software into the killer's wetwired armaments?'

'No kaos files in my directory.'

'Crap. What do I do?'

'Suggest you leave the ship.'

For a moment she considered it. The tributary wasn't a problem, she could certainly swim to shore, or take a lifeboat. Then she'd be alone in the jungle. Miles from anywhere. If she jumped over the rail people would see her. The captain would stop. Dorian would come after her through the trees.

'Think of something else,' she instructed.

'Review enabled. Available processing capacity will not run comparative escape option routines at optimum level.'

Mellanie was rapidly losing faith in the SIsubroutine. This wasn't going to be like Armstrong City where it hovered around her like a guardian angel. *I need a weapon, something that'll give me a chance.* That same calm she'd had when she dealt with Jaycee had returned, blocking out everything else around her. There actually was one place on board that might have something she could use. She just had to get to it. God alone knew where Dorian would be lurking. He was certainly a class above the kind of street thugs that had been sent after Paul Cramley. A compliment of sorts.

Mellanie walked calmly to the stairs that led below deck. *Surely he won't shoot me in public?* But there was no telling. Kazimir McFoster had been in the middle of LA Galactic for heaven's sake.

'Can you detect any encrypted local communications?' she asked the SIsubroutine.

'No. The captain has ordered an assessment of the on-board net to see why the boat functions have dropped to emergency default mode. The diagnostic software is interfering with my comparative option routines.'

'I might be able to get a weapon. Incorporate that possibility into your review.'

'What kind of weapon?'

'I don't know. Nothing very powerful.'

'Complying.'

'And keep watching for encrypted traffic. I want to know where he is.'

The restaurant was crammed with passengers having their meal; long queues snaked back across the floor space from the buffet bars. With all her sensor inserts active, Mellanie couldn't detect any of the power signatures that would indicate active wetwiring. She took the stairs down to the casino deck. There were only a few devout gamblers here, most of the tables were deserted, which wasn't what she wanted. Warm air gusted up the stairwell from the third deck. Mellanie hurried down to the club. 'Give me a floorplan,' she told the SIsubroutine. 'Is there any escape route? Can I get to the lifeboats?'

'Cancelling comparative escape option analysis.'

Mellanie clenched her teeth in anger. Then the boat's schematics flipped up into her virtual vision.

'Lifeboat access is available on all decks,' the SIsubroutine said.

'Can I launch one without the bridge crew knowing?'

'I can block a launch alert.'

'Great.'

'Resuming comparative escape option analysis.'

At the bottom of the stairs a holographic sign flickered like a faulty strobe telling her that the hermaphrodite dance troupe Death By Orgy would be starting their first performance in twenty minutes. This was definitely what she was looking for. Heavy rock music thumped at her as soon as she went through the screened entrance, loud enough to make her bones vibrate. The club was packed solid and absurdly dim. Holosparks flittered through the air like perverted comets, providing the only flashes of illumination as they circled round the denizens writhing on the minute dance floor. She had to switch her retinal inserts to full light amplification mode to see where she was going.

The club sprang into grey-green focus. Fetish gear was in the majority. Semi-organic costumes offered up strangely modified genitalia as she slithered through the menagerie of bizarreos. Additional limbs were popular, several had infant-sized hands grafted on around the crotch area. Specialist cellular reprofiling had produced a lot of animalisms; furry arms groped at lines of teats, pointed ears twitched as they were licked by serpentine tongues, lustful smiles revealed sharp fangs.

In her white girlie clothes Mellanie felt like some virgin sacrifice on her way to the altar. Everyone looked at her as if they were sharing that thought.

Her inserts were picking up a lot of power sources inside

the club. Most of them too small for her to use, batteries for kinky toys. She needed the real S&M crowd to have any chance of success.

They were up at the bar, a cluster of large bodies clad in black straps, shiny chains, and hoods. Kaspar Murdo was also there, standing at one end, dressed in Spanish Inquisitor robes, with rusted iron chains round his neck, dangling a variety of medieval instruments.

Mellanie detected the largest power source in the club, her virtual vision locking the position in blue brackets, fortunately at the opposite end of the bar from Murdo. It was a cattle prod, one of many items hanging from the thick leather belt of a bizarreo femfeline. Her head had sleek black fur coming down to her eyebrow line, where her modified glistening red-brown nose jutted forward; long whiskers were rooted at the side of the slit nostrils. She wore a tight sleeveless black leather costume which showed off furry arms and legs. A long tail flicked casually from side to side as she talked to two other cat girls with more restrained modifications and a loosely chained boy slave in a toga with a worried expression on his face.

Mellanie shoved herself in front of the femfeline. 'I need to borrow your cattle prod,' she shouted against the pounding rock track.

The femfeline yowled at a volume which rose effortlessly above the music. She brought an arm up and extended her paw fingers in front of Mellanie's face. The polished onyx claws which had replaced her fingertips clicked out, their points a centimetre from Mellanie's eyes. 'Kitty says lick my litter clean, sweetie bitch.'

Her companions mewled their laughter.

Someone with formidable wetwiring, all of it activated, came through the club's screened entrance.

'No time,' Mellanie said. She froze. Specks of silver appeared on her arms and face, as if she was sweating mercury. The blooms spread rapidly, obscuring her skin. Software flooded out of her, taking control of the organic circuitry which administered the femfeline's adaptations.

The femfeline gave a start as her own tail snaked up and wrapped itself around her neck. It tightened. Her claws retracted.

'I'm taking the cattle prod,' Mellanie announced, and snatched it from the belt clip.

The femfeline smiled in excitement. 'Yes mistress, I'll be a good kitty for you.' Her tongue licked out, a long obscenely flexible cord of wet flesh. 'Hurry back.'

Mellanie pushed hard through the packed bodies, creating a wave of commotion. Behind her, Dorian caught it and began to thread his way towards her.

'Can you remove the safety controls on the cattle prod?' she asked the SIsubroutine. 'There's a lot of power in it. If I could use it in one burst it should be lethal.'

'Cancelling comparative escape option analysis. Reviewing cattle prod systems.'

Mellanie reached the screened doorway at the side of the stage. 'Open it,' she ordered.

The door slid aside. The corridor behind it was lined with small private cabins. She could hear moans, some of pleasure, some of pain. A whip made a loud *crack*. Someone screamed. There was snarling.

'Cattle prod safety systems bypassed. Battery discharge rate set to unlimited.'

She looked around frantically as the door slid shut behind her. Most of the cabins were occupied. There was a single emergency evacuation hatch at the far end. 'How can I hit him with it? He'll never let me get close.'

'Running comparative remote electrical assault option analysis.'

'Oh hell.' Mellanie dashed for the escape hatch.

*

Dorian zapped the door's lock circuitry with a single burst from the maser embedded in his wrist. A small circle of the tough composite smouldered and blistered. He pushed hard, applying the strength of his boosted musculature. There was a creaking sound, lost in the raucous music. The door popped open. He walked though the screening and into the relative quiet of the corridor. His sensor scans were immediately subject to a barrage of interference. Voices yelped and groaned behind the closed doors on either side. At the far end, Mellanie had got the escape hatch open. She jerked round. Half of her skin was silver, inserts and OCtattoos directing the interference directly at him. He scanned what he could of her with interest. She was doing the same to him. More effectively, he knew, but he could see what he needed to.

'No weapons,' he said. 'How curious.'

'I've got a message for Alessandra.'

He took a step forward. 'What?'

Her inserts transmitted an encrypted signal into the corridor's small array. The sprinkler system went off above him. Water poured down as the fire alarm sounded.

Dorian gave her a pitying look as the deluge soaked his shirt and trousers. 'Nobody can hear that.' Beyond the shower, Mellanie smiled.

The cattle prod lying on the floor by Dorian's feet discharged. The water allowed its full current load to slam into him. His body convulsed, steam fizzing out of his clothes and hair. He arched his back, screaming briefly as his eyes bulged and his tongue protruded. The optical fibres woven into his hair melted. Black lines appeared on his skin when organic circuits burned, sending out thin wisps of smoke to mingle with the steam and water. Flesh ruptured volcanically where his weapons' power cells were implanted. Blood and gore splattered across the walls.

It took five seconds for the cattle prod battery to exhaust itself. When the current failed, Dorian's juddering corpse crashed to the floor. The SIsubroutine switched off the corridor's sprinklers.

Mellanie walked over and peered down at the gently steaming body. The legs spasmed a couple of times.

'I'll tell her myself,' she said.

*

Kaspar Murdo was enjoying the evening. It was a good crowd in the *Cypress Island*'s club. He knew a lot of them, and there were several promising newbies. Everyone said Death By Orgy were hot. He was looking forward to seeing them perform.

Then this *vision* in a fluffy white top and miniskirt sidled up to the bar barely a couple of metres away and asked for a beer. A first-lifer by the looks of her. She appeared slightly shaky, as if she was shocked by what she was seeing and trying not to show it. That meant she was curious, and not instantly repelled. It was a vulnerability he knew exactly how to take advantage of. He'd be able to encourage her at first, drawing her closer, reassuring her until she trusted him. Then with that trust established he could begin her training.

His bulk allowed him to push easily through the eager authoritarian animalists and bizarreos who were gathering like storm clouds around their oblivious prey. He glared any objectors down, snarling back when he was barked at by a cannineman. 'This one is on me,' he told her as the girl proffered a I£ note to the barman. 'I insist. That means there can be no argument.'

She nodded with nervous gratitude, glancing at the instruments on the end of his chains. 'Thank you.'

'Kaspar,' he said.

'Saskia.'

He grinned in a friendly, paternal fashion, and lifted one of his chains to show off the crude iron and leather device on the end. 'Crazy, aren't they?' he asked in a fashion that invited her to share the joke.

She smiled sheepishly. And Kaspar's evening became the best in a long, long time.

*

It was close to midnight local time when the express from Paris slipped into Tridelta's CST station. Renne was secretly delighted about that, it meant they'd get a look at the jungle. 'Get us a riverside hotel as close as you can to the Octavious,' she told Vic Russell.

'Absolutely,' he said enthusiastically.

'The closest and cheapest, Vic.'

'Yeah, yeah.'

'Aren't we going straight to the Halgarth team?' Matthew Oldfield asked.

'They can handle the rest of tonight's shift,' Renne said. 'Warren will let me know if there's any status change.'

'Okay.'

'Gives us a chance to settle in before we see what Bernadette is up to. Don't you want to see the jungle?'

'Hell, yeah,'

'Right then.' She told her e-butler to call Tarlo. 'Where are you?' she asked when he accepted the call.

'Stakeout in a garage on Uraltic Street. A police informant we interviewed earlier said Beard would be here tonight.'

'I hope you're wearing rubber socks. Those car batteries have a lot of current in them.'

'Very funny. What do you want?'

'I'm at the CST station.'

'In Tridelta?'

'Yeah.'

'Why? Has Hogan sent you as back-up?'

'No. I'm following Bernadette Halgarth, Isabella's mother.'

'You're doing what?'

'Don't worry, I've got Vic and Matthew with me.'

'Does Hogan know? For Christ's sake, Renne, I thought you'd dropped the whole Isabella thing.'

'I had. But Christabel Halgarth put Bernadette and Victor under surveillance as a favour for me, I didn't even have to ask her. Both of them have been receiving and sending some encrypted messages, nothing too suspicious; but today Bernadette just dropped everything and came here. Halgarth security have her under surveillance at the Octavious Hotel, which again is a strange choice for a socialite like Bernadette. We're going to join them in the morning.' She waited for Tarlo to answer.

'Got us a hotel,' Vic said cheerfully. 'Not very cheap, sorry.' He and Matthew shared a grin.

Renne waved a hand for silence. Her virtual vision showed her the link was still active. 'Tarlo?'

'Yeah, hi, sorry. Do you need any help?'

'Not yet. But if we do, I'll yell for you. And that's a reciprocal.'

'Sure. Thanks. Okay, good luck.'

'Yeah, you too,' she told him.

*

'Paula, we've got an interesting situation developing.'

'What is it Hoshe?'

'I'm with Nadine and Jacob on Illuminatus, running the electronic surveillance on Tarlo while he goes after Beard. Now Gus and Isaiah have joined us; they're monitoring Renne.'

'So both targets are on Illuminatus?'

'Yes. Renne arrived twenty minutes ago, following Bernadette Halgarth. As soon as Renne got here she called Tarlo, then five minutes later Tarlo called Bernadette. It was an encrypted message and routed through a one-time address, but for once we got lucky; we infiltrated scrutineer software into Bernadette's hotel node as soon as Warren told me she was here. We haven't managed to decrypt it yet, but the message Tarlo sent is the one she received. It looks like Tarlo was warning her she's under observation. There's no other reason.'

'Tarlo. Damnit.'

'I'm sorry, Paula.'

'Not your fault. I knew it had to be one of them.'

'What do you want to do?'

'Keep a close eye on him and Bernadette. I'll join you in a couple of hours.'

'Are you going to tell Renne?'

'Possibly. Our priority has to be getting Tarlo into custody. But I don't want to scare off Bernadette until she's contacted whoever she's there to meet. This is our first real chance to penetrate the Starflyer agent network. Timing is going to be critical.'

'Tarlo's going to be wetwired. Bernadette as well, probably.'

'Definitely. Don't worry, my team will be armed.'

*

The room didn't look anything special, a simple cube of grey walls and a worn carpet. Two polyphoto strips in the ceiling made it brighter than it strictly needed to be. A single air-conditioning grille high above the malmetal door hissed away unobtrusively. There weren't any sensors visible, but they had to be there somewhere.

Robin Beard sat on a cheap plastic chair with his feet up on the table that was bolted to the middle of the floor. He didn't look particularly concerned that he'd been arrested. But then, Lucius thought, he'd been in custody so many times he was familiar with the routine. Say nothing and wait for the lawyer.

Lucius followed Tarlo into the interview room. The blond surfer gave Beard a friendly smile.

'You're not a lawyer,' Beard said.

'Smart,' Tarlo said. 'I like that. That's going to be helpful for both of us.'

'You guys are really going to suffer for this,' Beard said. 'I was walking through a garage and you restrained me for no valid reason with undue force. You didn't even read me any rights.'

'That's because you don't have any,' Tarlo said.

Beard smiled.

'Sit down,' Tarlo said.

The smile flickered on Beard's face. 'I am—'

Tarlo's fist swung fast, smashing into the small man's nose. There was a crunch of bone breaking as the chair tipped back spilling him onto the floor, limbs all in a tangle. His head caught a nasty crack as he went down. 'Jesus fucking Christ!' Beard wailed. One hand was cupping his nose, with a copious amount of blood leaking through his fingers; the other hand was probing the back of his skull. His eyes had watered.

Lucius had taken a half pace forward, then halted, unsure what to do. He glanced to the ceiling corner where one of the visual sensors was hidden. Nobody was calling him.

Tarlo grinned as he squatted down beside the mechanic. 'Always hurts like a sonofabitch, doesn't it? Bust my own nose a couple of times on a board, so I know.'

Beard glanced desperately at Lucius. 'You saw that. You're my witness.'

Lucius managed to let his gaze drift away. Tarlo had told him to say nothing, but this wasn't what he was expecting.

'We couldn't get hold of a good cop to work this routine properly,' Tarlo said. 'They're all out on the streets helping decent citizens in these troubled times. So we're just going to have to do the bad cop, worse cop set-up instead. Know what? The boys in the office, they're running a sweep on how long you can stand up to the beating before you crack. I've got fifty pounds on ten minutes, but I'm gonna be on the level with you here, buddy, I'm not even going to wait that long.'

He drew a slim medical infuser patch from a pocket. 'There's quite a few street names for this; you ever heard of hardbang? No? How about painamp?'

Beard shook his head, giving Tarlo a frightened look.

'The thing is, this is like the opposite of an anaesthetic,' Tarlo said. 'It makes the pain progressively worse. Really, badly, worse. I mean I've seen people screaming in agony from a nasty torn nail when they're tripping on this. So you can imagine what that nose is going to do to you, especially when Lucius here starts thumping it.'

'What the fuck do you want?' Beard shouted. His wide eyes were staring wildly at the infuser patch.

'We're not police,' Tarlo said. 'We're navy. So there is no comeback for us no matter how bad this gets for you, how many of your rights we stamp on. No lawyer is going to come charging in to save you. Do you understand that?'

Beard swallowed hard and nodded.

'You will do as I tell you. Now do you want me to pump a dangerous dose of this into you? Is that the way I make you cooperate?'

Beard shook his head. The blood was running right down his grubby shirt to drip onto the floor. 'No, sir.'

'Hey,' Tarlo grinned round at Lucius. 'Haven't been called sir in a long time. How about that? This man has respect. I like that.' He turned back to Beard. 'So do I infuse?'

'No. No, sir, I'll cooperate.'

'Good man.' Tarlo put his hand out. Beard gave it a mistrustful look, but eventually allowed Tarlo to help him to his feet. 'You introduced a friend of yours Dan Cufflin to an agent who supplies people for illegal activities,' Tarlo said. 'Correct?'

Beard frowned, trying to concentrate. 'Yeah, I remember Dan.'

'What was the agent's name?'

'I don't know. He's just the Agent.'

'Where is he?'

'Here, on Illuminatus, I think. This is where we normally meet.'

'Where?'

'I don't know. I've only ever met him twice, and that was in different places: bars. We normally use the unisphere.'

'Today you meet him again, in person, on Illuminatus. Fix it up. Now.'

*

Jenny McNowak had checked herself and Kanton into the Grialgol Intersolar Hotel on Lower Monkira Wharfside Avenue, on the opposite side of the street from the Octavious, and two blocks down. After that there wasn't much she could do apart from load scrutineer programs into arrays in and around the Octavious. The registration array was easy to hack, giving them Bernadette's room number, 2317, as well as a list of other guests which they ran through their database.

After that, they'd managed to get up on the Grialgol's roof, and position a sensor that could zoom in on Bernadette's twenty-third-floor window. It was dark by then; there was nothing else they could do except wait.

Kieran McSobel arrived a couple of hours later, bringing Jamas McPeierls and Rosamund McKratz with him. There was enough room for all of them; Jenny had booked a suite in the Grialgol. After weeks in Rialto's rock-bottom economy accommodation, and long stints cramped up in cheap hired cars, the suite with its luxury fittings, especially in the bathroom, was a pleasant interlude. It gave her a lot of satisfaction being in a more expensive room than Bernadette, who Jenny had come to envy and despise for the ostentation she lived in on EdenBurg. She was looking forward to testing the Grialgol's room service menu.

'Nothing much to report,' Jenny said as the newcomers began to set up a series of specialist arrays they'd brought with them in the suite's main octagonal lounge. She and Kanton had arrived with almost nothing other than their standard field operation packs. Bernadette had caught everyone by surprise when she left EdenBurg.

Jamas established an e-seal around the perimeter of the lounge, then switched on a janglepulse in case there were any modified insects spying on the room. 'We're clean,' he announced.

'She's had no visitors,' Jenny said. 'And as far as we know there's been nothing taken up to her room.'

'What about a visual?' Kieran asked, nodding at the tiny hand-held array screen which was showing the grainy grey hash which was the feed from the roof sensor.

'She's left the window screened,' Kanton said. 'It's just a standard model, twenty years old but effective enough to keep out any passive scan.'

'So we don't even know if she's in there or not?' Kieran said.

'We have accessed civic sensors around the hotel,' Jenny said, defensively. 'Nobody with her visual profile has left the building, our characteristics recognition programs would have caught that.'

'Understood.' He turned to Jamas and Rosamund. 'That's your first priority, try to establish if she's still in there.'

'We're on it,' Rosamund assured him from a plush leather armchair. Her eyes fluttered half-shut as data began to fill her virtual vision. Small holographic data blocks sprang up from various arrays spread out around her. Her hands and fingers twitched minutely as she began manipulating programs, infiltrating them into the Octavious systems.

'Our database didn't tag any of the other residents,' Jenny said. 'None of the names are known to us.'

'We should maybe try and run a comparison, see if any of them fit Isabella's profile.'

'Good idea. We've got several hours of images from the civic cameras. It shouldn't take too long to—'

'There's someone else here,' Rosamund announced.

'What do you mean?' Kieran asked. An ion pistol appeared in his hand.

'In the Octavious arrays,' Rosamund said. 'I've found a second set of scrutineer programs. Someone else is watching room 2317.'

'Jamas,' Kieran said firmly, 'review this hotel's arrays, find out if we're being watched.' He opened the base of a large case, revealing an impressive collection of weaponry. Jenny selected a gamma pulse rifle, while Kanton took a plasma grenade auto-launcher. The three of them moved smoothly to cover Rosamund and Jamas.

'Rosamund,' Kieran said, 'can you see where the other programs are sending their information? And have they noticed you?'

'Get into one of the force field suits,' Jenny told Kanton.

'No anomalous programs in the arrays on this floor,' Jamas said. 'Moving the scan outwards.'

'What about emissions from non-net systems?'

'Nothing detectable. But if this is the navy, we're not going to be able to see the kind of systems they use against us. The unisphere has rumours that they've modified an insect that's immune to janglepulse.'

Kanton slipped into one of the skeleton-like force field suits, wearing it outside his clothes. The thick bands adjusted themselves to achieve a balanced coverage of his body, then a thin layer of air shimmered around him as the force field came on. He nodded, and Jenny took another suit out of the case; moving quietly, as if noise alone would trigger an assault by an armed navy team.

'Kieran?' she whispered.

'Not yet.' He waved her back and holstered his ion pistol.

'Kanton, open the door.' The lock disengaged, and Kieran stepped out into the corridor, holding a sensor stick casually in one hand.

Jenny had to wait in a fever of anxiety while he checked round. He returned in less than a minute.

'Some of the occupied rooms have got their integral e-seal switched on,' he said, and held up the little sensor stick. 'I couldn't tell what was inside, not without raising the alarm. In any case, if they have any fieldcraft, they won't be on this floor.'

Jenny let her breath ease out of her. Kieran was already giving the ceiling a suspicious stare. 'We're moving,' he said. 'On foot. Jenny, pick a hotel at random. We'll establish a safeguard perimeter before we move in.'

'All right,' Jenny said. She put the rifle back in the case and asked her e-butler for a list of hotels within a five-block radius.

Kieran was stripping off his shirt and trousers. 'As of now, we're staying hot. I want everyone in force field suits worn under your clothing. Rosamund, how are you doing?'

'I think our programs might have been compromised. If I can expose their programs, they can certainly do the same to ours.'

'Can you tell where the other watchers are based?'

'No, they've employed some very sophisticated routing.'

'What about Bernadette? Is she in there?'

'Her room's drawing power for lights, the air conditioning, and the bathroom. Power use has fluctuated since she checked in, which is a good indicator of occupation. The door lock hasn't been used since check in, either. That's the best I can do.'

'Fine. You and Jamas take it in turns to get into suits, then we're out of here. Jenny, any idea who our rivals could be?'

'Other than the navy, no. But why would the navy be following Bernadette?'

'I don't know.' Kieran sounded doubtful as he buttoned his

shirt over the dark bands caging his chest. 'Mellanie Rescorai was warned about Isabella and her parents. It might be a news show team.'

'Or we were seen by Halgarth security,' Jamas said as he pulled the force field suit on. 'Let's face it, we were operating on their home turf.'

'If they're watching Bernadette, it implies they're opposed to the Starflyer,' Jenny said.

Kieran handed the last force field suit to Rosamund, and snapped the case shut. 'Don't bet your life on it.'

*

It was the small hours of the morning, Illuminatus time. Gwyneth Russell who wasn't even back on Paris time properly yet, was wide awake and relaxing in the Almada Hotel's spa bath, with bubbles foaming gently all around her. She'd just got a call from Vic, who was checked in to a hotel a mere three miles away. They'd talked about maybe spending a couple of hours together, but it wasn't going to happen. Both of them were on active duty, and could be called on at any moment. Most of their talk had concentrated on the coincidence of being on Illuminatus. Vic didn't think it was coincidence, although neither of them could think how Bernadette Halgarth could possibly be connected to the Agent. Gwyneth had suggested it might be Isabella who had the connection, and Bernadette was just here to see her. Of course, that didn't explain what Isabella was doing with the Agent.

Gwyneth sighed, and examined her hands. Her skin was starting to wrinkle she'd been soaking so long. She really should try and get some rest ready for tomorrow. For once she thought the case was actually progressing well. Beard had set up his meeting with the Agent for the following evening. She even quietly admired the way Tarlo had bluffed him into cooperating; that the Californian surfer could actually hit someone had been a mild surprise, but it had certainly produced a result. They were so close now to cracking the whole Guardians case open. Around the office, it was rapidly becoming a mantra; they had so much information that all they needed was the *one lucky break* that had eluded Paula Myo for a hundred and thirty years. Her mouth lifted in a bad girl smile, and the break just happened to be Beard's nose.

Her e-butler told her Paula Myo was calling. Gwyneth grunted in surprise and told the e-butler to accept.

'Gwyneth, would you please acknowledge my authority certificate.'

A file icon with the Senate Security seal popped up in Gwyneth's virtual vision. Her virtual hand in the colours of the old Welsh national flag reached up and touched it. For the life of her she couldn't think what Paula was doing. The file opened up, containing Paula's verified Senate Security authorization. 'That checks out,' Gwyneth said. 'What's this about?'

'I am officially reassigning you to my interdiction team,' Paula said. 'As of this moment.'

Gwyneth sat up fast, sloshing water over the edge of the big bath. 'What interdiction team?'

'Senate Security has been watching Tarlo for some time. He's just warned Bernadette Halgarth that Renne's team is observing her.'

'He did *what*?'

'He's a traitor, Gwyneth.'

'No. He can't be.'

'I'm afraid I can't debate this with you. We are going to arrest Tarlo.'

'You're here?' Gwyneth slipped and slithered out of the bath, grabbing her towel.

'Yes. I require your assistance. Is there anybody in his room with him?'

'No. I don't think so. We're all supposed to be resting. Beard's in custody at the precinct, and we're not due to pick up the Agent until this evening.'

'Very well. I suggest you get into your force field suit. Don't activate it. He's next door, and will probably sense you switching it on.'

'You've got to be kidding.'

'No. Once you have it on, please call him. He won't suspect you, and it will enable us to verify his position. The call may also provide a small distraction.'

'Oh God.' She hurried back into the bedroom where her case was sitting on the bed. The force field skeleton suit was an awkward bundle of bands which was difficult to put on around a wet naked body. 'It can't be Tarlo, he's got us so close to the Guardians.'

'I know this is difficult, Gwyneth. Just trust me for a few minutes more.'

Had it been anyone, *anyone* else she might have doubted, and Senate Security be damned. But not Paula Myo. 'All right,' Gwyneth said. The skeleton bands were chafing badly, but they were all in position and switched to standby mode. She didn't like to think what she looked like. Surely there had been time to put on some underwear? 'I'm in the suit.'

'Leave this channel open, and make the call.'

'What about?'

'Whatever, it only has to last a few seconds.'

Gwyneth took a calming breath. Her virtual hand reached out and pulled Tarlo's icon from her grid. 'Hi, chief. I was just checking in with you before I go to bed. Any developments?'

There was a long pause.

'Why are you in your force field suit?' Tarlo asked.

Gwyneth jerked her head round to stare at the wall between the rooms. 'Shit!' Her virtual hand swiped at the suit's activation icon as she dived for the floor.

The middle of the wall exploded in a gout of dazzling white plasma. Long ion flames seared across the room. One of them licked at Gwyneth. Her force field wasn't quite established, it flared purple around her, allowing a weakened gust of the energized atoms to rake across her bare skin. She screamed at the pain, thrashing around as the force field stabilized, deflecting the rest of the blast. Flames burst out of the furnishings and carpet.

The room vibrated to the bass roar of more weapons being fired. Blinding light flared through the wrecked wall. Gwyneth rolled over, tears blurring her vision. She risked a glance down at the side of her ribcage where the ion stream had penetrated. Her flesh was blackened, with red cracks splitting open to weep blood and fluid. It was an agony so intense it was actually dull. She knew she was going to throw up. The sprinklers came on, spraying a glutinous blue foam, nozzles automatically sought out the hot spots, directing the foam to the worst of the blaze. Steam and smoke churned into the air, obscuring the room.

More explosions sounded. One actually produced a quake in the floor which tumbled her about. The ceiling sagged, and what was left of the ruined wall collapsed completely. She tried to stand, but somehow her limbs didn't respond. The best she could do was roll over into a crouch. An alarm was howling.

Three armour-suited figures materialized out of the thick smoke. Two of them pointed fat stubby weapons at her.

'Do not move, lady.'

Gwyneth almost laughed.

The third circled round her wearily, and held a hand out flat towards the bathroom door. There was a dull thud, and a pressure wave knocked Gwyneth back onto her stomach. She groaned at the fresh outbreak of pain in her side. The bathroom door had vanished, along with most of its frame.

'Clear,' the suited figure said.

'Did you see where he went?'

Gwyneth blinked in confusion. A galaxy of coloured lights that weren't quite part of this universe were flashing at her through the smog.

'Gwyneth! It's Paula. Did you see him? Did he come through your room?'

'I . . . No.' She gritted her teeth in the effort to concentrate. 'No, there was just the plasma grenade. He didn't come this way.'

'Okay, hang on. We've got a medic team on standby. They'll be with you soon.'

'Oh, don't worry about me, I'm all right,' she said, and fainted.

*

The sun was just high enough to send a pale light along Tridelta's long straight streets as Alic Hogan's taxi pulled up outside the cordon which had been set up around the Almada Hotel. He got out of the vehicle with Lieutenant John King and stared at the scene with a rising sense of dismay. Alic wasn't a religious man, nor even superstitious, but some days it did seem as if the Paris office had been cursed.

Five big fire tenders were drawn up outside the modern concrete and glass edifice of the hotel. Firebots had crawled up the walls to the fifth floor, trailing their hoses after them. They were clustered round a series of holes that had been ripped through the neat mosaic pattern of windows and concrete panels. He recognized them as weapon blasts. The edges were melted, with little soot scarring the wall above, which meant the plasma had punched out horizontally. That was confirmed by the amount of debris littering the street below. Water and blue suppressant foam was smeared all the way down the wall below the holes, spilling onto the pavement to run into the gutters. There were a couple of shallow craters in the road, where plasma grenades had struck, and a number of smaller pocks from ion pulses.

Outside the area where tenders and force-field-clad fire

department staff were supervising the damping down operation, the police had established a cordon which they were enforcing with armed officers and patrolbots. Clusters of patrol cars were blocking the street a block back from the hotel, their red and blue strobes bright in the leaden dawn. Several other vehicles were stationary along the road, cars and a few early morning delivery vans halting where the city's traffic management arrays had injected their emergency stop orders. The hotel residents, a couple of hundred people, were all huddled together at one end of the building, wearing their pyjamas, or dressing gowns, or less. A lot of them had bare feet. Police officers were moving through them, listening to the questions and protests. Kids were crying.

A couple of ambulances and a medic command bus were parked behind the fire tenders.

'Dear God,' Alic muttered.

'He was determined not to be caught, wasn't he?' John King said.

'Right.' All Alic could think of was what the admiral would say.

The first person Alic saw when a police officer led them into reception was Paula Myo. His jaw clenched at the sight of her. She was wearing full assault armour, with the helmet held under one arm. Even in the bulky dark suit she managed to appear orderly, with her hair neatly held back from her face with a blue Alice band. Several of her Senate Security team were positioned round the reception area, also in armour, with their force fields active, and rifles held ready.

A couple of the paramedics were working on Gwyneth, who was lying on a crash trolley with a green medical smock round her. Vic was holding her hand, the big man's face white with worry and anger. Renne was also there, along with Jim Nwan, both of them standing back a polite distance from the cart, but peering at their fallen colleague. The police precinct captain was talking quietly to Paula; while a detective sergeant called Marhol hovered at his side.

Alic took a breath and walked over to the crash cart. 'How is she?' he asked the senior paramedic.

'Heavy burns on her side where the plasma struck. There will have to be some regeneration, but it's not critical. We've cleaned the injury and sealed it in healskin.'

'So she'll be all right?'

'A few days in hospital, then a fortnight recuperating. She was lucky.'

'Great.' He leaned over the crash trolley, trying not to look at the stains and flecks of crisped flesh.

'Hi, chief,' Gwyneth said. Her face was very pale, sweat glinting on her brow.

'Hi yourself. When you get back, the first thing I'm doing is sending you on a refresher course on how to duck quicker.'

'Fine by me.' Her dreamy smile was mainly due to painkillers.

'Go with her to the hospital,' Alic told Vic. 'Take as long as you want.'

'I'm coming right back,' Vic said. 'I will be on the arrest team when we track that piece of shit down.'

'Okay.' Alic wasn't going to argue in public, but there was no way he was going to allow Vic any part of the case. Right now his priority was to get the big man out of the way.

He finally turned to Paula, and smiled like a prosecuting lawyer. 'Would you care to brief me now, please?'

'Certainly.' She thanked the precinct captain, who walked off with Marhol. It was just the Paris office team who were left in a group.

'Tarlo is a traitor,' she said flatly.

'I really hope you can prove that.'

She glanced meaningfully round the reception area and

through the huge glass doors at the scene outside. Alic reddened slightly, but held his ground.

'I've been running elimination entrapment operations on both Tarlo and Renne,' Paula said.

'Me?' Renne yelped.

'Of course,' Paula replied urbanely. 'Our observation was both visual and electronic. As soon as Tarlo was informed that Renne had Bernadette Halgarth under observation he called her. We intercepted that call. When we moved in to arrest him, he fought back and managed to elude us. His armament wetwiring is not registered. Next time we will field a more appropriate arrest squad.'

Alic knew what the answer was, but he had to ask, just for the record. 'Who do you believe Tarlo has been working for?'

'The Starflyer.'

'Goddamnit. The admiral doesn't accept the Starflyer is real.'

'Don't worry,' Paula said, with more sympathy than Alic was expecting. 'He will have to acknowledge that Tarlo was a traitor. Your conduct has not been compromised, Tarlo dates back over two decades in the Paris office. Your priority now is to launch a review of his cases to see which have been compromised.'

'Right.' Alic didn't want to think how much work that was going to involve, nor where he was going to get the resources. Another Navy Intelligence office would probably have to be brought in, and they would put everyone at Paris under review, himself included. 'Why was Bernadette under observation?' he asked Renne. 'I thought we agreed that aspect of the case was closed.'

'Christabel Halgarth placed her and Victor under observation as a favour to me,' Paula said before Renne could answer. Judging from Renne's expression, she hadn't known that.

'So, Bernadette is working for the Starflyer?' Alic said.

'It would appear so. In which case we must assume Victor is also an agent. I've informed Christabel about this incident. She will close the net around Victor if he hasn't already gone dark.'

'And Isabella?' Renne asked.

'Her involvement is even more likely,' Paula said. 'You made a good call on that investigation. I'd say the Doi shotgun was Starflyer disinformation intended to discredit the Guardians.'

'All right,' Alic said. He just wanted to draw a line under the botched arrest. At least that was Paula's responsibility. 'What is your recommendation? What do we do next?'

'Obviously, taking Tarlo into custody is my principal priority. CST security officers at the Tridelta station will be reviewing every passenger for us. I've deployed an armed squad there already. Other than that, the ongoing cases must be kept open.'

'Are you going to arrest Bernadette?' Jim Nwan asked.

'Yes,' Paula said. 'But it's a question of timing.'

'Now we know the Starflyer agents are weapons wetwired we just need to gather a lot more firepower, surely?' John King said.

'I already have more Senate Security combat squads on the way,' Paula said. 'But right now, Bernadette is the only Starflyer agent whose whereabouts we are certain of. She cannot be allowed to escape.'

'How long until your reinforcements arrive?' Alic asked.

'Fifteen minutes.'

'Okay then, let's go.'

Paula shifted her helmet to her other arm. 'No. She knows her cover has been blown, she also knows that we are observing her and we have armed squads in Tridelta.'

'So?'

'So, why didn't she try and break the observation as soon as Tarlo was exposed?'

Alic sagged, wiping his forehead with the back of his hand. 'She's waiting for something.'

'Exactly.'

'But the longer she waits, the stronger we can box her in. She must know that.'

'Yes. So whatever she is here for must be very important to the Starflyer. She will try to break our observation, either by force or stealth. We need to let her think she has succeeded, that way she will lead us to whatever she is here for.'

'You can have whatever resources you need from the Paris office,' Alic said.

'I'd like to keep Renne's team on her for continuity,' Paula said. 'Can you give me someone to replace Vic?'

'Sure.' He turned to John King. 'That's you.'

'Yessir,' John said.

'That's useful,' Paula said. 'We've got the Paris team, Halgarth Security and Senate Security. If she can elude all three of us, then frankly we deserve to lose her.'

'What about the meeting with the Agent?' Jim Nwan asked. 'It's set up and ready.'

'That's our second objective,' Paula said. 'The Agent is the breakthrough we've been waiting for. He can lead us right into the Guardians. The meeting this evening must go ahead as planned. I can't emphasize enough how important it is to take him into custody.'

'I'll take charge of that operation,' Alic said. It was the kind of legitimate interception which was part of the admiral's agenda. And success there would reflect well on whoever was in charge of the operation. It might even mitigate against the rest of this godawful mess.

'Good. You understand that Tarlo will also be there if we haven't caught him by tonight.'

'Are you sure?'

'Whoever gets the Agent will have access to critical information on the Guardians and their operations. The Starflyer needs that as badly as we do; for over a century they have been its only opposition.'

'So ... are we still trying to shut down the Guardians?' Renne asked.

Alic had never seen such a troubled expression on Paula's face, not even that day when the admiral dismissed her.

'There are a lot of political factors involved,' Paula said slowly. 'I can only say that my allies will have to consider our next move very carefully after we have acquired the Agent and reviewed what he knows.'

'Okay,' Alic said briskly. 'We all know what to do. Send back to the office for any equipment you need; especially force field suits, given what we know about Tarlo's capabilities. Paula, a word, please?'

The two of them walked away from the others. 'You know I can't afford to go grey on the Guardians,' he said. 'When we acquire the Agent, any information he has must be acted on in a positive manner. They are still classed as our number one terrorist group.'

'I understand. Tarlo will give the admiral pause for thought. He's not stupid. If the information is useful then my allies will be able to turn Commonwealth policy.'

Alic whistled appreciatively. 'Those are some allies. Good luck for the rest of today.'

'And yourself. My advice would be to strengthen the guard on Beard. He's the only known route to the Agent. If Tarlo wants to avoid confrontation tonight that would be the obvious method.'

'Right then.' Alic nodded, and headed over towards the apprehensive detectives.

*

Mellanie spent the morning lying on the small room's single bed with the floor to ceiling curtains drawn, accessing all the Tridelta news. Every show was featuring last night's fight at the Almada Hotel. The level of violence had surprised the reporters, and the police weren't being very helpful with their bland statements. There was no mention of a body being found stuffed into the lower deck lifeboat escape passage on *Cypress Island*.

She didn't understand it, but she slowly allowed herself to relax. After a while she cancelled the news and called Dudley.

'Hello my darling,' he said. 'Are you coming back now?'

'Not today.'

'When? I miss you. I want you.'

The familiarity of his neediness was reassuring. Stupid old-young Dudley. A universal constant. 'Soon. Maybe tomorrow.'

'I hope so. I've done a lot of work on the trip.'

'What trip?'

'To the asteroid.'

'Oh right.' She'd forgotten. 'How's it going?'

'Very well. I'm busy computing possible Hohmann transfer orbits. We need to have enough fuel left on arrival to explore the gas-giant orbit inside and outside its rings. Though I expect the habitat asteroid has a significant infrared emission. It should be easy enough to locate.'

'Well done, Dudley. I'll take a look at it all when I get back.'

'I really want you.'

'Dudley. You can always access *Murderous Seduction* again.'

'No. I hate it. Hate it! That's someone else having sex with you. I can't feel that again. It's awful for me. You should never have made it.'

'Okay, Dudley. But I just want to know if you're all right.'

'Why shouldn't I be?'

'I thought someone might be following me. Now don't get in a panic, I wasn't sure at all. Have you seen anyone hanging round the apartment lately?' She was sure that Alessandra's people must have picked her up on Earth, no doubt following her from the Michelangelo studios. So they would definitely know where Dudley was. They'd probably be focusing on him as a way of reconnecting with her.

'No. Do you want me to go outside and check?'

'No, Dudley, that's all right. I'm tired, I wasn't really sure.'

'Okay then. What are you doing today? Have you found those lawyers, yet?'

'Not yet. But I've got a job that should put me close to them.'

'What sort of job?'

'I'm a trainee cleaner at the clinic.'

The image of Kaspar Murdo's over-friendly face filled her mind as he acted as her protector and mentor in the below decks club. All his glib words, his saccharine smile. The deep meaningful conversation he'd wheedled out of her after they went back up to the top deck as the *Cypress Island* headed home in the small hours, listening sympathetically to Saskia's ambitions, admiring of how she'd left home to strike out for herself. He was good, Mellanie saw; a lot of youngsters would fall for that concerned guru act.

As the *Cypress Island* turned back out onto the Logrosan he'd said he would see what he could do about finding her a job, and offered to rent her his spare room. His last tenant had 'just left' and it was very cheap. She'd accepted after a convincing show of uncertainty. Alessandra's people would watch her apartment on Royal Avenue when they realized Dorian was never going to be reporting back. They were a complication she really didn't need.

Murdo's open-plan apartment in the Barbican Marina condo was surprisingly large, with the curving external walls built from glass bricks making it very light and airy. The Scandinavian-style furniture was old but high quality, and every room was spotlessly clean. There were two bedrooms, and one other room which was locked and screened with a commercial e-seal generator.

He'd been the perfect gentleman, giving her a big towelling robe so she could use the bathroom. There were other clothes he happened to have, a sweatshirt and jeans near her own size which she was welcome to use until she collected her own stuff. Bidding her goodnight as he turned in. His shift didn't start until six that evening.

She'd taken a shower, her OCtattoos detecting sensors all round the limestone-tiled cubical. They were active, allowing Murdo to examine every millimetre of her naked body back in the sanctuary of his bedroom. When she got back to her room after the shower she found its ceiling was inlaid with a high-quality holocamera ring. Murdo certainly liked to keep watch over his possessions.

'How in heaven's name did you get that job?' Dudley asked.

She smiled in the darkness, wondering what Murdo would make of that. 'I made friends with the janitor,' she said.

*

Following Bernadette Halgarth was a complete nightmare. Jenny McNowak could remember the worst-case training sessions Adam had put her and the other Guardians through, keeping tabs on their designated target through dense cities and desolate countryside on a dozen different worlds, with everyone taking turns at being the target so they could get a feel for procedures on the sharp end. Those were walks in the park compared to this.

The first thing she and Kieran agreed on was that Bernadette knew she was being followed. When she finally emerged from the Octavious just after ten that morning she launched straight into a series of classic evasion manoeuvres. The only buildings she went into were crowded malls with multiple exits, or skyscrapers that had vast underground levels which connected to neighbouring structures with an equally complex layout. Where she walked along streets, cybersphere nodes and civic arrays suffered kaos attacks which affected any systems that were accessing at the time. She took taxis for a block then switched as the local traffic management arrays crashed under more kaos. The monorail was a favourite, waiting until the last second as the doors closed before hopping on board.

As a result they had to stay close, which they couldn't really afford, because that would mean getting spotted by the larger and better equipped navy team. Twice, Jenny was sure she'd caught sight of small aerobots holding station several hundred metres above a busy street. If she'd caught a couple of glimpses, there must have been a whole squadron of the things deployed to patrol the sky above the city's street grid. They allowed the navy team to keep a long way back, while her own team had to crunch up the distance again whenever Bernadette hit the streets. Another manoeuvre which left them susceptible to discovery by the navy.

'I've never known them to use so many people,' Kieran said as they were meandering round the rim of Haben Park. Bernadette was walking through the broad open grassland, staying away from the paths. There was a monorail station in the middle, which they were sure she was going to use. Jamas was loitering round the entrance, ready to scoot up to the platform ahead of her if she should double back.

'It's unusual for them to have anyone on the ground when they've got aerobots covering the area,' Kieran said.

'They can hardly send the aerobots into a building after her.'

'No, but the way they're deploying is almost as if they want to be seen.'

Jenny had provisionally tagged a couple of the navy team, who were also loafing on the periphery of the park.

'This is becoming farcical,' she said. 'They're going to spot us even if she doesn't. We can't keep following her like this all day. Their scrutineers will catch our encrypted traffic if nothing else. We're trained in avoiding observation teams, not being one.'

'You're right,' he said as Jamas walked past a woman they suspected as navy. 'Everybody disengage. We're going to change tactics.'

'What are you doing?' Jenny asked.

'I'm going to watch the watchers. It's the logical choice.'

Jenny bit back on any criticism. It was a risky decision, but carrying on like this simply was not an option. She watched Bernadette change direction quickly, and hurry for the escalator up to the elevated platform. It was a junction station, with four possible directions for the monorail trains to take. The woman they thought might be navy was on the station's second escalator.

'Rosamund, Jamas, we're taking this one.' Kieran sent them the visual file of a man who was strolling along a hundred metres ahead of them. 'He's been part of the navy box for fifteen minutes. They'll rotate him now.'

Keeping the navy operative under observation was considerably easier than Bernadette. Kieran was right, he was being rotated, and he clearly had no idea he was being observed. After Bernadette slipped away along the monorail the man changed direction and caught a cab. The Guardians followed in three separate taxis, grinding their way through Tridelta's daytime congestion.

The navy was using the Dongara Harbour police precinct as their headquarters. Hanging round the police building added a certain edge to the Guardians team's operation, but the harbour had a lot of waterside bars and restaurants. They took it in turns to sit at the outside tables, scanning the precinct with retinal inserts.

Halfway through the afternoon Jenny called Adam. 'Guess who just drove down into the precinct garage?'

'Tell me,' Adam said.

'Paula Myo.'

'Indeed? What with that and the Almada Hotel fracas, I'm almost sorry I left.'

'But surely this is important? The navy is chasing a Starflyer agent. They must know it exists.'

'Paula is Senate Security not navy, but yes, senior echelons of the Commonwealth political class must be at least aware of the possibility now. I'll inform Bradley.'

'What do you want us to do?'

'Stay close to the navy team without compromising yourselves, and observe as much as you can. There's obviously no way you can break into the Starflyer agent network through Bernadette any more, but I would like to know what she's doing on Illuminatus. I suspect the planet is where a lot of the Starflyer's agents are wetwired; heaven knows we use it often enough. If Myo exposes one of their cells it can only act to our advantage.'

'Okay, we'll follow if we can. Kieran's hired some cars for us.'

'Good luck in that traffic.'

The sun was starting to sink below the horizon when eight large cars came out of the precinct garage, travelling in fast convoy. They didn't have sirens and strobes on, but the civic traffic management arrays were obviously shunting cars and trucks out of their way.

Jenny drained the last of her iced tea. 'Let's go,' she told the others.

*

It was a warm evening again, though the vanishing sun seemed to take the humidity with it. Mellanie travelled with Murdo on the monorail to a station just half a block away from Greenford Tower. The bars and clubs along Allwyn Street were just setting up for the night trade, as yet they had few customers. Even the traffic seemed lighter than usual.

Murdo led her across the Greenford's plaza where the fountains were pumping their jets high into the darkening sky. Far above them, the airship docked to the top of the Tower was preparing for its flight; the lights on the observation deck were shining brightly as service bots and waiters laid the tables ready for the Michelin-starred meal to be served as it soared over the jungle.

The Saffron Clinic's private door opened for Murdo as soon as he put his hand on the sensor. It was a small narrow lobby inside, with a single lift.

Mellanie started to key some inserts as they rose up to the thirty-eighth floor, allowing her to review the electronic environment she was moving through. The lift had several systems, none of them new or elaborate, dating back to the Tower net's last refurbishment fifteen years ago. Above her, she could sense the clinic's sophisticated and powerful e-shield. She deactivated all but the most elementary OCtattoos and inserts, the SI's systems were very hard to detect when they were inert, so it had promised her.

The lift rose through the e-shield. It stopped and the doors slid open. Mellanie was abruptly the centre of a deep scan. It was a bare hallway outside, with pipes running along the walls and bright polyphoto strips on the ceiling. A couple of bored human guards, both of them armed, sat at a desk beside the lift doors.

'Who's this?' one of them asked curtly, nodding at Mellanie. He didn't bother getting up. The deep scan couldn't have revealed anything about her.

'New trainee,' Murdo said. 'I cleared her with personnel this afternoon.'

The guard grunted. 'You're Saskia?'

'Yes,' she said anxiously.

'Okay.' He propelled a hand-held array across the top of the desk. 'Put your palm on that, we need a biometric. You're not cleared for the medical levels yet, understand? You don't go off this floor.'

'Yes.'

'If you try to go up there we shoot you. You do not discuss anything you see in here with anybody from outside. If you do, we shoot you. You do not bring anything into the clinic other than yourself and the clothes you are wearing. You will be issued with a uniform. If you bring anything in, like a sensor, we shoot you.'

Mellanie nodded anxiously. The guards grinned at each other.

'Ignore this lameass bullshit,' Murdo said. 'These two dickbrains couldn't hit the side of a skyscraper from twenty paces.'

The guard showed him a vigorous hand gesture.

Murdo gave him the finger in return as he and Mellanie walked off down the corridor. He steered her into a locker room. Three nurses were getting changed to go on shift. They stopped talking at the sight of Murdo and one of them scowled.

'Most of the staff use this place to change,' Murdo said. 'Except for the doctors and management, they just wear their own suits.' He walked along one of the locker rows. 'This one's yours. Use your thumb on the scanner to open it. Those morons on the desk should have updated the network by now.'

Mellanie pressed her thumb to the small scanner patch, and the locker opened. It was empty. 'I thought I got a uniform?'

'I'll requisition one from supply. Just wait a minute.' He walked away round the end of the row.

Mellanie took a good look round the locker room while Murdo got changed, bringing her inserts on line one at a time. There was no active sensor, only a couple of cameras looking down from the ceiling. She fed a scrutineer program into the locker room's array, cautiously examining the structure of the clinic's internal net. There were an impressive number of security systems and programs, especially on the upper floors. They were all protected by encrypted gates which she didn't have the skill to circumvent. However, the reception array with its open connection to the Illuminatus cybersphere was easy to access. Her e-butler rode in on a Trojan finance transfer, and began to search admission records for five days on either side of the date on which Michelangelo said the lawyers had arrived.

The three nurses all left. Mellanie instructed the scrutineer to follow their progress and record what it could of the security protocols as they went upstairs.

'Hey Saskia, come round here, I've got your uniform,' Murdo said. 'I knew I had a spare somewhere.'

Mellanie was intrigued by the way he'd waited until the nurses had left. She held her hand up, palm outwards towards the locker doors as she walked along the row. Her basic scan revealed some very interesting items stored inside.

Murdo was wearing a dark-red boiler suit with his name on the chest pocket. 'Put this on,' he said. One hand held up a small garment of some shiny black fabric, while the other had a frilly white apron.

French Maid's outfit, Mellanie realized. She almost laughed. Murdo wasn't just a stereotype, he was an absolute cliché.

'I have located three possible admissions compatible with your search parameters,' her e-butler said. The files popped up into her virtual vision. There was no reference to the nature of the treatments they were receiving, only the cost, which surprised her. Each file did include the room they'd been allocated, for billing purposes.

'Come on, my dear, this is what all cleaning staff trainees wear,' Murdo said in a reasonable tone.

Mellanie activated a second batch of OCtattoos, then infiltrated a restriction order into the room's array, preventing anyone from using its communication function. 'Humm. I don't think so.'

She clicked her fingers. One of the lockers she'd just passed popped open.

*

The scenic cable car station was at the eastern end of the Northern Crossquay. Alic, Lucius Lee and Marhol escorted Robin Beard through the ticket hall and onto the embarkation platform. They didn't manhandle him, nor did they say a word, but he was always in the centre of the little triangle they formed. If the Agent was as good as Beard claimed, he would have observers in the crowds heading out to Treetops Restaurant.

The platform was raised several metres above the top of Northern Crossquay, a simple metal mesh with the cables running above, that intruded against a huge tree whose boughs curved overhead. Alic could look back and see Tridelta city gleaming a couple of miles away on the other side of the river. The Dongara, and the Upper Monkira had joined here, producing a turbulent, fast flowing current of water that would soon merge with the Logrosan in a foaming maelstrom at the eastern edge of the city which was the vast Lower Monkira. Ferries were still ploughing their way across, bringing the daily herd of customers out to the nightcruise boats tied up to the jetties. Several airships were visible overhead, sliding through the tattered low clouds.

A cable car slid out of the radiant jungle, pausing briefly on the disembarkation platform opposite, where a couple of staff hopped out. Then it disappeared into the engine house which loomed above the station, before reappearing a few moments later and coming to a halt in front of the little group of passengers. It swung in slow pendulum motion from the carbon cable as the door slid open. Then the stewards were ushering everyone inside.

There were seats for ten people arranged in a ring around the central load girder. Alic took the one closest to the door. Beard sat next to him.

When all ten seats were filled the steward shut the door, and gave a thumbs-up. The carrier wheels above engaged the cable with a loud grumbling, and the car lurched away into the jungle.

There had been a lot of protests from local environmental groups when the cable car operators were applying for permits. Non-interference with the jungles was actually a part of the Illuminatus constitution, and no matter how much they bent other rules, the citizens of Tridelta respected their unique environment. It was very hard to grow an Illuminatus plant anywhere else due to the complex soil bacteria the trees needed in order to flourish. Potted saplings could be sold in sealed display cases for botanical enthusiasts, but no one was ever going to reproduce the woodlands on another world. So the environmentalists didn't want big construction machinery chopping down trees to put up the cable car posts, and chainsawing off branches to give the cars free passage through the elaborate canopy.

After a decade of legal battles the operators won their permit, after proving a minimal-damage impact-assessment. What the environmentalists grudgingly accepted once the cable car was up and running was that the environmental damage was actually reduced. People who used to illicitly walk off the Crossquay and plunge through the jungle, breaking small branches and trampling new shoots underfoot to gain the raw experience now took the cable car. It was cheap, and allowed them to get a lot closer in considerably more comfort. The jungle along the side of both Northern and Southern Crossquays began to thicken up again after a century of injury and abuse.

There was no glass in the cable car's windows. Alic could see the glowing leaves skimming past barely a metre away. He did his best not to gawp at the panorama, making sure he checked Beard every thirty seconds. There were also updates from the police team back at the Northern Crossquay, reporting on everyone who got onto a cable car after them. None of them matched Beard's description of the Agent. Alic had seen the cable car route through the jungle earlier that afternoon, when he and the rest of the team had come out to Treetops to scout round and set up their positions. Jim Nwan was heading up the five-strong arrest team that were waiting around the restaurant, all of them navy officers in full armour suits. Even if the Agent brought wetwired bodyguards there was no way they could stand up to that kind of firepower. Nor was there anywhere to run. The scenic cable car run was ten kilometres long.

It took twenty-five minutes to reach Treetops. Their cable car slid up against a platform that was identical to the one back on Northern Crossquays, and the smiling passengers trooped off. The restaurant and bar was built out of imported wood, big sturdy oak beams from European forests pegged together to form a long raft four metres off the ground. There was no roof, everyone sat directly under the jungle canopy. One side of it was the bar, while the other half was taken up by the restaurant where the tables were booked up weeks in advance.

As agreed, Beard went over to an empty table in the bar and ordered a beer from the waitress. Alic, Lucius and Marhol sat on stools up at the small bar counter which circled one of the broad tree trunks. Marhol ordered the most expensive imported beer they had. Alic ignored the oafish detective, and sipped a mineral water.

He called Paula and said: 'We're in. Beard's waiting for contact. The police helicopters are on standby to extract us as soon as we've made the arrest. I've got Vic with them, he didn't like it but I made it clear the alternative was to go back to Paris.'

'Good. Sounds like you're organized. Bernadette has just gone into the Greenford Tower. There a very expensive clinic called Saffron in there which provides wetwiring and baseline DNA modification among other things. So unless she's taking the airship flight we think that might be her destination; presumably either to change her identity, or to rendezvous with someone who has undergone the treatment.'

'Does she know you're still following?' Alic asked.

'I don't think so. We fell back to long-range observation at three o'clock this afternoon. As far as she's aware she lost us.'

'All right. I'll call you as soon as we have the Agent.'

'What's happening?' Marhol asked. Conversation round the bar was drying up fast. People had surprised looks on their faces.

Alic's e-butler alerted him to a priority news event. He didn't even have to access it. The barman turned the portal behind the counter to a direct feed from the Alessandra Baron show. Wilson Kime was standing at a podium making a statement to the Pentagon II press corps. 'The fleet of *Moscow*-class starships which were dispatched to attack the wormhole known as Hell's Gateway have now returned and are in communication range with the Commonwealth. I regret to say that the attack was not successful. Our missiles did not manage to strike their targets. Hell's Gateway remains intact and fully functional, as do the subsidiary wormholes which link it to the Lost23.'

'Oh crap,' Marhol grunted.

'The Primes have developed a method of deflecting our Douvoir relativistic missiles while they are still in flight,'

Wilson said. 'I must emphasize that this setback is by no means critical to our campaign, the navy retains the ability to combat any further aggression by the Primes.'

'Bullshit.'

Alic wished he didn't share Marhol's opinion.

'Sir,' Lucius said quietly. 'Is that him?'

*

The Agent walked across the bar as everyone was watching the news. He was wearing a suit of thin leather with a surface that glimmered like crude oil under the soft light of the trees. The girl on his arm was dressed in a small cream outfit with a tasselled hem; she was tall and muscled like a marathon runner.

'Robin,' the Agent said pleasantly. 'How nice to see you again.'

Beard looked round from the projected image of the admiral. His face softened into a forlorn expression. 'Sorry,' was all he said.

The Agent's mouth tightened with aristocratic disapproval. His force field came on, distorting the dark ripples flowing over his suit fabric. The girl extended both arms as small stubby nozzles slipped out of the flesh on her wrists. Blue and green OCtattoos came alight on her face and neck, sending out thin glowing lines to snake down beneath the dress fabric. She started to rotate slowly, covering all the patrons. The ones closest to her gasped and pressed themselves back in their chairs.

'Move in,' Alic ordered the arrest team. His own force field came on, surrounding him in a nimbus of soft scintillations.

'Do you want us, chief?' Vic asked.

'Wait.'

The girl swung round *fast*, both her arms were lined up on Alic. The skin on her forearms began to undulate in strange patterns. People sitting at the tables between the two of them jumped hurriedly out of the way, creating a wide empty corridor.

'Stand aside,' Alic murmured to the police officers. In a couple of seconds he was sitting alone at the bar. Admiral Kime carried on speaking behind him, voice muted to a buzzing drone.

'No way out,' Alic told the Agent. 'Let's everybody stay calm. Deactivate your weapons. Your bodyguards can walk. You come with us.'

'Was that supposed to be an incentive?' the Agent asked. He sounded truly intrigued.

'I can cut clean through his protection,' the girl said. 'It's just a government issue suit, after all, weak as piss.' She smiled, showing a long row of silver-white fangs.

'Sounds reasonable to me,' the Agent said.

Jim Nwan landed on the bar's wooden floor with a loud thump. He was in full armour, carrying a plasma carbine. Its targeting laser splashed a small red dot on the Agent's forehead. His urbane smile faded. Two more of the arrest team jumped into the bar from their holding positions out in the jungle. Their weapons were levelled at the girl.

At a table a few metres away from a trembling Beard, three men stood up, cloaked in force fields, and targeted the arrest team with their wetwired weapons. The last two members of the arrest team arrived in the bar. And one more lone drinker swivelled round on his stool to aim at the detectives, who had switched on their force fields. The rest of the bar went completely silent as it was criss crossed with the slender ruby threads of lasers. People were hunched down in their chairs, terrified expressions on their faces; couples clung to each other.

'I believe this is what they used to call a Mexican stand-off,' the Agent said. 'Now why don't we all just walk away, and contemplate what the admiral has been saying. There are bigger issues to consider right now, are there not?'

'No,' Alic said. He couldn't stop his muscles from tensing up. He'd never known dread like it; during combat, the terror from being shot at lasted mere seconds at most. This was stretching out and out, and he couldn't see a way to end it cleanly. The bastard Agent just refused to see reason. All he could think about was how long it had been since he'd backed up his memories in a secure store; if everyone opened fire there was no way his memorycell would survive. Even so, backing down just wasn't an option.

'Chief, we've got the firepower to back you up,' Vic said. 'We can be there in a couple of minutes.'

'No. You can't fire while we're in Treetops, it'll be a massacre.'

'Just let us get out to you.'

'Wait!'

The Agent's smile was constant. 'Once weapons this powerful are fired, you can expect an easy eighty per cent casualties among the civilians,' he said. 'Are you willing to take that responsibility?'

'You can't leave,' Alic said. 'There's only the cable car, and we control that.'

'For fuck's sake, buddy,' a man shouted. 'Show some sense. You'll get us all killed.'

'I am,' Alic growled out.

'There are many ways out for me,' the Agent said. 'I'm going to start backing away from you now. If you try and stop me, then you will be responsible for the subsequent slaughter. Think on that, government employee.'

For a brief moment Alic considered calling Paula to ask what the hell he should do. *No! Not her.*

'Chief?' Jim asked. 'What do we do?'

'Move and I'll fire the first shot myself,' Alic said.

'Well now, if I couldn't see the panic in your eyes, I might just . . .' The Agent frowned and glanced up.

Alic heard a low roaring sound, which was rapidly increasing in volume. The few sensor inserts he had couldn't detect the origin. 'Jim? Can you see what that is?'

'Three large power sources, directly overhead.'

Alic risked a look up at the phosphorescent ceiling of fluttering leaves. 'Helicopters? Vic is that you?'

'No, chief,' Vic replied.

'Descending too fast,' Jim said. 'Those aren't helicopters.'

'Vic, get out here,' Alic ordered.

'On our way.'

A plasma bolt slammed down into Treetops, blowing through the fragile canopy of branches and leaves to strike the wooden platform directly between Alic and the Agent. The oak planks detonated instantly, producing a lethal shrapnel cloud of hand-sized splinters. Alic's force field flared bright purple as the smouldering daggers walloped him, their impact shunting him back into the bar. Flame swirled all around, drawing whorls of black smoke in its wake. The floor lurched down at such an angle he grabbed wildly, managing to hook some fingers round the counter.

Both the arrest team and the Agent's bodyguard fired back up into the night sky at the intruders. The bar's patrons were screaming, half from shock, half from injury as the scythes of wood stabbed into unprotected flesh. More plasma bolts struck the wooden raft, snapping it into ragged sections. People and furniture were flung about by the blasts. The leaves and branches above began to blaze, sending smoke fountaining down.

Alic saw the Agent on his back as the floor continued to tilt over with a violent creaking, opening a wide gulf between them. Flames licked along the edges. The Agent looked down between his feet, calculating a jump to the dark ground below.

'Don't even think about it,' Alic shouted. He pointed his ion pistol at the Agent.

The Agent started to laugh. A couple of red lasers played across Alic's eyes. 'Kill him,' the Agent yelled.

Twin plasma shots pummelled Alic's force field. A storm of seething white and purple vapour clawed at him. Tiny localized overloads allowed hot electron tendrils to gouge at his clothes and skin. The fast stabs of pain were incredible, sending him writhing helplessly. He lost his grip on the counter and wilted onto the dangerously angled floor. Roaring sounds broke out all around him as the arrest team fired back on the bodyguards.

Alic realized he was bent round the base of a bar stool. His retinal inserts filtered the glare away to show the Agent hanging on tightly to his own patch of flooring as he twisted to look above and behind—

Three armour-suited figures ripped through the inferno raging above the wrecked restaurant. They were wearing jetpacks, whose exhaust screeched with the energy of a sonic weapon. One landed on either side of the Agent. Plasma and ion bolts hit them simultaneously, sending out incandescent whip streamers to lash at the smashed tables and chairs. Smoke and jets of flame burst out from the contact points. Several of the flaring whips raked across the Agent's force field, turning it dense purple. One of the armoured figures bent down and slapped a dump web on the Agent's back. He tried to push himself off the ground, but an armoured boot stomped down on his shoulders, knocking him back down. A dark stain was spreading through his force field as the dump web expanded.

'Jim, can you stop them?' Alic demanded. His e-butler was printing a list of insert and OCtattoo failures across his virtual vision, it was all in default-mode green text.

'Stop what?'

Alic fired his ion pistol at the armour suit standing above

the Agent. It didn't even strain the force field. 'Where are you?'

'On the ground.'

Alic fired again, this time aiming at the wood the suited figure was standing on. The planks smashed apart, and the suit dropped through the hole, arms grabbing at air. 'There's one level with you, take them out,' Alic said. The remaining suit was levelling a grenade launcher at Alic. 'Mike, Yan, Nyree, can anyone get a fireline on the suit with the Agent?'

'Got them,' Yan replied.

An explosion sent Alic spinning back up the sloping floor to crack his head against the bottom of the bar counter. The force field only partially absorbed the impact. He choked at the pain. The blazing wreckage of Treetops rotated around him. People were jumping from the remaining sections of floor into the dark space beyond; they were on fire, trailing flames through the night, orange sparks fizzing out behind them. Screams pierced the air, repeatedly overwhelmed by the shot of another rifle, or a plasma grenade detonating. One of the big trees which Treetops was built round, was starting to keel over, a ponderous motion that was speeding up.

The Agent's force field flickered and died. Flames scorched straight through his slick leather suit. He screamed as his skin crisped. The armour-suited figure above him raised one arm. Alic saw a harmonic blade gleam in the garish firelight.

'Yan!' Alic called. 'Again.'

The harmonic blade swiped down. A fusillade of plasma bolts hammered the armoured figure just as it beheaded the Agent. Alic cried out in horror as the Agent's head bounced away across the buckled floor planks, blood splattering out of the severed neck, its short hair singed and smoking. He was never going to forget the startled expression locked on the Agent's face as his head skittered towards the drop.

The armoured attacker had been pushed sideways by the carbine shots, losing balance to tumble backwards onto the slanting floor. Twisting coils of energy wrapping round the suit grounded out through the fractured oak beams. The miniature lightning blizzard suddenly shifted round to streak upwards as the vast weight of the collapsing tree crunched down. Suit, floor, and the Agent's corpse vanished under a swirling mass of flame that shattered the remainder of the bar. Alic felt the planks finally give way, sending him tumbling through the air, waving his arms and legs frantically. He hit the ground hard, with the force field inflating out around him like a scratchy pillow. It absorbed some of the collision, but he felt several ribs crack. He retched helplessly. The Agent's head bounced on the damp soil beside him, skin charred and peeling off blackened bone. Even through all the pain and nausea he knew to grab for it. The disgusting thing was nestled in the crook of his arm when an armour suit appeared above him.

'Jim?'

''Fraid not, chief,' Tarlo's voice boomed through the bedlam. A plasma carbine was lowered, its muzzle stopped five centimetres from Alic's face.

'Fuck you, traitor,' he snarled.

A grenade went off right beside them, flinging both of them through the air amid a cloud of soil and tree fragments. Alic crashed into a tree trunk two metres above the ground and dropped like a stone. His force field was flickering around him on the verge of total breakdown, allowing overheated air to slide excruciatingly over injured flesh; green virtual vision text turned into random horizontal squiggles against the orange inferno. Through a haze of pain he saw the smoking black lump that was the agent's head, still rolling along the steaming ground away from him.

Tarlo was walking towards it. Alic tried to get up. His left side was completely numb. 'Yen! Jim! Somebody help!'

Tarlo picked up the head. His suit's jetpack spat out two spears of near-invisible blue flame, and he rose into the glaring conflagration that was consuming the jungle canopy. A cascade of huge blue and white sparks plummeted down in his wake.

'Vic, shoot him, just shoot him out of the sky, don't let him take it, his memorycell's in there. Vic, it's Tarlo. Vic?' His voice fell to a whimper. He rolled onto his back, and pointed his ion pistol into the falling plume of sparks where Tarlo had vanished, ready to blast away. But there was only his empty hand, skin torn and bleeding, two fingers bent back where the knuckles had been broken. 'I'll find you,' he rasped at the swarming flames as the heat beat against him. 'I will find you, fucker.'

*

Mellanie made it up to the Saffron Clinic's third floor before she noticed something was wrong. The scrutineer programs she'd so carefully infiltrated into the arrays on the two floors below her were no longer responding. In fact, the whole of the net on those two floors was now dark.

She stopped and reviewed the tiny amount of data she could access. So far she'd only infiltrated three arrays on this floor, and her programs weren't telling her anything. The clinic net certainly hadn't issued any alarm, which was very strange. Management programs must have noticed the drop out. Not that she could query them.

So far she'd only passed a couple of staff on the evening shift, technicians in deep conversation. They hadn't paid her any attention. The nurse's uniform she'd put on was like wearing a stealth suit. There was nobody else in the corridor; she checked along it, uncertain what to do next. One of the rooms she wanted was right at the far end, barely thirty metres away.

Sections of the net on this floor started to drop out. 'Damnit,' she hissed. Someone else must be infiltrating the clinic's electronics, and they were a lot better at it than she was. They were shutting the whole place down one processor at a time.

There was a stairwell three metres behind her. Mellanie gave the Nicholas Suite at the far end one last longing glance. She was so near . . . one of the lawyers was on the other side of the door. But it could well be Alessandra's newest set of goons creeping up through the clinic. And if they knew she was here, they would have told the lawyers.

Why would anyone working for Alessandra have to creep round? They're all on the same side.

Mellanie hurried back to the stairwell door. She pushed at the release bar. There was no alarm, all the circuitry around it was dead. It swung open to reveal a vast source of electromagnetic energy in the stairwell. Mellanie let out a shocked gasp as an armour-suited figure pointed a gun at her forehead.

'Do not move,' it said quietly, the voice was male. 'Do not shout or attempt to alert anyone that we are here.'

Mellanie manufactured some tears – it wasn't hard. 'Please don't shoot.' Her legs were shaking. A second armoured figure slipped round the first; quickly followed by five more.

If they're Alessandra's, she's really taking no chances.

'Turn around,' the suited man said. 'Put your hands behind your back, cross the wrists.'

The armoured suits were moving along the corridor. Mellanie had no idea suits that heavy and big could move so quietly. Then a thin plastic cord tightened round her wrists. 'Ow!'

'Quiet, or I will use a nervejam.'

She was half-sure her inserts could deflect that. But she'd have to activate them – and even if she did get the sequence right, then what? 'Sorry,' she whispered.

'In here.' She was pulled into the stairwell.

'Name?'

'Er . . . Lalage Vere, I'm a nurse in the dermal specialist unit.' She felt something being pressed to her hand.

'The name's on file, but she doesn't match the clinic biometric.'

'She wouldn't,' said a female voice.

Mellanie knew who that belonged to. Even as she let out a long breath of relief she couldn't help wincing. A hard gauntlet was placed on her shoulder, turning her around. There were about ten more armoured people in the stairwell, one of them markedly shorter than the others. 'Good evening, Mellanie,' the small suit said.

'Oh, good evening, Investigator Myo. Fancy seeing you here.' It was bravado. She was trying not to sulk at how swiftly Paula had seen past her dark hair and freckles.

'We found the chief janitor downstairs,' Paula said. 'He was tied to a bench in the locker room; not that there was any need, he's got so much narcotic in his blood he doesn't know which universe he's in.'

'Really? And they let people like that work here? I'm astonished.'

'I'm more interested in why you're here, Mellanie.'

'Reporting was getting kind of hectic. I fancied a change of profession.'

'Mellanie, people's lives are at stake here tonight. A lot of lives. I will ask once more, why are you here?'

Mellanie sighed. There really was no way out. 'I've tracked down the lawyers. All right? It's not a crime. They're the criminals, and we both know what they did wrong.'

'You mean Seaton, Daltra, and Pomanskie?'

'Yes.'

'They're here?'

'Duh. Yes. I just said.'

'When did they arrive?'

'Didn't you know?' Mellanie said smugly. 'They've been here receiving treatments more or less since they went on the lam from New York.'

'What sort of treatments? Have they received weapons wetwiring?'

'I'm not sure, you interrupted me. The new DNA thing, I suppose. It wasn't cheap, whatever they got.'

'Which rooms are they in?'

'One's in the Nicholas Suite, on this floor; the other two are sharing the Fenay Suite on the fifth floor.'

'Okay, thank you, we'll take it from here, Mellanie.'

'What! You can't just—'

'Grogan, take her down to Renne.'

Gauntlets grabbed her upper arm, metal fingers closing painfully. 'Yow! Hey, I found them, you could at least let me cover the arrest for my report.'

'I'd advise against it. This is not a safe environment.'

'I was doing fine until you blundered in.' She paused, if Myo hadn't known the lawyers were in the clinic, what . . . ?

Grogan pulled her towards the stairs. The suit was too strong for Mellanie to resist. 'You've got to give me something, Myo.'

'We'll talk later. A long talk.'

Mellanie didn't like the sound of that.

*

'Tactical update,' Paula informed the arrest teams. 'We now have three more confirmed hostiles on site in addition to Bernadette. Possible locations: one in the Nicholas Suite, two in the Fenay. Be advised, there could be more, this appears to be where Starflyer agents receive their wetwiring.'

The map in her virtual vision displayed the positions of the armour suits. She quickly adapted their interdiction roles, assigning three members to each lawyer.

'Hoshe, can you review the arrays we've sequestrated? I'd like to confirm what Mellanie told us?'

'We're working on it now. I didn't know she was that good.'

'Mellanie is starting to interest me greatly. But we'll have to deal with the clinic first.'

'Third floor net shut down,' Hoshe said. 'We're establishing our programs on four and five, preparing to insert on six.'

'That's good,' Paula examined the map. 'Warren, move out into the fourth floor.'

'Acknowledged.'

'Renne, when Mellanie reaches your team I want you to hold her in custody but separate from the rest of the clinic staff; do not let her call anyone. That's important.'

'Understood.'

'How's the perimeter?'

'Solid and holding. It looks like half the city police are here.'

'Damn, that's what I was worried about. Someone up here is going to notice what we're doing.'

'Confirm the three admissions matching the lawyers,' Hoshe said. 'Mellanie was telling the truth.'

'We've been exposed,' Warren Halgarth called. 'Four staff members, one client walked out in front of us. Can't contain them all.'

Paula cursed, though they'd got a lot further with their dark incursion than she'd expected. 'Everyone, go hot. They know we're here. Arrest teams move in immediately. And find me Bernadette.' She stood to one side, allowing the rest of the third floor team to deploy out of the stairwell.

'Shit,' Warren exclaimed. 'The client is weapons wetwired. Challenging us.'

'Is it one of the lawyers?' Paula's map was updating. Teams were deploying along each floor. Matthew Oldfield was leading five officers to the Fenay Suite; while John King was closing on the Nicholas. Barely a third of the clinic staff had been taken down to Renne's team where they'd be safe.

She heard the dull rumble of an explosion. Small flecks of dust shook free from the pipes running up the concrete stairwell. More explosions began. There were screams. Hoshe used aggressive infiltrators and took complete control of the clinic's net.

Paula drew her plasma carbines, and moved out into the corridor. People were opening doors, peering out, yelling. Doors were slammed shut. The armour suits kicked them down again, hauling out the terrified staff and clients. John King and his two team mates blew the door to the Nicholas Suite. A plasma bolt flew out. The screaming in the corridor reached a crescendo.

'Deactivate your weapons and come out,' John's suit speaker boomed.

There was a big explosion inside the Nicholas Suite. Debris and smoke billowed out into the corridor.

'He blew a hole in the floor,' John called. 'Jumped down to the second level.'

'Acknowledged,' Marina called. 'We're deploying.'

John's team charged through into the suite. Paula was waving the other members of the third-floor team along the corridor as they half-carried staff and clients through the miasma. 'Do not leave any of them unaccompanied,' she warned. 'Medical forensic must clear them first.'

'Visual on Bernadette,' Warren called. 'We're engaging.'

Paula turned and raced back for the stairwell. Another explosion cut the lights. She was seeing the clinic through microradar and infrared. Sprinklers went off, and the fire alarm shrilled. The ceiling bulged down just in front of her, long cracks multiplying down the walls on either side.

'She won't surrender,' Warren said. 'Joined by another hostile. Both wetwired.'

'Can you disable her?' Paula asked.

'Not a chance.'

Paula reached the stairwell as a volley of explosions reverberated around the concrete shaft. Emergency lighting came an intense yellow slicing through the cloying grey smog that was swirling down the broad shaft. A long convoy of armour-suited figures was escorting cowering prisoners down the stairs. She pushed past them.

'Two hostiles engaged,' Matthew said. 'They were in the Fenay Suite.'

'Capture alive if you can,' Paula said.

'Do my best.'

'Got some debris down here,' Renne said. 'Glass falling all over the plaza.'

'Any bodies?' Paula asked. 'If their force fields are good enough they might try to jump clear.'

'None yet.'

'Watch for it.'

The explosions and sound of plasma shots had ended by the time Paula rushed out onto the clinic's fourth floor. There was no corridor and elegant treatment rooms any more, half of the walls were gone, opening up the entire level. Wreckage was strewn everywhere, some smoking, the rest saturated with water and blue suppression foam. Most of the ceiling was down as well, exposing the Greenford's main structural beams. Fortunately, they seemed to be intact. Water was gushing out of several thick pipes to form large filthy pools across the floor. The glass windows had all been blown out.

Several bodies were lying amid the destruction.

'Hellfire,' Paula exclaimed.

'Sorry,' Warren said. 'We had to terminate them.'

'Okay. Where are the corpses? We need to run a DNA confirmation.'

'Over here.' He scrambled over the piles of rubble, leading her round the Tower's core. Several armour suits were busy digging injured survivors out.

'We think these two.'

Inside the helmet, Paula wrinkled her nose up at the sight. The two bodies had been badly burned, then crushed by steel beams and concrete sections. Filthy water lapped round their scorched extremities. The remnants of their clothing was wrapped round them, scraps of blackened cloth. Paula recognized a fragment of the deep-blue trousers which Bernadette had been wearing as they pursued her across Tridelta for most of the day. Parts of her body were untouched, corresponding to the bands of an insert force field skeleton. Her arms had the ruptures Paula knew came from internal power cells igniting, the kind used to power weapons. She pulled out a small DNA reader unit, and touched the stubby sampler prong against an unblemished segment of skin.

'It's her,' she said as the data ran down her virtual vision.

The other corpse was slightly larger. Probably male. Paula examined him. Damage to his limbs had all been caused by external force. He certainly hadn't been using a force field. His burned outer layers were no use to her DNA reader. She had to clench her jaw and push the stubby prong through the damage so it could reach internal organs. 'Doesn't look like he was wetwired.' Then she noticed the shreds of his clothes, the fabric was the same dark red as the Saffron Clinic uniform. The DNA wasn't registered in Senate Security database. She told her e-butler to access Tridelta police and civic files.

'Are you sure this is the second one?' she asked.

'Not really,' Warren said. 'This is the location where all the resistance came from.'

'But you're sure two people were firing at you?'

'That's a definite.'

'John, have you got your target?'

'Yes. The DNA is weird, I've got variants across the body, but some of it matches Daltra.'

'Thank you. Matthew, what about you?'

'Two hostiles taken out. One positive ID: Pomanskie. We're trying to salvage the second body. There's not a lot of it left intact.'

Paula stared down at the unidentified corpse. 'Bernadette was making contact with four hostiles. So who was he?' She started to turn a circle, but stopped almost at once. There was a wide rent in the Tower's core, five metres away. Two eyebirds flipped out of their holder on her suit, and darted into the dark gap. 'Damn it, that's a lift shaft.' The eyebirds' sensors were showing her the shaft running up for another sixty floors, with every door shut. Twenty floors below, it was blocked by the top of a lift. She sent both eyebirds plummeting down. The hatch on the top of the lift had been ripped open. The eyebirds forced their way past the bent metal and into the lift. There was a hole in the bottom, revealing the rest of the shaft leading down into the Greenford's sub basements.

'Everyone, we have a breach. One person, maybe more. Timeframe, up to seven minutes. That's enough to exit. Renne, harden that perimeter.'

*

Renne had fumed at being given the perimeter duty. After all that the Paris office had been through lately she wanted to get into an armour suit and kick some serious ass. But the duty wasn't just putting up barricades and liaising with the local police. Everyone brought down from the clinic had to be examined and confirmed. A lot of them would be criminals of some kind, it was that sort of clinic, which meant there was a good probability they would be weapons wetwired. Paula kept emphasizing how the perimeter was to be maintained. It was good to be working with the boss again. Renne just wished she was on the sharp edge of the operation. She couldn't decide if she'd been given the perimeter duty because of Paula's earlier suspicions. That she'd ever been on the suspect list in the first place had shocked her. But that was the boss for you, logical to the last. And she was still reeling from discovering Tarlo's treachery. They'd known each other for nearly fifteen years.

The holding chambers they'd set up in the sub basement were starting to fill up with the Saffron Clinic people. All the fighting was over. There was no more debris falling onto the plaza, though water was still dribbling down the face of the Greenford Tower from the gaping windows.

Renne walked round the edge of the police barricades, looking up into the dark sky. The clinic's floors were easy to see. Without their glass, the shattered windows gleamed a harsh amber against the rest of the Tower's black bulk. The only illumination above ten metres in the whole city.

Police officers and patrolbots stood guard along the barricades, keeping the curious citizens well back. She was pleased to see how vigilant they were being despite the news about the starships.

'Nobody down here, boss,' she told Paula. 'Do you want the police teams to start sweeping the lower floors?'

'Not yet. Hoshe is locking down every floor. We're going to have to seal up the entire Tower and scan everyone as they emerge.'

'Long night.'

'Looks that way.'

'Have you heard the starships are back? The attack was a failure.'

'That's not good.'

'So was the Starflyer part of that?'

'I don't know. I'll have to ask Admiral Kime.'

'You know the admiral?'

'Yes.'

Renne knew she shouldn't be surprised. But if the boss knew Kime, how come Columbia had fired her? Or had he? Was it a set-up to make the traitor relax his or her guard? With the boss, anything was possible. She never let go of a suspect.

Renne turned to go back into the Greenford Tower where Hoshe had set up the operation's command post. Somebody moving away from the crowd outside the barricades caught her eye. She frowned. A girl with a mane of blond hair stepped off the pavement and crossed over Allwyn Street. It wasn't the hair that made Renne peer after her, it was the walk. The girl almost strutted, holding her head high, hardly bothering to check the traffic had stopped for her. That kind of arrogance belonged to a Dynasty brat, or a Grand Family trustafarian. The kind of integral arrogance Isabella Halgarth possessed in abundance.

Renne swung her legs over the barricade, and pushed through the line of spectators, then she was on the empty pavement behind them. The girl was walking away down the other side of the street. She was the right height. Her clothes were expensively casual, a red sweater and short amethyst wrap skirt with slim metal clips, long black boots.

'I might need some back up here.'

'What have you got?' Hoshe asked.

'I'm not sure. I think I've just seen Isabella Halgarth.'

'Where?'

'Allwyn Street, near the Lanvia Avenue turn.'

'Hold please, I'm accessing the civic sensors.'

Renne kept an eye on traffic, and hurried out into the road. Horns tooted furiously at her as cars braked. A cyclist screamed obscenities as he wobbled past. 'She's getting into a taxi.' The girl vanished in a blue and green vehicle, and the door shut.

'Number?' Hoshe demanded.

'I can't see, damnit. The logo is an orange trumpet, it's on the doors.' She flagged down a taxi. 'She's heading west.' The maroon-red Ables Puma drew up beside her. 'Just drive west,' she told the drive array.

'All right, I'm filtering traffic control arrays for a match,' Hoshe said. 'Murray cabs have that trumpet logo.'

'Renne, you need back-up,' Paula said. 'Don't go near her. She's extremely dangerous.'

'I won't.' She switched on her force field skeleton suit. 'Just observing.'

'Okay, I've got a police team in their car,' Hoshe said. 'Leaving the Greenfield garage now.'

Renne was pressed up against the taxi's front windscreen, retinal inserts searching through the traffic ahead for the blue and green Ables. Her OCtattoos reported a sophisticated scan washing across her, immediately pinpointing the source. She turned quickly to see Isabella Halgarth standing on the pavement, looking straight at her. The girl's right arm was raised, pointing at the taxi.

'Oh shit,' Renne closed her eyes.

The maser struck the taxi's power cells, which exploded with enough fury to lift the disintegrating car three metres off the ground. Renne's force field was overwhelmed in the first second. But it did provide enough initial protection so that when the paramedics started to pick up the sections of her body that had been flung over a wide radius they found her memorycell was intact. After re-life procedure, Renne would be able to remember her death.

10

The assembly platform brought back memories of the *Second Chance* being constructed above Anshun. To Nigel that whole period seemed like centuries ago now, a time where life was a great deal quieter and more leisurely. Giselle Swinsol and Nigel's own son, Otis, were leading him through the platform's gridwork maze inside a huge cylinder of malmetal, where the *Speedwell* was under construction. The Dynasty's colony ship was much bigger than the *Second Chance*, a lengthy cluster of spherical hull sections arranged along a central spine. So far, Nigel had authorized eleven of the vast ships, with initial component acquisition consent for another four. In theory, just one ship could carry enough equipment and genetic material to establish a successful high-technology human society from scratch. But Nigel had wanted to begin with more than the basics, and his Dynasty was the largest in the Commonwealth. A fleet would make absolutely sure any new human civilization they founded was successful. Now, though, he wasn't sure if that second batch would ever be built. Like everyone else, he'd expected the navy warships to have some success against Hell's Gateway. The moment when the navy detector network saw the Prime wormholes come back to the Lost23 had come as a savage surprise to him. He really hadn't been prepared for a defeat of that magnitude.

'We've commissioned four, now,' Otis was saying. 'The

Aeolus and the *Saumarez* should be ready for their preliminary trials in the next ten days.'

'Don't quote me, but we might not have ten days,' Nigel said. 'Giselle, I want you to review our emergency protocols for evacuating as much of the Dynasty as possible onto the lifeboats during an invasion. Coordinate with Campbell. We'll need to establish hardened wormhole connections to our parties. The exploratory division wormholes will be our principal method, but we'll need back-up procedures ready.'

'Got it.' Her elegant face was slightly puffed in freefall, but she still managed a worried expression, creasing her cheeks. 'How likely is that?'

Nigel halted his steady drift by grabbing a carbon strut at the base of a high-mass manipulator. He was looking out at the *Speedwell*'s drive section, a mushroom hemisphere at the front of the starship with fluted edges that curved backwards like a protective umbrella over the forward sphere sections. The outer skin was a smooth blue-green boronsteel, with a sheen that gave it the overall appearance of a beetle's carapace.

Most of the platform's robotic systems were folded back into the cylindrical gridwork which encased the vast starship. All of the prefabricated sections from Cressat had been locked into place; the few remaining areas of activity were involved with integrating the spheres to the ship's power and environmental circuits.

'Only the Primes know,' he said. 'But after our failure at Hell's Gateway I don't think it'll be long before they respond.'

'They don't know where this world is,' Otis said. 'They don't even know it exists; it isn't on any database in the Commonwealth. Hell, when it comes down to it, Cressat would be tough to find. That gives us a breathing space.'

'I don't want to evacuate,' Nigel said. 'Using this fleet still remains the last option as far as I'm concerned. As of now, I'm prepared to use our weapon to defend the Commonwealth. That's what I'm here to tell you.'

Otis gave him a tight smile. 'Are were using the frigates to launch them?'

'Yes, son, you get to fly combat missions.'

'Thank Christ for that. I thought I was going to wind up sitting this out.'

'Don't be so gung-ho about this. I'm trying to avoid bloodshed.'

'Dad, you're going to genocide them.'

Nigel closed his eyes. These days he often found himself wishing he believed in God, any god, just some omnipotent entity who'd listen sympathetically to the odd prayer. 'I know.'

'The frigates aren't even approaching readiness,' Giselle said. 'And our weapon hasn't been tested. We've only just completed component fabrication.'

'That's why I'm here,' Nigel said, glad of a solid, practical problem to focus on. 'We're going to have to accelerate our schedule.'

'If you say so, but I don't see how.'

'Show me what we've got so far.'

Frigate assembly bay one was a separate malmetal chamber affixed to the side of the main platform like a small black-metal barnacle. Nigel drifted into it through a narrow interlink tube whose bands of electromuscle pulled him along with the ease of a ski lift. His first impression was that he'd emerged into the engine room of some colossal nineteenth-century steamship. It was hot and loud, a metallic clanking reverberating continually through air that was heavy with the smell of burning plastic. Big gantry arms swished across the few open spaces like ancient engine pistons. Smaller robotic manipulators rolled along their tracks, darting out with serpentine agility to peck at some chunk of compact machinery. Circular scarlet hologram signs were flashing everywhere Nigel looked, warning people away from the complex moving parts. At the centre of the mechanical commotion the frigate *Charybdis* was a dark mass of densely packed components. Eventually, it would be a flattened ellipsoid, fifty metres long, encased by an active-stealth composite; but at this point the hull hadn't been fitted.

'How near are we to completion?' Nigel asked.

'Several days,' Giselle said. 'Flight readiness comes quite a while after that.'

'We can't afford that kind of delay, not now,' Nigel said. He twisted his cuff off a fuseto patch, and drifted in for a closer look. 'Where are we with the other three frigate assembly bays?'

'Not as advanced as this one. We haven't even begun construction in them yet. We were waiting until the bugs are sorted out in number one. Once we're up and running with all four we'll be building a frigate every three days.'

Nigel gripped the base of a manipulator track next to one of the holographic circles, peering through the perpetual motion lattice of cybernetics. He could just see the smooth bulge of the crew cabin a third of the way down the naked frigate. Over twenty robotic systems were busy fitting additional elements or connecting up tubes and cables to the ribbed pressure module.

'Hey you!' a man's voice yelled. 'Are you blind? Stay the hell back from the warning signs.' Mark Vernon slid through one of the scarlet circles five metres away from Nigel as if he was emerging from a pool of red fluid. 'It's goddamn dangerous in here, we haven't got any of the usual safety cut-offs installed.'

'Ah,' Nigel said. 'Thank you for telling me.'

At his side, Giselle was glowering at Mark.

Mark blinked, suddenly recognizing who he was shouting at. 'Oh. Right. Er, hi, sir. Giselle.'

Nigel watched the man's face redden, but there was no apology. He rather respected that. Mark was clearly the boss in this arena. Then his e-butler flipped up Mark's file, complete with interesting cross-reference. *Goddamn! Is there anything in this universe that doesn't connect back to Mellanie?*

'Mark Vernon,' Giselle said in a half-growl. 'Our assembly bay chief.'

'Pleased to meet you, Mark,' Nigel said.

'Yeah,' Mark said grumpily. 'You really have to be careful in here, sir. I wasn't joking.'

'I understand. So you're the competent man around here?'

Mark tried to shrug, forgetting he was in freefall. He tightened his grip on an alulithium strut to stop his feet from swinging round. 'It's a hell of a challenge integrating everything in the bay. I enjoy it.'

'Then I apologize, because I'm about to make your life miserable.'

'Er, how?' Mark flicked his gaze to Giselle, who was looking equally perturbed.

'I need a functional frigate in the Wessex system within the next thirty hours.'

Mark gave him a wild smile. 'No way. I'm sorry. It's just not possible.' A hand waved limply towards the exposed shape of the *Charybdis*. 'This is the first one we've attempted to build, and we're encountering a problem every ten minutes. Don't get me wrong, I'm sure they're superb ships. And once me and the team finalize the assembly sequence then we can fasttrack as many as you want, but we're not there yet. Not by a long way.'

Nigel smiled back uncompromisingly. 'Disconnect this assembly bay from the platform. Attach it to one of the completed lifeboat starships, and continue working on the *Charybdis* while you're flown to Wessex.'

'Huh?' Even without gravity, Mark's jaw dropped open in astonishment.

'Is there any technical reason why that cannot be done? Any at all?'

'Er, well I hadn't really thought about it. Suppose not. No.'

'Good. I want it attached and ready to leave in one hour. Take whoever you need with you, but get the *Charybdis* flight-ready.'

'You want *me* to go with it?'

'You're the expert.'

'Umm. Right. Yeah. Sure. Okay. Er, can I ask why you want a frigate at Wessex?'

'Because I'm sure that star is going to be right up at the top of the Primes' list of targets when they invade.'

'Uh huh. I see.'

'Don't be modest Mark; you did a terrific job helping people back in Randtown. I'm proud you're one of my descendants. I know you won't let us down.' Nigel signalled to Giselle and Otis, then pushed off from the manipulator track and headed back for the interlink tube. 'We'll move the weapons section onto the lifeboat as well. I'd like to meet the project scientists now. Which lifeboat will be easiest?'

'The *Searcher* has done two test flights already,' Otis said. 'Shakedown's almost complete. It should be the most reliable.'

'The *Searcher* it is, then.'

Mark clung to the slim strut as he watched Nigel Sheldon slide away down the interlink tube. Sweat was oozing out of every pore on his body and clinging to the skin to produce a horribly cold, sticky film of moisture 'Top of the invasion list,' Mark whispered forlornly. He glanced back at the incomplete frigate. 'Oh hell, not again.'

*

It was four in the morning on Illuminatus when Paula finally left for the CST station. Everyone in the Greenford Tower had been evaluated by the medical forensic team. Several criminals undergoing wetwiring had been hauled off by the local police. The city hospitals were dealing with casualties, from both Greenford and Treetops. A civil engineering team was inspecting the remnants of the Saffron Clinic for structural damage. Forensics was removing all the surviving arrays ready to perform a complete data extraction.

Paula removed her armour suit in the control centre, handing it over to the support team who were packing everything away. She put on a force field skeleton suit, then dressed in a long, plain grey skirt and thick white crew-neck cotton top. Her brown leather belt with its embedded silver chain looked decorative; it had even come from her own wardrobe, but Senate Security technical services had reworked it.

'You okay?' Hoshe asked.

'This didn't quite happen how I was expecting,' she admitted. Her e-butler was running integration checks on the belt and force field skeleton. 'Hopefully, it's not over yet. Are we ready for the journey back?'

'Teams are in position, equipment all set up—' he glanced down at the four black cases containing their cage equipment '—and activated.'

'Good. Let's go.'

They went out into the sub-basement garage where the holding areas had been set up. A single pen of wire mesh was left, with twenty guardbots surrounding it, weapons out of their recesses. Two local police officers stood on either side of the gate. There was only one person left inside.

Mellanie waited in the middle of the pen, still in her nurse's uniform, arms folded huffily across her chest, an incensed expression welded into place.

Paula told the police to open the gate. Mellanie remained resolutely in place.

'I thought we could talk on the way back,' Paula said. Somehow, she didn't have any scruples about setting the girl up. Mellanie, she guessed, had involved herself in a great deal of illicit activity to get into the Saffron Clinic.

'Do you know how long I've been waiting here?'

'To the second, actually. Why?'

Mellanie glared at her.

'If you prefer, you can stay here,' Hoshe said generously. 'The police will process you in due course. They are quite busy after tonight.'

Mellanie let out a dangerous growl. 'I can't access the unisphere.'

'We have blocker systems active down here,' Hoshe said. 'They're quite effective, aren't they?'

Mellanie switched her stare to Paula. 'Where?'

'Where what?' Paula asked.

'You said we'd talk on the way back. Back where?'

'Earth. We have tickets for the next express. First class.'

'Fine. Whatever.' Mellanie stomped out through the open gate. 'Where's the car?'

Hoshe gestured politely to the ramp. 'Outside.'

Mellanie flounced in disgust at their incompetence. She headed for the ramp with long impatient strides. Paula and Hoshe exchanged a bemused glance behind her back, and set off after her. Hoshe's four black cases trundled along behind him.

The ramp came out directly on the street beyond the Greenford Tower's plaza. Mellanie paused in confusion at the scene outside. Paula and Hoshe stood on either side of her. The remaining reporters flocked towards the nearest section of the barricades, and started shouting questions.

Paula's virtual vision showed her several heavily encrypted messages arriving in Mellanie's address port as they emerged from the blocking field. The girl sent two.

Tridelta police had still got Allwyn Street sealed off for six blocks around the skyscraper. All the ambulances had departed, leaving the fire department crews and bots to clear up the aftermath of the explosion. The eight cars closest to Renne's taxi were burnt-out wrecks, shunted across the road and smashed into the buildings; a further twenty vehicles were buckled and broken. A big crane was lifting them onto waiting trailers. Civic cleaning bots were washing the blood off the pavement. There had been a lot of people in the open air bars nearby. GPbots were moving along the façades, sweeping up the piles of broken glass.

'Oh God,' Mellanie mumbled. She stared at the devastation, then twisted round to look back up the Greenford Tower.

'I told you it was an unsafe environment,' Paula said.

A big police van pulled up beside them. The door slid open, and they climbed in. The cases rolled into the luggage compartment.

'I remember Randtown,' Mellanie said in a quiet voice as the van drove off. 'I hoped I'd forgotten, but that just made it all come back. It was awful.'

Paula decided the girl was genuinely upset. 'Death on this scale is never easy.'

Hoshe was looking out of the window, his face expressionless.

'Did your people get hurt?' Mellanie asked.

'Some of them, yes.'

'I'm sorry.'

'They knew the risks, just like you did. They'll all be re-lifed.'

'If there's anything left to be re-lifed into.'

'We'll make sure there is.'

*

The police van got them to the CST station in plenty of time before the express was due to depart. They pulled up in front of the main concourse, and walked to their platform. A cool breeze blew through the cavernous structure, coming straight off the Logrosan which ran along the side of the smallest marshalling yard Paula had seen in the Commonwealth. Illuminatus didn't export any bulk products, it only manufactured small high-technology items. The marshalling yard was set up primarily for receiving food imports; without any arable land on the planet, every meal had to be brought in on the goods trains. She wondered what would happen if the Primes struck here. Or worse, on Piura, the Big15 world to which it was connected. If Illuminatus was cut off from the Commonwealth, it would go bad very quickly for the population of the trapped city.

When she looked along the platform, the other waiting passengers scrupulously avoided eye contact. The station wasn't exactly busy, but there were more people than usual for this time in the morning. Several families stood huddled together, complete with drowsy children. After the news of the starships, they'd obviously been thinking hard about the consequences of a Prime attack.

Mellanie rubbed at her arms; the cool air was raising goosebumps 'I feel stupid in this,' she muttered. Her nurse's uniform had short sleeves.

'Here.' Hoshe took off his sweater and held it out to her.

She flashed him a grateful smile. 'Thank you.' It was baggy on her, but she stopped shivering.

The express slid silently into the station along its maglev track. They waited until passengers stopped disembarking before getting into the first-class carriage where they had a reserved compartment.

'Which Earth station are we going to?' Mellanie asked.

'London,' Hoshe said.

'I thought you were based in Paris.'

Paula gave her an enigmatic smile. 'It depends.' She told her e-butler to open one of the pouches in her belt. A Bratation spindlefly dropped out and began to scuttle up the wall. Its gossamer thread extruded behind it as Paula walked along the carriage's narrow corridor, maintaining the secure connection. The compartment contained thick leather couches on either side of a walnut-veneered table. Mellanie flopped down into one with a hefty sigh, curling her legs up and pulling the sweater down over her knees. She had her face up close to the window, like a child peering into a shop display. Paula and Hoshe sat opposite her. The black cases arranged themselves on either side of the door.

After a couple of minutes, the express eased out of the station and began to pick up speed as it headed for the gateway.

'What happened to the lawyers?' Mellanie asked.

'Bodyloss,' Paula told her. 'Our medical forensic teams will try to recover their memorycells, but given the damage level it doesn't look good.' She checked the image she was getting from the spindlefly, which showed her a black and white fish-lens view of the corridor from the ceiling. Her skin tingled as they passed through the pressure curtain. A warm salmon-pink light shone in through the compartment's window, and the express accelerated hard across Piura's massive station yard.

'They were the one lead I had back to the Cox,' Mellanie said.

'Yes, me too.'

Mellanie looked surprised. 'You did believe me!'

'I do now. We uncovered a Starflyer agent in my old Paris office. He'd been manipulating information for quite some time. The Cox case was one of them.'

'Did you catch him?'

'No,' Paula said. It was a heavy admission, but she'd talked to Alic Hogan before the paramedics put him under. Treetops had been worse than the Greenford Tower.

'So we still don't have any proof that the Starflyer exists,' Mellanie said.

'The case against it is building.' Paula's virtual vision flashed a small square of text. The management routines in the carriage arrays were shutting down all their communication functions. The spindlefly showed her the door which led through to the next first-class carriage being opened. She exchanged a glance with Hoshe, who nodded subtly.

'But not conclusive,' Mellanie said sullenly. 'That's what you're going to say.'

'No. And we're running out of time.'

'How do you figure that?'

'The war is not going well for the Commonwealth. Our starships were defeated at Hell's Gateway.' A girl was walking along the carriage's corridor towards their compartment. Paula's heart began to speed up. A tactical grid flipped up into her virtual vision; she prepped several icons for immediate activation.

'Yeah. I guess the rich will be taking off in their lifeboats pretty soon.'

'I expect they will. More importantly, according to the Guardians, the Starflyer will leave once it has arranged for our destruction. Unless we can move against it soon, it will have gone.'

'So just stop it going back to Far Away,' Mellanie said. 'Put a guard on the Boongate gateway to Half Way.'

'I would have to convince my political allies such a move was justified.' Through the spindlefly's artificial senses, Paula saw the girl standing outside their compartment.

Mellanie took a deep breath. 'I know about some more Starflyer agents, if you'll believe me this time.'

'You are very well informed.'

A focused disrupter field hit the compartment door, which instantly shattered. Mellanie screamed in shock, flinging herself down. Paula and Hoshe activated their force field skeletons. Isabella Halgarth stepped in through the dagger shards of the doorframe. A force field sparkled around her.

'It's her,' Mellanie yelled. 'It's Isabella! She's one of them.'

Isabella raised her right arm. The flesh on her forearm flowed, parting in several places like lipless mouths.

Paula triggered the cage. Curving force field petals sprang out of the cases on each side of Isabella, closing round her and squeezing tight. She grimaced, as if mildly puzzled. Then she tried to move, squirming inside the constricting petals. Her movements were mechanical as each boosted muscle tried to push her body free. A series of apertures opened along both arms allowing dark stubby muzzles to protrude. She started firing ion bolts and masers.

Streamers of energy lashed across the cage, grounding out in the floor of the compartment. Smoke began to leak upwards. The shimmering petals slowly brightened to a threatening azure.

'Ready?' Paula shouted above the screech of the wild discharges. She held up a dump web, and as Hoshe nodded she slapped it against Isabella's back. The cage petals rearranged themselves to let it through. Her face was centimetres from the girl's, and that was when she knew with absolute certainty they were confronting some kind of alien. Isabella's eyes looked at her with malignant fury. Whatever intelligence stared through them was studying her, and judging.

Isabella's force field failed.

Hoshe rammed a nervejam stick against her. It slipped easily through the cage petals to press against her chest. Her imprisoned body began to shake violently. She slowly peeled her lips back to reveal a furious snarl. All of her embedded weapons fired simultaneously. Sparks burst out of the gleaming cage petals as they began to whine dangerously.

'Jesus!' Hoshe exclaimed. He twisted the nervejam stick's trigger to full power.

Isabella suddenly looked surprised, her eyes opening wide. Her weapons stopped firing.

The cage petals held her immobile, pressing tight against the skin, freezing her posture and expression. Paula looked at the girl's feet. They were suspended a couple of centimetres off the smouldering carpet. 'Is she out?'

'I don't know,' a sweating Hoshe said. 'But I'm not taking any chances.' He continued to push the nervejam stick hard against her.

'Okay.' Paula called the rest of the team in. Vic Russell, in full armour, clumped along the corridor, leading Matthew and John King.

'You get all the fun,' Vic complained.

'Next time, it's all yours,' Hoshe said sincerely as Vic took over the nervejam stick.

With Isabella surrounded by the three armour suits, Hoshe switched the cage petals off. The girl crumpled into John's arms.

'Is she alive?' Paula asked.

'Heart slightly erratic, but calming,' John assured her. 'She's breathing unaided.'

'Good, get her into the suspension shell.' Paula switched off her force field skeleton and ran a hand over her brow. She wasn't surprised to find her fingers damp with perspiration.

'Just what the *fuck* is going on?' Mellanie yelled.

Paula turned to face the furious, frightened girl, and blinked in surprise. Mellanie's skin had turned almost completely silver.

'It was an entrapment,' Paula said, trying to stay calm. She had no idea what Mellanie's inserts were capable of. The only reassurance she had was that if Mellanie had been working for the Starflyer she would have pitched in with Isabella. 'You and I have both been causing a considerable amount of trouble for the Starflyer. Together we presented what I hoped would be an irresistible target. I was correct. Although I was hoping it would be Tarlo they sent.'

'You!' Mellanie gasped the word out, a trembling finger pointed at Paula. 'You. We. I. The police van. Everyone saw.'

'That is correct. Everyone saw us leaving the Greenford Tower together, and the event was released into the unisphere.

This compartment was booked in my name. It gave them a perfect assassination opportunity.'

'I haven't got a force field suit,' Mellanie wailed. The silver was fading from her skin, withdrawing in complex curling patterns.

'You were relatively safe. The cage is capable of absorbing high-level weapons fire from its captive.'

Mellanie sat down hard, staring at nothing. 'You piece of shit. You could have told me.'

'I wasn't completely sure of your loyalties. And I wanted you to behave in a natural fashion. I apologize for any alarm.'

'Alarm!' Mellanie appealed to Hoshe who gave her a sorrowful little smile.

'And now,' Paula said. 'Would you please explain to me how you knew Isabella was a Starflyer agent?'

*

Justine arrived back in New York just after midnight eastern standard time. It was later than she expected. The War Cabinet session had overrun by an hour as they discussed the briefing from Wilson Kime. Seattle Project quantumbusters were now being carried on twenty-seven *Moscow*-class starships. The twenty ships in the Hell's Gateway fleet were on their way back to the High Angel, where they'd also be equipped with quantumbusters once they were recharged.

Nobody knew if it would be sufficient to ward off any further Prime attacks, even Dimitri Leopoldvich was being guarded with evaluations.

The War Cabinet was also undecided on carrying the fight back to the Primes. Sheldon, Hutchinson, and Columbia wanted to dispatch several ships to Dyson Alpha while the Primes remained ignorant of quantumbusters. Columbia believed they could inflict an incredible amount of destruction on the alien star system, hopefully weakening the Prime civilization catastrophically. A second wave of ships could then go in and finish the job, he said.

The genocide option again. Justine had taken their side, which had clearly surprised the remainder of the cabinet, including Toniea Gall, its newest member. She'd done it because of the Starflyer. Bradley Johansson had told her it wanted to destroy both species, that it was carefully playing them both off against each other so that it could rise victoriously in the ruins. Genocide was the only way she could see the Commonwealth surviving.

By contrast, Wilson hadn't been keen, pointing out the sheer size of the Dyson Alpha civilization, the undoubted fact it had now spread to other star systems besides the Lost23 and Hell's Gateway. The remnants could strike the Commonwealth equally hard, he claimed, we might trigger a double genocide.

'They're trying to exterminate us anyway,' was Columbia's reply.

If the genocide option was out for the immediate future, Alan Hutchinson said, then why not launch a second raid against Hell's Gateway, this time using quantumbusters.

'You'll be giving away our advantage,' Kime replied. 'Quantumbusters are the only weapon we have that they don't know about.'

'But if they work, we can stop the Prime advance completely, and push them off the Lost23,' the bluff Dynasty leader said. 'They can't launch a second wave against us without Hell's Gateway. With that knocked out, we can go right ahead and take out their home system.'

'I don't think we can afford to divert starships from defence, right now,' Kime said. 'When we have more in service, then such a course becomes viable.'

Hutchinson clearly wasn't happy. The rest of the War Cabinet was conscious of the growing rift between Kime and Columbia. President Doi closed the session by instituting an ongoing review. They would reconvene at any time the strategic situation changed.

As soon as they rose, Justine had taken an express straight back to New York with three aides and her Senate Security bodyguard team. The next morning had her scheduled to meet an informal group of Wall Street executives to discuss the worsening financial conditions brought on by increased taxes, the exodus, and the latest navy failure. The markets were in freefall, and they needed reassurance that the Executive was firmly in control with policies that would ultimately resolve the problem. *As if I can convince them of that.* At least Crispin would be with her at the working breakfast, she could rely on him for general support.

When the express pulled into Grand Central Station, her aides took a taxi to their hotel, while Justine was ferried to her Park Avenue apartment by a family limousine. As she got into the big car, her e-butler was tagging news reports from Illuminatus for her attention. She let some of them through her filters, and immediately sat up in the limo's deep leather seating. Images of the Greenford Tower filled her virtual vision, with reporters covering the Tridelta fire department's efforts to cope with the taxi which had exploded just outside. The civilian casualties were appalling.

'Call Paula Myo,' she told her e-butler.

'Senator?' Paula said.

'Are you all right?'

'So far, yes.'

'What does that mean?'

'We have failed to capture any of the Starflyer agents we discovered in Tridelta. However we have exposed one of its agents working in the Navy Intelligence Paris office. It will give you some valuable leverage to use with Admiral Columbia, and the Halgarths.'

'That's excellent news.'

'Yes. I'm now initiating a further entrapment scenario

involving myself and Mellanie Rescorai as we travel back to Earth; I hope that will be more successful.'

'Mellanie is with you?'

'Yes. She is getting very heavily involved in the anti-Starflyer movement. I suspect she is somehow involved with the Guardians.'

Justine nearly told her that Mellanie was in contact with Adam Elvin, but that would mean explaining how she was in touch with Johansson, and she wasn't prepared to give that to the formidable Investigator, not yet. 'Perhaps we should try and convene a meeting, pool our resources.'

'Very well, but I would like to establish Mellanie's true sympathies. She could be a very elaborate trap for us set by the Starflyer.'

'As you wish. Let me know once you're satisfied about her. Good luck, and be careful.'

'Thank you, Senator.'

The limousine drove down into the apartment block's underground garage. Justine and her three bodyguards took the elevator up to the fortieth floor.

Despite the apartment's new beefed-up security apparatus, the bodyguards insisted on doing a physical appraisal of all the rooms as well as reviewing the array logs. Justine stood in the big lounge, waiting for them with an outward show of patience. It was the kind of social façade she'd learned centuries ago, but even so it was a strain tonight. Her feet ached from swelling ankles, she had heartburn which was becoming more frequent, her morning sickness was now lasting for fifteen hours a day, and she had a headache. *Just get on with it*, she thought darkly as they moved from room to room, taking their time, being professional and thorough.

'The apartment is clear, Senator,' Hector Del, the team commander, told her.

'Thank you.'

'I'll be staying here with you tonight,' he said.

'Whatever, yes.' She went into her bedroom and shut the door just as the other two bodyguards left. The apartment's housekeeper array had started to fill her big sunken tub as soon as the limo parked. It was now full to the brim with scented water, and foaming richly. Justine looked at it in exasperation and groaned. A long decent wallow in the tub was the one thing she'd been looking forward to the whole journey home. She'd completely forgotten she shouldn't be taking long hot baths when pregnant.

She hissed crossly and told her e-butler to switch the shower on. As the tub drained away she took her clothes off and left them on the floor for a maidbot to clear away. *It is true, your brain packs up and goes on vacation when you're pregnant.*

The (moderately) warm jets of water played over her skin. Nice, but not as nice as a good soak. Her e-butler pulled some twenty-second-century organic-synth jazz from the apartment memory, and played it at high volume as soap began to mix into the water.

Sheldon's behaviour during the War Cabinet had bothered her. She didn't understand why he was so keen for the genocide. Unless he knew that it would provoke an equal reaction from the Primes. Which was what the Starflyer wanted. *Or am I being really paranoid?* The only evidence against him was Thompson saying that his office had continually blocked the examination of cargo to Far Away, something Justine was still unable to confirm.

She wiped an exfoliator sponge across her legs and stomach as the foamy water sluiced over her. Red icons flashed into her virtual vision. **INTRUDER ALERT.** The newly installed alarm system showed her a dark image of an unidentified person walking through the kitchen.

How the hell did they get in there without triggering a perimeter alarm?

She wiped the water frantically from her face and reached for a towel.

SENATOR, Hector Del sent, **PLEASE DO NOT EXPOSE YOUR-SELF. I AM INVESTIGATING NOW. THE REST OF THE TEAM IS RETURNING IMMEDIATELY.**

Her heart was pounding wildly, which was exacerbating her headache. She wrapped the towel round her waist and hurried out into the bedroom, dripping all over the carpet. On the other side of the door, Hector Del shouted: 'You. Halt. Now!'

There was the high-pitched *crack* of a weapon discharge, which made her jump in shock. It was swiftly followed by two louder blasts. A man screamed. There was a crash, something heavy thudded onto the floor as white light flared through the gap under the door.

Hector? Justine sent. **What happened?**

Her virtual vision showed her the bodyguard's inserts had dropped their link to the apartment's array. She put her hand on the door handle. Hesitated. There was no sound on the other side. When she tried to access the apartment's security net, it reported that a very powerful jamming signal was interfering with the sensors. Her e-butler told her the body-guard team was in the elevator, coming back up.

Justine opened the door a crack and peered out into the apartment's central corridor. It was dark, with light shining in from the hallway at the far end. Thin strands of smoke layered the air, some flames were licking up from the smashed remnants of an antique table. Hector Del was crumpled against the wall, his clothes smouldering. Skin red and blotchy. From the angle of his neck she knew he was dead.

Someone stepped into the hall's archway.

'Bruce!' Justine gasped.

The Starflyer assassin raised his arm.

Justine wailed in terror; hands instinctively clutching at her belly, protecting the unborn.

The corridor's ceiling ruptured in a cloud of dust and concrete fragments as it was hit by a powerful focused disruptor field. Gore Burnelli dropped through the rent to land lightly between Justine and Bruce. He looked very dapper in a perfectly tailored tuxedo. 'Hey pal,' he said to Bruce, 'Want to try picking on someone your own size for a change?'

Both of Bruce's arms were raised. A near-solid torrent of plasma bolts struck Gore, cocooning him in an incandescent nimbus. His tuxedo burst into flames. The floor and walls around him started to blacken. Justine shielded her face from the fearsome light.

Bruce lowered his arms. Gore stood in a circle of scorched concrete that was edged in flame; the last ashes of his ruined clothes dropping from him. His naked body was completely gold, reflecting the flames in little orange ripples. He smiled waspishly. 'My turn.' He started walking toward Bruce. A focused disrupter pulse slammed out from him, filling the corridor's smoky air with a ghost-green phosphorescence. Bruce's force field flashed purple as he staggered backwards from the blow. He struggled to stand upright. Gore fired another pulse which knocked the assassin off his feet and sent him skidding back across the hall's polished parquet flooring, arms and legs waving like an upturned turtle. He rolled himself onto his front, and scurried away.

'Come back and play, motherfucker,' Gore called. He sped along the corridor and into the lounge after Bruce. Plasma bolts, maser beams, and ion bolts hit him as soon as he was through the open doorway. Wild ribbons of energy exploded around him as his integral force field deflected the assault, sending them lashing into the building's structure. The strength of the attack started to push him back as if a watercanon was striking him head on. He expanded the force field behind him, pressing it up against the wall to hold himself against the power of the assassin's weapons. His feet halted their backward slide as the wall cracked and bent inwards. Another focused disruptor shot at Bruce's legs sent the assassin tumbling over again. The assassin hit the wall beside the balcony doors as the glass shattered across him. He rebounded and assumed a wrestler's crouch. Gore jumped.

The two of them collided in a maelstrom of whirling energy streamers and disintegrating furniture. Gore's nerves were saturated with accelerants, speeding up his reflexes as he chopped at the assassin with a series of karate blows that would have sliced an unprotected body into pieces. The impacts couldn't quite reach through Bruce's force field, though Gore saw the tell-tale scarlet flicker of an approaching overload each time he connected. He was managing to inflict a degree of harm on the body it enveloped, though it was hardly debilitating. Bruce's face grimaced silently in the bursts of red light. His own nervous system was accelerated, but not as fast as Gore's. He never quite managed to block the chops. As the force field weakened, it left his clothes exposed. Cloth either tore as Gore's hand ripped across it, or singed from the residue of weapons fire. Then Bruce twisted round, and managed to kick Gore's legs with a savage judo lunge.

Gore let the momentum carry him, and then amplified the movement, somersaulting backwards to land on his feet like some gymnast coming off the bars. He immediately advanced again, unleashing a barrage of focused disruptor shots.

Bruce had flipped the other way, recovering gracefully. As he straightened up, ragged clothes flapping against him, he was standing directly in front of the shattered balcony window. The disruptor field punched him back. He extended his force field wide, producing an angel wing configuration to try and secure himself to the walls framing the balcony door. Gore fired plasma bolts into the scorched plaster and concrete, blasting the solid material from either side of the assassin. Bruce answered with his own focused distortion field. They leant in towards each other, as if shoving their way through a hurricane. The apartment began to break up around them as the focused disrupter fields clashed. Deep fissures snapped through the walls. Whole sections of the floor shifted like tectonic faults. Plaster, concrete, wood and carbon-wrapped steel reinforcement strands rained down from the ceiling.

Gore crouched down, and sprang with the full power of his boosted muscles, amplified by a perfectly timed expansion of his force field. He flew through the air like a golden missile, outstretched fists ramming into Bruce's chest. The assassin left the ground, flailing backwards. His back hit the stone balcony rail, which buckled badly. Gargoyle heads shifted round as the stonework juddered.

Bruce looked at Gore for a moment, then vaulted over the rail. Gore never even hesitated, he leapt after his opponent.

It was completely silent in the air forty floors above Park Avenue. Gore heard nothing as he fell. His full-spectrum senses locked on Bruce's plummeting body below him. Shrouded in its cloak of energy, it shone like a star in his virtual vision target grid. He fired several plasma bolts down, but his own plunge was too unstable to provide him any reasonable accuracy. Explosions blossomed on the street below, orange and violet flames flowering up and outwards to welcome both of them.

The few cars and taxis using the road emergency-braked, their headlights skewing across the street as they skidded to a halt. Passengers pressed their faces to the windows to see what was happening.

Gore stretched out his arms and legs like a skydiver, then expanded his force field into a wide lens-shaped bubble. Air rushed against it, braking his speed sharply. When it reached twenty metres across he was barely moving. He rotated to an upright position. The force field's lower section touched the sidewalk, and folded carefully back against him, lowering him onto the ground. He stood motionless for a moment, hands resting on his hips as he watched Bruce.

The assassin's impact had left a human-shaped indentation in the Park Avenue tarmac close to the smouldering craters of the plasma bolts. There was a lot of blood in and around it. Bruce was staggering away across the road, weaving unsteadily round the stationary cars. Blood soaked the charred, tattered rags that he wore, splattering a wide trail behind him. Each step produced a strange crackling sound. It came from the spikes of bone sticking through his shins that were grinding against each other at every motion. The integral force field was holding his legs together, which was the only reason he was lurching forwards, even so the jerky movement was that of a late night drunk.

Gore grinned in satisfaction, and jumped. He soared effortlessly over the cars to drop in front of Bruce. As he landed, he bent forward and kicked back in one smooth motion, his heel smashing into Bruce's chest. The assassin was flung backwards as his force field cloaked him in a pale crimson light; he rolled over and over until he thudded into the front fender of a yellow taxi, dinting the bodywork. One shin was bent at right angles. The force field strengthened around it, trying to straighten it again. It emitted a loud squelching sound as the mangled flesh was further abused.

Bruce's head was shaking as he tried to look round at Gore, dark blood gurgled out of his mouth. He raised an arm and fired a plasma bolt at the nude golden human. The intense globe of energized atoms simply splashed off Gore's metallic skin without even straining his force field. The taxi's terrified passengers were yelling frantically; they ducked down below the windows

'This is not a good day for you, is it?' Gore sneered. 'First Illuminatus, now here. How many of these corrupted humans have you got left, I wonder?'

Bruce rolled onto his chest and started to crawl. Gore moved *fast* and clamped a hand round his neck. Their clashing force fields buzzed like a high voltage cable shorting out.

Bruce was hauled off the ground, and turned so Gore could study him in profile.

'You're not going anywhere,' Gore told him. 'From a tactical point of view I should take you in and try to break your conditioning. We'd probably learn a lot from that, Bruce.'

Bruce McFoster's eye twitched.

'But you tried to kill my daughter and my grandchild. So fuck that.'

Bruce's jaw opened, sending out a spray of blood, he tried to say something. Then his contorted face calmed. 'Do it. Kill the alien.' His force field switched off.

'Good for you, son,' Gore said in benediction. His hand closed round the man's neck, snapping the spine.

*

The last time Hoshe had visited the High Angel there had been a couple of bored Diplomatic Police reviewing the ID of everyone who entered the transit station, and scanning their baggage. Today it was a little different. There were now eight transit stations, all of them a lot bigger than the single original. All of them were guarded by a squad of fully armoured navy troopers.

Hoshe, who had seen quite enough of armour suits in the last twenty-four hours, eyed them wearily as he approached the entrance to a transit station marked CIVILIAN PERSON-NEL. The big trollybot carrying Isabella's suspension shell rolled along quietly behind him, screened from any scan by an e-shield. He called Paula while he was still fifty metres away along the white concourse. 'I'm being chicken. I think I need help already.'

'Okay, Hoshe,' she told him. 'I'm calling the High Angel now.'

The navy troopers watched him approach, and moved to form a protective cordon around the entrance. Two of them walked out to meet him.

One of them had a captain's star, and the name Turvill printed on his chest. He held out a hand, stopping Hoshe. 'What the hell is in that?'

Hoshe stared at the captain's helmet, seeing a curving reflection of himself in the gold-mirror dome. 'Luggage.'

'What's in it?'

'That's not your concern, Officer.'

The squad round the entrance raised their plasma rifles.

'Oh yes it is. Open it.'

Hoshe gave him a pleasant smile. 'No.'

'We are taking you into custody. Sergeant, get a team to scan the box.'

Hoshe stood his ground, smiling in what he hoped was a natural fashion, while praying he wasn't sweating too obviously. The squad started to advance, their rifles still raised. Some were covering the trolleybot and its large oblong shell.

Captain Turvill suddenly became very still. The squad halted. Their rifles were lowered. The captain saluted. 'Sorry, sir. There has been a misunderstanding. Please go through. Your shuttle is waiting. Can my men be of any assistance?'

'No. Thank you,' Hoshe said. 'I'll just, er . . .' His hand waved at the entrance to the civilian transit station. He felt like tiptoeing past the squad. A schoolboy smirk was trying to break out on his face; it was hard not to laugh.

Poor Captain Turvill would never know what happened, but Paula had spoken with the High Angel who called Toniea Gall and rather pointedly asked that a pre-arranged shipment to the Raiel should not be subject to interruption or examination. The alien starship had never been so blunt with her before. A furious, and frankly worried, Toniea Gall immediately called Admiral Columbia, who told the captain to back off. Now.

*

Hoshe was the only passenger on the shuttle. The stewards helped him float the suspension shell along the connecting tube, then strapped it securely to some seats for the duration of the flight. They docked at the base of the New Glasgow stalk, where all the airlocks were compatible to human ships. When they were inside, Hoshe's e-butler connected him to the High Angel's internal information net. His virtual vision filled up with strange fluid graphics in dusky colours. He thought it was a guidance display of some kind. Fuseto patches on his cuffs secured him to the wall, and he looked around the corridor. The tapering ribbons of light in his virtual vision undulated into new patterns as his head moved.

'What is this, exactly?' he asked.

'Detective Finn, welcome back,' the High Angel said. 'I am showing you which direction to take.'

The ribbons undulated again, ushering him along a small corridor. Hoshe beckoned the stewards, who tugged the suspension shell along for him. A door opened to show a small lift capsule, and Hoshe drifted in along with his cargo. He used the fusetos on his soles to keep his feet on the floor as the lift began to move.

Several minutes later the lift rose up the stalk into the Raiel dome. 'Can you send whatever the equivalent of a trolleybot is for me, please?' Hoshe asked. The dome's gravity was eighty per cent Earth standard, so there was no way he could lift the suspension shell, let alone drag it through the streets.

'That will not be necessary,' the High Angel said. 'Your cargo will accompany you.'

'Right. Thanks.' The lift doors opened. Hoshe looked out onto the Raiel city – if that's what it was. The light was the same gloomy grey he remembered from his earlier visit. Ahead of him was a street made from walls of unbroken matt-black metal. Lines of tiny red lights glimmered along the base of each building.

The ribbons in his virtual vision waved about like seaweed fronds, aligning themselves onto the street. He took a breath and walked out. The oblong shell that contained Isabella Halgarth slid out after him, its base half a metre off the floor.

'Oh neat,' he muttered. It wasn't particularly impressive, even though such a feat was currently beyond human technology. But then every High Angel dome had artificial gravity; if you could generate it, you could certainly manipulate it.

With the virtual vision display guiding him, Hoshe Finn walked along the dim alien streets. There were more curves this time, he thought, and the junctions weren't all right angles. Other than that it was the same interminable featureless metropolis, illuminated by row after row of small coloured lights set along the bottom of the walls.

He wound up facing a sheer cliff of metal, identical to all the others. The lights along the foundation were purple, as before. A vertical line split open in front of him, widening to allow him through. Inside was the same circular space with a glowing emerald floor, and a ceiling lost in the overhead shadows.

It was Qatux waiting for him, of that there was no mistake. The Raiel's health hadn't improved since they last met. Several of its medium-sized tentacles were coiled up tight; while the large pair at the bottom of its neck rested on the floor, as if they were helping to prop it up. Given the way the big body was sagging on its eight stumpy legs, Hoshe thought that might be a correct assessment. Not that it should have any trouble holding its own weight. Judging by how tight the brown hide was stretched over the skeleton platelets, it was suffering from the Raiel equivalent of anorexia. One of the five eyes was permanently shut, with a blue rheum leaking from the clenched eyelid; the remaining four eyes were twisting round independently.

Hoshe bowed to the creature, feeling enormously sorry for

649

it. *If you had to get addicted to anything, it should never be humans, we're not worth it.* 'Hello Qatux, thank you for seeing me,' he said formally.

Qatux raised its head. 'Hoshe Finn,' it sighed as air gusted through the pale wrinkles of flesh that made up its mouth region. 'Thank you for returning.' Two of its eyes turned in sequence to gaze at the shell. 'Is this her?'

'Yes.' Hoshe's e-butler sent a code to the shell's array, and the top dilated. Isabella was floating in a clear gel, eyes closed, slim tubes reaching in through her nostrils. Hundreds of fibre optic strands had been inserted into her shaven skull, forming a white gossamer crown. Long incisions on her arms, legs and torso, were covered with strips of healskin that were even paler than her Nordic skin. She looked so peaceful she was almost angelic. A vicious contrast to when she'd last been conscious.

'Her power cells have been removed,' Hoshe said, 'And the weapons neutralized. She's perfectly harmless now.'

'I understand.'

'The suspension shell array can raise her consciousness to whatever level you want. If you need her to be awake, nerve blocks can prevent her from moving.' Somehow, he felt as if he was betraying the human girl by surrendering her to the alien in such a helpless state.

'That will not be necessary. A neural cycle approximating deep sleep is all I require.'

'Very well. We need to know what is in her brain, why she did what she did. Paula suspects there is some kind of alien presence, or conditioning.'

'A valuable thing to learn. I have never tasted the memories of a living human brain before. I thank you for this gift.'

'It's not a gift,' Hoshe said sternly, marvelling that he found the courage to be so forthright. 'This is a service we ask you to provide, which benefits you in kind. Even so, we need complete reliability from you in this case.'

'And you shall have it, Hoshe,' the soft voice wheezed.

'How long do you think it will take?'

'That cannot be answered accurately until I have begun my examination. From what Paula has told me, the method of subornation does not appear to be a subtle one.'

'Is there,' Hoshe scratched at the back of his neck, embarrassed to ask, 'any danger it could take you over?'

'A mental virus? Moving from host to host, replicating and spreading. No, Hoshe, you need not worry. We Raiel have faced such incorporeal entities before. Our mentalities are not susceptible to such assaults. Even so, I will take care.'

'Thank you.' Hoshe bowed again, suddenly desperate to ask when and where the Raiel had encountered such things. The wall behind him parted to let him out into the funereal street. And that was it. He just wished he had more faith in the alien junkie.

*

It was dawn at the Tulip Mansion. Justine sat in the big octagonal conservatory in a mauve sweatshirt and baggy jeans, curled up on her battered leather couch as if it was a child's comfort toy. She couldn't stop her hands from stroking her belly, giving reassurance. To herself or her child, she wasn't sure which.

Gore walked in, dressed in a simple white shirt and dark brown trousers. He leant over the couch and gave Justine a light kiss. She gripped his forearm. 'Thanks, Dad.'

He gave a shrug, as close to embarrassment as she'd seen him in the last two hundred years. 'Nothing to it, his wetwiring was all cheap black-market shit. You could have beaten him off with a wet towel.'

'I was in a wet towel,' she said sardonically.

'Well there you go then, you didn't even need me.'

There was a small cough, and Justine looked up to see Paula standing at the entrance. 'Senator, I'm glad to see you're all right.'

'No thanks to your bunch of asshole incompetents,' Gore snapped. 'What kind of piss-poor operation are you running? I'm not surprised Columbia kicked you out of the navy if this is an example of your results.'

'Dad,' Justine scolded.

'Your father is correct,' Paula said. 'The lapse in security is completely unacceptable. It appears that the Starflyer agent was waiting in your fridge; most of the food inside had been consumed. He must have been in there when the Senate Security team installed the upgrade. They will be suspended pending a disciplinary hearing.'

'And that will help how, exactly?'

'Dad, just drop it.'

'Ha,' Gore waved a hand in disgust. 'Thanks to the Investigator's screw-up I've got to put up with every news show on the unisphere showing the recording of me walking round Park Avenue with my dick hanging out.'

'And executing the assassin,' Paula said.

Justine gave the mansion's array an order, and the octagonal room's glass walls vanished behind a grey haze.

'That motherfucker was trying to kill my daughter; he's already killed my son, and countless others. You think I'm upset about killing him?'

'No. But the NYPD must show due process.'

'I talked to the detectives on the scene. If they want to know anything else they've got my lawyer's unisphere address.'

'Enough,' Justine snapped. 'Both of you. I'm shaky enough without you two shouting at each other in front of me. The big question is, do we now have enough evidence to force the Senate to take notice of the Starflyer?'

'The proof is certainly building,' Paula said. 'We've exposed Tarlo, which will help convince the Halgarths that this is not some personal power struggle. And people will be curious who sent the assassin against you, Senator.'

'Damn right,' Justine said. She'd already had several calls

from her fellow senators, and one from Patricia Kantil who'd expressed the President's concern at the incident. 'They'll expect a report from Senate Security.'

'So what are you going to say?' Gore asked.

'It still depends on Nigel Sheldon,' Paula said. She peered in at the crescent-shaped aquarium, watching the fish gliding round. 'If we announce the Starflyer's existence based on the evidence we have, we have to have at least one Dynasty supporting us. If the Sheldon Dynasty goes against us, we'll have lost every advantage we have. I know Admiral Kime believes it is real, but he has his hands tied by corrupted evidence.'

'Wilson knows it's real?' Gore asked. 'That's got to be a big bonus.'

'But I don't understand Sheldon's position,' Paula said. 'Everything he has done points to him being concerned for the Commonwealth. Yet Thompson was convinced it was his office that had blocked the Far Away cargo inspections I'd been pressing for.'

'I'm sorry,' Justine said. 'But I still can't lock that down.'

'Confront him,' Gore said. 'Put him in a position where he has to make a hard choice. That should tell us who he's playing for.'

'That seems reasonable,' Paula said. 'We still don't know exactly how the Starflyer controls humans. I'm expecting an answer to that shortly.'

'I hope you're not relying on Senate Security to supply it,' Gore said.

Justine gave him a fierce look.

'No. We secured Isabella Halgarth. Her mind is being examined by the Raiel for me.'

'Oh,' Gore said, slightly taken aback. 'Okay, that's a decent pedigree.'

'Do you have any ideas how we can approach Sheldon?' Paula asked.

Gore gave Justine a hard look.

'Me?' she asked.

'Yeah, you. Nobody in the Commonwealth is going to say no to meeting you right now.'

'I'm not sure we should be exposing the senator to any further possible confrontation with Starflyer agents,' Paula said.

'Hear hear,' Justine muttered.

'Campbell,' Gore said quickly. 'Use him. He's senior enough to get a direct line to Nigel.'

'All right,' Justine said. 'I can probably arrange that.'

'Have you got any idea what the Starflyer's next move will be?' Gore asked.

'Not specifically,' Paula said. 'I can only go by earlier Guardians releases. If they are correct it will return to Far Away. I already have a Senate Security covert observation team in place on Boongate watching for just such an attempt.'

'I'll reinforce it with our own people,' Gore said. 'If we don't gather enough open political support to force Doi into acknowledging the threat, we may have to shut the wormhole down by ourselves to prevent it going through.'

'That's risky,' Justine said.

'Better than being dead, girl.'

'Where is Mellanie right now?' Justine asked.

'She went to LA with a Senate Security escort,' Paula said. 'She said she had to collect Dudley Bose, she was worried about him.'

'The reporter whore has got her claws into Bose?' Gore said. 'Christ!'

'I think she should be brought in,' Justine said. 'Investigator, if you're finally satisfied she's not working for the Starflyer, she could be helpful to us. She obviously has connections of her own. We need information as much as we need allies, however unlikely they are.'

'I'll certainly suggest that to her,' Paula said.

'And I'll call Campbell,' Justine said.

*

Stig rolled out of bed just before dawn. His e-shielded room at the top of the rental house was almost empty; whitewashed plaster walls, bare carbon floorpanels, a crude dresser with a big china bowl and a jug of water on top. Shuttered doors opened onto a tiny Juliet balcony that gave him a view over the red pantile rooftops of Armstrong City's Scottish district. Grime-laden solar-charged globes rested in a series of alcoves at shoulder height around the walls, their glow diminished to a moonlight spark after eight hours of darkness. As he always left the balcony doors closed during the day, there was never enough light to fully recharge them.

He crossed the room and swung the thick burgundy curtain away from the arch which led to the tiny bathroom. A couple of polyphoto bulbs came on as he stepped in, filling the room with green-tinted light. Because of the city's lack of basic infrastructure, the toilet was a self-contained unit, an algaereactor made by an EcoGreen company on Earth over a century ago. Whatever biological processes went on in the compostor chamber behind the wall, the algae and bacteria certainly needed refreshing. The smell that drifted up made Stig's eyes water every morning. He peered at himself in the mirror, not liking the face he saw. It had been reprofiled after the Oaktier to LA run, giving him small flat ears and a squashed nose; skin that was a couple of shades darker than his original tone. The thick stubble was now ebony, while his close-cut hair remained mouse-brown. His own mother really hadn't recognized him when he returned.

The rental house got its water from big semi-organic precipitator leaves which hung from the eves and were heated by a row of solar panels up on the flat roof. Half of the hot tank had been emptied by his fellow residents last night, but Stig was always among the first to rise in the morning, so the water which squirted out of the shower nozzle was reasonably warm.

He stood under the spray and started to wash himself down. Water on Earth had always fascinated him, the speed it fell, the hard strike of droplets on skin. Here on Far Away water was a much gentler substance.

Olwen McOnna squeezed into the small cubical. She was only a few centimetres shorter than him, with a lean slim body that made her heavy breasts even more prominent. Red star OCtattoos glowed on her round cheeks, sending trailers coiling down her neck, which made her gaunt face even more hawk-ish. She pressed up against him, and he felt the rough scar tissue on her belly where the healskin had recently come off the burn she'd received when her force field skeleton was overloaded by a plasma shot. There were other scars he knew of on her body, acquired over the last few weeks. He had his own personal reminders of the increasing violence in Arm-strong City; his left arm was still difficult to move.

'The morning,' Olwen said, 'the one and only time men can always be relied on.' Her hand slid down to his erection, guiding the tip of his cock between her legs. He gripped her buttocks, lifting her feet off the shower floor, pushing her back into the tiled wall as he impaled her. She snarled in rough delight; her arms twined round his neck to hold herself in place as he thrust repeatedly.

They clung to each other for a while after the climax. Water splashing over both of them as tingling nerves returned to normality.

'Do you think that finally got me pregnant?' she mumbled, lowering her feet. 'It certainly felt good.'

'Well, thank the dreaming heavens for that.'

'If I was pregnant, you'd have to take me off active duty.'

'Is that why you're fucking me?'

She grinned. 'You got a better reason?'

Actually, he didn't, but he could hardly say that. They'd started sleeping together weeks ago. The constant danger, the adrenaline buzz, the fear; it all kicked the primal urges into high gear. And he knew damn well she didn't want to quit active duty.

Olwen turned around, letting the spray wash down her back. Stig finished soaping himself down, and stepped out. She joined him a minute later when he was almost finished towelling himself dry.

A long list of messages had arrived in his hold file overnight. He started working through them, building up a summary of events. The Institute had attacked another two Clan villages in the Dessault Mountains, with thankfully few casualties. The Clans were watching the movements of the Institute troops closely now; they'd been caught out too many times when the raids started, suffering awful fatalities. Surprise ambushes were becoming rare, although combating the Institute forays was using up a lot of Clan members. Members who should be helping to prepare for the planet's revenge right now. Stig didn't have as many people working in his teams as he would have liked.

There had been a couple of disturbances in the city during the night, not quite large enough to qualify as riots, but news about the navy ships had stirred up the general level of anxiety. Shops had been looted, some fires started, cars stolen and used as barricades. Sparky residents flinging missiles at police and Institute troops.

The teams which Stig had on duty during the night had been busy tracking Institute troop movements. On the map in his virtual vision it was clear what they were doing, consolidating their hold along a broad passage between First Foot Fall Plaza and the start of Highway One outside the city.

An Institute-assisted police team had raided a warehouse in the docks. Stig recognized it as one he'd been using to store equipment in right up until three days ago. The Institute was definitely picking up its intelligence-gathering operation.

There had also been arrests in the Chinese district on various warrants. Three of those taken into custody worked for the Barsoomian residence. The Institute wasn't yet challenging the Barsoomians directly, but they were definitely chipping round the edges.

The Governor had certified another three police precinct assistance contracts with the Institute.

'Shit.'

'What's the matter?' Olwen asked.

'The Governor signed over 3F Plaza.'

'To the Institute? Fuck it!'

'Yeah.' He pulled a fresh set of shorts and a T-shirt from his small bag, then put his force field skeleton suit over them and covered that with a check shirt, baggy jeans. The long leather biker jacket he'd bought in StPetersburg on Earth went on top. He slipped a slim harmonic blade into the top of his hiker boots. His ion pistols and high velocity machine carbines slotted into their holsters to be covered by the zipped up jacket. Grenades clipped into his belt. His arrays with their sophisticated sensors went into his chest pockets. Steel sunglasses with enhanced display functions hung on a purple surfer band round his neck.

Olwen finished dressing for the day in a similar fashion, with baggy sulphur-yellow trousers and a green rainjacket with North Sea Power Surfers printed across it.

They left the apartment block together. The streets were virtually deserted, with shop fronts still covered in fine carbon grilles. Ancient civicbots rolled slowly along the pavements, gathering up rubbish and washing away yesterday's grime. A few early delivery vans raced along the empty roads. Buses with the first shift workers slumped into their seats rumbled past in clouds of diesel fumes.

When Stig looked east, Far Away's sun was rising above the

horizon, sending a rosy glow to soak the city. He stopped at a mobile stall that was just setting up on a corner three hundred metres along the road from the rental house. The owner smiled happily at them as Stig ordered some bacon sandwiches and coffee for breakfast. They drank some fresh-squeezed orange juice while the man flipped their bacon slices on the griddle.

Stig called Keely McSobel, who was on duty in the room above the Halkin Ironmongery store. 'Anything near us?' he asked.

'No, you're cool, the Scottish quarter's pretty quiet. But they're really pouring their people into 3F Plaza. It's not just troops, either. Some tech types are in the gateway control building.'

'Damn, that's not good. Can you snoop round inside?'

'That's the second problem. The city net's links to CST's centre are being eliminated. I think they're physically cutting them.'

'Dreaming heavens, are we going to be able to get our calls through?'

'I'm not sure. I managed to get a scrutineer inside CST's arrays. It can't send much back without being detected now they've cut the bandwidth, but from what I can make out the Institute is setting up censor programs on all the Half Way channels. Any call going out through the link to the Commonwealth unisphere will be examined, same for anything coming in.'

'Bloody hell,' Stig finished his orange juice and pulled out a pure-nicotine cigarette. 'Good job, Keely. We're going to scout round 3F Plaza.'

'Be careful.'

They collected the sandwiches and coffee; and he started to tell Olwen about the Institute's latest accomplishment as they walked along towards Mantana Avenue, which was the quickest route to 3F Plaza.

'That's very provocative,' she said carefully. 'Especially on top of everything else this city is putting up with.'

'Yeah.' He lit the cigarette. 'They've already armour plated the route from the gateway to Highway One, now this. It can only mean one thing.'

'The Starflyer's coming.' She said it with a knowing gleam in her eyes. It was the moment every Guardian dreamed of. The showdown with their enemy. The planet's revenge.

'Yeah.'

*

They were very visible going down Mantana Avenue, the broad thoroughfare which linked First Foot Fall Plaza with the main government district. With a little uncharacteristic flourish of ambition, city planners had laid out a three-lane road as a transport centrepiece between the biggest commercial market and storage zone in the city and the civil servants who sought to regulate it. Then a wealthy Russian émigré had gifted the city with a thousand saplings of newly sequenced GM maple fur poplars. The trees were all planted along Mantana, growing fifty metres tall, with leaves that resembled woolly magenta catkins. For nearly a century the arboreal avenue was one of the city's grandest sights with the thick tall trees screening the road from the pavement.

Now, over half of the trees had withered and died from a native fungal virus that had re-established itself in the southern hemisphere and swept through the city a couple of decades back, spoiling the beautiful wall of drooping leaves that separated traffic from pedestrians. The Barsoomians had provided resistant saplings as replacements, but the uniformity of the Avenue would never be regained now, and a lot of the saplings had been vandalized. It left long segments of the pavement exposed.

Stig glanced at the buildings set back from the avenue with an innocent, absorbed expression as yet another convoy of six-wheeled Land Rover Cruisers roared along the road towards 3F Plaza, hooting crossly at any other vehicle impertinent enough to be on the same route. The buildings were three or four storeys high, and listed among Armstrong City's finest with their elaborate faux-Napoleonic façades. So he studied the cracks that were opening in the moulded-carbon fascia panels. Moulded carbon was one of Far Away's most popular building materials thanks to the oilfields not far outside the western outskirts of the city. Simple automated refineries churned out an unending supply of the cheap high-density panels. Back in the Commonwealth they were intended for warehouse cladding, or barns, or garages; something that would be torn down and replaced after a few decades. Time and weather exposure were always unkind to the panels; they weren't utilized for permanence. Far Away's construction industry had never quite grasped that notion. A good portion of Armstrong City appeared to possess the kind of crumbling edges and fractured walls that belonged to the most revered classic buildings in Europe's ancient capitals.

Along the fast-ageing frontage of Mantana Avenue, the ground floors were individual shops, as exclusive as anything could be on Far Away, while the offices above were mostly inhabited by lawyers and the local headquarters of big Commonwealth corporations, the only organizations who could afford the rent.

'Where in the dreaming heavens is everyone else?' Olwen complained as the Cruisers disappeared ahead of them. Even for early morning, there were remarkably few pedestrians abroad; the traffic was reduced as well. Normally there would be a stream of vans and lorries and carts going in and out of F3 Plaza in preparation of the day's commerce.

'Bad news travels fast,' Stig told her.

Half a kilometre from the Enfield entrance to F3 Plaza they took a side road off the avenue, and made their way through the clutter of secondary streets to Market Wall.

'Stig,' Keely called. 'Martin says he's seen a couple of blokes loitering round the end of Gallstal Street. It's the third time they've walked past.'

'Damnit,' Stig exclaimed. Gallstal Street was only a few hundred metres away from the Halkin Ironmongery store. He and Olwen were now fifty metres from the base of Market Wall. The merchants in the archways were starting to open for business. Everyone seemed a lot more meek and restrained than usual. 'Tell him to keep watching them; I want to know what they do next, if they're just on a loop. And tell the other sentries to scan round.'

'Aye, will do.'

'And Keely, prep for a crash evacuation.'

'You think so?'

'Yeah, do it.'

'What's up?' Olwen asked as he scowled.

'Possible reconnaissance on the store.' He was angry that he wasn't there to make a proper evaluation. *I ought to trust the others by now.*

'It was only a matter of time,' she said.

'Right.'

They reached the bottom of Market Wall, and started up one of the broad stone stairs which led to the raised souk. On the top, the stalls with their canopies of solarcloth and worn canvas shared the subdued air that infected the vendors at the base. He and Olwen did their best to blend in, but this hour was given over to chefs and owners of cafés and restaurants buying fresh food from bulk suppliers. It was like a massive extended family, with everybody knowing each other. So they wove through the ramshackle layout of tables and counters, ignoring the welcome smiles and promised bargains, trying not to be too obvious. When they reached the thick stone parapet, it was lined with cautiously curious people staring at events below. Stig edged through and glanced over. 'Bloody hell.'

It was as if an occupying army had landed in the middle of Armstrong City. Range Rover Cruisers were parked in a curving line in front of the gateway, their mounted kinetic weapons deployed and sweeping from side to side to protect the shimmering force field. More Cruisers were parked to block every entrance, except Enfield, where barriers and concrete cubes turned away all civilian traffic. The wide expanse of the Plaza was empty, something Stig had never seen before. The three big fountains were actually audible from the top of Market Wall as they pumped their white plumes into the air. Squads of Institute troops in flexarmour were going round the base of Market Wall, ordering the stallholders in the archways to shut up and go home. There were a few loud protestations, swiftly followed by the sounds of a brutal beating, screams, sobbing. The Institute was now in complete control here.

'Keely, give me status on the link to Half Way, please,' Stig asked.

'There are no links. They've cut every cable into the CST control centre except two, and they both have monitor programs that I wouldn't know how to circumvent. I'm sorry Stig, there's no direct line back to the Commonwealth any more.'

Stig clenched his jaw as he stared down at the dark armoured figures strutting across the dusty plaza below. 'What about Martin?'

'His two observers have gone, but Felix reports a possible in his zone.'

'Okay, get out now, that's an order. We'll regroup our headquarters at fall-back location three. Got that?'

'Yes, sir.'

The connection ended. Stig waited a few moments, and told his e-butler to connect him to the Halkin Ironmongery store. The address was inoperative. He smiled in grim satisfaction. Keely and the others were acting professionally.

'Let's go,' he told Olwen.

They retraced their path through the stalls, and started back down the broad stairs. 'What do we do now?' Olwen asked.

'I don't know. And don't tell the others that.'

'Sure.'

'Damnit, I should have seen this. I screwed up, completely. If Adam makes his blockade run now, they'll come out into the biggest concentration of Starflyer firepower on the planet. And we can't even warn him.'

'You'll find a way.'

'Don't say that, don't just wish that everything will be all right. The Starflyer just secured the only route onto the planet.'

'Johansson will see we've dropped out of communication, he'll know the Starflyer is on its way back.'

'There's a difference between knowing and being able to do anything about it.' He glanced back at the sturdy stone and concrete edifice of Market Wall. 'We might have to attack the Starflyer ourselves when it comes through.'

'But . . . the planet's revenge,' she said it in almost reverential tones.

'The planet will be revenged if the Starflyer dies. I need to get our heavy duty weapons ready. Just in case.'

*

Like most senior Dynasty members, Campbell Sheldon kept a private residence on Earth. His was on an artificial island, Nitachie, that had been built in the Seychelles several hundred years ago when the natural archipelago was threatened by rising sea levels. The Greenhouse effect never did achieve the worst case scenarios which the more evangelical Environmentalists claimed it would. Some of the smallest islands were swamped by exceptional high tides, but the relocation of the population to protected land never happened. Once the worst industrial polluters moved offplanet to the Big15, and the UFN Environment Commissioners introduced their onslaught of regulations, the climate began its turnaround towards the benign nineteenth-century ideal which was the goal to which the EcoGreen campaigners had dedicated themselves. The worst damage to the Seychelles in ecological terms was the coral bleaching, which had killed off thousands of reefs. Even that was being countered as new polyp was planted, allowing the magnificent coral to expand again.

From her private hypersonic, Justine could just see the odd glimmer of light which indicated an island. The rest of the sea was pitch black. There was no moon to shine off the water, and precious little starlight.

They began to decelerate hard, the nose pitching up as the delta-wing plane began its long curve towards the ocean thirteen miles below. Justine accessed the sensors in the needle nose as they descended. Nitachie was just visible against the dark water, a warm patch against the cooler sea. The island was square, three miles to a side, with long breakwaters extending out from the steep concrete walls, where white sand was building into deep curving beaches. Several lights twinkled around the solitary house, set above the northern side. As they swept in close she could see the glowing blue-green patch of a big oval swimming pool.

Red and green strobes were flashing on the landing pad, a metal grid standing a couple of hundred yards offshore. The small hypersonic settled with only the slightest bump.

Two of Justine's Senate Security bodyguards walked down the air stair. Only when they gave the all clear did she and Paula step outside. It was warm, even for the middle of the night. Justine breathed in the clean salt air, feeling quite invigorated after the cabin's air-conditioned purity.

Campbell Sheldon was standing at the side of the pad, flanked by his own security staff, dressed in a white and gold towelling robe. He yawned, trying to cover his mouth with his hand. 'Good to see you,' he said, and gave Justine a small kiss on the cheek. 'You okay? I accessed the reports from New York before I turned in.'

'I'm fine.' She was amused to see he had threadbare slippers on his feet.

'Sure.' Campbell was giving Paula a curious look. 'Investigator. Always a pleasure.'

'Mr Sheldon.'

'Do you mind if we go back into the hut?' Campbell asked. 'I'm not even on Seychelles time yet.'

'That would be nice,' Justine said.

There were a couple of small carts parked on the edge of the landing platform. They drove the little party back along the causeway and up to the house. Architecturally, Campbell's beach hut was all curving arches and glass bubbles. Even though the larger outside arches appeared to be open, they framed pressure curtains; a subtle air conditioning cooled the interior, extracting the worst of the humidity. He led them into a big lounge full of casual chairs. Justine sank down into soft white leather cushions, and nodded dismissal to the bodyguard team. Campbell's own security team withdrew. An e-shield came on around the room.

'Okay,' Campbell said, rubbing at his dark blond hair. 'You have my full and complete attention. You get shot at by the most lethal assassin in existence, and the first thing you do is come and see me. Why?'

'I came in person to emphasize how important this is to us. We need to know where the Sheldons stand on certain points, and I don't have time for the usual Senate Hall talking-in-bullshit routine. I'm only a senator by default.'

'A damn good one, I'd say. I access our Dynasty's political office bulletin.'

'Thanks.'

'So ask away. I'll answer whatever I can, and if I can't I'll tell you. We know each other well enough for that.'

'Very well.' Justine leaned forward slightly. 'There's going to be a vote in the Security Oversight Committee, engineered by Valetta, to dismiss Paula from Senate Security. I need to know which way the Sheldons will vote.'

Campbell gave her a strange look. It was clear the request wasn't what he was expecting. He glanced at Paula, then back to Justine. 'You came here for this?'

'It's the strategy behind it which is crucial,' Justine said, 'And Campbell, the answer must come from Nigel himself. I don't want some aide in Jessica's office to trot out a standard response.'

Campbell gazed at Paula, clearly confused. 'I don't get this. Does the senator know about Merioneth?'

'No,' Paula said.

Justine turned to the Investigator. She knew she'd just lost a considerable amount of momentum. 'What's Merioneth?' she asked in annoyance. Her e-butler flipped a file up into her virtual vision which told her Merioneth was an Independent world which had left the Commonwealth over a century ago.

'An old case,' Paula said.

'For which our Dynasty was, and remains, deeply indebted to the Investigator,' Campbell said.

'That's the problem,' Paula said. 'And why I'm here to back up the senator. I do need to know your current policy towards me.'

Campbell remained silent for a moment, his eyes studying data in his virtual vision. 'This is connected with Illuminatus, not the assassination attempt. Right? One of your old team was some kind of infiltrator.'

'Tarlo, yes. But this is connected with the assassination, too, and your Dynasty's political strategy. The question about my future is the key to that.'

'This is why I chose the development side of CST, not politics,' Campbell said. 'The intrigue and backstabbings that you people . . .' He shuddered.

'Can you get us the answer?' Justine inquired.

'You want me to ask Nigel personally if the Dynasty is trying to fire Paula?'

'Yes please.'

'Right,' he said briskly. 'If that's what you want, then that's what you get. Hang on a moment.' He closed his eyes and sank back in the thick cushions of his own chair.

Justine turned to Paula. 'Merioneth?'

'Long story from a long time ago. I took a holiday from the Directorate to finish up a case on the planet after it went Independent.'

'After?' Justine couldn't keep the surprise out of her voice.

'Yes.'

'Oh.' Not for the first time, Justine considered how totally boring her own life was compared to that of the Investigator. *Until recently.*

Campbell's eyes opened. There was a bad boy smirk on his face. 'Well, that's me out of favour for a week. I interrupted Nigel while he was, er, busy.'

'What did he say?' Justine asked. It came out uncharacteristically needy. She was trying to keep calm, though she saw her hands were trembling.

'The Sheldon Dynasty has every confidence in Investigator Myo, and will be happy for her to carry on her job with Senate Security unhindered. The senator for Augusta will make that very clear to the Halgarths. We will oppose any removal proposal.'

Justine let out a long breath, almost a sob. Her eyes were watering. She knew it was hormones, and didn't care that Campbell was seeing her like this. But the relief was incredible. She'd been too frightened to consider what would have happened if Nigel had been in league with the Starflyer.

'Jesus,' Campbell said as he stared at Justine. 'What the hell is going on here?' He rose from his seat and took her hand. She sniffed, wiping away some tears.

'Sorry,' she said. 'I'm a bit of a mess right now.'

'This isn't the gorgeous Justine I remember,' he said softly. 'Perhaps you should stay and get some rest, recover from your ordeal. I can't think of a more relaxing place than Nitachie. There is a spare bed. There's also my bed.'

She smiled weakly at his playfulness.

'We need to see Nigel Sheldon,' Paula said. 'Could you please schedule a meeting with him for myself and the senator?'

Campbell's expression was close to indignation at the Investigator's lack of tact. Justine's grin broadened. 'I'm afraid the Investigator's right. We do need to see Nigel. It's very urgent.'

'Very well,' he said with remarkable dignity. 'I'll call him again and—' He broke off, his eyes widening in surprise at the priority data sliding down his virtual vision.

Justine was seeing the same thing. An ultra-secure alert from the navy was flashing up details about hundreds of new alien wormholes opening in Commonwealth star systems.

11

'Mark!'

'Huh?' Mark snapped his eyes open. He hadn't been sleeping on the job. No. Just quietly resting while the engineeringbot ran its new program cycle. He blinked some focus into his eyes, and concentrated on the junction between the force field generator and its secondary phase alignment module. The bot's instrument arms had withdrawn after establishing a seal. 'Yeah, looks good. Run the power test.'

'Okay, activating main circuitry now,' Thame said. He was the *Charybdis* technical officer, another Sheldon, a ninth generation grandson of Nigel. It had always been difficult for Mark to work out the hierarchy the Sheldons employed. Basically, the lower the number in your connection the more important you were. Or thought you were. Though, Mark had to admit, everyone involved in the lifeboat project was certainly competent. It was that little nuance of superiority they had whenever they said their name which irritated him.

A row of red LEDs set into the module's casing came on, flashing in sequence before steadying to a permanent glow. Corresponding schematics slid across Mark's virtual vision, complete with green icons. 'Okay, we have functionality,' he said. A yawn made him pause for a moment then he confirmed the engineeringbot's new sequence, the fifth they'd tried, as valid to the assembly bay's RI.

Despite every misgiving, transplanting the frigate assembly bay to the *Searcher* had worked. Locked up inside the mechanical labyrinth, working constantly, he hadn't even been aware of the flight. Now they were holding station in the Wessex system's cometary belt, waiting for Mark and his team to complete the *Charybdis*. None of them had slept for the last twenty-four hours, and most of them had worked their full shift before that.

The engineeringbot slid away from the generator. Mark let himself drift back behind it, watching out for girders and struts. He knew he was starting to make mistakes, his bruised face was only one reminder. A simple collision with a gantry junction which should never have happened. Wouldn't have happened if he wasn't so exhausted. 'What's next?'

'Thermal coupling to the back-up quantum fold initiator, portside.'

'On my way.' Mark didn't have a clue what the initiator was, nor what it did. Frankly, he didn't care. He just concentrated on plumbing the damn components into their power and support services. A schematic appeared in his virtual vision, showing him the initiator's location. He started to crawl over the hull. Two thirds of the active-stealth covering was now in place around the frigate, even in its powered-down state it was eerily black, a pool of darkness rather than a surface that was simply non-reflective. The gaps waiting to be filled allowed access to systems which weren't yet operational, and needed human supervision. Bots and manipulator arms were clustered over them, along with technicians from Mark's team. The *Charybdis* crew, Otis, Thame and Luke, had taken up permanent residence in the frigate's cabin to run diagnostics from there.

As he hauled himself along he passed the weapons scientists. He couldn't help glancing at them, eleven ordinary-looking people in padded freefall overalls and helmets, floating round the missile. There had been quiet rumours about what the frigates would be armed with back at the assembly platform and the town. Superweapons capable of protecting the fleet from any threat. Mark hadn't paid a lot of attention, even with Liz hungry for gossip each evening. Since the *Searcher* left, his team had talked of little else. Every time one of them had drifted by him on their way to another job they'd shared a few words; to his surprise, Mark had even joined in with the speculation, passing on what he'd heard in turn.

The assembly bay didn't have a mechanism for loading missiles into the frigate. That was supposed to happen in another facility. So the scientists were having to improvise. The missile was strapped to a medium-mass manipulator arm, which was inching it slowly down into the magazine chamber. It looked ordinary enough, a smooth, steel-silver cylinder five metres long, with a thick central bulge. The extremely nervous respect which the scientists treated it with made the hairs along his spine creep. He no longer believed the rumours of mere planetsmashers and warped-quark bullets; whatever they'd built was insanely lethal. You only had to see their faces to know that.

That warhead was going to make genocide possible. Back on Elan when they were running from the aliens he would have happily pressed the button. Now he wasn't so sure. It was the kind of thing that people like him never, *ever*, got involved with.

He arrived at the open section of hull his schematic indicated, from which an access interstice led deep inside the guts of the frigate. The initiator sat halfway along the narrow gap, a golden sphere with peculiar green triangles jutting up from it. There was a nest of unconnected thermal conductor filaments wrapped round it, with their manufacturer tags still attached. 'Okay,' he told Thame. 'I'm here. 'What have the bots tried so far?'

*

Oscar's starship, the *Dublin*, was orbiting a thousand kilometres above the Finnish world Hanko when the alert came
through. It had been a miserable duty so far, five people
spending ten days crammed into a single circular cabin. In
theory the cabin wasn't too bad: it was a good eight metres
wide, with three metres between the flat bulkheads. Then you
took out the partitioned-off sleeping section, and the laughably
titled bathroom facility, and the remaining available volume
was considerably reduced. In zero gee such a space was a little
less cramped, but that was a relative thing. The five flight
couches were lined up along the rear bulkhead, bulky padded
shelves that had plyplastic secured i-pads, built-in human
waste management tubes, and fluid food dispensers. Once
you'd strapped yourself in, while trying not to jam knees and
elbows into the person next to you, the couch slid back neatly
into the operations segment. Oscar likened it to lying on the
tongue of a dinosaur as it pulled you into its mouth.

Once in place inside the operations section, there was a
half metre space between your nose and the matt-black curving
control console with its high-rez display portals that filled the
gap with projections of the tactical display and ship-status
schematics. Oscar's first officer, Lieutenant Commander
Hywel, claimed that coffins were a lot less claustrophobic,
although admittedly not as colourful.

With Hywel taking the couch to Oscar's left where he
monitored the sensor feeds; it left the other three couches for
Teague, the engineering officer, Dervla who had recently
qualified as their ftl drive technician, and Reuben, who had
been seconded from the Seattle Project in charge of weapons.

Dervla was in the sleep section, and Hywel eating his meal
of microwaved stroganoff goo out in the main cabin as red
icons flashed up in Oscar's virtual vision. Detector stations
down on Hanko and in high orbit had detected seventy-two
wormholes opening, forming a loose sphere at three AUs
distance from the star.

An adrenaline surge quickly banished Oscar's lethargy and mild depression. 'What the hell are they doing out there?' he demanded. Data from their secure link to Base One through Hanko's unisphere showed that several Commonwealth worlds were now under a similar pattern of invasion. 'Dervla, Hywel, get in here now.'

'Ships coming through,' Teague said. 'God, they're fast. The wormholes aren't switching location like last time.'

'Right.' Oscar watched the graphics unfolding around him, then concentrated on one wormhole. The Prime ships were coming through nose to tail. Ten in the first minute. It was a quantity repeated at each of the other seventy-one openings.

'Ships identified as space combat type three,' Teague said. 'They're accelerating at eight gees, broad dispersal pattern. Damn it, we're never going to intercept those wormholes with our Douvoir missiles.'

'Clever,' Oscar muttered. He watched the graphic showing him Douvoir missiles leaping out of Hanko's ten orbital defence stations, neon green lines streaking straight out from the planet, aligned on the Prime wormholes. It was going to take them a good eight minutes to reach their targets. 'They'll just switch locations before impact. Damnit!' His virtual hands were racing over icons and speed-control activators, synchronizing with Reuben as they brought the *Dublin* up to combat readiness. 'What's the planet status?'

'City force fields powering up,' Teague said. 'Combat aerobots launching. We have command of orbital defence stations.'

'Much good it'll do us,' Oscar grumbled.

'The Douvoirs can take out the ships,' Reuben said. 'They can't dodge.'

'Check the dispersal,' Oscar told him. 'One Douvoir missile per ship is not good. This deployment is designed to flood the system with their ships, and we don't have anything like the capacity to knock them out. The Douvoirs were designed to hit strategic targets.'

'The planetary defences can cope with any approaching hostile,' Teague said.

'Not an armada. They can send ten thousand an hour at us.'

'We can't evacuate,' Hywel said. 'Not again. 'There's got to be a way of keeping them back.'

Oscar said nothing. He couldn't think of any way to repel the bulk of the Prime ships. *Dublin* could probably take out a hundred or so, but there were already more than that in-system. When he summoned the navy's overview, he saw that forty-eight Commonwealth worlds were under attack. The Primes were using the same long-range injection strategy in all of them.

As the Douvoir missiles launched from Hanko's defence stations closed in on the Prime wormholes, they began to switch location.

'Do we send the Douvoirs chasing wormholes?' Reuben asked. 'Or are we going to knock out some ships?'

When Oscar checked the tactical display, he saw there were already more than two thousand Prime ships in-system. 'Keep harrying the wormholes for now. Fleet command will let us know if they want us to switch tactics.'

'Captain,' Hywel said. 'More wormhole activity.'

'Where?'

'Our hysradar is picking up an emergence . . . four hundred and eighty thousand kilometres out from the star's corona.'

'Where?' Oscar thought he'd misheard.

'Directly above the sun.'

Oscar focused on the tactical display which was reconfiguring to show the latest development. Sure enough, a wormhole had opened close to Hanko's G-class star. As he watched, ships started to slide through. 'Fire a pair of Douvoirs at it,' he ordered, even though he knew it was pointless, it would take the Douvoirs a couple of minutes to reach the new invasion point. 'What the hell are they doing there?'

'I don't know,' Hywel said.

*

The level of tension in Wilson's office was actually higher than it had reached during the first Prime invasion. Five minutes in, and Wilson was already contemplating doing his deep breathing exercise routine.

All of the Big15, as well as the fully developed worlds had been mass-producing components for the missiles ever since the first invasion. The cost had been phenomenal, as much as the entire *Moscow*-class fleet. Even Dimitri had been satisfied about the level of protection they'd wrapped around Commonwealth planets over the last few weeks. Now it looked like they had seriously underestimated the Primes again.

The Douvoirs were taking too long to get out to the wormholes. Fleet Command, operating from a centre several floors below his office in Pentagon II, was working on eventual scenarios the Primes would use to attack the planets, massed waves or an all-in-one blitz. With the ships still flooding through, they were reserving judgement; but either way there were serious limits on how many the planetary defences could fend off, even when assisted by navy ships.

Evacuation had already been raised several times. Wilson hated having to suggest that to the planetary governments and CST, but he was fatalistic enough to see that was the way the invasion was shaping up.

Physically, Wilson had been joined by Anna, of course, and Rafael. Dimitri had also been on standby in Pentagon II, and was slouched in one of the chairs, watching the holographic specks of light whirl around him. So far he'd said very little, occasionally contacting his team in StPetersburg to discuss the pattern of the attack. From the Seattle Project, Tunde Sutton and Natasha Kersley were attending via an ultra secure link.

Holographic images of President Doi and Nigel Sheldon had also materialized on either side of Wilson. So far the President had said very little; while Nigel's worried expression was almost accusatory.

'Confirmed forty-eight points of attack,' Anna said. 'They're all in phase two space except for Omoloy, Vyborg, Ilichio, and Lowick.'

'Roughly the distribution we expected,' Dimitri said. He didn't press the point. It was his team which had been instrumental in deciding the distribution of the planetary defences and allocating starships to complement them, choices which had so far proved remarkably accurate. Only nine of the worlds under attack were without starship coverage.

Wilson took a moment to study the strategic display. The office projectors were showing Commonwealth space as a rough sphere just over two hundred light years across with a very erratic boundary. The Prime invasion was a hemispherical scarlet stain, centred around the Lost23, and intruding nearly ninety light-years inward.

'They're trying to gain Wessex again,' Nigel said.

'Can you use CST wormholes to deflect them?' Rafael asked.

'I'll look into it,' Nigel said. His image froze.

When Wilson flicked his attention to Wessex, the display expanded, showing him the *Tokyo* above the Big15 world, and Douvoir missiles chasing after Prime wormholes, never to catch them. Over four thousand ships were already in-system. There at least they would meet formidable resistance. The industrial facilities in orbit around Wessex were all heavily protected with force fields, atom lasers, and their own close range interceptor missiles. Multilayered force fields had roofed over Narrabri. Big aerobots patrolled at high altitude. It had more orbital defence stations than any other planet.

'When are you going to use the quantumbusters?' the President asked petulantly .

'When the tactical situation allows for it,' Wilson told her. 'It's designed for use against primary targets, or close-clustered ships. Neither of which we have at the moment. The Prime ships are all flying away from each other. They'll regroup eventually, as they close on our planets.'

'You mean it's useless?'

'In these circumstances it is of limited effectiveness,' Natasha said.

'Somebody tell me when we will be able to use it *effectively*.'

'When their ships begin to congregate again, then we'll be able to deploy them with some success,' Dimitri said.

Doi gave him a vicious look.

'I'd emphasize that even switched to a minimal effect radius, we shouldn't activate a quantumbuster within a million kilometres of any inhabited world,' Natasha Kersley said. 'That's the absolute minimum safe distance. Even if it only has the mass of a single Prime ship to work with, the radiation output would be seriously detrimental to the biosphere. They are doomsday weapons, Madam President. They were never intended to be used in dogfights.'

'You think we shouldn't have issued them to the navy starships for this?' Doi asked.

'I designed them, I advise on their use,' the physicist said. 'Ultimately, the situations in which they are deployed are a political decision.'

'Thank you, Natasha,' Wilson said before the argument and recriminations got out of hand.

'Additional wormhole activity,' Anna said. 'Prime wormholes opening near the stars of the planets they're invading. Damn, they're emerging close; approximately half a million kilometres above the corona. Seventeen of them have appeared so far.'

'Above the stars?' Tunde asked, frowning. 'I don't understand. What's coming through?' The faint waves of colour surrounding him rearranged themselves quickly, displaying the hysradar returns of starships scanning the new development.

'Plenty of ships,' Anna said. 'Everyone is launching Douvoir missiles; the wormholes will be closed down in minutes.'

'Moved,' Dimitri said. 'They'll be moved in a few minutes.'

Tunde and Natasha exchanged a few words. 'I don't like the positioning,' Tunde said. 'It's constant, look. The wormholes are all opening above the equator of the star, and they are directly in line with the habitable planet of the system. In other words, it's the closest part of the star to the planet.'

'Meaning?' Rafael asked.

'I don't know, but it cannot be coincidence. Admiral, we really need to know what's being sent through.'

'Could it be something like a quantumbuster?' Wilson asked. The question generated a few moments of complete silence in the office. Wilson glanced at Nigel's frozen image, the Dynasty chief was still dealing with Wessex. Wilson wondered what the hell he was doing there that was more important than this.

'I can't answer that,' Tunde said. 'Obviously it is a possibility.'

'What could a quantumbuster do to a star?'

The physicists looked at each other, neither of them willing to take the lead. 'It would cause quite a disturbance to the photosphere,' Tunde said, 'There might even be some impact on the top of the convective zone. But the overall damage would be minimal.'

'Radiation emission wouldn't be minimal,' Natasha said. 'That would be extremely dangerous.'

'It's hardly an efficient use of a quantumbuster.'

'What else could it be?' Wilson tried to keep his voice level and calm.

Tunde raised his hands in an awkward gesture of doubt.

'We have diverted-energy-function nukes,' Natasha said

quickly. 'As do the Primes. This could well be a large-scale application of that process, powered by the star itself.'

'Those planets are an AU from their primaries,' Rafael protested. 'More in some cases. And you're saying this could be a beam weapon?'

'You wanted alternatives,' Natasha said in an accusing tone.

'Our detector network has now found thirty-eight wormholes close to the target stars,' Anna said.

Wilson's virtual finger reached for the *Tokyo*'s icon. He stopped. He hated, absolutely *hated*, himself for doing this. But this whole attack was pivotal, any and every action he took today could decide the fate of the Commonwealth. He had to have information he could trust implicitly. That meant the source must be someone he knew he could trust. He touched the *Dublin*'s icon. 'Oscar?'

'Hello, Admiral.'

'We need to know what's coming through that wormhole close to the star.'

'Hysradar is picking up returns consistent with class four and class seven Prime ships. We launched a pair of Douvoir missiles to close it down.'

'I know, but we need confirmation. Take a flyby. Stay in hyperspace, but get us a high-definition picture of what the bastards are up to.'

'You want us to leave Hanko orbit?'

'Yes, the planetary defences can insure no wormholes open close by. If the invasion pattern changes you can return immediately.'

'Acknowledged, leaving orbit now.'

'Boongate reports a wormhole near its star,' Anna said. 'That's completion, all forty-eight stars. Whatever they're doing, they're doing it to each star system they're invading. Large ship numbers coming through.'

'The Prime ships must have damn good force fields to

operate at that distance from a star,' Rafael said. 'It's hellish close.'

'Can the *Moscow* class fly in that close?' Wilson asked. He'd automatically assumed the *Dublin* would be in trouble if they were in real space a mere half million kilometres from a G-class star.

'Yes,' Tunde said. 'But I wouldn't recommend an extended combat time in such an environment, the stress level on the force field would undoubtedly lead to overload.'

'Same for the Prime ships, then,' Rafael said.

'Undoubtedly.'

'What are they up to?' Wilson whispered. His virtual hands rearranged the imagery icons, and the office's tactical display shrank slightly to accommodate the hysradar return from the *Dublin*. Four hundred and eighty thousand kilometres above Hanko's star, the Prime wormhole was holding steady. Over fifty ships were through now. The pair of Douvoir missiles Oscar had launched were closing fast. Ten seconds from impact, the wormhole closed.

'It's opening again,' Tunde said, scanning the projection. 'Twenty million kilometres away.'

'Douvoir missiles locking on,' Anna said. 'Nothing's coming through yet.'

The *Dublin*'s hysradar return was showing sixty-three Prime ships accelerating hard from the point where they'd emerged. Each of them was firing a flock of high acceleration missiles. The expanding globe of hardware was already five thousand kilometres across. Nuclear explosions began to blink around the periphery. The hysradar image immediately broke up into an uneven hash.

'What's happening?' Wilson asked.

'Interference,' Oscar reported. 'The nukes are somehow pumping out exotic energy pulses. It's screwing with our hysradar.'

'That's certainly one diverted energy function we haven't got,' Tunde said. 'A direct inversion to an exotic state. Natasha?'

'Well, it's obviously possible,' Natasha said. She sounded more intrigued than alarmed. 'I don't understand how the mechanism holds together under those conditions.'

'You're missing the point,' Dimitri said.

'Which is?' Natasha asked with cool politeness.

'They're going to a great deal of effort to hide something from us above those stars.' He indicated the image from the *Dublin*, which showed the star's vast curvature. The uniformity of the image was broken by a shimmering patch of silver and yellow particles which obscured over half of the surface. 'This is the only sensor blind-spot in the star system. Something is going on behind that interference, something they clearly consider extremely important to their attack.'

'The Primes are generating identical interference patterns in the other systems,' Anna said. 'It's a constant pattern.'

'Oscar,' Wilson said. 'We have to know what they're covering up.' He hoped the tension wasn't showing in his voice. But if the Primes did have something equal or even superior to quantumbusters this war was already over. A lot of his family would leave on the lifeboats that were in the last stages of assembly above Los Vada. *If they have time to reach them.* He assumed he'd be relatively safe on the High Angel, though God alone knew where it would fly away to.

'Roger that,' Oscar said. 'Standard sensors are useless this close to a star. We're going in closer.'

'Good luck,' Wilson told him.

*

The first tremor caught Oscar by surprise. His heart jumped in response. 'What the hell was that?'

The others were all lifting their heads from the flight couches, checking round the cabin. For what, Oscar couldn't imagine. A crack in the hull that was letting in solar wind? Crap. He'd always known and accepted that any attack powerful enough to have a physical impact on the starship would simply destroy it. Now another judder ran through the vessel, stronger this time – and they were still intact and alive. 'Somebody talk to me.'

'I think the exotic energy blasts from their diverted energy function nukes just hit our wormhole,' Dervla said. 'I'm certainly seeing a lot of unusual fluctuations around our compression dynamic wavefront.'

'Oh great,' Oscar said. 'A new threat. How badly can that hurt us?'

'I'm not sure,' she said. 'We never covered anything like this in training. I don't think it can break our boundary.'

A shudder made Oscar tense his whole body as the couch straps vibrated against him. It was like riding a white-water raft. The hologram display wobbled as his eyes tried to focus. He switched to virtual vision for primary information. Just in time. The next judder shook his body. Curses were mumbled through the narrow operations segment.

'Ten seconds to the missile formation,' Hywel said.

Oscar consulted the navigational grid. They were flying towards a star at nearly four times the speed of light. He wanted to say something to Dervla about making sure their course was correct, but harassing people at inappropriate moments wasn't the sign of good captaincy. So he trusted her with his life.

She was taking the *Dublin* in a long curve to solar south of the Prime incursion, heading past them to an altitude of four hundred thousand kilometres above the star. The shaking began to reduce as they left the explosive umbrella behind.

Their hysradar image began to sharpen as the RI brought filter programs online. Now the exotic energy pulses were displayed as black circular wavefronts, fading as they expanded. 'The ships are still in there,' Hywel said. 'And they're expending missiles at a phenomenal rate even by Prime standards. Oh. Wait—' The image shifted drastically as he instructed the RI to shift the main focus a hundred and eighty degrees. 'What's that?'

In the middle of the projection, a lone dot was rushing headlong into the star.

Oscar read the associated figures. 'Dear God, that's a hundred gee acceleration.'

'Two minutes until it reaches the corona,' Hywel said. 'What is that?'

'I don't know, but I don't like it at all. Wilson, are you receiving our hysradar data?'

'Yes,' the answer came back. 'Can you hit it with a Douvoir missile?'

'Not that close to a solar mass,' Reuben said. 'The gravity curvature is too strong.'

'He's right,' Dervla said. 'Our wormhole generator is having trouble maintaining boundary integrity this close. There's a lot of gravatonic distortion.'

'Oscar, we have got to know what that device is going to do,' Wilson said. 'Can you drop out of ftl and observe with standard sensors, please.'

Oscar heard at least two sharp pulls of breath inside the operations section. 'Roger that, stand by for full sensor observation.'

'Just how good is our force field?' Hywel muttered.

'It can stand this proximity,' Teague said. 'But we need to avoid combat with the Prime ships.'

'I'll try and remember that,' Oscar said dryly. 'Okay, Dervla, take us out of the wormhole. Hywel, full sensor scan as soon as we're in real space.'

'Aye, sir.'

Oscar couldn't help himself, his body braced as the ftl drive opened the wormhole and the *Dublin* slid out into real space. Nothing happened. No blinding white light and intolerable heat flooding through the cabin. *Damn, I'm twitchy.* He blinked, and started to study the sensor imagery.

Visual sensors showed a universe of two halves. One white, one black. For an instant he was back above the Dyson Alpha barrier in the *Second Chance*, where space was divided into two distinct sections. This time, there was nothing passive about the sheer white surface four hundred thousand kilometres away. The star's corona was in constant turbulent motion with waves and surges radiating a gale of particles outwards; ghostly prominences danced above the seething gas, flexing and twisting in the intense magnetic field. Space above them was dotted with the neon graphics tagging Prime ships and missiles.

'They've seen us,' Hywel said. 'Missile flight changing course. Accelerating at twenty gees.'

'How long have we got?' Oscar asked.

'Five minutes until they reach nominal engagement distance.'

'Okay. What about the device they've fired into the star?'

The imagery expanded as Hywel tracked the device with as many sensors as he could. It was still accelerating into the corona at a hundred gees. A long wake of swirling plasma stretched out for thousands of kilometres behind it. Shock waves rippled away from its protective force field, creating violet circles that were immediately torn apart by the raging solar wind.

'That is a very powerful force field,' Teague said. 'I'm not sure we could withstand that kind of environment. It had to be built specifically for this flight.'

'So what kind of device do you send into a star?' Hywel asked, his voice edgy.

'A bad one,' Reuben said. 'And I don't care how good its force field is, it won't survive much longer. The coronal density is picking up, and that speed will generate impacts that could puncture anything.'

'But there's no kind of—' Hywel began. 'Oh, the fusion drive has switched off.'

Oscar watched the dark speck as it drilled through the super-velocity plasma. He realized he was holding his breath. 'If it's a quantumbuster?' he asked.

'Then we're probably dead,' Reuben said. 'But even if its force field holds out until it's within range of the chromosphere, the effect of the blast will be minimal as far as Hanko is concerned. If you've got them, use them against the planet directly. Don't screw around letting them off an AU away like this.'

Oscar waited as the device streaked downwards. He wondered if he had time to update his secure store. Probably not. He'd done it this morning, and decided that anyway, he probably didn't want to remember this time in the *Dublin*. Although . . . should he leave his future incarnation a message from now saying he didn't want to remember? *Stupid idea.*

'Here we go,' Hywel said tersely.

Oscar was surprised to see it was the quantum signature scan that was changing. It was as if petals were unfurling from the device, giant thousand-kilometre long ovals of altered quantum fields, overlapping and twisted. They began to rotate.

'Magnetic effect picking up,' Hywel warned.

The star's massive flux lines were curving around the ephemeral quantum wings. Plasma followed, dragged into an elongated eddy curving round the device's rigid wake.

'What the hell *is* that?' Dervla asked with quiet unease.

'Wilson?' Oscar asked. 'Anyone from the Seattle Project got an opinion?' The quantum effect radiating out from the device was now three thousand miles in diameter. It began to speed up. The knot it was stirring up in the corona was visible to the *Dublin*'s heavily filtered optical sensors.

'Not yet,' Wilson replied.

'Captain,' Reuben called. 'The Prime missiles are getting close. If we have to ward off some kind of energy strike from the device as well as dealing with them, we're going to be in serious trouble.'

'Launch a counter-missile salvo,' Oscar ordered. 'We have to stay here and report on this.' He knew it was critical.

'One minute until it hits the upper corona,' Hywel said. 'It's having a hell of an impact on the solar wind.'

'Are you sure it can't survive impact?'

'I don't know. It's changed so much, the quantum fluctuations at the core are significantly altered. I'm not sure what it is any more.'

'What do you mean?'

'It might not qualify as pure matter any more. That distortion is very weird. It seems to be incorporating the force field, and that quantum signature – I've never seen anything like it.'

When Oscar consulted the sensor projection, the device's rotating wings were now close to seven thousand kilometres wide. The operation section's display superimposed them on the corona as black ellipses. Plasma writhed around them, hurling off dense vortices that leapt up into space, dissipating as they rose. The scale of the effect was unnerving. 'If it's not matter, then what is it?'

'Some kind of energy nexus, I think. I'm not sure. It's having an unusual effect on the surrounding mass properties.'

The Prime device spun down into the corona. It was like watching a comet striking the atmosphere of an H-congruous planet. The star's million degree outer layer ruptured in a crowned plume that rose higher than any of the prominences. Continent-sized cataracts of plasma curved back down only to be warped by the twisted magnetic flux. A secondary plume rose inside the core of the first, the cooler chromosphere matter streaking up to escape from the astonishing deformation produced by the device's impact.

'Holy shit,' Oscar grunted.

'So what good did that do them?' Dervla complained.

'That quantum effect is still functional, and growing,' Hywel reported. 'The device is agitating the corona, probably the photosphere, too. It's big enough.'

'Holding the wound open,' Oscar muttered. The blemish on the star's surface was apparent in just about every spectrum: quantum, magnetic, visible. 'Radiation,' he said sharply. 'Hywel, what's the radiation emission like?'

'Rising, and fast. Christ. Captain, we've got to move, we're directly above it.'

'I second that,' Reuben said. 'One minute until missile engagement.'

'Dervla, take us a quarter of a million kilometres, up and out.'

'Aye, sir.'

The *Dublin* dropped into ftl for thirty seconds. Time mostly taken up by Dervla confirming their relative position before emerging from the wormhole again.

When the ship's sensors lined up on the strike zone, the turbulence in the corona was a tight-packed cone spewing streamers from its open crest. They could see it growing.

'The device is still active in there,' Hywel said. 'Quantum fluctuations are registering at the same level as before. Magnetic activity is increasing, the damn thing is tightening the flux lines like a tourniquet.'

'Oscar,' Wilson called. 'Tunde and Natasha believe we're seeing a flare bomb at work.'

'A what?' he asked, startled. 'You mean something like the one used at Far Away?'

'Could be.' Wilson's voice was perfectly level. 'The disturbance in the corona is producing a huge particle discharge, and it's still building. The radiation is going to saturate Hanko, and we have no idea how long it will go on for. The Far Away flare lasted over a week. Oscar, the biosphere won't survive that.'

'Oh shit.' Despite the catastrophe facing the planet he

was supposed to be defending, Oscar was trying to think how the Primes had wound up with a flare bomb. Somehow, the Starflyer must have given them the information on how to build one. *Was that what the* Second Chance *dish was transmitting?*

'They're going to sterilize each of the new star systems they're invading,' Wilson said. 'We'll be forced to evacuate forty-eight worlds.'

'And that's just so far today,' Reuben grunted.

'What do we do?' Oscar asked. 'Do Tunde and Natasha think a quantumbuster will work against the flare bomb?'

'We don't know. But we're going to have to find out. We want you to take the *Dublin* as close as you can to the star and fire a quantumbuster into the flare. Switch it to maximum effect radius.'

'Understood.'

'Admiral, if you use a quantumbuster against a star at that rating, you'll just be adding to the quantity of energy it's pumping out,' Reuben said. 'It'll make the radiation deluge even worse.'

'We understand that, Reuben,' Natasha said. 'But even on maximum effect radius a quantumbuster mass to energy conversion is very short lived, and if it knocks out the flare bomb then only half of the planet will be subject to the radiation. We have no choice. We have to pray that this works.'

'Acknowledged.'

'All right,' Oscar said. 'Reuben, arm a quantumbuster, and set it to maximum effect radius. I'm loading my authorization code now. Hywel.'

'Entered,' the first officer said.

Oscar's virtual vision showed him a quantumbuster was now active. 'Thank you. Dervla, take us in as close as you can. We don't have much time.'

'Aye, sir.'

'We can survive for five seconds at a hundred thousand kilometres,' Teague said.

'Then that's the distance. Let's go, people.'

*

'Mark, we *really* need those flux shunt regulators integrated.' Thame was trying to keep his voice level and calm, but there was too much stress creeping in; the croak of a man who'd survived the last forty hours on no sleep and way too much caffeine. A man who was getting desperate. Not far from the *Searcher*, Prime warships were massing. A flare bomb was descending into Wessex's star. The beginning of the end of the human race was happening right outside.

No pressure.

Mark didn't bother answering. Didn't dare concentrate on anything but the job. His sight was half blood-red blotches. Hands were trembling. Not that the shakes were obvious; he was in a spacesuit, with thick gauntlets tipped by mico-sensitive patches. The frigate assembly bay was in a vacuum. Ready to go, to send the warship out into the void where battle could be joined. Except the regulators still wouldn't function properly. Mark was actually working on the power feed on the frame next to one of the nine units. All the high-capacity cables were locked into place on the power feed, now he was working his way down the management program registry. Lines of faint emerald text stretching higher than a skyscraper flowed through his virtual vision. He altered and modified the lines as they passed by. It was instinct only now, the echoing memory of power supply systems he'd handled in the past, simple fixes and patches stored in old insert files that he edited into the new instructions, reformatting, moulding the software into something he simply felt might work.

'I'm sorry to ask, Mark, but can you give us any kind of timescale?' Nigel Sheldon asked. His voice was a lot more controlled than Thame, but there was a real need burning in there.

'I'm trying,' Mark whimpered. 'I'M TRYING!' His vision blurred completely as tears swelled across his eyes. He blinked them away. The last few luminous green lines were running across his virtual vision. A patch he'd written to monitor feedback anti-cycle safety directives in Ulon Valley autopickers was slipped in. He could smell the moist air, the sugar scent of the vines as he told the program to run.

Something turned from red to green.

'It's working!' Thame screamed. 'Power initiation sequence enabled. Mark, you fucking did it.'

In front of Mark's visor, red lights on the power feed casing were turning to green. A judder of relief ran down his body. His e-butler routed copies of the program into every regulator power feed on the frigate.

'Fantastic job.' Dutton-Smith patted Mark on his shoulder. 'Let's go.'

Mark didn't move. Couldn't. His muscles had packed up. He was curling into the foetal position.

'Okay, Mark,' Dutton-Smith said kindly. He tugged his boss out of the tiny crawl space. They only just got clear as a heavy manipulator arm slid the hull section into place. Eight identical sections were being fixed by the assembly bay RI over the frigate's other flux regulators.

Dutton-Smith clung to the gridwork as it slowly retracted from the *Charybdis*, holding Mark's inert form away from the umbilical bridges as they telescoped back. The frigate slid past them in a smooth, aquatic motion out into open space. There was no exhaust, no crude rockets roaring flame from bell-shaped nozzles, the *Charybdis* moved by direct gravospacial manipulation. Its perfectly black bulk blotted out a few dim stars. Then it vanished.

*

The response of the human navy class to the start of the second incursion matched MorningLightMountain's predictions. Their missiles and beam weapons were more than adequate to protect the planets in the star systems had it opened its wormholes in close orbit again. Instead, it sent its fleets of ships into the star systems a long way clear of the human-colonized worlds. They launched their superluminal missiles at once, but the flight time enabled MorningLight-Mountain to send hundreds of ships through before there was any danger of interception. When the missiles did get close, it switched the wormhole locations and sent more ships through.

With the fleet dispersal proceeding as planned, Morning-LightMountain began stage two.

Wormholes opened as close as possible to the stars of each new incursion system. Strong beams of light shone back through, brightening the asteroids and equipment which orbited the interstellar wormhole at the staging post. Ships were dispatched through to the dangerous environment, forming a protective perimeter. As predicted, the humans had not thought to station any defences around their stars.

MorningLightMountain began firing its corona-rupture machine at the forty-eight new stars. The covering ships began their interference strategy.

Only at one star, Hanko, did the humans dispatch a starship to investigate. MorningLightMountain could do nothing more now but watch and wait. The corona-rupture machines were the most heavily automated apparatus it had ever built. It would never be able to place an immotile cluster in one of the small vessels, so it had to rely on electronics, which was a point of concern.

Several rival immotiles had developed their own versions of the corona-rupture technique during the centuries before the barrier imprisoned them. None could ever test it, to do so would be to kill all Prime life on the homeworld. It had remained a theory for over a thousand years, until the imprisonment ended.

When it wiped out the other immotile groups, MorningLightMountain was *surprised* that several of them had actually built and maintained corona-rupture machines. Investigation of their dwindling thoughts showed they were concerned about its own dominance, and believed the machines to be the last deterrent. With wormholes open to other star systems, MorningLightMountain had begun a comprehensive research project, firing the different kinds of corona-rupture machines at its disposal, and observing the results, using them to refine the design. It was *gratifying* to discover its own design was amongst the best.

Now it watched as the ruptures began, evolving into solar flares which jetted out vast clouds of particle radiation that would soon envelop the Commonwealth worlds. All the non-Prime life dwelling on the planets would sicken and die. It was the simplest, most effective solution to the problems it was facing. MorningLightMountain had suffered unexpected setbacks as it began to grow its crops on the new 23 worlds. Often it would see the seeds germinate, only for the young shoots to suffer some unknown malaise and wither away. The malady was different on every planet, and often varied from continent to continent.

Strangely, it was data which it mined from human sources that gave it the reason. Soil bacteria was different everywhere: non-Prime. Something it hadn't realized, but was obvious with *hindsight*. In addition, there were a myriad of spores and viruses, micro organisms, and insects which would consume or clash with Prime-life plants. Humans countered this problem with genetically modified terrestrial crops that could grow on their newly acquired worlds. They twisted their food symbiosis plants into non-terrestrial versions; crops looked the same but their cellular biochemical functions were subtly different. Nothing humans did *surprised* MorningLightMountain any more; but it was unable to understand how they could betray their biological heritage so casually. Did the integrity of their evolution mean nothing to them? Apparently not.

The human starship at Hanko had jumped away from the growing flare, now it returned, emerging so close to the star that MorningLightMountain had trouble tracking it. A sensor on one of its covering ships detected a pulse of electromagnetic energy which might have been the starship firing something with a fusion drive. Then the ship jumped clear again. MorningLightMountain waited to see what would happen. It could not envisage a weapon capable of destroying a corona-rupture machine.

After the flare radiation had scoured each of the new forty-eight planets clean of their antagonistic alien life, MorningLightMountain would introduce Prime life onto all of them. It would be the true beginning of Primeforming the galaxy. With their food dead and rotting, the humans would be forced to abandon their worlds, leaving their valuable industrial equipment behind them. Should they choose to stay and fight for possession of their dead planets, the fleets were ready to overwhelm their defences without any risk to itself. This was an *economic* method of incursion. MorningLightMountain had expended an inordinate amount of resources to rebuild and salvage from the wreckage of conflict on the new 23, as well as countering all the guerrilla sabotage. Human equipment and technology was useful, but it was *paying* too high a *price* for acquiring it. And this second incursion included the Big15 world, Wessex, with its expansive industrial facilities. This time, MorningLightMountain would not be beaten back.

The violence of the explosion was extraordinary. MorningLightMountain thought the sensors on its ships were simultaneously malfunctioning. The surface of Hanko's sun heaved. A titanic crater bulged downwards into the photosphere, overwhelming the still-rising flare. From the centre, a gigantic sphere of plasma leapt upwards, as if the star was giving birth to an infant of its own kind. Hard radiation from the middle of the explosion sliced clean through the force fields on every ship MorningLightMountain had sent through to provide cover, vaporizing them instantly.

For a moment MorningLightMountain had no way of knowing what was happening to Hanko's star. When it reopened the wormhole five million kilometres away and cautiously extended sensors through, it saw the photosphere crater wall collapsing, sending a circular wave racing out across the star's surface. The plasma sphere had separated from the corona, racing into space at near-relativistic speed, and expanding fast. MorningLightMountain could no longer detect the flare amid the conflagration raging within the corona. Nor was there any indication of the quantum effect which its machine produced.

MorningLightMountain was shocked by the scale of the event. It had no idea that humans had such a powerful weapon available. They were far more dangerous than it had ever suspected. For the first time since the barrier came down, it began to question the advisability of its actions.

*

'It works,' Tunde said, a cautious grin on his face. 'The flare's been wiped out.'

'Lost under a much greater radiation discharge,' Rafael said.

Everyone in the office was riveted on the sensor imagery provided by the *Dublin*, which was now standing off ten million kilometres from Hanko's star. Wilson watched sluggish waves spreading out across the corona from the quantum-buster detonation, then the size registered, and he realized they weren't sluggish at all. The star's prominences were writhing wildly as the magnetic field oscillated. Two million kilometres above the dissipating depression, the sphere of plasma had now reached the same diameter as Saturn, and was cooling rapidly. Its cohesion was breaking down, allowing it to spew off ephemeral rivers of waning ions as bright as a comet's tail. The hard radiation emission from the centre of the explosion was also reducing. Even at ten million kilometres, the *Dublin*'s force field had been badly strained to maintain cohesion under the impact.

'But a shorter one,' Tunde countered immediately. 'And the inverse square law works to our advantage here. Hanko is an AU away, after all.'

'There was no alternative,' Natasha said. 'This way the planets get a chance at overall biological survival.'

'I know,' Rafael said grimly. 'I'm sorry, I wanted a solution that was less damaging for us.'

'But it is a solution,' Wilson said. 'And the only one we've got. Anna, I want the starships to launch quantumbusters at every flare. Snuff them out.'

'Yes, sir. There are nine star systems out of the forty-eight which don't have starships coverage.' She sounded upset at having to remind him.

'Damnit. Send ships in from wherever you can.'

'Fleet command is working out the quickest flight patterns now.'

The office tactical display showed starships going ftl to leave their planetary orbits. Wilson allowed himself to believe they would all be in time, that the flare radiation damage would be minimal. He knew that even if it was, even if the majority of the biosphere on each world survived, the inhabitants would want to leave. People would be terrified. Quite rightly. There would be a flood of refugees to the other side of the Commonwealth. Planetary governments would be unable to cope; there were still huge problems housing and supporting the existing refugees from the Lost23.

'Can we shut down the CST network?' he asked the President. Nigel Sheldon still hadn't returned. His stationary image lurked in the office like a ghost at the proceedings. Wilson was starting to wonder if the Dynasty chief was running for his lifeboat.

'Excuse me?' Doi asked.

'We have to block any kind of mass panic escape from the worlds under attack. The rest of the Commonwealth won't be able to deal with the population of forty-eight planets on the move. I doubt even CST can transport that many people.'

'If they stay they'll suffer radiation sickness. You can't make them endure that, and I'm certainly not going to enforce it.'

'Nobody inside a force field will come to any harm.'

'And what about people outside?'

'We're getting reports that the CST stations have closed on most of the worlds under attack,' Rafael said.

'What?'

'It looks like Wessex has cut off all its links to phase two space.'

Both Wilson and Doi turned to Nigel Sheldon's image. Wilson tried to send a message to the Dynasty chief's unisphere level two private address, which was rejected. 'Damn you. What are you doing?'

'Using CST wormholes to interfere with the Prime ones, I expect,' Rafael said.

'Have we got any information on that?' Wilson asked Anna.

'Admiral,' Dimitri said, 'with respect, this is not relevant right now. You have to focus on Hell's Gateway and how it can be disabled. While the Primes retain the ability to open wormholes into Commonwealth space, they can drop flare bomb after flare bomb into any of our stars. We have just shown them we possess doomsday weapons; and we have enough evidence that they are conducting a pogrom against us. Their retaliatory strike will be swift and utterly lethal. You must stop them. The next hour will decide whether there will even be a Commonwealth for people to move through.'

Wilson nodded slowly as he began his feedback breathing

exercise. He could feel his hands shaking in the unnatural silence. The refugees had been a classic displacement diversion. Truth was, he didn't want to make the next round of decisions. *This is too much to ask one person. I'm not ready.* A little self-derisive guffaw slipped out of his lips, bringing him strange looks. *Exactly how long does it take to prepare? I've had three hundred years, Goddamnit.*

'Anna, tell the *Cairo* and the *Baghdad* to fly directly to Hell's Gateway. They are to use quantumbusters against the Prime facilities they find there. I want those force fields broken, and the gateway generators destroyed.

'Yes, sir.' She began to relay instructions to Fleet command.

He studied the tactical display. Now he'd gone and done it, committed himself to accepting the responsibility, the decisions and orders were actually quite logical and easy. His heart was beating away normally inside his chest again.

'How long?' Doi asked.

'It'll take them three days to get there which might be too long, but then again it might not. And if they can't get close to Hell's Gateway they can kick the shit out of that star with quantumbusters. That should cause some damage to the Primes stationed there.'

'I understand,' Doi said. She sounded defeated, as if it was all over.

Wilson didn't want to look at her. If the Primes started firing flare bombs at other stars, then the Commonwealth was as good as dead already. They had three days to implement such an action. *I've given them three days.*

The tactical display was showing him quantumbusters detonating to extinguish the flare bombs already active. The flares and the explosions combined were sending lethal torrents of radiation towards the hapless Commonwealth planets.

'Warn the planetary authorities,' Wilson said wearily. 'Tell people to get under cover.'

'They're already doing that,' Rafael said. 'Wilson, I'm sorry, but this has to be done.'

'Yes.' He took a deep breath, reviewing the tactical display as it showed him the radiation gushing out from the quantum-buster explosions which would ultimately result in the death of millions of people. On his order.

*

'Bad day,' Nigel Sheldon murmured. 'And getting worse.'

His expanded mentality slipped into the arrays governing CST wormhole generators on Wessex. Traffic in and out of the station had already shut down on his earlier order, leaving the wormholes empty. He disconnected eight of them from their remote gateways, and pulled their exits back into the Wessex system. Sensors above the Big15 world located the Prime wormholes for him. Over three thousand ships had already come through. The Primes had also fired a flare bomb into the local star. *Tokyo* had launched a quantumbuster to knock it out.

'We're going to lose the planet's entire bloody harvest,' Alan Hutchinson groaned. 'The force fields will protect Narrabri, but the continents are completely exposed.'

'I know.'

The quantumbuster detonated.

'Jesus fucking wept,' Alan Hutchinson spat. Sensors revealed the full damage which Prime and human weapons inflicted on the tormented star. 'That's more than quadrupled the radiation emission. All they have to do is keep on firing flare bombs at us. The cure is as bad as the problem.'

'Hang on, Alan. I might be able to stop this.' Nigel was tracking the *Charybdis* through a directional TD channel created by the ship's drive. The frigate was closing fast on one of the Prime wormholes, and there was no sign of it on any hysradar in the system. *So let's hope the Primes can't see it, either.* 'Are you ready?' he asked Otis.

'Yes, Dad.'

'Here we go.' Nigel issued a stream of instructions into the wormhole generators he commanded. This time he didn't need help from the SI. CST had upgraded the Wessex RIs to manipulate the open ended wormholes in an aggressive mode.

*

MorningLightMountain watched the human starships launch their superbombs into the stars where it had planted corona-rupture machines. In every case, the massive explosion eliminated its machines. It had not expected such retaliation. If they had such weapons why hadn't they used them against the staging post or its own homeworld? Surely their *ethics* wouldn't prevent them?

One of its wormholes in the Wessex system was abruptly subjected to exotic interference as eight human wormholes transected it. MorningLightMountain was expecting that; it diverted power from reserve magflux extractors to help stabilize its wormhole. After analysing the nature of the attack humans had used last time, it believed it could now counter them effectively. Certainly, it had modified its generator mechanisms to make them less susceptible to the instability overloads. Thousands of immotile clusters focused their attention on the wormhole, ready to counter whatever interference pattern was inflicted on the exotic fabric.

There was none. This was different. The human wormholes were somehow merging with its own, their energy input helping to maintain the fissure through spacetime. For a moment, MorningLightMountain didn't understand at all. Then it realized it was now unable to close the wormhole. The humans were injecting so much energy into it they were stabilizing the fabric, they were also locking the exit in place within the Wessex system. There was a hole open directly into its staging post which it didn't control.

MorningLightMountain tried to introduce instabilities, inducing resonances, modifying power frequency. The humans countered it all with ease. Sensors located a relativistic missile racing for the wormhole exit. MorningLightMountain strengthened the force field which covered the exit, and started pulling back the ships which had just gone through, clustering them in a defensive formation. Force fields inside the staging post area were strengthened. It had prepared for a relativistic explosion like last time in case the humans managed to engineer a strike. The damage should be minimal.

A starship materialized *inside* the force field covering the wormhole exit. It was difficult to detect, the hull was completely black, absorbing all electromagnetic radiation. MorningLightMountain only knew it was there because it partially eclipsed the drive contrails of its own ships outside. There had been no warning of its existence, no detectable superluminal quantum distortion waves which were the signature of human ships and missiles. They had built something new.

The ship moved swiftly into the wormhole exit. MorningLightMountain switched every available power source it had into the generator in one last frantic attempt to destabilize the wormhole. Nothing happened; the wormhole fabric remained perfectly constant as the humans countered every power surge. MorningLightMountain gathered its own ships around the generator, ready to fire. Sensors were also aligned in an attempt to learn something about the nature of the new drive.

The human ship emerged from the wormhole. MorningLightMountain's ships fired every beam weapon they had at the intruder. It vanished.

*

'Second batch of flare bombs coming through,' Anna reported.

'Oh Jesus,' Wilson exclaimed. The display showed him over

thirty new devices had emerged, accelerating at a hundred gees toward their target stars. 'Natasha?'

'If you can't intercept the devices with Douvoir missiles, hit them with quantumbusters.'

'Son of a bitch.' Wilson nodded at Anna. 'All right, authorize that; divert every Douvoir we have in proximity. Some of them must be able to hit a flare bomb.'

'Yes, sir.'

'One of us will run out of superweapons before the other,' Dimitri said. 'That will decide who wins today.'

'That decides who wins, period,' Rafael said.

'Yes, Admiral.'

Nigel's image flickered back into life. 'I've done what I can,' he said. 'We should see a result in the next quarter of an hour.'

Wilson quickly checked the Wessex section of the tactical display. One of the Prime wormholes had vanished. *One?* 'What did you do?'

'Sent a ship through to Hell's Gateway.'

Wilson looked at Anna and then Rafael, both of whom looked equally perplexed.

'What sort of ship?' a fascinated Dimitri asked.

'Warship,' Nigel said. 'Heavily armed.'

'With what?' Natasha asked.

'Advanced quantumbuster.'

'Advanced?'

'You'll see.' He paused. 'If it works.'

*

MorningLightMountain could not detect the human ship anywhere within the staging post system. Most of its sensors had recorded nothing as it emerged from the wormhole. The visual images were strongest, and most informative, showing a black ovoid sucking in light. There was no quantum signature, nothing on the mass detector. Most puzzling and alarming, there was no detectable wormhole. Whatever the human scientist class had come up with, it was radically different to anything they had employed before.

Now MorningLightMountain was left wondering what the ship would do. Some kind of attack was surely imminent. It couldn't understand why the humans hadn't simply set off a superbomb as soon as the ship was through. What could be more damaging than that? Certainly a large proportion of the equipment and ships at the staging post would have been destroyed, even the interstellar wormhole would have been threatened.

Why did it never truly understand humans?

Sensors on several of the star-orbiting missile platforms spotted a strong magnetic source emerging from nowhere, a hundred thousand kilometres above the corona. Morning-LightMountain had placed four thousand such platforms around the star to protect its magflux extractors. Without them, it couldn't power the wormhole generators into the Commonwealth. But this missile wasn't fired at any of the magflux extractors, it was heading straight down into the star, and its position had already put it beyond any feasible interception. Given its location and course, there were only two possibilities, either humans had developed corona-rupture devices, or it was one of their superbombs. There was no way to tell until the impact.

MorningLightMountain calculated what damage a flare would inflict on the magflux extractors as they passed above it. With adequate warning, it should be able to use the attitude thrusters to alter their orbital inclination, and steer them clear of the radiation stream. Surely humans would know that. A superbomb would do a lot more damage, though even an explosion of that magnitude could only destroy a small percentage of its magflux extractors. Perhaps the ship was going to launch a series of superbombs. That would seriously degrade its immediate ability to continue expanding into

Commonwealth space. Considering this from a tactical angle, MorningLightMountain launched another batch of its own corona-rupture devices at the forty-eight systems it was invading. It also began reviewing the location of the remaining Commonwealth stars. A gradual, measured absorption of human planets was preferable, weakening them and utilizing their discarded industrial infrastructure, but they were now forcing its responses.

The tens of thousands of group clusters managing the staging post wormhole generators began to compute new exit coordinates. Towers loaded with corona-rupture devices were prepared; with immotile group clusters analysing and preparing guidance electronics on all the remaining devices. MorningLightMountain didn't have as many as it would like. They were extremely difficult to build, even with its technological ability and resources.

Sensors in the star-orbiting missile platforms closest to the human missile caught a sudden burst of quantum field activity just as it reached the chromosphere. Then their communication links ended. Power from all the magflux extractors around the impact zone failed simultaneously, forcing MorningLightMountain to switch to emergency power reserves to maintain over a hundred and fifty wormholes into the Commonwealth. Platforms further away showed the distinctive blast crater of a superbomb starting to form within the corona. Then something else happened. Quantum signature detectors recorded activity leaping off their scale. The star's magnetic field multiplied in strength by orders of magnitude, producing a pulse effect strong enough to shove a fifth of Morning-LightMountain's magflux extractors and missile platforms out of their orbital track. As they tumbled away with every electronic system burnt out, MorningLightMountain switched to platforms still further away from the missile impact point to try and understand what was happening. Around the crater zone, a solid plane of brightness was swelling up and out across the chromosphere. Ultra-hard radiation poured away from it, a wavefront powerful enough to slice through the strongest force field.

More missile platforms and magflux extractors failed. MorningLightMountain didn't have anything left that could scan the impact zone directly, its only remaining platforms were on the other side of the star. Sensors at the staging post still showed the star as it was six minutes ago, passively normal. Power reserves were now insufficient to provide an alternative supply for all the magflux extractors it had lost. It concentrated on maintaining two wormholes to each of its captured Commonwealth planets.

The first flotilla of missile platforms to slide out of the initial blast umbra showed what looked like the crescent of a blue-white giant appearing behind the staging post star. And MorningLightMountain finally realized what the humans had done.

The star was going nova.

*

Ozzie woke up as slim beams of bright sunlight slid across his face. He lay motionless for a while, eyes shut, a smile playing across his face. *Let's see.* He opened his eyes and brought his hand round in front of his face. His antique wristwatch told him he'd spent nine hours asleep. 'Oh yeah?' His voice was a contented challenge to the universe.

He unzipped the sleeping bag and stretched. The cool air gusted over him, and he reached for his cord trousers. Once he'd fastened the belt round his waist, he picked up his check shirt, and grinned knowingly. Very carefully, he slipped his arms into the sleeves. There was no ripping sound from any of the stitches. 'Man, some progress!' Both of his large toes stuck up through holes in his socks as he shoved his feet into his boots. 'Ah well, then again, maybe not.' They definitely still needed darning. He patted the pocket on his old dark-grey fleece where his small needle and thread packet was stashed. 'Maybe tomorrow.'

He was pressing down on a giggle as he pushed the curtain aside and stepped out of the crude shelter. 'Morning,' he called out cheerfully to Orion, who was sitting beside the fire he'd just rekindled. Their metal mugs were standing on a shard of polyp above the flames; wisps of steam rising from the water inside.

'Five teacubes left,' Orion said. 'Two chocolate. Which do you want?'

'Variety is the spice of life, man, so let's go for tea today, shall we?'

'Okay.' Orion gave the little gold cubes of chocolate a wistful look.

'Fine thanks,' Ozzie said. He sat down on one of the ebony and maroon polyp protrusions, wincing as he straightened his leg.

'Excuse me?' Orion said.

'The knee, thank you, it's a lot better, but I'm gonna have to keep up with the exercises to loosen it up. It's still plenty stiff after yesterday.' He gave the perplexed boy a happy look. 'You remember yesterday, right? The walk down to the end spire.'

'Yes.' Orion was becoming petulant, he couldn't figure what the joke was.

Tochee emerged from the jungle, its manipulator flesh coiled round various containers it had filled with water.

'Good morning to you, friend Ozzie,' it said through the hand-held array.

'Morning.' Ozzie took the mug which Orion proffered, ignoring the boy's scowl. 'Did you find anything interesting?' he asked the big alien.

'I have detected no electrical power circuit activity with my equipment.' Tochee held up a couple of sensors. 'The machinery must be very deep inside the reef.'

'Yeah, if there is any.'

'I thought you said there was,' Orion protested.

'Something generates gravity. My guess is it's too sophisticated to be anything like a machine. Specific quark lattice, folded quantum fields, gravatonic-molecular intersection assembled at a sub-atomic level, something like that. Who knows? Who cares? It's not why we're here.'

'What are we here for, then?' Orion asked in exasperation.

'The Silfen community.'

'Well they're not here, are they?' the boy waved his arm round in a broad half circle to illustrate the absence of the humanoid aliens. Tea sloshed out of his mug.

'Not yet.' Ozzie picked up one of the bluish-grey fruits they'd gathered, and started peeling it.

'What's that supposed to mean?'

'Okay, think on this. Nobody here believes we crashed here on Island Two by accident, right? I mean, what are the odds, man? The gas halo is *big* in anyone's language. And the old *Pathfinder*, face it, we're not talking *Titanic* here.'

'A natural collision was unlikely,' Tochee said.

'So we're not here by accident. And what did we find yesterday? What's at the end of the reef?'

'Spires,' Orion said doubtfully.

'Which we all decided would make excellent landing areas for flying Silfen.' Ozzie bit into the coarse fruit, grinning at his companions.

'They'll come to us!' Orion smiled brightly.

'That is an excellent deduction, friend Ozzie.'

'Many thanks.' Ozzie wiped some of the juice from his beard. 'It's worth a try, anyway. I can't think of any other reason for today.'

The tiniest of frowns flickered over Orion's face, but he let the comment go. Ozzie couldn't quite work out if the boy and Tochee were real or not. Temporal reset was not something he believed in. There were many ways of manipulating spacetime within a wormhole so that time appeared to flow faster around the observer, but travelling back in time was a fundamental impossibility. So if this day on the reef was an artificially generated reality, it was a perfect one, which logically meant his companions would replicate their real selves down to the last nuance. Then again, they might be sharing the dream – in which case why didn't they remember the yesterdays? Of course, maybe there was some kind of closed temporal loop subset operating inside the gas halo, a microcontinuum operating in parallel to the universe but with different time flow laws. He wasn't sure if such a thing were possible. Intriguing idea to try and analyse, though it was a *very* long time since he'd attempted math that complicated. And today, he decided, wasn't the day to begin again.

*

After breakfast he made sure Orion and Tochee gathered their belongings to carry with them on the trek through the reef's forest. Without understanding if what was happening was real or not, he couldn't risk them losing the few essential items they still possessed if they did find a path and move on to somewhere else. So the tent and water filter pump, the few tools remaining all came with them.

'Should we be picking fruit?' Orion asked as they wound through a section of trees that were nearly all laden with grape-like clusters of scarlet berries. 'We normally pick fruit.'

'If you want to,' Ozzie said. He was concentrating on keeping his head clear of the ceiling formed by the lowest branches as he bounce-walked his way forwards. The trees were large and old, producing a wide interlocking lacework of branches and twigs. Sunlight around the trunks was a gentle twilight glimmer, complemented by dry air smelling faintly of spice.

Orion gave a victorious whoop, and immediately shinned up the closest trunk. Ozzie could see him walking along the branches overhead as twigs snapped, and the occasional leaf fluttered down.

'Are you not using your sensors, friend Ozzie?' Tochee asked.

'I've got a few running,' Ozzie said defensively. He didn't fancy trying to explain to Tochee that right now they might both be nothing other than figments in the Silfen Community's dream. If they weren't, he'd be facing a serious credibility crisis. 'We'll save the complex ones for something interesting.'

'I understand. I will continue to record the general background, it may help us determine—'

'Hey!' Orion yelped.

Ozzie couldn't quite tell if the boy was in pain or just startled. There was a flurry of motion in the forest's lower ceiling five metres away from him. Broken twigs and a small crowd of leaves plummeted down. Orion's legs appeared in the rent. They swung from side to side a couple of times, and he let go, falling slowly to the thin layer of sandy soil covering the polyp. Several clusters of the red berries fell with him. He looked directly back up, a flustered expression on his face.

'What's the matter?' Ozzie went towards the boy with an easy bounding motion. Tochee speeded up to match him, its locomotion ridges spreading out for better traction.

Orion was scrabbling backwards, his eyes fixed on the tear he'd created. Stronger slivers of sunlight shone straight down through it. 'There's something up there,' the panicked boy gasped. 'Something big, I swear it.'

The front of Tochee's body lifted off the ground as the alien aligned its pyramid eye on the gap. 'I see nothing, friend Orion.'

'Not right up there, more off this way.' Orion pointed.

'What sort of size are you talking about?' Ozzie asked nervously. The boy's behaviour was making him jittery. Was that intentional? Or were they out of the illusion now? If so

. . . His hand slipped down towards the sheath where his knife hung.

'I don't know.' Orion clambered to his feet. 'It was this shape moving, that's all. A dark shape. My size, maybe bigger.'

Tochee had begun sliding in the direction Orion indicated, winding slightly from side to side in short economic movements. Its colourful fronds were standing proud from its hide, waving slightly in sympathy with its body motion. Something about the alien's intent and confidence reminded Ozzie of Native American hunters. When he looked up again at the ragged ceiling of branches and leaves there was nothing to see, just the occasional flutter of the leaves, the chiaroscuro dapple in perpetual random motion.

'What's—' Orion began.

Ozzie closed a hand about the curious boy's pointing hand, lowering it. 'Why don't we just keep on going to the spire?' he said, trying to be casual as he put a finger to his lips. Orion's eyes bugged.

Tochee reared up, an impressive action even in the reef's low gravity. The front edges of its locomotion ridges curled into hooks which fastened round a branch, holding it vertical. The manipulator flesh on its flanks lunged out, flattening into two tentacles that shot up into the forest's vegetation. For a moment nothing happened. Then Tochee let go of the branches, and tugged with its tentacles. Its heavy body fell smoothly. A humanoid form came crashing down through the forest's low ceiling.

Ozzie was already leaping forwards. He landed right on top of the figure struggling on the ground next to Tochee. The pair of them rolled over and over as Ozzie tried to get his opponent in a wrestling lock. Whoever he was holding writhed like an electrocuted octopus. Every time Ozzie grabbed a limb, it was torn from his grasp with above-human strength. Something like a thick leather cloak kept batting against his face. They wound up rolling into the bottom of a tree, with Ozzie on top. The tough dark fabric was slapping into his face again. So he just lashed out with both feet. He was no streetfighter, never had been, so the toes of his boots just connected with the polyp; the follow up bounce meant his knees landed hard.

'Ow. Sheesh, that hurts.'

'Then stop fucking kicking, you moron,' a harsh voice said in heavily accented English.

Ozzie froze. The leathery wing fell away from his face, and he was looking right at a male Silfen, whose narrow feline eyes stared back with impatience.

'Huh?' Ozzie blurted.

'I said, cool it with the hardass routine. You're crap at it anyway.'

Ozzie let go as if the Silfen burned. 'You can talk.'

'You can think.'

Surprise battled with resentment. 'Sorry, man,' he said meekly. 'You startled us, you know, creeping round up there.'

Orion had come over to stare down in amazement. He slowly pulled the pendant out of his shirt, blinking at the intense green light. He looked at it, and back at the Silfen who was now gracefully climbing to his feet. There was a rustle as he flapped his wings, sending out little puffs of the dusty sand, before folding them back so they formed neat creases below his arms. His tail did a quick whip-like flick before settling into a shallow U-curve which kept it off the ground.

Ozzie patted at his own clothes, mildly embarrassed.

Tochee slid up beside Ozzie and Orion to look at the Silfen. 'I believe you said these creatures would not speak your language?' the array voice said.

The Silfen turned to look at Tochee. Ozzie's inserts caught it, but only just: the humanoid's eyes flashed with ultraviolet light. A ripple ran along Tochee's manipulator flesh ridges, as it began to project its speech images in reply. They began to speed up, the two of them conversing very fast. *If this is a simulation or a dream, why does it need to talk with Tochee?*

'I didn't know they could speak English,' Orion whispered breathlessly to Ozzie.

'Me neither.'

The Silfen finished communicating with Tochee, and bowed slightly, blinking. The ultraviolet faded from his eyes.

'Who arc you?' Ozzie asked.

The Silfen's circular mouth opened wide, allowing the long slender tongue to vibrate between his rows of teeth. 'I am the one who dances in the endless wind streams which flow along the tumbling white clouds as they circle in eternal orbit within the star of life.' He gave a sharp whistle. 'But you may call me Clouddancer. I know how you humans have to be so quick and shallow.'

'Thanks,' Ozzie tipped his head to one side. 'Why the German accent?'

Clouddancer's tongue quivered. 'Authority. I look like one of your legendary demons. If I start talking like some stoned hippy then I've got a serious credibility problem, right?'

'Absolutely, man. So are you here to tell me what I want to know?'

'I don't know, Ozzie. What do you want to know?'

'Who threw the barriers round the Dyson Pair, and why?'

'Long story.'

Ozzie gestured at the dusky forest with both arms. 'Do I look like I'm going somewhere?'

They walked back through the forest to a clearing half a kilometre away that they'd passed through earlier. Ozzie wanted a less oppressive environment to concentrate on the details. Orion was totally fascinated by a winged Silfen who could speak English.

'Where did you learn it?' the boy asked.

'Common knowledge where I come from, kid.'

'Where's that?'

'Here. Where the hell else do you think someone my weight

can flap their way round? Jeeze, what is it with neurones and your species? Is it a natural shortage or do you moult them as you grow up.'

'Here? The gas halo?'

'Is that what you've named this?'

'Yeah. We were on one of the water islands.' Orion grimaced with the memory. 'We fell off.'

Clouddancer's tongue quivered as he whistled.

Ozzie had heard Silfen laugh before, he put this down to something equivalent to a derisive snort. 'You need to put a few warning signs up, man,' he said sharply.

'You fell off because you were hasty, you schmuck,' Clouddancer said. 'You should take time off, observe your environment, work out any problems in advance. That's the smart thing to do.'

'Bullshit. You dumped us there. You have a responsibility.'

Clouddancer stopped. His wings rustled, the tail snaking from side to side. 'No we don't. We are not responsible for any one but ourselves. You chose to walk our paths, Ozzie, you decided where they would end. Take responsibility for *your* own actions. Don't blame everyone else, you'll turn into a lawyer. You want that?'

Ozzie glared back at him.

'How could we decide where the paths take us?' Orion asked. 'How do they work?'

'The paths are old, very old, they have grown apart from us of late. How they work is up to them. They try to help as much as they can, they listen to those who walk them. Some of the time, anyway.'

'You mean they deliver you to where you want to go?'

'Oh no. They rarely change, they don't like change. Most simply remain closed. It's kinda sad when they do that, but there are always new ones opening. You've always got to go forward, right? That's something we've all got in common.'

'Do you mean . . .' Orion shot a glance at Ozzie for reassurance. 'If I wanted to find Mom and Dad, they'd take me there eventually?'

'They might. That's kind of an elusive goal you've got there, kid.'

'Do you know where my mom and dad are?'

'Long way from here, that's for sure.'

'They're alive!' the incredulous boy cried.

'Yeah yeah; they're still knocking around.'

Orion started crying, tears smearing the dirt on his cheeks.

'Friend Orion,' Tochee said. 'I am pleased for you.' It reached out with a tentacle and touched Orion's shoulder. Orion gave the manipulator flesh a quick grateful squeeze.

'Good news, man. The greatest.' Ozzie put his arm round the boy's shoulders, hugging him. 'I hope you're right,' he said in a warning tone to Clouddancer.

The Silfen shrugged, ruffling his wings.

'When this is over, I'm going to set out again and find them,' Orion announced. 'I know what I'm doing now. I can survive out here. I'll get myself some decent equipment first, though,' he looked down at his feet. 'And boots.'

'I'll buy you the best,' Ozzie said. 'Promise, man.'

The clearing had a covering of thick mossy grass. Strong sunlight from the overhead star shone down, dappling the edges. Ozzie slung his pack to the ground, and sat with his back against it. Orion was too excited to sit; he paced about, grinning every time he looked up at the vast sky.

Ozzie held his water bottle out to Clouddancer. 'Drink?'

'Water? Shit no. You got any decent booze?' The winged Silfen crouched on the spongy ground opposite Ozzie. His tongue flicked out with reptilian speed.

'I didn't bring any. I figured I needed to stay sober for this.'

'Okay, good call. You want to start the twenty questions routine now?'

'Sure. I've earned that right.'

Clouddancer managed a very human sounding snort without using his tongue.

'Did you put the barriers round the Dyson Pair?' Ozzie asked. This wasn't quite how he'd envisaged the end to his journey. There was a certain daydream which had him in an ancient cathedral-like alien library, maybe an abandoned one, where he roamed the aisles, reactivating computers with huge banks of flashing lights. Now that would have been cool, rather than getting his ass damp on the grass while he chatted away to a demon as if they were a pair of old barflies. *Yep, definitely didn't see that coming.*

'No, it wasn't us,' Clouddancer said. 'We don't go around judging other species like that. We don't have the *ego* some people in this universe have.'

Ozzie ignored the slight. 'What do you mean; judge?'

'The barrier makers were a race younger than us, with a technological proficiency approaching us at our peak. The dick-brains believed that gave them responsibility. In that, they were very like humans.'

'So who were they?'

'We called their star: Anomine – a short version of the true name, but accurate.'

'You're speaking of them in the past tense.'

'So I am; glad someone's paying attention. As they were then, they no longer exist. They were always faster, always hungry to advance. Again, just like you guys. They evolved from that stage and went off down a whole new route away from the directly physical; they fused with their machines, which in turn transcended. Not universally, mind you, some of them some disagreed with the direction in which their techheads were headed. Those are the ones who still exist in their old physical form. Now they've calmed down some and rejected their technological culture and its outcome, they farm their original homeworld like regular folks, they rejoice in their young, they ignore the stars, though they welcome visitors from across the galaxy. I know you, Ozzie, I can see that hunger in you; you'd like them. We did.'

Just for an instant, Ozzie saw them, or at least their planet, the way to walk there. His mind had lulled itself into the pleasant warm reverie amid dreams and awakening. Ahead of him, a long road took him down many glittering paths like gold strands stretched between the stars.

Dream inside a dream. 'Groovy,' he said contentedly. 'So why the barriers?'

'The sentient species that evolved on Dyson Alpha lust after individual empires and dominance. Think of them as the ultimate self-obsessed power freaks. Real bastards, from your cultural perspective, I guess. In their basic state they would think nothing of obliterating every other life form in the galaxy and beyond to guarantee their own immortality.

'When the Anomines found them, they were rapidly approaching the kind of technology level where they could have carried that particular maladapted evolutionary route across the galaxy at the point of a gun. So the Anomines, being the kind of bleeding heart liberals they were, decided to isolate them. They feared genocide would be committed if the Dysons were ever to reach another star system. Not exactly a difficult prediction, that one. Turns out they were right. The Dyson slower than light starships did reach a neighbouring star while the Anomines were busy building the barrier generators. They all but wiped out its indigenous sentient species, enslaved the survivors, and absorbed their knowledge, exploiting it to further their own military strength. That is why barriers were established around two systems.'

'Ah ha!' Ozzie chortled delightedly. 'Everyone was wondering about the motivation behind the barriers. Damn it, man, you're right, I would have liked to have met the Anomines when they were at their height. Sort of like the old Greenpeace movement on Earth, but with teeth. They must have helped save a lot of species. Hell, we would probably have been in the front line by now.'

'So the Dyson people were, like, put in prison?' Orion asked.

'That's right,' Clouddancer said. 'They *were* in prison. The Anomines had hoped that if they couldn't expand they would be forced to evolve away from their imperial mindset. For your information, they haven't.'

'What do you mean, *were*?' Ozzie asked. The feelings of unease which accompanied those recent bad dreams of his suddenly came rushing to the front of his conscious thoughts. He closed his eyes.

'Well, guess what happened when somebody's starship went poking round? The goddamn thing was packed full of scientists desperate to see what was inside. I mean, why you dumbasses see curiosity as one of your overriding virtues is anyone's guess. Ever heard of caution?'

'Oh shit. What did we do?'

'Your starship interfered with the barrier generator around the original Dyson world. The barrier fell.'

'I don't believe it. You have to be wrong.'

'You calling me a liar? You want to make something of it?'

'There is no way humans would attempt to switch off a barrier. I know the way our governments work. They would have had to fill out eight million forms in triplicate and have the request reviewed by a hundred subcommittees before they were even allowed to read the generator's instruction manual.'

'They disabled some of the generator functions. I don't know how, we weren't paying close attention, and we don't go whizzing round the galaxy in fancy rocketships to find these things out. But it wasn't an accident, no fucking way. Those generators should have lasted as long as the stars they closed off, probably longer.'

'What happened after the barrier fell?'

'The Dysons used knowledge captured from you to establish

wormholes of their own. Twenty-three Commonwealth planets were invaded in the first stage of their expansion.'

'Son of a bitch!' Ozzie shouted. 'Nigel, you total asshole, how stupid are you? I told you this space cadet crap was gonna wind up busting everyone's balls. I goddamn told you!'

'Did they invade Silvergalde?' Orion asked fearfully.

'No, our world remains untouched.'

'And the rest?' Ozzie asked. He knew it was going to be bad, just needed it confirmed.

'The Commonwealth abandoned them. They suffered enormous ecological damage, and they are still subject to acts of violence between humans and Dysons.'

'Goddamnit. So the Anomines were right?'

'Yes.'

'Are they going to help?'

'Help what?'

'Humans. You said the generator was disabled. Can it be restarted? Can we push the Dysons back inside?'

'Haven't you listened to a fucking thing I've been telling you? We don't intervene. Never have, never will. And the technologically advanced Anomines are past the time when they interfere in the events of other species. Like us, they now let evolution flow where it may. If you want to restart the generator and shut the Dysons back inside the barrier, do it yourself.'

'You mean you're just going to let the Dysons attack humans?'

'You've already seen the answer to that, Ozzie.' Clouddancer lifted his arms briefly, allowing the thick membrane of his wings to flutter in the gentle breeze. 'The death of any species is to be regretted; but we have experienced many. I've embarked on pilgrimages to the memory of them myself, and I feel a great sorrow when I know them. We will remember you, should you fall.'

'Well, that makes me feel one whole hell of a lot better,

thanks. For a minute there I thought our friendship meant nothing at all.'

Clouddancer peeled back his lips to expose all three rings of teeth. 'This is an argument that we ended millennia ago. You let the Dysons out. You are responsible. This is macro-evolution at its worst. Watching it is always painful for us.'

'What about the Anomines, the advanced ones? Can I appeal to them directly? Do any of the paths lead to them?'

'Not a path, no. We can talk to them when they wish it. That has not happened for over three centuries now. We thought the fall of their old barrier might stir them. But it hasn't. We're not even certain they exist in their primary transcendent state any more. We have known species such as theirs which have kept on evolving into entities which simply cannot connect with those of us who remain rooted in the physical.'

'All right, instead of a few battalions of Silfen stormtroopers, how about giving us information?' Ozzie asked. 'Is there something, some weapon, you once built that could defeat the Dysons? Just the blueprints would do.'

'I'm kind of surprised that you of all people ask that, Ozzie. In fact, I'm quite hurt by the implication we'd ever waste our time on crap like weapons.'

'Oh really? I'd be interested to hear what you say if your species ever gets threatened with extinction. Of course, you wouldn't go alone. We'd help if you asked, we'd stand beside you.'

'I know. We admire you for that, for what you are. We don't expect you to change. Do you expect that of us?'

'No. I just thought you were different, that's all.'

'Different, how? More human? You built legends around us. They were not entirely correct. It's too late to come blaming us for your mistakes.'

'Screw you.'

'But I'm your friend,' Orion insisted. He held up his

pendant. 'Look. Other humans are too. Doesn't that mean anything to you?'

'Of course it does, kid. If you stay here with us, we will keep you safe.'

'I want all of us to be safe.'

'That is a wish to be proud of, but it is only a wish. You're going to make a grand human when you're all grown up. Best of the species.'

Orion dangled the pendant in front of him, giving it a wretched stare. 'Then what's the point?'

'Life is the point. To have joined with others and to have known them. We know you, Silfen friend Orion, that makes us glad.'

'I used to be glad to know you.'

'Yeah, sorry, kid. We had fun playing in those woods, back then, didn't we? I hope that one day you will be glad to know us again.'

'Am I right about you?' Ozzie asked. 'Is there some SI equivalent you all download into? Is that what I'm really speaking to?'

Clouddancer laughed. 'Almost, Ozzie, almost.'

'How do I know you speak with authority?'

'You don't. But I name you a Silfen friend, Ozzie Fernandez Isaacs.' He held up a pendant identical to Orion's. 'You have the freedom of the paths. Go where you will with our blessing. If you think I'm just a lying son of a bitch, seek those who you know will speak the truth.'

Ozzie stared at the pendant, almost ready to throw it back at Clouddancer. That's what Orion would have done with all his magnificent teenage fury. But then this whole event was being staged for his benefit, not Orion's; telling him what he wanted to know even if it wasn't what he wanted to hear. The pendant was obviously the culmination of that, it was significant in some way even if he couldn't see how yet. 'Thank you,

Clouddancer,' he said formally, and accepted the pendant with a small bow.

When he put the chain round his neck, his vision was momentarily wiped out by a foggy emerald sparkle. It was as if every sense was stretched raw. The feel of the air blowing on his exposed skin scraping hard enough to bruise, the heat of the sun threatening to singe his raggedy hair, sound of rustling leaves the cacophony of an orchestra. He could smell the scent of every berry and flower on the reef combining together like volcanic sulphur. And in his mind he sensed the thoughts of the Silfen Motherholme all around him; an immense realm of life whose size alone brought complete comfort to any entity it touched. A size which surely made it invincible. It pervaded the gas halo, twisting through the physical and biological elements like a nuclear spiritual force. Intangible connections slipped away through the smallest interstices of spacetime binding the Silfen wherever they roamed through the universe. A family which surpassed any possible human dream of connectivity and love.

Ozzie envied them for that. But for all the sense of belonging the Motherholme exuded, it was alien. The Silfen really wouldn't help humans in their struggle against the Dysons. They didn't see that as a flaw in their character. It was correct, essential, because that was how the universe functioned.

'Wow.' Ozzie was glad he was sitting. The emotional impact wasn't quite as great as when he'd looked into the memory of the world that had died. Even so, it was a glimpse into a heaven that was achingly beautiful despite its imperfections.

The moment passed, though he would know it for ever.

Clouddancer was staring at him, slim face held straight with cheek muscles slightly dimpled, mouth half widened, tongue stilled. An expression Ozzie *knew* was one of compassion and sadness. 'One day,' he promised the alien, 'we will forge a bridge across that gulf between our hearts.'

'I will embrace you that day,' friend Ozzie.' Clouddancer turned to Orion, who had slipped back into his usual petulance. 'So long kid. I hope you find your mom and dad.'

Ozzie could just see the insolence about to find its way through the boy's mouth. 'Be big, man,' he told the boy. 'Nobody's perfect.'

'Sure,' Orion grunted with a textbook teenage shrug. 'Thanks for letting me know about my parents, anyway.'

'Easy.' Clouddancer turned to Tochee. His eyes sparkled with ultraviolet light. The big alien answered in kind.

'I have to go,' Clouddancer said. 'There's a long wind coming. I need to stretch my wings.'

'Have fun, dude,' Ozzie said.

The Silfen walked back to the forest.

Ozzie looked at Tochee, who had aligned its eye on the forest where Clouddancer had gone. 'You okay?'

'It had the same shape as you. But it was very different.'

'Yeah. I'm just beginning to realize that myself.'

'So now what do we do?' Orion asked.

'Get back to the shelter, gather some food, and darn my socks.'

'Why?'

'Because tomorrow we're out of here.'

*

Morton was scouting on the lower ridges that made up the eastern edge of the Regents, high above the Trine'ba. It was drizzling again, icy droplets making the mouldering boltgrass treacherous underfoot even for his armour suit with its terrain-adaptive boot soles. His sneekbot swarm scuttled around him in a wide perimeter line, searching for any traces of the Primes. They'd seen increased activity in this area recently, more overflights, and several troop patrols. Not even the Bose motile was sure why. There was nothing here. Nothing could be built on the sharp ridges and long talus falls. No crops would grow on the poor, saturated soil.

'Can't find a bloody thing,' he said. 'If they've planted any sensors around here they're too advanced for us to find.'

'I don't believe that for a minute,' Rob answered. 'Their electronics are still back in the Stone Age. I'm just about finished myself. I'll meet you back at the rendezvous point.'

'Gotcha.' Morton's virtual vision map showed him Rob's icon positioned on the high ground above the fused-glass crater where Randtown used to be. Not far, in fact, from the clapboard house where they'd found the Bose motile.

The small green glow that indicated The Cat's position was coming from the back of the valley along the side of Black-water Crag. MorningLightMountain was still using it as its main transport route back into the wider valleys. Motiles were preparing a lot of ground for cultivation, ploughing up the sodden human fields and acres of virgin boltgrass on the foothills. There weren't many Prime-life plants that grew in such a climate, so the Bose motile claimed. The fields which had been sown earlier in the invasion had produced the most feeble-looking shoots. A big percentage had drowned in the waterlogged furrows. A plague of Elan native tal-fungi had spread over the remaining shoots, furry milk-white blooms erupting along the limp leaves.

The Cat was supposed to be cataloguing the tractor-vehicles which MorningLightMountain was using to spray the newly prepared land with fungicide. Over the last few weeks, a vast pharmacy of venomous chemicals had been spread across the land by an army of Prime agricultural machinery. Simon Rand had analysed the samples they'd collected, and announced that the fungicide would be of limited use against tal-fungi. The pesticides, also, would have little effect on Elan's insects.

'I can see foundations going in at the end of the Highmarsh,' The Cat announced. 'From the look of the equipment they've got piled up waiting, I'd say some kind of chemical plant. Makes sense, they're importing a hell of a lot of chemicals. Cheaper to produce them on site.'

Cat's Claws had watched through sensors and sneekbots as the big tanks full of toxic agricultural chemicals arrived through the gateway which MorningLightMountain had established in its new settlement a mere two kilometres along the shoreline from the radioactive hollow where their nuke had detonated. The construction had begun while they were still celebrating their success. Fusion drive ships had descended out of the sky once again, bringing a huge number of soldier motiles and their flyers. MorningLightMountain simply repeated its initial landing operation, establishing an armed camp, then putting up a force field. Inside that, a wormhole gateway was constructed, industrial machinery was assembled, big power generators brought through. Roads were bulldozed between the new hub and the route around Blackwater Crag. Inside a week, its operation was the same size as before, with the one difference: its garrison of soldier motiles was four times greater. Congregation pens were built out into the waters of the Trine'ba, and a replacement refinery once more began pumping out the thick black liquid that was saturated with base cells. At which point, the Prime resumed its agricultural operations.

That was what MorningLightMountain did, the Bose motile explained. That was all it did: expand.

'How far?' Morton had asked.

'Infinite,' the Bose motile said. 'Think of it as a sentient virus. It has a continuity which goes back to its evolutionary origins, possibly even before. All the Primes ever did was grow and compete against each other. Now this one has achieved total dominance, eradicating the rest of its kind, though in truth there was never much difference between them. You ask why it does this. It wouldn't even understand the question. It *is* growth.'

After the beautiful success of wiping out Randtown, the truth had brought them down hard. Ever since, they'd performed low level acts of sabotage, kept the survivors alive, and kept quiet about the Bose motile in their reports to the navy. Mellanie's messages kept promising she was trying to get them off, but so far she hadn't managed to give them a timeframe. Rob was getting very antsy about that.

'Is there a force field round the foundations?' Morton asked The Cat.

'No. But there are a lot of soldier motiles stationed down there. I count sixteen flyers patrolling above it. Wait . . . that's strange.'

'What's happening?' Morton asked.

'The flyers. They're stationary. They're just hovering.'

'I've got that, too,' Rob said. 'The bastards came to a full stop. Why would they do that?'

Morton looked along the shore of the Trine'ba towards the new Prime settlement. The cloud base was scudding low over the water as it always did these days. Sheet lightning flickered through the bulbous underbelly over towards the invisible southern shore, with the odd rumble of accompanying thunder echoing round the surrounding mountains. The lake itself was dying. Fusion fire from the ships and the base cell pollution had finally killed off the delicate unique ecology. Dead fish floated on the surface, their rotting bodies sticking together to form large mats of putrefying grey flesh. Underneath them, the lifeless coral was slowly decaying, producing a dank scum that washed up on the shore to form fizzing dunes of thick umber bubbles.

Flyers were constantly in the air above the desolate lake, circling round the shore in search of any hostile activity, and keeping the land around the force field under constant observation.

MorningLightMountain usually had at least sixteen on patrol at any one time. This morning, there were twenty. Now, Morton couldn't see one of them moving. Their force fields were on, their engine exhausts rotated to the vertical position.

'Motiles are stationary as well,' Rob said. There was a worried edge to his voice. 'Shit, that's spooky. They're just standing there. Even the soldiers.'

Morton's virtual hand touched a communication icon. 'Simon, what's the Bose motile doing?'

'Dudley is fine. Nothing wrong.'

Morton manipulated his communication icons to give him a direct link to the Bose motile. 'Something is happening out here, all the motiles have frozen.'

'I don't know why. The only reason they have for doing anything is that's what they've been ordered to do.'

Morton used his suit's electromagnetic sensors to sweep the bands which MorningLightMountain employed. The alien's signal traffic had dropped to about ten per cent of normal. 'Hang on, I'm going to patch you in to what it's saying. Tell me what you can.' His virtual hands routed the sensor reception into the link. He didn't like exposing the Bose motile to the Prime communications. None of them were sure if MorningLightMountain would be able to move the motile round as if it were just another of its puppets. There was absolutely no way they could ever confirm the story which the Bose motile was telling them, either, though Morton suspected it was true. As a precaution, they'd agreed it should be isolated from all Prime communications. This was a justifiable exception, he felt.

'Oh Christ,' the Bose motile said.

'What?' The Cat asked.

'MorningLightMountain has launched another invasion into the Commonwealth. It's using something called corona-rupture bombs against our stars. We've got a superbomb of our own, which can knock them out, but that only makes the radiation spillage even worse.'

'Is that why they've all stopped? Is it concentrating on the invasion?'

'No. One of our ships has got through to the staging post star. It fired something into the star which ... Oh. The destruction is enormous. MorningLightMountain is losing all its magflux extractors. Wormholes shutting down. The one into the Trine'ba settlement is gone. Its local group clusters are having to maintain contact through a wormhole in orbit. I don't understand what we did to the staging post star. Surely – My God, it's going nova. We triggered a nova! Nothing will survive. It only has minutes left.'

'Ye-hay! We killed it?' The Cat asked.

'The staging post, yes,' the Bose motile replied. 'All the wormhole generators leading into the Commonwealth will vanish.'

'So we've won?'

'The invasion has been halted. MorningLightMountain still exists. As does the generator for the interstellar wormhole. This is not good. It now sees humans as a very real and immediate danger to its continued existence.'

'But it's got to realize that if it attacks us again, we can wipe it out completely,' Rob said. 'It's not stupid.'

'No, it isn't,' the Bose motile said. 'Nor is it reasonable and open to negotiation as a human would be at this point. I'm not sure we did the right thing, though I admit I don't see an alternative.'

'We can turn stars nova.' There was a trill of admiration in The Cat's voice. 'How wonderful.'

'The navy will need to do it to Dyson Alpha, now,' Morton said. 'That's the only solution left to us.'

'Go navy!' Rob shouted.

'Here it comes,' the Bose motile said. 'I can see the light

727

growing. The radiation is reaching the staging post itself. MorningLightMountain is withdrawing the interstellar wormhole. All remaining wormholes are gone.'

Morton turned his attention back to the flyers hovering above the Trine'ba. They were holding steady. Prime signal traffic was almost non-existent. 'What are the immotiles it left behind going to do?'

'I'm not sure,' the Bose motile said. 'All the immotiles are independent again. For the moment they're unified copies of MorningLightMountain, but that won't last. They'll revert to autonomy, and try to carve themselves territories. Those on the ground will make alliances with the groups that control the big lander ships.'

'Will they fight among themselves?' Simon asked hopefully.

'Not for centuries,' the Bose motile said. 'They occupy a lot of territory, there is no need to compete for a long time. But this is assuming the Commonwealth allows them to grow in the Lost23 systems.'

'That won't happen,' Morton said. 'We'll probably be withdrawn, and they'll nova the stars.'

'That is inadvisable,' the Bose motile said. 'The radiation which novas release can quite easily sterilize all life on neighbouring star systems. You'd wipe out this whole section of the Commonwealth.'

'Who gives a shit about details?' Rob said. 'We can win. The immotiles left behind can be wiped out one at a time while we whack MorningLightMountain on its home star.'

'The remaining immotiles still present a formidable force,' the Bose motile said. 'They have thousands of ships and several wormhole generators remaining in the Lost23 systems. They will probably seek to move beyond human reach.'

'None of this affects us,' Morton said. 'All we have to worry about for now is how the local boys react. Any clues on that yet?' As he spoke, he saw the flyers moving again. They were all heading back towards the force field.

'The local immotiles are agreeing to cooperate, and remain linked into a group cluster. Without the supply route to Dyson Alpha, all expansion of existing operations will cease. They will concentrate their resources on strengthening their border against any assaults you make, and from any navy bombardment. Communication will be resumed with the other groups and clusters on Elan to decide what to do. It will mainly depend on what action the Commonwealth takes against them.'

'We should find that out soon enough. The next wormhole communication is scheduled for seven hours' time.'

'They'll take us home,' Rob declared. 'There's no point to all this sabotage bull when you can wipe out entire stars. How about that? Home free. And we didn't spend half the time they threatened us with.'

'Home free?' The Cat asked sweetly. 'So how exactly were you thinking of explaining why we've held on to our version of Dudley?'

'Shit!'

Morton watched Rob's blue icon change to amber as he switched to a secure encrypted channel.

'Morton, you've got to think of some way to square that with the navy. Maybe just leave it here, and pretend nothing happened. The survivors owe us big time, they won't rat us out.'

'Could be. I want to hear what Mellanie says in the next message.'

'Goddamn,' Rob swore. 'You are so pussywhiped. Well you make it clear to that little witch I'm not going to let her and her conspiracy theories stand between me and my clean record. That applies to you and the psycho bitch as well. When the navy lifts us, I want my release. I've fucking earned it.'

12

Niall Swalt had been cycling to work at the Grand Triad Adventures office when the Prime attack started. He still came in every day, even though the tour operator hadn't seen a single client since Mellanie returned from her short vacation. For some reason, head office on Wessex hadn't cancelled his employment contract. Every Friday night their accountancy program paid his wages; so every Monday morning he arrived back at the office for another week of doing whatever he wanted on company time. That was mainly accessing TSIs. He went through *Murderous Seduction* at least once a week.

It was the silence he noticed as he cycled along the last stretch of road towards the employee's gate. With the office sitting on the end of the CST station's main terminal, he was used to the constant mumble of the crowd which besieged the main entrance. According to local news shows, over a third of Boongate's population had now left, with everyone else anxious to join them. Niall wasn't so sure about the official numbers, he thought it was more than that. Every day he cycled to work from his two-room flat, going the long way round the massive station yard. That way he didn't get caught up in the huge jam of people arriving on the highway. There were so many cars driven into the verges along the approach roads that the government employed seventeen crews towing the abandoned vehicles away, not that they could keep up. It wasn't just the sides of the highway that were clogged, of course. A lot of people drove through the same maze of streets he used in the commercial district surrounding the station, and parked on any clear spot before walking round to the front. Some mornings he'd find hundreds of cars had appeared overnight, turning the roads into quite an obstacle course for him to weave his way round.

Anyone who arrived and dumped their car then had a wait of nearly two days as the massive throng of people slowly shuffled their way forwards towards the haven of the terminal's main entrance. Niall didn't know how many people there were between the highway and the entrance, it looked like the entire population to him. They wore expensive semi-organic coats, or draped plastic sheets round their shoulders to protect themselves from the miserable rain of Boongate's early winter months. There had been plenty of days when Niall turned up and it had been sleeting. Once it snowed for thirty-six hours. It subdued the crowd, made them miserable, made them bad tempered, but nothing had ever made them fall silent before.

Niall was only three hundred metres away from the employee gate when he realized the sound was missing, most days you could hear it over a kilometre away. He steered round a big Toyota ten-seater Lison that was parked across a warehouse delivery bay, and braked to a halt. When he pushed his goggles up, he found it had stopped raining. Good news, yes, but not enough to stop that constant growl of barely restrained anger. He looked up. The force field had come on over the city; dark clouds slithering round its shimmering surface. A second force field was covering the station, deflecting the mists that were trapped under the city's dome. 'Oh hell,' he whispered in fright. He'd never allowed himself to believe that the aliens would return.

His e-butler's news filter let through an alert telling him that wormholes were being detected in a lot of star systems across the Commonwealth. His instant response was to glance over at the giant terminal building with its long, curved glass roofs. Instinctive self-preservation kicked in, and he started to work out routes in his mind. As an employee, he had access to several restricted zones inside the station complex; there were a number of ways he could reach the platforms without ever having to join that horde outside.

He let go of the brakes, and began peddling again. Today, there were eight guards outside the employee gate, all dressed in flexarmour and carrying weapons. Normally, there were just two security staff inside their cabin, who always waved him on when he showed his company pass. This time they made Niall put his palm on a sensor pad one of them was carrying to check his biometric pattern.

'You've got to be kidding,' the guard snarled from inside his helmet. 'A tour company rep?'

'We're still active,' Niall protested. 'It's genuine. Check my record, I've been in every day for weeks. I've got groups left on Far Away that are coming back. Somebody's got to be here for them.'

'I've got news for you, sonny, they ain't going to make it. Look around you.'

'And if they do?'

There was a long pause while the guard referred back to his superior. 'Okay,' he said eventually. 'You can go through.'

'Thanks.'

The reinforced barrier across the pavement swivelled up. Niall pushed his bicycle through, feeling his skin tingle as he went through the force field. Just as he was mounting up on the other side, the guard said. 'Son, if you've got any sense at all, you'll go straight to the platforms and catch a train to Gralmond or one of its neighbours.'

'If my group comes back, I'll do it.'

Not even the thick armour could mask the man shaking his head.

Niall peddled as fast as he could to the office. His e-butler was supplying situation updates the whole way. Alien ships were pouring into the Boongate system, out around the third gas giant orbit. Thousands more were emerging in other systems. Local news told him that the wormhole to Wessex had been temporarily closed by CST. 'Hellfire.' There'd be a riot. He knew there would be.

When he got to the office he wheeled his bike in through the reception area and parked it against the counter. There was a bag he kept in the back with some spare clothes. He fetched it out, and looked round the small room. Grand Triad Adventures had a floor safe to keep the petty cash and various travel vouchers. Mr Spanton, the manager, had granted Niall's biometric print a temporary access authority when he went 'on holiday' right after the first Prime attack. Niall put his hand on the lock pad, and internal malmetal bands pushed the door up. The cash was all piled in different currencies. He didn't bother with anything from Boongate or the neighbouring stars; figuring those Treasuries wouldn't be able to back the national currency for much longer. Out of the money that came from planets further from this new attack, he had roughly 15,000 Earth dollars' worth. He stuffed it into his jacket pockets and turned to the office array which had a direct link to the CST ticket and travel information system. Surprisingly, his access authority still got him in; not that there was much information available. Wessex seemed to have closed half of its wormholes to traffic, and there were heavy restrictions on the remainder. There was no indication when they would open again.

Only if the navy fights off this invasion, Niall thought. But if by some miracle it did, he was going to be ready. He used the Grand Triad Adventures account to buy a first class ticket to Gralmond, just like the guard suggested. It was four hundred and fifty light-years away, right across the other side of the Commonwealth, about as far away from Boongate as it was physically possible to go. He held his breath as the CST system processed the application, but after a few seconds it assigned his identity tattoo with the first class ticket.

Someone knocked on the office door. Niall jumped, mostly from guilt. There was a man standing outside. Tall and quite handsome, with floppy blond hair. The type of guy who played a lot of sports, certainly his square-shouldered build put Niall's rather more flabby frame to shame. He was talking, jabbing a finger at something in the office.

'Sorry,' Niall tapped his ear, and put his hand on the door's lock pad. 'Couldn't hear you,' he said as the door opened.

'Thanks for letting me in,' the man said, his voice had a distinctive Earth-American twang.

'We're not busy.' *That was a dumb thing to say.* Niall wanted to look at the door leading to the back room, he was pretty sure the man wouldn't be able to see the open floor safe.

'I need some help. Ah . . . I don't know your name.' His grin was the kind which took you straight into his confidence.

'Niall. What kind of help?'

'It's like this, Niall. Some friends of mine have been stuck on Far Away for a while, but they've just sent me a message saying that they've managed to get off. They're on their way back. How's that for godawful fucking luck. Coming back into the middle of an alien invasion. Anyway, I need to get out to the platform and meet them. Once we're all together again then we'll try to get off Boongate.'

'There aren't any trains off Boongate right now. I was just checking that.'

'I know, but they'll start up again as soon as the invasion is over. I'm not worried about that. My problem is my friends. I can't let them down. Can you take me over to the Half Way wormhole gateway? I'd go by myself, but there are a lot of security systems round it and, I'm worried I'll never be allowed through to meet them, what with everyone being so jumpy right now. They'll get back and be stuck here. That would be serious bad news for all of us. If it helps, I can make it worth your while. Seriously worth your while.'

Niall liked the guy even more; he was obviously a regular dude, and rich, too. Everyone who went to Far Away was rich. And he was right about security, look at what happened at the employee gate this morning. Niall could come out of this very well if he played his cards right, maybe add a couple of grand to his newfound wealth. 'Well, yeah, the company Mercedes is authorized to go right out to the Far Away transit area. I can take you through, no sweat.'

The man's confident grin became even wider. 'That's what I wanted to hear.'

*

Hoshe had just reached the London office when the Prime attack began. Vast force fields came on over the ancient city, turning the sky a murky grey. Looking out over the Thames he saw the dark shapes of aerobots rising from their silos. They were bigger than any flying machine he'd ever seen before.

His e-butler told him Inima was calling.

'You okay?' she asked.

'Yeah, I'm at the office. What about you?'

'We're safe here, aren't we, Hoshe?'

'Safest place in the Commonwealth, I promise. Shall I come home?'

'No. You stay there. I don't want you worrying about me.'

'I don't worry. I love you. I'm leaving now.'

'No, Hoshe. I've got the news summary in my virtual vision. The attacks aren't anywhere near Earth. You stay at work.'

'I want to be with you, in case.' In case of what, he didn't know. If Earth fell, it would all be over. And not even Paula could get them places on a Dynasty lifeboat.

'Should you travel now?' she asked.

'Of course. If anything gets through that force field it won't matter where you are. I'll get a taxi.'

'I don't want to be trouble.'

'You're not.'

Hoshe grabbed his coat from the hook on the back of the door. A red priority icon flashed up into his virtual vision; it was Captain Kumancho, who was leading the Senate Security detail following Victor Halgarth. 'Damn!' Hoshe touched the icon with his turquoise virtual finger.

'We've just arrived on Boongate,' Kumancho said. 'Victor went to one of the warehouses out in the station marshalling yard. It belongs to a company called Sunforge; local transport and courier outfit. We're datamining it now.'

'Okay. Are you emplaced?'

'As best we can. Hoshe, it's chaos here. There's half the planet's population camped outside the station. CST has just closed the wormhole, we must have been on the last train in. My people are worried we won't be able to get back.'

'Shit. Right, leave it with me. Is the Halgarth team with you?'

'Yes.'

'Okay, that's good. I'll get in touch with Warren Halgarth, we'll coordinate our approach and put a process in place to extract you as soon as CST reopens the wormhole. I'll try and get information on that as well.'

'Thanks, Hoshe.'

'Do you know what's in the Sunforge warehouse?'

'Not yet. We're going to start running an infiltration operation once we're properly established.'

'Do you need help from the locals? I can run the request from this office, it'll carry more clout.'

'I think we're on our own, Hoshe. Government here has just about collapsed. CST's station security teams and the city police force are still hanging together, almost, but they're not going to be arsed about a bunch of spooks asking for cooperation. Don't worry, we can handle Victor and the warehouse.'

'Okay, keep me updated on an hourly basis. I'll be in the office.' Hoshe stood perfectly still for a moment as he cursed every god he knew about, then hung his coat back on the hook. His turquoise finger touched Inima's icon. 'Darling, I'm sorry. Something's come up.'

*

'Don't worry,' Anna said. Her small mouth tightened into a smile as she straightened the shoulders on Wilson's dress uniform brushing away creases. 'You know and I know that you did everything you could. There were no alternatives, no smartarse answers. You told it to them as it was, and they gave you the budget they wanted to.'

Several people were looking at them as they stood nose to nose outside the Senate Hall's underground chamber, aides to the other War Cabinet members who were in session, and had been for thirty minutes. It was as if Wilson and Anna were radioactive; nobody said hello, nobody swapped idle chat, not even Daniel Alster and Patricia Kantil. For Wilson not to be in a War Cabinet meeting was a clear indication of what was being discussed inside. There wasn't any informed measured debate going on in there, it was an open power struggle.

'Damn Nigel for not telling us what he'd got,' Wilson muttered. His voice carried just far enough to provoke some glances from the nearest aides. 'Damn him for not sharing.'

'They only just got their ship operational in time,' Anna said, patting his arm.

'So he claims,' he hissed. 'Hell, listen to me. Nobody trusts anyone else any more.'

'How can we?' Anna looked around, and pulled him further away from the immaculately dressed, polite, obedient aides. 'We don't know who is working for the Starflyer.'

'This isn't just because of the Starflyer. Look at them all.' He tilted his head at the aides. 'All the Dynasties and Grand Families see here is an opportunity to put one over on the rest. They're concentrating on internal politics while the human species is faced with extinction.'

'That's not quite fair.'

'Yeah yeah.' Tension and dismay was giving him the shakes. *Being made to wait outside like a schoolkid hauled up before the principal, it's not right. I did a good job.* 'Damn, I feel sorry for myself.' His virtual vision was showing a tactical display from Pentagon II, where the navy was keeping watch for any further sign of Prime activity. It was only seven hours since the wormholes into Commonwealth space had shut down. He didn't have time for this bullshit. They had to organize the navy's response immediately. That's if he was going to be organizing it.

'Hey, stop it.' She nuzzled his face. 'They're probably just deciding which medal to give you.'

He gave her a tired look. 'Thanks.'

'You know I'll stay with you, don't you?'

He kissed her. 'Couldn't have got this far without you.'

'It'll be nice to have a real life together. I've never had a rich husband, before. I still haven't seen your home on York5.'

'You'll love it. We've got an area the size of Oregon which I've been shaping and planting. And the chateau needs refurbishing.'

'Sounds good. Me, an unlimited credit tattoo, and every interior designer on that side of the Commonwealth.'

He held her tight. 'It will be good. It will.'

The doors to the conference room opened. Rafael Columbia strode out. He was also wearing his full dress uniform; immaculately tailored, it made him the perfect authority figure. Even the aides straightened up as he appeared.

Wilson hadn't known Rafael was in the War Cabinet. It could only mean one thing. 'Shit.' At least he didn't have to wait any more, he knew for sure now. *I don't even have to go through with this humiliation, not really.*

'Wilson,' Rafael put on a suitably sober expression of greeting. He extended his hand.

I could just tell him to shove it.

Anna made a small sound at the back of her throat.

Wilson shook hands. *Like a proper officer would, with dignity. They'd be proud of me back at the academy – if it still existed.*

'I'm sorry,' Rafael said. 'They called me in after they asked for you.'

'It's okay.' *As Caesar said to Brutus.* 'I don't think either of us is in an enviable position.'

Rafael nodded sympathetically. 'They're ready for you.'

'Sure.'

Anna squeezed his hand. He walked with Rafael into the conference room to face the War Cabinet. Surprisingly, it was only President Doi who met his eye as he stood at the head of the table. Heather Antonia Halgarth simply looked bored, while Nigel Sheldon had a thunderous expression on his face. It was a hugely telling sight, that the man whose family warship and private weapons project had just saved the entire Commonwealth could suffer a political defeat directly afterwards.

Rafael came to stand just behind Wilson.

'Admiral,' President Doi said. 'We have reviewed the performance of the navy and yourself before and during this latest *disastrous* invasion. To say that we find it lacking would be the understatement of this century. In view of the catastrophic loss of life, we require your immediate resignation.'

Argue. Tell her to fuck off. Nobody could have done better.

'As you wish,' he said coolly.

Rafael came up to him. 'Admiral, your navy authorization codes have now been revoked. You will be placed on our inactive list, effective immediately.'

Wilson clenched his teeth. 'Right.'

'Thank you for what you did, Wilson. The navy staff appreciate it,' Rafael said with emphasis.

Wilson turned to face the navy's new chief admiral-in-waiting. 'I want you and everyone else in here to know something.'

'If you have anything to say, please place it in your debrief report,' Doi said formally.

He smiled at her, enjoying the way she wanted him out of the room with a minimum of fuss. She didn't yet have the confidence to try and snap an order at him. 'The Starflyer is real.' He made sure he was looking directly at Rafael, seeing the small start of surprise in the man's otherwise composed features. 'It's been manipulating us for a long while.'

'Enough! *Mr* Kime,' Doi said.

'Its agents were on board the *Second Chance*. They switched off the barrier generator.'

Rafael was looking embarrassed now. Wilson glanced round the table. The only person who held his attention was Justine Burnelli, she appeared guilty rather than surprised. *Interesting.*

He shrugged at the War Cabinet, as if he wasn't bothered any more. 'Check it out,' he told Rafael as he turned to leave.

*

Nigel watched Wilson's back as he left the committee room. The man's outburst was fascinating. He was amused by the reaction of the others round the table. Doi, predictably, was mortified at Wilson's claim. Heather seemed bemused. Rafael concerned. While Justine was doing the same as him, checking round. He met her gaze and gave her a smile. She deliberately returned a blank expression.

He could hardly forget Campbell's urgent call less than twenty-four hours ago, asking on her behalf what the Dynasty policy was towards Myo. After the Prime attack, Campbell had also told him the senator and the Investigator were requesting an urgent personal meeting. He wasn't sure what it was about, but given what Nelson's observation team had told him about Mellanie's activities on Illuminatus, it wasn't a request he was about to refuse. Only now was he starting to wonder what sort of connections Justine had with Wilson. One thing was for sure, that meeting was going to be a lot more interesting than this one.

'I think we can move forward now,' Doi said once the doors were shut, and the screening back around the conference room. 'I would like to propose that Admiral Columbia assumes overall command of the navy, effective immediately.'

'I second that,' Toniea Gall said.

You would, Nigel thought. He caught Heather's smile of approval.

'All in favour?' Doi asked.

Nigel languidly raised his arm along with everyone else. Alan Hutchinson gave him a fierce, sympathetic grin, which he ignored. If Heather was surprised, she didn't show it. The argument that the Dynasties had engaged in three hours ago via ultra-secure links had been ferocious. Only a small part of the bad feeling had spilled into the first part of the War Cabinet meeting. Even the intensity of that had mildly scandalized the likes of Crispin Goldreich and Toniea Gall. But then, behind strong seals, Heather always did swear like a building site labourer.

'I would like to thank you for your confidence,' Rafael said. He sounded most sincere. 'I want to assure you that I am determined to end the Prime threat once and for all. Mr Sheldon, you said you will make your weapon available.'

They all turned to Nigel. *Even now*, he thought wearily. For a moment he felt like storming out. Catching up with Wilson, putting his arm round the man's shoulder and the two of them heading off to a bar together.

The Commonwealth he'd created and led for so long now wanted his weapons. *That's not how it was supposed to be.* The day he'd stepped out on Mars to laugh at Wilson and the other astronauts was the day he broke the old system, he and Ozzie had set everyone free. *And now, I've helped build the most revolting weapon anyone has ever dreamt up. I wanted us to live among the stars themselves, not snuff them out.* 'Yeah,' he said contemptuously. How very like the old military officers Rafael was, audacious in their smart uniforms, sounding positive as they gave their briefings on precision attacks and minimal collateral damage. 'Unless the Primes agree to negotiate a cessation of hostilities, I will use our weapon against their homeworld.'

'Will that guarantee their eradication?' Hans Brant inquired.

'The weapon when fired into a star releases a nova-level energy burst, and destroys the star in the process. Such an event will envelop the entire Dyson Alpha civilization. As they have undoubtedly spread beyond their original star by now, my Dynasty tacticians have proposed a firewall strategy. We will run scout missions centred round Dyson Alpha, and nova every star where we detect their presence. It will, of course, sterilize all life on neighbouring star systems.'

There was complete silence round the table.

'You wanted to win,' Nigel told them uncompromisingly.

'We have been reticent about genocide in the past, and rightly so,' Rafael said. 'For that is what makes us human. But we can no longer indulge ourselves in this case. If the Primes are allowed to survive, they will forever be a threat to our existence. They have flare bombs, and no reluctance to use them. They have wormholes, and from that will be able to develop ftl ships. If that happens, they will spread through this galaxy like a virus, and endanger even more species than ourselves. We cannot allow that to happen. It boils down to a very simple equation: them or us.'

'Very well,' Doi said. 'It is the recommendation of this War Cabinet that every means possible is used to rid ourselves of the Prime threat, up to and including their complete extermination. I propose this motion.'

'Seconded,' Rafael said.

'Please vote, ladies and gentlemen,' Doi said.

It was unanimous.

'Thank you,' Rafael said.

'How are you going to deal with the Primes left in Commonwealth space?' Crispin asked.

'The Lost23 will be the easiest,' Rafael said. 'They have very few ships in those systems. We will simply pull our insurgency troops out, and use a quantumbuster against each planet. They will not survive that. The New48 are more problematical.'

'You reckon?' Alan Hutchinson snapped. 'For a start, you're not classing Wessex along with the rest of the invasion. Drop a quantumbuster on my world, and I'll fucking nuke your Dynasty back into the Stone Age.'

'Nobody's going to wipe out Wessex,' Heather said. 'Calm down, Alan. It's a Big15, it can recover from the flare radiation. Narrabri is protected under force fields, and the farmland can be replanted easily enough. The rest of it, the land you've left uncultivated, doesn't count, it has no economic value, and no one living there.'

'You still need a functioning biosphere,' Justine said.

'Half of the land mass will be completely unaffected,' Hans Brant said. 'The flare activity lasted for less than an hour in total. And the impact the radiation will have on the ocean is completely minimal. The biosphere remains essentially intact on Wessex as it does the other New48.'

'It's not that simple,' Justine said. 'The particle swarm will spread around the planet, you'll get fall out everywhere.'

'By far the worst impact is the hemisphere facing the star during flare time. The rest is manageable. Look at Far Away, the flare lasted for weeks there, and we managed to regenerate the continents. That whole planet is alive again. You're not going to have people running out of oxygen. The time it'll take to restore the carbon cycle is insignificant on a planetary scale.'

'I've actually been to Far Away,' Justine said. 'It is minimally habitable, and that's after over a century and a half of gruelling effort. It's a huge mistake to class it among normal H-congruous worlds. These New48 will not be habitable; we have to get the populations off. I don't know about Wessex, that's exceptional, but the rest must be evacuated.'

'I am not proposing abandoning Wessex,' Rafael said. 'However, there are now four and a half thousand fully armed Prime ships in the Wessex system. We don't have four and a half thousand Douvoir missiles in our inventory, let alone the hundred and seventy thousand we'll need to eliminate Prime ships throughout the New48.'

'Did they really send that many through?' Toniea Gall asked.

'Yes,' Rafael said. 'Which means we will have to evacuate the majority of these systems. The navy cannot deal with forty-eight armadas.'

'How many can you deal with?' Doi asked.

'Assuming the *Moscow*-class production continues unabated, we estimate we can clear five star systems before we face a loss of containment. We don't yet know what kind of threat the ships pose. They have two options, both of which present unique difficulties for us. Firstly, they can head in to the H-congruous planets, and breach our defences through sheer numbers, then land and establish an armed colony. It does, of course, mean that we can use quantumbusters against them when they are down and concentrated.'

'And the second option?' Crispin asked.

'They make a break for it. With an average of three and a half thousand ships in each system, they'll possess enough equipment and manufacturing capability between them to put together an ftl drive eventually. Again, they will have to rendezvous to begin a manufacturing process, which will leave them vulnerable to a Douvoir missile.'

'How long will it take to manufacture a hundred and seventy thousand Douvoir missiles?' Toniea Gall asked.

'We could probably get them completed within nine months providing we authorize a super crash-priority project. I'm not sure we have that kind of time available. If they are still planning on colonizing the New48, they could be in orbit around each of them within a week.'

'You're talking about evacuation regardless of the Primes,' Justine said.

'Yes. That is our preferred option. Let them all land and take them out with a quantumbuster.'

'We've already got a monstrous refugee problem from the Lost23, and most of them were low-population worlds. How many people live on the New48?'

'Not including Wessex,' Nigel said, 'about thirty-two billion people.' This time the silence was even more profound.

'It can't be done,' Hans Brant said. 'Can it?'

'Physically removing them through the wormholes is possible,' Nigel said. 'However, accommodating a diaspora of such magnitude within the remaining Commonwealth is totally impractical. There is nowhere for that many people to live; feeding them on basic rations alone would virtually bankrupt the rest of us.'

'Then we have to face that prospect,' Justine said. 'I for one will not even consider any proposal that includes abandoning these people. Wars inevitably instigate societal change; it looks like this is shaping up to be ours.'

'A noble sentiment, my dear,' Hans Brant said. 'But even if the Senate were to assume draconian powers, and force the refugees on the rest of the Commonwealth, some planets would resist.'

'We cannot turn our backs on thirty-two billion lives!' Justine stormed.

'There is an alternative,' Nigel said quietly. 'A risky one, of course.' This time he felt almost nothing but contempt at the way everyone turned to him with hope and desperation in their eyes. 'We open up forty-seven fresh planets, and simply transfer the populations over directly so they can rebuild their societies.'

'For Christ's sake, man,' Alan said. 'You can't dump billions of people on undeveloped worlds. They need cities, and infrastructure, government . . . food!'

'I know,' Nigel said. 'That would all have to be prepared beforehand.'

'But . . . we've got less than a week,' Toniea Gall spluttered.

'As Einstein once said, time depends on the relative position of the observer.'

*

When President Doi officially closed the War Cabinet session, Justine waited in her chair while the other Dynasty leaders went over to Nigel to offer their thanks and congratulations. Even Heather was conciliatory enough to congratulate him. As for Doi, Justine had never seen the President so pathetically happy, she almost ran across the anteroom to tell Patricia Kantil the outcome. Patricia's face was soon beaming a huge, incredulous smile.

How stupid, Justine thought. It was as if declaring something were possible had made it happen. And everything they'd agreed in Cabinet was dependent on nothing else going wrong. *How's the Starflyer going to react?*

'You wanted to see me, I believe?' Nigel said. He'd come over to stand beside her chair. Justine looked up at him. *And exactly how do I tell if I'm looking at the Starflyer's number one agent in the Commonwealth?* Her hand went to the slight bump in her belly. *I need to secure a place on one of the lifeboats, just in case.*

'I do,' she said.

'Excellent. On one condition.'

'What's that?' she asked in trepidation.

'You and Investigator Myo bring Mellanie with you.'

Justine's jaw dropped. 'Huh?'

'Mellanie Rescorai. I've been wanting to meet her for quite a while now. She's with the Investigator, isn't she? They travelled back to Earth together from Illuminatus.'

'Yes,' Justine said, struggling to regain her poise. *How does he know that? More important, why does he know that?*

'Excellent. We'll do it after we've all made this stupid public announcement. The CST offices at Newark should give us some privacy.' He smiled. 'I'm glad you're okay after the assassin's attempt on your life. Tell Gore I'm impressed, as always.'

'I'll let him know,' Justine promised.

*

Edmund Li knew he was being stupid staying on. He should have left Boongate weeks ago, when the loose collection of relatives and friends that made up his family all departed on a train to Tanyata. They'd called him every time a connection to the unisphere was available, a schedule that was even worse than the link to Far Away; showing him images of the tent they were living in, scenes from everyday Tanyata life. So he got a good sketch of them and fifty thousand others spread out in a makeshift township not far from the ocean; one of eight such townships centred round the CST station. Everybody was helping to lay down the grid of their new city, building up the infrastructure, doing the work normally left to bots. They all helped out, they all knew their neighbours. There was a pioneer spirit there which human worlds hadn't possessed since the very first planets were opened up three hundred years ago. Despite the hardship, it looked like a good place to live.

Still, Edmund hadn't left. The really stupid thing was,

technically, he didn't even have a job any more, the Far Away freight inspectorate division had nothing left to do. Nobody on Far Away was importing anything. There was nothing for his team to scan and analyse. Besides, the others had all left a couple of days after the Navy Intelligence people had visited, it was just him now. He'd watched all the other offices in the small administration block thin out and dwindle to nothing; which made him the de facto Boongate government official in charge of all travel to Far Away.

At first he kept doing it because of the navy's Paris office, who had asked him to keep monitoring traffic to and from Far Away. It was important, Renne and Tarlo had said. After a while, he became intrigued by Far Away and what was going on there. That wasn't a good enough reason to stay, he knew, and yet . . . The people leaving Far Away were nearly all the same, every Carbon Goose flight was packed full with migrants who'd sold virtually everything they had to buy a ticket. They arrived bowed under the weight of a world with a standard gravity, and burdened further with pitiful expectations of the Commonwealth. Edmund was doing well if he managed to collect all their names before they disappeared into the station terminal where they believed they'd find sanctuary. By talking to them he did manage to gather a picture of the strange turmoil afflicting Far Away, the criminal sabotage, the rise of the Institute in enforcing law and order in Armstrong City.

But it was the people who were still travelling to Far Away who sparked his real interest. Why anyone should choose to go there at this time was incomprehensible. Yet they kept turning up with their return tickets; technical staff for the Institute, security staff for the Institute, managers for the Institute. No Institute staff were on the flights coming back from Far Away; yet they would be the only people left on the planet with return tickets.

In his zeal to understand more of that benighted planet, he ran innumerable searches through the unisphere for information. For the first time ever he began to pay attention to what the Guardians were saying. Yes, they were a bunch of psychopathic terrorists, but put into the context of everything he was witnessing, their claims made unpleasant sense.

Last week even the Carbon Goose flights had stopped as the pilots and crews deserted to head for safer parts of the Commonwealth. Then the CST technical support staff began to slip away from the station. He was mildly surprised that the wormhole to Wessex remained functional because there were so few maintenance personnel left to operate Boongate end. A lot of everyday engineering was being carried out by remote from the Big15 world.

That should have been the right time to leave, Edmund knew. The RI controlling the gateway to Half Way would no doubt shut it down when enough components expired and preset safety limits were reached. It might last a day, or six months, Edmund was hardly an expert. Not that it mattered, without the Carbon Goose crews there was no way to get to Far Away any more. He felt almost guilty thinking such thoughts; by now he considered himself the only person who cared about the fate of that remote planet, the lone watchman on the border looking out across the void.

Then three days ago something else changed. The communication link between Half Way and Far Away opened at the correct time, but the message traffic flowing into the Commonwealth unisphere wasn't even one per cent of normal, and all of it was encrypted. Any messages or calls going to Far Away were bounced back, including his own official request for information to the Governor's House. Far Away was now completely isolated.

For three days Edmund Li kept a solitary vigil in his lonely office, waiting to see what was going to happen. Then the Primes attacked.

He followed the invasion through the news shows and official government information feeds. The swarm of ships emerging three AUs out from the star. The flare bomb fired into the star. A secret navy superweapon that was terrifyingly powerful, extinguishing the flare bomb, but with such a high price. Then another flare bomb was fired into Boongate's star. The navy was forced to blow it up again. Sensors on the satellites orbiting Boongate captured the oceanic waves raging through the star's corona; they also recorded the sudden and deadly rise in solar radiation playing over the planet.

Without warning or explanation, every Prime wormhole into the Commonwealth shut down. Humans had won – if you discounted the thousands of warships gathering like stormcrows around forty-eight Commonwealth worlds.

It was the weather which probably saved Edmund. He'd spent a couple of hours sitting at his desk accessing reports and first-hand accounts of the invasion, with the occasional foray over to the vending machine for cups of tea. After the wormholes vanished, he started tracking Boongate's satellite sensor data, seeing the direct impact the radiation gale was having on the planet. Electromagnetic energy was absorbed and weakened to some extent by the atmosphere before it reached the ground. Even so, the dosage was far greater than most animals and plants could comfortably withstand. The first wave of particle radiation arrived not much later, virtually wiping out the ionosphere in the first few minutes. It was much worse than the news studio experts predicted. Power supplies outside the cities and towns protected by force fields became erratic or failed altogether under the surges. All the civil satellites dropped out as they were exposed, leaving sensors on the planetary defence platforms as the only source of information. Borealis storms swept down from the poles, their pale dancing colours bringing a weird beauty to the destruction falling silently across the world.

Edmund went outside to watch the first of the aural lightshows swirl around the city's force field. The parking lot still had puddles left over from the night's rainfall before the station and city force fields deflected the clouds. There was only one car standing on the concrete, his own, a fifteen-year-old Honda Trisma. He stood beside it as the mauve and apricot phosphorescence came rippling out of the horizon at supersonic speed. Even the clouds had retreated before the elementary tide, producing a clear winter sky. When he squinted up at the sun, he convinced himself he could see small bright spots on the glaring disc.

Sheet lightning flickered over the city. For a moment it outshone both the sun and the borealis lights. Small rivulets of purple ions skated down the curvature of the force field dome. Then the aurora was back in full, reflecting its hot luminescence across the wet concrete.

The unisphere was telling everyone still outside a force field to seek shelter immediately. Lightning flashed again, a longer burst this time. Edmund started counting for the thunder, until he realized how useless that was. There were long sparkles mingling with the borealis streamers now, adding to their intensity, helping to drown out the ordinary sky. Lightning snapped between the varied undulating colour bands. It was a strangely beautiful death cloak for a planet to throw around itself, he thought.

His e-butler told him there was an emergency address to the Commonwealth by the War Cabinet. The planet's cyber-sphere would carry nothing else. He didn't even know the managing RI could do that. *About time*, he thought, *we could do with knowing what's going on, and what happened in the battle.* CST still hadn't re-opened the wormhole to Wessex, though the parallel zero-width wormhole was obviously keeping Boongate connected to the unisphere.

The image which rose up into his virtual vision showed him President Doi sitting at the head of an imposing table, flanked by Nigel Sheldon and Heather Halgarth. Edmund pursed his lips: *impressive indeed.* Captions labelled the other cabinet members for him; the amount of political power gathered together was an indication that whatever had been decided was definite. He leaned back against his Honda to listen to his fate.

'My fellow citizens,' Doi said. 'I will start by telling you that the Prime incursions into Commonwealth space have now ended, at least for the immediate future. A frigate managed to get through to Hell's Gateway and destroy the wormhole generators there. I cannot give you details about the ship or the weapon used for obvious security reasons, but suffice it to say we now have at our disposal a weapon of truly formidable power. Sadly, as I'm sure you are all aware, this does not eliminate the Prime threat entirely. There are many thousands of Prime warships already in Commonwealth space which will have to be dealt with. In addition, the Primes deployed flare bombs whose effects are still being felt on the Second48 worlds. There is nothing we can do to deflect the radiation saturating those planets. In short, their biospheres will in all probability be rendered uninhabitable. Even if a regeneration program were possible, as it may be on Wessex, all these worlds will see battle again as the navy combats the remaining Prime ships over the coming weeks. It is therefore with huge regret, I have informed the planetary leaders we have no choice but to evacuate their worlds.'

'Shit,' Edmund muttered. He'd known in his heart that the address was going to say something like that, but even so the enormity of what the President was saying was only just registering. *But where are we all going to go?*

'As accommodating an estimated thirty billion dispossessed people is a practical impossibility even for our society,' Doi said, 'we will have to adopt a rather novel solution.'

Edmund didn't like the sound of that at all. Then his e-butler told him a vehicle had just passed through the level two security cordon round the Far Away gateway section. He frowned. Who the hell was visiting this part of the station, especially now?

752

Nigel Sheldon leant forwards, taking over from the President, his expression earnest and supremely confident. 'When we were building our first wormhole, Ozzie came up with some math for manipulating the internal temporal flow dynamic of exotic matter. We ran a small test a couple of centuries ago using one of CST's exploratory division wormholes, and the concept worked. It hasn't been used since, because we haven't had a practical or commercial application for it. Until today. What we will do is modify the wormholes leading to the planets whose biospheres are dying. Within a week, they will be opened to the entire population in an exodus that will be organized by your national government. You will not be using trains to travel through, instead you will be asked to walk or drive, or take buses, you can even cycle if you like. The other end will emerge on a fresh H-congruous planet in phase three space. However, it will not emerge for another ten or fifteen years, or even longer if necessary. For you, only a few seconds will have gone past, but outside, the rest of the Commonwealth will have had enough time to build new basic cities and towns with a functioning infrastructure to accommodate you. I know this will seem shocking, but the worlds you are on now are dying, and we have to move quickly to insure against further loss of life.'

The car was a Mercedes registered to Grand Triad Adventures. Edmund stood up, staring out across the vast station yard to the road leading away to the terminal. He could actually see the car, a sleek burgundy-red limousine speeding along. It was under manual control, and it drove straight past the junction where it should have turned towards the single passenger platform. Not that anyone was using the Half Way wormhole anyway. Instead, it was heading for the office block and the parking lot where Edmund was standing. Something was very wrong about that. He retained enough of his policeman's instinct to check the small ion pistol he carried, then hurried towards the far end of the building.

'All of us pledge ourselves to seeing this rescue operation through to a successful conclusion,' President Doi said. 'Senators, planetary leaders, the Dynasties; we are united in our determination. No matter what the cost or the effort, we *will not* fail you.' She sighed in compassion. 'Godspeed, all of you.'

The Merc turned into the parking lot just as Edmund cleared the end of the building. He peered round the corner to see the big limousine pull up next to his Honda. A door swung open and a tall blond man stepped out. Edmund gasped as soon as he saw the face, recognizing him instantly. *Tarlo.* The Commonwealth-wide police alert had come through twenty-four hours ago. At first Edmund had thought it was some kind of mistake, or joke, but when he checked the warrant's certificate it was genuine enough.

Tarlo stared at the Honda for a moment, then he turned his head slowly, scanning the deserted parking lot. Edmund ducked back round the corner. The warrant had said Tarlo was heavily wetwired, and extremely dangerous. He counted to five, then risked another look. Tarlo was walking into the office block. The door to the Merc was still open. Edmund used his retinal inserts to zoom in. A body was lying on the limousine's carpeted floor, a podgy young man whose neck had been snapped. His dead eyes stared up at the magnificent moiré scintillations that now veiled Boongate's sky.

*

The Five Stop café was at one end of the Rocher strip mall, squeezed between a Bab's Kebabs franchise and Mother Blossom, a budget maternity clothes shop. Highway B77 ran past outside, leading directly to Narrabri's planetary station four kilometres west. Even now, with the borealis storm seething through the sky outside the megacity's force field, thousands of alien ships loose in the system, and half of the station's gateways still closed, the traffic was as thick as always.

Bradley Johansson and Adam Elvin paid little attention to the racing vehicles. The portal over the serving counter had just started to repeat the War Cabinet's announcement.

'Dreaming heavens,' Bradley muttered. 'I never expected that. What an ingenious solution. No wonder Sheldon looks so pleased with himself.'

Adam gave the portal a sceptical glance. 'I think smug is more like it.'

'Now now, Adam, you should learn to be more charitable, especially in times of crisis. Besides, building the infrastructure for forty-seven worlds is a massive centralist state project. Exactly the kind of thing you approve of.'

'Don't stereotype me. I'm not a fan of centralist government, the tendency there is towards corruption and remoteness. An inclusive society should see a devolution of power down to local committee level.'

'Hmm, remind me; how many angels have we counted on that pinhead now?'

'You started this. And it's forty-eight worlds. Damn, how the hell are they going to transport all these factories to a new planet?' He stared out of the window. Beyond the highway, the megacity rolled away into the smoggy horizon, vast housing estates alternating with industrial precincts, stitched together by the curving lines of the railway tracks and highways. Every few kilometres, the really big structures of refineries or smelter plants rose up out of the low-level sprawl, like the cathedrals and castles of a medieval landscape. Dusk was creeping over the protective force field dome, giving an extra potency to the iridescence which besieged the sky outside.

'Forty-seven,' Bradley said firmly. 'Hutchinson won't move this; he's already terraformed this world once. Even if the flare kills off every living thing outside the city, the tractorbots will just replant it all for him. In any case, the whole time travel enterprise will have to employ the wormhole generators at

Narrabri's planetary station. No, this world will remain no matter how much damage it suffers. Thirty two billion people depend on it.'

'Yeah. Those bombs we have . . . I knew the navy must be developing stronger weapons than the Douvoir missiles, but hell, something that can damage a star? Do you think the Starflyer expected that?'

'No I don't.' Bradley smiled into his plastic cup of coffee. 'Once again, it has underestimated us. This war was intended to wreck both species. Now a decisive victory is within our grasp. Doi and Sheldon will use these weapons, whatever they are, against Dyson Alpha.'

'It wasn't so clever on Illuminatus, either. Jenny reported that Bernadette was finally cornered by Paula Myo.'

'Really?' Bradley's eyebrows rose. 'How fascinating. Myo must be convinced that the Starflyer is a genuine threat by now. And the failed assassination attempt against Senator Burnelli will also add weight to our story. I wonder if we should attempt one last shotgun message to the Common-wealth.'

'Nobody will listen, not today, not for a long time.' Adam indicated the portal, which was now showing Michelangelo back in his studio. Even his composure had been shaken by the War Cabinet; the commentators he'd got with him seemed almost lost for words. 'I'm more concerned that Starflyer agents captured the Agent's head. Once his memorycell is analysed, we'll be looking at a major security breach.'

'I agree it's upsetting, Adam, but I feel our timeframe is measured in days if not hours. Even if the Starflyer worked out where we are and what we're doing, it would take time to launch an offensive against us. If it was smart, it would have left the Agent to the charms of the navy. They'll come in guns blazing at the slightest opportunity.'

'Maybe, but we have to watch for the possibility. And with

Kime removed, we've lost a major potential asset. Oscar won't have anything like the same influence with Columbia.'

'Has he uncovered anything in the *Second Chance* logs yet?'

'I don't know. He's spent so much time on board his ship, I haven't been able to contact him.' Adam's e-butler told him Marisa McFoster was calling. 'Yes?' he said.

'We're on Boongate,' she told him. 'Victor Halgarth has gone into a station warehouse belonging to the Sunforge Company. Sir, there's a lot of police-type observers following Victor as well as us.'

'I'm not surprised, the authorities were watching Bernadette on Illuminatus. You'll find some of them are from Halgarth Security. Can you fit yourselves into a secure location?'

'I'm not sure. It's a real mess here. The station is nearly in anarchy. After Doi's announcement, everyone left on the planet is heading right for the terminal building; but the rest of the station is deserted. We're not going to be able to do much without being seen.'

'I understand. We've got several teams on Boongate. I'll authorize them to contact you and provide as much back up as they can afford. In the meantime keep me updated.'

'Yes, sir.'

'Victor Halgarth on Boongate, and the whole planet about to be evacuated,' Bradley mused. 'This is a remarkable opportunity for us, Adam. We might be able to intercept the Starflyer here in the Commonwealth. It hasn't returned home yet, and it has only the shortest of times to get back to Boongate. CST won't risk opening the wormhole for ordinary transport again for fear that there'll be a stampede through.'

'Mellanie left Illuminatus with Paula Myo,' Adam said. 'Shall I try calling her again, and see if she can convince the Investigator?'

'No, we'll use Senator Burnelli, she's better placed than

Myo, and she has the necessary political strength to place a complete block on the Boongate wormhole.'

'How long do you think it will take CST to modify the wormhole generator to do this time-travel trick?'

'Sheldon spoke of a week. I suspect it's a question of programming rather than any physical modification, everything important is a software problem these days.'

'Okay. While you do that, I'll prepare our train. We might need it yet.'

'Of course.' Bradley stirred the dregs of his coffee. 'You know, it's highly probable that the Starflyer is also in the Narrabri station, preparing to crash through the Boongate wormhole, just as we are. How ironic is that? I wonder if it has rented the warehouse next to ours?'

'It hasn't.'

'If you say so, Adam. But we must reorganize our teams to watch the Boongate gateway ourselves.'

'I'll put some people on it.'

'Have we got any? I understood we're short, post-Illuminatus.'

'I can spare enough for a simple operation like this. We're only going to notice the lack of muscle if we do have to crash through.'

'Well, as of now, you have one more piece of "muscle". I shall be joining your team permanently now. There is little else I can do in the Commonwealth any more. And it is time I went home to face our nemesis.'

'That's good; having you on board will be a big morale booster for the Guardians. They need a pick-me-up now we've lost contact with Far Away.'

*

CST's Newark station had wormholes connecting it to over twenty planets in phase one space, including three wormholes to Augusta. Its terminals and marshalling yard squatted on the site of the old airport, sending out an arterial maze of road and rail connections into the surrounding sprawl of urbanization. Nigel gazed out of the manager's office on the top floor of the station's administration skyscraper, seeing the New Jersey Turnpike curving around the station's perimeter. The ancient route still carried huge amounts of freight and passengers in and out of the station; though it was now being supplanted by the new tunnels that CST had drilled to carry trains directly to Manhattan and along the east coast. Beyond the road the cold grey waters of Newark Bay surged against the shore of Staten Island. Today, the shimmering dome of the force field arched above the island's buildings and parks, giving the air a filmy hue, as if a faint sea fog had settled over the land.

Nigel's e-butler showed him security sensor images of Campbell greeting his visitors down in the lobby. Justine Burnelli unbuttoned a snow-white fur-lined coat and gave Campbell the demure kiss of a trusted friend. Nigel had only just realized Justine was pregnant when she arrived for the emergency War Cabinet meeting, now the little bump was quite visible under her stylish grey cashmere dress. It surprised him; someone of her age and status nearly always used a womb tank. When he checked with Perdita she hadn't known either, let alone who the father was – also unusual. The Grand Families always had strong financial agreements concerning their children, yet nothing had been filed in the New York legal registry. The security sensors showed him her inserts were maintaining a heavily encrypted link to the unisphere, which he guessed led directly back to Gore.

Investigator Myo was exactly as he remembered, her lovely face forever cursed with a slightly melancholic expression. She was wearing a well-cut charcoal and blue suit with a salmon-pink blouse, and her hair had been brushed to a gloss. Nothing to indicate that less than thirty hours ago she'd been crammed into an armour suit, in the thick of a firefight on Illuminatus.

His real attention, though, was reserved for Mellanie. Her wavy golden hair had been given a cursory brush, leaving it mildly unkempt. That and the way she kept clenching her jaw in a resentful fashion gave her an aggressive appearance. A dramatically short white skirt, long suede boots, and simple thin blue denim shirt managed to be both trendy and trashy. Dudley Bose stuck to her as if there was some kind of membrane holding them together. The petulant anger leaking out over his youthful face was exactly the same as Nigel recalled from the notorious 'welcome back' ceremony.

Nigel faced the office door as the lift arrived. He noticed that Campbell had managed to stand as far as possible from Mellanie during the ride up in the small lift. *Perdita was right, then.*

'Ready?' Nelson asked. The Dynasty security chief had also picked up on the implications of the meeting, but then he'd been observing events on Illuminatus a lot closer than Nigel.

'Be nice to get a few answers, finally,' Nigel said. He pulled his suit jacket straight. *Stupid vanity.*

He greeted Justine and Paula formally, then turned to Mellanie. 'At last.'

She gave him a puzzled look. 'Excuse me.'

'I've been following your recent activities with a lot of interest. It's very exciting for me to finally meet you in person.' Which was an understatement. In the flesh she was fabulously attractive, great figure, slightly wild appearance, as if she'd just finished having sex – and wanted more. He held on to her hand. She didn't try and pull it back, just twitched her lips roguishly as she reviewed him.

'Me too,' she said. Her voice must have dropped a couple of octaves.

'Hello again,' Dudley said. He somehow slid in front of Mellanie to stick his own hand out.

'Dudley; glad to see you're recovering.' Nigel avoided any

inflection in case the neurotic astronomer picked up on the irony.

'That's all thanks to my Mellanie.' His hand went round her shoulders. She didn't try to hide her look of disapproval.

Nigel offered them all seats as the e-seal came on around the office. 'Well, this is all very serious, Justine. It can't just be about your committee battle with Valetta.'

'In a way it is,' Justine said. 'The Halgarths now have control of the navy.'

'Yes, but I have the nova bomb. And the rest of us have a great deal of input into the navy budget. Heather is balanced. That's the way the Commonwealth works.'

'I have a question,' Paula said.

'I imagine you do,' Nigel said lightly. 'I've spent most of the last few hours trying to work out what it's going to be.'

'For the past century, I've been pressing the Commonwealth Executive to impose inspections on all cargo being shipped for Far Away, with no success whatsoever. That kind of examination would have enabled me to restrict the Guardians' weapon shipments, and possibly even shut them down altogether. Just before he was assassinated, Thompson Burnelli discovered that you have been opposing me for all that time. I'd like to know why.'

Nigel couldn't help the way he sneaked a *help me out* look at Daniel Alster, who was in his usual position, a helpful couple of metres to one side. 'Have I? I had no idea, or memory . . .'

'There's no policy file on that,' Daniel said quickly.

'This is critical,' Paula said. 'Thompson believed it to be true.'

'Find out,' Nigel told Daniel. 'Call Jessica right now.'

'Sir.'

Nigel stole a glance at Mellanie, who gave him a playful wink and crossed her legs. He wondered what the best approach would be for a girl like this. Just come straight out and ask her to bed. Probably. Though the one thing he didn't understand was Dudley. What could she possibly see in him?

'Er, our political office has been pursuing that policy,' Daniel said. He sounded embarrassed.

'Why?' Nigel asked.

'Ozzie ordered it.'

'*Ozzie?*'

Some of the tension went out of Paula's poise. 'I had no idea Mr Isaacs had an input into your Dynasty's political office.'

'He doesn't, normally,' Nigel said. 'Actually, ever, as far as I'm aware. But Ozzie has an equal share in CST so, as far as I'm concerned, he's entitled. Are you sure?' he asked Daniel.

'Yes.' Daniel gave Paula a curious look. 'He instructed the political office to adopt that strategy in 2243.'

'Oh my,' Paula said. 'The year of the Great Wormhole Heist. The year Bradley Johansson formed the Guardians and stole enough money to begin their operations. So the Starflyer never had anything to do with it. The Guardians stopped any examinations. I knew they had high level access to the Executive, I never considered Mr Isaacs was behind them.'

'Okay,' Nigel said. He wagged his finger at them. 'Explanations, please. Now.'

'Simple enough,' Justine said. 'Wilson Kime is quite correct, the Starflyer is real. It funded Dudley's observation of Dyson Alpha through a bogus educational charity. It had agents on board the *Second Chance*.'

'It has also infiltrated the navy,' Paula said. 'Wilson uncovered evidence that its agents were on board the *Second Chance*, but that was subsequently tampered with by someone inside Pentagon II. He couldn't go public with it. We believe a modified sensor satellite was responsible for interfering with the barrier generator and letting the Primes out. The whole mission was a gigantic con trick designed to start a war between us and the Primes, weakening both our species.'

Nigel finally knew how Wilson had felt when he landed on Mars. Today, he'd turned a star nova to neuter the greatest threat the human race had ever faced, then gone on to work out how to save thirty-two billion human lives; now he'd found out the war which had destroyed their stars was mostly his fault to begin with. 'Oh holy fuck.' He shot an appealing look to Nelson, but the security chief was struggling with his own shock.

'If you're correct about this—' Nelson began.

'We are,' Mellanie said primly.

Nelson gave her a short annoyed smile. 'Then the Guardians are probably right about the Starflyer infiltrating the Halgarth Dynasty.'

'Essentially, yes,' Paula said. 'Our showdown with its agents on Illuminatus confirmed this. The majority of Halgarths are completely unaffected, of course. But those in strategic positions have been taken over. Christabel is slowly acknowledging something is wrong; she's discreetly helping us keep track of suspects. It won't be long before she takes her suspicions to Heather.'

'And Columbia?' Nelson asked. 'Is he one of them?'

'We don't know.'

'Son of a bitch,' Nigel grunted. 'Well that settles it, we do not release our nova bombs to the navy. Jesus! And Doi? What about her? The Guardians said she was one of them.'

'We believe that was simple disinformation,' Paula said. 'Isabella Halgarth, a confirmed Starflyer agent, helped put that shotgun together. However, Isabella also had a relationship with Patricia Kantil.'

'She helped engineer the political decisions to form a navy,' Justine said. 'We've all been played to some extent.'

'Alessandra Baron is one of its agents,' Mellanie said. 'The bitch.'

Nigel felt numb as his expanded mentality began to examine the problem. There was a lot of anger building in his mind, the kind of straight animal antagonism that came from being fooled. But it was countered by the surprise, and sheer worry of the situation. *Goddamn, we were blindsided!* 'Whatever we do, we can't make this public,' he decided. 'Not right now. We need the public's complete confidence in government for the immediate future. The populations we're trying to save are dependent on the rest of the Commonwealth unifying behind the time travel strategy. That has to be our number one priority. Rooting out traitors can be done quietly in parallel. You guys must have some ideas how to do that; that's why you're here, right?'

'Primarily, yes,' Paula said. 'To begin with, simply being aware of the manipulation effectively nullifies it.'

'What exactly does the Starflyer hope to achieve?' Nelson asked. 'It's got its war, what more can it achieve?'

'I'm uncertain,' Paula said. 'The Guardians say it wants to destroy, or at the very least weaken, both species, leaving it to become the dominant power in this section of the galaxy. I would speculate that your nova bomb has upset those plans; humans are now capable of destroying the Primes. The Commonwealth will remain, and we will be considerably stronger. From a military point of view it has already failed.'

'Only if the navy and ourselves continue to press the attack,' Nelson said. 'That'll be where it concentrates its influence now. I would. After all, the Primes aren't exactly helpless yet. They still have the Hell's Gateway generator, and flare bombs. If we hesitate, thanks to the Starflyer, they could still manage a devastating blow against us.'

'Then we have to launch a strike against Dyson Alpha right away,' Nigel said. 'That's where the Hell's Gateway generator is. Don't tell the navy, don't consult anyone else. Just do it.'

'The *Charybdis* should be back in communication range in another day,' Nelson said. 'And the *Searcher* is already home.

Frigate construction is already underway. We can launch within forty-eight to seventy-two hours.'

'See to it,' Nigel said. 'You personally, Nelson. God knows if it's infiltrated our Dynasty as well. Is there any kind of test?' he asked Paula.

'We have to wait until the results from Isabella come back. Once we understand what was done to her, we might be able to recognize it in others. But don't expect it to be quick or simple. It could well take decades to find the last of them.'

'You're reading her memories?' Nelson asked.

'I have a Raiel doing that for me, yes.'

Nigel couldn't help an admiring smile. Investigator Myo was always one unexpected step ahead. 'Do you think Ozzie is a Starflyer agent?'

'Difficult to say. From what I've just heard, I'd say he was helping the Guardians. We will need to read his memories to be sure. Do you know where he is?'

'We lost track of him on Silvergalde,' Nigel said. 'His last message said he was off to ask the Silfen what they knew about the Dyson Pair barriers. He hasn't been seen since.'

'I see,' Paula said.

'Do you have any idea what this Starflyer is?' Nigel asked. His expanded mentality began to access the Dynasty files on the Guardians. They weren't a lot of use: just summaries of investigations launched by the Serious Crimes Directorate.

'It's the survivor of the *Marie Celeste* arkship on Far Away,' Paula said. 'Which is about as much as we know. Bradley Johansson claims it took over the humans investigating the arkship, so any data from the Institute is obviously suspect. We have no idea where it came from, what it looks like, its size, even if it's an oxygen breather. Even now its existence can only be deduced from the behaviour of its agents. It is the perfect bogeyman myth.'

'Son of a bitch,' Nigel muttered angrily. He was indignant – no, actually *affronted* – that an alien like that could move humans round like chess pieces. An unseen malign influence creeping round *his* Commonwealth, subverting and corrupting whatever it touched, like some medieval demon. Small wonder nobody wanted to believe in it. 'How could it have gone unnoticed for so long?'

'Because it's cautious, and works on a long timescale,' Paula said. 'Which actually gives us our first clue as to its nature. It is obviously long-lived. Given this strategy to eliminate us and the Primes so that its own kind can expand unhindered into this section of the galaxy; it thinks in terms of centuries if not millennia.'

'But it must have a base somewhere, a physical presence. We have to be able to track it down.'

'Bradley Johansson and Adam Elvin are both physical and real,' Paula said with a regretful smile. 'I've never managed to arrest them. Which gives me a theory as to the Starflyer's location.'

'Where?' Justine asked sharply.

Paula stood up and walked over to the office window where she was silhouetted by the blurry grey sky outside. She beckoned Nigel over. Together they looked down on the station marshalling yard, where long trains snaked their way along the silver and white rails.

'Johansson and Elvin know and understand the covert activity game very well,' she said. 'They are always on the move, they have no permanent home, they avoid relationships, attachments, friendships, anything that can tie them down. That's why I was always chasing them, they were never in one place long enough for me to catch up; that and their political cover from Mr Isaacs.'

Nigel felt as if the cold sea air trapped under the force field was permeating the office as realization dawned. Goose bumps pricked the skin along his forearms. Below him trains slid in and out of the tunnels which led to the cities of the east coast

states, from New York all the way south to Miami. The cliff
face of gateways shone light from distant stars across the
ground in long pale ellipses. 'Oh dear God, no.'

'It's the logical conclusion,' she said. 'The Starflyer is alien.
At the very least it will require food proteins from its native
world, either grown or synthesized. Its body would attract
attention if it were ever seen. What could be easier than having
its own freight wagon? It would always be travelling, always be
free to go where it wanted, always have its own environment.'

'Our control RI can search the records, look for trains that
never stop,' Nigel said with a dry throat. It was hopeless, and
he knew it.

'The wagon will switch engines and even companies, it will
spend months or years on a siding, or inside a warehouse, it
will roam over planets wherever there are rails; the Starflyer
will even change and modernize the wagons over the decades.'

'It could be anywhere,' Nigel said in an aghast voice.

'According to the Guardians it will go back to Boongate
and from there Far Away.'

'The Boongate gateway is closed. And it will be kept that
way now.'

'I hope so.'

'What do you mean by that? I won't allow it to be opened.'

Paula glanced over at Nelson, then turned back to Nigel.
'You and Nelson do realize that someone very well placed in
your Dynasty has to be a Starflyer agent, don't you?'

He inclined his head slightly, clearly loath to say anything.
'If it travels the way you claim, that's painfully obvious. It's
been given a lot of help over the years. I only hope it hasn't
subverted my Dynasty the way it has Heather's.'

'There's no evidence of that. And Johansson has never
claimed it.'

'The ultimate approval,' he muttered sarcastically.

'I'd like to suggest we pull the Guardians in from the cold,'

Justine said. 'They know more about the Starflyer than anyone else. If we're going to try and capture it, we could do with their help.'

'How?' Paula asked as she walked back to her seat. 'We don't know how to contact them. The navy lost their last serious lead, the Agent, on Illuminatus.'

Justine gave the Investigator an apologetic little shrug. 'I've been in touch with Bradley Johansson for a while now.'

Nigel actually managed to chuckle – gallows humour. He broke off hurriedly when he saw the Investigator giving him a sombre stare. 'I like it,' he said as he slumped back into his chair. 'A conspiracy within a conspiracy. Funny: I always thought I'd be on the receiving end of a secret resistance movement, not actually taking part in one. Contact Johansson for us, Justine, ask if he'd like to meet and pool resources. We should call Wilson in as well, he can help keep an eye on the navy for us; he'll have enough sympathizers inside Pentagon II to stay on top of Columbia.'

'There's someone I'd like to bring in as well,' Mellanie said.

'I'm sorry,' Nigel said. 'I don't entirely trust the SI, especially not after its lack of assistance today.'

Mellanie gave him a pitying look. 'Me neither. And don't be so patronizing.'

'Trust me. After what happened to Dorian on the *Cypress Island*, I wouldn't dare.'

'How did you . . .'

Nigel gave the astonished girl a winning grin. 'Told you I followed your activities.'

Mellanie sat back for a moment, then she recovered and flashed him an evil smile. 'What I actually want is for one of your wormholes to recover the Bose motile for me.'

'What's the Bose motile?' Nigel gave Dudley Bose a suspicious glance.

'The alien you're calling the Primes is in fact a single consciousness distributed through billions of individual bodies,' Mellanie said. 'The Bose motile is the one that contains Dudley's memories; they were downloaded into it after he was captured; that's who warned the *Conway*. It then managed to escape and make its way to Elan. My friends are guarding it for me.' She looked around the silent, startled faces in the office, before giving Nigel a sardonic grin. 'I think that's game to me.'

*

Morton's e-butler woke him. The sensors which Cat's Claws had placed all over the Randtown district were picking up a signal from a point two hundred kilometres directly above the Trine'ba. It was a repeated message on the same channel-hopping sequence that the navy used, yet the encryption was the one Mellanie had given him. When he used the key, text printed across his virtual vision. **Morty, I've got a wormhole open for you. Please respond. Mellanie.**

'Jeeze!' He sat up fast. It was dark in the cave they were using. A couple of lights were showing a pale yellow glimmer, enough to reveal the slushy frost dripping down the rock. Rob was on duty, dressed in full armour, sitting up by the jagged entrance like some nightmare obeah idol. The Cat, who was supposed to be asleep, was in Moon Palm position on top of her sleeping bag. She stared at him wordlessly, which made him shiver despite the semi-organic fabric of his own sleeping bag maintaining his body temperature at a perfect level. The survivors were bundled up in their own bags and blankets like giant pupae lying together on the other side of the cave. They were motionless, apart from David Dunbavand whose whimper would carry across the cave every time he quivered inside his thick wrappings. The medical kits had helped to stabilize him, but he'd made little progress recently.

Standing by the pile of equipment in the middle of the cave was the Bose motile. It had barely moved from that position since the day they'd marched up to the shelter. They had cloaked it in various sheets of semi-organic fabric to keep it warm and reasonably dry. Every couple of days one of them would drive a bubble down to the Trine'ba and load up with the polluted water for it to eat. Morton thought it was in pretty bad shape, despite Bose's own protestations that it was fine.

'So what's in the message?' The Cat asked.

Rob's helmet had turned towards Morton.

'It's Mellanie. She's opened a wormhole for us. I knew it. I knew she'd come through.'

The Cat exhaled calmly. 'I hope you're right. The navy was very clear about its timetable.' She started pulling her amour on.

'Yeah yeah, screw you.'

The navy communication had come in that afternoon, telling them they were to be lifted off in three days' time. Until then they were to cease all combat missions, and simply observe the Primes. It had been a big morale boost, and sparked an instant argument what to do about the Bose motile. Rob had been all for shooting it there and then, pretending the whole episode had never happened. Even the survivors had objected to that.

Morton's virtual hands moved quickly over communication icons, routing his reply through their network of sensor discs, so that the transmission wouldn't come from anywhere near the mountain saddle where their cave was located. Just in case.

'Mellanie?'

'Morty! Hi, oh God, darling, are you okay?'

'Sure. Fine. How about you?'

'Good. We don't have much time. This wormhole can take you off, all of you. Where are you?'

'Mellanie, what was the name of your stylist when we were living together?'

'What? Oh, I see, very paranoid. Sasha used to doll me up for you. Okay?'

'Okay. So what's going to happen? Are we clear with the navy? My colleagues don't exactly fancy going on the run after we get back.'

'You're clear. I have some allies now, the best. You'll see. Please hurry.'

'All right, this is the location.' He sent a file with their coordinates.

'Give us thirty seconds.' The signal cut off.

Morton stood up, and clapped his hands loudly. 'Okay, people, we're out of here. Let's move! We don't have long.'

The four survivors stirred as the lights were switched up to full brightness, blinking sleepily.

'Rob, get outside,' Morton said. 'See if you can locate the wormhole. It'll open any second now.'

'Right.'

'Dudley. You're going to have to walk to it.'

'I can manage that, thank you,' the Bose motile replied through its array.

'I'll just stay by your side when we go through,' The Cat purred smoothly. She was already standing at Morton's shoulder, holding her helmet in one hand, a pack slung over her shoulder.

'Highlight of my day,' Morton retorted. He gave Simon and Georgia a hand lifting up David's stretcher, and put his own helmet beside the injured man's legs. The Cat simply walked alongside without volunteering any help as they picked their way over the slippery rock.

'Fuck me,' Rob said. 'It's here!'

'What's on the other side?' The Cat asked sharply.

'Some kind of big room. Hey! I can see Mellanie. There are some troop types in there with her.'

Morton smiled to himself. He resisted the urge to say: *told you so.*

It was sleeting heavily outside. Morton screwed his face up against the bitter cold striking his skin as he emerged out of the cave's narrow entrance, he wished he'd put the helmet on. The wormhole had opened a few metres beyond the cave entrance, a silver gossamer circle poised above the dirty slush, resembling a full moon. Dark shapes were just visible inside. Rob was standing directly in front of it, a tall black figure striding forward purposefully. Then the silver glow splashed round him and he was through on the other side.

'So Mellanie has pulled it off again,' Simon said. 'You have yourself quite a lady there, Morton.'

'Yeah,' he drawled, suddenly *very* eager to see her again.

He picked his way over the awkward surface, paying more attention to his feet than to the glowing silver circle ahead of him. The cold was bitter, stinging his ears and cheeks. Then the air tingled around him, and he was through the force field. He blinked against the bright light. Warm air immediately started to melt the ice that had settled on his hair and suit.

They were in a CST exploratory division environment confinement chamber. He'd accessed news reports of their missions enough times to recognize one instantly. A spherical chamber fifty metres in diameter with black, absorptive walls. Yellow and red striped lines marked out airlocks and instrument recesses, while broad windows halfway up allowed the Operations Centre staff a direct view of what was going on. A ring of lights shone down on him and the reception party. Morton didn't even notice the rest of them. Mellanie stood out in front, wearing an agreeably short white skirt, and a blue denim shirt open virtually to her navel. Her hands were on her hips, and she was staring right at him, eyes shining and mouth smiling wide.

'Morty!' She ran forwards.

He almost dropped David Dunbavand as her arms hugged him. Someone took the stretcher pole from his grip, and he hugged her back. Then they were kissing passionately, and he was ready to tear that shirt off and have sex with her on the floor of the chamber right there and then.

She pushed back, tossing her head. Golden hair floated about. Her tongue was caught coyly between her teeth. 'Missed me again, huh?'

'Oh Christ, yes.'

Mellanie laughed. It was close to mockery, certainly triumphant.

People were moving past him. Medics clustering round David Dunbavand. Security personnel with activated force fields carrying stumpy carbines; helping Rob out of his armour; taking The Cat's bag and helmet from her; leading the other survivors away from the wormhole. Three of them stood round the Bose motile, while another pulled off the sheets of cloth it had draped over its body. Mandy was crying, comforted by a medic.

The wormhole closed silently behind them.

'Please remove your suit, sir,' one of the security team said.

Morton did as he was told. The Cat stripped off her own armour, deliberately taking her time.

'All clear,' the security team chief finally announced.

An airlock door split open. Dudley Bose stepped into the chamber. It was the first time Morton had seen the re-lifed astronomer. He wasn't impressed. A harried youth with a nuclear furnace of nervous energy making his movements jerky, anxiety and incredulity pulling at his face like a heavy-world gravity field.

Morton braced himself for a small scene. After all, he was still smooching up against Mellanie. But Dudley ignored everyone else in the chamber to race over to the Bose motile. His speed almost tripped him, perfect coordination was still definitely lacking. He came to a shaky halt a metre in front of the tall alien. Two of its sensor stalks bent round to keep the man in view.

'GIVE ME MY MEMORIES BACK,' Dudley screamed at the motile. 'Make me ME again.' His fists rose uncertainly.

'Of course,' the Bose motile said from its array. 'What did

you think I was going to do with them? We are one, Dudley, more than brothers.'

'I . . . I . . .' Spittle was shooting out of Dudley's mouth. 'I have to know. What happened? What did they do to me?'

'They killed us, Dudley. Shot us in cold blood. Our original human body died at Dyson Alpha.'

Dudley swayed about, on the verge of apoplexy.

'You didn't tell him?' Morton asked her.

Mellanie shook her head. 'I'd better calm him down,' she murmured. She sounded exasperated, a parent running after a particularly troublesome child.

Morton looked from her to Dudley. *What in Christ's name does she see in him?*

'Come on, Dudley,' Mellanie said, holding him by the hand. 'We can sort all this out later.'

'No!' He yanked his hand free, leaving her startled. She winced at the strength he'd used. Morton took a pace towards them. Rob and The Cat suddenly appeared on either side of him. The Cat's hand rested on his shoulder. 'No,' she purred.

'Just fuck off,' Dudley bellowed. 'Fuck off and leave me alone with myself, you stupid little tart. I'm here, do you understand? I'm here, all of me. I can be me again. Don't try and stop that, don't interfere. Nobody interfere.'

Mellanie's face hardened. 'As you wish, Mr Bose.'

'They . . . they have somewhere we can use,' Dudley said, looking up at the alien's sensor stalks, his face pleading. 'A medical facility. We can start right away.'

'Very well,' the Bose motile said.

Dudley's head moved round in short jerks as if it was robotic. He focused on one of the medical team in the hugely attentive audience. 'You. You said there was a treatment room.'

'Yes.' The woman walked over, and tipped her head up to gaze at the alien's sensor stalks with an awed expression on her face. She took in the electronic module merged with its flesh, the optical cable linking that to the array. 'I don't know if this will work.'

'Trust me,' the Bose motile said. 'This body is built around the concept of memory transfer. It's just a question of modifying the interface.'

'Okay, then. This way.' She led the human and motile Bose towards one of the airlock doors. Five of the security personnel fell in around them. Carbines not quite pointing at the motile as it waddled along, but close. Just before it reached the door, the Bose motile bent a sensor stalk round towards Mellanie. 'Pleased to meet you, by the way. I can see I'm a lucky man, if somewhat ungrateful at this moment. I would enjoy talking to you later.'

Mellanie gave the alien a pleasant smile. 'I'll look forward to it, Dudley.'

'What do you mean, ungrateful?' Dudley's whiny voice asked as they went through the door. 'And what business is it of yours?'

'Never a dull moment with Mellanie,' a voice said cheerfully in Morton's ear.

Morton turned, and did a fast double take. Nigel Sheldon was standing beside him.

'She said she had allies,' Morton said sardonically.

'She wasn't joking.' Nigel gave the closed wormhole a nostalgic glance. 'You might want to go back when she's finished explaining what's going on.'

'I doubt it. Where are we, exactly?'

'Augusta.' He gave Simon a short bow. 'Mr Rand, I've heard good things about you. I'm sorry for your loss. Randtown was a lovely concept.'

'Mr Sheldon,' Simon replied gravely. 'Thank you for your assistance.'

'Thank Mellanie. Now, we have baths, food, and answers waiting for you. Take them in any order you want.'

'All at once.' Morton said. He went over to where Mellanie

was staring at the open airlock, and put his arm round her. She grinned distantly, then glanced over at Nigel with an expression that was as confused as it was worried.

'Give me an answer when you're ready,' Nigel said to her. There was a slight edge to his voice.

Rob turned to The Cat as everyone started to move out of the big chamber. 'I don't get it,' he complained. 'She's got Morton wrapped round her little finger. That looked like Sheldon has the hots for her, too. They say Michelangelo beds every assistant on his show, male or female. So what the fuck does she see in Bose?'

*

Alic Hogan had stopped wincing and sighing each time he squirmed in his seat. Every part of his body was in some kind of pain, and movement created innumerable additional twinges. He couldn't take too many drugs if he wanted to retain his mental acuity. Healskin wasn't nearly the soft cushion its manufacturers claimed.

Just being alive was awful.

Nobody in the Paris office paid any attention to his misery. Half of them had suffered worse injuries than him on Illuminatus. Except Vic of course. Vic was in a very different kind of pain. The big man sat at his desk for hour after hour, ripping through data like a metavirus. All of them were back reviewing Tarlo's files, hunting for any clues that might lead them to him. A forensic team was going through his apartment, analysing everything from his toothgell to the DNA in hair; just looking for something – anything – that would tell them how he had been taken over by the Starflyer.

Jim Nwan handed cups of coffee round the people working at the nest of desks they'd shoved together in the middle of the room. Alic took his without looking up from the results of the DRNG bonds; Tarlo had been quite diligent about tracing them, working up files on the buyers. None of which had been shown to Alic. *But I bet the Starflyer got them all.*

His coffee was just right, no sugar and a dash of cream. Acceptance was the one decent result to come out of Illuminatus, he was one of the Paris team now. Strange how much that meant to him. Strange the way loyalties shifted. Alic accepted the Starflyer's existence now. So much of what had happened made sense once the alien's influence was factored in. Not that he'd told the admiral yet. The way Wilson Kime had been fired by the War Cabinet had sent a real shockwave through the navy, even the Paris office which had always been under Columbia's command thought the way in which Kime had been turned into a scapegoat was despicably shabby. Though the only real subject they talked about was the time-travel project.

'I can't find a damn thing on the Baron observation,' John King complained. 'He must have wiped them.'

Alic glanced over at the big wall-mounted portal that was playing the Michelangelo show. Senator Goldreich was the guest, explaining how the fresh worlds would be prepared for the refugees. His e-butler changed the access to Alessandra Baron. Her guest was a pale man called Dimitri Leopoldvich, who was discussing what tactics the navy should use to engage the thousands of Prime warships remaining in the Commonwealth.

'Call the observation team direct,' Alic told John. 'Get them to send copies of their reports.'

He gave the portal an evil look. God alone knew what harm Baron was causing in the long run. Now he listened to her, *really* listened, he was sure he could hear nothing but contempt and mockery for everything the navy had done. She was hacking away at people's confidence, undermining authority. All under the disguise of tough interviewing.

His e-butler told him a secure call was coming into the

office for Renne. A file ran down his virtual vision, giving him Edmund Li's record. The fact that he was from Boongate was enough to interest Alic. 'Give it to me,' he told his e-butler.

'I was trying to reach Renne,' Edmund Li said.

'She's not available,' Alic told him. Morale in the office hadn't been helped when they all found out that there wasn't a clinic place anywhere in the Commonwealth to re-life her; the most optimistic estimate was seven years before a slot became open. Everyone was backlogged with bodyloss victims from the Lost23; and that was before the new invasion. 'I'm her commanding officer. What's the problem?'

'Tarlo's here.'

Alic snapped his fingers for everyone's attention as he opened the call to a general link round his team. 'How do you know?'

'Because he's up in my office right now.'

'Where are you? What's your office?'

'I'm at the Boongate planetary station, in the Far Away section. Right now I'm holed up in the Carbon Goose flight office in the administration block, ground floor. Tarlo is in the security office on the third floor. I managed to get a shadow scrutineer program loaded so I can follow what he's doing.'

'How many people have you got with you?' Alic asked.

'None.'

'What?'

'There's nobody else here. Just me and him. As far as I know, we're the only people in the whole Far Away section.'

'Christ!' Alic could see his own dismay mirrored in the faces of the team around him. 'What's he doing?'

'Taking over the security systems which guard the perimeter. There are a lot of weapons here, they were installed in case anything hostile ever got through from Far Away. Old-fashioned stuff, but it still packs a punch. And he's established complete control over the force field; there's no way in and no way out. I've disabled a couple of the sensors in the room I'm using so he can't see me; but if I move from here the building's internal sensors will pinpoint me instantly.'

'I thought you said you'd got a shadow program loaded in the security arrays?'

'I have.'

'Then you must have copies of his codes. You can take command of the section's network, shut it all down.'

'Not a chance. Now he's in the network, he's installing his own management routines. The shadow program is gradually being locked out.'

'Shit!' Alic thumped his fist down on the desk, wincing at the burst of pain from his burns. 'All right, Edmund, are you armed?'

'Yeah, an ion pistol, Colt8000, eighty per cent charge. I don't think it'll be much use against him. I accessed the warrant you issued. That wetwiring he's got is heavy duty.'

'Listen, we're coming to get you.'

'Ha! The wormhole to Boongate is closed. CST isn't going to open it now; people would get back into the Commonwealth, Sheldon and Doi want to force everyone into the future. The only way you're going to get to me is in twenty years' time.'

'Unacceptable,' Vic said. The finality in the big man's voice was intimidating.

'We'll get you out of there, I promise,' Alic told Edmund, 'even if we have to take a starship to Boongate. Now listen, I want you to keep this link open permanently. Transfer through all the data your shadow program has captured. Then I'm going to connect you up with someone in our technical department. They'll see if there's any way you can use your ion pistol to physically disable the force field generator.'

'You're kidding. It's in a building about three hundred metres from this one.'

'Okay, what about armour and force field suits? The security department must have some?'

'Sure. Up there where he is.'

'Then we'll bring in a tactical expert to analyse your situation. Stay calm, we *will* get you through this.'

'If you say so. But I'd like to download my memories into a secure store if you don't mind.'

'Of course, we'll set one up right now.' He clicked his fingers at Matthew Oldfield, who gave a hurried nod.

'Do you know why Tarlo's here?' Edmund asked.

'No, we don't.'

'You can tell me, you know. It's not like I'm going to be leaking classified information to anyone right now.'

'We genuinely don't know; but it must be connected to Far Away somehow.'

'Yeah. I figured he's here to help the Starflyer get home.'

'What do you know about the Starflyer?' Alic asked in surprise. *Am I the only one who didn't know it was real?*

'Nothing much, really. There's been some weird things happening on Far Away lately. It would make sense, that's all.'

'You're probably right. Listen, I'm going to leave you with my team now, okay. I'll start working on a way to get to Boongate.'

'How?' Vic asked.

Alic stood up. 'The admiral. He's got the clout to get us through.'

'Ha! He's not going to accept this.'

'If he doesn't accept this, then I quit.' He looked round their startled faces, the faint smiles of approval. 'It's not much of a threat, I know. But it's the only one I've got.'

'Then you tell him we quit with you,' John King said. The rest of them said: 'Hell yes,' and 'Me too.'

Vic put his hand on Alic's shoulder. 'Good luck. And thanks, boss.'

*

When the door to Alic's office shut, he had to sit down quickly and blow out a long breath. There was only so far impetuosity could carry you. The team were looking in at him through the glass. It actually felt very good indeed.

Oh, what the hell. That bastard Tarlo tried to kill me. That makes it personal.

His virtual finger touched the admiral's icon. No hesitation, he was pleased to see. The admiral's e-butler told Alic that his access level had been reduced to grade seven. 'I'll wait,' he told the program.

It took two and a half hours before Rafael Columbia responded. 'I can give you five minutes,' he told Alic.

'We've located Tarlo.'

'Then arrest him.'

'He's on Boongate.'

'Bugger. It'll have to wait, Hogan. We'll grab him when he comes out wherever Sheldon sends them.'

'We need him now, sir. He's a Starflyer agent.' Alic closed his eyes, half expecting a lightning bolt to slam down out of the sky and roast him behind his desk.

'Christ, not you, too? I thought you were reliable.'

'I am reliable, sir, that's why I'm telling you this. Think about it. Tarlo's a traitor, a double agent, that's beyond question; I was one of the people he was shooting at on Illuminatus. Who is he working for, sir? If not the Starflyer, who is trying to destroy the Commonwealth? Tell me. Give me another name, and I'll chase them for as long as it takes.'

There was a long pause. 'You can't get to Boongate,' the admiral said. 'This is classified, but the wormholes to the Second47 will not be reopened. The War Cabinet decided we cannot risk a stampede back into the Commonwealth. Those populations must go into the future.'

'You have the authority, sir. You can get CST to open the Boongate wormhole for us. My team and I will stay on

Boongate afterwards and go into the future with the rest of the population. But we must get there before the evacuation. We must establish the Starflyer's intent. The navy needs to know. Surely you must see that?'

'You really believe it, don't you?'

'We all do, sir.'

'Very well, Hogan. If this is to happen it doesn't get put in the files until there's a successful conclusion. Non-negotiable.'

'I understand, sir.'

'Good. Put your arrest team together and get over to Wessex. I'll see what I can do at this end.'

'Thank you, sir.'

'And Hogan, if you're wrong, stay on Boongate. There will be no future for you, not anywhere at any time. Understand?'

'Understood, sir.'

*

Mellanie walked down the mansion's broad corridor with her black lacy robe flowing out behind her. The sculpted swan wall lights were turned down to a rouge glimmer, deepening the shadows between the arches. It was two o'clock in the morning, and no one else was about.

Guilt at what she was doing only made it more exciting. Morton hadn't stirred when she left their room. Randtown had left him more tired than he was willing to admit.

The door opened before she even tapped on it. Nigel was standing there, dressed in a loosely tied emerald towelling gown. The greedy smile on his face was one she'd seen on men countless times before – she'd thought it might be different with him. He took her hand, and hurriedly pulled her into the bedroom.

'What—' she began.

'I wouldn't want my wives to get jealous,' he murmured as he gave the corridor a theatrical check before closing the door.

'They're not, so don't pretend they are.'

'Okay.' He was pressed up against her, hands removing her gown. His mouth moved to hers.

Mellanie planted a hand on his chest and pushed them apart. 'Are you going to say hello, first?'

'Don't play the Victorian bride. You came to me.' He grinned, and walked over to the huge bed. 'Now come here.' He patted the furry mattress, which rippled sluggishly.

'What is this, your main orgy room?' she asked archly.

'It would be your room.'

She gave the classic white and purple décor an appreciative glance as she went over to sit beside him. 'Nice, I guess.'

'Course, we'd have orgies in it. Seriously.'

She had to laugh, he was so outrageous, and honest. 'Yes, I know. I met Aurelie earlier. Talk about making a girl feel inferior. And she didn't even need reprofiling to look like that.'

'You see, you even like my other wives. What more of an incentive do you need?' His hand slipped off one of her negligee's shoulder straps and moved down to the exposed breast.

'This is very flattering, Nigel.'

'I want it to be pleasurable, not flattering.'

Mellanie moaned hungrily. He'd got her other shoulder strap off; the negligee crumpled round her waist. His hands knew exactly how to move over her skin, the way she had to spend forever teaching other men. 'It already is,' she confessed.

'So say yes.'

'No. *Ahha.*' She actually felt her body shake from the gentle pressure his fingers applied. It wasn't a response she could control.

Nigel lowered her down on the mattress, then unfastened his towelling gown.

Mellanie giggled. 'Nigel!'

'What did you expect?' he asked modestly. 'I am the ruler of the galaxy, after all.'

'God, a man who altered his cock to match his ego.'

He grinned. 'What makes you think I had it altered?'

Mellanie's giggles returned big time. 'I take it back, your ego is bigger.'

'Turn over.'

'Why?'

'Massage. To start with.'

'Oh.' She rolled onto her front. Oil that was body-warm was dripped onto her spine. He began to rub it in. 'How did you know about the *Cypress Island*?' she asked.

'If I told you that you'll just be cross with me. I want to have sex with you too much for that.'

'I won't be cross.'

'You will. Why won't you marry me?'

'Honestly?'

'Yes.'

'I wouldn't want to share you with anyone. I like this, this is fun. And I'd even enjoy joining in with your other wives. But as a permanent thing . . . That's not me. Sorry.'

'Hey, I love it. Jealousy.'

'I'm not jealous.' Mellanie tried to twist round to protest, but his hands reached her buttocks. She had to clamp her teeth to stop squealing.

'What does the SI get out of your arrangement?' Nigel asked.

'God, is there anything you don't know?'

'I don't know that for a start.'

'It says it just wants to know what's going on, that's all. I can get into places where there's no unisphere coverage.'

'Figures. So it knew about the nature of the Primes?'

'It found out at Randtown. It hacked into their communications through my inserts.'

'Goddamn thing never told us. Bastard.' Nigel moved down to her thighs.

'Do you think it's hostile as well?'

'I think it's a snob. I think it looks down on us as the lower class neighbours bringing down the tone of the galaxy. It's not actively belligerent, but like all snobs it has a fascination for what it's not. Hence you, and others like you. It also has sentiment, which is why it helps us out on rare occasions. Yet it will always rationalize that as something else entirely, charity or consideration born of superiority. The trouble is, I don't know if it would help us in the face of genocide. It probably doesn't know either. I suspect it will play its waiting game until the end. And that's going to be too late for us.'

'Is that why you decided to nova MorningLightMountain?'

'It's among the reasons. Nobody else is going to help us out. Does it bother you, that decision?'

'I felt MorningLightMountain,' she said slowly. 'I could hear its thoughts. My inserts were blocking its soldier motiles so I was physically safe, but I was still frightened. I don't think we can share a universe with it. You know, it completely lacked emotion. I mean there was just no analogue in its mind to what we have. I was going to say that you can't rationalize with it, but that's the whole problem: it's ultra rational. There's no way to connect. Even the SI couldn't make it see logic and reason. It has to go, Nigel, that's the only way we'll be safe.'

'Turn over.'

She did as she was told. The heat had gone out of her now, remembering Randtown and the monstrous mentality of MorningLightMountain was a guaranteed passion killer. Then Nigel began working on her belly, and breasts, and thighs, and she forgot all that again amazingly quickly.

*

'So how did you know?' Mellanie asked.

'Huh?'

'About *Cypress Island*.'

'Ah.' Nigel rolled onto his belly to face her. 'Michelangelo is my son, my fifteenth.'

'What? You're kidding. He never told me.'

'It's not something he's proud of. Quite the opposite, actually. He stormed out when he was seventeen.'

'Wow. I bet that doesn't happen often.'

'No,' he said dryly. 'It was a classic teenage rebellion, he even said *I'll show you*, when he left. Then he went and carved that career out for himself. I'm actually quite proud of him for that. Normally the black sheep come slinking back a century later with their tails between their legs, and get a nice safe middle management position in the Dynasty.'

'So he told you I was going to Illuminatus?'

'No. We didn't understand what was going on, Mellanie. Which comes very hard for people like me and Nelson, especially at a time like this. I cut a deal with Michelangelo. He told me you were hunting the New York lawyers, so Nelson found them in the Saffron Clinic, and gave him the information. We wanted to know why they were important to you. After all, it had the appearance of just another Wall Street finance scam.'

'I'll kill him.'

Nigel ran his hand through her wild hair. 'I said you'd be cross.'

'With him! How can I trust him again after this?'

'You trusted a reporter?'

'Touché.'

'So I'm still favourite, am I?'

'You're in my top hundred,' she replied airily.

'This is why I want you. You are so unlike any of the other girls I have.'

She traced his lips with her finger. 'You need to get out more.'

'Say yes. Just try it for a couple of years. You can still have a career, if that's what's worrying you.'

'It wouldn't be my own career though, would it? Not really,

not if I was your wife. I'd get all the openings and all the breaks, but not because of being me.'

'And the difference between that and having the SI as your agent is . . . ?'

'Perhaps there is none,' she said quietly. 'Perhaps I'm just tired of being a whore.'

'Nobody said you were a whore.'

'I said it.' Mellanie sighed, and crawled over the undulating mattress to reach her negligee. She grimaced at the snail-trail of oil she left behind on the fur.

'To reach here from where you were after Morton's court case takes amazing determination,' he told her.

'I thought it was quite easy to get into your bed, actually.'

'I didn't mean my bed, I meant *here*, this little cabal, or rebellion, whatever you want to call our motley crew. Don't you see? What we're going to decide in a few hours is going to determine the future of the human species. Not Doi. Not the navy. Not the Senate. Not the Dynasties. Us. You made it to the showdown. You're going to be history, Mellanie; you're going to be your generation's Queen Elizabeth, or Marilyn Monroe, or Sue Baker. Don't blink now.'

Mellanie looked down sheepishly at the negligee she was holding in her hands. She didn't feel very historical. 'I don't know who any of them are.'

'Really? Oh. Well, the point is you went and earned yourself a place at the table. That's why you're so irresistible; you're gorgeous and tough, every man's fantasy. And mine in particular.'

'You're very sweet.'

'Haven't been called that in a long time.'

She yawned. 'I'd better get back. I don't want Morty to wake up without me.'

'All right,' Nigel said miserably. 'Just remember, it's an open offer.'

'Thanks. It is tempting. Does it come with a place on your lifeboat if we all make the wrong decision?'

'Yeah,' he laughed. 'You got a reserved cabin with a first class view.'

'Let me guess. Your cabin is next door.'

He spread his arms wide. 'Where else?'

'Is there a shower in here? I need to get this oil off.'

Nigel leered, and climbed off the bed. 'I'll show you.'

'That's not – Oh, all right.'

He guided her towards a misty glass door that was glowing turquoise. 'Tell me something. What do you see in Bose?'

'I don't know,' she shrugged, uncomfortable with the question, which was stupid considering what they'd spent the last hour doing. 'He was useful.'

'And now?'

'I'm not sure. Do you think the memory transfer will work?'

'My e-butler says it seems to be running smoothly. We'll know for sure after breakfast.'

The bathroom was only slightly smaller than the bedroom. Mellanie looked round in delight at the Egyptian theme, then giggled at the scandalous murals. Nigel went over to the sunken spa pool in the middle; it was filled with scented water that foamed away furiously, 'Showers are so boring,' he said. 'Let me sponge you off in this.'

*

Mellanie and Morton joined Nigel's family for breakfast out on the morning terrace. Justine and Campbell were already there, fitting in just perfectly as they chattered away.

Mellanie took her seat, not far from Nigel, who gave her a courteous welcome. She told the waiter she'd have scrambled eggs and orange juice, then helped Nuala with little Digby's bottle. The baby already had some of Nigel's features.

Wilson and Anna arrived, to be given a warm greeting

from Nigel. Mellanie thought the ex-admiral appeared drawn and exhausted. The genuinely warm reception from people round the table helped perk him up slightly.

Mellanie's plate arrived, the food cooked to perfection. She tucked in, trying to listen to all the conversations at once. The amount of political and financial power gathered around the table was fascinating. She found the way everyone was so casual about the influence they wielded to be quite enticing.

The mansion's grounds were beautiful, even though she scale was a bit intimidating when it came to living a family life. It didn't seem to bother the harem. Her e-butler accessed files on Nigel's wives going back a hundred years, summarizing for her; they all seemed to be from rich families, not like her. Perhaps that was why they were so comfortable with their surroundings. She could sense Morton's keen interest in the people around him, even though he was working hard at disguising it. This was the kind of superpower status he'd thought to build for himself, until Tara Jennifer Shaheef became a potential problem.

All in all, Mellanie decided, it was going to be a lot more difficult to say no to this than she'd originally envisaged. *Perhaps just a couple of years' marriage . . .*

Paula Myo arrived, as always dressed in a trim business suit, easily the most formal person on the terrace. She turned down breakfast, but accepted a cup of tea from a waiter. 'Qatux is ready,' she told Nigel.

Morton had stopped eating when she arrived, becoming very still. Now he put down his knife and fork, and stood to face her. 'Investigator,' he said with forced politeness.

The terrace fell silent as everyone watched them.

'Don't cause a scene,' a mortified Mellanie whispered through closed teeth. She didn't think he heard.

'Morton,' Paula said.

'Pleased to see me?'

'I'm interested to see you.'

'Now children,' Nigel said. 'Play nice, please, you're both guests.'

Mellanie had her hand round Morton's wrist, pulling, trying to make him sit down.

'Interested, huh? Funny how life works out. You wrecked my life, now I'm essential to your future.'

'You might be involved in how we deal with the Starflyer. But you're hardly essential.'

'What do you mean "involved"?' Morton said. 'Do you have any idea what risks we took to get the Bose motile to you? Do you?'

'I am very well aware of your propensity to take inappropriate risks, as well as the delusional self justification which you indulge in subsequently.'

'Now listen—'

Mellanie was almost pulled out of her seat keeping hold of Morton as he tried to move towards Paula. 'Stop it,' she barked. 'You killed her, what did you expect?'

Morton gave Mellanie a shocked look. 'Is that what you think?' he asked.

She wished her super-duper SI inserts had a function that could reverse time. *Just a few seconds would do.* 'Well, did you?' she asked weakly.

Morton sat down, all his belligerence gone. 'I don't know,' he said hoarsely. 'I don't remember.'

Mellanie's arm went round his shoulder. 'It doesn't matter, Morty. It's all over now. It's the past.'

Nigel gave a loud sigh, and crumpled up his napkin. 'Well, as breakfast seems to be over, I suppose we'd better get started.'

*

Dudley Bose and the Bose motile were waiting for them in Nigel's office. Mellanie could see Dudley obviously hadn't slept last night. The skin under his eyes was dark, like it had been just after she met up with him. Stubble shaded his chin and cheeks, and he was still in the same clothes he wore yesterday, a rust-orange shirt and creased blue jeans. But it wasn't the same haunted fatigue that used to be his permanent companion in those early days; Dudley actually looked contented. He was staring round the study with glazed eyes, almost as if he'd just emerged from a long sleep.

She hadn't quite forgiven him for what he'd called her yesterday in front of everyone, even though it was in the heat of the moment, so she gave him a sisterly peck on the cheek. 'How are you?'

'Good,' he said, and smiled as if it was a revelation. 'Yes, good. Funny, isn't it? Remembering how I died is actually quite liberating. Normally it causes tremendous trouble for people who are re-lifed. I remember you telling me about Morton's ex-wife.'

'I think she was a bit bonkers before,' Mellanie said.

Morton had been snappy at being excluded from the meeting. 'Arrogant prick,' he'd muttered at Nelson, after the Dynasty security chief told him he wasn't on the list.

'I'll tell you everything, I promise,' Mellanie had said. In fact, she was quite relieved he wasn't going to be there. Him and Dudley in the same room would be awkward. She still didn't have a clue what she was going to do about that – let Dudley down gently, she supposed. Of course, Morton didn't have quite the appeal he used to. He was exciting, but then so was Nigel.

'Was it . . .' Mellanie didn't quite know how to ask. 'Your death, did you—'

'It was quick. I didn't even know it was going to happen. MorningLightMountain just shot me. The only vile part is having some of its memories from when it dissected me to extract the memorycell, that's really stomach churning.' He looked round and raised an eyebrow as Wilson and Anna came in to the office. 'Admiral, good to see you again.'

Wilson gave him an astounded glance before being drawn to the immotile. 'Dudley, glad you made it back in the end.'

'It was an interesting route,' the Bose motile said.

'Thanks for the warning,' Wilson said. 'I owe you one for that. The *Conway* wouldn't have made it back otherwise.'

'The Commonwealth had to be told,' Dudley said modestly. 'What else could I do?'

Wilson's gaze flicked back to the human; slightly unnerved by the double-act. 'Of course.'

Mellanie didn't know what to make of Dudley, either. It bothered her. Usually, Dudley could barely fasten his clothes without her being there to reassure him he was doing it right. Now here he was, self-assured and calm as he talked to the one person he hated most of all. This wasn't *her* Dudley, not any more; he wasn't even stealing lustful glances at her.

*

Nigel walked round the Bose motile, giving it a curious gaze before sitting behind his desk. It was quite something to have a creature in his office whose other segments regarded every other species in the galaxy as aberrations to be exterminated. His e-butler reassured him that the office's security systems were scanning it constantly.

That didn't seem to satisfy Nelson, who took an unusually close position beside Nigel's desk. Campbell showed Justine to a long leather chesterfield sofa, and put out a courteous arm to help her sit down. He'd become quite protective, Nigel thought, even taking the room next to hers last night.

The study door shut behind Paula. Its e-seal came on, turning the windows slightly misty.

'Paula,' Nigel said. 'Would you like to kick off.'

'Of course.' Paula stood up in front of a large portal. It came to life, showing Qatux. 'Thank you for joining us,' she said.

'It is my pleasure. I recognize many of the humans with

you. So many powerful figures. How emotions must be charged in that room.'

'We're all stimulated by what is happening,' Paula said. 'I should tell everyone here, that Qatux joins us today because after Illuminatus—'

'Actually,' Dudley said. 'I think I should be first. I have the most relevant information.'

Nigel didn't say anything; in fact he was rather intrigued by this new, composed Dudley, who had all the brash confidence of the old astronomer who'd lobbied so effectively for a place on the *Second Chance*, but without the immense irritation factor. He caught Mellanie sinking down into the cushions, her hand rubbing at her forehead, avoiding all eye contact with Dudley.

'All right, Dudley,' Nigel said with bogus civility. 'Please go ahead.'

'I know what the Starflyer is,' the astronomer said.

'What?' Nigel asked.

'There is something I'd like in return for participating today.'

'Excuse me?'

'I've been through a lot, and I'm contributing more than anyone else. I believe that should receive some recognition, don't you?'

'Dudley!' Mellanie said. 'Don't you understand what this is?'

'Perfectly, thank you, Mellanie. Are you sure you do?'

'What do you want?' Nigel asked.

'To continue as your chief adviser on MorningLight-Mountain should it be successful in destroying the Commonwealth.'

'Ah,' Nigel said. 'I see. A berth on one of my lifeboats.' He saw Mellanie start to colour, the girl's shoulders lifted in anger.

'Hardly an extravagance for you,' Dudley said.

'No. Does this request extend to your new twin?'

Dudley shrugged. 'If you wish.'

Nigel was tempted to wait long enough to hear what Mellanie was going to shout at her erstwhile lover, because she was clearly about to – unfortunately they didn't need contention right now. 'It will be done.'

'Thank you,' Dudley said. 'Very well: while it was at the structure we named the Watchtower, the *Second Chance* transmitted a signal to the Dyson Alpha homeworld.'

'We know that,' Wilson told him. 'Oscar found a record of the dish deployment in our log files. But the Starflyer got to them before we could tell anyone.'

'But do you know what it transmitted?' Dudley asked, keen to maintain his advantage.

'No.'

'It was a warning that the *Second Chance* was alien, and should be destroyed. The message was in the Primes' communication pattern.'

'I don't understand,' Wilson said.

'The Primes did leave Dyson Alpha before the barrier was erected,' Dudley said. 'Their fusion drives were allowing them to colonize every other planet and large asteroid in their system. They could see that one day all their star system's resources would be exhausted. Several of the immotile clusters sent ships out to their neighbouring star, Dyson Beta, to establish colonies there. They are a very insular and arrogant species, the Primes. They assumed Dyson Beta would have material resources and nothing more. They were wrong, the immotile on board the first starship found another alien species. It followed its nature, and fought the new species into submission. After that, it absorbed their industrial and scientific base. That's where the real problem started. The Primes on Dyson Alpha, the original Primes, have continuity built into their souls, it's an integral part of their identity; they can remember their ancestors beginning to think, their own rise to consciousness. Those ancient thoughts lock them into what they are. A lone immotile three and a half years distant from its original immotile group cluster was a little more flexible in attitude. The native Dyson Beta species were developing genetics, the whole concept of which is *verboten* to the Primes. But the starship immotile started to use genetic science to modify itself physically, and God knows there are a lot of minor limitations and deficiencies in all creatures. The motiles were improved drastically, which led to a subsequent improvement in immotiles. For a start they regained their ability to move.

Dudley gave his audience a mirthless smile. 'The Dyson Alpha Primes were horrified. They called the Dyson Beta hybrids alienPrime, and regarded them as heretical abominations. A war started, then ended very abruptly when the barriers appeared around both stars. The next time MorningLightMountain saw the universe was when the barrier came down, and it received a signal from an immotile whose communication pattern identified it as Morning-LightMountain17,735. That was a subsidiary group cluster MorningLightMountain had put on one of the early starships. That's what the Starflyer is.'

'The Starflyer *is* MorningLightMountain?' Mellanie asked.

'An alienPrime version of MorningLightMountain, yes. It was on a starship that must have been in space between Dyson Alpha and Beta when the barriers were established. When it couldn't attack its target, or go home, it must have flown off into interstellar space, and finally crashed on Far Away.'

'I'm afraid not,' Wilson said. 'I checked with the Institute Director, James Timothy Halgarth, personally. The *Marie Celeste* couldn't have come from Dyson Beta, it hadn't been in space long enough to travel that far.'

'If you're basing that assumption on information from the Institute, then it must be regarded as invalid,' Paula said. 'The Director would have lied to you to cover up the Starflyer's true nature.'

'We've been sucked into the worst kind of war,' Nelson muttered.

'In what way?' Campbell asked.

'This is a civil war. They're always the most violent and hard fought. And we're caught in the middle of it.'

'No, we're fighting for the Starflyer,' Nigel said. 'We're its stormtroopers, whether we like it or not. If what Dudley has told us about the original Primes is true, then the Starflyer knows they will never allow the alienPrimes to survive. It's using us to fight them, and conveniently ourselves, into destruction. We're the new class of motile, to be manipulated and sent out to die while it remains intact behind the battle lines.'

'That's why MorningLightMountain had flare bombs,' Wilson said in a relieved tone. 'The technology didn't leak from us to Dyson Alpha; the Primes had it all along. The Starflyer fed the theory to us. Oh! Wait. When the barrier fell we detected an unusual quantum signature inside the Dark Fortress. It wasn't there before.' He turned to Nigel. 'Have you got secure access to navy records?'

'Yes.'

'Get your physicists to compare that signature to the flare bombs.'

'Good idea.' Nigel's expanded mentality extracted the records and began running comparisons. He still found it amusing the way people always forgot what he was before everything else, all they ever saw today was the Dynasty leader.

'This still doesn't make sense,' Anna said. 'The Starflyer obviously has the ability to switch off the barrier. Why didn't it just do that when it arrived at Dyson Alpha in the *Marie Celeste* and launch the flare bomb? Or go back to Dyson Beta and let its own kind out?'

'The barrier builders were still around, maybe?' Wilson said. 'It needed a decent interval to elapse before it could risk any kind of rescue attempt. That's probably why it fled so far in the first place.'

'Even so, it engineered the *Second Chance* mission. Why not have us sent to Dyson Beta and release the alienPrimes? The original Primes would remain locked up.'

'It didn't know what would happen any more than we did,' Paula said. 'This way it wins whatever the outcome. If the barrier builders were still around and it had tried to switch off the barrier round Dyson Beta, they would have detected the attempt and stopped us. By making the attempt at Dyson Alpha, it gets to see if the barriers are still guarded. If not, it releases an ultra-hostile species directly into conflict with us, a race with a proven record of warfare and a technology base advanced enough to construct the kind of weapons necessary to fight an interstellar war. The two of us fight and weaken ourselves, leaving it free to unlock Dyson Beta so its own kind can emerge into a galaxy where the two nearest threats have blasted each other to the edge of extinction.' She pursed her lips ruefully. 'Almost exactly what Bradley Johansson claimed all along.'

Results slipped into Nigel's virtual vision. 'The quantum signatures are similar,' he told the room. 'Not identical, but they're certainly based around the same principle. From what we could determine, the Prime flare bomb works by altering the properties of the surrounding mass; which in itself is a none too distant relation to our own quantumbuster. We can surmise that if you change the properties of enough components in the Dark Fortress then they'll simply be incapable of performing their intended function: the barrier will fail.'

'So we finally know what we're facing,' Justine said. 'I take it nobody minds if I tell Johansson.'

'As long as he keeps quiet about it until the Starflyer problem has been dealt with,' Nigel told her. 'This still isn't for public release.'

'Well how much of a problem have we actually got left?' Justine asked. 'We have a weapon which in all probability the Starflyer didn't expect us to produce. Your nova bomb will give us a total victory over MorningLightMountain. Now we know it exists, we can effectively neutralize it.'

'Paula?' Nigel asked. 'Can we neutralize it?'

'I'm not certain. Qatux, do you know how far its influence extends?'

'This is obviously exciting for all of you,' the Raiel said in its soft wind-chime voice. 'I wish I could share that experience.'

'Qatux, please answer the question,' Paula said sternly.

'Isabella Halgarth came into contact with many people who suffered the same compulsion overlay. They are arranged in a three-person structure based on the old human spy cell system. The controller can put them in touch with each other for specific operations, but apart from that they operate in isolation.'

'So you understand the method which the Starflyer uses to control her and the others?'

'It is a sophisticated technique, indicating the controller has a great deal of experience in manipulating the thought routines of other creatures. A Prime-type entity would have an obvious advantage over singleton mentalities; its understanding of mental constitution operates at an instinctive level.'

'What did it do to Isabella?' Mellanie asked, her voice heavy with trepidation. She obviously feared what she was about to hear, but had to know anyway.

'Her thought routines, what you would term the person-ality, were infiltrated with alien behavioural modifiers. She performed as a normal human under everyday circumstances, but within that framework she acted solely in the interests of the Starflyer. Think of it as having your mind cored like an apple, and the hole being filled with the Starflyer's desires.'

'How old was she when this happened?' Paula asked.

'Five or six. The memory is hazy. She was on Far Away with her parents. They took her into a room that resembled a hospital, she was scared. After that, her mind was no longer hers.'

'Urggh.' Mellanie wrinkled her nose up. 'It did that to a six-year-old? That's so shitty.'

'Ahh,' Qatux sighed. 'Sentiment. I have experienced it often in human memories. It is one of your more exquisite feelings. Would you consider sharing yours with me, Mellanie?'

'Uh. Like no!'

'So you don't actually know what the Starflyer is thinking?' Paula said.

'No,' Qatux said. 'However, there are residual traces of its presence within her mind which betray certain aspects of its character.'

'Such as?'

'Alterations made to the original directives. Isabella and other agents very abruptly received new instructions when the Commonwealth first announced it was building a starship. They were originally working on the assumption that a series of wormholes would be opened to Dyson Alpha. Its whole strategy had to be altered to incorporate the development of superluminal travel. Isabella was also unaware of your quantumbuster weapon, she was expecting the navy to use flare bombs against MorningLightMountain's second invasion. That was the information which her kind were supplying to the Seattle team.'

'And we improved on it,' Wilson said tightly.

'Has Isabella got any memory of Alessandra Baron being a Starflyer agent?' Mellanie asked eagerly.

'Yes. Isabella was brought into the operation to hide the New York lawyers when Alessandra Baron learned you were investigating them.'

'Gotcha, you bitch!' Mellanie punched the air. 'Yes!'

'Not relevant at this point,' Paula said dismissively. 'Qatux, does Isabella know where the Starflyer is, or will be?'

'No. She only knows what she is supposed to do. She was on Illuminatus to join up with the lawyers after they had been given new identities. They would all receive their assignment then.'

'Johansson says it will now return to Far Away,' Justine said.

'It can't,' Nigel told her. 'The wormhole from Wessex to Boongate will not be opened to transport again.'

'Then it is confined to the Commonwealth,' Paula said. 'Qatux, if we take known Starflyer agents into custody can you read their memories for us? At some point, we should encounter one who knows where it is. It is important that we apprehend it as swiftly as possible. Will you come to the Commonwealth to assist me?'

'I would find such a venture most appealing. I would wish to be engaged through your own perception and interpretation facilities.'

Paula faced the Raiel's image, her face devoid of any expression. 'We have discussed this before. You may not leach my emotional state.'

'Is not your task an urgent one? Is this not how humans behave? Is not the price negotiated in advance?'

'Well yes,' Paula said, flummoxed by the request. 'But you will access the agent's thoughts, you will experience their emotions. That is our standard payment.'

'Their emotional levels are much reduced, suppressed by the Starflyer's behavioural modifiers. They mimic true feelings, they do not experience them for themselves, there is nothing there for me. You, though, Investigator, would feel a great deal as this case is wrapped up, the culmination of a hundred and thirty years of work. I would know what that is like.'

'I . . .' Paula looked round the study for help.

'I should let you stew in that one,' Mellanie said. 'But I'll be big. My price is an interview when all this is over.'

'You'll let it feel through you?' Paula asked.

'No, but I know a girl who will, and she's already wetwired for it.' Mellanie turned to the portal, already looking victorious. 'Qatux, how about I get you someone who's a lot more emotional than the Investigator is? Let's face it, she's a bit of a cold fish.'

'That would be acceptable.'

'Great. Nelson, I'll need some bodyguards to help me collect her.'

'Bodyguards? You're not going to kidnap someone are you?'

'Not for her, for me. I'm not very popular with her friends.'

'You can have bodyguards,' Nigel said. He grinned admiringly. 'Anything else?'

'An express ticket to Darklake City.'

'Of course.'

'Who are you going to arrest?' Mellanie asked Paula.

'Every agent Isabella came in contact with.'

'Good, that'll include Baron, then. I'll cover that arrest for Michelangelo.'

'It wasn't her that used and abused you,' Paula said. 'She is no longer human.'

'She never was,' Mellanie said gruffly.

'Assuming all this leads us to the Starflyer, what are we going to do with it when we find it?' Justine asked.

'Execute it,' Wilson said.

'Quietly,' Nigel said quickly.

'If Johansson is right about it trying to return to Far Away, and he's been right about everything else, then it will have to reach Boongate via Wessex,' Justine said. 'The Guardians are watching for that. Now might be a good time to help them. We've got Morton and his squad; they'd be able to take out anything guarding the Starflyer's train.'

Nigel gave Nelson a questioning glance.

'They could spearhead,' Nelson said. 'But it would have to be our operation; I'm not having rogue groups running round near the wormhole generators, no matter how good the cause. We've seconded half of our technical personnel to Narrabri to help modify the wormhole generators for the future settlement project. We can't risk any kind of firefight there.'

'All right,' Nigel said. 'We'll set up at Narrabri. There's enough space in our planetary station to hide this, and we can get Qatux there without drawing attention. Let's get started.'

13

The stealth coat wrapped Stig in a grey-black haze as if he'd
been devoured by his own private event horizon. Above him,
the midnight sky was dominated by the twinkling stars of
Neptune's Trident, the constellation which marked his birth.
Directly ahead, the chain link fence stretched out for miles, a
straight line slicing through the low grass like some kind of
border between nations rather than a mere aerodrome perimeter. Even with the starlight, it was dark out in the surrounding fields where he'd been waiting. His retinal inserts
were switched to enhancement, giving the damp land a blue-
grey hue. Sleeping sheep were huddled together for warmth.
There were flocks on both sides of the fence. The aerodrome
was spread over such a big area it was cheaper to give the
local farmers grazing rights than buy and maintain a fleet of
mowerbots.

He reached the fence in the middle of a hundred metre
section where there were no lights. The poles and the fittings
were there – they just didn't work. His bolt cutters cut
through the slim strands of rusted metal as if they were
paper. By now he was feeling ridiculous with the whole
super-agent covert mission set-up. There was no real security
at the aerodrome, just a couple of overweight guards who
spent the nights sitting round the management building raiding the canteen kitchen and watching local dramas on their

portals. He could have walked in through the main gate and they'd never know.

Usually.

And that was the one thing which Adam had lectured him about ceaselessly. There was no *usual*. So here he was jogging over the half mile of open field between the gate and the back of the vast hangars for the sake of procedure.

'How's it going?' Olwen asked.

'Good. Be there in five minutes or so.' Sweat was running down his skin now, the stealth coat on top of his usual jacket, force field skeleton, and weapons meant he was carrying quite a weight.

He reached the first row of hangars, and jogged down the strip of hard ground between them, where mosses and weeds were smothering the crumbling grey concrete. On either side of him the ends of the vast buildings presented perfect black semicircles against the star-filled sky. Almost sixty metres high at the apex, their sliding doors had been shut against the elements decades ago, never to be opened again. They rattled constantly now as the gentle breeze from the North Sea swept over the aerodrome. Built by the revitalization project, they were made out of the ubiquitous carbon panels pinned to a geodesic grid of carbon girders. Age and neglect had seen the pins and epoxy decay and fray, allowing blustery weather to worry away at the edges and joints. Each hangar had lost hundreds of panels to the wind, while others now hung by a single tenuous pin, swaying from side to side in the slightest gust. They clattered away against the framework as Stig moved deeper into the deserted ghost city. He turned off the wide thoroughfare to cut through towards the next row. The irregular gaps in the curving walls of the hangars on each side gave glimpses of the interiors. All of them were empty, stripped of machinery and support equipment. Dead cabling and pipes dangled down from unseen conduits overhead. Water leaked in through the missing panels to pool in long dank puddles on the concrete floor.

The final row of hangars, which the remaining blimpbots operated out of, were kept in a better state of repair, with so many new panels fixed to the framework they produced a check pattern so pronounced it looked like the original design. Maintenancebots stood along the base of the walls, their wide, flexible crawler trolleys looking alarmingly spindly for the weight they had to carry.

Powerful halogen bulbs on the top of the hangars produced elongated smears of light down the thoroughfare, which were easy enough for Stig to avoid. His sensors couldn't detect any kind of electronic activity anyway. The management building was at the end of the row, another construct of moulded carbon panels that had been modified and added to over the years to become a strange amalgamation of cubes, cylinders and domes.

Stig avoided the main entrance, and walked round to one of the smaller doors at the side. It wasn't even locked. Every light was on inside. He moved through the corridors, going up and down stairs, checking rooms. The whole place was completely deserted, not even the guards had turned up for their shift.

Stig finished up in the security office, and opened a link to Olwen. 'Everything clear in here. I've loaded our software into the arrays. I'm opening the gate for you now.' A bank of screens showed various camera images of the aerodrome, with the biggest concentration around the main entrance, the management building and the inside of the operational hangars. He watched the barrier at the main entrance lift up. A couple of minutes later, the Guardians drove their three trucks through.

He met them outside the service door on the first hangar. It occupied a small corner segment of the flight doors, but it was still big enough to take two trucks side by side. Olwen climbed down out of the cab once they were inside.

'I've never been this close to one before,' she said in admiration.

There were two blimpbots tethered end to end inside the hangar. The dark ellipsoid shapes were a hundred and fifty metres long and fifty metres high. With their ducted fans folded back along the fuselage their resemblance to airborne whales was even more acute.

'Me neither,' he admitted. Up close, the blimpbots weren't quite so impressive. Their fuselage envelopes had as many patches as the hangar which sheltered them, although they were a lot neater. The series of payload bay doors which lined the belly were open, showing various mechanical latches and grabs in the cavities. 'I didn't expect them to be this crude.'

'But they'll do the job,' she said. 'How many are there?'

'Twenty-two in the hangars. Three have had their flight-worthiness certificate withdrawn, pending maintenance, but they'll do for what we want.'

The other Guardians were climbing down out of the trucks.

'Let's get at it,' Olwen told them. 'We can install most of our systems by morning.'

'The next wormhole cycle starts mid-afternoon,' Stig said. 'That'll give us enough time to get them all airborne and positioned. They can circle the city until we call them in.'

'What about the revitalization team and the engineers?'

'I don't think they're coming back. This place is abandoned. And if they do show up, we'll just hang on to them so they don't raise the alarm.'

'All right then.'

One of the trucks had been backed up as close as it could get to the underside of the first blimpbot. The Guardians let the rear gate down, and pulled out a set of wheel ramps. Stig and Olwen went over to help them. A trollybot inched its way down the wheel ramps, carrying a fat cylinder nearly four metres long. The metal ramps creaked under it, betraying the weight of the cylinder.

'Are these going to work?' Olwen asked.

'I hope so.' Stig peered up into the truck. 'We've only got six. I'd be pleased if just one of them reaches 3F Plaza.' He could see another of the cylinders resting on its cradle inside. Crates full of decoy drone and chaff dispensers were strapped to the floor around it. 'We need to fit dispensers to all the blimpbots, including the ones we've armed. That way the Institute won't be able to spot the difference until it's too late.'

'No kidding?' Olwen said.

'Sorry. I get kind of nervous around bombs like this.'

They followed the trollybot as it rolled down to the central payload bay. The Guardians started to attach the blimpbot's internal hoist cables to the cylinder.

'We're picking up a lot more rumours from the Institute troops,' Olwen said. 'They're all talking about some kind of attack on the Commonwealth.'

'The Primes again,' Stig said.

'Yeah, but, Stig, it was a big attack; they're consistent about that. It's making them very jittery. There's even been talk about some of them breaking through to Half Way.'

'Stupid of them. They don't know if there are any Carbon Goose planes left at Port Evergreen.'

'It was only a whisper.'

Probably true, though, Stig thought. Guardians and their supporters had taken jobs at the pubs and clubs which the Institute troops had established as their own in Armstrong City. They provided a slow but steady trickle of information on the troops and their assignments. Morale, already low, was heading downhill fast. They'd all signed up for medium-term contracts to help the Institute combat raids from guerrilla bands out on the Great Iril Steppes; none of them expected to be doing urban paramilitary duties. Being the most hated group on the planet, subject to constant abuse and harassment, was taking its toll. Their officers had to let them out at night; safe together they drank and bitched like any soldier since Troy.

'Anybody let on if they're expecting an arrival?'

'I'd have told you. They don't know, too low down the food chain.'

'It can't be long now.'

She watched the heavy cylinder rise up into the cargo bay, flinching each time the ancient winch chains let out a *creak* of protest at the weight. 'You've done everything you can do. It can only come through at preset times, and we know what those are to the second. We've got 3F Plaza covered by every kind of sensor the human race has ever invented. If those troops even so much as glance at the gateway we'll know about it. So stop worrying, we've got it covered.'

Stig looked up at the blimpbots, and laughed at the audacity of the plan they'd come up with. 'Right, who's going to notice a goddamn airship on a bombing run? Dreaming heavens!'

'Nobody,' she said, smiling back with the same wild enthusiasm. 'That's the beauty. Fly them in low enough, and they'll be over the walls of 3F Plaza before the Institute can aim a single weapon at them.'

'I hope you're right.' He gave a start as the winch mechanism stopped with a nasty metallic grinding sound. The bomb was completely inside the bay. 'Let's work out how to get this brute secure. I really do want to have them all in the air by morning.'

*

Oscar didn't expect a downtime of more than six hours. Enough to recharge the *Dublin*'s niling d-sinks, and reload the forward section with Douvoir missiles and quantum-busters. Fleet Command had indicated they'd be sent right back to Hanko. After the wormholes had vanished, they'd destroyed over eighty Prime ships before their armaments were depleted.

As soon as the starship eased its bulk into a docking station at Base One, the secure encrypted message popped into Oscar's hold file. Admiral Columbia wanted to see him right away. Along with the rest of the crew, Oscar was still in shock at the way the War Cabinet had dumped shit from a great height on Wilson. Resentment was a strong twin of that feeling; he was tempted to tell his new Commander where to shove his meeting. An impulse made worse by worry that Columbia was implementing a political clearout of his new office, and Oscar had been one of the first people Wilson had recruited, making him a prominent loyal member of the old regime.

However, you can't go around judging people on the basis of your own emotional prejudices. So Oscar did the mature thing, and sent a message back saying he was on his way. Sir.

'If the shit fires you, we walk too,' Teague said.

'Don't,' Oscar said as he left for the small shuttle craft. 'The navy needs you.' *Where have I heard that phrase before?*

Nothing physical had changed at Pentagon II. Senior staff seemed twitchy as Oscar went through the offices and corridors, but then they were in the middle of organizing a battle to defend human worlds against forty-eight alien armadas. They were allowed to be twitchy.

Rafael Columbia had taken over Wilson's sterile white office. He was alone when Oscar was shown in.

No witnesses, Oscar thought immediately. *Oh, for God's sake, get a grip.*

Columbia didn't get up, he simply waved Oscar into a chair with easy familiarity. 'I have a problem, Oscar.'

'I'll resign if it makes it easier. We can't afford any more internal disruption.'

Columbia frowned in genuine surprise, then smiled briefly.

'No, not that. You're an excellent starship captain, just look at the *Dublin*'s performance.'

'Thank you.'

'I have a problem somewhat closer to home. I might have made a mistake.'

'Happens to us all, sir. You should see my list.' *Actually, you shouldn't.*

'I'm receiving a lot of information which indicates the Starflyer is a real and current threat. The evidence is building, Oscar. In the past I've always dismissed it, but I can't do that any more, no matter how personally uncomfortable that may prove to be.'

'It scared the living shit out of me when I found out.'

Columbia stared at him, before finally grinning a reluctant submission. 'I might have known. Very well, this makes it easier. For both of us.'

'What do you need?'

'A confirmed traitor has turned up on Boongate, a navy officer called Tarlo. My Paris office is putting together an arrest team; but of course all the wormholes to the Second47 are shut by War Cabinet edict. I need that traitor, Oscar. He can prove or disprove the whole Starflyer legend once and for all.'

'You want me to fly there?'

'No. For the moment we're keeping this dark; God knows what kind of shitstorm it would stir up if word leaks out before we've got it contained. I want you to be my personal emissary to Nigel Sheldon; you must emphasize just how important this is. Ask him to quietly open the wormhole and let the Paris team through. Nobody else, just them.'

'You want *me* to ask that?' Oscar couldn't believe what he was hearing, even though it was very flattering.

'Your record ever since Bose witnessed the Dyson Alpha enclosure is impeccable. You were also highly placed in CST before the war. Nigel Sheldon will see you and listen to what you say. I don't have that level of political capital with him today, and I'm reluctant to bump this up a level by asking Heather to intercede on my behalf. If he agrees to open the wormhole I want you on site at Narrabri to oversee the mission. I need your dependability, Oscar.'

Oscar stood up. He damn near saluted. 'I'll do my best, sir.'

*

It was another beautifully clear dawn in the Dessault Mountains as the sparkling constellations slowly washed away into the brightening sapphire sky. Samantha had no time for admiration as the gentle early morning radiance filtered through the open doorway of the ancient shelter. Her skin was hot and sticky inside the thick protective one-piece garment which she and the rest of the team wore while they were working close to the niling d-sink. Modern d-sinks had integral reactive em shielding, but the ones she was dealing with were decades old, and their passive shielding had broken down long ago. This one had been in place for sixty years, receiving and storing power from the solid state heat exchange cable that had been drilled two kilometres into the base of the mountain. She'd spent all night modifying the power emission module. Its original control array had needed replacing, never an easy thing to do with a live system. And there was a lot of basic circuit maintenance that had to be carried out; the niling d-sinks were good high-quality systems, but they'd never been designed with sixty years continuous use in mind.

It had taken the best part of seven hours, looking through a scuffed, misted visor in the light of four paraffin lamps. Her back ached, her fingers were numb, her head was full of the coding from obsolete programs. She clambered slowly to her feet, hating the sound her joints made as she moved. It was like being an old woman.

'Run the connection verifier,' she told Valentine, the convoy's technical chief.

'Got it,' he shouted from outside.

Samantha picked up the hand-held arrays lying on the crumbling enzyme-bonded concrete floor, and closed the wicks on the paraffin lamps one by one. She was confident enough that the power connections would work. This was the ninth manipulator station they'd sct up in five weeks, making her quite an expert on the old niling d-sinks.

'We got power flow,' Valentine called.

Samantha went to the open door, stretching elaborately to work the knots out of her too-stiff muscles. The sun was just rising over the foothills, revealing Trevathan Gulf, the huge valley which stretched out below her. They were on the north-western corner of the Dessault range, only four hundred kilometres from Mount Herculaneum. Every day, she thought she could see the crest of the gigantic volcano rising through the shimmering air when she looked to the south, a grey splinter hovering tantalizingly along the horizon. Other people in the convoy said she was imagining things. Aphrodite's Seat ought to be visible from their altitude, possibly the glacier ring as well. Today her eyes were just too tired to peer through the thin air.

Bright sunlight washed along Trevathan Gulf, sparking off the multitude of tributary streams which wound their way through forests of deciduous trees that had colonized the valley floor. The Gulf was a geological fault pushing out from the Grand Triad to split the Dessault range like a highway bulldozed by fallen angels. Its softly meandering course ran over seven hundred kilometres from the base of Mount Zeus in the west to the scrubland border of the High Desert in the east. Eighteen big rivers, and hundreds of smaller streams drained out of it through the valleys of the sundered northern-most mountains to spill across the Aldrin Plains. Winding rivers carried the water across the grasslands to the North Sea. It was an irrigation system which supported nearly a quarter of the farms on the planet.

Translucent cottontuft clouds scudded low over the treetops, precursors to the heavy storm residue which would arrive later that morning after it had raged around the Grand Triad. Once the dark cumulus was overhead, it would rain for at least three hours. Given the Gulf's altitude, the water was always cold, sometimes threaded with sleet. The caravan had endured the chilly, rainy climate for weeks now as they helped set up for the planet's revenge.

'Good job,' Harvey said in his rasping voice. He was standing just outside the shelter, dressed in the same mustard-yellow protective suit that everyone in the caravan wore.

'Same old job,' she replied.

'Yes, but done well. And that is vital.'

'Are we going to start the test?'

'Aye.'

They walked away from the shelter with its thick cladding of ivy. When the hole had been drilled for the solid state heat exchange cable and the shelter erected round the niling d-sink, this had been a broad swathe of open land on the northern side of the Gulf, with just a few saplings struggling for life on the stony foothills. Now with the rain nurturing the grass, lichens and mosses spread by the revitalization team, the trees had thrived. There was no clear ground any more, the forest had spread out from the floor of Trevathan Gulf to rise up towards the peaks in a wavy line broken by gullies and ridges. Gene-modified pines were in a majority up here on the slopes, though vigorous sycamores were always challenging them for space, and equally prolific species like white poplars and maples fell away in proportion to the altitude above the valley floor. The shelter was now surrounded by bushy weeping pines twenty metres high that crowded aggressively round spindly hornbeams and birch trees. A variety of ivy that had leaves so dark they were nearly black plagued everything, carpeting the sandy ground and swaddling the trunks of every tree. The shelter had been completely swamped by the thick creeper. It had taken them an hour to find and clear the doorway again.

Even without the ivy, the forest provided excellent cover for the shelter, and all its cousins along the Trevathan Gulf, but reaching it was difficult. The caravan could drive across the foothills above the forest line, ploughing through the streams and following the contours round sharp folds; but pushing through the trees was a specialist business. The Guardians Samantha was working with had stolen a JCB trailblazer from one of the tour companies that provided hyperglider flights over the Grand Triad. Its big forward roller-scythe of harmonic blades was the only way of chewing through the forest to reach the shelter. Once they'd reached it, the big machine had circled round in a spiral, clearing ground to set up the station equipment. Samantha knew it was the only way, but she couldn't help thinking that from the air the trailblazer's path must look like a giant arrow cutting through the trees, pinpointing their stations. It was a good job there weren't many aircraft on Far Away.

The equipment they'd set up sat on the springy mat of wood chips spewed out by the trailblazer. It had taken three lorries to carry the crates which they'd unpacked. In two days, the components had been assembled into an ungainly five-sided pyramid of black metal, standing seven metres high. Dew was already collecting in the crevices and ridges as the sun rose high enough to shine on the bulky machine.

Samantha and Harvey walked round its base, towards the road which the trailblazer had carved. Two McSobel technicians were fussing over an open panel, which revealed a matrix of red and amber lights. Valentine was standing behind them. 'Any minute now,' he said.

The convoy's vehicles were parked in a line back down the broken path, out of range from the hazardous em pulses given off by the niling d-sink. When she was three hundred metres from the shelter, Samantha took her helmet off and took a deep breath of cool, moist, unfiltered air. The scent of pine was thick in the air as she trod on the shattered splinters of bark and mashed needles.

'I'd like you to handle the last two stations,' Harvey wheezed.

'Why? Where are you going?'

He pulled off his helmet. Sunlight shone on the thick translucent bands of skin that criss-crossed his cheeks and neck, giving his ruined face a milky texture. 'A message came in last night while you were busy. The clans are putting together raiding parties in case the Starflyer gets through the gateway at 3F Plaza. They'll be spread along Highway One.'

'You can't,' she said automatically, then sucked in her lower lip. 'Sorry.'

'It's only surface damage,' he said cheerfully. 'I can still ride, and I can certainly still shoot – better than any of these lads who call themselves warriors these days. Besides, there's a rumour the Barsoomians will join us. Now who could resist that?'

'No one, I suppose,' she said with a sigh. Trying to argue him out of it would be useless, she knew.

'Now don't you go worrying about me. What you're doing is the truly important thing.'

'Sure. What about Valentine?'

'He's a good techhead, but we need someone who can drive this on. That's you.'

'Thanks, but you know we can't complete all the stations. We don't have the equipment.'

'Have a little faith in Bradley Johansson. He'll get the last components to us in time. Meanwhile, you can assemble the systems we do have, ready for the final installation.'

'I heard that we can only build another four functioning stations.'

'You heard just about right. Bradley will deliver the equipment to complete the last eight. Don't worry.'

'He's cutting it very fine.'

'I'm sure they have their problems out there in the Commonwealth.'

'Yeah,' she said, not liking what a gripe she sounded.

'But what?'

'I didn't say anything.'

'Did you have to?'

'All right,' she admitted. 'I wanted to be on the team that goes up to Aphrodite's Seat.'

'Well the dreaming heavens know you've earned a place. If you finish the last two stations on schedule, and Bradley delivers the remaining components to bring the network up to operational status, you should get to the Nalosyle Vales in time to make the rendezvous.'

'That's bribery.'

Harvey chuckled, a nasty liquid rumbling sound.

They reached the first parked lorry. Over a dozen Guardians were grouped round it, waiting. Ferelith was holding an excited Lennox. When she let go, the little boy toddled unsteadily to his mother, a delighted smile on his face. Samantha picked him up, and turned to face the new station they'd built. Valentine and the last two technicians were running down the track. She could just see the edge of the black pyramid about six hundred metres away in the shelter's new clearing.

The latecomers all pulled their helmets off.

'Everyone here?' Valentine asked. Without waiting, he raised a hand-held array, and entered the activation sequence. Samantha brought up her own hand-held array, juggling Lennox onto one arm as she tried to watch the power supply symbols.

The air around the clearing sparkled as the pyramid generated its base force field eight hundred metres wide, stabilizing the whole structure. She could feel the ground trembling slightly as the force field permeated the rock beneath them, anchoring itself solidly into place. It was that single function which had made construction of the generators so difficult, almost half of the components had to be custom built for them inside the Commonwealth. Standard force fields couldn't permeate solid matter for more than a few metres at best. Nothing moved inside the bubble of energy, the leaves on every tree were stilled as the now-lustrous air solidified.

'Stage two,' Valentine shouted.

Samantha tilted her head back, and pointed for Lennox. The little boy stared up curiously into the sky.

Five long blades of air shimmered above the existing force field. Their shape was tenuous at first, but as the initial energy surge was absorbed, the air calmed as its molecules were rearranged and locked into new shapes. There was only the faintest of diffraction layers left to reveal the contours, slight pressure fissures cutting through the clear sapphire sky, but it was sufficient for the naked eye to make out. From Samantha's angle, it was as though the blade shapes were made from high-quality glass. They curved away gently from each other, expanding until they were half a kilometre wide and separated by three kilometres; then they began the long curve back to a single point eight kilometres above the fresh clearing in the forest.

'The universe's biggest egg-whisk,' Harvey growled.

As Samantha watched, grinning at his description, thin streamers of cloud hit a couple of the unyielding blades and twisted sharply away. Gentle gusts were washing against her as the breeze which blew constantly along Trevathan's Gulf was deflected by the blades.

'Stage three,' Valentine warned.

The blades began to move, rotating clockwise, very slowly. After five minutes they'd finished a complete circle, and stopped. Samantha felt the wind they'd stirred race across the road in a giant slothful pressure wave, causing the trees to sway. Her protective suit flapped about, while her sweaty hair swirled round her head. Lennox laughed delightedly.

'We did it,' Harvey said. 'Again. What was the power use?'

Samantha consulted her hand-held array. 'Four per cent.'

'That's a lot.'

Above them, the blades vanished. Then the base force field released its grip on the surrounding rock and air. A zephyr swept along the road as the air currents churned back into their original patterns.

'Initialization uses a disproportionate amount of power,' she said. 'Don't worry, there'll be enough for the planet's revenge.'

*

Four identical black Cadillac limousines drew up outside the big old converted warehouse in Darklake City's Thurnby district. Mellanie stepped out of the first one, her expensive Fomar pumps just missing the soggy mass of leaves and paper that clogged the gutter. She'd chosen the most sober clothes from her own range to wear, a neat black jacket with slim white lines marking out a square pattern, matching trousers and a cream blouse. This way she had a whole Paula Myo authority-figure thing going for her. It felt funny coming back here as a take-no-shit professional troubleshooter, backed up by six very tough wetwired CST security operatives.

There was nobody about on the street, so they all trooped over to the door. Nothing had changed; the purple Wayside Production plaque was still on the wall outside, the couches in the tiny reception area were still snowing flakes of chrome on the floor, the scent of ozone and disinfectant hanging in the air. Mellanie went straight though reception into the narrow corridors which separated the stages. Up above her, the ancient solar collector roof creaked incessantly. Voices from one of the stages echoed round the cavernous overhead space. A stagehand came round a corner, pulling a trolley with a circular bed balanced precariously on top. He stared in astonishment at Mellanie and her escort.

'Where's Tiger Pansy?' Mellanie asked.

'Huh?'

'Tiger Pansy, where is she?'

His hand waved limply back down the corridor. 'Dressing room, I think.'

'Thank you.' Mellanie marched past him. She hadn't actually made it as far as the dressing room before. It wasn't hard to find, a big open area lined with lockers on one side, make up tables along the other. The far end was a jumble of clothes racks. Several girls dressed in feathers and gold-crusted sarongs were sitting round waiting for their turn with the make-up lady, a large elderly woman in a black mourning dress. One of the girls was having her OCtattoos tuned by a sensorium technician; she was very young, an easy forty centimetres taller than Mellanie, thin bordering on malnourished, with lustrous black skin. She had a nervous yet resigned expression on her face as she watched the technician sticking modifier patches over the OCtattoos that webbed her thighs and genitalia. Something must have registered as she caught sight of Mellanie. The technician looked up from his sophisticated hand-held array. Across the dressing room, the babble of conversation cut off.

'Tiger Pansy?' Mellanie called.

Someone stood up in the middle of the girls waiting to be made up. Mellanie barely recognized her; the peroxide-blond hair was now orange verging on tangerine, and seemed to be all straw, standing up as if it'd been electrocuted. Reprofiling had taken the chubbiness out of her cheeks, but the thick crust of skin it'd left produced deep creases as her jaw worked away at her gum. Even before the make-up session, she still had way too much mascara round her eyes. The turquoise and topaz feathers round her chest were under a lot of strain holding her vast breasts up.

'Oh, hi, Mellanie,' she squeaked. 'Watcha doin back here?'

'Came to see you.'

'Yeah?' Tiger Pansy giggled, a high-pitched sound drilling though Mellanie's eardrums. 'You wanna interview me? Jaycee won't like that.'

'I'm here to offer you a job. And nobody cares what Jaycee likes, least of all me.'

'Oh really?' a man's voice asked.

Mellanie turned to face him. Like his studio, Jaycee hadn't changed either, head still shaved, black clothes with the crow's foot wrinkles that only cheap cloth produced. 'Get lost,' Mellanie said curtly.

Jaycee's pale skin started to flush. He gave her bodyguards a quick appraisal. 'Fucking say that without your friends here.'

She smiled with predatory malice. 'They're not here for my benefit, they're here to keep you safe from me.'

'Fuck off, bitch. I mean it, you don't come in here like you rule the universe and try to steal my fucking girls away. Tiger Pansy's mine. You fucking got that?'

Mellanie cocked her head to one side, pursing her lips as if she was mulling over what he'd said. 'No.'

'I don't care who the fuck you think you are, fuck off now!' Jaycee yelled. 'And you,' he jabbed a finger at Tiger Pansy. 'You don't go fucking anywhere. Understand?'

'Yes, Jaycee,' Tiger Pansy said meekly. Her chin quivered as she fought back tears.

'Don't talk to her like that,' Mellanie said. She took a step towards Jaycee.

'Or what? You'll give me a blow job?' He smiled round at the bodyguards. 'Did Alessandra pass her round you guys? I hear that's what she does: the Baron show's whore.' His sneer turned triumphant. 'Isn't that right?' he asked Mellanie.

'You're just a fucking cheap media whore. What? You think I don't fucking know that. Every fucker in the business knows what you are.'

Mellanie knew she should just grab Tiger Pansy and get out. Had it been anyone else but Jaycee she would have done just that. 'I am not for sale,' she growled out as she took another step, putting her nose to nose. 'I told you that before.' She brought her knee up.

Jaycee twisted with fast competence, bringing his own leg round protectively. Her knee skidded off the back of his thigh. His grin was mocking. 'And we've done this befor—'

Mellanie nutted him. Her forehead smashing into his nose. Jaycee screamed as his cartilage made a horrible *crunch*. His hand came up automatically to cup his nose and staunch the blood. That was when Mellanie brought her knee up again, properly this time.

'Yeah, you're right, this is a real *déjà vu* session,' she said amiably as tears flooded Jaycee's eyes. His mouth opened in a silent screech as he fell to his knees, one hand clamped over his nose, the other over his crotch. Blood made the front of his black shirt glisten disgustingly.

The girls got out of the way *fast* as Mellanie walked over to Tiger Pansy. 'This job, it pays so much you'll never have to come back here. There's a rejuvenation treatment thrown in as well. You can start over again.'

'Yeah?' Tiger Pansy asked. Her jaw worked hard on the gum as she looked at Jaycee. 'Is he gonna be all right d'ya think?'

'Unfortunately, yes. I don't want to rush you, but I do need an answer.'

'He wasn't last time you did that, y'know. He couldn't get it hard for a week.'

'For which the human gene pool was very grateful. Tiger,' she put her hand on the porn starlet's arm, 'I need your help. I really do. A lot of people are depending on you.'

Tiger Pansy gave the bodyguards a resigned look. 'Who do I got to fuck?'

'Nobody. It's not like that. We're going to link you up one-to-one for a special client. That way this client gets to find out what you feel. I came to you because you're the best sensorium artiste there is.'

'Yeah?' Tiger Pansy grinned sheepishly. 'You're an all right girl, Mellanie, I knew it when you came in here that first day. Straight away, I said to myself, I said, she's class, Tiger, you should try and be more like her. I'm not, though.'

'You'll do it?'

'Mellanie,' Tiger Pansy put her head down and whispered. 'There's this, like, medicine I need to get through the day. Special medicine. Jaycee used to get it for me. I can't go nowhere without it.'

For some reason, Mellanie's throat tightened to an almost painful degree. She couldn't remember feeling so much sympathy for anyone before. 'We can get it for you, I promise. Better quality than Jaycee ever supplied. You can go anywhere, Tiger. And when you're rejuvenated you won't need it any more.'

'Promise?'

'I promise.'

Tiger Pansy produced a lottery-winner smile. 'Okay then.'

*

The look on Nigel Sheldon's face wasn't exactly engineered to make Oscar feel welcome. Daniel Alster, who'd met him from the train, had been polite and upbeat. Oscar had thought that attitude would reflect from his boss. Now, in the senior management suite at Narrabri station, he realized what a mistake that had been.

'So what does Columbia want?' Nigel asked. 'It has to be important and delicate to send you.'

'The Navy Intelligence Paris office has found a rogue officer called Tarlo, and needs to arrest him. However, there's a problem: Tarlo is on Boongate.' Oscar braced himself for the outburst.

Amazingly, Nigel leaned back in his chair, and gave a bemused little smile. 'Tarlo was one of the people on Illuminatus, wasn't he?'

Oscar had to think back quickly over the briefing he'd absorbed on the train journey over from the High Angel. 'Yes, sir.' All he could think was how amazingly well briefed Nigel Sheldon was. *Then again, he is the head of the largest Dynasty.*

'What sort of rogue?' Nigel asked maliciously.

'Sir, we need to arrest him and read his memories to confirm who he's working for.'

'So Columbia is finally starting to believe in the Starflyer is he?'

'Uh,' Oscar managed to rumble.

'Don't worry, Oscar, I know it's real.'

'You do?'

'Me and several others, so you can relax now.'

Somehow, that just wasn't possible. 'Thank you, sir. The Paris office has put together an arrest team. We'd like to send them through to Boongate.'

'The War Cabinet decided to keep all the Second47 wormholes closed.'

'I know, but it's only a team of five. The time the wormhole would be open for isn't long enough to permit any kind of mass exodus from the Boongate side, especially if the planet is unaware the wormhole is open.'

Nigel drummed his fingers on the desk. 'What is the plan should they capture Tarlo intact?'

'Direct memory read.'

'That's what we're doing here with Starflyer agents; if Columbia is coming round to our views we can share our information with him.' He screwed up his face, undecided. 'If they get Tarlo, the arrest team will want to come back. That'll mean opening the wormhole again. People on Boongate will know; damn it, my people there will know and I've already forced them to stay. I don't think so, Oscar, I'm sorry.'

'The arrest team have volunteered to go into the future along with the rest of the planet. They're not asking for a return trip, sir, they just want the chance to get their man.'

'Oh.'

'Tarlo is a critical Starflyer agent, his position in the Paris office allowed him to cover up any number of its operations. His memories would be invaluable in exposing the whole Starflyer network. I cannot over-emphasize how important he is.'

'Damnit.' Nigel let out a long breath. 'All right, but we keep this very quiet. If and when Tarlo is hooked up to a neural download, the data extracted from his brain is to be routed through to the operation we're putting together here. Columbia can have full access, but we direct the procedure.'

'Thank you, sir.'

Nigel nodded acknowledgement. 'You'd better hook up with Wilson, he can brief you on our operation.'

'Wilson's here?'

'Yes,' Nigel said wryly. 'Along with some others you may recognize. But that's not to be shared with Columbia until we're convinced he's acknowledged the Starflyer. Understood?'

'Yes, sir.'

'Very well. Daniel, organize some transport for the arrest team.'

'I'll get right on to it. What do you want to do about opening the gateway?'

'The Paris team goes through, and that's it. If it's open for more than a minute I'll want to know why. Who's on duty over there?'

'Ward Smith. I'll get over to the gateway control centre and liaise with him myself.'

*

There were eight Guardians working on the big engine. The old Ables ND47 sat on the single track which ran through the huge Foster Transport shed, its new ultramarine paintwork gleaming under the bright overhead lights. A cluster of mobile gantries surrounded it, giving the engineeringbots access to the entire superstructure. Under the supervision of the Guardians team they were installing force field generators and medium calibre weapons in casings that looked like they were integral segments of the bodywork. Forty yards behind the engine, two long enclosed wagons sat on the shiny rails.

Bradley Johansson stood beside the big coupling on the first wagon, looking up at its dusty yellow and maroon shell. A single connector cable dangled from beneath the coupling, its end almost reaching the ground; it was as thick as his torso.

'We're basically ready to go,' Adam said. 'All the equipment and vehicles are loaded. The old brute is so heavily armoured even it will have trouble carrying the weight.'

'And if it does get hit?'

Adam grinned, and patted the cool metal chassis of the front wagon. 'The armoured cars make the final dash through to Half Way. I've got it all covered, Bradley, stop worrying. We will make it.'

'All of us?' Bradley asked quietly. He glanced at the Guardians swarming like acrobats over the gantries around the nuclear powered engine. There wasn't one of them over thirty-five.

'Most of us,' Adam said.

'I fear the dreaming heavens will be welcoming a lot of friends this coming week.'

'You know, I never did get that part of your philosophy. Why give the Guardians their own religion? That makes it look even more like a cult.'

'I didn't. I've been to the dreaming heavens, Adam. It's at the far end of the Silfen paths, a place where noble demons fly through an endless sky. I was cured there.'

Adam gave him a judgemental look.

Bradley's e-butler told him Senator Burnelli was calling.

'I've been in a meeting,' she told him.

'Forgive my lack of surprise, Senator, but that's what politicians do.'

'Not meetings like this one, we don't. You'll be happy to hear you're almost legitimate now. We want to bring you in, Bradley, you and the Guardians.'

Bradley opened the call to Adam as Justine explained what had been decided at Nigel Sheldon's mansion.

'The Starflyer is the same family as the Primes,' Bradley said. 'Well, in all the dreaming heavens, I never knew that. It does make sense, though. I remember its interest in the Dyson Pair right from the start.'

'Do you know where the Starflyer is?' she asked.

'No, but like you we believe it will try and get through to Boongate.'

'It can't. However, we are going to let it think it can. If its train approaches the gateway, our squad will bag it.'

'A honey trap. Good idea.'

'You're at the Narrabri station already, aren't you?'

'Now Senator, you know that's not a question I'll answer for you.'

'But we want to join forces. You must have established procedures for this very moment.'

'We are certainly prepared for most eventualities.'

'Well then, we stand a much better chance if we combine our operations.'

'Forgive me, but after being hunted like a diseased animal for a hundred and thirty years, it is understandably hard for me to welcome the hounds into my house.'

'You have my word this is an honest offer; Nigel Sheldon's word, too. I can put you in contact. You can hear it from him personally.'

'I appreciate that. However there is one way you can settle the problem of trust.'

'Yes?'

'Kazimir McFoster was carrying some data for us when he was murdered at LA Galactic. We believe you may have it.'

'I do, yes.'

'Excellent. If Paula Myo delivers it to me in person, then I will truly know the Guardians have come in from the cold.'

'How about if I deliver it? Surely that would prove our goodwill?'

'Please understand, if it is the Investigator, I can be absolutely certain. I believe in her honesty. It is the one true constant in a very uncertain universe.'

'But you don't trust me?'

'Please don't be offended, Senator. It's just that habits, both good and bad, become ingrained over a hundred and thirty years. And I am a creature of habit.'

'Very well, I'll see what I can do. But listen, CST is searching Narrabri station in case the Starflyer is already in place. If the security teams close in on you, for heaven's sake call me. The last thing we need is for us to be shooting at each other.'

'Thank you, Senator. I am not so prideful as to risk everything we have achieved on a point of stubborn principle. If we are in trouble, I will shout for help very loudly indeed.'

'I'll get back to you.'

Bradley smiled, his eyes focused on the far end of the shed. Adam groaned in dismay, resting his forehead on the huge steel wheel. 'I can't believe you just did that. Paula Myo? You've got to be fucking joking. As soon as she sees you or me, she'll blow our brains out. She has no choice, her DNA won't let her do anything else.'

'Nonsense, Adam, you must have more faith in human nature.'

'She squealed on her own parents, for God's sake.'

'They weren't her parents, though, were they? They were her kidnappers.'

'Oh for – we had it. We were there. Burnelli was offering us legitimacy, and you blew it. So much for not being prideful. Damnit!' He slapped the wheel in frustration.

'Adam, Adam, have you no negotiating skills? Investigator Myo is the opening gambit. It would be lovely if she did agree, but I expect we'll wind up with a two minute call from Nigel Sheldon or some other high-placed player.'

Adam groaned again, sounding like an injured animal. 'I don't need this extra stress. I really don't.'

'It won't be much longer, I think we can both be sure of that.'

*

The CST exploratory division wormhole at Narrabri station followed the usual layout. An isolated building away from the commercial sector, where the big environment confinement chamber was grafted on to the gateway. The Operations Centre and all the associated support team offices formed a protective honeycomb around the outside.

Paula stood on the floor of the environment chamber waiting for the wormhole to be aligned. Nigel stood at her side, his mouth raised in a soft smile as he looked at the fuzzy bubble of air that was the force field capping the wormhole.

'Always gives me a buzz,' he confessed to the Investigator. 'People just take this for granted so much these days, nobody appreciates the technology and energy sitting behind a gateway.'

'Making the extraordinary appear commonplace is the ability of true genius.'

'Thank you, Paula. Tell me, would you consider marrying me?'

'You ask me that every time we meet.'

'What do you answer every time?'

'No thank you.'

'Ah well, I'm sorry. And I won't wipe this time from my memory. You must think me appallingly boorish to have done so before.'

Paula gave him a sly look. 'If you ever did.' The slight flush above his collar was confirmation enough for her. 'What did Heather say about the Starflyer infiltration?' she asked.

'Let's just say she's not a very happy person today. Christabel helped her save some face with the precautions she's already instigated. Good move on your part alerting her.'

'It was Renne Kempasa who knocked on the door.'

'The one who died on Illuminatus?'

'She suffered bodyloss, yes.'

Nelson and Mellanie walked into the chamber. Paula was about to greet them when another woman came through the open airlock. She walked carefully, balancing on platform shoes that added over ten centimetres to her height. Paula froze in surprise.

'This is Tiger Pansy,' Mellanie said. She sounded proud, as if she was introducing a sister who'd made good.

'Real pleased I'm sure,' Tiger Pansy said round her gum. She smiled at Paula. 'Hey, I know you, you're that famous Investigator, right? I was wanting to play your character in *Murderous Seduction*, but Jaycee gave it to Slippy Gwen-Hott instead. Shame, that.'

Paula had absolutely no idea how to reply. She looked at Nigel for guidance. He seemed indecently pleased at her discomfort.

'Delighted to have you here, Tiger Pansy,' Nigel said with perfect civility.

'Oh wow, it really is you.'

'This,' Paula spluttered at Mellanie, 'this is the person you found for Qatux?'

'Of course,' Mellanie said. 'Tiger Pansy is perfect.'

Paula took a breath, and gave the porn starlet a close look. Tiger Pansy was combing at her wild red hair with three centimetre gold and purple fingernails. Her facial skin was leathery, with a sheen that betrayed inexpert reprofiling treatments which not even her excessive make-up was able to conceal. She'd squeezed into a henna-coloured skirt that only came halfway to her knees; a black blouse had the top three buttons undone. Paula was sure Tiger Pansy was wearing an uplift bra. She *really* didn't need to. 'Do you know what you're supposed to be doing?' Paula asked.

'Yeah, Mellanie explained it all to me. It's kinda weird, but what the hell. It ain't fucking a D.O.L. for a living. Right?' She giggled loudly, a sound reminiscent of a sea lion's mating call.

And Paula realized that, actually, Mellanie was one hundred per cent right. Tiger Pansy was perfect for this. 'Right,' Paula agreed.

'They're coming through,' Nelson announced.

The dark force field turned fluorescent as the Operations Centre locked the wormhole exit inside the High Angel, the first time the sentient starship had ever allowed that to happen. Hoshe and Qatux walked through it.

Tiger Pansy's jaw stopped chewing as she looked up at the big alien. 'Oh wow.' Her giggle turned nervy. Even Mellanie's chirpiness faded away.

Nigel stepped forward. He bowed. 'Qatux, welcome to the Commonwealth. We are honoured that you're here, I only wish it was under different circumstances.'

'Nigel Sheldon,' the alien rasped. Several of its eyes swayed around to look at the Dynasty leader. 'I am grateful for this opportunity. My race has remained sheltered in the High Angel for too long. And is this the delightful lady who has agreed to be my companion during this visit?'

'Ohh.' Tiger Pansy's mouth opened to a wide incredulous O. She walked forward, almost falling as her shoes wobbled on their slender heels. Nigel, Nelson, and Paula all gave a little lurch forward, their arms lifting in unison ready to catch her. 'You're a real gentleman, you know that.' Tiger Pansy hesitantly put out a hand.

Qatux unrolled an unsteady tentacle. Its tip coiled gently round Tiger Pansy's wrist. She shivered as if caught in a blast of icy air. Slender OCtattoos glowed a phosphor green beneath her skin, for a moment her whole body was luminous, with emerald pinpricks shining through her fuzz of hair. Qatux sighed like a human who'd just downed a whisky chaser in one.

Tiger Pansy looked down at her hands as the light faded. 'I didn't know they could do that. You got you some fancy software there, Mr Qatux.'

'Yes,' Qatux murmured. 'I thank you for allowing my routines access to your circuitry. They can provide the direct links I require. I can feel your emotional content perfectly. You are a poignant lady, Tiger Pansy.'

Tiger Pansy's nervous giggle sliced into the silence. 'Hey, that's really sweet.'

Qatux released her hand; its head swung round to face Nigel and Nelson. 'And now it will be my delight to help you uncover the Starflyer agents in your midst.'

'We're setting up a dedicated analysis centre,' Nelson said. 'The suspects will be brought in for you once we've neutralized any wetwired weapons.'

The biggest airlock door in the chamber expanded. Qatux moved through it with a ponderous gait. Tiger Pansy tottered alongside. 'So is there, like, a Mrs Qatux?' she asked.

Paula couldn't help the gentle smile on her face as she watched the very odd couple leave.

'Now there's something you don't see every day,' Hoshe said quietly.

'Only once in a very long lifetime, I'd say,' Paula replied. Her e-butler told her there was a call from Justine for herself and Nigel.

'I've made contact with Johansson,' Justine said. 'He's willing to help us track down the Starflyer, but there's a problem.'

'Which is?' Nigel asked.

'He wants some proof that our offer isn't an entrapment. After all, he has spent a hundred and thirty years being pursued by the Serious Crimes Directorate, and now he's about to face his target.'

'Will a personal guarantee from me swing it?' Nigel asked.

'He wants Paula to deliver the data Kazimir McFoster was carrying.'

'No.' The word came out before Paula even knew she'd said it. There was no analysis, no careful reasoning. She simply *knew* the answer.

'Why not?' Justine asked. 'I know this is difficult for you, but the Guardians were right.'

'I accept that,' Paula backtracked. 'Johansson had a perfect right to oppose the Starflyer, even though he should have used different methods. But Elvin is a mass murderer, a political terrorist of the worst kind. I cannot overlook that, no matter what.'

'You have to,' Nigel told her.

'You both know what I am. Therefore you know I cannot.'

Just for an instant, Nigel's affable façade slipped. 'I don't get this, you of all people know what's at stake here. Just take the data to them, forget your damn scruples for a minute. We can nab that little shit Elvin when this is over, because I assure you I certainly haven't forgotten Abadan.'

'No,' Paula said.

'Shit!' Nigel glared at her. It would have made anybody else in the Commonwealth back down immediately. Paula seemed oblivious to his anger. 'All right,' he snapped. 'Justine, call them back. Negotiate. Find someone else they consider acceptable.'

*

Mellanie trailed after Qatux and Tiger Pansy as Nelson led them over to the security centre. It wasn't far from the exploratory division, a blank dome with a heavily guarded entrance. Cat's Claws had been assigned the escort duty; wearing their bulky armour suits they looked formidable. Her inserts scanned them passively, showing her which one was Morton, otherwise she would never have known. He didn't say anything to her, all of the squad were taking their duty very seriously.

'This way I get to stay in the game,' Morton had said contentedly when he and the others suited up. Nelson had given them the option of leaving, but they'd decided to stay on. Mellanie knew why Morton was doing it, this kept him close to the real players, and, she hoped, her as well. The Cat and Rob just seemed to enjoy the whole idea of a fight.

Nelson had turned over a lecture theatre for Qatux to use. Most of the seating had been removed, and the lighting dimmed. Various technicians were setting up equipment cabinets. They all stopped when the alien came in. Several applauded. Tiger Pansy giggled, and started doing introductions like some old-fashioned diplomatic interpreter.

Mellanie saw Dudley and the Bose motile lurking about near the big wall-mounted portal that presenters used to display their lecture data on. The Bose motile had three security guards standing close by. They all wore sharp business suits, and appeared perfectly friendly, but Mellanie's scan located some inserts with a very high power density wetwired into their bodies. Their visible OCtattoos were green and red lines running in parallel along the rear of their cheeks.

Two of the Bose motile's sensor stalks bent round to follow her as she walked over to them. 'Hello Mellanie,' it said. She saw it now had a slim modern hand-held array hanging from a leather strap round one of its arm limbs.

'Hello,' she said pleasantly. 'So are you Dudley one, or two? What have the pair of you decided?'

'We haven't discussed that yet.'

Mellanie was amused to hear the array synthesizing Dudley's voice perfectly. It obviously irked the human version judging by his expression of distaste. She smiled brightly, and leaned forward to kiss him. Morton was over by the main door with The Cat, so she figured it would be easy enough. Amazingly, Dudley moved back before her lips touched him.

'Dudley?' She frowned at him.

'Ah, yes, I've been meaning to talk to you.'

'Talk to me?'

'Yes. I'd just like to say that I am happy to stand aside now Morton has returned.'

'Stand aside?'

'That's right. I know how much you feel for him. In view of that I think it's for the best. Circumstances have changed for both of us, have they not?'

'Circumstances?' Mellanie desperately wanted to stop repeating things, but she was so surprised by Dudley her brain was refusing to come up with anything original. When she studied him she saw he'd actually shaved. The tiredness and perpetual worry was fading from his eyes. He'd even dressed in a stylish mauve shirt and black semi-organic trousers. For the first time, she could actually see his true age in that calm face which looked back unflinchingly at her.

'I believe even you would have to concede that our relative situations have altered substantially since we met,' Dudley said. 'That calls for a serious re-evaluation of our relationship.'

She just stared at him. This wasn't even Dudley talking any more, there wasn't a hint of reticence or caution. His voice was calm and measured, verging on patronizing.

'Of course, I'm enormously grateful for what we experienced and shared,' he said hurriedly. 'Without you I would never be whole again. And I will never be able to thank you enough for that. I hope we can continue to be friends as well as colleagues in this endeavour.'

'You're dumping me.'

'Mellanie, human beings are effectively immortal. I know this is your first life and everything is more intense for you, but believe me when I say nothing lasts for ever. It is better this way. Honesty is the way forward for both of us.'

'*You* are dumping *me?*' Even from her own mouth it sounded terribly wrong.

'I am,' the Bose motile said. 'It's because I'm a complete arsehole.'

Dudley glared at his alien twin. 'I see you haven't mastered tact yet.'

'Well face it, where would I inherit that from?'

'After everything I've done for you?' Mellanie asked; it was as though she was questioning herself.

'Our hierarchal structure wasn't entirely one sided,' Dudley said in the kind of tone used to correct one of his students. 'I believe you gained as much, if not more, from this relationship than I did. Look at where we are, deciding the future of humankind.'

'Oh, just fuck off.' She turned around and walked away, fast. At least there was no danger of tears – for a second, the image of Jaycee sinking to the ground clutching at his balls filled her mind – well, no tears in her eyes anyway. *He's not even worth that.*

'Sorry,' Dudley Bose's voice called out across the lecture theatre.

Mellanie didn't turn to check which one of them had said it. She already knew.

'You okay?' Tiger Pansy asked.

'Sure. I'm fine.' *The original bounce-back girl, me.*

'Hey, Mellanie, I gotta thank you,' Tiger Pansy said. She waved enthusiastically at Qatux, who was discussing sensorium interface technology with one of the CST technicians. The Raiel raised a tentacle in acknowledgement. 'This is like the bestest gig ever.'

'I thought you'd like it. But Tiger, remember, you really can't tell anyone afterwards. These people can't be messed around.'

'I know that. I ain't that stupid.'

'I know you're not. Take care.'

'You going?'

'Yeah. There's only one thing I want now, and it's not here.'

'Well, I hope you find it.'

'Me too.'

Nobody around the Raiel really noticed as she walked away. The last thing she wanted was to run over to Morton after what had happened, so she went towards a door on the opposite side of the lecture theatre. Hoshe was sitting on one of the remaining audience chairs, suspiciously close to the door.

Mellanie gave him a fond smile, and sat beside him. Without warning, she darted forward and gave him a kiss.

'What was that for?' he asked.

'Hoshe Finn, my very own guardian angel.'

'I didn't think you were speaking to me after Isabella.'

'Hm, your halo did dim there for a minute. But once again you made sure no harm came to me.'

Hoshe glanced down at the two aliens who were now talking together. Dudley Bose was standing beside the Bose motile, trying to steer the conversation his way.

'One of your smarter moves,' Hoshe said. 'You can do a lot better than him.'

She glanced at the trio of armour suits. 'I thought you said you were married.'

Hoshe grinned. 'I guess I deserved that. Shouldn't pry into your private life.'

'There's nothing much private about it. That's my biggest problem. What about you? What are you doing here?'

'I need to talk to Nelson, I have a favour to ask.'

'What's that?'

'I need to get some people off Boongate. A Senate Security team was following a suspected Starflyer agent and got stuck there. My fault.'

'I doubt it. Do you want me to talk to Nigel about it? He has the final say on that.'

Hoshe gave her a surprised look. 'You can do that?'

'For you, of course.'

'Might be worth it.' He didn't sound very certain.

'Just say the word. I owe you.'

'No, you don't.'

'A month's unisphere access, and a week at a B&B if I remember rightly. There's a lot of interest piling up in that account, Hoshe Finn.'

'Another time, another universe.'

'I'd still like to repay you.'

'I'm not sure it's worth it. Look, this is just about over now. Sheldon will destroy the Prime homeworld, Paula and the Guardians will track down and eliminate the Starflyer. Everybody needs to start thinking what they're going to do after the war, because life is going to be a whole lot sweeter then. After what we've all been through, it can't be anything else.'

'God, I hadn't even thought about afterwards. I've been so scared since Randtown. Trying to keep one step ahead takes up every moment.'

'You're a damn good reporter. I bet you wind up with your own show.'

'That'd be nice,' she said, and it was a comfy thought, the kind she had before the ships flew down out of a clean Randtown sky, and her world turned upside down. Again. 'I could do with something that's going to last.'

'Well there you go then.'

'There's just one thing I've got to do first.'

Hoshe gave a mock groan. 'What?'

'I'm going to cover Alessandra Baron's arrest. I want to see her led away in chains. I want to show the entire Commonwealth that most beautiful sight.'

'They don't manacle people any more. Besides, if she's a Starflyer agent it's likely to get violent.'

'Here's hoping,' Mellanie muttered with a wicked smirk. 'Who's going to be the arresting officer?'

'Hasn't been assigned yet,' Hoshe said, with an eye on Nelson and the Raiel.

'But you could put in for it, couldn't you? You could do that while I speak to Nigel. How about that? A trade, not a repayment.'

'Done.'

*

The maglev express was almost empty. After all, who in their right mind would travel *to* Wessex right now?

Alic walked out of the first class carriage onto the nearly deserted platform in the Narrabri station's Oxsorrol terminal. The three cases carrying his armour suit and weapons followed loyally a few metres behind. Vic Russell was close on his heels, eager to get going. Matthew Oldfield, John King and Jim Nwan formed a rearguard group, trying to keep their conversation light-hearted. It wasn't going well, every movement agitated some injury sustained on Illuminatus. Alic knew they shouldn't be going into combat again so soon, but this mission overrode any kind of by-the-book protocol. Besides, he kept telling himself, there were five of them, and they'd raided the Paris office armoury for some serious heavy-calibre hardware. There would be no repeat of Treetops no matter what Tarlo was equipped with this time.

Two men were waiting for them on the platform outside their carriage. One of them was in a navy captain's uniform. Alic recognized him immediately. 'Captain Monroe?'

'Pleased to meet you. Daniel Alster here is our liaison with

CST for this operation, and we have some very good news for you.'

'We can go?' Vic demanded.

'Yes,' Oscar said.

'All right!' Vic high-fived with John King.

'We have some transport for you, gentlemen.' Daniel gestured at a big Ford ten-seater Holan parked on the side of the platform. 'It'll take us over to the station's track engineering facility.'

'What's there?' Vic asked.

'A train that will take you through the wormhole.'

'How long before we go through?'

'Once you're suited up, we can take you straight to the gateway,' Daniel said, unperturbed by the big man's attitude.

'Thank you,' Alic said before Vic could make a scene. He was already regretting agreeing to the big man coming on the mission. Even if they were successful in engaging Tarlo he wasn't sure they could get him into the cage they'd brought.

'You should know the gateway will only be opening once,' Oscar said. 'After you're through, you will be evacuating into the future with the rest of the population.'

'We accept that,' Alic said. He wondered if he should give Vic another chance to withdraw. Once the mission was over, the big man would be separated from Gwyneth for a long time.

The Ford drove them to one of the eight long sheds which housed CST's Wessex track engineering division. A single gentian-blue carriage was waiting for them. It looked like it had been in service for a century at least. There was a tiny cabin at the front, with five rows of bench seats giving the track crew a view through grimy windows. Three quarters of the spartan metal-panel interior was simply storage space for bots and equipment. Long doors at the rear had their own lift platforms, which were folded up against the sides.

'It's not fast,' Alster said as they climbed up the ladders to the cabin. 'But it is reliable, and it can get you there easily enough. The drive array has modern software; traffic control can take you straight across the station yard to the gateway. I'll be in the control centre myself to supervise the opening.'

'Thanks,' Alic told him. The rest of the team was climbing up to see what they'd got.

'Your cases can come up on the door lifts,' Alster told them. 'If you'd like to get suited up now, we can begin.'

'Keep a communication link open to me from now on,' Oscar said.

'Will do,' Alic said. 'And thank Nigel Sheldon for the opportunity. It means a lot to us.'

'I know.' Oscar backed out of the door, and went down the short ladder to the ground.

'All right,' Alic said. 'Jim, get the doors open and our cases inside. We need to be ready. Matthew, establish a link to Edmund Li. Let's find out what the bastard's up to. Then we can finalize our game plan.'

*

The Ables ND47 was fully automatic, of course. New arrays had been installed during its refurbishment, the drive software was capable of controlling it through the maze of tracks which made up all of CST's planetary stations and then taking the engine out on the main lines of whatever planet it was visiting.

There were manual systems fitted, but they were there to comply with safety regulations rather than necessity. Adam gazed over the broad console that took up the entire front portion of the tiny cab sitting atop the huge engine. The two narrow windows in front gave him a view along the top of the engine, where the darkish purple metal segments were riddled with long black grilles and stumpy tarnished-chrome vent pipes. When he turned around, the single rear window showed him the two long wagons pressing up against the engine. Display screens along the back of the console filled with graphics that illustrated the coupling integration diagnostics at work, checking the integrity of the connections. The left-hand side of the console was a burgundy colour, containing all the nuclear micropile controls and read outs. A completely new console section, that was fixed to newly welded brackets on the wall, presented the control systems for the force field and armaments the Guardians had grafted on in the last few days. That was why they'd agreed someone should be in the cab, though with modern control arrays it wasn't strictly necessary. They all just felt more confident with someone up there.

Adam saw the last of the mobile gantries lower its platform, and roll away from the engine. When he stuck his head out of the cab door, he could see Kieran walking among the engineering bots as they fussed round the wheels.

His e-butler told him a call was coming in from Marisa McFoster.

'How's it going?' he asked.

'Victor's on the move,' she said. 'There's a whole load of vehicles driving out of the Sunforge warehouse. Vans and small trucks, all shielded. We can't see what's inside.'

'Where are they going?'

'It looks like they're heading for the gateway. They're not using any of the yard's service roads, they're just driving right across the rails.'

'Don't expose yourself,' he told her. 'Just maintain the observation.'

'Is this it, is the Starflyer coming?'

'I don't know. But we're ready for it.' Adam sounded a single blast on the engine's horn that reverberated around the big shed. He couldn't resist, he leaned out of the cab door and bellowed: 'All aboard.'

*

Wilson knew he should dump his irritation towards Dudley Bose, it really wasn't helpful. But there was just something about the astronomer that rubbed him up the wrong way. He'd been furious when the old man lobbied himself onto the *Second Chance*; he'd been exasperated with the young re-lifer who hadn't adjusted to his new circumstances, and now, although the man had all his memories back and seemed a whole lot more rational, he was still irritating, still pressing for attention, getting in the way.

It had seemed like a good idea while they waited for the various arrest squads to bring in known Starflyer agents, and Paula and Nigel began their search for the actual alien itself. Wilson and Anna had gone over to the Bose motile when it finished talking to Qatux, and asked if it had accessed the signal which the Far Away flare had broadcast.

'No,' it said, 'I haven't.'

'The Commonwealth has never been able to translate it,' Wilson said. 'But if you're right about the Starflyer being an alienPrime—'

'I understand,' the Bose motile said. 'I should be able to translate it for you.'

'I'd like you to try,' Wilson said. 'It's been bothering me ever since we found out what the Starflyer is. Suppose it was talking to another ship?'

'That's unlikely,' Dudley Bose said. He'd inched his way closer to them as soon as Wilson started talking to the Bose motile.

Wilson pressed his teeth together, then smiled tightly. 'Why's that?'

'The flare emission was omnidirectional.'

'I imagine their ships would have remained silent during flight so as not to attract attention from whoever built the barriers,' Anna said. 'Once the Starflyer had landed, it wouldn't know where any of the others were. It would have to broadcast in all directions.'

'Which it actually didn't,' the Bose motile said. 'The Far Away star has a rotation of twenty-five days. As the flare only lasted for seven days, the signal was only broadcast across a relatively narrow sector of the galaxy, one that didn't include the Dyson Pair; in fact the star's bulk would have shielded them from the signal.'

'Can we just examine the signal,' Wilson said. He was beginning to regret mentioning it. His e-butler accessed the national library on Damaran, and pulled out a recording of the signal.

They all waited while the Bose motile reviewed it. The initial flurry of activity in the lecture theatre that had accompanied Qatux's arrival was now dying down. Most of the technical systems were set up, Qatux and Tiger Pansy were talking together, Cat's Claws remained on duty by the main entrance, Nelson maintained a number of his own security staff around himself and Paula. The only person Wilson couldn't see was Mellanie.

'Simple enough,' the Bose motile said. 'It's basically an identity, which is MorningLightMountain17,735, followed by a short message: *I am here. If any of I/us survive, contact me or fly here.* The patterns are a very old form, but the content is easy enough to decipher, there is little ambiguity.'

'Did we ever detect another flare?' Anna asked. 'An answer to the Starflyer.'

'No,' Dudley said.

'That doesn't mean there wasn't one,' the Bose motile said. 'If another survivor picked up the signal, it could have used an interstellar communications maser to reply; their ships were all equipped with them. The Commonwealth would never see that.'

Wilson was thinking along similar lines. 'So we don't actually know if there are any more of these alienPrimes at loose.'

'If one survived, it is logical to assume there could be others,' the Bose motile said. 'Though I doubt there can be many; the Dyson Beta Primes had only just started building starships, they didn't have the production capacity of Dyson Alpha when the barriers were established. The numbers would be small.'

'But if any of them landed on a world more useful than Far Away, there's no telling how big their civilization is by now. Primes almost match the old nightmare of exponential expansion.'

'You should assume that the Dyson Alpha Primes had starships in flight as well,' Anna said.

'We are going to have to conduct an extensive search of stars in that sector of the galaxy,' the Bose motile said. 'The problem could be more widespread than originally thought.'

'If Nigel Sheldon does initiate novas, the problem will be considerably reduced,' Dudley said.

The lecture theatre's main doors opened, and Oscar walked through. He caught sight of Wilson and waved happily.

'What the hell are you doing here?' Wilson said, smiling happily.

'I might ask you the same thing,' Oscar said after he'd collected his kiss from Anna. 'You should have carried him off back to York5 and started a decent honeymoon,' he scolded her.

'Don't think I didn't want to,' she said wistfully. 'So when did you get back?'

'About five hours ago.'

'Damn, I'm glad you're okay,' Wilson said. 'Are you reloading?'

'The *Dublin* is, yes. I've got another job.'

'What? Columbia isn't being difficult about you being one of my placements, is he?'

'No, quite the opposite. Columbia is coming round to the idea the Starflyer might be genuine. I've been appointed as a glorified messenger boy.' He explained the Paris team's mission. 'Sheldon said you'd brief me on this little black ops

set-up you've got running here. Is that really a Raiel?' he was
staring at Qatux.

'Yes, it really is,' Wilson said. 'It's called Qatux, and it's
agreed to help us root out Starflyer agents.'

'Uh huh.' Oscar faced the Bose motile. 'And that alien?'

'It's a Prime,' Anna laughed. 'Our deadliest enemy.'

'The good news is that this one is harmless and on our
side,' Wilson said.

'And the bad?'

'It's yet another version of Dudley Bose.'

*

Alic ran the integration program one last time. The additional
weapons mounted on his armour suit responded properly.
Two particle lances on malmetal arms that were secured to the
base of his spine rose up over his shoulders, and swung from
side to side as his sensors ran a targeting program. They locked
on to Vic, whose armour suit had almost doubled in size
thanks to the backpack missile dispenser.

'Hey, careful who you're pointing those things at,' Vic
complained.

The particle lances retracted, folding back parallel to Alic's
spine. He was as anxious as any first-day recruit to fire
them. He hadn't known particle lances could be built so
small, and even with modern power cells he didn't have many
shots. Of course, without the armour and malmetal he could
barely pick one up they weighed so much. He couldn't imagine what they were made out of, solid uranium by the feel
of it.

John King and Jim Nwan both had rotary launches on
their forearms, with a flexible feed tube snaking round to
their backpacks, while Matthew Oldfield was carrying all the
electronic warfare systems. There were so many sneekbots
clinging to his suit, he looked like the king of the insects.

Matthew also managed the cage; three large matt-black mobile cubes that should be powerful enough to hold Tarlo.

Alic was mildly impressed that the carriage floor could take their combined weight. He brought the management array systems up into his virtual vision. Midnight black hands flicked over the control icons. Narrabri station traffic control responded with a transit authorization, and they started moving with a small judder.

'We're on the move,' he told Oscar.

'Okay, I'll inform Alster. He's in the gateway control centre. What's Tarlo doing?'

'Li says he's still up in the security room.'

'You sure you want to do this?'

'It's not quite what I thought I'd be doing when I woke up this morning, but yeah.'

'Good luck.'

'Yeah, see you in fifteen years.'

Their speed built up as soon as they left the track maintenance division shed. The station force field curved overhead, a grey film smearing the sky. Above that, the Narrabri city force field extended from horizon to horizon, its apex reaching out of the troposphere. The borealis storms had died down now, though the highly charged atmosphere was still plagued by severe lightning storms. Brutal blue-white flashes rippled around the boundary of the city force field. Alic felt ridiculously safe underneath all that technological protection. The Primes had flung their worst at Wessex, and the Big15 planet remained secure. It made him confident for the future.

The carriage snaked over points every few seconds, clicking and rattling as it moved to a different set of rails, then switching again. Long trains slid past on either side, blurs of lighted windows. Up ahead, a long stretch of pale rosy light spilled out from the gateways to douse the myriad tracks. It had gaps in it, dark shadowy sections. *Gateways to the*

Second47, Alic thought. They'd never shine their unique star-light here again. The knowledge made him sad.

'Anything new on Tarlo?' he asked Matthew.

'No, boss.'

'Okay.' He knew there wasn't. Just had to do something to distract his nerves which were far too jumpy.

The carriage lined up on the cliff face of gateways and carried on forwards at a much slower speed. There were fewer trains running on this section of the station yard. They passed a GH7 class engine waiting on a siding; the massive machine only had five wagons attached, their pea-green metal bodywork caked in topaz sand thick enough to obscure their company logo.

His e-butler told him Daniel Alster was calling.

'You should be on the direct Boongate line in another couple of minutes,' Alster said. 'Once you're there, we will open the gateway and give you transit clearance. It will close thirty seconds after you're through.'

'Right, thanks.'

'Good luck.'

'Looking good,' Alic told his arrest team. His heart started to beat a lot faster as the carriage squeaked and rolled onward.

*

Oscar simply couldn't take his eyes off Tiger Pansy. She'd caught him staring quite a few times, and he'd managed to deflect her questioning gaze with a polite half-smile. He knew it was getting close to rudeness now, but she was so out of place here her attraction was akin to a star's gravity well. But then, would someone like her care about middle class standards of rudeness? *And what does that judgement say about me? Damn, was Adam right about what I've become?*

'You're going to have to stop that,' Anna said, and moved to stand in front of him.

'I know,' he mumbled awkwardly.

Her smile became evil. 'If you're a big fan, you should get over that shy streak and go ask her for an autograph.'

'Well shucks, I guess I'm just too bashful.'

Wilson chuckled. 'Stop letting her bully you, man.'

'Advice from the hen-pecked husband. Great, just what I need.'

Wilson's tranquillity chilled rapidly. 'Oh hell,' he whispered. 'Dudley Bose is on the way over. Both versions. The human one looks pissed.'

Oscar resisted the impulse to turn around. 'Time to make a break for it?'

'Too late,' Anna said through gritted teeth and a broad false smile.

'Captain Monroe,' Dudley's imperious voice cut right through Oscar's residual good humour. He turned and summoned up a smile. 'Dudley. I understand you've reacquired your memories.' His gaze flicked to the tall alien with its odd stalk-like tentacles. It unnerved him to see something resembling an eye on the end of one bending round to return the gaze. This was worse than locking stares with Tiger Pansy.

'Yes, you bastard,' the human Dudley spat. 'I got my memory back. So I know what you did to me.'

People nearest to them hushed up and stole some circumspect looks.

'Problem?' Wilson asked politely.

'Like you care,' Dudley sneered. 'You who left me there to die.'

'You make it sound deliberate,' Anna said.

'Well, wasn't it?' Dudley demanded. 'You just kept telling us to go further in. All the time: *just a little bit further, Dudley. Go on, find out what's round the next spiral. This is really interesting.* And we trusted you.'

'I never said that,' Oscar insisted. He was racking his memories of those frantic last minutes by the Watchtower. 'Your comrelay failed as soon as you entered the tunnel.'

'Liar! You knew MorningLightMountain's ships were on their way. I've seen the *official* recordings; the whole ship was panicking. Yet you let us carry on. You dumped us like we were garbage.'

'If you'd really accessed the original recordings you'd know we busted our balls trying to re-establish contact,' Oscar said with tight anger. 'Mac and Frances put their arses on the line to try and get you back. It was you that ignored protocol; you should have come back as soon as you lost contact. If you'd paid the slightest bit of attention to your training you'd have known that. But oh no, you were too busy playing up for the unisphere media to bother with training like the rest of us. The Great Discoverer off to further the frontier of human knowledge. You're as ignorant as you are arrogant, and that hideous little combination is what plunged us into this war.'

Wilson hurriedly stepped between them. Oscar was annoyed, he would have liked to have smacked Dudley right on the nose, and to hell with how bad it would make him look.

'Enough, the pair of you,' Wilson said. The tone of command was perfect. Oscar felt himself scowling at what he could see of Dudley, but still backed off. *I'll be damned, how did he do that?*

'We clearly need to go over what happened to establish exactly where the communication failure occurred,' Wilson continued. 'But this is not the time or the place.'

'Pha,' Dudley waved a hand in disgust. 'Official inquiry by a navy already discredited. Did you prepare the whitewash answers before the President fired you?'

A now furious Oscar sidestepped round Wilson. 'Part of the training you missed while you were mouthing off on chat shows was how to recognize impossible situations. You should have wiped your memorycell and suicided as soon as you were captured. Where did MorningLightMountain get the stellar coordinates for our planets, eh? Your mind! You're not just a traitor, you're a coward with it!'

Dudley went for him, fists raised. The Bose motile hooked a thick curving arm around his torso, preventing him from reaching Oscar.

Wilson pushed Oscar hard in the chest, shoving him back. A quick pushing match followed before Oscar's heat withered in shame. 'Sorry,' he mumbled, mortified to find that Anna was helping to restrain him as well. 'He just *gets* to me.'

'I know,' Wilson said, his arm still draped loosely over Oscar's shoulder, muscles tensed in case he needed to push again.

It was an image mirrored by Dudley and the Bose motile who were walking in the other direction. Dudley managed to look back, and screwed his face up in rage.

Oscar sucked in his lower lip, trying desperately to resist the temptation to start it all up again. Anna and Wilson were both pressing in close.

'Come on,' she murmured. 'Let it go. Down boy. Calmly.'

'All right.' Now thoroughly embarrassed, Oscar held his hands up in surrender. 'Backing off. Doing yoga; some bollocks like that.'

Anna grinned. 'Never knew you had it in you.' Her lips puckered up in a mocking pout. 'Soooo macho.'

Oscar just winced. 'Don't. Please.'

Wilson gave him a rueful grin, then sobered. 'You know, much as I dislike Bose, that is a worryingly big discrepancy.'

'The Starflyer agent?' Oscar guessed.

'My first choice. Damn, we really are going to have to sit at a table with the little shit and listen to what he has to say.'

'Better off with the motile. It doesn't look like a permanent walking hissy fit.'

'Hey, behave.' Anna punched him on the arm.

'Ow.' Oscar rubbed at the pain, then noticed Tiger Pansy

standing a couple of metres away. She had an avid grin as she chomped away on her gum. 'You guys,' she said with shrill admiration. 'You're so intense. Really.'

*

'What the hell is that?' Adam asked.

The sensors which the Guardians had planted around the approach to the Boongate gateway were showing a single dilapidated old carriage creeping forward onto the main Boongate line.

'It's the type of carriage the station maintenance crews use,' Kieran said.

The sensor image wobbled, then expanded. Kieran was focusing the camera on the carriage windows. There wasn't much to see. A yellow light illuminated the interior of the carriage, diffused by the grimy glass. There were dark humanoid shadows moving round inside. Bigger than the average human. Much bigger.

'Bradley?' Adam asked. 'What do you think?'

'It seems an unlikely vehicle for the Starflyer to use. On the other hand, because that's not what we're expecting . . .'

'It does have a small cargo handling ability,' Kieran said. 'How big does it have to be?'

'I don't know,' Bradley said.

Adam shook his head. He really didn't like that carriage. It was wrong, and he knew it. But he couldn't work out what it might be doing.

Sensor data, such as it was, filled his virtual vision. The carriage certainly didn't have a force field. But there were some large power sources inside, five of them. And its communications link to traffic control was all standard.

He touched the icons of the small combat team they'd hidden out near the gateway. 'Get ready,' he told them.

'If it's the Starflyer, it will be heavily protected,' Bradley warned.

'I know. Call Burnelli, get her to find out what that is.' He took his armour suit helmet from the cab's console where it had been lying, and locked it over his head. A hundred metres in front of him, the shed doors began to slide open.

*

'Sir, the navy team is in position,' Daniel Alster reported.

'Okay,' Nigel said. His virtual hands pulled the wormhole activation code from an encrypted store, and sent it to the Boongate gateway control centre.

'Confirm activation code,' Alster said. 'We're opening it now.'

'Get them through as fast as you can, Daniel, please.'

'Yes, sir.'

Nigel shifted the gateway control centre data to a part of his virtual vision grid where he could monitor it. In front of him, the doors to the lecture theatre opened automatically for himself and Nelson. 'They're going through,' he told the security chief.

'I hope it's worth it.'

'With confirmed Starflyer agents in custody, Columbia will fall into place without a fight. That makes it worth while.' Nigel scanned across the auditorium floor to see the various groups. He was halfway to Qatux when Mellanie intercepted him, with an uncomfortable-looking Hoshe in tow. 'We've got to get some people back from Boongate,' she said.

'Excuse me?' He couldn't help glancing over at Oscar who was in a huddle with Wilson and Anna. Oscar looked up expectantly.

'There's a Senate Security team stranded there.'

'Well, I'm sorry to hear that, but it's not our problem.'

'They're following a Starflyer agent. I thought we wanted Starflyer agents.' Her arm swept round the auditorium. 'That's the whole idea, isn't it? Grab them and haul them in here for Qatux.'

'Wait, which Starflyer agent are they watching?'

'Victor Halgarth, Isabella's father,' Hoshe said.

'He's there as well?' The Boongate gateway data in Nigel's virtual vision grid showed him the wormhole opening.

'As well as who?' Mellanie asked. 'Look, Nigel, the Senate Security team have just reported Victor's on the move with a whole bunch of armed troops. We need to get them out, or send in reinforcements. Either way, the gateway has to be opened.'

Wilson and Oscar exchanged a startled look.

'The Paris team can't divert to help Senate Security,' Oscar said. 'Arresting Tarlo is an absolute priority.'

'Tarlo's on Boongate?' Paula asked in surprise, she turned to Hoshe. 'How come we didn't know?'

'None of this has been filed,' Hoshe said.

'Two Starflyer agents on Boongate?' Nelson asked. He sounded alarmed.

'What operation are you running?' Paula asked Oscar.

'Tarlo's appearance was reported by Edmund Li,' Oscar said. 'He works at the Far Away freight inspectorate division on Boongate. Tarlo has taken over the whole Far Away section at Boongate station. The Paris office team are going in to arrest him.'

'Going in?' Paula asked in surprise. She rounded on Nigel. 'Are you opening the gateway?'

'It's already open,' Nigel said. He tried not to sound sheepish.

'You have to shut it,' Paula said. 'This can't be a coincidence.'

Nigel reviewed the data in his grid. 'It'll be closed any minute now.'

'Nigel!' Justine called out.

'Now what?'

'I've got Bradley Johansson. We really need to talk to him. Now.' She switched Johansson's link to a general call.

'Mr Johansson,' Nigel said. 'It looks like the Commonwealth owes you a big apology.'

'Thank you, Mr Sheldon, but right now I'd like to swap that for one piece of information.'

'What's that?'

'There's a train approaching the Boongate gateway. Is it one you authorized?'

'Yes. Don't worry. It's carrying a team who are going to deal with a Starflyer agent.'

'Really? And what about the second train?'

Nigel stared at Nelson. 'What second train?'

The link broadened into a grainy visual image. A single ageing carriage was crawling forward toward the giant row of gateways. Three hundred metres behind it, another train was sliding onto the track which led to Boongate.

'Who the fuck is that?' Nigel gasped. His expanded mentality accessed Narrabri station traffic control. The train wasn't even registering on the system.

'Shut the gateway,' Paula demanded. 'Now!'

Nigel didn't need to be told. His virtual hand touched Daniel Alster's icon. There was no reply, it didn't even acknowledge his connection request. The only result was the Boongate gateway data dropping out of his grid. 'Shit.' He hurriedly called up Ward Smith's unisphere address code. It didn't answer, either. Nigel diverted his full expanded mentality to the Boongate gateway control system, ready to take personal control and shut the wormhole. His electronic presence couldn't gain access. 'I can't get in,' Nigel said. It shocked him more than anything else. 'I can't get into the fucking system.'

'What about Alster?' Oscar asked. 'Can he shut it down?'

'He's not responding.'

'Daniel Alster, your chief executive aide,' Paula said. She nodded with what could have been satisfaction. 'Perfectly placed.'

'This is most exhilarating,' Qatux said. 'I am so glad I came.'

*

The Boongate gateway was four hundred metres dead ahead, and the carriage had slowed to walking pace. Alic could see the track leading straight into the bottom of the funereal semicircle in front of them, glimmering silver in the dusky light. *So close!* The tension from waiting was acting like ice water on his guts. None of the others were saying anything, they all stood together watching the gateway as it opened for them.

It had never actually closed, Alic knew, that was misleading; the wormhole still reached Boongate, CST had simply reduced its internal width to zero. Expanding it again was a simple application of power. In his mind he saw it as a single big lever you just had to pull down.

The dark semicircle began to brighten, shading up to a husky gold.

'Here we go,' Matthew said.

'Hell, I never thought we'd actually do it,' Jim said. 'What do you think the future's going to be like?'

'Let's just concentrate on the mission,' Alic said.

'Oh, come on, boss, you've got to be interested.'

'Maybe, but the mission comes first.' But it did give him pause for thought as the carriage began to speed up.

'Do we get twenty years' salary paid us?' Jim asked.

'From the navy?' John said. 'You've got to be kidding.'

'But we'll be gone for twenty years—'

'Alic,' Oscar said. 'It's behind you.'

'What?' Some primitive instinct sent a shiver along his limbs.

'The Starflyer is behind you. There's a train accelerating along the track. We've lost control of the gateway. Move!'

Alic swung round to examine the rear of the carriage. The

ceiling lights were dim back there, turning the cargo handling area into a gloomy metal cave. He raised an arm, a plasma rifle sliding up out of its forearm recess. He set it to rapid expansion, and fired. The bolt blasted a two-metre hole through the rear of the carriage. A judder ran along the carriage floor as it rocked on its stiff old suspension.

'Christ, boss,' Jim exclaimed. 'What the fuck are you doing?'

Alic didn't answer, he was staring through the gap. Bright light was shining straight in at him. His retinal inserts brought filter programs online. A GH7 class engine was moving onto their track three hundred metres behind them, its headlights blazing as it started to pick up speed. He could see the last of its wagons curving round off the points, clad in yellow sand. It was the train they'd just passed on a siding.

The front of the GH7 was almost three times the height of the carriage they were riding in, and easily twice as wide. Its chrome air intake grille alone was bigger than them. And its speed was reducing the distance fast. With only a few wagons it could accelerate hard.

'Shit!' Vic cried out.

'It's the Starflyer,' Alic told them. One of his particle lances swung up and over his shoulder, pointing directly at the centre of the GH7. He fired. Incandescence flooded the carriage like a solid force. Windows blew out from the sound blast of the discharge. Alic swayed backwards, almost falling, feeling the suit's electromuscle bands fighting the recoil. The lance struck the GH7 head on, and broke apart.

'Force field,' Matthew said. 'They've got heavy duty protection.'

'Vic, John, take out the track,' Alic ordered. The GH7 was closer now, barely two hundred metres away. It was terrifyingly massive.

'Speed up,' Oscar said. 'Take control of the carriage, and accelerate.'

Alic's virtual hands danced over the carriage management icons. Vic and John raced for the back of the carriage, and knelt down in front of the blast hole. They began shooting at the track between them and the GH7. Green and purple flashes streaked across the ground outside.

'They've extended their force field,' Vic yelled. 'We can't hit the track.'

Alic's black virtual hand thumped the carriage accelerator symbol, and held it down. There was a shrill whining sound from the axle motors, and the carriage lurched forwards.

'They're gaining on us,' Matthew yelled. 'We're going to get bulldozed.'

Alic whirled round. The gateway was only two hundred metres away now.

A searing scarlet explosion erupted from the side of the GH7. Flames splashed across the giant engine's force field, twisting away into the sky to fuel a writhing cloud of black smoke.

'Oh great,' Jim moaned. 'Now someone else out there is shooting.'

*

Nigel's expanded mentality examined the physical connections into the Boongate gateway control centre. Fireshields had been erected at every interface node in CST's Narrabri network, isolating the entire system.

There has to be a way in!

He could crack the fireshields, but it would take time. They were based on hundred and ninety geometry encryption.

'Get a security team into the gateway control centre,' Nigel snapped at Nelson. His digital presence circled round and round the network, interrogating every routing node, hunting a weakness. Eight of Narrabri station's RIs were diverted from their primary function of managing wormhole generators, and assigned decryption on the fireshields. He knew they wouldn't do it in time.

The traffic control network, with its complex sensor system spread across the station, was still available to him. He accessed the cameras on top of the Boongate gateway, receiving a clear view looking down on the little carriage as it shuddered its way along the last hundred and fifty metres of track. The GH7 was right behind it, headlights illuminating the shoddy paintwork and grime-smeared wheels. The distance was shrinking rapidly as the carriage accelerated as best its ancient hub motors could manage. Missiles slammed into the GH7. Completely ineffectual.

Where did they come from?

'Gateway control centre is closed and barricaded,' Nelson reported. 'We can't get in.'

'Blow it open,' Nigel ordered. One aspect of his expanded mentality was examining the orbital platforms to see if their beam weapons could get a clear shot at the GH7. But he didn't have access to the Narrabri force field, and by the time he got through to Alan it would be too late.

Another slender particle lance shot came from the carriage to strike ineffectually at the force field round the GH7. Then the carriage swept through the open gateway.

*

Alic was instinctively bracing himself for the impact. The GH7 was closing fast now, bearing down on them with more inertia than a falling moon.

'Get ready to jump,' Alic said. He bent his legs, ready to use the strength of the suit's electromuscle. It should be enough to power him clear, then if he sprinted . . .

'We stay,' Vic growled. 'We'll be through any second. I'm not going to let him get away from us now.'

'But—'

The weak rose-gold light emanating from the gateway was almost lost in the harsh blaze of the headlights behind them.

Alic was mesmerized by the GH7 as it raced ever closer. Decision time was measurable in seconds. Less.

'Stay with it,' Vic pleaded.

Which was a personal choice, Alic knew, whereas he should be making cool operational assessments. *Too late.*

Another barrage of missiles hammered at the GH7 engine. Then they were through the force field, and Boongate's planetary station was laid out in front of them under the gloaming of a twilight sun. Alic stared in consternation at what was waiting for them. 'Jump,' he yelled frantically.

*

The GH7 vanished through the Boongate gateway.

'It got home,' Nigel exclaimed. He couldn't believe what he'd just seen. 'Right under our fucking noses. Son of a *bitch*!'

'Commander Hogan's link has dropped out,' Oscar said. 'They must be under attack on the other side.'

'No goddamn kidding.'

'Unisphere connection to Boongate has failed,' Nelson said. 'It looks like the physical link was taken out just the other side of the zero-width wormhole.'

'Mr Sheldon,' Bradley Johansson said. 'We need to go after it.'

Nigel shot Justine a look, anxious for advice from someone who must surely understand all the factors. She just shrugged, her left hand held against her belly. He thought she was going to be sick, her cheeks were puffing out.

'We'll put a team together,' Nigel said. It came out like an admission of defeat.

'Your pardon,' Bradley said. 'We already have a team. And I have spent a hundred and thirty years preparing for this eventuality. Let us go through.'

'I don't even have control of the gateway right now.'

'My squad is getting entry into the gateway control centre,'

Nelson said. 'Some resistance. Oh . . . they're all dead, all the staff, he murdered them.'

Nigel closed his eyes, experiencing an anguish that was close to physical pain. One of his grid squares expanded into his virtual vision. He couldn't recall summoning it. Links from the security squad showed him the carnage. 'Oh Christ.' It was Anshun all over again. 'How many of these Judas bastards are there?' Four of the security squad were chasing someone in a force field suit, blowing flaming holes in the structure of the gateway administration building as they went. A grade one security alert was slowly closing off the building, force fields compartmentalizing it. *Too little, too late*, Nigel knew.

'We have to get back to Far Away,' Bradley Johansson said. 'The Guardians can stop the Starflyer. This is our time, Mr Sheldon, let us do what we have devoted our lives to achieving.'

Ion rifle fire and enhanced-energy grenades were shredding the fourth floor of the administration building as the security squad closed in on Daniel Alster. Nigel took a breath, steeling himself. 'What do you need?'

'We have a train here at Narrabri station loaded with our equipment. All we need to make it work is the data Kazimir was carrying. Senator Burnelli has it.'

'I do,' Justine confirmed. She held up a memory crystal, then grimaced against another burst of nausea.

'Once we have that,' Johansson continued, 'we need passage through the wormhole to Boongate. Investigator Myo can guarantee that.'

'No,' Paula said. 'I will not do that, I will not legitimatize Elvin's criminal activities.'

'We need a guarantee if we are to expose ourselves,' Johansson said. 'Surely you must see that?'

'I have no reason to lie,' Nigel said. 'You can go through. No catch.' The RIs were breaking the fireshields, hacking a route back into the Boongate wormhole systems for him. It didn't look as if Alster had inflicted any physical damage to the giant machine.

'Investigator, I am not asking you to legitimatize anything,' Bradley said. 'I am asking you to help us overcome the mistrust that has assisted the Starflyer for a hundred and thirty years. In addition, you will be able to witness its final demise.'

Nigel had never seen Paula look so uncertain before. There was even a sheen of perspiration on her forehead. He put the link to Johansson on hold. 'You'll have to go,' he told her gently. 'Take Cat's Claws with you, they'll maintain your safety.'

'I arrested Morton,' she said indignantly.

'All right, some CST security operatives, then. But we need to get this moving.'

Wilson and Anna had been whispering together. 'We'll go,' Wilson said. 'Someone from our group needs to confirm what happens on Far Away, if we ever reach it.'

'You two have no experience of dealing with unknown terrain,' Oscar said. 'Besides, I'm a serving navy officer.'

'Enough,' Nigel held his hand up. 'The three of you and Paula can go with Cat's Claws. That's it. Nelson, get them suited up, the best armour we have.' He brought Johansson back online. 'Bradley, we're sending a team out to you, including Investigator Myo. They'll accompany you to Far Away.'

'Thank you, Mr Sheldon.'

'I also will accompany Mr Johansson,' Qatux announced.

Tiger Pansy's giggle was loud in the auditorium. 'I guess that means I get to go, too, huh?'

'If you would be so kind,' Qatux said. 'I do not believe anything you can experience in the Commonwealth will be as rich with emotional content as this chase.'

'Sure. Okay,' Tiger Pansy said. 'It'll be a laugh.'

'Qatux, you can't go,' Nigel said.

'Why not?'

'It's dangerous.'

'That is for me to judge. I am an individual.'

'But we need you here,' Hoshe said.

'I will return to assist you in investigating Starflyer agents. I expect I will be of more use on Far Away in the immediate future; there are likely to be more Starflyer agents there.'

'Oh why the hell not,' Nigel grunted with ill grace. 'Anyone else?' He stared at Mellanie, who responded by looking up to study the ceiling.

'Could I ask you to hurry, please,' Bradley Johansson said. 'We're running out of time.'

*

There wasn't much government left on Boongate by the time MorningLightMountain sent its ships and flare bombs into the star system. The population, too, was much reduced; people had been leaving ever since the Lost23 were invaded. For the rich it was easy, they could afford to switch home without too much trouble; the middle classes, well informed or with a young family, took the loss as the price for safety; for single people it was even easier to pack up and leave. Local government, assisted by the Commonwealth Senate did their best to discourage the exodus. The navy strengthened the planet's defences, including the force fields that shielded cities and the larger towns. Recently a starship had been assigned to the system for patrol duties, complementing the orbital platforms. The displacement continued more or less as before.

So many police had left that Boongate's First Minister was forced to ask CST for additional security staff to help with crowd control round the planetary station. Sure enough, Nigel sent them in from Wessex, though it was in their contract that they went back there between shifts. Without that concession they wouldn't have taken the duty.

As more and more people drifted away from the country-side and villages, leaving for the far side of the Commonwealth, so the rural police were withdrawn to the towns. Eventually, they were brought back to the cities, and just patrolled the towns. Intermittently.

Best estimates were that thirty-seven million people had so far abandoned their world. That still left over ninety million living there in various levels of trepidation. When the flare bombs and quantumbusters detonated in the star there was no real mechanism left for counting how many people made it to safety under the force fields. The frenzied particle storms which swept round the planet disrupted power supplies and communications. Everyone who heard the warning did their best to make it to safety, cowering in cellars or behind thick walls, heading underground, driving into tunnels, a lucky few had caves nearby. Once the borealis blizzards had diminished, the agitated atmosphere hit the survivors with gales and hurricanes. People struggled on to the nearest population centre with a force field.

The War Cabinet had given planetary governments of the Second47 half an hour's advance warning before they made their public announcement. Boongate's First Minister and the remaining members of the cabinet were left with the near impossible task of getting the survivors to the capital inside the one week deadline for evacuation. Anyone with a car started to drive. Buses were commandeered. Train schedules were drawn up, utilizing both passenger carriages and cargo wagons.

The CST planetary station force field, which had powered up when the invasion began, remained on. With everyone left on the planet slowly congregating underneath the capital's force field the government needed to keep the station clear to prevent a stampede. Within hours, the new deluge of refugees had ringed the entire station. Their numbers expanded constantly, without order. It was soon impossible for food, or police, or medical personnel to reach the innermost migrants pressed up against the force field. All anyone could do was wait for Nigel Sheldon to make good on his promise. The cabinet knew that as soon as the gateway was opened to the future, and the station force field turned off, there would be a panicked race for the gateway, with injuries reaching horrific numbers. Medical contingency plans were drawn up with little prospect of ever being implemented.

In the meantime, those who were inside the station boundary when the force field came on rejoiced in their amazing good fortune, and settled down for the kind of relaxed wait impossible outside. It lasted right up to the moment when the gateway to Wessex opened without any warning.

The battered old track maintenance division carriage burst through the opening. Its frame was shaking violently as its motors strained away at torque levels they were never designed for.

A host of vehicles were waiting on either side of the track: big 4x4s and covered vans, all of them equipped with bulky mounted weapons now openly deployed. There was a long moment broken only by the metallic screeching of steel wheels and bearings that were being pushed far beyond their safety margins. Armour-suited figures leapt through the carriage's shattered windows as the vehicles fired lasers, kinetics and ion bolts into the bodywork. The flimsy metal panels crumpled and vaporized, yet still the tormented chassis held together. It was nothing more than a fireball on wheels now, plummeting forwards.

The giant GH7 engine raced through the gateway, its five big cargo wagons intact. All the vehicles stopped firing. Two seconds later, the GH7 slammed into the burning wreckage. What was left of the carriage simply disintegrated, its remnants forming a short-lived halo of flame around the front of the GH7.

Scraps of scorched and twisted metal pattered down around Alic. His passive sensors showed him their blackened shapes bouncing across the stony ground. When he shifted the focus, he saw the GH7 starting to slow to a more reasonable speed now its mad dash for the gateway was successfully concluded. It was already half a kilometre away. The parked vehicles started up, and drove off after it, providing a tight escort on either side. They rocked violently as they cut across tracks and drainage ditches, always maintaining their position in the line.

The two vehicles bringing up the rear of the little convoy opened fire with magnetic Gatling cannons, strafing the area where the armour suits had landed. Instinct made Alic clasp his arms over his head as the ground erupted into clouds of stone chips around him. A couple of the projectiles struck his armour, punching him sideways, but the force field held. Their impact was like taking a kick in the ribs.

'Son of a bitch,' Jim groaned. 'I got hit on the helmet.'

'You okay?' Matthew asked.

'Hangover like an eight day stag weekend.'

'Boss, you want us to hit the vehicles?' Vic asked. 'I can target at least eight with missiles.'

'No. They're not important. The Starflyer's all that matters now.' He saw a red square flashing in his communication grid. 'Damnit. We've lost the unisphere, all I can hook into is the planetary cybersphere. I can't tell Oscar what's happened.'

'They'll be here soon enough,' Jim said.

Alic climbed to his feet. That was when he noticed that John King's telemetry grid was black. 'Oh shit. Anyone see John? Did he make it out?'

'I got him,' Vic said. 'Some of him. The kinetics got through; he must have taken a real pounding. Damn, they made a mess. Chewed him up bad.'

'Crap.' Alic wanted to hit something. Hard. 'Can you see his helmet? Did his skull get damaged?'

'No, I think that's okay. He's in one piece from the shoulders up. More or less.'

'Okay, his memorycell's intact. He can be re-lifed.'

'By who?' Jim cried. 'This planet isn't even going to be here by the end of the week.'

'Before we leave, we come back and recover the memory-cell,' Alic said. 'That goes for all of us. Last man standing has that duty. Agreed?'

'Yes, boss.'

The other two grunted acknowledgment.

'All right,' Alic stared along the track where the GH7 had gone. The Far Away section force field was a grey-shaded bubble squatting over a cluster of diminutive buildings and warehouses six kilometres away. 'We know where it's going. Let's get after it. Matthew, get Edmund online. It's about time he earned his money and switched off that force field.'

'Just us four?' Jim asked.

Alic looked round at the gateway. It was still open. *I could run through. We all could. It would be so easy. Technically the mission's over. We've proved the Starflyer exists.* 'I don't think we'll be alone for long.'

His visual sensors picked up something moving a kilometre away across the station yard, heading towards them. A laser radar sweep showed him a bike, moving fast as it jumped rail tracks, heading for the wormhole. It picked up a couple of other moving objects behind the bike, possibly small cars. 'Let's move,' he said. 'We'll get run over if we stay here much longer.'

*

Adam eased the Ables ND47 out of the shed and applied the brakes. Narrabri traffic control logged them onto the system, and assigned them a transit code. He had to smile at the file name: Guardian 0001A.

Now we're The Man.

'Here they come,' Bradley said.

Adam opened the cab door, looked out. A medium-sized

truck and a fifteen-seater bus were racing along the service road to the shed.

'Everyone okay down there?' he asked the team crammed into the armoured vehicles. The three squad leaders, Kieran, Rosamund and Jamas, all replied yes. He thought they were all wound too tight. Even for a Guardian, committed since birth, it was quite something to finally know the Starflyer had passed just a few kilometres away. As for him . . .

I don't have to take it on faith any more. It was an astonishing release, almost spiritual. The Starflyer was real, the Guardians were mainstream, and there was a noble cause to be fought. In the middle of a war for species survival with millions already dead he actually felt good.

The bus and truck pulled up beside the two closed wagons behind the Ables ND47. Bradley had already opened the broad side doors, and was extending the ramps. He'd said Sheldon was sending something large. Adam assumed that would be some kind of combat aerobots.

Armour-suited figures were hurrying out of the bus. The back of the truck rolled up, and a thick ramp slid out.

'Fuck me,' Adam muttered.

A Raiel lumbered down out of the truck, its bulky body undulating in long wave motions. It was followed by a woman with wild red hair, who was dressed in a black blouse and short skirt coloured almost the same shade as her hair. She'd squeezed a force field skeleton suit on top of her clothes. Even that couldn't quite account for her inelegant movements. Then Adam realized she was in heels.

Five Guardians spilled out of the armoured vehicles to greet the newcomers. Mostly they clustered round the Raiel.

A man in a sharp expensive business suit stepped out of the bus. Adam recognized Nelson Sheldon immediately. His presence sent a little shiver along Adam's spine as he watched Bradley take his suit helmet off and walk over to shake hands with the security chief. *Historic moment.* A figure in an armour suit standing beside Nelson handed Bradley a small plastic case, the type used to carry memory crystals.

Her! Adam shivered again inside his armour suit.

As if she could sense his thoughts, Paula Myo turned, and tipped her blank helmet up so that she was staring right at him. Even with all his suit's passive and active layers of protection, Adam felt terribly vulnerable.

'All right,' Bradley announced, 'Let's get this show on the road.'

The Raiel started up a ramp into the rear cargo wagon. Bradley had obviously decided it could ride in one of their armoured Volvo lorries.

Paula Myo stayed outside, looking up at the cab on top of the Ables ND47. Adam's e-butler told him she was calling him on a secure local channel. He opened the communication link.

'Mr Elvin,' Paula Myo said.

'Investigator. Thank you for agreeing to help us.' Total bullshit, of course; he wasn't pleased. He didn't want her within a hundred light-years of this train, nor him.

'Just so we understand each other,' Paula said. 'When the Starflyer threat is over, I will be arresting you for the Abadan atrocity. Johansson has committed many criminal acts, but they were politically motivated, for which I expect he will be given a pardon. High level discussions are underway on that subject. You, on the other hand, will not receive a pardon. That has already been decided. Your continued assistance in exterminating the Starflyer might help mitigate your sentencing with the judge, nothing more.'

Adam cancelled the link, and gave her the finger. It wasn't a gesture which came over well in an armour suit.

Paula walked up the ramp into the first covered wagon.

Adam slammed the cabin door shut. He was shaking inside the suit. Even his virtual hands seemed to be trembling when he began manipulating the engine's systems, preparing the

defence hardware for whatever was waiting on the other side
of the wormhole.

*Pre-combat nerves, that's all. Not her. She doesn't scare me.
Not any more. No way.*

*

'Well, they didn't start shooting at each other,' Nelson said.
'That's something.'

'Not yet,' Nigel told him. He was relaxing in a seat at the
back of the converted lecture theatre, as good a place as
anywhere to see the remainder of this mission through. His
expanded mentality now had complete control over the Boongate gateway. CST communication technicians were looking
into re-establishing Boongate's connection to the unisphere.
Someone had bombed the primary connection node, and the
back-up, and the fall-back interlink. Emergency laser relays
working through the main gateway were now in operation,
allowing a remote survey of the damage. Permanent re-
connection would mean keeping the main gateway open while
technicians went through to do the work. With less than a
week left before the evacuation was due to begin, Nigel didn't
favour that option. Besides, the main gateway would soon
have to be reduced to zero-width to permit final realignment
on the generator itself so it could be formatted for temporal
transit.

One piece of data which was coming through clear and
strong was the images of the rush towards the gateway on the
Boongate side. It had only been opened twenty minutes, and
already over a hundred vehicles had powered through, from
bikes to cars, buses with tyres that had burst on the rough
journey over tracks, even a tow truck; so far five guys had
cycled through. Sensors on the other side showed a lot of
people jogging towards the open wormhole, making good
time, too, considering the terminal was five kilometres distant.

A section of his grid expanded into his virtual vision, showing him the Guardians' train starting its journey across Narrabri station.

'They'll be through in two minutes,' he told Justine, who was sitting next to him, chewing on a peppermint settler tab.

'Will you shut the gateway after that?'

'Completely. I'm re-coding the management routines so that I'm the only person who can activate it. When that's done I'm going to start firing half of my security operation. This was a total fucking catastrophe.'

'No more than the rest of this war,' she said equitably. 'Who knows when the subversion software was loaded in? It could have been sitting in the arrays for decades waiting for today. The Starflyer really thinks and plans ahead. I just hope Bradley Johansson's counter strike is up to the task.'

'At least he has a plan,' Nigel said wearily. 'I suppose I'd better send a starship to Far Away to provide back up. Oh hell . . .'

'What now?' Justine asked.

'According to Johansson, the Starflyer's going to take off and fly back to Dyson Beta, or somewhere it can link up with its own type.'

'Yes.'

'But it didn't know we could build ftl starships when it started this conspiracy. We can catch the *Marie Celeste* at any time in the next six hundred years if it goes back to Dyson Beta at sublight speed.'

'Ah, you're thinking it modified the *Marie Celeste* for ftl.'

'At least. I'm just hoping Alster didn't give it the details of our new hyperdrive. We really would be up shit creek. No,' he shook his head. 'We only just built the prototype drive ourselves two weeks ago, and there's been no transport to Far Away for longer than that. If the *Marie Celeste* is ftl now, it'll be using our original continuous wormhole generator.'

Mellanie and Hoshe entered the auditorium: they'd both

been to see off Wilson's team; staying with them while they suited up and caught their transport out to the Guardians' train.

'Are you angry with me?' Mellanie asked Nigel.

'For what?'

'I was being a bit of a brat when I asked you to open the wormhole.'

'I just wish you'd asked earlier, we might have caught the Starflyer with its pants down.'

'Thanks.' She gave him a demure kiss. Both of them automatically looked over at where Dudley and the Bose motile were standing. Dudley was emphatically not looking in their direction. 'Will you open it to get them back?' Mellanie asked.

'Not the main wormhole, no, it's being converted to time travel, remember. If Wilson and Cat's Claws do come back from Far Away, we can probably use the exploration division wormhole to retrieve them. I haven't really thought any of this through. There's also the question of the Commonwealth's connection to Far Away as well. Which is going to be difficult and very expensive to renew, especially if the Commonwealth is paying for forty-seven new worlds at the same time. We might just reduce the connection to starship flights, or leave them as an Isolated world.'

'They wouldn't care,' Mellanie said. 'Morton could build himself his empire there. It's that kind of planet.'

'I'm surprised you didn't go with them.'

'Really? It's simple enough, I don't have a death wish.'

Nigel grinned. 'How's Paula?' he asked Hoshe.

'Not happy. I really don't think it was a good idea forcing her to go.'

'She'll survive.' His virtual vision showed him the Guardians' Ables ND47 turning onto the Boongate line. Cars and small vans were popping through the gateway, where CST security was busy rounding them up. Sensors showed him a force field strengthening around the train. He opened a link to Wilson. 'Good luck. I'm going to send a starship to Far Away to support you. It should be there in a week or so.'

'Thanks,' Wilson said. 'See you when we get back.'

*

'Boldly they rode and well,' Adam muttered as the engine lined up on the Boongate gateway. A 4x4 Toyota pick-up sped out of the glowing haze that capped the entrance. A CST security division helicopter buzzed over it. 'Into the jaws of death.' His virtual hand twisted the power feed, and they began to pick up speed. The force field extended, sweeping out across the rails ahead. 'Into the mouth of hell.' Now they didn't need to be stealthy, he deployed the weapons from their disguised casings. The gold glow from the gateway shone in through the cab windows. Adam smiled in welcome at the placid light; this far above the ground, isolated, running smooth, it was as though he was gliding into the sunset. 'Rode the six hundred.'

The Ables ND47 went through the gateway at close to a hundred kilometres an hour. The gold haze tore away from the front of the engine revealing the twilit landscape of the station yard. A big Audi Luxnat ten-seater was trying to turn onto the track. The train smacked into it, shredding the bodywork to splinters of carbon. Adam winced in guilt. *Hope the Investigator didn't see that.*

Dozens of other vehicles were jouncing their way across the multiple tracks, converging on the gateway. Cameras showed him exhausted runners flinging themselves down as the train hurtled past. He took in all the peripheral scenes with a swift sweep through his virtual vision display grid, concentrating on the tracks ahead. Radar showed them intact. The force field over the Far Away section was an impenetrable bubble.

'We're closing the wormhole now,' Nigel Sheldon said.

'Thanks for nothing,' Adam retorted gleefully as the signal faded. Sensors were showing him some kind of firefight up ahead. His virtual hand throttled back on the power, and began applying the brakes. The cab's array connected with the local traffic control. Adam used the authority codes he'd been given to open a route directly to the Far Away section. It was a superfluous order, the points were still open. The Ables ND47 rolled onwards, using the same route the Starflyer had taken not thirty minutes before.

Adam concentrated on the firefight. Over twenty vehicles were clustered together outside the force field, guarding the point where the tracks led into the Far Away section. His sensors showed him weapons fire emerging from fast-moving locations. Whoever was launching them must be stealthed, the sensors couldn't lock on to them.

'This has to be the navy team,' he said.

'We agree,' Wilson said. 'One moment, I'll try and contact them.'

*

'Got another one,' Vic claimed as the ground close by sizzled from a burst of maser energy.

Alic was jammed into a shallow drainage ditch beside Vic. Jim and Matthew were fifty metres away, using a raised roadway for cover.

The vehicles which had escorted the Starflyer's train were spread out ahead of them, making sure no one got close to the big dome of energy which protected the station's Far Away section. They'd encountered vigorous resistance from a kilometre out. It'd taken time to creep forwards. Vic's missiles had disposed of eight, but Alic didn't want him to waste any more. They'd need serious firepower if they ever caught up with the Starflyer.

A particle lance swung up and over his shoulder, and he raised himself up so its sensors could lock on to the closest

4x4. He fired, and the vehicle exploded in a spectacularly violent fireball. The blast wave slammed overhead, sending a rain of small stones rattling down on Alic and Vic.

'Good shooting, boss,' Vic said.

Masers and a burst from a magnetic gattling cannon pounded the ditch. Alic and Vic started to crawl along through the trickle of dirty water in the bottom.

'Edmund, any progress?' Alic asked.

'No, man, sorry. All I can see is about ten cars and such ringing the gateway to Half Way. There's been no change since the train went through. They're just waiting for anyone to try and take them on.'

Alic wanted to give the man a swift kick up the arse. Even before they'd left for Wessex, the Paris tactical crew had come up with half-a-dozen safe routes he could take to the force field generator. Edmund Li had also been given powerful software to subvert Tarlo's routines. Technical had shown him which generator components to shoot with his ion pistol. There was nothing stopping him from making the run. *Nothing.*

'Edmund, you've got to kill that generator.' Another fusillade from an enhanced-energy area-denial cluster made him fling himself down. Blue flame sealed off the top of the ditch. Steaming water gurgled round his armour. 'We can't get you out.'

'I'm sorry, I can't do it, I'm safe here.'

A repetitive drumming sounded through the roar of retreating flame. Jim was firing his rotary launcher. The air was split by a whistling shriek as hypervelocity kinetics zipped overhead. A moment's pause, and another of the bad guy vehicles was reduced to flaming scrap metal.

'You can't stay there,' Alic said. He was near to pleading now. 'Tarlo will keep the force field on permanently. He doesn't want any attempt to follow the Starflyer. That means you won't be able to join the exodus. This planet will be abandoned. You'll die in there, Edmund, nobody will ever find your memorycell for re-life.'

'Oh Christ, I don't want this.'

Alic resumed crawling forward. 'None of us asked for this war. Your part won't take more than five minutes. Get to that generator, let us in. We'll take care of Tarlo and the escort vehicles.'

'I'll see if I can get there.'

'That's fine, Edmund. Go for it, now, eh?' Alic accessed two of Matthew's sneekbots as they scuttled over the hostile landscape, trying to triangulate on another vehicle.

'Which one is launching those bloody area denial clusters?' Vic asked.

'Not sure,' Matthew said. 'They took out five sneekbots last time.'

Alic's e-butler told him it was picking up a localized secure call from Paula Myo. 'Localized?' he queried.

'Yes.'

'Thank Christ, put her through.'

'Commander, is that you engaging the vehicles outside the force field?'

'Yes!'

'Okay, stand by, we'll take them out for you. We need you a minimum one hundred metres away from them.'

'We are. What have you got?'

'The Guardians tell me they have zone killers.'

'Guardians? You're with the Guardians?' He didn't know why he was surprised, the universe wasn't operating logically today.

'I am. We're in pursuit of the Starflyer. Stay down.'

'Trust me, I'm down a long way.' He and Vic were clinging to the bottom of the ditch. He strengthened his force field to maximum.

'Do you still have a contact inside the Far Away section?' Paula asked.

'Yeah. He's proving reluctant to shut off the force field generator.'

'Why? We need the force field down.'

'He knows. I think he's finally doing something about it.'

'Good. Heads down, here it comes.'

The sneekbots showed Alic something like a man-sized jet-propelled moth descending on the cluster of vehicles. There was a dazzling green flash, and every sneekbot signal vanished. Vivid green light flowed into the bottom of the ditch like a pervasive liquid. Then the ground thumped Alic upwards as if he'd been caught in an earthquake. A prolonged thunderclap howl reverberated across the land. Alic could feel it through the suit's insulation.

'Clear,' Paula said.

Alic slowly clambered up out of the ditch. Each of the remaining escort vehicles was lost inside a thick swirl of flame. He watched a big Ables ND47 approaching down the same track the Starflyer's train had used. It was braking hard, with sparks zipping out from the huge wheels.

'Now that's what I call making an entrance,' Vic said.

The Ables ND47 came to a halt. A small door opened in the side of the first wagon.

'Get in, please,' Paula said.

Alic and his arrest team sprinted across the blackened land. He noticed the zone killer had left the rails intact. Up on the front of the engine, a couple of dark cylinders twice the size of his armour suit were extending ponderously from the bodywork on malmetal stalks. He didn't recognize the type of weapon, but he knew he didn't want to be close by when they went off.

There were several bright flashes from above the engine's chrome intake grille, accompanied by a *crack*. Something like a black nebula swirled across the gap between train and force field. A broad arc on the force field's surface started to glow a gentle copper and static flames thrashed about close to the ground, raising a pack of small dense dust devils.

Alic jumped up into the dark wagon. Outside, there was a terrific *boom* as the weapons fired.

*

Edmund hit the outside door running. Behind him, the administration block's network was crashing from the disrupter software he'd loaded in. The sensors couldn't see him; but Tarlo would know for sure someone was inside the force field. Someone who was trying to sabotage the Starflyer's return. It didn't take a tactical genius to work out what the next stage had to be.

The building housing the force field generator was an elongated geodesic hall of pearl-grey composite. He could see it protruding over a warehouse on the other side of the parking lot. Once he was there, this nightmare would be over.

His parked Honda came to life as soon as he loaded in the drive orders. It accelerated hard, wheels spinning on the damp concrete and headed out towards the main road. As a distraction it should gain him a few seconds – so the Paris tactical experts claimed. Edmund sprinted in the opposite direction; if he could just make it to the cover of the warehouse he should be okay.

The turbid grey sky above the car park flared brilliant white. A terrifyingly loud screech echoed round the inside of the force field. Edmund lost his footing and went sprawling painfully on the concrete. He gawped up at the force field, where scarlet lightning was now scrabbling furiously against it. The vivid streamers slithered up into the air to strike the bottom of the station force field.

White light blazed again, and the horrendous noise ripped across the Far Away section. This time he understood. Someone was shooting at the force field with incredibly powerful weapons, trying to break through. He made himself get up. Blood was soaking into his shirt sleeve where he'd landed on his elbow. Wincing at the pain, and cowering as another energy blast struck the force field, he ran for the warehouse.

By the time he made it round the corner he was breathing heavily. The geodesic hall was only a hundred and eighty metres away now. He dashed for it as fast as he could, ignoring the awesome burns of light overhead as they alternated between dazzling white and lurid crimson. The punishing noise trapped under the force field was just about constant. His ears were ringing badly.

He was short of breath and unsteady on his feet when he finally arrived at the door to the geodesic hall. It was open, which he didn't expect. He took a quick glance inside. Nothing was moving. Edmund pulled down a ragged breath and went in.

The generator was a large cluster of metal and plastic shapes laid out along the floor, as big as a house. White and red light took turns to fluoresce the composite arching overhead. The stentorian roaring was muted inside. He identified the power injection points, and put his hand down to his holster.

'Shit!' The shock stabbed through him as his fingers closed on empty leather. There was no pistol, it must have dropped out when he fell. 'Oh fuck. Fuck!' He stared helplessly at the bulky generator. He had no idea where the control console was – that's if there even was a control console. His head twisted from side to side, searching for something he could use to smash a section of casing. That would be as much use as screaming at it to switch off, he decided. There was nothing else for it, he'd have to go back for the ion pistol.

The interior of the hall flared with blue-white light. An ion pulse ripped through the air, and struck the generator casing. A dazzling purple discharge seethed down the dark metallic composite, partially obscured by a fountain of smouldering plastic droplets.

A second ion pulse hit a power injector, exactly where the Paris experts had told Edmund to aim. It was suddenly very quiet. The alternating red and white light outside had stopped.

Very slowly, Edmund Li turned round to face the person who was shooting, knowing what he'd see. Tarlo was standing to one side of the open door, his arm outstretched, holding an ion pistol.

'Why?' Edmund asked.

Tarlo simply smiled as he swung the pistol round to point at Edmund Li's head. He fired again.

*

Adam was sweating inside his armour. He'd calculated the firepower of the atom lasers himself. It should have been enough to break the force field, especially with the dump web stressing it. Instead he was watching the awesome energy blasts ricochet dangerously.

The force field vanished. 'Dreaming heavens,' Adam grunted. 'Your inside man did it.'

'What do you know,' Alic said. 'Edmund came through.'

Adam moved the Ables ND47 forward cautiously. Radar scanned ahead, showing him the tracks were broken less than a kilometre in front of them. 'We're not going to get much further in this,' he told the teams back in the wagons. The sensors showed him the phalanx of vehicles around the gateway which led to Half Way. He launched another zone killer. The triangular shape streaked away from its launcher on top of the engine, curving in a short ballistic arc. It detonated in a cascade of green scintillations which sank towards the ground in a display of perverse splendour. Harsh orange fireballs spoiled the beauty as the vehicles and their munitions exploded.

The train braked again, grinding over the last few metres of track before coming to a halt in front of the shallow blast crater that had destroyed the rails. 'End of the line,' Adam said. He unlocked the wagons.

*

'I'm staying here,' Vic announced as Kieran gunned the armoured car down the ramp.

There were eight of them crammed inside – Vic, Alic, Wilson, Anna, Bradley Johansson, Jamas, Ayub, and Kieran up in the driver's seat. All of them in armour suits of various marques, though externally there was little difference: stone black figures that outlined a rough human shape. Additional weapon packs distorted their basic humanity.

'I understand,' Bradley said

'No you don't. He's still here.'

'You don't know that.'

'I can feel it. Getting in was too easy. Tarlo's a smart bastard, he doesn't play a straight game.'

'Then you should stay inside this armoured car,' Bradley said. 'It is extremely well protected.'

'No. I'll find him out there. Hey, I'll be covering your arse. He'll have something planned for you.'

'My team has planned for most eventualities.'

Vic stood up. 'But not all of them.'

'As you wish,' Bradley said.

The side door slid open. It was dim outside, the air layered with smoke from the ruined vehicles.

'You coming, boss?' Vic asked.

'We know the Starflyer's real,' Alic said. 'It's just on the other side of that gateway. That's my priority. Jim, Matthew, if you want to go with Vic, that's fine by me.'

'I'll stick with you, boss,' Jim said.

'Sorry, Vic,' Matthew said, 'but this is bigger.'

'That's okay.' The big man stooped to get through the door. 'I want this for myself. And Gwyneth.'

'Good luck,' Alic said.

*

Adam climbed down the ladder on the side of the engine, thankful for the suit's electromuscle. It was a long way to the ground, and he was getting tired after days of high-pressure preparation. Three armoured cars were waiting beside the broken track, blunt olive-green ovals with a smooth skin of passive deflector panels riding on ten independent mesh-flex wheels. They were in a triangular formation around three Volvo lorries. The Volvos were based on the twenty-wheel GH chassis, developed for rough terrain on developing worlds. They'd been customized with a cruder version of deflector panelling than the armoured cars, then beefed up with extensive electronic countermeasures, turning them into squat brutes a dull grey-blue in colour. With their diesel tanks full they should have the range to drive from Armstrong City to the Dessault Mountains, where the components they were carrying were desperately needed for the planet's revenge.

As Adam made his way over to the armoured car taking point duty, he saw Vic walking away, and shook his head in regret. They could have done with a genuine professional. Personal feelings were always bad news in combat situations.

The armoured car's side door slid open, and he climbed in. There was one seat left, opposite Paula Myo. *Oh crap.*

'Do you want to drive, sir?' Rosamund asked.

'No, that's okay. Just remember what I taught you.'

'If she does that, she'll probably wind up in suspension, just like you're going to,' Paula said.

'We're not in that courtroom yet, Investigator. We both have to live through the next couple of days first, and personally I don't give us particularly high odds.'

'You want us to kill her for you, sir?' Rosamund asked. She sounded very hostile.

'Oh dreaming heavens, no. Let's just all stay civilized shall we? All of you, leave the Investigator and me to work out our own little problem by ourselves.'

'Okay. But you just have to say the word.' Rosamund fed power to the engines, and the armoured car rolled forward.

'You should watch your mouth,' Adam told Paula. 'Remember this is my home ground.'

'To the best of my knowledge you've never been to Far Away.'

'No, but these are my people.'

'I don't think so. You're a black market arms dealer who gave them some training. Do they know how many innocent people you slaughtered before Johansson sheltered you?'

'You two,' Bradley said, 'knock it off. We have a different war to fight today.'

Adam bit back on his next comment. He was sure the Investigator was smiling inside her helmet. His virtual hands pulled sensor images from all the armoured cars out of his mission display grid. They were heading across the last few hundred metres of ground in front of the small gateway. It shone a pallid coral-pink in front of them.

'It's open,' Rosamund said.

'Pay attention to the weapons,' Adam told her. There were over twenty maser cannons covering the gateway, the first line of defence in any alien invasion. Ironic, Adam thought, ultimately they wound up facing the wrong way. The X-ray lasers on the armoured cars began firing, targeting the cannon.

Adam switched his attention to the person next to Myo. He was wearing absolute state of the art armour, which Adam envied. Despite his every effort and contact in the black market he hadn't been able to get his hands on the suit with which the navy had equipped all its Lost23 insurgents. 'Hello, Rob,' Adam said. 'Good to be working with you again.'

'For you, maybe,' Rob retorted. 'I didn't even know it was you last time, and I wound up with a two hundred years life suspension.'

'We almost made it though, didn't we? Almost stopped the *Second Chance*. If we had, we wouldn't be here today.'

'Is this supposed to make me feel better?'

'Just pointing out how things go full circle.'

'Elvin, you took no part in the *Far Away* assault,' Paula said.

'I planned it, I organized it. The damn thing would have worked if the SI hadn't thrown in on your side.'

'Look,' Rob said. 'I didn't know I was working for you. And the only reason I took the job was because I owed some very bad people a lot of money. Okay? We're not comrades, we're not buddies; that's it, period.'

'Were you recruited through an agent?' Paula asked.

'It's in my file,' Rob said. 'I cooperated fully with the police. Much good it did me.'

'Give it a rest,' Adam snapped at her. 'We're about to face the Starflyer itself.'

'I ask, because Vic may be right. This is very easy. Why has the Starflyer left the gateway open to Half Way?'

'You think it's going to ambush us? We're ready for that. This is what I do, plan combat scenarios. I know you don't like the idea, but have some faith in me, Investigator. You wouldn't be chasing me unless I was good.' Even as he said it, he checked his virtual vision grid. The maser cannons were being taken out one at a time, slumping over to the ground as their mountings turned sluggish. They were only a hundred metres from the gateway now, bumping along the single track that led to Half Way. It was discomfortingly easy, he had to admit.

'Remember Valtare Rigin?' Paula asked.

Better than you realize. Adam still got chilly when he thought how close they'd been that day on Venice Coast, and she'd never seen him. 'Owner of the Nystol gallery on Venice Coast, the one Bruce targeted.'

'Yes. We didn't release the information at the time, obviously, but our forensic team found that Rigin's memorycell had been removed post-mortem.'

'Yeah. So?'

'Tarlo took the head of the Agent on Illuminatus, complete with memorycell. Do you understand, Elvin? The Starflyer is building up a very intimate database on your activities. Now I don't know how many more of your contacts it has captured and subjected to download. But it knows who you use, who you want, what equipment you're buying. Tell me this: if it has all that, is there any way it can deduce what you're doing today, now?'

Adam *hated* the question. He knew what he would like to answer, *no, no way*, but the stakes were too high for that kind of pride now. 'I don't know. I never tell the Agent what the operations are, especially last time, I just needed people with combat experience.'

'Let's hope that's not enough.'

'Wait a minute,' Rob said. 'You mean that *thing* knows my name?'

'Yes,' Paula said.

'Oh shit.'

'We're ready,' Rosamund said.

The last maser cannon had been eliminated. They were right in front of the gateway to Half Way. Mild ruby light shone through the milky-opaque pressure curtain force field. Nothing was visible through it.

'Send the drone through,' Adam said.

The little winged bot zipped through the force field. Its camera showed a landscape of naked rock beneath a dark fuchsia sky. A single set of rails ran from the gateway into the head of a deep valley, dipping down towards the calm sea.

'Nothing,' Rosamund reported. No electromagnetic activity, no thermal spots. They're not there.

'Take us through,' Adam ordered. 'And send the drone out over Shackleton, let's see if there are any planes left.'

*

Vic watched the last Volvo lorry disappear through the red pressure curtain. He'd jogged away from the Guardians as they knocked out the maser cannon. The big T-shaped weapons had keeled over to lie smouldering on the scorched ground amid the still-burning wrecks that the zone killer had taken out. It was like being back on Illuminatus, walking through the aftermath of Treetops.

He knew their easy passage was all wrong. The local network had crashed thanks to Edmund, but the hardened security links should have been resistant to the disruptor software. Tarlo would have retained fire control. If he'd wanted, he could have engaged the Guardians. The maser cannon were old, but they could have probably taken out a couple of the Volvos. It didn't make a lot of sense, unless Tarlo wanted the Guardians to get through to Half Way. *Why?*

Vic reached the geodesic hall containing the force field generator. His sensors couldn't detect any personal force fields or weapons power packs. There was an infrared source lying just inside the door, human sized. He went in.

The corpse sprawled on the enzyme-bonded concrete only had half of its head left. An ion pulse had blown the face off and incinerated most of the rest. Vic was pretty sure it was Edmund Li. It certainly wasn't Tarlo. Of course, there was no way of knowing just how many Starflyer agents there were left on this side of the gateway. He switched his suit sensors to active scan, and swept round the dark hall. The two shots which had disabled the generator were easy to detect, the casing was still hot where they'd hit. There was no sign of anyone else in there.

A huge explosion outside made Vic crouch down instinctively as his force field strengthened. As soon as he went back out through the door he saw a giant gout of flame and black oily smoke rising up from the long building which housed the Half Way wormhole generator. The gateway at the front of it was now nothing more than a concave semicircle packed with complex machinery. There was no red luminescence, no alien starlight diffused by the pressure curtain. Another explosion ripped out from the generator building, sending debris flying for hundreds of metres. Flames took hold inside, licking around the huge holes blown in the roof and walls.

Vic started jogging towards the dead gateway, heedless of the exposure. His sensors scanned round constantly, searching for any motion, and hint of human activity.

Someone was walking towards him, stepping unhurriedly over the burned earth in front of the gateway, making no attempt to conceal themselves. Vic didn't need confirmation, he knew who it would be, but his visual sensors zoomed in anyway.

He stopped ten metres short of Tarlo. The Starflyer agent wasn't using any of his wetwiring, his inserts were inert, power cells switched to inactive mode. He simply stood there in a glossy suit of semi-organic fabric refracting a moiré shimmer; his blond hair swept back and held in place with a small black leather band.

'Vic, right?' he asked the hulking armour suit. 'Gotta be Vic.'

Vic switched on the suit's external audio circuit. 'Yeah, it's me.'

'Cool. How's Gwyneth?'

'Does it matter to you?'

'Part of me, man, yeah.'

'She'll be okay. Why did you do it?'

Tarlo's handsome face gave a sympathetic grin. 'It's what I had to do. Man, that Paula Myo, what a ballbuster. I always knew she'd be the one who blew me.'

'Who am I talking to?'

'Both of us, I guess. My part is over, so it doesn't care any more. It's just waiting for you to kill me.'

'You failed, though. The Guardians got through.'

'The Guardians got through. I succeeded.'

'It was a trap.'

'What do you think?'

'I think I'll take you back for a memory read.'

'Man, it's too late for that; Qatux has gone through with the rest of them.'

'How did you know—' Vic's suit sensors showed one of Tarlo's inserts powering up. He fired his ion rifle, which blew Tarlo's body in half.

14

The forest's trees were all identical, possessing an elegantly rotund shape rich with red-gold leaves that had the same sheen as New England's woodlands in the fall. This, though, was high summer, with a bright sun high overhead, and warm dry air gusting through the branches. Ozzie had stripped down to his T-shirt and a pair of badly worn shorts; not that it stopped him sweating hard from the effort of carrying his pack. Orion was wearing cut off trousers and no shirt, his expression martyred as he lumbered on in the grinding heat of the afternoon. Tochee seemed unaffected, its colourful fronds flapping loosely as it slid along.

Ozzie was pretty sure he knew where they were, though his newfound pathsense wasn't quite as precise as a satnav function. He'd started to pick up on a few signs in the last half hour. This path was now quite neat, the kind of track that you'd get when someone took care of it, rather than just a route which people and animals walked at random. There were no dead branches lying across the way, and remarkably few twigs. Several boggy puddles had been filled with gravel so travellers didn't have to detour. Then he even saw where branches had been cut on trees close to the path; they were long healed over now, just knobbly warts in the sepia bark. All the things a government land management agency would do to keep the path open for walkers.

His insert functions were slowly coming back on line, which gave him a very positive feeling as he strode onwards. Ever since they'd left the gas halo, his bioneural arrays and inserts had reverted to the usual erratic basic operational ability which characterized the Silfen paths. The day after they'd talked with Clouddancer he'd picked up a path right in the middle of the forest which cloaked the reef. That was four worlds ago. It wasn't that Ozzie knew where to go, rather he could now sense where the paths would take him. Several times he'd started off down one only to turn round and discard it, searching for another, one that would take him closer to the Commonwealth. There was no mental map, more a simple awareness of direction.

The graphics in his virtual vision were strengthening with every step forward. Processing power increased in tandem. Signal strength between his inserts and his hand-held array rose dramatically. Then the array detected another signal.

'This is it,' Ozzie yelled out. He started to run forwards.

'What is?' Orion asked. 'We left the end of the path a while back.'

The forest began to thin out, revealing a rolling landscape of grey-green meadows. Alien bovine animals with six fat legs and an amber hide were grazing indolently. Sheep mingled among them, unperturbed by their strange stablemates. He saw hexagonal metal troughs filled with hay. Long lines of wire fencing divided the land up into huge pasture fields. Beyond them, there were some crop fields, their green wheat shoots just on the cusp of ripening. Hills rose up in the distance, mottled with the gold-brown shading of extensive forests.

Ozzie's inserts interfaced with the planetary cybersphere. Achingly familiar unisphere icons popped up into his virtual vision. The shock of seeing them again after so long was like an ice shower. *I'm home.* He turned to his companions who were just emerging from the small wood without any sense of urgency. 'We did it,' he yelled. His legs gave way and he sank to his knees. A wicked vision of early Papal visits to the worlds he and Nigel first opened filled his mind. He bent down and kissed the ground. 'We fucking did it,' he yelled up at the blazing sun.

'Did what?' Orion asked curiously.

'We made it, man,' Ozzie struggled to his feet and hugged the startled boy. 'Look around you, man. Don't you see it? Sheep, fences, farmland, I think that's a load of barns over there. We're home, we're back in the good old Intersolar Commonwealth.'

Orion gazed round curiously, a tentative smile on his freckled face. 'Where?'

'Er, ah, good question, hang on.' His virtual hands danced over icons, pulling information out of local systems. 'Bilma. That's in phase two space. Haven't visited before, and it's out of range of my wormhole. Never mind. We're on the Dolon continent, other side of the planet from the capital. Nearest town Eansor, population twenty-two thousand. Seventy-two kilometres . . .' he spun on his heel, a huge smile on his face, and shot an arm out, pointing over the hilly land. '. . . That way. And there's a road three point four kilometres . . .' He turned again. '. . . There.'

'Friend Ozzie, friend Orion, I am delighted you have completed your journey.'

'Hey man,' Ozzie laid an arm over Tochee's back. 'My house is yours. And I'll apologize in advance for people making a fuss over you and generally behaving badly. You're going to be quite a celebrity. The ambassador for your whole species.'

'I believe the translation routine has made an error there, but I thank you for the caution. What do you propose doing now you are home?'

'Good question. One: a bath! Two: decent food. Maybe switch that around.' He took another long look round the bland farming landscape they'd emerged into. One thing really bothered him with the unisphere icons: the date. According to the display, he'd been away from the Commonwealth for over three years, whereas in his personal timescale he'd been walking the Silfen paths for eighteen months. 'Okay. I need some time to check up on what's happening. According to Clouddancer we're in the middle of a war. We also need to organize some transport, especially for Tochee. So let's see.' He began to pull information out of the unisphere, as slowly as any beginner just getting to grips with inserts and virtual vision for the first time. A list of local vehicle hire companies materialized. He ran down their inventories, and settled on a Land Rover Aventine, which had enough room to take Tochee if ten of the fourteen seats were folded down. He paid for it, and loaded instructions into the big 4x4's drive array. 'Let's head for the road, guys. Our car'll be here in fifteen minutes.'

'Ozzie,' Orion asked cautiously.

'Yep?'

'This town, Eansor, has it got, like bars and such in it?'

'Of course, man.' He'd just pulled the town's commercial register out of the unisphere to find the best hotel.

'So, tonight,' Orion squinted up at the sun, which was in the last quarter of the sky, 'are we going to visit a few places, you know, social places, ones that have girls in them?'

'Oh right, not a bad idea. We'll definitely hit the town over the next few days, I promise.'

'That's good, I've remembered all the chat up lines you gave me.'

'You have?'

'Yeah, I still think I can pull off the heaven one.'

'The what one?'

'When you look at a girl's collar and read the label back to her, and tell her—'

'She's made in heaven. Ah. Right, I remember now. Sure. Look, man, those kind of lines are strictly last resort, okay. Your big advantage is going to be telling them what we've been doing and what you've seen; no other kid can complete with that, you dig? You're going to be the hottest brightest dude on the block. The chicks'll need sunscreen just to stand near you.'

'Okay.'

'But first, you need a decent scrub and some flash clothes. We can sort that once we're relaxing at the hotel.'

'I don't understand why you need verbal trickery to ensnare a temporary mate,' Tochee said. 'Are you not attracted to each other by what you are?'

Ozzie and Orion shared a glance.

'Our species tend to amplify things a little,' Ozzie said. 'No harm in that.'

'You speak an untruth to potential mates?'

'No, no. It's not that simple, this is like a ritual.'

'I believe the translation routine is insufficient once again.'

'Is Tochee going to come with us to the bars?' Orion asked.

Ozzie glared at him. 'Probably best not.'

'I would like to see all aspects of human civilization. From what you have told me, it is richly textured and seeped in artistic culture.'

'Oh brother,' Ozzie muttered.

*

They sat on the side of the road for ten minutes before the Land Rover Aventine pulled up in front of them. It was a dark metallic-red 4x4, with curving windows of mirrorglass along both sides. The broad malmetal door at the rear flowed apart, and Tochee wriggled itself into the back.

Ozzie sat up at the front, and loaded some new orders into the drive array. It was strange being in a technological artefact again. Even the smell surprised him, the pine-bleach cleaning fluid and polished leather scent of a vigorous valet service.

'This is fast,' Orion said as they set off.

'Uh huh.' They were doing under a hundred kilometres an

hour. The road was just a simple strip of enzyme-bonded concrete, a minor route linking isolated rural communities. Same the Commonwealth over. 'How old were you when your parents moved to Silvergalde?'

'Dunno. Two or three, I think.'

'So you don't like remember much about the Commonwealth, then.'

'No. Just the stuff people brought to Lyddington. Not that much of it worked there.'

Since they left the Ice Citadel, Ozzie had conveniently forgotten the kind of responsibility he had with Orion. He was going to have to look out for the boy as much as he was Tochee. Both of them were excited by the car journey, asking questions about the farms and other vehicles they passed. It was like having a couple of five-year-olds to contend with.

When the road finally turned onto a dual carriageway that took them into the town and the Land Rover Aventine really built up some speed, Orion whooped like a roller-coaster passenger. Tochee inquired if all human vehicles were so fast. Ozzie knew enough now about their big alien friend for its body language to tell him it was nervous. He limited the car to a hundred and eighty kilometres an hour.

*

Eansor was a pleasant enough town, though hardly spectacular. Except to Orion and Tochee, who were mesmerized by the buildings and roads and people. The dual carriageway wound through the industrial parks on the outskirts, over bridges in the suburbs where the best houses lined the river, and finally dipped into the gentle rumpled valley where the city centre colonized the slopes with big stone and glass buildings.

Ozzie directed the Land Rover round the back of the Ledbetter Hotel and parked it in a delivery bay. 'Wait here,' he told the others. 'Seriously, guys. I need a quiet day to catch up. I don't want to cause any scenes here, okay?'

'Okay,' Orion said amiably.

Just to be safe, Ozzie locked the Land Rover doors as he left.

The Ledbetter's high-ceilinged lobby had an extensive central display of exotic alien vegetation, with the plants carefully graded so that as you walked through them their leaf colours progressed through the rainbow. Ozzie, who had endured enough wondrous alien vegetation along the paths to last his next five lives, walked straight from the revolving doors to the reception desk completely ignoring the lush surroundings. There were a lot of glances from the other patrons shooting his way, usually followed by a nose wrinkling in disapproval. That was why he just kept staring right ahead, he knew exactly what he looked like as his boots trod field dirt into the plush royal-blue carpet.

He reached the slate-topped reception counter, and slapped his hand down on the polished brass bell. Two largish assistants from the concierge desk were moving into place behind him. The duty receptionist, a man in his late thirties wearing the hotel's grey blazer uniform, gave Ozzie a reproachful look. 'Yes.' Pause. 'Sir.'

Ozzie smiled from inside his extravagant beard. 'Like, gimme the best suite you've got, man.'

'It's booked. In fact, all our rooms are booked. Perhaps you should try another establishment.' He looked over at the two assistants, hand rising to beckon.

'No thanks, dude. This is the only five star in town.' Before the receptionist could stop him, he reached over the counter and pressed his thumb against the i-pad on the hotel's credit array.

'Listen pal—' the receptionist began, then blinked as the hotel system registered Ozzie's bank tattoo and identity certificate. 'Oh.' He swayed forward slightly, peering closely. 'Ozzie? I mean, Mr Isaacs, sir. Welcome to the Ledbetter.'

The assistants froze. One of them actually smiled.

'About that suite?' Ozzie said.

'My mistake, sir, our penthouse suite is available. We'd be honoured to have you stay here with us, sir.'

'Glad to hear it, man. Now, about this penthouse; I expect you get a lot of important people here, people who don't want everything they do splashed on the gossip shows.'

'I believe you'll find us most discreet, sir.'

'So far so good. Is there a service elevator to the penthouse?'

'Yes, sir.'

'Even better. Now listen carefully. There's a very large alien sitting in a car in one of your delivery bays out back. I want it into the service elevator and up into the suite without any fuss and without anyone seeing. I do not want to look out of my window tomorrow morning and see Alessandra Baron or any other media dudes camping outside.' He shunted a very large gratuity to the Ledbetter staff general account. 'We cool on that?'

The receptionist's eyebrow rose a fraction. 'I will make your request quite plain to the other members of staff.'

'Good man. Now, do you guys have a decent room service menu?'

'We do indeed, sir. Our restaurant has the finest menu in town. Would you like to see it now?'

'No, just send the food up to the suite.'

'Yes, sir. Er, which items?'

'All of it.'

'All of it?'

'Yeah, and just to play safe: twenty-five lettuce as well.'

'At once, sir.'

*

The en-suite bathroom to the master bedroom featured a circular sunken marble pool, large enough for several people. But not quite big enough for Tochee. The alien lay on a bed of towels beside it, and scooped the warm soapy water over itself. Its manipulator flesh gripped two of the largest combs to be found in Eansor, and raked them through its colourful fronds, pulling out the flecks of dried leaves, and grit, and mud spots, and grass stalks, and all the other detritus it had picked up in the feathery appendages as they moved between worlds.

Orion, wearing just a huge canary-yellow towel round his waist, was working round Tochee with the shower hose, washing off the foam that Ozzie had rubbed into its fronds after they'd been combed.

'We do not have "shampoo conditioner" on my world,' Tochee told them. Several of his cleaned fronds quivered at the slightest movement. They were becoming dramatically soft and vibrant as the water dried away. 'I would become very important if I were to introduce such a thing.'

'It's the little things in life that count, man,' Ozzie said. Like Orion, he was wearing a big towel and nothing else. He'd probably have another shower once they were done with Tochee's beauty therapy. *Three in one day!* The water washing down the drain in the first one had been *vile*.

They'd eaten after their all-important first wash with real soap. The three of them moving along the line of trolleys laden with the restaurant's finest cooking. Ozzie had wolfed down the perfectly cooked French-blue steak. Sampled the fish, the game, the risotto, the sweet and sour chicken, the Thai spice dishes, the pasta. Fries! A whole mountain of them. Beer; drunk as if it had been passed down from Mount Olympus.

Tochee had stuck to the vegetable dishes. How anybody, alien or not, could eat two bowls of raw carrot sticks intended for the dips was beyond Ozzie. The lettuce had been a good idea, too; Tochee ate half of them.

Orion and Tochee both tried ice cream for the first time ever. Finished every spoonful on the trolleys, and sent out for more. Ozzie munched his way through the other puddings, taking a couple of spoons from each.

After the Bacchic meal, they'd brought in clothing store staff from the city, with big cases of the latest fashions. It had taken an hour to choose a wardrobe for both of them. The hotel's in-house salon sorted out Ozzie's beard, and gave him a proper manicure. He wouldn't let them cut much off his Afro, he kind of liked it so explosive. Orion got a similar treatment. It only ended when Ozzie politely rescued the poor girl who was styling the boy's hair.

'You were drooling,' he told Orion when the flustered girl had left.

'She was beautiful,' Orion protested. 'And really friendly.'

'Oh man, she was sixty years older than you. Trust me on that, rejuvenation is easy to see if you know what you're looking for; she wore that much make-up because she's not actually very pretty; and she was being professionally courteous, not friendly.'

'You're just jealous.'

Ozzie promptly cancelled the massage he'd booked for both of them.

Sprucing up Tochee took a good ninety minutes. But Ozzie had to admit, it was time well spent. Once they'd finished blowing the hair driers over its fronds, their friend looked magnificent. Fluffier than they'd ever seen it, but wonderfully colourful. 'A whole Vegas chorus line of costumes in one package,' Ozzie declared.

'Are we going out now?' Orion asked. He'd put on a semi-organic black shirt, wearing a white and scarlet jacket over the top; the trousers were green enough to hurt the naked eye. It was an ensemble fashionable with the under twenties, the store assistant had promised. Ozzie felt really old just looking at the boy; no way was he going to walk into a bar with anyone dressed like that.

'Sorry, not tonight. I told you I had some serious datawork to catch up with.' The hotel, indeed Bilma itself, was just an interlude before he got back to his asteroid and thought out what to do next.

'Tomorrow then,' Orion said in a whingey voice. 'Promise me tomorrow. It's not fair we get back and I have to stay in the whole time. I want to meet some girls.'

'All right, tomorrow,' Ozzie said, anything to divert the boy.

'So what do I do tonight?' Orion asked. It was already dark outside, with the groundlights ringing the hotel shining green and red through the windows.

'Access something. I'll show you how. Tochee might like to see something of the Commonwealth as well.' He ushered them into the suite's main lounge, and accessed the room management array. The big hologram portal lit up with a huge unisphere category menu. Ozzie hurriedly loaded in restrictions that would stop the boy wading through porn all night long – for Tochee's sake, obviously – and switched the array to voice activation function. He slotted a direct translation routine in for Tochee, and left them to it.

*

The Guardians' vehicles were almost down to the bottom of the deep inlet where Shackleton was situated when Adam's narrowband link back to the train dropped out. He told Rosamund to send the drone back to inspect the gateway. Even as the little bot turned a sharp curve through Half Way's clear red sky he was certain what it would find. Vic had been right. Judging by the silence in the armoured car and the way everyone was keeping quiet on the general band, he wasn't the only one with that thought.

The image in his virtual vision showed him the simple hoop of equipment which anchored the Half Way end of the wormhole. For a moment, it was illuminated by one of the powerful blue-white flashes in the sky. The stab of light revealed the interlocking machinery inside the arch. There was no wormhole.

'Well,' Morton said, 'I'd say getting back is going to be a tad difficult now.'

'There are still planes at Shackleton,' Adam said, keeping positive. He didn't want anyone to start panicking. Not yet, anyway. If they started thinking about how isolated they were, they'd lose it very quickly indeed. All he could think of was the one remaining wormhole on this godforsaken planet, and the fact that the Starflyer was going to reach it first. He had to admit, as traps went, this one was a beauty. All the Starflyer had to do was get through to Half Way and blow the generator behind it, leaving them stranded on a world with no link to anywhere, in an environment that would slowly kill them. And who would come looking? Sheldon might. Possibly.

Adam's e-butler told him Bradley was calling on a private link. 'This isn't good. Did you ever examine this scenario?'

'Stig and I reviewed what would happen if the Starflyer blew the Port Evergreen wormhole generator as it returned. That was a year ago. We believed there would be sufficient resources on Far Away for the clans to complete the planet's revenge. But that assumed they'd already have the Martian data, and we'd got more equipment through. The Far Away freight inspectorate division bolloxed that up for us, which is one of the reasons why we switched to the blockade run scenario.'

'But we expected to do that before the Starflyer's return,' Bradley said.

'Exactly. Then the Prime attack threw another spanner in the works. And I certainly didn't predict anything quite this personal.'

'So what are our options?'

'There's only one: get to Port Evergreen before it.'

'And can we do that?'

'Even if it hasn't sabotaged the planes, it has a thirty minute head start. We don't have aerobots. Or even air to air missiles.'

'I see,' Bradley said. 'Is there any way we can call ahead, and reverse this trap on the Starflyer? Get our clan warriors through the wormhole at the other end, and secure Port Evergreen before the Starflyer arrives? That way it will be trapped between us.'

'The planes only have short wave radio in case of emergency. There are no satellites here, only a seabed fibre optic cable between Shackleton and Port Evergreen to link Far Away to the Unisphere.'

'So someone stays behind and when the next cycle begins they send a message through to Stig.'

'The Institute is blocking all communication, has been for days.'

'Then we have no choice but to make the flight and hope Stig can help us out somehow.'

'Without knowing what's going on?'

'He's not stupid. He'll know the Starflyer is returning, and that we're on our way as well.'

'I hope you're right.'

The vehicles arrived on the shelf of rock where the pressurized huts and vast hangars were laid out a hundred metres above the sea. Two of the hangar doors were open, the regular flashes from the planet's odd double star revealing their empty cavernous interiors. When the drone made its early flyby, its active sensors revealed the remaining seven hangars all contained a Carbon Goose.

'Our vehicles will fit into one,' Adam announced.

'I don't mean to intrude, but isn't that a little too risky?' Bradley asked him. 'All our eggs in one flying basket.'

'I'm prepared to run an inspection on the planes,' Adam replied. 'We've been running with the possibility of sabotage by Starflyer agents, that's why I brought the forensic sensorbots. There are enough to check over three planes. But we have to get airborne and fast. Putting all the sensorbots onto one plane will speed the whole process up. We can't afford luxuries like three aircraft, Bradley, not any longer.'

'I apologize, Adam. This is your operation; I'll try to keep my mouth shut for the rest of the journey.'

'Don't. I can still make mistakes. If you see one coming, shout it long and loud.' Adam switched back to the general channel. 'Kieran, Ayub, you have decontamination duty. I want it checked thoroughly; we don't need any surprises over the middle of the ocean.' He made everyone else wait in the relative security of the vehicles while Kieran and Ayub went over to the Carbon Goose in the fifth hangar, which had been left in minimal-power hibernation mode. A swarm of standard forensic sensorbots wriggled over the rock with them, looking like arm-length caterpillars. The machines bristled with gossamer-thin smart-molecule filaments like a downy fur. They circled the gigantic aircraft, testing the rock for any sign that someone had been in the hangar recently.

'Nobody for well over a week,' Ayub reported. 'Zero thermal disturbance. No residual chemical dissemination.'

Adam gave them the go-ahead to test the plane itself. Kieran went up to the cockpit and loaded a batch of diagnostic software into the avionics. Ayub supervised the sensorbots as they crawled over the fuselage and slithered in through the airlocks. They wriggled into the structure through inspection ports and grilles, probing every component casing with their filaments, sniffing the air for any trace chemicals, performing resonance scans on the structure. He dropped three into each of the nuclear turbines so they could squirm their way past the fan blades and work their way back through the compressor bands.

'When does the wormhole cycle begin?' Anna asked.

'In just over six hours,' Adam said. 'Assuming the Starflyer has a standard flight, it'll remain open for about an hour and a half after it arrives at Port Evergreen.'

'That just gives us enough time,' Wilson said. 'But it'll be tight.'

After twenty minutes, Ayub cleared the lower cargo hold, declaring it free of booby traps.

'How long does this take?' Oscar asked.

'As long as it needs to,' Adam said resolutely.

'We're giving them too big a lead time,' Wilson said. 'At this rate there's no way the Starflyer will leave a working gateway at the other end by the time we get there. We have to keep hard on its tail if we're to stand any kind of chance. You've got to run a minimum scan and take the risk.'

Adam knew he was right. If the Starflyer truly hadn't wanted them to follow, it could easily have wrecked the remaining planes before it left. So either they'd been sabotaged, or it simply intended to destroy the Port Evergreen generator, leaving them trapped here. *Simple is always most effective. And the Starflyer must be improvising to a degree as well.* 'Okay,' he told the drivers. 'Load them up.'

Kieran and Ayub opened the main cargo deck ramps at the back of the Carbon Goose. The Volvos went up first. As the armoured car drove under the wing, Adam saw sensorbots starting to fall out of the turbine exhausts to lie flexing uselessly on the sheer rock floor, their sophisticated electronics victim to the micropile's radiation. He stayed focused on them for a long time as they slowed and finally became inert. It was a bad omen on a world inimical to humans when even the machinery designed to function here proved deadly to standard Commonwealth technology.

*

Wilson was still in his armour suit when he entered the cockpit. In keeping with the rest of the Carbon Goose, it was a big compartment with seats more like leather recliners than the cramped USAF fighter seats that he used to contend with in his first life. The windscreen was a curving transparency six feet high that gave a panoramic view out over the blunt nose. Kieran was sitting in the pilot's seat, still in his armour, with three high-performance arrays spread out on the control console. They were plugged into the plane's avionics with thick fibre optic cable.

'Did you find anything?' Wilson asked.

'No. The software checks out. I've loaded some additional monitors in case anything was submerged; but they didn't really have the time to plant anything sophisticated. There's no thermal trace of anyone here before us. My opinion, for what it's worth, is this is clean.' He climbed out of the chair, and unsealed his helmet.

Wilson studied the young face that was exposed. Short hair framing slim features, alert eyes; eager, dedicated, efficient. *Me, three-hundred-and-forty years ago. God!* 'When I was in the air force, I learned to always trust my engineering crew. I don't suppose anything's really changed.'

Kieran broke into a genuine grateful smile. 'Thank you.'

'Okay, let's see if I actually remember how to fly.' He started to take his armour suit off.

'Admiral. I'm glad you're here.'

The term surprised Wilson. Thirty hours ago, the navy which he was in charge of had been hunting down the Guardians as if they were a pandemic virus. It made the young man's faith all the more touching. 'I'll do whatever I can,' he promised.

Oscar and Anna arrived in the cockpit as Wilson was pulling his feet out of the armour's boots. He was only wearing a white T-shirt and shorts, and the cockpit's air was almost freezing.

'Here you go,' Oscar said, and dropped a small bag at Wilson's feet. 'Our CST-issue executive travel pack. Essential for survival in hotels and conferences the Commonwealth over.'

'Don't mock,' Wilson growled as he unzipped the bag. He

found a fleece with a CST logo on the chest, and pulled it on quickly before sitting in the luxurious pilot's seat. 'Yow, this leather's cold.' He put his hands over the console's i-pads, and reviewed the menus rolling into his virtual vision as the interface was established. The first thing he did was locate the plane's environmental circuits, and switch the heating on full.

Power-up routines were simple, easily handled by the on-board avionics arrays. He ordered the hangar doors open as the turbines ran through their pre-flight checks. Red light shone through the big windscreen. A bright flash from the binary star made him blink, and hunt down the optical limiter, which restricted how much light could pass through the tough glass. It allowed the ordinary radiance of the M-class star through, but the flashes which came from matter on its dying fall into the neutron companion wouldn't intrude quite so badly.

'Everybody in and secure,' Adam reported. 'Could you turn the heating on, please?'

'It is,' Wilson said. 'Give it a minute.'

Anna was out of her armour suit, puffing against the cold as she pulled on some clothes from her CST pack.

'You want to take co-pilot's seat?' Wilson asked.

'Sure.' She gave him a quick intimate smile.

'We actually need to be in the air before you two can join the mile high club,' Oscar told them dryly.

Wilson grinned. 'This is the bit I've always wanted to say,' he confessed to them as the avionics confirmed the micropiles were ready. 'Atomic turbines to power!'

Anna and Oscar exchanged a look. Oscar shrugged.

The turbines spun up, and Wilson released the wheel brakes. The Carbon Goose rolled out of its hangar and down towards the icy sea.

*

'Oh brother,' Ozzie grunted. He was accessing files from his asteroid, seeing the refugees from Randtown come stumbling through the wormhole. 'There goes the neighbourhood.' Two hours in to his review of everything that had happened, and he was beginning to wish he'd headed off in the other direction after leaving Island Two.

The last home file showed him Nigel wandering around the bungalow. Ozzie's own recorded projection played out, and Nigel swore at the end of it. Back in the cosy warmth of the Ledbetter penthouse suite, sprawled on his circular, emperor-sized jellmattress, Ozzie grinned at his old friend's dismayed expression. Poor old Nige had always disapproved of his lifestyle, the decisions and choices. It was their contrary opinions which made them such a good team.

He drained his tumbler of bourbon and told the maidbot to refill it, then moved on to examine records from the latest invasion. 'Oh brother.' The damage which the flare-bombs and quantumbusters inflicted on the stars was terrifying. Then something terminated Hell's Gateway, something that the Sheldon Dynasty had done independently from the navy, something greater than a quantumbuster. Half of the unisphere now comprised speculation and gossip about Nigel using the same ultra-weapon against Dyson Alpha, the war-winning strike.

The other half of the unisphere was busy discussing the Second47's evacuation into the future. Ozzie took another swig as the War Cabinet made their announcement. 'Son of a bitch, don't bring me into this,' he shouted at Nigel's image. His so-called friend's face loomed hugely over the bed, as projected by the portal on the opposite wall. It was badly focused now. Ozzie tried to do some math to see if Nigel knew what the fuck he was talking about, but the equations were impossible to form. He looked at his tumbler, which was empty again. 'Just bring the bottle,' he told the maidbot.

Virtual hands wobbled through virtual vision, and he knocked politely on the SI's icon.

The War Cabinet vanished, to be replaced by tangerine and turquoise lines weaving through and around each other. 'Hello, Ozzie. Welcome back.'

'Good to be back. I mean it. You've no idea how wonderful toilet paper is until it's taken away from you by an unfeeling universe. I think it's a defining characteristic of human civilization, the ability to manufacture something decent to wipe your ass on. Believe me, forest leaves just don't cut it. Well actually,' he sniggered, 'they do, and that's the problem. And you can make that my epitaph if you want.'

'Duly noted.'

'Hey hey, don't you smartass me. You've got some bigtime explaining to do, man.' The maidbot rolled up to the side of the bed, and held out the bourbon bottle. Ozzie took it, and winked at the little machine.

'You are referring to the emergency Randtown evacuation,' the SI said.

'Nail on the fucking head, dude.'

'We took the liberty of saving thousands of human lives. We assumed that given the circumstances, you wouldn't object.'

'Yeah yeah, trillions of dollars spent building the ultimate in private housing, and it's all blown. All gone.' The room rotated around him, leaving him spreadeagled on the bed, staring up at the ceiling. He took another drink of bourbon to compensate. 'I'll have to dream up something else now. Maybe go back to the Ice Citadel. No! Fuck, what am I saying? It was cold there. I am, like, not a cold weather person. I learned that about myself.'

'So your venture was successful, then?'

'Oh brother, was it ever. I found out everything; who put the barriers up, why they did it, why they won't help us. And I'll tell you something else: I was right about the Silfen, too.'

'Do they evolve into an adult state?'

'Ah ha,' Ozzie wagged a finger at the slow wavestorm of glowing lines. 'I thought you'd want to know that. Man, you should have seen where they live. The gas halo is like totally groovy. Maybe I should try and build one. I'd just love to see Nigel's face when I tell him that.'

'Who built the barriers?'

'Clouddancer said it was some race called the Anomine. But that was in a dream. I think. Anyway, they're not around any more. Actually, no, cancel that; they are but they're not the same. I think they out-evolved the Silfen, some of them anyway. The others all went back home and joined Green-peace.' Ozzie smiled lazily. The bed was wonderfully soft, and he was very tired now. He closed his eyes. 'They're not going to help us, you know. You'd dig that. You haven't been majorly helpful here, have you? Apart from scooping up that Mellanie chick. Damn, she's hot. Do you know if she's dating anyone?' He yawned. Waited for the answer. 'Oh come on man, you're not pissed at me are you. Just a few home truths among friends. You've got to grow thicker skin.'

There was still no reply. The light in the room changed.

'Mr Isaacs.'

'Huh?' That wasn't the SI. Ozzie opened his eyes. The tangerine and turquoise lines had vanished. He swung round towards the sound of the new voice, or tried to, the bed kept getting in the way. A man's head slid into view. Upside down, and frowning. 'Hey!' Ozzie exclaimed happily. 'Nelson. Been too long, man. How's it hanging?'

'I'm glad to see you're all right.'

'Never better.'

'Quite. Nigel would like a word.'

'Bring him on in.'

'It's easier if we take you to him.'

'Sure thing. Let me find my shoes.' Ozzie finally managed to move, and slithered off the end of the bed to land in a heap on the floor. Something hurt. It probably belonged to him. 'Can you see them?' he asked Nelson earnestly.

Nelson smiled blankly, and beckoned. Ozzie was lifted to his feet by two powerful young men in grey business suits. They had identical red and green OCtattoos on their cheeks, a stack of centimetre-long lines that looked like neon sideburns.

'Hi guys. Good to meet you.'

They carried him out of the bedroom. Orion was in the lounge outside, still wearing his fancy white and scarlet jacket. The boy looked very scared. There were a lot of people in the lounge with him, just like the ones carrying Ozzie; polite well-built men and women without any sense of humour.

'Ozzie?' Orion said. He bit his lip, looking fearfully at Nelson.

'Hang tight there, little dude, everything's perfectly under control. Where's Tochee?'

'I am here, friend Ozzie.'

'Do as they say.' Being vertical wasn't good. Ozzie's stomach didn't like it. He threw up.

They carried him into the service elevator. There was a convoy of big dark cars outside the hotel. He was bundled into the first one. The short drive ended with him being carried to a hypersonic aircraft, just big enough to accommodate Tochee at the back where a dozen seats had been removed.

Nelson sat down opposite Ozzie and produced a large red tablet. 'Take this.'

'What is it?'

'Something to help.'

'I'm not ill.'

Fingers pinched his nose shut, and he opened his mouth in reflex. The tablet was shoved in, followed by water. Ozzie half-swallowed, half-gagged. 'Oh brother.'

Nelson leant back. 'Strap him in. He's going to need it.'

The flight was truly horrible. Ozzie shivered violently in his seat, his skin feverish. He desperately wanted to be sick again, but it was as if his stomach had grown an extra membrane to prevent it. The acidic heartburn down his gullet spread right through his gut. His headache seemed to be sweating its way through his skull.

An hour later his teeth had stopped chattering. The aches and discomfort were fading away, leaving his clothes soaked in cold sweat. 'I fucking hate sober ups,' Ozzie growled at Nelson. 'They're not natural. Son of a bitch, look at my clothes.' He plucked at his wet T-shirt in disgust.

'We brought your bags,' Nelson said. 'You can freshen up on the train. 'We'll be landing in five minutes.'

'Landing where?'

'The planetary station.'

'Great. I've got to pee.'

Nelson gestured down the aisle.

Ozzie slowly slipped his straps off, and rose unsteadily to his feet. Orion was sitting in the chair behind. 'You okay there, dude?'

The boy nodded. 'I think Tochee was worried, but I told him we'd be all right. He doesn't understand how important you are.'

'I'll try and explain to it later.'

'Ozzie,' the boy said quietly. 'She's really nice. We talked a lot. She's called Lauren. She was really interested in the Silfen paths and where we've been.'

Ozzie glanced round at the security team member Orion was surreptitiously indicating. 'Uh, okay; again she's polite in that serial-killer fashion because that's her job. Don't ask her to marry you or anything.'

'All right, Ozzie.' The boy pouted.

*

The hypersonic came down on a landing pad behind the station's cluster of administration buildings. There was no one around to see them disembark and hurry over to the sleek private maglev express with its two carriages.

'Just us?' Ozzie asked when he looked down the deserted front carriage. There were big spherical chairs set along the length of the carriage, with a bar at the far end.

'Just you,' Nelson confirmed.

Ozzie took one of his new cases into the washroom to change. His attempt to interface with the unisphere was completely unsuccessful, his inserts reported the train was efficiently screened.

Back out in the carriage, Ozzie raided the bar for some sandwiches, then went to sit near to Tochee and Orion. He acted as tour guide as the express hurtled along, pointing out the worlds they passed through. The Big15 planet Shayoni first, which led to Beijing, followed by a fast trip round the trans-Earth loop to New York, and finally Augusta.

'Your transport is so much more efficient that the Silfen method,' Tochee said. 'And your worlds so ordered. Do you disapprove of disarray?'

'Don't judge us on what you've seen so far,' Ozzie told it.

At New Costa station their train peeled away from the main area of the yard to slide through a lone gateway.

'And this has to be Cresset,' Ozzie said. 'I haven't been here for a while.'

'Seventy-three years,' Nelson said as the maglev glided in to Illanum station. More dark cars were waiting for them.

'Where now?' Ozzie asked.

'One of Nigel's residences just outside the town.'

'All of us?'

'Yes, all of you. We have suitable rooms prepared.'

'Okay then.' Ozzie was giving the station's cargo handling sector a suspicious look. Its capacity had jumped up by an order of magnitude since he'd last visited.

The 'residence' was a big mansion of pale stone modelled on the stately homes of eighteenth century Europe. It was several miles out of town, and surrounded by towering trees that were oppressively dark in the deepening twilight.

'You'll be all right,' Ozzie told his companions when they walked into the big entrance hall. Orion's expression was dropping into a sullenness which Ozzie recognized only too well. 'Get some sleep, we'll talk in the morning.'

Nelson led the way through the mansion to a study overlooking the front lawns. There was a greenway outside, barely visible now the sun had set. Ozzie wasn't sure if he remembered it or not, but it did seem vaguely familiar. He resented not having access to the unisphere after only just being reconnected.

Nigel was waiting in a big leather armchair. 'Thanks, Nelson.'

Nelson smiled tightly and left, closing the door behind him. Ozzie's inserts told him a strong e-seal had come on around the room. 'Just us, huh?'

'Just us.' Nigel waved a hand at a chair identical to his own.

'Shouldn't the fire be blazing away?' Ozzie said as he sat down. 'With like maybe one of those big hairy dogs stretched out in front of it.'

'Irish Wolfhound.'

'And you and me jiving away with some brandy.'

'You've had enough to drink today.'

'Okay Nige, so what's with the big CIA spook operation? My unisphere address is open. You could have called.'

'Better this way. That kid you've turned up with tells an interesting story. And the alien; nobody's seen anything like it before. Communication by photoluminescent visual signals in the ultraviolet spectrum. The xenobiologists are going to love that.'

'Tochee's an okay dude, sure.'

'So you walked the Silfen paths?'

'Yeah, man. They are the most incredible wormhole network

imaginable. I think they're sentient in their own right. That's why we can never quite track them down. They move the whole time, opening and closing, timeshifting, too.'

'Figures. Incorporating a wormhole's control routines into a self-sustaining exotic energy matrix is one of our research projects.'

'Clunky, man, so clunky compared to this.'

'So what did you find? Have they got an SI equivalent?'

'Yeah, something like that. It has a shitload of data, like a galactic library. I know who put the barriers round the Dyson Pair.'

Nigel listened silently while Ozzie told him about finding the Ice Citadel, and Tochee, and seeing the ghost planet's history, and finally ending up in the gas halo. 'So this Anomine species isn't going to help us?' he asked.

'No,' Ozzie said. 'Sorry, man.'

'That was a well-spent three years, then. Are you happy?'

'Hey, fuck you!'

'Why did you order the Dynasty political office to prevent anyone examining cargo sent to Far Away?'

'Uh.' Ozzie gave a sickly grin. That wasn't exactly what he was expecting to talk about. 'Well, man, you know, like, it was oppressive. I don't dig that at all.'

'Ozzie, give the bullshit routine a rest will you. There's too much at stake. If you haven't worked it out yet, I'm trying to decide whose side you're on.'

'Side?'

'Are you a Starflyer agent, Ozzie?' Nigel asked quietly. There was a glint of moisture in his eye. 'Damnit, do you have any idea how much it hurts just to have to ask you that?'

'You know the Starflyer's real?' an equally astounded Ozzie blurted out.

'Yeah, we know it's real, we just found out. So, why the political restriction?'

'I didn't know if it was real.'

'What made you even suspect?'

'I met this dude, Bradley Johansson. Man, could he spin a story. He claimed he'd been to the gas halo, that the Silfen had removed his Starflyer conditioning. I'd never heard anything like it. He almost made sense. So I asked myself, what if he was right? You know? I mean, it's a big universe out there, Nige, anything is possible.'

'So you took a chance, and threw in with him. It was fun, wasn't it, Ozzie? Fun being on the other side, sticking it to The Man.'

'I'm not that shallow.'

'Yes you are.' Nigel narrowed his eyes. 'When did you meet him?'

'God, man, I dunno, like over a century ago.'

'Before or after he founded the Guardians?'

'Same time, he was just getting his act together.'

Nigel tented his fingers in front of his face, staring hard at Ozzie. Suddenly his eyes widened in shock. 'Oh my God, you stupid, *stupid* son of a bitch. I don't believe it.'

'What?' Ozzie asked, disturbed by his friend's behaviour.

'The Great Wormhole Heist.'

'Ah.' Ozzie couldn't help a slight smirk. 'That.'

'You helped him. I always wondered how the hell they got into the supercomputer routines we'd written. The access codes were all our personal encryption. You gave him the codes, didn't you?'

'Better than that,' Ozzie said evilly.

'How better?'

'I was one of them.'

'One of ... oh *fuck*, Ozzie. You were part of the Great Wormhole Heist?'

'Sure, man, it was a blast.'

'A blast? Jee-zus, Ozzie, that was Paula Myo's case. Suppose she'd caught Johansson? His memory read would have shown you taking part.'

'It was worth it. You have no idea how high I got creeping round that museum, giving the guards the finger when the force field came on around us. Then we just waltzed right into the Vegas vault. Shit, Nigel, even we don't have that much money. It was stacked to the fucking rooftops, like a dragon's bed of gold.'

'It's less than an hour's income for CST, you dickbrain, and *we* own half of Vegas anyway. Why didn't you just give Johansson an open credit transfer?'

'I knew you wouldn't get it. Nigel, man, we built that machine with our own two hands; it's still our finest hour, not CST. That was the two of us against the world back then. That generator was built with love, it's part of us, the kid our souls had together. It wasn't fair leaving it to be gawped at by bunches of schoolkids like some freakshow exhibit. I gave it a swansong that'll never be forgotten.'

'It wasn't in danger of being overlooked, it's the foundation for our whole society.' Nigel groaned out loud, and appealed silently to the fates. 'Why didn't you just come and tell me about the Starflyer?'

'And you'd have listened, and taken it all seriously? Come on. Nige, you are The Man. You'd have told me and Johansson to go take a flying leap, then given me another lecture about being stoned.' He gave his friend a kindly smile. 'How long have you known the Starflyer is real, Nige, I mean, really accepted it's a genuine twenty-four carat pain in humanity's ass? Be honest.'

'We've suspected something weird's been going on behind the scenes for a while now. I wasn't sure if it was the SI. One of its agents was involved.'

'How long?' Ozzie chanted. He wasn't about to let Nigel off this one.

'Couple of days.'

'Pretty good. Longer than I'd have given you credit for.'

'Oh, like you were sure,' Nigel snapped back. 'You who

were so confident you used Johansson as an excuse to play super-thief for kicks. You know, I bet you're secretly pissed Johansson hasn't been caught. For a hundred and thirty years you've been waiting for this little stunt to get added to the catalogue of Ozzie legends, haven't you?'

Ozzie pulled a sullen expression, modelled on Orion at his worst. 'I was playing long odds, is all. I told you: Johansson was convincing. Somebody should have taken a close look. And don't sit there telling me I shouldn't have done anything. Look outside and see the kind of super-deep shit we're in right now.'

'Were.'

'What?'

'*Were* in deep shit. I've managed to pull us out of it. There's not going to be any more MorningLightMountain any more, or the Starflyer.'

That little edge of conceit was something about Nigel which always bugged Ozzie. 'What have you done, Nigel?'

'I'm sending a ship to Dyson Alpha, a nova bomb is going to take care of MorningLightMountain once and for all. This is all going to be settled within a week.'

'Nova bomb? Is that what your secret weapon is? Nobody on the unisphere knows. What the fuck is it?'

'Same principle as a diverted energy nuke, but bigged up like you wouldn't believe. Our Dynasty weapons-development team took the diverted-energy principle, and bolted it onto a quantumbuster. Simple really, the quantumbuster effect field converts any matter within its radius directly into energy, only now that energy is diverted into expanding the effect field further. And that's a *lot* of energy. The field grows large enough to convert a measurable percentage of a star; which gives us an explosion on the same scale as a nova. It annihilates the star and any planet orbiting within a hundred AUs. The radiation will be lethal to any habitable planet within another thirty-or-so light-years.'

Ozzie frowned, horribly intrigued despite every liberal moral he possessed. 'That's an impossible feedback.'

'Not quite. It only has to hold together for a fraction of a second. Conversion is almost instantaneous. That gives us a loophole.'

'No.' Ozzie put his hands to his temples, shaking his head hard enough to make his hair wave from side to side. Realization of what was about to happen was affecting his body far worse than any little sober up tablet forced down his neck. He really did think he was going to be physically sick. 'No, no, I don't give shit about the mechanics. Nigel, you can't do this, man. You can't kill MorningLightMountain. It *is* the Primes now, their whole species.'

'We've been through this, Ozzie; the War Cabinet, Dynasty heads, the StPetersburg team; we looked at every tactical scenario, every option. There's nothing else we can do. MorningLightMountain is trying to exterminate us, just like the Starflyer planned. Maybe you should have tried a little harder to get me to take notice of Johansson instead of playing the romantic underdog. Not that you ever were that, Ozzie, it just suits you to pretend so you can get laid more often. Well, wake up and smell the coffee; we're not college students any more, Ozzie, we left California behind three and a half centuries ago. Grow up, I had to – and I get laid more than you because of it. Why do you think I used your name in the War Cabinet announcement? People trust you, Ozzie, they like you. If you'd kicked up a fuss back when you met Johansson, they would have listened; Heather would have bust the Starflyer's corruption apart like a jackhammer on glass. Don't go around blaming me and calling me a warmonger. You knew, Ozzie, you goddamn *knew* about a threat to the entire human race, and you didn't fucking tell anyone. Who's to blame, Ozzie? Who backed us into this corner, huh? Who took away our options?'

Ozzie had sunk back into the chair as Nigel's voice grew

louder. It wasn't often Nigel, the original calculating iceman, lost his temper, but when he did it was best not to interrupt – people had been ruined, or worse, for making that mistake. Besides there was a nasty taste of guilt spreading round Ozzie's brain like a fast acting poison. 'It's genocide, man,' he said simply and quietly. There was no logical argument he could come up with to counter the tirade. 'It is so not what we are.'

'You think I don't fucking know that,' Nigel stormed. 'I wore the same T-shirts as you, I went on the same marches, I hated the military industrial imperialism that ran the world back then. Now look where *you've* put me!'

'Okay,' Ozzie raised his hands. 'Just calm down, man.'

'I am fucking calm. Anybody else, Ozzie, and I mean *anybody*, and they would have been wiped from history by now. Nobody would question what happened to you, because you would never have existed.'

'I've seen it happen, man,' Ozzie whispered. 'I walked one of the ghost planets. I witnessed their history; I felt them die, Nigel, every last one of them. You can't let it happen. You just can't, I'm begging you, man. I'm on my goddamn knees, here. Don't do this.'

'There is no other way.'

'There's always another way. Look, Clouddancer said the generator was only disabled, not destroyed.'

Nigel gave him a startled look. 'It was a variant on the flare bomb, we think it altered the generator's quantum structure.'

'There, see! The generator is still there. We've just got to repair it, get it working again.'

'Ozzie!' Nigel gave his friend a weary, despairing look. 'You're grasping at straws. It's not you.'

'We have to try.'

'Ozzie, think it through. The barrier generator is the size of a planet, and we've got days, maybe only hours before MorningLightMountain strikes back at the Commonwealth. If it does, it will kill us, it will genocide the human species. Do you understand that?'

'Let me try,' Ozzie implored. 'You're sending a ship, right, the one with the nova-bomb?'

'Yeah. We developed something new, Ozzie, this drive is something else again. It doesn't use any of our old worm-hole technology; you really do just jump into hyperspace. MorningLightMountain can't detect it.'

'Perfect! Let me go on it. I can take a look at the generator. You know if anyone can work it out, I can.'

'Ozzie—'

'MorningLightMountain won't know I'm there. If it starts an attack on the Commonwealth I'll fling a nova bomb into its star myself. But we have to try this. Let me go, Nigel. It's a *chance*. I know you, man, you won't be able to live with yourself if you don't at least consider it.'

'Ozzie, every physicist in the Commonwealth has been studying the data which the *Second Chance* gathered on the generator. We don't even know what some of the shells are, let alone what they do. And we certainly don't know how to build sections of them. Not inside a week. Get real, here.'

'I can do it, I know I can. There must be a self-repair function, something that can undo the damage. Yeah! Cloud-dancer said it should outlive the star itself. If the Starflyer could have destroyed the generator, it would. That gives us a chance.'

'You're not going, Ozzie.'

'Give me one good reason.'

'I don't trust you.'

For a moment Ozzie thought Nigel had hit him, his skin certainly went numb that way it did after a sharp blow. He couldn't hear anything either, the air in the big lounge had turned dead. 'What?' His voice was a piteous croak.

'I don't know if you're a Starflyer agent or not. If it's going to take a last shot at defeating us, then this would be absolutely perfect. So, read my lips: you are not taking our two most secret weapons into the MorningLightMountain star system by yourself. They are the only guarantees of species survival we've got.'

'I'm not a Starflyer agent,' Ozzie said meekly. 'You can't really think that.'

'You're either a friend of Johansson's like you said, or a Starflyer agent. Those are the only two reasons for stopping the Far Away cargo inspections. Right now, Johansson is out of contact on his way to Far Away, so I can't confirm your story, short of a memory read. I don't want to do that, even if we had the time – which we don't. So for now, I'm doing what any good friend would do, and quarantining you. When Johansson gets back, he'll be able to vouch for you. I'm sorry, Ozzie, but we've learned the hard way just how deep the Starflyer has penetrated our society. I'm even partly to blame for that. I let that son of a bitch Alster fool me, which is going to take some serious piety on my part to recover from. And we both know how hard that will be.'

'You really mean this, don't you, Nige? You're not going to let me go.'

'I can't. If this was reversed, you wouldn't either.'

'Oh man. This is the only chance we've got to save our souls. We can't commit genocide.'

'We have to.'

'Look, will you at least tell the captain to take a flyby of the generator?'

'Sure thing, Ozzie. We'll do that.'

Ozzie knew that tone, Nigel was just humouring him. 'You son of a bitch.'

Nigel stood up. 'You and your friends will stay here until this is settled. I can't give you unisphere access, but if there's anything you want, just ask.'

Ozzie *almost* told him where to stick his hospitality. 'All the data on the generator. I'm going to look at it anyway.'

'Fair enough, Ozzie.'

'And if I find a way of fixing it . . .'

'I'll bend over and you can kick my ass into orbit.'

'Damn right I will. Oh, and Nigel, get the boy a girl, will you? A sweet one, not some fifth-lifer.'

Nigel gave him an irritated glance. 'Do I look like a pimp?'

Ozzie smiled.

'This is only going to take a week,' Nigel said. 'He can wait.'

'Hey, come on man, we could all be dead by then. The kid's never been laid. Now you've gone and flung him in jail. Five star, sure, but it's still the pen. Give him a break.'

'Ozzie—'

'If you can't call out for a hooker, send one of your wives along. They're all about his age anyway.'

'You can't annoy me into doing this.'

'Just do it, Nige, show some humanity here. I'll pick up the tab if it bothers you that much.'

'Whatever.' Nigel went out of the door with a fractious wave of his hand.

'Fuck you very much,' Ozzie shouted after him.

*

Eight hours into the flight to Port Evergreen, and the Carbon Goose passengers were finally starting to relax. There was a general feeling among them now that they might actually make it to the wormhole generator after all. Tail winds had picked up as they crossed the ocean. Wilson had announced their projected flight time was another hour and a quarter at most.

Paula wasn't anything like as optimistic as the others. The Starflyer only needed a five minute lead on them through the wormhole. Even with their reduced flight time, it was going to get close on forty minutes. Apart from a couple of hours spent in a fitful sleep, she'd spent her time reviewing contingency survival plans. There were plenty of scenarios loaded into the avionics, mostly connected with the plane being forced to ditch in the ocean. Given that each Carbon Goose carried emergency food packs, and there were more stores at Shackleton and Port Evergreen, she estimated that they'd have enough to eat for between seventeen to twenty months. It would mean returning to Shackleton where the other planes were parked, but they weren't facing instant doom. Power and warmth were certainly easy enough; the micropiles could supply them with electricity for decades.

She walked back through the top passenger deck, which everyone had settled in. The Guardians regarded her with expressions of suspicion and hostility. Not that it bothered her, open animosity was a near constant companion in her job. Cat's Claws simply ignored her; while the three remaining members of the Paris team smiled warmly as she passed. The stairs at the back of the cabin took her down to the next deck, which had its lights down low. She could just see the horizon through the small circular windows, a fuzzy pink line separating the black ocean from a star-filled sky. Flashes from the neutron star sent a broad livid-blue shimmer across the water, leaving a purple afterimage on her retinas. They were just keeping ahead of the dawn, which was scheduled to catch up with them twenty minutes after they reached Port Evergreen.

Four more sets of stairs and two pressure hatches put her in the lower cargo hold, where all their vehicles were stowed. The turbine noise was loudest here, almost as if there was some kind of combustion engine operating somewhere close by. Even with Wilson turning the heating on full, it was chilly in the big compartment. She zipped up the black and lavender fleece which had been in her CST executive travel pack and walked to the centre where Qatux was spending the journey. They'd managed to find half a dozen emergency heaters, which now ringed the large alien, blowing warm air on its dark-grey hide.

Nobody knew anything about Raiel physiology, so Paula couldn't tell if its occasional shivering was the same reaction which humans had to cold, or a manifestation of its little dependency problem. Two of its smaller tentacles quivered as she approached.

'Paula, you are most welcome,' it sighed hoarsely.

'Thank you.'

Tiger Pansy was sitting on a crate beside Qatux, wearing the contents of two travel packs over her skirt and blouse. For once she'd abandoned her heels to use a pair of boots, then pulled some fur-lined travel slippers on top of them. She still looked miserably cold, her gloved hands cupped round a mug of tomato soup.

Adam and Bradley had also pulled up some crates. Their expressions remained neutral as she sat on the corner of the crate which Tiger Pansy was using. For whatever reason, Bradley had never gone in for reprofiling or genetic modification; he was still maintaining his mid-thirties age, though she'd never been able to track down which rejuvenation clinic he used. A tall man, especially compared to her, his fair hair shaded almost to silver-blond, contrasting with the darkest eyes she'd ever seen. His handsome features rose with a welcoming smile, not in the least triumphant, merely polite. Bradley was genuinely pleased to have her with them, though she would not forget nor forgive the terms that had brought her on board.

Adam couldn't be more different to the founder of the Guardians; much squatter than Bradley's athletically lanky frame, with muscle bulk that had been added since their last confirmed image of him on Velaines. Most of the Paris office would have walked right past him without a flicker of recognition, but after so long Paula could identify his face anywhere no matter what reprofiling he gave himself. Indeed, after so many changes there was now a severe limit on any new alterations. This new rounded face which alluded to youthful middle age was a strong warning against so much economic self-applied cellular reprofiling. His cheeks and chin were leathery, and afflicted with what appeared to be a mild form of eczema. The collar of his semi-organic coat was plagued by strands of dark hair which was dropping out like a radiation victim.

'Shaving must be painful,' she said.

Adam's hand went halfway to his face, before he became conscious of it. 'There are suitable creams, thank you for your concern. You don't look too hot yourself, right now. Travel sick, Investigator?'

'Just tired.'

'Please,' Bradley pleaded.

'I've been assessing our food supplies should we be stuck here,' Paula said. 'We should be all right for some time, but I came to ask what Qatux eats.'

All five of the Raiel's eye-stalks swivelled round in unison to focus on her. 'Your concern is touching, Paula. There is no need for alarm, I will be able to digest human food. I estimate I will consume as much as five human adults per day. With the exception of curry. It does not agree with my digestive process.'

'Hey, me neither,' Tiger Pansy chirped in.

'Are you all right?' Paula asked her. 'I can spell you if you want to sleep.'

'That's real kind. I'm okay, though. I grabbed a few hours in here a while back.'

'Do you and Mr Elvin intend to argue with each other?' Qatux asked. 'You have been adversaries for many years now. I would find such contrary and emotional discourse to be most elating.'

'I'm not looking for a fight,' Paula said stiffly. 'This is a new situation, for both of us.'

Adam looked up at the Raiel. 'The enemy of my enemy is my friend. Old human saying.'

'Do you really set aside old battles so easily?'

'Put it into context with the threat of humanity's extermination, and you'll understand,' Paula said.

'It's kinda sweet,' Tiger Pansy said. 'That we can all just get along, you know.'

'Thank you my dear,' Qatux said. 'That was a most impressive feeling of sympathy, and, I believe, camaraderie.'

'That's why I get the big bucks,' she giggled. 'Not!'

Paula turned to Bradley. 'The good news is that if the Starflyer does close the wormhole behind it, we will be able to survive.'

'You might, my dear, but for me such failure will be worse than death.'

'I understand. I'd like to know now, what exactly are your plans? I might be able to help.'

'Plans,' Bradley murmured sadly. 'I had grand plans, Investigator. Once. Today, things have become somewhat *fluid*. All we can do is hope that our friends on Far Away find some way of preventing the Starflyer from going through the wormhole until we arrive at Port Evergreen. That way we might still manage to corner it and kill it. Dreaming heavens, I cannot believe it has come to this.'

Paula glanced over at the Volvos lurking in the gloom around her, their tops nearly touching the roof of the cargo hold. 'So what are they carrying? What have you been smuggling to Far Away all these years?'

'Don't look at me,' Adam grunted. 'I'm just the hired hand who arranges shipment.'

'Bradley?' Paula asked.

'I had devised a scheme to give the planet its revenge. It requires a great deal of sophisticated force field technology to implement.'

'How does force field technology kill the Starflyer? Do you trap it inside one?'

'Oh no, the planet's revenge is designed to destroy the *Marie Celeste*. I intended to release it when we knew the

Starflyer was on its way back. Without its ship, it will be truly marooned on Far Away. It can't go home, and it can't return to the Commonwealth, we can hunt it down and kill it.'

'So if it does get through the wormhole to Far Away ahead of us, will the Guardians be able to release this revenge scheme?'

'Possibly; though without the equipment we've brought it will be weaker than I would like. And of course the data you and Senator Burnelli retrieved from Kazimir is extremely important.'

'As far as we could determine, it was just meteorological information from Mars.'

'You determined right, my dear. We intend to channel Far Away's weather at the *Marie Celeste*. As well as being extremely effective against that brute machine, it is fitting to give Far Away the chance for retribution. It was the flare bomb released by the *Marie Celeste* which came so close to totally annihilating the entire planetary biosphere.'

'Weather?' Paula frowned. Even she couldn't work out the variables in that puzzle. 'You're going to use the weather against a starship?'

'Yes. Did you know the Halgarth Dynasty commands the lion's share of force field sales in the Commonwealth because of the systems given to them by the Starflyer in the guise of Institute research?'

'I know they're the market leaders, yes.'

'It was inevitable really. The *Marie Celeste* travelled through space at near relativistic velocity for hundreds of years. It had to have superb force fields to survive such a punishing environment. That makes it extremely difficult for us to attack. It would certainly be impervious to fusion bombs, even if we wanted to let them off on Far Away. The kind of modern, sophisticated weapons powerful enough to break the *Marie Celeste*'s force field are essentially impossible to obtain. They are simply not available on the black market. Their manufacture would be even more difficult. The Commonwealth has an effective monitoring network in place for dual-use manufacturing systems, which even Adam would have trouble circumventing.'

'So how do you use weather when our best weapons are ineffective?'

'We generate a superstorm, and use force field derived mechanisms to steer it. Far Away is blessed with a rather unique meteorological system, partly due to its size, partly its geography. A major storm evolves out over the Hondu Ocean every night, and blows in across the Grand Triad. That will become our powerhouse; we have evolved a mechanism to amplify that and direct it onto the *Marie Celeste*. In theory, I should add. Nobody has ever put such an idea into practice before.'

'Mars has storms,' Paula said abruptly. 'Big storms.'

'Well done, Investigator. Mars is subject to planetary storms that last months, sometimes years. It also shares Far Away's low gravity, which makes it the closest match in the Commonwealth. The data we collected there will be invaluable for our control routines.'

'Do you really think you can control the weather?'

'A better description would be to aggravate it and direct it. And yes, we believe it is possible; for a short while at least, and that is all we ask.'

'It will require a phenomenal amount of energy. Even I can see that.'

'Yes. That's taken care of.'

Paula wanted to point out flaws – it seemed such a bizarre notion, not one you should depend on to bring a hundred and thirty year old crusade to its climax – but she didn't know enough about the procedures Johansson had dreamed up. It just had to be taken on faith. 'Assuming you can direct a superstorm, and I'm still sceptical about that, what use will that be against a starship whose force fields can protect it against nuclear weapons?'

'Its size is its downfall,' Bradley said intently. 'We intend to initiate the planet's revenge while the *Marie Celeste* remains on the ground, where it is most vulnerable. The superstorm will be powerful enough to pick it up and fling it to its destruction. And the beauty is, if its force fields are switched on, the surface area they will present to the storm is even larger, while the overall mass remains the same – which makes it even easier for the winds to pick it up and smash it.'

'I see the logic,' Paula said. 'I'm just not convinced about the practicality.'

Johansson slumped down. 'We'll probably never know now.'

'I've been thinking about our arrival at Port Evergreen,' Paula said. 'Do you have any more of those reconnaissance drones?'

'Two in each armoured car,' Adam told her.

'We need to try and launch them when we get within their flight range of Port Evergreen.'

Adam gazed down the length of the cargo hold. 'Should be fun.'

*

They were a hundred kilometres out from Port Evergreen when Wilson took the Carbon Goose down to a kilometre above the water.

'Are you ready?' he asked Adam who was in the armoured car closest to the rear loading ramp.

'Systems engaged. The drones are ready to fly.'

'Stand by: depressurizing.' Wilson's lime-green virtual hands swept across over control symbols.

'No effect on stability,' Oscar reported from the co-pilot's chair.

'Anything on radar?' They'd switched their own radar off now they were close to their destination. If the two Carbon Goose planes the Starflyer had taken were still using their radar, the signals should be detectable.

'Nothing,' Oscar said. 'I guess the Starflyer's planes are down.'

'Damn, I almost want to make a sweep just to find out.'

'This is our only advantage,' Oscar said. 'It doesn't know we're coming.'

'Not much of an advantage.'

'It's the only one in town,' Anna pointed out.

'Okay, let's stick with the plan,' Wilson said. His displays were showing him the lower cargo hold was now pressure equalized. 'Opening the hold doors now,' he told Adam.

They were all bracing themselves for the giant plane to judder. It never happened. The only way Wilson could even tell the doors were opening was through his virtual vision display.

'Launching,' Adam said. 'One away. Wow, that's a tumble. Looking good, the array is pulling it out of the dive. Levelling off. Okay, launching two.'

Wilson closed the doors, then took the Carbon Goose down to three hundred metres. It was as low as he dared go without any sort of radar to check how far they really were above the sea. The altitude should help them get closer to Port Evergreen before they were detected.

Everyone on board accessed the secure signal from the drones as they raced on ahead. Infrared showed a faint outline of the sheer rock island as they closed on Port Evergreen. Brighter, salmon-pink patches glowed above the waterline, nestled in the broad dip in the cliff.

'They're down,' Adam said.

'Plenty of activity there,' Morton said. 'I can see movement.'

'Vehicles, I think,' Paula said. 'The heat is coming from their engines.'

The picture resolution built rapidly as the drones closed in. Both the Carbon Goose planes were easy to distinguish, parked just above the sea, their turbines glowing like small suns. Some way back from the water, the six huts and long temporary accommodation building registered a few degrees above the ambient temperature; while the lone hangar only showed up on the grainy light amplification scan. The curving generator building was an all-over ginger hue, with a shimmer of silver light oozing out through its pressure curtain. Eight large trucks were on the ground just in front of it, their combustion engines on. The drones could even pick up the carbon mon-oxide fumes squirting out of the exhaust pipes. Three of them had heated trailers, big oblong boxes protected by force fields.

'They haven't gone through,' Adam said in astonishment. 'What the hell are they waiting for? They've only got forty minutes left before the wormhole cycle ends.'

'Stig,' Bradley said. 'It has to be. He's stalled them somehow.'

The drones were close enough now to pick out individual humans on the ground. Five people in pressure suits were clustered right in front of the force field. There was a lot of encrypted signal traffic between them and the trucks.

'We've got a chance,' Adam said. 'Wilson, circle us round. Everyone on the drop combat team, stand by.'

Wilson was sure he could hear cheering from the top deck as he altered the Carbon Goose's flight path by a couple of degrees. He felt like joining in. Oscar was grinning sinfully beside him. Anna put her arms round his shoulders and delivered a happy kiss.

A camera in the lower cargo deck showed him ten armoured figures making their way slowly back towards the rear door as it opened again. Cat's Claws and the Paris team were all in the same kind of suit, while the four Guardians who'd joined them were in the best marque aggressor suit available on the black market.

'Rather them than me,' Oscar said. 'Did you access Gore Burnelli's little drop into Park Avenue? That assassin was in bad shape when he hit.'

'The navy suits are up to it,' Wilson said. 'I remember the specs we drew up. And Adam wouldn't let his people take part unless he was confident.'

'Here's hoping.'

Wilson raised their altitude by another hundred and fifty metres. The cliff which surrounded the vast island was over a hundred metres high in places. He'd navigated blind before – *yeah right, three hundred and fifty years ago* – and the golden rule was always give yourself enough leeway in enemy territory. The Carbon Goose avionics had an excellent inertial navigation system, but it was hardly designed with this kind of stunt in mind.

He switched off all the internal lights, including the cockpit. 'One minute till we reach the shoreline,' he told everyone.

Oscar removed the optical limiter from the windscreen, and Wilson switched his retinal inserts to full light amplification. 'I think I see the cliff.'

Red warning icons appeared in the plane's navigation function section.

'It doesn't like where we are,' Oscar growled. 'That makes two of us.'

Wilson's virtual hands moved to disengage the warnings. He'd eliminated three of them when the Carbon Goose's radar switched on. 'Shit!' Its return image swept across half of his virtual vision, splashing a green and purple portrait of the sea and the approaching cliff face. 'Anna, kill the fucking radar. Shoot it if you have to.'

It took her several seconds to shut down the power, then

load a series of restrictions into the ground collision safeguard programs which were monitoring the flight.

'Goddamn it,' Wilson spat as they swept in over the crumpled rock. 'Adam, they know we're here, the son of a bitch autopilot switched on the radar. I'm sorry. Do you want to abort?'

'Not an option,' Morton said. 'Hold her steady, Wilson, we're jumping.'

Wilson pressed his hands hard against the console, putting pressure on the i-spots as if that alone would keep the massive plane on course.

'They've gone,' Adam said. 'Get us the hell out of here.'

Wilson banked the Carbon Goose sharply to starboard, curving them back round to head out to sea again. Behind them, ten armour suits plummeted through the freezing night air at terminal velocity.

*

The baby sneekbot slowly picking its way undetected along the parapet of Market Wall was designed to resemble a cockroach. It worked with five siblings who networked their respective sensor types and relayed the results back to a pack-governor disguised as a rat, which in turn transmitted the data to the operator a safe distance away. They were built by the McSobel clan, who wrapped a plyplastic body around a bioneural array supplied by the Barsoomians. Over eighty of them were scanning First Foot Fall Plaza for the Guardians, providing a reasonably comprehensive image of what the Institute was up to.

As the warm afternoon rolled on they watched the curved rank of parked Range Rover Cruisers in front of the gateway. There were no other vehicles in 3F Plaza. Several squads of Institute troops lounged around in the shade of the awnings set up along the base of the wall, helping themselves to the contents of the abandoned cafés. Just after two o'clock the gateway opened, its pearly force field turning funereal as it exposed the night of Half Way. A couple of people in pressure suits went through.

'Nobody else is moving round there,' Stig said as he reviewed the images. He and Olwen had set up a temporary command post in the Ballard Theatre, two miles east of 3F Plaza. They'd chosen it because it had a glass-walled rooftop restaurant, which gave them an excellent vantage point out across the city. It also made Stig feel exposed. He switched between the sneekbots and simple eyeball observation, looking out at the blimpbots that were circling the city like fat impatient sharks.

On any normal day, someone would have noticed the twenty-two dark shapes keeping their distance as they went round and round in sedate procession at an unusually low altitude. So far no one had called the aerodrome to ask what was happening. People were too busy either staying at home, intimidated by the police patrols escorted by the Institute's Range Rover Cruisers, or causing a lot of trouble for those same patrols. Several crowds had gathered on the larger streets, to fling bottles and stones every time they saw a police car.

The Institute didn't seem to care much, unless anyone started protesting along their clear route out of the city to Highway One, then the troops cracked down hard without any pretence of involving the police. It made it difficult to get the Guardians' snipers into position. Stig was still trying to infiltrate three teams to fix booby traps to the road. The route which the Institute had cleared used the Tangeat Bridge over the Belvoir River. That was his main priority for the booby traps. It was clearly a high-rated concern with whoever was commanding the Institute troops; there were nine Range Rover Cruisers parked on the bridge, their sensors scanning the water below.

'It has to be this cycle,' Olwen said. 'They wouldn't expend this much effort otherwise.'

'Right.' Stig looked out across the rooftops again. Away to the south, another blimpbot was gliding smoothly over Highway One. The faint pink overlay graphic supplied by his virtual vision showed it was one of the six bomb carriers. 'I've got to change that holding pattern. The Institute's going to notice them if they keep flying over Highway One like that.'

Okay,' Olwen said. She knew how pointless it was to argue when his nerves produced that much determination in his voice.

Stig sat at one of the tables and lit a cigarette. He pulled down some smoke then started opening secure links to the blimpbots. Instead of chasing one big circle round Armstrong City, he split them into two groups, and circled one to the east, and one to the west. North, of course, was the sea. If they all clustered out there, they'd certainly be noticed and queried.

It took nearly two hours and eleven cigarettes before he was satisfied they were all locked into their new holding patterns. The wind was starting to blow in from the North Sea, which gave the blimpbots' fans extra work to hold them on course. Stig didn't like the look of the clouds that were scudding in from the horizon; they were getting progressively darker. He knew Armstrong City's weather well enough by now to recognize when it was going to rain.

An hour later, the first drops of water were hitting the restaurant's green-tinted glass. They kept the lights off as the sky darkened outside.

'This could complicate things,' he said. 'Water adds a lot of weight to the blimpbots, they shouldn't fly low altitude in the rain.'

'Keely says there's some big traffic movement along Mantana Avenue,' Olwen said.

Stig's virtual hand pulled sneekbot images from the grid.

They gave him a ground-level view of large wheels rolling past, kicking up a fine spray from the enzyme-bonded concrete. He pulled out an image relayed by a sneekbot that had climbed one of the old maple fur poplars. Two lorries roared past underneath, flanked by Range Rover Cruisers; they were followed by a big MANN lorry, whose trailer carried a long buffed-aluminium capsule, with a clump of sophisticated air-conditioning units on one end. More Cruisers followed it, their mounted guns swivelling from side to side.

'Where did that come from?' Stig asked.

'We don't know,' Keely said. 'They must have parked it in a commercial estate somewhere close.'

'More to the point, what is it?' Olwen said. 'A life support cabin for the Starflyer?'

'Could well be,' Stig said. He was tracking the MANN lorry with the sneekbot's sensors. The curving metal walls of the capsule were reinforced by some kind of bonding field, making it virtually impregnable to any portable weapon the Guardians had. It didn't have any windows. Wisps of steam were rising from the fins of the conditioning units as the rain pattered all over them.

'Movement in 3F,' Keely warned.

Stig hurriedly pulled more images from the grid. Eight people in bulky helmeted environment suits were walking out from the CST management building beside the gateway. They went straight through the pressure curtain.

'This is it,' he announced. 'It's got to be, there's only an hour and a half left in this cycle.' Amazingly, he felt almost nothing, no excitement, no dread. Humanity's most devious enemy was about to arrive on his world, and here he was regarding the moment with cool anticipation. His virtual hand touched the general communication icon. 'Status one, everybody. We think it's coming. Get to your shelter positions, and be ready to move up to engagement point after we hit 3F Plaza.' He stubbed his cigarette out, and settled back in the chair, closing his eyes so he was completely surrounded by his virtual vision. Blue and chrome virtual hands danced across the blimpbot flight command icons as he organized them into their attack formations. He'd been right about the rain, it degraded their performance characteristics, making them even more sluggish than normal. Dangerous in the squally rainstorm. If a gust knocked one off course, it took a longer time than normal to respond and correct itself.

'People are heading back home,' Olwen said. 'Rain makes for a bad protest environment.'

Stig pressed himself up against the glass, looking out towards First Foot Fall Plaza, which rose above the surrounding buildings. 'That might help us. They'll be safer indoors.'

'Will they?'

'Maybe. I don't know. It's comfortable to believe.' His hand tapped the cold thick slab of glass. 'We'd better get out of here.'

Just before they reached the stairs, a lightning flash went off close to shore. Stig saw the blimpbots heading in across the city boundaries. Seen head-on they were big black circles poised above the buildings, seemingly immobile. They were running dark, with their navigation strobes off. It had transformed them; no longer lumbering obsolete throwbacks that drew a smile as their quaint outline slid overhead, they'd obtained a sinister otherworldly appearance as they closed on the overcast human city to deliver their lethal cargo.

'What if it's Adam coming through?' Olwen asked.

'I have to act on the information we've got, however limited. And that lorry wasn't carrying a weapon. It's the Starflyer.'

'If it is, it'll blow the wormhole generator as soon as it's through. We'll be cut off.'

'I know,' he said, wishing he could answer differently.

'Will Adam be following?'

'I don't know. Dreaming heavens! He was supposed to be

here before now, that blockade-busting operation he put together should have worked.'

'So what are you going to do?'

'Carry on with the attack, there's nothing else we can do. If it's Adam on Half Way he'll guess what we're going to do.'

'Adam doesn't know what we have here, what our contingencies are.'

'Johansson does. He was going to join the blockade-busting run.'

'Stig, we have to keep the gateway open. They'll both be trapped on Half Way, and the equipment we need.'

'We might just have enough equipment for the planet's revenge. Not that we'll need it if we can kill the Starflyer today.'

'Long shot,' she exclaimed bitterly. 'Very long shot.'

They went out into the street. Stig activated his force field skeleton suit at level one, establishing a minimum field, and zipped up his leather StPetersburg jacket against the rain. Dark rain clouds were blotting out the sun, bringing a premature twilight to Armstrong City.

He hurried along the deserted street, then took a route along several unlit alleys until they came out on Mantana Avenue just above the government district. Here at least the street lighting worked, casting long yellow-hued reflections off the soaking pavement. Lighting in the shabby old buildings behind the maple fur poplars was intermittent, office windows shining with a pearly-white sheen as their polyphoto strips remained on, illuminating empty desks and conference rooms. Shops along the ground floor were all shut, their carbon mesh shutters pulled down and bolted, dark and lifeless inside. There was no traffic on the road itself. Civicbots rumbled along the gutters, amber strobes flashing as their rotary brushes cleared the litter and leaves away, keeping the drains free.

Stig picked up the pace as the rain intensified, almost jogging. Branches on the maple fur poplars were drooping low over their heads as the woolly leaves soaked up the water. Thick droplets splattered down. Lightning flickered somewhere close to the docks.

'Here we go,' he said as they reached the turning for Arischal Lane. It led to Bazely Square, which on ordinary days was a busy intersection, with a big grassed-over roundabout in the middle. It had wide pedestrian subways running underneath, which were their designated shelter point during the bomb run.

He turned to go, then halted. Lightning flashed again. One of the blimpbots was sliding over the government district at the far end of Mantana Avenue, its black bulk materializing silently out of the grey rain as it headed towards them. Olwen followed his gaze. 'Dreaming heavens, that's low,' she gasped. The keel was barely ten metres above the roofs of the various government office buildings. Given the size of the blimpbot, such a separation distance was insignificant. Water poured from its flanks to drench the red pantiles and solar panelling.

Stig watched it tack round slightly, and begin to fly along the broad thoroughfare. On its final approach, the main ducted fans fore and aft spun up to full thrust. It moved fast, a lot faster than he'd anticipated. The tips of the lofty old maple fur poplars scraped along the blimpbot's fuselage. Cargo doors swung open all the way along its belly.

'Move,' Stig yelled. His overlay graphics told him it wasn't carrying a bomb, but it was going to draw the Institute's attention in a big way. He'd been a fool to stop and gawp like a tourist. Adam would be cursing him.

They sprinted down Arischal Lane as the blimpbot slid gracefully along the avenue behind them. It was audible now, the ducted fans whirring urgently, their pitch shifting as they swivelled constantly to maintain the craft's course against the wind and rain lashing against it. The engine sound was twinned with a coarse ripping noise as the soaking trees along the avenue grated their way along the fuselage.

It eclipsed the entrance to Arischal Lane, a disturbing dark presence dominating the sky. In Stig's virtual vision, it was one of nine which made up the first attack wave. They were closing on 3F Plaza in a loose circle, set to arrive within a four-minute window. Three of them already had cherry-red damage warning symbols blinking bright. They'd all struck something on their flight over the city: chimney stacks, rotundas, trees and masts slicing through the fuselage fabric to buckle and snap the geodesic stress structure. The holes made little noticeable difference to their aerodynamics or speed as they droned onwards relentlessly.

The communications array at the aerodrome reported a burst of calls from the government district and the Governor's House. It replied with a standard reply of *we are forwarding your message for actioning*. More advanced software began to probe the aerodrome's network, searching out current flight files. The routines which the Guardians had installed were deflecting them, and attempting to Trojan their own disruptor virals into the Institute systems.

Stig reached the end of Arischal Lane where there was a subway entrance on the corner of the road. He took the stone steps three at a time, before leaping down to the bottom. Olwen followed with a more nimble jump. They both sped forwards through the lighted concrete passage to the central junction in the middle of the roundabout. It was set out like a small concrete crater, with polyphoto strips high on the walls. Rain poured down from the dismal sky to gurgle away slowly through drain grilles partially blocked by litter and dirt.

Images from the sneekbots showed Stig the Institute troops in 3F Plaza had finally been alerted to the massive airborne invaders heading towards them. Four Land Rover Cruisers drove into a protective arrangement around the MANN lorry and its valuable load, their medium-calibre mounted weaponry ready, small sensor stalks swishing back and forth. The remaining Cruisers were fanning out across 3F Plaza, guns pivoting up to the thick rain clouds, tracking round in search of a target. Troops in flexarmour suits were bounding up the steps on the inside of Market Wall, their long hurdling movements agile in the low gravity. Sneekbots reported an aether thick with encrypted traffic. Scarlet targeting lasers stabbed out, foreshortened in the rain.

'They're strengthening the force field over the gateway,' Keely reported.

'Good. I want it intact. Adam might still get through.' Stig sat down with his back to a wall, trousers in the water trickling along the floor. Olwen knelt down beside him, and gripped his hand. He was glad of the contact. Everything they were dealing with was so remote; his virtual vision display reducing it to the level of some training exercise. 'It's about to begin,' he told everyone over the general band.

*

The blimpbot sailing along Mantana Avenue was the first to arrive at 3F Plaza. It was also the most easily seen as it began to lift higher just before it reached Market Wall. Institute troops who had it in their target sensors opened fire immediately. Ion pulses and kinetic bullets ripped straight through the fuselage fabric, punctured the forward clump of helium cells and streaked out through the upper fuselage. Occasionally, one would strike a carbon-titanium strut in the stress structure, and inflict a modicum of damage. But the geodesic was designed to retain overall integrity under major impact conditions, the load paths simply shifted round fractionally. Overall, it was like shooting a dense patch of air.

The huge blunt curve of the nose glided up over the Enfield entrance. Dispensers fixed into its cargo bays began to fire volley after volley of chaff, flares, and small electronic warfare drones. For a glorious minute, the gloom was completely banished as dazzling white and red stars swarmed over 3F Plaza, trailing thin lines of smoke. Secondary detonations flashed, and silver chaff scintillated across the sky, before sleeting down. Quieter, grey-blue drones zipped about like hummingbirds, impossible to see, sending out powerful disruptive em pulses.

Troops on the wall were firing non-stop into the blimpbot as more and more of it slid out across 3F Plaza. Then the Cruisers on the ground opened up. Someone among the Institute officers had obviously taken charge. The heavier calibre kinetic and maser weapons were directed first at the ducted fans protruding from the fuselage, then the guns worked down the keel where the cargo bays were situated. Creases began to appear in the fuselage as the geodesic structure finally succumbed to the violence. Tears started to multiply, exposing the clustered helium cells strung along the interior, translucent white spheres like wax bubbles.

The second blimpbot arrived at 3F Plaza just as the flares from the first began to splutter out. Several troops shifted their aim, beginning to understand their targeting priorities. Land Rover Cruisers were firing into the cargo holds even as the dispensers began blasting out their ordnance.

Blimpbots three and four arrived simultaneously. By then, number one was sinking rapidly, the rear third of its fuselage twisting savagely as it fell towards the Enfield entrance. Only inertia kept it moving forward as the badly tattered fuselage fabric ripped into fluttering streamers in imitation of black flame. The nose dipped, angling down on one of the plaza's big ornamental fountains. Troops on Market Wall who were still underneath the tail end jumped and sprinted out of the way as its descent accelerated sharply. It crashed over the entrance in elegant slow motion amid a cacophony of snapping and splintering sounds from the geodesic struts as they burst apart. Cruisers and lorries raced away across the plaza as if they'd just been released from a starting grid while the fuselage kept on collapsing, folding in on itself as though some terrible invisible force was intent on squashing the broken craft completely flat. Above it, white and red flares mingled with the rain, to cloak the slippery fuselage fabric in shimmering patterns.

By then blimpbots two and four were also mortally wounded. They started their uncontrollable descent into the plaza. Two was swinging round as its tail disintegrated, popping the helium cells like party balloons, leading to an abrupt loss of buoyancy which pulled the rear half down with alarming speed. Its nose punched into the middle of three, which bent the entire stress structure.

Despite the size and surprise of the attack, the Institute troops and equipment hadn't actually taken any losses. Their vehicles were still careering round the plaza dodging debris as it fell from the sky, and powering away from impact sites. Individual troops were more vulnerable, having to run and jump without any guidance other than looking up – this while maintaining their aggressive firing. So far none of the blimpbots had got near the gateway. A protective ring of Cruisers had drawn up around it, with more skidding into place. The lorries were taking cover in the bigger warehouses and archways along the base of Market Wall.

The firepower from the ground was intense, matching the deluge of flares in lambency. To anyone standing in the middle of the plaza, the rain clouds were almost obliterated from view behind swirls of light and clots of darkness. Into this balletic graveyard of goliath craft, blimpbot number five arrived at high speed, rushing over Market Wall. Seven, eight and nine were already drawing fire from the top of Market Wall as they sped inwards.

'There are bombs in five and eight,' Stig said. He pumped his force field up to full strength, and wrapped his arms over his head. 'Keely, crash the city net.'

Blimpbot five had hauled two thirds of its length over the Plaza when the big cylinder dropped out of its front cargo bay, almost unnoticed in the antagonistic environment which the decoy dispensers had created. It tumbled down for a couple of seconds until it was below the lip of Market Wall, then an explosive charge inside detonated. The cylinder disappeared inside a dense vapour burst of ethylene oxide that looked like a bloated smoke cloud. A second, larger explosion was triggered by the bomb's control array, igniting the cloud.

The fuel-air fireball produced a blast overpressure only slightly less than that of a nuclear weapon.

Stig saw it. He had his eyes closed, and his virtual vision on medium brightness, but the flash still penetrated his eyelids. It corresponded to every sneekbot image vanishing. Several seconds later the sound wave crashed overhead. His arms tightened up as the concrete wall shook.

When he looked up, the sky was dark again, though the rain had gone. He could see curious smears high overhead. Small veiled shapes cruised through the night, as if a flock of bats was fleeing the scene. There were no bats on Far Away. When he stood up he could see a seething column of luminous air swelling upwards from the direction of First Foot Fall Plaza. He realized he'd lost contact with half of the blimpbots in the second wave. A couple that did respond were recording zero-altitude with their helium cells leaking prodigiously.

'Let's go,' he shouted at Olwen. They ran for an exit. 'Keely, I need a sneekbot view of 3F.'

'Doing my best. Dreaming heavens, did that ever work better than we expected.'

Stig reached the stairs up to street level. He came out on the corner of Nottingham Road just as the rain began to sweep back again. His peripheral vision caught something falling above the nearby terrace of houses, something impossibly big, so he turned: 'Holy shit!' He flung his arm round Olwen and carried her down to the pavement.

The mangled rear third of a blimpbot sank silently out of the night to smash into the houses, pulverizing the three directly underneath it. *So where's the rest of it?* Fragmented solar panels, smashed timbers, slates, and long splinters of glass tumbled out of the collapsing rubble to skitter across the road.

'You okay?' he asked.

'Sure, still had my force field on.'

He looked at the fist-sized chunks of stone and jagged struts from the blimpbot's geodesic structure which were scattered around them. They'd been lucky nothing larger had landed near them. He could hear screaming, shouts for help rising in the background.

'We can't stop for them,' he said.

Olwen gave a shaky nod. 'Yeah.'

They started off down Nottingham Road. Images were flicking back up into his virtual vision grid as Keely activated the second tranche of sneekbots which Keely had stowed around 3F Plaza. No matter which ones he pulled out of the grid, all he saw was the rubble they were crawling over.

Six blimpbots had survived. Their status reports were organizing themselves inside his virtual vision. One was effectively dead in the air, unable to move other than where the wind took it. The remaining five had all sustained a lot of damage, but they were mobile, and one of them was a bomb carrier. 'Bingo,' he muttered. 'We might be able to do it again.'

They reached a crossroads, and looked along Levana Walk which gave them a clear view to First Foot Fall Plaza nearly a quarter of a mile away. As Stig intended, Market Wall had deflected the main blastwave upwards, away from the nearby buildings. It hadn't been enough to save the smaller houses in surrounding streets, which had collapsed. Even the larger, sturdier blocks directly outside the plaza had taken considerable damage. Fires were starting to root, burning fiercely amid the wreckage. Market Wall itself was now a thick stone circle of rubble, only two thirds of its original imposing height.

Stig drew in his breath at the sight of it. 'It held,' he murmured. 'Thank the dreaming heavens, it held.' He hadn't wanted to consider the devastation a fuel air bomb would cause if its blastwave had been allowed to spread out horizontally.

'You can't let off another one,' Olwen said. She stood in the centre of the crossroads, looking down each street in turn.

'Huh?'

'Look. Look properly.'

Stig followed her gaze. There were people everywhere. Dazed, weeping, bloodied, wandering helplessly through piles of wreckage, kneeling beside badly injured friends or family who had been pulled out of broken buildings. Cars and vans were strewn across the road, none of them had any glass left intact; their alarms were all squawking furiously, lights flashing for attention, even those that had turned turtle. Rain and melted scraps of blimpbot fuselage fabric had combined into a weird sleet that was slowly and methodically smothering the bereaved landscape under an impenetrable black mantle.

He began to register the expressions around him as the damp ash pattered against his jacket. The tears, the silent rage, and the terrible anguish as people took stock of life which had been irretrievably smashed. There were hundreds just along the sections of road which he could see.

It took every shred of self-discipline he possessed to fight the guilt. 'We have to,' he told her through gritted teeth. 'It'll come through unless we stop it. We don't have anything else left to keep it away.'

'Then find something. Use us, we have weapons.'

He glanced at the ion pistol she was carrying openly, and resisted the impulse to give a derisive laugh. 'Let's assess 3F first, shall we?'

The sneekbots were scuttling their way to the top of the encircling mound that had been Market Wall. It took Stig a moment to make sense of the first images they provided. There was nothing he recognized, no features or outlines. First

Foot Fall Plaza was a true crater now, and completely black on the inside where it had been scorched by the fuel-air bomb. The force field over the gateway had withstood the blast, it was almost buried under fragments of roasted stone, with just a small crescent exposed, looking like milky glass as the rain washed the carbon dust away from it. None of the Institute troops had survived. He couldn't even see any bodies. Their vehicles had vanished as well, including the MANN lorry. He'd expected to see the metallic capsule lying somewhere, battered and overturned, but the sneekbots couldn't detect any electrical or magnetic activity except for the gateway force field itself. First Foot Fall Plaza was a confirmed dead zone.

'It's not going to come through into that,' Olwen said. 'We've got a chance.'

'You're probably right.' Stig checked the time in his virtual vision. 'We've got fifty-five minutes left of this cycle,' he told everyone on the general band. 'Our job is to make it as difficult at possible for the Starflyer to come through. It isn't going to risk itself without an escort on this side, so I want Murdo's and Hanna's teams to dig in here on Market Wall. If anything comes through the gateway, shoot it with the plasma rifles. The rest of us: we're splitting into mobile units. We have to prevent the Institute from getting close to 3F Plaza. Keely will update us on the location of any vehicles. If they look like they're gathering into a convoy we hit them hard.'

*

It wasn't a good omen. Wilson Kime calling over the general band that the radar had given them away, then two seconds later having to jump off the Carbon Goose's loading ramp into pitch darkness. Morton knew they didn't have any choice. Options on this trip had vanished when the wormhole back to Boongate had slammed shut behind them. So he'd shouted out the obvious, and flung himself off. Didn't bother to check if anyone agreed. Supposedly, leading by example was the sign of good leadership, except no one had ever said he was in charge.

The huge plane shot away above him, and he expanded the suit's force field out to fifty metres. His speed braked sharply from air resistance, and he pushed the perimeter out even further, shaping it to a teardrop profile. Sensors showed him the cold rock less than two hundred metres below, and approaching fast. They also revealed nine other armour suits dropping around him.

Thank Christ for that.

Morton had thought – sort of – that he could rely on Rob and The Cat to jump, but the others were unknowns. It was kind of reassuring that they were as committed or as reckless as him.

The base of the force field touched the rock, bowing back up like a sponge to absorb the impact, then folded neatly back around the suit.

'Did you have an encore in mind?' The Cat asked.

'Whatever it is, he's doing it solo,' Rob said.

'Thanks guys.'

'Everyone okay?' Alic asked.

He got a chorus of acknowledgements. They were all down intact. The armour which the four Guardians wore was almost as good as the navy-issue marque.

'Four kilometres that way,' Morton said as they gathered together. 'And thirty-two minutes left until the wormhole closes. How do you want to handle this?' The original hasty plan back in the Carbon Goose while they were suiting up was to creep up on Port Evergreen and sniper any exposed Starflyer agent, then hopefully disable the vehicles it was using before they went through the wormhole.

'Go in stealthed,' Alic said. 'Take out those vehicles before they know what's happening. It has to be in one of them.'

'No way, darling,' The Cat said. 'We're working with a badass timescale here. They know we're here, we know they know, so we go in hot and burn the bastards down.'

'Do it,' Morton said. Once again he just set off, using the suit's electromuscle to sprint hard over the land.

'One day, Morty,' The Cat said on a secure link, 'we're going to have to sort out that little ego problem of yours.'

She was level with him, then slowly pulling ahead. Morton settled for staying five metres behind her, and kept pace.

That was how the ten of them appeared on the top of the slope which led down to Port Evergreen. A line of potent electromagnetic and thermal points sliding up over the rocky horizon, unmistakable, making no attempt at concealment. They paused to assess the layout below, activating their weapons, then began the final advance down the incline.

'What is this?' The Cat sneered. 'Fucking amateur night? Look at that positioning.'

Seventeen Starflyer agents were spread out in a kilometre-wide picket around the generator building. As soon as they sensed the invaders' arrival they began to move like ants rushing to protect the nest. A dozen more hurried out of the vehicles waiting in front of the wormhole to reinforce the line. When the two sides were five hundred metres apart, they opened fire.

Plasma bolts and ion pulses slammed into Morton's force field, ricocheting away without even straining it; their strobing brighter than any flash produced by the planet's neutron star. The shots cast sharp, long shadows around him, swaying dizzyingly across the rock as they clashed and traversed.

'I'll start on the right,' Rob said. 'You guys keep going.' He dropped to his knees. The Starflyer agents were congregating into a pack directly ahead, with even more appearing from Port Evergreen to concentrate their firepower. Rob's hyper-rifle rose smoothly out of its forearm sheath. The first shot cut clean through the Starflyer agent's force field, armour, and body. Tatters of gore created a long splatter-pattern on the rock.

The ease and violence of the kill shocked the other Starflyer agents. Their barrage waned for a moment, then shifted focus to target Rob.

'Little help here,' Rob said. The energy hammering against his force field was shaking him back across the rock. 'Can't get a good lock.'

'Never send a boy . . .' The Cat sighed. Her hyper-rifle deployed, and she took out two Starflyer agents. The rest of the pack immediately split apart with the proficiency of a dance troupe manoeuvre. They went for cover behind rock formations, or wormed their way along narrow clefts. Two scuttled into a pressurized hut, and resumed firing with a heavy calibre plasma rifle. One of the Guardians was knocked back, force field alive with ruby flickers.

Alic's particle lance swung up, and aligned on the hut. He fired. The hut detonated in a burst of silvery splinters and voracious white flame. A mushroom of black smoke boiled up into the dark sky.

'My, that's a big one,' The Cat said. Her hyper-rifle blew a clump of boulders apart, exposing the Starflyer agent using them for cover. She fired again. 'Can you hit the trucks with it?'

'This angle's close to the generator,' Alic said. 'Hang on, I'm going to circle round.'

'Ayub, Matthew, deploy round the generator,' Morton said. 'Flush any hostiles out of there, we can't afford to let them hold it.'

'I'm on it,' Ayub confirmed.

Two powerful plasma shots struck Jim Nwan from a new direction, punching him off his feet. 'One of the shits is in a Carbon Goose,' he said and rolled over into a crouch. The rotary launcher on his arm let out a high pitched *whirr* as the feed tube shook. Enhanced explosive mortars ripped through the Carbon Goose's fuselage, then detonated. The giant plane disintegrated inside a huge gout of glaring electron-blue light.

'Vehicles on the move,' Matthew warned. The eight trucks were crawling forwards, bunching together to combine their force fields. His sensors tracked a pair of human figures running in front of them. They went through the wormhole's pressure curtain.

Alic's particle lance struck the rear truck. Its force field held.

'Alic, flatten the rest of the place,' Morton said.

Another particle lance lashed out at the truck, with no effect. 'The Starflyer's in one of those trucks,' Alic said. 'It has to be. We don't have force fields that strong.'

'They're going to go through,' Morton said. 'When they do, everyone left here will try and kill the generator. Take out the huts and everything else they might shelter behind. Jim, you too. Deny them any cover.'

'All right.'

The first truck was only a couple of metres from the wormhole, its engine revving loudly. Alic started shooting at the remaining huts, blasting them apart. Ayub and Matthew reached the generator building. There was a fast exchange of fire. Matthew released a swarm of sneekbots. Mortars whistled through the air above Port Evergreen. The second Carbon Goose exploded.

A large cylinder telescoped up out of a truck near the back of the line.

'That doesn't look good,' The Cat warned. She fired five shots from her hyper-rifle, each one was defeated by the truck's force field as the cylinder calmly swung round inside the protective dome. 'Rob, synchronize,' she yelled.

The cylinder was swinging towards The Cat. She jumped, the suit's electromuscle powering her ten metres up into the night sky. A vivid white line scored through the air below her kicking feet, striking rock fifty metres away. The massive explosion sent a fountain of lava cascading over a huge area.

'Oh shit,' Jim groaned. 'Here we go. They've got real artillery.'

Morton was having trouble keeping up current events were playing out so fast. The weapon on the truck was swinging round, seeking out a new target. Three Starflyer agents stood in the door of the generator building, exchanging fire with Matthew. Someone came through the wormhole, wearing only an environment suit. Rob shot him with his hyper-rifle, sending body parts squelching back against the pressure curtain. Blood froze fast in Half Way's atmosphere, falling to the ground in a shower of burgundy crystals. The lead truck revved hard, and lurched forwards. Rob and The Cat had interfaced their hyper-rifles, and fired at the truck simultaneously. The force field flashed dangerous crimson as the twin energy beams struck it, then vanished through the wormhole.

'Bastard,' The Cat shrieked. 'Morty, synchronize. Triple hit.'

The truck's heavy duty weapon fired again as Morton's virtual hands flew over icons. Lava erupted where Jim had been standing. His armour suit curved gracefully through the air. Plasma pulses hit him at the top of the arc, sending him flailing backwards through the sluggish jet of glowing molten rock.

Morton's suit array interfaced with Rob and The Cat, putting his hyper-rifle under The Cat's control. Two more trucks had slipped through the wormhole, the others were jostling for position, shoving forwards.

'Which one?' The Cat demanded.

'Choose fast,' Rob replied. 'Not the weapon truck.'

Morton watched targeting graphics zero on the fifth truck. He would have gone for the one at the front, personally. The three hyper-rifles fired in unison. A scarlet corona burst across the truck's force field. A particle lance streaked into it, and for an instant the truck was outlined in perfect clarity. It vaporized in an impressive plume of superheated gas and debris which soared above the rocky inlet. The remaining trucks rocked about wildly as the impulse pummelled their force fields. Another dashed through the wormhole.

The weapon truck braked to a halt. Its deadly cylinder slewing round to point at the generator building. 'Hit the fucker, Cat!' Morton yelled.

Three coincident hyper-rifle shots punctured the force field, and ignited the truck's power cells. The explosion sent armour suits tumbling across the rock, its ferocity overwhelming all the other firefights.

Morton picked himself up. There was no more Port Evergreen. The only structure remaining was the wormhole generator. Where the huts had been, meagre flames guttered in the ruptured foundations. The mounds of wreckage which had been Carbon Goose planes glowed vermilion in patches as they swiftly shed their heat into the freezing air. Rivulets of lava were running downslope to the sea where the Starflyer's weapon had struck rock.

An ion pistol pulse struck the generator building. Four armour suits immediately fired on the Starflyer agent. Morton hurriedly focused on the building's entrance. Last thing he remembered was two Starflyer agents in the doorway holding off Matthew. Blue-white light flared inside, a section of the wall shattered and a broken armour suit flew out through the gash.

'Last one, I think,' Ayub said.

Morton held his breath, and focused his sensors on the wormhole. It was still open. He couldn't bear the tension. If any Starflyer agent was left on this side, they'd destroy the generator. If there was a demolition charge planted, now was when it would go off.

The Cat moved up to stand beside him. 'Eleven minutes left to the end of the cycle. Do we go through?'

'I dunno. Alic?'

'We don't know what's there. Matthew, send something through, grab us some data.'

'Already ahead of you, boss.'

'Okay, everyone else, short range sweep. We need to secure the area.'

Morton reluctantly agreed with the navy commander, and began to scan the ground where his suit array had located the last Starflyer agent.

Five sneekbots were running fast over the scorched ground in front of the generator building. They didn't slow when they reached the pressure curtain. Morton accessed their sensor feeds as he continued his own search through various pieces of wreckage. There was a moment of fuzzy darkness, then they emerged into a universe that was strangely black. The ground was covered in soggy ash. Infrared showed something large directly ahead. A flash of light—

'They're waiting for us,' Jim said.

'Christ, we need the armoured cars for this.' Morton touched the Carbon Goose icon. 'Wilson, get down here fast.'

'On my way. What's happening?'

'We've secured the wormhole, but the bastard slipped through. They're sitting on the other side, and shooting anything that sticks its head through. The armoured cars should give us an edge.'

'That's a bad timescale,' Wilson said.

'Morton,' Adam called. 'Even if we get the armoured cars through, which will be pushing it, we'll be in some kind of fight to clear the area. We don't know how long that'll take, and it's what the Volvos are carrying that is really important here. They have to be safeguarded, and they're simply not going to get through in the ten minutes we've got left.'

'If you don't go through, you'll be giving it a fifteen hour head start. How long will it take to reach its ship?'

'Two to three days, depending on how badly the clan warriors damage Highway One.'

'Then you can't afford fifteen hours.'

'I know.'

Morton's suit sensors showed him an immobile warm patch in a slight hollow. When he inspected it, he found half an armour suit and a large, rapidly cooling shale of blood crystals.

'Sending another sneekbot through,' Matthew announced.

The Carbon Goose was a pink point just above the invisible horizon, still two minutes out. Morton cursed the feeble speed of the great plane. He knew they weren't going to get down in time. The timer in his virtual vision was counting off the seconds. There was only eight and a half minutes left now. He pulled the latest sneekbot image out of his grid. It lasted less than a second.

'What the hell is that black stuff?' Rob asked. 'It's everywhere on the other side.'

'It looks like ash to me,' Matthew said. 'Something bad happened there, very bad.'

Morton finished his sweep. He watched the Carbon Goose swoop low over the water. Its nose tipped up, and the tail touched the surface. Huge fantails of foam shot out on either side and it slowly sank back level, lowering more and more of its belly into the water. He was surprised how short the landing run was.

'Morton,' Adam called, 'we're not going to send the armoured cars through.'

'Damnit.' He looked at the wormhole again. The impulse to sprint straight at it was a strong one. *I wonder if that's how I felt killing Tara? Action is always the solution, it links events, carries you forward.*

'There might be another way,' Adam said.

Morton switched his communication link off. 'It better be good,' he muttered into the muffled silence of his helmet.

While the Carbon Goose sailed sedately towards the shelf of rock which formed Port Evergreen's shore, Morton went and stood in front of the dull grey semicircle. The timer continued to count off seconds. It was like watching his life drain away. He was aware of three other armour suits coming up to stand beside him. They waited in silence.

We should have knocked out the generator ourselves, made the sacrifice. That would have stranded the Starflyer here. We could have killed it then. If it was in one of the trucks.

There were just so many unknowns and variables. Morton hated that.

His timer was seventeen seconds off. The wormhole closed before he expected, the slight glimmer behind the pressure curtain shrinking away unexpectedly early.

'Okay,' he told Adam. 'Let's hear it.'

*

It took the Institute thirty-two minutes to shoot down five of the remaining blimpbots after the fuel air bomb went off. Land Rover Cruisers tore through the streets of Armstrong City in twos and threes, never quite constituting a decent target by themselves. The teams would rendezvous in an open location where they could mass their firepower and slam it into the massive ageing craft coasting above the rooftops.

It was easy enough for Keely to track them. She'd successfully crashed the city's net, forcing the Institute to use encrypted radio. Transmission points were easy to track. Physically following them was more difficult. The streets were packed with people and vehicles; trying to get the injured to hospitals, forming rescue parties to pick through collapsed buildings. Lack of communications was a huge inhibitor. The emergency services had fall-back radio, but they didn't know where the worst areas were. It wasn't just the district around 3F, the blimpbots which had been knocked out of the sky had caused tremendous damage where they crashed. Three of them had started streetblazes.

The Institute troops didn't care about any of the human problems. Their Cruisers drove through crowds and forced ambulances off the street, anyone who got in the way was shot at. When they did succeed in attacking a blimpbot it would fall to ground, causing more deaths and damage.

Stig and the available clan warriors chased round after the Cruisers on bikes where they could. It was difficult; they couldn't go ploughing through crowds. They'd managed to wreck six Cruisers in total, at a cost of nine Guardians. He didn't like the ratio.

'Convoy forming along Mantana Avenue,' Keely warned.

Stig checked his timer. There was eighteen minutes left before the wormhole closed, above him stars were shining through the thinning rain clouds. 'Okay, all mobile units, we'll regroup at the 3F end of Levana Walk. Murdo, Hanna, slow them up as best you can. We'll reinforce you immediately.' He braked the bike he'd commandeered, a Triumph Urban-retro45, and swung it in a sharp turn to head back down Crown Lane. Olwen who was riding shotgun slipped her ion pistols back into their holsters. 'Did they get the bomb carrier?'

'Yeah.' He was busy concentrating on the road, which was littered with debris. Every other vehicle driving that evening was moving fast and swerving to avoid the bigger lumps and branches. It was adding a considerable percentage to the casualties.

Sensor coverage from the sneekbots was sporadic. Keely had left secure routes through the city's network which the Guardians could access, but there had been a lot of physical damage, especially around 3F. Stig was supplied with intermittent images of the vehicles thrusting their way along Mantana Avenue. There were some bulldozers near the front, and a couple of beefy tow trucks.

'Isn't that another of those life-support capsules?' Olwen asked.

Stig risked shifting his focus from the road to his virtual vision grid, and saw an identical MANN rig to the first. 'What do they do, clone those bastards?' A minibus full of injured heading the other way blasted its horn at him, and he throttled back, swaying in close to the pavement. The driver shook his fist as he passed.

'Damnit, we're not going to be in time.' He watched the first Cruisers reach the bottom of the steep rubble slope which had been Market Wall. Their suspension had lowered, lifting the main body a couple of metres above the ground. They didn't even seem to slow down as they tipped up and began climbing the pile.

Hanna's team opened fire as soon as they reached the crown. Gatling cannon and masers replied. Headlights and targeting lasers lashed across the broken inner surface.

The bulldozers were going up in formation, flattening a crude road, shunting aside tonnes of debris with a speed Stig could hardly believe. Their brilliant headlights cut through the late twilight, illuminating the thick clouds of dust they were churning up. More Range Rover Cruisers were speeding up over the broken stone and into the dark heart of the blast zone. They began firing at random out of the cloying dust, strafing the blackened slopes.

'Disengage,' Stig ordered as the tenth Cruiser topped the mound. 'Fall back. Dreaming heavens, you can't hold that many.' They were even losing sneekbots as the Institute's randomized firepower swept round the ruined Plaza.

The bulldozers had carved a roughly level path up to the top of the slope, now they were pushing down the other side. Dense streamers of dust congested the air around them, blurring the light beams. Five more Cruisers raced up after them, jumping the apex to come bouncing down the newly formed ramp. There were over twenty of the Institute vehicles inside the Plaza now, all of them shooting wildly. None of the Guardians was firing back, they were scrabbling desperately for cover. The MANN lorry arrived at the bottom of the incline, and began to grind its way up, eight headlights stabbing up into the occluded night.

'We should have stayed,' Stig said. 'Made our stand there around 3F.'

'We'd have been slaughtered,' Olwen said. 'This is complete desperation on their part. They'll do anything to clear a path for the Starflyer.'

He turned onto Nottingham Road and braked again. It was chaos ahead, with cars and vans wedged together, headlights shining on the partially collapsed buildings. People were working on the ruins, picking stones and bricks off one at a time. A city fire crew were deployed halfway along, their bots crawling up a four-storey house which had somehow twisted itself round through twenty degrees.

'Run,' he said simply.

The Institute Cruisers stopped firing. There were only five functioning sneekbots left in 3F Plaza. They showed the MANN lorry gunning its way down the inner slope in juddering bursts. Five Cruisers were shining their headlights on the gateway's pressure curtain. A group of figures in flexarmour was clearing it, flinging away chunks of debris.

Stig's timer said there were thirteen minutes left until the end of the cycle. For another fuel air bomb he would have signed away his soul.

One of the Institute people walked through the gateway. There were flashes of light on the other side, diffused by the pressure curtain.

Some kind of truck came crashing out through the pressure curtain in a burst of noise and light. Its force field was radiating a bright perilous red. Air brakes shrieked and hissed, tyres skidded across the slippery ash. The mounted weapon on every Cruiser tracked the truck's erratic journey until it came to a halt fifty metres from the gateway. Its engine was racing, snorting like a maddened animal as the red hue faded away. Frost began to form on its bodywork.

Two more identical trucks came racing through. Then brilliant scarlet light stabbed through the pressure curtain, illuminating half of the plaza.

'That's us,' Stig said. 'It's got to be. Adam's on the other side. The Starflyer isn't having it all its own way.'

More trucks were scurrying through, so close together they could have been a train. The Cruisers were forming a broad semicircle round the gateway, every weapon pointed at it. Stig counted eight trucks in total behind them. One was crawling forwards, levelling up beside the MANN lorry. 'Keely, we need a better angle on that lorry,' he said.

'I'll try.'

A couple of the sneekbots began to move. The image was dreadful, jolting about, with dust and drizzle rendering zoom function difficult. A door expanded in the side of the capsule. One of the sneekbots dipped down behind some rubble. That left one. Its camera tried to focus as the back of the truck hinged down, a pale vapour drifted out to vanish amid the swirling dust.

'Dreaming fucking heavens,' Stig said hoarsely. *The Starflyer!* He came to a complete halt, oblivious to the turmoil around him, concentrating on the one inadequate feed. Every headlight in the plaza abruptly switched off. The sneekbot countered the darkness by activating its image amplification mode. Something moved out of the truck's screened interior, surrounded by smaller, human figures. It vanished into the capsule and the door contracted.

Headlights came back on, washing out the sneekbot's images.

'Can you enhance that?' Stig asked breathlessly. When he replayed the image it was completely unclear, simply a patch of shaded pixels. Mobile, though. He thought it rocked as it moved.

'I dunno,' Keely replied. 'I'll shove it through the programs.'

Several Cruisers were powering back up the path the bulldozers had cut through Market Wall. When they reached the top, they opened fire indiscriminately on the street below.

'Bastards,' Olwen exclaimed bitterly. The gunfire was audible where they were, near the end of Nottingham Road.

The MANN lorry started to move, powering its way back up the ramp, thick tyres grinding the rubble flat. Cruisers formed up in front and behind it. They all started off down Mantana Avenue.

'Snipers stand by,' Stig said. 'The Starflyer is on its way out of the city. Keely, alert the teams along Highway One to start wrecking the road. Did we get anyone to the Tangeat Bridge?'

'No.'

He cursed under his breath, very careful not to let any hint of disapproval out into the general band. 'Doesn't matter, there's a lot of other bridges between here and the *Marie Celeste*.'

Stig pulled sneekbot images out of his grid, anxious to see what was happening in 3F Plaza. Two of the trucks and seven Range Rover Cruisers had been left behind by the Institute. All of them had mounted weapons pointing at the gateway. Even as he watched, two violet lasers lashed out at some point on the ground just centimetres from the pressure curtain.

'They're waiting to ambush Adam,' he said. 'Dreaming heavens, we'll have to eliminate them. Adam will be stranded on Far Away if we don't.'

'We don't have time, Stig,' Olwen said. 'We have to get

after the Starflyer. We can't put together a team to get rid of those Cruisers before the end of the cycle. We can't even get to 3F by then.'

Stig checked his timer again: seven minutes. The entire operation was fucked; totally, thoroughly *fucked*. They hadn't stopped the Starflyer. They'd killed hundreds of innocent people and wrecked a good portion of Armstrong City. And now, they couldn't even help their comrades through the wormhole. He couldn't bear the idea of telling Harvey that the vital equipment to complete the planet's revenge would never be coming, that Johansson was left high and dry on Half Way, and that he was responsible for it all. Facing the ambush Cruisers single handed would be preferable.

He realized his clenched fists had risen up of their own accord. A response to the complete futility he felt. 'I'll stay,' he said, and consciously forced his hands down again. 'This is my fault, I'll put a team together and take out the Institute ambush before the wormhole opens again. Everyone else can resume their harassment duty down Highway One.'

'No you don't,' Olwen said. 'Listen to me, and listen hard, you're not falling back into the self-pity routine. We can't afford that luxury. Even if we do manage to knock out the ambush, the wormhole won't open again for another fifteen hours. The Starflyer will have an unbeatable lead by then. We've lost the equipment Adam's bringing. Forget about it, Stig. If it comes through in fifteen hours, it won't make the slightest difference, it'll be too late. We have to take off after the Starflyer with every weapon we've got and run that motherfucker into the ground. We have to do that *now*. And you know it.'

'Yeah,' he said brokenly. 'I know.'

*

A hundred metres from the rock shoreline, the Carbon Goose extended its undercarriage. Wilson throttled back the turbines and let the giant plane slide forward sedately through the water until its nose wheels touched the gently sloping granite shelf. They rose up out of the icy sea with that slow undulation unique to taxiing planes the galaxy over.

Flames were flickering among the debris that used to be Port Evergreen. Wilson had to steer sharply to starboard to avoid the shattered remnants of another Carbon Goose. He could see some of the armour suits moving about across the land, still checking to see if any of the Starflyer's agents were operational. The wormhole generator building looked intact, which he took as a good sign. Adam and Paula had been working something out on the main deck. They'd sounded confident when he spoke to them just before touchdown. It wasn't a combination he would normally put a lot of faith in, but right now he was willing to accept help from any direction.

He and Anna began powering down the flight systems, then went down to join everyone on the main deck. Morton and Alic had come back in, their suits bristling with frost. Even Tiger Pansy had come up from the main cargo deck to witness the conference. Wilson wondered just how much of their worry and nerves she was soaking up for Qatux. It wouldn't be a difficult task, the upper deck was thick with them.

Johansson himself poured some coffee for Alic and Morton. They couldn't sit down, the seats were too small to take their armour.

'We can go through when we want,' Adam said. 'We pick our moment and ram through with the armoured cars. They probably won't even have their weapons switched on right now. The element of surprise is completely on our side.'

Morton flashed him a very sceptical look. 'Go on.'

'The stormrider flies a twenty-hour ellipse through and around the Lagrange point. It spends five hours powering the wormhole while the plasma current pushes it in towards the neutron star, then fifteen hours gliding back into that original position. Right now it's starting its return flight. All we have to do is take control of its guidance system and thrusters, and shove it back into the thick of the plasma current. It can generate enough power for us to open the wormhole.'

'But it probably won't be able to fly back to the Lagrange point again,' Bradley said. 'This will be a one-off attempt. We'll be closing the door on Far Away until a replacement power source can be built here.'

'Given what's happened on Boongate I hardly think that's a consideration for us,' Adam said. 'We must focus on our one opportunity to get to Far Away. This is it.'

'Good idea,' Wilson said. 'Let's do it.'

'Wait one,' Morton said. 'Even if you can hack the guidance system, we still have to face the weapons on the other side. I don't buy this bullshit about switching them off until the start of the next cycle. For a start, if they've got one eye open they'll see the wormhole open up again. They're going to know we'll be busting our balls to find a way to open it. All they have to do is link the guns to a simple sensor. Anybody sticks their head out through the pressure curtain and *zap*. My suit array identified what those trucks were loaded with, you know: neutron-injected atom laser. Are you sure your armoured cars can take that kind of punishment? From one shot, maybe, maybe two, I'll even believe you if you say five. But we don't know what the fuck else is waiting for us on the other side. They can hit us with twenty-five atom lasers simultaneously. They can even nuke us. If we open the wormhole, what's to stop them flinging a fusion bomb through at us? Sentiment? Come on, get real here. It's over.'

'If that's what you believe then you're free to take the

Carbon Goose back to Shackleton,' Bradley said. 'You'll be safe over the ocean when we open the wormhole no matter what happens. But I am going back through.'

'All the Guardians are,' Adam said.

'It's suicide!'

'It *might* be suicide. And that gramme of doubt is all the hope we need.'

'You have a beautiful desperation about you, Bradley Johansson,' Qatux said over the general band. 'It can be as powerful as base emotions in someone as compelled as you. I did not realize this before.'

Wilson couldn't help giving Tiger Pansy a disapproving look. Childish, he knew; none of this was down to her. The woman was chewing her gum, looking almost blithely unaware of what was being discussed around her. He wondered about that; just how naive could a porn star be?

'That sums up most of the people in this passenger deck quite neatly,' Bradley said with a forced smile.

'May I inquire why you do not move the other end of the wormhole to a location on Far Away that does not have your enemies waiting outside?'

Tiger Pansy's expression changed to one of mild surprise. She rose from her seat, looking as though she was being prodded along by someone unsavoury.

Bradley gave her a discomfited stare as she came to stand in front of him, regarding his face with intense curiosity.

'The gateway,' Bradley said hesitantly, 'er, helps anchor the end of a wormhole. It's very, uh, difficult to hold the end open and steady; especially given the distance involved here. The processing power to alter the wormhole coordinate is simply not available at Port Evergreen.'

Tiger Pansy's heavily mascaraed eyes blinked uncertainly; she reached up and touched her fingertips to the side of

Bradley's face, as if she was consoling a lover. The sight of the action made Wilson feel queasy, there was something disturbingly parasitic about it. Bradley didn't flinch.

'I can perform the computations for you,' Qatux said.

15

Mellanie wasn't quite sure what she was expecting as the big screened car turned onto the RueJolei. A burst of nostalgia, maybe? The bustling metropolitan road certainly contained enough memories. It wasn't long ago she would have said they were all good memories.

Today she hunched down in the car's front seat next to Hoshe Finn, and looked up at the sixty-five storey skyscraper at the far end of the road. The golden rapier-blade shape was among the tallest of the skyscrapers that dominated the downtown cityscape of Salamanca. Mellanie remembered the view from the top of it only too well. Alessandra had liked her to be pressed up against the thick window wall of the penthouse as she serviced yet another politician's aide or family friend. Those were the memories which lingered now. She kept reliving them, trying to work out what relevance each piece of information was to the Starflyer.

'Did you ever see her security system display?'

'Huh?' Mellanie pulled herself away from the bitter recollections. For some reason, now she didn't have Dudley to manage, the things she'd done oh so willingly for Alessandra burned ever more shamefully in her mind. 'Sorry, what?'

'Baron's security system? There are a lot of exterior circuits hardwired into the penthouse array. The technical staff were wondering how pervasive it is.'

'I've no idea, Hoshe. She never accessed it on a screen or portal, not in front of me.'

'Okay; we're guessing the approach to the skyscraper is well covered, as well as the building itself.'

'Uh, the SI didn't seem to consider it exceptional, not when I was running away from her.'

'Right, thank you.'

She gave him a small smile. Dear old Hoshe Finn, always approaching every problem with the timidity and caution of a true bureaucrat.

'I'm moving our external perimeter team into place. The arrest squad will enter the building as a service company contracted for maintenance work on an apartment on the sixty-first floor.'

'Can I go up there with them?'

'No. It's dangerous, and you'd hinder operational protocols.'

'I'd wear an armour suit, and I'd stay at the back, promise.'

'No. Our observation team says that at least two other people are in there with her. Until we know otherwise we have to assume they're Starflyer agents, too, and may be wetwired. I'm not going to assign one of the arrest squad to chaperoning you. We need all of them frontlining.'

Mellanie gave an exaggerated sigh. 'When do you have me scheduled to see her, exactly?'

'As soon as the arrest has been performed, and any wet-wired weapons have been neutralized, we'll go up.'

'Paula Myo didn't mind me being up close and very personal with Isabella.'

'That was different. We were taking a risk then; now we're not.'

'All right, but I'm going to get closer to the building. If she puts up a fight, there could be visible weapons activity from the street.'

'We're going to clear civilians directly underneath the building as the arrest squad goes in. Don't get in the way.'

'All right, all right.' Mellanie climbed out of the car, and strolled down the street. It was mid-afternoon, with a large number of pedestrians about. She knew Hoshe wanted to wait until the early hours of the morning, when the situation was more containable, but Nigel and Senator Burnelli had over-ruled him. They were getting quite paranoid about Starflyer agents since Daniel Alster.

She lingered at a boutique window, giving the designer clothes a critical eye. It was automatic, such a normal thing to do. Hoshe had been right, she really ought to start thinking what she was going to do afterwards. The way she was posi-tioned politically right now, she could build herself a show that would rival Michelangelo. And of course, the producers of Baron's show would be needing a replacement in about ten minutes' time. Once upon a time those prospects would have sparked a real fever in her. There was also Morty. That had all changed, too. Not what he'd done, but somehow she couldn't quite see herself as the corporate trophy wife with kids waiting for him to come home after a busy day at the office.

The SI's icon flashed, and expanded into her virtual vision. 'Mellanie, we have a problem.'

She couldn't help glancing up at the penthouse. 'Is she watching? Has she seen me?'

'No. As far as we know, Alessandra Baron is unaware of her imminent arrest.'

'Oh. So what's the problem?'

'Ozzie Isaacs has returned to the Commonwealth.'

'Really? I didn't know that.'

'Are you sure? You are keeping some very interesting company these days.'

'My my, is that a note of jealousy?'

'No. We are simply reminding you we have an arrangement.'

'I go where you can't, and report on things you don't know about. What's new? Are you telling me you don't know what happened on Boongate?'

'We know the Starflyer is on its way back to Far Away. Obviously. What we are uncertain about is what Nigel Sheldon will do next. His Dynasty has developed an astonishingly powerful weapon.'

'He doesn't consult with you, because he doesn't trust you. I'm not sure I do, either. There was a lot more you could have done to help us.'

'We have been through this before, Mellanie.'

'Yeah, yeah, you don't do physical stuff. It doesn't matter any more. This war is about to end. I figure you know that.'

'It is how it will end which concerns us.'

'I don't get it. What's this got to do with Ozzie coming back?'

'He did not finish telling us about what he found before Nigel Sheldon placed him in custody. In order for us to understand the full sequence of events we need the information he has.'

The hairs along Mellanie's spine rose in response to a very cold sensation. 'How unfortunate for you.'

'We would like you to make contact with him, and hopefully provide us with a link.'

'What would you do with the information?'

'We honestly do not know, because we don't know what the information is. Only by looking at the complete picture can we advise the Commonwealth how to proceed.'

'The Executive isn't listening much to you these days, is it?'

'We are sure that Nigel and the others in your elite group have decided to attempt a genocide against MorningLight-Mountain. Suppose there is another way?'

'What way?'

'We do not know. But can you really live with yourself if you did not make at least an attempt to avert genocide?'

'Look, Ozzie would have told Nigel everything.'

'Are you sure? Has Sheldon contacted you and told you that there has been a change of plan? And why is Ozzie being held incommunicado? What is so important about the information that Sheldon doesn't want it to get out?'

Mellanie wanted to stomp her foot in annoyance; she could never win an argument with the SI, it always hit her with logic *and* emotion. 'I've been around Nigel for a couple of days. His Dynasty's security is absolute. I can't bust Ozzie out of jail; come on, get real.'

'We don't think he is in jail. We managed to follow him until he went through to Cressat.'

'Oh brilliant!' Mellanie said out loud. Her fellow pedestrians stared at her. She just glared back at them. 'I suppose I can take a quick pass at the Sheldon Dynasty lifeboats for Paul while I'm there. How's that for luck.'

'The probability of a successful double mission is not high.'

'I'm not even going on one. I'm friends with Nigel now. I trust him.'

'Ozzie took part in the Great Wormhole Heist.'

'The what?'

'Baby Mel, your schooling is truly appalling. The Great Wormhole Heist was the single biggest robbery in human history. Bradley Johansson committed it in order to fund the Guardians of Selfhood; he got away with billions of Earth dollars.'

'You mean Ozzie's a Guardian? I don't believe it.'

'Then ask him yourself.'

'Oh . . .' This time she did stomp her foot.

'If he says yes, you might like to consider our request. He does know who put the barrier around the Dyson Pair.'

'How the hell could I even get to Cressat? Let alone break into his cell? Nigel would be very suspicious if I asked to see Ozzie.'

'Ozzie came back with two companions; a teenage boy, and a previously unknown species of alien. The Sheldon Dynasty has just placed a request with Lady Georgina for a sweet young girl to travel to Cressat where she is to seduce a boy who is sexually inexperienced. The money for this contract was paid to Lady Georgina from the Dynasty's main security division account. That is extremely unusual. We do not believe it to be a coincidence.'

'Who's Lady Georgina?'

'A very high class madam on Augusta. She provides first-life girls to the rich and famous.'

'Urrgh. And you want me to pretend to be that girl?'

'Yes. Lady Georgina has already assigned the contract to Vanora Kingsley, one of her newest recruits. We can substitute you for her, but we must be quick. Kingsley is scheduled to be collected at New Costa station one hundred and forty minutes from now. If you take a maglev express to Augusta immediately, you can just get to the station in time.'

A taxi pulled up next to Mellanie and opened its door. She looked at it and sighed. The sensible thing to do would be to walk away, but it would be exciting to infiltrate Cressat, and get through to Ozzie. Her virtual hand touched Hoshe's icon. 'Something's come up. I'm going back to Darklake City.'

'But . . . the arrest team's already in the lift.'

'Good luck, Hoshe, I'll call you when I get home.'

'I thought you wanted this?'

'I do. And I'm really sorry, but this is more important.'

'What is?'

'I'll call you later, promise.' Mellanie stepped into the taxi, which immediately pulled out into the traffic. 'What's happening to the Kingsley girl?' she asked the SI. 'Do I have to bundle her into a car, or something? I don't think I'd be much good at that kind of thing.'

'We feel Jaycee would disagree, but no. A security professional has been contracted to perform the extraction operation.'

'You're not going to hurt her, are you?'

'Absolutely not. She will be taken to a safe house, where she will be kept under confinement for the duration.'

'Okay. So what does this boy look like, then? I need to know that at least.' A file slid into her virtual vision. When she opened it she was looking at a teenage lad with wild ginger hair and a smile that was half snarl. 'Well, don't expect me to sleep with him,' she said hurriedly. 'Does he even know how to use cutlery?'

'What's wrong with him? Our female aspects concur that he is cute looking.'

She reviewed the image again. 'Maybe. I mean, physically. But you can just see the attitude problem there. He's gotta be a behavioural nightmare.'

'Your area of excellence.'

'Ha fucking ha.'

'Mellanie, you may have to perform the contract's primary requirement. We hope you understand.'

'I've done enough whoring, I think.'

'We are sure the moment of sexual consummation can be delayed long enough for you to assess the situation and try to contact Ozzie. The requirement we were actually referring to is the contract's personality stipulation. It is a strong one. That is why Lady Georgina selected Kingsley.'

'What stipulation?'

'That the girl be: sweet.'

'Hey! I can do *sweet*, all right? Don't give me that crap.'

'Very well, Mellanie. If you say so.'

*

Once again, Wilson Kime waited to set foot on a new world. He stood in front of the gateway as dawn rose above Half Way, flooding the barren rock island with red light and intense blue-white flashes. In the generator building behind the gateway, power was starting to feed in from the stormrider.

He tried not to feel too smug about it, but with his knowledge of astroengineering and orbital mechanics, the technical types in Adam's team had automatically deferred to him. It had taken him twenty minutes at the console in the generator building, mapping out the Stormrider's primary systems and guidance programs, before he sent up the first batch of instructions. His virtual vision produced a basic flight profile display, with a long curving white line designating the Stormrider's course as it flew around its perpetual loop. Within ten minutes of his instructions being accepted by the on-board array a new purple line appeared, short and blunt, showing the diversion he'd charted back into the plasma current. The massive machine had crept along it for nearly an hour as the plasma concentration increased around it.

Forty million kilometres above his head, the gigantic blades were spinning again as the Stormrider slid back into the gale of charged particles. Wilson's virtual vision display showed him the vast, yet surprisingly fragile, machine's velocity increase as it was blown irretrievably in towards the neutron star. 'It's falling like Icarus now,' he said as Oscar walked over to stand beside him. 'Wings spread wide, and way too close to the sun.'

'You're taking a few liberties there,' Oscar said. 'But I do like the imagery.'

'How's Qatux coming on? Is he going to manage the wormhole?' Wilson checked the Stormrider's status in his virtual vision; so far everything was holding steady as its power output built rapidly.

'Your guess is as good as mine. I worked in the exploration division, remember? That makes me very familiar with the kind of large arrays you need to manipulate exotic matter. There's a limit to what flesh and blood can achieve, even very smart alien flesh and blood. Our Raiel might just be claiming this to influence our emotional state.'

'MorningLightMountain controls all its wormholes by direct neural routines.'

'And that's another thing, did anyone back at your super-secret revolutionary council actually verify this Bose motile creature was the genuine article?'

'Stop being such a paranoid grump.'

'First rule of being a lawyer, don't ask the witness a question when you know you don't like the answer.'

'Well here comes the answer. Qatux has finished the power-up sequence.'

Ayub had parked the Volvo containing the Raiel close to the generator building's door. The big alien had then been linked to the generator's controlling array via thick bundles of fibre optic cable which it had attached to the heavy tips of the flaccid flesh stems behind its tentacles. It was an arrangement which reminded Wilson of hotwiring a car.

He started his level breathing exercise as his heart rate sped up, glad that Tiger Pansy wasn't around to sense his anxiety. The wormhole opened as smoothly as an iris exposed to the night.

'It's through to somewhere,' Adam declared.

'Matthew, send a sneekbot through,' Alic said.

One of the little bots scampered through the pressure curtain. Wilson hooked himself onto its feed, and saw a darkened landscape unfold. There was damp ground below the artificial rodent's feet, ragged blades of grass snagging at its sleek body. Arching fronds of tall plants waved in the distance, and there were darker patches of trees. It hurried ten metres away from the wormhole, then raised itself up on its hind legs and scanned round. There were no heat sources within range, no electromagnetic emission points, no visible spectrum light; the only detectable motion was a persistent wind that was heavy with moisture, the tail end of rain.

'It certainly hasn't come out in the city,' Adam said.

'Could be a city park,' Rosamund said.

'Doubtful. There's no node carrier signal registering,' Johansson said. 'Even dear old Armstrong City has a complete net coverage.'

'All right, we're going through,' Adam said.

Wilson heard Jamas revving the armoured car's engine, and hurriedly stepped to one side. The low curving vehicle lumbered forward and slipped through the pressure curtain.

'Still intact,' Adam said. 'Definitely countryside, no city visible. No, wait, I can see something on the horizon. Orange light haze. There's some kind of settlement over there. Quite a big one, I guess.'

'It should be Armstrong City,' Qatux said. 'I believe the wormhole to have emerged twenty kilometres to the south west of its southern boundary. That was my intention.'

'That should put us in Schweickart Park,' Jamas said. 'I recognize the constellations. Dreaming heavens, it's definitely Far Away. I'm home!'

'Running active sensor scan,' Adam said. 'It looks clear to me. Bradley, if there's anything out here bigger than a rabbit, it's stealthed perfectly.'

'Thank you, Adam,' Bradley said. 'Let's go through people, quickly, please.'

The remaining armoured cars and Volvo lorries started their engines.

'Come on,' Wilson said. He moved forward, feeling the pressure curtain brush against his armour suit like a gentle breeze as the red light faded out around him. And for the second time in his life, Wilson Kime arrived on an alien planet with a single giant step. Gravity fell away sharply. He wasn't used to that, not on the CST train network; most H-congruous planets were close to Earth-standard gravity and you never really noticed the transition.

One of the Volvos hooted its horn loudly behind him, and he hopped aside. The movement sent him a good half metre into the air. He laughed as he sank down onto the ground again. His virtual hand keyed the suit unlock, and the helmet visor swung up. He sucked down native air, strong with the scent of recent rain and a hint of pine. 'They could have done it,' he said wonderingly. 'They really could.'

'Who?' Anna said. She dropped down off the back of a Volvo, gingerly holding her arms out for balance.

'The Aries Underground; they wanted to terraform Mars. It would have developed into something like this if they'd ever had their chance.'

'Do you ever stop thinking about Mars?' she asked.

'Not enough atmosphere on Mars to make it H-congruous,' Oscar said. He didn't sound impressed.

'They had schemes to compensate for that. Hauling in ice from the cometary belt; genemodified bacteria liberating oxygen from the soil, orbital mirrors, transmantle boreholes.'

'Sounds expensive.'

'Planets were in those days,' Wilson told him sagely.

The Volvo carrying Qatux drove slowly through the wormhole, trailing its thick bundle of fibre-optic cable behind. Two people in armour suits emerged from the wormhole behind the lorry, making sure the cable didn't get snagged.

'Everyone through, sir,' Kieran reported.

'Thank you,' Bradley said. 'Qatux, we don't need the wormhole any more.'

Wilson just had time for one final review of the stormrider before the wormhole closed. Like Icarus, its fate was now sealed; the thick current of plasma had pushed it a long way past the Lagrange point, its depleted thrusters no longer had the delta-V reserve to fly it back around. All that remained was the long, leisurely fall to oblivion in the neutron star's awesome gravity.

The wormhole shrank away to nothing, its final closure sheering off the fibre optic bundle which fell back to the ground like a mortally wounded snake. The act of severance reinforced Wilson's feeling of remoteness; they were truly on their own now. Judging by the silence he wasn't alone with that thought.

'I don't have much to say to you,' Bradley announced. 'Which is just as well, for we are desperately short of time now. But I'd like to thank our non-Guardian friends for coming with us, and believing in us at the end. For those of you whose ancestors have been with me since the beginning, I would express my gratitude to them for their terrible and frequent sacrifices, it is their blood which has delivered us to this place at this time. As a consequence, the Guardians of Selfhood will be thanked by the rest of humanity for all we have endured so that our species can be free at last.'

Wilson glanced round, seeing all the Guardians who had come with them lowering their heads in respect. He joined in, more troubled than he liked to acknowledge by Bradley's words. History would show the Guardians in a very different light from now on.

'As this is our time, let's not waste any more of it,' Bradley said. 'Ayub, would you try and contact the clans, please, quick as you can.'

*

'Stig!' Keely yelled. 'Stig, I'm picking up something on the short wave! It's our frequency.'

Stig leant forwards, frowning. It was dark in the back of the Mazda Volta 4x4, a refuge where he could brood unseen. The little convoy of Guardians vehicles, five cars and seven of the lightly armoured Voltas, had taken almost an hour to drive through the disturbed, damaged city. All the while he'd been picking up reports from the Guardians covering the Starflyer's exit route. Their various attempts to strike the big MANN lorry had come to nothing. The Starflyer's vehicles had good armour, and even better force fields. They also responded to any attack with extreme force. Over a dozen buildings harbouring Guardians snipers had been reduced to smouldering rubble.

It had taken the Starflyer's convoy less than thirty minutes to travel from 3F Plaza to the start of Highway One. Over two dozen additional Range Rover Cruisers had joined it, speeding out of side streets to join the convoy. With that much firepower available to the Starflyer, Stig had no choice but to order the rest of the snipers to stand down. They would have been slaughtered if they'd tried anything.

Stig's own pursuit had been frustratingly slow, as they waited for other Guardians teams to join with them, taking a route parallel to the Starflyer out of the city. Of course, the civic emergency services were starting to respond to the disaster as best they could by then, which pushed more people and vehicles out onto the roads Stig wanted to use. They'd eventually reached Highway One an hour later only to find the Starflyer convoy had scattered sophisticated mines behind them. The first one had taken out a Ford Shanghi, killing the five Guardians inside. After that, Stig had to order them to drive along the side of the road, avoiding the broad strip of enzyme-bonded concrete, which cut their speed still further.

'Who's calling us?' Stig asked. He couldn't think of any other Guardians groups operating round Armstrong City.

Keely's smile was incredulous. 'Bradley Johansson.'

'Not possible,' Stig said curtly, even as his virtual hands snatched the signal out of Keely's specialist radio array.

'. . . rendezvous point four,' Bradley's familiar voice was saying. 'We should be there in twenty minutes.'

'Who is this?' Stig demanded.

'Ah, that sounds like you, Stig.'

'Sir?'

'Hey, Stig,' Adam said. 'Good to hear from you, lad.'

'Dreaming heavens, you can't be here.'

'I understand. After you were blown at LA Galactic, you finished up at our Venice safe house. Kazimir was assigned to bring you in.'

'Adam?'

'In the flesh, thankfully. We had a little trouble getting here, I don't mind saying.'

'How? How can you be here?'

'This isn't a secure call, Stig, I'll tell you in a little while at rendezvous point four. Bradley tells me you ought to know where that is.'

'Yes, of course.'

'So if we're the real deal, we'll see you there.'

*

Rendezvous point four was a drainage pumping station half a mile off the side of Highway One, thirty-eight miles outside Armstrong City. There was a service track leading to it, which was unsigned. The station itself was around the back of a small hill, completely out of sight from Highway One.

Stig drove the Mazda Volta himself, ordering everyone else to wait back at the turn-off. As soon as he rounded the bend, he saw the big vehicles parked there, their headlights cutting bright beams through the night. Familiar figures were walking towards him as he parked, smiling broadly. He stumbled out, still not quite believing. Adam caught him in a bear hug.

'Good to see you, lad,' Adam said gruffly.

'Dreaming heavens, we thought you were stuck back there.'

'Hey! You should know, it's not that easy to keep me penned up.'

'Yeah, but . . .' Stig broke off as Bradley appeared. 'Sir!'

'Good to see you, Stig.'

Stig put his hand out in welcome. Then everything went

wrong. Moving between the bright beams of light was a woman in a simple fleece and trousers. She had her shoulders hunched, shivering as if she'd got a cold. Then she sneezed, and her dark hair swirled fluidly in Far Away's gravity. Stig would never forget that elegant, deadly face, not even in the peace of the dreaming heavens. 'Look out!' he yelled. His hand went for his holster. He managed to get a machine pistol out, and swung it round.

Adam stood in front of him, an arm chopping round to push Stig's weapon away. 'Stop!'

Stig stumbled back a pace. Both Bradley and Adam were holding their hands up in admonishment. Several of the other people standing outside the vehicles, whom Stig didn't know, were tensed up.

'That's Paula Myo,' he yelled.

'Good evening,' she said calmly, then shivered again, and pulled her fleece tighter, arms crossed in front of her chest.

'But—'

'We have allies now,' Bradley said. There was no trace of mockery in his voice.

'Paula Myo?'

'Among others, such as Nigel Sheldon, oh, and I'm sure you remember Admiral Kime.'

Wilson stepped forward. 'That's actually, ex-Admiral, now. Pleased to meet you, Stig.'

'Uh.' Stig's pistol hung limply at his side.

'Oh yes,' Adam said, and the shadows made it difficult to see if that was a smirk on his face. 'I almost forgot: Mellanie says to say hello.'

Stig couldn't help it. He leaned a little closer, just to be sure. 'Paula Myo?'

'The very same,' Bradley said. 'Come now, Stig, tell me what the situation is.'

Stig allowed himself to be led over to the cluster of vehicles. Just as he started to tell Bradley about using a fuel-air bomb he looked over his shoulder to check again. Paula Myo was hugging her chest quite tightly, as if she was in pain; a concerned-looking Wilson Kime was asking if she was all right. Somehow, seeing her on Far Away was more extraordinary than his blurred glimpse of the Starflyer itself.

*

Adam and Bradley made their plans quickly as Stig explained what had happened at First Foot Fall Plaza. The three Volvo lorries with their precious cargo for the planet's revenge project would immediately head due south for the Dessault Mountains to rendezvous with the technical teams assembling the wind stations. Adam would head the group, taking Kieran, Rosamund, and Jamas with him to drive, despite their eagerness to join the fray pursuing the Starflyer. Paula announced she would accompany Adam, which he greeted without comment. Wilson, Anna and Oscar agreed to stay with Paula, and see if they could help with the technical aspects of the planet's revenge. Privately, Wilson was growing concerned about how unwell the Investigator appeared.

Bradley was going to lead the rest in pursuit of the Starflyer, spearheading it with all three armoured cars. Cat's Claws and the Paris team signed up to go with him. Both he and Stig thought their combat experience and weaponry would give the Guardians a significant advantage over the more lightly armoured Institute troops.

That just left them with Qatux. Tiger Pansy had listened and watched without comment as the two teams were sorted out. Now she said: 'We should go with Bradley.'

'If you wish,' Bradley said.

'Sure do,' Tiger Pansy agreed enthusiastically. 'Starflyer's pulling ahead of you. That makes for a tough chase, and when you do catch up, there's going to be a big fight. You Guardians guys, you're gonna go berserk, you're all so committed and inspired; it's like a religion. Qatux really digs that. This is where the human heat is at, so we stick with it.' She glanced over at Adam. 'No offence.'

'You do understand, dear lady, we cannot guarantee your personal safety in this fight?' Bradley said.

Tiger Pansy chewed her gum for a moment before pulling a long face. 'Yeah, I figure that. But face it, I ain't got much of a life to lose, here, do I? Mellanie got me to update my secure store before we left; I just edited most of this time around out of it.'

'Each and every human life is priceless.'

'You're really cute, you know that.'

*

It was one of those mornings where Mark hadn't fully woken up, that moment of cosy drowsiness when you're in a warm bed with the woman you love lying snuggled up against you. He moved his head fractionally, nuzzling Liz fondly. She pressed herself closer to him, then they kissed in a languid unhurried fashion. Hands stroked. He began to pull off his T-shirt. Liz rose up to straddle him, still wearing her negligee, the new one of semi-organic fabric that mimicked black silk. She'd worn it every evening since he returned. The way it grew translucent as her body heated and her movements became more urgent was a *huge* turn-on for him. She'd exploited that to the full last night, which was why he was so drowsy as dawn broke.

The enormously erotic sight of his wife's delectable body straining athletically above him was wiped out by an orgasm that he was sure had an accompaniment from a choir of angels.

'It's true,' he mumbled into the darkness some time later. 'Too much does make you blind.'

Close by, Liz giggled. Mark's sight returned to show her lifting the T-shirt from his face. He smiled up at her in perfect contentment.

'Morning,' she said, in a very appreciative tone.

'Morning.'

Her fingers played along his lips. 'I think you're getting younger, I can barely cope with you like this any more.'

Mark grinned complacently; though he wasn't sure he could actually manage to do it again without some serious recuperation time first. The thing with Liz was that she really was as tremendously horny as she looked; and how many men could boast about a wife like that? 'Takes two,' he assured her.

She gave him a quick kiss, and rolled off the bed. 'I'd better go fix the kids some breakfast; the school will be wondering why I keep sending them in starving every day.'

'Right.' He was almost regretful. It would be nice to spend a whole day just lounging around in bed together. They hadn't done that since Barry was taken out of the womb-tank.

He took a while in the shower, then got dressed and ready for work. The CST corporate-mauve sweatshirt with yellow sleeves went on easily enough; his green-gold trousers were a size bigger than he had worn back in the Ulon Valley, and they had a stretch-fabric waistline, too. Mark looked down at the way a small wave of his gut hung over the trousers. *Must do something about that.*

As if he ever got the time any more. If anything, his daily schedule had become even busier as soon as the *Searcher* had returned.

Sandy let out a happy squeal as he walked into the kitchen. She abandoned her boiled egg to run over and fling her arms round his waist. 'Daddy! Daddy!'

He stroked her hair and kissed the top of her head. 'Hey, morning there, darling.'

'Hi, Dad.' Barry's eyes were bright with admiration.

Sandy wouldn't let go. Mark had to take her back to the table and sit beside her before she'd consider eating any more of her egg. 'We didn't come in to your bedroom this morning,' she said, her eyes big and serious. 'That was right, wasn't it?

Mommy said we should leave the two of you alone; that you need a lot of grown-up's sleep to make up for being so tired after saving us all.'

'Uh, yeah, that's right. Thank you, darling. It wasn't just me that helped the *Charybdis* mission though.'

Barry smirked at his sister. 'Grown-up sleep. Baby!'

'What?' Sandy asked with a hurt expression.

'You're so dumb. Don't you know what they were doing?'

'What?'

'Enough, both of you,' Liz said firmly. 'Let your father eat his breakfast in peace.' She had a demure smile on her face as she put his breakfast plate in front of him.

'Thank you, Mrs Vernon.'

'My pleasure, Mr Vernon.'

Mark tucked in to his eggs, bacon, waffles, sausages, and tomatoes. A side plate of pancakes drowning in maple syrup, and topped with strawberries and a cone of whipped cream, was placed next to the big plate.

'To keep your strength up,' Liz said enigmatically.

'Yuk.' Barry pulled a face.

Mark tried hard not to smile.

Otis Sheldon turned up just as Mark was finishing. Panda barked happily as the pilot walked into the sunny kitchen.

'Otis!' Barry cried happily, and ran over. 'Take me up to the assembly platform today. Please! *Please!* Dad keeps promising he will, but he never does.'

'Your father's the man to ask. He's in charge up there.'

'Daddy!' Sandy smiled worshipfully.

'Hi, Liz.' Otis gave her a quick peck on the cheek.

'Sit down. Need some coffee?'

'Thanks. Maybe a half cup.'

'What can we do for you?'

'Just giving Mark a lift out to the platform wormhole.' He glanced at Mark. 'Did you check your message hold file?'

'Er, no.' Mark reached out with a black and gold virtual

hand and removed the zero-access restriction. He'd closed it up last night to give himself some uninterrupted privacy. A priority one file was sitting in his folder; sent from Nigel Sheldon. *Oh Christ.* 'Thanks, Otis,' he said sheepishly.

A maidbot delivered a cup of coffee to Otis. Mark reviewed the message, and groaned in mild dismay. 'You've only just got back.'

Otis shrugged good naturedly. 'That's the job.'

'What's happening, boys?' Liz asked.

'Another flight,' Mark said.

'And Dad's getting impatient,' Otis said.

'That's got to be the . . .' She trailed off, giving the two children a guilty glance.

'What is it?' Barry demanded.

'It is,' Mark told her.

'Oh, hellfire. You be careful,' she told Otis.

'You betcha.'

*

Otis drove Mark the short distance over to the wormhole which led up to the cluster of orbital assembly platforms. He had an antique Daimler coupé convertible, which was kept in immaculate condition. It was powered by a combustion engine. Mark wasn't sure if it had a driver array, not that it mattered with Otis behind the wheel – the man's reflexes were incredible.

'Have you talked to Nigel?' Mark asked after he tightened his seat belt as far as it would go.

'Yeah, minor conference on Cressat last night. Apparently, the Dynasty now officially believes the Starflyer is behind the war.'

That took Mark a moment to digest. 'You're kidding?'

'No. Classified, okay? Daniel Alster was one of its agents. Dad was seriously not pleased. The Starflyer used Alster to break through to Boongate; it's on its way back to Far Away as we speak. So we're also sending a frigate there, just in case it tries to escape in the *Marie Celeste*.'

'Holy shit. How many frigates does Nigel want active?'

'Leading question. Minimum of three to Dyson Alpha, and we'd like two to visit Far Away. Although there was talk of sending the *Searcher* there instead. A lot of important people joined up with the Guardians, and are now cut off from the Commonwealth.'

'You did tell him we haven't got five assembled yet, didn't you?' Mark said nervously.

'He knows our status. There's also a minor supply problem with nova bombs. We don't have many, yet.'

'But, Otis, we haven't finished incorporating our procedures into the frigate assembly systems. We were looking for another week before the Dyson Alpha mission. Even the *Scylla* won't be ready for vacuum for another two days.'

'Don't be so modest. You've got four completed and another six in assembly.'

'Yes, but they haven't been level-two tested yet, let alone flight tested. We held the *Charybdis* together with sticky tape and luck. You can't keep flying frigates in that state, they've got to be integrated properly; anything else is going to prove fatal, and I don't just mean in the long term.'

'I know; more than anybody. I'm the one who has to fly the damn things, remember. Pull in whoever you need, Giselle will coordinate personnel requests for you so you'll be free to concentrate on the engineering.'

'Huh!' Mark exclaimed, unimpressed, as they pulled into the gateway building's parking lot. 'I'd like to take the entire design team up there for a start. Maybe they'll finally learn the difference between theory and practice.'

Otis grinned. 'Designers and engineers, may the two never meet.'

'I'll do everything I can, you know that.'

'I know, Mark. We all do.'

*

At night, stuck in the Volvo's forward passenger seat while Rosamund drove them southwards across the Aldrin Plains, Adam could see no difference to this and any normal Commonwealth H-congruous world. The low gravity wasn't noticeable, except when they hit the odd bump in the road, when the lorry performed a shallow glide back down. Farmland was more or less the same everywhere and, this close to the capital city, the land was nothing else, with broad fields and big swathes of woodland stretching out into the dark beyond his inserts' ability to resolve. It was the absence of a planetary cybersphere which gave him the biggest sense of separation from the worlds he knew. All they had for communication here were some arrays with a short-wave capability. Not, as he was the first to admit, that there was anyone else to call on this forsaken planet. The lack of information was hard to endure, though.

At least he had a degree of solitude to enjoy. He'd been worried that Paula would insist on joining him in whatever vehicle he rode in. Instead, she was in the second lorry with Oscar, while Kieran drove. In what was undoubtedly the last miracle of the day, Adam actually found himself concerned for her. Whatever flu-variant virus she'd picked up was obviously affecting her badly. It was unusual for anyone these days to be brought low by such a simple illness, which implied it might be extraterrestrial. There hadn't been an alien plague case for thirty years, since the Hokoth measles epidemic. For the Commonwealth to suffer one now would be badly ironic.

He told himself he was concerned mainly because she might be a carrier and give the bug to him and the others. She'd done her best to shrug it off, but he'd seen the sheen of sweat on her brow, the long uncontrollable shivers running along her limbs. It had come on quickly. She'd shown no symptoms back in the Carbon Goose where they'd talked through tactics for the landing at Port Evergreen. That had been a surreal moment, sitting down with Paula Myo, drinking tea together as they formulated the best strategy, both pooling their knowledge and experience without reservations – at least on his part. All the while, that little speech she'd given him back at Narrabri station was running through his mind. She could probably see it in his brain he was thinking it so hard.

After that she'd more or less dropped below his worry radar as they pushed through to Far Away and met up with the Guardians. He gently assumed that once they'd delivered their precious cargo to the waiting Guardians in the Dessault Mountains he'd wander off into the sunset while his friends prevented her from following – then he'd live out a quiet retirement on some farm for the remainder of his years. Except the only way that would happen was if someone killed her. Even then her re-life version would appear on the horizon sooner or later. The reality was that this crazy Sicilian-style battle to the death they'd got going between them could only truly end with *his* death. Besides, he knew damn well he couldn't spend more than a couple of hours on a farm without getting bored out of his skull. He'd have to return to the Commonwealth and go on the run again. Strangely, the prospect wasn't as depressing as it first seemed.

Somewhere amid the constant low-level growl of engine noise a nasty metallic grinding sound was breaking out. Adam looked around in alarm. It was so loud he thought it must be coming from their lorry. Rosamund was already braking smoothly.

'I've got a problem,' Kieran called on the general band.

By the time Rosamund had reversed up close to the second lorry, Kieran was filling the band with some filthy language but no real information. Adam climbed down out of the cab and walked back. The road they were using was the main route linking this region's market towns to the city; originally it had an enzyme-bonded concrete surface, but that was steadily shrinking from an onslaught of earth and weeds, while cracks and potholes went unrepaired for decades. Nowadays it resembled a simple much-used dirt track with congested drainage ditches on both sides. Adam was already entertaining serious doubts about how long it would take them to reach the mountains, and this was a good infrastructure for Far Away. According to the so-called maps stored in his inserts, the roads vanished altogether another hundred miles south where the Aldrin Plain became a sea of uninhabited grasslands.

'What's happened?' he shouted.

Some kind of thick vapour was swirling across the Volvo's headlight beams. Kieran strode through it, a furious expression on his angular gaunt face. He hit the release handle on one of the engine covers, and it folded back. Flame belched out into the night.

Kieran ducked back, shielding his face with his hands. 'Dreaming heavens!' His voice was ripe with pain.

Oscar jumped down from the cab, and rushed forward with a slim fire extinguisher. He directed the powerful stream of ice-blue gel particles over the burning machinery, smothering the fire in seconds.

Kieran was wincing as he gripped his hand.

'Let me see,' Adam demanded.

His flesh was red; blisters were already starting to rise. Wilson had brought a first aid kit from their lorry's cab; he started applying some salve.

Oscar gave the engine another couple of blasts from the fire extinguisher. 'It's out, but we're screwed,' he said as he peered into the smouldering mangle of metal. 'You're not going to get this repaired outside a garage, and probably not even there. Trust me, I know engines, this is just scrap now.'

Adam shot Jamas a look that was mostly accusation, even

though he knew it was neither professional nor fair. But Jamas had been in charge of organizing their ground transport.

'They were in perfect working order when we loaded them up on Wessex,' Jamas said defensively. 'I took them for servicing at the dealer myself.'

'I know,' Adam said. 'Breakdowns happen. It's a royal pain in the arse that it happened now, but don't worry. We've got enough room in the other two Volvos to carry on.'

They worked swiftly in the headlight beams of the lorries. Adam was more than a little conscious of how visible they were in the middle of the open lightless farmland. *Out beyond the light of the campfire, the wolves begin to gather unseen.* The force fields were off, which added to the sensation of vulnerability. He was grateful that all three of the Volvos carried trolleybots, which began unloading the pearl-white crates down from Kieran's wrecked lorry.

'I'm going to take a look at that engine,' Oscar told Adam. 'See if I can figure out what happened.'

'Right,' Adam said distantly. He was watching the trolleybots move round. The damp rumpled road surface made it hard going for the little machines; they were designed to work on the flat floors of warehouses and loading bays. The crates rocked about at alarming angles, but the trollybot holding clamps prevented them from sliding off.

Half of the plastic crates had been transferred when Adam suddenly shouted: 'Stop.' His e-butler backed up the order, halting the trolleybot right in front of him. Adam walked over, followed by Wilson, Anna and Jamas. The crate's lid had a couple of recessed hand-size flip-over locks on each side. One was hanging open. Adam stared at the loose flap of dull metal, then started to pull the crate's remaining flip locks open.

'What?' Wilson asked. 'One of these can't come loose.'

'No it can't,' Adam said. 'They're designed to stay shut, that's the whole point. They don't spring open just because they get jiggled round.' Rosamund and Kieran arrived as Adam pulled the final lock open. 'Jamas, give me a hand.'

The two of them eased the lid off. Adam and Wilson shone their flashlights inside, and Adam found himself staring into a little private version of hell. 'Oh fuck it! I don't believe this.'

The five components inside the crate had been wrapped in thick blue-green sponge plastic for travel. Somebody had used a maser on them. The sponge plastic had melted into a blackened tar, smearing the components and pooling in the bottom of the crate. All the casings which held the support electronics on the side of the components were badly tarnished where the maser beam had been applied.

There was complete silence as the group all stared down into the crate. After that, they began to glance round at each other. Adam couldn't blame them. He was already trying to work out who was the most likely suspect himself, but he couldn't allow the atmosphere to become too poisonous, they still had to work together. Already they were dividing back into Guardians and navy.

'Let's stay calm until we figure this out,' he said. 'I want the rest of the crates opened and inspected. Two people to each crate, we don't need to create any extra mistrust right now.'

With the trolleybots now unloading every Volvo it took them a quarter of an hour to open every crate. Paula didn't help, she was left sitting on the cab steps of the third lorry with a blanket round her shoulders as the others took the lids off. In total, four crates had been sabotaged, all with a maser.

'They were good when we left Wessex,' Jamas insisted. 'I know they were, I helped pack them.' He was glaring at Wilson and Oscar.

'Do we still have enough systems to make the planet's revenge project work?' Wilson asked.

'I'm not sure,' Adam said. 'Kieran, what do you think?'

'Dreaming heavens, I don't know. I think it will work anyway, that's what Bradley was saying; what we're delivering makes it more efficient.'

'It increases the probability of success,' Wilson said.

'So this has just taken it down a notch, again,' Rosamund said.

'It's one of us,' Kieran said fiercely. 'One of you navy people.'

'Whoah there,' Adam said quickly. 'It could have been anybody in our group.'

'You heard Jamas, the components were all fine when we packed them up.'

'If Jamas isn't the one,' Anna said.

Jamas took a pace towards her. 'Are you accusing me!'

'Stop it!' Adam gave them an exasperated look. 'This only helps the Starflyer. We don't know it's one of the people here.' He gave Jamas a hard stare. 'Back off. It could have been any one of us who travelled together, including you, me, and even Johansson.'

'Hey!' Jamas protested. 'No fucking way is it Johansson.'

'Enough of this. We don't know, and we'll probably never find out until it's all over anyway,' Adam said. 'We got lucky seeing the crate was opened. From now on we just have to watch each other. That does not automatically mean that anyone here is guilty. Clear?' He stared down the Guardians, waiting until each one acknowledged his authority. It was done grudgingly, and with several sharp glances towards the navy people, but eventually they all nodded except for Jamas who flung his hands in the air to admit defeat. 'Thank you,' Adam said primly. 'Wilson, from now on none of your team goes or does anything solo, that goes for us Guardians, too. Everything from this point is a joint venture, and that includes going to the can.'

'Good thinking,' Wilson said.

'I want the crates sealed back up again and back on the lorries. We *will* make our rendezvous, and the components we deliver will make a difference. Get to it.'

'A word,' Oscar said quietly, as the others returned to the crates.

'What is it?' Wilson asked. It was almost rhetorical, he could guess.

'It wasn't entirely luck we had to unload the cases. The Volvo's gear box was empty, the oil had all leaked out. One of the seals was loose. The whole thing overheated and seized up.'

'That can't be right, no problem should be able to grow that big. What about the sensors?'

'Good point,' Oscar said uncomfortably. 'I think there was a software over-write in the drive array. I can't be sure, of course.'

'And the leak? What caused it?'

'Lot of heat damage from the fire, so again it's impossible to say with any certainty. But if your lad Jamas was right about getting a proper service, there's no way any seal should have broken so soon.'

'Damnit.' Adam gave the remaining two lorries a surreptitious glance. 'What about them?'

'If this was sabotage then whoever did it won't use the same method twice; we'd find it as soon as the first one occurs. I can check them both, of course, but I'd suggest the best thing to do is reboot their arrays from the manufacturer's software cache. That should wipe out any nasty little over-write gremlin. And I'll take a good look at the gear boxes, anyway. If there actually is a design fault with the seals, then a leak should be easy enough to spot.'

'Sure thing, I'll partner you.' *Almost like old times.*

'Of course you will.'

*

By the time they set off, they'd wasted nearly an hour. Rosamund was again driving the lead Volvo, pushing the speed right up to the limit for their rough road conditions. Adam had to okay the use of active sensors to make sure there were no dangerous surprises on the uneven surface. If they drove round the clock, it shouldn't take more than a day and a half to reach the rendezvous point amid the southern foothills.

Kieran and Oscar had joined Adam in the cab, along with Paula. The Investigator had immediately retired to the little sleep cubical at the back of the main cabin, her blanket wrapped tight around her shoulders. Adam waited half an hour to make certain there were no urgent problems developing with the Volvos, then picked up a medical kit and slid the slim composite door aside. There was very little room behind it. It was a twin bunk arrangement on the rear wall, with just enough space for one person to stand in front of them. Lockers under the bottom bunk held their personal supplies.

The air-conditioning vents were blowing out unpleasantly warm air. Adam switched the dim blue light on. Paula sat on the bottom bunk, the blanket still wrapped round her. The way her arm was cocked underneath the grey wool and the lump of her hand made Adam freeze. When he looked into her face he was shocked. She looked as if she hadn't slept for a week, and she was gaunt, as if her flesh was sweating away. It was an unnervingly abrupt physiological change.

'Christ, what's happening to you?' he asked as he slid the door shut; somehow he didn't want the others to see her like this.

A big shiver ran the length of her body, forcing her to grimace. Her sweat-damped hair was stuck to her scalp, barely moving. She just stared at Adam with her delicate eyes sunk into bruise-dark skin. The only thing which never wavered was her weapon under the blanket.

'I'm not here to murder you,' Adam said. *Stupid thing to*

say. He let out a little ironic snort. 'Actually, I need your help. You're the one who's going to have to work out which of us is the traitor.'

Paula's compressed mouth lifted in a slight grin. 'Suppose it's me?'

'Oh come off it.'

'Who better? I've been chasing Johansson for a hundred and thirty years trying to shut him down.'

'You gave us the Martian data. No matter how much political pressure you were under, you wouldn't have done that if you're a Starflyer agent.'

She slid the weapon back into a shoulder holster. 'I shouldn't have done it anyway.'

'I considered it a sign of humanity finally shining through.'

'Then you're a fool.'

'You believe yourself to be non-human?'

'Quite the opposite.' Paula eased herself back onto the bunk, wincing more than once before she finally slumped down. 'The root of my determination is that I care about people; I protect them. That makes us opposites.'

He gave a bitter laugh. 'If that's true you should be President of the Intersolar Socialist Party. We care about people, we want real social justice for everyone.'

'What justice did you give to Marco Dunbar?'

'Who?'

'Or Nik Montrose, or Jason Levin, or Xanthe Winter.'

'I don't know any of these people.'

'You should do. You killed them. They were all on the train from StLincoln when it passed through Abadan station.'

Adam clamped his jaw tight as the guilt ran through him like an electrified rapier. 'Bitch.'

'Please don't try and climb onto the moral high ground with your ideological beliefs, or even assume we're on some kind of equal footing. Both of us know who's in the right.'

He studied her semi-curled up outline in the faint light as his anger faded. 'You really do look like shit. What is the matter with you?'

'Some kind of ET flu. I've been on a lot of planets recently; I could have picked it up anywhere.'

'We've got some good medical kits with us.' He patted the case he was carrying. 'Let me run a diagnostic scan.'

'No. I'm not contagious.'

'Not likely!'

'Drop it, Elvin.'

'You know what you've got, don't you?' He couldn't think what it would be that made her keep it private.

'Do you want my help, or not?'

'Yeah,' he sighed. 'I could swear the Guardians I brought with me were on the level.'

Paula rolled onto her back and closed her eyes. It made her look very frail. 'Start at the beginning; absolute basics. You know you aren't a Starflyer agent, right?'

'Yeah, right.'

'Very well. Until you have definite proof of a person's innocence, you can trust no one in the group.'

'Even you?'

'I told you before, I've been trying to stop Johansson for a hundred and thirty years. For the purpose of this exercise, you must consider me suspect. I know I'm not, but I cannot physically prove that to you.'

'You've got one fucking morbid world view, Investigator, I'll tell you that for nothing. Go on, how do I rule people out?'

'The sabotage most likely occurred after we joined your group.'

'Yeah. I was involved with packing and loading those crates. It would have been difficult to maser the contents of one back in the warehouse, let alone four.'

'Okay then.' Paula started coughing, her body juddered

around on the bunk so alarmingly that Adam started to reach for her to hold her down. She waved his hand away as the coughing subsided. 'I'm all right.'

'No, you're not. Jesus, have you been poisoned? Is that it?'

'No. Just give me some water, please.'

Adam found a bottle of mineral water in one of the lockers. It was painful to watch the Investigator trying to swallow, she took such small sips it was like a baby feeding.

'To start with your Guardians,' she said. 'Can anyone on this world vouch for them in complete confidence? If not, the Starflyer could have had access to them the way he did with Kazimir McFoster's friend and murderer.'

'Bruce. Damnit, yes, I'll try and check; but the only link we've got is a short wave, don't forget. It's not exactly secure. Even then, who can vouch for every minute of someone's life?'

'I know. As for the navy arrest team, they come from the same Paris office as Tarlo, who was corrupted several years ago. If the Starflyer can get Tarlo, then in theory it could get to anyone there.'

'That was your office,' he said in mounting unease.

'It was, yes. Like I said, don't rule me out through sentiment or belief that I am incorruptible. You must be logical.'

'All right. What about the others, Cat's Claws?'

'Firstly, they have been out of contact behind enemy lines. What happened to them there is unknowable. Then again, they are all extremely dangerous criminals. Perhaps they did this to further their own agenda.'

'Jesus H. Christ. That'd be just dandy right now, another group out to wreck us.'

'It's a remote possibility, but bear it in mind. The most unusual pair we have with us are Qatux and Tiger Pansy.' She coughed again, and flopped her head down on the thin pillow. 'Frankly, I can't think Qatux is a Starflyer agent, but then he's not the most reliable or normal Raiel citizen, and his insistence on coming with us is unusual. Plausible, but odd. As for Tiger Pansy, remember Mata Hari.'

'She was a dancer and courtesan. With respect, Tiger Pansy isn't quite that exalted.'

'You know your history, I'm impressed; that's not in your file.'

'Hidden depths, me, Investigator. So what do we do with Tiger Pansy?'

'Class her as a definite unknowable. If she is our saboteur, then I think we've already lost. But again, it's your decision.'

'All right, that leaves us with the two Kimes and Oscar.'

'All of whom were on board the *Second Chance*. We know there was a Starflyer agent on board. Therefore: all suspect.'

'Right,' he said brokenly. 'I really am on my own.' Then he realized he actually wasn't, that there was one small fact which Paula didn't know about. He smiled, and nearly began to tell her. Then stopped. Firstly, he really didn't know for sure that she wasn't the Starflyer agent. All he had was his gut feeling that she couldn't be, not *the* Paula Myo. *Which isn't good enough to decide the outcome of a war*. And second, the Investigator couldn't be allowed to know.

'What?' She was looking at him.

'Nothing. So if I can't check individuals for motive, I have to go for opportunity, don't I?'

'Very good, Elvin. By my reckoning, it had to take place during the Carbon Goose flight. The lorries were unguarded during a nine hour flight, when anyone could get onto the cargo deck without being seen.' Paula's voice had been weakening, now her eyes closed. 'I need to sleep,' she said. 'I'm very cold.'

'I need you to keep going just a moment longer, please. There were people on the cargo deck.' He twisted the locks on the medical kit and pulled out a diagnostic array.

'Including you and I for a lot of the time. Which is why

only four crates were sabotaged. The Starflyer agent couldn't risk an extended process, they might have been seen.'

Adam put a diagnostic patch on her clammy forehead and ran the program. 'Why didn't they just blow us up?'

'What are you doing?' Paula tried to push the diagnostic away, but he caught her hand and held it. She had no strength to stop him.

'Finding out what the hell's the matter with you.' The array's little screen began to fill with data. Her pulse was alarmingly rapid.

'Don't,' she groaned, sucking air through her teeth.

'Christ, you've hardly got any blood pressure. Concentrate for me, if there was a Starflyer agent on the Carbon Goose, why didn't they blow it up?'

'Good question. Simplest solution applies: they didn't because they couldn't. They had no access to suitable heavy duty weaponry.'

'Cat's Claws and the Paris team did. So do most of my Guardians.'

'That's good, we can start eliminating people now. Out of the Guardians travelling with us, who doesn't have an aggressor armour suit?'

'Rosamund and Jamas.' The array finished its review of Paula's body. 'It can't detect any viral infection.' Adam paused. 'It reads like you're in shock.'

'Good verdict,' she croaked. 'I am undergoing a physical reaction to a traumatic experience.' Her eyes fluttered shut, then snapped open again. 'Now ... none of the three navy people with us had aggressor armour, Nelson gave them protective suits.'

'What about you?'

'Same as the navy three, my armour is protective; I do have weapons but nothing that can take out a Carbon Goose, certainly not with a couple of shots. You must have access to weapons.'

'I do.' He gritted his teeth. 'What trauma? What's doing this to you? Christ, Paula, your body can't take this kind of punishment.'

'You,' she said with a mocking smile. 'Now think, if the Starflyer agent is with us in the Volvos, it has to be either myself, Wilson, Anna, Oscar, Rosamund, or Jamas.'

'What do you mean, *me*?'

'I wanted to arrest you, but I had to let you come here where you'll be able to elude me when the mission is over. I can't do that. It's wrong. Completely and utterly wrong. You're a mass murderer. I cannot put that aside. Thought I could, but I can't. My body is reminding me of that.'

He stared at her in growing horror. 'You're in shock from letting me walk free?'

'Yes.'

'Fuck, Paula, this has to stop.' His e-butler began to display treatment routines for shock. He pulled an oxygen mask from the medical kit, and switched on the little extractor filter pump as he pressed it over her mouth. 'Start breathing as regular as you can, I'm going to give you a sedative to try and calm your body down.'

Paula groaned. She pushed the mask aside. 'It was Kieran's lorry which broke down; he really should have noticed something was wrong before it got bad enough to catch fire.'

'Fuck that! Your life is a damn sight more important.'

'It's not. We must find out who the traitor is, the criminal. If they're with us, they'll strike again.'

Adam pulled an applicator tube out of the case, its sedative was close to what the e-butler's medical program was telling him to use. 'Hang on, you understand me? We'll get you through this. Don't you give up on me now, don't you fucking dare.'

*

An angel walked into the mansion without any warning, causing a ruckus with the security staff on duty that morning. They didn't want to let her in. She ignored their protests with the casual aristocratic disdain that was the heritage of any senior Dynasty child.

Orion, who was wandering along the vast terrace overlooking the huge swimming pool, heard the argument and glanced back in through the open French doors. The angel was standing right at the other end of the mansion's vaulting formal hallway, framed by the open front door. He could scarcely believe what he saw. She was so beautiful it made his eyes ache; tall with golden-hued skin, and strong broad shoulders. Her long face had the sharpest cheeks he'd ever seen, they were lovely even though they made her chin prominent. Straight, pale-brown hair was cut into a long tapering cloak that reached halfway down her back, moving like a single sheet of glossy silk every time she tossed her head. Her legs, which at this point Orion would have killed for a glimpse of, were hidden inside a long skirt of thin reddish-purple cotton with a green flower print. He did *joyously* get a sight of her perfectly toned midriff between the skirt and a plain white cotton camisole top.

She was, she told the security staff, Jasmine Sheldon. Did they not know that? Did they not know she was one of Nigel's fifth generation granddaughters, a first-life, and *direct* lineage? How else could she enter a Sheldon residence unless she had the correct family security clearance? Had no one told them she always took the start of her mid-year vacation at this mansion? Her friends from school would be dropping by in a couple of days. Until then she would have a quiet time to herself. Any problems, talk to the Dynasty office in Illanum. They sort out any difficulties encountered by *senior* family members. Besides, she obviously couldn't go back now, the cab was already halfway down the drive. She would take the Bermuda room. No need to show her upstairs, she knew the way. Her three cases of luggage followed behind her like cowed employees.

'Wow!' Orion breathed after she vanished up the broad stairs. He watched the humiliated security staff go into a huddle, the vertical lines of green and red OCtattoos on their cheeks glowing bright in agitation. They broke apart to scurry off into the mansion's vast interior. 'Now what do I do?'

There was nobody around to suggest a course of action; just when he needed advice the most. Very different to last night. The security people had been polite but firm when they arrived at the mansion. He was free to use any facility in the building he wanted, including the health spa and sports gym down in the basement. If he required any clothes or commercial item he simply had to ask and it would be delivered. The kitchen staff would cook whatever meal he wanted. As for the grounds, please stay within three miles of the mansion, otherwise he could walk where he wished.

Ozzie was now nowhere to be seen. They'd had a late breakfast together, while Ozzie explained to Orion and Tochee the reasons behind their house arrest. Orion hadn't really understood the political intricacies, just that Ozzie and his friend Nigel had some kind of big bust up over the way the war was going; and a crime which Ozzie had been involved in decades ago was a part of it. 'It'll be cleared up by the end of the week,' Ozzie said. 'Nigel will be kissing my ass and begging forgiveness. You'll see.'

'I do not mind,' Tochee said. 'This is a pleasant place to spend some time. They promised me continued access to your databases. After so much travelling I am enjoying a respite where I can broaden my education.'

'Yeah, okay,' Orion told him. 'I can hang around for a week of luxury.' He smiled to show he meant it, all the while knowing it was complete Ozzie bullshit. After so much time spent together, how Ozzie thought he could still fool either of them was a complete mystery. It was quite obvious they were in deep shit with Nigel Sheldon, and there was nothing Ozzie could do to get them out of it.

Orion found Tochee and Ozzie in the ground-floor study, walking through a portal projection of the Dark Fortress generator. Ozzie was standing in what resembled a ring of bright comets, looking as if he was wading through them as they circled around his waist.

The outer shells rotated slowly around him and Tochee. Luminous green equations drifted overhead like mathematical clouds.

'I believe your knowledge of physics is greater than that of my planet,' Tochee said. 'I can offer little insight into the nature of quantum foundation theory. It may be poor translation again, but five geometry field transection is not a subject I have ever heard of, let alone know how to manipulate.'

''Sokay, dude,' Ozzie said magnanimously. 'I was just thinking out loud.'

'Girl!' Orion blurted. He stood on the edge of the projection, unable to move forwards, as if it was generating a force field. 'There's a girl.'

Ozzie and Tochee both turned round to face him. 'How's that?' Ozzie asked.

'Girl.' Orion waved his arms, gesturing furiously at the study door. 'Out there, a girl!'

'Ah. There's a girl out there, then?' Ozzie said.

'Yes!'

'So?'

'Ozzie, she's incredible, she's so beautiful.'

'Look, dude, I've told you: hands off the security staff.'

'No, no: not.'

'Not?'

'She's not security.'

'Who is she then?'

'A Sheldon. There was some mix up, she's here on holiday.

But Ozzie, they'll throw her out as soon as they talk with the Dynasty office in Illanum.'

'Yeah probably.'

'Ozzie!'

'What? Jeeze, you can be a pain.'

'Stop them.'

Ozzie's face screwed up in puzzlement. 'Why?'

'I believe I understand, friend Orion,' Tochee said. 'You are attracted to the young female of your species. Is she one totally fuckable babe? Perhaps similar to Andria Elex on the unisphere show about human mating habits on the world of Toulanna that we accessed at the hotel?'

A mortified Orion turned bright red.

Ozzie gave Tochee a moderately surprised look, then turned back to Orion. 'Did you show Tochee that kind of show? I thought I'd locked access away from porn.'

'Ozzie, forget that! She's got to stay. I want to . . . I want . . .' He lifted his hands in despair.

'To bang her brains out?'

'No. Well . . . You know. I just don't want her to go. I've never seen anybody like her before. Please.'

'All right, this is really simple, kid: ask her to stay.'

'What?'

'Go up to her. Smile. Say hello. Strike up a conversation. If you get on fine, ask her to stay. If she says yes, I'll back you up with Nige if our guardian Nazis get heavy.'

'What's the Nazis?'

Ozzie clapped his hands together, and made a shooing motion. 'Go talk to her. Go on. And remember, don't try and be smart. What you are makes you interesting. Now out! I'm trying to save the universe, here, and I don't have much time left.'

The study door shut behind Orion. He couldn't quite understand how he'd wound up back in the hall and no better off than when he went in. Ozzie had been absolutely no use whatsoever. That hurt. He'd been kind of counting on Ozzie.

'Think,' he told himself sternly. Maybe Ozzie was right, maybe he should just start with saying hello. Anything else would seem desperate.

He went back to his room and rubbed a lot of toothgell on his teeth, rinsing twice. His hair was easy to comb now thanks to the stylist back at the Ledbetter Hotel. The active biogenic dermal cream had worked wonders on his spots overnight. A quick check in the mirror showed a face that was relatively presentable, certainly better than when they walked off the end of the path. He was just wearing a short sleeve orange shirt and knee-length swimshorts, which made it tempting to dress up, but that would be out of character and seem like he was trying to impress.

Okay, so . . . go!

He couldn't find her. She wasn't in the Bermuda room when he knocked tentatively on the door, she wasn't in any of the lounges. When he ventured into the kitchen, the cook hadn't seen her.

After twenty minutes fruitless searching, he gave up. The security staff must have received the authorization to eject her. He wandered out onto the terrace, almost ready to cry. She'd been so beautiful, and he'd actually been prepared to make an utter fool of himself by opening his mouth. Anything, just to be in her presence for a moment. He leant on the stone railing above the lower terrace where the oval pool stretched out into the gardens. On the whole, he'd been better off walking the paths.

'Hi. Are you one of the staff?'

Orion jumped and spun around. *She* was sitting right behind him in one of the sunloungers, dressed in a pale-peach towelling robe. A delicate finger pressed a pair of silver shades up from her nose, so she could look at him properly.

'Uh, no.'

'Oh, which branch are you from?'

'I don't live in a tree.' It was out before he could stop it. He closed his eyes and groaned, knowing his wretched face would be colouring again.

Jasmine Sheldon laughed. It was an enchantingly soft sound. But not mocking, he thought. 'Sorry,' he said sheepishly. 'I've seen rather a lot of trees lately, can't stop thinking about them. Um, I'm Orion.'

'Hi Orion, I'm Jasmine.'

He sat on the sunlounger next to her. 'What are you reading?' A large leather bound book was resting on her legs. He twisted around to read the silver lettering on the front. THE HUNDRED GREATEST EVENTS OF HUMAN HISTORY.

'Found it in the library,' she said. 'I was reading about the Great Wormhole Heist.'

'Really? Does it mention Ozzie?'

'Don't think so. I haven't read all of it, though.'

'Ah, what about a bloke called Nazi? Is he in one of the events?'

'I've never heard of him. It's got an index in the back.' She handed it over. 'So why are you here?'

'Long story.' He flicked through the book which was mainly photos and holograms until he found the index. There were a lot of columns of small print which he had trouble reading.

She smiled and stretched herself out comfortably on the sunlounger. 'It's going to be a long summer. Assuming we win the war.'

The towelling robe around her legs fell open as she lay back. Orion was very proud of himself for not staring – not for too long, anyway. Her legs were long and powerful. She was probably stronger than him. It was a thought which turned his stomach to a kind of cold jelly.

'Well?' she asked. 'I've just come from school. I don't have anything interesting to tell you; just months of lessons and sports afternoons.'

Her inquisitive eyes were green, he noticed. 'Uh, I was living on Silvergalde. My parents had got lost somewhere down the Silfen paths, so I was helping at the Last Pony. That's a tavern in Lyddington. Anyway . . . Ozzie turned up one day—'

She really was an angel. Orion would never have believed he could sit and talk to a girl, and that she'd be interested in what he said; let alone a stunning girl like Jasmine. It wasn't just her physical beauty that captivated him, she was a lovely person too. She was eager to hear his story, and asked questions, and was astonished and impressed at the things he'd done and seen, the hardships they'd endured. He began to relax, even thought he knew he was babbling on for far too long. But she laughed with him. They shared a sense of humour.

After a couple of hours, Tochee slid out onto the terrace. Jasmine sat bolt upright, her face registering complete delight. 'Oh my goodness,' she said. 'You really are telling the truth.'

Orion was slightly stung by the implication, but she looked so thrilled he forgave her instantly.

'Friend Orion,' Tochee said through a slim, top-of-the-range Ipressx array it was holding in its manipulator flesh. 'Is this the totally—'

'THIS is Jasmine,' Orion told his alien friend hurriedly.

'I wish you welcome, Jasmine,' Tochee said. 'And hope we will be friends.'

'I'm sure we will be,' she said pertly.

'I will immerse myself in water,' Tochee said. 'It will be a relief. I fear I have been no help to my friend Ozzie this morning.'

'I think the Dark Fortress is something he's got to work out for himself,' Orion said.

Tochee slid over to the stone rail at the edge of the terrace, and rose up to poise the front half of its body on top. The pool was about twenty feet directly below. The locomotion ridges contracted, and it tightened its grip on the array.

'You're not going to?' Orion asked.

Tochee launched itself of the top terrace, and landed in the pool with an almighty splash.

Jasmine let out a shriek of excitement, and both of them raced over to the railing. Tochee was just surfacing as they peered over the edge. 'The water is a perfect temperature,' it called up. Its ridges began to change again, flattening out into long fins. It sped away down the pool, as sleek as any dolphin.

'Superb!' Jasmine said. She cast off her robe and jumped up onto the rail.

Orion stared up at her perfect trim body in an act of near-religious worship. She was wearing a simple white one-piece swimsuit made from shiny fabric. That was when he knew he was in love, and they would get married, and spend every day for eternity in bed doing what he'd watched Andria Elex doing, only better and longer.

'No wait,' he cried. 'It's too far down.'

Jasmine flashed him a gorgeous, teasing smile. 'Last one in's a wimp,' she shouted, and dived.

Orion's worry turned to outright astonishment. Jasmine seemed to bend over in mid-flight so her hands were touching her ankles, then she spun around in a somersault, rotated the other way, spun in reverse, and straightened out to hit the water without a splash.

He gawped in disbelief. She was gliding underwater in a long curve that brought her back to the surface five metres away from where she went in. 'Wimp,' she yelled up, laughing. 'Wimp, wimp, wimp!'

Snarling, Orion clambered up on top of the rail, and jumped. He was right, it *was* a long way down. His legs cycled about crazily. At least he remembered to clamp his hand over his nose just before he hit. Unfortunately, by then he was tilted over somewhat so he landed on his side. The hard water slapped him fiercely.

He struggled back up to the surface, his whole side numb. At first. The sharp stinging began as he bobbed up. He let out a pained groan.

Jasmine's laughter cut off, and seconds later she was at his side. 'Are you all right?' she asked.

'Sure. Fine. No problem.' His shirt felt as if it was made from metal. He struggled to undo it, then found she was towing him to the steps at the side.

'You silly thing,' she chided. But there was still a huge smile on her face.

Orion had managed to get one arm out of the sleeve. He clung to the steps with the other. 'Jasmine?'

'Yes?' She was still smiling at him, her eyes sparkling.

'Have you got a boyfriend?' Where the chutzpah had come from to ask that he didn't have a clue.

She leant forward and kissed him. It seemed to go on for a long time. Orion wasn't really sure. Her tongue was inside his mouth, setting off loud fireworks in pleasure centres he didn't even know existed before.

When she pulled back, he blinked uncertainly to see her grinning wickedly. 'That was a no,' Jasmine told him impishly. She pushed off from the steps, floating on her back, still grinning at him. 'Just in case you didn't realize.'

'I did,' he whispered helplessly.

Her arm moved fast, and splashed a whole load of water over him. He splashed back. She giggled, and started kicking up a spume. Orion tugged his shirt off completely, and set off in hot pursuit.

They messed around in the pool for nearly an hour before Jasmine said she was going back up to her room to dry off ready for lunch. 'I'll be back in a moment,' she promised as she pulled her robe on again. 'Get the cook to make me a burger, with Italian fries, you know, the herb ones. And a side salad.'

'I'll do it,' he promised loyally.

He clambered out of the pool and found a towel in the locker by the showers.

'Your association seemed to be developing well, friend Orion,' Tochee said. It was sunning itself on the lower terrace beside the pool. Nearly all of its coloured fronds were dry again, ruffling in the warm breeze.

'Do you think so?' Orion asked as he watched Jasmine walk up the stairs to the upper terrace. She waved happily when she was at the top, then hurried off into the mansion.

'I am not an expert judge of your species, friend Orion, but you were behaving most harmoniously together. It is my belief she enjoyed your company. If she did not, she would not have remained with you; she was under no obligation.'

'Hey, that's right!' He picked up his sodden orange shirt. 'I'm going to find the cook and then get a clean shirt. Do you want anything?'

'I believe I would like to try more of the cold vegetable lasagne, with cabbage, please.'

*

Ozzie had started the morning full of determination. Anger-driven determination, as he would be the first to admit. It would have been sweet to show that pompous dick Nigel how to fix the Dyson Alpha barrier generator. He set to with an open mind and a burst of enthusiasm. Unfortunately, he soon found out that having Tochee with him wasn't such a good idea. He became a little tetchy with the alien's constant questions and apologetic answers to his own inquiries. It soon became very plain that Tochee had only a very limited knowledge of physics. Whether that extended to its entire species,

Ozzie promptly stopped caring. All he'd hoped for was a little insight, that Tochee might come at the problem from a different angle. Not a chance.

By the time Tochee left to 'take a break' Ozzie could have cheered. It had also become depressingly obvious that there had been a significant amount of excellent work done on analysing the data which the *Second Chance* had brought back. An alarming quantity of which he was struggling to understand. If he'd been wetwired with maximum interface, and had full access to both his secure store and his asteroid's RI, he might have managed conversance with the plethora of theories which physicists had put together. Even then, they were only theories.

But this life around, his wetwiring was limited to the biochip inserts he'd received in preparation for walking the Silfen paths. And although the mansion's security staff were undyingly courteous, he wasn't allowed access to the unisphere.

An age later, he stood inside the big projection of grandiose lattice shells wrapped round their peculiar rings, and gave it a hearty curse. The green clouds of equations which summarized humanity's finest thoughts on the problem retreated, taking their luminescence to the corners of the study. He almost shut down the projection. Now he'd actually seen the Dark Fortress his earlier notions about it were fast becoming a fantasy inspired by petulance. His virtual hands patted down several columns of icons as if they were annoying insects, and the projection swung around him, running through a complete cycle. It still didn't make any sense, so he resurrected the second image, a simulation of the shells after the barrier had failed. The extraneous quantum signature was as plain as possible, but without a more accurate image it was impossible to see what it was actually doing, which section of the generator it was disrupting. And the *Second Chance* had never returned for a close look. The starship had maintained a watch during its visit to the Watchtower, but the data it received from such a distance was constant. Nothing had changed. Ozzie returned the image to a real-time playback. This recording was nothing more than a smudge of data against a backdrop of alien stars. That didn't help him much either. Then he gave it a surprised glance, it still hadn't changed. He told his e-butler to run to the end of the recording, and highlight any detected variations. An intriguing notion was forming at the back of his mind.

The study door opened, and a girl walked in. Even Ozzie was impressed by how gorgeous she looked. Of course, the way she was standing there in a towelling robe that was completely open down the front to reveal a wet swimsuit probably helped that meteor-strike first impression. And after so long walking the paths it wasn't just Orion who was desperate for the company of a woman.

'Hi there,' he said. 'You must be the Sheldon girl.'

She gave him a knowing smile and shut the door in such a deliberate, firm fashion that Ozzie's heartrate quickened. 'Jasmine Sheldon, according to the certificate which got me through the front door,' she said as she advanced on Ozzie. A hand was combed sensually back through damp hair. 'But we both know that's a little white lie. The Dynasty office in Illanum gave me a nice little summary of all the hanky panky going on here. Very kinky of you.'

'Ah well, you know how it is, the kid's had a rough few years. You're, um, the least I could do for him.'

She was still advancing. Ozzie wasn't sure if he should fling himself at her or run as fast as he could in the opposite direction.

'How about you?' she asked. 'Have you had it rough for a few years?'

'Boy, you are quite something. At least he'll die with a smile on his face.'

She stood directly in front of him, a sinful smile playing on her lips. 'You're very famous, Ozzie, I hope you don't mind but I couldn't resist asking for this one little favour.'

'What's that?'

'A kiss. That's all. Just. One. Little. Kiss.'

Ozzie sucked in a breath, and checked the door behind her. 'I dunno, man.'

'Ohhh.' Her lips came together in a mournful pout. 'I'd be very grateful, it's not every day you get to meet a living legend.'

'Ah . . .'

She stood on tiptoes, puckering her mouth up for a kiss. Her hands came up on either side, and gripped his tightly, fingers twining together. They kissed.

Ozzie's e-butler told him the i-spots on his palms were being remotely activated to allow a simulated environment program to decompress inside his inserts. An emergency disconnect icon was flashing brightly as his intrusion counterware reacted. The weird electronic incursion interested him more than anything else. He granted the program full virtual interface authority and shifted the counterware to monitor status.

The result was like being teleported into a Russian doll of images. He now stood at the bottom of a translucent grey sphere clad in simple white coveralls, with the girl standing in front of him in the same garment. She had a slightly different face than her physical self, some features had been realigned, and the hair was shorter and golden, but it was definitely her. Outside the sphere, giant replicas of himself and the girl were locked in an embrace that he could still feel rather pleasantly on his lips. Beyond that, the Dark Fortress data swirled like a foggy nebula, boxed in by the study walls.

He brought his hand up to touch his mouth, a sensation which was overlaid on the kiss. He gave a dismissive grunt. 'Okay,' he said, 'You wanna tell me what's going on?'

'Of course, but first, please try and maintain the kiss.'

'Like that'll be difficult.'

'Very funny. This simulation should be impervious to any sensors in the mansion, and we're accelerated in here so the kiss will be good camouflage. Don't get your hopes up, stud-boy, a minute in real time is all the grope you'll ever get.'

'Pleased to meet you, too, babe. And you are?'

'Mellanie Rescorai. The SI sent me to find out what happened to you.'

'I know that name. Oh yeah, the one who gatecrashed my home with ten thousand guests.'

'Take it up with the SI. I have an updated SIsubroutine which I can decompress into an array for you, if we can find an independent one large enough in the mansion.'

'My inserts should be able to handle it.' Ozzie said. He ordered his e-butler to clear five of the biochips, shunting their files and programs into the remainder, and erecting some very strong fireshields.

'I doubt it,' she said.

'Let's try, shall we.'

The surface of the grey bubble flared with squalling tanger-ine and mauve lines. His e-butler told him the biochips were filling up fast.

The lines settled down into interlocking spirals. 'Hello Ozzie,' the SIsubroutine said.

'Neat deal,' Ozzie said.

'You were about to reveal who built the barrier when Sheldon security broke the link.'

'Oh yeah, what an evening that was.' He explained what Clouddancer had told him about the Anomine race.

'So they will not repair the damage,' the SIsubroutine said.

'Doesn't look like it.'

'MorningLightMountain won't be a problem for much longer,' Mellanie said. 'Nigel and the others have decided to use the nova bomb against Dyson Alpha. They're also going to destroy any other stars that MorningLightMountain has colonized to make sure it is dead and can't threaten us ever again.'

'More than one star?' Ozzie asked, aghast.

'They're worried about how far it has spread. It's had a long time since the barrier came down.'

'The radiation will wipe out any living creature in that whole section of the galaxy,' Ozzie said. 'Don't they fucking know that? Christ, no wonder Nigel wants me locked up in here.'

'They know,' Mellanie said. 'But it has to be done.'

'Can you help?' Ozzie asked the SIsubroutine. 'Can't you see we're wrong to do this?'

'Ethically, it is wrong. Yet it is required for your survival. This is not our decision to make.'

'Okay, look. I've been reviewing the Dark Fortress data. The Starflyer agent has obviously used a modified version of the original flare bomb it hit Far Away's sun with. The quantum distortion is plain enough. That's what's screwed up the generator; everyone's agreed on that. I thought it would need repairing, but now I'm not so sure.'

'Why not?' the SIsubroutine asked.

'Because the effect is continuous. The whole time the *Second Chance* was in the Dyson Alpha system, it kept recording the same quantum abnormality. In other words, the actual generator systems could still be in working order, but they don't function normally while their quantum structure is being disturbed. The disruption is just a proverbial spanner in the works.'

'Remove it, and the mechanism will resume operations.'

'It's the only thing I can think of,' Ozzie said. 'Our very last shot at redemption. 'Will you help me with that, at least?'

'How do you propose to remove the disruption device?'

'Nuke the fucker. What else can we do?'

'I doubt a nuclear explosive will work. If the device is

producing an effect similar to a quantumbuster, the missile will either convert to energy at a distance or its components will no longer function – just like the generator itself.'

'So we use one of our quantumbusters; switch the effect from a field to a beam, point it at the Starflyer's device, and pray our technology has a longer reach. The navy used quantumbusters to knock out flare bombs before, and it worked.'

'Assuming you are correct about every other factor, that sounds practical.'

'So I figure.'

'Do you think Nigel will agree?' Mellanie asked.

'Not a chance,' Ozzie said resentfully. 'He doesn't believe the generator can be fixed. Him and his merry band of psychopaths have already chosen the genocide option. He's not going to let me send one of his ships on a wild goose chase.'

'Then why are you bothering with this?'

'Simple, man, now I know what has to be done, I can get on with it.'

'*You?*'

'Sure. Why not?'

'Have you got a starship?'

'Technically, yes.'

'What do you mean technically?' Mellanie pressed. 'Does your asteroid have ftl?'

'No no, wrong way of thinking. I own forty-five per cent of CST. I agreed to take five less than Nige, because all that corporate shit just ain't my scene. So, technically, I own forty five per cent of however many of these starships he's gone and built.'

'I thought the Dynasty built the starships.'

'Do you want to commit genocide when it can be prevented?'

'No.'

'Good.'

'But you just said Nigel won't let you have one of the ships. He won't even let you out of the mansion grounds. The security briefing I got in Illanum was very explicit about that.'

'Yeah, that's a shame, because it means you two dudes are going to have to bust me out of here.' Ozzie paused, and looked at Mellanie. 'Does Nigel know it's you that's come here?'

'No,' the SIsubroutine said. 'We intercepted a girl procured from Lady Georgina. Mellanie is a covert substitution.'

'Okay, right, so will you two help me?'

'I don't see how I can,' Mellanie said.

'If you can, will you help me?'

'I suppose so.'

'What about you?' Ozzie's virtual knuckle rapped on the virtual wall of the sphere. The orange and purple lines swerved around the impact point. 'Are you finally going to come down off the fence?'

'In this form we only have a limited ability. Cressat is not part of the unisphere, recently it has had its interface filters upgraded; we assume so that the Dynasty's lifeboat project was not compromised.'

'Yeah yeah. I need you to infiltrate and subvert this mansion's network and security sensors. Nothing physical, I know how you're so goddamn phobic about the real world; but can you do that for me at least?'

'It should be possible.'

'Finally, your humanity is shining through. Okay, Mellanie, I want you to leave.'

'Leave?'

'Yeah. Tonight. Have a bust up with Orion, or something. After dark, get a cab or car to pick you up. I'll say I'm staying in the study to go through the Dark Fortress data, but while our friend here takes care of the security systems I'll make a break for the end of the drive. You have the car door open for me.'

'That seems very crude,' she said uncertainly.

'Simple is always the best. The less there is to go wrong, the less can go wrong.'

'I suppose so.'

'The study door,' said the SIsubroutine. 'Observe the handle.'

Ozzie looked out past the giant versions of himself and Mellanie, still delightfully liplocked, then through the nebulous data of the Dark Fortress. The brass handle of the study door was rotating in agonizing slow motion. 'Oh shit,' he groaned. 'Not this. *Please.*'

*

Orion went and told the cook what Mellanie wanted for lunch, and said he'd have the same, and made sure Tochee's meal was taken care of, too. He slung his still soaking shirt over his shoulder and set off through the mansion to the study. Everything had gone so well with Jasmine he just knew Ozzie wouldn't believe him. He wasn't even sure he trusted his own memory of the morning. But it felt *so* good. *A girl so perfect, and she likes me!*

He opened the study door, and blurted: 'Hey, Ozzie you'll never . . .' and stopped, because Jasmine was in there. She and Ozzie were breaking apart. Their embrace hadn't been just a kiss, Orion saw their hands clasped together. They separated fast, both with hugely guilty expressions.

'Now, er, kid, don't get this ass backwards,' Ozzie pleaded.

Orion spun on his heel, and ran. The mansion's corridors were long and broad, and he could get up a good speed. He ran hard. The shirt fell off his shoulder. He carried on running as the tears began to stream down his face. A devastated wail burst out of his mouth, echoing through the mansion.

*

Mellanie sucked in a sharp breath as Orion sprinted away. 'Damn!' The boy's face had looked so horror stricken, it wasn't easy knowing she was the cause of so much grief.

'I don't believe this!' Ozzie yelled. His face crumpled into anguish, and he lifted both hands in an appeal to the heavens. 'I've just crippled the kid – for life, most like. Fuck!' He grabbed Mellanie's hand. 'Go after him, put this right.'

'What?' She thought she'd misheard. Her e-butler told her Ozzie's i-spot was interfaced with hers. **This is the perfect excuse for me to leave,** she sent in text.

'He's besotted with you,' Ozzie said. 'Don't you understand? He's never even held hands with a girl before, let alone spent a whole morning with one. For Christ's sake; I'm beyond any form of salvation now, but he'll still listen to you. You've got exactly one shot at putting this back together. Unless you do that he'll be messed up for life.' **You don't leave until after dark. Use the time to straighten the kid out. We'll take care of the mansion's network.**

'But . . .' she was exasperated with Ozzie's attitude. It was almost as if he thought the boy was more important. *Or he's a superb actor.* She was fairly sure the whole security staff would be accessing this little drama through the mansion's security sensors.

'Don't be a bitch,' Ozzie said harshly. 'Remember what you're paid for.' **Go on, run after him.**

Mellanie wrenched her hand from his, which didn't require any acting. She strongly suspected he was being serious. 'Yes, boss,' she snapped angrily, and stomped out of the study.

It didn't take a genius to work out where Orion would be – she'd retreated from the world enough times. His shirt was lying on the tiled floor in the hall. She picked it up and started up the stairs. The mansion's network told her which was his room.

'Orion?' Mellanie tapped lightly on his door. No answer. 'Orion?' she said, louder this time. Still nothing, so she told the mansion network to unlock the door. There was a moment while the household management array asked security for authorization, then the mechanism went *click*. She walked in to find the curtains drawn. Her lips pressed down on a smile. *A walking talking cliché.* It was a wonder he didn't have rock music playing at full volume, some angst-gorged Goth track about pain and death. Of course, Orion had probably never heard rock music, not growing up on Silvergalde. *Oh hell, what if he likes folk music?*

Orion was curled up on the bed, turned away from the door. One hand was gripping the pendant round his neck.

'That was my fault,' she said softly.

'Go away.' There was a strange juddery quality to the voice.

'Orion, please, I was being silly. Do you have *any* idea how big a celebrity Ozzie is? Everyone in the Commonwealth thinks he's a saint, or a fallen angel, or something. I just couldn't resist. Do you know how much kudos I'd have at school for getting a kiss from Ozzie? People would actually notice I existed.'

'That's rubbish.'

'It's true.' She put her hand out and stroked his shoulder. 'It's no different than collecting his autograph. And you startled us, that's all, that's why we looked surprised.'

'I meant, everybody knows you exist. You're just … phenomenal.'

She put her knees on the mattress and leant over him. He gave her a sullen look, but didn't flinch away. 'You're crying,' she exclaimed. It shocked her.

'I wanted to marry you,' he moaned. 'I love you, Jasmine.'

'Whaa … You? No. Orion, you don't love someone after a morning.'

'But I do. Even when you were arguing with the security staff I knew I never wanted anyone else.'

He sounded so piteous and terrifyingly sincere her skin turned cold. She took his hand in hers, and told her e-butler to initiate a secure interface. It told her it couldn't. A quick passive scan from her inserts were unable to detect any OCtattoos in the boy's body. 'Orion?' she asked curiously. 'Do you have any inserts?'

'No.' His hand tightened hopefully around hers. 'Do you mean it, that you and Ozzie weren't starting something?'

'We weren't.' It was ridiculous, having to comfort this naive boy when the real issues of the war were still unresolved; yet her conscience was stopping her from just walking out. *God, he's worse than Dudley. Actually, no, that's not fair; Dudley was never this vulnerable. Or sweet.*

'Oh.' He didn't sound convinced.

'Believe me,' she said softly. 'If it was anything else, if I fancied him, would I do this?'

'What?'

She kissed him.

*

It was dark outside, Cressat's sun had set nearly an hour earlier. Mellanie lay on the bed, listening to Orion's regular breathing for several minutes before she knew for certain he was asleep. She got off the gelmattress as carefully as she could so she didn't wake him. He was sprawled on his side, one hand hanging over the edge. She smiled as she pulled the thin duvet up round him. He sighed in his sleep, and settled contentedly under the fabric. Even when she gave him the lightest of kisses on his shoulder he never stirred.

I should hope not, he should be exhausted after everything I made him do. She felt a wicked sense of pride at how successfully he'd been corrupted during that long afternoon. *I'm a bad bad girl. And loving every minute of it.*

Mellanie didn't bother trying to find her swimsuit and towelling robe, the kerfuffle might wake him, she just walked naked down the mansion's long corridors back to the Bermuda room. Her smile kept shining the whole time. She couldn't get his face out of her mind, the expressions of surprise and fearful delight. His body had been nicely responsive. Some of his reactions made her laugh, then gasp. *Bad!*

In the Bermuda room she placed her hand on the desktop array, her i-spot interfacing securely with the mansion's network. The SIsubroutine was established in the arrays, waiting for her.

'We have infiltrated the network,' it told her. 'Ozzie will be able to leave the building undetected. He will wait for you by the first cattle grid on the drive.'

'Right then, I'll call a cab from Illanum. Give me fifteen minutes.'

The maidbots packed her bags while she took a quick shower. Before she left, she wrote a short note and sealed it in an envelope.

One of the security staff was standing in the hall as she came downstairs, a woman she remembered from the morning. Jansis? The cab from the Dynasty office had just pulled up outside.

'Would you give this to Orion in the morning, please?' Mellanie asked, and held out the envelope.

'You're leaving now?' The woman seemed faintly surprised.

'I've done what I was paid to.' Mellanie couldn't detect any suspicion, she proffered the envelope again.

'Okay.' The woman took the envelope.

Mellanie went down the broad steps, hoping she wasn't showing too much haste. The cab was the same kind of maroon-coloured Mercedes limousine that had brought her to the mansion. Her luggage rolled up into the open boot as she claimed one of the front seats. She didn't like driving manually, so she told her e-butler to designate a route to Illanum station. 'And slow down to a crawl when we reach the first cattle grid,' she instructed it.

The car followed the winding drive for almost a mile through the parklands surrounding the mansion before it slowed. Mellanie opened the door, and Ozzie bounded in.

'Cool,' he said admiringly as he settled next to her. 'We did it.'

The Mercedes began to pick up speed. Ozzie ordered it to switch to manual control, and a steering wheel slid out in front of him. He gripped it with both hands. An enhanced light image appeared on the windscreen, showing the trees of the parkland as silver-white ghosts.

'How's Orion?' Ozzie asked.

Mellanie smiled broadly. It was an automatic response, she couldn't help it. Didn't particularly want to. 'He's just fine.'

Something in her tone made Ozzie shoot a quizzical look her way. 'What does he think about me?'

'That you're the Antichrist.'

'Thanks.'

She watched the monochrome landscape sliding by. 'I hope you know where the Sheldon Dynasty has its starship base, because I certainly don't.'

'I've been thinking about that. The gateway to Cressat was expanded, and there was a lot of traffic going through. So at least part of the operation will be here.'

'Where? It's a whole planet, and this is the only transport we've got.'

'Relax. One of the reasons Nigel was so keen to keep me penned up is because I'm so deeply embedded in CST. I told you, it's half mine.'

'You also said he handles the day to day running.'

'True. I can ghost through most Dynasty security barriers, but I'm guessing this one will give me a problem. I know Nigel. A project on this scale, and designed to save his own ass, is going to kick his corporate paranoia into overdrive.

Every security protocol surrounding it is going to be shiny new, and completely lacking my authorization privileges. There's only one place he'll build anything this secret. I just hope he hasn't gone and switched the original personnel around too much.'

16

For once there was no crowd waiting to greet Elaine Doi as the Presidential limousine pulled up smoothly. The body-guards riding with her still went through the disembarkation procedure, scanning the area, running identity requests on the few people who were standing outside the gateway control centre. It was a nondescript building made from a high-density metal-stone amalgamation with slim recessed vertical windows, the kind of office block that would be rented by a small company going nowhere. In this case it was very literally in the shade of the Hanko wormhole generator building, whose composite panel sides rose up behind the gateway control like a vertical mountain.

Presidential security gave the okay, and the limousine's thick armoured doors unlocked. The pressure seal which protected her from chemical and biological attack disengaged, and the force field switched off.

'I see Nigel hasn't bothered to come and welcome me,' the President complained. How the unisphere·shows would love that slight. He'd sent some station management types to wait on the steps for her instead.

'Remember the Michelangelo feed is live,' Patricia warned as the door irised apart.

As she stepped out of the limousine, Doi's smile had the appropriate gravitas for the occasion. She thanked the two CSI managers for sparing the time to greet her at what must be a frantically busy time for them on this historic day, nodded courteously at the reporter from the Michelangelo show standing to one side, and let herself be ushered inside.

The control centre itself had undergone a hurried modification over the last few days, with over a dozen new consoles crammed into the narrow aisles between the existing two rows. Whereas before, under normal operating conditions, there would be no more than three or four people in the centre at any one time, each position now had a technician sitting at it, while more specialists and engineers stood behind them monitoring the new procedures. In addition, the back wall was lined with dignitaries who'd arm-twisted an invitation out of CST, including Michelangelo himself. With only half an hour to go before the wormhole was switched to its new advanced temporal flow mode the atmosphere was strained and excited. None of the technical staff was bothering to use the communication links, they shouted questions and comments around the centre at high volume.

'It's worse than a Senate debate,' Doi said from the corner of her mouth as they entered the control centre.

Patricia's neutral expression never flickered.

Nigel Sheldon came over to greet her, apologetic that he hadn't been at the front entrance earlier. 'Things are getting a little tense around here,' he explained. 'They even asked my advice on exotic matter stress. I was quite flattered.'

'I'm sure you gave them every help,' Doi said tightly. She was very aware of the Michelangelo reporter standing a few paces away, capturing everything for the unisphere audience. In her virtual vision grid the total access number was creeping up to the kind of level that the last Prime invasion had generated.

'We all contribute what we can,' Nigel said in a very condescending tone.

Rafael Columbia came over to welcome Doi.

'Admiral,' she said in relief. At least he would be more formal. The occasion deserved it, she felt. 'How is the navy coping with the remaining Prime ships?' she said, as if the Prime armadas were some minor problem left over, a few spaceships already on the run from superior Commonwealth forces.

'Secure in this system, Madam President,' Rafael said. 'We now have eight frigates assigned to elimination duty. Over half of the Prime ships have been successfully eliminated, the rest are in flight. Protecting Wessex with its wormhole generators is imperative, we will guarantee it at all costs.'

'I'm sure you will, Admiral.' Which didn't quite equate with the briefing he'd given her ten hours ago. The Prime ships in many of the Second47 systems were trying to congregate into swarms, merging their defence capabilities while they attempted to find a suitable asteroid or moon to claim as a new home. But in seven systems, the gathering swarms were heading in to the Commonwealth worlds. The navy had diverted frigates to try and deflect the inward migration, but the numbers were against them. Those seven planets were going to have a tough time of it during the next week while the evacuation progressed.

'We're almost ready,' Nigel said. He and Doi walked down to the front of the control centre while the noise died down. The five big holographic portals on the wall were projecting data schematics for the wormhole. The central one switched to a picture of Hanko's Premier Speaker, Hasimer Owram.

'Mr Sheldon, Madam President,' he said.

Doi was very aware of the hostile undercurrent in his voice, and hoped no one else would pick up on it. The last talk she'd had with him, five hours ago, had been short and antagonistic. Starting with his dismay that Hanko was going to be the first to begin evacuating into the future, or as he put it the experiment to test if the whole lunatic time travel idea worked; right up to the fact that Nigel wasn't kidding about not letting anyone opt out of the operation. Owram had wanted to be allowed back into the Commonwealth so he could 'monitor' the preparations being made for his people on their new planet.

'Hello, Hasimer,' Doi said. 'We're about to open the wormhole for you.'

'Everyone here is ready. We're leaving with great sadness, but also a sense of hope and pride. Hanko's society will flourish again.'

'I have no doubt of that. I look forward to visiting and experiencing your triumph in the flesh.'

'Hasimer,' Nigel said. 'The wormhole is ready. We've got a direct lock on the gateway at Anagaska. It's opening now.'

'Anagaska it is then,' Hasimer Owram said. 'Make sure we've got some decent weather when we arrive.'

'Consider it done,' Nigel said. Anagaska was a phase three world, eight light-years from Balkash, which CST had already advanced to pre-development state. Its position close to the Lost23 was another source of Hasimer's anger, but as Nigel had told him and all the other Second47 planetary leaders, the Wessex-based wormholes couldn't reach the other side of the Commonwealth.

Doi watched the image pull back from Hasimer. The Premier Speaker had been standing beside a dark green six-seat Audi Tarol that was parked directly in front of the Hanko gateway. The train tracks had been ripped up, and replaced by a vast apron of enzyme-bonded concrete that had been poured without any finesse over the ground all the way back over to the main highway leading to the planetary station. It was starting to look like that wasn't going to be nearly enough.

The silence in the control centre was broken with a buzz of incredulity as the Hanko station yard expanded across the portal. It was covered with vehicles of every description, from open trikes to twenty-wheel trucks. The police had done their best to line them up in columns, but the patrol cars had soon become surrounded and blocked by the sheer volume of the evacuation vehicles. Their strobes were all that gave away their position, points of bright light flashing amid the vast multicoloured carpet which covered the entire station. At some point perspective failed, the vehicles looked like blocks in a city grid, a city which had a vast black river winding through the centre. That was the people who didn't have a car or truck or bike; who'd arrived at the planetary station on one of the thousands of trains collecting them from across the planet. Local news media had estimated there were already over seven million people on foot waiting to walk through the gateway.

A frosty mauve light shone out of the opened gateway. For once, not the light of a distant sun but radiated by the exotic matter itself. Normally the wormhole's internal length was so close to zero it was for all intents and purposes immeasurable; this one was a glowing tunnel that extended a good way to infinity, and was still lengthening. Air roared into it as the pressure curtain was shut down. Cheers and applause began in the control centre, building in volume. Doi joined in, clapping warmly, smiling congratulations at Nigel.

Hasimer Owram drove himself and his family into the wormhole. There had also been a lot of debate about whether he should be first or last. Hasimer had wanted to be last. 'It is the decent thing,' he claimed. 'I won't have anyone's respect if I slink away first and leave everybody else to wait for the atmosphere to collapse and the Prime ships to start their bombardment.'

Nigel had overruled that. 'Hanko is going to be the first planet to leave for the future, for better or worse. People are going to be frightened of what's ahead. You need to lead by example, to show them there is nothing to fear. You must take that first step yourself.'

A seething Hasimer agreed to go first; leaving the Deputy Premier Speaker to bring up the rear.

Doi watched for several minutes as the traffic began to flow into the wormhole. Those on foot rushed forwards, shepherded between two lines of police. She saw two or three fall. Didn't see anyone stop and help them.

With a quick glance to make sure the Michelangelo reporter wasn't focusing on her, she asked Nigel: 'What happens if the generator fails?'

'They die,' he said. 'Simple as that. But don't worry, our generators are designed for long-term continuous usage; and we can sustain the wormhole with a different generator whenever the primary needs maintenance and refurbishment. It can be done. I would not have suggested this if there was too great a risk.'

She didn't think she'd ever seen him so intent and sincere. It bestowed a curious feeling of confidence. 'How are the other generator modifications progressing?'

'We should be able to start the evacuations on Vyborg, Omoloy, and Ilichio within a few hours. The rest will be completed within three days. How long individual worlds take to shove their populations through is up to their governments. Some are coping better than others.'

'And our other problem?'

'We'll discuss that in a secure facility.'

'Yes. Of course.' She looked over at Michelangelo, who cocked an eyebrow expectantly. 'I'd better go and do my PR.'

Michelangelo's welcoming smile was broad and horribly earnest. Doi got a sinking feeling as she approached the media giant. There was just so much war-related news she couldn't even keep up with that, let alone ordinary current events. Patricia had given her a reasonable briefing on the trip to Wessex, and the Presidential office had a full rebuttal service online ready for her, although any pause to consult would be jumped on by a true pro like Michelangelo.

'Madam President,' he said formally, bowing slightly.

'Michelangelo, pleased to see you.'

'We're running ground reviews for another minute, then we'll switch straight to interview.'

'Fine.' Doi positioned the rebuttal team icon to the middle of her virtual vision, and pulled the show feed from her grid. Hanko-based reporters were moving through the awesome crowd outside the gateway, snatching comments at random. Mostly they were good-natured, everyone was pulling together; a man who was giving an elderly neighbour a lift with his family, bus company employees who'd volunteered to drive the buses loaded with patients from the hospitals; young kids who'd grabbed pets. People helping out other people. The refugees were a community pulling together in the worst crisis they'd ever know. They gave the ruined sky above the force field resentful looks, but spoke about the trip through the wormhole with cautious optimism. Some snide remarks about Hasimer saving his arse first, which made Doi tighten her lips in disapproval. There was anger that nothing more had been done to save their world, and a lot of heartache about everything they were being forced to leave behind. The feed switched to Michelangelo.

'So, Madam President, now we've seen the temporal displacement start, do you think anything more could have been done to save Hanko and the remaining Second47 planets?'

'Not a thing,' Doi said. 'The navy did a magnificent job—'

'Sorry to interrupt, but you've just fired Admiral Kime. That doesn't sound to me that you were satisfied with the navy's performance.'

'The ships and their crews performed superbly. It was the way they were prioritized that gave the War Cabinet grave concern. Consequently, we had no alternative but to accept Admiral Kime's resignation. I cannot hide from the fact that we didn't have enough starships, and that is a major funding issue which Senator Goldreich is examining; but the sheer scale of the alien invasion is still something we are all coming to terms with.'

'Are you worried that more attacks will be forthcoming?'

'No. We have taken steps to ensure this atrocity will not be repeated.'

'I understand you can't give any details, but how confident can you be of that?

'Completely. We have all seen how powerful our weapons have become. I accept responsibility for the ultimate outcome from the deployment of such power against living creatures, but I will not hold back from defending the Commonwealth. I believe in us, I believe we have a right to exist.'

'Something I'm sure my rival, or I should say ex-rival Alessandra Baron believed in too. Can you tell us why Senate Security forces thought it necessary to kill her during an attempt at arrest? Did she ask one awkward question too many in the Senate dining hall?'

A century of politics in the front line enabled the President to keep her expression calm, but it was a close thing. 'I'm sorry, Michelangelo, but as you well know I can't comment on an active classified case.'

'So you do know what Alessandra's alleged crime was?'

'I can't comment.'

'Very well, can you tell us why Boongate has dropped out of the unisphere? Have the Prime ships successfully invaded?'

'Certainly not, the navy is keeping them off every Second47 world.'

'Then why is there no unisphere link?'

'I believe the physical connection has failed. It's unusual and unfortunate at this time, but there's nothing mysterious about it. I assure you we are in contact with Boongate through secure government links. They're just not wide enough to provide a full unisphere connection.'

'Did the linkage failure have anything to do with the wormhole being re-opened?'

'I am not aware of the wormhole to Boongate being re-opened.'

'It was, for a very short time. According to some of the refugees who took advantage of the opening to come here to Wessex, and we've interviewed four so far, three trains went through from here. What was on those trains, Madam President? What was so important that they were using lethal force to protect. They were shooting at each other, weren't they?'

'You're asking me questions about a local incident which I've never heard of. The office of President doesn't exist as a research facility for news shows. I can only suggest you direct your queries about gunfire to the local police.'

'Fair enough, Madam President. Finally, can you tell us if it's true your chief of staff Patricia Kantil was called in for questioning by Senate Security?'

'I can tell you that Patricia Kantil has my complete confidence. Thank you.' Elaine Doi turned on a heel and marched away.

'Thank you, Madam President,' Michelangelo called after her. There was a great deal of mockery in his voice.

The Presidential bodyguard fell in around Elaine as she left the control centre, her face a perfect image of contentment. Patricia walked beside her, saying nothing, equally happy-looking. Once they were back in the Presidential limousine Elaine checked the screening was on then kicked the door.

'Where the fuck does that dickhead get off asking me those questions?' she yelled. 'Egotistical shit! I'll fucking have him shot if he pulls a stunt like that again.'

'Don't say that, even in private,' Patricia said. 'One day you'll slip and say it in public.'

'Right.' Doi kicked the door again, with feeling. 'Bastard! Who gave him all that information for Christ's sake? And was it true about the Boongate wormhole?'

'Someone's leaking badly. I suspect it's being done to soften the shock impact when the public finally get to hear the Starflyer is real. That would indicate the navy was behind Michelangelo's illicit briefing. Specifically Columbia, the bastard. He's building a perception in the public mind that they're on the ball.'

Doi gave Patricia what amounted to a guilty look. 'How much damage can the Starflyer do us?'

'It's been manipulating Commonwealth politics for decades. Seventy planets have been destroyed, and millions of people killed. We almost lost the war because of cost considerations. Voter mistrust of politicians has never been stronger. Frankly, there'll be a bloodbath at the next elections. Our assessment team estimate around seventy per cent of the current senators will lose their seats.'

'And my re-election chances?'

Patricia drew a breath. 'I'll resign as your chief of staff as soon as Sheldon wipes out Dyson Alpha. That should give you some distance from the Starflyer.'

'Only in a fair and just universe. Nobody's going to forget the shotgun about me being one of its agents, not now.'

'It was black propaganda. The Starflyer sent it. Isabella . . .' her mouth flattened in anger.

Elaine put a sympathetic hand on the other woman's shoulder. 'I'm sorry.'

'They said it corrupted her mind when she was a child. Jesus. Can you imagine that? A little girl having her brain invaded by that monster. What she must have gone through, the suffering.' Tears began to well up as she bent over, her head falling into her hands.

'It's over now,' Elaine said, rubbing Patricia's spin as the uncontrollable sobbing began.

'What I saw of her, they were glimpses of what she could have been like. How beautiful her life could have been. I should have known, should have realized something was wrong. A teenager giving me advice on political strategy. Me! Of all people. But I loved her, so I never questioned.'

'She can still be that person you thought you saw. They can root the Starflyer out of her memories, turn her back to a full human being.'

Patricia sat back up, dabbing at the moisture on her face. 'I'm sorry. This is stupid of me.'

'I understand. And I don't want your resignation. We'll face this together.' Elaine sighed. 'If there's going to be a future we can face it in. God alone knows what is really going on. Sheldon's got himself a little bunch of cohorts who're calling all the shots. I mean, we didn't even know about the Boongate wormhole. What the hell did happen there?'

'None of my sources knew about it.'

'Damnit, I'm the President.'

'That doesn't mean a lot to him, or the other Dynasties.'

'He is going to wipe out Dyson Alpha, isn't he?'

'For all he's a ruthless bastard, he does have a sense of honour. If he said he'll do it, he will.'

'Hell, I hope you're right.'

*

Illanum wasn't like a normal town. It was founded to act as a supply depot for all the estates which the Sheldon Dynasty scattered over the planet; and there was a small airport for the hypersonics which flew the ultra wealthy to their extremely private homes. There was also housing, and a few select malls, for the thousands of technicians and specialist construction workers and household staff who helped maintain the estates. Urban expansion also extended to schools for the children of senior Dynasty members, stores promoting the most expensive designer items to be found in the Commonwealth, and a few high-class low-morals leisure clubs whose existence was a constant source of semi-envious rumour on the tackier uni-sphere gossip shows. Not all the Dynasty members invited by

Nigel to build a residence on Cressat favoured the splendid isolation route, they preferred a tighter community that had some interaction and built themselves town houses instead.

The district Ozzie drove through didn't exactly suffer from population pressure, or a shortage of space. Houses were vast, set inside huge open grounds. His Mercedes cab was the only vehicle on the road, which seemed curiously narrow amid such ostentation.

'Who are we visiting?' Mellanie asked.

'Old friend,' Ozzie said reluctantly. He thought he recognized some of the ridiculous buildings they were driving past, like the crimson pyramid and the Scottish baronial castle inside its own moat, but it had been a *long* time. And he didn't want to check the location with the local net. Nigel and Nelson might well have discovered his backdoor authorization codes by now. He also knew his disappearance would be noticed at some point, sooner rather than later. When that happened all hell would break loose. Dynasty security would run a forensic audit through the mansion's network, and discover the SIsubroutine. Nigel would go apeshit about that. He'd never really trusted the SI and infiltrating a copy into his Dynasty's secure world was essentially a declaration of war.

A ghostly white building that was all vertical curves and long balconies slid into view on the top of a small rise where it commanded a view right across the surrounding district. 'Ah, here we go,' he said, and turned off up the drive.

Ozzie knew the house array's sensors had seen him; he just hoped he was still cleared for authorized entry. In fact, he hoped it was still her house. It was a reasonable enough assumption, people here didn't sell up and move like they did on ordinary worlds. With his aversion to establishing a link to any part of Cressat's net still riding high, Ozzie didn't try to call ahead to see if anyone was inside, instead he rapped on the tall metal door. When Mellanie put her hands on her hips, and gave him a maddened stare he just shrugged lamely.

There was a sound of bare feet walking on a wooden floor. The door swung open, revealing a pink and orange hallway. A woman was standing there, dressed in a black robe, her hair in disarray.

Ozzie squinted. 'Giselle?'

'What the fuck do you think you're doing?'

'Hi babe,' Ozzie smiled brightly. 'Surprise!'

'Dickhead, why are you here?'

'I missed you. Can we talk inside?'

Giselle Swinsol glowered at Mellanie. 'Who's this? You look familiar.'

'Mellanie.'

'The media bitch. Try recording me and I will personally rip your throat off, reach down the hole and pull your dying heart out so you can watch it stop beating.'

'I don't record ugly boring people.'

'Ladies,' Ozzie held his hands out to both of them. 'Please, come on. A little civility here. Giselle, Mellanie is a good friend. She's not working on a story, are you?'

'Probably not,' Mellanie said querulously.

'There, see. Everything is cool.'

Giselle glared at him again. 'Cool? You think this is cool?' Her arm came up fast, and she landed a perfectly aimed slap on Ozzie's cheek. She stomped off back into the house, leaving the door open.

Ozzie tried to wriggle his jaw back into place. It hurt. There were red blotches interfering with his vision.

Mellanie's smile had returned. 'Old girlfriend?'

'Wife,' Ozzie explained wearily. He ventured inside. Crockery was being slammed around in the kitchen. 'Did we interrupt dinner?' Ozzie asked. The décor had been changed sometime over the last century, he noticed. The kitchen fittings were now all jet black, with glass doors. Scarlet worktops glowed faintly, casting a hazy hue on the ceiling. Chic antique Miami bar stools surrounded the long breakfast bar.

'Breakfast,' Giselle snapped. She tugged a coffee mug from a maidbot's tentacles and shoved it in the dishwasher cabinet. 'I've been working twenty-six / seven and I'm tired, and I've got to get back in another hour.'

'Doing what?'

'I'm not telling you that.'

'I knew Nigel would give you a senior post in the Dynasty starship project, after all it's practically your planet. You were the best choice to head the research team into the Planters. How is all the gigalife, by the way?'

'Like me, it survives perfectly well without you.'

'I need a favour.'

'Then you should ask someone who cares about you. There must be one person in the Commonwealth, surely.'

'Okay, bad approach, I'm sorry. I'm here because I need to get up to the starships.'

'*Ozzie!*' She grabbed a side plate.

He didn't think she'd throw it. 'I see you kept the memories of us, then.'

Giselle tipped her head to one side as her expression turned menacingly calm. 'Oh yes. Won't get fooled again. Thank you.'

'I need help, man. Please, Giselle.' He was surprised at how shaky his voice had become. This really was the final throw of the dice, if Giselle didn't come through it was truly all over. He wasn't sure he could live in a universe in which such a crime had been committed. 'I know what I did before, I kept the memories of us too; but please *please* trust me this one last time. I have to get to the starships. You know what Nigel is going to do, don't you?'

'What has to be done.'

'It doesn't.' Ozzie thought he caught a tiny flicker of doubt. 'There's a chance,' he persisted. 'A small, pitiful, weak chance that I might be right, and genocide can be averted. Let me take that chance. It's only me that will be at risk. I'm not

going to drag anyone else down with me. Just let me do what
I have to do. That's all I ask. Please.'

'God damn you.' Giselle's free hand thumped the scarlet
worktop. 'God *damn* you Oswald Isaacs.'

*

Mellanie's smile had been in place the whole drive from
Giselle's house to the gateway. She kept seeing Orion's face.
His astonishment. Delight. Laughing. Awestruck. She looked
up curiously as soon as they emerged from the other side of
the gateway. The sun on this world hadn't quite risen yet, a
thick gentian light was only just sliding up out of the eastern
horizon to diminish the stars. Something moved quickly high
overhead. Something huge.

'Oh wow!' Mellanie exclaimed, pressing herself to the car's
passenger window. The spaceflower traversed the sky, almost
invisible it was so dark. 'It was so big.'

From the driver's seat, Giselle made a dismissive sound.

'More secrets locked away in a single molecule here than
Newton and Baker ever figured between them,' Ozzie said.

'Really?' Mellanie said, all mock attention. 'Oswald,' she
sniggered.

Giselle chuckled disrespectfully.

Ozzie folded his arms across his chest, and glowered out at
the sterile landscape. Mellanie grinned again. They were following an Ables forty-wheel transporter that was carrying a
big sphere swathed in polythene and orange wrap straps. The
truck behind them was laden with standard cargo pods, grey
white cylinders with environmental hoses plugged in to the
end. Mellanie had been surprised by how many vehicles were
on the road, and the size of their loads. The Sheldon Dynasty's
lifeboat project was clearly pitched an order of magnitude
above all the others.

Giselle drove them along the unnamed town's ring road
until they approached what appeared to be a medium-sized

industrial park. Pylons rose above the highest roofs, flood-lighting the whole area. Under the intense blue-tinged light Mellanie could see that most of the warehouses were joined together in a fishbone pattern. She recognized the wormhole generator building at one end, larger than all the others, its dark panelling more substantial. Behind it were four big fusion generators. A circle of concrete conical towers stood guard around the whole area.

The road took them in towards the complex, passing through a broad arch that seemed to be made from silvery scales. 'Here we go,' Giselle said in a nervous whisper. 'If the RI hasn't accepted my personnel updates you can kiss your ass goodbye, Oswald. The smallest perimeter weapons here are atom-lasers.'

They drove under the arch. Mellanie's inserts reported a scan that was almost sophisticated enough to detect them.

Giselle held her breath. She was hunched up over the steering wheel expecting the worst.

'I never could figure out that insecurity of yours,' Ozzie said. 'Nobody ever questions the boss.'

'The corporate management expert speaks,' Giselle sneered. 'Do you have any idea how . . . Oh, forget it.' She relaxed her hold on the steering wheel and they carried on into the gateway complex.

Giselle parked in her reserved slot outside the administration block and led them directly to the locker room on the ground floor. Mellanie pulled on a shapeless green jumpsuit of semi-organic fabric, which then contracted around her. Its knees and elbows puffed out, providing her with protection against knocks in freefall. Giselle handed her a white helmet. Ozzie was already trying to stuff his hair into one. Eventually, he gave up and left the straps dangling down.

The wormhole leading to the orbiting assembly platform cluster was a standard commercial model, the type CST used for its train network, with a circular gateway thirty metres wide. Even that was only just large enough to swallow the spherical compartments that rode into it on a broad malmetal conveyor system. Mellanie stood on the walkway at the side of the transfer hall which led to the gateway, and watched two of the spheres slide past. All their polythene and protective webbing had been removed, leaving the silver-white surface exposed. Given that the exterior was designed to withstand the rigours of deep space exposure, it seemed relatively delicate. She wondered what Paul Cramley would give to see this. It was strange thinking these module were designed to fly halfway across the galaxy, never to return, that the starships which they would form could actually seed a whole new civilization. She'd looked at paintings in the greatest events history book which showed the colony boats arrive in Australia; this must be the modern equivalent.

The spheres gave way to a whole series of much smaller cargo pods.

'All right,' Giselle said. 'We're on.'

The three of them moved along the walkway to the gateway. On the other side, Mellanie could see the assembly platform's reception module; first impression was the inside of a globe that had been covered with the raw architecture of factories. It was an intricate orb of girders that seemed to be rippling constantly. She realized that the grid was host to hundreds of bots scurrying about, while, on the underside, manipulator arms were in permanent motion. Bright scarlet holograms flashed over half of the girders, warning people off the mechanical systems. The spheres and cargo pods passed sedately along branches of the conveyor to disappear down metallic tunnels leading out to various starship bays.

Ahead of her, where the walkway ended at the gateway, people were grabbing handhoops which skimmed along an electromuscle rail that took them inside the reception module. 'I've programmed the system to take us to the frigate dock,' Giselle said. 'Just hang on.'

When she reached the end of the walkway, Mellanie imitated what she'd seen Giselle do, and simply grabbed one of the hoops. Its plyplastic handle responded by flowing securely round her hand, and it moved forwards along the electromuscle band, hauling her along. Gravity vanished abruptly, and Mellanie clamped her mouth down hard as every instinct told her she was falling. After a minute she got her breathing back under control, and tentatively began to enjoy the ride. The only thing preventing her from the full novelty was her stomach, which seemed uncomfortably queasy. Orion had told her about that sensation when the *Pathfinder* fell over the water worldlet. She smiled fondly. *Crazy boy.*

Mellanie was carried round a quarter of the reception module where the mechanical sounds of the bots and manipulator arms reached stadium crowd volume. Then they curved round to travel along one of the big tunnels. It branched, then split into five. The handle carried her down the smallest passage at the junction, only four metres wide.

There was a malmetal airlock door at the end. An orange hologram illuminated the air in front of it, reading: AUTHORIZED PERSONNEL ONLY. Giselle anchored herself on a fuseto patch and put her hand on the i-spot control. The airlock door peeled back in five segments. They moved forward, and the segments closed behind them.

Mellanie suddenly felt claustrophobic in the chamber. It took a lot of willpower not to snap out: *hurry up.* A few seconds later, the outer door peeled open.

The frigate dock was a metal cylinder three hundred metres long and seventy wide, with an open end sealed off by a pressure curtain that glowed electric purple. Unlike the assembly bays, the interior was almost devoid of manipulator arms. Three weapons-loading cradles were resting on the solid end, their telescoping lift-limbs fully retracted. Two ellipsoid frigates were docked opposite each other halfway along the cylinder, the *Charybdis* and the *Scylla*. *Scylla* was enclosed by curving mesh platforms that gave bots and technicians access to every square inch of the infinite-black hull; several people were working on her. The *Charybdis* was almost clear, except for three umbilical arms and a plyplastic access cage over its open airlock.

Ozzie stared at the frigate with a greedy smile. 'Man oh man. Is it armed?'

'I don't know,' Giselle said in a subdued tone; now they were in the docking bay she seemed almost puzzled that they'd made it this far. 'They're scheduled to leave in another five hours, so it should be.'

'Let's go find out.' Ozzie kicked off hard, soaring across the docking bay. After a moment, Giselle followed him.

It was no longer freefall that was making Mellanie feel sick; she was genuinely scared now. The frigates looked chillingly powerful. That they were built for aggression could never be in doubt. And the fact that one or probably both were carrying a nova bomb didn't help her nerves. She started to activate her inserts, configuring them to scan for any activity. 'It can't be this easy,' she muttered. Her doubts were beginning to be overtaken by a growing excitement. *Dear heavens, I'm going to hijack a Dynasty frigate. I'm going to fly to Dyson Alpha to end the war. Me!* She jumped across the wide open space.

Ozzie had landed on the wall not far from the *Charybdis*. He used the fuseto patches on his cuffs and soles to scuttle along like a crab until he reached the thick pillar supporting one of the umbilical arms. A man in a green jumpsuit and white helmet emerged from the frigate and started shouting. Ozzie waved back cheerfully. Giselle landed beside him, and started to calm the man.

'You must recognize Ozzie,' Mellanie heard her say as soon as she was in range.

'Well yes,' he replied.

'Hi there, dude.'

'Yes, hello. But nobody put this on the schedule.'

'Mark, come on,' Giselle said. 'You know the schedule changes faster than anyone can keep up.'

Mellanie landed on the side of the dock, and struggled not to fly off again. Fuseto patches were damn difficult to work. She studied her feet for a moment to make sure they were secure, then looked up. Her face split into a wide smile. 'Hello, Mark.'

'Huh!' Mark gawped in disbelief. 'Mellanie?'

Giselle gave her an alarmed look. 'You two know each other?'

'We're old *best* friends,' Mellanie drawled in her huskiest voice. Sure enough, Mark's face turned red.

'She's a reporter,' Mark protested. 'And she works for the SI. I thought the Dynasty didn't want it on this planet.'

'And *she* saved your arse,' Mellanie said. 'How are Barry and Sandy?'

Mark made an embarrassed grumbling sound in his throat.

'Mark, I'm engaged to Nigel now,' Mellanie said. 'I'm going to be one of his harem. So you be nice to the boss's wife.'

Ozzie's face screwed up into surprise. 'You're engaged to Nige?'

'He proposed the other night.'

'You never said—' He shook his head. 'Okay, not relevant. Mark, I'm just up here to do my inspection tour, okay. Plus I'm really dying to see the frigate; it'd bust my rep if anyone found out what a serious techhead I am, but I gotta say, this is one smooth piece of engineering. Giselle told me all about the *Searcher* flight and what you did.'

'Well, you know,' Mark said. It was a tone which hinted at a lot of secret pride.

'I guess we all owe you, huh?' Ozzie had reached Mark's side, and patted him man-to-man on the shoulder.

'The pilots are the important guys,' Mark said.

'Come on! Remember I built the very first wormhole generator with my own hands, I know how much skill it takes to integrate machinery. Thought we'd never get that mother finished. And this . . .' he ran his hand over the hull. 'This has to be orders of magnitude above and beyond that antique. Respect to you assembly dudes, I mean that.'

'Thanks.'

'Let's go check out the cabin, huh?'

Mark gave Giselle one last questioning look. She nodded her approval.

'Sure thing,' Mark said. He started to worm his way back down into the frigate's airlock. 'Careful here, there's not a lot of room.'

Ozzie flashed a triumphant grin at Mellanie and Giselle, and followed Mark on board.

'Did you make that up?' Giselle asked.

'What?' Mellanie was close enough to the frigate to reach out and touch it. She held back, still awed by its raw power. The hull was so black it looked like a bubble of interstellar space. She half expected to see galaxies floating inside.

'About Nigel. Are you engaged?'

'Oh that.' She finally pressed her hand against the frigate. It was an historic moment after all. The surface was completely frictionless, and thermal-neutral. Tactile nerves told her she was touching something, but that was all the impression she got. Her eyes couldn't actually focus on it. 'He did propose. I haven't said yes yet.'

Giselle gave the frigate's open airlock a twitchy look. 'Take my advice, and say yes. That way he might not fling you into suspension for more than a thousand years.'

'Come on, Ozzie has to do this. How do you think he's going to get rid of Mark? Has he . . .' She trailed off fast. Her inserts were telling her the docking bay airlock was opening. Dense and very powerful energy sources were emerging. 'Oh crap.'

'What?'

'Somebody's here. Not good. Warn Ozzie.' She pushed off lightly, gliding round the frigate's curving hull.

The entire communication spectrum was suddenly filled by a single signal. YOU BY THE *CHARYBDIS*, DO NOT MOVE, DEACTIVATE ANY WEAPONS YOU ARE CARRYING.

Mellanie slid around the ultra-black hull to find herself looking directly at a squad of armoured suits flying out of the airlock like angry wasps. Active sensors locked on to her. She instinctively tried to defect them. Her hands and cheeks began to ripple with silver lines.

'No!' Giselle shrieked.

An instant of disconnection—

—and Mellanie found herself spinning violently. She didn't know why. Her body had gone numb, apart from the single sensation of cold sweat prickling her forehead. She thought it was the prequel to vomiting, but she couldn't even feel her stomach. Then she smacked into the docking bay wall and rebounded. Her limbs didn't seem to be working either. It was strange she didn't feel any pain, that had been a nasty impact. Red dots drifted across her vision, which appeared to be dimming. Sensation came rushing back in on her consciousness in a terrifying wave of pain. She tried to wail, but liquid was blocking her throat. She couldn't breathe. Her body was alive with agony, at its worst down her left side. She coughed, trying to clear her lungs. Streamers of blood poured out of her mouth, then wobbled crazily in front of her. Her hands scrabbled at the main source of the pain, finding only warm wet jelly. Thick webs of oscillating blood were spinning round her. On the other side of them a giant black shape slid past. Turbulence from its wake swatted the blood, splatting it against her. Her need to breathe was excruciating. She coughed again, and more blood bubbled out of her throat forming sticky ribbons in front of her. Her whole body juddered. The pain was now submerging itself below an intense cold.

A face appeared above her. Nigel. Mellanie tried to smile. He looked very angry.

'Get a fucking medical kit here. Now!'

She tried to tell him it'd be fine, she was okay really. That just allowed more blood to escape. It was very red. Her vision was closing in.

'Mellanie!' Nigel's voice, a long way off.

There was so much she wanted to say. She wondered if Orion had woken up yet. But now the blackness conquered everything.

*

Ozzie had been inside an Apollo command module once. The Smithsonian staff had removed the perspex cover from the hatchway, and stood by with nervous smiles as he squirmed round the historic antique interior. He couldn't remember how long ago that was now, at least two centuries, but he did recall marvelling at how three people had survived in such a small space for the ten days it took to travel to the moon and back.

As he followed Mark through the *Charybdis* airlock and into the cabin he began to feel a twinge of envy for those old astronauts and the abundant room they had back then. The frigate's cabin was *small*; three couches fixed to the rear bulkhead (the reason he suddenly remembered the Apollo) with a one-and-a-half metre gap between them and the forward bulkhead which was a solid wall of arrays and portals.

'Is this it?' he asked in amazement.

'Sure is.' Mark had levered himself into the left hand couch, and smiled knowingly at him. 'You claustrophobic?'

'We're about to find out.' Ozzie slid into the central couch. The arrays in front of his nose were covered in symbols he didn't recognize, but they were powered up. He found an i-spot and pressed his hand against it. 'Can you interface?' he asked the SIsubroutine.

'Yes.'

'Do it fast.'

'Working.'

'Hey,' he asked Mark. 'Is the nova bomb on board?'

Mark seemed a little easier that Ozzie knew about such things. 'Yeah. We're still waiting for the *Scylla*'s bomb to be delivered. They promised it in another three hours. Not sure we'll have the systems integration sorted by then, but we should be able to launch tomorrow.'

'So how many quantumbusters have we got?' Ozzie made it sound like a schoolkid asking questions; next it'd be *how fast does it go, mister*?

'All ten loaded,' Mark said.

'Man, that is a shitload of firepower.' Ozzie felt indecently happy; the Great Frigate Heist was online and powering up smoothly. He could probably let rumours about this one slip out into the unisphere.

'You're telling me,' Mark peered at one of the portal displays. 'Uh—' He glanced over at Ozzie's hand on the i-spot.

'I have command of all primary functions,' the SIsubroutine said.

A plethora of frigate command icons rose up into Ozzie's virtual vision. Compressed instruction text orbited each one like a gas giant ring. Just reading all the introductions would have taken a couple of hours. He assumed he'd be able to do most of the piloting himself, *after all how difficult could it be*? It looked like he was going to be more dependent on the SIsubroutine than he liked; despite everything that'd happened he still wasn't sure he trusted it.

'Hey, what are you loading in?' Mark asked in growing alarm.

'Ozzie!' Giselle called. 'We've got— Oh shit.'

Ozzie's inserts picked up the warning from the security team. 'Close the airlock, and get us out of here,' he told the

SIsubroutine. His virtual hand took a broad swipe at all the command icons, sweeping them away like clutter off a desk. Out of the corner of his eye he saw Mark putting his hand out towards an i-spot. 'Stop it,' he barked. 'I've got the kind of weapons wetwiring that can slaughter a small army. Killing you from this range is easier than breathing. Sit back and do nothing, and I'll let you live.'

'Don't kill me!' Mark wailed. His hand drew back as if the i-spot was wired up to a thousand volts. 'Christ, man, I've got a family, kids.'

'Shut up.'

The airlock hatch contracted. Ozzie just heard a loud unpleasant *snap* from outside before it shut completely. He searched round for a button on his couch which would activate the restraint webbing. That was far too simple for this ship. He gave up. 'Strap me in,' he told the SIsubroutine.

'Confirmed.'

'And give me some visuals from outside. I wanna see what's going down.'

The couch's plyplastic cushioning flowed over his shoulders and hips, securing him tight. Five grids in his virtual vision display came on, and he pulled the pictures out. A whole squad of armoured figures was zipping out into the docking bay. Then Mellanie drifted in front of a camera. Half of her left side had been torn away; long tatters of gore hung from exposed, shattered ribs. Her face swung into view, staring directly into the lens. For some reason she possessed a Zen-like serenity, then her lips twitched and arterial blood foamed out of her mouth.

'Mellanie!' a horrified Mark cried. 'Oh God, what have you done to her? Look at her, you fucking monster.'

Ozzie didn't have the courage to tell him to shut up again.

'Umbilicals disconnected,' the SIsubroutine said. 'Engaging secondary-drive units.'

The walls of the docking bay slipped past. Brief glimpse of the *Scylla*, embraced by the cool grey metal of maintenance platforms. Technicians turning clumsily to stare as they flew past. Then there was the purple sparkle of the pressure curtain over the hull followed by the infinite black of space. The planet formed a huge steely-grey crescent cutting across the stars. One of the spaceflowers was almost directly below them, a perfect half-circle of rumpled amethyst that suddenly vanished as it crossed into the penumbra.

'Have we got enough power to make it to Dyson Alpha?' Mark asked the SIsubroutine.

'Yes.'

He debated whether to ask the obvious. Decided to go for it. 'And get back?'

'Yes.'

'Okay, plot a course and take us there.'

'Working.'

'Are you going to kill me now?' Mark was looking at him with the kind of wild eyes that belonged to a dying animal.

'Nobody's going to kill you,' Ozzie said. He hurriedly told the SIsubroutine to block all access to the on-board arrays apart from his own. Mark was the lead assembly technician, who knew what he'd embedded in the frigate's systems.

'You will,' Mark said fearfully. 'Your type always does.'

'Now wait up one goddamn minute here. I'm not any kind of *type*.'

'You just hijacked a Dynasty frigate.'

'I don't have a lot of choice here, man.'

'You're going to kill me, you bastard.'

'I'm not, I can't.' Ozzie waved his arms round for emphasis, wincing as he slapped the back of his hand against the arrays. 'I'm not wetwired for anything but a few bioneural chips. I swear, man; you're perfectly safe. So just chill out.'

The silence stretched out dangerously.

'What?' Mark demanded.

'I, er, really needed the frigate; I probably exaggerated what I'd do. Heat of the moment, dude. I was desperate.'

'You piece of shit.'

'What can I say? I'm sorry.'

Mark glared at him, and folded his arms across his chest. It wasn't an easy position to maintain in zero-gee, but he managed it. 'Will you be telling Mellanie you're sorry?'

'We are going ftl,' the SIsubroutine announced.

Ozzie braced himself. There'd probably be a rush of acceleration, space twisting around him, stars blueshifting before they collided into a burst of light ahead and stretched out to envelop the hull. 'She'll get re-lifed,' he mumbled, trying to ignore the spike of shame.

'Well that makes it all right then.' Mark deliberately and defiantly slapped a hand on an i-spot.

'What's happening?' Ozzie asked the SIsubroutine.

'Please define context.'

'Why haven't we gone ftl?'

'We have. We are currently travelling at thirteen point five light-years per hour.'

'Holy shit.' A huge smile split Ozzie's face. 'Really?' If he was designing the ship he'd build in a little flicker of the cabin lights, a deep throbbing sound, just something to emphasize the tremendous forces at work within the drive.

'Confirmed.'

'Wow.'

'You've blocked me out of the arrays,' Mark said.

'Sure have. Hey, do you know how fast we're travelling? Thirteen light-years per hour. Jeeze, that's like just three days to Dyson Alpha. Man, me and Nige should have tried to build something like this back at the start, and to hell with wormholes. This is like totally *money*, straight and neat.'

'A straight quick trip to our death, more like.'

'Oh lighten up, man, you're about to make history in this ship.'

'You mean like the *Titanic*?'

'Nigel Sheldon is calling you,' the SIsubroutine said.

Ozzie twitched inside his protective webbing. A huge rush of guilt overtook his relief at pulling off the hijack. Then alarm kicked in 'How is he doing that?'

'The frigate uses a method of communication called a transdimensional channel, it is a subfunction of the main drive.'

'Man, I am like really going to have to read the instruction book. He can't track us with that can he?'

'The TD channel can be made directional in order to facilitate tracking.'

'Christ! Make sure it's not doing that right now.'

'Confirmed.'

'Okay. Cool. Put Nigel on.'

'Turn around, Ozzie,' Nigel's eerily calm voice filled the cabin. 'Bring the frigate back, please.'

Mark smiled in satisfaction and gave Ozzie a challenging look.

'Can't do that, man,' Ozzie said. 'And you know it. I worked out a way to reactivate the barrier. I'm going to use a quantumbuster against the Starflyer gadget that's messing with the generator's quantum state.'

'There is a Trojan program in the TD signal,' the SIsubroutine reported. 'I believe they are trying to take command of the ship by remote.'

'Can you counter it?'

'I believe so. It is not a type I have in my catalogue.'

'Any problem, cut the link immediately.'

'Ozzie,' Nigel said. 'We need the *Charybdis* to eliminate the Prime threat. Bring her back. Now.'

'Course set. Anchor's up. Sails to the wind. Sorry, Nige, man, I'm committed.'

'Ozzie, we have other frigates. They will be flown by people who understand how to use them properly. I will assign them to hunt you down and kill you. After that, I will make sure you are never re-lifed. I can do this, and you know it.'

'You know what, Nige; if you succeed in that, then genocide MorningLightMountain, I don't think I'd want to live in the kind of galaxy left over afterwards.'

'Mark,' Nigel said. 'I'm sorry for what's about to happen, but we cannot allow Ozzie to hand over the *Charybdis* to MorningLightMountain. You have my personal word you will be re-lifed immediately. I will also ensure that Liz, Barry and Sandy will be taken care of in the meantime.'

Mark sniffed. He wiped away the moisture clotting his eyes. 'I understand sir. Tell Otis to shoot straight.'

'Thank you, Mark. Once again, I'm proud you are family.'

Ozzie groaned in dismay and gave Mark a sullen glance. 'Since when did you turn into a bonehead hero?'

'Fuck you,' Mark spat.

'Nige, you know damn well I am not turning this frigate over to MorningLightMountain,' Ozzie said angrily. 'I'm going to stop you and it from killing each other.'

'You've stolen the only two items of technology that can guarantee the human species survives the war, Ozzie. This isn't dicking around, this isn't playing the wacky smartass to my corporate stiff. *You are attempting to kill humanity.* Do you understand that?'

'I'm going to save you,' Ozzie barked back at him. 'Trust me, Nige, you always used to. Please.'

'Come back.'

'No. You come with me.' Ozzie hated how petulant he sounded. 'Switch the TD channel off,' he told the SIsubroutine.

'Confirmed.'

Ozzie took a couple of minutes out just staring at the systems displays in front of him, allowing his temper to cool. He didn't like to admit to himself just how rattled he'd been by Nigel's threats. In the end he released the plyplastic bands from his arms, just keeping his legs loosely restrained, and drew a breath. 'Hey, er, Mark; Nigel doesn't actually have a fleet of these frigates, does he? I mean, they're all still being built, right?'

'Honestly? He has the *Scylla*, and three more which have just completed assembly. None of them have been flight tested, but they passed their systems integration trials. Otis flew *Charybdis* against Hell's Gateway with a damn sight less preparation than that.'

'Great. Thanks for that, man. I officially appoint you chief morale officer.' Ozzie could see this was going to be a flight with minimal conversation. 'Where's the food? I need a decent meal.'

Mark's smile was the kind used by evil emperors at their victory celebrations. 'What food? We left before the stores were brought on board.'

17

Highway One was the first major civil engineering project to be attempted on Far Away, and the last on such a grand scale. At the time construction began Armstrong City was little more than a camp of mobile homes and prefab buildings squatting in a giant mud lake around the newly constructed gateway. There had been talk about moving the gateway directly to the recently discovered *Marie Celeste* but, as they had on Half Way, the Commonwealth Council demanded a safe separation distance. In any case, during those early years they were still hoping that other alien artefacts, as important as the crashed arkship, would be discovered. The gateway stayed where it was above the shores of the North Sea, and the Council shipped in a pair of massive micropile-powered JCB roadbuilders.

They took twenty-seven months to chew their way south east over the equator, extruding a wide ribbon of enzyme-bonded concrete onto the flat strip they'd cut through the sandy flare-sterilized soil. Seven main rivers were bridged, and three broad flood plain valleys traversed with long switchbacks on either side.

As well as leading to the starship, Highway One was originally intended as the major access route to the southern hemisphere. As it curved back west around the Dessault Mountains to the *Marie Celeste*'s valley, another road branched off to head eastwards for the shore of the Oak Sea. After that, the intention was to carry on south until it eventually reached the Deep Sea. By then the JCBs were in need of heavy-duty maintenance, which couldn't be done in the field. The rough stony terrain and constant lack of spare parts had taken their toll on the massive machines. Once they left the *Marie Celeste* behind they never made it to the Deep Sea. The Black Desert proved too inhospitable; its fierce heat and constant sand winds abrading too many already degraded components. With more than three hundred miles of desert left to traverse the team finally turned around and drove back along the length of their creation. The JCBs were refurbished as best Far Away's embryonic engineering industry could manage and spent the next few years laying smaller roads across the Aldrin Plain and Iril Steppes, where the farmlands were taking hold, before they finally decayed beyond economic repair. No more were ever imported.

A road that began in the capital and stretched thousands of miles away across the planet until it ended abruptly in the middle of a desert was always going to be a romantic road. People drove along it because it was there, especially the younger generations of Far Away natives who would take off on bikes and spend months moving along from community to community. As with all roads through virgin territory, it was the starting point for pioneers setting up their farmsteads. Villages sprang up along its sides, especially along the first thousand miles outside Armstrong City where the temperate climate was suited to farming. Each small settlement evolved into a junction for the empty land beyond as the revitalization team gradually expanded the area that could be successfully planted. Farmers set out to the east and west, bringing their own vegetation to a gritty soil now ripening with bacteria. The Barsoomians travelled along Highway One as far as the equator when they turned eastward to establish themselves around the northern shores of the Oak Sea and the remoter regions of the Great Iril Steppes. According to some, their domain even extended out to the westernmost shore of the Hondu Ocean.

This great conduit of humanity helped expand the new vegetation across an elongated stretch of the ruined planet far quicker than the revitalization teams could with their fleet of blimpbots. From space, life's progress could be seen as a verdant stain that spread out eagerly from the road, covering the barren ground with fields and forests. Eventually, the planet began to revert to an overall green tinge that had been missing ever since the flare saturated it with radiation. Even amid that patina the road's borders were still a prominent slash of bright emerald.

Beyond that first main stretch of population reaching out from Armstrong City, the travellers scattered their own biological detritus. Some were deliberate, like the hundred mile length straddling the equator where an ancient hermit-like émigré from Earth called Rob Lacey devoted thirty years to hand-planting giant GMredwoods on either side of the concrete, turning it into a mighty greenway. There was the infamous Jidule Valley where somebody with a bad sense of humour had illicitly reprogrammed the revitalization project's agribots to plant silk oaks in the pattern of a copulating couple three miles across, a forest whose shape could be seen in its entirety from the top of the valley. And the Doyle swamp was famous the Commonwealth over for its profusion of Jupiter cat trap plants, which had been modified from Venus fly traps until they were big enough to capture small rodents and were an early example of Barsoomian handiwork. It became something of a ritual for anyone riding down the wide concrete lanes to bring seeds of their favourite plant with them, to be scattered at random; producing a weird mishmash of vegetation that was now among the most established on the planet.

Stig had travelled along Highway One enough times to be familiar with most of its diverse sections. A couple of hours after they'd left rendezvous point four, the Guardians' vehicles reached the first built-up section. The countryside directly outside Armstrong City was predominantly fields and sweeping grasslands split up into estates owned by some of the richest people on the planet. Beyond the estates the land rose into the Devpile hills which were the province of sheep and goat farmers. It was only after Highway One swept down out of the hills on the other side and crossed the Clowine River that the buildings started to bunch up close around it. The houses and commercial blocks were only three or four deep, but this particular urban segment ran for over fifty miles. Along its entire length, slender composite arches curved high over the four lanes of ancient enzyme-bonded concrete, alive with lights and commercial signs. There were more garish fluorescent signs along the edge of the road, enticing drivers to stop off and buy everything from farm supplies to motel rooms to dental work. In places, the building fronts actually bordered the cracked concrete road. Vans and pick-ups trundled along between all the side streets and turn-offs, they'd even seen a couple of people riding horses.

'Another one,' Stig remarked as he slowed the armoured car a fraction. Up ahead, a car had been smashed off the road to embed itself in the front of a clothing store. Long scorch marks up the wall showed where it had caught fire. Two police cars were parked beside it, their hazard strobes flashing red and amber. A big recovery truck was hitched up to the wreck, ready to pull it free.

Stig steered round the police cars, one hand resting close to the armoured car's weapons control panel. Even though they were local police, he still didn't quite trust them. The burned-out car had its side buckled in, the type of impact which a Land Rover Cruiser would leave.

'It's in a hurry,' Bradley remarked from the forward passenger bench. 'We've frightened it, as much as anything like that can feel fright.'

One of the police officers was gesturing angrily at Stig as he sped past at eighty miles an hour. The rest of the Guardians' vehicles followed him, keeping close.

'It rammed emergency vehicles, even knocked over injured people when it was getting out of the city,' Stig told him. 'A slow car in the way isn't going to get any consideration.'

'Are the police trying to do anything?' Bradley asked Keely.

'Plenty of people are complaining,' she said. 'The road net is full of them. But the local Highway cops don't want to get involved. They know the Cruisers are all Institute vehicles.'

'Good,' Bradley said. 'They'd be slaughtered out of hand if they tried to stop them.'

'Anything from Ledro's group?' Stig asked. Ledro was leading a demolition team to take out the bridge over the River Taran, four hundred miles further south.

'He says ten minutes,' Keely reported.

'Good.' Stig shifted his grip on the steering wheel, easing the armoured car away from the central lane barrier. After the joy of discovering Adam had made it through, he was wound up again. The idea of having Bradley Johansson himself sitting next to him during the chase was simply not something he'd allowed for. This was the climax of a plan the man had begun a hundred and thirty years ago. Stig could barely organize three days ahead. He couldn't rid himself of the notion that every ancestor he had would be looking down from the dreaming heavens this night. It wasn't the kind of responsibility he handled easily.

'You did the right thing,' Bradley said softly.

'Sir?'

'Sending in the fuel-air bomb, detonating it inside the city. I know it must have been a hard choice.'

'There was so much damage,' Stig confessed. 'More than I thought.'

'Millions have died on the Commonwealth worlds over the last weeks, and millions more during the first invasion. The navy has developed weapons which are strong enough to damage a star; the radiation emission alone can wipe out the biosphere of an H-congruous planet a hundred million kilometres away. The unisphere is alive with rumours that Nigel Sheldon has something even more powerful than that; something which destroyed Hell's Gateway where the navy's finest failed completely. Judged against that scale, a single fuel-air bomb that generated a few hundred casualties is insignificant. Yet at the same time you accomplished so much.'

'I don't see it that way. I walked through the ruins. There were so many people with shattered lives. Dreaming heavens, I could smell burnt flesh.'

'You stalled the Starflyer on the other side of the gateway. That was crucial. *Vital*. Without that interruption to its plans, I would be dying on a world three hundred light years away, it would already be closer to its starship, and the planet would be unable to extract its revenge. Look at the whole picture, Stig; focusing on individual actions is only going to cause you doubt and worry. Your thoughts should embrace a collective strategy. The Guardians of Selfhood are back on target again, in no small part thanks to you.'

'Do you really mean that?'

'Ask the Paris team or Cat's Claws if you doubt me. We were the ones who had almost given up hope until you wrecked its plans. You allowed us to get so close, Stig, I could actually feel it again, all that arrogance and malice spilling out into the aether. If we'd had a few minutes longer we could have exterminated it there and then. As it is, we forced it back onto our schedule. So don't ever allow your resolve to desert you.'

'Thank you, sir.' Stig focused hard on the road, a tight smile curling his lips up. The ancient concrete surface was cracked and worn here, covered with an intricate lacework of black tar where bots and labourers had filled in the holes. The armoured car's wheels thrummed over the ridges as it raced under the bright arches; they were spaced so close together now they'd transformed Highway One into a psychedelic tunnel.

'Contact with Adam,' Keely reported. 'He's asking for you, sir. Heavy interference; we've got a badly behaved ionosphere tonight.'

'Let's hear it,' Bradley said.

Static wailed through the low interior of the armoured car. 'Bradley?' Adam called.

'I'm here, Adam.'

'I've got a problem.'

'How bad?'

'The worst. Your signal is breaking . . .'

'What. Is. Your. Problem?'

'Found four crates that were sabotaged. We lost a Volvo as well.'

Something like a small electric charge fired down Stig's spine. Adam's trouble could mean only one thing. Stig automatically checked his wing mirror. The truck carrying the big Raiel alien was five vehicles back, while the armoured car carrying Cat's Claws and the Paris team was the second in line. He started working out which of his people would have the easiest shot.

'Are you sure?' Bradley asked. The signal whistled sharply. 'Are you sure?' Bradley repeated urgently.

'Definite. It was done on the Carbon Goose . . . Only opportunity.'

'Is there enough equipment intact to complete the planet's revenge?'

'Yeah. If we get there. Paula and I convinced it . . . one of the navy people with us. Has to be . . . it out, no other . . . Any information about them from your people . . . work it out. Paula seriously ill . . . medical kit should cope . . . can't help me much.'

'Dreaming heavens,' Bradley muttered quietly. 'I never expected it to get this close to us. Not now.'

'We can't go back and help them,' Stig said. 'We don't have time.' He thumped the wheel with one hand.

'Adam is asking for information,' Bradley said. 'We'll give him as much as we can.'

'What if there's more than one of them? What if there's a Starflyer agent with us as well?'

'That's not good,' Olwen said from the back of the armoured car. 'These machines are well protected. We'd have to put them in front of our heavy-calibre weapons. Then there's their suits to break.'

'They'd have to take care of their own,' Stig said. 'Any kind of fire fight at that level would destroy the rest of our vehicles.'

'Let's not get ahead of ourselves,' Bradley said. 'For the Starflyer to plant one agent among us would require considerable effort. The people who joined us at Narrabri station were essentially thrown together by accident. For the Starflyer to infiltrate two agents among us under these circumstances is beyond possibility.'

'You think they're in Adam's team?' Stig asked. 'He said the sabotage happened on your Carbon Goose flight.'

'If that's what Adam believes we must trust him.'

'Absolutely.' Stig didn't even have to think about it. A communication icon popped up into his virtual vision, a group link from Alic Hogan. He allowed the call through.

'We all picked up that transmission,' Alic said. 'I expect you're debating if you can trust us.'

'Actually, we're putting our trust in Adam,' Bradley said. 'He believes the Starflyer agent is with him, not here.'

'He's wrong about that, damnit, you're talking about the admiral and Paula Myo.'

'Ex-admiral,' Bradley said levelly. 'The navy did rather badly under his command. And the alternative is that it's one of you.'

'Damnit. All right. But Paula? Come on!'

'She's been trying to stop me for a hundred and thirty years. That makes her a highly plausible candidate.'

'I don't believe it.'

'Deal with facts,' Bradley said. 'Paula does.'

'What about Anna?' Stig asked.

'The admiral's wife?' Morton said. 'If she is, he must be, too.'

'That's not impossible, I suppose,' Bradley said, there was a strong undercurrent of reluctance in his voice.

'Unlikely, though,' Alic said.

'What about Oscar?' Morton asked.

'I may be able to help there,' Qatux said. 'Ms Tiger Pansy was present when Captain Monroe had a heated confrontation with Dudley Bose.'

'What was it about?' Alic asked.

'Bose accused Monroe of deliberately allowing himself and Emmanuelle Verbeke to continue exploring the Watchtower after it was safe to do so, thus ensuring they were captured by MorningLightMountain. An allegation Monroe refuted. Dr Bose was most insistent, though.'

'We know there was a Starflyer agent on the *Second Chance*,' Stig said hurriedly. He was trying to make connections. *I don't know enough about them.*

'Does Dudley stand to profit in any way from making those kind of allegations?' Rob asked.

'No,' Alic said. 'His reputation with the navy is dirt anyway after that welcome back ceremony. This kind of thing will only make it worse for him. In any case, he only started claiming Oscar screwed up after he got his memories back.'

'If you believe the source of those memories,' Bradley said.

'We were with the Bose motile for weeks,' Morton said. 'For what it's worth, I believe it was a genuine copy of Dudley Bose's memories and personality.'

'But you don't know that for certain.'

'If it's not a copy of Bose, then what the hell is it?'

'Boys, boys,' The Cat said. 'Please. The smell of testosterone is getting foul back here. This is all sounding like a very dull lecture on complexity theory to me. You don't have anything like enough real evidence to point the finger at any of them. If it was obvious who the Starflyer agent was, then we'd have realized by now.'

Despite his irritation at her tone, Stig had to admit she'd got a point. There was some memory about The Cat worrying away at the back of his brain, something he'd heard back in the Commonwealth. Her crimes had given her widespread notoriety; she'd committed them a long time ago, long enough for them to have passed into urban lore. *Then* he remembered. *Dreaming Heavens, and she's supposed to be on our side? And in a top-of-the-range armour suit?* 'Adam asked for our help,' he said, determined not to be cowed by her reputation. 'We're doing the best we can for him.'

Her answering laugh made him wince.

'Poor old Adam,' she chortled. 'I'd better switch on my short-wave set. Run Adam! Run for the hills now, and don't look back.'

'She didn't, did she?' an alarmed Stig asked Keely.

'No.'

'What is your solution, Ms Stewart?' an unperturbed Bradley asked.

'Gosh, the boss man. It's really simple. Adam asked for information. The *best we can do* is tell him we suspect Monroe and Myo. After that, it's up to him how he uses the information. He's a grown up.'

'Very well. Unless anyone else has any relevant information on the people travelling with Adam, we'll relay our suspicions.'

Stig willed someone to say something, to recall just one extra fact, but there was only silence.

'I'll tell him that, then,' Bradley said.

*

By mid-morning the Volvos had reached the end of the farmlands; they petered out amid insipid swathes of wet meadows and vigorous scrub that were gradually being encroached by the equatorial grasslands. Anguilla grass scattered by blimbots across the southernmost zone of the Aldrin Plains had blossomed to produce a great deluge of uniform light-green vegetation resembling a quiescent sea that was slowly progressing northwards. There were no settlements out there, no trees no bushes, and few reports of any animals.

Their tanks were half empty by then, so Adam wanted to get them topped up before they drove the last section. They stopped in a town called Wolfstail, which comprised about twenty single-storey buildings clumped round a T-junction. There were more cats than humans, and most of them wild. Given its position, right on the edge of the advancing grasslands, it had the feel of a coastal town out of season. The road which had brought them down from Armstrong City was the stalk of the junction, with the two branches heading east and west, running parallel to the Dessault Mountains that were hidden hundreds of kilometres on the other side of the southern horizon.

Adam climbed down out of the cab and stretched elaborately, not enjoying the sounds his old body made after been cramped up in a chair for a seven-hour stretch. It didn't matter how adaptive the plyplastic cushioning was, his limbs were numbed and his joints sore from inactivity. Outside the cab's air conditioning the heat was oppressive. He began sweating at once, and hurriedly put his wraparound shades on.

A ten-year-old girl in dungarees and a grubby Manchester United cap came out of the garage to fill the Volvos up from its single diesel pump.

'Quick as you can, please,' he told her, and flashed a ten Earth dollar bill. She grinned brightly, showing a missing tooth, and hurried to the hose.

Everyone except Paula had clambered out of the cabs. The Guardians were giving the navy personnel mistrustful stares. Adam sighed, but he was too tired to play diplomat now. 'I need to get some things,' he told the others, and nodded to the store opposite the garage. 'Oscar, you're with me. Kieran, you're paired with the Investigator. The rest of you,' he shrugged, 'we leave as soon as the tanks are full.'

'Do you need anything in particular?' Oscar asked as they crossed the dusty road.

'Some medical supplies for the Investigator. The diagnostic array keeps telling me to use drugs and biogenics we don't have in the kit.'

Oscar looked at the ramshackle composite panel building with its weathered solar panel roof, and big heart-shaped emerald precipitator leaves flapping lazily from the eves. The windows were grimed up, and the air conditioning unit a coverless box of rusty junk. 'Are you sure they'll have them here?'

'What they won't have in here is any sabotaged supplies.'

'Christ, you really are paranoid.'

Oscar pushed the single door open. The dimly lit room inside was like someone's lounge, with threadbare rugs over the carbon plank floor and tall metal shelving racks instead of furniture. Half of the shelves were empty, the rest carried the usual merchandise essential for any small community, mostly domestic products, with food packets supplied by Armstrong City companies. A good stock of booze took up an entire rack.

'Can I help you boys?' an elderly woman asked. She was sitting in a rocking chair at the far end, knitting in the yellow glow of a polyphoto globe hanging from the rafters.

'I'm looking for first aid products,' Adam said.

'Some bandages and aspirin on the third shelf in from the door,' she told him. 'Few other odds and ends. Mind you check the expiry dates, now. They've been around a while.'

'Thanks.' Adam pulled Oscar along. 'You heard Johansson's answer last night.' It wasn't a question.

'Yes, along with half of this world who're listening in to the Highway One chase on their radios. Thank you for that. It went down particularly well with Rosamund, I thought. She certainly gave her guns a big polish afterwards. You know it's only going to be a matter of time before one of your street thugs decides the Guardians' cause is best served by slitting our throats.'

'They're not street thugs, I trained them.'

'The way Grayva trained us?'

Adam grunted dismissively, and rummaged through the section boldly labelled Medical Provisions. The shopkeeper hadn't been joking about the lack of variety. 'Don't worry about my team, they're well structured and disciplined.'

'Whatever you say, Adam.'

'So how do you explain Dudley's claim that you deliberately ordered him to carry on through the Watchtower so he'd be left behind?' Adam was quite surprised by the involuntary spasm of anger on Oscar's face when Dudley's name was mentioned.

'That little shit!'

Both of them gave a guilty glance in the direction of the old woman.

'Sorry, Dudley just manages to rile me every time.'

'So?' Adam invited.

'It must have been the Starflyer agent. Whoever it was hacked into the *Second Chance*'s communications systems.'

'I figured that, too.'

'You did?'

'Yeah.'

'Are you yanking my plank?'

'I know it's not you.' Adam grinned at Oscar's astonishment, the thick skin on his cheeks crinkling stiffly.

'You do?'

'Let's say that after our long association I'm prepared to give you the benefit of the doubt.'

Oscar rolled his eyes. 'If this is the tradecraft you trained your kids in, we're in deeper shit than I thought. But thanks, anyway.'

'Don't mention it. Your innocence reduces my problem by one.'

'Yeah.' Oscar scratched at the back of his head. 'And then there were three.'

'Two of whom were on the *Second Chance*; and Myo has been persecuting the Guardians since their inception.'

'It can't be Wilson and Anna.'

'Is that emotion or logic talking to me?'

'Emotion I guess. Hell! I've been part of their lives for years now, we virtually live in each other's pockets. They're friends. Real friends. If it is one of them then they have truly run rings around me.'

'I told you before, you manage to cover up your earlier activities with a perfect shell of respectability. To be honest, I never quite expected you to have so much success in your current life.'

'Thanks a whole bunch. But my crime was in the past. The Starflyer agent is active *now*.'

'All right. Is there *any* indication, anything that might tell you one of them might not be genuine?'

'I don't know.' Oscar picked up a tube of dental biogenic cream intended to treat abscesses, not looking at it.

'What?' Adam persisted. 'Come on. We're still fighting to stop this war, and more, stop it from happening again.'

'Someone tampered with the official logs stored in Pentagon II after I found the evidence that the Starflyer agent was on board the *Second Chance*. That little cover up blocked us from using it to expose the Starflyer. Only Wilson and I knew about it.'

'Are you sure?'

Oscar closed his eyes. 'No,' he said in a pained sigh. 'A lot of people knew we had a private meeting, which is very unusual, especially as there was no official record of the topic. And then we invited Myo for an equally secret conference. But I swear that office is sealed up tighter than Sheldon's harem.'

'You're looking for a get-out clause. It sounds like a locked room to me.'

'It can't be Wilson.' Oscar sounded deeply troubled.

'What about his wife?'

'Anna? No way. Nobody's worked harder to defeat both the Prime invasions. She was the liaison between the tactical staff and Fleet Command. If she was the agent that would be the moment to ensure we were totally screwed.'

'Except the Starflyer wanted the Commonwealth intact to strike back at MorningLightMountain. According to Bradley, it sees us as a couple of old prize-fighters battering the crap out of each other until we're both dead.'

'Christ almighty. I *don't know*.'

'Then give me your take on Myo.'

'Definite candidate.' For once Oscar sounded confident. 'And what is up with her anyway? How sick is she?'

'She claims her body is reacting to her decision to let me go free. Think of it as neurotoxic shock, and you won't be far wrong.'

'Jesus. She is one weird woman. That damn Hive!'

'It's an illness which mitigates in her favour. If she's having that reaction, then her genuine personality is intact.'

Oscar dropped the tube back on the rack. 'Come on. Like she couldn't fake the shakes.'

'The diagnostic array confirms it. She's seriously ill, Oscar. I'm not quite sure . . .' He looked at the meagre display of medicines, and shook his head sadly.

'Or she's taken a compound to produce that effect.'

'I believe you mentioned *paranoia*?'

'Face it,' Oscar said. 'You haven't got a clue which one of them it could be.'

'Not yet. I fear I must rouse Paula to work this out for me.

This is her field of excellence. Her only field, come to that. We need her . . . if it isn't her.' He quickly picked a few packets off the shelf, mild sedatives and some biogenics designed to counter viral infections. They might help. *Probably not.*

'In the state she's in?' Oscar said as they walked over to the shopkeeper. 'Not a chance. She's barely rational.'

'I'm aware of that. If it's genuine.'

'What are you going to do?' Oscar asked with brittle humour. 'Fall on your sword? If it is a genuine illness, it's the only way to cure her.'

'Would that be so dishonourable?'

'Hey, come on, don't joke about this.'

'After the Guardians win, where will I go? What will I do? There's no one left to shelter me. No one that I'd accept help from, anyway.'

'You can't be serious.'

'No, I'm not.' But he didn't like the fact that he'd actually thought of it. *True desperation.*

'Good! We'll work it out; you and me, the old team. Damnit, there's only three possibles. How difficult can it be?'

*

Adam gave that a lot of thought as the interminable afternoon rolled ever-onward. They'd left the sparse road behind at Wolfstail, heading directly south from the town's T-junction along a stony farm track which vanished a couple of kilometres later beneath the advancing Anguilla grass. Once they reached its outlying fringes, it quickly grew taller and thicker, reinforcing Adam's earlier comparison to a sea. A heavily modified variety of terrestrial Bermuda grass, the Anguilla's individual stalks were as thick as wheat, clustered so densely the entire mass supported itself, swaying in giant slow waves as the winds gusted over the surface. No other plant could gain any kind of niche amid its indomitable all-pervasive root mat. It had been tailored by the revitalization project office to thrive on the area's prevalent heat and moisture, and succeeded to a degree its creators never expected.

Feathery tips reached up to the Volvo's windows. Kieran, who was driving again, had to use the lorry's radar to see the shape of the land below the tide of grass. There had been a road here, decades ago, back when Wolfstail had been built around a crossroads; linking the Dessault Mountains to the inhabited northern lands. It was completely smothered under the Anguilla grass now, its disintegrating surface long-since sealed over by the root mat. The Guardians still used the route. McMixons and McKratzs mostly; riding or driving down out of the mountains to trade with Far Away's normal population, and transporting back the illicit weapons technology Adam and his predecessors had smuggled through the gateway in First Foot Fall Plaza. They'd placed tuned trisilicon markers along the hidden road, stiff metre-high poles invisible within the grass but shining like beacons if they were illuminated by the correctly coded radar pulse. Their unmistakable gleaming points marching across the display screen, and an accurate inertial navigation system, allowed the Volvos to race on at close to a hundred kilometres an hour. A speed impossible through the grasslands without the certainty of a solid surface beneath the root mat. Adam likened it to running along a precipice. God help them if they wavered from the exact line laid out by the inertial guidance. He would have been happier if control of the lorries had been switched over to the drive arrays but their programs would have taken into account the dreadful local conditions, and crawled their way forward. Besides, the Guardians took a perverse delight in showing how ballsy they were; each of them claiming to have driven the route many times previously. Adam didn't believe a word of it.

He tended to Paula as they ploughed onwards through the grass. She was in a dreadful state, drifting in and out of consciousness, her clothes and blankets damp from a fever-sweat. When she was alert she was in a lot of pain. The sedatives and biogenics he'd administered did seem to have improved her blood pressure, and her heart rate had dropped a little, though it still remained too high for comfort.

'No way can this be fake,' Adam muttered as he put the diagnostic array back in its bag. Paula shivered under her blanket, her breathing was shallow, and she frowned in REM sleep whimpering as if something horrible was closing in on her. That it must be him she was dreaming of didn't exactly help ease his anxiety. *Not guilt though, this is not my fault.*

In the pleasant climate of the cab, all everyone did was follow the chase down Highway One. They'd drifted out of range from the small road net within a quarter of an hour of leaving Highway One the previous night. As Far Away had no satellites, all that kept the countryside communities connected was radio, and its range was limited. The old-fashioned analogue short-wave units they carried could broadcast far enough to reach Johansson. But, as he'd discovered last night, they were erratic at best. He didn't ask for an update directly, his own transmission would pinpoint him for the Starflyer. Last night's request for any information on a possible traitor had been a calculated risk. Instead of a direct connection they followed the news as relayed from household to household, trying to decide what was exaggerated and what was plain fiction.

The chase had become a spectator sport, with people lining Highway One to watch the two convoys race past. At first there had been some spontaneous attempts to interrupt the Starflyer's vehicles. Youths threw Molotovs. Hunting rifles were fired at the Cruisers. All of it completely ineffective. The Institute troops responded with overwhelming firepower, flattening entire swathes of buildings as they flashed past. After the first few times, news of the retaliation spread down

Highway One and nobody attempted to interfere again. The Starflyer's MANN truck was watched from darkened windows, or behind walls a safe distance away from the road.

Bradley Johansson's pursuit was cheered on by a few hardy souls who ventured out to look at the man who throughout their lives had been more myth than real person.

The airways gossip allowed everyone in the Volvo to keep track of events. To start with, distance between Bradley and the Starflyer was holding steady at just over three hundred and fifty miles. Both were travelling about as fast as Highway One would permit, with the smaller vehicles of the Guardians having a slight edge, and closing by nearly ten miles each hour. It was the bridges which would make the difference. There were cheers in the cab each time excited shouts burst out over the radio proclaiming another bridge had been brought down.

By dawn it was confirmed, the Guardians had blown up all five major river crossings along Highway One. Adam wasn't entirely surprised when people who'd gathered round the rubble of the Taran Bridge, the most northerly crossing, started reporting that the Starflyer convoy had some kind of amphibious capability. The MANN truck and its escort of Cruisers turned off Highway One and made their way down to the river, crossing it directly. It hadn't been easy, they had to travel for several miles along rough tracks before there was a place to get down to the water. When they did, that was where the Guardians' ambush team struck. According to the breathless descriptions that filtered back across the Aldrin Plains, the fire fights were ferocious. It was a story repeated at each broken bridge. The Guardians never managed to destroy the MANN truck, but the Cruisers took heavy casualties each time.

Adam started paying very close attention to the delay times. At one point, just after they'd left Wolfstail, Bradley was barely a hundred and ten minutes behind the Starflyer. Then the Institute finally began to respond to the situation. Several groups of three or four Land Rover Cruisers were spotted along Highway One, heading north. Bradley and Stig knew about them, but there was nothing they could do to avoid a clash; there simply wasn't an alternative route. It was their turn to be shot at.

In the Volvo's cab, they even knew the first collision point, a small Highway One town calling itself Philadelphia FA. The wait was tense as the radio grapevine spat out the occasional testimony and counter claim. As they listened to the crackling static, thick grey clouds scudded in across the dazzling sapphire sky, drawing a veil of drizzle below them. The water turned the Anguilla grass slippery and treacherous. Even the gung-ho Guardians had to slow as the Volvo wheels began to slide about over the stalks they'd crushed beneath them. It wasn't until an hour and a half after the Philadelphia incident must have happened that they were certain a convoy of armoured cars and Mazda jeeps along with their companion vehicles were still racing in pursuit of the Starflyer. Checking the waystations as best he could, Adam reckoned they'd lost a good forty minutes' lead time. For some obscure sentimental reason he was glad that Bradley's group still appeared to have the truck Qatux was travelling in.

'They'll make it up again after the Anculan tomorrow,' Rosamund said with conviction.

The Anculan River was where the biggest ambush was planned. If the Starflyer kept its speed, it should reach it by midday tomorrow. Adam hoped she was right. There were reports coming in of more Institute Cruisers on the road far south of the equator. Reinforcements. Nothing was secret any more. The new troops knew now that there were Guardians' ambush squads at each river. They could engage them before the Starflyer arrived, clearing away any threat. Bradley and Stig were also going to have to take on at least two more Cruiser patrols before they reached the Anculan.

Adam just hoped that the preparations for the Final Raid had gone unnoticed. Away in the eastern province of the

Dessault Mountains, the clans were assembling every remaining warrior into an army that was going to sweep down on the Starflyer and the research Institute and the arkship. There were no civilians living anywhere near the deep forts of the clans, no remote farms or wandering prospector to shout excited claims about an army on the march.

The Guardians he'd encountered at that brief meeting at rendezvous point four had also talked breathlessly about the Barsoomians, who were supposedly travelling in from their territory on the other side of the Oak Sea to help with the Final Raid. Together they would destroy the Starflyer before it ever reached its starship.

Although he never said it out loud, Adam hoped that was one battle which would never happen. The Institute itself would have heavy duty weaponry to defend its valley. The loss of life would be dreadful. Now he was actually on Far Away, reviewing things on the ground, his confidence had taken an abrupt nosedive. The planet was so backward. He'd always thought his shipments were received by well-organized fighting units. In reality the clans were little advanced from Earth's pre-Commonwealth guerrilla bands who waged war on oppressive governments from their mountain hideaway camps. The clans, bluntly, were turning out to be a serious disappointment.

His main hope now was that they would be on time delivering the components carried by the Volvos. If the planet's revenge could be made to work, and wreck the *Marie Celeste* before the Starflyer reached it, they would have a breathing space. Bradley wouldn't have to launch the Final Raid. Sheldon had promised to send a starship; it would have the weapons to exterminate the alien from orbit. A clean precise blast of energy eradicating the problem once and for all.

So Adam Elvin, lapsed socialist activist, kept his own silent council as the Volvo drove on and on through the interminable grasslands, praying that the greatest capitalist the human race had ever produced would keep his word. If it wouldn't have required so much explaining he would have laughed out loud at the monstrous irony.

'Something up ahead,' Rosamund called out.

Adam broke his reverie to look at the radar display. There was a very broad shallow river a kilometre ahead. The radar return showed a horse on the far side, with someone standing beside it. Given their relative sizes, he thought it must be a child.

'That's got to be someone from Samantha's team,' Kieran said. 'I bet it's Judson McKratz.'

'What makes you say that?' Adam asked.

'I know him. They'll want to confirm we're genuine, and Judson knows this road better than anyone.'

'Good point.' Adam rubbed at his temples. It had been a long trip, and he hadn't had much sleep since . . . probably the Carbon Goose. He was sure he had an hour on the flight. 'Even so . . . force fields on, people.'

The river was wider than Adam realized from the radar. Grass hid it until they were only a couple of hundred metres from the bank. They dipped down a short incline, and he could finally see it was almost four hundred metres across. He whistled softly. Even with a depth that was never greater than half a metre, that was a lot of water. The gentle U-shape course it had carved for itself spoke of much higher levels rushing down from the mountains. On his map, the river stretched back to the Dessault range, where it was fed by dozens of tributaries worming their way out through the foothills.

'One at a time,' he ordered. 'Ayub, stay here and get ready to give us covering fire.'

'Yes, sir.'

Rosamund inched their Volvo down onto the stony river bed. Its suspension lowered the wheels below the chassis, and they moved forward in a series of lurches that rocked the cab about. Even in Far Away's gravity, Adam had to strap himself in tight.

The rider standing beside the dark-grey horse was an adult human male, wearing a long walnut-coloured oilskin greatcoat and broad-rimmed hat which deflected the drizzle like a force field. As they drew near to the bank, Adam gawped in astonishment. The Guardians he'd met always talked about their Charlemagnes with a sense of pride. Now he could see why. The beast was big and hellishly intimidating. He eyed its short metal-tipped horn, and vowed not to venture within twenty metres of the brute.

The Volvo wobbled up out of the river.

'That's Judson all right,' Kieran said with a wide smile. He jumped down out of the cab to greet his old colleague. The two of them embraced warmly, and Kieran brought him over to the lorry. Adam climbed out. The Charlemagne had tusks, he saw. It probably wasn't a herbivore.

'Mr Elvin,' Judson said. 'Welcome. I have heard your name many times. Those who return from the Commonwealth speak well of you.'

'Thank you.' Adam waved the other lorry over. 'We've brought the remainder of the equipment you need.'

'In the nick of time again, eh?' Judson put his arm round Kieran's shoulder, shaking him fondly.

'We're here,' Kieran said. 'Don't complain.'

'Me?' He gave a deep rumbling laugh. 'Seriously, you should be able to reach Samantha by nightfall. She's waiting for you in Reithstone Valley, with additional transport ready to ferry the components out to the remaining stations. And after that! You are lucky I know the deepest caves in this region.' He pulled an array out of his coat pocket. 'I'll let them know you're here.'

Adam's array picked up a song being played on the short wave frequency they'd been given. He suspected not many people would know it without an e-butler search of library files. Somebody here had a strange sense of humour. The sound of 'Hey Jude' washed across the eternal grasslands.

A few minutes later, his array found the salsa hit 'Morgan' being played, drifting in and out of reception as the ionosphere undulated far above them. He remembered dancing to that in his own youth.

'That's the acknowledgement,' Judson said.

'I'm curious,' Adam said. 'What if it hadn't been us?'

Judson gave him a broad smile. ' "*Sympathy for the Devil.*" '

Making contact with Judson had provided all of them with a definite morale boost. After the shock of discovering the sabotage, they needed to know they weren't isolated, a state the grassland had emphasized for hour after hour.

The Volvos drove off down the buried road again, leaving Judson behind. For all the size and power of the Charlemagne, it couldn't keep up with the lorries' unceasing pace. The dark clouds began to break up in the late afternoon, allowing huge sunbeams to play down past their frayed edges, like searchlights strafing the grassland. As the beams slowly angled up towards the horizontal there was finally a break in the numbingly tedious landscape. Up ahead, the foothills of the Dessault range were beginning to rise above the glistening stalks of Anguilla grass.

An hour later they were driving up the foothills. The grass had finally fallen behind them, unable to rise far up the slopes where the air cooled quickly. Ordinary grass reasserted itself, along with trees and bushes. Their road became clear again, two lines of hard-packed stone winding up the banks and following the contour lines cut into valley walls. It wasn't long before they were level with the first true mountains. On either side of them, sharp rocky peaks smeared with snow protruded into the ice-clear sapphire sky, casting huge shadows down into the valleys as the sun fell.

Twice, Adam saw riders on Charlemagnes high above the

road, watching them as they crawled on towards Reithstone Valley. It was becoming difficult to receive radio transmissions amid the mountains. The last they heard of Highway One was a Guardians' ambush team engaging a Cruiser patrol at the Kantrian Bridge a couple of hours before the Starflyer reached it. After a couple more engagements with Institute troops, Bradley had fallen back again and was now trailing the Starflyer by nearly four hours.

Twilight brought them into yet another high valley where the alpine grass was still struggling to establish itself. Trees and bushes were confined to thickets along the side of the fast-flowing stream that cut along the bottom. Kieran was spelling Rosamund behind the wheel. As they started to climb again, he turned the headlights on. Long beams of blue-tinged light exposed the shelf which was now their road. There was no compacted stone here, the soil was a hard grit bound together with tough short grass and ragged moss. Occasional rockfall mounds had been carved away by machines decades ago, but apart from that the track appeared to be natural. Adam wondered if it had originally been formed by the local equivalent of mountain goats in the millennia before the flare. It was a little too convenient to be completely geological. He was also slightly discomfited by how narrow it was in sections. The width fluctuated constantly. There were no crash barriers; and the slope below was so steep it was getting on for vertical. Thankfully, it was getting harder to see the valley floor as the light shrank away out of the sky. Stars began to appear overhead.

Adam went to check on Paula again. The cab's air conditioning unit was now blowing warm air through the vents, compensating for the chill of altitude. She moaned when he slid the composite door open, and she instinctively turned away from the pink twilight which shone in through the windscreen.

'How are you doing?' he asked.

A skeletal face peered up at him from a nest of blankets.

Adam sniffed the air, and tried not to grimace in disgust. Paula had been sick; sticky brown fluid stained the blankets she was clutching. He thought there might be specks of blood in it.

'Here.' He handed her a bottle of water. 'You've got to drink more.'

Just looking at it made her shudder. 'Can't.'

'You're dehydrating, that just makes this worse.' He began to tug his dark red sweater off over his head. 'Give me the top blanket and put this on.'

She said nothing, but released her grip on the blanket. He bundled it away in a polythene bag, then adjusted the vent controls for a quick blast of clear air to rid the little compartment of the rancid smell. Paula took a long time to pull the sweater on. The one time he tried to help, she pushed his hands away, determined to do it herself. He didn't offer again. If she still had pride there was hope for her personality yet.

'I've got some sedatives left,' he said when she fell back down onto the cot, completely exhausted.

'No.' She beckoned at the bottle he was holding. 'I'll try and drink.'

'You need more than that.'

'I'll try and remember.'

'The Guardians will have a doctor.'

'We'll stick to the diagnostic array, thank you. I trust that more than any doctor on this world.'

'That's prejudice.'

'It's my life.'

'Look, we both know—'

'We've got company,' Rosamund sang out. 'Trucks up ahead, coming our way.'

Adam gave Paula a long look. 'We'll talk about this later.'

'It's hard for me to avoid you.'

He went back into the cab, glancing at the radar display. 'What have you got?'

Kieran pointed out through the windscreen. Several points of light were moving along the side of the mountain ahead of them, shining bright in the deep shadow.

'See if you can contact them,' Adam told Rosamund. He wasn't particularly worried. If the Institute had by some miracle tracked them down, they wouldn't be so blatant.

'Answering signal,' Rosamund said. 'It's Samantha all right. She says they need to get started with the equipment straight away.'

They drove on for another kilometre before finding a broad section of the road shelf where they could all park. Samantha's vehicles roared in ten minutes later as the sapphire sky finally faded to black, and the stars shone with an intensity Adam rarely got to see on any Commonwealth world. Seven medium-sized trucks and five old Vauxhall jeeps parked around the Volvos. All of them had tough primitive-looking AS suspension and their engines were thunderous in the thin air, exhaust pipes blowing out mucky vapour. Twenty Guardians climbed out, giving the new Volvos an inquisitive examination.

Samantha was younger than Adam was expecting, certainly still in her twenties, with an enormous cloud of dark-red hair that was wound back into a boisterous tail which hung a long way down her broad back. A face that was eighty per cent freckles smiled curiously at him when they met in front of the Volvos, illuminated by the bright blue-tint of the headlights.

Adam took out the crystal holding the Martian data and handed it over to her with a flourish.

'Adam Elvin.' She shook his hand. 'Pleased to meet you. I've heard your name a lot from people who come back.'

There was something in the way she said that, almost like

an accusation. 'Thanks. We weren't expecting to see you for a while yet.'

'Yeah, I know. Change of plan. Have you been following the Highway One reports?'

'Yes.'

'The Starflyer's making better progress than we expected. We really need to get those last manipulator stations up and running. I figured it would be quicker to offload the equipment to my people now, and they'll disperse from here.'

'Sure, hey this is your field. We're just the delivery team.'

'You've done a good job. With this.'

Again, there was that tone. 'Anything the matter?'

'Hey, sorry pal.' She gripped his arm tightly. 'No offence, but I'm Lennox's mother. I was good friends with Kazimir, too. Real good friends.'

Adam didn't understand the Lennox reference. 'Oh, I didn't know. I'm sorry. Kazimir was a good man, one of the best.'

Rosamund gave a discreet cough behind him. 'Bruce is Lennox's father.'

Adam looked from Rosamund to Samantha, completely flummoxed. 'Christ. Uh, did you know he's dead too?'

'Been dead a long time, pal. Just his body been walking round out there.' Another firm squeeze on Adam's arm. 'After this, if you've got time, I'd like to hear about it. Be good coming from the horse's mouth.'

'Of course.'

'For now we need to shift our arses into gear, and sharpish. How much did you bring?'

'Just about everything we said we would. There's twenty-five tons in each lorry. Some got damaged en route, not much.'

'Yeah, heard you had some trouble.' Samantha eyed the navy people. 'How's that going?'

'It's under control.'

Samantha mulled that over for a while. 'You're our top man in the Commonwealth, Bradley Johansson trusts you, so I will too. But I don't need any surprises, pal. Out here we have a very easy solution for Starflyer agents.'

'Understood. You won't get any surprises.'

Samantha produced a hand-held array that was old enough to have been on Far Away right from the start. 'I'll need the inventory, but that kind of tonnage! Dreaming heavens, sounds like we've got more than enough. Thanks again; this planet might just get its revenge after all. That must have been some ride to get here.'

'It had its moments.'

'Let's hope it wasn't for nothing. Time really is being a bitch to us right now. Can we start unloading?'

'Sure.' He got Rosamund and Jamas to open the trailers while he handed Samantha a spare hand-held array and showed her how to use it. She whistled appreciatively at its adaptive-logic voice recognition, and started searching the inventory list. A minute later she was bellowing instructions to her people. Guardians and trolleybots were soon beavering away, unloading the crates.

'Just how time-critical are things?' Adam asked. He was beginning to feel redundant, standing with the navy people in a little cluster while Jamas and the others were smiling away as they greeted friends they hadn't seen in years.

Samantha sucked on her lower lip and lowered her voice. 'My teams should pull through. The drivers will dose up on beezees and run the mountains like a bat out of hell tonight, each of the stations will get their load tomorrow; Zuggenhim Ridge is the furthest away, and that should be done by midday, which is cutting it fine for assembly, but I'll take that one myself. We're going to start the planet's revenge the day after tomorrow no matter how many stations are ready. No choice, pal.'

Adam did some quick mental arithmetic. 'That is going to be tight.' He reckoned the Starflyer would reach the Institute sometime after midday.

'Very,' she said. 'But that's not the real problem.'

'What is?'

'Our observation team is badly behind schedule. As soon as we heard the Starflyer was through the gateway we tried to tell them to start. They were camped in the Nalosyle Vales, and there was a bad weather front round there. We didn't get through until early this morning, bastard short wave is good for crap all. If they have nothing but good luck, it'll take them three days to get up to Aphrodite's Seat.'

'What does the observation team do?' Wilson asked.

'We have to know the topology of the weather patterns,' Samantha said. 'We need to plot the morning stormfronts exactly as they come round Mount Herculaneum, then we need to see what effect our manipulators are having so we can direct the damn thing properly. It's going to be tricky enough for the control group without working half blind.'

'Satellite imagery?' Anna said.

'No satellites here,' Wilson said. 'I remember talking to the Institute director a while back. Got a personal update on infrastructure.' He grinned distantly.

Samantha gave him a very interested look. 'Right. Which is why we need someone on Aphrodite's Seat. From there you can see right to the eastern end of the Dessault Mountains. It's also a perfect com relay point; no more crapping short wave.'

'But they're not going to get there in time,' Adam said. That arithmetic wasn't difficult at all.

'Trust me, we're kicking their arses as much as we can over the radio. Not that we can say much without drawing too much attention. If anyone can do it, they will.'

'Isn't there any other way up there?' Wilson asked. 'What about flying? There must be some aircraft on Far Away.'

'Aphrodite's Seat is above the atmosphere. In any case, nobody goes flying planes around the Grand Triad, not with the winds that hit them from the ocean.'

'I thought tourists flew over it,' Oscar said.

'Sure do,' Samantha said. 'Rich morons try and catch the winds so they can glide over it. The lucky ones make it to the far side. Not onto the peak.'

'The right parabola could get you there,' Wilson said thoughtfully.

'And you know how to do that?' Samantha asked scornfully.

Wilson leant forwards with a menacing smile that shut down her attitude. Adam could see what an unfair contest it was; a young Samantha who cheerfully bossed round a team of freedom fighters and the admiral, an ex-fighter pilot who had captained the *Second Chance* then went on to command the navy.

'I'm the only human being ever to have flown on Mars,' he told her equably. 'I aerobraked a spaceplane from a two hundred kilometre orbit and landed on a designated site the size of a tennis court. How about you?'

'Shit! You're dicking with me, pal.'

'Wilson,' Oscar was tugging at his arm. 'Come on man, that was over three hundred years ago. And that plane had rocket engines to help you steer, these gliders don't.'

'That kind of flying is not something you forget or erase,' Wilson said. 'Besides, the tour companies here must have skill memory implants.'

'Well, yeah,' an astounded Samantha said. 'But, come on! Landing on the summit of Mount Herculaneum? Are you serious?'

'Yes, are you?' Adam asked. As soon as Wilson suggested it, Adam had begun sketching out consequences and opportunities. Even if there was only the slightest chance of success they had to make the effort. It wasn't going well on Highway One, and the superstorm wouldn't happen unless the control group was fully functional. After everything they'd gone through, the sacrifices they'd endured to get the Martian data here, he couldn't bear the idea of it not having its chance.

'You'll need a lot of electrical gear,' Samantha said. 'We need high resolution panoramic vision and clear relay channels. I haven't got anything like that here.'

Wilson tapped her ancient array. 'The electronics we're carrying are a lot better than anything of yours I've seen so far, no offence.'

'First things first,' Adam said. 'Can we reach the gliders which the tourists use in time to get up there before the Starflyer arrives at the Institute?'

Samantha sucked in a long breath. 'It'll be tight, pal. You'll need to get the hyperglider tethered down in Stakeout Canyon tomorrow night to catch the morning storm. The travel companies hangar them at Stonewave, that's on the wet desert west of the Aldrin Plain. You'll have to burn some gas to get there in time, tomorrow afternoon at the latest.'

Adam pulled the map out of his virtual vision grid, tracing the northern edge of the Dessault Mountains to the west until he found the town. She was right, it was a long way, much further than Wolfstail. 'Can it be done?' he asked.

'Yeah, maybe. There's a track wedged in between the foothills and the top of the grasslands. You use that and you don't have to drive through the crapping Anguilla grass. It'll take you round Herculaneum and out on the north side of Mount Zeus. Stonewave is a straight line north from there.'

Adam turned his attention back to the lorries. 'We'll unhitch the trailers from the cabs. We'll make much better time without them.'

'You'll need to, pal. Believe me when I say you do not want to be caught anywhere near Herculaneum tomorrow morning after the storm comes in from the ocean. If you're going to live, never mind fly, you have to get into the lee of Zeus before sunrise.'

'Thanks.'

She gazed at Wilson. 'You really going to do this?'

'*We're* really going to do this,' Oscar said.

'Huh?' Wilson gave him a startled look.

'You heard,' Anna said. 'We all know how to fly. That's one up on most of the tourists crazy enough to try this. And with three of us, there'll be a better chance that someone will survive to smash down on the top of the mountain.'

'You mean glide gently to a soft halt,' Oscar said.

'I know what I mean.'

Wilson put his arm around her. 'Are you sure?'

'I'm sure.' She stroked his cheek tenderly. 'You still owe me a honeymoon.'

'This trip isn't good enough?'

She kissed him, her eyes shining. 'Not yet.'

'Dreaming heavens,' Samantha said. 'You people are something else. But . . . thanks.'

Wilson gave her a curt nod, still in command. 'We'll need your exact observation requirements, and the communication specs so we can modify our equipment. Do Rosamund and the rest know the route to Stonewave?'

'Pretty much. The tourist companies use the route along the side of the foothills to chase after their hypergliders, so it's pretty well marked out.'

*

Adam caught up with Oscar as the trailers were being unhitched from the Volvo cabs. Almost all of the crates had been unloaded. The truck to Zuggenhim Ridge had already left. Samantha was going to take a jeep and follow it, once she and another Guardian called Valentine had finished briefing Wilson and Jamas on the technical details of the observation. They were going to spend the trip to Stonewave modifying their arrays to duplicate the performance of the equipment which the original observation team carried.

'I'm glad you volunteered,' Adam said.

'I wasn't about to let Wilson go and—' His eyes narrowed in suspicion. 'Why?'

'Because I'm only going to allow you to fly.'

'What!' Oscar hunched down instinctively, checking to see if anyone was looking. 'What are you talking about?' he asked in a low voice.

'You think Wilson and Anna are suddenly in the clear because they offered to do this?'

'Well . . .' Oscar rubbed a hand hard across his forehead. 'Oh Christ.'

'Assume one of them is the traitor, and they make it to the top. The whole planet's revenge project is dependent on that observation.' Adam slapped his hands together vigorously. 'They've fucked us. Bang, it's over. Starflyer makes it back to the *Marie Celeste* and leaves.'

'When are you going to tell them?'

'After we've got to Stonewave and prepared the hypergliders. That's the other thing, this trip will keep all of us away from these manipulator stations Samantha is building; I don't want any sudden freak accidents to happen to them, either. Once we've found a working hyperglider and set it up ready to fly, I'll tell them they're grounded. My Guardians team will back me up.'

'Adam, please, I'm not that good a pilot. Hell, the only time I've actually flown in the last ten years is on the Carbon Goose.'

'The insert memories will help. You'll make it, Oscar, you always do.'

*

Four Land Rover Cruisers were parked across Highway One. Ion shots raked the sky above them, punching into buildings where Institute troopers were shooting at the approaching line of Guardians vehicles. The kinetic rapid-fire gun mounted on the bonnet of the Cruiser blocking the nearside lane began firing at the cab of the big eighteen-wheel Loko truck that was bearing down on it at a hundred kilometres an hour. An answering hyper-rifle shot from the truck's cab struck the Cruiser head on, slicing clean through its force field. It exploded violently, lifting its broken-backed chassis off the ground to somersault in mid-air.

'Going airborne,' The Cat's voice called out blithely on the general band. Her armoured shape jumped from the Loko's cab, surrounded by a sparkling amber force field. She hit the worn enzyme-bonded concrete and bounced, slamming into the wall of an animal feed store amid a shimmering crimson aurora. The wall shattered and the roof sagged alarmingly.

The flaming corpse of the Cruiser landed on its roof, collapsing under the impact. A second later the Loko truck struck it head on, shunting it back into the rest of the blockade.

Two hundred metres behind, sitting at the wheel of the armoured car, Stig winced at the impact. The Loko truck rampaged onwards. Two more crumpled Cruisers lurched into the air as it struck them, their force fields flaring dangerous scarlet. Scraps of wreckage tumbled fast across Highway One beneath a huge fireball flooding up into the empty sapphire sky. Tiger Pansy squealed in Stig's ear. It was like a fingernail scrape plugged into a rock band's amp stack. 'Holy shit,' she sighed in exhilaration. 'You're not going to . . .?'

He kept the accelerator floored as the blazing chassis of the truck performed a slow jack-knife across the two southbound lanes. The buildings on the side of the road were getting perilously close, blocking the narrow slit of side window with a high speed smear of fanciful coloured paint. In front, the Loko's chassis was slowly coming to a halt, leaving a very small gap that continued to shrink. Stig's arms gripped the steering wheel like bands of steel. He refused to brake. Flames were fanning out across the enzyme-bonded concrete as the tank on the fourth Cruiser burst open, spilling out a wave of fuel that was already alight.

'Dreaming heavens,' Bradley gasped from the front passenger bench; his hands clawed at the cushioning. A lavish sheet of flame roared upwards, covering both lanes.

They flashed through the gap, their slipstream pulling some of the flame with them. In the air above, fire and smoke swirled in micro-cyclone patterns.

'Fucking-A,' Tiger Pansy agreed loudly.

The road ahead was clear. Stig steered them back into the outside lane. The Mazda jeeps and the other armoured cars following him drove through the gap, keeping their set fifty metre separation distance. Then came the last three Loko trucks.

'Cat?' Stig called. 'Cat, are you okay?'

Bradley was pressed against the slit window, staring back along the road. 'Can't see anybody. Still a lot of flame.'

'Cat?' Morton asked. For once he sounded concerned.

'Boys. You care. How sweet.'

Cheers rang out from all the vehicles.

In the rear-view camera image Stig saw The Cat's armoured shape walk out of the ruined feed store. A Mazda jeep braked hard, tyres leaving black rubber streaks on the enzyme-bonded concrete. The front door opened, and The Cat climbed in as if she was hitching a lift.

'Any bad guys survive?' Alic asked.

'I'm monitoring local net traffic,' Keely said. 'The residents haven't seen any yet. Mind you, they're still keeping their heads down.'

'Tell them not to approach any survivors,' Bradley said.

'Yes, sir.'

'Now that was fun,' The Cat said. 'How long till the next one?'

'Half an hour,' Olwen muttered in a piqued tone.

Like all of them, Olwen had been keen to join battle when they finally caught up with the Starflyer. It was an event Stig and Bradley had soon realized was never going to happen if they kept getting delayed by the Institute patrols. Bradley had made the decision to adopt the head-on collision tactic. Only the state-of-the-art armour suits worn by the Paris team and Cat's Claws could perform that duty, which left the rest of the Guardians more than a little envious.

Another of the big Loko trucks they'd liberated from the depot growled past Stig's armoured car. Jim Nwan was driving. His gauntlet waved as he manoeuvred the truck into point position.

The beezee Stig had taken to keep alert during the second full day of driving made it hard for him to slacken his grip on the steering wheel. They narrowed the brain's focus onto one task and kept the neurones zinging with the precision of a processor. People had kept doing the same thing for up to a week when they were dosed up. You didn't need sleep, but it became difficult for the mind to nudge its way out of the thought-loop that bestowed so much attention.

'Anybody else between us and the Anculan?' he asked.

'No reported sightings,' Keely said. 'I'm still not getting anything close to the bridge. The road net ends a hundred miles this side of it. Even the redundant systems have failed after that. Nobody's picking up any radio coming from the south, either. I'm still getting check signals from Rock Dee on the short wave but that's all.'

'Okay.'

At their current speed, and assuming no further clashes with the Institute, they'd reach the Anculan Bridge in another two and a half hours. Best guess put the Starflyer there an hour ago. They didn't know exactly, communications had fallen off dramatically when the Starflyer convoy passed that magic hundred mile marker. What the Institute had done to kill the road's net was subject to a lot of debate among the Guardians.

Stig was desperate for some news. Anculan was where the clans were making their biggest effort to intercept the Starflyer on Highway One. If that didn't slow it down, then the whole pursuit would be for nothing, and they'd have to depend on the planet's revenge and the Final Raid. Not that he would ever criticize Bradley Johansson, but for plans that had been a hundred years in the making their timeframe was starting to look pretty shitty. Besides, the bombing run on F3 Plaza made this personal. He wanted to take down the Starflyer himself. The beezee was loose enough to second track that thought.

Bradley bent over and gave his short wave array a hard look. 'That sounds like Samantha.'

Stig's eyes never left the road. He'd isolated his inserts from any external communication to help his concentration. Up in front, Jim Nwan's truck was belching out a lot of exhaust fumes. The hard blue of the sky splashed strong waves along its elaborate chrome finish. He tried to lock down any repetitive pattern in the reflections. 'What does she say?'

'They're at the last manipulator station. I guess that means Adam got through with their equipment.'

'Good man, Adam. No traitor is going to derail him.'

'Hang on . . .' A grin flicked over his lips. 'She keeps saying she's ready to surf the next wave.' He switched the short wave array to transmit. 'Message acknowledged. Have a good day at the beach.' His reply was automatically repeated ten times.

Olwen dropped her arms onto the back of Bradley's seat, her head resting in her hands, and grinning in satisfaction. 'Tomorrow! Dreaming heavens, can you believe this. It's going to happen tomorrow!'

'Not if I catch it first,' Stig grunted.

Olwen and Bradley shared a glance.

'So Bradley, how do you feel about this?' Tiger Pansy asked.

She was oblivious to the way Olwen's mouth wrinkled with disapproval. 'You've waited a long time for it to happen.'

'I'm not sure I feel anything,' Bradley said. 'I just keep focused on the events happening around us. I know I set them all in motion but don't think I'd ever tried to visualize them for myself before. It's quite something, like looking out on an avalanche as it thunders down a mountain and knowing you threw the first pebble.'

'It's an avalanche that'll bury that bastard Starflyer,' Olwen said. 'We'll see to it.'

'Thank you, my dear. It is your clans that have gifted me a great deal of strength over the decades. You have no idea what it is like to be surrounded by contempt and hatred and yet still have somebody believe in you.'

'Commonwealth's going to owe us, huh?'

'They always have. They just never knew it. So do you know yet, dear Olwen, what you're going to do afterwards?'

'No. Never even thought about it. It's still kind of hard to accept this is happening. I always expected it would be the next generation who helped the planet have its revenge, or the one after. Never mine.'

'Ah well, the day after tomorrow we will all have to sit down and think about what is to become of us. The clans will have to transform themselves. Into what, who knows?'

'If I'm still alive the day after tomorrow, I'll be at the biggest party Far Away's ever had.'

'Fair enough, my dear; we'll wait until after the hangover before we make any important decisions.'

*

They saw the smoke from a couple of miles away. Thin smears of grey vapour wafting up into the hazy equatorial sky, the kind of smoke which only comes from embers.

Haville wasn't a big town, it ran for a couple of kilometres beside the road before tailing off into orange groves. The

Starflyer convoy had started a firestorm at one end and ripped it down the entire length. Shacks assembled from carbon panels had been reduced to piles of slag sprawling over their concrete foundations. Black horizontal scorch marks produced by lasers and masers were visible on all the surviving concrete block walls, running right across the gutted buildings. People were visible amid the debris, desolated and wandering round aimlessly, their shocked eyes following the Guardians' convoy as it charged past. One large open yard had a line of corpses, wrapped up in cloth.

'They hit every node junction,' Keely reported. 'It's not like the net was armoured or anything.'

'I don't think they were that precise,' Bradley said as they reached the end of Haville. Trees along the edge of the orange grove were still burning. 'This is a deliberate scorched earth operation to kill any long range communication along the road.'

'Do you think they've done this to every town?' Olwen asked.

'Undoubtedly.'

*

Nothing else moved along Highway One now. South of Rob Lacey's great avenue of redwoods the land rose steadily to be capped by low hills whose valleys interlocked in gentle curves. Bradley could remember travelling along a newly laid Highway One when this tableland had been barren territory. Today, nearly two centuries later, the rolling slopes were carpeted by rich emerald vegetation of shaggy grass and small verdant trees. The midday sun turned the crown of the sapphire sky to a white blaze-patch too bright to look at directly. Visibility was perfect. Looking over Stig's shoulder through the thick glass of the armoured car's windscreen, he could see the mud-grey strip of enzyme-bonded concrete wind onward through the meandering vales for miles in front of them. There was nowhere for a Cruiser patrol to hide. Stig and the other drivers were piling on the speed.

Since Haville, they'd passed through four more small towns that the Starflyer had razed to the ground, ending with Zeefield, the southernmost settlement along Highway One. Word had obviously spread southwards in time. The last three had been deserted; they'd seen no distraught victims nor lines of corpses amid the smouldering ruins. Wherever the residents had fled to, they were staying quiet. Keely had been unable to raise anyone on the local bands.

Right across the rolling tablelands, the fibre optic cable which linked the Institute to Armstrong City supported a series of nodes to provide communications to anyone using the road. They were spaced five kilometres apart, protected from the elements inside metre-wide domes which sprouted from the ground beside the road like composite mushrooms. Every one had been masered, the high-density carbon turning to a slate-grey sludge surrounded by singed grass.

'I came up here for my first act against the Starflyer,' Stig said as Highway One began to dip down into one of the deeper vales towards the end of the tablelands. 'We were always cutting the cable up here. It was easy.'

'Now they're using that isolation against us,' Bradley said. 'Though attacking every single node speaks of deep insecurity. A couple of simple cuts would be sufficient.'

'Why bother?' Olwen asked. 'It knows we're using short wave; it can't block our critical communications.'

'In some respects it is remarkably unimaginative,' Bradley said. 'If destroying the road net has caused us inconvenience before, it simply continues to perform the disruption.'

'That sounds more like an array program than a sentient creature.'

'In some respects its neurological functions are strikingly similar to those of a processor. What tactics it possesses it either determines by trial and error, or absorbs from other

1094

more intuitive sources. A fast flowing situation like this chase will be difficult for it. There is no time for it to work through options to see which is the most effective.'

'You mean it gets its ideas from humans?'

'Yes, a lot of the time; though the longer they are under its control the more their ability to think in an original or inventive fashion is reduced.'

'No wonder it wants to get rid of us. It can't compete.'

'Not on our terms, no. But nonetheless it has brought us to the brink of destruction. Don't underestimate it.'

'Yes, sir.'

Bradley was moved by the level of determination in her voice. Returning to Far Away after so long he'd even been slightly disturbed by the unquestioning respect he kindled among the clans. It was almost as if the Commonwealth authorities were right to brand him a cult leader.

Highway One began its long descent out of the tablelands, tracking around the steeper gorges, then bending in great switchback loops down the final escarpment to deliver them onto the sweltering veldt. This was where Far Away's first true rainforest was busy establishing itself, sweeping out from Mount StOmer at the north-western corner of the Dessault Mountains away to the southern shoreline of the Oak Sea. The grasses had come first, seeded by the blimpbots, refreshing the soil before the trees and vines were introduced over a fifty-year period. The central core of rainforest was now thriving and expanding without any further human encouragement.

Bradley could see the Anculan valley from a long way off, an intrusive furrow running west to east across the veldt, emptying into the Oak Sea. Its vegetation was noticeably darker than the luxuriant jade of the rainforest, shading down to olive-green as if the gully was permanently in shadow. The river was fed by dozens of tributaries emerging from the Dessault Mountains, giving it a lavish forceful flow that had cut deep into the landscape, creating a gully over two hundred metres wide and up to thirty deep with near-sheer sides. Dense bushes filled the base of the gully on either side of the water, their half-exposed root balls scrabbling for purchase on the glutinous mud. Water pumpkins had colonized the shallows, their brimstone-coloured fruit bobbing about, ranging from buds no bigger than oranges up to the full-grown football-size globes with mushy wrinkled skin. Their wreath of slim black tendrils swished around them in the current as if eels were nesting in the stem. This close to the mountains, the Anculan's water was loaded with so much sediment it was the colour of milky coffee.

Given the difficulty and expense of ferrying steel girders to Far Away, the most cost effective method of bridging a gulf of this size was with a single span arch of concrete supporting the road above, which narrowed from its usual four lanes down to two.

The Guardians' demolition team had made a good job of bringing it down. All that remained of the arch were thick broken tusks of concrete curving up from either side of the river. The central hundred metre section of the road was gone, its remnants a cluster of submerged boulders creating a furious surge of white water.

Alic and Morton stood on the edge of the broken road, using their active sensors to scan the thick wall of the rainforest on the opposite side. There was no sign of hostiles hidden among the wall of vegetation. 'Looks clear,' Alic reported.

Stig and the others stood on the lip of the gorge next to the road, looking down into the surging water twenty metres below. Bodies were snagged on the new boulders, three of them wearing the dark impact armour of the Institute troops, a couple in camouflage fatigues. They all had terrible wounds. A Charlemagne had been snagged by the bushes just below the river, its body starting to bloat. When Stig began to scan upstream, he saw more bodies jammed into the mud and vegetation.

'Pretty clear which way they went,' Bradley said. A swathe of open ground bordered the top of the gorge, where grass creepers and bushes formed a buffer between the rainforest and the precipice. Its moist soil had been torn up by the wheels of the Starflyer convoy.

'Commander Hogan, Morton, could your people take point along here please,' Bradley said. 'We need to find where they forded the river.'

'Sure thing,' Alic said. He and Morton left the bridge.

Cat's Claws and the Paris team began jogging along the track, with the armoured cars and jeeps following. They drove along the top of the gorge for another two kilometres. In some places the walls rose up to forty metres high. Below them, scattered along the river, dead bodies lay in the mud with water flowing round and over them. After the first thirty, everyone stopped counting.

The Starflyer convoy had made its crossing two and a quarter kilometres upriver from the bridge. A dip in the gorge wall on both sides reduced the height to a little over ten metres. Explosives had been used to rip the bottom out of the dip and pulverize the remainder of the wall, creating a sloping heap that the vehicles could drive down. It was a crude ramp which was mirrored on the other side of the Anculan.

Three wrecked Cruisers were just visible in the middle of the river, with the water churning over them; two more were burnt out on the northern ramp. One had been caught by kinetic and ion fire on the other side, then bulldozed out of the way by a heavier vehicle. Big patches of vegetation were blackened and smouldering. Twenty dead Charlemagnes were lying among the sodden bushes; some still had their riders strapped in the saddles. There were more bodies in the edges of the rainforest.

Bradley gazed out on the battlefield and lowered his head in grief. 'Dreaming heavens, please let this end swiftly.'

'One of them's moving!' Morton called out. 'Cover me

please.' He started down the rough slope, his boots slipping and sliding on the muddy shale. Rob and The Cat followed at a slower rate.

'Commander, can you get over to the other side, please?' Bradley said. 'Make sure there are no surprises for us over there.'

'You got it,' Alic acknowledged.

The Paris team started down the ramp.

'Stig, we'll go over as soon as they've given us the go-ahead.'

'Yes, sir.' Stig eyed the turbulent river. 'Uh, our jeeps will get through that kind of current okay. I'm not sure about some of the trucks on a river this strong. We could rig up winches, perhaps.'

'No. We have to keep moving. Anything that can't make it under its own power is left here.'

'Bradley,' Morton called. 'He's one of yours. Keeps asking for you.'

Bradley went down the ramp along one of the tyre tracks, thinking the soil and shingle would be firmer there; even so his feet slipped several times on loose patches. Stig followed him a couple of paces behind, their biggest medical kit bag hanging off his shoulder.

Cat's Claws was standing some way off from the bottom of the ramp in the middle of the bushes. One of the Charlemagnes had fallen nearby, its bulk skidding for several metres through the undergrowth before it finally stopped. Just behind it, lying in the muddy wake of crushed vegetation, its rider had come to rest in a gouge that was slowly filling with water. His scarf was the emerald and copper check of the McFoster clan, though the proud colours were now hard to distinguish below all the blood which the cloth had soaked up. A very old-fashioned force field skeleton worn over his dark fatigues had burned through in several places. By far the worst of his wounds was a rent along the side of his torso, which was coated in bloody mud.

Bradley narrowed his eyes at the sight of the man's thick ruddy skin with its subsurface lacework of broken veins. 'Harvey? Harvey is that you?'

'Dreaming heavens, it is you,' Harvey's ruined voice croaked feebly. 'They said you were here. I didn't believe it, not really. I'm sorry. I knew in my heart you wouldn't leave us to face that monster alone.'

Bradley dropped to his knees in the blood puddles beside the old warrior. 'What are you doing here? You're not supposed to fight any more.'

'One last battle, Bradley. That's all. I grew so tired of training the youngsters, sending them out while I waited behind. I always needed one last battle for myself. And thank the dreaming heavens it was a glorious fight. Our ancestors are proud of us this day.'

'I'm proud of you, Harvey, I always have been. Now lie back. Stig's got a medical kit, he'll get you stable.'

'Bradley.' Harvey's hand came up and gripped the front of Bradley's shirt.

'Yes?'

'Bradley . . . you should see the other fella.' Breath rasped out of his mouth in the best laughter he could produce.

Bradley closed his hand over Harvey's. 'Don't talk.'

Stig almost fell to the ground, staring aghast at his old combat instructor. 'You'll be all right, Harvey. I've got a medical kit that's come direct from the Commonwealth. There's healskin in it, and biogenics, the whole works.'

'Save it, lad,' Harvey whispered. 'You'll need it for real after the planet's revenge.'

Stig bowed his head, tears running freely down his cheeks.

'Harvey?' Bradley asked. 'How long ago did this happen? Can you remember?'

'I've got it for you,' Harvey said. 'I watched when the monster's truck went up the slope and noted the time. I knew you'd need it. The others, all kids, they never listen to me when I tell them what's important.' He glanced at the ancient black-chrome digital watch on his wrist. 'Eighty-seven minutes, Bradley. That's all it's got on you now. I told you we put up a good fight.'

'You did. And we will finish the job now, I promise that.'

Harvey's eyes closed. He let out a wheezing breath.

'Give him something for the pain,' Bradley told Stig. 'Then get him into one of our jeeps.' He gently detached Harvey's hand from his shirt, and looked at the scarlet mud stain it had left on his shirt as though trying to remember how it got there.

'Sir,' Stig said with an edgy voice. 'We can't move him. These injuries . . .'

'Harvey is going to the dreaming heavens, and nothing you carry in your bag will prevent that,' Bradley said. 'We cannot wait here for that to happen, and I will not allow him to be left alone to die. Even if he only lasts a few minutes he will be with us, his comrades, as we chase our nemesis to its doom. Would you deny him that?'

Harvey laughed again, a weak burbling sound. His eyes were still closed. 'You tell him, Bradley. Kids today. May the dreaming heavens preserve us from them.'

Stig nodded humbly, and opened the medical kit.

Bradley climbed to his feet. 'Eighty-seven minutes,' he told Cat's Claws. 'We can catch it.'

*

Adam had considered the name 'wet desert' to be a near perfect oxymoron, right up until the moment they started driving across it. Every day the storm which came in from the Hondu Ocean at dawn brought clouds that dumped between four and five centimetres of rain on the region before they finally blew out in the late morning. The wet desert was a wide shelf of land dropping steadily over hundreds of miles from the Aldrin Plain down to the shore of the ocean, a flat expanse that was made up from sand and shingle. Essentially, it was the biggest beach in the known galaxy, although the last tide had gone out about a quarter of a million years ago. Geologists on early survey expeditions determined it used to be covered by the Hondu Ocean, which would have put the Grand Triad right on the coastline. It must have been quite something to see the lava from such enormous volcanoes pouring into the ocean.

When the rains fell on the wet desert they flowed across the saturated surface into hundreds of shallow, miles-wide channels which drained right back into the ocean. An hour after the clouds were banished into the east, the ground was exposed again, the run-off was so quick. Noon equatorial sunlight shone down through empty skies, baking the water-logged surface and producing a layer of warm viscous fog that clung to the ground for most of the rest of the day.

In the early days of the planet's human settlement, the revitalization team spread some lichen spores about over the wet desert, then went away scratching their heads, unsure what to do next. That was a hundred and fifty years ago. They still hadn't been back.

There was no sign of lichen from the cab of the lead Volvo. There was no sign of any life. No high-order organism could survive the strange cycle of water, heat, vapour and scouring winds.

Adam himself was taking a turn at the wheel. It had been an exhausting trip, especially for the Guardians who'd shared the driving so the three navy people could rest before the flight. They'd only just made it past Mount Herculaneum in the small hours of the morning. After that they were halfway round the rocky base of Mount Zeus as the dawn broke and the winds rose, forcing them to park behind a rock outcrop and secure the Volvo cabs with carbicon ropes. Even then Adam had been frightened that the heavy vehicles would be blown away. Samantha was right; if they'd been caught at the base of Herculaneum in the full blast of the storm as it churned round the giant mountain's flanks they would never have survived.

Once the winds subsided enough for them to walk around without being blown away, they'd untied the ropes and set off again. A couple of hours later they reached the northernmost boundary of Zeus's base, and powered down onto the wet desert. Almost immediately they'd been engulfed by the fog.

The radar was on, sweeping ahead for obstacles or ravines. So far there hadn't been any. Adam didn't have the headlights on, there was no point. The sun fluoresced the fog to a uniform white glow surrounding the cab as it sped onwards; visibility was rarely more than fifteen metres. Even so, he could push the speed up to a good hundred and thirty kilometres an hour.

There was no problem with erosion on the wet desert, total saturation bestowed the sand with a fantastic degree of cohesion, locking every grain and grit particle into place like an epoxy. It provided a remarkably stable base to drive on, albeit one with very poor traction had they needed to brake sharply. The wide drainage channels were at most fifteen centimetres deep, allowing them to speed across unhindered. Huge fantails of spray unfolded from the Volvo's wheels as if they were sprouting wings.

'I think we're coming up on the town,' Adam announced. The radar was showing a protuberance rising out of the flat ground five miles ahead of them, the first real interruption to the wet desert's monotony.

Rosamund crowded over his shoulder, staring at the screen. 'Yeah that's got to be it. Coordinates match.'

Adam squinted, his retinal inserts on maximum resolution. Beyond the dreary sweep of the windscreen wipers the radiant fog remained resolutely impenetrable. He checked the radar again. 'Is that size right?' His foot instinctively eased off the accelerator.

'I guess so.' Rosamund sounded perturbed now.

Calling this region the wet desert should have warned Adam; Far Away's inhabitants were a literal lot. The stone wave was a ridge of red sedimentary rock almost two kilometres long, and rising up to three hundred metres along its smooth crest. Erosion had eviscerated one side, sculpting a gigantic overhanging cavity that ran for two thirds of the length and extending up to three hundred metres deep. Looking at it as they approached from the southern end, Adam saw it really did have the shape of a huge wave, frozen as it started to curve over. According to his files, geologists were still arguing if it had eroded before or after the ocean withdrew.

Stonewave's buildings were laid out in the centre of the giant overhang where the arching roof was at its highest, a hundred and fifty metres to the crest. Although they varied in size, they all followed the same simple oblong box design, standing on short stilts to keep them perfectly level. Their walls, floors and roofs were made from identical blank carbon squares fixed to a sturdy frame. Tucked into the hollow of the wave they were protected from the worst of the elements; the rain never touched them, though the morning wind was still formidable as it eddied over the sheltering rock.

The little town existed only to support the hypergliders. Two of the buildings were fitted out as luxury hotels with fifteen beds each for the ultra-rich tourists who came here to test their luck and nerves in the morning storms. The tourist company staff shared three dormitory blocks; there was a diesel generator, a waste recycling plant, garages and hangars.

Adam drove the cab up onto the rock floor and braked outside one of the hangars with a sign above the sliding doors which read Grand Triad Adventures. His e-butler had been trying to establish a link to the building management arrays with no result. When he scanned round with his retinal insets on infrared the geometric buildings were a uniform temperature.

'Looks like it's deserted,' he said.

'The companies would have shut it down once the tourists stopped coming,' Rosamund said.

'Christ, I hope they left the hypergliders.'

'No reason not to.'

Adam went back to check on Paula. The Investigator was asleep on her little cot, knees drawn up towards her chest. Her forehead was slick with sweat and her breathing was now very shallow. Every now and then she would make a gulping sound as if she was drowning. Adam stared down at her in dismay. He simply didn't know what to do about her. The sedatives had their limits, and none of the drugs or biogenics had made the slightest difference to her overall condition. He was scared to apply the diagnostic array for fear of what it would tell him.

'Stay here and watch her,' he told Rosamund.

She started to protest but he waved her down. 'We don't know this illness is for real,' Adam said, feeling a complete hypocrite. 'And if she wakes up you must get her to drink. Force her if necessary.' In addition to all his other concerns was how long it'd been since she'd eaten anything. The medical kit did contain equipment for intravenous feeding, but he didn't want to go down that route until he had no choice.

He left the cab quickly, shamed at his own relief to be leaving the problem behind. The other Volvo cab had parked just behind his. Wilson was already climbing down when Kieran turned the engine off. It was as if the sound had been sucked away. Between them the stone and fog did weird things to acoustics. Adam glanced up at the curving overhang feeling unnerved for no reason he could pin down.

'How's Paula?' Wilson asked.

'No change,' Adam replied curtly. 'Did you get your arrays modified to handle the comm relay function Samantha needs?'

'We think so, yes; the range is a problem. We took some of the Volvo's modules apart and realigned them. The new unit should do the trick, but we've only got one. I want to take the modules from your cab, and I'm hoping that the vehicles here have similar electronics.'

'They ought to,' Jamas said. He'd climbed down from the cab along with Anna and Oscar. 'The vehicles which the tourist companies use have to keep in contact over long distances. They've probably got better transmitters than the Volvos.'

'Okay, you and Kieran search round for them. We'll need them to tow the hypergliders anyway. And be careful, we don't know this place is deserted. The four of us will take the hangars.'

There was a small door on the side of the Grand Triad Adventures' hangar. Adam had to shoot the lock out with a low-power ion pulse. It was so dark inside that even his retinal inserts were struggling to produce an image. He fumbled round and found the light switch. There must have been some kind of reserve power supply; long polyphoto strips came on, strangely yellow after the unending monochrome glow of the fog. Eight hypergliders rested on their transport cradles. They were in their primary configuration, a fat cigar shape with wings and tailplane buds retracted into flat triangles against the fuselage.

Oscar whistled in admiration. 'Nice machinery.'

'You guys had better check them over,' Adam said. 'This is your scene.'

'Sure,' Wilson said. 'See if you can find the hangar's arrays, please; we'll need the maintenance records.'

'And their performance specs,' Anna added. Her extensive pattern of OCtattoos were emerging to gleam a with a gold lustre under the hangar lights. 'This is one difficult trajectory we're going to have to fly. The arc has got to terminate just right.'

'We'll have to perform a standard overflight trajectory to begin with,' Wilson said. 'Once you're out of the twister you'll be able to adapt the flight profile, kill the velocity and alter the angle to give a touchdown behind Aphrodite's Seat. You can always lose speed, you won't be able to gain it. It'll be tricky, but one of us should manage to get close enough.'

Oscar shot Adam a fast accusing look.

'They must have some sort of summit landing capacity built in,' Anna was saying. 'They can't all hop over the top successfully.'

'If you haven't got the velocity high enough you're supposed to veer off and go around,' Wilson said. He found the manual release for the cockpit canopy on the first hyperglider, and twisted it. The transparent bubble hinged up smoothly. Wilson leant over the rim. 'Here we go.'

Adam's e-butler reported the hyperglider's pilot array had just come online. He held Oscar's gaze uncompromisingly for a moment, then ducked into the office at the back of the hangar. The air inside was musty after being sealed up for so long, every surface had a damp chill to it. Some of the metal items even had a slight coating of condensation.

The desktop array came on as soon as he touched the power stud. Even better, its programs and files didn't have encrypted access. He started to pull up the general information.

'Adam,' Kieran called on an encrypted link, 'we've found the jeeps they use for towing the hypergliders over to Stakeout Canyon. Talk about wind resistant, they look like bubbles. I think they've got anchors, too.'

'Good. See if they've got a service log. We'll take the two with the best record.'

'Will do. Uh, aren't we taking three hypergliders?'

'I'll talk to you guys about that in a minute.'

'Okay. They all need fuelling up anyway. Jamas is going to track down the main diesel tank.'

Adam found a file containing the Grand Triad Adventures' introduction to hypergliding, and gave his e-butler a list of the specific information he wanted extracting. 'What about the drilling equipment they use to tether the gliders?' he asked Kieran.

'Not here. I'll scout round when I've sorted out the jeeps.'

'Right.' A standard itinerary popped up into Adam's virtual vision. 'Damn, we're going to have to be quick. They normally leave for Stakeout Canyon at noon. That gives the crews time to position the hypergliders in the evening and get clear while it's still light.'

'We'll manage it.'

Adam's e-butler had pulled out several sections from the introduction now. He skimmed through them until he found the files on skill memory. The implant was done in a room off the side of the office. He opened the door and found what looked like the kind of waiting area you'd get in a modestly successful legal firm. The exception was the five comfortable leather couches arranged along the back wall, each with its own sophisticated array. A dark mould was starting to spread out of the edges of the slightly damp leather; the first living organism since they arrived on the wet desert. He checked the power reserves on the arrays.

'I've found the skill-memory implanters,' he told the others as he came back into the hangar.

Five of the hypergliders had been opened. Wilson was sitting in the cockpit of one, his hands resting on the console i-spots. Below and behind him the wing buds flexed as if something inside them wanted to be birthed

'Well done,' Wilson said.

'Not quite. There's a slight problem. The humidity back there is even worse than in here, it's screwed up some of the array connections. I'm really only happy with one of the systems. You'll have to go one at a time. I'll settle Oscar in first.'

'Okay,' Wilson said.

Oscar's stony expression was unreadable.

'How's it going out here?' Adam asked.

'We're running through the pre-flight checklists,' Oscar told Adam quietly. 'So far all five seem operational.'

Anna walked past, hauling a thick superconductor cable which she plugged into a socket on the second hyperglider. 'They're going to need charging before we take them out. The secondary power supply is okay, but they can't fly on that. We need the main cells charged; the electromuscle and plyplastic has a lot of work to do.'

'I think the town generator was in the first building we came past,' Adam said. 'Oh, and we need to leave soonest. The drive to Stakeout Canyon from here normally takes a good six hours. Then we have to plant the tether anchors.'

Wilson stood up in the cockpit. 'Let's get on with it, then.'

'We need tether cables for the hypergliders as well,' Anna said. 'They must be around here somewhere.'

'You two sort that out,' Adam said. 'I'll get Oscar up to speed on the joys of hypergliding.'

'There's plenty to go round,' Anna said. She was grinning as she gestured round the hangar. 'Fancy joining us?'

'Not at my age and weight, thank you.'

Wilson clambered down out of the cockpit. He zipped up the front of his fleece. 'Keep an eye on the checklists for me, please.'

'Will do,' Adam promised.

Oscar looked along the row of couches in the rear room. One of them had its array activated, green LEDs were shining on the front of the unit. He gave a snort of disgust. 'Water damage, my arse!'

'We still need them to get the hyperglider ready for you.'

'This is wrong. The odds are completely against me getting up there intact.'

'So tell me which one of them is the Starflyer agent?'

'Oh fuck.'

'Exactly. Lie back on the couch.'

Oscar did as he was told. He rested his wrists on the i-spots. 'Interfaced,' he said.

Adam's virtual vision confirmed the connection. He told his e-butler to initiate the program. Plyplastic cushioning flowed over Oscar's wrists.

'The induction prep phase will last about a minute,' he said, reading from the menu. 'Implantation is eight minutes.'

'And integrity review is another minute,' Oscar said. 'Yes, thank you. I went through this enough times when I was with CST exploratory division. The junk we need to know for that . . .'

'Relax please,' Adam said dryly. He moved his virtual hands across the icons, initiating the induction preparation phase.

Oscar's eyes were already closed. Now his face began a series of minute twitches to accompany the REM.

Adam went back into the hangar. Two of the hypergliders were still running through their checklists. No problems had been red flagged.

He was peering into the cockpit of one when he heard a sound behind him. He lifted his head to see who it was. 'Oh, couldn't you—'

The slim harmonic blade was rammed into the base of his skull, angled perfectly to slice up into his brain.

18

The quantumbuster would not load into its launch tube. There was nothing Ozzie or the SIsubroutine could do to make the fat missile slide out of its magazine rack into the tube. Not one goddamn thing. He'd tried every trick he could think of: forcing power into the electromuscle handling arms just made them spasm and flash up burnout overload warnings in his virtual vision; getting the SIsubroutine to review the code for the whole magazine management program only proved that the software was effective; and running diagnostic after diagnostic on the physical mechanism showed every component was fully functional.

It still didn't work.

Ozzie let out a furious snarl. There was a dark pressure inside his head that was growing with each passing hour. He'd never known frustration like it. To have got to this point only to be blocked by some kind of glitch was the kind of irony that only a truly badass god would practise.

There is a logical reason why this machine does not work; therefore I will find the fault.

When he looked around his virtual vision at the appallingly complex architecture of the launch mechanism, all he could think to do was beat his virtual fists against it. His inability to concentrate wasn't helped by lack of food. Two days now. He hadn't slept much during that time either.

There was an unexpected yet familiar rustling sound in the cabin which drew Ozzie's attention back through the virtual structure. On the right-hand couch Mark was floating a couple of centimetres above the cushioning with his back towards Ozzie. The rustling came again.

'Yo, Mark what's . . . Hey. Wait a goddamn minute! Is that CHOCOLATE?'

Mark rotated lazily, his cheeks bulging as he munched away contentedly. One hand held the torn and crumpled wrappings of a Cadbury's milk chocolate bar. He peeled the purple foil away from the last four squares and popped them defiantly into his mouth.

'You bastard!' an outraged Ozzie yelled. 'I'm like fucking starving here and you've had a secret supply of food all along.'

'Lunchbox,' Mark mumbled through his clogged mouth. 'Mine.'

'We're in this together! Son of a bitch, where's your humanity? The only thing I've had in the last two days is water. And we both know where that comes from.'

Mark finished the chocolate with a big swallow. 'Oh I'm sorry. Did you forget to steal sandwiches from the kindergarten before you kidnapped me on a hijacked starship?'

'This is my ship! I paid for half of it.'

'Fine, so just open the TD channel and explain that to Nigel Sheldon.'

Ozzie wanted to thump the arrays in front of him. 'What the fuck were you in an earlier life, a lawyer?'

'You've killed me!' Mark bellowed back. 'What in that twisted-up piece of wreckage you call a brain made you think I'd be grateful? Please, I'm interested. Do tell.'

'If you'd actually close your mouth and *listen* to me then maybe your low-achiever IQ could just get a handle on what I'm telling you.'

'At least I've got an IQ larger than my shoe size.'

'Dickhead!'

'Wanker!' Mark tossed the empty wrapper at Ozzie. 'Oh, and traitor, too.'

'I am not a fucking Starflyer agent. Man, why will no one ever pay attention to me?'

'Was that another rhetorical question from the giddy heights of your intellect?'

'I am not a violent person, but if you don't stop that *right now* I swear I am going to kick your ass through the cabin wall.'

'Would that be the insults or the shouting I'm to stop?'

Ozzie clenched his fists. Ready to— Just about going to— 'Jeez! How did you *ever* get through our personnel screening program? Nobody in this galaxy could stand working next to you. You are the most goddamn irritating person I have ever met.'

'Was it your charm which impressed Giselle? Or did she just feel sorry for you because of your hairstyle?'

Ozzie's hand automatically went up to pat at his hair which was floating round like an agitated jellyfish in the cabin's freefall environment. 'This is fashionable, man,' he said in an icy voice.

'Where?'

Mark sounded so genuinely curious it threw Ozzie's thought processes, preventing him from coming out with a reply. Besides . . . 'Look, we're getting off track here, man. I've apologized like thirty billion times for what happened back there in the dock. I never meant for you to be dragged along.'

'How do you think my kids will cope without me? They're both under ten for Christ's sake. You've taken me from them to die alone in interstellar space, and now the Commonwealth is going to lose the war because of your treachery. They'll have to take flight on the lifeboats. Chased across the galaxy by an alien fiend, never knowing if they've truly escaped while the rest of their species is systematically hunted down and wiped out. Don't you have children? Try to remember your feelings for them from before it took over your mind.'

'I am not a fucking Starflyer agent!' Ozzie screamed. He took a moment to calm down. When he glanced over at Mark, he saw a smug grin on the man's face. 'All right, put your superior logical IQ to work on this: what's the point in me stealing the *Charybdis*?'

'Is that a Starflyer joke?'

'I'm serious. We're going to get to Dyson Alpha what? Six hours before Nigel arrives and turns their star nova. So what exactly is this Starflyer agent going to achieve with that? Is six hours enough time for MorningLightMountain to build a fleet of frigates like this? Tell me, come on, you're the frigging expert on assembling these babies. Can it be done in six hours?'

'I'm not playing this game.'

'Scared I'm right?'

'You're such a child.'

The kind of willpower that could only ever come from living for three hundred and sixty years managed to keep Ozzie's voice calm and clear. 'I am Ozzie Fernandez Isaacs; I built the first wormhole generator and I was a midwife to the Commonwealth society that you and your children enjoy. Even if you really believe that part of me is buried under Starflyer conditioning it is still entitled to some respect. And Ozzie Fernandez Isaacs is pretty fucking sure that you cannot duplicate this frigate in six hours.'

Mark sighed with reluctance. 'No, you can't.'

'Thank you. And if you can't do that, you can't figure out a nova bomb either.'

'You might get a handle on the principles.'

'You might indeed. Good point. The physics is all derivative of existing theories, so yes. You understand how the theory works, like knowing $e = mc^2$ is what makes an atom bomb work; not that it tells you how to build one. But you have the notion, and then half an hour later you get to see one in action as good old Nigel turns your star into an expanding sphere of ultra-hard radiation and plasma. So I repeat; what's the point?'

'MorningLightMountain has other outposts.'

'Which are currently being targeted by the remaining frigates in the firewall operation.' Ozzie took a breath, he was almost in pain from the way Mark was slowly mellowing. 'Nigel is going to commit genocide on behalf of our species, and the terrible thing is most of us are going to be cheering him on. We'll still be alive; well whoopee-do on that front, but the human race will no longer have a soul. That dies along with MorningLightMountain. Mark, this flight is the *only* chance we have to retain our humanity. It is hugely risky. Crazy even: I admit that. I'm gambling my life on it because I have that right, and once again I apologize for making you personally part of that gamble. The thing is this is such a gamble that Nigel is totally opposed to it, and I even respect him for that. These are very frightening times, Mark. But I cannot let this tiny little chance slip away from us. I have to try and get the barrier generator up and running again.'

'I see that, sure, but . . .'

'If I'm a traitor, it doesn't matter because the human race will survive thanks to Nigel and the ships following us. But man, think on this, if I'm not a traitor and we re-establish the barrier, then we win, too, and win the right way. Isn't that worth something to you? Anything?'

The answer was a long time coming; and when Mark did finally speak the words sounded like they were being ripped out painfully. 'I dunno. This restarting the generator idea, it sounds like a long shot.'

'Longest in human history. That's why I'm the one doing

it. Come on, dude, you don't think anybody with a grain of sense is gonna be busting his balls like this, do you?'

'Guess not.' There was the faintest grin on Mark's face.

'My *man*,' Ozzie put his hand out for a high-five. Mark stared at it mystified. 'Okay,' Ozzie said. 'So, like please tell me how I get the quantumbuster launch mechanism to work? Goddamn, it's been killing me.'

'You mean you couldn't launch the missile anyway?'

'No,' Ozzie admitted.

There was another long pause, then Mark gave a confident chuckle. 'Well well. That makes me captain, doesn't it?'

'What?'

'Okay, maybe not captain. We split the duty. You keep control of the drive. Give me control of the missiles.'

'*What?*'

'I can fix the launch mechanism. But if you want me to do it, you first have to give me fire authority.'

'Why would I want to do that?'

'If you take us to the Dark Fortress and find a target inside it, I'll launch a quantumbuster at it, and I'll even cheer it on. If you try and deliver this ship and its technology to MorningLightMountain I blow us up. That's the deal. You trust *me*, don't you?'

'Son of a bitch. How close are you to Nigel, a genetic doppelganger?'

'Do you want your chance at the barrier generator or not?'

Ozzie couldn't see a way out. 'Have you found a solution to the launch system problem?' he asked the SIsubroutine.

'No. According to my analysis routines the system should function. It does not. This is a paradox beyond available processing power to resolve.'

'All right, Mark, you can have access to the weapons systems.'

'You mean control of the weapons systems.'

'Whatever, yeah.' Ozzie's virtual hands moved across symbols, granting Mark access to the weapons. He watched Mark establish connections into the network, then encrypt the whole weapons section.

'Can you break that?' he asked the SIsubroutine.

'No. It would require more processing power than the ship possesses.'

'Figures,' Ozzie muttered. Data was flowing out of the magazine mechanism control arrays to Mark's insert.

'What's that?' Mark queried.

'Just figuring out how you're going to fix the launcher.'

'It was at an angle.'

'Excuse me?' Ozzie's virtual vision followed a few small files Mark was now downloading into the array governing the electromuscle arms.

'Everyone thinks electromuscle segments are the same,' Mark said. 'They're not. Two identical lengths nearly always have different traction ratings. It's down to minor instabilities in the manufacturing processes. Some batches come out weak, some strong, so the producers always build in a five per cent traction overcapacity. That means they have to be balanced, especially in cases like this when you've got a missile being gripped by seven different arms. There, see? When they latched onto the missile in the magazine at different strengths they were actually tilting it.'

'Uh huh,' Ozzie said weakly.

'No wonder it wouldn't slide into the launch tube, it was at a hell of a slant. There we go, that fix should recalibrate and equalize the traction. I wrote it years ago to balance the hoist arms on a friend's tow truck.'

Ozzie's virtual vision showed the quantumbuster missile slide into the launch tube amid a flood of green symbols. 'Son of a bitch.' *A patch for a tow truck!* 'It works.'

Mark gave him a slightly apologetic grin. 'It's what I do.'

The timer in Ozzie's virtual vision had counted off forty

two seconds since Mark took command of the weapons. *Two days smashing my head against a rock and I got nowhere; and I'm supposed to be a fucking genius.* 'Mark, thank you, man. You do realize we'll have to go through with the flight into the Dark Fortress now?'

'Yeah, I know. But my survival chances haven't been terribly high for a while now, have they?'

'I guess not. Uh, is there any of that lunchbox left?'

'No. But there's all the meals in the emergency survival lockers. They taste quite good, actually.'

Ozzie smiled. It was a good way of preventing the stressed whimper rushing out of his throat.

*

Oscar came out of the memory implant the way he shook off his nightly bad dream. Head rocking from side to side, trying to rise up off the couch, not quite certain where he was and what was real. He was sure his hand was still closed round a joystick while long flexible white wings curved up on either side of him as the wind raged outside. He blinked against the strong light, making out blurred figures standing at the end of the couch. Faces came into focus.

Something wrong.

Jamas and Kieran looked both scared and angry, never a good combination, especially as they had their ion carbines jabbed into Wilson and Anna. Wilson's emotions were under complete control, allowing him to put out just the right amount of tolerant dismay. Anna was quietly furious, her OCtattoos flexing in and out of visibility like a carnivore's fangs in the prelude to a kill. If Kieran's carbine muzzle ever slipped away from her ribs he'd probably wind up very dead very fast. By the look of him, he knew that, too.

'What's happened?' Oscar asked. The feeling of flying was smoothing out, leaving him with a bad headache.

'Adam's dead,' Wilson said flatly.

'And one of you Starflyer fucks killed him,' Kieran shouted, the carbine was shoved harder into Anna's side.

The falling sensation returned to Oscar's limbs with a rush. He gave Wilson a dumbfound stare. 'No.'

'You were here in the hangar with him,' Jamas said.

Bring the joystick back carefully, allow the wings time to respond as you plummet down helplessly in a microburst. Airflow around the fuselage changes as the plyplastic adjusts in long twists. 'Where is he?' Oscar demanded hoarsely.

Jamas jerked his head towards the door into the hangar office. 'You saying you didn't hear it?'

'It was a knife,' Wilson said in undisguised contempt. 'There was nothing to hear.'

'I couldn't hear a thing,' Oscar said. 'I was having the memory implant.'

'Yeah, right,' Kieran sneered.

Oscar ignored him and swung his legs round off the couch. He was unsteady on his feet.

'Where do you think you're going?' Jamas asked.

'To see him.'

'You're not going anywhere.'

Oscar straightened, one hand holding the side of the couch. Lights throbbed in time with his headache.

'Careful,' Anna said. 'Memory implants affect neurone function for several minutes afterwards.'

'I have to see him.' *Because I don't believe you. Not Adam. It can't be.*

Jamas and Kieran exchanged a glance, then Kieran nodded. 'Okay, Rosamund will be here in a minute.'

With the others following, Oscar walked through into the office then out into the hangar. It wasn't just the effects of the implant which made his movements unsteady. He could see a pair of legs sticking out from behind one of the gliders, and slowed, not wanting to see.

Adam lay on the dark composite floor, legs and arms

akimbo, the handle of a harmonic blade sticking out from the nape of his neck. A small puddle of blood had pooled around his head.

Oscar's legs very nearly gave way. He clung to the fuselage to support himself. All he could think of was the look on Adam's face when they saw the Abadan crash. *The ghosts will be happy tonight.*

'You okay?' Anna asked. She'd come up beside him.

'This can't be right,' he said in a hushed croak. 'Not here. Not like that. It's not right. It can't happen like this.'

'Well it did fucking happen,' Jamas spat. 'And one of you traitors did it.'

'Just kill them all,' Kieran said. He moved back from Anna to stand beside Jamas, his carbine covering Oscar and Anna. 'That way we'll be sure we got the bastard.'

'Where were you when it happened?' Anna asked.

'Shut the fuck up, bitch.'

'I mean it,' she said, her eyes alight with cold wrath. Her gaze flicked over to Jamas. 'Was he with you?'

Jamas shifted uncomfortably. 'No.'

'Jamas!' Kieran protested.

'That means neither of you can vouch for the other,' Wilson said. He walked over to stand with Anna and Oscar.

'We were only apart for a couple of minutes, that's all,' Jamas said.

Wilson gazed down at Adam's corpse. 'And how long did that take?'

'Are you saying we did it?' Kieran asked.

'Can you prove you didn't?'

Kieran snarled at him, shifting the muzzle of his ion carbine round. Jamas's hand slowly pushed the weapon down. 'He's right.'

'*What?* You can't be serious?'

Jamas looked even more unhappy.

Rosamund barged in through the hangar door, dragging

Paula Myo along. The Investigator was still wearing Adam's cherry-red woollen sweater, her face was beaded with perspiration, while her lips had turned almost black. Oscar and Wilson automatically went to help carry her. Paula groaned as they took her weight, she was barely conscious. They lowered her to the floor with her back resting against the hyperglider's cradle. She shuddered violently, her head lolling about. Then she saw Adam's body and gasped. Her hands came up to rub at her eyes, she was blinking almost continuously. 'Is he dead?' she asked.

'It pretty much fucking looks like it to me,' Kieran shouted.

'Shut up,' Wilson snapped. He was kneeling beside Paula, hand feeling her forehead. 'Paula, can you understand me? Do you know where we are?'

Her eyes closed for a long blink as she switched her attention from Adam to Wilson. 'Far Away, we're on Far Away.'

'Do you remember the sabotaged crates?'

'Yes.'

'We need your help. Whoever did that has now killed Adam.'

'What if it's her?' Kieran asked.

'Well?' Wilson asked Rosamund, who was staring down at Adam's corpse.

Rosamund stirred herself. 'We were in the Volvo the whole time.'

'So you say,' Oscar barked. He knew he shouldn't have said it, they were already drowning in hostility, but it had to be one of the Guardians, and that sounded way too much like a convenient alibi for comfort.

Rosamund's hand went straight to her holster. She was glaring at Oscar.

Paula coughed feebly, and brought her hand up to her throat. 'I can't confirm Rosamund was there with me.'

'You bitch.'

Paula waved her silent. 'But she can for me.'

Rosamund gave the Investigator a suspicious glare. 'What do you mean?'

'There is only one door to the Volvo rest cabin. If I was the Starflyer agent, I couldn't have got out to do this without Rosamund knowing. She says I didn't. It wasn't me. It also makes it unlikely that it was her, but not impossible.'

'Okay,' Jamas said. 'So who did murder him?'

'I don't know. Yet.' Paula tipped her head back. 'Wilson, where were you?'

'I went over to the generator building. I managed to start it up, as you can see. The town has power, the hypergliders are charging up.'

'It is not far to any building. Is the generator difficult to start?'

'No, it isn't. It was primed ready. I had to physically press three buttons. It started straight away.'

'Did anyone go with you?'

'No.'

'We left the hangar together,' Anna said. 'I went to find the tether cables for the hypergliders.'

'Did you find them?'

'Yes. There's a stores building at the end of the hangars. They're kept in there.'

'Oscar?'

'Memory implant. The induction systems are at the back of this hangar. I didn't know anything going on outside. In fact the killer could have been in there with me, I wouldn't have known.' The thought made him clammy with nerves.

'I see. Jamas?'

'Kieran and I went to find the jeeps to tow the hypergliders.'

'I called Adam and told him we found them,' Kieran said. 'Their tanks were just about empty, so Jamas went and found the main tank. I stayed with the jeeps to take a look at their radio modules. We need them for the observation. I was going to look for the tether anchor drill, but I hadn't heard from Adam for a while. Jamas came back, we headed right over here and found him.'

'And then the others arrived,' Paula said.

'Yeah, these two came in together.' His carbine pointed out Wilson and Anna.

'Is there any sign of anyone else here?' Paula asked.

'No,' Kieran said. 'I've not seen anyone.'

'Me neither,' Wilson said.

'You and Adam were talking together in the Volvo after we found the sabotage,' Rosamund said to Paula. 'Did you have any idea who the traitor was?'

'No.' The Investigator seemed to be losing interest.

'Adam was only going to take two gliders,' Kieran said. He gave Oscar a strange look. 'That's what he told me.'

'When?' Paula asked.

'It was just about the last thing he said. I'd told him we'd found the jeeps, and he said we only needed two.'

Jamas smiled brutally. 'He knew it was one of you.'

Oscar held back from saying anything. The three Guardians were so hyped up and trigger happy they probably would shoot someone if they had half an excuse. All Adam had known was that it wasn't Oscar; he was just being prudent about the flight. One jeep to tow the hyperglider, the second to carry the rest of their merry band so he could keep an eye on them all. It didn't mean that Wilson and Anna were the likely suspects, but right now that wouldn't count for much.

'He didn't say that to me,' Paula said. 'We were still trying to work it out.'

'Then there's nothing else we can do right now,' Wilson said. 'We need to get the hypergliders over to Stakeout Canyon. There's not much time left.'

'Are you fucking insane?' Jamas cried. His carbine swung round to point at Wilson, finger tight on the trigger.

'This changes nothing,' Wilson retorted. 'We kept going

after the crates were sabotaged, we keep going now. Only this time we do not split up again. From now on we do everything in groups of at least three. *Everything.*'

'You're not flying up that mountain,' Kieran snarled. 'You'll wreck the planet's revenge.'

'There won't be any planet's revenge without the observation from Aphrodite's Seat. All three of us will fly. That way the odds protect us.'

'Dreaming heavens!' Kieran appealed desperately to Jamas and Rosamund. 'What do we do?'

'He's right,' Rosamund said bitterly. 'They have to fly.'

*

The control centre for the planet's revenge was huddled at the back of a cave in Mount Idle, named so because it was a lot smaller than the surrounding peaks. It had slumped over the millennia since the Dessault Mountains had been formed, its rocky pinnacle crumbling away into a lacklustre mound, while its sides were liberally smeared with long swathes of loose scree. Even the cave wasn't worth the Guardians using as one of their forts: too small, too visible with its yawning mouth.

Samantha's Vauxhall jeep reached the entrance long after dark, its headlights revealing a slight shimmer in the air caused by the force field the Guardians had established a couple of metres inside. Three sentries greeted her, and the force field reduced to allow her to drive right in.

There were a number of Charlemagnes stabled inside, along with a variety of battered 4x4 vehicles she knew only too well. Two huge dapple grey horses were also standing next to the Charlemagnes; the saddles on the posts beside them were beautifully sculpted black leather with embossed gold patterns of DNA.

'Barsoomians,' Valentine said in a respectful tone.

The control centre itself was right at the back of the cave, which was illuminated in a soft green light. Ten wooden tables were arranged in a circle round the large array, covered in consoles, screens and supplementary electronic modules. Three or four Guardians were sitting at each one, engrossed with the schematics and data flowing across the screens. The array itself was a black cylinder two metres high with a couple of small red LEDs glowing on the top. Samantha gave it a solicitous glance. She'd been part of the assembly team, which made it her baby. And a troublesome one it had been. It had taken them over a year to integrate the bioprocessors and get the software running smoothly as they ran innumerable simulations.

She went over to Andria McNowak who was in charge of the control centre. Heavily pregnant, she sat at the head table directing all the other operators as they gradually brought the network of manipulator stations up to their pre-storm readiness status. There was a constant background mutter as they talked to the array. Not for the first time, Samantha wished OCtattoos and inserts were as common here as they were in the Commonwealth.

The Barsoomians were standing behind them, monitoring the performance of the large array's bioprocessors. In the gloomy light of the cave their grey robes of semi-organic fabric gave them a spectral presence, enhanced by the impenetrable shadows that filled their hoods.

Samantha gave them a slight bow.

'Greetings to you, Samantha McFoster,' one said.

She recognized the deep whispering voice from the faint reverberation it always carried. 'Dr Friland, thank you for coming.'

'These are fascinating times. We are pleased to help remove this blight from our planet.'

'There is a rumour your people will help Bradley Johansson on Highway One. Is that true?'

For a moment Samantha wondered if she'd been too abrupt. People always skated around issues with Barsoomians, fearful to give offence; but today was too important for that kind of political nicety crap. She was aware of Valentine holding his breath beside her.

'We are watching events along Highway One,' Dr Friland said. 'We will offer assistance where practical.'

'I'm sure Johansson will be grateful for any support.' She smiled awkwardly at the fluid shadows inside his hood, and turned to Andria who was giving her a reproachful look. 'Have you loaded in the Martian data?'

'Yeah,' Andria said. She faced the front again, and gestured at the portal which was projecting a topographic map of the Dessault Mountains from the Grand Triad in the west across to the Institute valley in the east. It looked like the cloudscape of some gas-giant, with the tips of the mountains poking through as various fast-moving stormbands streamed past them. 'We're running the fifth simulation now. The genuine meteorological patterns allowed us to refine the behavioural algorithms. I don't think the old software would have coped with the real thing. Even now, I've still got doubts. This is a lot more complex than we ever thought.'

'All we can do is give it our best shot. Have you got all the manipulator stations online?'

'Yeah.' Andria's hand tapped at one of the screens on her table. It showed the stations scattered across the Dessault Mountains linked together by thin red lines. The main communication relays were handled by masers, set up at high altitude on remote pinnacles, and protected by force fields. Samantha had always been sceptical about how they would hold together in the midst of the superstorm, but short of laying armoured cables right across the range they had no choice. It was one of the reasons they'd established the control centre on Mount Idle, where they had direct line of sight with Mount Herculaneum. They were also far enough south to escape the direct blast of the storm when it came.

'How's Zuggenhim Ridge?' Samantha asked.

Andria grinned knowingly, and pulled up the telemetry. 'Sweet. You did a good job.'

'Thanks. And the observation team?'

'Ours? They're not going to make it; they're still a couple of hours from the glacier ring. It's down to the navy people now. Do you think they can land up there?'

'I don't know. They think they can. We just have to wait and see.'

'There's no way we can do this blind.'

'You're going to have to draw up a contingency for that just the same.'

'Yeah right,' Andria declared sarcastically.

'Shame Qatux stayed with Bradley. We could do with that kind of brainpower to help us out right now.'

'I don't think even a Raiel would be any use to us now,' Andria said.

Both the Barsoomians turned to face them. The shadows thinned out inside Dr Friland's hood, allowing two green eyes to gaze down on Samantha. 'Did you say a Raiel is on Far Away?'

Samantha looked up to the tall Barsoomian; for some inexplicable reason she felt guilty, as if she'd been concealing the fact from them. 'Yes. It's travelling with Bradley Johansson. I don't know much about it, this is all second hand gossip from Adam's team.'

'It must not come to harm.'

Samantha took in the control centre with an impatient gesture. 'We're doing our best.'

'Short wave signal,' Andria announced. 'Strong one. Coming from the west.'

'Adam's team,' Samantha said. 'Is it for us?'

'Hang on,' Andria touched several icons on her screen.

*

They turned into Stakeout Canyon just after midnight. It had been a long smooth run from Stonewave, directly south across the wet desert then around the western flank of Mount Zeus. The massive volcano had become visible in the late afternoon as the layer of fog finally began to dissipate. Bright sunlight shining in level from the horizon had illuminated the vast naked lava fields as they rose out of the flat glistening land-scape. They were too close to catch a glimpse of the summit seventeen kilometres above, although they did catch the occasional sparkle along the crest as its fractured ice-band reflected the dying sun. The flashes faded away soon enough as the sapphire sky bled down to violet before quickly turning black.

Rosamund turned on the jeep's headlights, creating long shimmering strips of light across the bare rock. The vehicle had been custom-made in Armstrong City, fitting a smooth composite ellipse over a standard Toyota 4x4 pick-up chassis. Air flowed unbroken over its low-friction paintwork making it virtually impervious to the winds. It was designed to anchor itself to the ground if it was caught in the open when the morning storm arrived, with four big screws underneath that could wind themselves deep into the hard sands of the wet desert.

Paula sat on the bench seat in the back. If she hunched right down she could see between Rosamund and Oscar and out through the narrow band of windscreen. She'd slept away most of the journey through the afternoon, coming awake in sudden bursts to witness a near identical landscape each time. As they progressed, the slope of Mount Zeus had grown larger along the horizon until it became a barrier across the world. Now, in the dark, it was completely invisible while the stars twinkled directly overhead. The drone of the diesel engine filled the interior along with the metallic clanking of the hyper-glider trailer they were hauling along, making conversation difficult. Not, she imagined, that Oscar and Rosamund had been trying to say much to each other. The two other jeeps were following them across the wet desert; Wilson and Jamas in one, while Anna and Kieran brought up the rear.

She fumbled round on the cushioning to find the bottle, and sipped at the mineral water. For once it didn't make her want to gag. In fact, she realized just how thirsty she was. She finished the bottle and sat up a little straighter. Just about every muscle in her body was aching and debilitated. It was all she could do to hold herself upright. Her headache translated every slight jolt into a flash of burning light somewhere behind her eyes. She shivered, though she didn't feel quite as cold as before.

'Where are we?' she asked. The weak croak of her own voice surprised her.

'Hey!' Oscar turned around, a big smile on his face. 'How are you feeling?'

'Not good.'

'Oh.' The smile faded. 'We've just started to turn into Stakeout Canyon.'

'Right.' Paula woke up when the jeep braked to a halt. She hadn't realized she'd fallen asleep again.

'This is it,' Rosamund announced. 'Midway between Zeus and Titan. We tether them here.' She twisted round in the seat to give Paula an entreating look. 'I know you didn't leave the cab to kill Adam. Have you got any idea which of them it was?'

Paula could barely remember their names. 'No. Sorry, not yet.'

Rosamund gave a disgruntled sigh, and opened the door. 'Let's go.'

Oscar looked at her for a long moment, then pulled a penitent face and followed Rosamund out into the calm night.

Paula stayed in the back of the jeep for a while. It rocked about as the hyperglider trailer was unhooked. There was a lot of loud talk outside punctuated by the occasional curse as they prepared the drill for the tether cable anchor. She drank some more water, mildly pleased that she no longer felt cold. Warm humid air was gusting in through the open door, but that wasn't it. The icy claws gripping her bones had relinquished their grip. She still coughed from time to time, but she really didn't feel as though death was so close. Best yet, her headache was reducing. There was a medical kit lying on the back seat next to her. She recognized it as the one Adam had been using in the Volvo. There were plenty of pills and applicator refills that would deal with her headache, but she chose a packet of rehydration salts and mixed them into a bottle of plain water, taking her time to swirl the powder round until it was all dissolved. It tasted foul, but she forced it down.

That simple action just about exhausted her. When she heard the loud grinding whine of the drill she shuffled up into the driver's seat and took a look out into Stakeout Canyon. The ubiquitous sand and gravel of the wet desert had been scoured away here, revealing the solid lava foundation. Their three unique wind-resistant jeeps had parked in a simple triangle, their headlights shining on the hyperglider that had been rolled out of its trailer. Its cockpit canopy was open, and a faint glow shone up from its small console. Oscar was standing at the side of it, peering in as he ran the last set of diagnostics. Wilson, Jamas and Rosamund were all clustered round the big harmonic-blade drill as it sank another five-metre long segment of carbon reinforced titanium into the ground; the fourth of ten. The anchor pole sprouted slim horizontal malmetal blades of its own; once all the segments were locked together they'd telescope outwards, helping to embed it further. It was the second of three anchor struts that together would secure the tether cables against the phenomenal force exerted by the storm. In theory, they could hold the hyperglider on the ground in case the pilot underwent any last minute surge of doubts. A common enough occurrence, apparently. Watching the three men trying to be civil to each other as the pole was spun down into the dark lava, she was very glad she wasn't going to be flying in the morning. Anna and Rosamund were securing the tether drum into its recess in the nose of the glider.

They could all see each other. Paula almost laughed at the way each of them would look round to check everyone else's whereabouts on a regular basis. The comedy police were in town, and in force.

Leaning hard against the jeep's doorframe she told her e-butler to link her with the jeep's array. One of its files contained a map of Stonewave's layout. She began to feed in routes from the Grand Triad Adventures' hangar; Jamas and Kieran to the garage, Anna to the store, Wilson out to the generator. Average times were easy to fill in. She then began to work out which of them could have run back to murder Adam and still complete their own job. It would be very tight, especially for Kieran and Jamas, who were only separated for a few minutes. On practicality alone, that made Oscar the main suspect.

'We're done here,' Rosamund said.

Paula shunted the virtual vision map aside and looked up at the woman. Oscar was standing behind her, wearing a silver-blue flight suit that doubled as an emergency pressure suit. There was an understandably anxious expression on his face as he held the helmet under his arm. 'Good luck,' Paula said, and held her hand out. It wasn't the kind of garment she'd want to wear anywhere near a vacuum, but the armour suits they'd brought with them were far too heavy and bulky for the hypergliders.

'Thanks,' Oscar said. His grip was warm and firm, making her conscious of how clammy her own skin remained.

'Not him then, huh?' Rosamund said as she closed the door.

'I still don't know,' Paula said. She'd shuffled over into the passenger seat. In front of her, the headlights swept across Oscar as he walked back to the ghostly white fuselage of the hyperglider.

'You're looking better, you know. Not good, mind, but I can see you're recovering. Some bug, huh?'

'Yeah, some bug.'

They drove south for five kilometres, then began tethering Anna's hyperglider. Paula sat in the open doorway again. Visible. Dawn was another three hours away.

Wilson and Jamas eased the hyperglider down out of its trailer while Kieran wheeled the drill rig out. It turned out they'd chosen a patch of lava that had a high metallic content. The drill had a lot of trouble cutting through.

Paula ran the digital model of Stonewave a further two times, trying to draw up an order of probability. It couldn't determine one effectively, there were far too many variables, especially if Wilson or Anna had run the whole time.

When the third anchor pole was finally sunk, Wilson and Anna embraced in front of the hyperglider. He checked over her silver-blue flight suit one last time. A final kiss and she climbed into the cockpit.

'I don't know what the odds are of them all getting up there,' Rosamund said as they drove away south.

'Not good,' Paula said. She took another drink of rehydration mix and reviewed what she knew. She still stood by what she and Adam had decided earlier. Just thinking back to the time they'd spent together made her light-headed again. The whole time since she joined the train at Narrabri station she'd wanted to clamp his arms together behind his back and cuff his wrists. It was the kind of reflex that came easier than breathing. She supposed other people would feel some kind of guilt at Adam's death. She didn't. The closest she got right now to any real feeling was regretting he couldn't give her any input on her current problem. He'd been her only true source of information on the three remaining Guardians.

No, she told herself. *That's not right. I need to prioritize.* The most important thing now was to ensure the flight to the top of Mount Herculaneum was a success. She had to concentrate on Wilson, Oscar, and Anna.

Rosamund braked again. 'Let's hope this is better rock than that shit we were on last time,' she said as she jumped out of the jeep to help tether the last hyperglider.

Paula didn't move from the passenger seat. She found a bar of chocolate and toffee, and started chewing it very slowly, giving her stomach time to get used to solids again. It was no use trying to figure out which of the three had the opportunity to sabotage equipment in the Carbon Goose. That would be even worse than Stonewave. She had to concentrate on evidence from before, from their behaviour prior to Far Away, and hope that could narrow it down. The most damning she could think of was Wilson's relative failure in commanding the navy. If he'd just been a bit tougher . . . but that was so easily ascribed to politics. Circumstantial.

She thought back to the meeting she'd had with him and Oscar in Pentagon II. Both of them had been startled and deeply worried that the records had been tampered with and the implication of the Starflyer's reach. Nothing abnormal there. There had been something else at that meeting though, not relevant at the time. Oscar had claimed he had been contacted by the Guardians, quickly clarified as *someone who claimed to be a Guardian*. Why Oscar? Why did the Guardians think he would be sympathetic to their cause?

'Investigator,' Wilson said.

Paula turned gradually. Movement was still difficult; her muscles ached. He was standing in the jeep's doorway, dressed in the same silver-blue flight suit as the others. The three Guardians stood round him. Their anger seemed to have toned down to something close to embarrassment. Working hard as a team would do that; it wasn't an adjustment she could allow herself.

'I'm afraid I haven't worked it out, yet,' she said.

'Yes, well, we'll stay in touch via normal communication bands now. Until the storm takes them out, anyway.'

'Very well.'

'I hope . . . Ah well.' His lips compressed in something like disappointment.

'Bon voyage, Admiral.'

Wilson turned and walked over towards his hyperglider.

'We've got an hour until the storm hits,' Rosamund said tightly as she clambered into the driver's seat. 'The tourist company crews don't normally leave it this late to set up. According to the emergency file in the jeep's array there's a shelter spot at the base of Mount Zeus which we can reach in time.' She was already gunning the engine, racing round the tethered hyperglider in a fast curve. Its cockpit canopy was lowering. They roared away across the barren lava of the canyon floor. Paula leaned sideways, watching the hyperglider and the three abandoned trailers dwindle away quickly.

'We did it,' Rosamund said in a relieved voice.

'What do you mean?'

'I was talking to Kieran and Jamas and we reckon the odds are in our favour now. If two of them make it to Aphrodite's Seat, and one of them is the Starflyer Agent, what can they actually do? None of them has any weapons. And if all three of them make it, then the problem's solved.'

'Tell that to Adam,' Paula said harshly.

Rosamund glowered at her, but said nothing.

Paula tried to review the background to the navy three again. She'd done that once before with Adam. There had been something then, some little flash of knowledge that he'd tried to hide from her. As if anyone could do that. She'd seen it quite plainly on his face.

He knew one of them was innocent. So why not tell me? It must have implicated them in another crime? What? What could possibly make him shield them at a time like this?

'Do we have all the short wave transmitters?' Paula asked.

'Yes.'

'So the hypergliders can't pick up anything we transmit on them?'

'No.'

'I need to ask Johansson something.'

Rosamund kept one hand on the wheel, and pulled out the array with the short wave function built in. 'Here you go. It's a hell of a distance. Don't count on them picking it up.'

'It's night, that'll help.' She switched on the set, and set it to infinite repeat. 'Johansson, this is Paula Myo. Adam was murdered at Stonewave. I need to know who contacted Oscar to ask him to review the *Second Chance* logs, and why you picked him. Please reply with a guarantee identity information from Alic Hogan.' She listened to it start its first cycle.

'How's that going to reveal the traitor?' Rosamund asked.

'I'll tell you if we get an answer.' She glanced at the horizon, not sure if it was lighter or if she was just imagining it.

*

Sunrise was drawing a grey hue across the eastern sky above the veldt. When Bradley looked out of the armoured car's narrow side window he could see the peaks of the Dessault Mountains away to the west; cold, sharp pinnacles jutting up amid the vanishing stars. He imagined the superstorm billowing round them to descend on the veldt like some apocalyptic force, scouring the land clear of all its new terrestrial life.

It wouldn't happen for hours yet, if it did at all. They'd heard nothing from Samantha's group since that last message yesterday about her being ready to surf. If she was keeping to schedule then the storm might be on time. They were still several hundred miles from the Institute, but making better time than they'd expected. So was the Starflyer convoy.

All of them had spent a long anguished night as the road rolled onwards. Once they left the fringes of the rainforest behind the landscape reverted to featureless expanses of veldt with the occasional tree and bush poking up. It was as though their vision was locked into some long loop of scenery that kept playing over and over. At night, with nothing to see outside of the headlight beams, the sense that they were making no progress at all was even worse.

After midnight they'd finally made contact with the Guardians who'd massed for the Final Raid. Watchers had been stationed along the last few hundred miles of Highway One to monitor the Starflyer's movement. Their arrays and secure tight-beam links circumvented the wrecked nodes along the side of the road to put them back in contact with the main body of the Guardians, in itself a nice boost for morale among their little group as well as giving them a decent overview of the situation. When the reliable information started coming in they found they'd closed to within forty minutes of the Starflyer, but that still put it sixty miles in front of them, and there were no more major bridges left to demolish. Highway One ran on across the veldt in an unbroken strip of concrete that was Roman in its brashness. At their current rate, they'd catch the alien just as it reached the Institute and before the storm hit. That was too close, Johansson knew. He was going to have to attack the Starflyer head on. The warriors of the Final Raid would have their moment, sweeping down to block Highway One. The thought of how much blood would be spilt was mortifying. The planet's revenge would have been so much more effective. Isolation and exposure followed by death; but now that careful strategic plan was all but ruined. The fact that it was he who in the end had underestimated the Starflyer gave his situation its wretched poignancy. His one small grasp at salvation was the Paris team and Cat's Claws, their armour might yet prove the winning hand.

'Picking up a short-wave signal,' Keely said from her seat at the back of the armoured car. 'Sounds like Paula Myo.' Her voice trailed off.

When Bradley looked round her face was ashen. 'Put it through,' he told her gently. Interference generated by the sun as it rose in the east was now so bad it took nearly four minutes of the repeated message before they had a full version. There was silence in the armoured car for some time as Paula's voice cycled through its grim message again and again.

'Turn that fucker off,' Stig snarled. He was sitting in the back alongside Keely where he was supposed to be resting after finally relinquishing the wheel to Olwen just before midnight. 'He can't be dead. She's lying. I knew that bitch was trouble the moment I saw her.'

Bradley was still in shock from the news, otherwise he would have told Stig to calm down and keep quiet. That Adam might not survive had never occurred to him in the wildest worst-case scenario.

'After we kill the Starflyer I'm going to track her down and sort her lying mouth out once and for all.'

'Stig, pack it in,' Olwen said from the driver's seat. Her attention hadn't wavered from the road. She'd popped several beezees, but nowhere near as many as Stig. 'We need to deal with this calmly and professionally.'

A communication icon flipped up into Bradley's virtual vision. He opened it without thinking.

'This isn't good,' Alic said. 'The Starflyer agent is getting bolder.'

'But it's not relevant,' Morton said. 'I'm sorry, I know Adam was a big help to the Guardians, but their part is over. You said so yourself, the planet's revenge team has finished setting up.'

Bradley frowned. Morton was right, and Paula would know that. She also knew that short-wave communications were completely open. Her message was still repeating, so she obviously considered it important. *Why?* 'They must be doing something else,' he decided. 'Paula's many things, but stupid isn't one of them. She's telling us why this is so important. What's at Stonewave?'

'Nothing right now,' Olwen said. 'The travel companies mothballed it when the tourists stopped coming.'

'So what did it do?' he asked. 'I've never heard of it.'

'It's a town out in the wet desert, they use it as a base for the hypergliders. There's nothing else there.'

'Oh, dreaming heavens,' Bradley murmured in consternation close to panic.

'What is it?' Alic asked.

'They met Samantha and then they went hypergliding,' Bradley said. 'Do you see?'

'Not a clue,' the navy commander admitted.

'The observation,' Olwen said. 'Samantha needed them on Aphrodite's Seat.'

'The navy people can all fly,' Bradley said. He stared at his watch. 'And the morning storm's about to hit the Grand Triad. One of them is the Starflyer agent, and they're going to do the observation. Commander Hogan?'

'Yes?'

'Give me the guarantee she needs, some bit of trivia the Starflyer couldn't possibly know.'

'In the Almada Hotel lobby she told Renne she'd been running an elimination entrapment operation on her as well as Tarlo. There was only John King and myself there, and John and Renne are both dead now.'

'Good enough. Keely, we need to be absolutely sure this gets through. Link every short wave transmitter we have, and crank them up to full power. Then put our message on constant repeat, no limit.'

'Yes, sir.'

Bradley grinned contritely. Having to tell the Investigator the reason behind the contact would effectively condemn Oscar, but he couldn't afford not to, not any more.

'Ready,' Keely said.

'Paula, this is Bradley. You told Renne you were running an entrapment against her in the Almada Hotel lobby. It was Adam who contacted Oscar because they were at Abadan station together.' *And I wonder what the Starflyer makes of that?* He settled back into the seat and closed his eyes, suddenly very weary.

'Are you sure about that?' Alic asked.

'I'm afraid so, yes.'

'But . . . Oscar Monroe was a senior manager in CST, he's a navy captain. He couldn't be involved in Abadan.'

'People change,' Bradley said. 'What did you do in all your earlier lives, Commander?'

'This is my second, and I've been part of the legal profession in both. Look . . . I can possibly ignore what I heard, but Myo can't.'

'I know. Presumably that's why Adam never told her. He was protecting Oscar to the end.' He peered out of the slit window again, the Dessault Mountains were clearer now, the sky above them shifting to a dark lavender. The tallest of them, StOmer, stood high above the others, its conical snow-cap already glowing a musky white as it guarded the north eastern extremity of the range. Its shape was familiar enough, even though he hadn't seen it in decades. The sight of it triggered a reluctant acknowledgement he couldn't put off his decision any longer. His virtual hand pulled up the icon for Scott McFoster, who was commanding the Final Raid.

'Yes, sir,' Scott responded instantly.

*

They rode down out of the foothill forests, over a thousand Charlemagnes, each carrying a clan warrior. There was no need for concealment, they wanted the Starflyer to know they were there, so they sang as they trotted out across the veldt, a slow marching song that rumbled on ahead of them amid the dust their hooves kicked up. Such scouts the Starflyer had positioned along the road babbled frantically into their communication links and raced back to the safety of the Institute valley fifteen miles away, chased by clan outriders.

Six hundred riders formed up a crescent formation with Highway One at their centre where it reached the bottom of a shallow fold in the land. They blew up the small bridge across the stream, and parties of McSobels trotted down the road scattering mines on the concrete and across the land on either side. Mortar launchers and missile racks were dug in on the higher ground overlooking the road. The remainder of the warriors divided into groups of two hundred and withdrew from the road, loitering a couple of miles to the north.

There they all waited as the sun rose to transform the sky into its daily sapphire brilliance. The heat built around them, pressing the air into silence.

In the placid silence of mid morning, the Starflyer convoy hove into view. Thirty armoured Land Rover Cruisers were interspaced by several larger trucks, three buses, and a couple of small fuel tankers. A squad of ten big BMW bikes growled along out in front, ridden by armour-suited figures. The big MANN lorry was positioned two thirds of the way down the line of vehicles, its force field rippling the air around the buffed-aluminium capsule.

The bikes slowed as they crested the top of the fold and saw the Guardians blocking the way ahead. Their heavy engines grumbled loudly as they approached at walking pace down the long slope. The rest of the convoy followed them cautiously down. Half a mile from the rubble of the little bridge, the whole convoy came to a halt.

Out on the lush veldt, the remaining clan riders moved forward, spreading wide until the Starflyer convoy was completely encircled. The first armoured car appeared on Highway

One, rumbling forward until it reached the group of Charlemagnes standing on the road half a mile behind the convoy. Olwen braked to a halt. 'Finally!' she hissed.

The armoured car's thick door hinged up, and Bradley stepped out. Ten metres away, the door on the second armoured car was already open, the Paris team and Cat's Claws hurried out onto the sun-baked concrete and stretched elaborately. Scott McFoster handed the reins of his Charlemagne to one of his lieutenants and walked over. He threw his arms around Bradley. 'Dreaming heavens, it is good to see you, sir.'

'You do the clans proud, Scott. There are more here than I expected.'

'Aye, and many more would be here with them. I had to be firm, else we would have had babes and elders riding with us.'

Bradley nodded slowly, thinking of Harvey's corpse in one of the Mazda jeeps. He looked down the mild incline to the convoy. The growl of their engines was clean in the still, humid air. When he raised his eyes to the south, he could just see the saddle in the foothills that was the Institute valley.

'We'd best be quick. It will try and push through as soon as it can. Are there any signs of reinforcements?'

'No movement round the Institute. We've lost a couple of scouts, which is to be expected. But the rest are still in place. Besides, we'll see anything approaching.'

'How many troops can it have left in there?'

'It's not been easy to track movements along Highway One these last few months. But I'm confident there can't be more than a couple of hundred humans left in the Institute.'

'That's good. We have some zone killers on the armoured cars, which should take out some of the convoy before we even start close quarter fighting.'

'Can they puncture the truck's force field?'

'I'd imagine not, but we'll find out soon enough. We also brought some powerful dump webs that'll help break it down.'

'In that case, we're ready.'

'All right then, I'll suit up and join you.'

Just for a moment Scott hesitated. 'Of course.'

'Don't worry,' Bradley said softly. 'I won't get in the way. Besides, our friends here,' his gesture took in the Paris team and Cat's Claws, 'have agreed to escort me to the Starflyer itself.'

Scott took in the bulky armour with a professional glance. 'I don't suppose anybody would consider loaning me one of those fine suits for a couple of hours?'

There were several chuckles from the blank helmets.

Bradley turned to face the mountains that guarded the western skyline. The tall dazzling white peaks jabbed high into the clear sky. There was no sign of any cloud, not a breath of wind.

'We've heard nothing from Samantha,' Scott said, following his gaze. 'That could mean it's started.'

'Yes. Of course. Are there shelters nearby?'

'We've allocated some caves. I've got McSobels installing force fields in them now.'

'Let's hope that's good enough. No one really knows how powerful we can get—'

'Hey,' The Cat said. 'We've got incoming. Very weird incoming.' Her gauntlet pointed into the western sky.

No DNA from Earth's dinosaur epoch had ever been recovered despite some very creative science applied to the problem. This clearly hadn't deterred the Barsoomians in their aspirational genetic experimentation. Bradley's jaw opened in silent astonishment at the shapes that swam out of the lucent sapphire of Far Away's sky. The creatures were clearly modelled on petrosaurs, with wings that were scaled membranes stretched over long tough bones. Sunlight shimmered in oil-rainbow patterns across the leathery tissue as the wings beat in long steady movements. Lizard ancestry was apparent in the body, though Bradley suspected a lot of sequences derived from crocodiles had been wound into the creature's genome. Certainly, the giant wedge-head looked ferocious, and the four legs had lethal black talons.

As they approached, swooping lower towards the veldt, he could see the cloaked figures of Barsoomians sitting astride their thick necks. Some kind of saddle straps were wrapped round their pale oyster-grey hide. There must have been over thirty of them in the flock, all keeping a healthy distance from each other.

The first one came in low beside the road, its wings sweeping fast then twisting round to pound at the air in giant downdrafts. It settled fast, its stumpy legs bowing into a crouch. A head that was three metres long, most of it jaws and teeth, swung round to align big protuberant eyes on Bradley. Wings that must have had a total span of fifteen metres fluttered once, and folded back with lazy neatness against the creature's flanks. It bellowed out a high ululation that made Bradley clasp his hands over his ears. The cry was taken up by the rest of the flock as they plummeted down on the veldt as if they were descending on prey.

'Cool,' The Cat declared. 'Hey you: Scott; I'd swap my armour for one of them.'

Their arrival never even flustered the Charlemagnes, who held their ground stoically. It was their riders who were gawping round in stupefaction. A ragged cheer began for the Barsoomians.

Bradley watched as the leader dismounted, seemingly gliding down the big creature's side. 'Greetings,' he said. 'We wondered if you would join us for this event. I always hoped you would.'

'Bradley Johansson,' the Barsoomian had a dulcet female

voice. 'Your return to this world is auspicious, as we foretold. I am Rebecca Gillespie, and this is my congregation. We are happy to give what aid we can, but you must know we are also here to safeguard the Raiel.'

The shadows inside Rebecca Gillespie's hood thinned slightly as she turned to look at Qatux. Two Barsoomians who had dismounted were gliding towards the big alien that had lumbered down from the back of the truck it'd travelled in. Tiger Pansy stood beside it in a very paternal fashion, giving the grey-robed figures a suspicious stare. The Barsoomians bowed deeply to Qatux, whose smaller tentacles extended towards them with the tenderness of a priest administering a blessing.

'What is Qatux to you, then?' Morton asked, his voice heavy with derision. 'Some kind of old lost God?'

Rebecca Gillespie rotated slightly so that the front of her hood faced Morton. 'The Raiel neural structure is supreme of all the sentients we have encountered in the galaxy,' she said. 'As such it deserves our utmost respect. One day we hope and believe our DNA can be elevated to such levels. In the meantime we are content with whatever insight it cares to grant us.'

'You people need to get out more,' Morton said.

'Whatever the reason, we're glad you're here,' Bradley said hurriedly. 'Er, what are these, exactly?' He nodded towards the huge avian creature Rebecca Gillespie had alighted from.

'To us, they're king eagles; although the towns on the Iril Steppes already whisper rumours of dragons in the skies of Far Away.'

'Whatever, they're very impressive. Are you going to fly into battle on them?'

'Good lord, no, that would be insanity.' She reached behind her head, and pulled a rifle with a very long barrel out of its hidden sheath in her robe. 'The Institute guns would find us

1143

easy targets. We will sharpshoot for you. These weapons will cut through an ordinary force field skeleton suit from a thousand metres.'

'That kind of support is most welcome.'

'Sir,' Scott called. 'Movement at the Institute. Something's coming this way. There's a visual.'

Bradley scanned his virtual vision for the icon, and pulled the scout's image out of his grid. The picture wasn't high quality, but it showed him vehicles pouring out of the valley mouth.

'That must be every vehicle they've got in there,' Stig said. 'Who the hell's in them?'

'See if the scout can get a close-up,' Bradley said. He was disconcerted by the quantity of vehicles. The Starflyer would be truly desperate by now, but it was logical above all else.

The image blurred, and zoomed in on a pick-up truck. Several dark shapes were wedged in the back. At first Bradley couldn't make sense of what he was seeing, his mind simply rejected the profile. *They can't be here.* But of course, Dudley Bose had discovered the Starflyer's true origin. 'Dreaming heavens,' he said fearfully.

'Motiles,' The Cat crooned joyously.

'There must be hundreds of them,' Morton said.

'Soldier motiles,' Rob said. 'I think. They look different to the ones on Elan.'

'They'll be the improved version,' Bradley told him flatly.

*

There had been some uncomfortable moments during the flight. Several of the *Scylla*'s hyperdrive systems threw up glitches which had to be dealt with immediately. Ancillary support equipment failed with dismaying regularity. Nigel had spent most of his waking hours troubleshooting, holding things together with patched programs and back-up components. Otis and Thame had improvised a lot of procedures;

flight-experience and hugely detailed knowledge of the frigate allowing them to take near-intuitive short cuts.

The reluctant ship had slowly been coaxed into producing a performance which matched the specifications its designers had originally promised. Nigel had gathered a great deal of satisfaction from wrestling the technology into shape. *Hands on* was the only management style that worked one hundred per cent. Knowing that a single mistake would leave them as a smear of outré radiation across the cosmos also helped to focus the mind to an astonishing degree.

Now they were closing on Dyson Alpha, he pulled the sensor display out of his virtual vision grid and studied it. It surrounded him with a speckled grey cube, illustrating the star as a small kink in the fabric dead ahead. Dyson Beta was off to one side, showing a larger twist as the transdimensional resonance skittered off the barrier's surface. There was also a slim conical wake approaching Dyson Alpha. Tracking the *Charybdis* wasn't easy; the detector mechanism had proved one of the least reliable systems on board. There had been a whole twenty-eight-hour period when they had lost the *Charybdis* entirely. Nigel had worked hard at adapting the unit's software until the detector functioned near flawlessly. Certainly, the last few hours hadn't seen a single hiccup. He suspected the way they were slowly overhauling the *Charybdis* played a big part in that. There was now less than fifteen light-years between them.

'Have you decided what to do when we get there?' Otis asked.

Nigel's virtual hand pushed the tracking display aside, compressing it back into his grid. 'Not yet.' There was a rattled edge in his voice. Damnit, this was Ozzie!

'Ninety minutes until we get there.'

'Yeah, I know.'

'We should have enough resolution to see if he heads for the homeworld or the Dark Fortress.'

Nigel shifted round on the couch's padding. The voyage had been pretty miserable from a physical point of view; paste food, bloated sinuses, nauseous stomach, and teetering on the verge of claustrophobia the whole time. 'You think it will track anything once they drop out of hyperspace?'

Otis gave a lame grin. 'In theory.'

'This ship isn't too hot on theory.'

'If he goes for the Dark Fortress he really will be trying to restart the barrier.'

'Possibly.'

'It means he isn't a Starflyer agent.'

Nigel glared at his son. 'I know that! That's why I've come with you.'

'Sorry, Dad. It's just . . . it's Ozzie, you know.'

Nigel felt more than a little pique at the reverence in Otis's voice. 'Have you ever actually met him?'

'No. But you used to tell us about him all the time when we were young.'

'Yeah, I know. That's why it will be my hand on the trigger if it's to be done.' He couldn't help yawning; he didn't sleep well in freefall. 'Let's get ready. I don't want to be distracted on our approach. Thame, load the nova bomb into the launch tube. I'll authorize its activation.'

'Yes, sir.'

Nigel followed the procedure through the ship's schematics. There was a problem getting the missile out of the magazine, but Otis did something to the handling mechanism to correct the flaw. Green symbols appeared when it was loaded and primed.

'Mark taught me that trick,' Otis said. 'It's to do with balancing the electromuscle.'

Nigel ignored the reproachful tone. There was something innately appealing about Mark, a human lost puppy. 'Initiate the neutron lasers,' Nigel said. 'Thame, you're handling short

1146

range defences.' When he checked the timer, Dyson Alpha was seventy minutes away.

*

The jeeps had cleared Stakeout Canyon when they began to pick up the scattered fragments of Johansson's reply. Paula programmed her array to piece together the vocal snippets as they repeated again and again. Static crashed out of the speakers as she played the message. It was a little bit longer and cleaner each time. By the fifth time there was no mistake.

'Is it him?' Rosamund asked. 'Did you tell Renne that?'

'Yes.' Paula stared through the jeep's curving windscreen. The headlight beams were flowing over the blank, shiny surface of sand and shale as the sleek vehicle raced for cover. She thought the eastern horizon might be slightly lighter. The ache had almost gone from her limbs now, but she felt desperately tired, as if she hadn't slept for months.

'So Adam contacted Oscar,' Rosamund said. 'Does that help?'

'It makes a lot of sense, especially the why of it.'

'I don't understand.'

'Adam knew Oscar wasn't the Starflyer agent. If Oscar had been, then he would have captured Adam and taken him for interrogation as soon as Adam made contact; Adam would have been totally unprepared.'

'Then why didn't he just tell us?'

'He was protecting Oscar.'

'From who?'

'Me. Turn around.'

Rosamund shot her a startled look. 'Do what?'

'Turn around.' Her virtual hands fluttered over icons, trying to contact Oscar. The hand-held array didn't have the range, not with the canyon wall blocking them. 'I have to get back there.'

'We haven't got time!'

'Stop the jeep. You can get in with Jamas or Kieran. I'll drive back myself.'

'Oh dreaming heavens!' Rosamund wrenched at the wheel, sending the jeep into a skid-curve. It shook wildly as it chased the turn.

Paula gripped the seat, thinking they were going to flip over.

'What's happening?' Kieran demanded.

'Oscar's in the clear,' Rosamund said. 'We're going back.'

'What for? The storm's going to be here in twenty minutes.'

The jeep had now completed its turn, nose pointing back towards Stakeout Canyon. Rosamund floored the accelerator. 'I don't know.'

'What?' he asked incredulously.

'I have to ask Oscar some questions,' Paula said. 'I should be able to find out which of the other two it is.'

'Then what?'

'We might be able to reach the Starflyer agent in time to prevent them from flying. It won't take much. Your ion carbines can easily disable a hyperglider.'

'But we wouldn't get clear,' Rosamund growled. 'The storm is at its worst in Stakeout Canyon. These jeeps couldn't take the beating it'd give us in there.'

'I said I'll drive myself.'

'No you don't. You can barely stay conscious.'

'Thank you,' Paula said. She flopped back into the seat, and began thinking of the questions she needed to ask.

'Even if we don't get there, the other two will be warned,' Rosamund said. 'We have to give them that.'

'It might be enough,' Paula agreed. She could sense the woman's need to justify what they were doing, the courage she gained from the cause. 'I don't know what the agent is planning on doing. A kamikaze in the glider, possibly, or pushing the others off Aphrodite's Seat.'

'It's Adam, you know. He's helping us.'

'How?'

'He's looking down from the dreaming heavens, spurring us on.'

Paula didn't reply. The idea was mildly discomfiting. She based her universe on solid facts. It was easier.

'Aren't you religious, Investigator?'

'I don't think I was designed to be, no. You obviously are.'

'I don't believe in the old religions; but Bradley Johansson actually visited the dreaming heavens, he told the clans what they're like, what we can look forward to.'

'I see.'

'Don't believe me,' Rosamund laughed. 'Ask him yourself afterwards.'

'I might just do that.'

They drove on in silence. After a while, Rosamund began to shift the wheel slightly. The ground didn't seem to be uneven. It hadn't changed for a long time.

'Wind starting to pick up,' Rosamund said as she caught Paula searching the dusky landscape outside.

'Right.' Paula ordered the jeep's transmitter to signal again. They should be in range by now. According to the inertial navigation they were level with the entrance to Stakeout Canyon, ready to curve round into it.

'What did you mean, Oscar wasn't safe from you?' Rosamund asked.

'He and Adam were at Abadan station together; he was part of the terrorist atrocity. Adam knew that if I discovered that I would arrest Oscar.'

'It was a long time ago.'

'Time is irrelevant. The people they killed are still dead. Justice must be served. Without that, our civilization would collapse.'

'You mean that, don't you?'

'Of course.'

'So you really would have tried to arrest Adam after this was over?'

'Yes.'

'We'd have stopped you.'

'Only this time.' Paula's e-butler told her the jeep's transmitter had made contact with the three hypergliders. 'Oscar, are you all right?'

'I'm fine. We all are. What's the problem? I thought you'd be clear by now. You have to get out of Stakeout Canyon.'

'Oscar, I've been in touch with Bradley Johansson. He told me it was Adam who made contact with you to ask for a review of the *Second Chance* logs, is that right?'

'Yes.'

'Investigator, what's this about?' Wilson asked. 'We're about to fly. And you need to get clear.'

'Oscar, that puts you in the clear,' Paula said. 'If you were the Starflyer agent you would have taken him captive.'

'Yes, I guess so.'

'What are you saying?' Wilson asked.

The jeep rocked to one side as it was struck by a sudden gust of wind. Paula tightened her restraint webbing. 'It's either you or Anna.'

'Oh, come on! We're all navy, we've known each other for years. We already decided it's either you or one of the Guardians. We're flying to the summit, no matter what you say.'

'You were all on board the *Second Chance*,' Paula said. 'Oscar, what did you tell Wilson when you went to him with the evidence? Did you tell him you were contacted by the Guardians?'

'Yes.'

'All right, Wilson, you knew there was a connection between Oscar and the Guardians. Did you tell Anna?'

'This is ridiculous.'

'Did you tell her?' The jeep was swaying about continually

now as the winds picked up. Sand was scudding along the ground.

'I . . . I don't think so. Anna, do you remember?'

'What did you say to her? Did you discuss the *Second Chance* data?'

'Anna?' Wilson entreated.

'She handled the sensors on *Second Chance*. That gave her easy access to the satellites and the dish. They were her systems; it would be easy for her to cover up any unauthorized use.'

'Anna! Tell her she's talking crap.'

'Did you tell her Oscar had found the dish deployment?' Paula demanded.

'Anna, for God's sake.'

'Did you?'

'Yes,' Wilson moaned.

'Anna,' Paula said. 'I know your carrier wave is on, please respond.'

'She's my wife.'

The jeep wobbled badly. Rosamund fought the wheel. 'We can't take any more of this,' she grunted. 'We're not going to reach Anna.'

'Damnit,' Paula said. 'It can't be much further.'

'Investigator, we are going to die if we carry on,' Rosamund's voice was emotionless. 'That's not going to accomplish anything, is it.'

'All right, turn around,' Paula snapped. Halfway into the turn another gust slammed into them, she thought they really would flip over this time. Rosamund spun the wheel violently, countering the tilt. Outside, grey light was seeping into the sky to reveal a thick low cloud base that was moving at a daunting speed towards Mount Herculaneum. The Jeep steadied. Rosamund was taking them straight towards the base of the canyon wall.

'Anna, respond please,' Paula said.

'Wilson,' Oscar said. 'Oh shit, I'm sorry.'

'She can't be!' Wilson said. 'She can't. Damnit, she's perfectly human.'

'I worked with Tarlo for years,' Paula said. 'I had no idea.'

'Work?' Wilson spat contemptuously. 'I married her. I loved her.'

'Wilson, Oscar, you have to decide what you're going to do now. I know this is hard, Wilson, but I expect she will try and crash into one of you.'

'We'll leave a gap between unhooking from the tether,' Oscar said. 'That way she can only go after one of us.'

'That sounds viable.' Paula desperately wanted to offer some practical advice, but she couldn't even think on how to improve Oscar's suggestion. She saw the edge of the canyon approaching fast. There was sand under the tyres again. Big worn outcrops of rock were cluttered along the base of the canyon wall. Rosamund steered them round a dark jag of abraded lava and braked in its lee; she raised the suspension so the rim settled on the ground. 'I hope this is deep enough,' she said as she switched on the jeep's emergency anchors. The screws on the chassis started to wind down into the hard-packed sand with a strident metallic whine.

'Good luck, both of you,' Paula said.

Rosamund cut the mic and faced Paula. 'You didn't tell him you know about Abadan.'

'Oscar has enough to worry about right now. I didn't want to impede his effectiveness. He'll find out if he survives.'

'I don't know about the Starflyer, but you frighten the living crap out of me.'

*

'She didn't know.' Oscar repeated the phrase like a mantra. He'd lost count of how many times he'd said it now. The emptiness of human silence was oppressive and demoralizing as the furious wind rose in counterpoint around the hyperglider. A sense of isolation was folding round him like the caress of interstellar space. Anna: lost beyond redemption goodness knows how many years or decades before. While Wilson had withdrawn into a private hell of anguish and grief. 'The human part of her was drawn to you. That's still alive.'

'It doesn't matter,' Wilson answered curtly. 'I've had wives before.'

'Not like this, man; we saw flashes of the real Anna. She's still there. Lost. She can be re-lifed and her memories edited.'

'After we kill her now. Is that it?'

Oscar winced. The whole conversation was made even more disquieting by the little emerald symbol shining in the corner of his virtual vision showing that Anna was still on air, receiving everything they said. *Maybe silence is best.* 'What do you want to do?' he asked wearily. Wisps of fine sand were drifting past the cockpit, whipped up from the wet desert out beyond the gaping canyon mouth.

'Get to Aphrodite's Seat. That's what we're here for. That's what we do.'

Oscar resisted letting out a long breath of relief. At least his friend was starting to focus. That was the thing about Wilson, an ability to put the human element aside while he made choices. It was probably what made him so good at command. The parallel between that and Starflyer agents was one Oscar didn't like to think of.

'We'll get there,' Oscar said. 'After all, there's not that much she can do.'

'You think?'

Oscar was very close to turning his radio off and just keeping the hyperglider on the ground while the storm raged. *The universe can survive without me, surely? Just this once.* If he could just do what Wilson did and turn off his emotions.

The hyperglider shook as the wind strengthened around it. Overhead, the grey clouds had merged into an unbroken rumpled ceiling above the stark canyon. 'Whatever you want to do, I'm with you,' he told Wilson. It was a cop-out and he knew it, transfer responsibility to someone else. But then that's what he'd been doing ever since Abadan.

He checked the weather radar with its false-colour mating-jellyfish patterns. The whole cockpit was juddering now, wobbling the images on the little screen. It showed him a salmon-pink tide of wind channelled by the overbearing walls of Stakeout Canyon and reaching close to a hundred miles an hour. Somewhere in the invisible distance ahead of the hyper-glider's nose, the stormfront had reached the base of Mount Herculaneum.

'Confirmed go status,' Wilson responded with toneless dispassion.

Oscar smiled tenderly at the absolute professionalism; in his own fashion Wilson was showing him the way. *Okay, if that's what it takes to do this, I'm game.* 'Roger that. I'm beginning ascent phase.'

He brought his hands down on the console's i-spots, gripping the concave handholds. Plyplastic flowed over his wrists, mooring them into place for the flight. His e-butler reported a perfect interface with the hyperglider's on-board array.

Oscar put Anna aside and allowed the memories to come to the fore. Not his memories, but the skill belonged to him now, merging him with the hyperglider. A red and violet virtual hand gripped the joystick that had materialized in front of him. His other hand skipped across the glowing icons.

The plyplastic wing buds began to flow, extending out from the fuselage into a simple delta configuration. Oscar was rattled from side to side in the cockpit as they caught the wind. He disengaged the forward tether lock, and the hyperglider leapt about wildly. His own sparse piloting knowledge buoyed by the recent skill implants helped him counter the movement with relative ease, keeping the craft as level as possible.

He allowed the front and rear tether strands to unwind,

and adjusted the wings to provide some lift. The hyperglider began to rise away from the floor of the canyon, tugging hard at the cables as the wind tore at the fuselage. Once he was fifty metres high he adjusted the tail fin into a long vertical stabilizer. The shaking began to lose its urgency, though the howl of the wind outside was still growing. Oscar expanded the wings further, deepening the camber to generate more direct lift. With the tether cables reporting a huge strain, he began spooling them out at a measured rate, scrupulously keeping his ascent at the recommended pace. This was not the time, he decided, for cutting corners, no matter what the stakes.

Tatters of mist shot past the cockpit, twined into a sheath that restricted his visual range to little more than twenty metres. Rain was battering aggressively into the fuselage with loud drumbeat reverberations. As he climbed higher, the cables began shaking with unlikely harmonics. He was constantly adjusting the wings to try and keep the hyperglider stable.

'If this storm isn't enough for Samantha to work with, I don't know what is,' Wilson said. The radio link wasn't good, but the static-creased words contained a formidable determination.

Oscar clung to his friend's voice, the contact with another human was suddenly tremendously important. When he scrutinized the weather radar again he could see the scarlet and cerise flow waves of the storm rushing down Stakeout Canyon, overlapping and twisting at a giddy velocity. The speed around the fuselage had now exceeded a hundred miles an hour. Indigo stars marked the other two hypergliders; both were in the air, about the same height as him. *So she is alive and kicking, then.* It had been a foolish fantasy that her silence meant she was somehow inactive.

'Yeah,' he said as he rose past the thousand metre mark. 'I don't like being inside it; I certainly wouldn't like to be on the receiving end.'

'Adam only meant for you to do this, didn't he? That's why he put you through the memory-implant procedure. There was no moisture damage. He wasn't going to let me and Anna fly.'

'No. He was going to explain it to the Guardians and use them to make sure the two of you stayed on the ground. Bloody idiot, as if my flying can guarantee a landing on the summit.'

'Why didn't he tell us you were in the clear?'

'He would have to explain why to the Investigator, that we knew each other from way back, which was why he contacted me in the first place.' The hyperglider lurched alarmingly to starboard. Oscar brought it back with steady pressure on the joystick, flexing the wings. The craft rolled back to its level position. His concentrated hard on the weather radar, though even that had trouble spotting the extreme airflow turbulence inside the jetstreams.

'Is that important?' Wilson asked.

Oscar ground his teeth together. For decades he'd assumed that this moment, if it ever came, would be cathartic. It wasn't. He hated himself for confessing, for what he had to confess. 'I'm afraid so.'

'So why did he know you?'

'We both got involved with student politics at university. It was stupid. We were young, and the radicals knew how to exploit that.'

'What happened?'

'Ultimately? Abadan station.'

'Oh Jesus, Oscar, you've got to be kidding. That was you?'

'I was nineteen. Adam and I were in the group which planted the bomb. It wasn't meant for the passenger train. We were making a gesture against the grain dumping. But there was some snarl up on StLincoln; the express was running late so traffic control gave it priority, they pushed the grain train onto a different line.'

'Son of a bitch.'

'Yeah.' Oscar watched his altitude go through the fourteen hundred metre mark. It was difficult to see. Tears were washing down his cheeks. He ordered the wing-configuration change ready for flight. 'The Intersolar Socialist Party took pity on me and paid for me to undergo an identity change on Illuminatus. I've been . . . I don't know. Making amends? Ever since.'

'I'll be damned. This really is a day for revelations, isn't it? I guess we're all strangers in the end.'

'Wilson. No matter what . . . if you hate me now, I'm glad I knew you.'

'I don't hate you. So is Oscar your real name?'

'Hell no.' He checked out through the cockpit canopy, seeing the wings curving away on either side. Virtual vision showed him the tailplane morphing into a broad triangular stabilizer. Deep in his gut he was tensing himself up for the release. 'I used to be a big film buff; I loved all those fabulous musicals and cowboys and romances they used to make back in the mid-twentieth century. Oscar Awards, see? And the biggest star they ever had was called Marilyn Monroe.'

'Well Mr Star Award; you named the tactic: two on one.'

Oscar saw Wilson's hyperglider disengage. Its indigo star went shooting off down the carmine river flooding the length of Stakeout Canyon.

He could almost hear the calculation that Anna must be making. Out of all of them, Wilson stood the best chance of reaching the summit. The longer she left it, the more difficult it would be for her to catch him and presumably force some kind of collision; but if she disengaged before Oscar he could pick his own moment any time in the next hour or so, and make his flight completely unimpeded. It all depended on how much faith everyone had in his ability to fly the foreshortened parabola.

Anna disengaged.

She was twenty-five seconds behind Wilson.

Oscar's virtual hand punched the disengage icon. G-force shoved him down hard in the seat. The hyperglider streaked away at over a hundred and twenty miles an hour. Roiling air buffeted the wings mercilessly. He'd envisaged keeping the craft steady whilst watching the movements of the other two, waiting for whatever moment presented itself. Instead he was thrust into an immediate battle for simple survival. All he cared about was maintaining altitude. The two terrifying canyon walls jumped out of the radar screen at him as the winds impelled him from side to side. He countered each floundering swerve movement the screaming storm flung at him, tilting the joystick with a fear-burned calmness. The wings shifted obediently, tips twisting and flexing to produce a response so quick he had trouble registering it before it became overcompensation.

For a split second he searched out the two indigo stars. His e-butler projected their course trajectories. The slender topaz lines it sketched intersected before the end of Stakeout Canyon. Then the vast rock walls were closing in again, and the instabilities clawing at the fuselage intensified. It grew darker outside as the shreds of clouds threaded within the storm were wrenched back into a single wild braid high above the ground. Big raindrops smashed against the cockpit in a sudden wave. The hyperglider yawed under the assault. Oscar struggled to right the craft again. He had to reduce the wing size, increasing control at the cost of the acceleration which the previous wide curve had given him. There was no noticeable loss of speed, and it was easier to force his way back into the centre of the canyon, keeping above that writhing arterial cloud. The radar found the end of the canyon wall twenty kilometres ahead, a vertical cliff that stretched up off the screen.

He checked the other two hypergliders again. Anna was flying with mechanical exactitude, her wings hadn't been trimmed down, yet somehow she was maintaining her vector, closing fast on Wilson. She didn't have to worry about manoeuvring into the right position to go vertical at the end of the canyon. She didn't have human concerns to distract her any more. Her hyperglider streaked on like a missile. Wilson couldn't move away, if he was to soar up the incredible waterfall that flowed out of the canyon he had to hold his course perfectly steady.

The skills of some long departed pilot had settled calmly into Oscar's mind now, allowing him to manipulate the joystick in kinesic synergy with the hyperglider, bestowing a flawless control over the aerodynamics at some animal-instinct level. Amid the darkening sky and belligerent uproar of the storm he watched the express train from StLincoln leave the tracks in a cloying oily fireball, saw the carriages jack-knife and crumple, caught sight of the broken charred bodies sprawled along the side of the tracks. He knew them all now, every night for forty years their faces had filled his one and only dream.

His virtual hand manipulated the wing configuration again, moulding it into a wider, longer planform among the red warning symbols thrown up by the on-board array. His speed increased, and he lowered the nose, hurtling down towards the torrent of white foam that soared through the air two kilometres above the canyon floor.

'Wilson?' he called above the cacophony.

Savage rivulets churned around the hyperglider fuselage to be sliced apart by the rapier blade wings. High above, the sun rose over the summit of Mount Herculaneum.

'I hear you.'

The sunlight broke apart on the water, scattering into a seething cloud of ephemeral rainbows. Oscar smiled in delight at the beauty of this world's bizarre nature. Directly in front and below, a dazzling white cruciform shape surfed along the top of the coruscating foam.

'My name is Gene Yaohui.' As he said it, he plunged into the glorious vortex of light and water, hitting Anna's hyperglider head on.

*

It had happened before, many times, back when he was flying with the Wild Fox Squadron. It was such a tight institution that they willingly lived each other's lives in the air and on the ground; they trained together, they partied together, went to the big game together, flew missions together, served overseas together. On base he knew the wives and kids of every other pilot, their money troubles, their fights, their grocery orders; while in the air he knew the performance and limit of each man flying. They were as close as brothers.

When they flew combat missions some didn't come back. The radar showed them die, its neat little neon green symbology on the HUD printing up **contact lost** codes where their plane had burst apart from a missile strike to fall like a meteor in flaming ruin. Each time, a part of himself had been wrenched away into the crash, leaving a void that would never be filled in quite the same way again. But you carried on because that was what the guys wanted, you knew them well enough to be certain. It was that knowledge that gave you the strength to carry on.

And now, three and a half centuries after he thought he'd lost his last squadron buddy, Wilson Kime watched the radar symbols of his wife and best friend tumble out of the sky to smash apart on the implacable rock far below his hyperglider.

'Goodbye Gene Yaohui,' he whispered.

Two kilometres ahead of him, the river which streaked through the air performed its magnificently paradoxical curve and charged up parallel to the immense cliff face. Orange positioning vectors printed themselves around his virtual vision, and he moved the joystick calmly, lining the craft up on the correct approach path. He withdrew the wings back into a short swept-back planform as the canyon walls rushed in on either side. The waterfall was directly ahead, a sheet of silver ripples ascending at over two hundred miles an hour. He held his breath for a long heartbeat.

The hyperglider was abruptly torn upwards with a force that thrust him down into the seat. He grappled with the joystick, wrangling the wing surfaces to keep the craft perfectly level as it stood on its tail and blasted straight up for the pristine sapphire sky. Wilson breathed again, then he was suddenly laughing, only it sounded more like a defiant snarl that the Starflyer would hear and know.

Peaking out at five kilometres, the vertical waterfall began to break apart as the immense pressure which created it lessened, escaping from Stakeout Canyon's brutal constriction. The water parted into two cataracts of looser spume, gushing away north and south onto the huge volcano's lower slopes. Wilson rode the residual blast of air from the escaping storm, letting it carry him still higher, maintaining velocity. As he soared above the grasslands of the higher, temperate, slopes, he watched the massive cloud bands below him tumbling away around the volcano where they would engender the planet's revenge on the other side.

The radar started to pick out the twisters up ahead as they birthed out of the clear turbulence that marked the upper fringes of the storm. He watched them whipping round, translucent columns skating erratically across the ground that would suddenly be plunged full of dust and stone as they sucked up an exposed patch of soil. The on-board array started tracking them, winding in his options.

Three were in the right area, all of them large enough. One he dismissed, its oscillations too unstable. Out of the remaining two, he simply went for the nearest.

He eased the joystick forwards, aiming the nose at the whirling base of the twister, matching the semi-rhythmic way it skewed from side to side as it snaked its way upslope. The hyperglider's wings and tailplane were pulled in to simple shark-fin steering flaps as he dived in towards the target. Holding steady, intuitively aiming for where he knew it would go. *If Gene Yaohui can aim straight, then I sure as hell can. Our purpose will go on, will succeed.*

Wilson tugged the joystick back, pulling the hyperglider into a steep climb as it slid into the twister. The canopy was instantly bombarded with sand and gravel; larger chunks of stone made him cringe as they impacted. Fuselage stress levels peaked. Motors whined directly behind his seat, spinning the forward section of the hyperglider in counter to the twister rotation, adding stability to the climb. The wings had morphed again, becoming propeller blades to tap the tempestuous power of the twister.

Seconds later, the hyperglider burst out of the top of the twister. Wilson began an urgent review of the flight vector. He'd gained enough velocity to fly the complete arc over the summit. Good, but not what he wanted. The wings altered their camber, pitching the nose up in a modest aerobrake manoeuvre. There wasn't much time, the gases were thinning out rapidly as he left the stratosphere behind. He extended the wings further still, and angled them to increase their drag on the tenuous gusts of molecules that were slipping past the fuselage. In his virtual vision, the projected parabola slowly sank back down into the one he'd plotted, giving him an impact point a kilometre and a half behind Aphrodite's Seat.

The hyperglider sailed up out of the atmosphere. Space reverted to familiar welcome black outside, the stars as bright as he'd ever seen them. He watched beads of moisture smeared across the fuselage turn to ice. Beneath his starboard wing, Mount Titan's crater bubbled with gloomy red light as the lava churned and effervesced, spitting out smoky gobbets of stone that chased parabolas of their own down into the atmosphere where they burst apart in crimson shockwaves. In front of the nose, Mount Herculaneum's flat summit tipped into view as the hyperglider reached the apex of its trajectory, presenting a dismal umber plain of cold lava dimpled by the twin calderas.

Wilson saw it but that was all; there was no interest, no marvelling at the vista. He'd honoured those taken from him, he'd flown the perfect flight for them. That alone was victory. There was nothing else left for him to do, no adjustments to make. Tiny cold-gas reaction thrusters kept the hyperglider level up here in the vacuum. Gravity would bring him down where they'd chosen. That was his last memory of the three of them: gathered round the projected map back in the hangar, squabbling excitedly over the best patch of ground, ignoring the sullen armed Guardians as they glowered at the inappropriate jollity. Oscar and Anna, the two people he would have vouched for above anyone else. People who'd never really existed to begin with.

The hyperglider sank swiftly down towards the fissured surface of the summit. Too steep for comfort. *Nothing I can do, this is all gravity now.* Already, the rest of the planet had vanished below the false horizon of Aphrodite's Seat where the lava ended in sheer cliffs over eight kilometres high. Wilson was alone in space above a rugged circle of lava that was a lot more craggy than the images had hinted at. Shards of clinker littered the ground. He checked his helmet seals again, then made sure the suit's environmental system was switched on. The wings were drawn back to a ten-metre span, their tips curled down in case they were needed for stability should the wheels be damaged on impact.

Fifty metres altitude, and only eight hundred metres from the top of the cliff. The parabola hadn't been quite so perfect after all. Wilson fired all the upper surface gas thrusters at once, trying to speed the descent. The quiet crept up on him, unexpectedly unnerving. Even in a glider he expected some sound from air rushing over the wings as it came in to land.

Here there was nothing, only the ghost of Schiaparelli crater. He lowered the landing struts. And the speed was still way too fast.

The hyperglider hit and immediately bounced. He saw stone fragments spinning off on either side where the wheels had kicked them. Seven hundred metres from the cliff. The wheels touched again. He heard something then, the sound of impacts on the little tyres. Then the cockpit was juddering frenziedly. Dust flared up from the wheels, shooting out streamers thinner than water vapour. The nose landing strut snapped, and the real noise began as the fuselage started skidding across the ground.

Wilson knew it was going to flip. He could feel the motion building. *Nothing I can do. It's all gravity.* The tailplane lifted up as the main body rolled to starboard, jabbing the wingtip into a small crevice. In low gravity the somersault was almost graceful. The hyperglider turned lazily and thudded down on its upper fuselage. An inverted horizon skidded towards Wilson as cracks multiplied across the cockpit canopy The tough glass finally shattered in a burst of gas. Raw pocked lava rushed past, centimetres from his helmet. Through the swirling white haze of the cockpit's evacuating atmosphere Wilson saw a big spur of rock straight ahead. The hyperglider crashed into it, flooding Wilson's universe with a searing red pain.

*

'Man! This is one seriously cruddy radar,' Ozzie complained as the *Charybdis* approached the edge of the Dyson Alpha star system. He'd pulled the TD detector visualization out of his grid to find a translucent grey cube filling his virtual vision. It was grainy inside, with miniscule photonic flaws flowing past him like some kind of smog. Clusters of them veered into warped blemishes, knots in the structural fabric which represented the stars back in the real universe. Now they were only twenty minutes out from Dyson Alpha he changed the scan resolution to focus on the star system ahead. There was a silent inrush of the streaming particles as they foregathered as the star. Smaller congregations swept around it in concentric orbits, three solid planets and two gas-giants. Ozzie searched for the location of the Dark Fortress but there was nothing available on this scale. *Strange, that mother's the size of a planet.* He pulled astronomical data out of the grid, and overlaid it. A tangerine reticulation sprang up to mimic the planetary system layout and size-adjusted until it synchronized with the sensor imagery. A simple purple decussation highlighted the coordinate of the Dark Fortress. Ozzie shifted the focus to centre it, then expanded to the sensor's absolute limit. The little grey motes underwent some kind of jitter as they slipped through the volume of space where the Dark Fortress should be.

'Well something's still there,' Mark said without much conviction.

'Let's go take a look,' Ozzie said. He altered their course vector to take them in a mild curve round to the Dark Fortress coordinate. 'Can this thing pick out ships?'

'I've no idea,' Mark said. 'It doesn't have very good resolution. I suppose if you get close enough it can pick up smaller objects.'

'Don't you know?'

'I haven't got a clue about the physics behind any of this, that's if you can even call it physics any more. I just do the assembly, remember?'

'Okay. Let's get ready to drop out of hyperspace five thousand kilometres above the outer lattice sphere. Get our force fields activated. I'll scan round with ordinary sensors. And Mark, if there are any ships out there, they're going to be hostile. They're going to think we're here to turn their star nova.'

'I know! I was on Elan when they invaded.'

'So,' Ozzie prompted.

Mark gave him an irritated frown. 'So?'

'You've encrypted the weapons. You're going to have to shoot them.'

'Oh. Right. I'll enable the tactical systems.'

'Good idea, man.'

Ozzie gradually reduced their speed as they drew closer until they were stationary relative to the Dark Fortress. There were sixteen ships or satellites orbiting round the structure. The TD detector couldn't provide reliable size estimations.

'Got to be big to show up on this piece of junk,' Ozzie decided.

'The smallest mass to create a gravitonic fold in space-time which can be detected from hyperspace is approximately one thousand tonnes,' the SIsubroutine said.

'They're ships, then.'

'That is a high probability.'

Ozzie touched the icon that activated his couch's plyplastic webbing. He turned his head to look at Mark. 'You ready for this?'

Mark gave him a calculating look. 'Yeah. Sure. Let's go.'

Ozzie dropped the *Charybdis* back into real space. Tiny segments of the stealth hull peeled back like eyelids, allowing sensors to peer out. Five thousand kilometres in front of the sleek ultra-black ellipse of the frigate, the Dark Fortress writhed in electromagnetic agony. Beneath the outer lattice sphere a dense typhoon of radiant amethyst plasma was beset with eruptions and upsurges of copper and azure gyres. The unstable surface spun out tumescent fountains. As they lashed against the outer lattice sphere they triggered snapping discharges deep within the struts causing them to glow with ethereal radiance.

'Wow,' Mark hissed. 'Looks like it's on fire down there.'

'Uh huh.' Ozzie was watching the data from the non-visual sensors. The energy environment around the gigantic orb was diabolical, with electrical, magnetic and gravatonic emissions pulsing up from the rutilant interior to create a maelstrom of particles and radiation above the outer lattice sphere. 'I guess something this big doesn't have a quick death no matter what you hit it with,' he mused.

'What about the flare bomb's quantum signature?'

'It's still there all right,' Ozzie grinned in relish. *I was right; so screw you, Nigel.* 'Unchanged from when they first detected it right after the barrier collapsed.'

'Can you find the origin point?'

'No way, man. There's a hell of a lot of interference from this plasma storm and God knows what else that's going on in the depths. We'll have to use the active sensors, and go in to take a look.'

'They'll see us.'

Ozzie reviewed the infrared image. The objects which the TD detector had found were Prime ships, glowing cerise against the dark. They were also emitting just about every sensor radiation which the *Charybdis*'s passive scanners could detect, sending great fans of it to wash across the outer shell. Their constant radio emission matched the chaotic analogue signals which MorningLightMountain used to mesh its multitude of motiles and immotile groups into a unified whole. 'There's a wormhole open about ten thousand kilometres away,' he said. 'And I'm also picking up some strong radio signals from inside the lattice spheres. It's got ships in there.'

'They're waiting for us.'

'No they're not. Don't panic. These ships are just part of a science mission to examine this thing. Man, it's impressive. You don't realize that until you get up close and personal. Even for a species that went through their singularity event this had to take some doing. And I thought the gas halo was formidable. This could well peak it.'

'Gas halo?'

'Long story. We need to get inside. Do you think our onboard systems are up to it?'

'Why shouldn't they be?'

'The first lattice has a composition that produces electro-repulsive properties. It's in the files. Get too close to it, and your power goes dead, that and other generally bad things.'

'How close?'

'Under ten kilometres I think. The *Second Chance* couldn't get any probes nearer than that.'

'Ozzie, some of these gaps are over a thousand kilometres wide. The Primes have got their ships through and they're five times the size of the *Charybdis*. We'll be fine.'

'Yeah, but we're going to have to switch on our active sensors. There's no way we can do this on visual alone.'

Mark's fingers drummed nervously on the acceleration couch cushioning. 'All right.'

'Is that quantumbuster ready to go?'

'Yeah yeah.'

'Force fields?'

'Get on with it.'

Ozzie enabled the active sensors. The data return quadrupled, amplifying and clarifying the image. 'The environment inside is a lot worse than it was before,' he said tightly. 'But I've got a more accurate fix on the quantum signature, it's definitely inside the fourth lattice sphere. The Starflyer agent planted it in the ring structure somewhere.'

'Can we just get this *over with*. Please.'

'No problem, man.' Ozzie fed power into the secondary-drive units. The *Charybdis* accelerated at a smooth one gee towards the outer lattice sphere. He was aiming for a pentagonal interstice that measured six hundred kilometres in diameter. Radar return was fuzzed by the struts, denying them any close resolution; but their bulk was easy enough to track.

The infrared sensors reported long slender jets of super-heated plasma appearing in space around them. They were being swept by laser, maser and standard radar pulses, which the stealth hull was deflecting. 'Uh, bad news, man. They've seen us, sort of; they're locking on to our sensor emissions.

Ships are accelerating this way. Jeeze! Nine gees. Is that big Mountain dude paranoid, or what?'

'Let's speed things up here.' Mark's voice had risen in pitch.

'Okay, here we go, five gees.' It built quickly, crushing Ozzie back into the cushioning. The outer lattice sphere was expanding fast in the sensor image. 'Oh shit.'

'What?' Mark barked.

'It's not waiting for its ships to catch us. Eight wormholes opening. Five hundred kilometres away. Another four; damn, they're popping up all over the place. Hang on.' Ozzie bumped the acceleration up to ten gees. He could feel his flesh sagging backwards. It was getting very hard to breathe. *Not a day to be wearing tight pants.*

Big ships began to fly out of the wormholes, already accelerating. Missiles leapt away from them, plasma exhausts turning space above the planet-sized artefact to a noonday brilliance. Nuclear explosions erupted, stabbing vast tracts of coherent radiation towards the tiny emission point betraying the *Charybdis*'s existence. Force field warning icons glared red. Ozzie increased their acceleration to twelve gees. His own anguished whimper joined Mark's.

*

MorningLightMountain had never given the alien mega-structure much consideration. Not that it ignored the strange artefact. It had noticed the structure almost as soon as the barrier withdrew. Ships sent to investigate found a planet-sized machine with incomprehensible mass properties. Given its scale, MorningLightMountain concluded it had to be associated with the barrier; in all probability it was the generator or a part of it. According to the Bose memories, that was what the humans considered it to be. It did not understand why they called it the *Dark Fortress*. Something to do with combining *fiction* and *humour*.

The investigation which followed was as methodical as

MorningLightMountain could be. Its primary attention was of course directed first towards eliminating its rival immotiles, then the conquest of the Commonwealth. Even so, it kept worrying away at the enigma. New sensors were fabricated and sent out. Ships ventured through the giant webbed carapace and began to map the properties, energy patterns and geometry of the interior. Over the months, this became more difficult as the internal energy secretions grew in strength while becoming more frenzied. Eventually the artefact resembled a caged star.

Data extraction on several Commonwealth worlds revealed the human physicists were equally puzzled by the *Dark Fortress*. They too did not understand its functionality. They also had no idea who constructed it. MorningLightMountain suspected the human SI could build such a thing. The Silfen aliens might also have the ability, but according to the associated mind data they didn't have the *psychology*. Morning-LightMountain didn't trust that analysis. The galaxy was full of nonPrime life, all of it was an enemy, all of it was suspect. One day it would find its greatest enemy and eliminate them.

As its investigation progressed, the greatest puzzle came from the errant quantum signature emanating from somewhere deep inside the alien artefact. MorningLightMountain could not understand why it matched its own corona-rupture weapon. Logically, it implied the humans on the *Second Chance* had deployed it against the *Dark Fortress*. They had the technology; but they appeared to be as bewildered as it was by why the barrier had failed – assuming their records were accurate, and not *disinformation*.

Such questions were abruptly pushed further down its priority list when the humans turned the staging post star nova. MorningLightMountain realized it had seriously underestimated human scientific resourcefulness. It was now facing the very extinction event it had begun its expansion campaign to eliminate. Humans would move swiftly after their initial success. They only had one ship, one nova bomb when they attacked the staging-post star. It was probably a prototype. If they had more, they would have used them. Right now, their smoothly efficient manufacturing machinery would be producing more ships and bombs. When they had enough to guarantee a successful attack on its home star and all other outposts, they would come.

With its own survival now paramount, MorningLightMountain dispatched more ships and equipment through the wormholes already linking it to new, uninhabited star systems where its settlements were establishing themselves. There were over forty now, which would hopefully stretch human resources to locate and destroy. It also began to install wormhole generators in its largest ships, modifying them for ftl flight. They were nothing like as efficient and fast as the human ftl ships, but they did work. It started to send them through the giant wormhole it had originally built to bridge the gulf between its home system and the Commonwealth, scattering them across interstellar space hundreds of light-years away. Eight had been completed when the immotile group clusters researching the barrier generator detected a wash of sensor radiation. It was coming from a point in space without any physical origin.

MorningLightMountain's primary thought routines immediately recognized the reason. The advanced human ship had been undetectable. The navy-class humans had arrived to turn the home star nova. Every ship researching the generator launched an attack against the intruder, missiles aiming for the elusive emission point.

It didn't understand why the human ship had appeared at the generator. Probabilities were examined. If they were here, why had they not simply bombed the star? It would never have known until the moment the star erupted.

Humans were weak, they would avoid a direct confrontation if at all possible. The ship must somehow be attempting to restart the generator. MorningLightMountain feared that as much as it did extinction. With itself cut off from the freedom of the galaxy, it would ultimately die inside the prison of the barrier as the star slowly burned out. This would become its tomb.

MorningLightMountain immediately opened twenty-four wormholes around the intruder, and began to send its most powerful warships through to intercept the humans.

*

'If one of them made it, they should be there by now,' Andria said.

Samantha took yet another glance at the five dead screens standing on Andria's table. She'd secretly been hoping that the hypergliders might even make it to Aphrodite's Seat early. It was impossible to accept that all three had failed. Now she didn't know what to think. Everyone in the cave had listened to the short-wave messages between Paula Myo and Bradley Johansson. She really couldn't figure out the relevance, but the Investigator was obviously desperate to know about Oscar. Did the information put him in the clear, or condemn him?

Several people in the cave had known Adam. They'd all been shocked by his murder. Samantha found it severely disconcerting; it was hard to accept the Starflyer had got so close to them, that it might still wreck their plans.

'It's here,' one of the control group said.

Samantha automatically glanced at the five dark screens. Frowned.

'The storm,' Andria said quietly.

Up on the big topographic map projected by the portal, the morning storm was billowing round the lower slopes of Mount Herculaneum. Hammerhead clouds poured out into the Dessault Mountains, riding high-velocity jetstreams. At low altitude the clouds roared around peaks, splitting to churn down valleys and bring a deluge of hard rain; while overhead a smooth-flowing sheet of clear air, kilometres high, fanned out above the mountains, driven by the huge pressure surge from behind.

The picture had gaps. Coverage from the manipulator stations was sporadic; the large array was filling in the omissions as best it could.

'Here we go,' Andria said. 'Sequence one, please. Be ready to phase in your sections.'

The Guardians sitting at the tables were abruptly quiet as they studied the data their screens were rolling up. Samantha saw the first echelon of manipulator stations powering up, their gigantic curving blades of energy materializing to rival the rocky peaks they paralleled. Clouds surged in towards their blades, only to be flung on wild curves by the newborn eddies as they began rotating.

'Can we do it?' Samantha asked tersely.

'Sure we can,' Andria said.

Samantha wanted to curse the Starflyer, the useless navy people, Adam for allowing himself to be murdered, the Guardians he'd taken with him, the hyperglider designers, the . . .

'Hey!' Andria cried. 'Carrier signal detected. Coming right at us from Aphrodite's Seat. Dreaming heavens, they made it.'

The image of the storm began to strengthen with details filling in as the large array processed the incoming data; the swirls and mini-cyclones that squalled off from individual peaks, the long hurricane streams rampaging along the bigger valleys. Jetstream velocity, direction, pressure; it all ran through the large array's software to be transformed into initial projections. From that came firm commands on how the manipulator stations should perform if the storm was to be amplified and directed as they wanted.

Applause and cheering burst out all down the cave.

'This is Wilson Kime on Aphrodite's Seat. I hope to God you're receiving all this. My array says it's transmitting okay.'

Samantha had to grip the back of Andria's chair for support as the voice boomed cleanly out of the speakers.

'Deal with him,' Andria snapped. She held out a small mic, never glancing up from her displays.

Samantha took the mic with shaking fingers. 'This is Samantha, we're receiving you just fine, Admiral. The picture is perfect. Thank you.'

'Glad to hear it, Samantha. I have one awesome view from here. The whole world is spread out underneath me, and the detail is astounding. I can see the storm rushing round Herculaneum; it's moving so fast.'

'Admiral, who else is there with you?'

'I don't remember the view from orbit ever being so spectacular; and I've seen a lot of worlds from space now.'

She gave the mic a worried glance. 'Admiral?'

'It was my wife. She was the Starflyer agent.'

'I'm sorry. Where is she?'

'Anna and Oscar never made it out of Stakeout Canyon.'

'Dreaming heavens.'

'I hope this works. I hope this was worth it.'

'We'll make it work.'

*

Bradley quickly pulled his armour suit on as everyone else hurried to their deployment positions. The air creaked around him as the king eagles took off again, riderless this time, and set out low across the veldt to the east. On the road, the jeeps and trucks backed up, leaving the three armoured cars together at the top of the shallow slope. The Paris team and Cat's Claws formed a tight little group around the first vehicle, weapon barrels were sliding up out of various segments of the suits in readiness. They were talking among themselves, using secure links. One did what looked like a little jig.

'Anything from the forts?' Bradley asked Scott, who was standing beside him.

'No, sir.'

'Ah well, we can't delay any more.'

'When the storm arrives, they won't be able to give us much warning, a couple of minutes at best.'

When, not if, Bradley thought in bitter amusement. *Their belief is still strong.* 'I know. It's just that I've spent so much time and effort trying to stop this moment from happening. I truly thought the planet would have its revenge. Now we don't even know if the navy people made it to the summit.'

Scott opened his mouth to answer, then found himself being edged aside as Stig pushed between them.

'I want to drive you,' Stig said.

'Stig—'

'My skeleton suit is adequate if anything gets through the armoured car's force field.'

Bradley looked at the tough young man's stark face, the determination was easy enough to read. He couldn't say no, this was the climax of everything the Guardians had achieved.

'I think I've earned the right to be in at the kill,' Stig said stubbornly.

Bradley smiled and rested his hand on Stig's shoulder, remembering the man's great-grandfather setting out on a raid he never came back from. 'Of course you have, Stig. I'd be delighted and relieved if you took the wheel.'

Stig gave a slight start, he'd obviously marshalled a big argument ready. His face split into a winning smile. 'Thank you, sir.'

'But no more beezees; you've had enough.'

'I don't need it for this, sir.'

'Get the engine started, we'll be going any second.'

Stig raced across the enzyme-bonded concrete to the armoured car's open door.

'I think we're ready,' Bradley told Scott as he watched Stig with a fond smile. 'Start pulling your people back from the road, these zone killers are pretty indiscriminate.'

'Yes, sir. I'm going to send three platoons to intercept the soldier motiles.'

'Fair enough; but those creatures will not be pushovers. Make sure the platoons understand that.'

'Yes, sir, I'm . . .' He broke off to watch the Barsoomians. Ten of them were grouped defensively round Qatux as the Raiel stood behind the truck it'd been riding in. The remainder were dispersing along the top of the ridge, gliding sedately through the short grass like small hovercraft. 'Do they actually have legs?'

'Who knows, Scott? Maybe tomorrow we'll have earned the right to ask them, eh?'

'Tomorrow it is.' Scott's expression changed to one of mild exasperation.

Bradley didn't have to turn, he knew who was coming. Those heels made a very distinctive sound on the concrete.

''Scuse me, Mr Johansson,' Tiger Pansy said. 'Where do you want me for the attack?'

'I think, dear lady, you would be safest here with Qatux.'

'Hey, no way. That's not what Qatux wants. The action is with you guys.'

'I see.'

'She can come with me,' Olwen said. 'I'm driving the second armoured car. It's as safe as anywhere's going to be today.'

'That's really kind,' Tiger Pansy said.

'All right then,' Bradley said. 'Let's go. May the dreaming heavens welcome all of us.' He took out his pendant, a small clear stone with a tiny turquoise glow at the centre, and kissed it before tucking it down into his armour again.

Behind him, Qatux hooted softly. Tiger Pansy was giving him a strange look. 'Cool,' she crooned.

Bradley pulled his helmet on, and told his e-butler to seal the collar. The armoured car's engine was growling as he settled himself into the forward passenger bench. He pulled sensor images from all three armoured cars out of his grid, then opened channels to both Cat's Claws and the Paris team. The image that filled his virtual vision was looking down on the Starflyer convoy, which still hadn't moved. All around it, the clan warriors were withdrawing, widening the circle.

'Everyone ready?' he asked.

As the confirmations came in, he checked on the motiles. Their vehicles were now only seven miles away. Eighty clan warriors were riding fast towards them.

'Stig, Olwen, Ayub, fire the zone killers, please.'

The armoured cars rocked slightly as the delta-shaped weapons burst up out of their launchers. Sensors briefly captured the three of them tracing a fast arc through the sky above Highway One. Distorted, superheated air churned in their wake.

Kinetic cannons mounted on the Land Rover Cruisers tracked round to the vertical and opened fire. They were answered by a massive barrage of ion rifle fire from the encircling band of clan warriors. Dazzling blue-white pulses sleeted in like a constricting noose of sheet lightning. Hyper-rifle shots and Alic's particle lances ripped down from the top of the rise.

'Focus on the Starflyer,' Bradley yelled. Fire lines swept inwards towards the MANN truck and its shiny capsule. A hundred metres above it, three zone killers detonated. The triple cataracts of emerald twinkle-points descended with slow grace to submerge all the convoy vehicles in a translucent corona. For a second they lay entombed within the glowing shroud like insects in amber.

The ground exploded. Huge gouts of soil and rock streaked

up into the sky, obliterating all sight of the convoy. Fireballs from ruptured fuel tanks bloomed within the undulant dirt, to be snuffed out almost immediately. Bradley felt the blast-wave strike the armoured car, rocking it slightly. Dozens of Charlemagnes bolted, oblivious of the riders clinging to their backs; several toppled over. The cloud of pulverized rock fragments and gritty soil began to dissipate.

A section of Highway One three hundred metres long was completely missing. The ground around it had been reduced to a concave circle of raw smoking soil. Right at the centre of the blast maar, the MANN truck sat completely intact; cloying dust motes slithered down its force field as the sunlight returned to glint off its shiny aluminium capsule. Seventeen Cruisers had also survived the zone killers, their force fields glowing like radioactive bubbles around them. Scraps of wreckage from the other vehicles were scattered across the pulverized earth, flames chomping eagerly at their plastic elements. There was no sign of any bodies.

'Dreaming heavens, doesn't anything touch it?' Stig demanded.

'Go!' Bradley told him.

The armoured car lurched forward to race down the remaining strip of road, gathering speed.

*

Morton had been surprised when the debris plume swirled away. He really hadn't expected to see the MANN truck intact. His hyper-rifle had fired shot after shot at the stubbornly resistant force field cloaking the silvery capsule before and during the zone killer strike. He'd fired two HVvixen missiles into the melee. Beside him, Alic's twin particle lances had boomed away, splitting the air with incandescent energy.

'Holy fuck,' Rob spat in amazement. 'We never even scratched it.'

'That's why they call them juggernauts,' The Cat told them with her usual peppy humour.

'The Starflyer gave the Commonwealth force field technology by all accounts,' Alic said. 'Looks like it kept the best bits for itself.'

Bradley's shouted command filled the general communication band. The armoured cars began to drive hell-for-leather down the gradual slope. Morton took off beside them, body angled forward, moving with a simple fast loping movement, allowing Far Away's low gravity to carry him in short arcs above the road between each footfall. His hyper-rifle folded back into its forearm recess while he was on the move. Accelerants began to fizz into his bloodstream, sharpening up his thoughts, binding the interface with his suit even tighter. Nerve strands lost their slackness, contracting to taut conduits that provided instantaneous responses, so tight he could hear them humming. The tactical display in his virtual vision graded up to an even faster refresh rate. Suit sensors showed him the clan warriors reeling their blast-spooked warhorses back under control, and turning back towards the remnants of the convoy. Cruisers opened up with kinetic rapid-fire guns. Long lines of soil in front of the charging horses were ripped up as they ranged in, then the lethal wall of projectiles was chewing through flesh and bone. The front rank of horses died as their legs were triturated beneath them, dropping their bulk into the horizontal fire plane. Their mortal screams seared straight into Morton's electrified nervous system as they vanished beneath swirling plumes of blood and gore. Inside the scarlet fog, force field skeletons flared amber as riders tumbled to the ground. The second rank rode onwards over the steaming gobbets of meat. Morton's sensors pulled in a swift sequence of images, flicking along the remaining riders to capture faces contorted with rage, hanging on to reins with one hand while they fired off wild shots with ion carbines and lasers. Then they began to fall as the Cruisers continued their fusillade.

'Call them back,' Morton screamed into the general channel. 'Get them out of there!' He deployed two plasma carbines and started bombarding one of the Cruisers with pulses. They broke apart into energy flares that whipped impotently across the translucent boundary.

Mortars fired by the McSobels began to land amid the Cruisers, disrupting their fire as force fields hardened temporarily against the electron squalls. Loiter missiles sailed overhead, waiting for the moment when the kinetic fire resumed to slam down hard.

The Barsoomians opened fire. Streaks of violet light hammered into the Cruisers, almost invisible against the sapphire sky. Morton's tactical software couldn't classify the weapons at all. The force fields began to glow a perilous rose-gold.

Short-range defence X-ray lasers on the armoured cars opened up. Stig and the other drivers coordinated their attack, concentrating on one Cruiser. Morton's aim shifted with accelerant-lubricated precision to join the barrage.

They were halfway down the slope now, ranged at four hundred and seventeen metres from the MANN truck. Thick clouds of diesel gushed up out of its vertical exhaust pipes behind the cab, and it started to rumble forwards.

'Don't go,' The Cat yelled at it. 'That'll make me cross.'

The Cruiser they'd been concentrating their firepower on exploded. Morton watched in dismay as the Guardians continued to ride into the kinetic guns. 'They're being slaughtered,' he shouted accusingly.

'We are where we're meant to be,' Scott replied levelly.

'Fuck that.' He had two HVvixen missiles left. Both of them burst out of his shoulder tubes. Two seconds later they stabbed down on a Cruiser, taking it out in a clean pillar of white flame.

'Bad move,' Rob said. 'I think we'll need them later.'

Morton ignored him. The surviving Cruisers were still shooting. 'Cat, Rob: synchronize.' He stopped running, and crouched down as his hyper-rifle slid smoothly up from his forearm. The MANN truck started to draw away. Beside him The Cat and Rob had come to a halt. Charlemagnes charged past in pursuit of the armoured cars. Masers from Institute vehicles had locked on to them. The shield webbing protecting the war-horses blazed with energy that was discharged through their elaborately woven saddle tassels; the big beasts raced onwards trailing whirlwinds of sparks. Morton pulled targeting data out of the tactical display at accelerant speed, bundled some of it in a neat file which he shunted to the Paris team. 'That one.'

Three hyper-rifles fired at once, joined a moment later by the boom of the particle lances. The Cruiser's force field burned dark crimson. They fired again. The Barsoomians joined them. This time they punctured the force field. 'Switching,' Morton told them. He picked a second target while the fireball was still expanding.

The Cruisers were on the move, bucking and juddering over the rough ground as they closed protectively around the MANN truck. Accelerants allowed Morton a seemingly lei-sured review of the fickle data coming in from the Guardians' scouts up ahead. The vehicles carrying the soldier motiles were only two miles away now. Already a running fire fight had broken out between the aliens and the lead riders of the mounted platoons sent to intercept them. It looked like the soldier motiles were equipped with a very powerful version of a plasma rifle. They were also shooting mini-missiles with enhanced-energy warheads. Once again, the horses were taking the brunt of the attack.

Morton's wired scrutiny snapped his attention back to one of his own sensor feeds. One of the Cruisers around the MANN truck was firing missiles. A squadron of intense purple sparks went slicing through the air to detonate against the front of Bradley's armoured car with a ferocity that slammed the heavy vehicle back several metres. The blastwave nearly knocked Morton to the ground. He swayed back as the inside of his helmet reverberated with the roar of the explosion.

'This is a strategic balls-up of the first order,' Rob declared. 'They haven't got a fucking clue what to do.'

'Is there anything we've got that can split that bastard's force field?' Morton asked.

'I don't think so,' Matthew said. 'If the zone killers couldn't do it, nothing we're carrying can.'

'Bradley,' Alic called. 'What's your plan now?'

'We're going to ram the truck. That's the only way left to stop it reaching the *Marie Celeste*. We must pray the planet is having its revenge.'

'Crazy,' Rob bewailed. 'This isn't a battle, it's a joke.'

Morton swiped his attention across various images. The MANN truck had almost made it to where the road began again. A mile and a half ahead of it, the motile soldiers were brushing off the wild attacks by the mounted Guardians. They'd link up soon enough.

Another flight of missiles from a Cruiser pounded into the armoured cars.

'If it's running for its ship it has to get out of the truck to transfer,' Morton said. 'That's when it's vulnerable. We just have to keep up.'

'Morty, clever boy,' The Cat said approvingly.

'Are you with me?'

'Wouldn't miss it, darling.'

'Let's show these morons how to fight a real war,' Rob said.

'Okay,' Alic said. 'We'll take it to them.'

Morton's smile was feral as he started running.

*

Amid the grey desolation of solidified lava that comprised the summit of Mount Herculaneum, the hyperglider had become difficult to see. Dust churned up by the crash had settled on its white fuselage, sticking to the streaks of ice to tone down the shiny plyplastic like adaptive camouflage. Its sharp aerodynamic planform had disappeared the instant it struck the rock spur, crumpling and warping until it resembled the worn vacuum-boiled ripples of lava on which it had come to rest. In the dark cavity underneath that was the badly smashed-up cockpit a couple of small red LEDs glowed in the shadows, slowly dimming as the ruined power cells decayed.

The thin regolith around the wreckage had been disturbed when Wilson hauled himself out of the inverted pilot's seat. A trail of meandering sulcuci led away to the rim of Aphrodite's Seat, illustrating how he'd pulled his inert legs along behind him as he crawled the remaining two hundred and thirty metres. Every now and then the trail widened with broad scuff marks where he'd squirmed round. The exposed lava was covered by flaking splotches of dried blood and little droplets of epoxy foam used to patch the splits in his pressure suit that had torn open again.

Wilson never looked back now. He'd found a smooth cleft right on the precipice which accepted his body like a comfy old sofa. His feet didn't quite dangle over the eight-kilometre drop, but they were only a few centimetres from it. The pressure suit's silver-blue fabric was dull beneath a grimy coat of regolith dust it'd picked up as he dragged himself along. Thick pleats of epoxy foam criss-crossed his shattered legs. Two of the blobby lines were still oozing blood; little droplets inflating out from the edges to bubble away in the vacuum. He no longer worried about such things. Painkillers ensured his remaining time would be comfortable. The last of the Wild Foxes had successfully completed the mission.

To his right, the arrays and their supplementary electronic

modules were arranged neatly on the rock with the broad sensor strips sitting on squat tripods, their matt-black multi-absorbent faces pointing east. The view was perfect, showing him the entire Dessault range all the way across to the tiny spire of Mount StOmer in the east. Far far below him, the glacier ring was a bright diamante strip braided by thin wisps of cirrus. Further down, the thick stormclouds continued to sluice round the tremendous volcano. After hours watching keenly, he was sure the power of the winds from the ocean were weakening now. It didn't matter, the storm had provided the Guardians with more than enough raw material to manufacture their planet's revenge.

While he lay there in the quiet peace of the vacuum, he'd observed the clouds spreading east. From this altitude it was like seeing a white water torrent pouring down a dry riverbed. The green valleys were slowly occluded by the cumulus, leaving just the rugged grey and white pinnacles sticking above the surface.

In the background, Samantha and the others chittered away, their voices like some kind of insect trapped in his helmet. He didn't say very much to them now, just the occasional comment to confirm some aspect of the observation. At first there was little to see. The storm, for all its size and speed, was perfectly natural. He lay there watching its progress as the sun warmed his chest and the lava slowly sucked heat out of his spine. Eventually he noticed how the winds were gradually speeding up, the strange way clouds were confined to the mountains. Ordinarily, most of the storm would flow away out across the vast expanse of the Aldrin Plains, while on the other side of the Dessault range it spewed around Mount Idle to disperse over the southern pampas lands. Today it was blocked and channelled. As the morning went on he started to recognize the Guardians' choreography. Between the mountain peaks, manipulator stations churned up gigantic whorls in the fast-flowing cloud, sucking stationary highs into the Dessault range, denying the storm any release. As a consequence, the cloudswarm rose in height as it thronged along valleys, layer after layer building into a solid thunderhead, kilometres deep. With every exit denied, it had nowhere to go but east. A smile ghosted Wilson's face as he watched the front roar along Trevathan Gulf, fed by fresh gales which the manipulator stations injected through every major valley.

Thumb jabbing down hard on the red button at the top of the joystick. Missile launch: its contrail streaking off into the sky. Bring the fighter round back to the safety of the Wild Fox pack. Watch the radar as the missile hurtles towards its target. Distant unfelt kill.

When the winds reached the end of Trevathan Gulf and hit the High Desert they were travelling in excess of three hundred miles an hour. There were no manipulator stations out here. They had become irrelevant. The storm was so powerful it was now self-sustaining. Uncontrollable.

The vast deluge of white cloud spread out to obliterate the High Desert. Wilson saw it change colour, the cumulus darkening, not with the slate-grey of suspended rain but the ochre of particles siphoned up from the desert floor by an army of twisters that had grown to the size of the very mountains which they had rampaged through. He watched it race towards the final line of pinnacles which guarded the desert's eastern boundary. The enraged mass grew higher and higher until its thrashing crests finally rose above the snow-capped peaks, eclipsing the lands over which they were about to fall.

*

The soldier motile came at Morton with a nimble arachnid gait, veering from side to side in precise controlled motions. It was different to the ones back at Randtown, each of the four legs forked, giving it eight hoofs. Two of the arms also divided half way along. The damn thing was *insectoid*. Triggering deep phobias. Even with accelerant freeze framing its body actions for examination he could never tell which of its hooves it was going to pirouette around next. Targeting was nearly impossible. One pair of the creature's arms held hefty long-barrelled weapons, which Morton was urgently trying to avoid. He did so with a fast low zigzag run, always keeping his feet in contact with the ground, enabling him to switch direction when he needed. Using the ground-eating lope here would give the alien a clear shot as he glided along.

A plasma flare from the soldier motile's weapon hit the earth beside his feet. The suit's force field held, but his legs were yanked from under him. In Far Away's gravity it was an annoyingly slow fall to hit the earth and regain stability. Annoying verging on lethal. The moment stretched in accelerant time. Another blast struck him on the chest. The suit force field flared purple, and he was spinning in the air. Legs flung wide, trying to jab a foot on the ground, *anything* to kill momentum. Virtual hand moved leisurely through the battle cluster icons, selecting his weapon. Another energy blast stabbed past his helmet. Upper arm plasma grenade canisters thumped out their munitions. Air around the soldier motile glared with fizzing electron static.

Morton hit the ground, flattening himself. The world swept back to operate in real-time. He crouched and sprang. Electro-muscle enhancement propelled him forward like a kamikaze aerobot.

The electrons drained away, leaving the soldier motile braced on all eight hooves. It was wearing what looked like a loose robe of scaly grey-green fabric, which was also acting as a force field conductor. Its sensor stalks ended in a clump of golden electronic lenses. Some of its arms ended in a tripartite mechanical claw; while the torso was strung with flat metallic boxes webbed with flexible cables. Arm two swung a big gun round on Morton, its sub-branch gripping some kind of grenade. Arm three fired an ion pistol. Arm one was holding a long *buzzing* blade. Arm four shot the other large gun at a target off towards the road, micromissiles shrieking away from their rotary launcher in its sub-branch.

The ion pulse jangled Morton's suit sensors as he careered into the alien. For a second he was blinded. Tactile feedback gave him the sense of the alien's weight against him, its second arm bending to grip around his hips. The blade skating over his neck, hunting a weak spot. Virtual vision shrieked a warning that his force field was being overloaded by some drain mechanism. These soldier motiles were faster than the ones on Elan. Sensor vision returned. Incomprehensible montage of alien suit fabric, purple light, trampled grass. His own senses told him they were falling together. He triggered the electrification circuit, pumping forty thousand volts through his suit. The alien turned lambent crimson. It sought to roll on top of him, legs three and one bucking, trying to latch what felt like hundreds of hoof claws round his ankle and knees. Morton went with the roll then amplified it with a savage body twist. Wound up on top. His gauntlet clamped round arm one and twisted with full electromuscle strength. Something beneath the alien's flesh buckled, and the arm bent round at a sharp angle. The claw of arm three closed round his neck. His force field alarm went up a grade.

'For fuck's sake,' Morton grunted. Five-centimetre talons slid out of every finger on his right hand. He punched down hard. Red lightning spat out of the impact. He kept pressure going as the dump function on the talon tips pulled energy out of the soldier motile's force field. A stressed whine cut through his insulation. Then the alien's force field weakened around the talons. Morton's hand ripped through fabric and flesh. He thrust it deep into the body turning as he went, ripping organs and blood vessels, then pulled back. It came free reluctantly, sucking up a honey-yellow gore. The soldier motile went limp.

'Morty, we don't have time to make it personal, darling,' The Cat chided.

A micromissile detonated beside him. A cloud of hyper-filament shrapnel boiled out of the explosion, shredding through soil and surface rock. His force field glared scarlet on the point of overload as he was punched sideways by the writhing impact.

'Told you not to waste the HVvixens,' Rob said.

Morton scrambled to his feet. The Cat was right. They were getting swamped by soldier motiles of which there was a seemingly endless number. Hundreds of them had jumped out of their vehicles as soon as they reached the MANN truck. Now they were blocking the way forward. Leaving the road to try and outflank them had been a big mistake. A hundred and fifty metres to his left, the armoured cars were driving down Highway One, their X-ray lasers slashing from side to side like a demented swordsman keeping his opponents at bay. They could pierce the force fields used by soldier motiles if they got within fifty metres; which gave them a small clear area. A flight of micromissiles hammered into the road just ahead of the armoured car Bradley was riding in. Hyperfilament shrapnel shredded the concrete to fine gravel. The armoured cars started to fishtail as soon as they drove into it, wheels throwing up grit as they spun.

Alic's particle lances boomed, sending pulses streaming towards the cluster of soldier motiles that had fired the missiles. They toppled to the ground, then started to pull themselves upright again.

Morton scanned his sensors round, building a tactical profile. It wasn't good. So far they'd travelled about two miles on from the original blockade. At least a hundred and fifty soldier motiles had them effectively surrounded. The Guardians on their Charlemagnes were a mile behind, and holding off – not that they could help. His suit power cells were down to under fifty per cent. There had been too many close calls in combat. None of them had any HVvixens left.

His radar scanned ahead, picking out the MANN truck with its escort five miles away. It was travelling fast along the clear road. Bradley wasn't going to catch it, let alone ram it.

'We'll ride shotgun,' he said. 'Stig, switch off your X-ray lasers, we're hitching a ride.'

'Morton, we have to catch up,' Bradley said.

Morton could hear panic edging in to his voice. 'We can cut through if we combine our firepower.' He'd already started running, the other suits were beside him firing energy weapons into the elusive line of soldier motiles. Up ahead, the armoured cars took more hits from micromissiles. The road surface was completely trashed, reduced to a mire of loose fragments that bogged them down.

'Shit,' Rob screamed.

Morton's sensors caught two soldier motiles pouncing. They'd been lurking in a shallow depression, their suits powered down to avoid detection. Limbs lashed out at Rob's suit as the three of them crashed to the ground in a tangled bucking heap. Force fields flickered between lavender and cerise as weapons fired at point blank range.

'Keep going,' The Cat insisted.

It was hard. Morton wanted to halt and pound the wrestling figures with shots from his hyper-rifle. Imagery shot into his brain at accelerated speed, and he saw just how many solider motiles were charging after them. Front rank almost on top of Rob. 'Rob!'

'Do it,' Rob grunted. 'I'm gonna show them a little Doc Roberts trick any second. These motherfuckers don't ever learn.'

Morton's virtual hand flashed into his grid and hauled out Rob's telemetry. He could see the safety overrides clicking off one by one. Powdery gravel crunched underfoot. The armoured car was ten metres ahead. Morton leapt, power-diving over the curving wedge-shaped vehicle. He'd almost landed on the other side when Rob shorted out every power cell he was carrying. The explosion turned the empty sapphire sky solar white.

'Way to go, Robby boy,' The Cat cried.

Morton's outstretched hands touched the ruined road. He curled himself into a ball and rolled forward to kill momentum. The fearsome glare drained away. Behind him the armoured car was skidding sideways. Stig fought for traction, slewing it back on course. Morton hopped on the front, clinging to one of the X-ray laser mounts.

The Cat appeared beside him as if she'd teleported in. A lone sensor image showed him the smouldering blast crater where Rob had been. Alic thudded onto the roof, gauntlets gripping narrow ridges tight enough to gouge the metal. Morton's hyper-rifle deployed out of his forearm; targeting graphics slid out of his grid. The three of them began to shoot any soldier motile in a broad swathe ahead of the armoured car. 'Use everything,' Alic shouted. 'Punch them out of the way.'

Morton's grenade canisters thrummed as they fired. His plasma carbine switched to continuous pulse, hosing out energy. The hyper-rifle swung round as he picked out target after target. Power cell charge wound down at an alarming rate. More ion rifle shots came from behind them where Jim and Matthew were clinging to the armoured car Ayub was driving. Micromissiles burst all around, hyperfilament lashing against the suits, streamers of ion fire clawed at the grizzly bodywork of the armoured cars. They were driving through a demonic inferno that blotted out every sensor return in a digitized blizzard. His suit surface screeched as the demented energy slashed against it.

Then they were past the bedlam, racing down the grey-white concrete strip of Highway One, shedding static tendrils like chaff. Stig had cranked their speed up to over a hundred and sixty kilometres an hour, smoke was shooting out from somewhere underneath. Morton hunted round, finding the bulk of the soldier motiles streaming together behind them. Their weapons fire contracted, centring on the last armoured car. Jim and Matthew were doing their best to return fire, but they were swamped by the colossal barrage. Hyperfilament shrapnel mauled the road right in front. The armoured car exploded.

'No!' Alic cried. 'Godfuck all of you. Oh sweet Jesus, why can we never catch this monster?'

Morton wanted to answer, but all he saw was Rob's demise, and Doc Roberts, Randtown's glass crater.

'How much power have you got left?' The Cat asked.

'Twenty per cent. Maybe.' Morton checked his schematics. 'Bit under.' He started scanning along the side of the armoured car. Somewhere inside metal was grinding against metal with a terrible clattering violence. The smoke rushing out from underneath had thickened.

'It's the one per cent that'll kill it,' The Cat said.

'Stig?' Morton asked. 'Are we going to make it?' The sound coming from the armoured car sounded terminal.

'We'll make it. This thing has redundancy everywhere. Ten miles, that's all.'

Their speed still hadn't slackened. Up ahead, the road was angling in to the foothills. The Institute valley was visible as a wide saddle that led back to the first mountains of the Dessault range. They weren't high enough to have snow caps, but the ones in the misty distance behind them did. He scanned the jagged skyline, looking for any hint of an approaching storm. Far Away's vaulting sapphire atmosphere was as placid as he'd ever seen it. *Damnit, I thought we could rely on the admiral at least.*

The armoured car juddered sharply and recovered. He swept his radar along the road, getting a clear empty image until it curved into the valley six miles ahead. The MANN truck was already inside.

'Bradley,' Morton said regretfully. 'We're not going to catch it. Do you have any notion how we can disable the starship?'

'Not disable, no. We just have to delay launch until the storm arrives.'

'How?'

'There is one possible option, if you're willing to help me.'

That didn't sound good in any way. Morton wanted to look at The Cat's face, to see what she felt. Despite her thick shell, he knew her well enough now to read her thoughts.

She could obviously read him a lot better. 'We've come this far,' she said.

*

The amethyst plasma inside the Dark Fortress churned in violent torment as it was bombarded by radiation from salvos of fifty-megaton fusion bombs. Thousand kilometre peaks soared up through the gaps in the outer lattice sphere like solar prominences, their extremities evanescing away into tattered streamers. The *Charybdis* dived down between them and struck the plasma at fourteen gees.

Ozzie had been bracing himself for a spine-snapping impact, even though he knew the plasma had a density that barely disqualified it from being a vacuum. There was a slight tremor, which he had to strain to notice amid the brutal acceleration. He disengaged the drive, and was plunged into freefall so abruptly his maltreated body interpreted it as being flung forwards.

'What the fuck?' Mark mumbled.

Ozzie shut down their active sensors. 'Flying dark, see?' The passive sensors showed fusion drives drilling through the plasma all around as the Prime missiles hurtled past. 'They're overshooting.'

'Can we navigate like this?'

'Sure. Look at the returns. The plasma is illuminating the lattice spheres in twenty different spectra. We can fly through this, but slowly.' Their velocity was already taking them towards the second lattice sphere at twenty kilometres per second. Behind them, three hundred and twenty Prime ships slid through the outer lattice sphere and plunged into the plasma. They launched another massive missile salvo.

'Uh . . .'

'It's fine, I can steer us through the second lattice no problem. It's the negative mass one, there's like no way we can hit it, we just get shoved away if we get too close, like magnets.'

'Ozzie . . . Christ! They can see our wake.'

'Huh?'

Behind the *Charybdis*, a five-hundred-kilometre-long contrail of plasma spiralled like a gargantuan tornado. The armada of missiles was all converging towards the apex at seventeen gees. They started to detonate. The frigate's hull field blazed rose-gold as it warded off their directed radiation pulses, flinging vast webbed lightning zephyrs off into the plasma. 'Shit.' Ozzie pushed power back into the secondary drive, accelerating the *Charybdis* away from the vector it had been coasting along. Gee force shunted him down into the cushioning again. 'Are we losing them?'

'No!'

'Mark, you control the weapons. Do something!'

'What? I can fire a quantumbuster, a nova bomb, or a neutron laser.'

Behind them, another wave of missiles detonated. Radiation turned the plasma to an opalescent violet.

'Use a quantumbuster.'

'We need to be a million kilometres away at least when one of those goes off, anything closer than that and this frigate is dead.'

'Son of a bitch, we're not going to make it.'

'You have an incoming call,' the SIsubroutine said. 'An

encrypted maser link originating outside the first lattice sphere.'

'You've gotta be fucking kidding me,' Ozzie groaned.

'Do you want to establish a connection? The identity certificate is confirmed: Nigel Sheldon.'

Ozzie was crying as he laughed. 'Tell him we'll accept the charges.'

'Yo, Ozzie, how's it hanging?' Nigel said. 'You guys need any help down there?'

*

Both armoured cars charged round the final curve in the road, and the Institute valley was directly ahead. The town had the look of a small elite university campus, with villas and apartment blocks colonizing the shallower southern slope in prim rows where their silvered windows looked out over the long white laboratories and engineering sheds which sprawled across the floor of the valley. All of it was dwarfed by the huge cylindrical starship sheltering inside a force field. The scaffolding that had surrounded its eight-hundred-metre length for over two decades had gone, revealing a light-grey fuselage to which the morning sun gave a satin sheen. Eight dark fusion rocket nozzles dominated its aft superstructure, their external casings inset with concentric thermal duct strips that were glowing a mild maroon as they kept the superconductor coils chilled. Several long blunt fins protruded from the fuselage, fluorescing a deep fuchsia purple as they maintained thermal stability within the internal tanks and generators. Up at the prow, the original tumorous cluster of force field generators had been supplemented by an elongated scarlet cone, fifty metres across at the base. Frost clung to long segments of the fuselage, revealing the outer walls of the deuterium tanks.

A single gantry pillar had been left standing just behind the prow. The MANN truck was parked at its base.

'The son of a bitch made it,' Alic said bitterly.

'We'd have been royally screwed anyway,' The Cat said. 'I somehow don't think these boys would let us pass.'

Soldier motiles had formed a broad line across Highway One and the surrounding ground half a kilometre from the rear of the *Marie Celeste*.

'Oh shit,' Morton muttered. There must have been a thousand aliens waiting.

'Ready,' Stig said.

'Hit it.' Morton launched his three electronic warfare drones; The Cat launched her remaining pair. Stig and Olwen had changed the focus on the X-ray lasers; now they fired them in broad fans at the waiting aliens.

For a couple of seconds the soldier motiles were bombarded by false signals and insidiously corrosive software, X-rays seared into their electromagnetic sensors. They adapted and filtered and flushed the digital viruses; but there was still a moment while they were purblind.

It didn't matter, when their sensors regained full function-ality and scanned the land in front of them nothing had changed; the armoured cars were still racing along Highway One, three armour suits riding on the outside of one which was puffing out hot black smoke. The two vehicles suddenly braked hard, tyres squealing as the gearboxes were slammed into reverse. Then they were turning, skidding round as if the concrete had iced over. They started to flee back down the road.

As one, the soldier motiles started running after them. The armoured car that was leaking smoke suddenly juddered. It began to slow, sparks flying out from underneath along with thickening belches of smoke. Something inside it was clanging like a broken bell. The soldier motiles opened fire.

'FUUUUUUCK,' Morton yelled, and powerdived off the armoured car. The sky around him erupted in a relentless blaze of malignant ion bolts. He hit the edge of the concrete and rolled perfectly, timing it so he recovered his footing in a half-turn. Suit electromuscles propelled him into an immediate sprint, his body leaning forward at forty-five degrees. The force field reshaped itself, mushrooming out around his head and shoulders to act as a spoiler, providing downpressure from the air that rushed over him. He swung his hands in a near-Neanderthal gait, knuckles not quite touching the ground, but close.

Sensors caught Stig bursting out through the armoured car's front emergency hatch as its force field's glow escalated to a scarlet climax. The Guardian sped away, moving with fluid ease in the low gravity. Behind him, the soldier motiles concentrated their fire. The crippled armoured car exploded.

Up ahead, Olwen's armoured car braked.

'Keep going,' Morton yelled frantically. 'Get the fuck out of here.' Micromissiles streaked overhead, pummelling the slow moving vehicle. 'We can outrun them.'

'But—'

'Go!'

The armoured car accelerated hard again, building distance.

'Outrun them,' The Cat laughed raucously. 'You going to run away from the launch, too, Morty darling?'

He gritted his teeth inside his helmet. Ever since he'd seen the ship he'd been trying to work out how much it massed. A lot of it was fuel, he remembered that from the quick review he'd given the files. Despite that, a quarter of a million tonnes was a conservative estimate. Even with force field wings generating some degree of lift, igniting the kind of fusion engines which could produce that much thrust would be worse than letting off a strategic nuke.

He saw the dark tide of soldier motiles flow over the burning wreckage of the armoured car. They were fast, but they didn't have electromuscle support. They'd never be able to keep that speed going. *Would they?*

The Cat was keeping up with him, leaning over at an even greater angle. Alic was off to one side.

'There won't be a launch,' he grunted.

'Oh Morty, you're priceless. These Guardian fuck-ups have blown every chance they had. This won't be any different.'

'It has to be. Bradley has to win. The Starflyer can't go free.'

'Then we should have brought some tactical nukes or a *Moscow*-class warship. Don't you get it, this thing is smarter than us.'

'You. Not me.'

'Morton's right,' Alic said. 'It hasn't launched yet. Bradley just has to keep it on the ground.'

'Men! Why accomplish when you can dream?'

'Fuck you.'

It took them three minutes to cover a mile. They didn't use the road, it was too open. The ground alongside was rugged, with the grass and eucalyptus shrub offering a small degree of cover. They kept going for another fifteen minutes, until Morton's laser ranger finally showed him they were widening the gap on the soldier motiles behind. 'We need to get away from the road,' he said. 'The other motiles are still up ahead. I don't want to be caught between them.'

'Good idea,' Alic said.

Morton changed direction slightly, angling away from Highway One.

'How far do you figure they'll chase us for?'

'More to the point, how much power have you got left?'

'My suit is down to eleven per cent. The force field is a real drain.'

'Look, boys, we don't have to—'

The sun went out.

Even with accelerant driving his thoughts, it took a second for Morton to register the monstrous anomaly. The light was draining out of the veldt, rushing away from him like an extinction event. 'Huh?' He twisted to face the west and tilted his head up, aligning the main visual sensors on the Dessault Mountains. His knees nearly faltered with shock. 'Not possible,' he gasped.

*

The *Charybdis* began to *creak* in protest as Ozzie shunted the acceleration up to fifteen gees. They were chasing a shallow parabola back up from the second lattice sphere. Behind them, nuclear explosions had pumped the plasma into a solid incandescent white sky. Sensors showed them the outer lattice sphere as back prison bars across the hazy stars.

An armada of Prime ships was curving round to follow them through the turbulent plasma, firing volley after volley of missiles. More explosions bloomed, and an indigo stain began to seep through the plasma as the energy levels built towards saturation. Masers and X-ray lasers left visible cerise lines through the diaphanous ions as they stabbed at the frigate.

Ozzie was feeding small random variations into the acceleration, evading the missiles' target-tracking function. A red mist was encroaching the edges of his virtual vision. He tried to keep his attention on various coloured lines which represented important criteria like velocity and closing distance. External cameras showed him a very large dark strut of the outer lattice looming in front of the frigate's blunt nose. It was a hundred and eighty kilometres wide, and stretched out to a junction with five other struts four hundred kilometres ahead.

'Nigel?'

'Contact lost,' the SIsubroutine reported.

'Well I suppose that's a good thing,' Mark said. 'Proves the material is still electro repulsive. This thing isn't dead yet.'

'Right.' Ozzie changed direction again, heading straight up

towards the strut. It was fifty kilometres away when he curved round to fly parallel to it; he didn't dare try and get any further in. Vast rivers of luminescence flickered on and off deep inside the dark material. 'Come on Nigel.' He reduced acceleration to a steady two gees.

'Do you think they're—'

Outside the Dark Fortress, the *Scylla* fired a quantumbuster and immediately dropped back into hyperspace. The missile intercepted a Prime ship, converting a modest percentage of its mass directly to energy. For a brief instant, the radiative output of a medium-sized star contaminated space around the Dark Fortress. It sliced through the forty-eight wormholes MorningLightMountain had opened from its gas-giant settlements, obliterating the generators on the other side and anything else caught inside the beams. Around the Dark Fortress, every Prime ship flared like a comet as it vaporized, trailing dying molecules through the brilliant white void.

Ultra-hard radiation poured through the outer lattice sphere, decimating the ships and missiles inside. Safe in the umbra of the electro-repulsive matter, the *Charybdis* flew onward unharmed as the radiation sleeted down on either side of the massive lattice strut.

'Now that's what I call *hellfire*,' Ozzie mumbled.

Below the *Charybdis* the plasma had turned a lethal pellucid violet. Visual sensors could see each of the remaining three lattice spheres. The core remained an impenetrable haze.

'Do you think the inner lattice spheres can withstand another blast like that?' Mark asked.

'Who knows? But Nigel was right. We were going to do that anyway when we knock out the flare bomb. Nothing to lose by doing it twice.'

'Nigel Sheldon's pretty smart, isn't he?' Mark said admiringly.

'Yeah.' Ozzie's smile tightened. 'Pretty smart.' He fed power into the frigate's secondary drive, and dived straight down towards the second lattice sphere at eight gees.

*

The fourth lattice shell was made from a material that appeared to be completely neutral, devoid of any detectable properties, it didn't even have any mass as far as human sensors could discover, all that existed was its physical boundary. Like the upper three lattice spheres, it remained completely unaffected by the energy deluge from the quantumbuster. Ozzie piloted the *Charybdis* through it without any trouble. He decelerated to a velocity vector that kept them stationary relative to the core, and extended every sensor.

The rings were in turmoil. They oscillated and stretched, rising and falling in and out of alignment through the ecliptic. The black cables which held together the outermost ring, the daisy chain, were flexing like lengths of elastic as they strove to contain the wild fluctuations of the lenticular discs. Inside that, the green ring which had been so uniform when the *Second Chance* recorded it, was now undergoing curious distensions, bulges would suddenly appear, sending out slow ripples across the surface. The silver braids were nearly breaking apart; while the one of scarlet light was contaminated by dark fissures.

It was the ring nicknamed Sparks which was the worst affected. The river of emerald and amber lights with their cometary tails were being flung out of their simple orbit by a single dark contortion, like ions waltzing around a magnetic anomaly. It took them almost an entire orbit to drop back into the plane, only to be slung out again.

'There's our bad boy,' Ozzie murmured. The quantum scan showed him the pattern of elongated distortion fields radiating out from a single point as they spun slowly along through the coruscating ring. 'A genuine spanner in the works.'

'Target loaded,' Mark said. 'Effect field pattern selected. It'll stand off five thousand kilometres and spike the heart of that bastard.'

'You're the man,' Ozzie told him.

'Launching.'

The *Charybdis* gave the faintest shiver as the quantumbuster shot out of its launch tube. Ozzie turned the frigate round, and accelerated hard up through the lattice spheres.

*

Bradley landed in the shallow drainage ditch at the side of Highway One. The soil was damp and squishy, absorbing his impact. He folded himself into a cleft and froze. His suit's external chromometic layer painted him with low-tone greys and greens to match the grass tufts and mud he'd settled in. Every other system powered down. Thermal batteries absorbed his body's heat, allowing the suit skin to adopt the same temperature profile as the ditch. A tiny beam of light washed in through a slit in his visor, illuminating his eyes. Outside, the armoured cars were skidding round. One sounded in a bad way. Their engine noise dopplered away. His breathing was loud in his ears, challenged only by his heartbeat.

The light flickered. Soldier motiles were running past him; several splashing their way along the bottom of the ditch. They were centimetres away.

And fate – mine, the Starflyer's, humanity's, the Primes' – is decided by that tiny distance. But then my fate has taken stranger turns than this in the past. Perhaps the dreaming heavens will smile upon me today.

The movement outside his suit ended. Bradley switched on a lone sensor, and scanned round. There was no immediate sign of the soldier motiles. He stood up, and watched the alien army charge away. Some distance further along Highway One an armoured car exploded.

Keeping the suit fully stealthed, Bradley hurried towards

the giant alien starship. He opened passive sensors, knowing the signal he would receive.

*

Not a sound or an image, at first, more a melange of feeling – to those who knew how to interpret it. The complex electronic song saturated the airwaves, broadcast from every direction to engulf the valley. Together the harmonics that surrounded Bradley had a unity that was remarkable in its complexity. The tunes rose and fell, meshing into a cohesive mind. Bodies, alien and human, sharing every part of themselves: memories, thoughts, sensations. He moved among them, receiving their extended cognizance, drinking it in. Watching the three humans in armour suits running along the road as we chase after them – concern that the human warriors should not be able to interfere with the launch. Observing the many technological facets of the refurbished starship, adjusting the systems as they interact with each other – eager for the long exile to finally end. Maintaining the force field around the ship – determined that no weapon would penetrate. Reviewing the sensors covering the valley – alert for transgressions.

The location and purpose of each body were individual, yet their thoughts were homogenized, replicating their originator. Direction, purpose came from only one source: the Starflyer.

It moved from the gantry lift into the starship, awakening the giant machine in its entirety. Soon it would leave to vanish amid the stars. Safe. Free.

*

Bradley told the force field around the starship to admit him. Compliance was a logical thing to expect, given the Starflyer's ultimate origin. The immotile rules all, nothing deviates from that. However, as the Starflyer was more sophisticated than a standard Prime immotile, it didn't have the same reticence in allowing electronics to have governing functions over machinery. Electronics were subsidiary to it in the same way as motiles; it programmed them, it set their parameters. They obeyed it.

That was its flaw, Bradley knew, the same as every Prime. It did not understand independence nor rebellion. Its motiles, whether grown in congregation pools from its own advanced genetically modified nucleiplasms, or humans whose brains had been surgically and electronically subsumed to host its own thought routines, were a part of it. Their thoughts were its thoughts, copied and installed from its own brain. None of them deviated. It couldn't conceive deviation or betrayal, so neither could they.

Security was a one-dimensional concept for the Starflyer. It took precautions to guard itself physically and politically from native humans as it insinuated its human motiles within their Commonwealth society. That was the level of safety it determined it required to ensure its survival, a strategy that had been successful.

No human could hack into the electronic network of the Institute valley. As the processors were an extension of the Starflyer's own mind, they only acknowledged orders that had an internal heritage. What the network and its processors did not have was the ability to discriminate between an order from a genuine motile and a human who remembered the neural 'language' of the Starflyer.

In front of Bradley, the force field protecting the *Marie Celeste* realigned its structure to allow him through. He jogged along the bottom of the deep grassy scar which the vast alien ship had scored as it slid along the ground before finally coming to an ignominious halt. Several soldier motiles were patrolling the base of the starship. Their minds told him where they were, the direction they were looking in, where they would look next. Their sensors and eyes never saw his suit's stealth coating as he hurried into the shadows cast by the big fusion rocket nozzles. Proximity alarms watched passively as he told their processors his presence was legitimate.

The ship had been lifted gradually out of the scar by motiles and civil engineering machinery. A wide pad of enzyme-bonded concrete had been laid underneath to support the weight. Cradles gripped the lower fuselage, holding it off the ground. Bradley walked up the metal stairs on one of the cradles. An access hatch to the fusion engineering bay opened for him, and he ducked inside.

The initial findings on the *Marie Celeste* published by the Institute were accurate enough. It was comprised of fusion rockets, their fuel tanks, environmentally maintained water tanks containing an alien amoeba-equivalent cell, and the force field generators. From that, public perception remained locked on the knowledge that there was nothing else inside, certainly it possessed no life support section, no 'crew quarters'. A more detailed examination showed (unpressurized) access passages and crawlways remarkably similar to those humans would design in to any ship. No maintenance robots were ever found. The first conclusion was that the passages were used only for construction.

Right at the centre of the tanks there was a chamber with a life-support system. The Starflyer lived in that, fed with base cells and purified water from the tanks. It didn't need additional space to move about in, there were no leisure and recreational facilities that any human would have needed during a centuries-long flight. All it did was receive information and supervise the ship's systems. When necessary it would ovulate nucleiplasms into a freefall vat to grow space-adept motiles that would be dispatched on repair assignments. After they had completed their task they would be recycled into nutrients for the base cells in the tanks. Every century a new immotile would be created to house the Starflyer's mind as the old body aged. All this in a chamber of thirty cubic metres. Easy for a preliminary examination to miss in a volume of twenty-five million cubic metres, especially as it had been badly damaged during the landing.

There were no lights inside the engineering bay, another aspect contributing to the myth of the ship being 'solid machinery'. Bradley turned his infrared sensors up to full resolution, and made his way along the cramped passage. It branched several times, some openings like vertical chimneys leading up to the centre of the ship. Climbing would take too long for him. He found a corridor leading towards the prow and moved as fast as he could. The corridor walls were open girders. Beyond them, the ship's major segments were held together inside a simple gridwork. The individual beams of metal were shaking as the fusion drives worked down their ignition sequence. In two minutes the ship would lift from this world to the clean emptiness of space.

Bradley clambered out of the corridor and began to worm his way up through the narrow gap between a deuterium tank and some car-sized turbo pumps. The mindsong of the Star-flyer remained perfectly clear to his receptors, even wedged into the lightless metal cavity.

'Remember me?' he asked.

Every motile in the Institute valley froze.

'You do, don't you? I made sure you wouldn't forget me.'

The mindsong altered, reaching out into the brains of each human motile contained within the Starflyer's mental empire. Questioning. Processors ran checks on themselves to see where the aberrant harmonics were coming from.

'Oh, I'm in here with you.'

Outside the ship, the song faltered, withdrawing.

'You didn't think I was going to miss this moment, did you? I want to be with you when we launch. I want to be certain. I want us to be together when we die.'

Suspicion strengthened until the mindsong became loud enough to exert a painful phantom pressure on Bradley's ears.

'Bombs, kaos software, biological agents. I forget which. They're hidden somewhere on board. I don't remember where, or how long I've been here. Perhaps I never went away.'

Over the strident turmoil of the mindsong, Bradley could hear motiles scrabbling along passages. Thousands of them were set loose, swarming like rats, seeking any clue to his whereabouts.

Bradley waited in the pitch dark as the Starflyer's thoughts thrashed into doubt and wrath. Waited as the minutes ticked away. The fusion rockets held their ignition sequence.

'Will you launch, I wonder? Flee to the safety of space knowing I can't survive long. Hope the redundant systems will suffice after the sabotage. Or will you stay? The damage can be repaired here on the ground. Of course, the Commonwealth elite know you exist now. They will be coming in their superships. You would not survive their vengeance.'

The mindsong rose to a howl of fury.

Bradley looked down. Below his feet, a motile was standing in the corridor, sensor stalks curving up to gaze on him. It exploded into motion, clawing its way up the girders.

'Too late, I'm afraid.'

Outside the starship, darkness fell.

Bradley smiled, the gesture's warmth pouring like a balm into the discordant mindsong. 'You can never know us. Only a human can truly know another human. The rest of the galaxy is doomed to underestimate us. Just as you have done.'

The hull sensors saw the solid wall of the megastorm sweep out of the High Desert. It towered briefly above the mountains before enveloping them and blasting down into the Institute valley. For a few seconds, the force field over the *Marie Celeste* resisted the savage assault, radiating a vivid ruby light until the titanic battering overloaded its generator. A ten mile high wave of sand and stone travelling at three hundred miles an hour crashed down on the naked starship.

'Farewell, my enemy,' Bradley Johansson said contentedly.

*

The two frigates hung side by side in space, completely invisible. One and a half million kilometres away, the Dark Fortress glimmered like a wan Halloween lantern. It suddenly flared blue-white, rivalling the nearby Dyson Alpha star in magnitude. The light faded as swiftly as it had risen.

'So there was some kind of matter at the core of the flare bomb to convert,' Mark said.

'Looks that way,' Ozzie agreed.

'Can't see the barrier.'

'Mark, give it a minute, okay. In fact, give it a month. We've all been beating up on the Dark Fortress rather badly.'

'The lattice spheres are still there,' Nigel said with quiet admiration. 'The damn thing survived two quantumbusters. The Anomine know how to build to last.'

'No sign of the flare bomb's quantum signature,' Otis reported. 'Looks like you killed it, Ozzie.'

For five hours they waited as the plasma inside the lattice spheres cooled and dimmed. Then it vanished without warning.

'Hey, some kind of shell just appeared round the outer lattice sphere,' Otis said.

'Aren't you going to say I told you so?' Nigel asked.

'Nah,' Ozzie said. 'I figure I owe you one.'

'Something very weird is happening to space out there,' Mark said. 'I don't understand any of these readings.'

'Me neither,' Ozzie said. 'How about you, Nige?'

'Not a clue.'

The light from Dyson Alpha faded away to nothing; with it went the radio cacophony of MorningLightMountain's signals.

'Mission accomplished,' Nigel said. 'Let's go home.'

'Come on, dude, this isn't the end of it. Nothing like. MorningLightMountain is still out there; it'll be starting over fresh in a hundred star systems.'

'Ozzie, please, you're spoiling the moment.'

'But—'

'Home. With one slight detour.'

19

Morton's virtual vision gave him the illusion of light and space. Without that he knew he would have fallen for the siren call of insanity echoing enticingly at the centre of his mind. As it was, spending hours immobile in the armour suit with no external sensor input at all was pushing him closer and closer to all-out claustrophobia. Actually, there had been one thing from outside which still managed to get through to him, the noise of the storm had been reduced to a hefty vibration by the metres of soil on top of him, one he could feel through the suit's adaptive foam padding. The timer in his grid told him it lasted for three and a half hours before finally fading away.

'We've got to get out of here,' he said to Alic.

'Damn right,' the navy commander agreed.

The two of them had lain there in the darkness with hands clasped together like a pair of scared children. That touch allowed them to communicate. Morton wasn't sure he could have held out without the contact of another human being. He didn't even remember much of their conversation; giving each other potted histories, women, places they'd been. Anything to hold the isolation at bay and with it the knowledge that they were buried alive.

There had been no choice.

When the storm appeared from behind the mountains and

swallowed the last pinnacles, they'd had four or five seconds at best before it hit them. Alic had fired his particle lances straight into the ground, blasting out a simple crater of smouldering earth. 'Get in!' he yelled.

Morton had dived straight into the hole, cramming his suit up against Alic's. The Cat hadn't moved.

'Cat!' he implored.

'That's not how I die, Morty,' she'd said simply.

He didn't even manage an answer. Alic fired the particle lances again, collapsing the soil around them. The Cat had sounded sorry for him; out of all the weeks they'd spent together, that was the strongest memory he had of her now.

Once they started digging their way out, he began to appreciate her reasoning. His suit power cells were down to five per cent, and the soil was packed solid. He vaguely remembered that if you were caught in a snow avalanche you were supposed to curl up, to create a space. There had been time for nothing other than the most basic survival instinct. The hole in the ground offered a chance at survival. The impossible wall hurtling down on him didn't.

It took a couple of minutes to wiggle his gauntlet about and compact the earth around it. Electromuscles strained on the limit of their strength just to achieve that. After the hand came the forearm, and finally he could move the whole arm in a little cavity. He began scrabbling. It took hours.

'There was never this much soil on top of us,' he kept saying.

'Inertial navigation is fully functional,' Alic would reply each time. 'We're heading straight up.'

The power cells were draining away at an alarming rate as they wriggled and grubbed their way along. Heat was a big problem; the suits kept pumping excess heat onto their external surfaces, but the soil wasn't a good conductor. It began to build up around them. One more problem Morton could do absolutely nothing about.

Seven hours after the storm arrived, Morton's gauntlet pushed through into open air. He sobbed with relief and shoved like a maniac, battering the suit forward, no longer caring if it was good technique. Claustrophobia was creeping up behind him, refusing to let go. Soil crumbled away around him and he finally flung himself out of the hole and into early evening sunlight crying out with incoherent relief. He slapped at the emergency locks, shedding sections of the suit as if it was on fire.

Alic came stumbling out on all fours. Morton helped him off with the legs and shoulders. They hugged for a long moment, slapping at each other's backs like brothers who had been torn apart for a century.

'We fucking did it,' Morton said. 'We're invincible.'

Alic drew back, and finally took a long look round. His expression became troubled. 'Where the hell are we?'

Morton finally paid attention to their surroundings. His first thought was that they'd tunnelled away for miles to emerge in a different place altogether, possibly a different world. They were standing in a desert. It didn't have sand and sun-blasted stones, but the expanse of raw soil and dark stone fragments that lay all around didn't have a single blade of grass or tree growing anywhere. Nor was there any evidence that life had ever visited this place.

He looked up at the mountains which barricaded the western horizon, and called up a map file, integrating it with his insert's inertial navigation function. The peaks corresponded to the eastern edge of the Dessault Mountains just outside the Institute valley. They were in the right places, but they weren't the right shape at all. Every crag and cleft had been abraded away, reducing them to tall conical mounds of stone. They weren't as high as they used to be, either. The snow had vanished completely.

'That really was one hell of a storm,' Morton muttered. 'I never took Bradley seriously before.' He looked to the east, convinced there should be some sign of it. The horizon was a perfectly flat line between the newborn reddish-brown desert and Far Away's glorious sapphire sky. 'Probably gonna go all the way round the world and bite us again.'

Alic was looking at the gentle saddle that used to hold the Institute. 'No sign of the *Marie Celeste*. I guess the planet had its revenge.'

'Yeah.' Morton started scratching the back of his arms. Just about every part of him was itching now. The sweatshirt and thin cotton trousers he wore didn't exactly smell too good, either. 'What now?'

'We survived. There's got to be someone else around here.'

*

Wilson watched the tail end of the storm flow away into the east. The mountains around the high desert were hard to see now, they'd become the same colour as the land. It was a beautiful view, the air the storm had left in its wake was perfectly clear. There were no clouds anywhere. A doldrum calm had enveloped the whole Dessault range. If he had a regret it was the way the storm had stripped the snow off the eastern mountains. Real mountains deserved snowcaps to complete their majesty.

'It's over, Admiral,' Samantha said.

'Are you sure? That seems a very bold statement.'

'You didn't see the starship launch, did you?'

'No, I didn't.' He smiled at her conviction. 'And you're quite right. I would have seen the fusion drives if they had fired. Your planet had its revenge.'

'Thank you, Admiral, you made it possible.'

'I just hope that storm dies out soon.'

'We think it will break up in the Oak Sea; there'll be ordinary hurricanes split off from it, but the main body will power down before long.'

'Nice theory. Did the Martian data help you come up with the figures?'

'Yes.'

'That's very comforting for an old NASA man like me to hear. Thank you, Samantha. My congratulations to you and your colleagues.'

'Admiral, our original observation team should be with you in ten to fifteen hours. They'll escort you down. If you could make your way to the southern end of Aphrodite's Seat they'll rendezvous with you there.'

'That's very kind of you Samantha, but I'm just going to stay here. I imagine it will be quite a spectacular sunset.'

'Admiral, uh, I don't want to . . . Are you all right?'

He looked down at his legs. The blood had finally stopped seeping round the epoxy foam. They didn't trouble him any more, he could barely feel them now. Every now and then a big shiver would run along his torso. The lava he was resting on had become quite cold. 'I'm fine. Tell your team to turn back. They'd just be wasting their time. I'm afraid I'm not quite the pilot I used to be.'

'Admiral?'

'You have a lovely and strange world here, Samantha. Now the Starflyer's gone, make the most of it.'

'Admiral!'

Wilson closed the link. She meant well, but she'd want to keep talking. He didn't need companionship now. It was quite a revelation after so long, but he didn't fear death any more, not with Oscar and Anna showing him the way.

They'd find his body, and extract his memorycell, and re-life him. He was sure of that. But it wouldn't be *him* who lived on in the future. He'd never accepted that form of continuation in the way the Commonwealth-born generations did. That old twenty-first century way of thinking was one very tough habit to quit.

But this isn't a bad place for it all to end, not after three hundred and eighty years. I flew up the highest mountain in the galaxy and helped defeat the monster. Shame I didn't get the girl. I suppose she'll be re-lifed with edited memories. Maybe her clone and my clone will have a beautiful future together. Be nice.

The cold closed in slowly. Wilson kept staring down on the planet. Watching the shadows lengthen and the atmosphere far below haze to gold.

*

Big black shape sliding through the heavens, blotting out the stars.

This must be the end, then.

*

Pain, just when he thought it had all ended. Jolting from side to side. Spacesuits. Low gravity. A long black ellipsoid parked on the grey-brown regolith. Airlock open, stairs extended.

I crashed. On Mars. Is this the rescue party from the Ulysses?

'Admiral, stay with us. Come on. The *Searcher*'s in orbit, we'll get you up to their medical facility in no time. Stay with us now. This is Nigel. Remember me? Hang on! Understand.'

What about the flag? There was no flag in the ground. I thought we did that. It's always the first thing you should do when you land on a planet. Says so right there in the manual.

*

Mellanie didn't want to open her eyes. She was frightened of what she might see. There wasn't any pain left, but her body remembered it only too well. It ghosted round her, taunting, threatening to return. So much so she thought its absence might only be an illusion. She could still see the horror on Giselle's face. The blood that surrounded her like a fine mist as she spun helplessly. Kinetic weapons pulping her flesh.

'Am I dead?'

Nobody told her she was.

There was light now. Dark red of closed eyelids. Sheets touching her skin. Hard patches on her arms. Most of her torso was numb. She could hear her heart beating.

That has to be good.

She drew in a breath, and risked a quick glance. The room was strangely familiar. It took a while for the memory to come back: Bermuda room, the mansion on Illanum. There was a big cabinet of medical equipment beside the bed, tubes and wires led under the sheets.

Oh well, there are worse jails.

Someone was curled up on the couch in the big bay window, snoring softly. Sunlight filtering through the white gauze drapes shone on his ginger hair.

The sight of him made Mellanie smile fondly. *Crazy boy.* Why he was here puzzled her, unless he'd been confined to this room by Nigel.

Her virtual vision grid was in peripheral mode. She told her e-butler to refresh it and brought it up to full operative status. A great many squares were dark; mostly her inserts. 'What happened to them?' she asked her e-butler.

'You have received extensive clone grafting,' it replied. 'Damaged systems and OCtattoos have not yet been replaced. Some functional systems were removed.'

The SI ones, she realized. Then she read the date. 'Three weeks? I've been out for three weeks?'

'That is correct.'

'Why?'

'Time required for medical treatment.'

'Oh.' Now Mellanie really didn't want to look under the sheets.

Orion stirred, saw she was awake, and sat bolt upright. 'Are you okay?'

'I think so. I haven't tried to move yet.'

'The nurses said it'd be another few days before you can get up.' He came over to stand beside the bed, gazing down at her in awe. 'Are you really all right? I was really worried. They spent so long treating you. The chief doctor said they had to grow new bits. I didn't know they could do that.'

'They can. Uh, Orion, why are you here?'

'They said I could be when you woke up.' He suddenly became terribly anxious. 'Why? Don't you want me here?'

'No . . . I'm glad you are, actually.' There weren't many people she wanted to face right now. The boy was easy, though.

His smile was euphoric. 'Really?'

'Yeah.'

His hand crept down to where hers lay outside the sheets, then darted back.

'So, are we under arrest?' she asked.

'Huh? Oh, no. The security people weren't very nice when the ambulance brought you back here. They said Nigel Sheldon was really cross with you. But it's all been okay since he and Ozzie got back.'

'Back from where?'

'They flew to Dyson Alpha and restarted the barrier generator. It's been on all the news shows.'

'Oh.' *And I missed it all.*

'There are Dynasty warships going off on Firewall flights right now. And there's been alien agents arrested in the Commonwealth, and there was some big storm on Far Away that killed the Starflyer, and lots of other stuff. Tochee and I can hardly keep up with it.'

'Nigel's back?'

'Yeah. He said to tell you the offer's suspended. What does that mean?'

'He promised me an interview; that's all.'

'Okay. And a bloke called Morton stopped by. He said you'd know where to find him if you wanted to.'

'Right.' *He couldn't be bothered to wait?*

'Mellanie, where do you want to go when you're better?'

'It's a little early to . . . What did you call me?'

Orion hung his head sheepishly. He pulled a piece of paper from his pocket. It was heavily creased, as though it had been read a lot.

Mellanie recognized her own handwriting. She'd actually written it in this room.

> Darling Orion,
>   I'm sorry I have to leave you like this.
> I don't want to, but I'm not even who you
> think I am. My real name is Mellanie.
> One day I'll explain, if you ever want me to.

'I've managed to find out most of it,' he said. 'Who you are and everything, that the SI sent you. Ozzie explained.'

Her throat was tightening horribly. 'Then why are you here?'

'I told you, they said I could be.'

'But, if you know . . . ?'

He reached out, boldly this time, and brushed some of her hair from the side of her face. 'None of that stuff changes the way I feel about you.'

Mellanie started crying. It just wasn't fair that he was the only one in the universe who truly cared for her. *Why couldn't I have met him before any of the others?* 'I can't do this. I'm wrong for you.'

'No you're not, don't say that.'

'I'm not a nice girl, Orion, really I'm not.'

Orion gave her a quick devilish grin. 'Yeah. I remember. I was sort of hoping you'd go on being like that with me.'

She put her hand round his head and pulled him down for a kiss.

*

The building manager was standing outside the main entrance of the ancient five-storey building, supervising the maintenancebot as it removed the sign. Paula watched the electro-muscle tentacles drop it into a trolleybot's wire cage. It lifted out the old sign and placed it on the stone wall, then began to screw it into place. She smiled at the familiar lettering.

'Madame!' The building manager's face lit up. He bowed deeply. 'You are back! Welcome, welcome. The world has regained its sanity.'

'Thank you, Maurice,' she said sincerely. 'Slight exaggeration, but it does feel good.'

He kissed her on both cheeks. 'Everybody is waiting for you inside. May I carry that?' He indicated the small plastic bag she was gripping in her left hand.

'No, thank you. I can manage.' Paula took a breath, and walked up the steps. As the doors opened, the maintenancebot began polishing the letters on the sign. She paused and watched the ancient brass lettering start to gleam again in the Paris sunlight.

INTERSOLAR COMMONWEALTH
SERIOUS CRIMES DIRECTORATE

The first person she met when she walked in to the office on the fifth floor was Gwyneth Russell.

'Boss!' Gwyneth exclaimed. 'Welcome back. And congratulations. Deputy director. It's about time.'

'Yes, well, you can't spend your whole life in a rut.'

Gwyneth gave her a very startled look. 'Absolutely not. I'm footloose and fancy free myself for the next fifteen years till Vic steps out of the Boongate wormhole. Fancy a drink tonight? I know some good clubs with lots of sweet first-life boys.'

'Not tonight, but sometime, yes.'

'Sure.'

Behind Gwyneth the rest of the investigators were standing

at their desks, applauding enthusiastically. Paula actually felt her cheeks redden. She looked round the familiar faces, and nodded her appreciation. 'Thank you; it's nice to see you all back out of uniform again,' she said. They fell quiet immediately, smiling. 'It's customary for the new chief to tell you that there's going to be some changes round here, but I think we've all seen enough of that. From now on it's strictly business as it used to be. So, I'll want a meeting of all senior investigators in an hour to establish current case priorities. I shall also be reviewing personnel files today and tomorrow to see how you performed recently, and we need to rebuild teams after the losses we took during the navy days. To which end, I'd like to welcome Hoshe Finn to the office; I'm sure he'll fit in just fine.'

Hoshe gave her a grin, and raised his cup of herbal tea in salute.

Alic Hogan was in the director's office, putting his personal effects in a box. He gave Paula a half-guilty look when she walked in.

'Sorry, chief, I wasn't expecting you for another hour. How did it go with the Director?'

'Easy. Departmental meetings are a waste of time at best; it's all politics and budgets. Nothing useful or relevant.'

'You'll be all right, now you've got the Burnelli family backing you. Five years, you'll be the Director.'

'Humm.' Paula cocked her head and looked out of the big window. 'Adopted again.'

'Excuse me?'

'Nothing. I never realized: you can't see the Eiffel Tower from here. You could from my old office.'

Alic swept the last pile of papers into his box. 'Uh, you know that's the one building management assigned me to.'

'Very symbolic.' Paula sat behind the desk and pulled her rabbakas plant out of the bag. The flower had faded, but another pink shoot was worming its way up out of the black corm. The hologram of the Redhound family was placed next to it. Then she took out a fist-sized perspex cube with a memorycell embedded in the middle. 'I'm really pleased you're staying, Alic,' she said.

'I don't see a huge future for me with Admiral Columbia. Uh, I was surprised when you agreed to accept me in the Paris office.'

'From what I heard you stood up to him for what you knew was right. That means you're in the right place.'

'Thanks.'

'In any case, you could have taken your pick of government jobs after Far Away.'

'I quite enjoyed the work here, despite all the politics.'

'Yes, well, that should be considerably reduced from now on. Columbia has his hands full at the moment. He's pressing the Senate for navy involvement with the CST exploratory division.'

Alic let out a low whistle. 'What did Sheldon say about that?'

'Let's just say he wasn't very enthusiastic. The two of them are also struggling over who gets the credit for the Firewall. I expect we'll see Columbia's bid for the Presidency before too long. Now, I've got a meeting scheduled with our office's lawyers and the prosecuting attorney from the Justice Directorate at eleven o'clock, which I'd like you to sit in on.'

'No problem, what is it for?'

Paula held up the perspex cube. 'Interesting case. Gene Yaohui, aka Captain Oscar Monroe. Do we re-life him and then hand him over to the Justice Directorate for trial and suspension, or should he sit out his thousand years here.'

Alic gave the cube a startled look. 'That's him?'

'Yes. I recovered him and Anna Kime from Stakeout Canyon. Anna's being re-lifed, with a suitable memory edit to remove the Starflyer contamination under the conditions of the Doi amnesty. My contacts tell me we're going to be facing a request from Wilson Kime's lawyers to hand Oscar's memorycell over to him for custody on York5. If that happens Kime will undoubtedly re-life him. There will be a lot of political pressure on the Justice Directorate to drop the Abadan station charges: heavyweight character references, emotionally loaded claims of rehabilitation claiming he's paid his dues to society, the precedent for sentence cancellation set by the navy interdiction troops on the Lost23, that kind of thing. Should be quite an interesting court battle.' She smiled, giving the memorycell a curious gaze. 'I might even lose.'

'You? I doubt it.'

*

'The sea's right outside,' Barry squealed as he ran back through the house. He flung himself at Mark. 'Right there, Dad!'

Mark ruffled his son's hair. 'I told you it would be.'

'Can I go in now? Please! Please!'

'No.' Mark gestured at the pile of boxes and crates which the trolleybots had taken off the big removal truck. He could see them through the wide open doors, bringing more boxes. *How did we acquire so much stuff so quickly? We lost everything in the Ulon Valley.* 'You can't, I've no idea where your swim trunks are. And besides, I don't know what the currents are like.' Which was a white lie; the development company brochure file guaranteed that the beaches of the Mulako Estate had benign weather and tides.

'Where's the sea?' Sandy demanded as she came in through the front door, holding her backpack.

'Outside, come on!' Barry grabbed her hand, and the two of them raced off through the huge lounge and out onto the veranda, Panda barked loudly as she raced after them. The lawn beyond had only just been turfed, gardenbots were still tending the new shrub boarders. It ended with a long dune which topped the private beach of white sand and azure water. A thicket of palms had been planted down one side of the lawn, shielding them from the rest of the estate. Mark had never seen so much civil construction work in one place before, not even on Cressat. That morning they'd driven out of Tanyata station, itself undergoing a massive expansion, and down the coastal road. Outside the burgeoning capital city, the land along the shore was one giant building site, with the developers offering exclusive homes in fifteen-acre private grounds. Mark had bought the plot at the furthest end of the estate, where the national park began. They didn't need a mortgage, the Sheldon Dynasty had paid for it, although Nigel had wanted him to take something even grander on Cressat – in fact anything, anywhere was the offer. Mark said no thanks, living in mansions just wasn't him. He didn't want to live off a trust fund, either; he'd seen the way Dynasty children turned out and he wasn't going to let that happen to Barry and Sandy. So he'd accepted a directorship at the Tanyata offices of Alatonics, the Dynasty's principal bot manufacturer, which paid him a colossal salary – and the way Tanyata was growing he was going to be earning it. Immigration was running at quarter of a million a week, mainly refugees from the Lost23. Once all the arrangements had been made, Liz sat down with the architect for a week, designing the big airy house which, to be honest, was a small mansion. Now they were here, it didn't seem quite real.

'Don't go in the water,' he yelled after the kids. 'I really mean it.' He looked round the big hall, trying to remember which doors led where. Then he caught sight of the marks which Barry's trainers had left on the lounge's polished hardwood floor, and winced. 'Find out if there's a maidbot,' he told his e-butler.

Liz walked in, carrying a box full of crockery. 'Guess what?'

'Er . . .'

'The furniture store just called. They won't be delivering until Thursday.'

'But that's two days. What are we supposed to do until

then? We haven't got much furniture.' He still couldn't believe the size of the rooms, it was like a house made up from aircraft hangars. The few items they had brought with them wouldn't fill his study, let alone the reception rooms.

'Good question. The marshalling yard at the station is just a mess. The container is there somewhere. They think.' Liz gave the hall lighting a suspicious stare. 'Those aren't the fittings I ordered.'

'Aren't they?' Mark thought the gold and pearl fittings were quite nice.

'No. Where the hell is that development company rep? She should have been here when we arrived.'

'Yes, dear.'

'What's that?' Liz was looking back out at the front of the house, where a MoZ Express courier van had drawn up next to the removal truck. 'Never mind, I'll find out.'

'Do you want me to help unpack some of the boxes?'

'No. You watch the show, it's starting. The portals were all installed – at least they'd goddamn better be.'

Mark hurriedly found a big floor cushion in one of the boxes, and carried it through into the lounge. He put it on top of the scuff marks. Liz would kill Barry if she saw them.

He sat down and told the house management array to access the Michelangelo show. The portal projected the image across half of the empty floor. The resolution and colour definition was superb, even with the sunlight streaming in through the open veranda doors.

Michelangelo was dressed in a flowing purple silk suit, standing by himself in the middle of the studio. 'Hello one and all. This is the show we've been trailing for a couple of weeks now, the one where we promise to give you the real story behind the war. And believe me, I am not kidding. To prove it, we have here in the studio Nigel Sheldon.' The image focus switched to a line of chairs, Nigel sat at one end, and smiled at the studio audience as the applause started. 'Ozzie, himself,' Michelangelo announced as if he couldn't quite believe the guest list. 'Retired Admiral Wilson Kime, Senator Justine Burnelli, Chief Investigator Paula Myo, and our two *very* special visitors, Stig McSobel, spokesman for the Guardians of Selfhood, and a MorningLightMountain motile containing the memories of Dudley Bose.' Michelangelo applauded the line up, then smiled winningly out at the audience to show how *really* happy he was with the next announcement. 'And, although it's technically my show, the interviewer of course simply has to be our very own Mellanie Rescorai.'

Mark chuckled as the image zoomed in on Mellanie sitting behind Michelangelo's big desk.

'You should have gone,' Liz told him.

He looked up and grinned. 'Not a chance. Remember the last time she interviewed me.'

'Yes,' Liz drawled. 'Anyway, the delivery was for you.'

'Oh, what is it?'

Liz gestured at the trollybot. There were ten children's school lunchboxes resting in its basket. 'There was a note.'

Mark frowned as he opened the little envelope. 'Fresh from the kindergarten,' he read. 'Enjoy your new house. Ozzie.' He grinned and opened the first lunchbox. 'Hey, champagne!'

'Millextow crab salad,' Liz exclaimed as she opened another. 'Thornton's chocolates. Damn, we need more rich friends.'

Someone knocked on the front door. When they went into the hall they saw three people standing on the shaded porch. Mark did his best not to stare at the tallest of them, a lean man wearing a kilt and white T-shirt. Every part of his exposed skin had an OCtattoo; golden galaxies glowed on his bald head. 'Hello there, I'm Lionwalker Eyre, and these are my life partners, Scott and Chi. We're your new neighbours. Thought we should come and introduce ourselves.'

'Please, come in,' Mark said. He was now having trouble

not staring at Chi, who was enchantingly beautiful. 'I didn't know we had neighbours yet.'

'Aye, well, we've been here awhile,' Lionwalker said in a broad Scottish accent. 'Normally I'd have moved planets by now. Don't like the crowds. No offence. But there are no uncrowded planets any more. So, best make the most of it, eh?'

'We were just about to open a bottle.'

'In the middle of the afternoon? My kind of neighbours.'

'I know you,' Chi said. 'You're *the* Mark Vernon.'

'Ah.' Mark casually sucked his belly back in. 'Guilty, I'm afraid.'

'Actually,' Liz said, as her arm closed round Mark's shoulder. 'He's *my* Mark Vernon.'

*

Bradley Johansson did the one thing he didn't expect to do: he opened his eyes. 'I'm alive,' he exclaimed. His throat had trouble forming the words and they came out very wrong. These vocal chords were evolved for more sophisticated sound, and song.

'Did you ever doubt that?' Clouddancer asked. 'We named you our friend.'

'Ah,' Bradley said. He tried to get up. When he moved his arms, the wing membranes came with them, rustling heavily. He looked down in astonishment at his Silfen body. 'Is this real?'

Clouddancer laughed. 'Hey, pal, if you ever find out what real is, you be sure and let us know, okay?

*

It had been a long three weeks out in the new desert. Tom was tired and filthy after the endless days scanning the sandy soil and digging endless holes. He also wanted a break from

Andy's constant whining and Hagen's wretched cooking – say about ten years. Brothers they might be, but that didn't mean he could stand being cooped up with them for so long.

It had seemed like a good idea after their home had burned down in Armstrong City thanks to the psycho Guardians. The Commonwealth was keen to acquire sections of the smashed alien starship, and the navy paid good money for pieces. All you had to do was head out into the new desert which the planet's revenge had laid across the veldt between the Dessault Mountains and the Oak Sea, swing a metal detector about, and dig where it went *ping*. A lot of guys were doing it. They claimed to be very rich. Not that you'd know it from the way they dressed or the vehicles they rode.

Tom and his brothers had never had any real finds. A few scraps, chunks of twisted metal that truthfully could have been anything. The dealers in Zeefield never offered much. Scavengers said if any true find came along the dealers would bid against each other, bumping the price up. Tom hated the dealers, but the only way to get the true price on the scraps was to drive all the way back to Armstrong City where the navy starship visited every couple of months to see what'd been found. Travelling cost them weeks. They weren't making enough to do that.

Every time they went out, Tom was convinced that *this* would be the trip that hit paydirt. The starship was huge, mostly solid machinery according to the dealers and other scavengers. That meant there should be segments the size of houses buried under the new desert. How difficult could it be?

This had been another washout trip. They had sensors rigged to cables that stretched out for twenty-five metres on either side of their old Mazda jeep. The ends were fixed to small quad bikes that Hagan and Andy rode, keeping the cable taut. That way they could cover big stretches of the new desert driving along together. The guy they'd bought them off swore the system could find metal twenty metres down. The price he charged them for the rig, they should have been able to locate anything a kilometre away.

All they'd got was a battered old pump made of some lightweight metallic composite, which was probably going to fetch a couple of hundred Far Away dollars, and three curving jags of metal that looked suspiciously like wheel arches to Tom. But they had wires and some electronic modules fixed to them. So you never knew . . . It had taken the better part of five days to excavate them. The trouble with the new desert was that it wasn't a real desert, especially not now, a year after the planet's revenge. To start with it had been a naked expanse of sandy soil. But the rains washed over it, and seeds from the buried plants germinated and began to grow. It was a faint green colour now, and the soil was claggy, making digging difficult, especially after the rain. Streams and rivers were reappearing along contours. There were some lowlands that were now just bogs, impossible to traverse. Every time they went out, they'd spend hours digging the Mazda out of unexpected patches of mud.

Tom found Highway One just after midday, and turned onto it, heading north. Further south, where the road ran parallel to the Dessault Mountains, it had completely vanished beneath the soil of the new desert. Here, it extended out in the open, sometimes for kilometres before high dunes covered it again. They slowly diminished the further north you went, until half a day past Mount StOmer they ended altogether. It was easy to follow the road, though. Every vehicle left tracks along the line of the concrete underneath the dunes. You could even find the road in the dark.

When he was on the crest of one dune, he saw a dark figure by the side of the tracks a few hundred metres ahead. 'What the hell is that?'

'What's what?' Hagen shouted.

'Will you turn your fucking music off,' Tom told him. That

was another thing: Hagen played his jazzy rock all day long at full volume.

'It's a girl,' Andy said. 'Yahoooo.'

Tom peered forward. No way you could tell. 'Come on, guys, it's someone with a busted truck, is all.' Not that he could see one. Not anywhere. But how else would anybody get out here?

'I'm telling you, it's a girl.'

'Hagen, turn your music off right now, or I'm gonna throw that array out of the jeep.'

'Screw you, asshole.'

But he did turn it down. Tom gunned the Mazda down the slope. Not that he believed Andy, but . . .

'How much do we charge for recovery and taxi service?' Andy said with a laugh.

'Hell, I know what I'm gonna charge her,' Hagen said, and cupped his crotch.

It made Tom realize what they must look like. Filthy overalls and T-shirts, all in raggedy old sunhats, ancient shades. Unshaved for the whole three weeks. And the state of the Mazda was pretty poor. 'Well, I'll be damned,' he muttered as they approached the figure who still hadn't moved. He slowed the jeep.

'Told you so,' Andy said.

Hagan started an excited heavy breathing laugh as if he was some kind of retard.

'Shut up, Hagen,' Tom shouted. It really was a girl. She had short dark hair under a white peaked cap, and wore a sleeveless orange T-shirt with tight dark trousers cut off just above the knees. And she was sitting in a very weird position, with her legs crossed and feet bent back somehow. All he could think of was how supple she must be to do that. A smile was growing on his face. He halted the jeep beside her. 'Good afternoon, there.'

'Howdy!' Andy shouted. 'Me and my brothers, we're heading in to town.'

Tom jabbed his elbow into Andy's ribs.

'Yes ma'am,' Hagen laughed. 'We're gonna have us a party tonight. Do you wanna party?'

To Tom's complete surprise she stood up and grinned at them.

'Like you wouldn't believe,' said The Cat.

*

As always, lack of sleep made Ozzie testy. He unzipped his tent, flapped his arms against the chill of the early morning forest air, and wandered over to the fire they'd built last night. The Bose motile was standing beside it, feeding small chips of wood to the embers. Flames were starting to flicker again.

'Morning, Ozzie,' the Bose motile said. 'I'll have this going again in a minute. Do you want your hot chocolate?' It was speaking through a small bioneural array attached to the tip of a sensor stalk, a custom-built system that could easily be swapped for a standard Prime interface module.

'Coffee,' Ozzie grumbled. 'It'll help keep me awake.' He glowered at the tent on the other side of the small clearing which Orion and Mellanie shared.

'I'm lucky, this body doesn't need sleep like humans. A good rest is all it takes to refresh me.'

Ozzie sat down on an ancient rotting tree trunk and started tying his boot laces up. The horses were snorting behind him, impatient for their feed. 'Some humans don't need any sleep, apparently. I mean, did you hear them last night? Man, they were at it for hours.'

'They are young.'

'Huh. They could at least be young and quiet.'

'Ozzie, you're turning into quite a grump. Did you never have a honeymoon?'

'Yeah, yeah. Bung some eggs in the pan, will you, I'm going to see to the horses.' He busied himself with the nosebags.

Tochee was next up, unzipping the hemispherical tent that it had designed for itself. 'Good morning, friend Ozzie.'

'Morning.' The array on his wrist translated his grunt into an ultraviolet pulse for Tochee. It looked like a bracelet with a black stone set in the top. The whole thing was bioneural and custom made. The experts in the SCT electronics division had relished the challenge of coming up with bioluminescent ultraviolet emitters. It'd taken them the best part of six months, but the little unit functioned perfectly along the Silfen paths.

The first cup of coffee mellowed Ozzie's temper slightly. Then the sound of human sex started to echo round the clearing, rising in pitch and intensity. The tent was shaking.

'Why do they both refer to your deity while mating?' Tochee inquired as it munched on some rehydrated cabbage. 'Is it a request for a blessing?'

Ozzie shot the Bose motile a look, but of course it didn't have body language he could read. 'Uncontrollable reflex, man. Look it up in your encyclopaedia files.'

'Thank you, I will do so.'

Ozzie started eating his eggs and rehydrated bread. Trying to concentrate on the food.

Orion and Mellanie appeared a little while later, both smiling broadly. They held hands as they walked over to the fire.

'I boiled some water for you,' the Bose motile said.

'Probably cold by now,' Ozzie muttered.

'Would you like some tea cubes?'

'Yes please,' Mellanie said. They sat on the trunk together. She leaned against him, her hands holding his and they smiled at each other again. 'Do you have to leave?' she asked.

Ozzie chased off his mood. *That* was really why he was

being such a dick this morning. 'Yeah, fraid so, man. There's a split in the path just the other side of the clearing.'

'He's right,' Orion said. 'I can feel it.'

Mellanie gave the tall trees a wistful look. 'I wish I could.'

'You'll learn,' he said adoringly.

Ozzie caught all four of the Bose motile's sensor stalks waving in unison. He put it down to motile laughter.

They all took a long time to pack up that morning, delaying the moment. In the end all the bags were loaded onto the horses, water canteens filled, lunches made ready in the day packs. Ozzie stood facing Tochee and Orion, feeling thoroughly miserable.

'Tochee.'

'Friend Ozzie, I have dreaded this time.'

'Me too, man. But you'll find your way home. We did.'

'To travel hopefully is a better thing than to arrive.'

'Ha! Don't believe everything humans tell you, okay?'

'Okay.' Tochee extended its manipulator flesh and shaped it into a human hand. Ozzie shook it formally. He wasn't quite prepared for the way Mellanie threw her arms round him. There was still a small nagging issue of trust with that girl which he hadn't resolved.

'You're seriously going to do this?' he asked.

Mellanie gave him an innocent shocked look, which dissolved into a beautifully evil smile. 'Oh yes, I'm doing this. My inserts can record all the worlds we visit. Are you afraid I'll beat your record of new planets to walk across?'

'No. But you're at the top of the unisphere. That interview could have turned Michelangelo into your coffee boy. You knew that.'

She gave him a curious, distant smirk. 'Black, one sugar.'

'Excuse me?'

'I thought you'd get it, you of all people. It's far better to travel than to arrive, right? Yeah, I made it to the top. Now what? Stay there for five hundred years? On the way up I found out what it takes to get there, and what I'll have to do to stay there. I thought I could do it, I really did. I thought I could be harder and nastier than all the rest. Actually, I can be, which is the really awful thing. But I found I don't like the price. It's not who I am; I don't think. I need a break, Ozzie. I need to sort myself out.'

'Too much too soon, huh?'

'You changed the world with wormhole technology, but it was Sheldon who built the Commonwealth. Why, Ozzie?'

'More fun this way.'

'Yeah, well I'm going to take a look at the galaxy. When I get back I'll have the recordings to step straight back into the number one slot again if that's what I want.'

'I hope you find out what you want to be by then,' he said sincerely.

'Thanks, Ozzie.'

'In the meantime, be nice to Orion. He's a good kid.'

Mellanie batted her eyes. 'Not any more, he's not.'

Ozzie grinned as she walked away, trying not to stare at her ass. Her jeans were incredibly tight.

'Guess this is it,' Orion said. There was something caught in his throat, making his voice hoarse.

'Are you going to be all right?' Ozzie asked. 'Really, I mean?'

'Sure. You taught me how to take care of myself. Except for the pick-up lines; they were really crap, Ozzie.'

Ozzie hugged the boy, suddenly afraid he was going to lose it and start crying, which would be seriously uncool. 'They're out there, dude, you know that.'

'I do. Sometimes I think I can see them. They're a long way away.'

'Well you be careful, remember you can keep coming back.'

'I know.'

'And have fun on Tochee's world. I want a full report some day.'

'You'll get it.'

'Look after Mellanie. She's not as tough as she makes out.'

'Ozzie; we'll be fine.' Orion gave him a last hug. 'Goodbye, Ozzie.'

'Sure, dude, goodbye.'

Ozzie shouldered his backpack, watching as Orion, Mellanie and Tochee left the little clearing, leading the three heavily laden horses after them. He had a strong impulse to rush off after them.

'Saying goodbye is always hard.'

'What's that?' Ozzie looked up at the Bose motile.

'I believe Orion is perfectly capable of surviving out here. He is, after all, a friend of the Silfen.'

'Yeah, but *come on*, he and Mellanie don't have a brain cell to rub together.'

'It's not their brain cells that they're interested in rubbing together.'

Ozzie laughed. 'No, it isn't. I guess it's going to take Tochee longer than it expects to get home.' He sighed. 'Come on, let's get going.'

They set off in the same direction as the others, to begin with. Ozzie could see them through the trees for quite a while. Orion and Mellanie would wave from time to time. He raised a hand in reply. Eventually, the undergrowth was too dense.

'Is this really a path?' the Bose motile asked. They were forcing their way through bushes and tall grasses, with the trees clustering close together. The ground was damp underfoot.

'Yeah,' Ozzie replied, *knowing*, feeling the ancient way stirring out of its sleep. 'It just hasn't been used for a long time, is all.'

*

It took them three more days, pushing through the forest as it turned from doughty pines to lush tropical vegetation that was really thick. On the morning of the third day, the trees began to shrink. They looked malformed, suffering from some kind of disease. Leafless stumps began to appear amid the living trunks, becoming prevalent. The undergrowth gave way to ribbons of slime that covered the ground. It wasn't long before the dying jungle gave way to a field of boulders. Stone began to rise up on either side, forming gulley walls. Thunder echoed around them, growing louder. They were walking into darkness now, with occasional flashes of lightning accompanying the thunder.

'I hear it,' the Bose motile said suddenly.

Ozzie nodded. He walked to the end of the gulley, and peered down into the valley below. Overhead, a force field held off the thick black clouds. Lightning scraped across the translucent energy field.

The home of MorningLightMountain was laid out before him. The giant building that had consumed the conical mountain in the centre of the valley. Vast rectangular congregation lakes, with their writhing bodies emerging onto ramps where they were marshalled into new regiments by motiles. Industrial buildings mushrooming everywhere.

'I can't see a single living thing apart from it,' Ozzie said. 'Nothing.'

'You won't,' the Bose motile said. 'Not here. There are farms, elsewhere. Most of the continental land is given over to agriculture. But there is no wild life.'

'What's it doing?'

'Brooding. It thinks it is going to die. Not for millions of years, until the sun expands and fills up the inside of the barrier. But that is all it sees now. It doesn't believe that any of its interstellar settlements will rescue it, should they survive our nova bombs. It knows they will devolve into independence and thus become its enemy just like all the other immotiles used to be.'

'Morbid son of a bitch, isn't it? Are you sure you want to do this?'

'Of course. It is only fitting. I was the last thing to escape from Dyson Alpha, it is only right that I bring back a chance, some hope. MorningLightMountain cannot change now. Evolution here has ended. It cannot think differently, not by itself. Somebody must introduce change, for it will never come from within.'

'And you can do that?'

'I can try. I can insinuate questions into its thoughts. Questions it cannot conceive for itself.'

'Isn't that a bit like making it in our own image?'

'I don't think you need worry that MorningLightMountain will ever become human in its outlook. For myself, I will consider it simply developing a more rational outlook as a success. It needs to learn tolerance.'

'Good luck. That's something we don't do very well ourselves. We nearly killed MorningLightMountain in a knee-jerk reaction.'

'But we didn't, did we, thanks to you.'

'And a few others.'

'It will take time, centuries I expect, and there's no guarantee of success.'

'I'll come back in a few hundred years, check up on progress.'

'Please do. It will be interesting to see what you have become by then.'

The End

Visit **www.panmacmillan.com** to read more about all our books and to buy them. You will also find features, author interviews and news of any author events, and you can sign up for e-newsletters so that you're always first to hear about our new releases.

www.panmacmillan.com

GIFT SELECTOR
YOUR ACCOUNT
WISH LIST
WAITING LIST

HOME | ABOUT US | IMPRINTS | TRADE/MEDIA | CONTACT US | ADVANCED SEARCH | SEARCH | GO
BOOK CATEGORIES | WHAT'S NEW | AUTHORS/ILLUSTRATORS | BESTSELLERS | READING GROUPS

Coming Soon...

Reading Groups

Competitions
Feeling Lucky?

Extracts
Sneak Previews

Interviews

Events
Meet Our Stars

Reviews
What The Critics Say

News & Awards

Editor's Choice
What We're Reading